CAEDMON'S SONG
&
AFTERMATH

Peter Robinson grew up in Yorkshire, and now lives in Canada.

His critically acclaimed Inspector Banks series has won numerous awards in Britain, the United States, Canada and Europe.

The Inspector Banks series

GALLOWS VIEW

A DEDICATED MAN

A NECESSARY END

THE HANGING IN THE VALLEY

PAST REASON HATED

WEDNESDAY'S CHILD

DRY BONES THAT DREAM

INNOCENT GRAVES

DEAD RIGHT

IN A DRY SEASON

COLD IS THE GRAVE

THE SUMMER THAT NEVER WAS

PLAYING WITH FIRE

STRANGE AFFAIR

Also by Peter Robinson

NOT SAFE AFTER DARK AND OTHER WORKS

PETER
ROBINSON

CAEDMON'S SONG
&
AFTERMATH

PAN BOOKS

Caedmon's Song first published 1990 by Penguin Canada.
First published in Great Britain 1990 by Viking.
First published by Macmillan 2003 and simultaneously in paperback.
First published by Pan Books 2004.
Aftermath first published 2001 by Avon Books, New York.
First published in Great Britain 2001 by Macmillan.
First published in paperback by Pan Books 2002.

This omnibus first published 2005 by Picador
an imprint of Pan Macmillan Ltd
Pan Macmillan, 20 New Wharf Road, London N1 9RR
Basingstoke and Oxford
Associated companies throughout the world
www.panmacmillan.com

ISBN 0 330 44376 3

Maps designed by Brian Lehan

1 3 5 7 9 8 6 4 2

A CIP catalogue record for this book is available from the British Library.

Typeset by IntypeLibra, London
Printed and bound in Great Britain by
Mackays of Chatham plc, Chatham, Kent

CAEDMON'S SONG

For Sheila

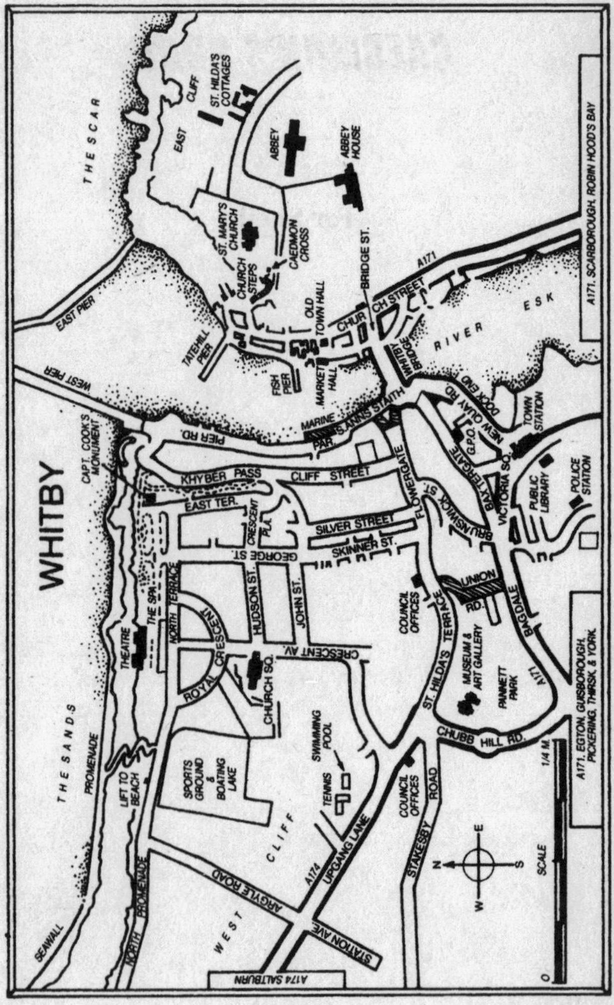

Map by Brian Lehen

CAEDMON'S SONG

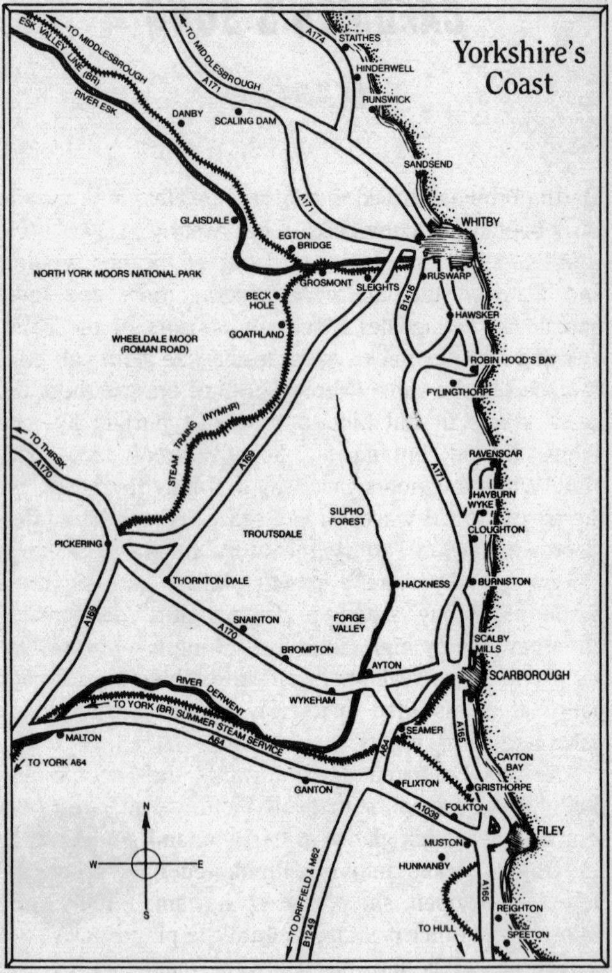

Map by Brian Lehen

1

MARTHA

Martha Browne arrived in Whitby one clear afternoon in early September, convinced of her destiny.

All the way, she had gazed out of the bus window and watched the landscape become more and more unreal. On Fylingdales Moor, the sensors of the early-warning missile-attack system rested like giant golf balls balanced at the rims of holes, and all around them the heather was in full bloom. It wasn't purple, like the songs all said, but more delicate, maroon laced with pink. When the moors gave way to rolling farmland, like the frozen green waves of the sea it led to, she understood what Dylan Thomas meant by 'fire green as grass'.

Sea and sky were a piercing blue, and the town nestled in its bay, a pattern of red pantile roofs flanked on either side by high cliffs. Everything was too vibrant and vivid to be real; the scene resembled a landscape painting, as distorted in its way as Van Gogh's wheat fields and starry nights.

The bus lumbered down towards the harbour and pulled up in a small station off Victoria Square. Martha took another quick glance at her map and guidebook as the driver backed into the numbered bay. When the doors hissed open, she picked up her small holdall and followed the other passengers onto the platform.

Arriving in a new place always made Martha feel strangely excited, but this time the sensation was even more intense. At first, she could only stand rooted to the spot among the revving buses, breathing in the diesel fumes and salt sea air. She felt as if she was trying the place on for size, and it was a good fit. She took stock of the subtle tremors her arrival caused in the essence of the town. Others might not notice such things, but Martha did. Everyone and everything – from the sand on the beach to a guilty secret in a tourist's heart – was somehow connected and in a state of constant flux. It was like quantum physics, she thought, at least in so far as she understood it. Her presence would send out ripples and reverberations that people wouldn't forget for a long time.

She still felt queasy from the journey, but that would soon pass. The first thing was to find somewhere to stay. According to her guidebook, the best accommodation was to be had in the West Cliff area. The term sounded odd when she knew she was on the *east* coast, but Whitby was built on a kink in the shoreline facing north, and the town was divided neatly into east and west by the mouth of the River Esk.

Martha walked along the New Quay Road by Endeavour Wharf. In the estuary, silt glistened like entrails in the sun. A rusted hulk stood by the wharf – not a fishing trawler, but a small cargo boat of some kind – and rough, unshaven men wearing dirty T-shirts and jeans ambled around on deck, coiling ropes and greasing thick chains. By the old swing bridge that linked the east and west sides of the town stood a blackboard with the times of high tides chalked in: 0527 and 1803. It was a few minutes before four; the tide should be on its way in.

She walked along St Ann's Staith, sliding her hand on the white metal railing that topped the stone walls of the quay. Small craft lay beached on the mud, some of them not much more than rowing boats with sails. Ropes thrummed and flimsy metal masts rattled in the light breeze and flashed in the sun. Across the narrow estuary, the white houses seemed to be piled haphazardly beside and on top of one another. At the summit of the cliff stood St Mary's Church, just as it had, in one form or another, since Abbot William de Percy built it between 1100 and 1125. The abbey beside it had been there even longer, but it had been crumbling away for over four hundred years, since Henry VIII dissolved the monasteries, and now there was nothing left but a sombre ruin.

Martha felt a thrill at actually seeing these places she had only read about. And she also had a strange sense of coming home, a kind of déjà vu. Everything seemed so damn familiar and *right*. This was the place; Martha knew it. But she'd have plenty of time to explore East Cliff later, she decided, turning her attention back towards where she was going.

The pubs, seafood stalls and souvenir shops on her left gave way to amusement arcades and a Dracula Museum; for it was here, in Whitby, where the celebrated Count was said to have landed. The road veered away from the harbour wall around a series of open sheds by the quayside, where the fish were auctioned before being shipped to processing plants. Obviously, the catch hadn't come in yet, as nothing was going on there at the moment. Martha knew she would have to come down here again and again and watch the men as they unloaded their fish into iced boxes and sold them. But, like everything else, it could wait. Now she had made up her mind, she felt she had plenty of time. Attention to detail was important, and it would help overcome whatever fear and uncertainty remained within her.

She stopped at a stall and bought a packet of shrimps, which she ate as she carried on walking. They sold whelks, winkles and cockles, too, but Martha never touched them. It was because of her mother, she realized. Every time the family had visited the seaside – usually Weston-super-Mare or Burnham-on-Sea – and Martha had wanted to try them, her mother had told her it was vulgar to eat such things. It was, too, she had always believed. What could be more vulgar than sticking a pin in the moist opening of a tiny, conch-like shell and pulling out a creature as soft and slimy as snot? It wouldn't bother her now, though. She had changed. Her mother didn't know it, but she had. Now she could probably even rip apart a lobster and suck out the meat. But her mother's words still stuck in her mind. The more she thought about it, the more she realized that it was not so much the act itself that her mother thought vulgar, but its class associations. Only the lower classes went around at seaside resorts sticking pins in whelks and winkles.

A bingo caller from one of the arcades interrupted her stream of thought: 'All the fives, fifty-five . . . Legs eleven, number eleven.' The amplified voice echoed through the empty auction sheds.

Martha passed the bandstand and took Khyber Pass up to West Cliff. At the top, she walked under the enormous whale's jawbone, set up like an archway into another world. It was a hot day, and by the time she had climbed the steep hill she was sweating. She ran her hand along the smooth, warm, weather-darkened bone and shuddered. If this was just the jaw, how gigantic the creature must have been: a true leviathan. And as she passed under its shadow, she fancied she was like Jonah being vomited forth from its mouth. Or was she going the other way, entering the whale's belly?

She could picture the old Sunday school illustrations of the Bible story: inside the whale had looked as vast and gloomy as a cathedral, with the ribs mimicking its vaulting. And there sat poor Jonah, all alone. She imagined how his cries must have echoed in all that space. But could there really be so much emptiness inside a whale? Wasn't it all a twisted congestion of tubing and swollen, throbbing organs like it was inside people?

She tried to remember the story. Hadn't Jonah attempted to escape his destiny by running off to Tarshish when he was supposed to go and cry against the wickedness in Nineveh? Then a great tempest had raged and the sailors threw him overboard. He spent three days and three nights in the belly of the whale, until he prayed for deliverance and the beast spewed him forth onto dry land. After that, he accepted his destiny and went to Nineveh. She couldn't remember what happened next. There was something about the people there repenting and being spared, which didn't please Jonah much after all he'd been through, but Martha couldn't recall the ending. Still, it seemed remarkably apt. She had struggled against her fate, too, at first, but now she had accepted her destiny, the holiness of her task. She was headed for Nineveh, where evil thrived, and no matter what, there would be no mercy this time.

Captain Cook's statue looked confidently out to sea just beyond the jawbone, rolled-up charts under his arm. Cook had learned his seamanship on the Whitby coal ships, Martha had read, and the vessels he had commanded on epic voyages to the South Seas had been built here, where that rusted hulk lay at anchor in the lower harbour. The *Endeavour* and the *Resolution*. Good names, she thought.

Royal Crescent, curved in an elegant semicircle facing the sea, offered a number of private hotels with vacancies, but the prices were too high. She might have to stay a week or two, and over ten pounds a night would be too much. It was a shame, because these hotels were probably a lot more comfortable than what she was likely to get. Still, a room with a bath and a colour television was too much to ask for. And you always had to pay more if you wanted to see the sea. How often did people on holiday actually sit in their rooms and admire the view? Martha wondered. Hardly at all. But it was the reassurance that counted, the knowledge that it was there if you wanted to look. And that privilege cost money.

The promenade along West Cliff was lined with huge Victorian hotels of the kind that were built in most seaside towns when holidays at the coast came into vogue. Martha knew none of these were for her, either, so she turned down Crescent Avenue to find a cheap bed and breakfast place on a nondescript street.

As it happened, Abbey Terrace wasn't entirely without charm. It sloped steeply down to the estuary, though it stopped at East Terrace before it actually reached the front, and boasted a row of tall guesthouses, all bearing recommendations from the RAC or AA. Many of them even had their rates posted in the window, and Martha chose one that cost nine pounds fifty per night.

Wiping the sweat from her brow with the back of her hand, she opened the wrought-iron gate and walked up the path.

2

KIRSTEN

'Come on now, let's be 'aving yer! Ain't yer got no 'omes to go to?' The landlord of the Ring O'Bells voiced his nightly complaint as he came over to Kirsten's table to collect the glasses. 'It's half past eleven. They'll have my licence, they will.'

'Pray cease and desist,' said Damon, holding up his hand like a stop sign. 'Dost thou not ken 'tis the end of term? Know'st thou not 'tis the end of our final year in this fair city?'

'I don't bloody care,' the landlord growled. 'It's time you all pissed off home to bed.' He snatched a half-empty glass from the table.

'Hey, that was my drink!' Sarah said. 'I haven't finished it.'

'Yes you have, love.' He stood his ground, not a big man, but quick and strong enough to outmanoeuvre a bunch of drunken students. 'Out, the lot of you. Now! Come on!'

Hugo stood up. 'Wait a minute. She paid for that drink and she's got every bloody right to finish it.' With his curly blond hair and broad shoulders, he looked more like a rugby player than a student of English.

Kirsten sighed. There was going to be trouble, she could sense it. Damon was drunk and Hugo was proud and foolish enough, even sober, to start a fight. Just what she needed on her last night at university.

The landlord tapped his watch. 'Not at this time, she hasn't. Not according to the licensing laws.'

'Are you going to give her it back?'

'No.'

Behind him, the cellarman, Les, an ex-fighter with a misshapen nose and cauliflower ears, stood poised for trouble.

'Well, fuck you, then,' Hugo said. 'You can have this one too.' And he threw the rest of his pint of Guinness in the landlord's face.

Les moved forward but the landlord put out an arm to stop him. 'We don't want any trouble, lads and lasses,' he said in an icily calm voice. 'You've had your fun. Now why don't you go and have your party somewhere else?'

'Might as well, Hugo,' said Kirsten, tugging at his sleeve. 'The man's right. We'll get nothing more to drink here and there's no sense starting a fight, not tonight. Let's go to Russell's party.'

Hugo sat down sulkily and frowned at his pint glass as if he regretted wasting the stout. 'All right,' he said, then glared at the landlord again. 'But it's not fair. You pay for your drinks and that bastard just snatches them off you. We ought to get our money back, at least. How long have we been coming here? Two years. And this is how we get treated.'

'Come on, Hugo.' Damon clapped him on the shoulder and they all got up to leave. ''Twould indeed be a great pleasure to drown yon varlet in a tun of malmsey, but . . .' He pushed his glasses back up the bridge of his nose and shrugged. '*Tempus fugit*, old mate.' With his short haircut and raddled, boyish complexion, he looked like an old-fashioned grammar-school kid. He whipped his scarf dramatically around his neck and the end tipped over a glass on the table. It rolled towards the edge, wobbled back and forth there, undecided, then stopped for a moment before dropping to the floor. The landlord stood by patiently, arms folded, and Les looked ready for a fight.

'Fascist bastards,' Sarah said, picking up her handbag.

They beat a hasty and noisy retreat out of the pub, singing 'Johnny B. Goode', the song that had been playing on the jukebox when the landlord unplugged it.

'Russell's is it, then?' Hugo asked.

Everyone agreed. No one had any booze to take along, but good old Russell always put on a good spread. He had plenty of money, what with his father being such a whiz on the stock market. Probably a bit of insider-trading, Kirsten suspected, but who was she to complain?

And so the four of them walked out into a balmy June evening – only Damon wearing a scarf because he affected eccentricity – and made their way through the deserted campus to the residence buildings. There were Hugo, Sarah, Kirsten and Damon, all of them final-year English students. The only person missing from the close-knit group was Galen, Kirsten's boyfriend. Just after exams, his grandmother had died and he'd had to rush down to Kent to console his mother and help out with arrangements.

Kirsten was feeling a little tipsy as they hurried to Oastler Hall and up the worn stone steps to Russell's rooms. She missed Galen and wished he could be here to celebrate, too – especially as she had got a First. Still, she'd had enough congratulations to make her thoroughly bored with the whole business already. Now it was time to get maudlin and say her farewells, for tomorrow she was heading home. If only she could keep Hugo's wandering hands away . . .

The party seemed to have spilled over into the corridor and adjoining rooms. Even if they wanted to, which was unlikely, Russell's neighbours would hardly have been able to get to sleep. The newcomers pushed their way through the crowd into the smoky flat, calling greetings as they went. Most of the lights were off in the living room, where The Velvet Underground were singing 'Sweet Jane' and couples danced with drinks in their hands. Russell himself leaned by the window talking to Guy Naburn, a trendy tutor who hung around with students rather than with his colleagues, and welcomed them all when they tumbled in.

'Hope you've got some booze,' Hugo shouted over the music. 'We just got chucked out of the Ring O'Bells.'

Russell laughed. 'For that, you deserve the best. Try the kitchen.'

Sure enough, half-finished bottles of red wine and a couple of large casks of ale rested on the kitchen table. The fridge was full of Newcastle Brown and Carlsberg Special Brew, except for the space taken up by litre bottles of screw-top Riesling. The four latecomers busied themselves pouring drinks, then wandered off to mingle. It was hot, dim and smoky. Kirsten went to stand by an open window to get some air. She drank cold lager from the can and watched the shadows prance and flail on the dance floor. Smoke curled up and drifted past her out of the window into the night.

She thought about the three years they had spent together and felt sad now they were all going their separate ways in the big, bad world beyond university – the *real* world, as everyone called it. What an odd bunch they'd made at the start. That first term, they had circled one another warily and shyly, away from home for the first time, all lost and alone, and none of them willing to admit it: Damon, the witty eighteenth-century scholar; Sarah, feminist criticism and women's fiction; Hugo, drama and poetry; herself, linguistics, specializing in phonology and dialects; and Galen, modernism with a touch of Marxism thrown in for good measure. Through tutorials, department social evenings and informal parties, they had made their tentative approaches and discovered kindred spirits. By the end of the first year, they had become inseparable.

Together, they had suffered the vicissitudes, the joys and the disappointments of youth: Kirsten consoled Sarah after her nasty affair with Felix Stapeley, her second-year tutor; Sarah fell out with Damon briefly over a disagreement on the validity of a feminist approach to literature; Galen stood up for Hugo, who failed his Anglo-Saxon exam and almost got sent down; and Hugo pretended to be miffed for a while when Kirsten took up with Galen instead of him.

After being close for so long, their lives were so intertwined that Kirsten found it hard to imagine a future without the others. But, she realized sadly, that was surely what she had to face. Even though she and Galen had planned to go and do postgraduate work in Toronto, things might not work out that way. One of them might not be accepted – and then what?

One of the dancers stumbled backwards and bumped into Kirsten. The lager foamed in the can and spilled over her hand. The drunken dancer just shrugged and got back to business. Kirsten laughed and put her can on the window sill. Having got the feel of the party at last, she launched herself into the shadowy crowd and chatted and danced till she was hot and tired. Then, finding that her half-full can had been used as an ashtray in her absence, she got some more lager and returned to her spot by the window. The Rolling Stones were singing 'Jumpin' Jack Flash'. Russell sure knew how to choose party music.

'How you doing?' It was Hugo, shouting in her ear.

'I'm all right,' she yelled back. 'A bit tired, that's all. I'll have to go soon.'

'How about a dance?'

Kirsten nodded and joined him on the floor. She didn't know if she was a good dancer or not, but she enjoyed herself. She liked moving her body to the beat of fast music, and the Stones were the best of all. With the Stones she felt a certain earthy, pagan power deep in her body, and when she danced to their music she shed all her inhibitions: her hips swung wildly and her arms drew abstract patterns in the air. Hugo danced less gracefully. His movements were heavier, more deliberate and limited than Kirsten's. He tended to lumber around a bit. It didn't matter to her, though; she hardly ever paid attention to the person she was dancing with, so bound up in her own world was she. The problem was, some men took her wild gyrations on the dance floor as an invitation to bed, which they most certainly were not.

The song ended and 'Time Is on My Side' came on, a slower number. Hugo moved closer and put his arms around her. She let him. It was only dancing, after all, and they were close friends. She rested her head on his shoulder and swayed to the music.

'I'll miss you, you know, Hugo,' she said as they danced. 'I do hope we can all still keep in touch.'

'We will,' Hugo said, turning his head so that she could hear him. 'None of us know what the hell we're going to be doing yet. On the dole, most likely. Or maybe we'll all come out and join you and Galen in Canada.'

'If we get there.'

He held her more closely and they stopped talking. The music carried them along. She could feel Hugo's warm breath in her hair, and his hand had slipped down her back to the base of her spine. The floor was getting more crowded. Everywhere they moved, they seemed to bump into another huddled couple. Finally, the song ended and Hugo guided her back towards the window as 'Street Fighting Man' came on.

When they'd both cooled down and had something to drink, he leaned forward and kissed her. It was so quick that she didn't have time to stop him. Then his arms were around her, running over her shoulders and buttocks, pulling her hips towards him. She struggled and broke away, instinctively wiping her mouth with the back of her hand.

'Hugo!'

'Oh, come on, Kirsten. It's our last chance, while we're still young. Who knows what might happen tomorrow?'

Kirsten laughed and punched him on the shoulder. She couldn't stay angry with him. 'Don't pull that "gather ye rosebuds" stuff with me, Hugo Lassiter. I'll say this for you, you don't give up trying, do you?'

Hugo grinned.

'But it's still no,' Kirsten said. 'I like you, you know that, but only as a friend.'

'I've got too many friends,' Hugo complained. 'What I want is to get laid.'

Kirsten gestured around the room. 'Well, I'm sure

you've got a good chance. If there's anyone here you haven't slept with already.'

'That's not fair. I know I've got a reputation, but it's completely unfounded.'

'Is it? How disappointing. And here was me thinking you were such an expert.'

'You could find out for yourself, you know,' he said, moving closer again. 'If you play your cards right.'

Kirsten laughed and wriggled out of his grasp. 'No. Anyway, I'm off home now. I've got to be up early to pack in the morning, especially if I'm to have time for lunch.'

'I'll walk you.'

'No you won't. It's not far.'

'But it's late. It's dangerous to walk out by yourself so late.'

'I've done it hundreds of times. You know I have. No thanks. You stay here. I don't want to end up fighting you off out there. I'd rather take my chances.'

Hugo sighed. 'And tomorrow we part, perhaps forever. You don't know what you're missing.'

'Nor do you,' she said, 'but I'm sure you'll soon forget all about it. Remember, tomorrow for lunch in the Green Dragon. Remind Sarah and Damon, too.'

'One o'clock?'

'That's right.' Kirsten pecked him on the cheek and skipped out into the warm night.

3

MARTHA

The room was perfect. Usually, a single room in a bed and breakfast establishment is nothing more than a cupboard by the toilets, but this one, clearly a converted attic with a dormer window and white-painted rafters, had been done out nicely. Candy-striped wallpaper brightened the walls, and a salmon-pink candlewick bedspread covered the three-quarter bed. Just to the left of the window stood the washstand, with clean white towels laid neatly over a chrome rail. The only other furniture consisted of a small wardrobe with metal hangers that jangled together when Martha opened the flimsy door, and a bedside lamp on a small chest of drawers.

The owner leaned against the door jamb with his arms folded while she made up her mind. He was a coarse man with hairy forearms and even more hair sticking out over the top of his white open-necked shirt. His face looked like it was made of pink vinyl, and six or seven long fair hairs curled on his chin.

'We don't get many girls staying by themselves,' he said, smiling at her with lashless blue eyes. It was obviously an invitation to state her business.

'Yes, well I'm here to do some research,' Martha lied. 'I'm working on a book.'

'A book, eh? Romance, is it? I suppose you'll find plenty of background for that here, what with the abbey ruins and the Dracula legends. Plenty of romance in all that history, I'd say.'

'It's not a romance,' Martha said.

He didn't pursue the matter further, but looked at her with a fixed expression, a mixture of superior, mocking humour and disbelief that she had often seen men use on professional women.

'I'll take it,' she said, mostly to get rid of him as quickly as possible. She didn't like the way he leaned against the doorway, arms folded, watching her. Was he hoping she'd start taking out her underwear to put in the drawers? The room began to feel claustrophobic.

He stood up straight. 'Right. Well, here's the keys. That big one there's for the front door. Come in any time you want, but try not to disturb the other guests. There's a lounge with a colour telly on the ground floor. You can make yourself a cup of tea or instant coffee there, too, if you like. But be sure to wash out your cup afterwards. The wife has enough on. Breakfast's at eight-thirty sharp. If you want an evening meal, let the wife know in the morning before you go out. Anything else?'

'Not that I can think of.'

He closed the door behind him as he left. Martha dumped her holdall on the bed and stretched. The sloping ceiling was so low at that point that her fingers touched the plaster between the beams. She poked her head out of the window to see what kind of view you got for nine pounds fifty a night. Not bad. On her right, very close, at the top of the street, loomed St Hilda's Church with its high, dark tower, like one of the monoliths from *2001*; to her left, on the opposite hillside over the estuary, stood St Mary's, built of lighter stone, with a smaller, squarish tower and a white pole sticking up from it like the mast of a ship. Beside it stood what was left of the abbey, where, according to her guidebook, the Synod of Whitby took place in 664 AD, when the churches in England dumped their Celtic ways and decided to follow Roman usages. The poet Caedmon had lived there at the time, too, and that was more interesting to Martha. After all, Caedmon was the one who had called her here.

She unpacked her toilet bag and went over to the sink to brush her teeth. The shrimp had left fibres between them and a salty taste in her mouth. As she spat out the water, she glimpsed her face in the mirror. It was the only part of her that hadn't changed much over the past year or so.

She wore her sandy hair cut short more for convenience than anything else. As she never had any reason to do herself up to look nice for anyone, it was far easier just to be able to wash it and forget about it. She didn't have to wear any make-up either, and that made for less fuss. Her complexion had always been clear anyway, and the smattering of freckles across her nose was hardly a blemish. Her eyes were a little Oriental – slanted almonds, and about the same light brown colour. Her nose tilted up slightly at the end – snub, they called it – and revealed the dark ovals of her nostrils. She had always thought it was her ugliest feature, but someone had once told her it was sexy. *Sexy!* Now *there* was a laugh! She had her mother's mouth: tight, thin-lipped, downturned at the edges.

All in all, she thought she looked haughty, stiff and aloof – prissy, in fact – but she knew well enough that her appearance had diverse effects on men. Not so long ago, she had overheard a conversation in a pub between two lads who had been giving her the eye all evening.

'Now there's a bird looks like she needs a bloody good fuck,' the first one had said.

'Rubbish,' his mate had replied. 'I'll bet she's had enough cock to pave the road from here to Land's End – ends up!' And they had laughed at that.

So much for her looks. Perhaps men just saw in her what they wanted to see. They used her as a mirror to reflect their own vile natures, or as a screen onto which they projected their obscene fantasies.

She put her toothbrush in the chrome holder on the wall and turned away from the mirror. It was early evening now. The tide would be on its way in.

She had enough money with her to survive away from home for far longer than she needed to, and though she was almost certain that this was the place where she would find what she was looking for, she knew there was always a chance she could be wrong. It might be one of the smaller fishing villages along the coast: Staithes, Runswick Bay or Robin Hood's Bay. No matter: she would check them all out if she had to. For now, Whitby felt right enough.

She was tired after her long journey. Maybe later, around sunset, she would go out and explore the town and find something to eat, but for now a nap was her best bet. First, though, she took what clothes she'd brought with her out of the holdall and put them in the drawers by the bed. There wasn't much, all of it casual: jeans, cords, denim shirts, a jersey, underwear. The grey quilted jacket in case of chilly evenings, she hung in the wardrobe.

Finally, she took out the most important thing she'd brought and smiled to herself at how it seemed to have become a ritual object, a talisman, and how simply handling it gave her a sense of awe and reverence.

It was a small, globe-shaped glass paperweight, flattened at the bottom, smooth and heavy on her palm. Ten pounds she'd paid for it at the craft centre. For ages she had stood there in the heat of the kilns and watched the man making the glassware he sold, explaining the process as he went along. He thrust the long blow-pipe into the white-hot heart of the furnace and brought out a blob of molten glass. Then he dipped this in the dishes of bright colours: vermilion, aquamarine, saffron, indigo. Martha had always thought you were supposed to keep blowing down the tube, but he had simply blown into it quickly and then covered the end with his hand. When the air heated, it expanded and puffed out the glass. She never did find out how he got the colours inside the paperweight, though, or how he made it so heavy and solid. This one was all dark shades of red: carmine, crimson and scarlet. The folds and curves they made looked like a rose. When Martha turned it in the light, the rose seemed to move slowly, as if under water. If ever she felt herself slipping away from her mission, denying her destiny, she knew that all she had to do was reach for it, and the smooth, hard glass would strengthen her resolve.

She placed it beside her on the bedspread and lay down. The rose seemed to open and pulse in the changing light as she stared into it. Soon she was sleeping soundly beside it.

4

KIRSTEN

Kirsten lingered on the pavement outside Oastler Hall and took a deep breath. She could still hear the music – Led Zeppelin's 'Stairway to Heaven' – above the muffled talk and laughter behind her. Taking stock of herself, she found that she didn't feel any more tipsy than she had earlier – less so, if anything. At the party she had drunk only about a can and a half of lager, and the dancing seemed to have driven much of the alcohol out of her system. She must have sweated it out, she supposed, considering the way her blouse was sticking to her.

The night was warm and muggy. There was no breeze to speak of, just an occasional breath of warm air such as one feels on opening an oven. Everything was still and quiet.

Kirsten headed for the park. She had crossed it plenty of times before, day and night, and never had any cause to worry about the journey. The worst that ever happened was that the gang of skinheads who hung out there early in the evening might hurl an insult or two at passing students. But the skins would all be tucked up safely in bed at this time of night.

Most of the houses in the area were old and far too large for one family these days, so they had been bought by landlords and divided into flats and bedsits for the students. It was a comfortable neighbourhood, Kirsten thought. No matter what time of day or night, if you had a problem or just wanted a cup of tea and a chat, there was always likely to be someone you knew burning the midnight oil not much more than five or ten minutes' walk away. Like a village within the city, really. Even now, soft, inviting lights burned behind many of the windows. She would miss it all very much. This was the place where she had grown up, lost her virginity, changed from a shy, awkward teenager into a wiser, more confident woman.

The park was a large square bordered on all sides by well-lit roads. Tree-lined avenues criss-crossed the cropped grass. In the daytime, students would lie out in the sun reading or playing makeshift games of cricket or football. Up near the main road were the public toilets – said to be a favourite haunt of local homosexuals – and colourful flower beds. At the centre of the park, thick shrubbery grew around the bowling green and the children's playground.

At night the place felt a little spookier, perhaps because there was no lighting in the park itself. But you could always see the tall, amber street lights on the roads, and the sound of nearby traffic was comforting.

Kirsten's trainers made no sound on the tarmac as she followed the path under the dark trees. There was very little traffic about. The only thing she could hear was the odd car revving up in the distance and the sound of her shoulder bag brushing against her hips. Somewhere, a dog barked. The sky was clear and the stars, magnified by the haze, looked fatter and softer than usual. How different from winter stars, Kirsten thought, all cold and sharp and merciless. These ones looked like they were melting. She looked up and turned her head in all directions but couldn't find a moon. It had to be there somewhere – perhaps behind the trees.

Yes, she would miss it all. But Canada would be exciting, especially if Galen came, too, as he intended. Neither of them had ever crossed the Atlantic before. If they could save enough money, they would take a few months after completing their courses and travel the continent together: Montreal, New York, Boston, Washington, Miami, Los Angeles, San Francisco, Vancouver. Even the names sent shivers of excitement up Kirsten's spine. Three years ago she could never have imagined doing such a thing. University hadn't only given her a first-class education, it had given her freedom and independence, too.

Soon she got to the centre of the park, near the bowling green. The whole tract of land was slightly convex, and this was the highest part. She could see lights in all directions, defining the valleys and hillsides upon which the city was built. Because of the warm, moist air, the far-off street lights all had haloes.

Just off the path stood a statue of a lion with a serpent coiled around it. Kirsten had noticed the other day that some idiot – perhaps the skinheads – had spray-painted its head blue and scrawled filthy graffiti in red all over its body. That didn't matter in the dark, though, and she decided to give in to an impulse she had often felt.

Swishing over the grass, she went up to the statue and ran her hand over the still-warm stone. Then, with sudden resolve, she jumped astride it.

The lion was small enough that her feet easily touched the ground. Down the path, she could see through the trees to the lights on the main road and the turning into her own street, only a few hundred yards away. To think she had been here all this time and had always wanted to sit on the lion but hadn't done so until now, her last night. She must have passed it at least a thousand times. She felt silly, but at the same time she was enjoying herself tremendously. At least nobody was watching.

She gripped the smooth mane and pretended she was riding through the jungle. In her mind, she could hear screeching cockatoos, chattering monkeys, humming and clicking insects, and snakes slithering through the undergrowth. She raised her head to look for the moon again, but before she could find it, she noticed a strange smell and, a split second later, felt a rough hand cover her mouth and nose.

5

MARTHA

The tide was in when Martha walked back under the whale's jawbone to Pier Road, and the small fishing boats bobbed at their moorings in the harbour. The sun was going down behind West Cliff, and, at the top of the hill opposite, St Mary's Church shone warm gold in the last rays.

There was still nothing happening in the auction sheds, but some of the locals seemed to be pottering around on their own small boats.

Martha leaned against the railing on St Ann's Staith and watched two men in navy-blue jerseys washing the deck of a red sailboat. She had brought her quilted jacket with her, but the air was still so warm that she carried it slung over her shoulder. As night came in, the fishy smell of the place seemed to grow stronger.

Something about the air made her crave a cigarette. She had never smoked before the past year, but now she didn't care one way or another. Whatever she felt like, she would do, and damn the consequences.

She went into a small gift shop near the Dracula Museum and bought ten Rothmans; that would do for a while at least. Then she went back to the railing and lit a cigarette. One of the men down in the boat glanced up at her admiringly from time to time, but he didn't call out or whistle. She was waiting for them to speak. Finally, one said something technical to the other, who replied in equally incomprehensible jargon, and Martha moved on.

She was hungry, she realized, dropping the cigarette and grinding it out with the ball of her foot on the stone quay. Down by the bridge she saw people ambling along, eating from cardboard cartons of fish and chips. She hadn't noticed any other kind of food available so far; the place was hardly crammed with French, Italian or Indian restaurants, and she hadn't even seen a McDonald's or a Pizza Hut yet. Clearly, it was a fish-and-chips-or-nothing kind of town.

At the first fish bar she found, she bought haddock and chips and wandered around by the bus station as she ate. The fish was fried in batter, of course, and had a kind of oily taste because the skin had been left on. It was good, though, and Martha licked her fingers when she'd finished, then carefully dumped the carton in a litter bin.

It was almost dark now. She stood on the bridge for a while, smoking another cigarette to take away the greasy taste. In the lower harbour, the rusted hulk she had seen earlier was still at dock. On the north side of the bridge, where the estuary widened towards the sea, strings of red and yellow quayside lights reflected in the dark water, twisting and bending as it lapped, like people's reflections in funfair mirrors. On its cliff-top, St Mary's stood floodlit against the dark violet sky.

Martha walked over the bridge to Church Street, in the oldest section of town just below East Cliff, stopping to buy a newspaper on her way, just before the shop closed. It was that quiet time after dinner and before bed. Places like Whitby shut down early. Martha was thirsty, but already the Monk's Haven cafe was shut; there was nowhere you could just drop in for a cup of tea or coffee. She also needed to sit down and think for a while.

The Black Horse pub across the street looked inviting enough. Martha went in. Antique brass fixtures attached to the walls shed real gaslight on the small, wainscoted room. The lounge was cosy, with narrow, pew-like wooden benches and scored oblong tables. It was also quiet.

Martha bought a half of bitter and found a free corner. A few years ago, she would never have thought of even entering a pub by herself, let alone sitting in one. But this place felt safe enough. The few people who were there seemed to know each other and were already involved in conversation. There were no lone wolves on the lookout for female flesh; it clearly wasn't a pick-up joint.

She glanced quickly through the copy of the *Independent* she'd bought. Finding nothing of interest, she folded the paper and put it aside. What she really had to do, she thought, was work out some kind of plan. Nothing too detailed or elaborate, because she had recently learned that serendipity and intuition played a greater part in events than anyone imagined. And she had to remember that she wasn't alone in her task; she had spirits to guide her. Nonetheless, she couldn't just wander the place aimlessly for days. Right now, it was all right; she was finding her way around, becoming familiar with the environment. There were certain spots she needed to know about: sheltered places, isolated paths, the shadows of the town. But she needed a plan of action.

Taking out a small notebook and her guidebook, she set to work. First of all, she scanned the map and made a note of places that looked like they were worth exploring: the beach area, St Mary's graveyard, the abbey grounds, a long cliff walk towards Robin Hood's Bay.

Then she turned her mind to a more serious problem: where could she find someone who actually *lived* and worked in Whitby? Where would he be likely to live, for example? So far she had seen no one but holidaymakers and those residents who ran guesthouses, pubs and shops. Nobody else actually seemed to live around the harbour area, where the men worked on their boats.

She flipped back to her map to see how far the town spread. It was small, with a population of about thirteen thousand, and East Cliff didn't seem to extend much at all beyond St Mary's. That left the southern area, further inland along the Esk estuary, and West Cliff itself. Up there, according to her map, housing estates seemed to stretch almost as far as Sandsend. And then there were smaller places nearby, like Sandsend itself, and Robin Hood's Bay. They weren't exactly suburbs, but it was possible that some people lived there and commuted to and from Whitby.

At one time, she might have felt as if she was looking for a needle in a haystack. After all, she had so little to go on. But she trusted her instincts now. There could be no doubt about it; she would know when she had found the one she was looking for. Her spirits would help guide her towards him. And Whitby felt like the right place; she could sense his nearness.

Martha sipped her beer. Somebody put an old rock and roll song on the jukebox and it reminded her of something a long time ago, another evening listening to old songs on a jukebox. She shut it out. Memories and sentiment were luxuries she couldn't afford these days. She stuck her hand in her holdall and felt for the smooth, hard sphere.

6

KIRSTEN

A long, oily blackness punctuated by quick, vivid dreams. A figure hunched over her, dark and hooded, and a blade flashed. It seemed to slice at her skin. Long cuts flapped open and blood welled, but there was no pain. She saw, as if from a great distance, the sharp steel pierce the pale flesh of her thigh. It went in deep and when it slid out, blood oozed around the edges of the gash. But she felt nothing at all. Then the darkness came again.

This time it was a figure all in white, a human shape with no face. The same things happened. The knife was different, but it cut just like the other, and again there was no sensation.

They were all just dreams. She couldn't possibly see these things, could she? Her eyes were closed. And if they had really happened, then she would have screamed out in agony from the pain, wouldn't she?

7

MARTHA

A loud shrieking woke Martha at four o'clock in the morning. She turned over in bed and frowned as she looked at the luminous dial of her watch. The row went on. It sounded very close. Finally, she realized it was the seagulls. They must have found a shoal of fish, or perhaps a cat had spilled the dustbin at the back of one of the fish bars and they had zoomed in on that. It was a terrible noise: the sound of raw hunger and greed. She pictured the gulls ripping dead fish apart, blank white faces speckled with blood.

She sighed and turned over again, pulling the sheet up around her ears. The gulls had woken her from a dream. Maybe she could get back to it. All her dreams were good these days – technicolour jaunts of indescribable beauty, full of ecstasy and excitement, visits to alien worlds, flying easily through space and time.

They hadn't always been like that. For a long time she had suffered from terrifying nightmares, dreams of blood and shadows, and then for a while she hadn't seemed to dream at all. The good dreams only started when the dark cloud in her mind disappeared. At least, she had always thought of it as a cloud, or perhaps a bubble. It was opaque, and whichever way she looked at it, it always deflected the light so that she couldn't see inside. She knew it was filled with all her agony and anger, yet it refused her entry.

For so long she had walked around on the edge because of that cloud inside her. Always on the verge of violence, despair or madness. But then one day, when she found the right perspective, she saw inside and the darkness dispersed like a monster that vanishes when you discover its true name.

The seagulls were still wailing over their early breakfast when Martha drifted off to sleep again and dreamed about her secret lake. Its waters flowed from the fountain of youth, clear and sparkling in the sun that never stopped shining, and she had to swim through narrow coral caverns to get to it. Only she knew about the lake. Only she could swim so effortlessly so far without the need for breath. And as she swam, the sharp, pinkish coral cut thin red lines across her breasts, stomach and thighs.

8

KIRSTEN

The first thing Kirsten saw when she opened her eyes was a long curving crack in the white ceiling. It looked like an island coastline or the crude outline of a whale. Her mouth was dry and tasted bad. With difficulty, she swallowed, but the vile taste wouldn't go away. Around her she could hear only quiet sounds: a steady hissing; a high-pitched, rhythmic bleeping. She couldn't smell anything at all.

She moved her head and glimpsed shadowy figures sitting beside her bed. It was difficult to focus from so close, and she couldn't make out who they were. Then she became aware of muffled voices.

'Look, she's coming round . . . she's opened her eyes.'

'Careful . . . don't touch her . . . she'll wake up in her own time.'

And someone bent over her: a faceless figure all in white. Kirsten tried to scream, but no sound came out. Gentle hands touched her brow and pushed her shoulders firmly back onto the hard bed. She let her head fall on the pillow again and sighed. The voices were clearer now, like a finely tuned radio.

'Is she all right? Can we stay and talk to her?'

'She'll talk if she wants to. Don't push her. She's bound to be feeling disoriented.'

Kirsten tried to speak but her mouth was still too dry. She croaked, 'Water,' and someone seemed to understand. An angled straw neared her mouth and she sucked greedily on it. Some of the water dribbled down the edges of her dry, cracked lips, but she managed to swallow a little. That felt better.

'I must go and fetch the doctor.'

The door opened and hissed shut slowly.

'Kirstie? Kirstie, love?'

She turned her head again and found it easier to focus this time. Her mother and father sat beside her. She tried to smile but it felt like it came out all crooked. Her teeth felt too big for her mouth. Her mother looked beside herself, as if she hadn't slept for days, and her father had dark heavy bags under his eyes. He looked down on her with a mixture of love and relief.

'Hello, Daddy,' she said.

He reached out and she felt his soft hand close on hers, just like when they used to go for walks in the woods when she was a child.

'Oh, Kirstie,' her mother said, taking out a handkerchief from her handbag and dabbing her eyes. 'We were so worried.'

Her father still said nothing. His touch told Kirsten all she needed to know.

'What about? Where . . .'

'Don't try to speak,' her father said softly. 'It's all right. It's all over now. Everything's going to be all right.'

Her mother was still patting away at her eyes and making little snuffling noises.

Kirsten rolled onto her back again and stared at the scar on the ceiling. She licked her dry lips. Sensation was returning to her bit by bit. Now she could catch the clean, white, antiseptic smell of the hospital room. She could also feel her body. Her skin felt taut, stretched too tightly over her flesh and bones. In places, it pinched at her as if it had snagged on something and puckered.

But worse than that was the burning ache in her breasts and in her loins. She had no sensation of the tight flesh there, just of a painful, throbbing absence.

The door opened and a white-coated man walked over to her. She flinched and tried to roll away.

'It's all right,' she heard someone say. 'The doctor's here to take care of you.'

Then she felt her sleeve pulled up, and a cool swab touched her arm. She didn't feel the needle going in, but it made a sharp prick when it slid out. The pain began to recede. Warm, soothing waves came to carry it far out to sea.

Her senses ebbed and the long darkness advanced to reclaim her. As she slipped away, she could still feel her father's hand in hers. She turned her head slowly and asked, 'What's happened to me, Daddy? My skin feels funny. It doesn't fit right.'

9

MARTHA

When Martha got downstairs for breakfast the next morning, the other guests were already seated. Only one small table, set for two, remained. Beyond the bay window, the sun was shining on Abbey Terrace, and the sky was blue again.

By the door stood a help-yourself trolley: jugs of orange or grapefruit juice; milk and miniature packets of Corn Flakes, Special K, Rice Krispies, Alpen and Frosties. Martha took some Alpen, poured herself a glass of juice and sat down. She helped herself to a cup of tea from the stainless-steel pot on the table. Judging by its colour, the tea had been stewing too long. She looked at the place opposite her and hoped that no one would join her for breakfast. Never very cheerful first thing in the morning, she had just about managed to nod and say hello to the others. Conversation would be out of the question.

As she sipped the bitter tea, she cast her eyes around the room. In the bay window sat an old couple. The man's dark brown hair was swept straight back from his wrinkled forehead and plastered down with Brylcreem. He had smiled when she came in, showing a set of stained and crooked teeth. His greyish face had the lined and hollow look of a fifty-a-day man, and his breath came in short emphysematic gasps, confirming the diagnosis. His wife hadn't smiled. She had simply stared at Martha with suspicious, beady eyes, as if to say, 'I know your type, young lady.' Blue-grey hair hovered around her moon-shaped head like mist.

By the opposite wall sat a young couple, probably on their honeymoon, Martha guessed. They both looked very serious. The man was thin, swarthy, bearded, and precise in his tea-pouring; the woman's face, as she sat bowed forward, was almost completely hidden by a cascade of glossy black hair. When she looked up at him, a shy, secret smile lit her eyes. They hadn't even noticed Martha come in.

Most of the noise came from the third table, near the serve-yourself trolley, where a tired-looking young woman and an equally exhausted man both struggled to put on a brave face as they tried to control two finicky youngsters. The children looked like twins: same blond colouring, same whiny voices: 'I don't *like* Shreddies, Daddy! Why aren't there any Sugar Puffs? I want Sugar Puffs!' 'Have some Frosties,' the pale mother said, trying to placate them, but to no avail. She glanced up and smiled weakly at the others. The father, dressed for a day on the beach in white slacks and a pale blue sports shirt showing the curly ginger hairs on his forearms, looked over and gave Martha a what-can-you-do-with-them shrug.

The owner's wife came in to take their orders. Not that there was much choice: you could have your eggs soft or hard, your bacon medium or crispy. There was a determined set to the woman's mouth, and she moved about her business with a brusque, no-nonsense certainty, all the while managing to smile and respond to small talk about the weather. Perhaps if anyone wore the pants around here, Martha thought, it was the wife. Her husband probably had a day job and only happened to be around because Martha had arrived late in the afternoon. Perhaps he was even a fisherman. If she could get a chance to chat casually with him, she might be able to find out something about how the local operation worked.

Just after she had given her order for crispy bacon and medium-poached eggs, the final guest came down, ordered and helped himself to cereal and juice, which he brought over to Martha's table and plonked down opposite her. He was tall and athletic-looking, probably a jogger, with a deep suntan, thin face, aquiline nose and lively blue eyes. His short, curly black hair still glistened from the shower. He smelled of Old Spice aftershave.

He poured some tea and grinned broadly, showing a perfect set of dazzling teeth, the kind one rarely sees in English mouths. My God, Martha thought, a morning person. Probably been for a run around the town before breakfast. She managed to muster a tiny, brief smile, then looked away again to see how the couple were coping with the two kids.

'Sleep well?'

'Pardon?'

The young man leaned forward again and lowered his voice. 'I said, did you sleep well?'

'Fine, thank you.'

'I didn't.'

'Oh?'

'Just put me right next to the bathroom, didn't they? Six o'clock the blooming parade starts – one after the other – and they all have to flush the loo. I think the pipes run right through my bed. Talk about clatter and bang. Keith's the name, by the way.' He stuck out his hand and smiled. 'Keith McLaren.' His accent was

Australian, certainly, Martha thought, but as she had specialized only in regional British accents, she couldn't pin it down to any specific area.

Martha took his hand reluctantly and gave it a quick, limp shake. 'Martha Browne.'

'And before you ask, yes, I'm an Aussie. I'm just taking a little time off from university to travel this lovely country of yours.'

'You're a student?'

'Yes. Master's degree in surfing and sunbathing at Bondi Beach University.' He laughed. 'Not true. Wish it were. I'm studying law, not half as interesting. I'm making my way up the coast to Scotland. Got some family there.'

Martha nodded politely.

'Seagulls, too,' Keith said, apropos of nothing, as far as Martha could make out.

'What?'

'Bloody seagulls kept me awake too. Didn't you hear them?'

'Seagulls, you say?' The owner's wife arrived at their table and set down two plates, which she held with worn oven gloves. 'Mind, they're hot. Seagulls, eh? You get used to them if you live here. Have to.'

'They never wake you up?' Keith asked her.

'Never. Not after the first couple of months.'

''Fraid I won't be here that long.' He looked at Martha again. 'Moving on tomorrow. Travelling by local buses whenever I can. Walking or hitching if I can't.'

'Well, good luck to you,' the woman said, and moved on.

Keith stared at his plate and prodded a dark medallion of reddish black stuff with his fork. 'What's that?' he asked, turning up his nose and leaning forward to whisper. 'Whatever it is, I don't remember asking for it.'

Martha examined the contents of his plate. They were the same as hers: bacon, egg, grilled tomato and mushrooms, fried bread, and the thing that Keith was pointing to. 'Black pudding, I think,' she said. 'Must be today's special.'

'What's it made of?'

'You don't want to know. Not at this time in the morning.'

Keith laughed and tucked in. 'Well, it sure tastes all right. That's what I like about staying at these places. They always give you a breakfast that sets you up for the entire day. I won't need much more than a sandwich till the evening meal. Are you eating here?'

'Not in the evenings, no.'

'Oh, you should. I usually come back. Well, I say usually, but this is only my third day. They do a decent spread. Good value, too.'

When he went back to his food he stopped talking and left Martha in peace. She ate quickly, hoping to get away before he started up again, even though she knew a rushed meal would give her indigestion. Across the room, one of the children flicked a slice of tomato at the wall with his spoon. It splattered on the faded rose-patterned paper and slithered down, leaving a pink trail behind. His father reddened and took the spoon from him angrily, and his mother looked as if she was about to die from embarrassment.

Martha pushed her chair back and stood up to leave. 'Excuse me,' she said to Keith. 'Must be off. Lots to do.'

'Aren't you going to finish your cup of tea?' Keith asked.

'I've had two already. Anyway, it's stewed.' And she hurried upstairs to her room. There, she locked the door, opened the window and enjoyed a cigarette as she leaned on the sill and looked at the small white clouds over St Mary's.

After she'd finished the Rothmans and paid a visit to the toilet, she picked up her holdall and set off down the stairs again. At the first-floor landing, she bumped into Keith coming out of his room. Just my luck, she thought.

'Want to show me around?' he asked. 'What with both of us being alone here . . . Well, it seems a shame.'

'I'm sure you know more about the place than I do. I've just arrived, and you've been here three days already.'

'Yes, but you're a native. I'm just a poor ignorant foreigner.'

'I'm sorry,' Martha said, 'but I've got work to do.'

'Oh? What would that be, then?'

'Research. I'm working on a book.'

They were walking down the last flight of carpeted stairs to the hallway. Martha couldn't just break away from him. She wanted to see which way he turned in the street so that she could walk the other way.

'Well, maybe we can have a drink this evening, after you've finished work and I've worn out my poor feet?'

'I'm sorry, I don't know what time I'll be finished.'

'Oh, come on. Say seven o'clock, all right? You know what they say: "All work and no play . . ." There's a nice, quiet little pub just on the corner at the end of the street. The Lucky Fisherman, I think it's called. Is it a date? I'm away tomorrow anyway, so you'll only have to put up with me the once.'

Martha thought quickly. They had passed the door

now and were already walking down the front steps to the path. If she said no, it would look very odd indeed, and the last thing she wanted was to appear conspicuous in any way. It was bad enough being a woman by herself here. If she acted strangely, then this Keith might just have cause to remember her as some kind of oddball, and that wouldn't do at all. On the other hand, if she did agree to have a drink with him, he would no doubt ask her all kinds of questions about her life. Still, she thought, there was no reason why she couldn't tell him a pack of lies. That should be easy enough for a woman with her imagination.

'All right,' she said as they reached the gate. 'Seven o'clock in the Lucky Fisherman.'

Keith smiled. 'Great. See you then. Have a good day.'

He turned left, and Martha turned right.

10
KIRSTEN

When Kirsten drifted out of the comforting darkness for the second time, she noticed the vases of red and yellow flowers and the cards standing on her bedside table. Then she turned her head and saw a stranger sitting at the other side of the bed. She gripped the sheets around her throat and looked around the rest of the room. The white-smocked nurse still hovered in the background – that, at least, was reassuring – and sitting against the wall by the door was a man in a light grey suit with a notebook on his lap and a pencil poised, ready to write. Kirsten couldn't focus all that clearly on him, but he looked too young to be as bald as he seemed.

The man beside her leaned forward and rested his chin on his fists. He was about her father's age – early fifties – with short, spiky grey hair and a red complexion. His eyes were brown, and a tiny wen grew between his right eye and his nose. Wedged between his left nostril and his upper lip was a dark mole with a couple of hairs sprouting from it. He wore a navy-blue suit, white shirt and a black and amber striped tie. His expression was kindly and concerned.

'How are you feeling, Kirsten?' he asked. 'Do you feel like talking?'

'A bit groggy,' she replied. 'Can you tell me what's happened to me? Nobody's told me anything.'

'You were attacked. You've been hurt, but you're going to be all right.'

'Who are you? Are you a doctor?'

'I'm Detective Superintendent Elswick. The bright young lad over by the door there is Detective Sergeant Haywood. We're here to see if you can tell us anything that might help us catch whoever did this.'

Kirsten shook her head. 'It's all dark . . . I . . . I can't . . .'

'Stay calm,' Elswick said softly. 'Don't struggle with it. Just relax and let me ask the questions. If you don't know the answers, shake your head or say no. Don't get worked up about it. All right?'

Kirsten swallowed. 'I'll try.'

'Good. You were at a party the night it happened. Do you remember that?'

'Yes. Vaguely. There was music, dancing. It was the end of term bash.'

'That's right. Now, as far as we can gather, you left alone at about one o'clock. Am I right?'

'I . . . I think so. I don't remember the time. I did go out by myself, though. It was a lovely warm night.' Kirsten remembered standing by the door of Oastler Hall and breathing in the honeyed air.

'And then you walked through the park.'

'Yes. It's a short cut. I've done it lots of times. Nothing ever—'

'Relax, Kirsten. We know. Nobody's blaming you. Don't get upset about it. Now, did you notice anyone else around at all?'

'No. It was quiet. There was no one.'

'Did you hear anything?'

'Only the cars on the road.'

'Nobody left the party and followed you?'

'I didn't see anyone.'

'Were you aware at any time of someone following you?'

'No. I suppose I might have run if I had been. But no.'

'What about earlier in the evening? As I understand it, you were at a pub with some friends: the Ring O'Bells. Is that right?'

Kirsten nodded.

'Did you notice anyone taking an unusual interest in you, anyone who seemed to be watching you closely?'

'No.'

'Any strangers there?'

'I . . . I don't remember. It was busy earlier, but . . .

'There was some trouble, wasn't there? Could you tell me about it?'

Kirsten told him what she could remember about the incident with the landlord. It seemed so silly now; she felt embarrassed to think of it.

'So you and your friends were the last to leave?'

'Yes.'

'And you didn't see anyone hanging around outside?'

'No.'

'What about the attack itself? Do you remember anything about how it happened?'

Kirsten closed her eyes and confronted only darkness. It was as if a black cloud had formed somewhere in her mind, and inside it was trapped everything that this man wanted to know. The rest of her – memories, feelings, sensations – could only circle the thick darkness helplessly. It was a chunk of her life, a package of pain and terror that had been wrapped up and hidden away in the dark. She didn't know if she could penetrate it, or if she wanted to; inside, she sensed, lived horrors too monstrous to confront.

'I was looking for the moon,' she said.

'What?'

'I sat on the lion – you know, that statue in the middle of the park – and I threw my head back. I was looking for the moon. I know it sounds silly. I wasn't drunk or anything. It's just that it was my last night and I'd always wanted to . . . to just . . . sit. That's all I can remember.'

'What happened?'

'When? What do you mean?'

'You were sitting on the lion looking for the moon. What happened next?'

Superintendent Elswick's voice was soft and hypnotic. It was making Kirsten feel sleepy again. Now that she had come round fully, she could feel her aching body with its tight skin, and she wanted to sail out on the tide again and leave it behind.

'A hand,' she said. 'That's all I remember. A hand came from behind, over my nose and mouth. I couldn't breathe. And then it all went black.'

'You didn't see anyone?'

'No. I'm sorry . . . I . . . There was something . . .'

'Yes?'

Kirsten frowned and shook her head. 'It's no good. I can't remember.'

'Don't worry about it, Kirsten. Just take it slowly. You can't remember anything at all about the person who attacked you, no matter how insignificant it might seem?'

'No. Only the hand.'

'What was the hand like? Was it big or small?'

'I . . . I . . . it's hard to say. It covered my nose and mouth . . . It was strong. And rough.'

'Rough? In what way?'

'Like someone who's done a lot of hard work, I suppose. You know, lifting things. I don't know. I've never felt a hand that rough before. We had a gardener once, and his hands looked like this one felt. I never touched them, but they looked rough and calloused from doing manual work.'

'This gardener,' Elswick said, 'what's his name?'

'It was a long time ago. I was just a little girl.'

'Do you remember his name, Kirsten?'

'I think it was Walberton. My daddy called him Mal. Short for Malcolm, I suppose. But I don't see why—'

'At this point, Kirsten, we know nothing. We need everything we can get. Everything. No matter how absurd it seems. Is the gardener still around?'

'No, not any more. Daddy knows. He'll tell you.'

'All right. Is there anything else?'

'I don't think so. I can't remember what happened after the hand grabbed me. How long have I been here?'

'Ten days. That's why we have to act as quickly as we can. The more time goes by, the harder it is to pick up a trail. Can you think of anyone who might have wanted to harm you? Any enemies? An angry boyfriend, perhaps?'

Ten days! It was hard to believe. What had she been doing here for ten days? Just sleeping and dreaming? She shook her head. 'No, there's only Galen. There's no one who'd do something like this. I don't understand it. I never did any harm to anyone in my life.' Tears began to trickle from the corners of her eyes into the fine hair above her ears. 'I'm tired. I hurt.' She felt herself fading again and didn't want to stop.

'That's all right,' Elswick said. 'You've been very helpful. We'll go now and let you get some rest.' He stood up and patted her arm, then nodded to Sergeant Haywood that it was time to go. 'I'll come back and see you again soon, Kirsten, when you're feeling better. Your mother and father are still here, waiting outside. Do you want to see them?'

'Later,' Kirsten said. 'Wait. Where's Galen? Have you seen Galen?'

'Your boyfriend? Yes,' Elswick said. 'He was here. He said he'd come back. He left those flowers.' He pointed to a vase of red roses.

When Elswick and Haywood left, the nurse came over to straighten the bed. Just as the door was closing, Kirsten could hear Elswick saying, 'Better keep a man here twenty-four hours a day . . . Might come back to finish what he started.'

Before the nurse could move away, Kirsten grabbed her wrist.

'What's happened to me?' she whispered. 'My skin feels tight and twisted. Something's wrong.'

The nurse smiled. 'That'll be the stitches, dearie. They do pull a bit sometimes.' She ruffled the pillow and hurried out.

Stitches! Kirsten had had stitches before when she fell off her bicycle and cut her arm on some broken glass. It was true, they did pull. But those stitches had been put in her arm; she had felt only very minor, localized pain. If stitches were the cause of her discomfort this time, then why did her whole body feel as if it had been sewn tightly and ineptly around its frame?

She could have a look, of course. Ease down the covers and open her nightdress. Surely nothing could be simpler. But the effort was too much for her. She could manage the movements all right, but what really stopped her was fear: fear of what she might find. Instead, she welcomed oblivion.

11
MARTHA

There were no names on the gravestones. Martha stood in the cliff-top cemetery by St Mary's and stared in horror. Most of the stones were blackened around their edges, and where the chiselled details should have been, there was just pitted sandstone. On some of them, she could see faint traces of lettering, but many were completely blank. It must be the salt wind, she thought, come from the sea and stolen their names away. It made her feel suddenly and inexplicably sad. She looked down at the ruffled blue water and the thin line of foam as waves broke along the beach. It didn't seem fair. The dead should be remembered, as she remembered them. Shivering despite the heat, she wandered over to the church itself.

It was an impressive place inside. She skipped the taped lecture and, instead, picked up a printed guide and wandered around. At the front stood a huge, three-tier pulpit, and below it stretched a honeycomb of rectangular box pews said to resemble the ''tween-decks' of a wooden battleship. Some of the boxes had engraved brass nameplates screwed to their doors, marking them out as reserved for notable local families. Most of these were at the back, where the minister would have a hard time seeing because of all the fluted pillars in the way. The rich could sleep with impunity through his sermons. But at the front, right under his eyes, some boxes were marked FREE, and others, FOR STRANGERS ONLY.

That's me, Martha thought, opening the catch on one and stepping inside: a stranger only.

When the latch clicked behind her, the small enclosure gave her an odd sense of isolation and sanctuary within the busy church. All around her, tourists walked and cameras flashed, but the box seemed to muffle and distance the outside world. A fanciful idea, to be sure, but it was what she felt. She ran her finger along the worn green baize that lined the sides of the box and the pew bench itself. There was even a red carpet, and patterned cushions to kneel on. Martha's knees cracked as she knelt. Now she was even further away from the world outside. It would make a good place to hide, if things should ever come to that, she thought. Nobody would be able to find her in a box pew marked FOR STRANGERS ONLY. It was just like being invisible. She smiled and let herself out.

Through the car park by the abbey ruin was a footpath, part of the Cleveland Way. According to Martha's map, it would take her all the way from East Cliff to Robin Hood's Bay. For the moment, she decided to explore just a short stretch of it. As she walked, she kept her eyes open for Keith McLaren, just as she had done while touring the cemetery and church. She already had a good idea of the story she would tell him that evening, and if he did happen to see her walking around St Mary's and the cliff-top, then her lies would gain even more credibility. She didn't want to run into him by accident, though.

A narrow boardwalk ran right along the edge of the high cliffs. In places, some of the cross-boards were missing, and erosion had eaten away the land right up to the path itself. There was a fence between the walk and the sheer drop, but even that was down here and there, and signs warned people to tread carefully and to walk in single file. It was dizzying to look down on the sea swirling around the sharp rocks way below.

When she got to Saltwick Nab, a long knobbly finger of rock jutting out into the sea, Martha noticed ramshackle wooden stairs and a path leading down. Slowly, she made her way to the pinkish-red rock. It started near the base of the cliff as a big hump, then dropped so that it was hardly visible above the water for a short distance, and finally rose to another knob – rather like a submerged camel with a long way between humps, she thought – further out to sea. There was nobody else around, so Martha sat down on the sparse grass for a rest. In the distance, between the humps, a white tanker was slowly making its way across the horizon. Waves caught the low section of the nab sideways on and spray cascaded over it in a shower of white.

Martha lit her second cigarette of the day. It tasted different out in the fresh, salt air. She crossed her legs and contemplated the rhythms of the sea as it swelled and slapped against the rock. Soon, she could see the waves coming and predict how hard they would break.

She had got the feel of the place now; so much so that she felt quite at home. There were no problems as far as she could see – except perhaps for the Australian. But even he seemed naive and harmless enough. She could string him along over a couple of drinks, and tomorrow he'd be gone. All she had to do now was find the one she was looking for. It might take a day or two, but she would succeed. He was close; of that there could be no doubt. Again, she felt a shiver of fear, and her confidence wavered. When the time came, she would have to summon up the nerve and do what had to be done. She slipped her hand into the holdall and felt for her talisman. That would help her, of course – that and her guiding spirits.

After a while, she flicked her cigarette into the sea and stood up. Fear is for the passive, she told herself. When you act, you don't have time to feel afraid. She brushed the grass and sand from her jeans and headed back towards the footpath.

12

KIRSTEN

The nurse popped her head around the door. 'A visitor for you, dearie.' Beyond her, Kirsten could make out the shoulder of the uniformed policeman sitting outside her room. Then the door opened all the way and Sarah walked in.

'Sarah! What are you doing here?'

'Some welcome! Actually, it wasn't easy. First I had to get permission from that bloody detective superintendent. And as if that wasn't enough, I had to get past Dixon of Dock Green out there.' She jerked her thumb towards the door, then pulled up a chair and sat beside the bed. For a long moment, she just looked at Kirsten, then she started to cry. She leaned forward and the two of them hugged as best they could without dislodging the intravenous drip.

'Come on,' Kirsten said finally, patting her back. 'You're hurting my stitches.'

Sarah moved away and managed a smile. 'Sorry, love. I don't know what came over me. When I think of everything you must have been through . . .'

'Don't,' Kirsten said. The way she felt, she needed Sarah to be her usual self: outrageous, down-to-earth, solid, funny, angry. She was sick of sympathy; even less did she want empathy. 'It's no wonder you had a hard time getting in, dressed like that,' she hurried on. Sarah wore her usual uniform of jeans and a T-shirt. This one bore a logo scrawled boldly across the front: A WOMAN NEEDS A MAN LIKE A FISH NEEDS A BICYCLE. 'They probably think you're a terrorist.'

Sarah laughed and wiped her eyes with the back of her hand. 'So how are you, then, kid?'

'I'm all right, I suppose.' And it was partly true. That day, Kirsten did feel a bit better – at least physically. Her skin felt more like its old self, and the frightening internal aches had diminished during the night. She felt numb inside, though, and she still hadn't found the courage to look at herself.

'Do I look a mess?'

Sarah frowned and examined her features. 'Not so bad. Most of the bruises seem to have gone, and there's no permanent damage to your face, no disfigurement. In fact, I wouldn't say you look much worse than usual.'

'Thanks a lot.' But Kirsten smiled as she spoke. Sarah was clearly back to normal after her brief bout of tears.

'You must have taken a hell of a beating, though.'

'I must?'

'You mean you don't know?'

'Nobody's told me what happened.'

'That's typical of bloody doctors, that is. I suppose he's a man?'

'Yes.'

'Well, there you are, then. What about the nurse?'

'She seems too timid to talk much.'

'Frightened of him, I should think. He's probably a real tyrant. Most of them are.'

'The police have been, too.'

'They're even worse.'

'Do *you* know what happened?'

'All I know, love, is what it said in the paper. You were

attacked by some maniac in the park and stabbed and beaten.'

'Stabbed?'

'That's what it said.'

Perhaps that explained the stitches and the way her skin had felt puckered and snagged. She took a deep breath and asked, 'Did it say if I was raped as well?'

'If you were, the newspaper didn't report it. And knowing the press, they'd have made a field day out of something like that.'

'It's just that I feel so strange down there.'

'Really!' said Sarah. 'Bloody doctors act like they own your body. They ought to tell you what's wrong.'

'Maybe I haven't pushed hard enough. Or maybe they don't think I'm strong enough yet. I've been feeling very weak and tired.'

'Don't worry, love. You'll soon get your strength back. You know, I'm sure if you refuse to take your pills or start screaming in the night, they'll tell you what's wrong. Would you like me to tackle the doctor for you?'

Kirsten managed a weak smile. 'No, thanks. I need him in one piece. I'll try later.'

'All right.'

'You didn't answer my question.'

'What question's that?'

'What are you doing here? I thought you were going home for the summer.'

Sarah reached out and took Kirsten's hand. Her own was small and soft with long fingers and short, bitten nails. 'Someone's got to look out for you, love,' she said.

'But seriously.'

'Seriously. That's the main reason, I tell no lie. Oh, it'd only be rows at home anyway. You know how much my parents approve of me. I lower the tone of the neighbourhood. Besides, who wants to spend a bloody summer in Hereford, of all places.'

'Lots of people would,' Kirsten said. 'It's in the country.'

Sarah shrugged. 'Maybe I'll pay a brief visit, but that's all. I'm here to stay. We're getting a feminist bookshop together where that old second-hand record shop used to be. Know what we're going to call it?'

Kirsten shook her head.

'Harridan.'

'Harridan? But doesn't that mean—'

'Yes, a bad-tempered old bag. Remember all that fuss when Anthony Burgess said Virago was a poor choice of name for a woman's press because it meant a fierce or abusive woman? Well, we're going a step further. We'll show them that feminists can have just as much sense of irony as anyone else.' She laughed.

'Or bad taste,' Kirsten said.

'Often the same thing. Now what are we going to do about you?'

'What do you mean?'

'When you get out of here.'

'I don't know. I suppose I'll be going home. I don't really feel right, Sarah. My mind . . . I'm very mixed up.'

Sarah squeezed her hand. 'Bound to be. It'll pass, though. Probably the drugs they're giving you.'

'I have terrible nightmares.'

'You don't remember what happened, do you?'

'No.'

'That'll be it, then. Temporary amnesia. The brain blanks out painful experiences it doesn't like.'

'Temporary?'

'It might come back. Sometimes you have to work at it.'

Kirsten looked away towards the window. Outside, beyond the flowers and the get-well cards on her table, she could see the tops of trees swaying slowly in the wind and a distant block of flats, white in the July sun. 'I don't know if I want to remember,' she whispered. 'I feel so empty.'

'You don't have to think about it yet, love. Rest and get your strength back. And don't worry, I won't be far away. I'll take good care of you, I promise.'

Kirsten smiled. 'Where's Galen? The police said he'd been here.'

'Yes. I phoned him and he dashed up to see you as soon as I told him the news. He stayed for three days. He'd have sat by your bedside all the time if they'd let him. Anyway, his mother's having a really hard time getting over his grannie's death so he had to go back. Apparently she's on the edge of a nervous breakdown. Very highly strung woman. He said he'd come again, though, when you regained consciousness. He's probably on his way right now.'

'Poor Galen.'

'Kirsten.'

'What?'

'I wouldn't expect too much. I mean . . . Oh, shit, never mind.'

'What? Tell me.'

'All I mean is that, sometimes, when things like this happen, men go funny.'

'How?'

'They can't deal with it. They just act strange . . . ashamed, embarrassed. They get turned off. That's all.'

'I'm sure Galen will be all right.'

'Of course he will, love. Of course he will.'

'Sarah, I'm thirsty. Will you pass me some water please? I've got these damn tubes in one arm and the other's just too tired.'

'Sure.' Sarah picked up the plastic bottle from the bedside table and held it for Kirsten, tilting it so that she could suck on the straw easily. 'Like being a bloody baby again, isn't it?'

Kirsten nodded, then removed the straw from her mouth. 'Okay, that's enough. Thanks. I hate feeling so helpless.'

Sarah put the bottle back and took her hand again.

'What's been happening in the outside world?' Kirsten asked.

'Well, we haven't had a nuclear war yet, if that's what you're worried about. And the police came and questioned us all about you.'

'How did they find out who I am?'

'They found your bag. Look, you don't know any of this, I can see, so I might as well tell you what I know. Do you want me to?'

Kirsten nodded slowly. 'But not about . . . you know . . . the attack.'

'All right. Like I said, I don't know what actually happened, but apparently a man taking his dog for a walk found you in the park and acted quickly. They reckon he saved your life. As soon as the police found out who you were from your student card, they were round at the university asking questions about your friends. It didn't take them long to find out about the party, so we all got a visit from PC Plod the next day. I suppose they thought one of us might have followed you and tried to do you in, but no one left the party for a long time after you. I stayed till two, and Hugo was still there trying to put his hand down my knickers. They even found out about the row in the Ring O'Bells. I'll bet that fascist landlord and his simian sidekick got a good grilling, too.'

Kirsten nodded. 'Yes, the superintendent mentioned that. The police moved fast, didn't they?'

'Well, what do you expect? You *are* a poor, innocent student, and your father *is* managing director of that hush-hush government electronics firm. Connections, love. It's not as if you were just some street tart touting for rough trade, is it?'

'Don't be so cynical, Sarah.'

'I'm sorry. I didn't mean to sound callous. But it's true, isn't it?'

'I don't know. I'd like to think they do everything in their power to catch someone who does things like this, no matter who to.'

'So would I, but dream on, kid.'

'What about the others? How are they?'

'Hugo dropped by a couple of times, and Damon put off his summer job for a week to come and see you, but you were out to the world then. They left flowers and cards.' She gestured towards the bedside table.

'Yes I know. Thank them for me, will you?'

'You'll be able to thank them yourself. I'm sure they'll be back now they know you're in the land of the living again.'

'Where are they now?'

'Hugo dashed off home to Bedfordshire, no doubt to sponge off his parents and bonk the local milkmaids for the rest of the summer, and Damon's going hop-picking in Kent. Imagine that, poor Damon getting those lily-white hands dirty!'

'So they're all gone.

'Yes, love. All but me. And you won't get rid of me that easily.' Kirsten smiled and Sarah squeezed her hand again. 'They'll be back. Just wait and see. Anyway, I think I'd better go now. You look all in.'

'You'll come again soon?'

'Promise. Get some rest.' Sarah bent and kissed her forehead lightly, then left.

As Kirsten lay there, she tried to take in all that Sarah had told her. Of course, she couldn't expect the others to stick around for so long, and a visit from the police must have given them a scare. Hugo probably thought they were after that gram of coke he'd bought to celebrate the end of term. But all the same, she felt deserted, abandoned. She knew they all had to go their separate ways. In fact, she remembered, that had been very much on her mind that last night. (Why did she call it her 'last' night? she wondered.) But it wasn't as if she had the plague or anything. Was there something in what Sarah had hinted? Were Damon and Hugo embarrassed by what had happened to her? Ashamed even? Afraid to face her? But why should they be? she asked herself. They had work to do. They would be back as soon as they could get away, just as Sarah had said. And Galen was probably on his way right now.

Sarah's visit had renewed her spirits a little. It had also inflamed her curiosity. Obviously, there was more to this whole business than she was aware of. Could she really get the doctor to open up if she kept nagging at him or having screaming fits?

At least there was one thing she could do right now.

Tentatively, she pushed down the bedclothes and started to unbutton the top of her nightgown. It was a slow job, as her good arm was hooked up to an IV machine and she had to fumble with the weak and awkward fingers of her left hand, the one she hardly ever used. She didn't really believe that she'd get very far, but, to her surprise, she found once she'd started she couldn't stop, no matter how difficult and painful the movements were.

Finally, she managed to get the first four buttons undone. It was hard to bend her head forward and look down, so she shuffled herself back against the pillows and slumped against the headboard. From there, she could just tilt her head forward without straining her neck too much. At first, she couldn't see anything at all. The nightgown still seemed to cling around her breasts. She rested a moment, then pulled at it with her free hand. When she looked down again, she started screaming.

13

MARTHA

The Lucky Fisherman, a bit off the beaten track, turned out to be an unpretentious little local frequented mostly by townspeople. Martha didn't notice any real difference between the public bar and the lounge; both had the same small round tables and creaky wooden chairs. The woodwork was old and scratched, and one of the embossed glass panels in the door between the bars was broken. At one end of the room was a dartboard, which no one was using when she walked in at five past seven.

There were only a few other customers in the place, most of whom leaned easily against the bar chatting to the landlord. Keith was sitting at a table in the far corner under a framed photograph, an old sepia panorama of Whitby in its whaling days, with tall-masted ships in the harbour and chunky men in sou'westers – like the man on the packets of Fisherman's Friend cough lozenges – leaning against the railing on St Ann's Staith and smoking stubby pipes. The fence had been made of wood in those days, Martha noticed: one long beam held up by occasional props.

'Good day?' Keith said, standing as she came up to him.

'Good day,' Martha answered.

He laughed. 'No, I mean did you *have* a good day? We don't all talk like Paul Hogan, you know.'

Martha put her holdall on a vacant chair and sat down opposite him. 'Who?'

'Paul Hogan. *Crocodile Dundee*. A famous Aussie. Lord, don't you ever go to the movies or watch television?'

Martha shook her head. She vaguely remembered the name, but it seemed centuries ago, and she could recall no details. Her mind seemed to have no room left for trivia these days.

'What *do* you do for entertainment?'

'I read.'

'Ah. Very sensible. Drink?'

'Bitter. Just a half, please.'

Keith went to the bar and returned with her beer and another pint for himself.

'So how *was* your day?' he asked again.

'Good.' It was a long time since Martha had talked like this with a boy – a man, really – or conversed with anyone, for that matter. She seemed to have lost all her skill at small talk. She must have had it once, she assumed, though she couldn't remember when. All she could do was let Keith take the lead and follow as best she could. She dipped into her bag for her cigarettes and offered him one.

'No, I don't,' he said. 'But please go ahead.'

She lit the Rothmans, noting that she would soon need another packet, and reached for her drink again.

'Well . . .' Keith said.

Martha got the impression that she was supposed to say something, so she forged ahead. 'What about you? Where did you go?'

'Oh, I just walked around, visited the usual places. Sat on the beach for a while. I even went for a dip. I'm not used to it being so warm over here.'

'It is unusual,' Martha agreed.

'I'm making my way up the coast to Scotland. I think I told you.'

Martha nodded.

'Anyway, it's a complete holiday. No papers, no radio, no TV. I don't want to know what's going on in the world.'

'It's not usually good,' Martha agreed.

'Too true. And what about you? I'm curious. Why are you here all by yourself, if it's not a rude question?'

Martha thought of saying that yes, it was a rude question, but that would only get his back up. It was much easier to lie. She realized that she could tell him anything she wanted, anything under the sun – that she lived in Mozambique, for example, and was taking a rest from organizing safaris, or that she had run away from her husband, an Arabian prince to whom she had been sold as a young girl and shut away in a harem. She could tell him she was travelling around the world alone, as stipulated in the will, on a legacy left by her billionaire arms-dealer father. It was an exhilarating feeling, a feeling of tremendous power and freedom. Best keep it simple and believable, though, she decided, and told him she was doing research for a book.

'You a writer, then?' he asked. 'Silly of me, I suppose you must be, if you're working on a book.'

'Well, I'm not famous or anything. It's my first one. You won't have heard of me.'

'Maybe one day, who knows?'

'Who knows? It's a historical book, though, more of an academic study, really. I mean, it's not fiction or anything.'

'What's it about?'

'That's hard to say. It's partly about early Christianity, especially on the east coast here. You know, Bede, Caedmon, St Hilda, the Synod of Whitby.'

Keith shook his head slowly. ''Fraid you've lost me. I'm just a simple Aussie law student. Sounds fascinating, though.'

'It is,' Martha said, glad to have lost him. With luck, there would be no more questions about what she was doing. She finished her cigarette, then drained her glass. Keith immediately went for refills.

'Do you know anything about the fishing industry here?' Martha asked when he came back.

He squinted at her. His eyes really were a sharp blue, as if he had spent so much time staring into blue skies and oceans that they had taken their colour from the water and air. 'Fishing industry? That's a funny question. No, I can't really say I do.'

'I just wanted to see them bring in the catch, that's all,' she said quickly. 'It's supposed to be very interesting. They take them to that long shed down by the harbour and auction them off.'

'That'll be on Friday,' Keith said.

'Fish on Friday? Is that a joke?'

Keith laughed. 'No. What I mean is, I heard they go out on a Sunday and come back Friday, so that's when the catch comes in. That's the big boats. Little boats, like keel boats and cobles, come and go every day, but they've so little to sell it's all over before the sun comes up.'

Martha thought for a moment, making mental calculations, trying to remember what happened on which day. The person she was looking for must have a small boat of his own, she concluded. That might be easy to trace if she knew where to look. There should be a register of some kind . . .

'It's only a couple of days,' Keith said. 'Pity I won't be here. You'll have to get up early in the morning to see the boats come in, but the auctions go on for quite a while.'

'What? Sorry.'

'To see the boats come in. I said you'll have to get up early. They come in before dawn.'

'Oh, well, I'm sure the seagulls will wake me.'

Keith laughed. 'Noisy little blighters, aren't they? Tell me, do you come from this part of the country?'

'Yorkshire? No.'

'I thought your accent was different. Where you from, then?'

'Exeter,' Martha lied.

'Never been there.'

'You've not missed much. It's just a city, like all the rest. Tell me about Australia.'

And Keith told her. It seemed to suit both of them. Keith could find suitable expression for his homesickness in talking about Sydney life, and Martha could pretend to be interested. The whole evening was beginning to seem like a farce to her, and she wondered why she had bothered to agree to meet him at all. It brought back disturbing memories, too, mostly of her years as a teenager, pretending to be interested in what the boys said as they showed off, and then, later, fending off their wandering hands for as long as it seemed proper to do so. Would Keith turn out to be just like the rest, too? She put that last thought right out of her head.

'. . . as flash as a rat with a gold tooth,' Keith was saying. 'But that's just what people from Melbourne say.

It's hardly surprising Sydney's like a flashy whore to them. Melbourne's more like an old maid in surgical stockings . . .'

The place was filling up. Already most of the tables were taken, and three men had just started to play darts. Martha nodded in all the right places. She soon found that she'd finished her second half-pint.

'Another?' Keith asked.

'Are you trying to get me drunk?'

'Why would I want to do that?'

'To take advantage of me.'

Keith blushed. 'I wasn't . . . I mean I—'

She waved dismissively. 'Doesn't matter. Yes, I'll have another, if you like.'

It was while he was away at the bar that Martha first heard the voice. It made her hackles rise and her throat constrict. Casually, she looked around. Only two men were playing darts now, and it was one of them who had spoken. He was small and swarthy and wore a navy-blue fisherman's jersey. He looked as if he hadn't shaved for a couple of days, and his eyes seemed to glitter unnaturally, like the Ancient Mariner's, under his ragged fringe. He caught Martha looking and returned her gaze. Quickly, she turned away.

Keith came back with the drinks and excused himself to go to the gents.

Martha turned her head slowly again, trying to catch the man in her peripheral vision. Had he recognized her? She didn't think so. This time he was so absorbed in throwing the dart that he didn't notice her looking. Could it really be him?

'Do you know him?'

Martha almost jumped at the sound of Keith's voice.

She hadn't seen him come back. 'No. What makes you ask that?'

Keith shrugged. 'Just the way you were looking at him, that's all.'

'Of course I don't know him,' Martha said. 'This is my first day here.'

'You just seemed to be staring rather intently, that's all. Maybe it's someone you thought you recognized?'

'I've told you, I don't know what you're talking about. Just drop it, will you?'

'Are you sure you're all right?'

'Yes, I'm fine,' Martha said. And it was probably the truest thing she'd said to him all evening. Now she had something concrete to work on, her mind seemed more able to focus and concentrate. On the other hand, she felt herself drifting further and further away from Keith. It was becoming harder for her to follow his conversation and respond in the appropriate way at the right time. He began to seem more like an irritating fly that she kept having to swat away. She needed to be alone, but she couldn't escape just yet. She had to play the game.

'You a student, then?' he asked.

'Yes. I'm doing postgraduate work at Bangor.'

'And this book, is it your doctoral thesis?'

'Sort of.'

It was excruciating, like some awful interview she had to go through. As she answered Keith's inane questions, Martha was conscious all the time of the darts match going on behind her. Her skin was burning and her pulse beat way too fast.

Finally, the game drew to a close. The man she had been watching walked over to the bar, where she could see him out of the corner of her eye, and put his empty glass down on the counter. 'Well, that's my limit for tonight,' he said to the barman. 'See you tomorrow, Bobby.' The accent was right, the voice hoarse.

'Night, Jack,' said the barman.

Martha watched Jack walk towards the exit. He glanced briefly in her direction before he opened the door, but still showed no sign that he recognized her. She looked at her watch. It was a quarter to ten. For some reason, she got the impression that what had just happened was a kind of nightly ritual: Jack finishing his game, putting his glass on the counter and making some remark about the lateness of the hour. If he was a fisherman, then he would probably have to be up early in the morning. But shouldn't he already be out at sea? It was all so confusing. Still, if it was his habit to do this every night, she could come back tomorrow, when Keith was out of the way, and . . . Well, the next move would take careful planning and a lot of grace, but she had plenty of time.

'Want to go?'

With difficulty, like focusing on something from a great distance, Martha turned her attention back to Keith. She nodded and reached for her holdall. Outside, the warm fresh air felt good in her lungs. A bright half-moon hung high over St Mary's.

'Want to go for a walk?' Keith asked.

'Okay.'

They walked along East Terrace by the row of tall, white Victorian hotels, towards the Cook statue. As they passed the whale's jawbone, Keith stopped and said, 'That must have been exciting, setting off after whales.'

'I suppose I'd have been one of the waiting women,' Martha said, 'hoping to see the jawbone of a whale nailed to the masts.'

'What?'

'It was a sign. It meant everyone was safe. The women used to walk up here along West Cliff and look out for the ships coming home.' Martha looked at the huge arch of bone. From where she stood, it framed the floodlit St Mary's across the harbour as perfectly as if the whole set-up had been contrived by an artist.

'It's hard to imagine you doing that,' Keith said, moving on slowly. 'Pacing and waiting.'

'Why do you say that?'

'Well, I can't really say I *know* you of course, but you give me the impression that you're a modern woman, liberated or whatever. You'd have been more likely to be out there on the ships.'

'They didn't take women.'

'I don't suppose they did. But you know what I mean.'

Martha didn't. It had been his first really personal remark and it took her aback. How could someone just sit and talk about inconsequential things for an hour or two and then come out with a statement like that? She hadn't even been paying attention to him most of the time. Could he really see into her character? She hoped not. He wouldn't like what he saw.

By the Cook statue, they sat on a bench and looked out to sea. A cool breeze ruffled her hair and the moon's reflection seemed to float somewhere far in the distance, yet its eerie white light spread over all the ripples and billows of the water as far as the eye could see.

Martha thought of the passage from Lawrence's *Women in Love*, where Birkin threw pebbles at the moon's reflection in a pond. It was supposed to symbolize something, or so her English teacher had said, but nobody really knew what. Symbols, to her, had always stood for things you felt but couldn't explain. And now she felt like throwing pebbles at the rippling white sea.

'Do you have a boyfriend?' Keith asked.

'What do you think? You seem to know what kind of person I am. What would you say?'

'I'd be surprised if you didn't. But if I was him I wouldn't let you go away by yourself like this.'

'Why not?'

'Stands to reason, doesn't it? A pretty girl like you . . .'

A pretty girl! Martha almost laughed out loud. From where they sat, at the top of the cliff and back a little bit from its fenced edge, she couldn't see the waves break on the beach below. She could hear them though, and the deep grumbling hiss as one withdrew filled the silence before Keith spoke again.

'There's something disconcerting about you, though,' he said.

'Oh? What's that?'

'Well, for a start, you're not easy to get to know.'

Martha looked at her watch. 'We've been together about three hours,' she said. 'How much do you expect to get to know about someone in that time?'

'It's not time that counts. Some people you can get to know real quickly. Not you, though. There's hidden depths to you.'

'Why am I disconcerting?' Martha asked. Despite herself, she was becoming interested in his perception of her.

'Oh, I don't know. You seem so distant. And you don't get my jokes. It's like you've spent the last few years on another planet. I mean, if I make a little joke, you don't laugh, you ask a question.'

'Like what?'

Keith laughed. 'Like that!'

Martha felt herself blushing. It wasn't a feeling she enjoyed. She smiled. 'I suppose you're right. It's just curiosity.'

He shook his head. 'No, it's not. It's more like a form of defence. You're very evasive. You've got a lot of defences, Martha. You're hiding in there somewhere, behind all the walls and barbed wire. Why?'

Martha became aware of Keith's arm slipping around her shoulder. It made her stiffen. Surely he must sense her resistance, she thought, but he didn't remove it. 'Why what?' she asked.

'Why do you need to protect yourself so much, to hide away? What's there to be afraid of?'

'There's a lot to be afraid of,' Martha said slowly. 'And what makes you think I'm protecting myself from the world? Maybe I'm protecting the world from me.'

'Now that really is choice. I'm not sure I understand you, not at all. But I do find you intriguing, and very attractive.'

A ship's light blinked far out to sea. Keith leaned over and kissed her. Martha managed to contain her boiling rage and let him. It was a soft, tentative kiss, not a violent, tongue-probing attack. A small price to pay, she told herself amid her anger, for appearing normal. She knew she wasn't responding with the enthusiasm he expected, but there was absolutely nothing she could do about that.

'It's a shame I have to go tomorrow,' he said, breaking away gently. Clearly her response, or lack of it, didn't mean very much to him. 'I'd like to spend more time with you, get to know you a bit better.'

Martha said nothing. She just stared out at the rippling moon on the water and watched the ship's light move across the horizon like a star through the sky. He kissed her again, this time more passionately, exploring her teeth with his tongue. When she felt his other hand slip up over her side and reach for her breast, she pulled away.

'No,' she said, as calmly but firmly as she could. 'What do you think I am? We've only just met.'

'I'm sorry,' Keith said, 'really I am. I didn't mean to offend you. I just thought . . . I mean I hoped. Oh God, you can't blame a bloke for trying, can you?'

Martha could, but she didn't say so. Instead, she tried to placate him despite the rage she felt. 'It's not that I don't like you,' she said. 'It's just too soon. I guess I'm not the kind of person for a holiday quickie.'

Now Keith seemed offended. 'That's not fair. That's not what I had in mind.'

But it was, Martha knew. Oh, Keith was a nice enough boy, not too pushy, but all it came down to was that he wanted to go to bed with her. He would make out that he didn't usually do such things, and she was supposed to say the same. Then he would tell her how it was different with her, really special. He was a wolf, all right, but a tame one. Getting the brush-off just made him sulk and become petulant. They weren't all as easy as him to fight off.

'Come on,' Martha said. 'Let's go back. It's getting chilly.'

Hands in pockets, head down, Keith walked beside her back to the guesthouse.

14

KIRSTEN

'It's *my* body. I have a right to know.'

Kirsten leaned back on the pillows. Her eyes were puffed up, and the tear-tracks had dried on her cheeks. The doctor stood by the bottom of the bed, and her parents sat beside her.

'You were in no state to be alarmed,' the doctor said. 'You've been suffering from severe trauma. We had to avoid upsetting you.' For the first time, Kirsten actually looked at him. He was a short, dark-skinned man with a deeply etched frown that converged in a V between his thick black eyebrows. Somehow, the lines made him look like a short-tempered person, though Kirsten had seen no evidence of this. If he had tried to keep the full extent of her injuries from her, he had at least been gentle.

'I'm already alarmed,' she said. Her nightgown was buttoned up again now, but the memory of what she had seen still frightened her. 'Look, I'm not a little girl. Something's wrong. Tell me.'

'We didn't want to upset you, dear.' Her mother echoed the doctor. 'There's plenty of time to go into all the details later, when you're feeling better. Why don't you just rest now? The doctor will give you a sedative.'

Kirsten struggled to sit up. 'I don't want a bloody sedative! I want to know now! If you don't tell me, I'll only imagine it's worse than it is. I feel awful, but I don't think I'm going to die, am I? What else could be so bad? What could be worse than that?'

'Lie back and keep calm,' the doctor said, gently pushing her down. 'No, you're not going to die. At least not until you've had your three-score and ten. If you were, you'd have done so before today.' He moved back to the end of the bed.

'So tell me what's wrong.'

The doctor hesitated and looked towards her father. 'Go on,' he said quietly. 'Tell her.'

Kirsten wanted to let him know that his permission wasn't required. She was twenty-one; she didn't need his approval. But if this was the only way to find out, so be it.

The doctor sighed and stared at a spot on the wall above the top of her head. 'What you saw,' he began, 'is the result of emergency surgery, the sutures. It looks bad now, but when they heal, it will be better. Not like new, but better than now.'

Anything would be better than now, Kirsten thought, picturing her red and swollen breasts covered with stitch marks like zips, like something out of a Frankenstein movie.

'When you were brought in,' the doctor went on, 'one breast was almost severed. We counted thirteen separate stab wounds to the mammary region alone.' He shrugged and leaned forward, gripping the metal bedframe. 'We did the best we could under the circumstances.'

'Alone? You said *alone*. What else was there?'

'You'd been beaten around the face and head and, all in all, you had thirty-one stab wounds. It's a miracle that none of them hit a major artery or organ.'

Kirsten gripped the top of the bedsheet and held it

tight across her throat. 'What did they hit then, apart from my tits?'

'Kirsten!' her mother gasped. 'There's no need to speak like that in front of the doctor.'

'It's all right,' the doctor said. 'I suppose she has every right to be angry.'

'Thank you,' Kirsten said. 'Thank you very much. You were saying?'

The doctor fixed his gaze on the wall again. 'Most of the other entry points were in the region of the abdomen, thighs and vagina,' he went on. 'It was a vicious attack, one of the worst I've ever seen – at least on a victim who survived. There were also shallow slashes across the stomach, and something that looked like a cross with a long vertical had been cut from just below the breasts to the pudenda. The cuts weren't deep, but they needed stitching nonetheless. That's why your skin feels so tight.'

Kirsten lay silent and relaxed her grip on the sheets. It was even worse than she had thought. Thirty-one stab wounds. That terrible ache between her legs. She gulped and struggled to force back the tears. She was damned if she was going to prove them right and react like a baby. 'If I'm not going to die,' she said, 'why are you all looking like undertakers? What's the bad news you're hiding from me? What is it you're all trying to save me from? Am I disfigured for life? Is that it?'

'There will be some disfigurement, yes,' the doctor said, glancing at Kirsten's father again for the go-ahead. 'Chiefly of the breasts and the pubic area. But that's not the main damage. There's always the possibility of further surgery to correct some of the disfigurement. The real problems are internal, Kirsten,' he said, for the first time using her Christian name, and saying it softly. 'When you came in, you were unconscious. We had to operate immediately to put things right, to save your life, and we had to do it quickly, because there's always considerable anaesthetic risk when a patient is unconscious.'

'Well?'

'You were suffering from severe internal bleeding, and there was a strong chance of infection, of peritonitis. We had to perform an emergency hysterectomy.'

'I know what that means,' Kirsten said. 'It means I can't have children, doesn't it?'

'It means surgical removal of the uterus.'

'But it means I'll never be able to have babies, doesn't it?'

The doctor nodded.

Kirsten's mother began to sob into a handkerchief. Her father and the doctor looked solemn. One machine beside her bleeped rhythmically, another hissed, and colourless fluid dripped into her arm from the IV. Everything in the room seemed white, apart from her father's charcoal-grey suit.

'It wasn't something I'd planned for the immediate future anyway,' she said with a little laugh, showing them she could put a brave face on things. But this time she couldn't stop the tears from flowing. Her father and the doctor were both staring down at her.

'Why are you looking at me like that?' she shouted, turning her face to the wall. 'Go away! Leave me alone.'

'You insisted I tell you everything, Kirsten,' the doctor said, 'and you'd have to have been told eventually. I said I thought it was too soon.'

'I'll be all right.' Kirsten reached for a Kleenex. 'How

did you expect me to react? Jump for joy? Is there anything else? Now you've started, you might as well get it all over with.'

There was a short pause, then the doctor said, 'Some of the stab wounds perforated the vagina.'

Her mother turned away to face the door. Such frank talk was clearly too much for her. Vaginas, breasts, penises and the rest had always been forbidden subjects around the house.

'So?' Kirsten said. 'I'm assuming you patched *that* up as well.'

The doctor nodded. 'Oh, yes. We had to close the lacerations, stop the bleeding. But as I said, it was an emergency patch-up.'

'Are you trying to tell me you made some kind of mistake because you were in a hurry? Is that it?'

'No. We followed standard emergency procedure. I told you. You were unconscious. We had to act fast.'

'So what *are* you trying to say?'

'Well, there was some tissue loss, and the damage could be serious enough to cause permanent problems.'

'*Could* be?'

'We just don't know yet, Kirsten.'

'And where does all this leave me?'

'Intercourse might be a problem,' the doctor explained. 'It could be painful, difficult.'

Kirsten lay silent for a moment, then she laughed and said, 'Oh, wonderful! That's just what I was feeling like right now, a really good fuck.'

'Kirsten!' her father snapped, showing the first signs of anger she had seen in him in years. 'Listen to the doctor.' Her mother started crying again.

'There's a chance that reconstructive surgery sometime

in the future might help,' the doctor went on, 'but there are no guarantees.'

It finally dawned on Kirsten what he meant – more from his tone than what he actually said – and she felt a chill shoot through her whole being. 'This could be for ever?'

'I'm afraid so.'

'And a hysterectomy can't be reversed, either, can it?'

'No.'

Kirsten turned towards the window and noticed it was raining outside. The tree-top leaves danced under the downpour and the distant flats had turned slate grey. 'For ever,' she repeated to herself.

'I'm sorry, Kirsten.'

She looked at her father. It was odd to be discussing such things as her sex life in front of him; she had never done so before. She didn't know what he assumed about her activities at university. But now here he was, looking sad and sympathetic because she couldn't make love, perhaps never would again. Or maybe it was the bit about no children that hit him the hardest, she being an only child.

She didn't know which was worse herself; for the first time in her life, the two things converged in a way they never had before. She had been on the pill for two years and had slept regularly with Galen, only her second lover. They had never thought about children and the future, but now, as she remembered their gentle and ecstatic love-making, she couldn't help but think of new life growing inside her. How ironic that it took the loss of the ability both to enjoy sex and to bear children to make her see how intimately connected the two functions were. She laughed.

'Are you all right?' her father asked, coming forward to take her hand. She let him, but hers lay limp.

'I don't know.' She looked at him and shook her head. 'I don't know. I feel sort of empty inside, all dried out and dead.'

The doctor was still hovering at the foot of the bed. 'As I said, there is a chance that reconstructive surgery might help. It's something to think about. I don't know if you understand this, Kirsten,' he said, 'or at least if you realize it yet, but you really are very lucky to be alive.'

'Yes,' said Kirsten, rolling on her side. 'Lucky.'

15

MARTHA

The next morning the honeymooners were gone, leaving one empty table, but Keith sat with Martha anyway. He made polite conversation over breakfast but demonstrated none of the ebullience and energy he'd shown the previous day, when he had first found himself at the table with her. Enforced celibacy, she guessed, had seriously dampened his spirits. It would be best to say nothing about last night, she decided. After all, it *was* Keith's last day; perhaps tomorrow she would be able to eat alone.

A particularly near and noisy flock of seagulls had awoken most of the guests at about three-thirty in the morning, and that provided a safe and neutral topic of conversation over the black pudding and grilled mushrooms that again augmented the usual bacon and egg.

Martha ate quickly, wished Keith a good journey, and hurried upstairs. She hadn't slept well. It wasn't only the scavenging gulls that had disturbed her, but thoughts and fears about what she had to do next. For weeks she had planned it and dreamed of it, gone over it all so often in her mind that she could perform the act in her sleep. Now that it was close, she felt terrified. What if something went wrong? What if, when the time came, she couldn't go through with it? Even the holiest have their doubts, she reminded herself. Faith would see her through.

Across the harbour, a few woolly clouds hung over St Mary's, but they were drifting slowly inland. The sun lit up the cottages that straggled up the steep hillside. Beyond St Hilda's, closer at the other end of the street, the sky was clear. A light breeze wafted through the window, bringing the salt and fishy smell of the sea.

Martha didn't know what to do with herself all day. She couldn't act until after dark, and she had already got the lie of the land. It would look suspicious if she stayed in her room, though, especially on such a lovely day at the seaside. Spells of warm, sunny weather were rare on the Yorkshire coast. Whatever she did, she would have to go out.

She waited until she had heard the other guests leave for the day, hoping that Keith was among them, then crept down the stairs and out into the morning sun. Already, courting couples strolled hand in hand along Skinner Street, content after a night of love set to the music of screeching gulls. Families paused and glanced idly at the racks of postcards and guidebooks outside the gift shops. Children in shorts and striped T-shirts, swinging bright plastic buckets and spades, demanded ice creams. Babies slept in their prams, oblivious to the noise and bustle of life going on all around them.

Martha went into the first newsagent's she came across and bought *The Times* and a packet of twenty Benson and Hedges. The ten Rothmans, a brand she hadn't liked all that much anyway, hadn't lasted very long, and she had a feeling she wouldn't want to be caught without. For twenty-one years she hadn't smoked a single cigarette. Now, within about a year, she had become addicted.

She wandered down busy Flowergate, a narrow street

crammed with shoppers, towards the estuary. Overhead, flocks of gulls screamed and flashed white in the sun. When she reached the bridge, she checked the high-tide times chalked on the board: 0639 and 1902. It was ten o'clock now; that meant the tide would be well on its way out. She jotted the times down in her notebook in case she should forget.

One problem with the guesthouse was that the manager's wife made awful coffee. Martha would have preferred it to tea in the morning, but she had no stomach for a pot of powdered Nescafé. Now she craved the caffeine that only a cup of strong, drip-filter coffee could provide.

She crossed the bridge and turned left along Church Street, joining the procession heading for the 199 steps up to Caedmon's Cross, St Mary's and the abbey ruin. A short distance along the narrow cobbled street, just before the marketplace, she found the cafe she had noticed before, the Monk's Haven, near the Black Horse pub. The cafe was meant to look very olde worlde. A painted sign, much like a pub sign, in Gothic script hung above the entrance, and pots of bright red geraniums ranged along the top of the frontage above the mullioned windows with their white-painted frames.

Martha ordered a cup of black coffee and sat down to struggle with *The Times* crossword. While mulling over clues, she watched the ebb and flow of people beyond the windows: more couples pushing babies in prams; toddlers hanging onto mummy's hand; stout old women with grey hair and sensible shoes. Outside the music shop opposite, a skinny young man clad in jeans and a checked shirt, who looked like he hadn't slept for a month or combed his hair for at least as long, started singing folk songs in a nasal voice. Some people dropped coins into the hat that lay on the pavement beside him.

When she had done as much of the crossword as she could, Martha read through the paper. She found nothing of interest. Waiting was no fun. It must be like this for soldiers, she thought, just before they know they are going into action. They sit around in the trenches, or on landing craft, smoking and keeping very quiet. She had no idea what she would do when it was all over. That was an aspect of the business she had left completely to instinct. Because she didn't know how she would feel when it was done, she couldn't make any plans about what to do. She just hoped that possibilities would present themselves when the time came.

She wandered up and down Church Street gazing at the displays of jet-ware, beautiful polished black stones set in gold and silver, or larger chunks carved into ornamental chess pieces and delicate figurines. By noon she was hungry again. So much for the staying power of black pudding and bacon. Desperate for an alternative to fish and chips, she nipped into the Black Horse and ordered a steak and kidney pie, which she washed down with a half of bitter. Then she smoked a cigarette and struggled for a while longer with the crossword. By half past one she was out on the street again wondering what to do with the rest of the day. She didn't want to go up to St Mary's again, and there was no sense in simply tramping the streets all day.

Close to the junction of Church Street and Bridge Street stood a small bookshop. The bell pinged as Martha went inside, and a plump, bespectacled girl smiled at her from behind a counter stacked with invoices and orders. The place had a large and comprehensive paperback fiction section, which Martha browsed through methodically, starting with A: Ackroyd, Amis, Austen, Burgess, Chatwin, Dickens, Drabble, Greene, Hardy . . .

'Can I help you?' the assistant asked, coming out from behind her counter and raising her glasses.

'No,' Martha said, flashing her a quick smile. 'Just browsing. I'll find something.'

The woman went back to her paperwork and Martha carried on scanning the titles. She wanted an ordered world she could lose herself in for a while. Nothing modern would do; twentieth-century literature, with its experiments in style, its self-conscious artistry and its lack of morality and order, had never much interested her. At one time she had liked to escape into the occasional crime novel – Ruth Rendell, P. D. James – but such things held no appeal for her now. For a moment she considered *Moby Dick*. She had never read it, and the seaside, especially an old whaling centre, would be the ideal place to start. But when she got to the Ms, she found they hadn't a copy left in stock. The only Melville book they had was *Pierre*, and she was in no mood for that. Finally, she settled for Jane Austen's *Emma*. She had read it at school, for her A-Levels, but that seemed a lifetime ago. With Jane Austen, you could count on nothing more to ruffle the ordered surface than an occasional social gaffe or mistaken romantic intentions.

What better to do, then, than spend an afternoon on the beach reading *Emma*? She just hoped Keith wasn't there. He had said he was moving on, but he could have changed his mind.

She made her way back over the bridge. With the tide out, the River Esk was reduced to a narrow channel in the sand. Boats leaned in the silt at odd angles. Martha walked along St Ann's Staith, thinking of the old days in the photograph when the railing was made of wood. She passed the amusement arcades, seafood stalls and Dracula Museum, then at the end of Pier Road she took the steps down to the beach.

Whitby Sands runs below West Cliff, and over the centuries, the sea has carved small caves and caverns in the sheer rock wall. Martha poked her head inside one. It didn't go very deep, but it was a dank, gloomy place, full of slimy rocks, smelly seaweed and dead, dried-out molluscs that crunched underfoot. She shivered and turned away.

The beach itself was crowded – only to be expected on such a fine day – but Martha managed to find a spot where she could lean back against the rock and stretch her feet out. Children screamed and splashed in the water, bravely taking it in turns to stand fast as waves came in and bowled them over. Anxious parents kept one eye on the knitting or the newspaper, and the other on the kids. Some children were busy constructing elaborate sandcastles with turrets, battlements, moats and drawbridges.

Some people were even sunbathing. A couple of teenage girls wearing skimpy bikinis lay flat out on towels. A group of boys about the same age, playing cricket nearby, kept hitting the ball in their direction just to make an excuse to chat the girls up.

What Martha was watching, she realized, was another way of life, another world completely – or one she had once known but lost. If she felt like a visitor from outer space when she watched lovers walk hand in hand, parents push babies in prams, and children play in the foam, she felt even more so when she watched the elaborate contact and courtship rituals of these teenagers bursting with hormones.

The first couple of times the cricket ball kicked up a little sand on the girls' bare stomachs, they responded with abuse. Anyone watching would think they didn't like getting sand in their navels. After a while, though, they started to join in the spirit of the game. They would pick up the ball and throw it towards the sea, or run off and bury it in the sand, laughing and making fun of the boys. Martha had never before noticed the importance of sheer repetition and persistence in the human mating ritual.

It was like watching a species of animal or insect, Martha thought, putting Jane Austen aside and lighting a cigarette. No matter how much progress we seem to have made, we still dance to primitive patterns so deeply imprinted that we wouldn't recognize them if they tripped us up in the street. Which they often do. Though we have the miracle of language, we still make more sense with meaningless sounds, gestures, looks and silences.

And beneath all the elaborate courtship rituals, Martha thought, lay pure animal desire and the scarcely recognized impulse to perpetuate the species. Just like Keith last night. He had wanted Martha. He had wanted to take her to his bed naked and enter her for the pleasure it gave him. All that fuss over five minutes of grunting sounds – or was it squelching sounds? – someone had once said. People would do anything for it: lie, cheat, steal, maim, kill, even die.

The whole human drama seemed so sad and pointless to Martha that day on the beach. People amounted to nothing more than puppets manipulated by forces they didn't understand or, worse, even perceive. Shakespeare was right, as usual— 'As flies to wanton boys, are we to th'gods; They kill us for their sport.' Martha included herself, too. Hadn't she experienced the 'sport' of the gods? And just how much choice did she really have in this tragedy or farce she was acting out? She was jumping to strings as much as anyone else. Different strings, perhaps, with more sinister pullers, but beyond her control nonetheless. Despite the heat, she shivered.

Finally, she managed to pull herself out of the philosophical gloom. She told herself she was just getting nervous, that was all, and that the weak and cowardly part of her nature was trying to sap her confidence. She had to be strong. It was no good giving in to a sense of futility; only one thing kept her going, and until that was done, she couldn't afford to reflect on life. Besides, who was she to make such judgements anyway?

She crossed her legs and picked up Jane Austen. It was a hot day on the beach, and there she lay in jeans and a shirt buttoned up to the neck. She was too warm, but she couldn't take her clothes off and lie almost naked like the teenage girls in their bikinis. And the rituals and consummation of courtship were beyond her, too. But for her, she thought, there was another kind of consummation devoutly to be sought. And seek it she would. Tonight.

16
KIRSTEN

Like most people who hear bad news, Kirsten went through all the textbook stages, including the belief that a second opinion would prove the doctor wrong, and that what he had told her was gone forever would somehow be miraculously restored. The first night, she convinced herself that it was all a bad dream; it would pass. But it didn't. Even in the mild light of the next morning everything was the same: her stitches, her aches, her wounds, her loss.

The nightmares of painless, almost bloodless, slashing and slicing continued. She never woke up screaming, but sometimes she would open her eyes suddenly at some ungodly hour of the morning to escape the relentless images and to puzzle over them.

Other times, she lay awake all night. Especially when it was raining. She liked to try and empty her mind and pretend that her hard hospital bed was really a pallet of pine needles deep in the woods behind her parents' house in Brierley Coombe. The rain pattered gently on the leaves outside her window, and for short periods she could imagine it falling, soft and cool, on her eyelids, and she could almost escape the horror of her condition.

At least she wasn't dead. In a way, the doctor had been right: she was lucky. If that man hadn't been walking his dog so late and hadn't got curious when it started to growl and scratch around in the shrubbery, then she would have simply bled to death on a summer's night out in the park, only a hundred yards or so from home. But the man had stopped, and for that she should be grateful.

Now she was a cripple with all her limbs intact – external limbs, anyway. Her sense of violation and loss was almost unbearable at times; that most intimate part of herself had been stolen and destroyed. She cried, prayed and even, at one time, fell into a fit of hysterical laughter. But ultimately, she accepted the truth, and depression bore down on her. At its heart was that thick cloud, an opaque mass swelling like a tumour in her mind, repelling all light and taunting her with its darkness and its heaviness.

The doctor and nurses ministered as best they could to her healing body. The stitches dissolved, leaving the flesh bunched up and corrugated around her breasts. Livid scars quartered her, like the doctor had said, in the shape of a cross with a long vertical bar and a short horizontal, from just below the breasts to her pubic hair – at least to where that hair *had* been, for the nurse had shaved her down there and now all she had was itchy stubble. Externally, the pubic region didn't look too bad. She glimpsed it for the first time when she was able to walk to the toilet alone. It was red and sore, covered in a lattice of fading stitchwork, but she had expected worse. It was inside where most of the damage had been done.

Her parents came in and out, her mother still too upset to say very much and her father taking the burden stoically. Superintendent Elswick dropped by again, but to no avail. She still couldn't remember what had happened or give them any information about her attacker, beyond the feel of his calloused hands.

Sarah visited again, too. She said she'd take on the small flat if Kirsten was going home to convalesce. Kirsten agreed. It would save a lot of trouble moving stuff when her parents took her home. She didn't tell Sarah about the full extent of her injuries. Maybe later. At that time, she couldn't bear to talk about it. She did, though, ask her to try and keep the others away for a while.

And then, a full week after she had been given the news, Galen turned up, breathless, from the station, lank dark hair flopping over his ears, concern etched in every feature of his thin, handsome face. He sat beside her and grasped her hand. At first neither of them knew what to say.

'I came before,' Galen told her, finally. 'They said you were unconscious and they didn't know when you'd come round. I phoned every day. I couldn't stay. My . . .'

Kirsten squeezed his hand. 'I know. I understand. Thank you for coming back.'

'You look a lot better. How are you feeling?'

'I can get up and walk around now. They tell me I'll be able to go home soon.' She touched her face gingerly. 'The bruises have all gone now. The swelling's gone down.' How much did he know about what had happened to her? She didn't want to give anything away.

Galen lowered his head and shook it, his face darkening. He smashed his fist into his palm. 'If I could get my hands on the bastard—'

'Don't,' Kirsten said. 'Just . . . don't. I'd rather not talk about it.'

'I'm sorry. You can't imagine how I feel. I've been blaming myself ever since it happened. If only I'd been there, like I should have been.'

'Don't be silly. It's not your fault. It could have happened to anyone at any time. You can't be expected to guard me night and day.'

Galen looked into her eyes and smiled. His grip tightened on her hand. 'I will from now on,' he said. 'After you've recovered and all that. I promise I won't let you out of my sight.'

Kirsten turned her head aside and looked out at the dazzling tower blocks rinsed by last night's rain, and the sunlight dancing in the polished leaves. 'What are you going to do?' she asked.

Galen shrugged. 'I don't really know. I suppose I'll just hang about at home for the rest of the summer. Mother's still taking it very badly – grandmother's death. And I'll come and visit you in Brierley whenever I can. It's not too far away and I'll have the car.'

'It might be better if you didn't visit me,' Kirsten said slowly. 'At least, not for a while.'

Galen frowned and scratched his earlobe. 'Why? What do you mean?'

'Just that I need some time by myself, to recover.' She managed a smile. 'Call it post-operative depression. I wouldn't be very good company.'

'That doesn't matter. You'll need me, Kirstie. And I want to be there for you.'

She rested her free hand on his forearm. 'No. Not for a while. Please. Just let me get myself sorted out.'

Galen got up and wandered over to the window, hands in pockets. His shoulders slumped the way they always did when he was disappointed about something. Just like a little boy, Kirsten thought.

'If you say so,' he said, with his back to her. 'I suppose it's the . . . er . . . the psychological effects that are worse than even the physical ones, is it? I mean, I don't know. I couldn't know, could I, being a man? But I'll do my best to understand.' He turned around again and looked at her.

'I know you will,' Kirsten said. 'I just think it's best if we don't see each other for a while. I'm all confused.'

She still wasn't sure how much they had told him. He knew that she'd been attacked, that was clear enough, but had they been vague about the nature of the assault? Perhaps he assumed that she'd been raped. Had she been? Kirsten wasn't too sure about that, herself. As far as the doctor had been able to make out, there had been no traces of semen in the vagina. It had been such a mess, however, that she didn't see how he could possibly be so certain. Did penetration by a short, sharply pointed metal object count as rape? she wondered. In the end, she just had to settle for the general opinion that people who do what this man did to her are usually incapable of real sexual intercourse.

'What about Toronto?' Galen asked, returning to the chair and hunching over her.

'I don't know. I just can't see myself going, not the way things are now. Not this year, at least.'

'But it's still a month or so off. You'll probably feel better by then.'

'Maybe. Anyway, you go ahead. Don't worry about me.'

'I wouldn't go without you.'

'Galen, don't be so stubborn. There's no point sacrificing your career because of me. I can't promise you anything right now. I can't even—' And she almost told him then, but pulled herself back just in time. 'I just don't know how things are going to go.' She started crying. 'Can't you understand?'

The effort of letting him down gently and hiding her feelings and her disability from him at the same time was proving too much. She wished he would just leave. When he bent down to comfort her, she felt herself freeze. The reaction surprised her; it was something she'd never done before. And it came from deep inside; it was completely involuntary, like a twitch or a reflex action. Galen felt it, too, and he backed off, looking wounded.

'I understand,' he said stiffly. 'At least, I'll try.' He patted her hand. 'Let's just leave it be for now, okay? Plenty of time to think about our future later on, when you're fully recovered.'

Kirsten nodded and wiped the tears away with the backs of her hands. Galen passed her a Kleenex.

'Is there anything you want,' he asked, 'anything at all I can bring you?'

'No, not really.'

'A book?'

'I've not felt much like reading. I can't seem to concentrate. But thank you very much. You'd better go, Galen, go back home and take care of your mother. I'm glad you came. I know I don't seem it, but honestly I am.'

He looked disappointed, as if he had been summarily dismissed. Kirsten knew she hadn't managed to sound very convincing. Her breasts ached and she felt close to tears again. He took hold of her hand, with that little-boy-lost expression on his face, and didn't seem to want to let go.

'I'll come again,' he said. 'I promise. I'll be up here for a couple of days sorting things out, anyway.'

'All right. But I'm tired now.'

He leaned forward and kissed her gently on the lips. She caught the toothpaste smell on his breath. He must have brushed his teeth on the train, she thought, or as soon as he got to the hospital.

When he left, she gave in and let the tears fall. There just seemed to be no future. Certainly there would be no life for him with her. If he was lucky, they would drift apart and he would go to Toronto in September. He might even meet someone else.

Kirsten had no idea what her full recovery would feel like, or even if such a thing were possible. The doctor hadn't sounded very hopeful about reconstructive surgery. Presumably, she would feel fine on the outside, though the scars would remain and have to be covered up. Was she just supposed to get used to her new state, put her past behind her and get on with life? Go to Toronto with Galen, even?

He would be very understanding about her disability, at least for a while. Perhaps he would even marry her out of love and pity, and as time went on she would considerately turn a blind eye to the bits on the side he needed to give him what she could no longer supply. She would be grateful just because he was self-sacrificing enough to love a cripple.

No. It didn't sound right. Such a life could never be, *should* never be. Without really telling him why, she would have to ease Galen out of her life for his own good.

The depression was on her, in her, a kind of numbing fatalism that would admit no light, no comfort. She couldn't imagine it ever ending, things getting back to normal. Already the carefree, cheerful young graduate who had stepped out of Oastler Hall, enjoyed the warm air and scanned the night sky for the moon as she sat on the stone lion was gone. Utterly. Irredeemably.

And who or what was going to take her place? Kirsten wondered. She felt vague and disturbing forces moving inside her, like flitting shadows in places so deep and dark she had not known they existed. And she felt powerless to do anything about them, just as she had when Galen had tried to hold her and she'd frozen on him. She was no longer in control.

But it was more, even, than that. She knew she only controlled enough of herself to give the comforting illusion of being in command. At best, like most people, she could control certain aspects of her behaviour. It was mostly a matter of manners, like not burping at the dinner table. But her habits and mannerisms shouldn't change so dramatically unless she made a great conscious effort to alter them. She surely wouldn't just wake up one morning and no longer bite her nails under stress or stop blushing when she overheard someone talking about her. No more than Galen could stop his shoulders slumping when he didn't get what he wanted, or Sarah sucking on her upper lip with deceptive calm before responding sharply to a remark that had offended her.

Yet that seemed to be just what had happened. What Kirsten had done when Galen had reached for her – before she had even had time to think about it – was something that had never been in her repertoire of responses. It was her habit always to return the embrace of a friend or a loved one. But that part of her – the part, perhaps, that responded to affection and love – was gone now, changed. She no longer recognized herself.

It would be typical of the doctors, she thought, to put it down to what had happened to her. It's like, they would say, touching a hot coal and flinching the next time the hand nears another. Once bitten, twice shy. Conditioning. One of Pavlov's dogs. Naturally, they would go on, anyone who has suffered and survived such a vicious attack is bound to react with suspicion when another man, however familiar, approaches her in any intimate way.

Well, maybe they were right. Perhaps it would pass in time. Animals and humans who are used to being ill-treated often strike out at first when someone finally offers them love, but in time they come to accept it and trust those who give it. Surely she, too, could re-learn the right responses? But Kirsten wasn't convinced. For some reason, she believed that this new instinctive and frightening reaction to her lover's concern was only the beginning, that there were other changes going on, other powers at work, and that she had no control over any of them.

What was she going to become? All she could do was wait and see. Even then, she realized, she would probably be none the wiser, for she would have shed her old self and would have nothing left to compare the new one with. After all, she wondered, does a butterfly remember the caterpillar it used to be?

17
MARTHA

Martha found a pizza place to eat in that evening. Oddly enough, instead of giving her butterflies in her stomach, nervousness was making her hungry. Upstairs was a take-away, where busy white-jacketed cooks prepared orders, but downstairs was a tiny cellar restaurant with only four tables, each bearing a red-checked tablecloth and a candle burning inside a dark orange glass. Very Italian. Martha was the only person in the place. The white-washed stone walls arched over to form the curved ceiling, and the way the candles cast shadows over the ribbing and contours made the place look like a white cave or the inside of that whale Martha had imagined herself entering the first time she passed under the jawbone on West Cliff.

The menu offered little choice: pizza with tomato sauce, with mushrooms or with prawns. When the young waitress came, Martha settled for mushrooms.

'What's the wine?' she asked.

'We've got white or red.'

'Yes, but what kind is it?'

The waitress shrugged. 'Medium.'

'What does that mean? Is it dry or sweet?'

'Medium.'

Either she hadn't a clue, or she was clearly taking no chances on offending anyone. Martha sighed. 'All right, I'll have a glass of red.' She hoped it was dry, whatever the quality.

She lit a cigarette and settled to wait. It was chilly in the cellar, despite the warm evening outside, and she put her quilted jacket over her shoulders. She had used it as a headrest during her afternoon on the beach, and when she lifted it, a few trapped grains of sand fell on the tablecloth. She swept them onto the stone floor, wincing at their gritty feel against her fingertips.

She had read until the incoming tide had driven her away from the beach, then she had gone back to the guesthouse for a bath. She had got sweaty sitting in the sun all afternoon with her jeans on and her shirt buttoned up to the neck. After that, feeling restless and edgy, she had gone walking nowhere in particular for a couple of hours, until hunger had driven her in search of somewhere to eat.

While she waited for her pizza, she rummaged in her holdall for the smooth, hard paperweight for the umpteenth time that day. Yes, it was still there. She needed to touch it, her talisman, to bolster her resolve.

At last the waitress returned with a small, thin-crusted pizza and a glass of wine. It was dry: some kind of cheap and ordinary Chianti, but at least drinkable. The pizza was barely edible. The crust was like tough cardboard, and about six slices of canned mushroom lay on top of a watery spread of tomato sauce – completely lacking in spicing or herbal ingredients – that dribbled over the edge when she cut into it. Still, it wasn't fish and chips; she had that, at least, to be grateful for.

She ate as much as she could manage, and soon found herself getting full. A young couple came in, looked around the cavern suspiciously, and took a corner table in the shadows. They held hands and made eyes at one another in the candlelight. Martha felt sick. She ordered a cappuccino, wondering how that would turn out, and lit another cigarette. She still had time to kill.

The cappuccino turned out to be half a cup of Nescafé with what tasted like condensed milk, all churned up by a steam machine and dusted with a few grains of chocolate. The lovers talked in whispers, occasionally laughing and stroking one another's bare arms on the tablecloth.

Martha could stand it no longer. She demanded the bill rather snappily as the waitress was dashing off with the couple's order. It was still a good ten minutes before it arrived. Not bothering to leave a tip, Martha took the slip of paper upstairs and paid a sullen young man, who actually did look Italian, at the till.

Outside, it was already getting dark; the narrow channels of water left in the harbour rocked and twisted the strings of red and yellow lights in their oily mirror. It was almost nine o'clock, and the tide was well on its way out.

The man called Jack had left the pub at a quarter to ten the previous evening. Though the whole scene had the appearance of a ritual to Martha, she couldn't be sure he would leave at exactly the same time again, or even if he'd be in the pub. For one thing, the darts game – part of the ritual – might last longer. What was even worse was that he might leave with his friend. Still, Martha planned simply to follow him, if she could, and find out where he lived. Even if he didn't leave alone, he was bound to go home eventually.

It was her intention to lean against the iron railing close to the pub, near the jawbone at the top of West Cliff, and wait for him to come out. She would take note of which way he walked and would follow. She had thought of going inside the Lucky Fisherman again, alone this time, but that would only draw attention to her. He might even talk to her and try to pick her up, then everybody would see them. That was too dangerous to be worth the risk.

If she got there for nine-thirty, she would probably be all right. He would hardly leave before then. More likely later than earlier. That left her time for a quick nip to calm her nerves. She went into the first pub she saw, a bustling tourist place, and ordered a double whisky. She drank it slowly so it wouldn't go straight to her head. The last thing she needed was to get drunk. But the card-board pizza should be enough to soak up anything that came along in the next hour or so.

At quarter past nine, when she could wait no longer, she set off for the Lucky Fisherman. It was dark by then, and the town's usual illuminations were all on. It took her five minutes to reach her waiting place. Once there, she leaned forward on the railing and looked over first at St Mary's, basking in its sandy light directly opposite, then to her left, out to sea beyond the pincer-like piers, where all was dark. She could see the thin white line of waves breaking on the sand.

She looked at her watch. Nine-thirty-five. It seemed to be taking for ever. Time for a cigarette. No one but the occasional courting couple ambled by. They would pause for a moment, arm in arm, look out to sea by Captain Cook's statue, perhaps kiss, and then walk around the corner by the white hotels along North Terrace. A strong fishy smell drifted up from the harbour. Martha remem-bered it was Thursday evening. The fishing boats would be coming in tomorrow.

Nine-forty-six. He was late. Must be having trouble

getting that last double twenty or whatever it was he needed. She pictured him carrying his empty glass over to the bar and saying, 'Well, that's my limit for tonight. See you tomorrow, Bobby.' Yes, he *would* be there! He had actually said so, she remembered: 'See you *tomorrow*, Bobby.' And Bobby would say, 'Night, Jack,' as usual. Any moment he would be walking out of that door. Martha was hardly breathing; her chest felt tight with excitement and apprehension. She ground out the cigarette and glanced over at the pub.

At ten o'clock, it happened. The door rattled open and one man – *her* man – walked out in his dark jersey and baggy jeans. She stayed where she was, as if rooted to the spot, her hands frozen to the railing. She must try to look like a casual tourist, she told herself, just admiring the night-time view: St Mary's, the abbey ruin, the lights reflected in the harbour. A slight breeze ruffled her hair and brushed along her cheek like cold fingers.

He was walking in her direction, towards the Cook statue. She turned her head to watch him coming. How it happened, she wasn't sure. Perhaps it was just the sudden movement, or maybe the light from a street lamp had caught her face as she turned. But he saw her. She could have sworn that he smiled and his eyes glittered more than usual. He started walking towards her.

She felt pure terror, as if her very bone marrow had turned to ice. He walked up beside her and rested his hands on the railing too.

'Hello,' he said, in that familiar, hoarse voice. 'Lovely night, isn't it?'

Martha could hardly catch her breath. She was shaking so much that she had to clutch the railings tight to stay on her feet. But she had to go through with it. It was too late to back off now. She turned to face him.

'Hello,' she said, in a voice that she hoped wasn't trembling too much. 'Don't you remember me?'

18

KIRSTEN

The doctor insisted that Kirsten leave the hospital in a wheelchair, though by then she was quite capable of walking unaided. The demand was made even more ridiculous when she reached the top of the front steps and had to get up out of the chair and walk down them.

Her father's Mercedes was parked right outside. With Galen in front, carrying her things, and one parent on each side, Kirsten made her way towards it.

At the car, Galen – who, true to his word, had visited her almost every day that week – shook hands with her father, said goodbye to her mother, who inclined her head regally, and gave Kirsten a peck on the cheek. He had learned, she noticed, not to expect too much from her physically, though she still hadn't told him the full extent of her injuries.

'Are you sure I can't offer you a lift anywhere?' her father asked him.

'No, thank you,' Galen said. 'The station's not much of a walk, and it's out of your way. I'll be fine.'

'Back or front?' her father asked Kirsten.

'Back, please.'

In the spacious rear of the car she could stretch out, her head propped up against the window on a cushion, a blanket over her knees, and watch the world go by.

'Are you sure you want me to go ahead?' Galen asked her through the open window.

Kirsten nodded. 'Be sensible, Galen. There's no point missing the start of term. If you do that, you might as well not bother.'

'And I can't persuade you to come with me?'

'Not yet, no. I told you, don't worry about me. I'll be okay.'

'And you'll join me soon?'

'Yes.'

She had finally managed to convince him to go to Toronto, partly by insisting that she was fine and needed only rest, and partly by promising to join him as soon as she felt well enough. When he agreed, she wasn't sure if it was due to the logic of her arguments or because she had given him an easy way of getting off the hook. He had acted a little stranger each day – distant, embarrassed – and Kirsten had come to believe that perhaps there was something in what Sarah had hinted about men friends turning 'funny' when women became victims of sexual attacks. Also, Hugo and Damon had sent more flowers and messages through Sarah, but they hadn't visited again. Kirsten was beginning to feel rather like a pariah. In a way, it suited her, for at the moment what she wanted above all was to be left alone.

Galen stretched his arm through the window and patted Kirsten's hand. 'Take care,' he said. 'And remember, I want to see a full recovery soon.' Kirsten smiled at him and the car pulled away. She watched him waving as the Mercedes headed down the road, until it turned a corner and she could see him no longer.

Her father cleared his throat. 'I suppose you'd like to drop by the flat first and pick up a few things,' he suggested.

Kirsten didn't, in particular, want to set foot in her

tiny bedsit again, but neither did she want her parents to think she had lost all interest in life. Even if some of her deepest feelings were numb and her instincts were beyond her control, she could still make an effort to behave in the normal, accepted manner. They seemed dispirited enough as it was. Her mother had more or less accused her already of not trying hard enough to 'snap out of it', and her father had become more and more resigned and distant. If she showed no interest at all in her possessions, they would only worry more. So she said yes and offered directions. Appearances were important to her parents.

The car slid smoothly away from the gloomy Victorian hospital and towards the student area of town: rows of tall, old houses in which entire families and servants once used to live. Blackened by two hundred years of industry, and emptied by a succession of changes – the break up of the family unit, the Great War, the Depression, the inability of most people to afford servants – they had fallen into the hands of local businessmen, who transformed the once magnificent rooms, with their high ceilings and fixtures where the chandeliers used to hang, into small flats or bedsits – as many to a building as they could manage – and rented them to students.

Kirsten had an attic room in a cul-de-sac near the park. After spending her first year feeling miserable in a bright, noisy student residence, she had been happy there for the last two years. As the three of them got out of the sleek, silver-grey car, she noticed people along the street looking out through their curtains. It must be quite a spectacle, she supposed, finding a Mercedes parked in such a place, where the cobbles still stuck through the various attempts at tarmac.

Torn newspapers, chip wrappers, empty cigarette packets and cellophane paper littered the pavement and gutters; weeds and unmown grass consumed the garden. In the hallway, which looked as if it hadn't been swept for a month, neat piles of mail lay on a rickety old table.

The time-switch Kirsten pressed revealed a bare bulb on each landing and cobwebs in the high cornices. The walls were painted a colour somewhere between eggshell blue and institutional green – painted, that is to say, some years ago – and the high ceilings were puce – what Sarah called 'puke'. In the light of the unshaded sixty-watt bulbs, the place looked even worse than it was.

As they climbed the stairs, Kirsten was aware of her mother's stiff disapproval. On entry, she seemed to have held her breath and not let it out for fear of having to breathe in again.

Feeling foolish as she did so, Kirsten knocked on her own door. She still had a key, but the room was officially Sarah's now and she couldn't just barge in. She hoped Sarah didn't have a naked man in her bed.

The door opened. Kirsten noted with relief the empty room behind Sarah, who wasn't even wearing one of her calculatedly offensive T-shirts that day. Instead, she wore white trousers and a baggy blue sweatshirt with UCLA printed across the front.

'Kirstie, love!' she yelled. Her fine, porcelain features broke into a smile anyone would have expected to shatter them, and she flung her arms around Kirsten.

Kirsten returned the embrace, then broke away gently. She didn't react as badly as she had to Galen's touch, but she still felt herself drawing back inside, holding in.

'My mother and father.' She stood back and introduced her parents, who hovered in the doorway.

'Cup of tea?' Sarah asked.

'That'd be lovely.' Kirsten looked at her father, who nodded. Her mother shook her head slightly and looked at her watch. 'Not for me, thank you, dear. We really must set off soon if we're to be home this evening.' She directed the comment at her husband.

'Oh, we've time for a cup of tea,' he said, smiling at Sarah and sitting down in the scuffed red armchair with winged arms. It was Kirsten's favourite, the spot where she had sat to do her reading and make notes for essays.

The L-shaped room was just about large enough to hold four people: all it contained were the two matching armchairs in front of the gas fire, a three-quarter mattress on the floor beneath the window, a small clothes cupboard set in the wall, and a desk and bookshelves by the other wall. A portable stereo cassette player stood on one of the shelves beside a rack of tapes. Sarah was playing Bruce Springsteen singing 'Nebraska'. She turned down the volume before she went to put the kettle on in the kitchenette, which was tucked away in the short end of the L and separated from the rest of the room by a thin red curtain.

Kirsten sat on the mattress, which had always had to double as a sofa when she had guests. She gazed over at the poster on the wall above the pillows – a print of Van Gogh's *Sunflowers* – and remembered the first time she and Galen had made love on that very mattress the night after the English Department Christmas dance at the start of their second year. As she thought about it, and about all the other wonderful times they had slept there together, her loins ached with longing and loss. She could still see him standing by the roadside waving. Of course, she would never see him again. It was for his own good.

Her mother made a point of standing by the window with her arms tightly folded. Whether it was the sight of the park – the scene of the crime – at the end of the street that intrigued her, or whether she was just keeping an eye on the Merc, Kirsten didn't know. She could sense her mother's disapproval of the bedsit. Nose in the air, she seemed only a hair's breadth away from running her finger down the wall to see how much dirt came off. If she did that, Kirsten thought, she would run off screaming for the maids in two seconds flat.

Her parents had never visited the room – or even the city – before. The rough and ready atmosphere and basic living conditions must have been just as much of a shock to their tender southern sensibilities as they had been to hers at first. Over two years, though, she had had a chance to get used to it. At her age, too, she was more concerned about parties, books, films, plays and love than she was about living in a spotless mansion. Unlike her mother, Kirsten had never been particularly houseproud. Even her room at home had always been a mess. Surfaces hadn't mattered too much as long as she had been having fun. She washed the dishes regularly, dusted and went to the launderette once a week: that was it. Besides, these houses were so old and decrepit you couldn't do much with them even if you tried. They were only temporary: places to pass through, not to make nests in.

Sarah came back with the cracked teapot and three mugs. Kirsten's father accepted his sugarless tea graciously, and her mother continued to stand like a statue by the window. Her father made small talk with Sarah while Kirsten made a pretence of searching the room for the things she was supposed to want. She picked up the small pile of mail – mostly junk – from the desk and shoved a few clothes and a random selection of books into the old suitcase in the cupboard. Then she sat down to finish her tea, which had cooled by then.

'Is that all you want?' Sarah asked.

'For the moment. I've got plenty of stuff back home – clothes and that.'

'But the books . . . ?'

'Hang on to them for me, will you? I think I need a rest from literature.'

Sarah eyed the shelves, still more than three-quarters full. 'I suppose it's about time I read Shelley and Coleridge,' she said, smiling. 'Though I'd planned on a summer with Thomas Hardy and George Eliot. I don't know about the linguistics and phonetics stuff, though. You know I never could understand all that.'

Kirsten shrugged and took one book down for her. 'That's a good one. The prof who wrote it is supposed to be able to tell what village you come from just by your accent. They say he's usually accurate within ten miles or so. I never got as good as that, but . . .'

'Thanks,' said Sarah. 'I'll give it a try.'

They must all, Kirsten thought, be conscious of her mother looming over them, radiating waves of discomfort. Were the circumstances different, she might have gone into one of her 'Why did you have to leave a clean, decent home?' spiels. Even her father might have reminded her of how he had tried to persuade her to go to a university closer to home instead of moving so far away. But she'd had to fly the coop. She knew she wouldn't have been able to stand living at home while all the other students were free to live their own lives for the first time. How humiliating it would have been to have to run off back to Mummy and Daddy's in time for tea after the Milton lecture. And the further the better, she had thought, while offering convincing arguments about the quality of teaching and the reputations of professors.

'I think we really should go, dear,' her father said finally, looking for somewhere to put down his mug.

Kirsten got up, took it from him and carried it into the kitchen. She was ready, too. She'd had enough of this tension and pretence. If everyone was going to treat her as if she were made of glass for the rest of her life, then she wanted out. She began to get an inkling of what the physically handicapped must feel like: everyone acting so embarrassed, condescending and pitying, and trying so hard not to offend them or refer to their disability in any way. Sex and babies would now be unmentionable subjects back home, she realized, along with all the other dirty words. Taboo. 'Don't mention you-know-whats,' her mother would whisper to visitors at the door, 'or you'll upset poor Kirsten.' She was tired. All she wanted to do was crawl in the back of the car and be chauffeured home quickly and quietly.

Sarah came down the stairs with them and hugged Kirsten again on the doorstep. 'Don't worry,' she said, 'I'll take care of everything. Oh, I forgot, what about your tapes?'

'It's all right, Sarah, you hang on to them. I've got as much music as I want at home.' And it was true. She had a deluxe stereo in her spacious bedroom, the one her father had bought her for her eighteenth birthday. It was too bulky and expensive to cart all the way up to university, so she had made do with the portable system and kept the other at home to enjoy on holidays.

Sarah said she would write soon and come down to visit when she could, and with that they were off. Necks craned behind windows to watch them go. Perhaps, Kirsten thought, it's not so much the posh car as her new celebrity status: 'There's the girl that nearly got herself killed by that maniac,' they would be saying to themselves. How odd the words sounded in her mind: *'Got herself killed.'* As if what happened had been, somehow, her own fault.

Her mother was clearly relieved to be out of the room and back in the more congenial and appropriate environment of the Mercedes. The two of them had, her father told her, been staying in the big hotel near the station all the time she had been in hospital. Poorer or less powerful people, Kirsten knew, would have been able to spare neither the time off work nor afford the luxury. She had always taken her family's wealth and status for granted, as the young do, but now, for the first time, she was conscious of privilege: the private room in the hospital; the family home, a renovated Tudor mansion in Brierley Coombe, near Bath; and the comfortable Mercedes that glided down the M1 towards it.

Through a thin drizzle, she watched the dull South Yorkshire landscape of slag heaps and motionless pit wheels flash by, and soon they were passing turn-offs for Nottingham and Derby. Kirsten's father was a motorway driver as a rule; even if it meant more mileage, he would generally stick to the motorways and drive as fast as he could get away with. But this time, she realized, as he turned off the M1 near Northampton, before it swung south-east towards London, they were taking the scenic route. Perhaps he thought a good dose of the green and pleasant land would prove therapeutic. As if to prove the point, the rain slackened off and the sun burst through before they had even skirted the south Midlands.

Kirsten was comfortable in the back. The Mercedes seemed to float on air without making a sound, and after a few attempts at making conversation, her parents had fallen quiet, too. Her father switched on Radio Three and Kirsten relaxed to the Busoni piano music that was playing. They passed through Banbury and Chipping Norton and soon entered the Cotswolds. By then, it was indeed a perfect day in the English countryside: blue sky, one or two fleecy white clouds drifting over, rounded green hills and quaint villages. Sunlight warmed the weathered limestone cottages, with their flagged roofs and gardens full of roses.

They drove straight through Stow-on-the-Wold, which was jampacked with parked cars and tourists, and finally stopped for a pub lunch at a small sixteenth-century inn near Bourton-on-the-Water. Kirsten's mother seemed at ease there, back in her natural environment of gentility and well-polished brassware. Kirsten picked at a ploughman's lunch. After the intravenous drip and so long on hospital food, she seemed to have lost her appetite.

After lunch, they took a stroll around the town, walked along by the river, and then set off for the last leg of the journey.

Kirsten dozed uneasily as an interminable Mahler symphony played, disturbed even during the clear daylight hours by her dreams of the dark man and the light man cutting at her body, and then, on the long hill that wound down into Bath, she felt the first twinge of fire deep in her loins. She ignored it and looked on the familiar city, its light stone glinting in the sun below. But before they even reached Pulteney Road, the fiery, shooting pains between her legs had her almost doubled up, gritting her teeth in the back of the car.

19
MARTHA

'Remember you?' The man looked puzzled. Then he smiled and jerked his thumb back towards the pub. 'You were in the Fisherman last night with your boyfriend. I remember that.'

'He's not my boyfriend,' Martha said. 'Besides, he's moved on now.'

Martha didn't know whether to feel angry or glad that he didn't remember her. It was an insult, yes, but one that she could use to her advantage. She had stopped shaking now, and her blood was warming a little. All she had to do was keep reminding herself what he was, what he had done, and she would find the courage she needed from her anger and disgust. This was her destiny, after all, her mission; it was the reason she had survived what many had not.

She still found it difficult to look at him, but when she did she noticed, in the dim glow of a street light, that he was not as old as she had first thought: late twenties, perhaps, or early thirties at the most. For some reason, she had expected him to be older. He stood just an inch or so taller than she, with a shaggy thatch of dark hair and the kind of facial growth that looks like a perpetual five o'clock shadow. Just as on the previous evening, he was wearing a navy-blue Guernsey jersey and baggy dark pants made of some heavy material. He had a strong local accent. The voice was right, she was certain. And the face. She had to trust in faith and instinct now; logic alone could never be enough to lead visionaries to their Grails.

'On holiday?' he asked, leaning easily against the railing beside her.

'You could say that.' Martha looked straight ahead as she spoke. Over the water, St Mary's stood squat, as bright as polished sand, in its floodlight. The red and blue and amber lights twisted like oil slicks in the dark harbour below. Footsteps clicked behind her – a woman in high-heeled shoes – and further away, down in the town itself, a group of noisy kids came out of a pub shouting and whooping. Out to sea, something splashed in the water.

'It's just that most people who live here don't really notice its beauty,' the man went on. 'I mean, when it's all around you, the sea and all, you hardly bother to stand and gawp at it.'

'Am I so obvious?'

He laughed. 'I stand and look myself sometimes, especially way out where it's all dark and you just get a tiny speck of light moving across in the distance. I often wonder what it must be like out on the boats like that, in the dark.'

'You're not a fisherman?'

'Me? Good Lord, no! Whatever gave you that idea? I have a small boat and I go out sometimes, but just for myself, and always during the day.'

'I just . . . oh, never mind.'

'As a matter of fact I'm a joiner by trade. Do a lot of work for the theatre, too, in season – chief scenery fixer and bottle washer.'

Martha was confused. She had so much expected her

quarry to be a fisherman. Now she thought about it, though, she didn't know how she had got that idea fixed in her mind in the first place. Perhaps it was the smell, the fishy smell. But anyone who lived by the sea might pick that up easily enough. And he *did* say he went fishing from time to time. No, she told herself, she had to be right. No excuses. Instinct.

'Have you been doing it long?' she asked.

'What – the joinery or the theatre?'

Martha shrugged. 'Both, I suppose.'

'Since I left school. The only thing I was any good at was woodwork, and I've always been interested in the theatre. Not acting, just the practical stuff – the illusions it creates. And you?'

'Have you worked anywhere else, or are you here all the time?'

'I've travelled a fair bit. The provinces. There's not enough work to keep me here all the time, but it's where I live. Home, I suppose.'

'Born and brought up?'

'Aye. Born and bred in Whitby. You didn't answer my question.'

Martha felt a chill in the wind off the sea and put her jacket over her shoulders again. 'What question?'

'I asked about you.'

Martha laughed and pushed back a lock of hair that the breeze had displaced. 'Oh, I'm not very interesting, I'm afraid. I'm from Portsmouth, just a dull typist in a dull office.'

'You'll be used to the sea, then?'

'Pardon?'

'The sea. Portsmouth's a famous naval base, isn't it?'

'Oh yes, the sea. The most I've had to do with it is a

hovercraft trip to the Isle of Wight. And even that made me feel sick.'

He laughed. 'Look, would you like to go for a drink somewhere. I hope you don't think me forward or anything, but . . .'

'Not at all, no.' Martha thought quickly. She couldn't go to a pub with him, that was for certain. So far her only link with him was the lounge of the Lucky Fisherman, and she didn't imagine anyone but Keith had noticed their fleeting eye contact the previous evening. But to go about publicly would be courting disaster.

'Well?'

'I don't really fancy a drink. It's far too lovely an evening to spend sitting in a noisy, smoky bar. Why don't we just walk?'

'Fine with me. Where?'

Martha wanted to avoid the town, where the pubs would soon be disgorging groups of drink-jolly tourists and locals who might just remember seeing the two of them together. If they stuck to quieter, dimly lit streets, nobody would notice them. And she had to get him alone somewhere, somewhere private. No doubt he would have the same thing in mind. He was certainly a cool one. No matter what he pretended, though, she was certain that he must remember her. How could he forget? And how could she forget what he was? She thought of the beach and the caves.

'Let's wander down towards the pier,' she said, 'and take it from there.'

'Okay. By the way, I'm Jack, Jack Grimley.' He stuck out his hand.

'Martha. Martha Browne.' She shook the hand; it

was rough with callouses – from sawing and planing planks of wood, no doubt – and touching it made her shudder.

'Pleased to meet you, Martha.'

They took the steps and cut across Khyber Pass down to Pier Road. It was after ten-thirty now, and all the amusement arcades had closed for the night Only a few pairs of young lovers strolled by the auction sheds, and they were all absorbed in one another.

They walked out on the pier and sniffed the sea air. Martha lit a cigarette and wrapped her jacket a little tighter around her throat against the chill out there. Jack hadn't tried to touch her or make any kind of a pass so far, but she knew it was bound to happen soon. For now, he seemed content to stand quietly as she smoked, watching the distant lights out in the dark sea. She wondered when he would pounce. The pier was too open. It was dark all around them, but the whole thing stood out rather like a long stone stage in the water. It was the kind of place where he might make his first move, though – a fleeting caress or a comforting arm around the shoulders to lull her into a false sense of security.

'Fancy the beach?' she asked, dropping her cigarette onto the pier and stepping on it. 'I like to listen to the waves.'

'Why not?'

He walked beside her back towards Pier Road and down the stone steps to the deserted beach. A thin line of foam broke along the sands, and after that came the sucking, hissing sound of the sea drawing back. The moon, now almost three-quarters full, stood high and shed its sickly light on the water. It seemed to float there like an incandescent jellyfish just below the water's surface.

They walked close to the rock face, where the sand was drier. It was pitch dark down there, apart from the moon. They were hidden from the town by the slightly concave curve of the cliffs.

At last, Jack took hold of her arm gently. This is it, she thought, tensing. She tried to act normally and not freeze as she usually did when a man tried to touch her. She had to distract him for a moment.

'Are you sure you don't remember?' she asked, dipping her free hand into her bag.

'Remember what?'

'Me.' It still seemed the ultimate insult that he pretended not to remember her after all that had happened.

'I looked a bit different,' she said, her hand closing on the paperweight. Warmth and certainty flooded her senses.

He laughed. 'Martha, I'm sure I'd remember if I'd seen you bef—'

'Martha wasn't my name then.'

It wasn't at all as she'd imagined, the way she had made it happen so many times in her mind's eye. He was supposed to just fall down neatly and that was that. But he didn't. When the heavy paperweight smacked into his temple and made a dull crack, he only dropped to his knees, groaned and put his hand up to the wound in disbelief. Blood bubbled between his fingers and glistened in the moonlight. Then he turned and stared at her, his glittering eyes wide open.

For a moment, Martha froze. She just stood there, hesitating, sure that she couldn't go on. She had been through this situation so many times, both in her waking mind and in her dreams, but it wasn't happening the way it was supposed to. Then, out of fear and outrage, she hit out again and heard an even louder crack. This time he pitched forward into the sand. But he wouldn't lay still. His body jerked and convulsed in spasms like a marionette out of control; his stubby fingers clawed at the sand. Martha stood and watched, horrified, as the prone figure danced on the sand. His arms twitched and his whole body seemed to shudder as if it was about to explode and shatter. Then, all of a sudden, it stopped and he lay still at last. The blood around his head looked viscous in the faint white light.

Martha bent forward and put her hands on her knees. She took a few deep breaths and tried to slow her racing heartbeat. She had almost blown it. Reality never happened the way she thought it would. She had left so much of the business to her instinct and imagination that she should have known to allow for things not going exactly as planned. At least it was done now, and he lay at her feet, even if the deed itself had been more horrible and frightening than she had expected. But it wasn't over yet. She couldn't just leave him out here on the beach, and she couldn't stay in the open herself any longer. Glancing around nervously, Martha steeled herself and set to work.

Gasping for breath, she struggled with the heavy body and slowly dragged it into the mouth of the nearest cave. The opening was a rough arch about six feet high, but it narrowed quickly the further in it went. In all, it only extended about fifteen feet into the cliff, curving as it went and ending almost in a point, but that was enough for Martha's purposes. The dark walls glistened with slime, as if the very rock itself were sweating in anticipation.

As soon as she had hauled the body inside the opening, Martha paused and listened. It was after eleven now. The pubs would have closed and some people might fancy a drunken walk on the beach. Moments later, someone giggled by the pier, and then she could hear voices coming closer. Quickly, she braced herself and heaved the body by its ankles back into the cave as far as it would go, just beyond the slight bend in the middle. She almost screamed when she snagged a broken nail on one of his woollen socks and couldn't free it without a struggle.

Finally, she got him as deep in the cave as she could. The effort exhausted her – sweat beaded on her forehead – but at least she was safe now. The slanting moonlight only illuminated the first four or five feet of the interior, and beyond that it was cut off by the top of the arched entrance. Nobody could see them so far back, behind small boulders set in the sand past the kink in the wall.

Cautiously, Martha peered from behind a boulder and saw a young couple framed in the cave's opening. She held her breath. They were about thirty yards away, down by the breaking waves. Even at that distance she could catch fragments of their conversation.

'. . . late. Let's go . . .'

'. . . a minute . . . peaceful . . . give me . . .'

'No! . . . cold . . . Come on!'

Then there was more laughter, and the boy started chasing the girl back towards the steps.

Martha breathed out. It was quiet again. Just to make sure that no other revellers were going to come and spoil her work, she waited, hardly breathing, for about fifteen minutes. When nothing else had happened by then, she pulled the body forward into the patch of moonlight near the cave's entrance to make sure he was dead.

Grimley's body crunched over the dead and dried-out shellfish that gleamed like tiny bones in the moonlight. Strands of dry seaweed crackled under Martha's feet, and the smell of sea-wrack, salt and rotten fish was strong in her nostrils. A small, dark shape scuttled over the sand back in the shadows. She shuddered. Outside there was only the even, quiet rhythm of waves breaking and retreating.

First, Martha washed the paperweight in a small rock pool, dried it off on her shirt and put it back in her bag. She checked her hands and clothing, but could see no blood. She would have to look more closely later, when she got back to her room.

Lastly, she forced herself to look at the body. Blood veiled one side of his face, where his eye bulged from its socket and seemed to stare right at her. His left temple was shattered. In horror, Martha put a finger to it and felt the bone fragments shift under her touch like broken eggshell. The second blow had caught the top of his skull, and she could trace the deep indentation. Again, the bones had splintered, and this time her finger touched something squelchy and matted with hair. She shivered and a cry caught in her throat as she began to heave. Kneeling beside him, she vomited on the sand until she thought she would never stop.

The ancient, rotten sea smell stuck in her nostrils, and the blood and brain matter were smeared all over her fingers. When she could catch her breath again, she washed her hands in the rock pool and knelt there gasping until she had controlled her heartbeat. She couldn't bear being close to the body any longer. Crawling to the mouth of the cave, she listened for a few moments. It was all quiet on the beach, except for the crash and hiss of the waves. Martha slipped out of the cave like a ghost in the moonlight and set off back to the guesthouse.

20

KIRSTEN

'You'll have to expect a bit of pain now and then,' said Dr Craven, writing on her prescription pad with a black felt-tip pen. 'Traumatic injuries often cause extreme pain. But don't worry, it won't last forever. I'll prescribe some analgesic. It should help.' She sat back and handed the slip of paper to Kirsten.

Behind the doctor, a brusque woman in her early forties, with severely cropped grey hair, steady blue eyes and a beak of a nose, Kirsten could see the small Norman church and the village green, with its two superb copper beeches, rose beds, little white fence and benches where the old people sat and gossiped. She could even hear the finches and tits twittering beyond the open window. Brierley Coombe. Home.

The previous evening she had managed to keep the pain from her parents. She had simply claimed tiredness after the journey, then taken four aspirins and a long, hot bath before going to bed. The pain receded, and she had actually slept well for the first time since the attack.

Dr Craven leaned forward and tapped a blue folder. The stethoscope around her neck swung forward and clipped the edge of the desk. 'I've got all your details, Kirsten,' she said, 'and I've been on the telephone to Dr Masterson at the hospital. If anything at all bothers you, please don't hesitate to come and see me. And I'd like you to drop by once a week anyway, just to see how you're doing. All right?'

Kirsten nodded. Dr Masterson? She hadn't even known his name, the man who had probably saved her life. One of her benefactors, anyway. She didn't know the name of the person who had so fortunately been walking his dog on the night of her attack either. But Dr Masterson? She remembered his dark complexion and his deeply lined brow, how he always looked cross but acted shyly and kind. She had even invented stories about him to pass the time. His father must have been an army officer serving in India, she had decided – a captain in the medical corps, most likely – and he had married a high-caste Indian woman. After independence, they had come to England . . .

The ease with which she could make up stories about people on so little evidence always surprised her. It was a skill, or a curse, that she had had since early childhood, when she had filled notebooks with stick drawings and family histories of invented characters. If she could make up lives for others, she thought, then she could probably do the same for herself. That would certainly be preferable to telling the truth to everyone she met. Already, on her way to the doctor's surgery that morning, she had noticed neighbours – people who had known her since childhood – giving her those pitying looks. What was worse was that one of them – Carrie Linton, a stuck-up busybody she'd never liked – had given her a different kind of look: more accusing than pitying.

'Kirsten?'

'What? Oh, sorry, Doctor. I was daydreaming.'

'I said make sure you eat well and get plenty of rest.

The healing process is doing very nicely, or Dr Masterson wouldn't have approved your coming home, but you're still convalescent, and don't forget it.'

'Of course.'

'And if you have any difficulty at all in adjusting to your condition, I can recommend a very good doctor in Bath, a specialist.'

Adjusting? Condition? Good Lord, thought Kirsten, she makes it sound as if I'm pregnant or something.

'I mean psychologically and emotionally,' Dr Craven went on, her eyes fixing on the diagram of the human circulatory system on the wall. 'It might not be an easy road, you know.'

'A psychiatrist?'

Dr Craven tapped her pen on the desk. 'Only if you feel the need. They can help, you know. There's no stigma attached these days, especially . . .'

She's embarrassed, Kirsten thought. Just like all the rest. They don't know what to do with me. 'In cases such as mine?' she offered, finishing the sentence.

'Well, yes.' Dr Craven seemed to miss the irony in Kirsten's voice. The corners of her lips twitched in one of her rare, brief smiles. 'You are rather unique, you know. Few women, if any, have ever survived an attack from such a maniac.'

'I suppose not,' Kirsten said slowly. 'I hadn't really thought of it that way. Like Jack the Ripper, you mean? Did anyone survive him?'

'I'm afraid I don't know. Criminology isn't my forte.' She leaned forward. 'What I'm saying, Kirsten, is that there may be some resultant emotional trauma. I want you to know that help is available. You only have to ask for it.'

'Thank you.'

The doctor sat back in her chair and peered at Kirsten over the top of her half-moon glasses. 'How *do* you feel?' she asked.

'Feel? Not so bad. The pain's eased a little now.'

'No, I mean emotionally. What do you feel?'

'What do I feel? I don't know really. Just blank, numb. I can't remember anything about the attack.'

'Do you keep running over events in your mind?'

'Yes, but I still can't remember. It keeps me awake sometimes. I can't concentrate for it. I can't even sit down and read a book. I used to love reading.'

'The amnesia may only be temporary.'

'I don't know if I *want* to remember.'

'That's understandable, of course. As are all your feelings. You've suffered a tremendous shock, Kirsten. Not just to your body but to your whole being. All your symptoms – emotional numbness, bad dreams, inability to concentrate – they're all perfectly normal given the circumstances. Awful, but normal. In fact, I'd be worried if you *didn't* feel like that. You feel no anger, no rage?'

'No. Should I?'

'It'll come later.'

'I suppose I do feel that I'd like to kill him, the man who did this to me, but it's more of a cold feeling than an angry one, if you can understand what I mean.' She shrugged. 'Still, I don't imagine I'll get the chance, will I? I wouldn't know him from Adam.'

'No. But let's hope the police find him soon.'

'Before he can attack anyone else?'

'Such people don't usually stop at one. And the next victim might not be so lucky.' Dr Craven stood up and held out her hand. 'Don't forget what I said. Take good care of yourself, and I'll see you next week.' Kirsten shook her hand and left.

Outside, the sun was shining in a clear blue sky. The rounded hills that fringed the village seemed to glow bright green with some kind of inner light, as if they formed the backdrop to a painter's vision. Kirsten put her hands in her pockets and ambled along the High Street. Not much there, really: a pub, the village hall (an 1852 construction, the newest building in Brierley Coombe), the shops (converted cottages, most of them) – post office, grocer's, butcher's, chemist's, newsagent's.

The village stood on the edge of the Mendips, between Bath and Wells, and it had its share of thatched roofs and award-winning gardens. Orderly riots of roses, petunias, periwinkles, hollyhocks and nasturtiums assaulted Kirsten's senses as she walked by the trim fences. The place always reminded her of those picture-postcard villages in English murder mysteries – Miss Marple's St Mary Mead, for example – where everyone knew his or her place and nothing ever changed. But no one ever got murdered in Brierley Coombe.

Kirsten took the prescription from her pocket and walked into the chemist's. It was only a small place, more decorative than functional, and one of the few chemist's shops that still kept those huge red, green and blue bottles on a shelf high in the window. The sunlight filtered through them onto Mr Hayes's wrinkled face. He had a good dispensary, Kirsten knew, especially for female ailments.

'Hello, Kirsten,' he said with a smile. 'I noticed you'd come back. Sorry to hear about your trouble.'

'Thank you,' Kirsten said. She hoped he wasn't going to go on and tell her how you couldn't be too careful these days, could you. He was that kind of man. But perhaps something in her voice or expression put him off his stroke. Anyway, he just looked puzzled and went to fill the prescription immediately.

With the painkillers in her pocket, Kirsten headed for the house. Brierley Coombe had been her home ever since the family had moved from Bath itself when she was six. Although the village was equidistant from Bristol and Bath, they had always frequented the latter for shopping and entertainment. Her mother regarded Bristol – big city, once-busy port – as too vulgar, and Kirsten had consequently only been there twice in her life. It hadn't seemed so bad to her, but then neither had the north of England.

Kirsten had no friends left in Brierley Coombe, and the way she felt now, that was a blessing; the last thing she wanted was to have to go around explaining herself to people. Indeed, she had to think hard to remember ever having friends or even seeing any young people there at all. That was another way in which it resembled an Agatha Christie village – there were no children, nor could she remember any. It was absurd, she knew, as she had been a child there herself and played with others then, but there was no village school, and, try as she might, she couldn't bring to mind the voices of children playing on the green. Over the years, they had all drifted apart. They went to prep schools first, of course, then on to public schools as boarders, as she had done, for there were no poor people in Brierley Coombe. After that, it was university – usually Oxford or Cambridge – and a profession in the City. Perhaps when they had inherited their parents' houses and made their fortunes or retired from public office, they would come home to spend their remaining days tending the garden and playing bridge.

The peace and quiet that Kirsten had enjoyed at home during the long summer and Easter holidays had always suited her after the hectic social life up at university. She was a bright and studious girl and managed to get plenty of work done – but she was easily distracted by a good film, a party or the chance of a couple of drinks and a chat with friends. At home, she had usually been able to catch up with her work and read ahead for the next term.

But what would she do with her time now? Her student days were over; her life was utterly changed, if not ruined entirely. She didn't know if she would be able to pick up the pieces, let alone put them back together again. Come to that, she didn't know if there were any pieces left. Perhaps she didn't even care.

She was still thinking about it when she opened the gate and walked down the broad path to the house – more of a mansion than a cottage. Her mother was in the garden doing something nasty to the honeysuckle with her secateurs. Gardening and bridge, they were the strict borders of her mother's existence.

When she saw Kirsten coming, she wiped her brow and put down the clippers, which flashed in the light, and shielded her eyes from the sun as she looked up at her daughter. A difficult smile slowly forced the corners of her lips up, but it didn't reach her eyes. It was going to be a long haul, this recovery, Kirsten thought with a sudden chill of fear. It wasn't going to be easy at all.

21
MARTHA

The seagulls were grotesquely distorted, no longer sleek, white bullet-faced birds. Their feathers were mottled with ash-grey, and their bodies were bloated almost beyond recognition. They could hardly stand. Their wiry legs, above webbed feet as yellow as egg yolk, couldn't support their distended bellies, which were stretched so tight that a pattern of blue veins bossed through the grey and white markings. Their wings creaked and flapped like old, moth-eaten awnings in a storm as they tried to fly.

But mostly it was their faces that were different. They still had seagull eyes – cold, dark holes that knew nothing of mercy or pity – but their beaks were encased in long, gelatinous snouts smeared with blood.

They still sounded like seagulls. Even though they could no longer fly, they waddled on the dark sands and keened like the ghosts of a million tortured souls.

Martha woke sweating in the early dawn. Outside, the gulls were screeching, circling. They must have been at it for a while, she thought as her heartbeat slowed. She must have heard them in her sleep, and her mind had translated the sound into the pictograph of a dream. It was like dreaming of searching for a toilet when you've had a bit too much to drink and your body is trying to wake you up before your bladder bursts.

Just the thought of moisture made Martha thirsty. She

got up and drank a glass of water, then crawled into bed again, the sour taste of vomit still in her mouth. Unable to get back to sleep immediately, she found herself thinking of the gulls as her allies. She could imagine them with their sharp hooked beaks picking and pulling at the body in the cave, snatching an eyeball loose or making an ear bleed. Did they never stop? For them, life seemed nothing more than a long-drawn-out feast: one for which you had to go out and catch your own food and tear it to pieces while it was still alive. Had she become like them?

Martha glanced at her watch: 6.29. That day, she remembered, high tide was chalked in as 0658, so the gulls couldn't have found the body unless it was floating on the water's surface. Already the cold North Sea would have stuck its tongue into the cave and slurped Jack Grimley's corpse into its surging maw.

Shivering with horror at what she had done, Martha turned on her side, pulled the covers up to her chin, and drifted back into an uneasy sleep with the paperweight in her hand and the harsh music of squabbling gulls echoing in her ears.

22

KIRSTEN

They came back again that night, the dreams of slashing and slicing, to invade Kirsten's childhood room. The white knight and the black knight, as she had come to call them, both without faces. This time, they seemed to be trying to teach her something. The black knight handed her a long ivory-handled knife, and she plunged it herself into the soft flesh of her thigh. It sank as if into wax. A little blood bubbled up around the edges of the cut, but nothing much. Slowly, she eased out the blade and watched the edges of torn skin draw together again like lips closing. A pinkish bubble swelled and burst. And all the time she didn't feel a thing. Not a thing. Somehow, she knew the faceless white knight was smiling down at her.

23

MARTHA

The dead fish stared up at Martha with glazed, oily eyes. Pinkish-red blood stained their gills and mouths, and sunlight glinted on their silvery scales and pale bellies. The fishy smell was strong in the air, overpowering even the sea's fresh ozone. Holidaymakers paused as they walked along St Ann's Staith and took photographs of the fish sales. The people involved, no doubt used to being camera-fodder for tourists, didn't even spare them a glance.

The auction sheds that Friday morning were hives of activity. Earlier, while Martha had still been sleeping, the boats had come in, and the fishermen had unpacked their catches into iced boxes ready for the sales. Crab pots were stacked and nets lay spread by the sheds. As Martha watched, a man hosed fish scales from the stone quay. Gulls gathered in a raucous cloud, and occasionally one swooped down after a dropped fish.

Of course, Martha realized, they only *sold* the fish here; they didn't clean them and gut them. That must be done elsewhere – in canning factories, perhaps, where the loaded lorries were headed. How little she really knew about the business.

It didn't matter now, though, did it? Odd that he had turned out not to be a fisherman, after all. But you can't be right about everything. Even so, as she walked by and watched the sales, she scanned the groups of fishermen by the railings and the auctioneers and buyers in the open sheds. It was what she had planned to do, and she was doing it anyway, even though there was no longer any point.

Martha felt strangely dazed and light-headed as she walked down the staith towards the bridge. She hadn't slept well after the gulls had woken her, and the thought of what she had done haunted her. At breakfast time she'd been very hungry and had even eaten the fried bread she usually left.

The old couple at the window table were still there, he grinning and even, now, winking, while his wife glared with her beady eyes. But all the others were gone, or had changed into someone else. Martha was finding it hard to keep track. The guests were all starting to look the same: serious young honeymooners; tired but optimistic couples with mischievous toddlers; old people with grey hair and morning coughs. She felt the same way she had on the only occasion she had tried marijuana. She could see more, sense more, each line on the face, the flecks of colour in the eyes, but ultimately it all added up to the same. The more individual the people became to her, the more they became alike.

She crossed the bridge, bought a newspaper, and turned up Church Street. It was becoming a routine. Still, this morning she needed waking up even more than usual: there were important decisions to be made. In the Monk's Haven, she sipped strong black coffee and smoked a cigarette while she flexed her brain on the crossword. Then she flipped through the headlines to see if there was anything interesting going on in the world. There wasn't.

Only for a short while, when she had finished with the paper and still had some coffee and cigarette left, did she allow herself to think of the previous evening. It had been awful, a million times worse than anything she had imagined. She could still feel the loose fragments of bone shifting under her fingers, and that soft, pulpy mass, like a wet sponge, at the top of his head. She didn't feel sorry – he had deserved everything he got – but she was appalled and amazed at herself for really going through with it. After leaving the body in the cave, she had run down to the sea and rinsed her hands and her paperweight again before going back to the guesthouse. She hadn't seen a soul on the way. The door opened smoothly on its oiled hinges and the carpet muffled her ascent to her room. Once safe, she had brushed her teeth three times, but still hadn't been able to get rid of the bitter taste of vomit. Even now, after the breakfast, coffee and cigarettes, she felt herself gagging as she recalled Grimley's body jerking on the sand and those long minutes in the dank, stinking cave: the blood, the staring eye.

The tide would have carried the body out to sea by now. She wanted it to be found soon, wanted to be there to enjoy all the fuss. It wasn't because she was conceited or proud or anything, but because the discovery was all part of the same event. To go now would be like leaving a book unfinished. And Martha *always* finished the books she started, even if she didn't like them. Surely, when they found out the dead man's identity, they would go to his home and find something to connect him with the atrocities he had committed? A man like that can't avoid leaving some kind of evidence behind. And Martha wanted to be around when the full story hit the newspapers. Even if there was a little risk involved, she wanted to stay to hear the gossip and whispers in the pubs and along the staith – to *know* that she was the one who had rid the world of such a monster.

She knew nothing of the tides and currents, but hoped the body would wash up soon somewhere nearby. It would be too much to expect it to land back on Whitby Sands, but it might drift only a short way up the coast to Redcar, Saltburn, Runswick Bay or Staithes, or even further down to Robin Hood's Bay, Scarborough, Flamborough Head or Bridlington. Wherever it turned up, she hoped it wouldn't take long.

She finished her coffee and stubbed out her cigarette. It was eleven o'clock already. Now that she had fulfilled the main part of her purpose here, time was beginning to hang heavy; all she could do was wait, a much more passive activity than searching and planning.

To kill time until lunch, she found herself again mounting the 199 steps to St Mary's and the abbey ruins. There were even more people about this time: children racing one another to the top, counting out loud as they did so – 'Eighty-four, eighty-five, eighty-six . . .' – old folk in elastic stockings, wheezing as they went, dogs with their tongues hanging out running back and forth as if they didn't know up from down.

Martha climbed steadily, counting under her breath. Again, it came to 199, though legend said it was hard to get the same figure twice. At the top stood Caedmon's Cross, a thin twenty-foot upright length of stone, tapering towards the top, where a small cross was mounted.

The length of it was carved with medieval figures – David, Hilda and Caedmon himself – like some sort of stone totem pole, and at the bottom was the inscription, 'To the glory of God and in memory of Caedmon the father of English sacred song fell asleep hard by 680.' Martha knew it wasn't that old, though; it had been carved and erected in 1898, not in the real Caedmon's time. But it still had power. She particularly loved the understated simplicity of 'fell asleep hard by'. When she had to die, that was the way she would like to go. Again, she thought of Jack Grimley and shivered as if someone had just walked across her grave.

Getting her breath back after the long climb – it came less easily since she had started smoking – she paused in the graveyard and looked at the town spread out beyond and below the cross. She could easily pick out the dark, monolithic tower of St Hilda's at the top of her street, and the stately row of white four-storey hotels at the cliff-side end of East Terrace. She could see the whale's jawbone, too, that entry to another world. The rough, sandy gravestones, with their burnt-looking knobbly tops, stood in the foreground; the trick of perspective made them look even bigger than the houses over the harbour.

Martha turned and wandered into the church again. A recorded lecture was in progress in the vestry. It sounded tinny from constant playing. She found herself drifting almost unconsciously towards the front of the church, where, below the tall, ornate pulpit she slipped into a box marked FOR STRANGERS ONLY. It was the same one she'd been in before, and again she felt that sense of luxurious isolation and well-being. Even the sounds of the tourists in the church, with their whispered comments and clicking cameras, were barely audible now. In the hush, she ran her fingertips over the green baize and knelt on a red patterned cushion. There, cut off from the rest of the world, she offered up a prayer of a kind.

24
KIRSTEN

Kirsten lay in bed late the next morning. Outside her window the birds sang and twittered in the trees and the village went about its business. Not that there was much of that. Occasionally, she could hear the whirr of bicycle wheels passing by, and once in a while the thrum of a delivery van's engine.

She put the empty coffee cup back on the tray – breakfast in bed, her mother's idea – and went to open the curtains. Sunlight burst through, catching the cloud of dust motes that swirled in the air. It's all dead skin, Kirsten thought, wondering where on earth she'd heard that. Probably one of those educational television programmes, science for the masses. She opened the window and warm air rushed to greet her, carrying the heavy scent of honeysuckle. A fat bee droned around the opening, then seemed to decide there was nothing for him in there and meandered down to the garden instead.

Kirsten's room reflected just about every stage of her transition from child to worldly student of language and literature. Even her teddy bear sat on the dressing table, propped against the wall. Stretching, she wandered around touching things, her feet sinking deep into the wall-to-wall carpet. The walls and ceiling were painted a kind of sea-green, or was it blue? It really depended on the light, Kirsten decided. Those greeny-blue colours often looked much the same to her: turquoise, cerulean, azure, ultramarine. But today, with the light shimmering on it as on ripples in the ocean, it was definitely the colour of the Mediterranean she remembered from family visits to the Riviera. The walls seemed to swirl and eddy like the water in a Hockney swimming-pool painting. When Kirsten stood in the middle of the room, she felt as if she were floating in a cave of water, or frozen at its centre like a flower in a glass paperweight.

It was two rooms, really. The bed itself, with a three-quarter-size mattress far too soft for Kirsten's taste, was set in a little recess up a stair from the large main room, just below the small window. Also tucked away in there were the dresser and wall cupboards for her clothes. Down the step was the spacious study-cum-sitting room. Her desk stood at a right angle to the picture window, so that she could simply turn her head and look out at the round, green Mendips as she worked. There, she had written essays during her summer vacations and made notes as she read ahead for the following term.

Above the desk, her father had fixed a few bookshelves to the wall on brackets. Apart from some old childhood favourites, like *Black Beauty*, *The Secret Garden*, *Grimm's Fairy Tales* and a few Enid Blytons – *Famous Five*, *Secret Seven* – most of the books were to do with her university courses. They were either for subjects she had studied over the past three years, brought home to save space in her bedsit, or books she had bought second-hand, usually in Bath, for courses she had intended to take in the future. Like the ones on medieval history and literature – including Bede's *An Ecclesiastical History of the English Nation*, Julian of Norwich's *Revelations of Divine Love*, and the anonymous *The Cloud of Unknowing*. But Kirsten had never taken that course. Instead, she had chosen at the last moment special tutorials on Coleridge with a visiting world expert in the field, an American academic who had turned out to be a crashing bore far more interested in trying to look up the front-row women's skirts than in the wisdom of *Biographia Literaria*.

By the side of the shelves was a corkboard, still spiked with old postcards from friends visiting Kenya, Nepal or Finland, photos of her with Sarah and Galen, and poems she had clipped from the TLS. There were no posters of pop stars in the room. She had taken them all down last year, thinking herself far too mature for such things. The only work of art that enhanced her wall was a superb Monet print, which looked wonderfully alive in the sunlight that rippled over it.

She also had an armchair with a footrest, for reading in, and the expensive stereo system. Her records were mostly a mixture of popular classics – Beethoven's Ninth, Tchaikovsky's *Pathétique* (which she had bought after seeing Ken Russell's *The Music Lovers* at the University Film Society) and the soundtrack of *Amadeus* – and a few dated pop albums: Rolling Stones, Wham, U2, David Bowie, Kate Bush, Tom Waits. She wasn't interested in any of these now, and had a hard time choosing the music she wanted to listen to. Finally, she settled for the *Pathétique*, and dressed as the music swelled and surged from its slow and quiet beginning.

But she couldn't stand it. As soon as the lush romantic theme came in, she snatched the needle from the turntable, scratching the record's surface as she did so. The burning pain in her loins had receded, but she had a headache that made music difficult to bear. She was sure it was caused by that dark mass lodged in her mind.

If she closed her eyes, she could even see it, a globe blacker than the rest of the darkness behind her eyes: a black hole, perhaps, that sucked everything in and turned it inside out; or the beginning of an emotional or spiritual cancer about to spread through her whole being.

Kirsten sat down cross-legged on the carpet, holding her head in her hands. With the music gone, she could hear the birds again. Someone called a greeting out in the lane. She could even hear her mother pottering around downstairs.

It was after ten o'clock and such a beautiful day outside that she felt she ought to go for a walk. Any other day, she would have been up before breakfast and down to the woods at the back of the house for a leisurely stroll under the light-dappled leaves. Not today, though. After ten and she still had no idea what to do with herself.

She tried to look ahead into the future, but it was all darkness. Before that night in the park, she had never really given it a thought. Somehow, she had always believed, the future would take care of itself and would be just as privileged, as bright and exciting as the past. But now she had no idea what to do with her life. Whenever she thought of such things her head began to ache even more, as if the bubble were growing inside it and pushing at the inside of her skull. She couldn't concentrate well enough to read a book. She couldn't bear to listen to music. What the hell was she supposed to do? She put her fists to her temples and tensed up. The headache was pounding inside her. She wanted to scream. She wanted to crack open her skull and claw her brain out with her fingernails.

But the rage and the pain ebbed away. Slowly, she got to her feet and walked up the step to the bedroom. There, she took her clothes off again, dry-swallowed three prescription analgesics and crawled back into bed.

25

MARTHA

Saturday brought Martha two important pieces of news: one that she had been expecting, and another that changed everything.

The day started as usual with a wink from the old man and a glare from his wife at breakfast. Martha wasn't very hungry, so she skipped the cereal and just picked at her bacon and eggs. She was wondering whether to move out that day and find somewhere else in another part of the town. It seemed a good idea. People were getting far too used to her here, and there might come a time when awkward questions would be asked.

After breakfast, she went back up to her room and packed her gear in the holdall. She had one last smoke there, leaning on the window sill and looking left and right, from the close and overbearing St Hilda's to the distant St Mary's. It was the first overcast day in the entire week. A chill wind had blown in off the North Sea, bringing the scent of rain with it. Already a light drizzle was falling, like a thin mist enveloping the town. Visibility was poor, and St Mary's looked like the blurred grey ghost of a church on top of its hill.

After checking the room once more to make sure she had forgotten nothing, Martha padded downstairs and found the proprietor helping his wife carry the dirty dishes through to the kitchen.

'I'd like to settle up now, if that's all right,' she said.

'Fine.' He wiped his hands on the grubby white apron he was wearing. 'I'll make out the bill.'

Martha waited in the hallway. The usual flyers about Whitby's scenic attractions, restaurants and entertainments lay on the polished wood table by the registration book. On the wall above was a mirror. Martha examined herself. What she had done hadn't changed her appearance. She looked no different from when she had arrived: same too-thin lips, tilted nose and almond eyes, the same untidy cap of light brown hair. All she needed was pointed ears, she thought, and she might be able to pass for a Vulcan.

'Here you are.' The man eyed her with amusement as he handed over the bill. Martha checked the total and pulled the correct amount from her purse.

'Cash?' He seemed surprised.

'That's right.' She didn't want to use cheques or credit cards; they could be too easily traced. She had cashed her father's cheque and emptied her bank account before she set off for Whitby, so she had quite a bit of money – not all of it so obviously bulging out of her purse, but hidden away in the holdall's 'secret' pockets.

'I suppose you'll need a receipt?'

For a second she was puzzled. Why would she want a receipt?

'For tax purposes,' he went on.

'Oh. Yes, please.'

'Hang on.'

Tax purposes? Of course! She was supposed to be a writer here to do research. She could deduct her expenses from her income tax. She was slipping, forgetting the details.

The man returned and handed her a slip of paper. 'I hope the book's a success,' he said. 'Certainly plenty of atmosphere in Whitby. I don't read romances myself, but the wife does. We'll look out for it.'

'Yes, please do,' Martha said. She wanted to tell him it was an academic, historical work, but somehow that just didn't seem important now. It was all lies anyway: romance or history, what did it matter? 'Thank you very much,' she said, and walked out of the door.

It really was cool outside. She had been intending to carry the quilted jacket over her arm, but she put it on instead as she set off on her usual morning trek to the Monk's Haven. She wasn't sure what to do with the rest of the day. Maybe go up to St Mary's again and shut herself in the box pew. She hadn't felt as safe and secure in years as she had the previous day up there. And then she would have to find another B&B to stay at.

The rain smelled of dead fish and seaweed. Browsers on Silver Street and Flowergate wore plastic macs or carried brollies, and fathers held onto their children's hands. Martha thought that was odd. When the sun shone, everyone seemed more relaxed and the children ran free, swinging their buckets and spades, dancing along the pavement and bumping into people. But as soon as it rained, pedestrians drew in and held on tight to one another. It was probably some primordial fear, she decided, a throwback to primitive instinct. They weren't aware they were doing it. After all, man was just another species of animal, despite all his inflated ideas about his place in the great chain of being. People had no idea at all why they behaved the way they did. Most of the time they were merely victims of forces beyond their control and comprehension, just as she had been.

You could only depend on reason and organization to a certain degree, Martha had discovered, and beyond that point lived monsters. Sometimes you had to cross the boundary and live with the monsters for a while. Sometimes you had no choice.

At her usual newsagent's on the corner just past the bridge, she bought a local paper and the *Independent* and headed for warmth, coffee and a cigarette.

First, she picked up the local paper and found what she was looking for on the front page. It wasn't much, just a small paragraph tucked away near the bottom, but it was the seed from which a bigger story would soon grow. BODY WASHED UP NEAR SANDSEND, the small-caps headline ran. Sandsend was only about four miles away. That was better than she'd hoped for. She thought it would have been carried further than four miles, and such an event might not seem so important in a large town like Scarborough. She read on:

> The body of man was discovered by a young couple on an isolated stretch of beach near Sandsend last night. So far, police say, the man has not been identified. Chief Superintendent Charles Kallen has asked anyone with information about a missing person to come forward and contact the police immediately. Time of death is estimated at no earlier than Thursday, and the body appears to have been drifting in the sea since then. Police had no comment to make about the cause of death.

They didn't know very much. Or if they did, they weren't saying. Martha would have thought it was obvious how the man had met his death. But the sea did strange things, she reminded herself. The police would probably think that his head injuries had been caused by rocks. The forensic people were clever, though, and they would soon discover at a post-mortem examination what had really happened.

A little disappointed at the thinness of the story, Martha ordered another black coffee and lit her third cigarette of the day. Should she stay in town until the real news broke? she wondered. This story just seemed so flat and anti-climactic. She should hang on at least until he was identified. On the other hand, that news would make the national dailies, which she could read anywhere. No, it was best to stay. Stick close to the action. She had gone so far that it would be futile to pull out now.

Next she turned to the *Independent*. She didn't expect to read anything about the discovery of Grimley's body there, but she looked just the same. At the bottom of the second page, tucked away like a mad relation in a cellar, was a short paragraph that caught her eye. It appeared under the simple heading, ANOTHER BODY FOUND. Perhaps that was it. Martha folded the paper and read on.

> Police last night say they found the body of a nineteen-year-old female on a stretch of waste ground near the University of Sheffield. Evidence suggests that the girl, a student at the university, was killed shortly after dark on Friday evening. Detective Superintendent Elswick, in charge of the field investigation, told reporters that evidence indicates the unnamed woman is the sixth victim of the killer who has come to be called the 'Student Slasher'. All his victims have been female students at northern universities. Police refused to reveal the exact nature

> of the girl's injuries. The killer has been operating in the north for over a year now, and there has been much criticism of the police's handling of the investigation. When asked why the killer hadn't been caught yet, Superintendent Elswick declined to comment.

Martha felt herself grow cold. The conversations going on around her turned to a meaningless background hum. All she could hear clearly was the litany of names running through her mind: Margaret Snell, Kathleen Shannon, Jane Pitcombe, Kim Waterford, Jill Sarsden. And now another, name unknown. Hands shaking, she lit another cigarette from the stub of her old one and read the article again. It said exactly the same, word for word. The 'Student Slasher' had struck again. She had been mistaken in Grimley. She had killed the wrong man.

Choking back the vomit, she crushed out her cigarette, rushed to the tiny toilet and locked the door behind her. After bringing up her breakfast, she splashed icy water on her face and leaned against the sink breathing fast and deep. She still felt dizzy. Everything was spinning around her as if she was standing on a high balcony suffering from vertigo. Her skin felt cold and clammy; her mouth tasted dry and sour. She took a deep breath and held it. Another. Another. Her pulse began to steady.

The wrong man, she thought, sitting down on the toilet and holding her head in her hands. And she had been so damn *sure*. The hoarse voice, the accent, the calloused hands, the low, dark fringe, the glittering eyes – it had all been right. So where did she go wrong? She couldn't have been thinking clearly at all. It had already occurred to her that her original theory – that he was a fisherman – must have been wrong, but she had gone ahead anyway. Her search had been based on slender enough evidence from the start. Anyone else would have said that she was looking for a needle in a haystack and, what's more, that she had no idea *which* haystack it was supposed to be in. But Martha had trusted her instincts. She had been sure that she would find him and that she would know him when she did. Well, so much for her bloody instincts.

Looking back, she could see that she should have known, that her perception had been flawed. He was too young, for a start, and though the voice was close, certainly in accent, it was pitched lower and had less of a rasp. The eyes and hands were the same, but there had been no deeply etched lines on his face.

How could she have let herself get carried away? This made her a murderer, pure and simple. There was no excuse. She remembered with a shudder his body twitching on the sand in the moonlight, the shattered bone and the sticky brain matter beneath her fingertips and the stifling sea-wrack smell of the cave. She had killed an innocent man. A man who would probably have forced himself on her eventually anyway, true – but an *innocent* man. And now she had to live with it.

She got up, drank some water from the tap and washed her face. She looked pale, but not enough that people would really notice. Taking another deep breath, she unbolted the door and walked back to her table. She seemed steady enough on her feet. She hoped nobody in the cafe had seen the way she had panicked. Still, they would have no idea why. Her coffee had cooled down, but the cigarette, improperly stubbed out, still smouldered in the ashtray. The story in the folded paper stared up at her. She turned it over and looked out of the window. Holidaymakers drifted by like shades in limbo. 'I had not thought death had undone so many,' she found herself thinking, but she couldn't remember where the words came from.

Should she call the hunt off, then, go back home to the shell of a life she had made for herself? No. Even now, at such a low point, she knew she must not do that. If she did, then it all came to nothing. Grimley would have died for nothing. Only if she fulfilled her purpose, set out to do what she had to, would any of it mean anything. She was still convinced she had got the right place: she would find her man in Whitby, or somewhere very close by. He was still here.

She grieved for Jack Grimley, would do anything to undo what she had done. But, she reminded herself, this was a war of a kind, and in war there are no innocent bystanders. Grimley might have been a good person, but he was still a man. To Martha, all men were potentially the same as the one she sought. Grimley, given the chance, would have led her into one of those caves and tried to rip her clothes off and . . . It didn't bear thinking about. Men were all the same, all violators and murderers of women. No doubt the real 'Student Slasher' was an ordinary, well-respected citizen on the outside. Maybe he even had a wife and children. But Martha didn't care about that. She just wanted to kill him.

Why did he travel inland so often? Was it just because that was where the universities were, or was it something to do with his work? She could no longer bank on his being a fisherman, after all, so maybe he was a travelling salesman based in Whitby. This was the kind of thing she had to do now – think again, plan again, act again. She couldn't let herself get dragged down by one mistake, no matter how horrifying it was. She had simply been too eager, too sure of herself, too impatient. She would have to focus more clearly on the task ahead, bring her intellect into harmony with her instinct. So start by *thinking,* she told herself. He travels inland frequently. Why? There, at least, was something concrete, a place to start.

'Anything else, love?'

'What?'

It was the waitress clearing away the empty table next to hers. 'Another cup of coffee?'

'Yes, all right.' Her last one had gone cold, anyway, Martha remembered.

'You stay there and I'll bring it over, love. You're looking a bit peaky. Had a shock?'

Martha shook her head. 'Thank you. No, no. Nothing serious.' She would have to watch herself, she realized. It wouldn't do at all if she went around town making a spectacle of herself. People would remember her.

When the waitress had brought the coffee, Martha returned to her thoughts. She knew that Superintendent Elswick and his minions would be wasting their time trying to figure out the killer's motives and come up with a psychological profile. It hadn't got them very far yet, had it? But she didn't give a damn about the man's unhappy childhood or the time he'd been forced to kiss his dead grandmother. Maybe his mother had abandoned him and gone to university. Perhaps that was why he always attacked young female students. Perhaps he had a daughter who had been corrupted as a student. Or maybe he just thought university campuses were dens of iniquity, full of sluts and sex-crazed bitches, the kind of place he was most likely to find loose women – and liberated women, careless or foolish enough to walk home alone in the dark. Again, she didn't care. When she found him she wasn't going to psychoanalyse him. She was going to kill him. Simple as that.

The rush of thoughts lifted Martha's spirits. It proved that her mind was working clearly again and that she could harden herself against experience, as she had to. When she looked back on what she had done the other night, keeping the grotesque images at bay, she saw that there was good in it, too. It hadn't really been a wasted effort at all. If she looked at it from a positive viewpoint, she could see killing Grimley as a kind of dress rehearsal for the real thing. A horrible thought, perhaps, but at least now she knew she could go through with it. Grimley's murder had also been an initiation of a kind, a baptism in blood. She had killed once; therefore, she could kill again. Only next time, she thought, fingering the paperweight in her holdall, she would be certain to get it right.

26

KIRSTEN

Kirsten remembered how she used to love the gossamer light in the woods, green and silver filaments dancing in the leaves, and the way it shot through gaps in the foliage here and there and lit up clumps of bluebells or tiny forget-me-nots by the brook, making them seem like still-life paintings rather than living, growing plants.

Today, though, she felt no elation as she trudged along the winding path under the high trees. After two days of hiding in her room, she had made the effort to go out – more for her parents' sake than for her own. Her father was beginning to look even more haggard than ever, and her mother was getting more impatient by the minute. They were almost at their wits' end with her, she knew. They wanted to tell her to put the unpleasantness behind her, stop moping and get on with her life. Only pity prevented them. They still felt sorry for her, and it was a sorrow they couldn't give voice to. So she had come to the woods to get them off her back. If she pretended all was well, they wouldn't know any different.

And it had worked. As soon as she had come downstairs the previous evening, they had cheered up, offered her a drink and sat companionably watching television with her. That morning, her father had returned to work, albeit reluctantly, and her mother had said she was going to Wells to do some shopping, as Bath was getting far too shabby and touristy of late.

But nature did nothing for Kirsten. As she walked, she remembered a passage from Coleridge's ode 'Dejection':

> A grief without a pang, void, dark, and drear,
> A stifled, drowsy, unimpassioned grief.
> Which finds no natural outlet, no relief.
> In word, or sigh, or tear.

Looking at the flowers in the light, she felt for Coleridge when he wrote, 'I see, not feel, how beautiful they are! . . . I may not hope from outward forms to win / The passion and the life, whose fountains are within.' Too true, Kirsten thought. The light that danced among the leaves could give her nothing, and her inner fountains had all dried up, had all been sucked through the dark star in her mind and turned to blood.

There was no point going on. About halfway along her usual route, she turned around and headed back home. Her room was the best place to be, and the house would be quiet with everyone out. Maybe in a few weeks the emptiness and the pain would go away and she would find herself back to normal. Already, though, she was finding it hard to remember what normal was.

Two black and white cows watched her with their big mournful eyes as she crossed the narrow stretch of grass between the woods and the back gate of the house. Her head still ached, and the depression suddenly gripped her more tightly than before.

Back in the house, she wandered aimlessly from room to room for a while, thought of making a sandwich, then decided she wasn't hungry. Getting drunk seemed like a good idea at first, but she had an even better one.

First she took a plastic bag from the cupboard under the stairs, then went up to the bathroom and opened the cabinet. Inside were the usual things: aspirin, antihistamine, antacid tablets, cold capsules, cough medicine and some old prescription antibiotics. Leaving only the cough mixture, she emptied the rest into the bag.

Next she crept into her parents' room. They kept their various pills in the top drawer of the bedside dresser. She took out her mother's tranquillizers and Mogadons and her father's blood-pressure tablets and poured them all into the plastic bag too.

In her own room, she opened her shoulder bag and found the prescription analgesic the doctor had given her for her pain. It was the same bag she'd been carrying the night of the attack, and she realized that she had never really wondered what had happened to it before. The police must have been through it, then had probably returned it to her room at the hospital while she was still unconscious. Emptying it on her bed, she found half a month's supply of birth-control pills still left. Smiling at the irony, she added them to her bagful and carried the lot back downstairs.

The living room was a huge split-level affair. At the front was a bay window that looked out on the lawn, the honeysuckle, the rose beds and the High Street beyond the white fence; at the back, French windows opened out onto the large garden, with its central copper beech, more flower beds and a croquet lawn. Beyond that was the woods. Kirsten opened the windows to let the sun slant in and sat on the carpet in its rays. She had taken a bottle of her father's best whisky from the cocktail cabinet – Glen-where-am-I, he always called it – and set it down beside her.

She picked up the plastic bag and poured the collection of pills onto the carpet in front of her. They were all the colours of the rainbow, and more besides: blue, green, red, white, yellow, pink, orange. Then she picked a few up, trying to get a nice selection of colours in her palm, swallowed them, and washed them down with a belt of Scotch straight from the bottle.

It was idyllic, sitting cross-legged there in the honeyed sunlight as the bees droned from flower to flower outside the French windows. Kirsten hadn't eaten all day, and she soon began to feel light-headed – light except for the dark cloud, which was far more dense than possible for something so small. At least it was small today. Sometimes it swelled up like a balloon, but today it was a nasty black marble. If she held it in her hand, she thought, it would probably burst right through her flesh with its weight.

A red one, a blue one, a yellow one, and a gulp of fiery whisky. So it went on; the level in the bottle dropped and the pile of pills on the tan carpet diminished handful by handful. Soon, Kirsten's head was swimming. Specks of light danced behind her closed eyes. When she opened them and looked out onto the sunlit garden again, she could have sworn it was snowing out there.

27
MARTHA

After Martha got off the bus at the station near Valley Bridge Road in Scarborough at about one o'clock in the afternoon, the first thing she did was grab a ham and cheese sandwich and a half-pint of lager and lime in the nearest pub, a quiet, run-down place with sticky tables.

She felt much calmer than she had earlier in the day. The news had hit her so hard she had almost given up, but in the end it had only strengthened her resolve. She couldn't go back without finishing her business on the coast. But now she knew that her precious instinct wasn't infallible, she would have to be much more certain the next time. How she could find proof beyond what she remembered of his appearance and voice, she didn't know. Perhaps she would have to lure him on and confront him. When Grimley had said he didn't remember her, he had been telling the truth. The real killer most likely *would* remember her, and if she could get him to admit to that, then she would be sure. She didn't want to leave a string of bodies behind her before she got the right one. She shivered at the thought of turning into the kind of monster she was out to destroy.

She stubbed out her cigarette and got up to leave. Things weren't as simple as they had been a couple of days ago. Now there was a chance that the police would soon identify Grimley and start looking into his death. Martha couldn't let herself get caught. She had already moved out of the Abbey Terrace room, but there were a few other things she could do to preserve her freedom before returning to Whitby.

She walked past the train station, then turned right down Westborough, where there seemed to be plenty of activity. The street guide she'd bought in Whitby gave her some sense of direction as she explored the side streets, but it didn't mark the main shopping areas. From what she could see, however, she was close to what she needed. The weather was just as grey as it had been earlier in Whitby, though the drizzle had stopped and it was warm enough now for her to take off her quilted jacket and carry it over her arm.

What she needed first was a big department store. Marks & Spencer would do fine, she thought, noticing the frontage: the clothes there were well made and reasonably stylish, but not too expensive. After wandering around the ladies' wear floor and flicking through the racks, she chose a plain, pleated black skirt, which hung well below her knees, and some black patterned tights to go with it. For the top, she bought a cream cotton blouse which buttoned up to the throat. She also picked out a navy-blue cardigan in case it got cool again.

In the shoe department, she chose a pair of no-nonsense pumps – sensible shoes, her mother would have called them – durable enough and easy to walk in. As soon as she had made her purchases, she went outside to a public toilet and changed, storing her old gear – jeans, T-shirt, sneakers and quilted jacket – in the holdall. No point throwing the stuff away, she thought. Nobody was likely to want to search her bag, and she could certainly wear the clothes again. She studied herself in the mirror and approved of the result. Nice girl, secretary perhaps, or receptionist. It was just the right inconspicuous, anonymous effect she was after. To improve the new look, she could also start wearing her glasses instead of contact lenses.

The sun had bored a few ragged holes through the cloud covering, and families were heading down Eastborough towards the South Beach. The children no longer hung onto their parents' hands, but dawdled and squabbled, swinging bright plastic buckets and spades. The occasional courting couple ambled by, hand in hand, in no hurry to be anywhere as long as they were with each other.

Martha found a Boots and made a beeline for the make-up counter. There she bought the basics: lipstick, eye-shadow, mascara, foundation, blusher – all in perfectly ordinary, conservative colours. In a cafe toilet across the street, she stood next to another woman who was also doing her face. The woman smiled and made small talk about the weather and the way men always complained about how long a woman spent in the toilet.

'And do you know,' she went on, squinting as she applied thick mascara, 'I don't even think they notice the difference when we come back. What do they think we're doing in here all that time? Do they think our bladders take longer to empty or something?' She chuckled, then sighed. 'Is it worth it? I ask myself.' She put on a coating of glossy red lipstick and patted her lips with a Kleenex to remove the excess. Then she sucked and pursed them a few times, just to make sure.

Martha looked at her and noticed the red stain on her front teeth. It made her think of vampires. 'I don't know,' she replied. 'I suppose it depends on what you want.'

This was too philosophical for the woman. She

crumpled the smeared tissue and dropped it in the bin, then frowned, sighed again, patted her hair and left.

Martha did the best she could. She had never been very good with cosmetics, never used them much except for dances and parties. The object this time, though, was not so much to turn herself into an irresistible beauty, but simply to look different from the young woman who had left Whitby that morning. This turned out to be surprisingly easy. The eyeshadow and mascara accentuated her eyes, but helped to disguise their shape. Blusher highlighted her cheekbones, and the shadows it cast below altered the planes of her face. The lipstick thickened and lengthened her lips just enough to make her mouth look larger and fuller. All in all, she thought, admiring the result, it was a success. Already she looked like a different person, and she hadn't even finished yet. She decided against wearing her glasses for the time being. Why go too far?

In the next department store, she headed for the small wig section. She didn't want anything showy, like platinum blonde or jet black, but something perhaps just a little darker than her natural colour. It had to be longer, though, and it had to look real.

'Can I help you, madam?' an assistant asked.

'Just browsing.' Martha didn't want anyone helping her on and off with wigs and making up her mind for her. That was the kind of thing a shopgirl might remember. Luckily, another customer came along, an older woman with tufts of hair missing, as if she'd been undergoing chemotherapy for cancer, and the assistant sidled up to her. The two of them began an involved discussion on exactly what was required, and the assistant led the woman over to a chair in front of a mirror.

Martha had never bought a wig before; she had never even tried one on. Gingerly, she picked up a long ash-blonde one just to see what it looked like on her. The effect was astonishing. The make-up alone had done a good job, but the addition of the wig changed her looks completely: it turned her into an entirely new person with a different history and personality. Martha stood and stared at herself, making up a story about the young woman she saw there: born in King's Lynn, Norfolk, educated at an exclusive girl's boarding school; sexy, independent, the owner of a chain of boutiques, perhaps, and often abroad on buying trips. Suddenly, afraid that people might be watching her, she snapped out of the game and got back to business.

After trying on a number of other hairpieces when she was sure nobody was paying her much attention, Martha finally found one that suited her. It was chestnut-coloured, but not unrealistically shiny, and curled under just above her shoulders. A short fringe fell over her forehead, too, and somehow this made her eyes look even more different. She carried the wig over to the nearest till, paid and took it away with her.

She took the escalator to the women's toilets on the fourth floor. When she pushed the door open, a frail-looking woman with a scrawny body and a large head jumped up from where she'd been sitting on the edge of a sink and quickly stuck her hand behind her back. Martha noticed that she was wearing a sales assistant's uniform – blue suit and white blouse, with a brass name-tag on the jacket identifying her as Sylvia Wield – and she looked as guilty as a schoolkid caught smoking behind the cycle sheds. When she saw it was only a customer, she relaxed and put her free hand to her chest.

'You gave me the fright of my life,' she said. 'I thought it was the supervisor. Do you know, we're not even allowed to smoke in our own lounge these days? That's why I have to sneak in here whenever I want a fag. It's usually quiet up here in furnishing.'

Martha smiled in understanding, then she went and sat in a cubicle until the saleswoman had gone. The shock of the meeting had made her own heart beat faster, too. When all was quiet again, she put on the wig and, looking around the door on her way out to make sure she wasn't noticed, she slipped down the nearest staircase back into the street.

She knew she should get back to Whitby soon and check into a different bed and breakfast place, but while she was in Scarborough, she couldn't resist a walk down to the harbour, just in case.

There wasn't much activity there. The lobster pots were stacked on the quay, and only one or two locals stood around, painting their boats or fiddling with the engines. The smell of fish was even stronger there than it was in Whitby. Mixed with the stink of diesel oil, it made her feel nauseated. As soon as she became aware of a young lad leaning nearby against the wall and giving her the eye, she decided she was wasting her time and headed for the bus station.

On the journey back to Whitby, she read *Jude the Obscure*, which she had bought at the same little bookshop on Church Street after finishing *Emma*. Within half an hour or so, it was time to get off again. This time, instead of climbing up to West Cliff, she turned into the area behind the station, another part of the town noted for its holiday accommodation. On a terrace of tall, dark guesthouses facing the railway tracks, all with VACANCY signs in their windows, she chose the middle one.

Moments after she had pushed the doorbell, a stout young woman with rubbery features came rushing from somewhere out the back and opened the door. Her hands were wet, and she looked tired and flustered, as if she was trying to juggle ten domestic chores at once, but she managed a smile when Martha said she'd like a room. She was probably only in her twenties, Martha thought, but hard work, children and worry had aged her.

'Single, love?' Her voice had a sing-song, whining quality.

'Yes, please. An attic will do, if you've got one.' Martha liked being high up in rooms with beams and slanting ceilings.

'Sorry, love,' the woman said, drying her hands on her pinafore. 'The only single we've got is a small room at the back.'

'I'll take a look,' Martha said.

It was on the second floor, a depressing little room with white stucco-effect wallpaper, looking out on back-yards full of dustbins and prowling cats.

'It's quiet,' the woman said. 'Being at the back, like, you can't hardly hear the trains. Not that there are many these days.'

She seemed anxious to please. Martha reckoned that she and her husband probably hadn't been in the place long and were finding it difficult to make ends meet. The woman had clearly made an effort to make the hall and rooms appear cheerful, but the house itself was drab and old; it gave the impression of being damp and chilly even though it wasn't, and its proximity to the railway tracks must surely put people off. Martha didn't mind, though.

It was hidden, anonymous. Even if it didn't boast a view of St Mary's, it would make a cosy retreat. And she liked this woman, with her tired eyes and wash-reddened hands, felt sorry for her. In a way, Martha saw herself as perhaps a champion of women like this one – not just the obviously abused, attacked and assaulted, but the weary, the downtrodden and the dispirited.

'How much is it?' she asked.

'Eight pounds fifty, love. And we don't do evening meals. I'm sorry.'

'That's all right. I'm usually out then, anyway.' Martha thought it over quickly: it was cheap, obscure, and the woman hadn't asked her any awkward questions about what she was doing in Whitby all alone. There would be a husband around, no doubt, but he'd probably have a day job and, with luck, she wouldn't see much of him. Even the husband at the other place had stayed out of the way except when she had arrived and left. 'I'll take it,' she said, dropping her holdall on the pale green bedspread.

The woman looked relieved. 'Good. If you'll just come down and register, I'll give you the keys.'

Martha followed her back down, noticing as she went how the stairs creaked here and there. That could be a problem if she had to sneak in late like before. But if she did a bit of discreet checking on her way up and down in the first day or so, she could find out exactly which stairs to avoid.

The hall was much shabbier than the one in Abbey Terrace. There was no mirror, and even the advertising flyers looked dusty and curled at the edges.

'I'm Mrs Cummings, by the way,' said the woman, giving Martha a card to fill in. 'Sorry if I seem to be rushing you, but my husband's usually out on the boats so I've got to run the place more or less by myself.'

'Boats? Is he a fisherman?'

'Well, sort of. He takes groups of tourists out for morning and afternoon fishing trips. It's not as if they catch enough to sell or anything, some of them just want a ride out in a boat. But he makes a decent living in season. Still, it means he's up before dawn and often not back till after teatime. Depends on the tides, like, and how many want to go out. There's good days and bad. We get by.'

It would have been too ironic to be true, Martha thought, if she had actually found herself staying in the same house as the man she wanted. But at least he might know where the fishermen hung out and what other local industries had close links to fishing. She could only question him casually, like an interested tourist, but it might be worth a try.

'Breakfast is eight to eight-thirty,' Mrs Cummings said. 'I have to get it all over and done with quickly so I can get the kids off to school. And here are the keys.' She handed Martha two keys on a ring. 'The big one's for the front door. We always lock up at about half past ten but you can come in when you want, and the Yale's for your room. There's a small lounge on the ground floor – it's marked – with a kettle and a telly. Only black and white, I'm afraid. But there's teabags and a jar of Nescafé. You can brew up there any time you like.'

'Thank you,' Martha said with a smile. 'I'm sure everything will be fine.'

Mrs Cummings took the card Martha had given her. 'Going out now, are you?'

'Yes, I thought I'd just have a little walk before dinner.'

'Good idea. Well, see you later . . . er . . . ' She looked at the card. 'Susan, is it?'

'Yes, that's right. Bye for now.' And Susan Bridehead walked out into the late Whitby afternoon.

28

KIRSTEN

'Yes, I *am* sure that Kirsten doesn't need her stomach pumped,' Dr Craven repeated patiently. 'You saw for yourself, she brought up the tablets before they had time to work their way into her bloodstream. At worst she'll feel a little sick and dizzy for a while – which is no more than she deserves – and she'll probably have a heck of a headache.'

They stood in Kirsten's room, where she lay tucked up in bed. Her mother was flapping about and wringing her hands like a character in a Victorian melodrama.

'You're upset, understandably,' the doctor went on. 'Perhaps it would be best if you were to take a tranquillizer and lie down for a while yourself.'

'Yes.' Kirsten's mother nodded, then she frowned. 'Oh, but I can't.' She looked at her daughter. 'She took them all.'

It wasn't meant as an accusation, Kirsten knew, but she was made to feel once again that she had done nothing but make a nuisance of herself since she got back home: first she had refused to go out, then she had been sick all over the living-room carpet, and now she was depriving her mother of the oblivion the poor woman so desperately needed in order to cope with the nasty twists of fate that had disrupted her life of late.

Luckily, Dr Craven reached for her bag and came to the rescue.

'Samples,' she said, tossing over the small foil and cellophane package. Inside were four yellow pills, each in its own compartment. 'And I'll give you another prescription to replace the ones you lost. Kirsten needs rest now.'

She scribbled on her pad, ripped off the sheet and passed it over. The brusqueness of her tone and gesture got through even to Kirsten's mother, who normally seemed impervious to hints that her company wasn't required.

'Yes . . . yes . . .' Clutching the package and the prescription, she drifted towards the door. 'Yes . . . I'll just go and get a glass of water and have a lie-down . . .'

When she had finally gone, the doctor sighed and sat on the edge of the bed beside Kirsten. 'She means well, you know,' she said.

Kirsten nodded. 'I know.'

Dr Craven let the silence stretch for a while before she said, in a tone far gentler than Kirsten would have believed possible for her, 'But it *was* a silly thing to do, wasn't it?'

Kirsten didn't answer. She wasn't sure.

'Look,' Dr Craven went on, 'I can't pretend to know what you feel like after what happened. I can't even imagine what you went through, what you're still going through, but I can tell you this: suicide isn't the answer. Why did you do it?'

'I don't know,' Kirsten said. 'It just seemed like a good idea at the time. I'm not being facetious. I didn't know what else to do.'

Dr Craven looked puzzled. 'What do you mean?'

'I didn't enjoy being outside. I wasn't really hungry. I didn't fancy reading a book or watching television. I was just at a loose end. Then I thought I'd get drunk, then . . . I've not been sleeping well.'

'There *are* other options, Kirsten. That's what you've got to remember. I don't suppose I should be all that surprised you tried something foolish. As I said, I can't imagine how you feel, but I know it must be terrible. What you have to do now is understand that there's no quick and easy way back to health. Your body is taking care of itself well enough, but your emotions, your feelings are damaged too, perhaps even more than we realize. Rest will help, of course, and time, but you won't be able to go on hiding for ever. There'll come a time when you have to make the effort to start living again, to get out and about, meet people, get involved in life. I know it probably sounds terrifying just at the moment, but you must make that your goal. If you let your fears dominate you, then you've lost. You mustn't give in, you have to fight it. Do you understand what I'm trying to tell you?'

'I think so,' Kirsten said. 'I . . . I just don't know if I can. I don't know how.'

'Sermon over.' Dr Craven's lips twitched in a smile again. 'Now back to practicalities. Nobody can make you, but I strongly suggest that you see a specialist in Bath, someone who knows about the kinds of things you're feeling. I can recommend just the right person.'

'A psychiatrist, like you mentioned before?'

'Yes. I feel it's even more important now. I'll set up an appointment for you, but what I want to know, Kirsten, is will you go?'

Kirsten turned her head aside and looked through the small window at the sky and tree tops. At least it had stopped snowing, she thought. That had been the last thing she had registered before coming over faint and retching on the carpet: how odd that it was snowing in August. It hadn't been snowing at all, of course; it had just been her vision going haywire.

She turned back to Dr Craven. 'All right,' she said, 'I'll go. I don't suppose I've got anything to lose.'

'You've got quite a lot to gain, young lady,' the doctor said, patting her hand. 'Good. I'll fix up an appointment and let you know. Now are you sure you're feeling all right physically? No ill effects?'

'No, I'm fine. Just a bit woozy. Mostly I feel silly.'

'And so you jolly well should.' Back to her normal self, the doctor stood up and walked to the bedroom door. Just before she left, she turned and said, 'You can stay in bed till tomorrow morning, that's quite reasonable for someone who's done what you just did, but after that I want to see you up and about. Understood?'

Kirsten nodded. Left alone, she pulled the sheets up to her chin and stared at the long, faint crack in the ceiling. Her head was still throbbing and her stomach felt sore, but apart from that, everything seemed in working order, considering the mixture of pills and the amount of alcohol she had taken. As Dr Craven had said, none of the tablets had had time to do any damage, and she was suffering more from the effects of the Scotch, which was all the stomach wall had had time to absorb.

She would go to the specialist in Bath, she decided. Though she had little faith in psychiatrists, having studied and dismissed both Freud and Jung in a first-year general studies course, she felt desperate enough to try anything. If only he could get that dark cloud out of her mind and give her something – anything – to replace the terrible cold emptiness that she felt about everything. It wasn't fear that kept her indoors, in her bed, it was just apathy. There was nothing she wanted to do, nothing at all. She felt foolish and despised, and that was about it. With a bit of luck, perhaps the specialist really could help. Maybe he could give her something to live for.

29
SUSAN

During the night, the seagulls by the lower harbour were just as noisy as the ones on West Cliff, but breakfast at Mrs Cummings's establishment was an altogether less elaborate affair. For a start, there was no cereal, just a small glass of rather watery orange juice for each person. Nor was there a choice between tea or coffee, only tea. The main course consisted of one fried egg with the white still runny, two thin rashers of bacon and a slice of fried bread; there were no grilled tomatoes, mushrooms or slices of black pudding. There was, of course, plenty of cold toast and marmalade.

And the whole meal seemed to be taking place at fast forward. Sue was a little late coming down, as she had her face to fix and her wig to secure. No sooner had she sat down than the plate appeared in front of her. The tea had already been mashing for some time, and it tasted so bitter by then that she had to resort to sugar. She never had time to get around to the orange juice.

The only other guests in evidence were a bedraggled-looking bachelor in a grey sleeveless V-neck pullover, who hadn't either shaved or combed his hair, and two bored teenage girls with multicoloured spikes of hair and warpaint make-up. Sue finished quickly, went up to her room to smoke a cigarette and pick up her bag, then wandered out.

It was another grey day outside, but the thin light was

piercingly bright. Weather like this always puzzled Sue. There was no sun in sight, no blue sky, no dazzle on the water, but she found that she had to screw up her eyes to stop them from watering. She considered buying sunglasses and perhaps a wide-brimmed hat, but decided against it. Enough was enough; there was no point in going overboard and ending up *looking* like someone in disguise.

First she bought cigarettes and newspapers at the closest newsagent's, then she found a different cafe on Church Street in which to enjoy her morning coffee. She had read in crime novels about people changing their appearance but still getting caught because they were stupid enough to stick to the same inflexible routines.

When she looked at the local newspaper, she noticed that it was a Saturday late edition she hadn't seen. Of course! Today was Sunday; there would be no local papers, only the nationals. In the stop-press section at the bottom of the left-hand column on page one, she saw an update on the Grimley story:

> Police are not satisfied that the body washed up on Sandsend beach last night, now identified as that of Mr Jack Grimley, died of natural causes. Detective Inspector Cromer has informed our reporter that a post-mortem has been ordered. Mr Grimley was last seen alive when he left a Whitby pub, the Lucky Fisherman, at about 9.45 p.m. Thursday evening. Anyone with further information is asked to get in touch with the local police as soon as possible. Mr Grimley, 30, was a self-employed joiner and part-time property assistant at Whitby Theatre. He lived alone.

Sue chewed on her lip as she read. Slowly but surely, they were stumbling towards the truth, and the police always knew more than they told the newspapers. She felt a vacuum in the pit of her stomach, as if she were suspended over a bottomless chasm. But she told herself she mustn't panic. There might not be as much time left as she had hoped for, especially if she were racing against the police investigation, but she must stay calm.

She lit a cigarette and turned to the *Sunday Times*. This was hardly the place to look for salacious, sensational and scandalous news, but surely they would at least report the latest developments in the Student Slasher case. And so they did. Police simply confirmed that the Friday evening murder was the work of the same man who had killed five other girls in the same way over the past year. They refused to discuss details of the crime, but this time they gave a name. Susan added it to the other five she knew by heart, another spirit to guide her: Margaret Snell, Kathleen Shannon, Jane Pitcombe, Kim Waterford, Jill Sarsden and now the sixth, Brenda Fawley.

Sue idled over the rest of the paper, hardly paying attention, and by mid-morning she had come up with a plan for the day. It was time to start checking out the nearby fishing villages. First, she headed back across the bridge and picked up a timetable at the bus station. It took her a while to figure out the schedule, but in the end she discovered that there were no buses going up the coast on Sundays. The service ran between Loftus and Middlesbrough, further north, and that was it.

She thought of renting a car, though she knew that might also be difficult on a Sunday. Even if she could get one, she realized, it might cause all kinds of problems with identification – licence, insurance, means of payment – and that was exactly the kind of trail she didn't want to leave behind her.

There was no train line, so it had to be a bus, then, or nothing. Turning to the Scarborough–Whitby service, she found that there were buses to Robin Hood's Bay. They ran regularly at twenty-five past the hour and took less than half an hour. Coming back would be simple, too. She could catch a bus at Robin Hood's Bay Shelter, which would be up on the main road, at 5.19 or 6.19 in the evening, or even later, right up to 11.19 p.m.. Robin Hood's Bay it would have to be.

Sue wasn't sure what she would find there, but the place had to be checked out. She was certain that her quarry came from Whitby and that he had something to do with fishing, but it was quite possible that he lived in town and worked in one of the smaller places nearby, or vice versa, for that matter.

Besides, she also felt the need to get away from Whitby for a while. She knew the town too well now and was becoming tired of tramping its streets day in, day out. The place was beginning to feel oppressive; it was closing in on her.

Breakfast at the Cummingses' had been a depressing and suffocating affair, too – the obvious poverty; the noise of children; the lack of cleanliness (the teacups were stained, and there had been one or two spots of dried egg that hadn't been washed off her plate properly); and the sense of hurry and bustle that even now was causing her heartburn. Yes, another day trip out of Whitby would be a very good idea.

Checking her timetable again, she found that she had missed the 10.25. Never mind, she thought, finishing her

Kenco coffee, she was in no hurry. There were the papers to read, crosswords to do, plenty to keep her occupied. She could even go up to St Mary's and spend a while in her favourite box if she wanted.

30

KIRSTEN

'Come in, Kirsten. Sit down. Make yourself comfortable.'

Dr Henderson's office was on the second floor of an old house, and the window, which was open about six inches, looked out over the River Avon towards the massive abbey. The last of the great medieval churches to be built in England, it was still very much in use.

Instead of a couch, Kirsten found a padded swivel chair opposite the doctor, who sat at the other side of her untidy desk with her back to the window. Filing cabinets stood to Kirsten's right, and glass-enclosed bookcases to her left, many of them filled with journals. From one shelf, a yellowed skull stared out. It seemed to be grinning at her. Behind her was the door, and beside that, an old hat stand.

Dr Henderson leaned back in her chair and clasped her hands on her lap. Of course it had to be a woman, Kirsten realized; they wouldn't have sent her to a male psychiatrist after what happened. But she hadn't expected such a young woman. Dr Henderson looked hardly older than Kirsten herself, though she must surely have been at least thirty. She had short, black hair, neatly trimmed so as not to be a nuisance, which complemented the angles of her face and emphasized her high cheekbones. She had dark blue eyes, kind but glinting with an edge of mischievous humour. Her voice was soft, husky and deep, with just a trace of a Geordie accent, and her lips were turned up slightly at the corners, as if always on the verge of a smile. A smattering of freckles covered her small nose and the tight skin over her cheekbones.

Kirsten made herself comfortable in the swivel chair, and after glancing around nervously at the office she turned to face the doctor, who smiled.

'Well, Kirsten, how do you feel?'

'All right, I suppose.'

Dr Henderson opened a file on her desk and pretended to read. Kirsten could tell she knew the contents already and was just doing it for effect. 'Dr Craven has passed on the full medical details, but they're not what interest me. Why don't you tell me what happened in your own words?' Then she leaned back and clasped her hands again. The springs in her chair creaked as she moved.

Kirsten felt her mouth turn dry. 'What do you mean? What details?'

Dr Henderson shrugged. 'Perhaps you could start with the attack itself.'

'I was just walking home and somebody grabbed me, then everything went black. That's all.'

'Hmm.' The doctor started playing with a rubber band, stretching it between her fingers like the silence she was stretching in the room. Kirsten shifted in her seat. Outside on the River Avon a young couple rowed by. Kirsten could hear them laugh as their oars splashed water.

'Well?' Kirsten said, when she could bear the tension no longer.

Dr Henderson widened her eyes. 'Well what?'

'I've told you what happened. What do you think? What advice have you got for me?'

'Now hold on a minute, Kirsten.' Dr Henderson put the rubber band down and spoke softly. 'That's not what I'm here for. If anybody has given you to believe that you're coming to me for some kind of magic formula and – hey presto! – everything's back to normal again, then they've seriously misled you.'

'What *are* you here for then?'

'The best way to look at the situation is that you are here, and that's what's important. You're here because you've got problems you can't deal with alone. I'm here to help you, of course I am, but you're the one who'll have to do all the work. Your description of what happened, for example – a bit thin, wasn't it?'

'I can't help it, can I? I mean, I can only tell you what I remember.'

'How do you feel about it?'

'How do you think I feel?'

'You tell me. Your description sounded curiously flat and unemotional.'

Kirsten shrugged. 'Well, I suppose that's how I feel.'

'How are you getting along with your parents?'

'I don't see what that's got to do with anything.'

'Have you told them about your feelings?'

'I told you, I don't see what that's got to do with anything. Of course I haven't told them. Do you think I . . .?'

'What?'

'Nothing.'

'Kirsten, have you ever been able to talk to your parents about your feelings?'

'Of course I have.'

'When?'

'What do you mean?'

'Give me an example of something you've discussed with them.'

'I . . . I . . . well, I can't think of anything offhand. You're making me flustered.'

'All right.' Dr Henderson sat up straight. 'Let's take it easy then, shall we?' And she smiled again. Kirsten found herself relaxing almost against her wishes. The doctor took out a packet of ten Embassy Regal from her desk drawer. 'Mind if I smoke?'

Kirsten shook her head. She was shocked to find a real doctor smoking – especially, for some reason, a young female doctor – but she didn't mind. Dr Henderson turned in her chair and opened the window a little further.

'Can I have one?' Kirsten asked.

'Of course.' The doctor pushed the packet towards her. 'I didn't know you smoked.'

Kirsten almost said, 'I don't,' but she managed to stop herself. 'Sometimes,' she said, then lit up. Though the first few drags hurt a bit, she didn't make a fool of herself and start coughing and spluttering and crying. She had smoked once or twice before, just to see what it was like. The smoke made her feel a little dizzy and sick at first, but her system seemed to adapt quickly.

'And my first name's Laura,' the doctor said. 'I want us to be friends.' She poured two cups of coffee from a Thermos on the desk and pushed one towards Kirsten. 'Milk? Sugar?'

Kirsten shook her head.

'Black, then. So, I take it you haven't really been able to talk to anyone about what happened to you?'

'No. I can't remember, you see, I really can't. It's like

there's a heavy black cloud inside my head where it's all stored, and I can't see inside it.'

'I don't mean the event itself so much as your feelings about it now,' Laura said.

'I don't think I feel anything.'

'Why did you take all those pills? Was it because of this cloud?'

'Partly, I suppose. But it's mostly because I don't feel I'm really living. I mean, I don't enjoy things like before. Reading . . . company . . . and I don't sleep well. I have bad dreams, over and over again. I thought it might just be better if I . . .'

'I see.' Dr Henderson made a note in the file. 'How important are sex and children in your life, Kirsten?'

Kirsten swallowed, shocked by the sudden change of direction. Her mouth turned dry again and the bitter coffee made it worse. She turned away. 'Never thought about them. I don't suppose one does till . . . till . . .'

'Till they're gone?'

'Yes.'

'Had you ever considered having children?'

Kirsten shook her head. 'One day. I imagined I'd have some one day. But not for a long time.'

'What about sex? Were you sleeping with your boyfriend regularly?'

In spite of herself, Kirsten blushed as she told Dr Henderson about Galen and about how she was now trying to cut him out of her life. The doctor listened, then made more notes in her file.

'As far as I understand it,' she said, 'Dr Masterson told you that sexual intercourse would be painful, if not impossible. Am I right?'

Kirsten nodded.

'But that's not all there is to sex, is it?'

'What do you mean?'

'What I mean,' said the doctor, 'is that perhaps you should start thinking about the pleasurable things you *can* do, rather than the ones you can't. I'm not going to embarrass you by explaining them, but there are manuals available. What I'm saying is that you have to accept the loss of your full sexuality, yes, but that you mustn't think that means the end of your entire sensual and erotic life. It's important to know that you can still have those feelings and can still satisfy them in some ways – you can still touch and you can still feel.'

Kirsten stared down at the floor. She hadn't thought about this, had tried not to think about sex at all since leaving the hospital, and she didn't know what to say. It was probably best to let it go by for the time being.

'Just think about what I've said, anyway,' the doctor said. 'It might be a long haul, Kirsten, but if you stick with it we'll get you there. And if at any time you feel the need to talk to someone, please call me. Any time. Do you understand?'

Kirsten nodded.

'What about dreams? You said you've been having bad dreams about what happened?'

Kirsten told her about the black and white figures slashing and slicing at her in the recurring dream.

'Are you talking about nightmares?' Laura asked. 'Do you wake up screaming?'

'No, nothing like that.'

'How do you react, then?'

'I don't really. It's all very ordinary. A bit frightening, I suppose, but there's no pain. It's like I'm detached from it all, just watching.'

'Why do you think you keep having that dream?'

'I don't know. I suppose it's some version of what happened. But I didn't see anything, so it can't be real.'

'Why are there two figures, a black one and a white one?'

'They're both doing the same thing.'

'Yes, but why two?'

'I don't know. Like I said, it can't be anything to do with what happened. I didn't see anything.'

The doctor stubbed out her cigarette and drank some more coffee. 'The mind's a curious thing,' she said. 'It remembers things that happen even when you're asleep or unconscious. Obviously, if your eyes are closed you can't see, but you can hear and smell, for example. Some of those things that happen come up in dreams. What the imagination does is translate them into pictures, based on what the sensations were and what you feel about them. I'm not a Freudian, but I do think dreams can tell us a lot. These two figures cutting you, who do you think they are?'

'I suppose one of them – the black one – must be the man, the one who . . . you know. Or maybe they both are.'

'White and black?'

'Yes. But if what you say is true, and I remember things even when I'm unconscious, then maybe the white one's the doctor. They operated on me for a long time, cutting in the same way I suppose. White and black. One for good, one for evil.' She felt pleased with herself, as if she had finally cracked a particularly obscure code, but Laura didn't seem impressed. 'Perhaps,' she said. 'Now what's in this cloud, do you think?'

'I don't know. Everything.'

'Everything?'

'What happened that night.'

'Do you believe that you were conscious for part of the time? That you saw the man and struggled, and that you've repressed the memory?'

'I don't know for certain, but I must have, mustn't I? Otherwise why would I feel there's something in me I can't get at?'

'Do you want to get at it?'

Kirsten crossed her arms and drew in on herself. 'I don't know.'

'It might be necessary. If you're to make any progress.'

'I don't know.'

The doctor made some more notes in the file, then closed it and put it in an overflowing tray – whether it was 'In', 'Out' or 'Pending', Kirsten couldn't tell. She suspected that Laura Henderson had no such efficient system for dealing with paperwork.

'Well,' said Laura, 'I don't suppose it matters for the moment. You'll come again?'

'I have a choice?'

'Yes. You must come of your own free will.'

'All right.'

'Good.' Laura stood up and Kirsten noticed how slim and healthy her figure looked, even under the loose white coat. It made her feel unattractive herself. In hospital, her skin had acquired that yellowish-grey pallor that sick people get, and the stodgy food had done her figure no good at all. Later, when she had lost her appetite, she had lost weight again, and now her skin felt wrinkly and loose. Her face was spotty too, as it hadn't been since she was fourteen, and even her hair seemed to hang lifeless and dry.

They walked over to the door, which Laura opened for her. 'And Kirsten,' she said finally, 'remember this: it's all right to feel things, even bad things. It's all right to feel hatred and anger towards whoever did this to you. In fact, if you want to get better, you must. The feelings are there, in you, and you have to admit them to yourself.'

Kirsten nodded and left. She felt, even as she walked out and crossed Pulteney Bridge to Grand Parade, that the doctor's words had planted the seeds of a recovery in her. As she watched the daring canoeists go through their paces in the wild water down by the city weir, she reminded herself of the doctor's last words: 'It's all right to hate him, it's all right to hate him.' And she did. Something inside her began hardening into a cold enduring hatred for the man who had shattered her future and crippled her sex. Below, the canoeists manoeuvred deftly, tracing crazy patterns on the water. Kirsten joined the crowd and watched them for a while longer. For some reason, they reminded her of Yeats's lines: 'Like a long-legged fly upon the stream / His mind moves upon silence.' It was an image she found strangely comforting.

31

SUSAN

Monday morning found Sue riding up the coast towards Staithes on the 10.53 bus. Her plan was to have lunch there, look around, then walk the three miles or so along the Cleveland Way to Runswick Bay for tea. From there she could get a bus back to Whitby at 6.25 in the evening.

Robin Hood's Bay, though quaint enough with its hotchpotch of pastel cottages almost sitting on top of one another, had proved disappointing. Not only had Sue seen no evidence of fishing there, she had felt very strongly that this was not the place she should be wasting her time in.

That evening, she had ventured into the lounge alone to watch TV and make a cup of instant coffee, and Mr Cummings had joined her for a while. He was a pleasant, ruddy-faced young man, more than willing to talk about fishing in the Whitby area. It turned out that there were more jobs connected with the industry than Sue had imagined – canning, freezing, processing, shipping – and some of them might be worth looking into. But Staithes was a strong fishing community, so she couldn't afford to overlook it.

The coast road to Staithes cut across a landscape of rolling farmland that ended abruptly in sheer cliffs at the North Sea. To the west lay a patchwork quilt of hedged fields. Some were brown after harvest, some still pale gold with uncut wheat and barley, while others were plain green pastures where black and white cows grazed. The bus passed a far-off village, a cluster of light stone houses with red pantile roofs, almost hidden by a clump of trees in a hollow. The weather had turned sunny again, and the colours of the landscape were saturated with light, like a colour transparency. On the seaward side, in a field next to a local rubbish dump, hundreds of white gulls squatted fat and replete after feeding. The sight disgusted Sue and made the bile rise in her throat. She looked beyond them to the clear blue sea, where the sun glinted silver on distant ships.

The bus stopped in the modern part of the village up on the main road, and Sue had to walk about a mile down to the village itself. The street, by Roxby Beck, was so steep that cars weren't allowed down it. Below her, the houses, a mixture of different stones, colours and styles, seemed to tumble over one another down to the sea. On the way, she stopped at a newsagent's and bought a local paper and a *Daily Mirror*.

The village at the foot of the hill was penned in on both sides by high headlands, huge skulls of grass-topped rock, where the horizontal strata of light sandstones and reddish-brown clays had been bared by the wind and rain over the centuries. The only view from the promenade was of the cliffs looming on each side, or out to the sea itself. There was nobody about; the place was deathly quiet. Even the gulls seemed to be swooping in silence, and the air was thick with the smell of rotten fish.

First, Sue wandered into the Cod and Lobster, a white-washed pub right on the seafront above the thick stone wall. She ordered a lager and lime and, surprised to find they didn't do meals, sat down for a cigarette and a read. There weren't many people in: a man in a Yorkshire Dales T-shirt scratched the neck of his red setter, two lads in navy jerseys, baggy jeans and wellingtons chatted up the young barmaid, and that was it. In fact, she hadn't seen many tourists at all, even on her way down the hill. Staithes seemed to be much more of an isolated, working village than Robin Hood's Bay. It seemed to be the kind of place where she might have more luck in finding the man she wanted.

As she smoked, Sue examined the photographs on the walls. Some of them showed a terrible storm that had hit Staithes in 1953 and damaged the pub badly. Others showed groups of local fishermen, and Sue studied them keenly. She knew she could rely on her visual memory least of all in her quest, but she *had* glimpsed him briefly in the moonlight and remembered the thick black eyebrows meeting in the middle, the Ancient Mariner eyes and the thatch of dark hair. No one in the photographs resembled him, so she turned to her newspapers.

There was nothing more on the Sandsend body in the local paper. Obviously, the police were stuck and the reporters couldn't justify repeating the same story day after day. It didn't mean that the investigation had come to a dead end, though, she realized. The police would still be working on it, questioning people, digging around for evidence. The very idea that they might be drawing closer gave her butterflies in her stomach.

She had bought the *Mirror* because she thought it might have more news about the Student Slasher. She found a whole page recapping his exploits, with the familiar blurred photos of the victims' faces taken from old students' union cards or passports (not Sue's, of course, for she had never been officially identified as his first victim). There they were: Kathleen Shannon with her long, wavy hair; Jane Pitcombe with her large, far-apart eyes; Margaret Snell with her lopsided smile . . . and the three others. Apart from veiled hints about what he did to the nubile young bodies (suggesting, between the lines, that some of them asked for it), and a number of editorial calls for the police to get a move on and catch him ('This could happen to *your* daughter, too!'), there was no real information at all. Sue stared at the six faces. She had never met any of the women, but she felt closer to them than she did to anyone else. Sometimes late at night, she had even fancied she heard them whispering in her ear. They helped her, guided her when she felt weak and lost, and for them, if not for herself, she had to carry on to the end.

Feeling hungry, she stubbed out her cigarette and finished her drink. Outside, a little further around the harbour from the Cod and Lobster, was a cafe attached to a private hotel. She walked in and found the small room crowded with full tables and only one waitress trying to deal with all the orders. Though she was obviously rushed off her feet by a recent influx of six or seven customers, the woman managed everything as quickly as she could, and with a smile. From the glimpses Sue got when the kitchen door swung open, there was only one cook, too. The menu offered little choice. The special of the day was cod and chips. Sue ordered it.

Smoking was not allowed in the cafe, so she passed the twenty minutes or so she had to wait for lunch doing the crosswords and reading about the sexual exploits of famous TV personalities and pop stars in the *Mirror*.

When the meal finally came, it was good. Sue realized that she had spent too much energy avoiding fish and chips in Whitby – because it seemed that that was the only food available – as she actually enjoyed it, at least in moderation.

As she ate, she remembered the local chippie near the university, where she and her friends had often stopped on their way home from the pub and eaten out of newspaper as they walked. If only her mother could have seen her; she'd have had a fit. But the north seemed so full of fish and chip shops, what could you do? Though she had never thought about it at the time, she guessed now that much of the fish came from places like Whitby and Scarborough, and even the smaller villages like Staithes. It came? Well, obviously it was delivered. It didn't fly there by itself. A whole fleet of vans must be constantly rushing back and forth from the coast to service inland towns and cities. Sue paused with her fork in the air as the simplicity of it all came to her: the final piece of the puzzle. Of course! How could she be so stupid? Now she knew exactly what to do next.

When she had finished eating, she pushed the empty plate aside and lit a cigarette. One or two fellow diners gave her nasty looks, but no one actually walked over and asked her to stop. The waitress also ignored her. She had much more on her mind than telling a patron to stop smoking. Eventually Sue got the bill, paid it, and walked out into the sea air. Its rotten-fish smell now seemed mingled with the odours of seaweed and ozone, and just a trace of diesel fuel from the boats.

There was no point remaining in Staithes any longer, she thought as she walked along the harbour wall. She had always been certain, in her heart of hearts, that

Whitby was the place where she would find him. Now even logic backed up her instinct.

Still, it was pleasant enough walking in the sun and watching the placid blue sea. The place seemed less oppressive now that she had decided to leave it soon. She could at least wait until she had digested her lunch. The only discomfort she felt was a hot and itchy scalp under her wig.

She sat down on the sea wall and let her legs dangle over the edge. Stretching her arms out behind her and resting her palms on the warm tarmac, she leaned back and let the sun warm her closed eyelids. One more cigarette, she decided, then back up the long hill to the bus stop. Shifting position, she checked her timetable and found out that there was a bus at 2.18. It was twenty past one now, so she had just missed the one before. Plenty of time.

As she sat watching a distant tanker move across the horizon, she became aware of someone staring at her. The hackles at the back of her neck, under the wig, stood on end. At first, she brushed off the feeling as ridiculous. Hadn't she just decided that she would find her man in Whitby? He couldn't be here. Then, for a moment, she panicked. What if it was the police? What if they had somehow got on to her? Or were they just following her, watching? She could bear it no longer. Turning her head slowly and casually towards the rail in front of the Cod and Lobster, where she thought the watcher was standing, she picked out the tall, tanned figure.

It was Keith McLaren, the Australian she'd met at the Abbey Terrace guest house. And he recognized her. Even as she looked, he waved, smiled and started to walk towards her.

32
KIRSTEN

August gave way to September and the nights turned cooler. As the weeks passed, Kirsten began to look forward to her sessions with Laura Henderson. They smoked and sipped terrible coffee together in that cosy room overlooking the River Avon. The immediate sights beyond the window became as familiar to Kirsten as if she had looked out on them all her life: Robert Adam's Pulteney Bridge, with its row of shops along each side, all built of Cotswold stone; the huge square late-Gothic tower of the Abbey; the Guildhall and municipal buildings. Often she stared over Laura's shoulders during the long silences or stood at the window as Laura sought out an article in a journal. Some evenings, when their sessions ran late, Laura would take a bottle of Scotch from her filing cabinet and pour them each a drink.

They talked more about Kirsten's childhood, her parents, her feelings about sex. Laura said that Kirsten was making progress. And so she was. She still didn't like going out or meeting people, but she began to enjoy the simple things again: mostly solo pursuits like a walk in the woods, music, the occasional novel. She even found that she could concentrate and sleep well again. Though she no longer flirted with suicide, she hung on to her cold hatred, and the dark cloud still throbbed inside her mind. Sometimes it made her head ache. She and Laura didn't talk about the attack. It would come,

Kirsten knew, but only when Laura thought she was ready.

At home, her mother continued to fuss and fret, and she often seemed to regard her daughter with a combination of embarrassment and pity. But Kirsten grew used to it. The two of them kept out of each other's way as much as possible. It wasn't difficult. With her garden, her croquet, her bridge parties and her myriad social engagements, Kirsten's mother managed to keep busy.

Hugo and Damon sent get-well cards, and Galen phoned several times during August. At first, Kirsten instructed her mother to tell him she was out. Soon, however, she realized that wasn't fair. She spoke to him and tried to respond to his concern without encouraging him too much. One Friday, he paid a visit and tried again to persuade Kirsten to go with him to Toronto. They walked in the woods and she let him take her hand, though her flesh felt dead to his touch. It wasn't too late, he said, they had both been accepted and term didn't begin for a few weeks yet. Gently, she put him off, told him she would join him later, and sent him away partially appeased. Finally, at the beginning of September, he went to Canada and sent her a postcard as soon as he got to Toronto. She had never told him what was really wrong with her; nor had she mentioned the suicide attempt.

If anyone sustained Kirsten outside Laura Henderson's office, it was Sarah, who phoned almost every week and wrote long, entertaining letters in between. Always outrageous, funny and compassionate, she made Kirsten laugh again. When she asked if she might visit over Christmas, when her own parents would be touring Australia, Kirsten jumped at the chance. Her father saw that it was a good idea, too, but her mother, perhaps recalling her only meeting with Sarah in the dingy northern bedsit, was reluctant at first. Christmas was a family time, she said. She didn't want strangers around. Her husband argued that it wasn't a very big family anyway. Kirsten's grandparents, two uncles and aunts usually came for Christmas dinner, then her parents visited friends in the village for drinks on Boxing Day. Surely, he argued, it would be good for Kirsten to have a friend of her own age around. Finally, her mother gave in and it was settled. Sarah was due to arrive on 22 December, and Kirsten would pick her up at the station after her late-afternoon session with Dr Henderson. She would have her mother's Audi, as usual.

One day in early October, when the elegant old city looked grey and a cold wind drove the rain through its Georgian crescents, circles and squares, Kirsten forsook her usual walk by the Avon and drove straight home from Laura's office. When she arrived, she noticed a strange car parked in the drive and her mother peeking out from behind the lace curtains – something she didn't usually do – and her heart began to beat faster. Something was wrong. Was it her father? she wondered as she hurried to the door. Her ordeal had taken a terrible toll on him, and though he did seem stronger and happier of late, the bags still hung dark under his eyes and he had lost his boyish enthusiasm for things. Was his heart weak? Had he had an attack?

Her mother opened the door before Kirsten even had time to fit her key into the lock. 'Someone to see you,' she said in a whisper.

'What is it?' Kirsten asked. 'Is father all right?'

Her mother frowned. 'Of course he is, dear. Whatever gave you that idea?'

Kirsten hung up her coat and dashed into the split-level living room. The two men sat close to the French windows, near the spot on the carpet, now dry-cleaned back to perfection, where Kirsten had had her Scotch and pills picnic. One of the men she recognized, or thought she should, but the memory was vague: spiky grey hair, red complexion, dark mole between left nostril and upper lip. She'd seen him before. And then it came to her: the policeman, Superintendent . . .

'Elswick, Miss,' he said, as if reading her mind. 'Detective Superintendent Elswick. We have met before.'

Kirsten nodded. 'Yes, yes of course.'

'And this is Detective Inspector Gregory.'

Inspector Gregory stretched out his hand, which was attached to an astonishingly long arm, and Kirsten moved forward to shake it. Then he disappeared back into the chair – her father's favourite armchair, she noticed. Gregory was probably in his mid-thirties, and his dark hair was a bit too long for a policeman. He was dressed scruffily, too, with brown corduroy trousers, threadbare from being washed too many times, a tan suede jacket, and no tie. Kirsten thought he seemed a bit shifty. She didn't like the way he looked at her. Superintendent Elswick wore a navy-blue suit, a white shirt and a black and amber striped tie. It was the same one he wore last time, she remembered. Probably from an old school or regiment; he looked like an ex-military type.

'How are you, Kirsten?' Elswick asked.

Kirsten sat down on the sofa before answering. Her mother hovered over them and asked if anyone would like more tea.

'I haven't had any yet,' Kirsten said. 'Yes. I'd like some, please.'

The two policeman said they wouldn't be averse to another cup, and Kirsten's mother walked off promising to make a fresh pot.

Kirsten looked at Elswick. 'How am I? I suppose I'm doing fine.'

'Good. I'm very glad. It was a nasty business.'

'Yes.'

They sat in tense silence until Kirsten's mother returned with the tea tray. Having deposited it on the mahogany coffee table before the stone hearth, she disappeared again, saying, 'I'll leave you to it, then.'

After her sessions with Dr Henderson, Kirsten was used to silence. At first it had disconcerted her, made her fidgety and edgy, but now they sometimes sat for as much as two minutes – which is a *very* long time for two people to be silent together – while Kirsten meditated on something Laura had said, or tried to frame a reply to a particularly probing and painful question. Elswick and Gregory were easy meat. There was something they wanted, obviously, so all she had to do was wait until they got to the point.

Gregory played 'mother', clearly an unsuitable role for him, and spilled as much tea in the saucer as he got in the cups. Elswick frowned at him, and added milk and sugar. Then, when they were settled again, Gregory crossed his long legs and took out a black notebook. He did his best to pretend he was part of the chair he was sitting in.

'Kirsten,' said Superintendent Elswick, 'I should imagine you've guessed that I wouldn't come all this way unless it was important.'

Kirsten nodded. 'Have you caught him?' For a moment she panicked and thought the attacker might actually be someone she knew, someone from the party. She didn't know if she would be able to handle that.

'No,' said Elswick, 'no, we haven't. That's just the point.'

It was obviously very difficult for him to talk to her, Kirsten realized, but she didn't know how to make it any easier.

Finally, he managed to blurt it out, 'I'm afraid there's been another attack.'

'Like mine?'

'Yes.'

'In the park?'

'No, it took place on some waste ground near a polytechnic not far away. Huddersfield, in fact. I thought you might have read about it in the papers.'

'I haven't been reading the papers lately.'

'I see. Anyway, this time the victim wasn't quite as lucky as you. She died.'

'What's her name?'

Elswick looked puzzled. 'Margaret Snell,' he answered.

Kirsten repeated the name to herself. 'How old was she?' she asked.

'Nineteen.'

'What did she look like?'

Elswick tipped the tea from his saucer into his cup before answering. 'She was a pretty girl,' he said finally, 'and a bright one too. She had long blonde hair and a big crooked smile. She was studying hotel management.'

Kirsten sat in silence.

'The reason we're here,' Elswick continued, 'is to see

if you've remembered anything else about what happened. Anything at all that might help us catch this man.'

'Before he does it again?'

Elswick nodded gravely.

'Does that mean there's some kind of maniac, some kind of ripper, running loose up there?'

Elswick took a deep breath. 'We try to avoid alarmist terms like that,' he said. 'It was a vicious attack, much the same as the one on you. From our point of view, we're pretty sure it was the same man, so it looks like we've got a serial killer, yes. But the newspapers don't know that. They don't know anything about the similarity between your injuries and those of the dead girl, and we're certainly not going to tell them. We're doing our best to prevent anyone linking you to the business.'

'Why?' Kirsten asked, suddenly apprehensive.

'All the bad publicity. It would upset your parents, make your life a misery. You've no idea how persistent those damn reporters can be when they get on the scent of a juicy story. They'd be up here from London like a shot.'

Kirsten could tell he was lying. He wouldn't look her in the eye. 'It's because you think he might come after me, isn't it?' she said. 'You're worried that if he knows you connect him to two victims and he knows one is still alive, then he'll want to finish me off in case I know something, aren't you?'

'It's not as simple as that, Kirsten.' Elswick shifted in his chair. 'When you were in hospital—'

'He's already tried?'

'Yes. You must have noticed that we had a man on the door all the time. As soon as news of your survival hit the papers, the attacker came back. Apparently he must have entered the hospital dressed as an orderly. He can't have been all that bright, otherwise he'd have known we'd be guarding you. Anyway, when he turned the corner, he spotted the constable and ducked quickly back the way he came. Our man was good. He saw from the corner of his eye that someone was behaving suspiciously, but he had orders not to leave his post. A more headstrong bobby might have done just that. But if he'd gone chasing after the intruder, looking for the glory of an arrest, then he could easily have got lost in the maze of corridors and chummy could've nipped back in and . . .'

'Finished me off?'

'Yes. Instead, the constable stayed put and called in on his radio, but by the time we got there our man was long gone. We didn't even get a description.'

'And he never tried again?'

'No. Not as far as we know.'

'Does he know where I live?'

'I don't think so. How could he? The press details were sketchy. The local police have been warned to keep a lookout for any strangers in the area, but I don't think you've got anything to worry about.'

Kirsten thought of all her walks in the woods, all the times she had lingered in the streets of Bath after sessions with Dr Henderson. She felt a sudden chill. 'Why didn't you tell me all this before?' she asked.

'We didn't want to alarm you.'

'Thanks a lot.'

Elswick leaned forward and rested his palms on his knees. 'Believe me, Kirsten, you've been perfectly safe. I can understand how you feel, but look at it this way. Whoever attacks you is worried when he hears you've survived, so he rushes over to the hospital with some half-baked scheme of trying to silence you. He fails. Time goes by, he no doubt loses track of you when you come down here, and lo and behold, it's already three months ago and nothing's happened to him. He's still free as a bird. So obviously, from his point of view, you can't know anything, you're not a threat.'

'Until he strikes again?'

'I still don't think you're in any danger. We'll keep an eye on you, don't worry, but it's more for form's sake than anything else.'

Kirsten felt a little relieved. There was some truth in what Elswick had said. If anything was going to happen, it would have happened long before now. And she wasn't about to start walking around in fear of her life; it wasn't worth that much. Though she no longer felt suicidal, she did feel reckless sometimes and often drove the car too fast or walked alone after dark in streets she shouldn't visit. Even genteel Bath had its seedy characters and sleazy areas. So she wasn't going to give in to fear. She had determined not to spend the rest of her life jumping at every sound and running from every shadow. If he found her, so be it; may the best person win. More than anything, she was angry at the police for being so useless and for joining the growing list of people who didn't want to 'alarm' her by telling her the truth.

'Why does he do it?' she asked. 'Mutilate women like that. Why does he hate us so much?'

Elswick shook his head. 'If we knew the answer to that we might have an easier job stopping him. Usually it's a him, and that's about all we can be sure of. Who can say what sets them off? We have people in to do profiles and doctors write books, but who knows really?

Often it's prostitutes they go after, but this time it seems to be female students, if we're reading the pattern correctly. No doubt there's a million unresolved conflicts from his childhood on, that have turned him into what he is. Perhaps he was sexually abused. But plenty of other people suffer from cruel parents and don't turn into killers. We don't know what the trigger is that makes the odd one different.' He shrugged. 'I suppose it comes down to fear, really. People like him are terrified by women, whatever the reason, and the only thing they can do about it, because of the kind of people they are, is strike out and despoil and kill.'

'How do you know it's the same person?' Kirsten asked. 'You said something earlier about the similarity of injuries.'

Elswick looked at her grimly. 'Do you really want to know?' he asked.

Kirsten wasn't sure, but she certainly didn't intend to give in. 'Considering that so much else has been kept from me, I think I have a right, don't you?'

Elswick sat back and studied her face for a moment. 'All right,' he said. 'The wounds were the same, the areas he used his knife on were the same; there was also bruising about the face consistent with punching and slapping. And that strange cross he cut, with the long vertical and short horizontal just below the breasts, that was found on her body, too. Do you want me to go on?'

Kirsten nodded.

'When he was with you, he was disturbed. The dog, we assume. Up to that point your injuries are identical with those of the other victim.'

'What killed her, then?'

'She was strangled.' Elswick pinched his nose, then scratched the mole lightly. 'Oh, she'd no doubt have died of loss of blood or internal bleeding, but just to make sure, the bastard strangled her. And according to our forensic experts, he did this *after* he had inflicted the other injuries.'

'Are you saying that she was conscious while he did all . . . what he did to me?'

Elswick shook his head. 'We don't know. It would have been difficult for him if she'd been able to struggle. The blows to the face and head were probably enough to cause loss of consciousness, and it seems that they were the first injuries. He grabbed her from behind, threw her down onto the ground, straddled her, pinning her arms down with his knees, and then began beating her about the face. Perhaps it wasn't until she was unconscious that he went on to the more serious business. And this time he wasn't disturbed.'

Kirsten felt sick. She could feel the blood drain from her cheeks. She struggled to control herself. She wasn't going to be sick. She wasn't going to let Elswick say, 'I told you so.' She wouldn't appear as the weak woman in front of these men who were intimate with every aspect of her brutalization. To cover up her discomfort, she poured another cup of tea. Inspector Gregory shook his head quickly when offered some. He was so still and silent he seemed really to have become part of the chair.

'What we were wondering,' Elswick went on slowly, 'was whether you'd remembered anything else, no matter how insignificant or unimportant it might seem to you.'

Kirsten shook her head. 'No, I haven't. I've tried, of course, but after what I told you, it's all still a blank.'

'You see,' Elswick persisted, 'what we think is that the victim must have still been conscious, at least at the time he threw her onto her back. And if that's so, then it might have been the same with you. You might have got a glimpse of his face. Maybe he was wearing a mask or a stocking, but even that could help us. Or maybe he said something. Anything.'

'I'm sorry,' Kirsten said, 'really I am. But I just can't remember. You might be right. Maybe I did see his face, maybe he did talk to me. But I *can't remember*. Do you think I don't want to? Of course I'd like to help you, but I can't. After that rough hand closed over my mouth, I can't remember a thing.' She felt tears in her eyes and fought to hold them back.

'There was a moon that night,' Elswick said.

'Yes. I was looking for it when . . . before. But I couldn't see it.'

'It was there, behind you, just over the tops of the trees. We've checked.'

'Why?'

'Light. Because if you were conscious when he pushed you down to the ground, there would have been just enough light to make out at least something about his appearance. It was a clear night – a bit hazy maybe – and there was a full moon.'

'But I can't have been conscious,' Kirsten said. 'I don't remember.'

'Never mind, then.' Elswick glanced over at Inspector Gregory, who slipped his notebook back in the inside pocket of his tan jacket, and both men swung forward in their chairs, preparing to leave. 'I'm sorry to have brought such bad news and stirred up painful memories,' Elswick went on, getting to his feet. His knees cracked and he put his hand to the small of his back as if it hurt. 'Getting old. I hear you've been seeing a doctor, Kirsten.'

'There's not much you don't know, is there?' Kirsten said. 'As a matter of fact, yes, I have. Her name's Laura Henderson and she's a psychiatrist.'

Elswick smiled indulgently. 'Yes, we know.'

'Don't tell me – you checked her out?'

'It's standard procedure in cases like this.' Elswick followed her out of the room down to the hall. 'Doing you any good?'

'Yes, I think she is. She says my loss of memory might be anterograde amnesia, caused by the trauma.'

'Hmm, yes, we'd heard. And it's consistent with the facts. All you remember is the hand, and you've blotted out all the violence, all the pain. According to our medical experts, the memory may or may not come back.'

'You've certainly done your homework, haven't you, Superintendent?'

Elswick seemed embarrassed again. He changed moods remarkably quickly for a policeman, Kirsten thought. One minute he was all confident and superior, the next he was avuncular, and then he got all tongue-tied. This time she decided to help him.

'What is it you want?' she asked. 'Do you want to talk to her? Do you want access to her records of our sessions? They won't tell you anything, you know.'

'Er, no, no, that won't be necessary,' Elswick said as Kirsten handed them their coats from the hall cupboard. She sensed from his hesitation that he might already have had such access or could easily get it if he wanted, and she felt a surge of anger towards Laura.

'What I was wondering was,' he went on, scratching

his mole again – Kirsten felt like telling him to get it seen to before it turned cancerous – 'was, well, with the doctor's permission, of course, I was wondering if you'd consider trying hypnosis?'

33
SUSAN

'It was partly the way you smoke your cigarette,' Keith said. 'Everybody's different. You hold it straight out between your first two fingers like a real lady, or like you're just pretending to smoke.' He grinned. 'But why the change in appearance? You look so *feminine*. I mean, not that you didn't before, it's just . . .' He slowed to a halt.

Sue smiled and flicked her cigarette end onto the sand. 'You know what they say: a change is as good as a rest.' Why the hell did he have to turn up? she asked herself. And what am I supposed to do about him?

'Did you need a rest?'

'No, I needed a change.'

They both laughed.

'But seriously, Martha,' he persisted, 'it's almost as if you're trying to avoid someone. You aren't, are you?'

'It's nothing but a skirt and a blouse. You're acting as if I'm dressed like Richard III or something.'

'There *is* the wig.'

Sue touched the false hair. 'I was sick of having it short. I couldn't wait.'

'And the make-up.'

'Can't a girl put a bit of lipstick on any more?'

Keith smiled. 'I'm still not convinced. I think you're a spy. I just don't know whose side you're on.'

He seemed happy to meet up with her again, despite

the sour note they had parted on, but she could tell he was suspicious by the way he studied her. He had recognized her without much difficulty, that was clear enough. Maybe it was because he fancied her, and when you fancy someone you notice little things like how they hold their cigarettes and the way they walk. She was sure that strangers, people she had passed in the street or sat near in a pub, wouldn't connect her with the short-haired, tomboyish Martha Browne. But Keith could be a problem.

'What are you doing up here?' he asked.

'Just taking a break for the day. And you? I'd have thought you'd be in Edinburgh by now.'

'Oh no, I'm moving very slowly. First Sandsend, then Runswick Bay, now Staithes.' Sue noticed again how pronounced his Australian accent was: Staithes came out as Stythes. 'I'm in no hurry,' he went on. 'I might never see these places again. And the weather's been so bloody good. Another first in England from what I've heard. You still in Whitby?'

'Yes.'

'Still in the same bed and breakfast?'

'Yes.'

'Still get black pudding for breakfast?'

'Most days.'

Sue's mind was working fast. She didn't want to be noticed with him in public, for a start, and they could hardly get more public than here on the sea wall. Luckily, though, there was hardly anyone around at the moment. One or two people sat on the beach, but they were facing the sea, and two blonde children, dressed identically in white shorts and blue and red striped T-shirts, stood eating ice-cream cones near the Cod and

Lobster. Everyone else was either in the pub, at the shops, or waiting for lunch in the restaurant. The steep hill down to the village probably put a lot of older visitors off, too, Sue thought. No matter how warm it was, people so much liked to sit in their cars right beside the sea, but they couldn't do that here. Though it was easy enough getting down to the beach, the walk back up the hill was no doubt too great a price for many to pay for a day at the seaside.

So far, no one had so much as glanced at them. The first thing to do was get Keith away somewhere off the beaten track, then she would be able to think clearly. She didn't like the idea that was forming, forcing itself on her, but she hadn't thought of another way out yet.

'What are your plans?' he asked.

'Well,' Sue said, 'I was intending to walk along the coast to Runswick Bay, then catch the bus back to Whitby. What do you think? Is it too far?'

'No, it's not far at all. I've done it myself. Nothing to it. Tell you what, if you've no objection, I'll come with you. There's an even better walk in my guidebook, though. You walk along the cliffs to Port Mulgrave, then cut back inland through some woods and circle around to the main road. That'll take you to your bus stop, and me back to Staithes. How about it?'

'All right. Are you sure you don't have anything else you want to do?'

'I told you, I'm on holiday. No plans, no newspapers, no television. A vacation from the world.'

Sue remembered the bit about not reading newspapers from their last meeting. It made her feel a little safer – especially as he had made no mention of Jack Grimley's death – but there were still too many ways that someone like Keith could come across a local news story: a photo of Grimley and a request for information in some pub or cafe up the coast, for example; or from the newspaper used to wrap his fish and chips one evening. Perhaps someone might be watching a local news programme on the TV in the lounge of his guesthouse just as he walked in to make a cup of tea. And he would remember, that was the problem. He recognized her, even in disguise, so he would surely recognize Jack Grimley, the man he had caught her staring at in the Lucky Fisherman. Then he might remember how he had thought she knew Grimley. The more she worried about what Keith knew, the more she realized she didn't feel safe at all. Why hadn't he gone straight up to Scotland, or taken the plane back to Oz?

Keith took her silence for hesitation. 'Look, Martha,' he said, scratching his earlobe and looking out to sea. 'I know I was out of order, like, before when . . . you know . . . and I'm sorry. I want you to know I'm not on the make. I just think it'd be nice to go for a walk with you. I won't try anything. Honest.'

Sue got to her feet and brushed the sand from the back of her long skirt. She was forming a plan and a little inducement would go a long way. 'It's all right,' she said. 'I didn't mean to seem so brusque with you before. It's not that I'm a nun or anything. It was just too soon. I mean, I hardly knew you.' She smiled at him.

Keith looked surprised. 'Yes, well . . . er . . . shall we be off?'

'Haven't you got your gear?'

'Gear? Good Lord, you don't need gear for a simple walk like this.' He looked her up and down. 'You could even do it dressed like that, though I wouldn't recommend it. No, all I've got is my Ordnance Survey guide.' He patted the back pocket of his jeans.

'No, I mean your stuff, your rucksack and all that.'

'It's back at the B&B. I was only having a little stroll around the village. No, what you see is what you get.' He spread his arms and stood before her, tall, slim, thin-faced and tanned. His curly, black hair still looked glossy, as if he had just stepped out of the shower, and his eyes reflected a bluer ocean than the one that stretched before them.

'What did you mean about me not being dressed right?' Sue asked.

'I was only joking really. It's not a hard walk. It's just that skirts tend to snag on thorns and things, and those pumps will take a hell of a beating.'

'Wait here a minute.'

Sue hurried into the public toilet, made sure that no one was around and went into a cubicle to change. First she took off her wig, scratching her head in relief when she had done so, then she put on her jeans, a dark-blue checked shirt and her trainers. Carefully, she rolled up the wig, long skirt, white blouse and cardigan and placed them in the holdall. Sometimes, she thought, it was a nuisance having to carry the damn thing everywhere with her, but it was light enough, and she could adjust the strap and carry it over her shoulder if she wanted.

She put the quilted jacket on top of everything in case it got chilly high up on the cliffs. Finally, she combed her hair in the cracked and grimy mirror above the sink and examined her make-up. It wasn't bad. She hadn't put too much on that morning as she had intended to be out of Whitby for the day anyway, and now there was no point in standing here and washing it all off. Someone might come. Quickly, she gave her lips a dab with a Kleenex, then dashed back outside to join Keith.

'Lead on,' she said, bowing and standing aside for him.

Keith laughed. 'Are you *sure* you're not a spy or an actor or something?'

'Not at all.' Sue gave him what she intended to be an enigmatic smile, and they set off.

They wound their way up by the Mission Church of St Peter the Fisherman, then followed the signs for the Cleveland Way past some farm buildings, over a couple of stiles and right up the hill to the cliff edge. The village lay spread out below them. Even though it was a clear, warm day, smoke drifted lazily from some of the chimneys. Up on the cliff top, there was a cool breeze from the sea. Pausing for breath, Sue put on the quilted jacket she'd been carrying in her holdall.

'What have you got in that thing?' Keith asked. 'Your life's work?'

'Something like that.'

The unfenced path ran close to the edge of the cliff, and the drop was sheer. After Keith had stopped to point out Boulby cliffs further up the coast, they started walking in single file. The pathway was rough, though mostly level, and they soon got into a comfortable rhythm. Keith was talking most of the time, half turning his head to look at her. He talked about how he was loving England but still felt homesick, and about a body that had been washed up on the beach at Sandsend while he was staying there. No, he hadn't got a good look at it. By the time he had noticed that something was happening quite a crowd had gathered and the police had arrived.

Sue realized now that she would have to kill him. He was just too much of a liability to let go free. She didn't know how the police were progressing on the Grimley investigation, but she was sure that, without Keith, they couldn't link her to the dead man. Keith might not have seen the body, but there was a chance he might find out who it was and, if questioned, remember that strange girl who had acted as if she recognized the man . . . the girl who kept changing her appearance.

But she didn't know if she could do it. Keith had done her no harm; he had only tried to kiss her. But he could give her away before she'd finished, and she couldn't afford to let that happen – not after everything else. Grimley had been a mistake in the first place, and one that almost sent her screaming back home. Now Keith. All she had wanted to do was find the man who had hurt her and murdered the other girls and kill him, put a stop to his carnage once and for all, but she was so deep in blood already and she hadn't even found him yet. How much further would she have to go?

With an effort, she pulled her mind back from this negative track. It wasn't as if she had any choice in the matter, she told herself. Somehow, from somewhere, she would have to dredge up the courage. He was a man, after all, wasn't he? When it came down to it, they were all the same underneath. Hadn't he tried to force himself on her, and wouldn't he do the same again? She shuddered at the thought.

It would be easy to do it up here. Just a gentle push over the edge, or quick kick at the ankles to make him stumble and fall. An accident. But it was too open, and she could see two other walkers approaching from the opposite direction. As it was, they turned out to be serious hikers with binoculars, boots and rucksacks, far more interested in distant seabirds than in fellow human beings, but there must be no witnesses and no probing, time-consuming inquest. As the men passed, Sue looked the other way. So far she was sure that nobody would remember seeing her with Keith, but there was no point in being careless.

Gulls swooped low, flashing white in the sun, and curious insects buzzed around Sue's head. Before long, she could see the crumbling jetty of Port Mulgrave way below, and they began their descent into the tiny village. Keith wanted to stop for a cup of tea and a sandwich at the Boat House Tea Room, but Sue urged him on, saying she was still full from lunch. She was nervous now she had made her decision, and that made her cautious. When she took his hand, he gave in quite easily and they set off up the road to Hinderwell.

Soon they were on a rough track approaching a caravan site, then they turned right, crossed some more fields, and walked down a steep hill to a footbridge over a beck. It was a dramatic change of landscape, from coast to inland valley. They walked through brambles and blackberry bushes, and Sue could see what Keith had meant about snagging her skirt on the thorns. Even in jeans she had to walk carefully. The smell was different here, too. Rotten fish and seaweed were distant memories, replaced by crushed berries and wild garlic in the honeyed air droning with insects.

Beyond the brambles, they entered the woods. The path was bounded on both sides by dense thickets and tall trees. They passed an elderly couple, who smiled and said hello, then after a few minutes walking in the quiet woods, Sue suggested that maybe it was time for a rest.

'But there's nowhere to rest here,' Keith said. 'Just the path.'

'There's the woods, isn't there?' Sue broke free and ran off through the undergrowth. 'Come on, it's nice in here!' she called back. 'Cool and dark. I'm sure we'll find somewhere to sit down.' Keith ran after her.

When they'd gone far enough that they couldn't be seen from the path, Sue pointed to a concave patch of ground between two trees. 'There. Perfect.' She sat and leaned back against a tree trunk. Filtered green light streamed down through the leaves and birds called to one another from their high nests, passing on warnings that intruders had come. Keith lowered himself down beside Sue, so close that their arms touched.

It wasn't long before his hands started wandering, as she had expected, just touching her hair and throat at first. The tension inside her was almost unbearable, but she tried not to stiffen up. Then he kissed her. She let him. She took off her quilted jacket to make a pillow against the rough bark and he started fiddling with the buttons on her shirt. She let him. One button, two buttons, three buttons . . . she had one arm around him and the other groping in her holdall. Her mouth was dry and it still tasted of greasy cod. Four buttons. Now her bra was exposed and he bent forward and kissed the dark cleavage. She sighed. His fingers quickened and soon unbuttoned the shirt right down to her waist. Without bothering to take it off, he pulled the bra up over her breasts. She let him. Her free hand stroked the nape of his neck and tears ran down her flushed cheeks.

Suddenly, he froze.

'My God, Martha! What happened? What on earth happened?'

He pulled back and stared in horror at the puckered zigzags across the skin of her breasts. They looked like an old hag's dugs, as Sue well knew. Her hand closed on the paperweight.

'Nothing,' she said softly. 'Nothing for you to worry about. Why, does it turn you off?'

'Well, no,' he said awkwardly. 'I didn't mean that. I just . . .'

'Go on then, Keith. Go ahead. Kiss them if you like.'

She put her free hand on the back of his head and drew him towards her. As she felt him resist, she pushed harder. She could feel his oily black hair under her fingers and the strength in the knotted muscles at the back of his neck as he shoved against her hand. Tears of anger burned in her eyes. His lips brushed the dead skin where the severed nerve ends had never knit back together. He strained back, but she kept pushing him down. When his mouth reached the place where her right nipple used to be, she brought the paperweight down on the side of his head.

He didn't jerk and twitch like Jack Grimley, and for that she was grateful. She didn't know if she would have been able to stand that without going mad. He just slumped forward into her arms. She rolled him off and he fell onto his back at her feet. Blood bubbled over his ear through his glossy hair onto the earth. She wasn't going to make the mistake of touching the wound this time. Her heart was beating wildly, but at least she didn't feel sick. Perhaps, like everything else, murder got easier with practice.

Sue raised the paperweight again, but the sound of rustling in the undergrowth stopped her. Heart thudding, she looked up straight into the eyes of a large panting collie. The dog just stared at her with its tongue hanging out and its head cocked to one side, as if it wondered what the hell was going on. Sue felt more naked under its gaze than she had under Keith's, and she quickly pulled down her bra and began to button up her shirt. The dog just stood there, watching her with that pained and puzzled expression in its eyes.

Then she heard a faint cry in the distance. The dog's ears pricked up and with a final, despairing glance at her, it turned and ran off through the thicket towards two distant figures standing on the path. This place was too dangerous; she had to get out before someone else came. First, she took Keith's Ordnance Survey guide from his back pocket. She would need that to find her way back to the main road. Then she felt for his pulse. She didn't really know where to look, except from programmes she'd seen on television, but she couldn't feel anything on his wrist. Quickly, she hit him once more, just to make certain. Surely one of the blows must have fractured his skull, she thought. She wiped the paperweight carefully on his shirt, wrapped it in paper handkerchiefs and put it back deep in her holdall.

Next she piled all the loose brush and dead leaves she could find over Keith's body. He looked so innocent lying there, such a babe in the woods. Then she remembered the pressure of his muscles as he had pushed himself away from her, rejected her, and that split second of balance when their strength had been equal and she had killed him. She patted her hair and brushed the leaf mould and twigs from her jeans, then hurried back towards the path. Looking behind her, she couldn't see anything of Keith, just a small mound that looked like an old tree stump. She followed the map about three-quarters of a mile to the main road without passing another soul. Not that it mattered anyway. If anyone did recollect her, it would be Martha Browne they remembered. The police might find Keith soon, and they would make enquiries and track down the bus driver too. But it would be Martha Browne he remembered. And as soon as she got to the toilets near Whitby bus station, Martha Browne would disappear for ever and Sue Bridehead would return.

At the bus stop, she caught her breath, then sat on the warm brick wall at the bottom of someone's garden, where she watched the ants and smoked a cigarette as she waited for the 4.18 back to Whitby.

34

KIRSTEN

'You realize it might take several sessions,' said Laura Henderson, brushing some ash off her white coat, 'and even then there's no guarantee?'

Kirsten nodded. 'But you can do it?'

'Yes, I can do it. About ten per cent of people aren't susceptible to hypnosis, but I don't think we'll have much trouble with you. You're bright, and you've got plenty of imagination. What did Superintendent Elswick say?'

Kirsten shrugged. 'Nothing much. Just asked me if I'd give it a try.'

Laura leaned forward. 'Look, Kirsten,' she said. 'I don't know what's on your mind, but I sense some hostility. I want to remind you that what goes on between us in this office is confidential. I don't want you thinking that I'm somehow just an extension of the police. Naturally, they're keeping tabs on you, and when they found out you were seeing me they made enquiries. I want you to know, though, that I haven't told them anything at all about our sessions, and nor would I, without your permission.'

'I believe you,' Kirsten said. 'Besides, there's been nothing to tell, has there?'

'Hypnosis might change that. Do you still trust me?'

'Yes.'

'And even if we do come up with something, even if the man told you his name for some reason, and you remember it, none of what we discover will be of any legal use.'

'I know that. Superintendent Elswick just said that I might remember something that would help them catch him.'

'Right,' Laura said, relaxing again. 'I just don't want you to expect too much, that's all – either from the hypnotherapy or from the police.'

'Don't worry, I won't. Are you going to get your watch out and swing it in front of my eyes?'

'Have you ever been hypnotized before?'

'Never.'

Laura grinned. 'Well, I'm sorry, but I don't carry a pocket watch. I'm not going to make hand passes at you, either. And my eyes won't suddenly start to glow bright red. You do need something to fix your attention on, true, but I think this'll do fine.' She picked up the heavy glass paperweight from on top of a pile of correspondence. Inside, caught in the glass globe, was what looked like a dark green tangle of seaweed and fronds. 'Do you want to start now?'

Kirsten nodded. Laura got up and closed the blinds on the grey afternoon so that the only light left shone from a shaded desk lamp. Then she took off her white coat and hung it on the stand.

'First of all,' she said, 'I want you to relax. Loosen your belt if it's too tight. It's important to feel as comfortable as possible physically. Okay?'

Kirsten shifted in her chair and tried to relax all her muscles the way she had done in yoga classes at university.

'Now I want you to look at that globe, concentrate, stare into it. Stay relaxed and just listen to me.'

And she started to talk, general stuff about feeling at ease, heavy, sleepy. Kirsten stared into the globe and saw a whole underwater world. The way the light caught the glass, the green fronds seemed to be swaying to and fro very slowly, as if they really were seaweed at the bottom of the sea, weighed down by so much pressure.

When Laura said, 'Your eyelids are heavy,' they were. Kirsten closed her eyes and felt suspended between waking and sleep. She could hear a distant buzzing in her ears, like bees in the garden one childhood summer. The soft voice went on, taking her deeper. Finally, they went back to that night last June. 'You're leaving the party, Kirsten, you're walking out into the street . . .'

And she was. Again it was that muggy night, so vivid that she really felt as if she was there. She entered the park, aware of the soft tarmac path yielding under her trainers, the amber street lights on the main road, the sound of an occasional car passing by. And she could almost recapture the feelings, too, that sense of an ending, the sadness of everyone going his or her own way after what seemed so long together. A dog barked. Kirsten looked up. The stars were fat and blurred, almost butter-coloured, but she couldn't find the moon.

She was at the centre of the park now, and she could see haloed street lights on the bordering roads. She felt a sudden impulse to sit on the lion. The grass swished under her feet as she walked over and touched the warm stone of the mane. Then she mounted it and felt silly but happy, like a little girl again. She thought of cockatoos, monkeys, insects and snakes, then she threw her head back to look for the moon again, and felt herself choking.

Laura's voice cut through the panic, steady and calm,

but Kirsten was still struggling for breath as she tried to drag herself out of the trance. She could feel the calloused hands with their stubby fingers over her mouth, and she was being turned around, pulled off the lion's back onto the warm grass. The world went dark and she couldn't breathe. The cloud in her mind hardened and gleamed like jet, blotting everything out. She felt her back pushed hard against the grass, a great weight on her chest, then she burst up to the surface, gasping for air, and Laura reached forward to hold her hand.

'You're all right,' Laura said. 'It's over. Take a deep breath . . . another . . . That's right.'

Kirsten glanced around her, terrified, and found she was back in the familiar office with its glass-enclosed bookcases, filing cabinets, grinning skull and old hat stand.

'Will you open the blinds?' she asked, putting a hand to her throat and rubbing, 'I feel like I'm at the bottom of the sea.' She was still gulping for breath.

Laura pulled the blinds up, and Kirsten walked over to look out hungrily on the twilit city. She could see the river below, a slate mirror, and the people walking home from work. It was just after five o'clock and the street lights had come on all over the city. She stood there taking in the ordinariness of the scene and breathed deeply for a couple of minutes. Then she sat down opposite Laura again.

'I could do with a drink,' she said.

'Of course.' Laura fetched the Scotch from the cabinet, poured them each a shot, and offered her a cigarette. 'Are you all right now?'

'Better, yes. It was just so . . . so *vivid*. I felt as if I was really living through it all again. I didn't expect it to be as real as that.'

'You're a very imaginative woman, Kirsten. It's bound to be that way for you. Did you learn anything?'

Kirsten shook her head. 'No, it all went black when he turned me around and dragged me to the ground.'

'He did that?'

'Yes, of course he did.'

Laura tapped a column of ash into the tin ashtray. 'That's not what you said before.'

'What do you mean?'

'Don't you remember? Before, you could only remember up to the point of the hand coming from behind. You said nothing about being dragged down.'

Kirsten frowned. 'But that's what must have happened, isn't it?'

'Yes, but this time you actually relived it.'

It was true. Kirsten had remembered the sensation of falling, or of being pushed, onto her back on the ground, and the soft warmth of the grass as it tickled the nape of her neck . . . then the darkness, the weight. 'I didn't see anything, though,' she said.

'Perhaps not. I told you this might take several sessions. The point is that you've made progress. You remembered something you didn't remember before, something you'd buried. It might not be much, and it might not tell you anything, but at least it proves that you can do it, you *can* remember.'

'There's something else, too,' Kirsten said, reaching for her Scotch. 'It's true that I didn't see anything new this time, but you're right, I did get further than I've been before. It's not just images, visual memories, but there are feelings, too, that come back, aren't there?'

'What kind of feelings do you mean? Fear? Pain?'

'Yes, but not just that. Intuitions, inklings . . . it's hard to describe.'

'Try.'

'Well, what I felt was that I *did* see his face. I don't mean now, today, but when it happened. I know I saw him, but I'm still blocking the memory. And there was something else as well. I don't know what it was, but there was definitely something else about him. It was almost there, like a name on the tip of your tongue, but I resisted. I couldn't breathe, and it was so dark I just had to come out.'

'Do you want to carry on?' Laura asked, offering the bottle again. 'You don't have to. Nobody can make you. You know how painful it can be.'

Kirsten tossed back the last of her Scotch and held her glass out. The experience had terrified her, true, but it had also given her something she hadn't felt before: a resolve, a sense of purpose. Her cold hatred had crystallized into a desire to see her attacker. It was all connected, in some strange way, with the dark cloud that weighed down her mind.

When she finally spoke, her eyes were shining and her voice sounded strong and sure. 'Yes,' she said. 'Yes, I do want to carry on, whatever happens. I want to know who did this to me. I want to see his face.'

35

SUSAN

The newspapers had nothing much to report the next morning. Sue sat in her new cafe on Church Street, drinking coffee to get rid of the taste of Mrs Cummings's tea. She knew she would be better off not drinking the vile brew in the first place, but she needed something hot and bitter to wake her up. It was drizzling outside, and the cafe was full of miserable tourists keeping an eye on the weather, spinning out a pot of tea and a slice of gateau until the rain stopped and they could venture out again.

Sue hadn't slept well. She had already been awake when the seagulls started at a quarter to four. Even under the blankets and the bedspread, she had been trembling with delayed shock at what she had done to Keith McLaren. She could still see his stunned, innocent face, the blood pouring over his tanned cheek. She told herself he was just like the rest, like all men, but she still couldn't help hating herself for what she had been forced to do.

When she came to analyse her actions, it was mostly the way she had deliberately set up the situation that disgusted her. Because she didn't see herself as a cold-blooded killer, she had lured Keith into the woods and forced him to put her in a position from which she could strike out in self-righteous anger. In a way, it had been as cold-blooded as any execution; she had just needed to get herself excited enough to kill, and to that end she had seduced Keith, seduced him to death. There was a perverse logic in that somewhere that made even Sue twist her lower lip in the semblance of a smile the next morning, but the night had been dreadful, full of self-loathing, recrimination, loss of nerve. Even the talisman and the litany of victims had offered scant comfort in the small hours.

She had also worried. As it happens when you lie awake during those dreadful hours of the not quite morning with something on your mind, one fear leads directly to another. The disturbed mind seems to toss up terrors with the prolific abandon of a tempestuous ocean. By killing Keith, she had more than doubled her chances of getting caught before she finished what she had set out to do. With two murders to investigate, the police would surely spot the similarities and start stepping up their search. Somebody might have seen her with Keith in Staithes, Port Mulgrave or Hinderwell, and then someone else might remember seeing her with Grimley outside the Lucky Fisherman. Her only hope was that Keith's body would remain undiscovered in the woods until she had finished her task, and that was what she prayed for as she tossed and turned and finally slipped into an uneasy sleep, lulled by the cacophonous requiem of the gulls.

The coffee and cigarette helped her wake up. There was nothing in the nationals about the Student Slasher, but according to the local paper, the police were now certain that Jack Grimley had been murdered. Detective Inspector Cromer said that they were looking into his past for anyone who might have a grudge against him, and they still wanted to know if anyone had seen him after he left the Lucky Fisherman on the night of his death. Clearly no one had come forward so far. Sue remembered that night. She was sure nobody had noticed them, and once they had gone down to the beach and the cave, no one had even known they were there.

Sue's hands shook a little as she combed the rest of the paper for news of Keith's body. Thank God, there was nothing; they clearly hadn't found him yet. But she would still have to move quickly. With the police stepping up their search and Keith's body lying out in the woods for anyone to find, time was no longer on her side.

She knew what she had to do next, but it was still too early in the day. A short distance inland, on the eastern edge of town by the River Esk, stood a factory complex. There, much of the locally caught fish was cleaned, filleted and otherwise processed for resale. Some of it was frozen. The factory employed about a hundred and fifty workers, an even mix of men and women. If the person she was looking for was not a fisherman but was still connected with the industry, that had to be the place to look. She was thinking much more clearly now after the mistake with Jack Grimley.

Even though she knew where to look, she still wasn't sure how to go about it. She could hardly hang about outside the factory gates, check everyone's appearance and ask all likely suspects to say a few words. But what else could she do but watch? She had thought of applying for a job there to get her foot in the door, but that would raise questions of identification, references and National Insurance stamps. She couldn't afford that. Another alternative was to find out if the workers had a favourite pub. Whatever she decided, she would have to start with hanging around the place at five o'clock, when the workers left for the day. Then she could take it from there.

Much as she wanted to, she *couldn't* rush things. The plan left so much time on her hands, and time was a gift to the enemy. Also, today was not the kind of day for sitting on the beach reading, and her room at Mrs Cummings's was far too depressing to spend a whole day in. She had the perennial problem of the English person at the seaside: what to do on a rainy day. She could always look for a cinema that showed afternoon matinees, she thought, or spend her time and money on the one-armed bandits in an amusement arcade. Then there were the Museum and Art Gallery, and Captain Cook's house. There would also be bingo, of course, last resort for the truly desperate.

But Sue knew she wouldn't be able to concentrate on things like that. She had to be actively engaged in her search or her fears would get the better of her. At least she could walk up to the factory and reconnoitre; that would be a positive step. It was in a part of the town that she had never seen before, and she needed to know its layout, its dark corners, its entrances and exits. She also had to find a suitable spot to watch from. There was a chance that she might even need binoculars, though they would look a bit too suspicious if she had to use them in the open.

But first, she realized, there was something else she must do: something she had decided on during her restless, guilty, paranoid hours awake in the night. She needed something to replace her holdall. It wasn't especially conspicuous, just a khaki bag with side pockets and an adjustable strap, but she had been carrying it all the time she had been staying in Whitby, whether as Martha Browne or as Sue Bridehead. It was exactly the kind of mistake that could get her caught. Far better, she thought, to buy something else, fill the holdall full of stones and dump it in the sea along with all her Martha Browne gear – jeans, checked shirt, quilted jacket, the lot. It would be a shame to throw away such good-quality clothing, but it would be dangerous not to. Apart from those few moments on the front at Staithes, it was only as Martha Browne that she could be linked with Keith McLaren and Jack Grimley, so Martha Browne would have to disappear completely.

She paid her bill, then crossed the bridge and walked up to one of the department stores on Flowergate. There she bought a smaller, dark grey shoulder bag – she wouldn't have as much bulky clothing to carry around – a lightweight navy-blue raincoat, and a transparent plastic rainhood. In the toilet, she transferred all the things she would need – paperweight, money, make-up, underwear, book – into the new shoulder bag, and put the old one in the empty plastic bag bearing the store's logo. Anyone who noticed her would think she was simply carrying her shopping. That would do for the moment, but sometime soon she would have to go for a walk along the cliffs and get rid of the holdall permanently.

She walked back over the swing bridge, and instead of turning left onto the touristy part of Church Street, she went right and continued about half a mile along, past New Bridge, which carried the A171 to Scarborough and beyond over the River Esk. To her right, rain pitted the grey surface of the river, and on her left she came to one of those functional, residential parts of town that every holiday resort tucks away from public view. Consulting her map, she turned sharp left, perpendicular to the river, and walked a hundred and fifty yards or so up a lane at the southern edge of a council estate. Finally, she turned right and found herself in the short cul-de-sac that ended at the large mesh gates of the fish-processing plant.

It was the kind of street that would look drab and uninviting whatever the weather. Terraced houses stood on both sides, set back from the road by small gardens complete with privet hedges and wooden gates with peeling paint. The houses were pre-war, judging by the crust of grime and the white patches of saltpetre that had formed on the grey-brown brick. On the road surface, the ancient tarmac had worn away in spots, like bald patches, to reveal the outline of old cobbles beneath. To Sue's left, a short section of the terrace had been converted into a row of shops: grocer, butcher, newsagent-tobacconist, video rental; and on the right, about twenty yards from the factory gates, stood a tiny cafe.

Certainly from the outside there was nothing attractive about the place. The white sign over the grimy plate-glass window was streaked reddish-brown with rusty water that had spilled over from the eaves, and the R and the F of ROSE'S CAFE had faded to no more than mere outlines. Hanging in the window itself was a bleak, handwritten card offering TEA, COFFEE and SANDWICHES. The location was ideal, though. From a table by the window, Sue would just about be able to see through the film of dirt, and she would have a fine view of the workers filing out of the gates down the street. As far as she could tell, there was no other direction they could take.

She walked all the way up to the gates themselves.

They stood open, and there was no guardhouse or sentry post. Obviously, national defence wasn't at stake, and a fish-processing plant had little to worry about from terrorists or criminal gangs. A dirt path ran a hundred yards or so through a weed- and cinder-covered stretch of waste ground to the factory itself, a long two-storey prefab concrete building with a new red-brick extension stuck on the front for clerical staff. Inside the glass doors was what looked like a reception area, and the windows in the extension revealed offices lit by fluorescent light. Apart from the front, the only other side of the factory that Sue could see was the one closest to the river, and it was made up entirely of numbered loading bays. Several white vans were parked in the area and drivers in blue overalls stood around talking and smoking.

As Sue stood by the gates memorizing the layout, a loud siren sounded inside the building and a few seconds later people started to hurry out towards her. She looked at her watch: twelve o'clock, lunch hour. Quickly, she turned back and slipped into the cafe. A bell pinged as she entered, and a wrinkled beanpole of a woman in curlers and a greasy smock glanced up at her from behind the counter, where she had been buttering slices of thin white bread for sandwiches.

'You must have nipped out early, love,' the woman said cheerfully. 'Usually takes them all of thirty seconds to get here after the buzzer goes. Them as comes, that is. Now the Brown Cow up the road does pub lunches, there's plenty 'as deserted poor Rose's. Don't hold with lunchtime drinking, myself. What'll you have then? A nice cup of tea?'

Was there any other kind? Sue wondered. 'Yes, thanks, that'll do fine,' she said.

The woman frowned at her. 'Just a cup of tea? You need a bit more than that, lass. Put some meat on your bones. How about one of these lovely potted-meat sandwiches? Or are you one of them as brings her own lunch?' Her glance had turned suspicious now.

Sue felt flustered. It was all going wrong. She was supposed to slip into the place unobtrusively and order from a bored waitress who would pay her no attention. Instead, she had gone and made herself conspicuous just because she had run for cover when the siren went and everyone had started hurrying towards her. She was too jumpy, not very good at this kind of thing.

'I'm on a diet,' she offered weakly.

'Huh!' the woman snorted. 'I don't know about young 'uns today, I really don't. No wonder you've all got this annexa nirvana or whatever they calls it. Cup of tea it is, then, but don't blame me if you start having them there dizzy spells.' She poured the black steaming liquid from a battered old aluminium pot. 'Milk and sugar?'

Sue looked at the dark liquid. 'Yes, please,' she said.

'New there, are you?' the woman asked, pushing the cup and saucer along the red Formica counter.

'Yes,' said Sue. 'Only started today.'

'Been taking time off for shopping already, too, I see,' the woman said, looking down at Sue's carrier bag. 'Don't see why you'd want to shop in that place when there's a Marks and Sparks handy.' She looked at the bag again. 'Pricey that lot are. They charge for the name, you know. It's all made in Hong Kong anyroads.'

Would she never stop? Sue wondered, blushing and thinking frantically about what to say in reply. As it happened, she didn't have to. The woman went on to ask an even more difficult question: 'Who d'you work for, old Villiers?'

'Yes,' said Sue, without thinking at all.

The woman smiled knowingly. 'Well take my advice, love, and watch out for him. Wandering hands, he's got, and as many of 'em as an octopus, so I've heard.' She put a finger to the side of her nose. The door pinged loudly behind them. 'Hey up, here they come!' she said, turning away from Sue at last. 'Right, who's first? Come on, don't all shout at once!'

Sue managed to weave her way through the small crowd and take the table by the window. She hoped that old Villiers and his friends were among the people who had deserted Rose's for the Brown Cow. If they were management, it was very unlikely that they spent their lunch hour eating potted-meat sandwiches and drinking tannic tea in a poky cafe.

Still, it was a bloody disaster. Sue had thought she could come to this place every day at about five o'clock for as long as it took without arousing much attention. After that, providing the weather improved and the police didn't catch up with her, if she needed to stay any longer she could buy some cheap binoculars and watch from the clump of trees just above the factory site. But now she had been spotted and, what's more, she had lied. If the woman found out that Sue didn't work at the factory, she would become suspicious. After all, Rose's Cafe was hardly a tourist attraction. She would have to spy from the woods now, whatever the weather. The only bright spot on the horizon was the Brown Cow. If workers went there at lunchtime, perhaps some also returned in the evening after work. It was easier to be unobtrusive in a large busy pub than in a small cafe like Rose's.

Annoyed with herself and with the weather, Sue lit a cigarette and examined the faces of the other people in the cafe, making the best of what time she had. Calm down, she told herself. It won't take that long to find him if he's here. It can't.

36

KIRSTEN

'What else did you remember?' Sarah asked, leaning forward over the table and cupping her chin in her hands.

'That's just it,' Kirsten said. 'Nothing. It's so frustrating. I've had two more sessions since then and got nowhere. Every time I pull back at the same point.'

It was seven o'clock in the evening. Kirsten had parked the car off Dorchester Street and met Sarah at the station about an hour earlier. They had walked up to the city centre in the lightly falling snow and now sat in a pub on Cheap Street near the Abbey. The place was busy with the after-work crowd and Christmas shoppers taking a break. Kirsten and Sarah had just managed to squeeze in at a small table.

'Are you going to carry on?' Sarah asked.

Kirsten nodded. 'I've got another session in the morning.'

'So you *do* want to know?'

'Yes.'

'You know there's been another one, don't you, just before the end of term? That makes two now – three including you.'

'Kathleen Shannon,' Kirsten said. 'Aged twenty-two. She was a music student. I only wish . . .'

'What?'

'Nothing.'

'Come on, Kirstie. It's me, Sarah, remember?'

Kirsten smiled. 'You'll probably think I'm mad. I feel so empty sometimes and then I get so angry. I keep thinking of those two others. And there's this block, like a huge black lump or a thick cloud in my mind, and the whole memory's locked in there. I don't think it will go away, Sarah, even if the police do get him. What if they find him and they can't prove he did it? What if he gets off with probation or something? He might even slip away from them.'

'Well, that's their problem, isn't it? You know I'm not the police's greatest fan, but I suppose they know their job when it comes to things like this. After all, it's respectable middle-class girls getting killed, not prostitutes.'

'Maybe. But I just wish *I* knew who it was. I wish I could find him myself.'

Sarah stared at her and narrowed her eyes. 'And what would you do?'

Kirsten paused and drew a circle on the wet table with her finger. 'I think I'd kill him.'

'Vigilante justice?'

'Why not?'

'Have you ever thought that it might turn out the other way round, that he'd be the one killing you?'

'Yes,' Kirsten said quietly. 'I've thought of that.'

'Don't tell me you're feeling suicidal?'

'No, that's gone. Dr Henderson, Laura, helped a lot. They all say I'm making wonderful progress, and I suppose I am really, but . . .'

'But what?'

Kirsten fumbled for a cigarette. Sarah raised her eyebrows, but said nothing. The couple beside them left and two young men took their place. Someone put a U2 song on the jukebox and Kirsten had to speak louder to make herself heard. 'They don't know what it feels like to be me, do they? Living half a life, in limbo. I don't feel that I'll get out of it until I've met him again and I know he's dead.'

'That's ridiculous,' said Sarah. 'Besides, you wouldn't know where to look for him any more than the police do.'

'No, I wouldn't. Not yet, anyway.' She took a long deep drag on the cigarette and blew the smoke out slowly. 'Shall we have another drink? Then you can tell me all about the others and how Harridan's doing.'

Sarah nodded and Kirsten made her way to the bar. She didn't have to wait long to get served. The crowd had thinned out a bit now, as many of the after-work drinkers had gone home and the evening regulars hadn't arrived yet. The two lads at the next table were still there, though, talking enthusiastically about girls. Kirsten ignored the way they looked at her as she walked back, and sat down again.

'What about Galen?' Sarah asked.

'I got a Christmas card from him. He seems to be doing all right.'

'Are you two . . .?'

Kirsten shook her head. 'It's not his fault, really. He tried – God, how he tried – but I put him off. I don't think I could handle a relationship with a man right now.' She remembered that she had never told Sarah the full extent of her injuries and wondered whether she should do so. Not now, she decided, but perhaps sometime over the next few days. Sarah had stuck by her; she deserved to know. Kirsten also remembered the small pile of unopened letters, most of them from Galen, that she had put away in her drawer.

As they chatted about old friends, the bookshop and the bedsit, Kirsten noticed the two lads looking at her again and talking to one another. During a lull in the conversation, the old Kinks song on the jukebox ended and she overheard them.

One said something about her looking stuck up and needing a really good fuck. The other laughed and said something she could only catch the end of: '. . . enough cock to pave the road from here to Land's End – ends up!' And they burst into laughter.

Kirsten whirled round and flung the rest of her lager at them. As they recoiled in shock, their knees knocked the table and their glasses tipped over, rolled onto the stone floor and smashed. Beer spilled all over the place. In a flash, the landlord rushed over. 'Hey! I don't want no trouble.' Before they knew what had happened, Kirsten and Sarah found themselves back out in Cheap Street. They had no idea where the two boys had got to.

Kirsten leaned against a lamppost to catch her breath, and Sarah stood beside her, laughing. 'Well, you really showed them, didn't you? And I thought getting chucked out of pubs was my speciality.'

'Did you hear what they said?'

'Yeah, some of it. Come on, love, let's walk a bit. Their kind's not worth bothering about. Besides, it's not as far from here to Land's End as it is from up north.'

'I suppose that does water down the insult a bit,' Kirsten said. 'Lancashire, I'd say, from the way they talked. Probably Manchester.'

Sarah raised her eyebrows. 'I'm impressed. I've already forgotten most of what I learned last year, but you still remember that linguistics stuff.'

Kirsten managed a smile. 'I suppose it's like riding a

bike. You never forget. Anyway, we should be going home soon. I said we wouldn't be late.'

The snow was still falling. Now the flakes were bigger and fatter, and an inch or two had settled on the roads and pavements, where it was soon churned up into grey slush by cars and pedestrians. They walked past the floodlit Abbey and turned right onto Pierrepont Street. Beyond Parade Gardens, the river reflected the strings of red and green Christmas lights, and snowflakes drifted down to melt on the water's surface. There were still plenty of shoppers about with huge carrier bags full of presents.

'Nice,' said Sarah, when she saw the Audi.

Kirsten took a scraper from the boot and wiped the snow from the windscreen, then she negotiated the one-way system onto Wells Road. Soon they had left the city behind and turned off the main road onto the narrow country lanes. Here the snow lay undisturbed before the car's wheels, a pristine white carpet glittering in the headlights. Thick flakes fell and stuck to the window, melting before the wipers could brush them away.

Almost without realizing it, Kirsten found herself pressing her foot down on the accelerator. She knew these winding roads like the back of her hand. They were all so narrow that drivers had to pull into the frequent passing places if they met someone coming in the opposite direction, and the hedgerows were so tall that no one could see what was around the next corner. Kirsten felt the car going faster and faster, the snow rushing at the windscreen like a blizzard. She started to slip a little on the corners. The needle edged higher and adrenalin surged in her veins. She couldn't stop herself even if she wanted to.

After a while, she became aware of a distant voice and felt a hand shaking her. It was Sarah yelling for her to slow down. She looked terrified. All of a sudden, Kirsten felt herself snap back, and eased her foot off the accelerator. She felt drained. Sarah was still ranting on about getting them killed and asking her if she was crazy. Finally, Kirsten just had to stop. She pulled into the first passing place she came across, put on the brakes and turned off the engine. Her hands were shaking on the wheel.

'Are you trying to get us both killed?' Sarah yelled.

Kirsten couldn't speak.

'Well, it's all right with me if you want to kill yourself,' Sarah went on angrily, 'but just leave me out of it, all right? I'd rather bloody well walk, even though I don't know where the hell I am.' And she reached for the door handle.

Kirsten leaned over to stop her. 'Don't,' she said urgently. 'I'm sorry, Sarah, I . . . I don't know . . .'

Sarah paused and turned back, concern showing in her fine, pale features. 'You all right?'

Kirsten's hands still gripped the wheel so tightly that her knuckles shone as white as the snow. She shook her head. She could feel the intense silence and darkness outside the car. Without lights, the snow only showed up as a faint pearly sheen on the road and hedges. The Mendip Hills were lost somewhere in the night. Inside, their breath misted the windows.

'Kirstie?' Sarah asked again. 'Are you all right, love?'

Kirsten let go of the wheel and threw herself towards Sarah with a strength and desperation that almost sent them both flying out of the door.

'No,' she cried. 'No, I'm not all right at all.'

She hung on tight and felt Sarah's arms close around her, holding her and muttering soft words. For the first time since it happened, she began to really cry. The warm salt tears didn't just trickle down her cheeks, they welled up in her eyes and poured over onto Sarah's shoulder as Kirsten clung on and sobbed.

37

SUSAN

After two days without success, Sue almost gave up. There seemed to be too many obstacles in her way, and she was making too many mistakes. For a start, the conversation with the woman in Rose's Cafe worried her, then she overheard two workers talking and learned that the factory operated on a shift system. Only the office workers came teeming out of the mesh gates at five o'clock. Most of the people on the shop floor worked one of the shifts: noon to eight, eight to four, and four to noon. Finding him now seemed like an impossible task. She could hardly turn up there at four in the morning and stand gawking as the workers filed out.

Even the weather continued to work against her. It rained on and off, and the temperature dropped low enough that she had to wear her cardigan under the raincoat. She was quite prepared to spend some of her fast-dwindling money on binoculars and go up to the woods, even though the ground would be wet, but fortunately it didn't come to that. A couple of pieces of good luck kept her going.

The first evening at five, she approached the gates again, and when she passed the cafe she noticed a different woman behind the counter. This one was younger, with long, stringy blonde hair. There were a few people sitting in the place already, so Sue entered, head bowed like someone just seeking refuge from the rain, bought a cup of tea without having to answer any questions, and took the window seat. Perhaps the woman she had met there before only worked lunchtimes? She wouldn't need to spend so much of her money on binoculars and end up catching pneumonia in the damp woods after all.

The problem of the shifts remained, and Sue didn't know how to get around that one. She certainly couldn't afford binoculars with infrared lenses, so the four a.m. changeover was beyond her. That left noon and eight at night, both of which she could cover from the Brown Cow.

Cheered by the turn in her fortunes, Sue left Rose's Cafe just after five-thirty on the first day, treated herself to cannelloni and salad in a rather expensive restaurant on New Quay Road near the station – a place that didn't specialize in fish and chips – and then went back over the Esk at a quarter to eight to find the Brown Cow. Instead of turning right at the cul-de-sac that led to the factory, she continued up the lane past the edge of the council estate and found the pub about a hundred yards further on. It was an undistinguished modern red-brick place with a Tetley's sign hanging outside.

The doors opened into a large lounge, completely lacking in character: dull beige wallpaper and a stained brown carpet, sticky and worn in patches. The tables were made of some kind of tough black plastic, and the moulded seats were uncomfortable. It was a functional place. Clearly the only people who went there were those who lived on the nearby estate. Factory workers might drop by at lunchtime, Sue thought glumly, but they weren't likely to make an evening of it there when the shift ended at eight o'clock.

However depressing the Brown Cow seemed to Sue, though, it was certainly busy enough. Well over three-quarters of the tables were occupied, and everyone seemed to be having a good time. The obligatory jukebox had a tendency towards ancient Engelbert Humperdinck and Tom Jones songs, and the row of one-armed bandits and video games winked seductively by the far wall like a line of tarts in a brothel. Plump women smoked and gossiped while plump men smoked and shoved coins into the machines.

In her raincoat and hood, Sue thought she looked drab and anonymous enough not to attract too much attention in her dim corner. As it turned out, though, she didn't have to stay long. When no crowd of workers had turned up by twenty-five past eight, she felt her suspicions confirmed and left. Like most seaside cafes, Rose's had closed at six o'clock, just about the time when people were ready for dinner, so there was nowhere else to watch from.

Lunchtime on the second day seemed more promising. Not only did several of the office workers call in at the Brown Cow, but quite a few of the factory men came in for a pie and a pint at the end of their shift. Sue still didn't see the man she wanted, and she began to wonder how much longer she could go on. Though Keith's body hadn't been found yet and nothing new had appeared in the papers, she was beginning to worry that the police might be getting close. Her money wouldn't last for ever, either, and she hardly dared contemplate the consequences if she was wrong about her quarry's origins. She had put so much energy into the search, gambled so much of herself on the outcome, that failure didn't bear thinking about.

Especially now that two innocent people lay dead because of her.

She went to Rose's Cafe again that evening around five and turned up at the Brown Cow at eight. Still nothing. By the third day she was thoroughly discouraged and depressed by the endless shuttling between two such awful environments. The world she now seemed to inhabit, though no more than a mile or so from the beach, the whale's jawbone, Captain Cook's statue, St Mary's and the twee shops of Church Street, was so drab and anonymous that it could have been almost anywhere in any English city.

It was also a world of shadows. She was getting jumpy, thinking people were following her and watching her. It was silly, she told herself. She was the one doing the watching. But she couldn't get the feeling out of her mind. She hardly slept at night, and not only because of the gulls. She started to think that her days in the sun on West Cliff had been a dream; now she had passed through the whale's jawbone into its dark, dank, dripping belly and there was no way out. Then, on the third day, she saw him.

38
KIRSTEN

The green fronds began to sway and Kirsten felt the weight of the ocean on her eyelids. Laura's voice murmured in the distance, urging her deeper, pressing her on, and then she heard the buzzing in her ears and she was walking out into the street one muggy June night aeons ago . . .

She could feel the tarmac path, softened by the day's heat, yield like a pile carpet under her feet and hear the swishing of her jeans as she walked. A car droned in the distance. A dog barked. Kirsten looked up. The stars were fat and blurred, almost butter-coloured in the haze, but she couldn't find the moon. It must be behind those high trees, she thought as she hurried on.

She stood at the centre of the park, where she could see the glow of the haloed street lights beyond the trees, and felt an urge to sit on the lion. She walked across the narrow patch of grass and mounted it. Images of cockatoos, monkeys, insects and snakes ran through her mind. She laughed and tossed her head back to look for the moon again behind the trees, then she felt the rough hand over her mouth and nose.

Her chest was tight and she knew she was kicking and struggling for air as someone manoeuvred her off the lion onto her back. Long grass tickled the nape of her neck.

And suddenly there was a moon. It was shining

through a gap between the trees on the spot where she had been dragged. And it lit up his face. It was dim and ghostly in the pale light, but a face nonetheless: deeply lined, with a short, black fringe low on the broad forehead and dark eyebrows that met in the middle. And his eyes. Even in the poor light she could see how they glittered and how they were far beyond reason.

For a moment, the image seemed to freeze and two time frames superimposed. She lay pinned to the ground, looking up into his face, but at the same time she seemed to be facing him directly through a haze. The vision disappeared almost as soon as it had formed. Again she lay on the ground fighting for breath as he shoved a coarse oily rag in her mouth. She was gagging, suffocating, she couldn't go on . . . The next thing she heard was Laura's voice slowly drawing her up from the depths.

Kirsten opened her eyes and took several deep breaths. Laura poured her a cup of coffee. As usual after the hypnotherapy sessions, Kirsten was grateful for the big window and its view of the city. She felt she had been lost in a deep airless vault and needed some air in her lungs, to see horizons again. Laura always waited a while before speaking, but this time Kirsten broke the silence.

'Did you get it all down?'

Laura nodded. She looked pale. 'You went further than you've ever been before.'

'I know. This time it was different. I couldn't stop myself going on even if I'd wanted to. Until he put that awful smelly rag . . . I couldn't breathe. I was choking.' She put her hand to her throat as if she still felt the pain.

'Your voice wasn't always easy to catch,' Laura said.

'You spoke very quickly, and sometimes you mumbled. Could we go over some of the details?'

Kirsten nodded, and Laura took notes as they analysed the session. When it was over, Kirsten wandered out into the grey day and stood watching the Avon churn down by the city weir. She felt curiously detached from the bustling city life around her. She knew that she could have gone on reliving the experience if it hadn't been for the choking sensation. That had felt too real to suffer through. But she did remember something else now, something she hadn't been quite able to grasp at the time. Hands in pockets, she sauntered towards High Street to meet Sarah for lunch.

The pub was warm and noisy. Conversations swirled around Kirsten like the buzzing of insects. She felt as if she was floating. It was a pleasant sensation, though; it had been a long time since she had felt grateful for the atmosphere of a crowded pub. Sarah was sitting close to the side door, a half of lager in front of her and a paperback in her hand. Kirsten waved to her, stopped at the bar for drinks and went over. Sarah shifted some parcels from the chair next to her and put them on the floor. Kirsten sat down.

'Christmas presents,' Sarah said.

Kirsten sipped her double Scotch and reached for her cigarettes.

'Are you all right?' Sarah asked. 'You look a bit pale.'

'I'm fine,' Kirsten said. 'I just had a bit of a shock, that's all. I feel dazed.'

'What was it? The hypnosis?'

Kirsten nodded. 'I remembered, Sarah. I remembered what he looked like.' Her voice sounded shaky and far away to her.

Sarah put her hand on Kirsten's arm. 'You don't have to talk about it—'

'No, it's all right. I don't mind. At least not with you anyway . . . a friend. Laura's a doctor. She's being paid to help me, however nice she is. I mean, I like her and I'm very grateful to her, but . . .'

'It doesn't go any deeper?'

'No. When it's not me in the office, it's someone else, isn't it? And she's probably just the same with them. It's nothing special; it's impersonal, like the police.' And she told Sarah about finally seeing her attacker.

'How old do you think he was?' Sarah asked.

'I never really thought. About forty, forty-five, I suppose. Pretty old. It's just that he had this lined face, you know, rough-hewn, lines from the edges of the nose and the mouth.' She drew them with her fingers on her own face, then she shuddered. 'It was awful, Sarah. It was like going through the whole thing again, but I couldn't stop myself. I didn't want to.'

'What happened next?'

'Laura brought me out of it.'

'Have you told the police what he looked like?'

Kirsten sipped some Scotch and glanced towards the bar. Things were coming into clearer focus now; her feet were touching the ground.

'Not yet. Laura's going to phone them and send a report.'

'Are you sure you're telling me everything?' Sarah asked.

'Why?'

'You sound vague, and you've got that shifty look on your face. I've known you long enough to tell when you're holding something back. What is it?'

Kirsten paused and swirled her drink in her glass before answering. 'There was something else . . . just an impression. I can't really be sure.'

'What was it?'

'When he put the gag in my mouth, I was too busy struggling, trying to catch my breath, to really notice at the time.'

'Notice what?'

'The smell. There was a smell of fish. You know, like at the seaside.'

'Fish?'

Kirsten nodded. 'It probably doesn't mean anything.'

'What did the doctor say?'

'Nothing.'

'What do you mean?'

'I didn't remember it until I'd left her office, when I was coming here to meet you.'

'Why don't you phone her?'

Kirsten shrugged. 'Like I said, it's probably not important.'

'But that's not for you to decide.'

Kirsten toyed with her cigarette in the large blue ashtray, shaping the end in one of its grooves. She felt herself starting to drift again like the smoke that curled and twisted in front of her. 'I don't know,' she said. 'It just seems that I keep feeding them bits of my memory, you know, things I've had sweated out of me, and nothing happens. They're so impersonal, just a big bureaucratic machine. I mean, two more girls have been killed since my . . . *two*. I can't explain myself, Sarah, not yet, but it's me and him. I feel I've got it in me to find him. It's as if he's inside me and I'm the only one who can flush him out.'

'And then what?'

'I don't know.'

'Jesus Christ! Kirstie. If you ask me you're turning a bit batty. It must be all that solitude and country air.' She put her hand on Kirsten's arm again. 'You really should tell the police everything you can remember. Like you said, he's killed two women already, and there's bound to be more. People like him don't stop till they're caught, you know.'

'Do you think I don't know that,' said Kirsten, pulling her arm away angrily. 'Do you think I don't feel for those women? I have to live what they died.'

'Come again?'

'It doesn't matter. I'm sorry if I seem so touchy about it. I can't explain. I'm not even sure what I mean myself.'

Kirsten sipped some more Scotch and looked around the pub again. The people looked indistinct; their conversations were just meaningless sounds. Sarah changed the subject to shopping.

As she half-listened and let herself be lulled by the buzz of talk around her, Kirsten came to a decision. People didn't understand her, it seemed. Not even Sarah. People didn't understand how *personal* it was. Not just for her, but for Margaret Snell and Kathleen Shannon too. Doctors, police . . . what did they know? In future, she would have to be careful just how much she told them.

When she tasted that foul rag he had stuffed in her mouth and smelled his rough stubby fingers, she recognized the saltwater taste as well as the fishy odour. The rag tasted as if it had been dipped in the sea. Wasn't there, then, a good chance that he had come from a coastal town?

And there was something else. Not only had she

remembered the smell, but when he had thrown her to the ground and put the rag in her mouth as she stared up at him in the moonlight, his mouth had been moving. He had been talking to her. She couldn't hear any sounds or words, but she knew he had spoken, and if she could bring that back, there was no knowing what it might tell her about him. It might even lead her to him.

39

SUSAN

As Susan approached the Brown Cow at lunchtime on the third day, she saw two white factory vans parked in front, and before she had even got near the entrance, two men came out of the pub and walked over to them. It was impossible to be sure from such a distance, but one of them matched the image in her memory: low, dark fringe, the thick eyebrows meeting in the middle. She had to get closer to see if he had deep lines on his face and, most of all, she needed to hear his voice.

When they started their vans and pulled out, she followed on foot. At least she could see which way they turned as they drove down the lane. If they went left, they would be on their way to the factory, and if they carried on down to the main road, they would be off making a delivery somewhere. She was in luck. They turned left.

Sue hurried after them. She didn't know what she was going to do, but there was no point in hanging around the Brown Cow any longer. When she reached the turning, the vans had already pulled up outside the loading bays a hundred yards beyond the mesh gates, and the drivers were nowhere in sight. She walked along the street as far as the row of shops. She couldn't just wander through the factory gates and go looking for the man;

nor could she sit in the cafe where the inquisitive woman would be on duty. What could she do?

Before she had time to come up with a plan, she noticed the man walk out of the glass doors of the office building. He seemed to be slipping a small envelope of some kind into his pocket. A pay packet, perhaps? Whatever it was, he looked as though he had finished for the day. If he was a driver, the odds were that he had just returned from an overnight run, padded his time sheet with an hour or so at the Brown Cow, and was now on his way home.

He was walking towards her, only about forty yards away now on the dirt track that led out of the factory. She had nowhere to hide. She couldn't just stand there in the street until he came level with her. What if he recognized her? She had changed a lot since their last meeting, lost a lot of weight, though her wig was about the same length as her hair had been then. Surely he couldn't have got a much clearer impression of her looks than she had of his? But she couldn't stand rooted to the spot.

There was only one thing to do. She rushed forward and ducked into the newsagent's. She needed her morning papers anyway, as she had been so absorbed in her new routine that she hadn't even spent her usual hour in the Church Street cafe. She hadn't looked for news of Keith, and she was still feeling nervous about the Grimley investigation, though no one had knocked on her door in the middle of the night yet.

The newspapers were arranged in small, overlapping piles on a low shelf just inside the window, below the rack of magazines. From there, as she pretended to make her selection with her back turned to the newsagent, she could get a closer look at the man as he went past. She bent and pretended to leaf through the stack, as if she were scanning the front pages for the best headlines, when suddenly he appeared right outside. He didn't walk past as she had expected. Instead, he patted his pockets, turned and came inside.

Sue kept her back to the counter and examined the *Radio Times* and *Woman's Own* in the rack above the papers.

'Afternoon, Greg,' she heard the woman say. 'In for some baccy, I suppose?'

'Yes, please.' The man's voice sounded muffled and Sue couldn't hear him clearly.

'Usual?'

'Aye. Oh, and I'll have a box of matches, too, please, love. Swan Vestas.'

'Finished for the day?'

'Aye. Just got back from the Leeds and Bradford run. Can't leave the poor beggars without their fish and chips, can we?'

The newsagent laughed.

Sue gripped the rack of magazines to keep herself from falling over. Her heart was beating so fast and loud that she thought it would burst. At the very least, both the newsagent and the man in the shop must be able to hear it. Her face was flushed and her breath was hard to catch. Everything seemed to swim and ripple in front of her eyes like motes dancing in rays of light: the magazine covers, the grim terraced houses across the street. And all the while she struggled to stay on her feet; she couldn't let these two people see that there was anything wrong with her. They would rush over to help, and then . . .

Sue held on and fought for control as the voice, the horrible, familiar voice that had been whispering hoarsely in her nightmares for a month, carried on making small talk as if nothing terrible had ever happened.

40

KIRSTEN

When Kirsten stood on the platform and watched the Intercity pull out at 12.25 on 3 January, she felt frightened and desolate. Despite an awkward beginning, Christmas at Brierley Coombe that year had turned out to be the best time she had enjoyed since the assault. She had been glad to have Sarah around, especially as a counter to all the uncles, aunts and grandparents who had treated her as if she were a half-witted invalid.

The village itself looked like a Christmas-card illustration. The snow that began on 22 December went on for almost two days and settled a treat, particularly out in the country, where there was little traffic and no industry to spoil it. It lay about two feet thick on the thatched roofs, smooth and contoured around the eaves and gables; and in the woods, where Kirsten often took Sarah for early-morning walks, the snow that rested on twigs and branches created an image of two worlds in stark contrast, the white superimposed on the dark.

They went into Bath once more to do some shopping at the Boxing Day sales and have drinks with Laura Henderson, whom Sarah liked immediately. One night they shocked the locals in the village pub. Sarah wore her FISH ON A BICYCLE T-shirt, and everyone looked embarrassed. There she was: the careless tangle of blonde hair, the pale complexion and exquisite features that looked as if they had been expertly worked from the finest porcelain, then smoothed and polished to perfection, and, to cap it all, that great advertisement for the redundancy of the male sex scrawled across her chest.

Nobody bothered them, like the Lancashire lads in Bath had, but the village men glanced over and muttered nervously among themselves, some of them smiling superciliously. It was the most uncomfortable evening of the holiday for Kirsten. Her enjoyment of crowded pubs didn't seem to have lasted long. She could relax with Laura and Sarah, but the proximity of men still made her tense and angry. And when they looked over with those superior smiles on their faces, her cheeks burned with fear and anger. After all, a man had taken what other men wanted from her. Somehow, she reasoned, they were all implicated in that.

On New Year's Eve, Kirsten's parents went to a party. Kirsten and Sarah were invited, but neither of them fancied spending the evening with a bunch of drunken old stockbrokers, their bored wives and yuppie offspring, so they decided to stay at home and celebrate by themselves.

The cocktail cabinet was well stocked, a log fire blazed in the hearth, and they turned out the lights and lit candles instead. The open curtains of the French windows revealed the snow-covered garden and trees. Kirsten brought some of her records and tapes down from her room to play on her father's stereo, and everything seemed perfect. They sat on the thick rug in front of the spitting fire, listening to Mozart, with the cognac bottle beside them.

'What are you going to do?' Sarah asked as she poured out their second drinks.

'With my life, you mean?'

'Yes.'

'I don't know. I haven't made any plans.'

'You can't just stay here for ever, you know.' Sarah looked around the room, where the candles and fire tossed shadows like dark sails in a storm, and out of the windows at the fairy-tale garden in the snow. 'Nice as it is, it isn't real life. Not yours.'

'And what is my life?'

'For Christ's sake, you got a First, a good one. You're not going to waste your education, are you?'

Kirsten laughed. 'Listen to yourself. You sound like a bloody guidance counsellor or something.'

Sarah bit her lip and looked away.

'I'm sorry.' Kirsten reached out and touched her shoulder. 'I didn't mean that. It's just that I haven't thought about it. I suppose I've put the future off and I resent being made to dwell on it.'

'Why don't you go back to university, do your MA? It needn't be up north if you don't want. There's plenty of other places would be glad to have you.'

Kirsten nodded slowly. 'I won't say it hasn't crossed my mind. But I couldn't start till the next academic year. What would I do in the meantime?'

Sarah laughed. 'How the hell should I know? What do you think I am, a guidance counsellor? But seriously, you could get a job, something in Bath. Just to keep you going and take you out of yourself. You've got too much time to brood on the past hanging around this village. What about a bookshop, for example? You'd probably like that.'

'But what would my mother think?' She put on a finishing-school accent: 'I mean, it's *awfully* common being a shopgirl, dear.'

Sarah laughed. 'Is that why she's so frosty towards me? Maybe I should tell her my father owns half of Herefordshire. Think that would help?'

'I'm sure it would. She's such a snob.'

'Seriously though, Kirstie, you've got to do something, get out of here. What about Toronto? You could go out there and join Galen.'

Kirsten topped up both their drinks. It was eleven-thirty. Mozart's *Requiem* had just ended and the world outside was silent and still.

'Well?' Sarah repeated. 'What about it? Or is it over between you?'

Kirsten stared into the fire. Flames licked the wood like angry tongues. If I don't tell her now, she thought, I probably never will. She looked at Sarah, so lovely in the winter firelight with red and orange and yellow flames dancing in her eyes and flickering over her face. Her skin looked almost transparent, especially where the fire seemed to shine a delicate coral through her nostrils and over her cheekbones. And she had it all: not just the looks, but a whole body. She could make love and have orgasms and have children.

'What is it?' Sarah asked softly.

Kirsten realized that a tear had trickled from the corner of one eye. Quickly, she wiped it away. She would have to stop this crying business. Once was all right, it had helped drain her of tension, but it mustn't become a habit, a weakness.

Over another cigarette, she finally told Sarah all about the damage to her body. Sarah listened in horror and couldn't find anything to say. She poured more cognac. They leaned back against the sofa, and Sarah put her arm around Kirsten and held her close. There were no more tears. They sat like that, content and silent for a while, sipping Rémy. Finally, Sarah swore softly: 'Shit, it's ten past twelve. We've forgotten the new year.'

Kirsten looked up and the spell was broken. Her back ached from the position she'd been sitting in. 'So it is. Never mind. I'll get the Veuve Clicquot and we'll have our own new year a bit late.' She stood up, rubbed her aching muscles, and went into the kitchen.

And so they had poured champagne, sung 'Auld Lang Syne' and wished each other a Happy New Year at twenty past twelve.

And now Sarah was gone. Kirsten walked aimlessly around Bath, its streets quiet with post-seasonal depression, and thought over what Sarah had said about the future. She decided that she would resume her studies, or at least apply for next year. It would be a good cover, and it would keep her parents off her back.

In the meantime, she was going to attempt to find out who had crippled her. It might take months, she realized, but at least now she had discovered that the knowledge was there, locked inside her. Of course, she must take care that no one suspected what she was really up to; she had to appear as if she was simply getting on with her life and putting the past behind her. She didn't know yet what she was going to do if she did discover anything, but she had to find the key, unlock the voice, and then . . . First, though, she had a lot of thinking and a lot of planning to do.

41

SUSAN

By the time the man had left the newsagent's, Sue had managed to get her breathing under control. She bought her papers and a packet of cigarettes, then walked back out into the drizzle.

He had reached the end of the street and turned left, down the lane towards the water. Without really considering what she was going to do, Sue started following him. She half expected him to turn into the council estate, assuming that was where he lived, but he didn't. Instead of walking down to Church Street, however, he turned right along a narrow road that ran parallel to it.

There were no houses on the right-hand side of the street, just a stretch of waste ground that sloped up to the southern edge of the council estate, almost hidden beyond the convex swell of the land. On the left stood a row of small, detached cottages. They were nothing much really – just red brick with slate roofs – but each had its own front and back gardens. Their rear windows would also look out over the harbour towards West Cliff, and a good view always costs money.

Sue had tried to hang back a reasonable distance behind the man, and she didn't think he had spotted her. Beyond the row of cottages lay another open tract of weeds and nettles, where the street itself petered out into a narrow dirt path that veered left, eventually to join

Church Street by the Esk. It might be difficult to follow him over open land, Sue thought. Although she looked ordinary enough in her long navy-blue raincoat and hood, if he turned he might just recognize her from the shop. And then he would wonder what a tourist was doing following him through such an unattractive part of town.

Before she had time to decide whether to go on or turn back, however, she saw him walk down the path to the last cottage in the row. She paused, taking cover behind a parked van, and watched him put the key in the lock and enter. So that was where he lived. She wondered if he lived alone. If he really was the man who had attacked her, and she had been certain as soon as she heard his voice that he was, he probably did.

Then she thought of Peter Sutcliffe, the Yorkshire Ripper who had lived with his wife, Sonia, throughout the period he had killed and butchered thirteen women. And hadn't there been two or three others who had survived his attacks? Sue wondered what had become of them. Anything was possible, but somehow she couldn't bring herself to believe that the man she was after shared his life with a woman.

When he had disappeared inside the cottage, Sue turned and walked back down the lane to the road. There was nothing more she could do at the moment. A little careful planning, at least, was called for now. She couldn't just go barging in and kill him; she had to lure him to an isolated open place after dark. Because she had been attacked in just such a place, she felt that she would have more chance of succeeding somewhere similar when the tables were turned. He was stronger than her, so she would have to use cunning. She couldn't see it happening in a house or on a street. But she knew where he lived now, and that was comforting knowledge. It gave her an advantage.

As if to mark her entry into tourist Whitby, the drizzle stopped and the clouds began to break, allowing a few feeble rays of sun through here and there. She was on the narrow, cobbled part of Church Street again, north of Whitby Bridge. The world went on as normal there: families and courting couples wandered down the road as usual, pausing to look in the windows of the jet shops and the little gift shops that sold flavoured fudge or sachets of Earl Grey tea and Colombian coffee.

It was one-thirty, and Sue hadn't eaten yet. She was also eager to read the papers. She went into the Black Horse, bought a half of lager and ordered a steak and kidney pie. The place was moderately busy, mostly with young couples eating lunch, mackintoshes strewn on the seats beside them and umbrellas propped up against the wall. She managed to find a small corner table and sat down to read the papers while she ate.

There was nothing about the Student Slasher in the *Independent*. It had, after all, been almost a week since he had last struck. Unless the police caught him or found an important clue, there would be nothing more about him until he had slashed and strangled his next victim. Sue meant to see that that never happened. She glanced quickly at the headlines – war, lies, corruption, misery – and then turned anxiously to the local paper.

The news was on the front page, staring her right in the face:

CRIMES LINKED?

Police in Whitby are attempting to establish whether there is any link between the murder of Whitby man, Jack Grimley, and the serious wounding of an Australian national, Keith McLaren, whose unconscious body was discovered by a wildlife worker in some woods near Dalehouse late last night. Mr McLaren, suffering from serious head injuries, is presently in a coma in St Mary's Hospital, Scarborough. Doctors refuse to comment on his chances of recovery but one hospital spokesman admitted there is a strong risk of permanent brain damage. When asked if the attacks could have been carried out by the same person a police spokesman told our reporter, 'It is too early to say. We are looking at two different cases, both with similar head wounds, but so far there is no evidence of a connection between these two men.' Police are still anxious to interview anyone who might have seen Grimley after he left the Lucky Fisherman last Thursday. They are also interested in discovering the identity of a woman seen with McLaren in Hinderwell last Monday afternoon. She is described as young, with short light-brown hair, wearing jeans, a grey jacket and a checked shirt. Police are eager that anyone who can identify her come forward at once.

Sue put the paper down on the table and tried to control her shaking hands. He wasn't dead! Keith wasn't dead. She should have known she hadn't hit him hard enough. Instead of finishing the job, she had been frightened by that damn dog and hurried away without making sure. Perhaps she had felt sorry for him, too, and that had made her soft. But it had never entered her mind that she might not have killed him. What could she do now? What if he were to come round and tell the police who she was? They already had a description of Martha Browne.

Sue pushed the rest of her pie aside and lit a cigarette. She had no appetite left. It was time to get a grip on herself. She went to the bar, bought a double brandy, then settled down to re-read the article carefully. She must be careful not to panic, not now that she had the scent of her true prey. She had to think clearly. The description of the girl was vague, for a start, and it certainly didn't resemble the way she looked now. But would the proprietor of the Abbey Terrace guesthouse remember her? And what about Grimley's pals in the Lucky Fisherman? She had been dressed much the same that night, she recalled, as when she had walked in the woods with Keith. Would the men remember seeing her sitting with the Australian, glancing over at Grimley as if she knew him? And had anyone seen her with Keith in Staithes? She had been wearing her new outfit at first, before she had changed in the toilet, so what if someone could connect the one girl with the other?

The police could be getting very close indeed, she realized. She would have to act quickly. There was no sense in staying around to get arrested for killing Jack Grimley when she had now caught up with the man she really wanted. Time was definitely working against her, its winged chariot snapping at her heels. And what about Keith? He might recover consciousness at any moment. Would he still be able to identify her, or would his memory of the incident be gone, as hers had been for so long? She didn't know. All she knew was that she had her man in sight, and she had better find a way of luring him into the open soon, or the whole mission would be at risk.

A tweedy woman who had just come to sit at the next table gave her a curious look. It was probably time to change her haunts. She had been to this pub and the nearby cafe far too often.

She sipped some more brandy; it warmed her throat and settled her fluttering stomach. Should she go to the hospital in Scarborough, creep into Keith's room and put the pillow over his face? Could she do it? Did she have the nerve? But she remembered that her attacker had tried to get to her in a similar situation and he hadn't succeeded. There would be police guards; security would be far too tight for her to be able to get through to him. No, that was out of the question. All she could do was hope that he wouldn't recover.

There was still the holdall back in her room. She hadn't got rid of it yet. That was something she could do while she worked out a plan to deal with 'Greg'. Then she would have to leave town quickly, no foolish hanging around to wallow in the outcome of her actions. She would have to read about and savour her success at a distance, like everyone else.

42

KIRSTEN

With Sarah gone, Kirsten had only her fears and a growing sense of mission to keep her going. In late January, the killer claimed his fourth victim, a second-year biology student called Jane Pitcombe. Carefully, Kirsten cut out her picture and all the details she could find and put them in the scrapbook she had started to keep track of the victims.

Also that month, she told Laura Henderson that she wanted to stop the hypnotherapy sessions as they were becoming too painful for her. In reality, she was worried that she would give away to Laura whatever she discovered and that the police would find the killer first. She had come to realize shortly after Sarah left that she wanted him for herself. It was the only way to heal her wounds and put the spirits of Margaret, Kathleen and Jane to rest. It wasn't difficult to convince Laura to stop the hypnotism; after all, the police had got as good a description of the killer as they were likely to.

It was important to try to keep everyone happy, so to this end she finally read Galen's letters and wrote him a long, cheery but noncommittal reply. She apologized for not writing sooner, but said she had just come through a lengthy period of depression. She also told him she was going to resume her studies, probably back up north. Canada just seemed too far away from home for her to consider yet. She was sure he would understand.

February, bleak and cold, came and went. Kirsten spent much of the time in her room brooding on the dark places in her mind, trying to find ways to make the cloud yield up its secrets. This was her main problem. Without Laura's hypnotherapy, she couldn't get at her censored memories. She bought a book on self-hypnosis and practised with some success. She could relax easily enough and induce a light trance, but she couldn't get beyond the fishy odour. Nonetheless, she intended to keep at it until she dispersed the cloud.

Towards the end of that month and until well into April, she found some solace in *The Cloud of Unknowing*, the fourteenth-century masterpiece of Christian mysticism, which she picked off her shelf to help her set her mind on university studies again. Yet Kirsten very much doubted that she read it the way its author intended. The words seemed to address her own problem in a startlingly direct way, and the irony wasn't lost on her:

> When you first begin, you find only darkness, and as it were a cloud of unknowing. You don't know what this means except that in your will you feel a simple steadfast intention reaching out towards God. Do what you will, this darkness and this cloud remain between you and God, and stop you both from seeing him in the clear light of rational understanding, and from experiencing his loving sweetness in your affection. Reconcile yourself to wait in this darkness as long as necessary but still go on longing after him whom you love.

It was a kind of inversion of what Kirsten felt – certainly it wasn't God she was seeking, nor did she love the object of her quest – but the words gave her sustenance, nonetheless, and helped her through the darkness, both internal and external.

The book also helped describe what she was experiencing in a way that even Laura Henderson hadn't been able to get at:

> Do not think because I call it a 'darkness' or a 'cloud' it is the sort of cloud you see in the sky or the kind of darkness you know at home when the light is out . . . By 'darkness' I mean 'a lack of knowing' – just as anything that you do not know or may have forgotten may be said to be 'dark' to you, for you cannot see it with your inward eye.

It was exactly like the dark bubble, or cloud, she felt in her mind. It came between her and the Devil, the man who had maimed her, and it wasn't so much an object or an element as a feeling, a sense of something impenetrable anchored deep in her mind.

The book offered more in the way of practical advice, too, and Kirsten began to wonder how she had ever sustained herself for so long without it. Especially the fifth meditation, which read:

> If ever you are to come to this cloud and live and work in it, as I suggest, then just as this cloud of unknowing is as it were above you, between you and God, so you must also put a cloud of forgetting beneath you and all creation. We are apt to think that we are very far from God because of this cloud of unknowing between us and him, but surely it would be more correct to say that we are much further from him if there is no cloud of forgetting between us and the whole created world.

Kirsten had to distance and detach herself from the everyday world if she wanted to follow through with her purpose. There was no use clinging to sentimental notions of good and evil. She had to learn to exist in a detached, rarefied world where the object of her quest had supreme importance and everything and everyone else was lost, for as long as it took, in a cloud of forgetting. But nobody must know this. She had to appear to be making progress as far as family and friends were concerned.

The book was arranged into seventy-five short numbered chapters, or meditations, and it was not the kind of text one could read for hours on end. Kirsten read a chapter a day, occasionally skipping a day to read a novel, so she managed to stretch the book out for over two months, as winter turned into spring.

Soon, bluebells and forget-me-nots grew in the woods again, and dandelions and buttercups gilded the open fields. The bitter air warmed and released the scents of the countryside from its wintry grip: grass and tree bark after rain; wild garlic rubbed between the fingers; damp earth recently ploughed over. As she walked and took it all in, Kirsten remembered last autumn, when she had felt dead inside and nothing could touch her. Now that she had a purpose, a sense of mission, she could enjoy the world again.

The book continued to convince her of the holiness of her task and seemed to promise success. When, on the final page one fresh, bright morning in mid-May, she read that 'it is not what you are or have been that God looks at with his merciful eyes, but what you would be,' she knew without doubt that she would succeed. 'All holy desires grow by delays; and if they fade because of these delays then they were never holy desires.' Tenacity. Determination. They were the qualities she had to nurture in order to prove her desires holy. Her need would not fade; it was with her, part of her, day and night.

Throughout this period, she still continued to visit Bath and see Laura, too, though not as frequently as before. Once a fortnight seemed enough for what they had to talk about. The main topic towards the end was Kirsten's feelings about being a 'victim'.

Some schools, Laura explained, hold that there are people who are born victims, who somehow attract killers. When the circumstances are right, they will get what they were born for. Things happen to us because of what we are, some psychologists maintain, and because of this, some of us keep making the same mistakes time after time – marrying the wrong man or woman, for example, or seeking out situations in which we are abused, asking for trouble. It wasn't masochism, Laura said, but something rooted deep in a person's unconscious that led him or her to keep making the same wrong choices.

Did Kirsten think she was one of those people? Did she feel guilt over what had happened to her? Did she feel as if she had asked for it?

The whole subject puzzled Kirsten at first. For a long time, she had simply assumed that it had been her bad luck to be in the wrong place at the wrong time, the unfortunate victim of a random assault. It had never, in fact, occurred to her that she might have been asking for it. That was the rapist's common defence, wasn't it, that his victim had been asking for it because she had dressed in a certain way or smiled at the wrong time? Kirsten couldn't accept that.

If she had given in to Hugo's advances that night and gone home with him, none of this would have happened. If she hadn't had to get home reasonably early and sober to pack for the next day, then she might have stayed at the party longer and walked across the park with a group of drunken friends. If she hadn't walked across the park that night but had taken the well-lit roads around it, if she hadn't strayed from the path to sit on the lion like a silly girl . . . and so it went on, nothing but a lot of ifs. And on the plus side, if that man hadn't been walking his dog at precisely the right time, then Kirsten would have died like the later victims had.

But the more she talked about it with Laura, the more she realized that things could only have been different had she been a different kind of person. Those schools were right, in a way. The roots of what happened were tangled up with who she was. She could easily have given in to Hugo, for example. He was attractive enough, and plenty of her friends would have done so; indeed, most of them had, at one time or another. But no, she wasn't 'that kind' of girl. And she did habitually cross the park alone after dark, no matter how often people expressed concern. Also, it would never have occurred to her not to give in to that childish impulse to ride the lion unless she had been with company. In other words, maybe she did think of herself as a born victim and she just hadn't admitted it before. But she didn't tell Laura this. She could sense that Laura was testing her, trying to find out how sensitive she was, so she gave what she thought were the right answers. Laura seemed relieved.

But Kirsten continued to question herself. Why did she cross the park by herself in the dark, for example? Was she looking for something to happen? She certainly hadn't been making any kind of a feminist gesture. When women want to make a point about their right to walk the streets and parks in safety, they do so in large, well-publicized groups – the sensible way. But Kirsten often did it alone. Why? Was she inviting destruction?

Somehow, a simple chain of causality wasn't enough to explain what had happened to her. She had been living in a dream ever since the attack had occurred simply because she had accepted it in such a shallow way and had never really contemplated the deeper implications. That was no acceptance at all. *The Cloud of Unknowing*, her last talks with Laura Henderson: both of these gave a shape and depth to her quest that she had never imagined possible before; they concentrated her resolve and acted like a magnet forming a rose-pattern from iron filings.

It all meant something – everything happened for a reason – and the more she thought about it, if there was a part of her deep inside that made her the victim – just as hatred twisted deep inside the man made him a killer – then the person who had found her must have been destined to be her saviour. He had found her for a purpose, she now realized. She hadn't died like the others; she had been delivered from that. And this was when the compelling idea of fate, destiny and retribution started to occur to her. If she had been a victim not by blind chance but for a reason, then she was still alive for a reason. She bore her stigmata for a reason. She carried within her the means of destroying this evil force. In a sense, she was his nemesis. And that was destiny, too.

She never told Laura all this; like the true nature of the cloud or bubble in her mind, it would have been too difficult to put into words. Besides, she wasn't at all clear about it herself at first. It didn't evolve as a fully fledged theory, like a Pallas Athene sprung from the head of Zeus, but the ideas took shape over time. It was something that she thought about a lot in the spring months of May and June while she re-read old novels, ploughed through Julian of Norwich's *Revelations of Divine Love*, and considered which university to apply to and which area of study to concentrate on. It would probably be best, she decided, to apply to several places – say the north, where Sarah suggested they share a flat together, and to Bath and Bristol, where her parents wanted her to go. Then, when the time came, she could see how she felt and make her choice.

In early June, the killer, the man the press were now calling the 'Student Slasher', claimed yet another victim: Kim Waterford, a petite brunette with a twinkle in her eyes that even the poor-quality newspaper photograph couldn't dim. Well, he had dimmed it, hadn't he? Now her eyes would be dull and lifeless as dead fish. Kirsten pasted the picture and articles in her scrapbook and worked even harder at self-hypnosis.

One glorious day in late June when Bath was filled with tourists again and boaters splashed and laughed on the Avon outside the half-open window, Laura smiled at the end of the session, offered Kirsten a cigarette and said, 'I think we've gone as far as we can go together. If you need me, I'll be here. Don't hesitate to call. But, really, I think you're on your own now.'

Kirsten nodded. She knew she was.

43

SUSAN

Still clutching her holdall in the carrier bag, Sue returned to the shops again that afternoon and spent a few pounds of her fast-dwindling funds on some dark grey Marks & Spencer slacks and a blue windcheater with a zip-up front. She spent a good while in front of the toilet mirror on her make-up, changing the emphasis a little here and there, and found that it was possible to fasten her wig back in a ponytail without revealing any of her own hair. Her glasses also went well with the new outfit. Now she looked just different enough not to spark any memories among those who might have noticed her ghost-like presence. She was no longer just the plain, primly dressed, 'nice girl' in the raincoat; nor was she the short-haired tomboy in jeans and a checked shirt. She looked more like a family holidaymaker taking a break from her parents' company for a while. The new clothes would also be more suitable for hanging around in the woods watching over the factory, if it came to that.

She was annoyed about the holdall. When she had got to Saltwick Nab, she found that the tide was coming in, not going out. She would have to go back later in the evening, or perhaps it would be easier to throw it from the top of West Cliff or somewhere closer. There would be too many people around in that area, though. Someone might see her. She shoved the raincoat and hood along with everything else in the holdall and took it back to her room. At least it was coming in useful now she had more stuff to get rid of.

She thought about Keith a lot too. Lying in that hospital in Scarborough with tubes and needles stuck in him, just as she had lain over a year ago. She had dismissed the idea of trying to get to him – security would be too tight, and she wasn't sure she could go through with it in cold blood – but she couldn't stop worrying. The police might be looking for her at that very moment. All the more reason to hurry up.

At a quarter to five, she dropped in at Rose's Cafe. The stringy blonde behind the counter showed no interest in her beyond taking her money. Sue needed some idea of what her man's hours were. When could she expect to find him walking alone in the dark? When did he make his deliveries? When did he sleep? She assumed that he had either made a morning delivery that day, or had set off the night before and stayed over. If the latter, then the odds were that he would be at home tonight. It annoyed her that she couldn't find out for sure. She certainly couldn't ask anyone. No doubt the drivers worked very irregular hours, taking loads when they were ready and standing in for mates who were ill or had driven too many hours. All she could really do was watch a little longer, and she didn't know how much time she had left.

Over the next two days, the weather, though still chilly, continued to improve. Sue took to hanging around the area by the factory almost constantly. All the time she felt as if she were looking over her shoulder for the police, when she was the one who should be doing the watching. She read the papers every morning, but they reported no change in Keith's condition or in the state of the police investigation. In a way, though she still felt nervous and paranoid at times, she took heart that nothing had happened yet. Surely they must have reached a dead end or they would have been on to her already? Nothing could stop her now. She was meant to succeed. Her task was holy.

She kept a low profile in Rose's and the Brown Cow, but found that now she had the man in sight, she could even recognize his squat, dark figure from the woods above the factory. She also investigated another pub, called the Merry Monk, at the bottom end of the council estate, and found that from one of its small windows in a dark corner she could just about see across the waste ground down to his cottage at the end of the row. As she had expected, his comings and goings were irregular, and as far as she could make out, he lived alone. She would have to know her opportunity when it arose and grab it without hesitation.

First, she wanted him to *know* that she had found him. When she finally lured him to his death, she wanted him to know who was doing it, and why. He would be asking for it. But she had to do this without causing undue danger to herself. Also, though she was certain this time, after her mistake she wanted more confirmation. She needed proof. If she killed or wounded another innocent man in the area, her chances of success would be practically nil. Slowly, as she watched him, she began to form a plan.

She almost bumped into him on her way back to town from Rose's Cafe at five-thirty-five on her second day of full surveillance. He was walking the other way, back towards the factory. She averted her face, but for a moment she could have sworn that he noticed her. He didn't know who she was – she would have felt that kind of recognition jolt her like an electric shock – but perhaps he connected her with the woman he'd seen yesterday in the newsagent's. Or perhaps, given what he was, he looked at all women that way. Sue hurried on with her head down and didn't stop until she got to the end of the street. From there, hidden by the wall of the corner house, she saw him in the distance by the loading bays talking to a man in a white smock and trilby, probably a foreman, who gave him some papers. Her man got in his van and drove off.

Sue carried on walking down the lane. She hadn't got far before he passed her, then he turned right, towards the junction for the main Scarborough road. It didn't mean that he was going to Scarborough, of course, as it was one of the few ways out of the town and could lead to York or to the Leeds area. But one thing was for certain: he was out on a job and he wouldn't be home for a while. Sue hurried down to the main road, but he was nowhere in sight. She walked north a little way on the pavement, then doubled back on the dirt path that eventually curved around past his cottage.

Sue's heart felt as if it were in her throat as she approached the cottage. Coming from that direction across the waste ground, she couldn't be seen from any of the other houses on the row. Luckily, too, there were no buildings on the other side of the street, only the scrub ground that sloped up to the council estate. She could be seen from her little window in the pub, but it was still early in the evening for drinkers, and there was no reason why anyone enjoying a pint and a chat in the Merry Monk should make the effort of looking out of that particular window, especially as it meant pulling the curtain aside a little. Even if they did, what they saw would mean nothing to them.

She had thought of waiting until dark, but that meant she would need a torch, which would, in the long run, give her much more risk of being spotted. No, this was better: a blind approach at a time when most people would be busy preparing their evening meals anyway. She had already noticed that he kept his curtains closed whenever he was out, and that would keep her hidden, should anyone pass by, while still giving her enough light to search by.

There was only one small window in the side of the house that faced the waste ground, and that was too high to reach. A kitchen extension built on the back, which also shielded her from the neighbours' view, looked more promising. The back door itself was solid and locked, and the curtained window that probably led into the living room or dining room also proved impossible to open. The kitchen window looked like a better possibility. The wood was old and the unfastened catch had been painted over in the open position long ago.

Sue wedged the heels of her hands against the crossbar and pushed up. At first nothing happened and she thought that perhaps the window too had been painted shut. But the paint was cracked and peeling on the outside, and before long it began to shudder upwards. Sue paused after she had made a space big enough to enter, but there was no sound; nobody had heard her. Nimbly, she slipped in over the kitchen sink and closed the window behind her. The palms of her hands felt sore and sweaty from the effort.

She had no idea what she expected to find – walls daubed in blood, perhaps, or heads on spikes and violent red graffiti scrawled over whitewashed walls: 666 and THE WHORE MUST DIE – but she wasn't prepared for the sheer ordinariness of the place. The only uncurtained window was the one through which she had climbed, and that let plenty of light into the kitchen. Everything was in its place; the washing-up lay in the draining rack; glasses and plates shone like new. The surfaces were all clean, too, and the room smelled of lemon washing-up liquid. A refrigerator she could see her reflection in hummed; cans of soup and tins of spaghetti stood in an orderly row on a shelf above the dining table, with its salt and pepper set out neatly on a mat at its centre. Even the small cooker was spotless.

The living room, where light filtered in pale blue through the thin curtains, was just as tidy. Magazines stood in the vertical rack by the hearth, corners and pages aligned so they looked like one solid block as thick as a telephone directory. A pipe rack hung above the mantelpiece, and the air was acrid with the smell of stale smoke. In the corner near the window was a television on a stand with a video on the shelf beneath it and, next to that, a cassette storage rack with a varnished wood finish – and not a speck of dust in sight. What did this man watch? Sue wondered. Pornography? Snuff movies?

But when she examined the cassettes, she saw they were all ordinary enough. He had labelled each one in clear print, and most of them were simply tapes of recent television programmes he must have missed while out driving: nothing more interesting than a couple of episodes of *Coronation Street*, no doubt taped while he was out on a delivery, a BBC2 wildlife special, a few American cop programmes, and two movies rented from a local shop: *Angel Heart* and *Fatal Attraction*. They weren't exactly *Mary Poppins*, but they weren't hard-core pornography either.

An old sofa sat in front of the fireplace, its beige upholstery protected by lace antimacassars, and one matching armchair stood at a precise angle to it. Like the rest of the house, the room was small and spotless, and as far as Sue could make out in the faint light, the walls were painted light blue, rather than papered. The only thing that struck her as at all odd was the complete absence of photographs and personal knick-knacks. The mantelpiece was bare, as were the solid oak sideboard and the walls.

There was, however, a small bookcase by the kitchen door. Most of the titles were on local history, some of them large illustrated volumes, and the only novels were used paperbacks of blockbusters by Robert Ludlum, Lawrence Sanders and Harold Robbins. Bede's *History* was there, of course. Sue picked it up, and noticed that the old paperback had been well thumbed. One passage, in particular, had been heavily underscored. Sue shivered and put the book back.

Upstairs revealed nothing different about the owner of the cottage. In the bathroom, every fixture, fitting and surface looked in shining pristine condition, and in the bathroom cabinet, various pills, potions and creams stood in orderly rows like soldiers at attention. There was only one bedroom: his. The bed was made, covered in yellow nylon sheets, and there was nothing in the drawers and cupboards but carefully ironed shirts, a couple of sports jackets, one pressed suit, and neatly folded underwear and socks. The place seemed to have no personality at all. Was he really her man? Surely there ought to be *some* sign beyond the book.

Back downstairs, Sue looked for a cellar door but couldn't find one. Perhaps it was just as well, she thought. She was feeling edgy being there at all; if she found a body in the cellar she didn't know how she would react. But that was silly, she told herself, just nerves. He didn't take the bodies home with him.

She opened the doors of the sideboard and found a little port, sherry and brandy, along with glasses of various shapes and sizes, place mats and a white linen tablecloth. In one of the top drawers were the everyday odds and ends one needs around a house: fuse wire, string, candles, matches, penknife, extra shoelaces, pencil stubs.

When she opened the second drawer, though, Sue's breath caught in her throat.

There, laid out neatly in a row on a lining of faded rose-patterned wallpaper, were six locks of hair, each bound in the middle by a pink ribbon. Six victims, six locks of hair. Sue felt dizzy. She had to turn away and support herself by gripping the back of an armchair. When she had fought back the vertigo and nausea, she turned to look again at the sight she found so gruesome in its simplicity and ordinariness. Nothing too grotesque for this man: no severed breasts, ears or fingers, just six locks of hair laid out neatly in a row on a lining of faded rose-patterned wallpaper. And, further back in the drawer, a pair of scissors, a roll of pink satin ribbon, and a long knife with a worn bone handle and a gleaming stainless-steel blade.

But it was the hair that really captured Sue's attention. Six locks. One blonde, three brunettes, two redheads. She reached out and touched them, as she would stroke a cat. She could even put names to them. One of the red locks, the darkest, was Kathleen Shannon's; the blonde was Margaret Snell's; the curly brunette lock had belonged to Kim Waterford; and the straight, jet-black strand was Jill Sarsden's. None of them was Sue's. He must have been disturbed before he got around to taking it, she realized. No doubt it was the last thing he did, take a souvenir. And the police had never said anything about it – which meant either that they didn't know, or that they were keeping the knowledge up their sleeves to deter copycats and check against phoney confessions, and, of course, to verify the true one, if it ever came.

Well, Sue thought, here was an oversight she could rectify easily enough. She pushed back her wig, picked up the scissors, and carefully snipped off a lock about two inches long, exactly the same length as the others. She then bound it neatly with a piece of ribbon and placed it in line with the rest.

Now, she thought, pleased with herself, just wait till he notices that. She was convinced that he drooled over his trophies every day, and what a bloody shock he'd get when he found another lock of hair there. Not only would he know there was someone on to him, he would probably know who it was. And that was just what Sue wanted.

The house was silent except for the sound of Sue's heart beating, but she still felt uneasy. It was time to get out before he came back. She slid the drawer shut and hurried back to the kitchen window.

44

KIRSTEN

That summer, Kirsten took long, brooding walks in the woods and reckless drives in the countryside. Close to the end of the university term, about the same time she had been attacked a year ago, the killer found his sixth victim – the fifth to die – in a quiet Halifax nursing student called Jill Sarsden. Kirsten pasted the photo and details in her scrapbook as usual.

At home, she pretended all was well. The dark cloud still troubled her, bringing painful headaches and bouts of depression that were difficult to hide. But she managed to convince Dr Craven that she was making excellent progress since discontinuing the analysis, and the doctor's opinion helped to reassure her parents. If she was occasionally quiet and withdrawn, well, that was only to be expected. Her parents knew that she had always valued her solitude and privacy anyway.

In her room each night, she kept at the self-hypnosis, but got no further. The directions she had read in the book were simple enough: roll your eyeballs up as far as you can, close your eyes and take a deep breath, then let your eyes relax, breathe out and feel yourself floating. She had even delved back into earlier memories of pain as practice – the time her finger got trapped in a door when she was six; the day she fell off her bicycle and needed stitches in her arm – but still she couldn't get beyond the odour of fish without feeling overcome by a sense of choking panic.

One hot, bright day in late July, she stopped in a Cotswold village for a cold drink. Walking back to the car, she noticed a craft centre in an old stone cottage and decided to have a look inside. The cottage had been extended at the back and part of it converted into a glass-blowing studio. Kirsten watched entranced as the delicate and fragile pieces took shape from molten glass at the end of the tube. Afterwards, as she browsed around the shop, she noticed a row of solid glass paperweights, like the one in Laura's office, with colourful abstract designs trapped inside them. The rose pattern appealed to her most, and she bought it, feeling great satisfaction at the smooth, slippery weight in her palm. And it gave her an idea.

That evening in her room, she prepared for self-hypnosis again, doing breathing exercises and relaxing each muscle in turn. When she was ready, she sat before her desk, where the paperweight lay between two candles, drawing and twisting their light into its curved scarlet petals. Her book had mentioned that there were many ways of self-hypnosis, and she had chosen the method said to be the most effective. But whether there was something about the connection with her early sessions with Laura, or something special about the paperweight itself, Kirsten found she had much more success this way. Though the first attempt led to no great breakthrough, she got a strong feeling that she would soon find what she wanted if she persisted.

It happened a week later. She had been taking herself further and further back from the attack and moving forward slowly. This time she started with her preparations for the evening: a long bath, the lemon-fresh scent of her clean comfortable clothes, the pleasant walk to the Ring O'Bells with Sarah. As usual, she drew back at the oily rag and the fishy smell, but this time she heard his voice. Not all the words – just fragments about a 'dark one' and a 'song of destruction' – but it was enough. With her training in linguistics and dialect, Kirsten could place the accent easily enough.

When she came out of the light trance, her heart was thumping and she felt as if she had just been dropped into an icy bath. She breathed deeply, fully alert now, and poured herself a glass of water. The raspy voice still sounded clear in her mind. He was from Yorkshire. She couldn't be certain, but she didn't think he had a city accent or the broad speech of the Dales and the Pennine Moorlands. When she added this new knowledge to the salt smell of raw fish that had covered his fingers and palms, then she knew he was from the Yorkshire coast – a holiday resort or a fishing village perhaps. The more she thought about it, replayed the voice and remembered her lessons, the more sure she became.

She jumped up and pulled down the old school atlas from her bookshelf. From what she could see, the coastline stretched from around Bridlington Bay in the south to near Redcar in the north. County boundaries were no sure guide, though, especially as they had been changed in the seventies. She didn't think he was from as far north as Middlesbrough, where a Northumbrian strain subtly infused the local speech, but she would have to include the Humberside area as far south as the Humber estuary. That left more than a hundred miles of rugged coastline. It was useless, she thought. Even if she were right, she would never be able to find him in such a large area. She dropped the atlas on the floor and threw herself onto the bed.

The next day, she tried the same self-hypnosis technique again, and again she heard the voice, the flat vowels and clipped consonants. She felt something about the words this time, something that rang a bell deep inside her mind. Try as she might, though, she couldn't identify them. He had been reciting a poem or a song of some kind. She had read somewhere that such killers sometimes do that, talk while they work, often quoting fragments of the Bible. But she didn't think it was from the Bible. He had said something about 'leaving a feast' because someone had asked him to sing a song and he couldn't. She knew the words; she had heard them before at some time in her studies, but she couldn't for the life of her remember where.

She slept badly that night, haunted by the fragmented speech and the raspy tone of his voice, but in the morning she felt no closer to her goal. She didn't know how it could help, but she needed to know exactly what he had said. She had to *think*, to work at it. The source was old – certainly pre-Renaissance by the sound of it – and that probably meant something from medieval literature. People were always singing and attending feasts then. There was only one thing to do: read.

And so she set to reading medieval literature on warm days in the garden: Sir Gawain, Chaucer, Piers Plowman, anthologies full of religious lyrics. She read them all to no avail. All she got for her pains was that awful feeling of trying to find a quotation you have on the tip of your tongue but can't pin down, or the frustration of looking for a phrase in Shakespeare when you can't even remember what play it comes from. Outwardly, Kirsten seemed fine, preparing to go back to university, optimistic about her future. She even told her parents that she was considering the restorative surgery that the doctor had mentioned might be possible. But inside she was seething with anger and frustration.

One golden day in late August she sat out on the back lawn under the copper beech with hardly a breeze to stir her hair from her brow. She had given up on medieval literature as a source and gone back even further, to Anglo-Saxon, which she had studied in her first year. So far, she had read translations of *Beowulf* and 'The Seafarer' and was now working her way through Bede's *An Ecclesiastical History of the English Nation*. It was an old translation that she had bought in a second-hand bookshop, attracted by the worn blue binding, the gilded page edges, and a pleasantly musty smell that reminded her of the local library. Inside the flyleaf, in faded, copper-coloured ink, was written, 'To Reginald, with Love from Elizabeth, October 1939. May God go with you.'

Despite the translator's flowery language, the Venerable Bede came through as far more human to her than many of his austere colleagues in the early church, and she could picture him out on the lonely island of Lindisfarne poring over illuminated manuscripts as he suffered through a wild Northumbrian winter. About two-thirds of the way through the book, she came to the passage about England's 'first' poet, Caedmon, who had been unable to sing. Whenever the harp was passed around at dinners, and everyone was expected to contribute a song, Caedmon always stole away.

One evening, after he left a feast to care for the horses in the stables, he had a vision in which a man came and spoke his name and asked him to sing. Caedmon protested, but the stranger paid no attention to his excuses. 'Yet shall ye sing to me,' he insisted. When Caedmon asked what he should sing about, the man replied, 'Praise ye Creation.' And Caedmon found his inspiration.

There was no blinding flash of light, but as Kirsten read, the dark cloud that had lodged itself in her mind since the attack seemed to disperse. In addition to her own silent voice, she could hear another voice reading along with her a perversion of Bede's words: 'And, lo, I asked, "Of what shall I sing?" and the Dark One told me, "Sing of Destruction".' It was the story *he* had told her as he beat her and slashed at her in the park that night. The summer garden turned to mist around her like a place filmed through a greasy lens, and her book slipped onto the grass. She took a deep breath and closed her eyes. After-images of light and leaves danced before her eyelids, then the memories flowed back unbidden.

She could see his face now, in shadow, with the moon over his shoulder catching one lined cheek, as he smeared the smell of fish all over her lips and nostrils. He stuffed a piece of oily rag in her mouth and it made her feel sick. Then he started slapping her, back and forth across her face, and talking in that raspy sing-song voice about how he had left the Feast of Whores one night and had a vision of the Dark One, to whom he confessed his impotence. The Dark One, he said, gave him the power to sing to women. That's what he was doing with his knife; he was singing to her, just like that old poet from his town, who had suddenly been blessed with the gift of poetry late in life.

The images went on. She could easily recall every painful moment of consciousness now. But she held herself back and pulled out with a sharp gasp when the unbearable image of the knife blade flashing in moonlight took shape.

When she had breathed in the warm air and run her fingers over the tree's smooth bark to bring herself back to earth, she remembered that he had actually said, 'just like the old poet from my town'. She could play the words back now as if they were on a tape inside her mind. She picked up the book and found that, according to Bede, Caedmon came from a place called Streanaeshalch. Of course, that would be the Anglo-Saxon name; Bede often used the Roman or Saxon names. Flipping through the index, Kirsten found it in no time: 'Streanaeshalch: *see* Whitby.' So he came from Whitby. It made perfect sense. It all added up: the fishy smell, the accent, and now the reference to Caedmon, poet of his town.

He had had no reason to assume that Kirsten would survive the attack; her continued existence had not been his intention. Hadn't Superintendent Elswick said something about him trying to get to her at the hospital, too? That must have been because he was worried that she might remember what he had said in his ritual chant. And as time went by and nothing happened, he must have realized that she had lost her memory and that he had nothing more to worry about. Then, he had continued blithely with his mission, singing his song with a knife on a woman's body.

So now she knew. What was she to do next? First, she hurried inside to find one of her father's old *AA Members Handbooks*. He usually kept a couple along with the telephone directory in the bureau drawer in the hall. She turned to the maps at the back and found Whitby. It was on the coast between Scarborough and Redcar, and it didn't look too big. She ran her finger down the Ws in the gazetteer: Whimple, Whippingham, Whiston – there it was, 'Whitby, population 13,763.' Bigger than she thought. Still, if the man she was after had such rough hands and smelled of fish, then she would probably find him around the docks or on the boats. She thought she would be able to recognize him, and now the voice would confirm it.

And she had guidance in her mission – Margaret, Brenda, Kim and the rest – they wouldn't let her fail, not now she had come so far. There was a *holiness* about what she had to do, a reason why she, out of all of them, had been saved. She had been chosen as his nemesis; it was her destiny to find him and face him. She couldn't picture the actual occasion of their meeting, what would happen. It would be in the open and it would take place at night; that was all she knew. As for the outcome: one of them would die.

But even a nemesis, she thought wryly, has to plan and deal with practical realities. The AA handbook also gave information about distances from London, York and Scarborough, and listed market days. There followed a selection of hotels, most of which would probably be too expensive for Kirsten. No matter, she could go into Bath and buy a local travel guide that would probably list bed and breakfast accommodation.

Excited and nervous at the prospect of the hunt, Kirsten settled down to make preparations. She would visit Sarah first and go to Whitby from there. She wouldn't take much with her, just a handy holdall, jeans, a couple of shirts, and whatever she needed to do the job. It would have to be something small, something she could conceal in her hand, as she knew she might have to act quickly.

Kirsten shuddered at the thought and began to doubt herself. Then she reminded herself again of all that she had suffered and survived, and the reason for that. She had to be strong; she had to concentrate on practical matters as far as she could and trust to instinct and fate to take care of the rest.

Two days later, after she had bought a Whitby guide and written to Sarah, she informed her parents that she had decided to go back up north to university. They both expressed concern and displeasure, but that was balanced by relief that she seemed to have come out of her long depression and decided to get on with her life.

'I won't say I'm happy you're going away,' her father said with a sad smile, 'but I will say I'm happy that you've decided to go. Do you know what I mean?'

Kirsten nodded. 'I suppose I must have been a bit of a pest. I haven't been very good company, have I?'

Her father shook his head quickly as if to dismiss her apology. 'You know you're welcome here,' he said, 'for as long as you want to stay.'

All the time, her mother sat stiffly, twisting her hands in her lap. She'll be glad to see the back of me, Kirsten thought, but she'll never admit such a horrible thought to herself. Her mother's life, Kirsten realized, was dominated by the need to keep all unpleasantness at a distance, look good in the eyes of her neighbours, and savagely maintain the borders of her closed and narrow world.

'I thought I'd go up before term, just to get my bearings again. I think it'd do me good to get out and about a bit. Sarah and I might do some walking in the Dales.'

'The *Yorkshire* Dales?' her mother said.

'Yes. Why?'

'Well, dear, I'm just not sure it's a very suitable environment for a well-brought-up girl such as yourself, that's all. It's so very . . . well, so very bleak and muddy, I hear, and so uncivilized. I'm not sure you even have the proper clothes for such an excursion.'

'Oh, Mother,' Kirsten said. 'Don't be such a snob.'

Her mother sniffed. 'I was only thinking of your comfort, darling. Of course, I dare say your friend is used to such a . . . a rough life. But not you.'

'Mother, Sarah's family owns half of Herefordshire. She's not quite the bit of rough you seem to think she is.'

Her mother looked at her blankly. 'I don't know what you mean, Kirsten. Breeding shows. That's all I'm saying.'

'Well, I'm going, anyway. And that's that.'

'Of course you must go,' her father said, patting her knee. 'Your mother's only concerned about your health, that's all. Make sure you take plenty of warm clothes and some sensible hiking boots. And stick to the pathways.'

Kirsten laughed. 'You're almost as bad,' she said. 'Anyone would think I was off to the North Pole or somewhere. It's only a couple of hundred miles north, you know, not a couple of thousand.'

'All the same,' her father said, 'the landscape can be quite treacherous in those parts, and it does rain an awful lot. Just be careful, that's all I'm asking of you.'

'Don't worry, I will.'

'When are you planning on going?' he asked.

'Well, I'll have to wait till I hear from Sarah first and make sure she can put me up and get some time off, but I thought I'd go as soon as I can.'

'And you'll be coming back before term starts?'

'Oh yes. That's not until the beginning of October. I'll come back and pick up my books and stuff. I'm hoping I can find a flat up there first, too. Perhaps Sarah and I can share.'

'Do you think that's wise?' her mother asked.

'It'll be better than being on my own, won't it?'

Her mother could offer no argument against that.

'So,' her father said, 'you're off on an adventure. Well, good for you. You must have known there were times when your mother and I . . . we . . . we didn't know what the future was going to bring.'

'I'm all right, Daddy,' Kirsten said. 'Really I am.'

'Yes, of course. Will you be seeing Dr Masterson at all while you're up there? About the . . . you know?'

Kirsten nodded. 'Probably,' she said. 'It won't do any harm to ask about it, will it?'

'No, I don't suppose it will. I'm afraid I won't be able to give you a lift up there. We've got a very important project on at the moment and I just can't take time off. Perhaps you could rent—'

'That's all right,' Kirsten said. 'I was planning on taking the train. I have to learn to get around on my own.'

'Well, that's fine, as long as you feel comfortable with the idea. You'll be needing some money, won't you?' he said, and went over to the top right-hand drawer of the sideboard to fetch his cheque book.

45

SUSAN

Sue got out of the house easily enough without anyone seeing her and went to celebrate her first housebreaking with veal scaloppine, garlic bread and a bottle of Chianti at the expensive restaurant on New Quay Road. After that, she stopped off at her room, then walked about a mile along the coast and threw her holdall, weighted down with heavy pebbles, into the sea. She stood and watched as the tide first threw it back, then sucked it out again and swallowed it. Even if it did turn up somewhere, she thought, it wouldn't be of any interest to anyone.

Now it was time to put the final stage of her plan into operation. First, let him sweat for a while.

And sweat he did. The first time Sue saw him on the day after she had broken into his cottage, he looked harried and preoccupied as he walked in to work. It was raining, and he kept his hands deep in his pockets and his head down, but his glittering eyes swept the street and the windows of the houses all around him. He must have noticed her sitting in the front of Rose's Cafe, Sue thought, but his eyes just flicked over her as they did everything and everyone else. He was nervous, on edge, as if he was expecting an ambush at any moment.

After he had gone by, Sue turned back to the local newspaper. There was no change reported in Keith's condition and the police seemed to have got nowhere in their search for Jack Grimley's killer. So far, so good. It would soon be over now.

Near lunchtime on the second day, from the same vantage point, Sue saw him slip into the newsagent's. Quickly, she left her tea and crossed the street to go in after him. He wouldn't recognize her. This time, she was dressed differently; also, she wore glasses, and her hair was tied back in a ponytail. He glanced around with a start at the bell when she entered, her head lowered, then turned his gaze back to the newsagent.

'All right today, love?' the woman asked. 'You look a bit peaky.'

'Not enough sleep, that's all,' he mumbled.

'Well, you take good care of yourself, you never know what germs are going round these days.'

'I'm all right,' he said, a little testily. 'Just tired, that's all.' Then he paid for his tobacco and left without even glancing at Sue, who bent over the newspaper and magazine section as before. She picked up the local paper and the *Independent*. When she took them over to the counter to pay, the woman clucked her tongue and said, 'I don't know what's the matter with him. Show a bit of polite interest and he damn near bites your head off. Some people can't even be bothered to be civil these days.'

'Maybe he's worried about something,' Sue suggested.

The woman sighed. 'Aye,' she said. 'We've all got plenty to worry about, haven't we, what with nuclear war and pollution all over t'place. But I still manage to find a smile and a good morning for my customers.' She went on, almost to herself, as she counted out Sue's change, 'Not like Greg Eastcote, that isn't. Usually such a pleasant chap.' Then she shrugged. 'Ah, well, maybe he is just tired. I could do with a bit of a lie-down myself.'

'I'm sure that's it,' said Sue, folding the newspapers under her arm and walking over to the door. 'He's just tired.'

'Aye. No rest for the wicked, is there, love? Bye now.'

As Sue walked along the street, Eastcote's van passed her by and took the same route out of town as it had before. Another delivery. Whether he would be back later or would be staying out overnight, she had no idea. She could imagine, though, that he would be loath to leave his cottage empty for very long. In fact, if she were in his shoes, she would make sure she was back before dark. After all, he didn't know that she had broken in during daylight.

She wondered what he had made of the extra lock of hair. Did he know it was hers? Surely he must suspect? Or perhaps he thought he was being haunted, that the supernatural was responsible for the sudden appearance of a seventh lock? Like the seventh daughter of a seventh son was supposed to be powerful in magic. One thing she did know: he had seen her, as one would notice any stranger in the street, but he didn't know who she was. Maybe when he got over the shock, he would start to think clearly again and count the times he'd glimpsed her from the corner of his eye; perhaps he would connect the girl in the navy-blue raincoat with the girl in glasses and a ponytail. But by then it would be too late.

Sue walked by the river towards town. The good weather seemed to have made a return. It was a beautiful day, with plenty of that intense blue sky you sometimes get at the seaside, and just enough plump white clouds drifting over to give a sense of depth and perspective. Beyond the greenish shallows, the sea reflected the sky's bright ultramarine. Sue stood on the swing bridge and looked around at the harbour. It was like another world to her now, after so long spent in the other, dingier part of town.

The tide was well out, and some of the light boats rested almost on their sides, with their masts at forty-five-degree angles to the slick mud. To Sue's left, beyond the high harbour wall, stood the buildings of St Ann's Staith, a mixture of architectural styles and materials: red brick, gables, chimneys, black and white Tudor-style fronting, even millstone grit. Further along, towards the sheds where the fish were auctioned, the jumble of buildings rose all the way up the hillside to the elegant white terrace of hotels that formed East Terrace.

People walked by, carefree and smiling: a courting couple, the man with his arm so low around the girl that it was practically in the back pocket of her tight jeans; two elderly ladies overdressed in checked tweeds and lace-up shoes, one carrying a walking stick; a pregnant woman, glowing with health, her husband walking proudly beside her.

All this normality, Sue thought. All these ordinary people going about their business, enjoying themselves, eating ice-cream cones and bouncing garish beachballs in the street, and they have no idea about the monster walking among them.

They have no idea that Greg Eastcote murdered six women and maimed one, that he slashed at their sexual organs with a sharp, bone-handled knife, and just to make sure they were dead, he strangled them. When he'd done that, when he'd finished his crude surgery, he carefully cut off a single lock of hair from each bruised and bleeding body, took it home with him, tied it up in a pink ribbon and placed it neatly in his sideboard drawer. Six of them all in a row. Seven now.

According to the press clippings that Sue had saved, he hadn't raped any of his victims. Clearly he was incapable of that, and the rage he felt towards women for causing his condition partly explained his actions. But only partly. There was an enormous chasm between his motives and his deeds that nobody could fathom. In a vision, the Dark One had appeared to him in a perversion of the Caedmon story and told him to sing his own song. And so he had. Only his accompanying instrument wasn't a lute, it was a knife, and the tune it played was death.

Sue wanted to jump up on the bridge rail and shout all this out to the complacent holidaymakers heading for the beach or the amusement arcades. They would shove their coins into slots, listen to the bingo caller, or sit on the beach in the sun on striped deck-chairs, newspapers shielding their faces, edging back every so often as the tide came in closer. Then, late in the afternoon, they would go to one of the many fish and chip restaurants and eat.

None of them knew about the man with the oily smell of fish on his fingers – probably the last thing his victims smelled – the Ancient Mariner eyes and the raspy voice. She wanted to tell them all about Greg Eastcote and the atrocities he had committed against women, all about the blood, the pain, the utter degradation and humiliation, and the way she had been imperfectly sewn back together again. All the king's horses and all the king's men . . . That man there, the balding one with the crying toddler in his arms, she wanted to assure him that she was here to restore the balance. But she wasn't crazy; she knew she couldn't say anything. Instead she just watched the people passing back and forth over the bridge for a while, wondering whether they were truly innocent or just indifferent, then she went to find a quiet pub.

She soon found a place on Baxtergate. Three bored-looking punks with green and yellow hair sat in the lounge playing the jukebox, but through a corridor by the side of the bar, separated from the lounge by swing doors, was a much quieter room, all dark varnished panels, hard chairs and benches. Sue realized that not only hadn't she looked at the papers yet, she hadn't even eaten since her meagre and greasy breakfast at Mrs Cummings's. The tea was so bad at Rose's that she hadn't felt inclined to find out what the food was like. All the pub served was cold snacks, so she ordered a crab sandwich and a half of lager and lime.

When she had eaten, she sat back with her drink and lit a cigarette, turning to the local paper first to see if there was any news of Keith. A brief report told her that police were continuing their inquiries into the suspicious death of Jack Grimley and the 'brutal assault' on a young Australian tourist, who was still in a critical condition at St Mary's Hospital, Scarborough. Apparently, Keith had not yet regained consciousness.

Then, under the heading HAVE YOU SEEN THIS GIRL? she suddenly noticed an artist's impression of her. She hadn't spotted it at first because it looked nothing like her. Perhaps there was a faint resemblance to Martha Browne, but even that would be pushing it a bit. The shape of the head was all wrong, far too round, and the eyes were too close together, the lips too thick. Still, it was enough to make her pulse race. It meant they were on the right track and they were getting closer. All the caption said was that police were anxious to talk to this girl, who had been seen with the Australian in Hinderwell, as she 'may have been the last person to see him before the attack.'

Sue folded the paper and turned to the crossword, but she found herself too preoccupied to concentrate on the clues. She knew that the police in general told little of what they knew to the papers. If she read between the lines, it seemed likely that they had also found the bus driver who had picked her up near Staithes. But all he could tell them was that she had got off at Whitby bus station. After that, Martha Browne had disappeared for ever.

Could they also track her to the lodgings on Abbey Terrace? Certainly if they traced Keith's movements, as they would surely be doing, then the odds were that they would check the register there, get a better description of her from the owner or his wife, and mount a full-scale search for 'Martha Browne'. Why, she wondered, were they taking so long? They must have found out where Keith had been staying in Staithes quickly enough. From there, it surely wouldn't have taken them long to work their way back to Whitby, unless there was no evidence among his belongings to say where he'd been – no journal, no brochures, no postcards unsent. What if they did know and every policeman in Whitby was on the lookout for her already? Nervously, she glanced over at a young couple by the bar, but they were only interested in one another.

Still, she told herself, she had no real cause to worry. Martha Browne no longer existed. She could have gone anywhere from Whitby bus station – Scarborough, York, Leeds – and why not on to London, Paris or Rome? Surely nobody would expect her to hang around in the area after she had attacked Keith McLaren? Even if they did know who they were after, they wouldn't centre their search in Whitby. She had told Keith that she came from Exeter, but she couldn't remember what she had written, if anything, in the register at the guesthouse. She wondered how long it would take the police to discover that Martha Browne had never existed in the first place. And what would they do then?

Of course, she knew that all this was nothing but speculation. Even if they could link her to Keith via Abbey Terrace, the Lucky Fisherman and Hinderwell, they still couldn't prove that she had done anything wrong. She could say that Keith had wanted to lead her into the woods but she had refused and left him, taking the bus back to Whitby. It probably wouldn't come to that, but if it did, she knew they couldn't prove anything. If the worst came to the worst, she could say he had tried to rape her and she had defended herself, then got scared and run away.

The only real problem was that it would look very odd indeed if they found her and discovered that Martha Browne and Sue Bridehead were the same person, and what's more, that she was really Kirsten, the only surviving victim of the Student Slasher. That would certainly look incriminating, especially when they found his body. But would it be enough to convict her of anything? Perhaps. Still, she had known from the start that the whole business was fraught with risks, though she hadn't expected it to turn into such a mess.

There was also a chance that the police might find out

about the wig and clothes she had bought in Scarborough, but that was very unlikely. She had purposely chosen large, busy department stores, and none of the shop assistants had paid her very much attention. Since she had been in, they would have served hundreds of other customers. Then she remembered the scrawny woman with the large head, the smoker she had startled in the ladies' toilet. She might remember. But so what? All she knew was that Sue had gone to the toilet in a Scarborough department store. Nothing unusual in that. There had been another woman who had spoken to her too that day. She remembered putting on make-up next to a woman who joked about her husband saying she always took so long to go to the toilet. But none of it mattered. She had spoken to lots of people during her time in Whitby, as anybody would.

No, there was nothing to worry about. Besides, she had divine protection, at least until she had fulfilled her destiny. Her spirit guides would hardly allow her to fail after she had got so far. Nonetheless, it was wise to be cautious, get it done quickly and leave town. There was no sense in jeopardizing the main reason for her visit just for the pleasure of toying with her prey a bit longer and watching Greg Eastcote grow more paranoid day by day. She wasn't in this for cruelty, for pleasure. Besides, he would be growing more and more cautious. Best get it done tonight, then, if she could.

The Student Slasher seemed to have disappeared completely from the pages of the *Independent*, as Sue had suspected he soon would. And he wouldn't appear there alive again. With luck, when she had killed him, the police would search his house and find the seven locks of hair. They would check the dates and places of his overnight deliveries, and they would find out who he was and what he had done. Also with luck, they would probably assume that a victim had got the better of him this time, and they wouldn't employ all their resources trying to find out exactly who she was.

After lunch, Sue returned to the factory area. Eastcote could be on a short local run and might come back at any time. She watched from the woods, lying on her stomach, then at evening opening-time she went to the Merry Monk and took her usual table by the window. By pulling back the curtain just a little when nobody was looking, she could see straight down the convex slope of waste ground to Eastcote's cottage. She would wait for him to come home, then she would somehow lure him away. He hadn't struck in his own town before, perhaps due to caution, but this time he wouldn't be able to resist.

Shortly after seven, Sue saw him arrive home. The lights went on behind the pale blue curtains in the cottage. Uncertain how to draw him out, she finished her drink and left the pub. Instead of returning to the lane, walking downhill and turning right onto Eastcote's street, she walked straight across the waste ground, from where she could easily be seen. Sunset was almost over now, and the western sky glowed in even striations of deep violet, scarlet and purple. A jet's trail snaked right across the western horizon, losing shape quickly, and one or two clouds blushed in the last light. Nettles and thistles stung Sue's legs as she brushed her way through the weeds, but the pain felt distant, unreal.

She could knock on his door, or telephone perhaps. But she hadn't seen a phone when she had been inside his house. Knocking on the door was too risky. He might react quickly and drag her inside. Instead, she just walked slowly down to the street and paused when she got to the end of the low garden wall. The curtains were still drawn. She thought she could see a shadow move behind them. She stood for a few moments, certain that they were looking at one another with only the thin blue curtains between them, then moved on, taking the dirt path across the scrub land that led down to the main road. As she walked, she felt a strange drifting sensation, as if she was floating an inch or two above the grass.

Sue stopped and just stood there, about a hundred yards from his house. It was uncanny, the certainty she felt that he had been aware of her standing outside his cottage and that he would open his door and look. And he did. She stood there in the middle of a piece of waste land, nettles, weeds and thistles all around, silhouetted by the sunset. He walked to the end of his garden path, turned his head in her direction, and slowly opened the gate.

46
KIRSTEN

Kirsten stared out of the window at the landscape beyond her reflection. The rounded green hills of the Cotswolds soon gave way to the fertile Vale of Evesham, where barley and wheat looked ready for harvest in the fields, and apples, pears and plums hung heavy on their trees in the hillside orchards.

Then came the built-up landscape of the Midlands: cooling towers, the sprawling monotony of council estates, allotments, greenhouses, a red-brick school, a football field with white goal posts. When the train crept into Birmingham and she could feel the huge city pressing in on all sides, she began to feel nervous. This was, after all, her longest journey in ages, and she was making it alone. For over a year she had been living in a soft, comfortable, familiar world, shuttling between the Georgian elegance of Bath and the bucolic indifference of Brierley Coombe.

Now it was grey and raining and she was in Birmingham, a big, rough city with slums, skinheads, race riots and all the rest. Luckily, she didn't have to get off the train there. She hoped Sarah would be at the station to meet her when she arrived at her destination.

After a twenty-minute stop, the train pulled out and lumbered past twisting concrete overpasses into another built-up area: the derelict warehouses with rusty zigzag fire escapes, and the messy factory yards stacked high with crates and pallets that always seemed to back onto train tracks in cities. It ran alongside a busy commuter road, a dirty brown canal, and a dark brick embankment wall scrawled with graffiti. Next came a few green fields with grazing cows, and then the train settled into a steady, lulling clickety-click through Derbyshire into South Yorkshire, with its slag heaps and idle pit wheels, a landscape in which all the green seemed to have been smudged by an inky finger that was now running in the rain.

Kirsten closed her eyes and let the rhythm carry her. She would stay with Sarah for a day or two perhaps, until she felt it was time to go. Despite what she had told her parents, she had not suggested that Sarah take time off work. Kirsten would say she was going to the Dales walking for a few days alone. If that sounded odd – after all, she *had* spent the last year in the countryside, much of the time alone – then it was too bad. But Sarah would take her word. It was surprising how eager people were to believe her about anything after what had happened to her.

The rain had stopped when Sarah met her at the station later that evening. They allowed themselves the luxury of a taxi to take them back to the bedsit. All the way, Sarah chatted about how glad she was that Kirsten had decided to come back, and how they would look for a flat together as soon as Kirsten had got her bearings again. Kirsten listened and made the right responses, glancing left and right out of the window like a nervous bird as familiar sights unfolded around her: the tall, white university tower, the terraces of sooty red-brick student housing, the park. Washed and glistening after the rain, it all took her breath away with its combination of familiarity and strangeness. For fifteen months it had been simply a landscape of the mind, a closed-off world in which certain things had happened and been filed away. Now that she was actually riding through it again in a taxi, she felt as if she had somehow drawn her surroundings from deep inside herself, from her imagination. She was no longer in the real world at all; she was in a painting, an imagined landscape.

It was getting dark outside when they arrived at the flat. Kirsten followed Sarah up the stairs, remembering with her body rather than in her mind how often she had made this journey before. Her feet remembered in their cells the cracked linoleum they trod, and her fingertips seemed to hold within them the memory of the light switch she pressed.

When she entered her room itself, she had that sensation, however mistaken, of being at a journey's end. It was something she had felt so often before, arriving home after lectures or tiring exams. She remembered the occasional day spent ill in bed with a cold or a sore throat, when she would read and watch the shadows of the houses opposite slowly crawl up the far wall and over the ceiling until the room grew so dark that she had to put the reading lamp on.

She dropped her holdall in the corner and looked around. Some of her belongings were still in their original places: a few books and cassettes in the main room and mugs and jars in the little kitchen alcove. All Sarah had done was clear space for her own things. There was no problem with clothes, of course, as Kirsten had emptied the cupboard of most of hers, but Sarah had filled one cardboard box with some of Kirsten's books and papers to make room for her own on the shelves and the desk.

'Well?' Sarah said, watching her. 'Not changed much, has it?'

'No, it hasn't. I'm surprised.'

'Does it upset you, being back here again?'

'No,' said Kirsten. 'I don't think so. I'm not sure. It's just a very odd feeling, hard to explain.'

'Well, don't worry about it. Just sit down for now. Do you want some tea? Or there's wine. I got a bottle of plonk. Thought you might like that better than going out on the first night.'

'Yes, that's great. I don't much fancy going out. I'm a bit tired and shaky. But some wine would be nice.'

Sarah took the bottle from the small refrigerator and held it up. It was a pale gold colour. 'Aussie stuff,' she said. 'A Chardonnay. Supposed to be good.' She picked up two glasses from the dishrack and searched for the corkscrew in the kitchen drawer. Finally, everything in hand, she filled their glasses and brought them through. 'Cheese? I've got a wedge of Brie and some Wensleydale.'

'Yes, please.'

Sarah brought in the cheese with a selection of biscuits on a Tetley's tray, liberated from the Ring O'Bells. They toasted the future and drank. Kirsten helped herself to some food, then picked up a book she noticed lying on the floor by the armchair. It was a thick biography of Thomas Hardy. 'Is this what you're reading right now?' she asked.

Sarah nodded. 'I'm thinking about doing my PhD in Victorian fiction, and you know how I love biographies. It seemed a pleasurable enough way of getting back into academic gear.'

'And is it? I mean, Hardy's hardly a light, cheerful read, is he?'

Sarah laughed. 'I don't know about a pessimist, but he was certainly a bloody pervert.'

'How?' asked Kirsten. 'I've only read *Far from the Madding Crowd* for that novel course in first year. I don't even remember much about that except some soldier showing off his fancy sword-play. I suppose that was meant to be phallic?'

Sarah laughed. 'Yes, but that's not what I meant. All writers do that kind of symbolism thing to some extent, don't they?'

'What *do* you mean?'

'Well, for one thing,' Sarah went on, 'do you know he used to like attending public executions when he was in his teens? Especially when women were being hanged.' She reached for the book and turned the pages slowly as she talked. 'There was one in Dorchester and he told someone about it when he was much older . . . ah, here it is . . . 1856. Martha Browne was the woman's name, and she was hanged for murdering her husband. She caught him with another woman and they got into a fight. He attacked her with a whip and she stabbed him. Hanging her was the Victorians' idea of justice. Anyway, Hardy went along and wrote about it.' She pushed the book under Kirsten's nose. 'Just look at that.'

Kirsten read: 'What a fine figure she showed against the sky as she hung in the misty rain, and how the tight black silk gown set off her shape as she wheeled half round and back.'

'I mean, really,' Sarah went on, 'the poor woman was swinging at the end of a bloody rope and Hardy makes out as if she was entering some kind of wet T-shirt contest. Would you credit it?'

Kirsten read over the description; it was certainly tinged with eroticism.

'Am I right?' Sarah asked, pouring more wine. 'Don't you get the feeling that Hardy got some kind of kinky sexual pleasure from watching the woman get snuffed?' She put a hand to her mouth quickly. 'Oh. I'm sorry, love. I . . . I put my foot in it. Must be the wine going to my head. I mean, I wasn't thinking. I didn't mean to . . . you know.'

Kirsten waved her hand. 'It's all right. I'd rather you say what you like than walk around handling me with kid gloves. I can take it. And anyway, you're right, it *is* sexual.'

'Yes. And what's more, did you notice how he turns her into some sort of convenient image for a poem. As if her life was only important because he got a charge from watching her get hanged. She wasn't even a person, an individual, to him.'

'I wonder what she was like,' Kirsten said abstractedly.

'We'll never know, will we?'

'I suppose not. But it's not as odd as all that, is it? The way Hardy uses her, I mean. We all tend to see other people as bit players in our own dramas, don't we? I mean we're all self-centred.'

'I don't think so. Not to that extent.'

'Maybe not. But you might be surprised.' She held her glass out and Sarah emptied the bottle. Kirsten was beginning to feel a little tipsy. After the journey and the disorienting effect of coming back to her old room, the wine was affecting her more than it usually would. Still, it wasn't an unpleasant sensation. She helped herself to another chunk of Wensleydale.

Sarah shook the wine bottle, grinned and jumped up, ruffling Kirsten's short hair as she passed by. 'Fear not,' she said. 'I suspected we might need more than the usual amount of alcoholic sustenance. How about some music? All right?'

Kirsten shrugged. 'Fine.'

Sarah turned on the cassette player and disappeared behind the curtain into the kitchen. She must have been playing the tape earlier because one song was just fading out, and then 'Simple Twist of Fate' began to play. It was the second track on Bob Dylan's *Blood on the Tracks*, Kirsten remembered, and it used to be one of her favourites; now, as she listened to Dylan's hoarse, plaintive voice while Sarah was busy opening the second bottle, she realized that the strange lyrics didn't mean what she used to think they did. Nothing did any more.

Sarah returned with a larger bottle, lifting it up with a flourish. 'Da-da! More your cheaper kind of plonk, really, but I'm sure at this stage it'll do.'

Kirsten smiled. 'Oh, it'll do fine.'

'What did you mean,' Sarah asked when she had filled the glasses and sat down, 'when you said I'd be surprised? What would I be surprised by?'

Kirsten frowned. 'I was thinking of the man who attacked me,' she said. 'I wasn't a person, an individual, to him, was I? I was just a convenient symbol of what he hated or feared.'

'Would it have made any difference?'

'I don't know. Would it have made any difference if it had been someone I knew? I can think of one way it would have: I'd know who it was.'

'And?'

'I'd bloody well kill him.' Kirsten lifted her glass of wine too quickly and spilled some down the front of her shirt. She patted herself on the chest. 'Doesn't matter' she said. 'It'll dry.'

'An eye for an eye?'

'Something like that.'

Sarah shook her head slowly.

'I'm not crazy, you know,' Kirsten went on. 'I mean it. Oh, there've been times . . . Sometimes I think it's some sort of contagious disease he gave me, like AIDS, only in the mind. Or like vampirism. Can you imagine all those ripped-up women coming back from the grave to prey on men? Of course, I didn't die, but maybe a part of me did. Maybe I have a little bit of the undead in me.'

'That's cuckoo talk, Kirstie. Or drunk talk. You're not going to convince me you're turning into some sort of vampire version of Joan of Arc.'

Kirsten looked hard at her and felt the focus blurring. My God, she thought, I'm losing it. I almost told her. She laughed and reached for a cigarette. 'You're right,' she said. 'I'm not. It's all academic anyway, isn't it?'

'Thank God for that,' Sarah said. The music stopped and she got up and turned over the tape.

As the two of them chatted, Kirsten glanced out now and then at the windows of the bedsits and flats over the street, just as she had in years past. At some point, she noticed 'Shelter from the Storm', another of her favourites, was playing, and her eyes burned with tears. She held them back.

Around midnight, Kirsten began to yawn in the middle of one of Sarah's stories about a retired brigadier-general who had strayed into Harridan by mistake.

'Boring you, am I?' Sarah asked.

'No. I'm just tired, that's all. It must be the wine and the travel. How about sleeping arrangements?'

Sarah yawned too. 'Look, now you've got me at it. How about I take the chair and you have the bed?'

'Oh no, I couldn't do that.'

'It *is* your room, after all. I've just been caretaking.'

'It *was* my room. No, I'll put a couple of cushions on the floor and sleep there.'

'But that's stupid. You'll be so uncomfortable. Hell, it's a three-quarter bed, let's share it.'

Kirsten said nothing for a moment. The suggestion made her feel nervous and shy. She knew that Sarah wasn't offering any kind of sexual invitation, but the thought of her own patched-up body next to Sarah's smooth, whole skin made her cheeks burn.

'I haven't brought a nightie,' she said.

'Not to worry. I've got a spare pair of pyjamas. Okay?'

'All right.' Kirsten was too tired to argue, and the idea of sleeping in what had once been her own bed was inviting. When she stood up, she felt herself sway a little. She really had drunk too much.

They prepared themselves for bed and drew the curtains. Kirsten watched Sarah pull her T-shirt over her head and struggle with her tight jeans, then stand there naked and unselfconsciously brush her blonde hair in front of the mirror. Her breasts bounced lightly with the motion of her arm, and below her flat stomach, the spun-gold hair between her legs caught the light.

Kirsten undressed last, in the dark, so that Sarah couldn't see her scars, and when she slipped between the crisp sheets, she found herself staying as close to the edge of the bed as possible to avoid any unconscious contact.

But she needn't have worried. Sarah lay with her face turned to the wall below the window, and soon her breathing settled into a slow, regular pattern. Kirsten listened for a while, feeling slightly dizzy and nauseated and cursing herself for almost telling Sarah everything she knew, not to mention what she intended to do about it. Eventually, she drifted off to sleep and dreamed of Martha Browne, that unknown woman in black swinging back and forth at the end of a rope in the misty Dorchester rain over a hundred years ago.

The next day, Sarah went into the bookshop, and Kirsten spent the morning revisiting her old campus haunts: the coffee lounge where she had met friends between lectures, the library where she had worked so hard for the final exams. She even wandered into an empty lecture theatre and imagined Professor Simpkins droning on about Milton's *Areopagitica*.

Though she had avoided it on her way over, taking the roads instead, Kirsten walked back through the park. As her feet followed the familiar tarmac path through the trees she felt nothing at all, but when she reached the lion, its head still spray-painted blue and the red graffiti still scrawled all over its body, her hands started shaking. Unable to stop herself, she walked over to the sculpture.

It was a little after twelve. Children played on the swings and seesaw nearby. The clack of bowls came from the green behind the low hedge, and one or two people sprawled out on the grass, listening to portable cassettes or reading. But Kirsten still felt extreme unease, as if she had somehow stumbled on a taboo place, an evil spot shunned by natives. She couldn't help herself when she sat astride the lion, drawing amused glances from two students playing cards on the grass nearby. It all happened so quickly. The fishy smell began to suffocate her and the world darkened at the corners of her vision. Then she saw him and heard his raspy voice and saw the blade flash in the moonlight. She leapt off and hurried on her way, trembling.

As she walked on down the avenue of trees, she cursed herself for giving in to fear. She would need all the courage and strength she could get for what she had to do, and jumping at shadows was a poor start. Still, she told herself, somehow shadows were more frightening to her now than substance. That must be a good sign. It was time to go.

First she went back to the flat and left a note for Sarah, then she went into town. After shopping for one or two essentials she needed for her trip, she headed for the bus station. About three hours later, Martha Browne arrived in Whitby on a clear afternoon in early September, convinced of her destiny.

47

SUSAN

Like some shadowy female figure out of Hardy standing on a blasted heath waiting for her lover, Sue stood on the waste land in the thickening darkness and watched Greg Eastcote shut his garden gate and take the path towards her.

Before he had got far, while Sue was still about sixty yards ahead, she turned her back to him and started walking along the rough path. When she got to the main road, there were few people about, but the street was well lit. Sensing him behind her, rather than seeing him, Sue continued along until she had passed the intersection with Bridge Street, where the road narrowed. This was the tourist area again, the cobbled street of gift shops, the Monk's Haven, the Black Horse. At this time of evening though, all the shops were closed. Polished jet gleamed in its gold and silver settings in the windows, and the enamel trays that had been covered with coffee- or mint-flavoured fudge all day lay empty. All the happy holiday families were back at the guesthouses watching television, or they had managed to put the kids to bed and gone out to the pub for a quiet pint alone. Only lovers and vampires walked the streets.

Hands in the pockets of her windcheater, Sue walked on purposefully. She had known where she was heading all along, she realized, but she had known it in her instinct and her muscles, not in her conscious mind. He was still behind her, moving more cautiously now, not hurrying to catch up with her. Perhaps he was getting worried. When she got to the steps, she turned and started climbing, counting by habit as she went. It was dark and deserted up the hill, with no street lights to light her way. But St Mary's was floodlit, like a beacon, and high above the church a waning three-quarter moon shone in the clear sky, surrounded by stars. At the top of the hundred and ninety-ninth step, where Caedmon's Cross stood silhouetted against the bright sand-coloured church, Sue turned through the graveyard of nameless stones. She could tell he was following her, that he would soon appear at the top and look around to see which way she had gone. She slowed down. She didn't want to disappoint him.

In the light of St Mary's, she followed the path through the graves around the seaward side of the church and across the deserted car park, where the world turned dark again. She found the coast path and stopped for a moment by the gate. Yes, he was there, just coming out of the cemetery and looking in her direction.

She turned back to the path and hurried on. She was high on the cliff now, the sheer part known as the Scar, walking in the general direction of Robin Hood's Bay. The raised boardwalk underfoot creaked in places, and she had to slow down in case of missing boards. A barbed-wire fence came between the path and the drop, but it had collapsed here and there where erosion had eaten the rock away.

Now that she was further away from the church's interfering floodlights, the moonlight shone more clearly, dusting the grass on one side and the sea on the other with its ghostly silver light. Sue thought she might lead him as far as Saltwick Nab and down the steps, out towards the knuckled rocks that pointed to the sea. But he was getting closer. She could hear his footsteps on the boardwalk, and when she half-turned her head, she could see him outlined faintly by the moonlight.

He was walking faster. She would never make it that far before he caught up with her, and she didn't intend him to attack her from behind. As she walked, she reached her hand into her shoulder bag and felt for the paperweight. There it was, smooth and heavy against her sweating palm.

He was almost so close now that she could hear his laboured breathing. The climb up the steps must have tired him. When she could bear it no longer, Sue stopped abruptly and turned to face him. In the moonlight, she could just about make out his features: the low, dark brow, wide, grim-set mouth and the eyes glittering like stars reflected on the water's surface. He had stopped, too. Only about five yards lay between them, and at first nobody said a word; neither of them even seemed to be breathing. Sue found that she was shaking. Suddenly, she remembered with perfect clarity all the pain she had suffered the last time she had seen this ghostly face in the moonlight.

Finally, she found the courage to speak, 'Do you remember me?'

'You,' he said, in that familiar raspy whisper. 'You were in my house.'

'Yes,' she said, gaining strength as they talked, feeling the hardness of the solid glass in her hand.

'Why? What are you trying to do to me?'

Sue didn't answer. Now that she had found him, she had said all she wanted to.

'Why?' he repeated.

She noticed that he was moving towards her very slowly, closing the gap as he talked.

'You know what you are,' she said, bringing her hand out of the shoulder bag. Then she took a sudden step towards him and shouted, 'Come on, then! Here I am. Come on, do it. Finish me!'

She could see the confusion and horror on his face as she continued moving towards him. 'Come on. What's wrong with you? Do it!'

But he kept on backing away as Sue edged closer, paperweight out in her hand now. He stretched out his arms before him as if to ward her off, and immediately she knew. She knew that he needed surprise to succeed. He was a coward. And what must she look like, she wondered, coming towards him with a fist of thick glass held out and all the rage of a ruined life in her face and voice? It didn't bear thinking about. The miserable bastard was terrified and his fear unnerved her for a moment.

He must have sensed her confusion like an animal scents its prey, for he began to smile as he slowed his retreat. In a moment he would start walking towards her again. But he had already gone too far. On his next slow step backwards, one of the rotten boards shifted under him and he wobbled at the edge. He waved his arms like a semaphorist, a look of terror on his face, and Sue almost reached forward to help him. Almost. But he regained his balance and again she saw that *other* face, the one his human mask barely hid. She took a pace forward and kicked out hard at him. Her foot connected with his groin and he tottered back towards the edge of the cliff with a scream.

The fence was low there, only about a foot or so off

the ground, and the post stood at an odd angle, crooked, pointing out to sea. As he fell backwards, his clothing snagged on the rusted barbed wire and he managed to turn himself around. He was half over the edge but his hands clawed at the thick tufts of grass. The more he struggled, the more the wire seemed to wrap him up, and when she moved closer, Sue could see blood seeping through his clothes. He grunted and snatched at the sods as he tried to stop himself from slowly sliding over. Sue knelt down and smashed at his hands with the paperweight. The fence post twitched like a dowsing rod as he howled and struggled, snatching at the barbed wire now, anything to get a grip, his hands coming away crushed, ripped and bloody. Only his head and shoulders showed above the edge now. The wire had torn one sleeve right off his jacket and its barbs stuck in the skin beneath. The post was almost out of the ground, pointing out to sea, and the more he struggled the more he slipped.

At last he managed to find a foothold in the cliff face just below the edge, but his hands were so badly damaged that all he could do was push himself up with his feet and flail his arms about. The barbed wire tied him to the edge but his feet pushed him away. Sue stood up, raised the paperweight and hit him on the side of his head. The jolt ran all the way up her arm. Blood filled his eye. She hit out again, this time catching him over the ear. He screamed and put one hand to the wound. The post broke free of its shallow pit and shot over the cliff side, taking him with it. Sue knelt right at the edge and saw him twist around in the wire like an animal in a trap before he tore free and plunged.

Far below, the sea lapped and spumed around the rocks at the base of the cliff, and the body, arms and legs whirling, hit them with a thud louder than the breaking waves themselves. Sue could see him down there, slumped and broken over the sharp dark rocks, where the foaming waves licked at him like the tongues of madmen.

It was done. Sue looked back towards the distant church and thought of the normal, day-to-day world that lay below it in the town. What would she do now that it was over? Should she follow him? It would be so easy just to relax and let herself slide over the edge to oblivion.

But no. Suicide wasn't part of her destiny. Her own death had been her stake, what she had risked, but it was not part of the bargain if she won. She had to accept her fate, whatever it might be: live with the guilt, if such she felt, or pay for her crimes if she was caught. But there was no giving in to suicide. She was free of her burden now, come what may.

She had no idea if the police were close to discovering her identity. Perhaps they were already waiting back at Mrs Cummings' to arrest her. And then there was Keith McLaren, still in a coma. What if he woke up and remembered everything? On the other hand, he might have brain damage or amnesia. If so, was it possible that he would spend his days trying to piece together the fragments of his memory by himself, and, if he succeeded, would he hunt down the woman who had so suddenly and without provocation wrecked his life? She didn't know. She might have created another like herself, someone with a bit of the undead in him.

But no matter how bleak some of the possibilities seemed, she felt free at last. More than that, she was Kirsten again. Even imprisonment would be a kind of freedom now. It didn't really matter what happened because she had done what had to be done. Now she was free.

Certainly her best bet would be to get out of town and back to Sarah first thing in the morning and destroy anything that might link her to the place. That's what she would do. Perhaps she could also tint her hair and make sure she looked like none of the girls who had been in Whitby.

All Kirsten really wanted to do at the moment, she realized, looking towards the church, was crawl into one of those box pews marked FOR STRANGERS ONLY, kneel and offer a prayer of sorts, then curl up on the green baize and sleep. But the place would be locked up for the night.

As she got to her feet, the paperweight slipped out of her sweaty palm, bounced on the springy grass and fell over the edge. She leaned forward to watch and saw the glass shatter against a rock in a shower of white powder like a wave breaking. Free of its cage, the rose seemed to drift up on a current of warm air. Its crimson petals opened, pale in the moonlight, then slowly it floated back down and a departing wave carried it out to sea.

afterword

'8th September 1987
Coast road, Whitby–Staithes. Rolling farmland, patchwork of hedged fields (cows grazing) light brown after harvest & wheat-coloured barley etc. End abruptly at cliffs, pinkish strata, sea clear light blue, sun glinting silver on distant ship. Flock of gulls on red-brown field. Clumps of trees in hollows. Cluster of village houses, light stone, red pantile roofs: ". . . arrived at the small coastal town at 11.15 a.m. in early September, her mind made up." '

Such were the humble origins of *Caedmon's Song*, I discover, looking back over my notebook for August 1987, to March 1988. I wrote the book in the late eighties, then, after my first four Inspector Banks novels. I remember I needed a change; a novel in which the police played a subsidiary role. Ever since reading about the Yorkshire Ripper, I'd had an idea for a story about someone who had survived a serial killer's attack setting out for revenge.

The idea lay fallow, as these things often do, until one September day in 1987, when we crested the hill into Whitby, shortly before the above-described trip to Staithes, when the original opening revealed itself. There lay Whitby, spread out below. The colours seemed somehow brighter and more vibrant than I remembered:

the greens and blues of the North Sea, the red pantile roofs. Then there was the dramatic setting of the lobster-claw harbour and the two opposing hills, one capped with a church and a ruined abbey, the other with Captain Cook's statue and the massive jawbone of a whale. I knew immediately that this was where the story had to take place, and that it began with a woman getting off a bus, feeling a little travel-sick, trying the place on for size.

When I heard that Macmillan planned to publish this novel in 2003, I toyed with the idea of rewriting it and updating it. After all, isn't it every writer's dream to get another chance years later at improving something one wrote in one's early days? But the more I thought about it, the more I realized that it just wouldn't work, that the world has changed so much since 1987, and that the events in *Caedmon's Song* couldn't happen in a world with mobile phones, e-mail, a McDonald's or Pizza Hut on every corner, and the current techniques of DNA testing. Genetic fingerprinting existed back then, as Joseph Wambaugh's *The Blooding* demonstrates very well, but it was still in its infancy. Besides, I was supposed to be leaving the police behind. Given the advances in forensic science since 1987, it seemed that if I were to update the book for 2003, it would be almost impossible to keep them in the background. Whitby has changed, too, especially the footpath along the top of the cliffs which plays such an important role in the book.

In the end, I settled for correcting a few minor points, changing a character's name, getting rid of an obtrusive comment about Margaret Thatcher. That sort of thing. In all other respects it's the original novel, now a period piece of sorts, a slice of late twentieth-century history, set in a time when you could smoke anywhere, get bed and breakfast for £9.50 a night and *Crocodile Dundee* was all the rage!

AFTERMATH

To Bob and Louise,

with many thanks for your
friendship and support

'The evil that men do lives after them'

William Shakespeare, *Julius Caesar*

PROLOGUE

They locked her in the cage when she started to bleed. Tom was already there. He'd been there for three days and had stopped crying now. He was still shivering, though. It was February, there was no heat in the cellar, and both of them were naked. There would be no food, either, she knew, not for a long time, not until she got so hungry that she felt as if she were being eaten from the inside.

It wasn't the first time she had been locked in the cage, but this time was different from the others. Before, it had always been because she'd done something wrong or hadn't done what they wanted her to do. This time it was different; it was because of what she had become, and she was really scared.

As soon as they had shut the door at the top of the stairs, the darkness wrapped itself around her like fur. She could feel it rubbing against her skin the way a cat rubs against your legs. She began to shiver. More than anything she hated the cage, more than the blows, more than the humiliations. But she wouldn't cry. She never cried. She didn't know how.

The smell was terrible; they didn't have a toilet to go to, only the bucket in the corner, which they would only be allowed to empty when they were let out. And who knew when that would be?

But worse even than the smell were the little scratching sounds that started when she had been locked up only a few minutes. Soon, she knew, it would come, the tickle of sharp little feet across her legs or her stomach if she dare lie down. The first time, she had tried to keep moving and making noise all the time to keep them away, but in the end she had become exhausted and fallen asleep, not caring how many there were or what they did. She could tell in the dark, by the way they moved and their weight, whether they were rats or mice. The rats were the worst. One had even bitten her once.

She held Tom and tried to comfort him, making them both a little warmer. If truth be told, she could have done with some comforting herself, but there was nobody to comfort her.

Mice scuttled across her feet. Occasionally, she kicked out and heard one squeak as it hit the wall. She could hear music from upstairs, loud, with the bass making the bars of the cage rattle.

She closed her eyes and tried to find a beautiful retreat deep inside her mind, a place where everything was warm and golden and the sea that washed up on the sands was deep blue, the water warm and lovely as sunlight when she jumped in. But she couldn't find it, couldn't find that sandy beach and blue sea, that garden full of bright flowers or that cool green forest in summer. When she closed her eyes, all she could find was darkness shot with red, distant mutterings, cries and an appalling sense of dread.

She drifted in and out of sleep, becoming oblivious to the mice and rats. She didn't know how long she'd been there before she heard noises upstairs. Different noises. The music had ended a long time ago and everything was silent apart from the scratching and Tom's breathing. She thought she heard a car pull up outside. Voices. Another car. Then she heard someone walking across the floor upstairs. A curse.

Suddenly all hell broke loose upstairs. It sounded as if someone was battering at the door with a tree trunk, then came a crunching sound followed by a loud bang as the front door caved in. Tom was awake now, whimpering in her arms.

She heard shouting and what sounded like dozens of pairs of feet running around upstairs. After what seemed like an eternity, she heard someone prise open the lock to the cellar door. A little light spilled in, but not much, and there wasn't a bulb down there. More voices. Then came the lances of bright torch light, coming closer, so close they hurt her eyes and she had to shield them with her hand. Then the beam held her and a strange voice cried, 'Oh God! Oh, my God!'

1

Maggie Forrest wasn't sleeping well, so it didn't surprise her when the voices woke her shortly before four o'clock one morning in early May, even though she had made sure before she went to bed that all the windows in the house were shut fast.

If it hadn't been the voices, it would have been something else: a car door slamming as someone set off for an early shift; the first train rattling across the bridge; the neighbour's dog; old wood creaking somewhere in the house; the fridge clicking on and off; a pan or a glass shifting on the draining-board. Or perhaps one of the noises of the night, the kind that made her wake in a cold sweat with a thudding heart and gasp for breath as if she were drowning, not sleeping: the man she called Mr Bones clicking up and down The Hill with his cane; the scratching at the front door; the tortured child screaming in the distance.

Or a nightmare.

She was just too jumpy these days, she told herself, trying to laugh it off. But there they were again. Definitely voices. One loud and masculine.

Maggie got out of bed and padded over to the window. The street called The Hill ran up the northern slope of the broad valley, and where Maggie lived, about halfway up, just above the railway bridge, the houses on the eastern side of the street stood atop a twenty-foot rise that sloped down to the pavement in a profusion of shrubs and small trees.

Sometimes the undergrowth and foliage seemed so thick she could hardly find her way along the path to the pavement.

Maggie's bedroom window looked over the houses on the western side of The Hill and beyond, a patchwork landscape of housing estates, arterial roads, warehouses, factory chimneys and fields stretching through Bradford and Halifax all the way to the Pennines. Some days, Maggie would sit for hours and look at the view, thinking about the odd chain of events that had brought her here. Now, though, in the pre-dawn light, the distant necklaces and clusters of amber street lights took on a ghostly aspect, as if the city weren't quite real yet.

Maggie stood at her window and looked across the street. She could swear there was a hall light on directly opposite, in Lucy's house, and when she heard the voice again she suddenly felt all her premonitions had been true.

It was Terry's voice, and he was shouting at Lucy. She couldn't hear what he was saying. Then she heard a scream, the sound of glass breaking and a thud.

Lucy.

Maggie dragged herself out of her paralysis, and with trembling hands she picked up the bedside telephone and dialled 999.

•

Probationary Police Constable Janet Taylor stood by her patrol car and watched the silver BMW burn, shielding her eyes from its glare, standing upwind of the foul-smelling smoke. Her partner, PC Dennis Morrisey, stood beside her. One or two spectators were peeping out of their bedroom windows, but nobody else seemed very interested. Burning cars weren't exactly a novelty on this estate. Even at four o'clock in the morning.

Orange and red flames, with deep inner hues of blue and green and occasional tentacles of violet, twisted into the darkness, sending up palls of thick black smoke. Even upwind, Janet could smell the burning rubber and plastic. It was giving her a headache, and she knew her uniform and her hair would reek of it for days.

The leading firefighter, Gary Cullen, walked over to join them. It was Dennis he spoke to, of course; he always did. They were mates.

'What do you think?'

'Joyriders.' Dennis nodded towards the car. 'We checked the number-plate. Stolen from a nice middle-class residential street in Heaton Moor, Manchester, earlier this evening.'

'Why here, then?'

'Dunno. Could be a connection, a grudge or something. Someone giving a little demonstration of his feelings. Drugs, even. But that's for the lads upstairs to work out. They're the ones paid to have brains. We're done for now. Everything safe?'

'Under control. What if there's a body in the boot?'

Dennis laughed. 'It'll be well done by now, won't it? Hang on a minute, that's our radio, isn't it?'

Janet walked over to the car. 'I'll get it,' she said over her shoulder.

'Control to 354. Come in please, 354. Over.'

Janet picked up the radio. '354 to Control. Over.'

'Domestic dispute reported taking place at number thirty-five, The Hill. Repeat. Three-five. The Hill. Can you respond? Over.'

Christ, thought Janet, a bloody domestic. No copper in

her right mind liked domestics, especially at this time in the morning. 'Will do,' she sighed, looking at her watch. 'ETA three minutes.'

She called over to Dennis, who held up his hand and spoke a few more words to Gary Cullen before responding. They were both laughing when Dennis returned to the car.

'Tell him that joke, did you?' Janet asked, settling behind the wheel.

'Which one's that?' Dennis asked, all innocence.

Janet started the car and sped to the main road. 'You know, the one about the blonde giving her first blow job.'

'I don't know what you're talking about.'

'Only I heard you telling it to that new PC back at the station, the lad who hasn't started shaving yet. You ought to give the poor lad a chance to make his own mind up about women, Den, instead of poisoning him right off the bat.'

The centrifugal force almost threw them off the road as Janet took the roundabout at the top of The Hill too fast. Dennis grasped the dashboard and hung on for dear life. 'Jesus Christ. Women drivers. It's only a joke. Have you got no sense of humour?'

Janet smiled to herself as she slowed and kerb-crawled down The Hill looking for number thirty-five.

'Anyway, I'm getting sick of this,' Dennis said.

'Sick of what? My driving?'

'That, too. Mostly, though, it's your constant bitching. It's got so a bloke can't say what's on his mind these days.'

'Not if he's got a mind like a sewer. That's pollution. Anyway, it's changing times, Den. And we have to change with them or we'll end up like the dinosaurs. By the way, about that mole.'

'What mole?'

'You know, the one on your cheek. Next to your nose. The one with all the hairs growing out of it.'

Dennis put his hand up to his cheek. 'What about it?'

'I'd get it seen to quick, if I were you. It looks cancerous to me. Ah, number thirty-five. Here we are.'

She pulled over to the right side of the road and came to a halt a few yards past the house. It was a small detached residence built of redbrick and sandstone, between a plot of allotments and a row of shops. It wasn't much bigger than a cottage, with a slate roof, low-walled garden and a modern garage attached at the right. At the moment, all was quiet.

'There's a light on in the hall,' Janet said. 'Shall we have a dekko?'

Still fingering his mole, Dennis sighed and muttered something she took to be assent. Janet got out of the car first and walked up the path, aware of him dragging his feet behind her. The garden was overgrown and she had to push twigs and shrubbery aside as she walked. A little adrenalin had leaked into her system, put her on super alert, as it always did with domestics. The reason most cops hated them was that you never knew what was going to happen. As likely as not you'd pull the husband off the wife and then the wife would take his side and start bashing you with a rolling pin.

Janet paused by the door. All quiet, apart from Dennis's stertorous breathing behind her. It was too early yet for people to be going to work, and most of the late-night revellers had passed out by now. Somewhere in the distance the first birds began to chatter. Sparrows, most likely, Janet thought. Mice with wings.

Seeing no doorbell, Janet knocked on the door.

No response came from inside.

She knocked harder. The hammering seemed to echo up and down the street. Still no response.

Next, Janet went down on her knees and looked through the letterbox. She could just make out a figure sprawled on the floor at the bottom of the stairs. A woman's figure. That was probably cause enough for forced entry.

'Let's go in,' she said.

Dennis tried the handle. Locked. Then, gesturing for Janet to stand out of the way, he charged the door with his shoulder.

Poor technique, she thought. She'd have reared back and used her foot. But Dennis was a second row rugby forward, she reminded herself, and his shoulders had been pushed up against so many arseholes in their time that they had to be strong.

The door crashed open on first contact and Dennis cannonballed into the hallway, grabbing hold of the bottom of the banister to stop himself from tripping over the still figure that lay there.

Janet was right behind him, but she had the advantage of walking in at a more dignified pace. She closed the door as best she could, knelt beside the woman on the floor and felt for a pulse. Weak, but steady. One side of her face was bathed in blood.

'My God,' Janet muttered. 'Den? You okay?'

'Fine. You take care of her. I'll have a look around.' Dennis headed upstairs.

For once, Janet didn't mind being told what to do. Nor did she mind that Dennis automatically assumed it was a woman's work to tend the injured while the man went in search of heroic glory. Well, she *minded*, but she felt a real concern for the victim here, so she didn't want to make an issue of it.

Bastard, she thought. Whoever did this. 'It's okay, love,' she said, even though she suspected the woman couldn't hear her. 'We'll get you an ambulance. Just hold on.'

Most of the blood seemed to be coming from one deep cut just above her left ear, Janet noticed, though there was also a little smeared around the nose and lips. Punches, by the looks of it. There were also broken glass and daffodils scattered all around her, along with a damp patch on the carpet. Janet took her personal radio from her belt-hook and called for an ambulance. She was lucky it worked on The Hill; personal UHF radios had much less range than the VHF models fitted in cars, and were notoriously subject to black spots of patchy reception.

Dennis came downstairs shaking his head. 'Bastard's not hiding up there,' he said. He handed Janet a blanket, pillow and towel, nodding to the woman. 'For her.'

Janet eased the pillow under the woman's head, covered her gently with the blanket and applied the towel to the seeping wound on her temple. Well, I never, she thought, full of surprises, our Den. 'Think he's done a runner?' she asked.

'Dunno. I'll have a look in the back. You stay with her till the ambulance arrives.'

Before Janet could say anything, Dennis headed off towards the back of the house. He hadn't been gone more than a minute or so when she heard him call out, 'Janet, come here and have a look at this. Hurry up. It could be important.'

Curious, Janet looked at the injured woman. The bleeding had stopped and there was nothing else she could do. Even so, she was reluctant to leave the poor woman alone.

'Come on,' Dennis called again. 'Hurry up.'

Janet took one last look at the prone figure and walked towards the back of the house. The kitchen was in darkness.

'Down here.'

She couldn't see Dennis, but she knew that his voice came from downstairs. Through an open door to her right, three steps led down to a landing lit by a bare bulb. There was another door, most likely to the garage, she thought, and around the corner were the steps down to the cellar.

Dennis was standing there, near the bottom, in front of a third door. On it was pinned a poster of a naked woman. She lay back on a brass bed with her legs wide open, fingers tugging at the edges of her vagina, smiling down over her large breasts at the viewer, inviting, beckoning him inside. Dennis stood before it, grinning.

'Bastard,' Janet hissed.

'Where's your sense of humour?'

'It's *not* funny.'

'What do you think it means?'

'I don't know.' Janet could see light under the door, faint and flickering, as if from a faulty bulb. She also noticed a peculiar odour. 'What's that smell?' she asked.

'How should I know? Rising damp? Drains?'

But it smelled like decay to Janet. Decay and sandalwood incense. She gave a little shudder.

'Shall we go in?' She was whispering without knowing why.

'I think we'd better.'

Janet walked ahead of him, almost on tiptoe, down the final few steps. The adrenalin was really pumping in her veins now. Slowly, she reached out and tried the door. Locked. She moved aside, and Dennis used his foot this time. The lock splintered, and the door swung open. Dennis stood aside, bowed from the waist in a parody of gentlemanly courtesy, and said, 'Ladies first.'

With Dennis only inches behind her, Janet stepped into the cellar.

She barely had time to register her first impressions of the small room – mirrors, dozens of lit candles surrounding a mattress on the floor, a girl on the mattress, naked and bound, something yellow around her neck, the terrible smell stronger, despite the incense, like blocked drains and rotten meat, crude charcoal drawings on the whitewashed walls – before it happened.

He came from somewhere behind them, from one of the cellar's dark corners. Dennis turned to meet him, reaching for his baton, but he was too slow. The machete slashed first across his cheek, slicing it open from the eye to the lips. Before Dennis had time to put his hand up to staunch the blood or register the pain, the man slashed again, this time across the side of his throat. Dennis made a gurgling sound and went to his knees, eyes wide open. Warm blood gushed across Janet's face and sprayed onto the whitewashed walls in swirling abstract patterns. The hot stink of it made her gag.

She had no time to think. You never did when it really happened. All she knew was that she couldn't do anything for Dennis. Not yet. There was still the man with the knife to deal with. Hang on, Dennis, she pleaded silently. *Hang on.*

The man still seemed intent on hacking at Dennis, not finished yet, and that gave Janet enough time to slip out her side-handled baton. She had just managed to grip the handle so that the baton ran protectively along the outside of her arm, when he made his first lunge at her. He seemed shocked and surprised when his blade didn't sink into flesh and bone but was instead deflected by the hard baton.

That gave Janet the opening she needed. Bugger technique and training. She swung out and caught him on the temple. His eyes rolled back and he slumped against the wall, but he didn't go down. She moved in closer and cracked down on the wrist of his knife-hand. She heard something break. He cried out and the machete fell to the floor. Janet kicked it away into a far corner, then she took the fully extended baton with both hands, swung and caught him on the side of the head again. He tried to go after his machete, but she hit him again as hard as she could on the back of his head and then again on his cheek and once more at the base of his skull. He reared up, still on his knees, spouting obscenities at her, and she lashed out one more time, cracking his temple. He fell against the wall, where the back of his head left a long dark smear on the whitewash as he slid down, and rested there, legs extended. Pink foam bubbled at the side of his mouth, then stopped. Janet hit him once more, a two-handed blow on the top of his skull, then she took out her handcuffs and secured him to one of the pipes running along the bottom of the wall. He groaned and stirred, so she hit him again. When he fell silent, she went over to Dennis.

He was still twitching, but the spurts of blood from his wound were getting weaker. Janet struggled to remember her first aid training. She made a compress from her handkerchief and pressed it tight against the severed artery, trying to nip the ends together. Next she tried to make the 10-9 call on her personal radio – officer in urgent need of assistance. But it was no good. All she got was static. A *black spot*. Nothing to do now but sit and wait for the ambulance to arrive. She could hardly move, go outside, not with Dennis like this. She couldn't leave him.

So Janet sat cross-legged and rested Dennis's head on her lap, cradling him and muttering nonsense in his ear. The ambulance would come soon, she told him. He would be fine, just wait and see. But it seemed that no matter how tightly she held the compress, blood leaked through to her uniform. She could feel its warmth on her fingers, her belly and thighs. Please, Dennis, she prayed, *please* hang on.

•

Above Lucy's house, Maggie could see the crescent sliver of a new moon and the faint silver thread it drew around the old moon's darkness. ***The old moon in the new moon's arms.*** An ill omen. Sailors believed that the sight of it, especially through glass, presaged a storm and much loss of life. Maggie shivered. She wasn't superstitious, but there was something chilling about the sight, something that reached out and touched her from way back in time when people paid more attention to cosmic events such as the cycles of the moon.

She looked back down at the house and saw the police car arrive, heard the woman officer knock and call out, then saw her male partner charge the door.

After that, Maggie heard nothing for a while – perhaps five or ten minutes – until she fancied she heard a heart-rending, keening wail from deep inside the bowels of the house. But it could have been her imagination. The sky was a lighter blue now and the dawn chorus had struck up. Maybe it was a bird? But she knew that no bird sounded so desolate or godforsaken as that cry, not even the loon on a lake or the curlew up on the moors.

Maggie rubbed the back of her neck and kept watching. Seconds later, an ambulance pulled up. Then another police car. Then paramedics. The ambulance attendants left the front door open, and Maggie could see them kneeling by someone in the hall. Someone covered with a fawn blanket. They lifted the figure onto a wheeled stretcher and pushed her down the path to the ambulance, back doors open and waiting. It all happened so quickly that Maggie couldn't see clearly who it was, but she thought she glimpsed Lucy's jet-black hair spread out against a white pillow.

So it was as she had thought. She gnawed at her thumbnail. Should she have done something sooner? She had certainly had her suspicions, but could she somehow have prevented this? What could she have done?

Next to arrive looked like a plainclothes police officer. He was soon followed by five or six men who put on disposable white overalls before they went inside the house. Someone also put up white and blue tape across the front gate and blocked off a long stretch of the pavement, including the nearest bus-stop, and the entire side of the road number thirty-five stood on, reducing The Hill to one lane of traffic in order to make room for police vehicles and ambulances.

Maggie wondered what was going on. Surely they wouldn't go to all this trouble unless it was something really serious? Was Lucy dead? Had Terry finally killed her? Perhaps that was it; that would make them pay attention.

As daylight grew, the scene became even stranger. More police cars arrived, and another ambulance. As the attendants wheeled a second stretcher out, the first morning bus went down The Hill and obscured Maggie's view. She could see the passengers turn their heads, the ones on her side of the road standing up to get a look at what was happening, but she couldn't see who lay on the stretcher. Only that two policemen got in after it.

Next, a hunched figure shrouded in a blanket stumbled down the path, supported on each side by uniformed policemen. At first Maggie had no idea who it was. A woman, she thought, from her general outline and the cut of her dark hair. Then she thought she glimpsed the dark blue uniform. *The policewoman.* Breath caught in her throat. What could have happened to change her so much so fast?

By now there was far more activity than Maggie had ever thought the scene of a domestic argument could engender. At least half a dozen police cars had arrived, some of them unmarked. A wiry man with close-cropped dark hair got out of a blue Renault and walked into the house as if he owned the place. Another man who went in looked like a doctor. At least, he carried a black bag and had that self-important air about him. People up and down The Hill were going to work now, driving their cars out of their garages or waiting for the bus at the temporary bus-stop someone from the depot had put up. Little knots of them gathered by the house, watching, but the police came over and moved them on.

Maggie looked at her watch. Half past six. She had been kneeling at the window for two and a half hours, yet she felt as if she had been watching a quick succession of events, as if it had been done by time-lapse photography. When she got to her feet she heard her knees crack, and the broadloom carpet had made deep red criss-cross marks on her skin.

There was far less activity outside the house now, just the police guards and the detectives coming and going, standing on the pavement to smoke, shake their heads and talk in low voices. The group of haphazardly parked cars outside Lucy's house were causing traffic back-ups.

Weary and confused, Maggie threw on jeans and a T-shirt and went downstairs to make a cup of tea and some toast. As she filled the kettle, she noticed that her hand was shaking. They would want to talk to her, no doubt about that. And when they did, what would she tell them?

2

Acting Detective Superintendent Alan Banks – 'acting' because his immediate boss, Detective Superintendent Gristhorpe, had shattered his ankle while working on his drystone wall and would be off work for at least a couple of months – signed the first officer's log at the gate, took a deep breath and walked into thirty-five The Hill shortly after six o'clock that morning. Householders: Lucy Payne, aged twenty-two, loans officer at the local NatWest up near the shopping precinct, and her husband, Terence Payne, aged twenty-eight, schoolteacher at Silverhill Comprehensive. No kids. No criminal record. To all intents and purposes, an idyllic, successful young couple. Married just one year.

All the lights were on in the house, and the SOCOs were already at work, dressed – as Banks was – in the obligatory white sterile overalls, overshoes, gloves and hoods. They looked like some sort of phantom house-cleaning crew, Banks thought: dusting, vacuuming, scraping up samples, packaging, labelling.

Banks paused a moment in the hall to get the feel of the place. It seemed an ordinary enough middle-class home. The ribbed coral-pink wallpaper looked new. Carpeted stairs to the right led up to the bedrooms. If anything, the place smelled a bit *too much* of lemon air-freshener. The only thing that seemed out of place was the rust-coloured stain on the cream hall carpet. *Lucy Payne*, currently under observation by both doctors and police in Leeds General Infirmary, just down the corridor from where her husband, Terence Payne, was fighting for his life. Banks hadn't a lot of sympathy to spare for him; PC Dennis Morrisey had lost his struggle for life far more quickly.

And there was a dead girl in the cellar, too.

Most of this information Banks had got from Detective Chief Inspector Ken Blackstone over his mobile on the way to Leeds, the rest from talking to the paramedics and the ambulance crew outside. The first phone call to his Gratly cottage, the one that woke him from the shallow, troubled and restless sleep that seemed to be his lot these days, had come shortly after half past four, and he had showered, thrown on some clothes and jumped in his car. A CD of Zelenka trios had helped him keep calm on the way and discouraged him from taking outrageous risks with his driving on the A1. All in all, the eighty-mile drive had taken him about an hour and a half and, if he hadn't had too many other things on his mind, during the first part of his journey he might have admired the coming of a beautiful May dawn over the Yorkshire Dales, rare enough so far that spring. As it was, he saw little but the road ahead and barely even heard the music. By the time he got to the Leeds Ring Road, the Monday morning rush-hour was already underway.

Circumventing the bloodstains and daffodils on the hall carpet, Banks walked to the back of the house. He noticed someone had been sick in the kitchen sink.

'One of the ambulance crew,' said the SOCO busy going through the drawers and cupboards. 'First time out, poor sod. We're lucky he made it back up here and didn't puke all over the scene.'

'Christ, what did he have for breakfast?'

'Looks like Thai red curry and chips to me.'

Banks took the stairs down to the cellar. On his way, he noted the door to the garage. Very handy if you wanted to bring someone into the house without being seen, someone you had abducted, perhaps drugged or knocked unconscious. Banks opened the door and had a quick glance at the car. It was a dark, four-door Vectra, with an 'S' registration. The last three letters were NGV. Not local. He made a note to have someone run it through the DVLA at Swansea.

He could hear voices down in the cellar, see cameras flashing. That would be Luke Selkirk, their hotshot crime scene photographer, fresh from his army-sponsored training course up at Catterick Camp, where he had been learning how to photograph scenes of terrorist bombings. Not that his special skill would be needed today, but it was good to know you were working with a highly trained professional, one of the best.

The stone steps were worn in places; the walls were whitewashed brick. Someone had put more white and blue tape across the open door at the bottom. An inner crime scene. Nobody would get beyond that until Banks, Luke, the doctor and the SOCOs had done their jobs.

Banks paused at the threshold and sniffed. The smell was bad: decomposition, mould, incense, and the sweet, metallic whiff of fresh blood. He ducked under the tape and walked inside and the horror of the scene hit him with such force that he staggered back a couple of inches.

It wasn't that he hadn't seen worse; he had. Much worse: the disembowelled Soho prostitute, Dawn Whadden; a decapitated petty thief called William Grant; the half-eaten body parts of a young barmaid called Colleen Dickens; bodies shredded by shotgun blasts and slit open by knives. He remembered all their names. But that wasn't the point, he had come to learn over the years. It wasn't a matter of blood and guts, of intestines poking out of the stomach, of missing limbs or of deep gashes flapping open in an obscene parody of mouths. That wasn't what really got you when it came right down to it. That was just the outward aspect. You could, if you tried hard, convince yourself that a crime scene like this one was a movie set or a theatre during rehearsals, and that the bodies were merely props, the blood fake.

No, what got to him most of all was the *pity* of it all, the deep empathy he had come to feel with the victims of crimes he investigated. And he hadn't become more callous, more inured to it all over the years as many did, and as he had once thought he would. Each new one was like a raw wound reopening. Especially something like this. He could keep it all in check, keep the bile down in his rumbling gut and do his job, but it ate away at him from the inside like acid and kept him awake at night. Pain and fear and despair permeated these walls like the factory grime that had crusted the old city buildings. Only this kind of horror couldn't be sandblasted away.

Seven people in the cramped cellar, five of them alive and two dead; this was going to be a logistical and forensic nightmare.

Someone had turned an overhead light on, just a bare bulb, but candles still flickered all over the place. From the doorway Banks could see the doctor bent over the pale body on the mattress. A girl. The only outward signs of violence were a few cuts and bruises, a bloody nose and a length of yellow plastic clothes-line around her neck. She lay spread-eagled on the soiled mattress, her hands tied with the same yellow plastic line to metal pegs set into the concrete floor. Blood from PC Morrisey's severed artery had sprayed across her ankles and shins. Some flies had managed to get in the cellar, and three of them were buzzing around the blood clotted under her nose. There seemed to be some sort of rash or blistering around her mouth. Her face was pale and bluish in death, the rest of her body white under the bulb's glare.

What made it all so much worse were the large mirrors on the ceiling and two of the walls that multiplied the scene like a funfair trick.

'Who turned the overhead light on?' Banks asked.

'Ambulance men,' said Luke Selkirk. 'They were first on the scene after PCs Taylor and Morrisey.'

'Okay, we'll leave it on for the time being, get a better idea of what we're dealing with. But I want the original scene photographed, too, later. Just the candlelight.'

Luke nodded. 'By the way, this is Faye McTavish, my new assistant.' Faye was a slight, pale, waif-like woman, early twenties perhaps, a stud through her nostril and almost no hips at all. The heavy old Pentax she had slung around her neck looked too big for her to hold steady, but she managed it well enough.

'Pleased to meet you, Faye,' said Banks, shaking hands. 'Only wish it could be in better circumstances.'

'Me, too.'

Banks turned to the body on the mattress.

He knew who she was: Kimberley Myers, aged fifteen, missing since Friday night, when she had failed to return from a school dance only a quarter of a mile from her home. She had been a pretty girl, with the characteristic long blonde hair and slim, athletic figure of all the victims. Now her dead eyes stared up at the mirror on the ceiling as if looking for answers to her suffering.

Dried semen glistened on her pubic hair. And blood. Semen and blood, the old, old story. Why was it always the pretty young girls these monsters took? Banks asked himself for the hundredth time. Oh, he knew all the pat answers, he knew that women and children made easier victims because they were physically weaker, more easily cowed and subdued by male strength, just as he knew that prostitutes and runaways made easy victims, too, because they were less likely to be missed than someone from a nice home, like Kimberley. But it was much more than that. There was always a deep, dark sexual aspect to these sorts of things, and to be the right kind of object for whoever had done this, the victim needed not only to be weaker, but needed breasts and a vagina, too, available for her tormentor's pleasure and ultimate desecration. And perhaps some aura of youth and innocence. It was despoliation of innocence. Men killed other men for many reasons, by the thousands in wartime, but in crimes like this, the victim always had to be a woman.

The first officer on the scene had had the foresight to mark out a narrow pathway on the floor with tape, so that people wouldn't walk all over the place and destroy evidence, but after what had happened with PCs Morrisey and Taylor, it was probably too late for that anyway.

PC Dennis Morrisey lay curled on his side in a pool of blood on the concrete floor. His blood had also sprayed over part of the wall and one of the mirrors, rivalling in its pattern anything Jackson Pollock had ever painted. The rest of the whitewashed walls were covered with either pornographic images ripped from magazines, or childish, obscene stick figures of men with enormous phalluses, like the Cerne Giant, drawn in coloured chalk. Mixed in with these were a number of crudely drawn occult symbols and grinning skulls. There was another pool of blood by the wall next to the door, and a long dark smear on the whitewash. *Terence Payne.*

Luke Selkirk's camera flashed and snapped Banks out of his trance-like state. Faye was wielding her camcorder now. The other man in the room turned and spoke for the first time: Detective Chief Inspector Ken Blackstone of the West Yorkshire Police, looking immaculate as ever, even in his protective clothing. Grey hair curled over his ears, and his wire-rimmed glasses magnified his sharp eyes.

'Alan,' he said, in a voice like a sigh. 'Like a fucking abattoir, isn't it?'

'A fine start to the week. When did you get here?'

'Four forty-four.'

Blackstone lived out Lawnswood way, and it wouldn't have taken him more than half an hour to get to The Hill, if that. Banks, heading the North Yorkshire team, was glad that Blackstone was running West Yorkshire's part of their joint operation, dubbed the 'Chameleon' squad because the killer, thus far, had managed to adapt, blend into the night and go unnoticed. Often, working together involved ego problems and incompatible personalities, but Banks and Blackstone had known each other for eight or nine years and had always worked well together. They got on socially, too, with a mutual fondness for pubs, Indian food and female jazz singers.

'Have you talked to the paramedics?' Banks asked.

'Yes,' said Blackstone. 'They said they checked the girl for signs of life and found none, so they left her undisturbed. PC Morrisey was dead, too. Terence Payne was handcuffed to the pipe over there. His head was badly beaten, but he was still breathing, so they carted him off to hospital sharpish. There's been some contamination of the scene – mostly to the position of Morrisey's body – but it's minimal, given the unusual circumstances.'

'Trouble is, Ken, we've got two crime scenes overlapping

here – maybe three if you count what happened to Payne.' He paused. 'Four, if you count Lucy Payne upstairs. That'll cause problems. Where's Stefan?' Detective Sergeant Stefan Nowak was their Crime Scene Co-ordinator, new to the Western Division HQ in Eastvale, and brought into the team by Banks, who had been quickly impressed by his abilities. Banks didn't envy Stefan his job right now.

'Around somewhere,' said Blackstone. 'Last time I saw him, he was heading upstairs.'

'Anything more you can tell me, Ken?'

'Not much, really. That'll have to wait until we can talk to PC Taylor in more detail.'

'When might that be?'

'Later today. The paramedics took her off. She's being treated for shock.'

'I'm not bloody surprised. Have they—'

'Yes. They've bagged her clothes and the police surgeon's been to the hospital to do the necessary.'

Which meant taking fingernail scrapings and swabs from her hands, among other things. One thing it was easy to forget – and a thing everyone might *want* to forget – was that, for the moment, probationary PC Janet Taylor wasn't a hero; she was a suspect in a case of excessive use of force. Very nasty indeed.

'How does it look to you, Ken?' Banks asked. 'Gut feeling.'

'As if they surprised Payne down here, cornered him. He came at them fast and somehow struck PC Morrisey with that there.' He pointed to a bloodstained machete on the floor by the wall. 'You can see Morrisey's been slashed two or three times. PC Taylor must have had time enough to get her baton out and use it on Payne. She did the right thing,

Alan. He must have been coming at her like a bloody maniac. She had to defend herself. Self-defence.'

'Not for us to decide,' said Banks. 'What's the damage to Payne?'

'Fractured skull. Multiple fractures.'

'Shame. Still, if he dies, it might save the courts a bit of money and a lot of grief in the long run. What about his wife?'

'Way it looks is he hit her with a vase on the stairs and she fell down them. Mild concussion, a bit of bruising. Other than that, there's no serious damage. She's lucky it wasn't heavy crystal or she might have been in the same boat as her husband. Anyway, she's still out and they're keeping an eye on her, but she'll be fine. DC Hodgkins is at the hospital now.'

Banks looked around the room again, with its flickering candles, mirrors and obscene cartoons. He noticed shards of glass on the mattress near the body and realized when he saw his own image in one of them that they were from a broken mirror. *Seven years' bad luck.* Hendrix's 'Roomful of Mirrors' would never sound quite the same again.

The doctor looked up from his examination for the first time since Banks had entered the cellar, got up off his knees and walked over to them. 'Dr Ian Mackenzie, Home Office pathologist,' he said, holding his hand out to Banks, who shook it.

Dr Mackenzie was a heavily built man with a full head of brown hair, parted and combed, a fleshy nose and a gap between his upper front teeth. Always a sign of luck, that, Banks remembered his mother once telling him. Maybe it would counteract the broken mirror. 'What can you tell us?' Banks asked.

'The presence of petechial haemorrhages, bruising of the

throat and cyanosis all indicate death by strangulation, most likely ligature strangulation by that yellow clothes-line around her throat, but I won't be able to tell you for certain until after the post mortem.'

'Any evidence of sexual activity?'

'Some vaginal and anal tearing, what looks like semen stains. But you can see that for yourself. Again, I'll be able to tell you more later.'

'Time of death?'

'Recent. Very recent. There's hardly any hypostasis yet, rigor hasn't started, and she's still warm.'

'How long?'

'Two or three hours, at an estimate.'

Banks looked at his watch. Sometime after three then, not long before the domestic dispute that drove the woman over the road to dial 999. Banks cursed. If the call had come in just a short while earlier, maybe only minutes or an hour, then they might have saved Kimberley. On the other hand, the timing was interesting for the questions it raised about the reasons for the dispute. 'What about that rash around her mouth? Chloroform?'

'At a guess. Probably used in abducting her, maybe even for keeping her sedated, though there are much more pleasant ways.'

Banks glanced at Kimberley's body. 'I don't think our man was overly concerned about being pleasant, do you, Doctor? Is chloroform easily available?'

'Pretty much. It's used as a solvent.'

'But it's not the cause of death?'

'I wouldn't say so, no. Can't be absolutely certain until after the post mortem, of course, but if it is the cause, we'd expect to find more severe blistering in the oesophagus, and there would also be noticeable liver damage.'

'When can you get to her?'

'Barring a motorway pile-up, I should be able to schedule the post mortems to start this afternoon,' Dr Mackenzie said. 'We're pretty busy as it is, but . . . well there are priorities.' He looked at Kimberley, then at PC Morrisey. 'He died of blood loss, by the looks of it. Severed both his carotid artery and jugular vein. Very nasty, but quick. Apparently his partner did what she could, but it was too late. Tell her she shouldn't blame herself. Hadn't a chance.'

'Thanks, Doctor,' said Banks. 'Appreciate it. If you could do the PM on Kimberley first . . .'

'Of course.'

Dr Mackenzie left to make arrangements, and Luke Selkirk and Faye McTavish continued to take photographs and video. Banks and Blackstone stood in silence taking in the scene. There wasn't much more to see, but what there was wouldn't vanish quickly from their memories.

'Where does that door over there lead to?' Banks pointed to a door in the wall beside the mattress.

'Don't know,' said Blackstone. 'Haven't had a chance to look yet.'

'Let's have a butcher's, then.'

Banks walked over and tried the handle. It wasn't locked. Slowly, he opened the heavy wooden door to another, smaller room, this one with a dirt floor. The smell was much worse in there. He felt for a light switch but couldn't locate one. He sent Blackstone to get a torch and tried to make out what he could in the overspill of light from the main cellar.

As his eyes adjusted to the darkness in the room, Banks thought he could see little clumps of mushrooms growing here and there from the earth.

Then he realized.

'Oh, Christ,' he said, slumping back against the wall. The

nearest clump wasn't mushrooms at all, it was a cluster of human toes poking through the dirt.

•

After a quick breakfast and an interview with two police detectives about her 999 call, Maggie felt the urge to go for a walk. There wasn't much chance of getting any work done for a while anyway, what with all the excitement over the road, though she knew she would try later. Right now, she was restless and needed to blow the cobwebs out. The detectives had stuck mostly to factual questions, and she hadn't told them anything about Lucy, but she sensed that one of them, at least, didn't seem satisfied with her answers. They would be back.

She still didn't know what the hell was going on. The policemen who talked to her had given away nothing, of course, had not even told her how Lucy was, and the local news on the radio was hardly illuminating, either. All they could say at this stage was that a member of the public and a police officer had been injured earlier that morning. And that took second place to the ongoing story about the local girl, Kimberley Myers.

As she walked down her front steps past the fuchsias, which would soon be flowering and drooping their heavy purple-pink bells over the path, Maggie saw the activity at number thirty-five was increasing, and neighbours were stood in little groups on the pavement, which had now been roped off from the road.

Several men wearing white overalls and carrying shovels, sieves and buckets got out of a van and hurried down the garden path.

'Oh, look,' called out one of the neighbours. 'He's got his bucket and spade. Must be off to Blackpool.'

Nobody laughed. Like Maggie, everyone was coming to realize that something very nasty indeed had happened at thirty-five The Hill. About ten yards away, across from the narrow, walled lane that separated it from number thirty-five, was a row of shops: pizza takeaway, hairdresser, mini-mart, newsagent, fish and chips, and several uniformed officers stood arguing with the shopkeepers. They probably wanted to open up, Maggie guessed.

Plainclothes police officers sat on the front wall, talking and smoking. Radios crackled. The area had fast begun to resemble the site of a natural disaster, as if a train had crashed or an earthquake had struck. Maggie remembered seeing the aftermath of the 1994 earthquake in Los Angeles, when she went there once with Bill before they were married: a flattened apartment building, three storeys reduced in seconds to two; fissures in the roads; part of the freeway collapsed. Though there was no visible damage here, it *felt* the same, had the same shell-shocked aura. Even though they didn't know what had happened yet, people were stunned, were counting the cost; there was a pall of apprehension over the community and a deep sense of terror at what destructive power the hand of God might have unleashed. They knew that something momentous had occurred on their doorsteps. Already, Maggie sensed, life in the neighbourhood would never be the same again.

Maggie turned left and walked down The Hill, under the railway bridge. At the bottom was a small artificial pond in the midst of the housing estates and business parks. It wasn't much, but it was better than nothing. At least she could sit on a bench by the water and feed the ducks, watch the people walking their dogs.

It was safe, too – an important consideration in this part of the city, where old, large houses, such as the one Maggie was staying in, rubbed shoulders with the newer, rougher council estates. Burglary was rife, and murder not unknown, but down by the pond, the double-deckers ran by on the main road just a few yards away, and enough ordinary people came to walk their dogs that Maggie never felt isolated or threatened. Attacks occurred in broad daylight, she knew, but she still felt close enough to safety down there.

It was a warm, pleasant morning. The sun was out, but the brisk breeze made a light jacket necessary. Occasionally, a high cloud drifted over the sun, blocking the light for a second or two and casting shadows on the water's surface.

There was something very soothing about feeding ducks, Maggie thought. Almost trance-like. Not for the ducks, of course, who seemed to have no concept of what sharing meant. You tossed the bread, they scooted towards it, quacked and fought. As Maggie crumbled the stale bread between her fingers and tossed it onto the water, she recalled her first meeting with Lucy Payne just a couple of months ago.

She had been in town shopping for art supplies that day – a remarkably warm day for March – then she'd been to Borders on Briggate to buy some books, and afterwards she found herself wandering through the Victoria Quarter down towards Kirkgate Market, when she bumped into Lucy coming the other way. They had seen one another before in the street and at the local shops, and they had always said hello. Partly through inclination and partly through her shyness – getting out and meeting people never having been one of her strong points – Maggie had no friends in her new world, apart from Claire Toth, her neighbour's schoolgirl daughter, who seemed to have adopted her. Lucy Payne, she soon found out, was a kindred spirit.

Perhaps because they were both out of their natural

habitat, like compatriots meeting in a foreign land, they stopped and spoke to one another. Lucy said it was her day off work and she was doing a bit of shopping. Maggie suggested a cup of tea or coffee at the Harvey Nichols outdoor café, and Lucy said she'd love to. So they sat, rested their feet and their parcels on the ground. Lucy noticed the names on the bags Maggie was carrying – including Harvey Nichols – and said something about not having the nerve to go inside such a posh place. Her own packages, it soon became clear, were from British Home Stores and C&A. Maggie had come across this reluctance in northern people before, had heard all the stories about how you'd never get the typical Leeds anorak and flat-cap crowd into an upmarket store like Harvey Nichols, but it still surprised her to hear Lucy admit to this.

This was because Maggie thought Lucy was such a strikingly attractive and elegant woman, with her glossy black, raven's-wing hair tumbling down to the small of her back, and the kind of figure men buy magazines to look at pictures of. Lucy was tall and full-breasted, with a waist that curved in and hips that curved out in the right proportion, and the simple yellow dress she was wearing under a light jacket that day emphasized her figure without broadcasting it out loud, and it also drew attention to her shapely legs. She didn't wear much make-up; she didn't need to. Her pale complexion was smooth as a reflection in a mirror, her black eyebrows arched, cheekbones high in her oval face. Her eyes were black, with flint-like chips scattered around inside them that caught the light like quartz crystals as she looked around.

The waiter came over and Maggie asked Lucy if she would like a cappuccino. Lucy said she'd never had one before and wasn't quite sure what it was, but she would give it a try. Maggie asked for two cappuccinos. When Lucy took her first sip, she got froth on her lips, which she dabbed at with a serviette.

'You can't take me anywhere,' she laughed.

'Don't be silly,' said Maggie.

'No, I mean it. That's what Terry always says.' She was very soft-spoken, the way Maggie had been for a while after she had left Bill.

Maggie was just about to say that Terry was a fool, but she held her tongue. Insulting Lucy's husband on their first meeting wouldn't be very polite at all. 'What do you think of the cappuccino?' she asked.

'It's very nice.' Lucy took another sip. 'Where are you from?' she asked. 'I'm not being too nosy, am I? It's just that your accent . . .'

'Not at all, no. I'm from Toronto. Canada.'

'No wonder you're so sophisticated. I've never been any further than the Lake District.'

Maggie laughed. Toronto, *sophisticated*?

'See,' said Lucy, pouting a little. 'You're laughing at me already.'

'No, no, I'm not,' Maggie said. 'Honestly, I'm not. It's just that . . . well, I suppose it's all a matter of perspective, isn't it?'

'What do you mean?'

'If I were to tell a New Yorker that Toronto is sophisticated, she'd laugh in my face. The best thing they can say about the place is that it's clean and safe.'

'Well, that's something to be proud of, isn't it? Leeds is neither.'

'It doesn't seem so bad to me.'

'Why did you leave? I mean why did you come here?'

Maggie frowned and fumbled for a cigarette. She still

cursed herself for a fool for starting smoking at thirty when she had managed to avoid the evil weed her whole life. Of course, she could blame it on the stress, though in the end it had only contributed more to that stress. She remembered the first time Bill had smelled smoke on her breath, that quick-as-a-flash change from concerned husband to *Monster Face*, as she had called it. But smoking wasn't that bad. Even her shrink said it wasn't such a terrible idea to have the occasional cigarette as a crutch for the time being. She could always stop later, when she felt better able to cope again.

'So why did you come here?' Lucy persisted. 'I don't mean to be nosy, but I'm interested. Was it a new job?'

'Not exactly. What I do, I can do anywhere.'

'What is it?'

'I'm a graphic artist. I illustrate books. Mostly children's books. At the moment I'm working on a new edition of Grimm's fairy tales.'

'Oh, that sounds fascinating,' said Lucy. 'I was terrible at art in school. I can't even draw a matchstick figure.' She laughed and put her hand over her mouth. 'So why *are* you here?'

Maggie struggled with herself for a moment, stalling. Then a strange thing happened to her, a sense of inner chains and straps loosening, giving her space and a feeling of floating. Sitting there in the Victoria Quarter smoking and drinking cappuccino with Lucy, she felt an immediate and unheralded surge of affection for this young woman she hardly knew. She wanted the two of them to be friends, could see them talking about their problems just like this, giving each other sympathy and advice, just as she had with Alicia back in Toronto. Lucy, with her gaucheness, her naïve charm, inspired a sort of emotional confidence in Maggie: this was someone, she felt, with whom she would be safe.

More than that; though Maggie may have been the more 'sophisticated' of the two, she sensed that they shared more than it appeared. The truth was difficult for her to admit to, but she felt the overwhelming need to tell someone other than her psychologist. And why not Lucy?

'What is it?' Lucy said. 'You look so sad.'

'Do I? Oh . . . Nothing. Look, my husband and I,' Maggie said, stumbling over the words as if her tongue were the size of a steak. 'I . . . er . . . we split up.' She felt her mouth drying up. Despite the loosened bonds, this was still far more difficult than she had thought it would be. She sipped some more coffee.

Lucy frowned. 'I'm sorry. But why move so far away? Lots of people split up and they don't move *countries.* Unless he's . . . oh, my God.' She gave her cheek a little slap. 'Lucy, I think you've just put your foot in it again.'

Maggie couldn't help allowing herself a thin smile, even though Lucy had touched upon the painful truth. 'It's all right,' she said. 'Yes, he was abusive. Yes, he hit me. You can say I'm running away. It's true. Certainly for a while I don't even want to be in the same country as him.' The vehemence of her words when they came out surprised even Maggie herself.

A strange look came into Lucy's eyes, then she glanced around again, as if looking for someone. Only anonymous shoppers drifted up and down the arcade under the stained-glass roof, packages in hands. Lucy touched Maggie's arm with her fingertips and Maggie felt a little shiver run through her, almost like a reflex action to pull away. A moment ago, she had thought it would do her good to admit to someone, to share what happened with another woman, but now she wasn't so sure. She felt too naked, too raw.

'I'm sorry if it embarrasses you,' Maggie said, with a hard edge to her voice. 'But you *did* ask.'

'Oh, no,' said Lucy, grasping Maggie's wrist. Her grip was surprisingly strong, her hands cool. 'Please don't think that. I asked for it. I always do. It's my fault. But it doesn't embarrass me. It's just . . . I don't know what to say. I mean . . . *you?* You seem so bright, so in control.'

'Yes, that's exactly what I thought: *How could something like that happen to someone like me?* Doesn't it only happen to other women: poor, less fortunate, uneducated, stupid women?'

'How long?' Lucy asked. 'I mean . . .?'

'How long did I let it go on before I left?'

'Yes.'

'Two years. And don't ask me how I could let it go on for so long, either. I don't know. I'm still working on that one with the shrink.'

'I see.' Lucy paused, taking it all in. 'What made you leave him in the end?'

Maggie paused a moment, then went on. 'One day he just went too far,' she said. 'He broke my jaw and two ribs, did some damage to my insides. It put me in hospital. While I was there I filed assault charges. And do you know what, as soon as I'd done it I wanted to drop them, but the police wouldn't let me.'

'What do you mean?'

'I don't know what it's like over here, but in Canada it's out of your hands if you bring assault charges. You can't just change your mind and drop them. Anyway, there was a restraining order against him. Nothing happened for a couple of weeks, then he came round to the house with flowers, wanting to talk.'

'What did you do?'

'I kept the chain on. I wouldn't let him in. He was in one of his contrite moods, pleading and wheedling, promising on his mother's grave. He'd done it before.'

'And broken his promise?'

'Every time. Anyway, then he became threatening and abusive. He started hammering at the door and calling me names. I called the police. They arrested him. He came back again, stalking me. Then a friend suggested I move away for a while, the further the better. I knew about the house on The Hill. Ruth and Charles Everett own the place. Do you know them?'

Lucy shook her head. 'I've seen them around. Not for a while, though.'

'No, you wouldn't have. Charles was offered a year's appointment at Columbia University in New York, starting in January. Ruth went with him.'

'How did you know them?'

'Ruth and I are in the same line of work. It's a fairly small world.'

'But why Leeds?'

Maggie smiled. 'Why not? First there was the house, just waiting for me, and my parents came from Yorkshire. I was born here. Rawdon. But we left when I was a little girl. Anyway, it seemed the ideal solution.'

'So you're living across the road in that big house all alone?'

'All alone.'

'I thought I hadn't seen anyone else coming and going.'

'To be honest, Lucy, you're pretty much the first person I've spoken to since I got here – apart from my shrink and my agent, that is. It's not that people aren't friendly. I've just been . . . well . . . stand-offish, I suppose. A bit distant.'

Lucy's hand still rested on Maggie's forearm, though she wasn't gripping at all now.

'That makes sense. After what you've been through. Did he follow you over here?'

'I don't think so. I don't think he knows where I am. I've had a few late-night hang-up calls, but I honestly don't know if they're from him. I don't think they are. All my friends back there swore they wouldn't tell him where I was, and he doesn't know Ruth and Charles. He had little interest in my career. I doubt that he knows I'm in England, though I wouldn't put it past him to find out.' Maggie needed to change the subject. She could hear the ringing in her ears, feel the arcade spinning and her jaw aching, the coloured-glass roof above her shifting like a kaleidoscope, her neck muscles stiffening, the way they always did when she thought about Bill for too long. *Psychosomatic*, the shrink said. As if that did her any good. She asked Lucy about herself.

'I don't really have any friends, either,' Lucy said. She stirred her spoon around the dregs of her cappuccino froth. 'I suppose I was always rather shy, even at school. I never know what to say to people.' Then she laughed. 'I don't have much of a life, either. Just work at the bank. Home. Taking care of Terry. We haven't been married a year yet. He doesn't like me to go out by myself. Even today, my day off. If he knew . . . That reminds me.' She looked at her watch and seemed to become agitated. 'Thank you very much for the coffee, Maggie. I really have to go. I have to get the bus back before school comes out. Terry's a teacher, you see.'

Now it was Maggie's turn to grasp Lucy's arm and stop her from leaving so abruptly. 'What is it, Lucy?' she asked.

Lucy just looked away.

'Lucy?'

'It's nothing. It's just what you were saying earlier.' She lowered her voice and looked around the arcade before going on. 'I know what you mean, but I can't talk about it now.'

'Terry hits you?'

'No. Not like . . . I mean . . . he's very strict. It's for my own good.' She looked Maggie in the eye. 'You don't know me. I'm a wayward child. Terry has to discipline me.'

Wayward, Maggie thought. *Discipline*. What strange and alarming words to use. 'He has to keep you in check? Control you?'

'Yes.' She stood up again. 'Look, I *must* go. It's been wonderful talking to you. I hope we can be friends.'

'I do, too,' said Maggie. 'We really *have* to talk again. There's help, you know.'

Lucy flashed her a wan smile and hurried off towards Vicar Lane.

After Lucy had gone, Maggie sat stunned, her hand shaking as she drained her cup. The milky foam was dry and cold against her lips.

Lucy a fellow victim? Maggie couldn't believe it. This strong, healthy, beautiful woman a victim, just like slight, weak, elfin Maggie? Surely it couldn't be possible? But hadn't she sensed something about Lucy? Some kinship, something they had in common. That must be it. That was what she hadn't wanted to talk to the police about that morning. She knew that she might have to, depending on how serious things were, but she wanted to put off the moment for as long as she could.

Thinking of Lucy, Maggie remembered the one thing she had learned about domestic abuse so far: it doesn't matter *who* you are. It can still happen to you. Alicia and all her other close friends back home had expressed their wonder at how such a bright, intelligent, successful, caring, *educated* woman like Maggie could fall victim to a wife-beater like Bill. She had seen the expressions on their faces, noticed their conversations hush and shift when she walked in the room. There must be something wrong with her, they were all saying. And that was what she had thought, too, still thought, to some extent. Because to all intents and purposes Bill, too, was bright, intelligent, caring, educated and successful. Until he got his Monster Face on, that is, but only Maggie saw him like that. And it was odd, she thought, that nobody had thought to ask why an intelligent, wealthy, successful lawyer like Bill should feel the need to hit a woman almost a foot shorter and at least eighty pounds lighter than he was.

Even when the police came that time he was hammering at her door, she could tell they were making excuses for him – he was driven out of his mind by his wife's unreasonable action in taking out a restraining order against him; he was just upset because his marriage had broken up and his wife wouldn't give him a chance to make it up. Excuses, excuses. Maggie was the *only one* who knew what he could be like. Every day she thanked God they had no kids.

Which was what she was thinking about as she drifted back to the present, to feeding the ducks on the pond. Lucy was a fellow sufferer, and now Terry had put her in hospital. Maggie felt responsible, as if she should have done something. Lord knows, she had tried. After Lucy's subsequent tale of physical and psychological abuse at the hands of her husband had unfolded during their many furtive meetings over coffee and biscuits, with Maggie sworn to absolute secrecy, she *should have done something*. But unlike most people, Maggie knew exactly what it was like. She knew

Lucy's position, knew that the best she could do was try to persuade her to seek professional help, to leave Terry. Which she did try to do.

But Lucy wouldn't leave him. She said she had nowhere to go and no one to go to. A common enough excuse. And it made perfect sense. Where *do* you go when you walk out on your life?

Maggie had been lucky she had the friends to rally around her and come up with at least a temporary solution. Most women in her position were not so fortunate. Lucy also said that her marriage was so new that she felt she had to give it a chance, give it some time; she couldn't just walk out on it; she wanted to work harder at it. Another common response from women in her position, Maggie knew, but all she could do was point out that it wasn't going to get any better, no matter what she did, that Terry wasn't going to change, and that it would come to her leaving sooner or later, so why not leave sooner and spare herself the beatings?

But no. Lucy wanted to stick it out a while longer. At least a little while. Terry was so nice afterwards, so good to her; he bought her presents, flowers, swore he would never do it again, that he would change. It made Maggie sick to hear all this – literally, as she once vomited the minute Lucy left the house – the same damn reasons and excuses she had given herself and those few close friends who knew about her situation all along.

But she listened. What else could she do? Lucy needed a friend, and for better or for worse, Maggie was it.

Now this.

Maggie tossed the last crumbs of bread into the pond. She aimed for the scruffiest, littlest, ugliest duckling of them all, the one way at the back that hadn't been able to get at the feast so far. It made no difference. The bread landed only inches from his beak, but before he could get to it, the others had paddled over in a ferocious pack and snapped it right from under his mouth.

•

Banks wanted to get a look at the whole interior of thirty-five The Hill before the SOCOs started ripping it apart. He didn't know what it would tell him, but he needed to get the feel of it.

Downstairs, in addition to the kitchen with its small dining area, there was only a living room, containing a three-piece suite, stereo system, television, video and a small bookcase. Though the room was decorated with the same feminine touch as the hallway – frilly lace curtains, coral pink wallpaper, thick pile carpet, cream ceiling with ornate cornices – the videos in the cabinet under the TV set reflected masculine tastes: action films, tape after tape of *The Simpsons*, a collection of horror and science fiction films, including the whole *Alien* and *Scream* series, along with some true classics such as *The Wicker Man*, the original *Cat People*, *Curse of the Demon* and a boxed set of David Cronenberg films. Banks poked around but could find no porn, nothing home-made. Maybe the SOCOs would have better luck when they took the house apart. The CDs were an odd mix. There was some classical, mostly Classic FM compilations and a best of Mozart set, but there were also some rap, heavy metal and country and western CDs, too. Eclectic tastes.

The books were also mixed: beauty manuals, *Reader's Digest* condensed specials, needlecraft techniques, romances, occult and true crime of the more graphic variety, tabloid-style biographies of famous serial killers and mass murderers. The room showed one or two signs of untidiness – yesterday's evening paper spread over the coffee table, a couple of videos left out of their boxes – but on the whole it was clean and neat. There were also a number of knick-knacks around the place, the sort of things that Banks's mother wouldn't have in the house because they made dusting more difficult – porcelain figures of fairy-tale characters and animals. In the dining area stood a large glass-fronted cabinet filled with Royal Doulton chinaware. Probably a wedding present, Banks guessed.

Upstairs were two bedrooms, the smaller one used as a home office, along with a toilet and bathroom. No shower, just sink and tub. Both toilet and bathroom were spotless, the porcelain shining bright, air heavy with the scent of lavender. Banks glanced around the plug-holes but saw only polished chrome, not a trace of blood or hair.

Their computer expert, David Preece, sat in the office clacking away at the computer keys. A large filing cabinet stood in the corner; it would have to be emptied, its contents transferred to the exhibits room at Millgarth.

'Anything yet, Dave?' Banks asked.

Preece pushed his glasses back up his nose and turned. 'Nothing much. Just a few pornographic Web sites bookmarked, chat rooms, that sort of thing. Nothing illegal yet, by the looks of it.'

'Keep at it.'

Banks walked into the master bedroom. The colour scheme seemed to continue the ocean theme, but instead of coral it was sea-blue. Azure? Cobalt? Cerulean? Annie Cabbot would know the exact shade, her father being an artist, but to Banks it was just blue, like the walls of his living room, though a shade or two darker. The queen-size bed was covered by a fluffed-up black duvet. The bedroom suite was assemble-it-yourself blond Scandinavian pine. Another television set stood on a stand at the bottom of the bed. The cabinet held a collection of soft-core porn, if the labels were to believed, but still nothing illegal or home-made, no kiddie stuff or animals. So the Paynes were into porn videos. So what? So were more than half the households in the country, Banks was willing to bet. But more than half the households in the country didn't go around abducting and killing young girls. Some lucky young DC was going to have to sit down and watch the lot from start to finish to verify that the contents matched the titles.

Banks poked around in the wardrobe: suits, shirts, dresses, shoes – mostly women's – nothing he wouldn't have expected. They would all have to be bagged by the SOCOs and examined in minute detail.

There were plenty of knick-knacks in the bedroom, too: Limoges cases, musical jewellery boxes, lacquered, hand-painted boxes. The room took its musky rose and aniseed scent, Banks noticed, from a bowl of pot-pourri on the laundry hamper under the window.

The bedroom faced The Hill, and when Banks parted the lace curtains and looked out of the window he could see the houses atop the rise over the street, half hidden by shrubs and trees. He could also see the activity below, on the street. He turned and looked around the room again, finding it somehow depressing in its absolute sterility. It could have been ordered from a colour supplement and assembled yesterday. The whole house – except for the cellar, of course – had that feel to it: pretty, contemporary, the sort of place where the up-and-coming young middle-class couple about town *should* be living. So ordinary, but empty.

With a sigh, he went back downstairs.

3

Kelly Diane Matthews went missing during the New Year's Eve party in Roundhay Park, Leeds. She was seventeen years old, five feet three inches tall and weighed just seven stone. She lived in Alwoodley and attended Allerton High School. Kelly had two younger sisters: Ashley, aged nine, and Nicola, aged thirteen.

The call to the local police station came in at 9.11 a.m. on the first of January. Mr and Mrs Matthews were worried that their daughter hadn't come home that night. They had been to a party themselves, and hadn't arrived back until almost three a.m. They noticed that Kelly wasn't home yet but weren't too worried because she was with friends, and they knew that these new year parties were likely to go on until the wee hours. They also knew she had plenty of money for a taxi.

They were both tired and a little tipsy after their own party, they told the police, so they went straight to bed. When they awoke the following morning and found that Kelly's bed had still not been slept in, they became worried. She had never done anything like this before. First they telephoned the parents of the two girlfriends she had gone with, reliable in their estimation. Both Kelly's friends, Alex Kirk and Jessica Bradley, had arrived home shortly after two in the morning. Then Adrian Matthews rang the police. PC Rearden, who took the call, picked up on the genuine concern in Mr Matthews's voice and sent an officer around immediately.

Kelly's parents said they last saw her around seven o'clock on the thirty-first of December, when she went to meet her friends. She was wearing blue jeans, white trainers, a thick cable-knit jumper and a three-quarter length suede jacket.

When questioned later, Kelly's friends said that the group had become separated during the fireworks display, but nobody was too concerned. After all, there were thousands of people about, buses were running late and taxis were touting for business.

Adrian and Gillian Matthews weren't rich, but they were comfortably off. Adrian oversaw the computer systems of a large retail operation and Gillian was assistant manager of a city centre building society. They owned a Georgian-style semi-detached house not far from Eccup Reservoir, in an area of the city closer to parks, golf courses and the countryside than to factories, warehouses and grim terraces of back-to-backs.

According to her friends and teachers, Kelly was a bright, personable, responsible girl, who got consistently high marks and was certain to land in the university of her choice, at the moment Cambridge, where she intended to read law. Kelly was also her school's champion sprinter. She had beautiful gold-blonde hair, which she wore long, and she liked clothes, dancing, pop music and sports. She was also fond of classical music and quite an accomplished pianist.

It soon became clear to the investigating officer that Kelly Matthews was a most unlikely teenage runaway, and he instituted a search of the park. When, three days later, the search parties had found nothing, they called it off. In the meantime, police had also interviewed hundreds of revellers, some of whom said they thought they'd seen her with a man and others with a woman. Taxi drivers and bus drivers were also questioned, to no avail.

A week after Kelly disappeared, her shoulder-bag was found in some bushes near the park; in it were her keys, a diary, cosmetics, a hairbrush and a purse containing over thirty-five pounds and some loose change.

Her diary yielded no clues. The last entry, on the thirty-first of December, was a brief list of new year's resolutions:

1. Help Mum more around the house.
2. Practise piano every day.
3. Be nicer to my little sisters.

Banks stripped off his protective clothing, leaned against his car out in the street and lit a cigarette. It was going to be a hot, sunny day, he could tell, only the occasional high cloud scudding across the blue sky on a light breeze, and he would be spending most of it indoors, either at the scene or at Millgarth. He ignored the people on the other side of the road, who stopped to stare, and shut his ears to the honking horns from the snarl of cars up The Hill, which had now been blocked off completely by the local traffic police. The press had arrived; Banks could see them straining at the barriers.

Banks had known it would come to this eventually, or to something very much like this, from the very first moment he had agreed to head the North Yorkshire half of the two-county task force into the series of disappearances: five young women in all, three from West Yorkshire and two from North Yorkshire. The West Yorkshire Assistant Chief Constable (Crime) was in overall charge, but he was at county headquarters in Wakefield, so Banks and Blackstone rarely saw him. They reported directly to the head of CID, Area Commander Philip Hartnell, at Millgarth in Leeds, who was the official Senior Investigating Officer, but who left them to get on with the job. The main incident room was also at Millgarth.

Under Banks and Blackstone came several detective inspectors, a whole host of detective constables and sergeants, culled from both west and north county forces, skilled civilian employees, Crime Scene Co-ordinator DS Stefan Nowak and, acting as Consultant Psychologist, Dr Jenny Fuller, who had studied offender profiling in America with the National Center for the Analysis of Violent Crime at the FBI academy in Quantico, Virginia, and didn't look a bit like Jodie Foster. Jenny had also studied with Paul Britton in Leicester and was recognized as one of the rising stars in the relatively new field of psychology combined with police work.

Banks had worked with Jenny Fuller on his very first case in Eastvale, and they had become close friends. Almost more, but something always seemed to get in their way.

It was probably for the best, Banks told himself, though he often couldn't convince himself of that when he looked at her. Jenny had such lips as you rarely saw on anyone but a pouting French sex symbol, her figure tapered and bulged in all the right places, and her clothes, usually expensive silky clothes, mostly in green and russet, just seemed to flow over her. It was that 'liquefaction of her clothes', that the poet Herrick wrote about, the dirty old devil. Banks had come across Herrick in a poetry anthology he was working his way through, having felt a disturbing ignorance in such matters for years.

Lines like Herrick's stuck with him, as did the one about 'sweet disorder in the dress', which made him think of DS

Annie Cabbot, for some reason. Annie wasn't so obviously beautiful in the way Jenny was, not as voluptuous, not the kind to draw wolf whistles on the street, but she had a deep, quiet sort of beauty that appealed very much to Banks. Unfortunately, because of his new and onerous responsibilities, he hadn't seen much of Annie lately and had found himself, because of the case, spending more and more time with Jenny, realizing that the old feelings, that odd and immediate spark between them, had never gone away. Nothing had *happened* as such, but it had been touch and go on occasion.

Annie was also consumed with her work. She had found a detective inspector's position open in Western Division's Complaints and Discipline Department, and had taken it because it was the first opportunity that came up. It wasn't ideal, and it certainly didn't win her any popularity contests, but it was a necessary step in the ladder she had set out to climb, and Banks had encouraged her to go for it.

DC Karen Hodgkins edged her little grey Nissan through the opening the police made in the barrier for her and broke off Banks's chain of thought. She got out and walked over. Karen had proved an energetic and ambitious worker throughout the whole investigation, and Banks fancied she would go far if she developed a flair for police politics. She reminded him a bit of Susan Gay, his old DC, now a DS in Cirencester, but she had fewer sharp edges and seemed more sure of herself.

'What's the situation?' Banks asked her.

'Not much change, sir. Lucy Payne's under sedation. The doctor says we won't be able to talk to her until tomorrow.'

'Have Lucy and her husband been fingerprinted?'

'Yes, sir.'

'What about her clothes?' Banks had suggested that they

take the clothes Lucy Payne had been wearing for forensic examination. After all, she wouldn't be needing them in hospital.

'They should be at the lab by now, sir.'

'Good. What was she wearing?'

'Nightie and a dressing gown.'

'What about Terence Payne? How's he doing?'

'Hanging on. But they say that even if he does recover he might be . . . you know . . . a vegetable . . . there might be serious brain damage. They've found skull fragments stuck in his brain. It seems . . . well . . .'

'Go on.'

'The doctor's saying that it seems the PC who subdued him used a bit more than reasonable force. He was very angry.'

'Was he, indeed?' *Christ.* Banks could see a court case looming if Payne survived with brain damage. Best let AC Hartnell worry about it; that was what ACs were put on this earth for, after all. 'How's PC Taylor coping?'

'She's at home, sir. A friend's with her. Female PC from Killingbeck.'

'Okay, Karen, I want you to act as hospital liaison for the time being. Any change in the status of the patients – either of them – and I want to know immediately. That's your responsibility, okay?'

'Yes, sir.'

'And we're going to need a family liaison officer.' He gestured towards the house. 'Kimberley's parents need to be told, before they hear it on the news. We also need to arrange for them to identify the body.'

'I'll do it, sir.'

'Good of you to offer, Karen, but you've got your hands full already. And it's a thankless task.'

Karen Hodgkins headed back to her car. If truth be told, Banks didn't think Karen had the right bedside manner for a family liaison officer. He could picture the scene, the parents' disbelief, their outpouring of grief, Karen's embarrassment and brusqueness. No. He would send roly-poly Jonesy. DC Jones might be a slob, but he had sympathy and concern leaking out of every pore. He should have been a vicar. One of the problems with drawing a team from such a wide radius, Banks thought, was that you could never get to know the individual officers well enough. Which didn't help when it came to handing out assignments. You needed the right person for the right job in police work, and one wrong decision could screw up an investigation.

Banks just wasn't used to running such a huge team, and the problems of co-ordination had given him more than one headache. In fact, the whole matter of responsibility was weighing very heavily on his mind. He didn't feel competent to deal with it all, to keep so many balls up in the air at once. He had already made more than one minor mistake and mishandled a few situations with personnel. So much so that he was beginning to think his people skills were especially low. It was easier working with a small team – Annie, Winsome Jackman, Sergeant Hatchley – where he could keep track of every little detail in his mind. This was more like the kind of work he had done on the Met down in London, only there he had been a mere constable or sergeant, given the orders rather than giving them. Even as an inspector down there, towards the end, he had never had to deal with *this* level of responsibility.

Banks had just lit his second cigarette when another car came through the barrier and Dr Jenny Fuller jumped out, struggling with a briefcase and an overstuffed leather shoulder-bag, hurrying as usual, as if she were late for an important meeting. Her tousled red mane cascaded over her shoulders and her eyes were the green of grass after a summer shower. The freckles, crow's feet and slightly crooked nose that she always complained ruined her looks only made her appear more attractive and more human.

'Morning, Jenny,' Banks greeted her. 'Stefan's waiting inside. You ready?'

'What's that? Yorkshire foreplay?'

'No. That's "Are you awake?" '

Jenny forced a smile. 'Glad to see you're on form, even at this ungodly hour.'

Banks looked at his watch. 'Jenny, I've been up since half past four. It's nearly eight now.'

'My point exactly,' she said. 'Ungodly.' She looked towards the house. Apprehension flitted across her features. 'It's bad, isn't it?'

'Very.'

'Coming in with me?'

'No. I've seen enough. Besides, I'd better go and put AC Hartnell in the picture or he'll have my guts for garters.'

Jenny took a deep breath and seemed to gird herself. 'Right,' she said. 'Lay on, Macduff. I'm ready.'

And she walked in.

•

Area Commander Philip Hartnell's office was, as befitted his rank, large. It was also quite bare. AC Hartnell didn't believe in making himself at home there. This, the place seemed to shout, is an *office* and an office only. There was a carpet, of course – an area commander merited a carpet – one filing cabinet, a bookcase full of technical and procedural manuals and on his desk, beside the virgin blotter, a sleek black laptop computer and a single buff file folder.

That was it. No family photographs, nothing but a map of the city on the wall and a view of the open-air market and the bus station from his window, the tower of Leeds Parish Church poking up beyond the railway embankment.

'Alan, sit down,' he greeted Banks. 'Tea? Coffee?'

Banks ran his hand over his scalp. 'Wouldn't mind a black coffee, if it's no trouble.'

'Not at all.'

Hartnell phoned for coffee and leaned back in his chair. It squeaked when he moved. 'Must get this bloody thing oiled,' he said.

Hartnell was about ten years younger than Banks, which put him in his late thirties. He had benefited from the accelerated promotion scheme, which was meant to give bright young lads like him a chance at command before they became doddering old farts. Banks hadn't been on such a track; he had worked his way up the old way, the hard way, and like many others who had done so, he tended to be suspicious of the fast-trackers, who had learned everything but the nitty-gritty down-and-dirty of policing.

The odd thing was that Banks liked Phil Hartnell. He had an easy-going manner, was an intelligent and caring copper, and let the men under his command get on with their jobs. Banks had had regular meetings with him over the course of the Chameleon investigation and, while Hartnell had made a few suggestions, some of them useful, he had never once tried to interfere and question Banks's judgement. In appearance, good looking, tall and with the tapered upper body of a casual weight-lifter, Hartnell was also reputed to be a bit of a ladies' man, still unmarried and tipped to remain that way for a while yet, thank you very much.

'Tell me what we're in for,' he said to Banks.

'A shit storm, if you ask me.' Banks told him about what they had found so far in the cellar at number thirty-five The Hill, and the condition of the three survivors. Hartnell listened, the tip of his finger touched to his lips.

'There's not much doubt he's our man, then? The Chameleon?'

'Not much.'

'That's good, then. At least that's something we can congratulate ourselves on. We've got a serial killer off the streets.'

'It wasn't down to us. Just pure luck the Paynes happened to have a domestic disagreement and a neighbour heard and called the police.'

Hartnell stretched his arms out behind his head. A twinkle came to his grey-blue eyes. 'You know, Alan, the amount of shit we get poured on us when luck goes against us, or when we seem to be making no progress at all no matter how many man-hours we put in, I'd say we're entitled to claim a victory this time and maybe even crow a little about it. It's all in the spin.'

'If you say so.'

'I do, Alan. I do.'

Their coffee arrived and both took a moment to sip. It tasted wonderful to Banks, who hadn't got his usual three or four cups down his gullet that morning.

'But we do have a potentially serious problem, don't we?' Hartnell went on.

Banks nodded. 'PC Taylor.'

'Indeed.' He tapped the file folder. 'Probationary PC Janet Taylor.' He looked away a moment, towards the window. 'I knew Dennis Morrisey, by the way. Not well, but I knew him. Solid sort of bloke. Seems he's been around for years. We'll miss him.'

'What about PC Taylor?'

'Can't say I know her. Have the proper procedures been followed?'

'Yes.'

'No statement yet?'

'No.'

'Okay.' Hartnell got up and stared out of the window for a few moments, his back to Banks. When he spoke again he didn't turn round. 'You know as well as I do, Alan, that protocol demands the Police Complaints Authority brings in an investigator from a neighbouring force to deal with a problem like this. There mustn't even be the slightest hint of a cover-up, of special treatment. Naturally, I'd like nothing better than to deal with it myself. Dennis was one of ours, after all. As is PC Taylor. But it's not on the cards.' He turned and walked back over to his chair. 'Can you imagine what a field day the press will have, especially if Payne dies? Heroic PC brings down serial killer and ends up being charged with using excessive force. Even if it's excusable homicide, it's still the dog's breakfast as far as we're concerned. And what with the Hadleigh case before the court right now . . .'

'True enough.' Banks, like every other policeman, had had to deal more than once with the outrage of men and women who had seriously hurt or killed criminals in defence of their families and property and then found themselves under arrest for assault, or worse, murder. At the moment, the country was awaiting the jury's verdict on a farmer called John Hadleigh, who had used his shotgun on an unarmed sixteen-year-old burglar, killing the lad. Hadleigh lived on a remote farm in Devon, and his house had been broken into once before, just over a year ago, at which time he had been beaten as well as robbed. The young burglar had a record as long as your arm, but that didn't matter. What mattered most was that the pattern of shotgun pellets covered part of the side and the back, indicating that the boy had been turning to run away as the gun was fired. An unopened flick-knife was found in his pocket. The case had been generating sensational headlines for a couple of weeks and would be with the jury in a matter of days.

An investigation didn't mean that PC Janet Taylor would lose her job or go to jail. Fortunately there were higher authorities, such as judges and chief constables, who had to make decisions on such matters as those, but there was no denying that it could have a negative effect on her police career.

'Well, it's *my* problem,' said Hartnell, rubbing his forehead. 'But it's a decision that has to be made very quickly. Naturally, as I said, I'd like to keep it with us, but I can't do that.' He paused and looked at Banks. 'On the other hand, PC Taylor is West Yorkshire and it seems to me that *North* Yorkshire might reasonably be considered a neighbouring force.'

'True,' said Banks, beginning to get that sinking feeling.

'That would help keep it as close as we can, don't you think?'

'I suppose so,' said Banks.

'As a matter of fact, ACC McLaughlin's an old friend of mine. It might be worthwhile my having a word. How's your Complaints and Discipline Department? Know anyone up there?'

Banks swallowed. It didn't matter what he said. If the matter went to Western Division's Complaints and Discipline, the burden would almost certainly land in Annie Cabbot's lap. It was a small department – Annie was the only detective inspector – and Banks happened to know that her boss, Detective Superintendent Chambers, was a lazy sod with a particular dislike of female detectives making their way up the ranks. Annie was the new kid on the block and she was also a woman. Not a hope of her getting out of this one. Banks could almost see the bastard rubbing his hands for glee when the order came down.

'Don't you think it might seem just a bit *too* close to home?' he said. 'Maybe Greater Manchester or Lincolnshire would be better.'

'Not at all,' said Hartnell. 'This way we get to be seen to do the right thing while still keeping it pretty close to us. Surely you must know someone in the department, someone who'll realize it's in his best interests to keep you informed?'

'Detective Superintendent Chambers is in charge,' said Banks. 'I'm sure he'll find someone suitable to assign.'

Hartnell smiled. 'Well, I'll have a word with Ron McLaughlin this morning and we'll see where it gets us, shall we?'

'Fine,' said Banks, thinking *she'll kill me, she'll kill me*, even though it wasn't his fault.

•

Jenny Fuller noted with distaste the poster as she went through the cellar door, with DS Stefan Nowak right behind her, then she put her feelings aside and viewed it dispassionately, as a piece of evidence. Which it was. It marked the keeper of the portal to the dark underworld where Terence Payne could immerse himself in what he loved most in life: domination, sexual power, murder. Once he had got beyond this obscene guardian, the rules that normally governed human behaviour no longer applied.

Jenny and Stefan were alone in the cellar now. Alone with

the dead. She felt like a voyeur. She also felt like a fraud, as if nothing she could say or do would be of any use. She almost felt like holding Stefan's hand. Almost.

Behind her, Stefan switched off the overhead light and made Jenny jump. 'Sorry. It wasn't on at first,' he explained. 'One of the ambulance crew turned it on so they could see what they were dealing with, and it just got left on.'

Jenny's heartbeat returned to normal. She could smell incense, along with other odours she had no desire to dwell on. So this was his working environment: *hallowed, church-like*. Several of the candles had burned down by now, and some of them were guttering out, but a dozen or more still flickered, multiplied into hundreds by the arrangement of mirrors. Without the overhead light, Jenny could hardly make out the dead policeman's body on the floor, which was probably a blessing, and the candlelight softened the impact of the girl's body, gave her skin such a reddish-gold hue that Jenny could have almost believed Kimberley alive were it not for the preternatural stillness of her body and the way her eyes stared up into the overhead mirror.

Nobody home.

Mirrors. No matter where Jenny looked, she could see several reflections of herself, Stefan and the girl on the mattress muted in the flickering candlelight. *He likes to watch himself at work*, she thought. Could that be the only way he feels *real*? Watching himself doing it?

'Where's the camcorder?' she asked.

'Luke Selkirk's—'

'No, I don't mean the police camera, I mean his, Payne's.'

'We haven't found a camcorder. Why?'

'Look at the set-up, Stefan. This is a man who likes to

look at himself in action. It'd surprise me a great deal if he didn't keep some record of his actions, wouldn't it you?'

'Now you come to mention it, yes,' said Stefan.

'That sort of thing's par for the course in sex killings. Some sort of memento. A trophy. And usually also some sort of visual aid to help him relive the experience before the next one.'

'We'll know more when the team's finished with the house.'

Jenny followed the phosphorescent tape that marked the path to the anteroom, where the bodies lay, still untouched, awaiting the SOCOs. In the light of Stefan's torch, her glance took in the toes sticking through the earth, and what looked like a finger, perhaps, a nose, a kneecap. His menagerie of death. Planted trophies. His *garden*.

Stefan shifted beside her, and she realized she had been holding his arm, digging in hard with her nails. They went back into the candlelit cellar. As Jenny stood over Kimberley noting the wounds, small cuts and scratch marks, she couldn't help herself and found she was weeping, silent tears damp against her cheek. She wiped her eyes with the back of one hand, hoping Stefan didn't notice. If he did, he was gentleman enough not to say anything.

Suddenly, she wanted to leave. It wasn't just the sight of Kimberley Myers on the mattress, or the smell of incense and blood, the images flickering in mirrors and candlelight, but the combination of all these elements made her feel claustrophobic and nauseated standing there observing this horror with Stefan. She didn't want to be here with him, or with any man, feeling the things she did. It felt obscene. And it was an obscenity performed by man upon woman.

Trying to conceal her trembling, she touched Stefan's

arm. 'I've seen enough down here for now,' she said. 'Let's go. I'd like to have a look around the rest of the house.'

Stefan nodded and turned back to the stairs. Jenny had the damnedest sensation that he knew exactly what she was feeling. Bloody hell, she thought, the sixth sense she could do without right now. Life was complicated enough with the usual five at work.

She followed Stefan past the poster up the worn stone stairs.

•

'Annie. Got much on right now?'

'As a matter of fact, I'm wearing a mid-length navy blue skirt, red shoes and a white silk blouse. Do you want to know about my underwear?'

'Don't tempt me. I take it you're alone in the office?'

'All on my little lonesome.'

'Listen, Annie, I've got something to tell you. Warn you about, actually.' Banks was sitting in his car outside the Payne house talking on his mobile. The mortuary wagon had taken the bodies away, and Kimberley's stunned parents had identified her body. The SOCOs had located two more bodies so far in the anteroom, both of them in so advanced a state of decomposition that it was impossible to make visual identification. Dental records would have to be checked, DNA sampled and checked against the parents'. It would all take time. Another team was still combing through the house, boxing up papers, accounts, bills, receipts, snapshots, letters, anything and everything.

Banks listened to the silence after he had finished explaining the assignment he thought Annie would be getting in the near future. He had decided that the best way to deal with it was to try to put it in a positive light, convince

Annie that she would be good for the job and that it was the right job for her. He didn't imagine he would have much success, but it was worth a try. He counted the beats. *One. Two. Three. Four.* Then the explosion came.

'He's doing *what*? Is this some kind of sick joke, Alan?'

'No joke.'

'Because if it is you can knock it off right now. It's not funny.'

'It's no joke, Annie. I'm serious. And if you think about it for a minute you'll see what a great idea it is.'

'If I thought about it for the rest of my life it still wouldn't seem like a great idea. How dare he . . . You know there's no way I can come out of this looking good. If I prove a case against her, then every cop and every member of the public hates my guts. If I don't prove a case, the press screams cover-up.'

'No, they won't. Have you any idea what sort of monster Terence Payne is? They'll be whooping for joy that populist justice is served at last.'

'Some of them, perhaps. But not the ones I read. Or you, for that matter.'

'Annie, it's not going to bury you. It'll be in the hands of the CPS well before that stage. You're not judge, jury and executioner, you know. You're just a humble investigator trying to get the facts right. How can that harm you?'

'Was it you who suggested me in the first place? Did you give Hartnell my name, tell him I'd be the best one for the job? I can't believe you'd do this to me, Alan. I thought you liked me.'

'I do. And I haven't done anything. AC Hartnell came up with it all by himself. And you and I both know what'll happen as soon as it gets into Detective Superintendent Chambers's hands.'

'Well at least we're agreed on that. You know, the fat bastard's been chomping at the bit all week because he hasn't been able to find anything *really* messy for me to do. For crying out loud, Alan, couldn't you *do* something?'

'Like what?'

'Suggest he hand it over to Lancashire or Derbyshire. *Anything.*'

'I tried, but his mind was made up. He knows ACC McLaughlin. Besides, this way he thinks I can hold onto some degree of control over the investigation.'

'Well he can bloody well think again about that.'

'Annie, you can do some good here. For yourself, for the public interest.'

'Don't try appealing to my better nature. I haven't got one.'

'Why are you resisting so strongly?'

'Because it's a crap job and you know it. At least give me the courtesy of not trying to soft soap me.'

Banks sighed. 'I'm only the advance warning. Don't kill the messenger.'

'That's what messengers are for. You're saying I've no choice?'

'There's always a choice.'

'Yeah, the right one and the wrong one. Don't worry, I won't make a fuss. But you'd better be right about the consequences.'

'Trust me. I'm right.'

'And you'll respect me in the morning. Sure.'

'Look, about the morning. I'm going back to Gratly tonight. I'll be late, but maybe you could come over, or I could drop by your place on my way?'

'What for? A quickie?'

'Doesn't have to be that quick. Way I'm sleeping these days it could take all night.'

'No way. I need my beauty sleep. Remember, I've got to be up bright and early in the morning to drive to Leeds. Bye.'

Banks held the silent mobile to his ear for a few moments, then put it back in his pocket. Christ, he thought, you handled that one really well, Alan, didn't you? *People skills.*

4

Samantha Jane Foster, eighteen years old, five foot five and seven stone three, was a first-year English student at the University of Bradford. Her parents lived in Leighton Buzzard, where Julian Foster was a chartered accountant and Teresa Foster a local GP. Samantha had one older brother, Alistair, unemployed, and a younger sister, Chloe, still at school.

On the evening of the twenty-sixth of February, Samantha attended a poetry reading in a pub near the university campus and left alone for her bedsit at about 11.15 p.m. She lived just off Great Horton Road, about a quarter of a mile away. When she didn't turn up for her weekend job in the city centre Waterstone's bookshop, one of her co-workers, Penelope Hall, became worried and called at the bedsit during her lunch-break. Samantha was reliable, she later told the police, and if she wasn't going to come into work because of illness, she would always ring. This time she hadn't. Worried that Samantha might be seriously ill, Penelope managed to persuade the landlord to open the bedsit door. Nobody home.

There was a very good chance that the Bradford Police might not have taken Samantha Foster's disappearance seriously – at least not so quickly – had it not been for the shoulder-bag that a conscientious student had found in the street and handed in after midnight the previous evening. It contained a poetry anthology called *New Blood*;

a slim volume of poetry signed 'To Samantha, between whose silky thighs I would love to rest my head and give silver tongue' and dated by the poet, Michael Stringer, who had read in the pub the previous evening; a spiral notebook full of poetic jottings, observations, reflections on life and literature, including what looked to the desk officer like descriptions of hallucinogenic states and out-of-body experiences; a half-smoked packet of Benson and Hedges; a red packet of Rizla cigarette papers and a small plastic bag of marijuana, less than a quarter of an ounce; a green disposable cigarette lighter; three loose tampons; a set of keys; a personal CD player with a Tracy Chapman CD inside it; a little bag of cosmetics; and a purse containing fifteen pounds in cash, a credit card, student union card, shop receipts for books and CDs, and various other sundry items.

Given the two occurrences – an abandoned shoulder-bag and a missing girl – especially as the young DC who was given the assignment remembered something similar had happened in Roundhay Park, Leeds, on New Year's Eve – the inquiry began that very morning with calls to Samantha's parents and close friends, none of whom had seen her or heard of any change in her plans or normal routine.

For a brief time, Michael Stringer, the poet who had been reading his work at the pub became a suspect, given the inscription he had written in his book of poems for her, but a number of witnesses said he carried on drinking in the city centre and had to be helped back to his hotel at around three-thirty in the morning. The hotel staff assured the police that he hadn't seen the light of day again until teatime the following day.

Inquiries around the university turned up one possible witness, who thought she saw Samantha talking to someone through a car window. At least the girl had long blonde hair and was wearing the same clothes Samantha was when she left the pub – jeans, black calf-high boots and a long, flapping overcoat. The car was dark in colour, and the witness remembered the three last letters on the number plate because they formed her own initials: Kathryn Wendy Thurlow. She said she had no reason to believe that there was any problem at the time, so she crossed over to her street and carried on to her own flat.

The last two letters of a car number-plate indicate the origin of its registration, and WT signifies Leeds. The DVLA at Swansea were able to supply a list of over a thousand possibles – as Kathryn hadn't been able to narrow the search down to make or even colour – and the owners were interviewed by Bradford CID. Nothing came of it.

All the searches and interviews that followed turned up nothing more about Samantha Foster's disappearance, and rumblings were starting on the police tom-toms. Two disappearances, almost two months and about fifteen miles apart were enough to set off a few alarm bells but not a full-blown panic.

Samantha didn't have many friends, but those she did have were loyal and devoted to her: in particular, Angela Firth, Ryan Conner and Abha Gupta, who were all devastated by Samantha's disappearance. According to them, Samantha was a very serious sort of girl, given to long reflective silences and gnomic utterances, with no time for small talk, sports and television. She had a level head on her shoulders, though, they insisted, and everyone said she wasn't the type to go off with a stranger on a whim, no matter how much she talked about the importance of experiencing life to the full.

When the police suggested that Samantha might have wandered off under the influence of drugs, her friends said it was unlikely. Yes, they admitted, she liked to smoke a joint occasionally – she said it helped her with her writing – but she didn't do any harder drugs; she also didn't drink much and couldn't have had more than two or three glasses of wine the entire evening.

She didn't have a boyfriend at the moment and didn't seem interested in acquiring one. No, she wasn't gay, but she had spoken of exploring sexual experiences with other women. Samantha might appear unconventional in some ways, Angela explained, but she had a lot more common sense than people sometimes imagined on first impressions; she was just not frivolous, and she was interested in a lot of things other people laughed at or dismissed.

According to her professors, Samantha was an eccentric student with a tendency to spend too much of her time reading outside the syllabus, but one of her tutors, who had published some verse himself, said that he had hopes she might make a fine poet one day if she could cultivate a little more self-discipline in her technique.

Samantha's interests, so Abha Gupta said, included art, poetry, nature, Eastern religions, psychic experiences and death.

•

Banks and Ken Blackstone drove out to the village of Tong, to the Greyhound, a low-beamed rustic pub with Toby jugs all around the plate racks, about fifteen minutes from the crime scene. It was going on for two o'clock, and neither of them had eaten yet that day. Banks hadn't eaten much in the past two days, in fact, ever since he had heard of the fifth missing teenager in the wee hours of Saturday morning.

Over the past two months, he had sometimes thought his head would explode under pressure of the sheer amount of detail he carried around in it. He would awaken in the early hours of the morning, at three or four o'clock, and the thoughts would spin around his mind and prevent him from going back to sleep. Instead, he would get up and brew a pot of tea and sit at the pine kitchen table in his pyjamas making notes for the day ahead as the sun came up and spilled its liquid honey light through the high window or rain lashed against the panes.

These were lonely, quiet hours, and while he had got used to, even embraced, solitude, sometimes he missed his previous life with Sandra and the kids in the Eastvale semi. But Sandra was gone, about to marry Sean, and the kids had grown up and were living their own lives. Tracy was in her second year at the University of Leeds, and Brian was touring the country with his rock band, going from strength to strength after the great reviews their first independently produced CD had received. Banks had neglected them both, he realized, over the past couple of months, especially his daughter.

They ordered pints of Tetley's bitter and the last two portions of lamb stew and rice at the bar. It was warm enough to sit outside at one of the tables next to the cricket field. A local team was out practising, and the comforting sound of leather on willow punctuated their conversation.

Banks lit a cigarette and told Blackstone about AC Hartnell giving North Yorkshire the PC Taylor investigation, and his certainty that it would go to Annie.

'She'll love that,' said Blackstone.

'She's already made her feelings quite clear.'

'You've told her?'

'I tried to put a positive spin on it to make her feel better, but . . . it sort of backfired.'

Blackstone smiled. 'Are you two still an item?'

'I think so, sort of, but half the time I'm not sure, to be honest. She's very . . . elusive.'

'Ah, the sweet mystery of woman.'

'Something like that.'

'Maybe you're expecting too much of her?'

'What do you mean?'

'I don't know. Sometimes when a man loses his wife he starts looking for a new one in the first woman who shows any interest in him.'

'Marriage is the last thing on my mind, Ken.'

'If you say so.'

'I do. I haven't bloody time, for a start.'

'Talking about marriage, how do you think the wife, Lucy Payne, fits in?' Blackstone asked.

'I don't know.'

'She must have known. I mean she *was* living with the bloke.'

'Maybe. But you saw the way things were set up back there. Payne could have sneaked anyone in through the garage and taken them straight into the cellar. If he kept the place locked and barred, nobody need have known. It was pretty well soundproofed.'

'I'm sorry, but you can't convince me that a woman lives with a killer who does what Payne did and she hasn't a clue,' said Blackstone. 'What does he do? Get up after dinner and tell her he's just off down to the basement to play with a teenage girl he's abducted?'

'He doesn't have to tell her anything.'

'But she *must* be involved. Even if she wasn't his accomplice, she must at least have *suspected* something.'

Someone gave the cricket ball a hell of a whack and a cheer went up from the field.

Banks stubbed out his cigarette. 'You're probably right.

Anyway, if there's anything at all to connect Lucy Payne to what happened in the cellar, we'll find out. For the moment, she's not going anywhere. Unless we find out differently, we'd better remember that she's a victim first and foremost.'

The SOCO teams might be spending weeks at the scene, Banks knew, and very soon number thirty-five The Hill would resemble a house undergoing major structural renovations. They would be taking in metal detectors, laser lights, infra-red, UV, high-powered vacuums and pneumatic drills; they would be collecting fingerprints, flaked skin, fibres, dried secretions, hairs, paint chips, Visa bills, letters, books and personal papers; they would strip the carpets and punch holes in the walls, break up the cellar and garage floors and dig up the gardens. And everything they gathered, perhaps more than a thousand exhibits, would have to be tagged, entered in HOLMES and stored in the evidence room at Millgarth.

Their meals arrived and they tucked right in, waving away the occasional fly. The stew was hearty and mildly spiced. After a few mouthfuls, Blackstone shook his head slowly. 'Funny Payne's got no form, don't you think? Most of them have *something* odd in their background. Waving their willies at schoolkids, or a touch of sexual assault.'

'More than his job's worth. Maybe he's just been lucky.'

Blackstone paused. 'Or we've not been doing our jobs properly. Remember that series of rapes out Seacroft way two years or so back?'

'The "Seacroft Rapist"? Yes, I remember reading about it.'

'We never did catch him, you know.'

'You think it might have been Payne?'

'Possible, isn't it? The rapes stopped, then girls started disappearing.'

'DNA?'

'Semen samples. The Seacroft Rapist was an excretor and he didn't bother wearing a condom.'

'Then check them against Payne's. And check where he was living at the time.'

'Oh, we will, we will. By the way,' Blackstone went on, 'one of the DCs who interviewed Maggie Forrest, the woman who phoned in the domestic, got the impression that she wasn't telling him everything.'

'Oh. What did he say?'

'That she seemed deliberately vague, holding back. She admitted she knew the Paynes but said she knew nothing about them. Anyway, he didn't think she was telling the complete truth as far as her relationship with Lucy Payne went. He thinks they're a lot closer than she would admit.'

'I'll talk to her later,' said Banks, glancing at his watch. He looked around at the blue sky, the white and pink blossoms drifting from the trees, the men in white on the cricket pitch. 'Christ, Ken, I could sit here all afternoon,' he said, 'but I'd better get back to the house to check on developments.'

•

As she had feared, Maggie was unable to concentrate on her work for the rest of that day and alternated between watching the police activity out of her bedroom window and listening to the local radio for news reports. What came through was scant enough until the area commander in charge of the case gave a press conference, in which he confirmed that they had found the body of Kimberley Myers, and that it appeared she had been strangled. More than that, he wouldn't say, except that the case was under investigation, forensic experts were on the scene and more details would be available shortly. He stressed that the investigation was not yet over and appealed for anyone who had seen Kimberley after eleven o'clock on Friday evening to come forward.

When the knock on her door and the familiar call, 'It's all right, it's only me', came after half past three, Maggie felt relieved. For some reason, she had been worried about Claire. She knew that she went to the same school as Kimberley Myers and that Terence Payne was a teacher there. She hadn't seen Claire since Kimberley's disappearance but imagined she must have been frantic with worry. The two were about the same age and surely must know one another.

Claire Toth often called on her way home from school, as she lived two doors down, both her parents worked, and her mother didn't get home until about half past four. Maggie also suspected that Ruth and Charles had suggested Claire's visits as a sneaky way of keeping an eye on her. Curious about the newcomer, Claire had first just dropped in to say hello. Then, intrigued by Maggie's accent and her work, she had become a regular visitor. Maggie didn't mind. Claire was a good kid, and a breath of fresh air, though she talked a mile a minute and Maggie often felt exhausted when she left.

'I don't think I've ever felt so awful,' Claire said, dropping her backpack on the living-room floor and plonking herself down on the sofa, legs akimbo. This was odd, for a start, as she usually headed straight for the kitchen, to the milk and chocolate chip cookies Maggie fed her. She pulled back her long tresses and tucked them behind her ears. She was wearing her school uniform, green blazer and skirt, white blouse and grey socks, which had slipped down around her ankles. She had a couple of spots on her chin, Maggie noticed: bad diet or time of the month.

'You know?'

'It was all around school by lunchtime.'

'Do you know Mr Payne?'

'He's my biology teacher. And he lives across the street from us. How *could* he? The pervert. When I think of what must have been going through his mind while he was teaching us about reproductive systems and dissecting frogs and all that stuff . . . ugh.' She gave a shudder.

'Claire, we don't know that he did anything yet. All we know is that Mr and Mrs Payne had a fight and that he hit her.'

'But they've found Kim's body, haven't they? And there wouldn't be all those policemen over the road if all he'd done was hit his wife, would there?'

If all he'd done was hit his wife. Maggie was often amazed at the casual acceptance of domestic violence, even by a girl-child such as Claire. True enough, she didn't mean it the way it sounded and would be horrified if she knew the details of Maggie's life back in Toronto, but still, the language came so easily. *Hit his wife.* Minor. Not important.

'You're quite right,' she said. 'It *is* more than that. But we don't know that Mr Payne was responsible for what happened to Kimberley. Someone else might have done it.'

'No. It's him. He's the one. He killed all those girls. He killed Kim.'

Claire started crying and Maggie felt awkward. She found a box of tissues and went to sit next to her on the sofa. Claire buried her head in Maggie's shoulder and sobbed, her thin veneer of teenage cool stripped away in a second. 'I'm sorry,' she said, sniffling. 'I don't usually act like such a baby.'

'What is it?' Maggie asked, still stroking her hair. 'What is it, Claire? You can tell me. You were her friend, weren't you? Kim's?'

Claire's lip trembled. 'I just feel so awful.'

'I can understand that.'

'But you don't. You can't! Don't you see?'

'See what?'

'That it was my fault. It was my fault that Kim got killed. I should have been with her on Friday. *I should have been with her!*' And when Claire buried her face in Maggie's shoulder again, there came a loud knock at the door.

•

DI Annie Cabbot sat at her desk still cursing Banks under her breath and wishing she had never accepted the appointment to Complaints and Discipline, even though it had been the only divisional opening available for her at the level of inspector after passing her boards. Of course, she could have stayed in CID as a detective sergeant, or gone back to uniform for a while as an inspector in Traffic, but she had decided that C & D would be a worthwhile temporary step up until a suitable position became available in CID, which Banks had assured her wouldn't be long. The Western Division was still undergoing some structural reorganization, part of which involved staffing levels, and for the moment CID was taking a back seat to more visible on-the-street and in-your-face policing. But their day would come. This way, at least, she would gain experience at the rank of inspector.

The one good thing about the new appointment was her office. Western Division had taken over the building adjoining the old Tudor-fronted headquarters, part of the same structure, knocked through the walls and redone the interior. While Annie didn't have a large room to herself like Detective Superintendent Chambers, she did have a partitioned space in the general area, which gave her some degree of privacy and looked out over the market place, like Banks's office.

Beyond her frosted-glass compartment sat the two detective sergeants and three constables who, along with Annie and Chambers, made up the entire Western Division Complaints and Discipline department. After all, police corruption was hardly a hot issue around Eastvale, and about the most serious case she had worked on so far was that of a beat policeman accepting free toasted teacakes from the Golden Grill. It turned out that he had been going out with one of the waitresses there and she was finding the way to his heart. Another waitress had become jealous and reported the matter to Complaints and Discipline.

It probably wasn't fair to blame Banks, Annie thought, standing at the window and looking down on the busy square, and perhaps she was only doing so because of the vague dissatisfaction with their relationship that she was already feeling. She didn't know what it was, or why, only that she was beginning to feel a little uncomfortable with it. They hadn't seen one another that often because of the Chameleon case, of course, and Banks had sometimes been so tired that he'd fallen asleep even before . . . but it wasn't *that* that bothered her so much as the easy familiarity their relationship seemed to be attaining. When they were together, they were behaving more and more like an old married couple and Annie, for one, didn't want that. Ironic as it seemed, the comfort and familiarity were making her feel distinctly *uncomfortable*. All they needed was the slippers and the fireplace. Come to think of it, in Banks's cottage they even had those, too.

Annie's phone rang. It was Detective Superintendent Chambers summoning her to his office next door. She knocked and went in when he said 'Enter', the way he liked it. Chambers sat behind his messy desk, a big man with the waistcoat buttons of his pinstripe suit stretched tight across his chest and belly. She didn't know if his tie was covered with food stains or if it was supposed to look that way. He had the kind of face that seemed to be wearing a perpetual sneer, and small piggy eyes that Annie felt undress her as she walked in. His complexion resembled a slab of rare beef and his lips were fleshy, wet and red. Annie always half expected him to start drooling and slobbering as he spoke, but he hadn't done it yet. Not one drop of saliva had found its way onto his green blotter. He had a Home Counties accent, which he seemed to think made him posh.

'Ah, DI Cabbot. Please be seated.'

'Sir.'

Annie sat as comfortably as she could, careful to make certain that her skirt didn't ride too high over her thighs. If she'd known before she left for work that she was going to be summoned to see Chambers, she would have worn trousers.

'I've just been handed a most interesting assignment,' Chambers went on. 'Most interesting indeed. One that I think will be right up your alley, as they say.'

Annie had the advantage over him but didn't want to let it show. 'Assignment, sir?'

'Yes. It's about time you started pulling your weight around here, DI Cabbot. How long have you been with us now?'

'Two months.'

'And in that time you've accomplished . . .?'

'The case of Constable Chaplin and the toasted teacakes, sir. Scandal narrowly averted. A satisfactory resolution all around, if I might say so. . .'

Chambers reddened. 'Yes, well, this one might just take the edge off your attitude, Inspector.'

'Sir?' Annie raised her eyebrows. She couldn't stop herself baiting Chambers. He had the kind of arrogant, self-important bearing that cried out for pricking. She knew it could be bad for her career, but even with the rekindling of her ambition, Annie had sworn to herself that her career wasn't worth anything if it cost her her soul. Besides, she had an odd sort of faith that good coppers like Banks, Detective Superintendent Gristhorpe and ACC McLaughlin might have more say in her future than pillocks like Chambers who, everyone knew, was a lazy slob just waiting for retirement. Still, she hadn't been a lot more careful with Banks at first, either, and it was only her good fortune that he had been charmed and seduced by her insubordination rather than angered by it. Gristhorpe, poor man, was a saint, and she hardly ever saw Red Ron McLaughlin, so she didn't get a chance to piss him off.

'Yes,' Chambers went on, warming to his task, 'I think you'll find this one a bit different from toasted teacakes. This'll wipe the grin off your face.'

'Perhaps you'd care to tell me about it, sir?'

Chambers tossed a thin folder towards her. It slipped off the edge of the desk onto Annie's knees and then to the floor before she could catch it. She didn't want to bend over and pick it up so that Chambers could have a bird's eye view of her knickers, so she left it where it was. Chambers's eyes narrowed and they stared at one another for a few seconds, but finally he eased himself out of his chair and picked it up himself. The effort made his face red. He slammed the file down harder on the desk in front of her.

'Seems a probationary PC in West Yorkshire has overdone it a bit with her baton and they want us to look into it.

Trouble is, the chappie she overdid it with is suspected to be that Chameleon killer they've been after for a while, which, as I'm sure even you will realize, puts a different complexion on things.' He tapped the folder. 'The details, such as they are at the moment, are all in there. Do you think you can handle it?'

'No problem,' said Annie.

'On the contrary,' said Chambers. 'I think there'll be plenty of problems. It'll be what they call a high-profile case, and because of that my name will be on it. I'm sure you understand that we can't have a mere inspector still wet behind the ears running a case of this importance.'

'If that's the case,' said Annie, 'why don't you investigate it yourself?'

'Because I happen to be too busy at the moment,' said Chambers, with a twisted grin. 'Besides, why own a dog and bark yourself?'

'Absolutely. Why, indeed? Of course,' said Annie, who happened to know that Chambers couldn't investigate his way out of a paper bag. 'I understand completely.'

'I thought you would.' Chambers stroked one of his chins. 'And as my name's on it, I want no cock-ups. In fact, if any heads roll over this business, yours will be the first. Remember, I'm only a hair's breadth away from retirement, so the last thing on my mind is career advancement. You, on the other hand . . . Well, I'm sure you catch my drift.'

Annie nodded.

'You'll be reporting to me directly, of course,' Chambers went on. 'Daily reports required, except in the event of any major developments, in which case you're to report to me immediately. Understood?'

'I wouldn't have it any other way,' said Annie.

Chambers narrowed his eyes at her. 'One day that mouth of yours will get you into serious trouble, young lady.'

'So my father told me.'

Chambers grunted and shifted his weight in his chair. 'There's one more thing.'

'Yes?'

'I don't like the way this assignment was delivered to me. There's something fishy about it.'

'What do you mean, sir?'

'I don't know.' Chambers frowned. 'Acting Detective Superintendent Banks from CID is running our part of the Chameleon investigation, isn't he?'

Annie nodded.

'And if my memory serves me well, you used to work with him as a DS before coming over here, didn't you?'

Again, Annie nodded.

'Well, it might be nothing,' said Chambers, looking away from her, at a point high on the wall. 'Summat and nowt, as they say up here. But on the other hand . . .'

'Sir?'

'Keep an eye on him. Play your cards close to your chest.'

He looked at her chest as he spoke and Annie gave an involuntary shudder. She stood up and walked over to the door.

'And another thing, DI Cabbot.'

Annie turned. 'Sir?'

Chambers smirked. 'This Banks. Watch out for him. He's got the reputation for being a bit of a ladies' man, in case you don't know that already.'

Annie felt herself flush as she left the office.

•

Banks followed Maggie Forrest into the living room, with its dark wainscoting and brooding landscapes in heavy gilt frames on the walls. The room faced west, and the late-afternoon sun cast dancing shadows of twisted foliage on the far walls. It was not a feminine room, but more like the kind to which the men withdrew for port and cigars in BBC period dramas, and Banks sensed that Maggie was uncomfortable in it, though he wasn't quite certain what gave him that impression. Noticing a whiff of smoke in the air and a couple of cigarette ends in the ashtray, Banks lit up, offering Maggie a Silk Cut. She accepted. He looked at the schoolgirl on the sofa, head lowered, bare knees close together, one of them scabbed from a recent fall, thumb in her mouth.

'Aren't you going to introduce us?' he asked Maggie.

'Detective . . .?'

'Banks. Acting Detective Superintendent.'

'Detective Superintendent Banks, this is Claire Toth, a neighbour.'

'Pleased to meet you, Claire,' said Banks.

Claire looked up at him and mumbled hello, then she took a crumpled packet of ten Embassy Regal from her blazer pocket and joined the adult smokers. Banks knew this was no time for lectures on the dangers of smoking. Something was clearly wrong. He could see by her red eyes and the streaks on her face that she had been crying.

'I've missed something,' he said. 'Anyone care to fill me in?'

'Claire went to school with Kimberley Myers,' said Maggie. 'Naturally, she's upset.'

Claire grew edgy, her eyes flitting all over the place. She took short, nervous puffs on the cigarette, holding it affectedly, straight out with her first two fingers vertical, letting go as she puffed, then closing her fingers. She didn't seem to be inhaling, just doing it to look and act grown-up, Banks thought. Or perhaps even to *feel* grown up, because only God knew what turbulent feelings must be churning inside Claire right now. And it would only get worse. He remembered Tracy's reaction to the murder of an Eastvale girl, Deborah Harrison, just a few years ago. They hadn't even known each other well, had come from differing social backgrounds, but they were about the same age, and they had met and talked on several occasions. Banks had tried to protect Tracy from the truth for as long as he could, but in the end the best he could do was comfort her. She was lucky; she got over it in time. Some never do.

'Kim was my best friend,' Claire said. 'And I let her down.'

'What makes you think that?' Banks asked.

Claire flicked her eyes towards Maggie, as if seeking permission. Maggie nodded almost imperceptibly. She was an attractive woman, Banks noticed, not so much physically, with the slightly long nose and pointed chin, though he also admired her elfin looks and her trim, boyish figure, but it was the air of kindness and intelligence about her that struck him. He could see it in her eyes, and there was an artist's grace in the economy of her simplest movements, such as flicking ash from her cigarette, in her large hands with the long, tapered fingers.

'I should have been with her,' Claire said. 'But I wasn't.'

'Were you at the dance?' Banks asked.

Claire nodded and bit her lip.

'Did you see Kimberley there?'

'Kim. I always called her Kim.'

'All right: Kim. Did you see Kim there?'

'We went together. It's not far. Just up past the roundabout and along Town Street, near the rugby ground.'

'I know where you mean,' said Banks. 'Silverhill Comprehensive, right?'

'Yes.'

'So you went to the dance together.'

'Yes, we walked up there and . . . and . . .'

'Take your time,' said Banks, noticing that she was about to cry again.

Claire took a final puff at her cigarette, then stubbed it out. She didn't do a good job, and the ashes continued to smoulder. She sniffled. 'We were going to walk home together. I mean . . . people had said . . . you know . . . it was on the radio and television and my father told me . . . we had to be careful, stick together.'

Banks had been responsible for the warnings. There was a fine line between panic and caution, he knew, and while he wanted to avert the kind of widespread paranoia that the Yorkshire Ripper case had whipped up for years in the early eighties, he also wanted to make it clear that young women should be cautious after dark. But short of instituting a curfew, you can't force people to be careful.

'What happened, Claire? Did you lose sight of her?'

'No, it wasn't that. I mean, not really. You don't understand.'

'Help us to understand, Claire,' said Maggie, holding her hand. 'We want to. Help us.'

'I should have been with her.'

'Why weren't you?' Banks asked. 'Did you have an argument?'

Claire paused and looked away. 'It was a boy,' she said finally.

'Kim was with a boy?'

'No. *Me*. I was with a boy.' Tears streamed down her cheeks, but she pressed on. 'Nicky Gallagher. I'd fancied him for weeks and he asked me to dance. Then he said he wanted to walk me home. Kim wanted to leave just before eleven, she had a curfew, and normally I'd have gone with her, but Nicky . . . he wanted to stay for a slow dance . . . I thought there would be lots of people around . . . I . . .' Then she broke down in tears again and buried her head in Maggie's shoulder.

Banks took a deep breath. Claire's pain and guilt and grief were so real they broke over him in waves and made his breath catch in his chest. Maggie stroked her hair and muttered words of comfort, but still Claire let it all pour out. Finally, she came to the end of her tears and blew her nose in a tissue. 'I'm sorry,' she said. 'Really, I am. I'd give *anything* to live that night over again and do it differently. I *hate* Nicky Gallagher!'

'Claire,' said Banks, who was no stranger to guilt himself. 'It's not his fault. And it's certainly not yours.'

'I'm a selfish bitch. I had Nicky to walk me home. I thought he might kiss me. I *wanted* him to kiss me. See? I'm a slut, too.'

'Don't be silly,' said Maggie. 'The superintendent is right. It's not your fault.'

'But if I'd only—'

'*If. If. If*,' said Banks.

'But it's true! Kim had no one, so she had to walk home by herself and Mr Payne got her. I bet he did awful things to her before he killed her, didn't he? I've read about people like him.'

'Whatever happened that night,' said Banks, 'is not your fault.'

'Then whose fault is it?'

'Nobody's. Kim was in the wrong place at the wrong time. It could have been—' Banks stopped. Not a good idea. He hoped Claire hadn't picked up on the implication, but she had.

'Me? Yes, I know that. I wish it had been.'

'You don't mean that, Claire,' said Maggie.

'Yes, I do. Then I wouldn't have to live with it. It was because of me. Because she didn't want to be a gooseberry.' Claire started crying again.

Banks wondered if it *could* have been Claire. She was the right type: blonde and long-legged as so many young northern girls were. Was it as random as that? Or had Payne had his eyes on Kimberley Myers all along? Jenny might have some theories on that.

He tried to picture what had happened. Payne parked in his car, near the school, perhaps, knowing there was a dance on that night, knowing the one he'd had his eye on would be there. He couldn't count on her going home alone, of course, but nothing ventured, nothing gained. There was always a chance. A risk, of course, but it would have been worth it to him. His heart's desire. All the others were practice. This was the real thing, the one he had wanted right from the start, there at school under his very eyes, tormenting him, day after day.

Terence Payne would also have known, as Banks did, that Kimberley lived about two hundred yards further down The Hill than her friend Claire Toth, under the railway bridge, and that there was a dark, desolate stretch of road there, nothing but a wasteland on one side and a Wesleyan Chapel on the other, which would have been in darkness at that hour, Wesleyans not being noted for their wild late-night parties. When Banks had walked down there on Saturday afternoon, the day after Kimberley had disappeared, following the route she would have taken home from the dance, he had thought it would have made an ideal pick-up place.

Payne would have parked his car a little ahead of Kimberley and either jumped her or said hello, the familiar, *safe* Mr Payne from school, somehow manoeuvred her inside, then chloroformed her and taken her back through the garage to the cellar.

Perhaps, Banks realized now, Payne couldn't believe his luck when Kimberley started walking home alone. He would have expected her to be with her friend Claire, if not with others, and could only hope that the others would live closer to the school than Kimberley did and that she would end up alone for that final short but desolate stretch. But with her being alone right from the start, if he was careful and made sure that nobody could see, he could even have offered her a lift. She *trusted* him. Perhaps he had even, being the good, kind neighbour, given her a lift before.

'*Get in the van, Kimberley, you know it's not safe for a girl your age to be walking the streets alone at this hour. I'll take you home.*'

'*Yes, Mr Payne. Thank you very much, Mr Payne.*'

'*You're lucky I happened by.*'

'*Yes, sir.*'

'*Now, fasten your seatbelt.*'

'Superintendent?'

'I'm sorry,' said Banks, who had been lost in his imaginings.

'Is it all right if Claire goes home? Her mother should be back by now.'

Banks looked at the child. Her world had shattered into pieces around her. All weekend she must have been terrified that something like this had happened, dreading the moment when the shadow of her guilt was made substance, when her nightmares proved to be reality. There was no reason to keep her here. Let her go to her mother. He knew where she was if he needed to talk to her again. 'Just one more thing, Claire,' he said. 'Did you see Mr Payne at all on the evening of the dance?'

'No.'

'He wasn't at the dance?'

'No.'

'He wasn't parked outside the school?'

'Not that I saw.'

'Did you notice anyone at all hanging around?'

'No. But I wasn't really looking.'

'Did you see Mrs Payne at all?'

'*Mrs* Payne? No. Why?'

'All right, Claire. You can go home now.'

'Is there any more news of Lucy?' Maggie asked after Claire had left.

'She's comfortable. She'll be fine.'

'You wanted to see me?'

'Yes,' said Banks. 'Just a few loose ends from this morning's interview, that's all.'

'Oh?' Maggie fingered the neck of her T-shirt.

'Nothing important, I shouldn't think.'

'What is it?'

'One of the officers who interviewed you gave me the impression that he thought you weren't telling the full story about your relationship with Lucy Payne.'

Maggie raised her eyebrows. 'I see.'

'Would you describe the two of you as close friends?'

'Friends, yes, but close, no. I haven't known Lucy long.'

'When did you last see her?'

'Why? Do you think I'm in danger? You said Terry—'

'Not that sort of danger. The press. They can be very persistent, and I wouldn't want you telling them what you've just told me.'

'Yesterday. She dropped by in the afternoon.'

'What did you talk about?'

Maggie looked down at her hands on her lap. 'Nothing, really. You know, the weather, work, that sort of thing.'

Kimberley Myers was tied up naked in the cellar of the Payne house and Lucy had dropped by to talk about the weather. Either she really was innocent, or her evil went way beyond anything Banks had experienced before. 'Did she ever give you any cause to suspect that anything was wrong at home?' he asked.

Maggie paused. 'Not in the way you're suggesting. No.'

'What way am I suggesting?'

'I assume it's to do with the murder? With Kimberley's murder?'

Banks leaned back in his armchair and sighed. It had been a long day, and it was getting longer. Maggie wasn't a convincing liar. 'Ms Forrest,' he said, 'right now anything at all we can find out about life at number thirty-five The Hill would be useful to us. And I mean *anything*. I'm getting the same impression as my colleague, that you're keeping something back.'

'It's nothing relevant.'

'How the hell would you know!' Banks snapped at her. He was shocked by the way she flinched at his harsh tone, at the look of fear and submission that crossed her features and the way she wrapped her arms around herself and drew in. 'Ms Forrest . . . Maggie,' he said more softly. 'Look, I'm sorry, but I've had a bad day, and this is becoming very frustrating. If I had a penny for every time someone told me their information was irrelevant to my investigation I'd be a rich man. I know we all have secrets. I know there are some things we'd rather not talk about. But this is a murder investigation. Kimberley Myers is dead. PC Dennis Morrisey is dead. God knows how many more bodies we'll unearth there, and I have to sit here and listen to you tell me that you know Lucy Payne, that she may have shared certain feelings and information with you and that you don't think it's *relevant*. Come on, Maggie. Give me a break here.'

The silence seemed to go on for ages, until Maggie's small voice broke it. 'She was being abused. Lucy. He . . . her husband . . . he hit her.'

'Terence Payne abused his wife?'

'Yes. Is that so strange? If he can murder teenage girls, he's certainly capable of beating his wife.'

'She told you this?'

'Yes.'

'Why didn't she do something about it?'

'It's not as easy as you think.'

'I'm not saying it's easy. And don't assume that you know what I think. What did you advise her?'

'I told her to seek professional help, of course, but she was dragging her heels.'

Banks knew enough about domestic violence to know that its victims often find it very difficult to go to the authorities or get out: they feel shame, feel it's their own fault, feel humiliated and would rather keep it to themselves, believing it will turn out all right in the end. Many of them have nowhere else to go, no other lives to live, and they are scared of the world outside the home, even if the home is violent. He also got the impression that Maggie Forrest knew first hand what she was talking about. The way she had flinched at his sharp tone, the way she had been so reluctant to talk about the subject, holding back. These were all signs.

'Did she ever mention that she suspected her husband of any other crimes?'

'Never.'

'But she was frightened of him?'

'Yes.'

'Did you visit their house?'

'Yes. Sometimes.'

'Notice anything unusual?'

'No. Nothing.'

'How did the two of them behave together?'

'Lucy always seemed nervous, edgy. Anxious to please.'

'Did you ever see any bruises?'

'They don't always leave bruises. But Lucy seemed afraid of him, afraid of putting a foot wrong. That's what I mean.'

Banks made some notes. 'Is that all?' he asked.

'What do you mean?'

'Is that all you were holding back, or is there something else?'

'There's nothing else.'

Banks stood up and excused himself. 'Do you see no
he said at the door, 'that what you've told me *is* relev
after all? Very relevant.'

'I don't see how.'

'Terence Payne has serious brain injuries. He's in
from which he may never recover and, even if he
might remember nothing. Lucy Payne will m
easily. You're the first person who's given us any i
at all about her, and it's information from whic
benefit.'

'How?'

'There are only two questions as regar
First, was she involved? And second, did sh
quiet about it? What you've just told me
that tips the scales in her favour. By talk
done your friend a service. Good eveni
make sure there's an officer keeping an

5

Leanne Wray was sixteen when she disappeared from Eastvale on Friday, thirty-first March. She was five feet two inches tall, weighed just six stone twelve, and was an only child living with her father, Christopher Wray, a bus driver, and her stepmother Victoria, who stayed home, in a terrace house just north of Eastvale town centre. Leanne was a pupil at Eastvale Comprehensive.

Leanne's parents later told police that they saw nothing wrong in letting their daughter go to the pictures that Friday night, even though they had heard of the disappearances of Kelly Matthews and Samantha Foster. After all, she was going with her friends and they said she had to be home by half past ten at the latest.

The one thing Christopher and Victoria might have objected to, had they known about it, was the presence in the group of Ian Scott. Christopher and Victoria didn't like Leanne hanging around with Ian. For one thing, he was two years older than she was, and that meant a lot at her age. For another, Ian had a reputation as a bit of a trouble-maker and had even been arrested twice by the police: once for taking and driving away and once for selling Ecstasy in the Bar None. Also, Leanne was a very pretty girl, slim and shapely, with beautiful golden blonde hair, an almost translucent complexion and long-lashed blue eyes, and they thought an older boy like Ian could be interested in her for only one thing. That he had his own flat was another black mark against him.

But Leanne just liked to hang out with Ian's crowd. Ian's girlfriend, also with them that night, was Sarah Francis, aged seventeen, and the fourth in the party was Mick Blair, aged eighteen, just a friend. They all said they had walked around the centre for a while after the film, then gone for a coffee at the El Toro – though the police discovered on further investigation that they had actually been drinking in the Old Ship Inn, in an alley between North Market Street and York Road, and lied about it because both Leanne and Sarah were under age. When pressed, they all said that Leanne had left them just outside the pub and headed home on foot at about a quarter past ten, a journey that should have taken her no more than ten minutes. But she never arrived.

Leanne's parents, though angry and worried, gave her until morning before calling the police, and an investigation, headed by Banks, soon went into full swing. Eastvale was papered with posters of Leanne, everyone who had been at the cinema, in the Old Ship Inn and in the town centre that evening was questioned. Nothing. They even ran a reconstruction, but nothing came of it. Leanne Wray had vanished into thin air. Not one person reported seeing her since she left the Old Ship.

Her three friends said they went to another pub, the Riverboat, a crowded place that stayed open late, and ended up at the Bar None on the market square. The closed-circuit TV cameras showed them turning up there at about half past twelve. Ian Scott's flat was given the full SOCO treatment to see if any evidence of Leanne's presence could be found there, but there was nothing. If she had been there, she had left no trace.

There were hints of tension in the Wray home, Banks soon discovered, and according to a school friend, Jill Brown, Leanne didn't get on well with her stepmother. They argued a lot. She missed her real mother, who had died of cancer two years ago, and Leanne had told her friend that she thought Victoria ought to go out and get a job instead of 'sponging off her dad', who didn't make a lot of money anyway. Things were always a bit tough financially, Jill said, and Leanne had to wear sturdier clothes than she thought fashionable and make them last longer than she would have wished. When she was sixteen, she got a Saturday job in a town centre boutique, so she was able to buy nice clothes at a discount.

There was, then, the faintest hope that Leanne had run away from a difficult situation and somehow hadn't heard the appeals. Until her shoulder-bag was found in the shrubbery of a garden she would have passed on her route home. The owners of the house were questioned, but they turned out to be a retired couple in their seventies and were soon exonerated.

After the third day, Banks contacted his Assistant Chief Constable, Ron McLaughlin, and discussions with Area Commander Philip Hartnell of West Yorkshire Police followed. Within days, the 'Chameleon' task force was created and Banks was put in charge of North Yorkshire's part. It meant more resources, more man-hours and more concentrated effort. It also meant, sadly, that they believed a serial killer was at work, and this was something the newspapers lost no time in speculating about.

Leanne was an average pupil, so her teachers said. She could probably do better if she tried harder, but she didn't want to make the effort. She intended to leave school at the end of the year and get a job, maybe in a clothes shop or a music shop like Virgin or HMV. She loved pop music, and her favourite group was Oasis, no matter what people said about them. Leanne was a loyal fan. Her friends thought her a rather shy but easy-going person, quick to laugh at people's jokes and not given much to introspection. She also suffered from mild asthma and carried an inhaler, which had been found along with the rest of her personal things in the abandoned shoulder-bag.

If the second victim, Samantha Foster, was a little eccentric, Leanne Wray was about as ordinary a lower-middle-class Yorkshire lass as you could get.

•

'Yeah, I'm all right to talk, sir. Really. Come on in.'

PC Janet Taylor didn't *look* all right to Banks when he called at her flat after six that evening, but then anyone who had, that morning, both fought off a serial killer and cradled her dying partner's head on her lap had every right to look a bit peaky. Janet was pale and drawn, and the fact that she was dressed all in black only served to accentuate her pallor.

Janet's flat was above a hairdresser's on Harrogate Road, not far from the airport. Banks could smell the setting lotion and herbal shampoo inside the ground floor doorway. He followed her up the narrow staircase. She moved listlessly, dragging her feet. Banks felt almost as weary as Janet seemed. He had just attended Kimberley Myers's post mortem and while it had yielded no surprises – death by ligature strangulation – Dr Mackenzie had found traces of semen in the vagina, anus and mouth. With any luck, DNA would link that to Terence Payne.

Janet Taylor's living room showed signs of neglect typical to a single police officer's dwelling. Banks recognized it all too well. He tried to keep his own cottage clean as best he could, but it was difficult sometimes when you couldn't afford a cleaning lady and you didn't have time yourself. When you did have a bit of free time, the last thing you wanted to do was housework. Still, the small room was cosy enough despite the patina of dust on the low table and the T-shirt and bra slung over the back of the armchair, the magazines and occasional unwashed teacups. There were three framed posters of old Bogie movies on the walls – *Casablanca*, *The Maltese Falcon* and *The African Queen* – and some photos on the mantelpiece, including one of Janet looking proud in her uniform, standing between an older couple Banks took to be her mother and father. The potted plant on the windowsill looked to be on its last legs, wilting and brown around the edges of the leaves. A television set flickered in one corner, the sound turned down. It was a local news programme, and Banks recognized the scene around the Payne house.

Janet moved the T-shirt and bra from the back of the armchair. 'Sit down, sir.'

'Can we have the sound on for a minute?' Banks asked. 'Who knows, maybe we'll learn something.'

'Sure.' Janet turned the volume up, but all they got was a repeat of AC Hartnell's earlier press statement. When it was over, Janet got up and turned off the TV. She still seemed slow in her movements, slurred in her speech, and Banks imagined it was something to do with the tranquillizers the doctor would have given her. Or maybe it was the half-empty bottle of gin on the sideboard.

A plane took off from Leeds and Bradford Airport, and while the noise didn't actually shake the flat, it was enough to rattle a glass and make conversation impossible for a minute or so. It was also hot in the small room, and Banks felt the sweat gather on his forehead and under his arms.

'It's why the place is so cheap,' Janet said after the noise had waned to a distant drone. 'I don't mind it that much. You get used to it. Sometimes I sit here and imagine I'm up there in one of them, flying off to some exotic country.' She got up and poured herself a small gin, adding some tonic from an open bottle of Schweppes. 'Fancy a drink, sir?'

'No, thanks. How are you coping?'

Janet sat down again and shook her head. 'The funny thing is, I don't really know. I'm all right, I suppose, but I feel sort of numb, as if I've just come round from an anaesthetic and I'm still all padded in cotton wool. Or like I'm in a dream and I'm going to wake up tomorrow morning and everything will be different. It won't, though, will it?'

'Probably not,' said Banks. 'It might even be worse.'

Janet laughed. 'Well, thanks for not giving me a load of bollocks.'

Banks smiled. 'My pleasure. Look, I'm not here to question your actions, but I need to know what happened in that house. Do you feel up to talking about it?'

'Sure.'

Banks noticed her body language, the way she crossed her arms and seemed to draw in on herself, and guessed that she wasn't up to it, but he had to press on nonetheless.

'I felt like a criminal, you know,' she said.

'What do you mean?'

'The way the doctor examined me, bagged my clothes, scraped under my fingernails.'

'It's routine. You know it is.'

'I know. I know. That's not what it feels like on the receiving end, though.'

'I suppose not. Look, I'm not going to lie to you, Janet. This could be a serious problem. It could be over in no time at all, a minor bump in the road, but it could stick around, cause you problems with your career—'

'I think that's pretty much over, don't you, sir?'

'Not necessarily. Not unless you want it to be.'

'I must admit I haven't given it a lot of thought since . . . you know.' She gave a harsh laugh. 'Funny thing is, if this was America, I'd be a hero.'

'What happened when you first received the call?'

Janet told him about the car fire and the call and finding Lucy Payne unconscious in the hallway in short, halting sentences, occasionally pausing for a sip of gin and tonic, once or twice losing her thread and staring towards the open window. Sounds of evening traffic came up from the busy road and occasionally a plane landed or took off.

'Did you think she was seriously hurt?'

'Serious enough. Not life threatening. But I stayed with her while Dennis checked around upstairs. He came back with a blanket and a pillow, I remember that. I thought that was nice of him. It surprised me.'

'Dennis wasn't always nice?'

'It's not a word I'd use to describe him, no. We disagreed a lot, but I suppose we got on okay. He's all right. Just a bit of a Neanderthal. And full of himself.'

'What did you do next?'

'Dennis went in the back, the kitchen. I mean, someone had hit her and if it was her husband, the odds were he was still in the house somewhere. Right? Probably feeling sorry for himself.'

'You stayed with Lucy?'

'Yes.'

'Then what happened?'

'Dennis called me, so I left her. She was as comfortable as I could make her, with the blanket and the pillow. The bleeding had pretty much stopped. I didn't think she was in any real danger. The ambulance was on its way . . .'

'You didn't sense any danger in the house?'

'Danger? No, not at all. I mean, no more than you do in any domestic. They can turn on you. It's happened. But no.'

'Okay. What made you go down to the cellar? Did you think her husband might be there?'

'Yes, I suppose we must have.'

'Why did Dennis call you?'

Janet paused, clearly embarrassed.

'Janet?'

Finally she looked at him. 'You've been there? Down the cellar?'

'Yes.'

'That picture on the door. The woman.'

'I saw it.'

'Dennis called me to see it. It was his idea of a joke. That's what I mean. Neanderthal.'

'I see. Was the door open? The door to the cellar?'

'No, it was closed. But there was light showing under it, a sort of flickering light.'

'You didn't hear anyone in there?'

'No.'

'Did either of you call out before you went in, identifying yourselves as police officers?'

'I don't remember.'

'Okay, Janet. You're doing fine. Carry on.'

Janet's knees were pressed tight together and she was twisting her hands on her lap as she spoke. 'Like I said, there was this flickering light.'

'The candles.'

Janet looked at him and gave a little shudder. 'There was a bad smell, too, like drains.'

'Did you have any reason to be afraid at this point?'

'Not particularly. It was creepy, but we were proceeding cautiously, as we always do in such situations. Routine. He could have been armed. The husband. We were aware of that possibility. But if you mean did we have any inkling of what we'd find in there, then no. If we had we'd have been out of there like a shot and brought in the troops. Dennis and me, we're neither of us the hero types.' She shook her head.

'Who went in first?'

'I did. Dennis kicked the door in and stood back, like, you know, making a bow. Taking the piss.'

'What happened next?'

She gave a sharp jerk of her head. 'It was all so fast. It was a blur. I remember candles, mirrors, the girl, crude drawings on the walls, things I saw out of the corners of my eyes. But they're like images from a dream. A nightmare.' Her breathing became sharper and she curled up on the armchair, legs under her, arms wrapped around herself. 'Then he came. Dennis was right behind me. I could feel his breath warm on my neck.'

'Where did he come from?'

'I don't know. Behind. A corner. So fast.'

'What did Dennis do?'

'He didn't have time to do anything. He must have heard or sensed something to make him turn, and the next thing I knew he was bleeding. He screamed out. That's when I pulled my baton. He cut Dennis again, and the blood sprayed over me. It was as if he hadn't noticed me, or he didn't care, he'd get to me later. But when he did, I had my baton out and he tried to slash me but I deflected it. Then I hit him . . .' She started to sob and rubbed the backs of her hands against her eyes. 'Sorry. Dennis, I'm so sorry.'

'It's all right,' Banks said. 'Take it easy, Janet. You're doing fine.'

'He had his head on my lap. I was trying to hold the artery closed, like they teach in first aid. But I couldn't do it. I'd never done it before, not with anyone real. The blood just kept seeping out. So much blood.' She sniffed and ran the back of her hand across her nose. 'Sorry.'

'That's okay. You're doing fine, Janet. Before that. Before you tried to save Dennis, what else did you do?'

'I remember handcuffing the man to one of the pipes.'

'How many times did you hit him?'

'I don't remember.'

'More than once?'

'Yes. He wouldn't stop coming, so I hit him again.'

'And again?'

'Yes. He kept getting up.' She started sobbing again. When she'd calmed, she asked, 'Is he dead?'

'Not yet.'

'The bastard killed Dennis.'

'I know. And when a man's partner is killed he's supposed to do something about it, right? If you don't, it's bad for business, bad for detectives everywhere.'

Janet looked at him as if he were crazy. 'What?'

Banks looked up at Bogart as Sam Spade. Clearly the posters were there for show, not as a result of any great passion for the films themselves, and his pathetic attempt at lightening things up fell flat. 'Never mind,' he said. 'I was just wondering what went through your mind.'

'Nothing. I didn't have time to stop and think. He'd cut Dennis and he was going to cut me. Call it self-preservation if you like, but it wasn't a conscious thought. I mean, I didn't think I'd better hit him again or he might get up and cut me. It wasn't like that.'

'What *was* it like?'

'I told you. A blur. I disabled the killer, handcuffed him to one of the pipes and then I tried to keep Dennis alive. I didn't even look in Payne's direction again. To be honest, I didn't give a damn what shape he was in. Only Dennis.' Janet paused and looked down at her hands clasped around the glass. 'You know what really gets me? I'd just been nasty to him. All because he'd been telling his damn sexist jokes to that fireman.'

'What do you mean?'

'We'd been arguing, that's all. Just before we got to the house. I told him his mole was probably cancerous. It was cruel of me. I know he's a hypochondriac. Why did I do that? Why am I such a horrible person? Then it was too late. I couldn't tell him I didn't mean it.' She cried again and Banks thought it best to let her get it all out. It would take more than one tearful session to purge her of her guilt, but at least it was a start.

'Have you been in touch with the Federation?'

'Not yet.'

'Do it tomorrow. Talk to your rep. They'll be able to help with counselling, if you want it, and . . .'

'Legal representation?'

'If it comes to that, yes.'

Janet got to her feet a bit more unsteadily and went to pour herself another drink.

'Are you sure that's wise?' Banks asked.

Janet poured herself a stiff measure and sat down again. 'Tell me what else I should be doing, sir. Should I be going to sit with Dennis's wife and kids? Should I try to explain to them how it happened, how it was all my fault? Or should I just smash up my flat and go out on the town and pick a fight in some anonymous pub somewhere, the way I feel like doing? I don't think so. This is by far the least harmful alternative to *anything* else I'd rather be doing right now.'

Banks realized that she had a point. He had felt that way himself more than once, and had even given in to the urge to go out on the town and pick a fight. It hadn't helped. He would be a hypocrite if he said he didn't understand plenty about finding oblivion at the bottom of a bottle. There had been two periods in his life when he had sought solace that way. The first was when he felt he was fast approaching burnout those last few months in London, before the transfer to Eastvale, and the second was more than a year ago, after Sandra had left him.

The thing was, people said it didn't work, but it did. As a short-term solution, for temporary oblivion, there was nothing to match the bottle, except perhaps heroin, which Banks hadn't tried. Maybe Janet Taylor was right, and tonight drinking was the best thing she could do. She was hurting, and sometimes you had to do your hurting by yourself. Booze helped dull the pain for a while, and eventually you passed out. The hangover would be painful, but that was for tomorrow.

'Right you are. I'll let myself out.' On impulse, Banks leaned over and kissed the top of Janet's head as he left. Her hair tasted of burnt plastic and rubber.

•

That evening, Jenny Fuller sat in her home office, where she kept all the files and notes on the investigation on her computer, no office having been made available to her at Millgarth. The office looked out over the Green, a narrow stretch of parkland between her street and the East Side Estate. She could just see the lights of the houses through the spaces between the dark trees.

Working so closely with Banks had made Jenny remember a lot of their history. She had once tried to seduce him, she recalled with embarrassment, and he had resisted politely, claiming to be a happily married man. But he was attracted to her; she knew that much. He wasn't a happily married man any more, but now he had 'The Girlfriend', as Jenny had come to call Annie Cabbot, though she had never met her. That had come about because Jenny had spent so much time out of the country and hadn't even been around when Banks and Sandra separated. If she had been . . . well, things might have been different. Instead, she had embarked on a series of disastrous relationships.

One of the reasons she had spent so much time away, she had finally admitted to herself after coming back from California this last time with her tail between her legs, was to get away from Banks, from the easy proximity to him that tormented her so much while she pretended to be casual about the whole thing, and much cooler than she felt. And now they were working closely together.

With a sigh, Jenny returned her attention to her work.

Her main problem thus far, she realized, had been an almost complete lack of forensic and crime scene information, and without them it was damn near impossible to produce a decent threshold analysis – an initial review that could serve as an investigative compass, help the police know where to look – let alone a more complex profile. About all she had been able to work on was the victimology. All this, of course, had given her detractors on the task force – and they were legion – plenty of ammunition.

England was still in the Dark Ages as far as the use of consultant psychologists and criminal profiling went, Jenny believed, especially as compared to the USA. Partly this was because the FBI is a national force with the resources to develop national programmes and Britain has fifty or more separate police forces all operating piecemeal. Also, profilers in the USA tend to be cops and are therefore more readily accepted. In Britain, profilers are usually psychologists or psychiatrists and, as such, are distrusted by the police and the legal system in general. Consultant psychologists would be lucky to make it to the witness box in an English court, Jenny knew, let alone be accepted as expert witnesses, the way they are in the USA. Even if they did get in the box, whatever evidence they gave would be looked at askance by judge and jury, and the defence would wheel in another psychologist with a different theory.

The Dark Ages.

When it came right down to it, Jenny was well aware that most of the police she worked with regarded her as perhaps only one step up from a clairvoyant, if that, and that they only brought her in because it was easier than not doing so. But she struggled on. While she was prepared to admit that profiling was still, perhaps, more of an art than a science, and while a profile could rarely, if ever, point the finger at a specific killer, she believed that it could narrow the field and help focus an investigation.

Looking at pictures on a screen just didn't do it for Jenny, so she spread out the photographs again on her desk, though she knew them all by heart: Kelly Matthews, Samantha Foster, Leanne Wray, Melissa Horrocks and Kimberley Myers, all attractive blonde girls between the ages of sixteen and eighteen.

There had been too many assumptions for Jenny's liking right from the start, the prime one being that all five girls had been abducted by the same person or persons. She could, she had told Banks and the team, make out almost as a good a case for their not being linked, even on such little information as she possessed.

Young girls go missing all the time, Jenny had argued; they have arguments with their parents and run away from home. But Banks told her that detailed and exhaustive interviews with friends, family, teachers, neighbours and acquaintances showed that all the girls – except perhaps Leanne Wray – came from stable family backgrounds and, apart from the usual rows about boyfriends, clothes, loud music and what have you, nothing unusual or significant had happened in their lives prior to their disappearances. These, Banks stressed, were not your common or garden teenage runaways. There was also the matter of the shoulder-bags found abandoned close to where the girls had last been seen. With the botched Yorkshire Ripper investigation still hanging like an albatross around its neck, West Yorkshire was taking no chances.

The number became four, then five, and no traces whatsoever could be found of any of the girls through the usual channels: youth support groups, the National Missing Persons Helpline, *Crimewatch UK* reconstructions, *Missing Can-U-Help* posters, media appeals and local police efforts.

In the end, Jenny accepted Banks's argument and proceeded as if the disappearances were linked, at the same time keeping clear notes of any differences between the individual circumstances. Before long, she found that the similarities by far overwhelmed the differences.

Victimology. What did they have in common? All the girls were young, had long blonde hair, long legs and trim, athletic figures. It seemed to indicate the type of girl he liked, Jenny had said. They all have different tastes.

By victim number four, Jenny had noticed the pattern of escalation: nearly two months between victims one and two, five weeks between two and three, but only two and a half weeks between three and four. He had been getting needier, she thought at the time, which meant he might also become more reckless. Jenny was also willing to bet that there was a fair degree of personality disintegration going on.

The criminal had chosen his haunts well. Open-air parties, pubs, dances, clubs, cinemas and pop concerts were all places where you were very likely to find young people, and they all had to get home one way or another. She knew that the team referred to him as the 'Chameleon' and agreed that he showed a very high level of skill in taking his pick of victims and not being seen. All had been abducted at night in urban settings, desolate stretches of city streets, ill-lit and deserted. He had also managed to stay well beyond the range of the CCTV cameras that covered many city centres and town squares these days.

A witness said she saw Samantha, the Bradford victim, talking to someone through the window of a dark car, and that was the only information Jenny had about his possible method of abduction.

While the New Year's party, the Harrogate pop concert, the cinema and university pub were common knowledge, and obvious hunting grounds, one question that had bothered Jenny since Saturday morning was how the killer had known about the school dance after which Kimberley Myers had been abducted. Did he live in the neighbourhood? Had he simply happened to be passing at the time? As far as she knew, these things weren't advertised outside the immediate community, or even beyond the school.

Now she knew: Terence Payne lived just down the street, taught at the local comprehensive. Knew the victim.

Also, now, some of the things she had learned that day were making sense of some of the other puzzling facts and questions she had gathered over the weeks. Of the five abductions, four had occurred on a Friday night, or in the early hours of Saturday morning, which had led Jenny to believe that the killer worked a regular five-day week, and that he devoted his weekends to his hobby. The odd one out, Melissa Horrocks, had bothered her, but now that she knew Payne was a schoolteacher, the Tuesday, eighteenth April abduction made sense, too. It was the Easter holidays and Payne had more spare time on his hands.

From this scant information – all this before the Kimberley Myers abduction – Jenny had surmised that they were dealing with an abductor who struck opportunistically. He cruised suitable locations looking for a certain type of victim, and when he found one, he struck as fast as lightning. There was no evidence that any of the girls had been stalked either on the evening of, or prior to, their abductions, though it was a possibility she had to bear in mind, but Jenny was willing to bet that he had scouted the locations, studied every way in and out, every dark nook and cranny, all the sight lines and angles. There was always a certain level of risk involved in things such as this. Just enough, perhaps, to guarantee that quick surge of adrenalin that was probably part of the thrill. Now Jenny knew that he had used chloroform to subdue his victims, that decreased the level of risk.

Jenny had also not been able until now to take into account any crime scene information because there hadn't been a crime scene available. There could be plenty of reasons why no bodies turned up, Jenny had said. They could have been dumped in remote locations and not discovered yet, buried in the woods, dumped in the sea or in a lake. As the number of disappearances increased, though, and as time went on and *still* no bodies were found, Jenny found herself moving towards the theory that their man was a collector, someone who plucks and savours his victims and perhaps then disposes of them the way a butterfly collector might gas and pin his trophies.

Now she had seen the anteroom, where the killer had buried, or partially buried, the bodies, and she didn't think that had been done by chance or done badly. She didn't think that the toes of one victim were sticking through the earth because Terence Payne was a sloppy worker; they were like that because he wanted them that way, it was part of his fantasy, because he *got off on it*, as they said back in America. They were part of his collection, his trophy room. Or his *garden*.

Now Jenny would have to rework her profile, factoring in all the new evidence that would be pouring out of number thirty-five The Hill over the next few weeks. She would also have to find out all she could about Terence Payne.

And there was another thing. Now Jenny also had to consider Lucy Payne.

Had Lucy known what her husband was doing?

It was possible, at least, that she had her suspicions.

Why didn't she come forward?

Because of some misguided sense of loyalty, perhaps – this was her *husband*, after all – or fear. If he had hit her with a vase last night, he could have hit her at other times, too, warned her of the fate that awaited her if she told anyone the truth. It would have been a living hell for Lucy, of course, but Jenny could believe her doing that. Plenty of women lived their whole lives in such hells.

But was Lucy more involved?

Again, possible. Jenny had suggested, tentatively, that the method of abduction indicated the killer might have had a helper, someone to lure the girl into the car, or distract her while he came up from behind. A woman would have been perfect for that role, would have made the actual abduction easier. Young girls wary of men are far more likely to lean in the window and help when a woman pulls over at the kerb.

Were women capable of such evil?

Definitely. And if they were ever caught, the outrage against them was far greater than against any male. You only had to look at the public's reactions to Myra Hindley, Rosemary West and Karla Homolka to see that.

So was Lucy Payne a killer?

•

Banks felt bone-weary when he pulled up in the narrow lane outside his Gratly cottage close to midnight that night. He knew he should have probably taken a hotel room in Leeds, as he had done before, or accepted Ken Blackstone's offer of the sofa, but he had very much wanted to go home tonight, even if Annie had refused to come over, and he didn't mind the drive too much. It helped relax him.

There were two messages waiting for him on the machine. The first was from Tracy, saying she'd heard the news and hoped he was all right, and the second was from Leanne Wray's father, Christopher, who had seen the press conference and the evening news and wanted to know if the police had found his daughter's body at the Payne house.

Banks didn't answer either of them. For one thing, it was too late, and for another, he didn't want to talk to anybody. He could deal with them all in the morning. Now that he was home, he was even glad that Annie *wasn't* coming. The idea of company tonight, even Annie's, didn't appeal, and after all he'd seen and thought about today, the idea of sex held about as much interest as a trip to the dentist's.

Instead, he poured himself a generous tumbler of Laphroaig and tried to find some suitable music. He needed to listen to something, but he didn't know what. Usually he had no trouble finding what he wanted in his large collection, but tonight he rejected just about every CD he picked out. He knew he didn't want to listen to jazz or rock or anything too wild and primitive like that. Wagner and Mahler were out, as were all the Romantics: Beethoven, Schubert, Rachmaninov and the rest. The entire twentieth century was out, too. In the end he went for Rostropovich's rendition of Bach's cello suites.

Outside the cottage, the low stone wall between the dirt lane and the beck bulged out and formed a little parapet over Gratly Falls, which was just a series of terraces, none more than a few feet in height, running diagonally through the village and under the little stone bridge that formed its central gathering place. Since he had moved into the cottage the previous summer, Banks had got into the habit of standing out there last thing at night if the weather was good enough, or even sitting on the wall, dangling his legs over the beck, and enjoying his nightcap and a cigarette before bed.

The night air was still and smelled of hay and warm grass. The dale below him was sleeping. One or two farmhouse lights shone on the far valley side, but apart from the sounds of sheep in the field across the beck and night animals from the woods, all was quiet. He could just make out the shapes of distant fell sides in the dark, humpbacked or jagged against the night sky. He thought he heard a curlew's eerie trill from high up on the moors. The new moon gave sparse light, but there were more stars than he had seen in a long time. As he watched, a star fell through the darkness leaving a thin milky trail.

Banks didn't make a wish.

He felt depressed. The elation he had expected to feel on finding the killer somehow eluded him. He had no sense of an ending, of an evil purged. In some odd way, he felt, the evil was just beginning. He tried to shake off his sense of apprehension.

He heard a meow beside him and looked down. It was the skinny marmalade cat from the woods. Starting that spring, it had come over on several occasions when Banks was outside alone late at night. The second time it appeared, he had brought it some milk, which it lapped up before disappearing back into the trees. He had never seen it anywhere else, or at any other time than night. Once, he had even bought some cat food, to be more prepared for its visit, but the cat hadn't touched it. All it would do was meow, drink the milk, strut around for a few minutes and go back where it came from. Banks fetched a saucer of milk and set it down, refilling his own glass at the same time. The cat's eyes shone amber in the darkness as it looked up at him before bending to drink.

Banks lit his cigarette and leaned against the wall, resting his glass on its rough stone surface. He tried to purge his mind of the day's terrible images. The cat rubbed against his leg and ran off back into the woods. Rostropovich played on, and Bach's precise, mathematical patterns of sound formed an odd counterpoint to the wild roaring music of Gratly Falls, so recently swelled by the spring thaw, and for a few moments at least, Banks succeeded in losing himself.

6

According to her parents, Melissa Horrocks, aged seventeen, who failed to return home after a pop concert in Harrogate on the eighteenth of April, was going through a rebellious phase.

Steven and Mary Horrocks had only the one daughter, a late blessing in Mary's mid-thirties. Steven worked in the office of a local dairy, while Mary had a part-time job in an estate agent's office in the city centre. Around the age of sixteen, Melissa developed an interest in the kind of theatrical pop music that used Satanism as its main stage prop.

Though friends advised Steven and Mary that it was harmless enough – just youthful spirits – and that it would soon pass, they were nonetheless alarmed when she started altering her appearance and letting her school work and athletics slip. Melissa first dyed her hair red, got a stud in her nose, and wore a lot of black. Her bedroom wall was adorned with posters of skinny, Satanic-looking pop stars, such as Marilyn Manson, and occult symbols her parents didn't understand.

About a week before the concert, Melissa decided she didn't like the red hair, so she reverted to her natural blonde colouring. There was a good chance, Banks thought later, that if she'd kept it red, that might have saved her life. Which also led Banks to think that she hadn't been stalked before her abduction – or at least not for long. The Chameleon wouldn't stalk a redhead.

Harrogate, a prosperous Victorian-style North Yorkshire city of about 70,000, known as a conference centre and a magnet for retired people, wasn't exactly the typical venue for a Beelzebub's Bollocks concert, but the band was new and had yet to win a major recording contract; they were working their way up to bigger gigs. There had been the usual calls for a ban from retired colonels and the kind of old busybodies who watch all the filth on television so they can write letters of protest, but in the end this was to no avail.

About five hundred kids wandered into the converted theatre, including Melissa and her friends Jenna and Kayla. The concert ended at half past ten and the three girls stood around outside for a while talking about the show. The three of them split up at about a quarter to eleven and went their separate ways. It was a mild night, so Melissa said she was going to walk. She didn't live far from the city centre and most of her walk home took her along the busy, well-lit Ripon Road. Two people later came forward to say they saw her close to eleven o'clock walking south by the junction of West Park and Beech Grove. To get home, she would turn down Beech Grove and then turn off after about a hundred yards, but she never got there.

At first there was a faint hope that Melissa might have run away from home, given the ongoing battle with her parents. But Steven and Mary, along with Jenna and Kayla, assured Banks this could not be the case. The two friends, in particular, said they shared everything, and they would have known if she was planning on running away. Besides, she had none of her valued possessions with her, and she told them she was looking forward to seeing them the next day at the Victoria Centre.

Then there was the Satanic element, not to be lightly dismissed when a girl had disappeared. The members of the band were interviewed, along with as many audience members as could be rounded up, but that went nowhere, too. Even Banks had to admit when examining the statements later that the whole thing had been pretty tame and harmless, the black magic merely theatre, as it had been for Black Sabbath and Alice Cooper in his day. Beelzebub's Bollocks didn't even bite the heads off chickens on stage.

When Melissa's black leather shoulder-bag was found in some bushes two days after her disappearance, as if it had been tossed from the window of a moving car, money still intact, the case came to the attention of Banks's 'Chameleon' task force. Like Kelly Matthews, Samantha Foster and Leanne Wray before her, Melissa Horrocks had disappeared into thin air.

Jenna and Kayla were devastated. Just before Melissa had walked off into the night, they had joked, Kayla said, about perverts, but Melissa pointed to her chest and said the occult symbol on her T-shirt would ward off evil spirits.

•

The incident room was crowded at nine o'clock on Tuesday morning. Over forty detectives sat on the edges of their desks or leaned against the walls. Smoking was not permitted in the building, and many of them chewed gum or fidgeted with paper clips or rubber bands instead. Most had been on the task force since the beginning, and they had all put in long hours, invested a lot of themselves in the job, emotionally as well as physically. It had taken its toll on all of them. Banks happened to know that one unfortunate DC's marriage had broken up over the hours he spent away from home and the neglect he displayed towards his wife. It would have happened some other time, anyway, Banks told himself, but an investigation like this one can put the pressure on, can push events to a crisis point, especially if that crisis point isn't too far away to start with. These days, Banks also felt that he was approaching his own crisis point, though he had no idea where it was or what would happen when he got there.

Now there was at least some sense of progress, no matter how unclear things still seemed, and the air buzzed with speculation. They all wanted to know what had happened. The mood was mixed: on the one hand, it looked as if they had their man; on the other, one of their own had been killed and his partner was about to be put through the hoops.

When Banks strode in somewhat the worse for wear after another poor night's sleep, despite a third Laphroaig and the second disc of Bach's cello sonatas, the room hushed, everyone waiting to hear the news. He stood next to Ken Blackstone, beside the photographs of the girls pinned to the cork-board.

'Okay,' he said, 'I'll do my best to explain where we are with this. The SOCOs are still at the scene, and it looks as if they'll be there for a long time yet. So far, they've uncovered three bodies in the cellar anteroom, and it doesn't look as if there's room for any more. They're digging in the back garden for the fourth. None of the victims has been identified yet, but DS Nowak says the bodies are all young and female, so it's reasonable to assume for the moment that they're the young girls who went missing. We should be able to make some headway on identification later today by checking dental records. Dr Mackenzie performed the post mortem on Kimberley Myers late yesterday and found that she had been subdued by chloroform but death was due to vagal inhibition caused by ligature strangulation. Yellow plastic fibres from the clothes-line were embedded in the wound.' He paused, then sighed and went on. 'She was also raped anally and vaginally and forced to perform fellatio.'

'What about Payne, sir?' someone asked. 'Is the bastard going to die?'

'The last I heard was that they had to operate on his brain. Terence Payne is still in a coma, and there's no telling how long that might last, or how it will end. By the way, we now know that Terence Payne lived and taught in Seacroft before he moved to west Leeds in September the year before last, at the start of the school year. DCI Blackstone has him in the frame for the Seacroft rapist, so we're already checking DNA. I'll want a team to go over the casework on that one with the local CID. DS Stewart, can you get that organized?'

'Right away, sir. That'll be Chapeltown CID.'

Chapeltown would be hot to trot on this, Banks knew. It was a 'red inker' for them – an easy way of closing several open case files at one fell swoop.

'We've also checked Payne's car registration with DVLA in Swansea. He was using false plates. His own plates end in KWT, just like the witness in the Samantha Foster disappearance saw. The SOCOs found them hidden in the garage. That means Bradford CID must have already interviewed him. I'd imagine it was after that he switched to the false ones.'

'What about Dennis Morrisey?' someone asked.

'PC Morrisey died of blood loss caused by the severing of his carotid artery and jugular vein, according to Dr Mackenzie's examination at the scene. He'll be doing the PM later today. As you can imagine, there's getting to be quite a queue down at the mortuary. He's looking for assistance. Anyone interested?'

Nervous laughter rippled through the room.

'What about PC Taylor?' one of the detectives asked.

'PC Taylor's coping,' said Banks. 'I talked to her yesterday evening. She was able to tell me what happened in the cellar. As you all probably know, she'll be under investigation, so let's try to keep that one at arm's length.'

A chorus of boos came up from the crowd. Banks quieted them down. 'It's got to be done,' he said. 'Unpopular as it is. We're none of us above the law. But let's not let that distract us. Our job is far from over. In fact, it's just beginning. There's going to be a mountain of stuff coming out of forensic examinations at the house. It'll all have to be tagged, logged and filed. HOLMES is still in operation, so the green sheets will have to be filled out and fed in.'

Banks heard Carol Houseman, the trained HOLMES operator, groan, 'Oh, *bugger* it!'

'Sorry, Carol,' he said, with a sympathetic smile. 'Needs must. In other words, despite what's happened, we're still very much in business for the time being. We need to gather the evidence. We need to prove beyond a shadow of a doubt that Terence Payne is the killer of all five missing girls.'

'What about his wife?' someone asked. 'She must have known.'

Just what Ken Blackstone had said. 'We don't know that,' said Banks. 'For the moment she's a victim. But her possible involvement is one of the things we'll be looking into. We're already aware that he *might have had* an accomplice. She should be able to talk to me later this morning.' Banks glanced at his watch and turned to DS Filey. 'In the meantime, Ted, I'd like you to put a team together to go over all the statements and re-interview everyone we talked to when the girls were first reported missing. Family, friends, witnesses, everyone. Okay?'

'Right you are, Guv,' said Ted Filey.

Banks hated being called 'Guv' but he let it go by. 'Get some photographs of Lucy Payne and show one to everyone you talk to. See if anyone remembers seeing her in connection with any of the missing girls.'

More muttering broke out, and Banks quieted them down again. 'For the moment,' he said, 'I want you all to keep in close touch with our office manager, DS Grafton here—'

A cheer went up and Ian Grafton blushed.

'He'll be issuing actions and TIEs, and there'll be plenty of them. I want to know what Terence and Lucy Payne eat for breakfast and how regular their bowel movements are. Dr Fuller suggested that Payne would have kept some sort of visual record of his deeds – video most likely, but maybe just ordinary still photographs. Nothing's been found at the scene yet, but we'll need to know if the Paynes ever owned or rented video equipment.'

Banks noticed a number of sceptical looks at the mention of Jenny Fuller. Typical narrow-minded thinking, in his opinion. Consultant psychologists might not be possessed with magic powers and able to name the killer within hours, but in Banks's experience, they could narrow the field and target the area where the offender might live. Why not use them? At best they could help, and at worst they did no harm. 'Remember,' he went on, 'five girls were abducted, raped and murdered. *Five* girls. You don't need me to tell you any one of them could have been *your* daughter. We think we've got the man responsible, but we can't be sure he acted alone, and until we can *prove* it was him, no matter what shape he's in, there'll be no slacking on this team. Got it?'

The assembled detectives muttered, 'Yes, sir,' then the

group started to split up, some drifting outside for a much-needed cigarette, others settling back at their desks.

'One more thing,' said Banks. 'DCs Bowmore and Singh. In my office. Now.'

•

After a brief meeting with Area Commander Hartnell – who *definitely* gave her the eye – and Banks, who seemed uncomfortable about the whole thing, DI Annie Cabbot read over PC Janet Taylor's file as she waited in the small office assigned her. Hartnell himself had decided that as Janet Taylor was coming in voluntarily, and as she wasn't under arrest, an office would be a far less threatening environment for the preliminary talk than a standard grungy interview room.

Annie was impressed by PC Taylor's record. There was little doubt that she would find a place in the Accelerated Promotion Course and make the rank of inspector within five years if she was cleared of all charges. A local girl, from Pudsey, Janet Taylor had four A-levels and a degree in sociology from the University of Bristol. She was just twenty-three years old, unmarried and living alone. Janet had high scores on all her entrance exams, and in the opinions of those who had examined her she showed a clear grasp of the complexities of policing a diverse society, along with the sort of cognitive skills and problem-solving abilities that augured well for a detective. She was in good health and listed her hobbies as squash, tennis and computers. Throughout her student career she had spent her summers working for security at the White Rose Centre, in Leeds, both manning the cameras and patrolling the shopping precinct. Janet had also done voluntary community work for her local church group, helping the elderly.

All of this sounded quite dull to Annie, who grew up in an artists' commune near St Ives surrounded by oddballs, hippies and weirdos of all sorts. Annie had also come late to the police, and though she had a degree, it was in art history, not much use in the force, and she hadn't got on the APC because of an incident at her previous county, when three fellow officers had attempted to rape her at a party following her promotion to sergeant. One succeeded before she had managed to fight them off. Traumatized, Annie had not reported the incident until the following morning, by which time she had spent hours in the bath washing away all evidence. The DCS had accepted the words of the three officers against hers, and while they admitted that things had got a little out of hand, with a drunken Annie leading them on, they said they had retained their control and no sexual assault had taken place.

For a long time, Annie hadn't much cared about her career, and no one had been more surprised than she had at the rekindling of her ambition, which had meant dealing with the rape and its aftermath – more complicated and traumatic than anyone but her really knew – but it had happened, and now she was a fully fledged inspector investigating a politically dodgy case for Detective Superintendent Chambers, who was clearly scared stiff of the assignment himself.

A brief tap at the door was followed by the entry of a young woman with short black hair, which looked rather dry and lifeless. 'They told me you were in here,' she said.

Annie introduced herself. 'Sit down, Janet.'

Janet sat and tried to make herself comfortable on the hard chair. She looked as if she hadn't slept all night, which didn't surprise Annie in the least. Her face was pale and there were dark semicircles under her eyes. Perhaps beyond the ravages of sleeplessness and abject terror, Janet Taylor was an attractive young woman. She certainly had beautiful eyes, the colour of loam, and the kind of cheekbones that models hang their careers on. She also seemed a very serious person, weighed down by the gravity of life, or perhaps that was a result of recent events.

'How is he?' Janet asked.

'Who?'

'You know. Payne.'

'Still unconscious.'

'Will he survive?'

'They don't know yet, Janet.'

'Okay. I mean, it's just that . . . well, I suppose it makes a difference. You know, to my case.'

'If he dies? Yes, it does. But don't let's worry about that for the time being. I want you to tell me what happened in the Paynes's cellar, then I'll ask you a few questions. Finally, I want you to write it all down in a statement. This isn't an interrogation, Janet. I'm sure you went through hell down in that cellar and nobody wants to treat you like a criminal. But there are procedures to be followed in cases like this and the sooner we get going the better.' Annie wasn't being entirely truthful, but she wanted to set Janet Taylor as much at ease as possible. She knew she would have to push and prod a bit, maybe even go in hard now and again. It was her interrogation technique; after all, it was often under pressure of some sort that the truth slipped out. She would play it by ear, but if she needed to badger Janet Taylor a bit, then so be it. Damn Chambers and Hartnell. If she was going to do the bloody job, she was going to do it properly.

'Don't worry,' said Janet. 'I haven't done anything wrong.'

'I'm sure you haven't. Tell me about it.'

As Janet Taylor spoke, sounding rather bored and detached, as if she had been through this all too many times already, or as if she were recounting someone else's story, Annie watched her body language. Janet shifted in her chair often, twisted her hands on her lap, and when she got to the real horror, she folded her arms and her voice became flatter, lacking expression. Annie let her go on, making notes on points she thought relevant. Janet didn't so much come to a definite end as trail off after she said she had settled to wait for the ambulance, cradling PC Morrisey's head on her lap and feeling the warm blood seep through on her thighs. As she spoke about this, her eyebrows rose and wrinkled the centre of her forehead, and tears formed in her eyes.

Annie let the silence stretch for a while after Janet had fallen silent, then she asked if Janet would like a drink. She asked for water and Annie brought her some from the fountain. The room was hot and Annie got some for herself, too.

'Just a couple of things, Janet, then I'll leave you alone to write your statement.'

Janet yawned. She put her hand to her mouth but didn't apologize. Normally Annie would have taken a yawn as a sign of fear or nervousness, but Janet Taylor had good reason to be tired, so she didn't make too much of it on this occasion.

'What were you thinking about while it was happening?' Annie asked.

'Thinking? I'm not sure I was thinking at all. Just reacting.'

'Did you remember your training?'

Janet Taylor laughed, but it was forced. 'Training doesn't prepare you for something like *that*.'

'What about your baton training?'

'I didn't have to *think* about that. It was instinctive.'

'You were feeling threatened.'

'Damn right I was. He was killing Dennis and he was going to kill me next. He'd already killed the girl on the bed.'

'How did you know she was dead?'

'What?'

'Kimberley Myers. How did you know she was dead? You said it all happened so fast you barely caught a glimpse of her before the attack.'

'I . . . I suppose I just assumed. I mean she was lying there naked on the bed with a yellow rope around her neck. Her eyes were open. It was a reasonable assumption to make.'

'Okay,' said Annie. 'So you never thought of yourself as saving her, as rescuing her?'

'No. It was what was happening to Dennis that concerned me.'

'And what you thought was going to happen to you next?'

'Yes.' Janet sipped some more water. A little of it dripped down her chin onto the front of her grey T-shirt, but she didn't seem to notice.

'So you got your baton out. What next?'

'I told you. He came at me with this crazy look in his eye.'

'And he lashed out at you with his machete?'

'Yes. I deflected the blow with my baton, the side against my arm, like they taught us. And then when he'd swung, before he could bring it back into position again I swung out and hit him.'

'Where did the first blow land?'

'On his head.'

'Where exactly on his head?'

'I don't know. I wasn't concerned about that.'

'But you wanted to put him out of commission, didn't you?'

'I wanted to stop him from killing me.'

'So you'd want to hit him somewhere effective?'

'Well, I'm right-handed, so I suppose I must have hit him on the left side of his head, somewhere around the temple.'

'Did he go down?'

'No, but he was dazed. He couldn't get his machete in position to strike again.'

'Where did you hit him next?'

'The wrist, I think.'

'To disarm him?'

'Yes.'

'Did you succeed?'

'Yes.'

'What did you do next?'

'I kicked the machete into the corner.'

'What did Payne do?'

'He was holding his wrist and cursing me.'

'You'd hit him once on the left temple and once on the wrist by this time?'

'That's right.'

'What did you do next?'

'I hit him again.'

'Where?'

'On the head.'

'Why?'

'To incapacitate him.'

'Was he standing at this point?'

'Yes. He'd been on his knees trying to get the machete, but he got up and came at me.'

'He was unarmed now?'

'Yes, but he was still bigger and stronger than me. And he had this insane look in his eyes, as if he had strength to spare.'

'So you hit him again?'

'Yes.'

'Same spot?'

'I don't know. I used my baton in the same way. So yes, I suppose so, unless he was half turned away.'

'Was he?'

'I don't think so.'

'But it's possible? I mean, it was you who suggested it.'

'I suppose it's possible, but I don't see why.'

'You didn't hit him on the *back* of his head at any point?'

'I don't think so.'

Janet had started to sweat now. Annie could see beads of it around her hairline and a dark stain spreading slowly under her arms. She didn't want to put the poor woman through much more, but she had her job to do and she could be hard when she needed to be. 'What happened after you hit Payne on the head a second time?'

'Nothing.'

'What do you mean, nothing?'

'Nothing. He kept coming.'

'So you hit him again.'

'Yes. I took the baton in both hands, like a cricket bat, so I could hit him harder.'

'He had nothing to defend himself with at this time, right?'

'Only his arms.'

'But he didn't raise them to ward off the blow?'

'He was holding his wrist. I think it was broken. I heard something crack.'

'So you had free rein to hit him as hard as you liked?'

'He kept coming at me.'

'You mean he kept moving towards you?'

'Yes, and calling me names.'

'What sort of names?'

'Filthy names. And Dennis was groaning, bleeding. I wanted to go to him, to see if I could help, but I couldn't do anything until Payne stopped moving.'

'You didn't feel you could restrain him with handcuffs at this point?'

'No way. I'd already hit him two or three times, but it seemed to have no effect. He kept coming. If I'd gone in close and he'd got a hold of me he'd have strangled the life out of me.'

'Even with his broken wrist?'

'Yes. He could have got his arm across my throat.'

'Okay.' Annie paused to make some notes on the pad in front of her. She could almost smell Janet Taylor's fear, and she wasn't sure if it was residual, from the cellar, or because of present circumstances. She drew out the note-making process until Janet started shifting and fidgeting, then she asked, 'How many times do you think you hit him in all?'

Janet turned her head to one side. 'I don't know. I wasn't counting. I was fighting for my life, defending myself against a maniac.'

'Five times? Six times?'

'I told you. *I don't remember.* As many times as I needed. To make him stop coming. He just wouldn't stop coming at me.' Janet broke into sobs and Annie let her cry. It was the first time emotion had broken through the shock and it would do her good. After a minute or so, Janet collected herself and sipped some more water. She seemed embarrassed to have broken down in front of a colleague.

'I've almost finished now, Janet,' said Annie. 'Then I'll leave you be.'

'Okay.'

'You managed to get him to stay down, didn't you?'

'Yes. He fell against the wall and slid down.'

'Was he still moving then?'

'Not very much. He was sort of twitching and breathing heavily. There was blood on his mouth.'

'Final question, Janet: did you hit him again after he went down?'

Her eyebrows shot together in fear. 'No. I don't think so.'

'What did you do?'

'I handcuffed him to the pipe.'

'And then?'

'Then I went to help Dennis.'

'Are you sure you didn't hit him again after he went down? Just to make sure?'

Janet looked away. 'I told you. I don't think so. Why would I?'

Annie leaned forward and rested her arms on the desk. '*Try* to remember, Janet.'

But Janet shook her head. 'It's no good. I don't remember.'

'Okay,' said Annie, getting to her feet. 'Interview over.' She pushed a statement sheet and a pen in front of Janet. 'Write out what you've told me in as much detail as you can remember.'

Janet grasped the pen. 'What happens next?'

When you've finished, love, go home and have a stiff drink. Hell, have two.'

Janet managed a weak but genuine smile as Annie left and shut the door behind her.

•

DCs Bowmore and Singh looked shifty when they walked into Banks's temporary Millgarth office, as well they might, he thought.

'Sit down,' he said.

They sat. 'What is it, sir?' asked DC Singh attempting lightness. 'Got a job for us?'

Banks leaned back in his chair and linked his hands behind his head. 'In a manner of speaking,' he said. 'If you call sharpening pencils and emptying the wastepaper baskets a job.'

Their jaws dropped. 'Sir—' Bowmore began, but Banks held up his hand.

'A car number-plate ending in KWT. Ring any bells?'

'Sir?'

'KWT. Kathryn Wendy Thurlow.'

'Yes, sir,' said Singh. 'It's the number Bradford CID got in the Samantha Foster investigation.'

'Bingo,' said Banks. 'Now, correct me if I'm wrong, but didn't Bradford send us copies of all their files on the Samantha Foster case when this team was set up?'

'Yes, sir.'

'Including the name of everyone in the area who owned a dark car with the number-plate ending in KWT.'

'Over a thousand, sir.'

'Over a thousand. Indeed. Bradford CID interviewed them all. And guess who's among that thousand.'

'Terence Payne, sir,' answered Singh again.

'Bright lad,' said Banks. 'Now, when Bradford CID were

working on that case, did they have any links to any similar crimes?'

'No, sir,' answered Bowmore this time. 'There was the girl went missing from the New Year's party in Roundhay Park, but there was no reason to link them together at the time.'

'Right,' said Banks. 'So why do you think I issued an action shortly after this task force was set up to go over all the evidence on the previous cases, including the disappearance of Samantha Foster?'

'Because you thought there was a link, sir,' said DC Singh.

'Not just me,' said Banks. 'But, yes, three girls, as it was then. Then four. Then five. The possibility of a link was becoming stronger and stronger. Now guess who was assigned to go over the evidence in the Samantha Foster case.'

Singh and Bowmore looked at one another, then frowned and looked at Banks. 'We were, sir,' they said as one.

'Including re-interviewing the list of car owners Bradford CID got from the DVLA.'

'Over a thousand, sir.'

'Indeed,' said Banks, 'but am I correct in assuming that you had plenty of help, that the action was split up and that the letter "P" was among those alphabetically assigned to you? Because that's what it says in my files. P for Payne.'

'There were still a lot to go, sir. We haven't got around to them all yet.'

'You haven't got around to them yet? This was at the beginning of April. Over a month ago. You've been dragging your feet a bit, haven't you?'

'It's not as if it was the only action assigned us, sir,' said Bowmore.

'Look,' said Banks, 'I don't want any excuses. For one reason or another, you failed to re-interview Terence Payne.'

'But it wouldn't have made any difference, sir,' Bowmore argued. 'I mean, Bradford CID didn't exactly mark him down as their number one suspect, did they? What was he going to tell us that he didn't tell them? He wasn't going to decide to confess just because we went to talk to him, was he?'

Banks ran his hand over his hair and muttered a silent curse under his breath. He was not a natural authoritarian – far from it – and he hated this part of the job, dishing out bollockings, having been on the receiving end of plenty himself, but if anyone ever did, these two prize pillocks deserved the worst he could give. 'Is this supposed to be an example of you using your initiative?' he said. 'Because if it is, you'd have been better advised to stick to procedure and follow orders.'

'But, sir,' Singh said, 'he was a schoolteacher. Newly married. Nice house. We *did* read over all the statements.'

'I'm sorry,' said Banks, shaking his head. 'Am I missing something here?'

'What do you mean, sir?'

'Well, I'm not aware that Dr Fuller had given us any sort of profile of the person we were looking for at this point.'

DC Singh grinned. 'Hasn't given us much of anything when you get right down to it, has she, sir?'

'So what made you think you could rule out a recently married schoolteacher with a nice house?'

Singh's mouth opened and shut like a fish's. Bowmore looked down at his shoes.

'Well?' Banks repeated. 'I'm waiting.'

'Look, sir,' said Singh, 'I'm sorry but we just hadn't got around to him yet.'

'Have you talked to *any* of the people on your list?'

'A couple, sir,' muttered Singh. 'The ones Bradford CID had marked down as possibles. There was one bloke had a previous for flashing, but he had a solid alibi for Leanne Wray and Melissa Horrocks. We checked that out, sir.'

'So when you'd nothing better to do, you'd fill in a bit of overtime by ticking a name or two off the list, names that Bradford CID had put question marks beside. Is that it?'

'That's not fair, sir,' Bowmore argued.

'Not fair. I'll tell you what's not bloody fair, DC Bowmore. It's not bloody fair that at least five girls that we know of so far have most likely died at the hands of Terence Payne. That's what's not fair.'

'But he wouldn't have admitted it to us, sir,' Singh protested.

'You're supposed to be detectives, aren't you? Look, let me put it simply. If you'd gone around to Payne's house when you were supposed to, say last month, then one or two more girls might not have died.'

'You can't put that down to us, sir,' Bowmore protested, red in the face. 'That's just not on.'

'Oh, isn't it? What if you'd seen or heard something suspicious while you were in the house interviewing him? What if your finely developed detective's instinct had picked up on something and you'd asked to have a look around?'

'Bradford CID didn't—'

'I don't give a damn what Bradford CID did or didn't do. They were examining a single case: the disappearance of Samantha Foster. You, on the other hand, were investigating a case of serial abductions. If you'd had any reason at all to look in the cellar you'd have had him, believe me. Even if you'd poked around his video collection it might have raised your suspicions. If you'd looked at his car, you'd have noticed the false plates. The ones he's using now end in NGV, not KWT. That might have rung a few alarm bells, don't you think? Instead you decide on your own that this action isn't worth rushing on. God knows what else you thought was so much more important. Well?'

They both looked down.

'Nothing to say for yourselves?'

'No, sir,' muttered a tight-lipped DC Singh.

'I'll even give you the benefit of the doubt,' said Banks. 'I'll assume that you were pursuing other angles and not just skiving off. But you still screwed up.'

'But he must've lied to Bradford CID,' Bowmore argued. 'He'd only have lied to us, too.'

'You just don't get it, do you?' said Banks. 'I've told you. You're supposed to be *detectives.* You don't take anything at face value. Maybe you'd have noticed something about his body language. Maybe you'd have caught him out in a lie. Maybe – God forbid – you might have even checked one of his alibis and found it didn't hold up. Maybe just something might have made you a little bit suspicious about Terence Payne. Am I making myself clear? You had at least two, maybe three, more things to go on than Bradford had, and you blew it. Now you're off the case, both of you, and this is going on your records. Clear?'

Bowmore looked daggers at Banks, and Singh seemed close to tears, but Banks had no sympathy for either of them at that moment. He felt a splitting headache coming on. 'Get the hell out of here,' he said. 'And don't let me see you in the incident room again.'

•

Maggie hid herself away in the sanctuary of Ruth's studio. Spring sunshine spilled through the window, which she opened an inch or two to let in some air. It was a spacious room at the back of the house, originally the third bedroom, and while the view through the window left a lot to be desired – a grotty, litter-strewn back passage and the council estate beyond – the room itself was perfect for her needs. Upstairs, in addition to the three rooms, toilet and bathroom, there was also a loft, accessed by a pull-down ladder, that Ruth said she used for storage. Maggie didn't store anything there; in fact, she never even went up there, as she felt disturbed by spidery, dusty, neglected places, the mere thought of which made her shiver. She had allergies, too, and the slightest hint of dust made her eyes burn and her nose itch.

Another bonus today was that upstairs at the back of the house she wasn't constantly distracted by all the activity out on The Hill. It was open to traffic again, but number thirty-five was screened off and people kept coming and going, bringing out boxes and bags of God knew what. She couldn't quite put it out of her mind, of course, but she didn't read the newspaper that morning, and she tuned the radio to a classical station that had few news breaks.

She was preparing to illustrate a new coffee-table selection of Grimm's fairy tales, working on thumbnails and preliminary sketches, and what nasty, gruesome little stories they were, she discovered on reading through them for the first time since childhood. Back then, they had seemed remote, cartoonish, but now the horror and the violence seemed all too real. The sketch she had just finished was for 'Rumpelstiltzskin', the poison dwarf who helped Anna spin straw into gold in exchange for her first-born. Her illustration was a bit too idealized, she thought: a sad-looking girl-child at a spinning-wheel, with just the suggestion of two burning eyes and the distorted shadow of the dwarf in the background. She could hardly use the scene where he stamped so hard his foot went through the floor and his leg came off as he tried to pull it out. Matter-of-fact violence, no dwelling on blood and guts the way so many films did these days – special effects for the sake of it – but violence nonetheless.

Now she was working on 'Rapunzel' and her preliminary sketches showed the young girl – another first-born taken from her true parents – letting her long blonde hair down from the tower where she was held captive by a witch. Another happy ending, with the witch being devoured by a wolf, except for her talon-like hands and feet, which it spat out to be eaten by worms and beetles.

She was just trying to get the rope of hair and the angle of Rapunzel's head right, so that it would at least *look* as if she might be able support the prince's weight, when the telephone rang.

Maggie picked up the studio extension. 'Yes?'

'Margaret Forrest?' It was a woman's voice. 'Am I speaking to Margaret Forrest?'

'Who's asking?'

'Is that you, Margaret? My name's Lorraine Temple. You don't know me.'

'What do you want?'

'I understand that it was you who dialled in the emergency call on The Hill yesterday morning? A domestic disturbance.'

'Who are you? Are you a reporter?'

'Oh, didn't I say? Yes, I write for the *Post*.'

'I'm not supposed to talk to you. Go away.'

'Look, I'm just down the street, Margaret. I'm calling on

my mobile. The police won't let me near your house, so I wondered if you'd care to meet me for a drink or something. It's almost lunchtime. There's a nice pub—'

'I've nothing to say to you, Ms Temple, so there's no point in our meeting.'

'You *did* report a domestic disturbance at number thirty-five The Hill early yesterday morning, didn't you?'

'Yes, but—'

'Then I *have* got the right person. What made you think it was a domestic?'

'I'm sorry, I don't understand. I don't know what you mean.'

'You heard noises, didn't you? Raised voices? Breaking glass? A thud?'

'How do you know all this?'

'I'm just wondering what made you jump to the conclusion that it was a domestic disturbance, that's all. I mean, why couldn't it have been someone grappling with a burglar, for example?'

'I don't know what you're getting at.'

'Oh, come on, Margaret. It's Maggie, isn't it? Can I call you Maggie?'

Maggie said nothing. She had no idea why she didn't just hang up on Lorraine Temple.

'Look, Maggie,' Lorraine went on, 'give me a break here. I've got my living to make. Were you a friend of Lucy Payne's, is that it? Do you know something about her background? Something the rest of us don't know?'

'I can't talk to you any more,' Maggie said, and then she did hang up. But something Lorraine Temple had said struck a chord, and she regretted doing so. Despite what Banks had told her, if she were to be Lucy's friend, then the press might prove an ally, not an enemy. She might have to speak to them, to mobilize them in Lucy's support. Public sympathy would be very important, and in that the media might be able to help her. Of course, all this depended on the approach the police took. If Banks believed what Maggie had told him about the abuse, and if Lucy confirmed it, as she would, then they would realize that she was more of a victim than anything else and just let her go as soon as she was well again.

Lorraine Temple was persistent enough to call back a couple of minutes later. 'Come on, Maggie,' she said. 'Where's the harm?'

'All right,' said Maggie, 'I'll meet you for a drink. Ten minutes. I know the place you mean. It's called the Woodcutter. At the bottom of The Hill, right?'

'Right. Ten minutes. I'll be there.'

Maggie hung up. While she was still close to the phone, she took out the Yellow Pages and looked up a local florist. She arranged to have some flowers delivered to Lucy in her hospital bed, along with a note wishing her well.

Before she left, she had one last quick look at her sketch and noticed something curious about it. Rapunzel's face. It wasn't the all-purpose fairy-tale princess sort of face you saw in so many illustrations; it was individual, unique, something Maggie prided herself on. More than that, though, Rapunzel's face, half turned to the viewer, resembled Claire Toth's, even down to the two spots on her chin. Frowning, Maggie picked up her rubber and erased them before she went off to meet Lorraine Temple from the *Post*.

•

Banks hated hospitals, hated everything about them, and he had done so ever since he'd had his tonsils out at the age of nine. He hated the smell of them, the colours of the walls, the echoing sounds, the doctors' white coats and the uniforms the nurses wore, hated the beds, thermometers, syringes, stethoscopes, IVs, and the strange machines glimpsed behind half-open doors. *Everything*.

If truth be told, he had hated it all since well before the tonsil experience. When his brother Roy was born, Banks was five, seven years too young to be allowed inside a hospital at visiting time. His mother had some problems with the pregnancy – those unspecified *adult* problems that grown-ups always seemed to be whispering about – and spent an entire month there. Those were the days when they'd let you hang on to a bed that long. Banks was sent away to live with his aunt and uncle in Northampton and went to a new school for the whole period. He never settled in, and being the new boy, he had to stick up for himself against more than one bully.

He remembered his uncle driving him to the hospital to see his mother one dark, cold winter's night, holding him up to the window – thank God she was on the ground floor – so he could wipe the frost off with his wool mitten and see her swollen shape halfway along the ward and wave to her. He felt so sad. It must be a horrible place, he remembered thinking, that would keep a mother from her son and make her sleep in a room full of strange people when she was so poorly.

The tonsillectomy had only confirmed what he already knew in the first place, and now he was older, hospitals still scared the shit out of him. He saw them as last resorts, places where one *ends up*, where one goes to die, and where the well-intentioned ministrations, the probing, pricking, slicing and all the various *-ectomies* of medical science only postpone the inevitable, filling one's last days on earth with torture, pain and fear. Banks was a veritable Philip Larkin when it came to hospitals, could think only of 'the anaesthetic from which none come round'.

Lucy Payne was under guard at Leeds General Infirmary, not far from where her husband lay in intensive care after emergency surgery to remove skull splinters from his brain. The PC sitting outside her room, a dog-eared Tom Clancy paperback on the chair beside him, reported no comings or goings other than hospital staff. It had been a quiet night, he said. Lucky for some, Banks thought, as he entered the private room.

The doctor was waiting inside. She introduced herself as Dr Landsberg. No first name. Banks didn't want her there, but there was nothing he could do about it. Lucy Payne wasn't under arrest, but she *was* under the doctor's care.

'I'm afraid I can't give you very long with my patient,' she said. 'She has suffered an extremely traumatic experience, and she needs rest more than anything.'

Banks looked at the woman in the bed. Half her face, including one eye, was covered with bandages. The eye that he could see was the same shiny black as the ink he liked to use in his fountain pen. Her skin was pale and smooth, her raven's-wing hair spread out over the pillow and sheets. He thought of Kimberley Myers's body spread-eagled on the mattress. That had happened *in Lucy Payne's house*, he reminded himself.

Banks sat down beside Lucy, and Dr Landsberg hovered like a lawyer waiting to interrupt when Banks overstepped his PACE bounds.

'Lucy,' he said, 'my name's Banks, Acting Detective Superintendent Banks. I'm in charge of the investigation into the five missing girls. How are you feeling?'

'Not bad,' Lucy answered. 'Considering.'

'Is there much pain?'

'Some. My head hurts. How's Terry? What's happened to Terry? Nobody will tell me.' Her voice sounded thick, as if her tongue were swollen, and her words were slurred. The medication.

'Perhaps if you just told me what happened last night, Lucy. Can you remember?'

'Is Terry dead? Someone told me he was hurt.'

The concern of the abused wife for her abuser – if that was what he was witnessing – didn't surprise Banks very much at all; it was an old sad tune, and he had heard it many times before, in all its variations.

'Your husband was very badly injured, Lucy,' Dr Landsberg cut in. 'We're doing all we can for him.'

Banks cursed her under his breath. He didn't want Lucy Payne to know what kind of shape her husband was in; if she thought he wasn't going to survive, she could tell Banks whatever she wanted, knowing he'd have no way of checking whether it was true or not. 'Can you tell me what happened last night?' he repeated.

Lucy half closed her good eye; she was trying to remember, or pretending she was trying to remember. 'I don't know. I can't remember.'

Good answer, Banks realized. Wait and see what happens to Terry before admitting to anything. She was sharp, this one, even in her hospital bed, under medication.

'Do I need a lawyer?' she asked.

'Why would you need a lawyer?'

'I don't know. When the police talk to people . . . you know, on television . . .'

'We're not on television, Lucy.'

She wrinkled her nose. 'I know that, silly. I didn't mean . . . never mind.'

'What's the last thing you remember about what happened to you?'

'I remember waking up, getting out of bed, putting on my dressing-gown. It was late. Or early.'

'Why did you get out of bed?'

'I don't know. I must have heard something.'

'What?'

'A noise. I can't remember.'

'What did you do next?'

'I don't know. I just remember getting up and then it hurt and everything went dark.'

'Do you remember having an argument with Terry?'

'No.'

'Did you go in the cellar?'

'I don't think so. I don't remember. I might have done.'

Covering all the possibilities. 'Did you *ever* go in the cellar?'

'That was Terry's room. He would have punished me if I went down there. He kept it locked.'

Interesting, Banks thought. She could remember enough to distance herself from whatever they might have found in the cellar. Did she know? Forensics ought to be able to confirm whether she was telling the truth or not about going down there. It was the basic rule: wherever you go, you leave something behind and take something with you.

'What did he do down there?' Banks asked.

'I don't know. It was his own private den.'

'So you never went down there?'

'No. I didn't dare.'

'What do you think he did down there?'

'I don't know. Watched videos, read books.'

'Alone?'

'A man needs his privacy sometimes. That's what Terry said.'

'And you respected that?'

'Yes.'

'What about that poster on the door, Lucy? Did you ever see it?'

'Only from the top of the steps, coming in from the garage.'

'It's quite graphic, isn't it? What did you think of it?'

Lucy managed a thin smile. 'Men . . . men are like that, aren't they? They like that sort of thing.'

'So it didn't bother you?'

She did something with her lips that indicated it didn't.

'Superintendent,' Dr Landsberg cut in, 'I really think you ought to be going now and let my patient get some rest.'

'Just a couple more questions, that's all. Lucy, do you remember who hurt you?'

'I . . . I . . . it must have been Terry. There was no one else there, was there?'

'Had Terry ever hit you before?'

She turned her head sideways, so the only side Banks could see was bandaged.

'You're upsetting her, Superintendent. I really must insist—'

'Lucy, did you ever see Terry with Kimberley Myers? You do know who Kimberley Myers is, don't you?'

Lucy turned to face him again. 'Yes. She's the poor girl that went missing.'

'That's right. Did you ever see Terry with her?'

'I don't remember.'

'She was a pupil at Silverhill, where Terry taught. Did he ever mention her?'

'I don't think so . . . I . . .'

'You don't remember.'

'No. I'm sorry. What's wrong? What's happening? Can I see Terry?'

'I'm afraid you can't, not at the moment,' said Dr Landsberg. Then she turned to Banks. 'I'm going to have to ask you to leave now. You can see how agitated Lucy is becoming.'

'When can I talk to her again?'

'I'll let you know. Soon. Please.' She took Banks by the arm.

Banks knew when he was beaten. Besides, the interview was going nowhere. He didn't know whether Lucy was telling the truth about not remembering or whether she was confused because of her medication.

'Get some rest, Lucy,' Dr Landsberg said as they left.

'Mr Banks? Superintendent?'

It was Lucy, her small, thick, slurred voice, her obsidian eye fixing him in its gaze.

'Yes?'

'When can I go home?'

Banks had a mental image of what *home* would look like right now, and probably for the next month or more. *Under construction*. 'I don't know,' he said. 'We'll be in touch.'

Outside in the corridor, Banks turned to Dr Landsberg. 'Can you help me with something, Doctor?'

'Perhaps.'

'Her not remembering. Is that symptomatic?'

Dr Landsberg rubbed her eyes. She looked as if she got about as much sleep as Banks did. Someone paged a Dr Thorsen over the PA system. 'It's possible,' she said. 'In cases like this there's often post-traumatic stress disorder, one of the effects of which can be retrograde amnesia.'

'Do you think that's the case with Lucy?'

'Too early to say, and I'm not an expert in the field. You'd have to talk to a neurologist. All I can say is that we're pretty certain there's no physical brain damage, but emotional stress can be a factor, too.'

'Is this memory loss selective?'

'What do you mean?'

'She seems to remember her husband was hurt and that he was the one who hit her, but nothing else.'

'It's possible, yes.'

'Is it likely to be permanent?'

'Not necessarily.'

'So her complete memory might come back?'

'In time.'

'How long?'

'Impossible to say. As early as tomorrow, as late as . . . well, maybe never. We know so little about the brain.'

'Thank you, Doctor. You've been very helpful.'

Dr Landsberg gave him a puzzled glance. 'Not at all,' she said. 'Superintendent, I hope I'm not speaking out of turn, but I had a word with Dr Mogabe – he's Terence Payne's doctor – just before you came.'

'Yes.'

'He's very concerned.'

'Oh?' This was what DC Hodgkins had told Banks the day before.

'Yes. It seems as if his patient was assaulted by a policewoman.'

'Not my case,' said Banks.

Dr Landsberg's eyes widened. 'Just like that? You're not at all concerned?'

'Whether I'm concerned or not doesn't enter into it. Someone else is investigating the assault on Terence Payne and will no doubt be talking to Dr Mogabe in due course. My interest is in the five dead girls and the Paynes. Goodbye, Doctor.'

And Banks walked off down the corridor, footsteps echoing, leaving Dr Landsberg to her dark thoughts. An orderly pushed a whey-faced, wrinkled old man past on a gurney, IV hooked up, on his way to surgery by the look of things.

Banks shuddered and walked faster.

7

One good thing about the family-style chain pubs, thought Maggie, was that nobody raised an eyebrow if you only ordered a pot of tea or a cup of coffee, which was all she wanted when she met Lorraine Temple at the Woodcutter that Tuesday lunchtime.

Lorraine was a plump, petite brunette with an easy manner and an open face, a face you could trust. She was about Maggie's age, early thirties, wearing black jeans and jacket over a white silk blouse. She bought the coffees and put Maggie at ease with some small talk and sympathetic noises about the recent events on The Hill, then she got down to business. She used a notebook rather than a tape recorder, Maggie was glad to see. For some reason, she didn't like the idea of her voice, her words, being recorded as sounds, but as squiggles on the page, they hardly seemed to matter.

'Do you use shorthand?' she asked, thinking nobody used that any more.

Lorraine smiled up at her. 'My own version. Would you like something to eat?'

'No, thanks. I'm not hungry.'

'Okay. We'll start, then, if that's all right with you?'

Maggie tensed a little, waiting for the questions. The pub was quiet, mostly because it was a weekday and the bottom of The Hill was hardly a tourist area or a business centre. There were a couple of industrial estates near by, but it wasn't quite lunchtime yet. Pop music played on the jukebox at an acceptable level, and even the few children in the family room seemed more subdued than she would have expected. Maybe the recent events had got to everyone in one way or another. It felt as if a pall lay over the place.

'Can you tell me how it happened?' Lorraine asked first.

Maggie thought for a moment. 'Well, I don't sleep very well, and maybe I was awake or it woke me up, I'm not sure, but I heard noises across the street.'

'What noises?'

'Voices arguing. A man's and a woman's. Then a sound of glass breaking and then a thud.'

'And you know this was coming from across the street?'

'Yes. When I looked out of the window, there was a light on and I thought I saw a shadow pass across it.'

Lorraine paused a moment to catch up with her notes. 'Why were you so sure it was a domestic incident?' she asked, as she had done over the phone.

'It just . . . I mean . . .'

'Take your time, Maggie. I don't want to rush you. Think back. Try to remember.'

Maggie ran her hand over her hair. 'Well, I didn't *know* for certain,' she said. 'I suppose I just assumed, from the raised voices and, you know . . .'

'Did you recognize the voices?'

'No. They were too muffled.'

'But it *could* have been someone fighting off a burglar, couldn't it? I understand there's quite a high burglary rate in this area?'

'That's true.'

'So what I'm getting at, Maggie, is that maybe there was some other reason you thought you were witnessing a domestic argument.'

Maggie paused. Her moment of decision had arrived, and when it came, it was more difficult than she had thought it would be. For one thing, she didn't want her name splashed all over the papers in case Bill saw it back in Toronto, though she very much doubted that even he would come this far to get at her. There was little likelihood of such exposure with a regional daily like the *Post*, of course, but if the national press got onto it, that would be another matter. This was a big story, and the odds were that it would at least make the *National Post* and the *Globe and Mail* back home.

On the other hand, she had to remember her goal, focus on what was important here: Lucy's predicament. First and foremost she was talking to Lorraine Temple in order to get the image of *Lucy the victim* in people's minds. Call it a pre-emptive strike: the more the public saw her that way from the start, the less likely they were to believe that she was the embodiment of evil. All people knew so far was that the body of Kimberley Myers had been found in the Paynes's cellar, and a policeman had been killed, most likely by Terence Payne, but everyone knew they were digging there, and everyone knew what they were likely to find. 'Maybe there was,' she said.

'Could you elaborate on that?'

Maggie sipped some coffee. It was lukewarm. In Toronto, she remembered, they would come round and refill your cup once or twice. Not here. 'I might have had reason to believe that Lucy Payne was in danger from her husband.'

'Did she tell you that?'

'Yes.'

'That her husband abused her?'

'Yes.'

'What do *you* think of Terence Payne?'

'Not much, really.'

'Do you like him?'

'Not particularly.' *Not at all*, Maggie admitted to herself. Terence Payne very much gave her the creeps. She didn't know why, but she would cross the street if she saw him coming rather than meet, say hello and make small talk about the weather, all the time with him looking at her in that curiously empty, dispassionate way he had, as if she were a butterfly pinned to a felt pad, or a frog on the table ready for dissection.

As far as she knew, though, she was the only one to feel that way. He was handsome and charming on the surface, and according to Lucy he was popular at school, both with the kids and with his colleagues on the staff. But there was still something about him that put Maggie off, an emptiness at his centre that she found disturbing. With most people, she felt that whatever it was she communicated, whatever radar or sonar beam went out, bounced off something and came back in some manner, made some sort of blip on the screen. With Terry, it didn't; it disappeared in the vast, sprawling darkness inside him, where it echoed for ever unheard. That was the only way she could explain how she felt about Terry Payne.

She admitted to herself that she might be imagining it, responding to some deep fear or inadequacy of her own – and God knew, there were enough of those – so she had resolved to try to like him for Lucy's sake, but it had been difficult.

'What did you do after Lucy told you this?'

'Talked to her, tried to persuade her to seek professional help.'

'Have you ever worked with abused women?'

'No, not really. I . . .'

'Were you a victim of abuse, yourself?'

Maggie felt herself tightening up inside; her head started to spin. She reached for her cigarettes, offered one to Lorraine, who refused, then lit up. She had never talked about the details of her life with Bill – the pattern of violence and remorse, blows and presents – with anyone here except her psychiatrist and Lucy Payne. 'I'm not here to talk about me,' she said. 'I don't want you to write about me. I'm here to talk about Lucy. I don't know what happened in that house, but it's my feeling that Lucy was as much a victim as anything else.'

Lorraine put her notebook aside and finished her coffee. 'You're Canadian, aren't you?' she asked.

Surprised, Maggie answered that she was.

'Where from?'

'Toronto. Why?'

'Just curious, that's all. I've got a cousin lives there. That house you're living in. Tell me, but doesn't it belong to Ruth Everett, the illustrator?'

'Yes, it does.'

'I thought so. I interviewed her there once. She seems like a nice person.'

'She's been a good friend.'

'How did you meet, if you don't mind my asking?'

'We met professionally, at a convention a few years ago.'

'So you're an illustrator, too?'

'Yes. Children's books, mostly.'

'Perhaps we can do a feature on you and your work?'

'I'm not very well known. Illustrators rarely are.'

'Even so. We're always looking for local celebrities.'

Maggie felt herself blush. 'Well I'm hardly that.'

'I'll talk with my features editor, anyway, if that's okay with you?'

'I'd rather you didn't, if that's all right.'

'But—'

'Please! No. Okay?'

Lorraine held her hand up. 'All right. I've never known anyone turn down a bit of free publicity before, but if you insist . . .' She put her notebook and pencil in her handbag. 'I must be going now,' she said. 'Thank you for talking to me.'

Maggie watched her leave, feeling oddly apprehensive. She looked at her watch. Time for a little walk around the pond before heading back to work.

•

'Well you certainly know how to pamper a girl,' Tracy said as Banks led her into the McDonald's at the corner of Briggate and Boar Lane later that afternoon.

Banks laughed. 'I thought all kids loved McDonald's.'

Tracy nudged him in the ribs. 'Enough of the "kid", please,' she said. 'I'm twenty now, you know.'

For one horrible moment Banks feared he might have forgotten her birthday. But no. It was back in February, before the task force, and he had sent a card, given her some money and taken her out to dinner at Brasserie 44. A very expensive dinner. 'Not even a teenager any more, then,' he said.

'That's right.'

And it was true. Tracy was a young woman, now. An attractive one at that. It almost broke Banks's heart to see how much she resembled Sandra twenty years ago: the same willowy figure, with the same dark eyebrows, high cheekbones, hair in a long blonde ponytail, stray tresses tucked behind her delicate ears. She even echoed some of Sandra's mannerisms, such as biting her lower lip when she was concentrating and winding strands of hair around her fingers as she talked. She was dressed like a student today: blue jeans, white T-shirt with a rock band's logo, denim jacket, carrying a backpack, and she moved with assurance and grace. A young woman, no doubt about it.

Banks had returned her phone call that morning, and they had arranged to meet for a late lunch, after her last lecture of the day. He had also told Christopher Wray that they hadn't found his daughter's body yet.

They stood in line. The place was full of office workers on afternoon break, truant schoolkids and mothers with prams and toddlers taking a break from their shopping. 'What do you want?' Banks asked. 'My treat.'

'In that case, I'll have the full Monty. Big Mac, large fries and large Coke.'

'Sure that's all?'

'We'll see about a sweet later.'

'It'll bring you out in spots.'

'No, it won't. I *never* come out in spots.'

It was true. Tracy had always had a flawless complexion; school friends had often hated her for it. 'You'll get fat, then.'

She patted her flat stomach and pulled a face at him. She had inherited his metabolism, which allowed him to live on beer and junk food and still remain lean.

They got their food and sat at a plastic table near the window. It was a warm afternoon. Women wore bright sleeveless summer dresses, and the men had their suit jackets slung over their shoulders and their shirt-sleeves rolled up.

'How's Damon?' Banks asked.

'We've decided not to see each other till after exams.'

There was something about Tracy's tone that indicated there was more to it than that. Boyfriend trouble? With the monosyllabic Damon, who had spirited her off to Paris last November, when Banks himself should have been with her instead of hunting down Chief Constable Riddle's wayward daughter? He didn't want to make her talk about it; she would get to it in her own time, if she wanted to. He couldn't make her talk, anyway; Tracy had always been a very private person and could be as stubborn as he was when it came to discussing her feelings. He bit into his Big Mac. Special sauce oozed down his chin. He wiped it off with a serviette. Tracy was already halfway through her burger, and the chips were disappearing quickly, too.

'I'm sorry I haven't been in touch very often lately,' Banks said. 'I've been very busy.'

'Story of my life,' said Tracy.

'I suppose so.'

She put her hand on his arm. 'I'm only teasing, Dad. I've got nothing to complain about.'

'You've got plenty, but it's nice of you not to say so. Anyway, apart from Damon, how are *you*?'

'I'm fine. Studying hard. Some people say second year's harder than finals.'

'Any plans for the summer?'

'I might go to France again. Charlotte's parents have a cottage in the Dordogne but they're going to be in America and they said she can take a couple of friends down if she wants.'

'Lucky you.'

Tracy finished her Big Mac and sipped some Coke through her straw, looking closely at Banks. 'You look tired, Dad,' she said.

'I suppose I am.'

'Your job?'

'Yes. It's a lot of responsibility. Keeps me awake at night. I'm not at all certain I'm cut out for it.'

'I'm sure you're just wonderful.'

'Such faith. But I don't know. I've never run such a big investigation before, and I'm not sure I ever want to again.'

'But you've caught him,' Tracy said. 'The Chameleon killer.'

'Looks that way.'

'Congratulations. I knew you would.'

'I didn't do anything. The whole thing was a series of accidents.'

'Well . . . the result's the same, isn't it?'

'True.'

'Look, Dad, I know why you haven't been in touch. You've been busy, yes, but it's more than that, isn't it?'

Banks pushed his half-eaten burger aside and worked on the chips. 'What do you mean?'

'You know what I mean. You probably held yourself personally responsible for those girls' abductions, the way you always do, didn't you?'

'I wouldn't say that.'

'I'll bet you thought that if you relaxed your vigilance for just one single moment he'd get someone else, another young woman *just like me*, didn't you?'

Banks applauded his daughter's perception. And she did have blonde hair. 'Well, there may be a grain of truth in that,' he said. 'Just a tiny grain.'

'Was it really horrible down there?'

'I don't want to talk about it. Not at lunch. Not with you.'

'I suppose you think I'm being nosy for sensation like a

newspaper reporter, but I worry about you. You're not made of stone, you know. You let these things get to you.'

'For a daughter,' said Banks, 'you do a pretty good impersonation of a nagging wife.' Immediately the words were out of his mouth he regretted them. It brought the spectre of Sandra between them, again. Tracy, like Brian, had struggled not to take sides in the break-up, but whereas Brian had taken an immediate dislike to Sean, Sandra's new companion, Tracy got along with him quite well and that hurt Banks, though he would never tell her.

'Have you talked to Mum lately?' Tracy asked, ignoring his criticism.

'You know I haven't.'

Tracy sipped some more Coke, frowned like her mother, and stared out of the window.

'Why?' Banks asked, sensing a change in the atmosphere. 'Is there something I should know?'

'I was down there at Easter.'

'I know you were. Did she say something about me?' Banks knew he had been dragging his feet over the divorce. The whole thing had just seemed too hurried to him, and he wasn't inclined to hurry, seeing no reason. So Sandra wanted to marry Sean, make it legal. Big deal. Let them wait.

'It's not that,' Tracy said.

'What, then?'

'You really don't know?'

'I'd say if I did.'

'Oh, shit.' Tracy bit her lip. 'I wish I'd never got into this. Why do I have to be the one?'

'Because you started it. And don't swear. Now, give.'

Tracy looked down at her empty chip carton and sighed.

'All right. She told me not to say anything to you yet, but you'll find out eventually. Remember, you asked for it.'

'Tracy!'

'Okay. Okay. Mum's pregnant. That's what it's all about. She's three months pregnant. She's having Sean's baby.'

•

Not long after Banks had left Lucy Payne's room, Annie Cabbot strode down the corridors of the hospital to her appointment with Dr Mogabe. She hadn't been at all satisfied with PC Taylor's statement and needed to check out the medical angle as far as it was possible to do so. Of course, Payne wasn't dead, so there would be no post mortem, at least not yet. If he had done what it very much seemed that he had, then Annie thought it might not be such a bad idea to carry out a post mortem on him while he was still alive.

'Come in,' called Dr Mogabe.

Annie went in. The office was small and functional, with a couple of bookcases full of medical texts, a filing cabinet whose top drawer wouldn't shut, and the inevitable computer on the desk, a laptop. Various medical degrees and honours hung on the cream-painted walls, and a pewter-framed photograph stood on the desk facing the doctor. A family picture, Annie guessed. There was no skull beside it, though; nor was there a skeleton standing in the corner.

Dr Mogabe was smaller than Annie had imagined, and his voice was higher in pitch. His skin was a shiny purple-black and his short curly hair grey. He also had small hands, but the fingers were long and tapered; a brain surgeon's fingers, Annie thought, though she had nothing for comparison, and the thought of them poking their way through the grey matter made her stomach lurch. Pianist's fingers, she decided. Much easier to live with. Or artist's fingers, like her father's.

He leaned forward and linked his hands on the desk. 'I'm glad you're here, Detective Inspector Cabbot,' he said, with a voice straight out of Oxford. 'Indeed, if the police hadn't seen fit to call, I would have felt obliged to bring them in myself. Mr Payne was most brutally beaten.'

'Always willing to be of service,' said Annie. 'What can you tell me about the patient? In layman's terms, if you please.'

Dr Mogabe inclined his head slightly. 'Of course,' he said, as if he already knew the élite, technical mumbo-jumbo of his profession would be wasted on an ignorant copper such as Annie. 'Mr Payne was admitted with serious head wounds, resulting in brain damage. He also had a broken ulna. So far, we have operated on him twice. Once to relieve a subdural hematoma. That's—'

'I know what a hematoma is,' said Annie.

'Very well. The second to remove skull fragments from the brain. I could be more specific, if you wish?'

'Go ahead.'

Dr Mogabe stood up and started walking back and forth behind his desk, hands clasped behind his back, as if he were delivering a lecture. When he came to name the various parts, he pointed to them on his own skull as he paced. 'The human brain is essentially made up of the cerebrum, the cerebellum and the brainstem. The cerebrum is uppermost, divided into two hemispheres by a deep groove at the top, giving what you have probably heard called right brain and left brain. Do you follow?'

'I think so.'

'Prominent grooves also divide each hemisphere into lobes. The frontal lobe is the largest. There are also parietal, temporal and occipital lobes. The cerebellum is at the base of the skull, behind the brainstem.'

When Dr Mogabe had finished, he sat down again, looking very pleased with himself.

'How many blows were there?' Annie asked.

'It's difficult to be specific at this stage,' said Dr Mogabe. 'I was concerned merely with saving the man's life, you understand, not with conducting an autopsy, but at an estimate I'd say two blows to the left temple, perhaps three. They caused the most damage to begin with, including the hematoma and skull fragments. There is also evidence of one or two blows to the top of the cranium, denting the skull.'

'The *top* of his head?'

'The cranium is that part of the head which isn't the face, yes.'

'Hard blows? As if someone hit directly down on it?'

'Possibly. But I can't be a judge of that. They would have been incapacitating, but not life-threatening. The top of the cranium is hard, and though the skull there was dented and fractured, as I said, the bone didn't splinter.'

Annie made some notes.

'Those weren't the most damaging injuries, though,' Dr Mogabe added.

'Oh?'

'No, the most serious injury was caused by one or more blows to the back of the head, the brainstem area. You see, that contains the medulla oblongata, which is the heart, blood vessel and breathing centre of the brain. Any serious injury to it can be fatal.'

'Yet Mr Payne is still alive.'

'Barely.'

'Is there a possibility of permanent brain damage?'

'There already *is* permanent brain damage. If Mr Payne recovers, he may well spend the rest of his life in a wheelchair in need of twenty-four hour a day care. The only good thing is that he probably won't be aware of that fact.'

'This injury to the medulla? Could it have occurred as Mr Payne fell back against the wall?'

Dr Mogabe rubbed his chin. 'Again, it's not my place to do the police's job, or the pathologist's, Detective Inspector. Suffice it to say that in *my* opinion these wounds were caused by the same blunt instrument as the others. Make of that what you will.' He leaned forward. 'In the simplest layman's terms, this man received a most vicious beating about the head, Detective Inspector. Most vicious. I hope you believe, as I do, that the perpetrator should be brought to justice.'

Shit, thought Annie, putting her notebook away. 'Of course, Doctor,' she said, heading for the door. 'You will keep me informed, won't you?'

'You can count on it.'

Annie looked at her watch. Time to head back to Eastvale and prepare her daily report for Detective Superintendent Chambers.

•

After his lunch with Tracy, Banks wandered around Leeds city centre in a daze thinking of the news she had given him. The matter of Sandra's pregnancy had hit him harder than he would have expected after so long apart, he realized as he stood and gazed in Curry's window on Briggate, hardly taking in the display of computers, camcorders and stereo systems. He had last seen her in London the previous November, when he was down there searching for Chief Constable Riddle's runaway daughter, Emily. Looking back, he felt foolish for the way he had approached that meeting, full of confidence that because he had applied for a job with the National Crime Squad that would take him back to live in London, Sandra would see the error of her ways, dump the temporary Sean and run back into Banks's arms.

Wrong.

Instead she had told Banks that she wanted a divorce because she and Sean wanted to get married, and that cathartic event, he thought, had flushed Sandra out of his system for ever, along with any thoughts of moving to the NCS.

Until Tracy told him about the pregnancy.

Banks hadn't thought, hadn't suspected for a moment, that they wanted to get married because they wanted to have a baby. What on earth did Sandra think she was playing at? The idea of a half brother or sister for Brian and Tracy, twenty years younger, seemed unreal to Banks. And the thought of Sean, whom he had never met, being the *father* seemed even more absurd. He tried to imagine their conversations leading up to the decision, the love-making, the maternal desire rekindled in Sandra after so many years, and even the shadowiest of imaginings made him feel sick. He didn't know her, this woman in her early forties who wanted a baby with a boyfriend she had hardly been with for five minutes, and that also made Banks feel sad.

Banks was in Borders looking at the colourful display of bestsellers, and he didn't even remember walking into the shop, when his mobile rang. He went outside and ducked into the Victoria Quarter before answering, leaning near the entrance across from the Harvey Nichols café. It was Stefan.

'Alan, thought you'd like to know ASAP, we've identified the three bodies in the cellar. Got lucky with the dentists. We'll still run the DNA, though, cross-check with the parents.'

'That's great,' said Banks, snapping back from his gloomy thoughts of Sandra and Sean. 'And?'

'Melissa Horrocks, Samantha Foster and Kelly Matthews.'

'What?'

'I said—'

'I know. I heard what you said. I just . . .' People were walking by with their shopping and Banks didn't want to be overheard. To be truthful, he also still felt like a bit of a dickhead talking on his mobile in public, though from what he saw around him, nobody else did. He had even once witnessed a father sitting in a Helmthorpe café phone his daughter in the playground across the road when it was time to go home, and curse because the kid had switched her mobile off so he had to walk across the road and shout to her instead. 'I'm just surprised, that's all.'

'Why? What's wrong?'

'It's the sequence,' Banks said. 'It's all wrong.' He lowered his voice and hoped that Stefan could still hear him. 'Working backwards: Kimberley Myers, Melissa Horrocks, Leanne Wray, Samantha Foster, Kelly Matthews. One of the three should be Leanne Wray. Why isn't she there?'

A little girl holding her mother's hand gave Banks a curious look as they passed him by in the arcade. Banks switched off his mobile and headed towards Millgarth.

•

Jenny Fuller was surprised to find Banks ringing her doorbell that evening. It was a long time since he had visited her at home. They had met many times, for coffee or drinks, even lunch or dinner, but rarely had he come here. Jenny had often wondered whether this was anything to do with that clumsy attempt at seduction the first time they had worked together.

'Come in,' she said, and Banks followed her through the narrow hall into the high-ceilinged living room. She had redecorated and rearranged the furniture since his last visit and noticed him glancing around in that policeman's way of his, checking it out. Well, the expensive stereo was the same, and the sofa, she thought, smiling to herself, was the very same one where she had tried to seduce him.

She had bought a small television and video when she got back from America, having picked up the habit of watching there, but apart from the wallpaper and carpeting, nothing much else had changed. She noticed his gaze settle on the Emily Carr print over the fireplace, a huge dark, steep mountain dominating a village in the foreground. Jenny had fallen in love with Emily Carr's work when she was doing postgraduate work in Vancouver and had bought that print to bring back as a reminder of her three years there. Happy years, for the most part.

'Drink?' she asked.

'Whatever you're pouring.'

'Knew I could count on you. I'm sorry I don't have any Laphroaig. Is red wine okay?'

'Fine.'

Jenny went to pour the wine and noticed Banks walk over to the window. The Green looked peaceful enough in the golden evening sunlight, long shadows, dark green leaves, people walking their dogs, kids holding hands. Perhaps he was remembering the second time he visited her, Jenny thought with a shudder as she poured the Sainsbury's Côtes du Rhone.

A drugged-out kid called Mick Webster had held her hostage with a handgun and Banks had managed to defuse the situation. The kid's mood swings had been extreme, and the whole thing had been touch and go for a while. Jenny had been terrified. Ever since that day she had been unable to listen to *Tosca*, which had been playing in the background at the time. When she had poured the wine, she shook off the bad memory, put a CD of Mozart's string quartets on and carried the glasses over to the sofa.

'Cheers.' They clinked glasses. Banks looked as tired as Jenny had ever seen him. His skin was pale and even his normally sharp and lean features seemed to be sagging on the bone the way his suit sagged on his frame, and his eyes seemed more deeply set than usual, duller, lacking their usual sparkle. Still, she told herself, the poor sod probably hasn't had a decent night's sleep since he was put in charge of the task force. She wanted to reach out and touch his face, smooth away the cares, but she didn't dare risk rejection again.

'So? To what do I owe the honour?' Jenny said. 'I'm assuming it's not just my irresistible company that's brought you here?'

Banks smiled. It made him look a little better, she thought. A little. 'I'd like to say it was,' he answered, 'but I'd be a liar if I did.'

'And God forbid you should ever be a liar, Alan Banks. Such an honourable man. But couldn't you be a bit *less* honourable sometimes? The rest of us human beings, well, we can't help the occasional untruth, but you, no, you can't even lie to give a girl a compliment.'

'Jenny, I just couldn't stay away. Some inner force drove me to your house, compelled me to seek you out. I just knew I had to come—'

Jenny laughed and waved him down. 'All right, all right.

That's enough. Honourable is much better.' She ran her hand through her hair. 'How's Sandra?'

'Sandra's pregnant.'

Jenny shook her head as if she had been slapped. 'She's *what*?'

'She's pregnant. I'm sorry to state it so abruptly, but I can't think of a better way.'

'That's all right. I'm just a bit gobsmacked.'

'You and me both.'

'How do you feel about it?'

'You sound like a psychologist.'

'I *am* a psychologist.'

'I know. But you don't have to sound like one. How do I feel about it? I don't know yet. When you get right down to it, it's none of my business, is it? I let go the night she asked for a divorce so she could marry Sean.'

'Is that why . . .?'

'Yes. They want to get married, make the kid legal.'

'Did you talk to her?'

'No. Tracy told me. Sandra and I . . . well, we don't communicate much any more.'

'That's sad, Alan.'

'Maybe.'

'There's still a lot of anger and bitterness?'

'Funnily enough, there isn't. Oh, I know I might sound a bit upset, but it was the shock, that's all. I mean, there was a lot of anger, but it was sort of a revelation when she asked for the divorce. A release. I knew then that it was really over and that I should just get on with my life.'

'And?'

'And I have done, for the most part.'

'But residual feelings surprise you sometimes? Creep up behind you and hit you on the back of your head?'

'I suppose you could say that.'

'Welcome to the human race, Alan. You ought to know by now that you don't stop having feelings for someone just because you split up.'

'It was all new to me. She was the only woman I'd been with for any length of time. The only one I wanted. Now I know what it feels like. Naturally, I wish them all the best.'

'*Meow.* There you go again.'

Banks laughed. 'No. Really, I do.'

Jenny sensed that there was something he wasn't telling her, but she also knew that he guarded his feelings when he wanted to and she would get nowhere if she pushed him. Best move on to the business at hand, she thought. And if he wants to say anything more about Sandra, he'll say it in his own time. 'That wasn't why you came to see me, either, was it?'

'Not really. Maybe partly. But I do want to talk to you about the case.'

'Any new developments?'

'Just one.' Banks told her about the identification of the three bodies and how he found it puzzling.

'Curious,' Jenny agreed. 'I would have expected some sort of sequence, too. They're still digging outside?'

'Oh, yes. They'll be out there for a while.'

'There wasn't much room in that little cellar.'

'Just enough for about three, true,' said Banks, 'but that still doesn't explain why it isn't the most *recent* three. Anyway, I'd just like to go over some stuff with you. Remember when you suggested, quite early on, that the killer might have had an accomplice?'

'It was only a remote possibility. Despite the inordinate amounts of publicity your Wests and Bradys and Hindleys get, the killer couple is still a rare phenomenon. I assume you're thinking of Lucy Payne?'

Banks sipped some wine. 'I talked to her at the hospital. She . . . well, she said she didn't remember much about what happened.'

'Not surprising,' said Jenny. 'Retrograde amnesia.'

'That's what Dr Landsberg said. It's not that I don't believe in it – I've come across it before – it's just so damn . . .'

'Convenient?'

'That's one way of putting it. Jenny, I just couldn't get over the feeling that she was waiting, calculating, stalling in some way.'

'Waiting for what?'

'Waiting to see which way the wind was going to blow, as if she can't work out what to say until she knows what's happening with Terry. And it would make sense, wouldn't it?'

'What would?'

'The way the girls were taken. A girl walking home on her own would be most unlikely to stop and give directions, say, to a male driver, but she might stop if a woman called her over.'

'And the man?'

'Crouched down in the back seat with the chloroform ready? Jumps out the back door and drags her in? I don't know the details. But it makes sense, doesn't it?'

'Yes, it makes sense. Have you got any other evidence of her complicity?'

'None. But it's early days yet. The SOCOs are still going through the house and the lab boys are working on the clothes she was wearing when she was assaulted. Even that might come to nothing if she says she went down in the cellar, saw what her husband had done and ran away screaming. That's what I mean about her waiting to see which way the wind blows. If Terence Payne dies, Lucy's home free. If he lives, his memory could be damaged irretrievably. He *is* very badly hurt. And even if he recovers, he might decide to protect her, gloss over what part she played.'

'If she played a part. She certainly couldn't rely on his memory being damaged, or his dying.'

'That's true. But it might have given her the perfect opportunity to cover up her own involvement, if there was any. You had a look around the house, didn't you?'

'Yes.'

'What was your impression?'

Jenny sipped some wine and thought about it: the magazine-perfect décor, the little knick-knacks, the obsessive cleanliness. 'I suppose you're thinking of the videos and books?' she said.

'Partly. There looked to be some pretty raunchy stuff, especially in the bedroom.'

'So they're into porn and kinky sex. So what?' She raised her eyebrows. 'As a matter of fact, I've got a couple of soft porn videos in my bedroom. I don't mind a little kinkiness, now and then. Oh, don't blush, Alan. I'm not trying to seduce you. I'm simply pointing out that a few videos featuring three-way sex and a bit of mild, consensual S & M don't necessarily make a killer.'

'I know that.'

'And while it is true,' Jenny went on, 'that, statistically, most sex killers are into pornography of an extreme kind, it's false logic to argue the opposite.'

'I know that, too,' said Banks. 'What about the occult

connection? I wondered about the candles and incense in the cellar.'

'Could be just for atmosphere.'

'But there *was* a sort of ritual element.'

'Possibly.'

'I was even wondering if there could be some connection there with the fourth victim, Melissa Horrocks. She was into that Satanic rock music stuff. You know, Marilyn Manson and the rest.'

'Or maybe Payne just has an extreme sense of irony in his choice of victims. But look, Alan, even if Lucy did get off on the kinky stuff and Satanism, it's hardly evidence of anything else, is it?'

'I'm not asking for court evidence. At the moment I'll take anything I can get.'

Jenny laughed. 'Clutching at straws again?'

'Maybe so. Ken Blackstone reckons Payne might also be the Seacroft Rapist.'

'Seacroft Rapist?'

'Two years ago, between May and August. You were in America. A man raped six women in Seacroft. Never caught. It turns out Payne was living there, single, at the time. He met Lucy that July, and they moved to The Hill around the beginning of September, when he started teaching at Silverhill. The rapes stopped.'

'It wouldn't be the first time a serial killer was a rapist first.'

'Indeed not. Anyway, they're working on DNA.'

'Have a smoke if you want,' Jenny said. 'I can see you're getting all twitchy.'

'Am I? I will, then, if you don't mind.'

Jenny brought him an ashtray she kept in the sideboard for the occasional visitor who smoked. Though a non-smoker herself, she wasn't as fanatical about not allowing any smoking in her house as some of her friends were. In fact, her time in California had made her hate the nico-nazis even more than the smokers.

'What do you want me to do?' she asked.

'Your job,' said Banks, leaning forward. 'And the way I see it now is that we've probably got enough to convict Terry Payne ten times over, if he survives. It's Lucy I'm interested in, and time's running out.'

'What do you mean?'

Banks drew on his cigarette before answering. 'As long as she stays in hospital, we're fine, but as soon as she's released we can only hold her for twenty-four hours. Oh, we can get extensions, maybe in an extreme case like this up to ninety-six hours, but we'd better damn well have something solid to go on if we're going to do that, or she walks.'

'I still think it's more than possible that she had nothing to do with the killings. Something woke her up that night and her husband wasn't there, so she looked around the house for him, saw the lights in the cellar, went down and saw . . .'

'But why hadn't she noticed before, Jenny? Why hadn't she been down there before?'

'She was afraid to. It sounds as if she's terrified of her husband. Look at what happened to her when she did go down.'

'I know that. But Kimberley Myers was the fifth victim, for God's sake. The *fifth.* Why did it take Lucy so long to find out? Why did she wake up and go exploring only *this* time? She said she *never* went down in the cellar, that she didn't dare. What was so different about this time?'

'Perhaps she didn't *want* to know before. But, don't forget, the way it looks is that Payne was escalating, unravelling. I'd guess he was fast becoming highly unstable. Perhaps this time even she couldn't look away.'

Jenny watched Banks take a contemplative drag on his cigarette and let the smoke out slowly. 'You think so?' he said.

'It's possible, isn't it? Earlier, if her husband was behaving strangely, she might have suspected that he had some sort of horrible secret vice, and she wanted to pretend it wasn't there, the way most of us do with bad things.'

'Sweep it under the carpet?'

'Or play the ostrich. Bury her head in the sand. Yes. Why not?'

'So we're both agreed that there are any number of possibilities to explain what happened and that Lucy Payne might be innocent?'

'Where are you going with this, Alan?'

'I want you to dig deep into Lucy Payne's background. I want you to find out all you can about her. I want—'

'But—'

'No, let me finish, Jenny. I want you to get to know her inside out, her background, her childhood, her family, her fantasies, her hopes, her fears.'

'Slow down, Alan. What's the point of all this?'

'You might come across something that implicates her.'

'Or absolves her?'

Banks held his hands out, palms open. 'If that's what you find, fine. I'm not asking you to make anything up. Just dig.'

'Even if I do, I might not come up with anything useful at all.'

'Doesn't matter. At least we'll have tried.'

'Isn't this a police job?'

Banks stubbed out his cigarette. 'Not really. I'm after an

evaluation here, an in-depth psychological profile of Lucy Payne. Of course, *we'll* check out any leads you might stumble across. I don't expect you to play detective.'

'Well, I'm grateful for that.'

'Think about it, Jenny. If she's guilty, she didn't just start helping her husband abduct and kill young girls out of the blue on New Year's Eve. There has to be some pathology, some background of psychological disturbance, some abnormal pattern of behaviour, doesn't there?'

'There usually is. But even if I find out she was a bed-wetter, liked to start fires and torture animals, it *still* won't give you anything you can use against her in court.'

'It will if someone was hurt in the fire. It will if you find out about any other mysterious events in her life that we can investigate. That's all I'm asking, Jenny. That you make a start on the psychopathology of Lucy Payne, and if you turn up anything we should investigate further, you let us know and we do it.'

'And if I turn up nothing?'

'Then we go nowhere. But we're already nowhere.'

Jenny sipped some more wine and thought for a moment. Alan seemed so intense about it that she was feeling browbeaten, and she didn't want to give in just because of that. But she *was* intrigued by his request; she couldn't deny that the enigma of Lucy Payne interested her both professionally *and* as a woman. She had never had the chance to probe the psychology of a possible serial killer up close before, and Banks was right that if Lucy Payne were complicit in her husband's acts, then she hadn't just come from nowhere. If Jenny dug deeply enough, there was a chance that she might find something in Lucy's past. After that . . . well, Banks had said that was the police's job, and he was right about that, too.

She topped up their wine glasses. 'What if I agree?' she asked. 'Where do I start?'

'Right here,' said Banks, digging out his notebook. 'There's a friend from the NatWest branch where Lucy Payne worked. One of our teams went and talked to the employees, and there's only one of them who knows her well. Name's Pat Mitchell. Then there's Clive and Hilary Liversedge. Lucy's parents. They live out Hull way.'

'Do they know?'

'Of course they know. What do you think we are?'

Jenny raised a fine, plucked eyebrow.

'They know.'

'How did they react?'

'Upset, of course. Stunned, even. But according to the DC who interviewed them, they weren't much help. They hadn't been in close touch with Lucy since she married Terry.'

'Have they been to see her in hospital?'

'No. Seems the mother's too ill to travel and the father's a reluctant care-giver.'

'What about *his* parents? Terry's.'

'As far as we've been able to work out,' Banks said, 'his mother's in a mental asylum – has been for fifteen years or so.'

'What's wrong with her?'

'Schizophrenia.'

'And the father?'

'Died two years ago.'

'What of?'

'Massive stroke. He was a butcher in Halifax, had a record for minor sex offences – exposing himself, peeping, that sort of thing. Sounds a pretty classic background for someone like Terry Payne, wouldn't you say?'

'If there is such a thing.'

'The miracle is that Terry managed to become a teacher.'

Jenny laughed. 'Oh, they'll let anyone in the classroom these days. Besides, that's not the miracle.'

'What is?'

'That he managed to hold on to the job for so long. And that he was married. Usually serial sex offenders such as Terence Payne find it hard to hold down a job and maintain a relationship. Our man did both.'

'Is that significant?'

'It's intriguing. If I'd been pushed for a profile a month or so ago I'd have said you were looking for a man between twenty and thirty, most likely living alone and working at some sort of menial job, or a succession of such jobs. Just shows how wrong one can be, doesn't it?'

'Will you do it?'

Jenny toyed with the stem of her glass. The Mozart ended and left only the memory of music. A car passed by and a dog barked on the Green. She had the time to do as Banks asked. She had a lecture to give on Friday morning, but it was one she had given a hundred times, so she didn't need to prepare. Then she had nothing until a string of tutorials on Monday. That should give her plenty of time. 'As I said, it's intriguing. I'll need to talk to Lucy herself.'

'That can be arranged. You *are* our official consultant psychologist, after all.'

'Easy for you to say that now you need me.'

'I've known it all along. Don't let a few narrow-minded—'

'All right,' said Jenny. 'You've made your point. I can take being laughed at behind my back by a bunch of thick plods. I'm a big girl. When can I talk to her?'

'Best do it as soon as possible, while she's still only a

witness. Believe it or not, but defence lawyers have been known to claim that psychologists have tricked suspects into incriminating themselves. How about tomorrow morning? I've got to be down at the hospital for the next post mortem at eleven, anyway.'

'Lucky you. Okay.'

'I'll give you a lift if you like.'

'No. I'll go straight over to talk to the parents after I've talked to Lucy and her friend. I'll need my car. Meet you there?'

'Ten o'clock, then?'

'Fine.'

Banks told her how to find Lucy's room. 'And I'll let the parents know you're coming.' Banks gave her the details. 'You'll do it then? What I'm asking?'

'Doesn't look as if I have much choice, does it?'

Banks stood up, leaned forward and kissed her swiftly on the cheek. Even though she could smell the wine and smoke on his breath, her heart jumped and she wished his lips had lingered a little longer, moved a little closer to her own. 'Hey! Any more of that,' she said, 'and I'll have you up on sexual harassment charges.'

8

Banks and Jenny walked past the police guard into Lucy Payne's room just after ten o'clock the following morning. There was no doctor standing over them this time, Banks was happy to note. Lucy lay propped against the pillows reading a fashion magazine. The slats of the blinds let in some of the morning sun, lighting the vase of tulips on the bedside table, forming a pattern of bars over Lucy's face and the white bedsheets. Her glossy black hair was spread out on the pillow around her hospital-pale face. The colours of her bruises had deepened since the previous day, which meant they were on the mend, and she still wore half her head swathed in bandages. Her good eye, long-lashed, dark and sparkling, gazed up at them. Banks wasn't sure what he saw in it, but it wasn't fear. He introduced Jenny as Dr Fuller.

Lucy looked up and gave them a fleeting wisp of a smile. 'Is there any news?' she asked.

'No,' said Banks.

'He's going to die, isn't he?'

'What makes you think that?'

'I just have this feeling he's going to die, that's all.'

'Would that make a difference, Lucy?'

'What do you mean?'

'You know what I mean. If Terry died, would it make a difference to what you might care to tell us?'

'How could it?'

'You tell me.'

Lucy paused. Banks could see her frown as she thought about what to say next. 'If I were to tell you, you know, what went on. I mean, if I knew . . . you know . . . about Terry and those girls and all . . . what would happen to me?'

'You'll have to be a bit clearer than that, I'm afraid, Lucy.'

She licked her lips. 'I can't really be any clearer. Not at this point. I have to think of myself. I mean, if I remembered something that didn't show me in a good light, what would you do?'

'Depends what it is, Lucy.'

Lucy retreated into silence.

Jenny sat on the edge of the bed and smoothed her skirt. Banks gave her the go-ahead to pick up the questioning. 'Do you remember anything more about what happened?' she asked.

'Are you a psychiatrist?'

'I'm a psychologist.'

Lucy looked at Banks. 'They can't make me have tests, can they?'

'No,' said Banks. 'Nobody can force you to undergo testing. That's not why Dr Fuller's here. She just wants to talk to you. She's here to help.' *And the cheque's in the post*, Banks added silently.

Lucy glanced at Jenny. 'I don't know . . .'

'You've got nothing to hide, have you, Lucy?' Jenny asked.

'No. I'm just worried that they'll make things up about me.'

'Who'll make things up?'

'Doctors. The police.'

'Why would they want to do that?'

'I don't know. Because they think I'm evil.'

'Nobody thinks you're evil, Lucy.'

'You wonder how I could have lived with him, a man who did what Terry did, don't you?'

'How *could* you live with him?' Jenny asked.

'I was frightened of him. He said he'd kill me if I left him.'

'And he abused you, is that right?'

'Yes.'

'Physically?'

'Sometimes he hit me. Where the bruises wouldn't show.'

'Until Monday morning.'

Lucy touched her bandages. 'Yes.'

'Why was it different that time, Lucy?'

'I don't know. I still can't remember.'

'That's okay,' Jenny went on. 'I'm not here to force you to say anything you don't want. Just relax. Did your husband abuse you in other ways?'

'What do you mean?'

'Emotionally, for example.'

'Do you mean like putting me down, humiliating me in front of people?'

'That's the kind of thing I mean.'

'Then the answer's yes. Like, you know, if something I cooked wasn't very good or I hadn't ironed his shirt properly. He was very fussy about his shirts.'

'What did he do if his shirts weren't ironed properly?'

'He'd make me do them again and again. Once he even burned me with the iron.'

'Where?'

Lucy looked away. 'Where it wouldn't show.'

'I'm curious about the cellar, Lucy. Detective Superintendent Banks here told me you said you never went down there.'

'I might have been there the once . . . you know . . . the time he hurt me.'

'On Monday morning?'

'Yes.'

'But you don't remember?'

'No.'

'You never went down there before?'

Lucy's voice took on a strange keening edge. 'No. Never. Not since we first moved in, anyway.'

'How long after that was it that he forbade you to go there?'

'I don't remember. Not long. When he'd done his conversions.'

'What conversions?'

'He told me he'd made it into a den, his own private place.'

'Were you never curious?'

'Not much. Besides, he always kept it locked and he carried the key with him. He said if he ever thought I'd been down there he'd thrash me to within an inch of my life.'

'And you believed him?'

She turned her dark eye on Jenny. 'Oh, yes. It wouldn't have been the first time.'

'Did your husband ever mention pornography to you?'

'Yes. He sometimes brought videos home, things he said he'd borrowed from Geoff, one of the other teachers. Sometimes we watched them together.' She looked at Banks. 'You must have seen them. I mean, you've probably been in the house, searching and stuff.'

Banks remembered the tapes. 'Did Terry have a camcorder?' he asked her. 'Did he make his own tapes?'

'No, I don't think so,' she said.

Jenny picked up the thread again. 'What sort of videos did he like?' she asked.

'People having sex. Girls together. Sometimes people tied up.'

'You said you watched the videos together sometimes. Did *you* like them? What effect did they have on you? Did he force you to watch them?'

Lucy shifted under her thin bedsheets. The outline of her body stirred Banks in ways he didn't want to be stirred by her. 'I didn't really like them much,' she said in a sort of husky, little girl voice. 'Sometimes, you know, though, even so . . . they . . . they excited me.' She moved again.

'Did your husband abuse you sexually, make you do things you didn't want to do?' Jenny asked.

'No,' she said. 'It was all just normal.'

Banks was beginning to wonder if the marriage to Lucy was just a part of Terence Payne's 'normal' façade, something to make people think twice about his real proclivities. After all, it had worked on DCs Bowmore and Singh, who hadn't even bothered to re-interview him. Perhaps he went elsewhere to satisfy his more perverse tastes – prostitutes, for example. It was worth looking into.

'Do you know if he went with other women?' Jenny asked, as if reading Banks's mind.

'He never said.'

'But did you suspect it?'

'I thought he might have done, yes.'

'Prostitutes?'

'I don't know. I didn't like to think about it.'

'Did you ever find his behaviour bizarre?'

'What do you mean?'

'Did he ever shock you, make you wonder what he was up to?'

'Not really. He had a terrible temper . . . you know . . . if he didn't get his own way. And sometimes, during school holidays, I didn't see him for days.'

'You didn't know where he was?'

'No.'

'And he never told you?'

'No.'

'Weren't you curious?'

She seemed to shrink back into the bed. 'Curiosity never did you any good with Terry. "Curiosity killed the cat," he'd say, "and if you don't shut up, it'll kill you too." ' She shook her head. 'I don't know what I did wrong. Everything was fine. It was just a normal life. Until I met Terry. Then everything started to fall apart. How could I be such a fool? I should have *known*.'

'Known what, Lucy?'

'What kind of person he was. What a monster he was.'

'But you did know. You told me he hit you, humiliated you in public and in private. You did know. Are you trying to tell me you thought that was normal? Did you think that was how everybody lived?'

'No, of course not. But it didn't make him the sort of monster you think he is.' Lucy looked away again.

'What is it, Lucy?' Jenny asked.

'You must think I'm such a weak person to let him do all that. A terrible person. But I'm not. I'm a nice person. Everybody says I am. I was frightened. Talk to Maggie. She understands.'

Banks stepped in. 'Maggie Forrest? Your neighbour?'

'Yes.' Lucy looked in his direction. 'She sent me those flowers. We talked about it . . . you know . . . about men abusing their wives, and she tried to persuade me to leave Terry, but I was too frightened. Maybe in a while I might have found the courage. I don't know. It's too late now, isn't it? Please, I'm tired. I don't want to talk any more. I just want to go home and get on with my life.'

Banks wondered whether he should tell Lucy that she wouldn't be going home for some time, that her *home* looked like the site of an archeological dig and would be in the police's hands for weeks, perhaps months, to come. He decided not to bother. She would find out soon enough.

'We'll go now, then,' said Jenny, standing up. 'Take care, Lucy.'

'Would you do me a favour?' Lucy asked as they stood in the doorway.

'What is it?' Banks asked.

'Back at the house, there's a nice little jewellery box on the dressing-table in the bedroom. It's a lacquered Japanese box, black with all kinds of beautiful flowers hand-painted on it. Anyway, it's got all my favourite pieces in, earrings I bought on our honeymoon on Crete, a gold chain with a heart Terry bought me when we got engaged. They're my things. Would you bring it to me, please? My jewellery box.'

Banks tried to hold in his frustration. 'Lucy,' he said as calmly as he could manage. 'We believe that several young girls were sexually abused and murdered in the cellar of your house, and all you can think about is your jewellery?'

'That's not true,' said Lucy, a hint of petulance in her tone. 'I'm very sorry for what happened to those girls, of course I am, but it's not *my* fault. I don't see why it should stop me having my jewellery box. The only thing anyone's let me have from there is my handbag and purse, and I could tell someone had even been searching through them first.'

Banks followed Jenny out into the corridor and they

headed for the lifts. 'Calm down, Alan,' said Jenny. 'Lucy's dissociating. She doesn't realize the emotional significance of what's happened.'

'Right,' said Banks glancing at the clock on the wall. 'That's just bloody fine and dandy. Now I have to go and watch Dr Mackenzie do his next post mortem, but I'll do my damnedest to remember that none of it is Lucy Payne's fault and that she's managing to dissociate herself from it all, thank you.'

Jenny put her hand on his arm. 'I can understand why you're frustrated, Alan, but it won't do any good. You can't push her. She won't be pushed. Be patient.'

The lift came and they got in. 'Trying to have a conversation with that woman is like trying to catch water in a sieve,' Banks said.

'She's a weird one, all right.'

'Is that your professional opinion?'

Jenny grinned. 'Let me think about it. I'll talk to you after I've talked to her co-worker and her parents. Bye.' They arrived at the ground floor and she hurried off towards the car park. Banks took a deep breath and pressed the 'down' button.

•

Rapunzel was going much better today, Maggie decided as she stood back and examined her work, tip of her tongue between her small white teeth. She didn't look as if one good yank on her hair would rip her head from her shoulders, and she didn't look a bit like Claire Toth.

Claire hadn't turned up as usual yesterday after school, and Maggie wondered why not. Perhaps it was only to be expected that she didn't feel very sociable after what had happened. Maybe she just wanted to be alone to sort out her feelings. Maggie decided she would talk to her psychiatrist, Dr Simms, about Claire, see if there was something that ought to be done. She had an appointment tomorrow which, despite the events of the week, she was determined to keep.

Lorraine Temple's story hadn't turned up in the morning newspaper, as Maggie had expected it to, and she had felt disappointed when she had searched through every page and not found it. She assumed that the journalist needed more time to check her facts and put the story together. After all, it had only been yesterday when they talked. Perhaps it would be a long article focusing on the plight of abused women, a feature in the weekend paper.

She bent over the drawing-board and got back to work on the Rapunzel sketch. She had to turn her desk light on as the morning had turned overcast and muggy.

A couple of minutes later, her phone rang. Maggie put her pencil aside and answered it.

'Maggie?'

She recognized the soft, husky voice. 'Lucy? How are you?'

'I'm feeling much better now, really.'

Maggie didn't know what to say at first. She felt awkward. Despite her sending the flowers and defending Lucy to the police and with Lorraine Temple, she realized they didn't know one another well and came from very different worlds. 'It's good to hear from you,' she said. 'I'm glad you're feeling better.'

'I just wanted to thank you for the flowers,' Lucy went on. 'They're lovely. They make all the difference. It was a nice thought.'

'It's the least I can do.'

'You know, you're the only person who's bothered with me. Everyone else has written me off.'

'I'm sure that's not true, Lucy.'

'Oh, but it is. Even my friends from work.'

Though Maggie could hardly bring herself to ask, it was only polite. 'How's Terry?'

'They won't even tell me that, but I think he's very badly hurt. I think he's going to die. I think the police are going to try to blame me.'

'What makes you think that?'

'I don't know.'

'Have they been to talk to you?'

'Twice. Just now there were two of them. One was a psychologist. She asked me all sorts of questions.'

'About what?'

'About things Terry did to me. About our sex life. I felt like such a fool. Maggie, I just feel so frightened and alone.'

'Look, Lucy, if I can help in any way . . .'

'Thank you.'

'Have you got a solicitor?'

'No. I don't even know any.'

'Look, Lucy. If the police come bothering you again, don't say *anything* to them. I know how they can twist your words, make something out of nothing. Will you at least let me try to get you someone? One of Ruth and Charles's friends is a solicitor in town. Julia Ford. I've met her, and she seems nice enough. She'll know what to do.'

'But I don't have that much money, Maggie.'

'Don't worry. We'll sort it out with her somehow. Will you let me call her for you?'

'I suppose so. I mean, if you think it's for the best.'

'I do. I'll call her right now and ask her to drop by and talk to you, shall I?'

'Okay.'

'Are you sure there's nothing else I can do for you?'

Maggie heard a defeated laugh over the line. 'Pray for me, perhaps. I don't know, Maggie. I don't know what they're going to do to me. For the moment, I'd just like to know there's someone on *my* side.'

'Count on it, Lucy, there is.'

'Thank you. I'm tired. I have to go now.'

And Lucy hung up the phone.

•

After attending Dr Mackenzie's post mortem on the sad pile of bones and decaying flesh that had once been a young and vibrant girl with hopes and dreams and secrets, Banks felt twenty years older but none the wiser. First on the slab was the freshest because Dr Mackenzie said it might tell him more, which seemed logical to Banks. Even so, the body had been partially buried under a thin layer of soil in Payne's cellar for about three weeks, Dr Mackenzie estimated, which was why the skin, hair and nails were loose and easy to pull off. Insects had been at work, and much of the flesh was gone. Where skin remained, it had burst open in places, revealing the glistening muscle and fat beneath. Not much fat, because this was Melissa Horrocks, weighing just a little under seven stone, whose T-shirt bore symbols to ward off evil spirits.

Banks left before Dr Mackenzie had finished, not because it was too gruesome for him, but because these post mortems were going to go on for some time yet, and he had other business to attend to. It would be more than a day or two, Dr Mackenzie said, before he would be able to get down to a report, as the other two bodies were in an even worse state of decomposition. Someone from the team had to sit through the post mortems, but this was one job Banks was happy to delegate.

After the sights, sounds and smells of Mackenzie's post mortem, the bland headmaster's office at Silverhill Comprehensive came as a relief. There was nothing about the uncluttered and nondescript room that indicated it had anything to do with education, or anything else, for that matter; it was much the same as any anonymous office in any anonymous building, and it didn't even smell of much except a faint whiff of lemon-scented furniture polish. The head was called John Knight: early forties, balding, stoop-shouldered, dandruff on his jacket collar.

After getting a few general details about Payne's employment history, Banks asked Knight if there had been any problems with Payne.

'There *have* been a few complaints, now that you mention it,' Knight admitted.

Banks raised his eyebrows. 'From pupils?'

Knight reddened. 'Good Lord, no. Nothing like that. Have you any idea what happens at the merest *hint* of something like that these days?'

'No,' said Banks. 'When I was at school the teachers used to thrash us with just about anything they could lay their hands on. Some of them enjoyed it, too.'

'Well, those days are over, thank the Lord.'

'Or the law.'

'Not a believer?'

'My job makes it difficult.'

'Yes, I can understand that.' Knight glanced towards the window. 'Mine, too, sometimes. That's one of the great challenges of faith, don't you think?'

'So what sort of problems were you having with Terence Payne?'

Knight brought himself back from a long way away and sighed. 'Oh, just little things. Nothing important in themselves, but they all add up.'

'For example?'

'Tardiness. Too many days off without a valid reason. Teachers may get generous holidays, Superintendent, but they *are* expected to be here during term time, barring some serious illness, of course.'

'I see. Anything else?'

'Just a general sort of sloppiness. Exams not marked on time. Projects left unsupervised. Terry has a bit of a temper, and he can get quite stroppy if you call him up on anything.'

'How long has this been going on?'

'According to the head of science, only since the new year.'

'And before that?'

'No problems at all. Terence Payne is a good teacher – knows his stuff – and he seemed popular with the pupils. None of us can believe what's happened. We're stunned. Just absolutely stunned.'

'Do you know his wife?'

'I don't know her. I met her once at the staff Christmas party. Charming woman. A little reserved, perhaps, but charming nonetheless.'

'Does Terry have a colleague here called Geoff?'

'Yes. Geoffrey Brighouse. He's the chemistry teacher. The two of them seemed pretty thick. Went out for a jar or two together every now and again.'

'What can you tell me about him?'

'Geoff's been with us six years now. Solid sort of fellow. No trouble at all.'

'Can I talk to him?'

'Of course.' Knight looked at his watch. 'He should be

over in the chemistry lab right now, preparing for his next class. Follow me.'

They walked outside. The day was becoming more and more muggy as the clouds thickened, threatening rain. Nothing new. Apart from the past few days, it had been raining pretty much every day on and off since the beginning of April.

Silverhill Comprehensive was one of the few pre-war Gothic redbrick schools that hadn't been sandblasted and converted into offices or luxury flats yet. Knots of adolescents lounged around the asphalt playground. They all seemed subdued, Banks thought, and a pall of gloom, fear and confusion hung about the place, palpable as a pea-souper. The groups weren't mixed, Banks noticed; the girls stood in their own little conclaves, as if huddled together for comfort and security, staring down and scuffing their shoes on the asphalt as Banks and Knight walked by. The boys were a bit more animated; at least some of them were talking and there was a bit of the usual playful pushing and shoving. But the whole effect was eerie.

'It's been like this since we heard,' said Knight, as if reading Banks's mind. 'People don't realize how far-reaching and long-lasting the effects will be around this place. Some of the students may never get over it. It'll blight their lives. It's not just that we've lost a cherished pupil, but someone we put in a position of trust seems to be responsible for some abominable acts, if I'm not speaking out of turn.'

'You're not,' said Banks. 'And abominable only scratches the surface. But don't tell the papers.'

'My lips are sealed. They've been around already, you know.'

'Doesn't surprise me.'

'I didn't tell them anything. Nothing *to* tell, really. Here we are. The Bascombe Building.'

The Bascombe Building was a modern concrete and glass addition to the main school building. There was a plaque on the wall near the door, which read: 'This building is dedicated to the memory of Frank Edward Bascombe, 1898–1971.'

'Who was he?' Banks asked, as they went in the door.

'A teacher here during the war,' Knight explained. 'English teacher. This used to be part of the main building then, but it was hit by a stray doodlebug in October of 1944. Frank Bascombe was a hero. He got twelve children and another teacher out. Two pupils were killed in the attack. Just through here.' He opened the door to the chemistry lab, where a young man sat at the teacher's desk in front of a sheaf of notes. He looked up. 'Geoff. A Detective Superintendent Banks to see you.' Then he left, shutting the door behind him.

Banks hadn't been in a school chemistry lab for thirty years or more, and though this one had far more modern fixtures than he remembered from his own schooldays, much of it was still the same: the high lab benches, Bunsen burners, test tubes, pipettes and beakers, the glass-fronted cabinet on the wall full of stoppered bottles containing sulphuric acid, potassium, sodium phosphate and such. What memories. It even smelled the same: slightly acrid, slightly rotten.

Banks remembered the first chemistry set his parents bought him for Christmas when he was thirteen, remembered the fine, powdered alum, the blue copper sulphate and bright purple crystals of potassium permanganate. He liked to mix them all up and see what happened, paying no regard to the instructions or the safety precautions. Once he was heating some odd concoction over a candle at the kitchen table when the test tube cracked, making a mess all over the place. His mother went spare.

Brighouse, wearing a lightweight jacket and grey flannel trousers, not a lab coat, came forward and shook hands. He was a fresh-faced lad, about Payne's age, with pale blue eyes, fair hair and a lobster complexion, as if he'd been able to find some sun and stayed out in it too long. His handshake was firm, dry and short. He noticed Banks looking around the lab.

'Bring back memories, does it?' he asked.

'A few.'

'Good ones, I hope?'

Banks nodded. He had enjoyed chemistry, but his teacher, 'Titch' Barker, was one of the worst, most brutal bastards in the school. He used the rubber connecting lines of the Bunsen burners in his thrashings. Once he held Banks's hand over a burner and made as if to light it, but he backed off at the last moment. Banks had seen the sadistic gleam in his eye, how much effort it had cost him not to strike the match. Banks hadn't given him the satisfaction of a plea for mercy or an outward expression of fear, but he had been shaking inside.

'Anyway, it's sodium today,' said Brighouse.

'Pardon?'

'Sodium. The way it's so unstable in air. Always goes down well. The kids these days don't have much of an attention span, so you have to give them pyrotechnics to keep them interested. Luckily, there's plenty of scope for that in chemistry.'

'Ah.'

'Sit down.' He pointed towards a tall stool by the nearest

bench. Banks sat in front of a rack of test tubes and a Bunsen burner. Brighouse sat opposite.

'I'm not sure I can help you in any way,' Brighouse began. 'I know Terry, of course. We're colleagues, and good mates to some extent. But I can't say I know him well. He's a very private person in many ways.'

'Stands to reason,' said Banks. 'Look at what he was doing in private.'

Brighouse blinked. 'Er . . . quite.'

'Mr Brighouse—'

'Geoff. Please. Call me Geoff.'

'Right, Geoff,' said Banks, who always preferred the first name, as it gave him an odd sort of power over a suspect, which Geoff Brighouse certainly was in his eyes. 'How long have you known Mr Payne?'

'Since he first came here nearly two years ago.'

'He was teaching in Seacroft before then. Is that right?'

'Yes. I think so.'

'You didn't know him then?'

'No. Look, if you don't mind my asking, how is he, by the way?'

'He's still in intensive care, but he's hanging on.'

'Good. I mean . . . oh, shit, this is so difficult. I still can't believe it. What am I supposed to say? The man's a friend of mine, after all, no matter . . .' Brighouse put his fist to his mouth and chewed on a knuckle. He seemed suddenly close to tears.

'No matter what he's done?'

'I was going to say that, but . . . I'm just confused. Forgive me.'

'It'll take time. I understand. But in the meantime I need to find out all I can about Terence Payne. What sorts of things did you do together?'

'Mostly went to pubs. We never drank a lot. At least I didn't.'

'Payne's a heavy drinker?'

'Not until recently.'

'Did you say anything to him?'

'A couple of times. You know, when he was in his car.'

'What did you do?'

'I tried to take his keys away.'

'What happened?'

'He got angry. Even hit me once.'

'Terence Payne hit you?'

'Yeah. But he was pissed. He's got a temper when he's pissed.'

'Did he give you any reason why he was drinking so much?'

'No.'

'He didn't talk about any personal problems he might be having?'

'No.'

'Did you know of any problems other than the drinking?'

'He was letting his work slip a bit.'

The same thing Knight had said. Like the drinking, it was probably more of a symptom than the problem itself. Jenny Fuller would perhaps be able to confirm it, but Banks thought it made sense that a man who was doing, who felt *compelled* to do, what Payne had been doing would need some sort of oblivion. It seemed almost as if he had *wanted* to be caught, wanted it all to be over. The abduction of Kimberley Myers, when he knew he was already in the system because of his car number-plate, was a foolhardy move. If it hadn't been for DCs Bowmore and Singh, he might have been brought to Banks's attention earlier. Even if nothing had come from a second interview, his name would have leaped out of HOLMES as soon as Carol Houseman had entered the new data, that Kimberley Myers was a pupil at Silverhill, where Payne taught, and that he was listed as the owner of a car whose number ended in KWT, despite the false NGV plates.

'Did he ever talk about Kimberley Myers?' Banks asked.

'No. Never.'

'Did he ever talk about young girls in general?'

'He talked about girls, not particularly young ones.'

'How did he talk about women? With affection? With disgust? With lust? With anger?'

Brighouse thought for a moment. 'Come to think of it,' he said, 'I always thought Terry sounded a bit sort of domineering, the way he talked about women.'

'How so?'

'Well, he'd spot a girl he fancied, in a pub, say, and go on about, you know, how he'd like to fuck her, tie her to the bed and fuck her brains out. That sort of thing. I . . . I mean, I'm not a prude, but sometimes it was a bit over the top.'

'But that's just male crudeness, isn't it?'

Brighouse raised an eyebrow. 'Is it? I don't know. I honestly don't know what it means. I'm just saying he sounded rough and domineering when he talked about women.'

'Talking about male crudeness, did you ever lend Terry any videos?'

Brighouse looked away. 'What do you mean? What sort of videos?'

'Pornographic videos.'

It wasn't possible for someone as red as Brighouse to blush, but for a moment Banks could almost have sworn that he did.

'Just some soft stuff. Nothing under the counter. Nothing you can't rent at the corner shop. I lent him other videos, too. War films, horror, science fiction. Terry's a film buff.'

'No home-made videos?'

'Of course not. What do you think I am?'

'The jury's still out on that one, Geoff. Does Terry own a camcorder?'

'Not that I know of.'

'Do you?'

'No. I can just about manage a basic point and shoot camera.'

'Did you go to his house often?'

'Once in a while.'

'Ever go down in the cellar?'

'No. Why?'

'Are you sure about that, Geoff?'

'Damn it, yes. Surely you can't think . . .?'

'You do realize we're carrying out a complete forensic examination of the Paynes's cellar, don't you?'

'So?'

'So the first rule of a crime scene is that anyone who's been there leaves something and takes something away. If you were there, we'll find out, that's all. I wouldn't want you looking guilty simply for not telling me you were there on some innocent mission, like watching a porn video together.'

'I never went down there.'

'Okay. Just so long as you know. Did the two of you ever pick up any women together?'

Brighouse's eyes shifted towards the Bunsen burner, and he fiddled with the test tube rack in front of him.

'Mr Brighouse? Geoff? It could be important.'

'I don't see how.'

'Let me be the judge of that. And if you're worried about splitting on a mate, you shouldn't be. Your mate's in hospital in a coma. His wife's in the same hospital with a few cuts and bruises he inflicted on her. And we found the body of Kimberley Myers in the cellar of his house. Remember Kimberley? You probably taught her, didn't you? I've just been to the post mortem of one of his previous victims and I'm still feeling a bit off colour. You don't need to know any more, and believe me, you don't *want* to.'

Brighouse took a deep breath. Some of the bright red colouring seemed to have leached from his cheeks and brow. 'Well, okay, yeah, we did. Once.'

'Tell me what happened.'

'Nothing. You know . . .'

'No, I don't know. Tell me.'

'Look, this is . . .'

'I don't care how embarrassing it is. I want to know how he behaved with this woman you picked up. Carry on. Think of it as confiding in your doctor over a dose of clap.'

Brighouse swallowed and went on. 'It was at a conference in Blackpool. In April, just over a year ago.'

'Before he got married?'

'Yeah. He was seeing Lucy, but they weren't married then. Not till May.'

'Go on.'

'Not much to tell. There was this cracking young teacher from Aberdeen, and one night, you know, we'd all had a few drinks at the bar and got to flirting and all. Anyway, she seemed game enough after a few gins so we went up to the room.'

'The three of you?'

'Yes. Terry and I were sharing a room. I mean, I'd have

stayed away if it was his score, like, but she made it clear she didn't mind. It was her idea. She said she'd always fancied a threesome.'

'And you?'

'It had been a fantasy of mine, yes.'

'What happened?'

'What do you think? We had sex.'

'Did she enjoy it?'

'Well, like I said, it had been mostly her idea in the first place. She was a bit drunk. We all were. She didn't object. Really, she was keen. It was only later . . .'

'What was only later?'

'Look, you know what it's like.'

'No, I don't know what it's like.'

'Well, Terry, he suggested a Greek sandwich. I don't know if you—'

'I know what a Greek sandwich is. Go on.'

'But she didn't fancy it.'

'What happened?'

'Terry can be very persuasive.'

'How? Violence?'

'No. He just doesn't give up. He keeps on coming back to what he wants and it just wears down people's resistance in the end.'

'So you had your Greek sandwich?'

Brighouse looked down and rubbed his fingertips on the rough, scratched lab bench. 'Yeah.'

'And she was willing?'

'Sort of. I mean, yes. Nobody *forced* her. Not physically. We'd had a couple more drinks and Terry was at her, you know, just verbally, about how great it would be, so in the end . . .'

'What happened afterwards?'

'Nothing, really. I mean she didn't kick up a fuss. But it soured the mood. She cried a bit, seemed down, you know, as if she felt betrayed, used. And I could tell she didn't like it much, when it was happening.'

'But you didn't stop?'

'No.'

'Did she scream or tell you to stop?'

'No. I mean, she was making noises but . . . well, she was a real screamer to start with. I was even worried about the people next door telling us to keep the noise down.'

'What happened next?'

'She went back to her own room. We had a few more drinks, then I passed out. I assume Terry did the same.'

Banks paused and made a jotting in his notebook. 'I don't know if you realize this, Geoff, but what you've just told me constitutes accessory to rape.'

'Nobody raped her! I told you. She was willing enough.'

'Doesn't sound like it to me. Two men. Her by herself. What choice did she have? She made it clear that she didn't want to do what Terence Payne was asking for, but he went ahead and did it anyway.'

'He brought her round to his way of thinking.'

'Bollocks, Geoff. He wore down her resistance and resolve. You said so yourself. And I'll also bet she was worried what might happen if she didn't go along with him.'

'Nobody threatened her with violence.'

'Maybe not in so many words.'

'Look, maybe things went just a little too far . . .'

'Got out of hand?'

'Maybe a little.'

Banks sighed. The number of times he'd heard that excuse for male violence against women. It was what Annie

Cabbot's assailants had claimed, too. He felt disgusted with Geoffrey Brighouse, but there wasn't much he could do. The incident had taken place over a year ago, the woman hadn't filed a complaint as far as he knew, and Terence Payne was fighting for his life in the Infirmary anyway. Still, it was one worth noting down for future reference.

'I'm sorry,' said Brighouse. 'But you must understand. She never told us to stop.'

'Didn't seem as if she had much chance to do that, sandwiched between two strapping lads like you and Terry.'

'Well she'd enjoyed everything else.'

Move on, Banks told himself, before you hit him. 'Any other incidents like that?'

'No. It was the only time. Believe it or not, Superintendent, but after that night, I was a bit ashamed, even though I did nothing wrong, and I would've been uncomfortable getting into a situation like that with Terry again. He was too much for me. So I just avoided the possibility.'

'So Payne was faithful to his wife from then on?'

'I didn't say that.'

'What do you mean?'

'Just that the two of us didn't pick up any more girls together. Sometimes he told me, you know, about picking up prostitutes and all.'

'What did he do with them?'

'What do you think?'

'He didn't go into detail?'

'No.'

'Did he ever talk about his wife in a sexual way?'

'No. Never. He was very possessive about her, and very guarded. He hardly mentioned her at all when we were together. It was as if she were part of a different life altogether. Terry's got a remarkable ability to compartmentalize things.'

'So it would seem. Did he ever suggest abducting young girls?'

'Do you seriously believe that I'd have anything to do with that sort of thing?'

'I don't know, Geoff. You tell me. He talked to you about tying them up and fucking their brains out, and he certainly raped that teacher in Blackpool, no matter how willing she might have been to have regular sex with the two of you earlier. I don't know what to think of your part in all this, Geoff, to be quite honest.'

Brighouse had lost all his colour now, and he was trembling. 'But you can't think that I . . .? I mean . . .'

'Why not? There's no reason you couldn't have been in it with him. More convenient if there were two of you. Easier to abduct your victims. Any chloroform in the lab?'

'Chloroform? Yes. Why?'

'Under lock and key, is it?'

'Of course.'

'Who has a key?'

'I do. Terry. Keith Miller, the department head, Mr Knight. I don't know who else. Probably the caretaker and the cleaners, for all I know.'

'Whose prints do you think we'd find on the bottle?'

'I don't know. I certainly can't remember the last time *I* used the stuff.'

'What did you do last weekend?'

'Not much. Stayed home. Marked some projects. Went shopping in town.'

'Got a girlfriend at the moment, Geoff?'

'No.'

'See anyone else over the weekend?'

'Just neighbours, you know, people from the other flats, in the hall, on the stairs. Oh, and I went to the pictures Saturday night.'

'On your own?'

'Yes.'

'What did you go to see?'

'New James Bond, in the city centre. And then I dropped in at my local.'

'Anyone see you?'

'A few of the regulars, yes. We had a game of darts.'

'How late were you there?'

'Closing time.'

Banks scratched his cheek. 'I don't know, Geoff. When you get right down to it, it's not much of an alibi, is it?'

'I wasn't aware I'd be needing one.'

The lab door opened and two boys poked their heads in. Geoff Brighouse seemed relieved. He looked at his watch, then at Banks, and gave a weak smile. 'Time for class, I'm afraid.'

Banks stood up. 'That's all right, Geoff. I wouldn't want to interfere in the education of the young.'

Brighouse beckoned the boys in, and more followed, swarming around the stools at the benches. He walked with Banks over to the door.

'I'd like you to come down to Millgarth and make a statement,' Banks said before leaving.

'A statement? Me? But why?'

'Just a formality. Tell the detective exactly what you just told me. And we'll also need to know exactly where you were and what you were doing at the times those five girls were abducted. Details, witnesses, the lot. We'll also need a fingerprint scan and a sample of DNA. It won't be painful, just like brushing your teeth. This evening after school will do fine. Say five o'clock? Go to the front desk and ask for DC Younis. He'll be expecting you.' Banks gave him a card and wrote down the name of the bright, if rather judgemental, young DC he had that very second chosen for the task of taking Brighouse's formal statement. DC Younis was active in his local Methodist Chapel and a bit conservative, morally. 'Cheers,' said Banks leaving a stunned and worried-looking Geoff Brighouse to teach his class the joys of unstable sodium.

9

Pat Mitchell took a break when Jenny turned up at the bank, and they walked to the café in the shopping centre over the road, where they sipped rather weak milky tea as they talked. Pat was a vivacious brunette with damp brown eyes and a big engagement ring. All she could do at first was shake her head and repeat, 'I still can't believe this. I just can't believe this is happening.'

Jenny was no stranger to denial, either as a psychologist or as a woman, so she made sympathetic noises and gave Pat the time to compose herself. Once in a while, someone from one of the other tables would give them a puzzled look, as if he or she recognized them but couldn't quite place them, but for the most part the café was empty and they were able to talk undisturbed.

'How well do you know Lucy?' Jenny asked when Pat had stopped crying.

'We're pretty close. I mean, I've known her for about four years, ever since she started here at the bank. She had a little flat then, just off Tong Road. We're about the same age. How is she? Have you seen her?' All the time she talked, Pat's big brown eyes continued to glisten on the brink of tears.

'I saw her this morning,' Jenny answered. 'She's doing well. Healing nicely.' *Physically*, anyway. 'What was she like when you first met?'

Pat smiled at the memory. 'She was fun, a laugh. She liked a lark.'

'What do you mean?'

'You know. She just wanted to enjoy herself, have a good time.'

'What was her idea of a good time?'

'Clubbing, going to pubs, parties, dancing, chatting up lads.'

'Just chatting them up?'

'Lucy was . . . well, she was just *funny* when it came to lads back then. I mean, most of them seemed to bore her. She'd go out with them a couple of times and then she'd chuck them.'

'Why do you think that was?'

Pat swirled the greyish tea in her cup and looked into it as if she were seeking her fortune in the leaves. 'I don't know. It was as if she was *waiting* for someone.'

'Mr Right?'

Pat laughed. 'Something like that.' Jenny got the impression that her laugh would have been a lot more ready and frequent had it not been for the circumstances.

'Did she ever tell you what her idea of Mr Right was?'

'No. Just that none of the lads around here seemed to satisfy her in any way. She thought they were all stupid and all they had on their minds was football and sex. In that order.'

Jenny had met plenty of lads like that. 'What was she after? A rich man? An exciting one? A dangerous one?'

'She wasn't interested in money particularly. Dangerous? I don't know. Maybe. She liked to live on the edge. Back then, like. She could be quite over the top.'

Jenny made some notes. 'How? In what way?'

'It's nothing, really. I shouldn't have spoken.'

'Go on. Tell me.'

Pat lowered her voice. 'Look, you're a psychiatrist, right?'

'Psychologist.'

'Whatever. Does that mean if I tell you something it goes no further? It stays between you and me and nobody can make you name your source? I mean, I wouldn't want Lucy to think I'd been talking out of turn.'

While Jenny might have some valid defences for not turning over her patients' files without a court order, in this instance she was working for the police and couldn't promise privacy. On the other hand, she needed to hear Pat's story, and Lucy would probably never find out about it. Without resorting to an outright lie, she said, 'I'll do my best. I promise.'

Pat chewed on her lower lip and thought for a moment, then she leaned forward and gripped her teacup in both hands. 'Well, once she wanted to go to some of those clubs in Chapeltown.'

'West Indian clubs?'

'Yes. I mean, most nice white girls wouldn't go near places like that, but Lucy thought it would be exciting.'

'Did she go?'

'Yes, she went with Jasmine, a Jamaican girl from the Boar Lane branch. Of course, nothing happened. I think she might have tried some drugs, though.'

'Why? What did she say?'

'She just hinted and did that, you know, that *knowing* sort of thing with her eyes, like she'd *been* there and the rest of us had only seen it on television. She can be quite unnerving like that, can Lucy.'

'Was there anything else?'

'Yes.' Once Pat was in full flow, it seemed, there was no stopping her. 'She once told me she'd acted as a prostitute.'

'She'd *what*?'

'It's true.' Pat looked around her to make sure no one was interested and lowered her voice even more. 'It was over a couple of years ago, before Terry came on the scene. We'd talked about it in a pub one night when we saw one – you know, a prostitute – wondering what it would be like and all, doing it for money, just as a bit of a laugh, really. Lucy said she'd like to try it and find out and she'd let us know.'

'Did she?'

'Uh-huh. That's what she told me. About a week later, she said the night before she'd put on some slutty clothes – fishnet tights, high heels, a black leather miniskirt and a low-cut blouse and she sat at the bar of one of those business hotels near the motorway. It didn't take long, she said, before a man approached her.'

'Did she tell you what happened?'

'Not all the details. She knows when to hold back, does Lucy. For effect, like. But she said they talked, very business-like and polite and all that, and they came to some financial arrangement, then they went up to his room and . . . and they *did* it.'

'Did you believe her?'

'Not at first. I mean, it's *outrageous*, isn't it? But . . .'

'Eventually you did?'

'Well, like I said, Lucy's always capable of surprising you, and she likes danger, excitement. I suppose it was when she showed me the money that tipped the balance.'

'She showed you?'

'Yes. Two hundred pounds.'

'She could have got it out of the bank.'

'She could, but . . . Anyway, that's all I know about it.'

Jenny made some more notes. Pat tilted her head to see what she was writing. 'It must be a fascinating job, yours,' she said.

'It has its moments.'

'Just like that woman who used to be on television. *Prime Suspect.*'

'I'm not a policewoman, Pat. Just a consultant psychologist.'

Pat wrinkled her nose. 'Still, it's an exciting life, isn't it? Catching criminals and all that.'

Excitement wasn't the first word that came to Jenny's mind, but she decided to leave Pat to her illusions. Like most people's, they wouldn't do her any real harm. 'What about after Lucy met Terry?'

'She changed. But then you do, don't you? Otherwise what's the point of getting married? If it doesn't change you, I mean.'

'I see your point. How did she change?'

'She became a lot more reserved. Stopped home more. Terry's a bit of a homebody, so there was no more clubbing. He's the jealous type, too, is Terry, if you know what I mean, so she had to watch herself chatting up the lads. Not that she did that after they were married. It was Terry, Terry, Terry all the way then.'

'Were they in love?'

'I'd say. Dotty about each other. At least that's what she said, and she seemed happy. Mostly.'

'Let's back up a bit. Were you there when they met?'

'She says so, but I can't for the life of me remember them meeting.'

'When was it?'

'Nearly two years ago. July. A warm, muggy night. We

were on a girls' night out at a pub in Seacroft. One of those really big places with lots of rooms and dancing.'

'How do you remember it?'

'I remember Lucy leaving alone. She said she hadn't enough money for a taxi and she didn't want to miss her bus. They don't run late. I'd had a few drinks, but I remember because I said something about her being careful. The Seacroft Rapist was active around then.'

'What did she say?'

'She just gave me that look and left.'

'Did you see Terry there that night? Did you see him chatting her up?'

'I think I saw him there, by himself at the bar, but I don't remember seeing them talking.'

'What did Lucy say later?'

'That she'd talked to him when she went to the bar for drinks once and quite liked the look of him, then they met again on her way out and went to some other pub together. I can't remember. I was definitely a bit squiffy. Anyway, whatever happened, that was it. From then on it was a different Lucy. She didn't have anywhere near enough time for her old friends.'

'Did you ever visit them? Go for dinner?'

'A couple of times, with my fiancé, Steve. We got engaged a year ago.' She held up her ring. The diamond caught the light and flashed. 'We're getting married in August. We've already booked the honeymoon. We're going to Rhodes.'

'Did you get along with Terry okay?'

Pat gave a little shudder. 'No. I don't like him. Never did. Steve thought he was all right, but . . . That's why we stopped going over, really. There's just something about him . . . And Lucy, she was sort of like a zombie when he was around. Either that or she acted like she was on drugs.'

'What do you mean?'

'Well, it's just a figure of speech. I mean, I know she wasn't *really* on drugs, but just, you know, overexcited, talking too much, mind jumping all over the place.'

'Did you ever see any signs of abuse?'

'You mean did he hit her and stuff?'

'Yes.'

'No. Nothing. I never saw any bruises or anything like that.'

'Did Lucy seem to change in any way?'

'What do you mean?'

'Recently. Did she become more withdrawn, seem afraid of anything?'

Pat chewed on the edge of her thumb for a moment before answering. 'She changed a bit over the past few months, now you come to mention it,' she said finally. 'I can't say exactly when it started, but she seemed more nervy, more distracted, as if she had a problem, a lot on her mind.'

'Did she confide in you?'

'No. We'd drifted apart quite a bit by then. Was he really beating her? I can't understand it, can you, how a woman, especially a woman like Lucy, can let that happen?'

Jenny could, but there was no point trying to convince Pat. If Lucy sensed that would be her old friend's attitude towards her problem, it was no surprise that she turned to a neighbour like Maggie Forrest, who at least showed empathy.

'Did Lucy ever talk about her past, her childhood?'

Pat looked at her watch. 'No. All I know is that she's from somewhere near Hull and it was a pretty dull life. She couldn't wait to get away, and she didn't keep in touch as much as she should, especially after Terry came on the scene. Look, I really have to get back now. I hope I've been of help.' She stood up.

Jenny stood and shook her hand. 'Thanks. Yes, you've been very helpful.' As she watched Pat scurry back to the bank, Jenny looked at her watch, too. She had enough time to drive out to Hull and see what Lucy's parents had to say.

•

It was several days since Banks had last stopped in at his Eastvale office, and the amount of accumulated paperwork was staggering since he had temporarily inherited Detective Superintendent Gristhorpe's workload. Consequently, when he did find time to drop by the station late that afternoon, driving straight back after his interview with Geoff Brighouse, his pigeonhole was stuffed with reports, budget revisions, memos, requests, telephone message slips, crime statistics and various circulars awaiting his signature. He decided to clear up some of the backlog of paperwork and take Annie Cabbot for a quick drink at the Queen's Arms to discuss her progress in the Janet Taylor investigation, and maybe build a few bridges in the process.

After leaving a message for Annie to drop by his office at six o'clock, Banks closed the door behind him and dropped the pile of papers on his desk. He hadn't even changed his *Dalesman* calendar from April to May, he noticed, flipping over from a photo of the stone bridge at Linton to the soaring lines of York Minster's east window, pink and white may blossom blurred in the foreground.

It was Thursday, the eleventh of May. Hard to believe it was only three days since the gruesome discovery at number thirty-five The Hill. Already the tabloids were rubbing their hands with glee and calling the place 'Dr Terry's House of

Horrors' and, even worse, 'The House of Payne'. They had somehow got hold of photographs of both Terry and Lucy Payne – the former cropped from a school class picture, by the look of it, and the latter from an 'employee of the month' presentation to Lucy at the NatWest branch where she worked. Both photos were poor in quality, and you'd have to know who they were before you'd recognize either of them.

Banks turned on his computer and answered any e-mail he thought merited a response, then he picked away at the pile of paper. Not much, it seemed, had happened in his absence. The major preoccupation had been with a series of nasty post-office robberies, in which one masked man terrorized staff and customers with a long knife and an ammonia spray. No one had been hurt yet, but that didn't mean they wouldn't be. There had been four such robberies in the Western Division over a month. DS Hatchley was out rounding up his ragbag assortment of informants. Apart from the robberies, perhaps the most serious crime on their hands was the theft of a tortoise that happened to be sleeping in a cardboard box nicked from someone's garden, along with a Raleigh bicycle and a lawn mower.

Business as usual. And somehow Banks found an odd sort of comfort in these dull, predictable crimes after the horrors of the Paynes's cellar.

He turned on his radio and recognized the slow movement from a late Schubert piano sonata. He felt a tight pain between his eyes and massaged the spot gently. When that didn't work he swallowed a couple of Paracetamol he kept in his desk for emergencies such as this, washed them down with tepid coffee, then he pushed the mound of paper aside and let the music spill over him in gentle waves. The headaches were coming more frequently these days, along with the sleepless nights and a strange reluctance to go to work. It reminded him of the pattern he went through just before he left London for Yorkshire, when he was on the edge of burnout, and he wondered if he was getting in the same state again. He should probably see his doctor, he decided, when he had time.

The ringing telephone disturbed him, as it had so often before. Scowling, he picked up the offending instrument and growled, 'Banks.'

'Stefan here. You asked me to keep you informed.'

Banks relaxed his tone. 'Yes, Stefan. Any developments?' Banks could hear voices in the background. Millgarth, most likely. Or the Payne house.

'One piece of good news. They've lifted Payne's prints from the machete used to kill PC Morrisey, and the lab reports both yellow plastic fibres from the rope in the scrapings taken from under Lucy Payne's fingernails, along with traces of Kimberley Myers's blood on the sleeve of her dressing-gown.'

'Kimberley's blood on Lucy Payne's dressing-gown?'

'Yes.'

'So she *was* down there,' Banks said.

'Looks like it. Mind you, she could explain away the fibres by saying she hung out the washing. They did use the same kind of clothes-line in the back garden. I've seen it.'

'But the blood?'

'Maybe more tricky,' said Stefan. 'There wasn't very much, but at least it proves that she was down there.'

'Thanks, Stefan. It's a big help. What about Terence Payne?'

'The same. Blood and yellow fibres. Along with a fair quantity of PC Morrisey's blood.'

'What about the bodies?'

'One more, skeletal, out in the garden. That makes all five.'

'Skeletal? How long would that take?'

'Depends on temperature and insect activity,' said Stefan.

'Could it have happened in just a month or so?'

'Could have, with the right conditions. It hasn't been very warm this past month, though.'

'But is it possible?'

'It's possible.'

Leanne Wray had disappeared on the thirty-first of March, so there was at least some possibility that it was her remains.

'Anyway,' Stefan went on. 'There's plenty of garden left. They're digging very slowly and carefully to avoid disturbing the bones. I've arranged for a botanist and an entomologist from the university to visit the scene tomorrow. They should be able to help us with time of death.'

'Did you find any clothing with the victims?'

'No. Nothing of a personal nature.'

'Get to work on identifying that body, Stefan, and let me know the minute you have anything, even if it's negative.'

'Will do.'

Banks said goodbye to Stefan and hung up, then he walked over to his open window and sneaked a prohibited cigarette. It was a hot, muggy afternoon, with the sort of tension in the air that meant rain would probably come soon, perhaps even a thunderstorm. Office workers sniffed the air and reached for their umbrellas as they headed home. Shopkeepers closed up and wound back the awnings. Banks thought about Sandra again, how when she used to work at the community centre down North Market Street they would often meet for a drink in the Queen's Arms before heading home. Happy days. Or so they had seemed. And now she was pregnant with Sean's baby.

The Schubert piano music played on, the serene and elegiac opening of the final, B flat sonata. Banks's headache began to subside a little. The one thing he remembered about Sandra's pregnancies was that she hadn't enjoyed them, hadn't glowed with the joys of approaching motherhood. She had suffered extreme morning sickness and though she didn't drink or smoke much, she continued to do both because back then nobody made such a fuss about it. She also continued to go to galleries and plays and meet with friends, and complained when her condition made it difficult or impossible for her to do so.

While pregnant with Tracy, she had slipped on ice and broken her leg in her seventh month and spent the rest of her confinement with a cast on. That more than anything had driven her crazy, unable to get out and about with her camera the way she loved to do, stuck in their poky little Kennington flat watching grey day follow grey day all that winter while Banks was working all hours, hardly ever home. Well, perhaps Sean would be around for her more often. Lord only knew, perhaps if Banks had been . . .

But he didn't get to follow that thought to the particular circle of hell he was sure must be reserved for neglectful husbands and fathers. Annie Cabbot tapped at his door and popped her head around, giving him a temporary escape from the guilt and self-recrimination that seemed to be so much his lot these days, no matter how hard he tried to do the right thing.

'You did say six o'clock, didn't you?'

'Yes. Sorry, Annie. Miles away.' Banks picked up his jacket, checking the pockets for wallet and cigarettes, then cast a backward glance at the pile of untouched paperwork on his desk. To hell with it. If they expected him to do two, three jobs at once, then they could wait for their bloody paperwork.

•

As Jenny drove through a shower and looked out at the ugly forest of cranes that rose up from Goole docks, she wondered for the umpteenth time what on earth had induced her to return to England. To Yorkshire. It certainly wasn't family ties. Jenny was an only child and her parents were retired academics living in Sussex. Both her mother and father had been far too wrapped up in their work – he as a historian, she as a physicist – and Jenny had spent more of her childhood with a succession of nannies and au pairs than with her parents. Given their natural academic detachment, too, Jenny often felt that she had been far more of an experiment than a daughter.

It didn't bother her – after all, she didn't know any different – and it was very much the way she had lived her life, too: as an experiment. Sometimes she looked back and it all seemed so shallow and self-centred that she felt herself panic; other times it seemed just fine.

She would turn forty that coming December, was still single – had never, in fact, been married – and while a bit shop-soiled, battered and bruised, she was far from down and out for the count. She still had her looks and her figure, though she needed more and more magic potions for the former and had to work harder and harder at the university gym to keep those excess pounds from creeping on, given her taste for good food and wine. She also had a good job, a growing reputation as an offender profiler, publications to her credit.

So why did she sometimes feel so empty? Why did she always feel she was in a hurry to get somewhere she never arrived at? Even now, with the rain lashing against her windscreen, the wipers going as fast as they could go, she was doing ninety. She slowed down to eighty, but her speed soon started creeping up again, along with the feeling that she was late for something, always late for something.

The shower ended. Elgar's *Enigma Variations* was playing on Classic FM. To the north, a power station with its huge corset-shaped cooling towers squatted against the horizon, the steam it spewed almost indistinguishable from the low cloud. She was nearing the end of the motorway now. The eastbound M62 was like so many things in life; it left you just short of your destination.

Well, she told herself, she came back to Yorkshire because she was running away from a bad relationship with Randy. Story of her life. She had a nice condo in West Hollywood, rented at a most generous rate by a writer who had made enough money to buy a place way up in Laurel Canyon, and she was within walking distance of a supermarket and the restaurants and clubs on Santa Monica Boulevard. She had her teaching and research at UCLA, and she had Randy. But Randy had a habit of sleeping with pretty 21-year-old graduate students.

After a minor breakdown, Jenny had called it a day and come running back to Eastvale. Perhaps that explained why she was always in a hurry, she thought – desperate to get *home*, wherever that was, desperate to get away from one bad relationship and right into the next one. It was a theory, at any rate. And then, of course, Alan was in Eastvale, too. If he was part of the reason why she had stayed away, could he also be part of the reason why she had come back? She didn't want to dwell on that.

The M62 turned into the A63, and soon Jenny caught a glimpse of the Humber Bridge ahead to her right, stretching out majestically over the broad estuary into the mists and fens of Lincolnshire and Little Holland. Suddenly, a few shafts of sunlight pierced the ragged cloud cover as the 'Nimrod' variation reached its rousing climax. A 'Yorkshire moment'. She remembered the 'LA moments' Randy was so fond of pointing out in their early days when they drove and drove and drove around the huge, sprawling city: a palm tree silhouetted against a blood-orange sky; a big, bright full moon low over the HOLLYWOOD sign.

As soon as she could, Jenny pulled into a lay-by and studied her map. The clouds were dispersing now, allowing even more sunlight through, but the roads were still swamped with puddles and the cars and lorries swished up sheets of water as they sped by her.

Lucy's parents lived off the A164 to Beverley, so she didn't have to drive through Hull city centre. She pressed on through the straggling western suburbs and soon found the residential area she was looking for. Clive and Hilary Liversedge's house was a nicely maintained bay-window semi in a quiet crescent of similar houses. Not much of a place for a young girl to grow up, Jenny thought. Her own parents had moved often throughout her childhood and though she had been born in Durham, she had at various times lived in Bath, Bristol, Exeter and Norwich, all university towns, and all full of randy young men. She had never been stuck in a dull suburban backwater like this.

A small plump man with a soft grey moustache answered the door. He was wearing a green cardigan, unbuttoned, and dark brown trousers which hugged the underside of his rounded gut. A belt wouldn't be much good with a shape like that, Jenny thought, noticing the braces that held the trousers up.

'Clive Liversedge?'

'Come in, love,' he said. 'You must be Dr Fuller.'

'That's me.' Jenny followed him into the cramped hall, from which a glass-panelled door led to a tidy living room with a red velour three-piece suite, an electric fire with fake coals, and striped wallpaper. Somehow, it wasn't the kind of place Jenny had imagined Lucy Payne growing up in; she couldn't get any sense of Lucy living in this environment at all.

She could see what Banks meant about the invalid mother. Pale skin and raccoon eyes, Hilary Liversedge reclined on the sofa, a wool blanket covering her lower half. Her arms were thin and the skin looked puckered and loose. She didn't move when Jenny entered, but her eyes looked lively and attentive enough, despite the yellowish cast of the sclera. Jenny didn't know what was wrong with her, but she put it down to one of those vague chronic illnesses that certain types of people luxuriate in towards the ends of their lives.

'How is she?' Clive Liversedge asked, as if Lucy had perhaps suffered a minor fall or car accident. 'They said it wasn't serious. Is she doing all right?'

'I saw her this morning,' Jenny said, 'and she's bearing up well.'

'Poor lass,' said Hilary. 'To think of what she's been through. Tell her she's welcome to come here and stay with us when she gets out of hospital.'

'I just came to get some sense of what Lucy's like,' Jenny began. 'What sort of a girl she was.'

The Liversedges looked at one another. 'Just ordinary,' said Clive.

'Normal,' said Hilary.

Right, thought Jenny. Normal girls go marrying serial killers every day. Even if Lucy had nothing at all to do with the killings, there *had* to be something odd about her, something *out of* the ordinary. Jenny had even sensed that during their brief chat in the hospital that morning. She could couch it in as much psychological gobbledygook as she wanted – and Jenny had come across plenty of that in her career – but what it came down to was the feeling that Lucy Payne was definitely a sausage or two short of the full English breakfast.

'What was she like at school?' Jenny pressed on.

'Very bright,' answered Clive.

'She got three A-levels. Good marks, too. As and Bs,' added Hilary.

'She could have gone to university,' Clive added.

'Why didn't she?'

'She didn't want to,' said Clive. 'She wanted to get out in the world and make a living for herself.'

'Isn't she ambitious?'

'She's not greedy, if that's what you mean,' Hilary answered. 'Of course she wants to get on in the world like everyone else, but she doesn't think she needs a university degree to do it. They're overrated, anyway, don't you think?'

'I suppose so,' said Jenny, who had a BA and a PhD. 'Was she studious when she was at school?'

'I wouldn't really say so,' said Hilary. 'She did what she had to do in order to pass, but she wasn't a swot.'

'Was she popular at school?'

'She seemed to get on all right with the other children. We got no complaints from her, at any rate.'

'No bullying, nothing like that?'

'Well, there was one girl, once, but that came to nothing,' said Clive.

'Someone bullying Lucy?'

'No. Someone complaining she was being bullied *by* Lucy, accused her of demanding money with threats.'

'What happened?'

'Nothing. It was just her word against Lucy's.'

'And you believed Lucy?'

'Yes.'

'So no action was taken?'

'No. They couldn't prove anything against her.'

'And nothing else like that occurred?'

'No.'

'Did she take part in any after-school activities?'

'She wasn't much of a one for sports, but she was in a couple of school plays. Very good, too, wasn't she, love?'

Hilary Liversedge nodded.

'Was she wild at all?'

'She could be high spirited, and if she got it in her mind to do something, there was no stopping her, but I wouldn't say she was especially *wild*.'

'What about at home? How did you all get along?'

They looked at each other again. It was an ordinary enough gesture, but it unnerved Jenny a bit. 'Fine. Quiet as a mouse. Never any trouble,' said Clive.

'When did she leave home?'

'When she was eighteen. She got that job at the bank in Leeds. We didn't stand in her way.'

'Not that we could have,' added Hilary.

'Have you seen much of her lately?'

Hilary's expression darkened a little. 'She said she's not been able to get over here as much as she'd have liked.'

'When was the last time you saw her?'

'Christmas,' answered Clive.

'Last Christmas?'

'The year before.'

It was as Pat Mitchell had said; Lucy had become distanced from her parents. 'So that's seventeen months?'

'I suppose so.'

'Did she telephone or write?'

'She writes us nice letters,' said Hilary.

'What does she tell you about her life?'

'About her job and the house. Just normal, ordinary sorts of things.'

'Did she tell you how Terry was doing at the school?'

This exchanged look *definitely* spoke volumes. 'No,' said Clive. 'And we didn't ask.'

'We didn't approve of her taking up with the first boy she met,' said Hilary.

'Did she have other boyfriends before Terry?'

'Nobody serious.'

'But you thought she could do better?'

'We're not saying there's anything *wrong* with Terry. He seems nice enough, and he's got a decent job, good prospects.'

'But?'

'But he seemed to sort of take over, didn't he, Clive?'

'Yes. It was very odd.'

'What do you mean?' Jenny asked.

'It was as if he didn't *want* her to see us.'

'Did he or she ever say that?'

Hilary shook her head. The loose skin flapped. 'Not in so many words. It was just an impression I got. *We* got.'

Jenny made a note. To her, this sounded like one of the stages of a sexually sadistic relationship that she had learned about at Quantico. The sadist, in this case Terry Payne, starts to isolate his partner from her family. Pat Mitchell had also suggested the same sort of progressive separation from her friends.

'They just kept to themselves,' said Clive.

'What did you think of Terry?'

'There was something strange about him, but I couldn't put my finger on it.'

'What sort of person is Lucy?' Jenny went on. 'Is she generally trusting? Naïve? Dependent?'

'I wouldn't really describe her in any of those terms, would you, Hilary?'

'No,' said Hilary. 'She's very independent, for a start. Headstrong, too. Always makes her own decisions and acts on them. Like about not going to university and getting a job instead. Once she'd made her mind up, she was off. It was the same with marrying Terry. Love at first sight, she said.'

'You weren't at the wedding, though?'

'Hilary can't travel any more,' said Clive, going over and patting his wife's inert form. 'Can you, love?'

'We sent a telegram and a present,' Hilary said. 'A nice set of Royal Doulton.'

'Do you think Lucy lacks confidence, self-esteem?'

'It depends on what you're talking about. She's confident enough at work, but not so much around people. She often becomes very quiet around strangers, very wary and reserved. She doesn't like crowds, but she used to like going out with a small group of friends. You know, the girls from work. That sort of thing.'

'Would you say she's a loner by nature?'

'To some extent, yes. She's a very private person, never told us much about what was going on or what was going through her mind.'

Jenny was wondering whether she should ask if Lucy tortured animals, wet her bed and set fire to the local school, but she couldn't find an easy way to get around to doing it. 'Was she like that even as a child?' she asked. 'Or did her need for solitude develop later in life?'

'We wouldn't know the answer to that,' said Clive, looking over at his wife. 'We didn't know her then.'

'What do you mean?'

'Well, Lucy wasn't our daughter, not our *natural* daughter. Hilary can't have children, you see. She's got a heart condition. Always has had. Doctor said childbirth could kill her.' Hilary patted her heart and gave Jenny a rueful look.

'You adopted Lucy?'

'No. No. We fostered her. Lucy was our foster child. The third and last, as it turned out. She was with us by far the longest and we came to think of her as our own.'

'I don't understand. Why didn't you tell the police this?'

'They didn't ask,' said Clive, as if that made it all perfectly reasonable.

Jenny was stunned. Here was an essential piece of information in the puzzle that was Lucy Payne, and nobody else on the team knew it. 'How old was she when she came to you?' Jenny asked.

'Twelve,' said Clive. 'It was in March 1990. I remember the day as if it were yesterday. Didn't you know? Lucy was one of the "Alderthorpe Seven".'

•

Annie lounged back in her hard wooden chair as if it had been moulded to fit her shape, and stretched out her legs. Banks had always envied the way she managed to seem so centred and comfortable in almost any environment, and she was doing it now. She took a sip of her Theakston's bitter and almost purred. Then she smiled at Banks.

'I've been cursing you all day, you know,' she said. 'Taking your name in vain.'

'I thought my ears were burning.'

'By rights they should have both burned off by now.'

'Point taken. What did Superintendent Chambers have to say?'

Annie gave a dismissive wave. 'What you'd expect. That it's *my* career on the line if there's any fallout. Oh, and he warned me about you.'

'About me?'

'Yes. Said he thought you might try to pump me for information, to play my cards close to my chest. Which he examined rather too closely for my comfort, by the way.'

'Anything else?'

'Yes. He said you're a ladies' man. Is that true?'

Banks laughed. 'He did? He really said that?'

Annie nodded.

The Queen's Arms was busy with the after-work crowd and tourists seeking shelter, and Banks and Annie had been lucky to get seats at the small, dimpled copper-topped table in the corner by the window. Banks could see the ghostly images of people with umbrellas drifting back and forth on Market Street beyond the red and yellow panes of glass. Rain spotted the windows, and he could hear it tapping in the pauses between words. Savage Garden were on the jukebox claiming that they loved someone before they met her. The air was full of smoke and animated chatter.

'What do you think of Janet Taylor?' Banks asked. 'I'm not trying to pry into your case. I'm just interested in your first impression.'

'So *you* say. Anyway, I quite like her, and I feel sorry for her. She's a probationary PC with limited experience put in an impossible position. She did what came naturally.'

'But?'

'I'll not let my feelings blinker my judgement. I haven't been able to put it all together yet, but it looks to me as if Janet Taylor lied on her statement.'

'Deliberately lied or just didn't remember?'

'I suppose we could give her the benefit of the doubt on that. Look, I've never been in a situation like she was. I can't begin to imagine what it must have been like for her. The fact remains that, according to Dr Mogabe, she must have hit Payne with her baton at least seven or eight times *after* he was beyond any sort of retaliatory action.'

'He was stronger than her. Maybe that's what was required to subdue him. The law allows us *some* latitude on reasonable force in making an arrest.'

Annie shook her head. She stretched out her legs sideways from the chair and crossed them. Banks noticed the thin gold chain around her ankle, one of the many things he found sexy about Annie. 'She lost it, Alan. It goes way beyond self-defence and reasonable force. There's another thing, too.'

'What?'

'I spoke to the paramedics and ambulance attendants who were first at the scene. They hadn't a clue what had happened, of course, but it didn't take them long to work out it was something really nasty and bizarre.'

'And?'

'One of them said when he went over to PC Taylor, who was cradling PC Morrisey's body, she looked over at Payne and said, "Is he dead? Did I kill the bastard?" '

'That could mean anything.'

'My point exactly. In the hands of a good barrister it

could mean she had intended to kill him all along and was asking if she had succeeded in her aim. It could signify intent.'

'It could also just be an innocent question.'

'You know as well as I do there's nothing *innocent* about this business at all. Especially with the Hadleigh case on the news every day. And don't forget that Payne was unarmed and down on the floor when she aimed the final few blows.'

'How do we know that?'

'PC Taylor had already broken his wrist, according to her statement, and kicked the machete into the corner where it was found later. Also, the angles of the blows and the force behind them indicate she had the advantage of height, which we know she didn't have naturally. Payne's six foot one and PC Taylor's only five foot six.'

Banks took a long drag on his cigarette as he digested what Annie had to say, thinking it wouldn't be a hell of a lot of fun to tell AC Hartnell about this. 'Not an immediate threat to her, then?' he said.

'Not from where I'm looking.' Annie shifted a little in her chair. 'It's possible,' she admitted. 'I'm not saying that wouldn't freak out even the best-trained copper. But I've got to say that it looks to me as if she lost it. I'd still like to have a look at the scene.'

'Sure. Though I doubt there's much left to see now the SOCOs have been in there for three days.'

'Even so . . .'

'I understand,' said Banks. And he did. There was something ritualistic in visiting the scene. Whether you picked up vibrations from the walls or what, it didn't really matter. What mattered was that it *connected* you more closely with the crime. You'd *stood* there, in that place where evil had happened. 'When do you want to go?'

'Tomorrow morning. I'll call on Janet Taylor after.'

'I'll arrange it with the officers on duty,' said Banks. 'We can go down there together if you like. I'm off to talk to Lucy Payne again before she disappears.'

'They're releasing her from hospital?'

'So I've heard. Her injuries aren't that serious. Besides, they need the beds.'

Annie paused, then she said, 'I'd rather make my own way.'

'Okay. If that's what you want.'

'Oh, don't look so crestfallen, Alan. It's nothing personal. It just wouldn't look good. And people *would* see us, no matter what you think.'

'You're right,' Banks agreed. 'Look, if there's any chance of a bit of spare time Saturday night, how about dinner and . . .?'

The corners of Annie's mouth turned up, and a gleam came to her dark eyes. 'Dinner and what?'

'You know.'

'I don't. Tell me.'

Banks glanced around to make sure no one was eavesdropping, then he leaned forward. But before he could say anything, the doors opened and DC Winsome Jackman walked in. Heads turned: some because she was black, and some because she was a gorgeous, statuesque young woman. Winsome was on duty and Banks and Annie had told her where they would be.

'Sorry to disturb you, sir,' she said, pulling up a chair and sitting down.

'That's all right,' said Banks. 'What is it?'

'A DC Karen Hodgkins from the task force just phoned.'

'And?'

Winsome looked at Annie. 'It's Terence Payne,' she said.

'He died an hour ago in the Infirmary without recovering consciousness.'

'Oh, shit,' said Annie.

'Well, that should make life interesting,' said Banks, reaching for another cigarette.

•

'Tell me about the Alderthorpe Seven,' said Banks into his phone at home later that evening. He had just settled down to Duke Ellington's *Black, Brown and Beige*, the latest copy of *Gramophone* and two fingers of Laphroaig when Jenny phoned. He turned down the music and reached for his cigarettes. 'I mean,' he went on, 'I vaguely remember hearing about it at the time, but I can't remember many details.'

'I don't have a lot yet, myself,' said Jenny. 'Only what the Liversedges told me.'

'Go on.'

Banks heard a rustle of paper at the other end of the line. 'On the eleventh of February 1990,' Jenny began, 'police and social workers made a dawn raid on the village of Alderthorpe, near Spurn Head on the East Yorkshire coast. They were acting on allegations of ritual Satanic abuse of children and investigating a missing child.'

'Who blew the whistle?' Banks asked.

'I don't know,' said Jenny. 'I didn't ask.'

Banks filed it away for later. 'Okay. Carry on.'

'I'm not a policeman, Alan. I don't know what sort of questions to ask.'

'I'm sure you did just fine. Please, go on.'

'They took six children from two separate households into care.'

'What exactly was supposed to have been going on?'

'At first it was all very vague. "Lewd and libidinous behaviour. Ritualistic music, dance and costume".'

'Sounds like police headquarters on a Saturday night. Anything else?'

'Well, that's where it gets interesting. And sick. It seems this was one of the few such cases in which prosecutions went forward and convictions were gained. All the Liversedges would tell me was that there were tales of torture, of kids being forced to drink urine and eat . . . Christ, I'm not squeamish, Alan, but this stuff turns my stomach.'

'That's all right. Take it easy.'

'They were humiliated,' Jenny went on. 'Sometimes physically injured, kept in cages without food for days, used as objects of sexual gratification in Satanic rituals. One child, a girl called Kathleen Murray, was found dead. Her remains showed evidence of torture and sexual abuse.'

'How did she die?'

'She was strangled. She'd also been beaten and half starved, too. That was what sparked the whistle-blower, her not turning up for school.'

'And this was proven in court?'

'Most of it, yes. The killing. The Satanic stuff didn't come out in the trial. I suppose the CPS must have thought it would just sound like too much mumbo-jumbo.'

'How did it come out?'

'Some of the children gave descriptions later, after they'd been fostered.'

'Lucy?'

'No. According to the Liversedges, Lucy never spoke about what happened. She just put it all behind her.'

'Was it followed up?'

'No. There were similar allegations and raids in Cleveland, Rochdale and the Orkneys and pretty soon it was all over the papers. Caused a hell of a national outcry. Epidemic of child abuse, that sort of thing. Over-zealous social workers. Questions in the House, the lot.'

'I remember,' said Banks.

'Most of the cases were thrown out, and nobody wanted to talk about the one that *was* true. Well, Alderthorpe wasn't the only one. There was a similar case in Nottingham in 1989 that also resulted in convictions, but it wasn't widely publicized. Then we got the Butler-Schloss report and revisions of the Children's Act.'

'What happened to Lucy's real parents?'

'They went to jail. The Liversedges have no idea whether they're still there or what. They haven't kept track of things.'

Banks sipped some Laphroaig and flicked his cigarette end into the empty grate. 'So Lucy stayed with the Liversedges?'

'Yes. She changed her name, too, by the way. She used to be called Linda. Linda Godwin. Then, with all the publicity, she wanted to change it. The Liversedges assured me it's all legal and above board.'

From Linda Godwin to Lucy Liversedge to Lucy Payne, Banks thought. Interesting.

'Anyway,' Jenny went on, 'after they'd told me all this I pushed them a bit more and at least got them to admit life with Lucy wasn't quite as "ordinary" and "normal" as they'd originally said it was.'

'Oh?'

'Problems adjusting. Surprise, surprise. The first two years, between the ages of twelve and fourteen, Lucy was as good as gold: a quiet, passive, considerate and sensitive kid. They were worried she was traumatized.'

'And?'

'Lucy saw a child psychiatrist for a while.'

'Then?'

'From fourteen to sixteen she started to act up, come out of her shell. She stopped seeing the psychiatrist. There were boys, suspicions that she was having sex, and then there was the bullying.'

'Bullying?'

'Yes. At first they told me it was an isolated incident and came to nothing, but later they said it caused a few problems with the school. Lucy was bullying younger girls out of their dinner money and stuff like that. It's fairly common.'

'But in Lucy's case?'

'A phase. The Liversedges worked with the school authorities, and the psychiatrist entered the picture again briefly. Then Lucy settled down to behave herself. The next two years, sixteen to eighteen, she quieted down, withdrew more into herself, became less active socially and sexually. She did her A-levels, got good results and got a job with the NatWest bank in Leeds. That was four years ago. It seemed almost as if she were planning her escape. She had very little contact with the Liversedges after she left, and I get the impression that they were relieved.'

'Why?'

'I don't know why. Call it intuition, but I got the feeling that they ended up being *scared* of Lucy, for the way she seemed able to manipulate them. As I say, it's just a vague feeling.'

'Interesting. Go on.'

'They saw even less of her after she hooked up with Terence Payne. I thought when they first told me that he might have been responsible for isolating her from her family and friends, you know, the way abusers often do, but now it seems just as likely that she was isolating herself.

Her friend from work, Pat Mitchell, said the same thing. Meeting Terry really changed Lucy, cut her off almost entirely from her old life, her old ways.'

'So she was either under his thrall or she'd found a new sort of life that she preferred?'

'Yes.' Jenny told him about the incident of Lucy's prostitution.

Banks thought for a moment. 'It's interesting,' he said. '*Really* interesting. But it doesn't prove anything.'

'I told you that would probably be the case. It makes her *weird*, but being weird's no grounds for arrest or half the population would be behind bars.'

'More than half. But hang on a minute, Jenny. You've come up with a number of leads worth pursuing.'

'Like what?'

'Like what if Lucy was involved in the Alderthorpe abuse herself? I remember reading at the time that there were cases of some of the older victims abusing their own younger siblings.'

'But what would it mean even if we *could* prove that after all this time?'

'I don't know, Jenny. I'm just thinking out loud. What's your next step?'

'I'm going to talk to someone from the social services tomorrow, see if I can get the names of any of the social workers involved.'

'Good. I'll work it from the police angle when I get a spare moment. There are bound to be records, files. Then what?'

'I want to go to Alderthorpe, nose around, talk to people who remember.'

'Be careful, Jenny. It's bound to be a very raw nerve out there, even after all this time.'

'I'll be careful.'

'And don't forget, there might still be someone who escaped prosecution worried about new revelations.'

'That makes me feel really safe and secure.'

'The other kids . . .'

'Yes?'

'What do you know about them?'

'Nothing, really, except they were aged between eight and twelve.'

'Any idea where they are?'

'No. The Liversedges don't know. And I *did* ask them.'

'Don't be defensive. We'll make a detective of you yet.'

'No, thanks.'

'Let's see if we can find them, shall we? They might be able to tell us a lot more about Lucy Payne than anyone else.'

'Okay. I'll see how much the social workers are willing to tell me.'

'Not much, I'll bet. Your best chance will be if one of them's retired or moved on to some other line of work. Then spilling the beans won't seem like such a betrayal.'

'Hey, I'm supposed to be the psychologist. Leave that sort of thinking to me.'

Banks laughed over the phone. 'It's a blurred line sometimes, isn't it? Detective work and psychology.'

'Try and tell some of your oafish colleagues that.'

'Thanks, Jenny. You've done a great job.'

'And I've only just begun.'

'Keep in touch.'

'Promise.'

When Banks put the phone down, Mahalia Jackson was singing 'Come Sunday'. He turned up the volume and took his drink outside to his little balcony over Gratly Falls. The rain had stopped, but the downpour had been heavy enough to swell the sound of the falls. It was just after sunset and the deep vermilions, purples and oranges were dying in the western sky, streaked with dark ribs of cloud, while the darkening east went from pale to inky blue. Just across the falls was a field of grazing sheep. In it stood a clump of huge old trees where rooks nested and often woke him early in the morning with their noisy squabbling. Such ill-tempered birds, they seemed. Beyond the field, the daleside sloped down to the River Swain and Banks could see the opposite hillside a mile or more away, darkening in the evening, rising to the long, grinning skeleton's mouth of Crow Scar. The runic patterns of the drystone walls seemed to stand out in relief as the light faded. Just a little to his right, he could see Helmthorpe church tower poking up from the valley bottom.

Banks looked at his watch. Still early enough to stroll down there and have a pint or two in the Dog and Gun, maybe chat with one or two of the locals he'd become friendly with since his move. But he decided he didn't fancy company; he had too much on his mind, what with Terence Payne's death, the mystery of Leanne Wray, and the revelations Jenny Fuller had just come through with as regards Lucy's past. Since taking on the Chameleon investigation, he realized, he had become more and more of a loner, less inclined to make small talk at the bar. Partly, he supposed, it was the burden of command, but it was also something more, the proximity to such evil, perhaps, that tainted him somehow and made small talk seem like a completely inadequate response to what was happening.

The news of Sandra's pregnancy was also still weighing on his mind, bringing back some memories he had hoped to forget. He knew he wouldn't be good company, but nor would he be able to get to sleep so early. He nipped inside and poured another shot of whisky, then picked up his cigarettes and went back outside to lean against the damp wall and enjoy the last of the evening light. A curlew piped up on the distant moors and Mahalia Jackson sang on, humming the tune long after she had run out of words.

10

Friday morning started badly for Maggie. She had spent a night disturbed by vague and frightening nightmares that scuttled away into the shadows the minute she awoke screaming and tried to grasp them. Getting back to sleep was difficult not only because of the bad dreams, but also because of the eerie noises and voices she could hear from across the road. Didn't the police ever sleep?

Once, getting up to go for a glass of water, she looked out of her bedroom window and saw some uniformed police officers carrying cardboard boxes into a van waiting with its engine running. Then some men carried what looked like electronic equipment through the front door, and a short while later Maggie fancied she could see a strange ghostly light sweeping the living room of number thirty-five behind the drawn curtains. The digging continued in the front garden, surrounded by a canvas screen and lit on the inside, so that all Maggie could see was enlarged and deformed shadows of men silhouetted against the canvas. These figures carried over into her next nightmare, and in the end she didn't know whether she was asleep or awake.

She got up a little after seven o'clock and headed for the kitchen, where a cup of tea helped soothe her frayed nerves. This was one English habit that she had slipped into easily. She planned to spend the day working on Grimm again, perhaps 'Hansel and Gretel', now that she had satisfactory sketches for 'Rapunzel', and trying to put the business of number thirty-five out of her head for a few hours at least.

Then she heard the paperboy arrive and the newspaper slip through her letterbox onto the hall mat. She hurried out and carried it back to the kitchen, where she spread it on the table.

Lorraine Temple's story was prominent on the front page, beside the bigger headline story about Terence Payne's dying without recovering consciousness. There was even a photograph of Maggie, taken without her knowledge, standing just outside her front gate. It must have been taken when she was going down to the pub to talk with Lorraine, she realized, as she was wearing the same jeans and light cotton jacket as she had worn on Tuesday.

HOUSE OF PAYNE: NEIGHBOUR SPEAKS OUT, ran the headline, and the article went on to detail how Maggie had heard suspicious sounds coming from across The Hill and called the police. Afterwards, calling Maggie Lucy's 'friend', Lorraine Temple reported what Maggie had said about Lucy's being a victim of domestic abuse, and how she was scared of her husband. All of which was fine and accurate enough, as far as it went. But then came the sting in the tail. According to sources in Toronto, Lorraine Temple went on to report, Maggie Forrest herself was on the run from an abusive husband: Toronto lawyer, William Burke. The article detailed the time Maggie had spent in hospital and all the fruitless court orders issued to stop Bill going near her. Describing Maggie as a nervous, mousy sort of woman, Lorraine Temple also mentioned that she was seeing a local psychiatrist called Dr Simms, who 'declined to comment'.

Lorraine ended by suggesting that, perhaps because of Maggie's own psychological problems, Maggie had been gullible, and that her identification with Lucy's plight may have blinded her to the truth. Lorraine couldn't come out and say that she thought Lucy was guilty of anything – the laws of libel forbade that – but she did have a very good stab at making her readers think Lucy might just be the sort of manipulative and deceitful person who could twist a weak woman like Maggie around her little finger. It was rubbish, of course, but effective rubbish, nonetheless.

How could she *do* that? Now everybody would know.

Every time Maggie walked down the street to go to the shops or catch the bus into town, the neighbours and shopkeepers would look at her differently, with *pity* and perhaps just the merest hint of *blame* in their eyes. Some people would avoid looking her in the eye and perhaps even stop talking to her, associating her too closely for comfort with the events at number thirty-five. Even strangers who recognized her from the photograph would wonder about her. Perhaps Claire would stop coming to see her altogether, though she hadn't been since the time the policeman turned up, and Maggie was already worried about her.

Perhaps even Bill would find out.

It was her own fault, of course. She had put herself in harm's way. She had been trying to do a favour for poor Lucy, trying to garner her some public sympathy, and the whole thing had backfired. How stupid she had been to trust Lorraine Temple. One lousy article like this and her whole new fragile, protected world would change. Just like that. It wasn't fair, Maggie told herself as she cried over the breakfast table. *It just wasn't fair.*

•

After a short but satisfying night's sleep – perhaps due to the generous doses of Laphroaig and Duke Ellington – Banks was back in his Millgarth cubby-hole by eight-thirty on

Friday morning, and the first news to cross his desk was a note from Stefan Nowak informing him that the skeletal remains dug up in the Paynes's garden were *not* Leanne Wray's. Had Banks been harbouring the slightest hope that Leanne might still be alive and well after all this time, he would have jumped for joy, but as it was, he rubbed his forehead in frustration; it looked as if it was going to be another one of those days. He punched in Stefan's mobile number and got an answer after three rings. It sounded as if Stefan was in the middle of another conversation, but he muttered a few asides and gave his attention to Banks.

'Sorry about that,' he said.

'Problems?'

'Typical breakfast chaos. I'm just trying to get out of the house.'

'I know what you mean. Look, about this identification . . .'

'It's solid, sir. Dental records. DNA will take a bit longer. There's no way it's Leanne Wray. I'm just about to set off back to the house. The lads are still digging.'

'Who the hell can it be?'

'Don't know. All I've been able to find out so far is that it's a young woman, late teens to early twenties, been there a few months and there's a lot of stainless steel in her dental work, including a crown.'

'Meaning?' Banks asked, a faint memory beckoning.

'Possible Eastern European origin. They still use a lot of stainless steel over there.'

Right. Banks had come across something like that before. A forensic dentist had once told him that Russians used stainless steel. 'Eastern European?'

'Just a possibility, sir.'

'All right. Any chance of that DNA comparison between

Payne and the Seacroft Rapist turning up before the weekend?'

'I'll get onto them this morning, see if I can give them a prod.'

'Okay. Thanks. Keep at it, Stefan.'

'Will do.'

Banks hung up, more puzzled than ever. One of the first things AC Hartnell had instituted when the team was first put together was a special squad to keep tabs on all missing persons cases throughout the entire country – 'mispers' as they were called – particularly if they involved blonde teenagers, with no apparent reasons for running away, disappearing on their way home from clubs, pubs, cinemas and dances. The team had monitored scores of cases every day, but none had met the criteria of the Chameleon investigation, except one girl in Cheshire, who had turned up alive and contrite two days later after a brief shack-up with her boyfriend, about which she just happened to forget to tell her parents, and the sadder case of a young girl in Lincoln who, it turned out, had been run over and had not been carrying any identification. Now here was Stefan saying they'd probably got a dead Eastern European girl in the garden.

Banks didn't get very far with his chain of thought before his office door opened and DC Filey dropped a copy of that morning's *Post* on his desk.

•

Annie parked her purple Astra up the street and walked towards number thirty-five The Hill, shielding her eyes from the morning sunlight. Crime scene tape and trestles blocked off that section of pavement in front of the garden wall, so that pedestrians had to make a detour onto the tarmac road to get by. One or two people paused to glance over the garden gate as they passed, Annie noticed, but most walked to the other side of the road and averted their eyes. She even saw one elderly woman cross herself.

Annie showed her warrant card to the officer on duty, signed in at the gate and walked down the garden path. She wasn't afraid of seeing gruesome sights, if indeed there were any left inside the house, but she had never before visited a scene so completely overrun with SOCO activity, and just walking into it made her edgy. The men in the front garden ignored her and went on with their digging. The door was ajar, and when Annie pushed gently, it opened into the hall.

The hallway was deserted and at first the house seemed so quiet inside that Annie thought she was alone. Then someone shouted, and the sound of a pneumatic drill ripped through the air, coming up from the cellar, shattering her illusion. The house was hot, stuffy and full of dust, and Annie sneezed three times before exploring further.

Her nerves gradually gave way to professional curiosity, and she noted with interest that the carpets had been taken up, leaving only the bare concrete floors and wooden stairs, and that the living room had been stripped of furniture, too, even down to the light fixtures. Several holes had been punched in the walls, no doubt to ensure that no bodies had been entombed there. Annie gave a little shudder. Poe's 'The Cask of Amontillado' was one of the more frightening stories she had read at school.

Everywhere she went she was conscious of the narrow, roped-off pathway she knew she was supposed to follow. In an odd way it was like visiting the Brontë parsonage or Wordsworth's cottage, where you could only stand and look beyond the rope at the antique furniture.

The kitchen, where three SOCOs were working on the

sink and drains, was in the same sorry state, tiles wrenched up, oven and fridge gone, cupboards bare, fingerprint dust everywhere. Annie hadn't thought anyone could do so much damage to a place in three days. One of the SOCOs looked over at her and asked her rather testily what she thought she was doing there. She flashed him her warrant card and he went back to ripping out the sink. The pneumatic drill stopped and Annie heard the sound of a vacuum cleaner from upstairs, an eerily domestic sound amid all the crime scene chaos, though she knew its purpose was far more sinister than getting rid of the dust.

She took the silence from the cellar as her cue to go down there, noting as she did so the door open to the garage, which had been stripped as bare as the rest of the house. The car was gone, no doubt in the police garage being taken apart piece by piece, and the oil-stained floor had been dug up.

She sensed herself becoming hypersensitive as she approached the cellar door, her breath coming in short gasps. There was an obscene poster of a naked woman with her legs spread wide apart on the door which Annie hoped the SOCOs hadn't left there because they enjoyed seeing it. That must have unnerved Janet Taylor to start with, she thought, advancing slowly, as she imagined Janet and Dennis had done. Christ, she felt apprehensive enough herself, even though she knew the only people in there were SOCOs. But Janet and Dennis hadn't known what to expect, Annie told herself. Whatever it was, they hadn't expected what they got. She knew far more than they had, and no doubt her imagination was working overtime on that.

Through the door, much cooler down here, trying to feel the way it was, despite the two SOCO officers and the bright lighting . . . Janet went in first, Dennis just behind her. The cellar was smaller than she had expected. It must have happened so quickly. Candlelight. The figure leaping out of the shadows, wielding a machete, hacking into Dennis Morrisey's throat and arm because he was the closest. Dennis goes down. Janet already has her side-handled baton out, extended, ready to ward off the first blow. So close she can smell Payne's breath. Perhaps he can't believe that a woman, weaker and smaller than him, can thwart him so easily. Before he can recover from his shock, Janet lashes out and hits him on the left temple. Blinded by pain and perhaps by blood, he falls back against the wall. Next he feels a sharp pain on his wrist and he can't hold onto the machete. He hears it skitter away across the floor but doesn't know where. He rears up and goes at her. Angry now because she knows her partner is bleeding to death on the floor, Janet hits him again and again, wanting it to be over so she can tend to Dennis. He scrabbles after where he thought the machete went, blood dripping down his face. She hits him again. And again. How much strength does he have left by now? Annie wondered. Surely not enough to overpower Janet? And how many more times does she hit him now he's down, handcuffed to the pipe, not moving at all?

Annie sighed and watched the SOCOs shifting their drill to dig into another spot.

'Are you going to start that thing up again?' she asked.

One of the men grinned. 'Want some ear-muffs?'

Annie smiled back at him. 'No, I'd rather just get out of here before you start. Can you give me another minute or so?'

'Can do.'

Annie glanced around at the crude stick figures and

occult symbols on the walls and wondered how integral a part of Payne's fantasy they were. Banks had also told her that the place was lit by dozens of candles, but they were all gone now, as was the mattress they had found the body on. One of the SOCOs was on his knees looking at something on the concrete floor over by the door.

'What is it?' Annie asked him. 'Found something?'

'Dunno,' he said. 'Some sort of little scuff marks in the concrete. It hardly shows at all, but there seems to be some sort of pattern.'

Annie knelt to look. She couldn't see anything until the SOCO pointed to what looked like small circles in the concrete. There were three of them in all, pretty much equidistant.

'I'll try a few different lighting angles,' he said, almost to himself. 'Maybe some infrared film to highlight the contrasts.'

'Could be a tripod,' Annie said.

'What? Bugger me – sorry, love – but you could be right. Luke Selkirk and that funny little assistant of his were down here a day or two ago. Maybe they left the marks.'

'I think they'd have been more professional, don't you?'

'I'd better ask them, hadn't I?'

Annie left him to it and walked through the far door. The ground had been sectioned into grids and the soil had been dug up. Annie knew that three bodies had been found there. She followed the narrow, marked path across to the door, opened it and walked up the steps into the back garden. Crime scene tape barred her entrance at the top of the steps, but she didn't need to go any further. Like the anteroom in the cellar, the overgrown garden had been divided into grids and marked out with rope. Most of them had already been cleared of grass and weeds and topsoil, but some, further back, remained overgrown. At the far wall, a large waterproof sheet used to protect the garden from yesterday's rain lay rolled up like a carpet.

This was a delicate job, Annie knew from watching the excavation of a skeleton at the village of Hobb's End. It was far too easy to disturb old bones. She could see the hole, about three feet deep, where one body had been dug up, and now there were two men gathered around another hole, taking off the soil with trowels and passing it to a third man who ran it through a sieve as if he were panning for gold.

'What is it?' Annie asked from the top of the cellar steps.

One of the men looked up at her. She hadn't recognized Stefan Nowak at first. She didn't know him well, as he hadn't been at Eastvale's Western Divisional Headquarters for long, but Banks had introduced them once. Stefan was the man, ACC Ron McLaughlin had said, who would drag North Yorkshire kicking and screaming into the twenty-first century. Annie had found him rather reserved, a bit mysterious even, as if he were carrying around a grave secret or a great weight of past pain. He affected a cheery enough demeanour on the surface, but she could tell it didn't run very deep. He was tall, over six foot, and handsome in a clean-cut, elegant sort of way. She knew his background was Polish and had often wondered if he were a prince or a count or something. Most of the Poles she had ever met said they were descended from counts or princes at one time or another, and there was something regal and stately in Stefan's bearing.

'It's Annie, isn't it?' he said. 'DS Annie Cabbot?'

'DI, now, Stefan. How's it going?'

'Didn't know you were on this case.'

'One of them,' Annie explained. 'Terence Payne. I'm with Complaints and Discipline.'

'I can't believe the CPS will even let that one see the light of day,' said Stefan. 'Justifiable homicide, surely?'

'I hope that's how they'll see it, but you never know with them. Anyway, I just wanted a look at the place.'

'I'm afraid we've made rather a mess,' said Stefan. 'It looks as if we've just found another body. Want a look?'

Annie ducked under the tape. 'Yes.'

'Be careful,' said Stefan. 'Follow the marked path.'

Annie did as he said and soon found herself standing beside the partially excavated grave. This one was a skeleton. Not quite as stained and filthy as the one she had seen at Hobb's End, but a skeleton nonetheless. She could see part of the skull, one shoulder and part of the left arm. 'How long?' she asked.

'Hard to say,' Stefan answered. 'More than a few months.' He introduced the two men who had been poring over the grave with him, one a botanist and the other an entomologist. 'These lads should be able to help with that. And we're getting Dr Ioan Williams to come over from the university and give us a hand.'

Annie remembered the young doctor with the long hair and the prominent Adam's apple from the Hobb's End case, the way he had caressed Gloria Shackleton's pelvic bone and leered over it at Annie.

'I know this isn't my case,' Annie said, 'but isn't this one body too many?'

Stefan looked up at her and shielded his eyes from the sun. 'Yes,' he said. 'It is. Rather throws a spanner in the works, doesn't it?'

'Indeed it does.'

Annie walked back towards her car. There was nothing more to be gained from hanging around The Hill. Besides, she realized, glancing at her watch, she had a post mortem to attend.

•

'What the hell do you mean talking to the press like that?' said Banks. 'Didn't I warn you about it?'

'This is the first I've heard we're living in a police state,' said Maggie Forrest, arms folded over her chest, eyes angry and tearful. They stood in her kitchen, Banks brandishing the *Post* and Maggie in the midst of clearing away her breakfast dishes. After seeing the article at Millgarth, he had headed straight for The Hill.

'Don't give me that adolescent crap about police states. Who do you think you are, a student protesting against some distant war?'

'You've no right to talk to me like this. I haven't done anything wrong.'

'Anything wrong? Have you any idea of the wasp's nest you could be helping to stir up?'

'I don't know what you mean. All I wanted to do was tell Lucy's side of the story, but that woman twisted it all.'

'Are you so naïve that you didn't expect that?'

'There's a difference between being naïve and caring, but a cynic like you probably wouldn't understand it.'

Banks could see that Maggie was shaking, either with anger or fear, and he was worried that he had given too free a rein to his anger. He knew she had been abused by her husband, that she was a bruised soul, so she was probably scared stiff of this man raising his voice in her kitchen. It was insensitive of him, but damn it, the woman irritated him. He sat at the kitchen table and tried to cool things down a bit. 'Maggie,' he said softly. 'I'm sorry, but you could cause us a lot of problems.'

Maggie seemed to relax a little. 'I don't see how.'

'Public sympathy is a very fickle thing, and when you mess with it, it's like dancing with the devil. It's just as likely to reach out and eat *you* up as anyone else.'

'But how would people find out what Lucy went through at her husband's hands? *She* won't talk about it, I can guarantee you that.'

'None of us know what went on in Lucy's house. All you're doing is jeopardizing her chance of a fair trial, if—'

'Trial? Trial for what?'

'I was going to say "if it comes to that".'

'I'm sorry, but I don't agree.' Maggie put the electric kettle on and sat opposite Banks. 'People need to know about domestic abuse. It's not something that should be swept under the carpet for any reason. Especially not just because the police say so.'

'I agree. Look, I understand you're prejudiced against us, but—'

'Prejudiced? Right. With your help I ended up in hospital.'

'But you have to understand that in many of these matters our hands are tied. We're only as good as the information we have and the laws of the land allow.'

'All the more reason for me to speak out about Lucy. After all, you're not exactly here to *help* her, are you?'

'I'm here to find out the truth.'

'Well, that's all very high and mighty of you.'

'Now who's the cynic?'

'We all know the police only want convictions, that they're not overly concerned with the truth, or with justice.'

'Convictions help, if they keep the bad guys off the street. Too often they don't. And justice we leave to the courts, but you're wrong about the rest. I can't speak for anyone else, but I'm very much concerned with the truth. I've worked day and night on this case since the beginning of April, and every case I work on I want to know what happened, who did it and why. I don't always find out, but you'd be surprised how much I do learn. Sometimes it gets me into trouble. And I have to live with the knowledge, take it into my life, take it home with me. I'm that snowball rolling down the hill, only the pure snow's run out and I'm picking up layer after layer of dirt and gravel just so that you can sit safe and warm at home and accuse me of being some sort of Gestapo officer.'

'I didn't mean it like that. And I wasn't always safe and warm.'

'Do you know that what you've just done actually stands a good chance of warping the truth, whatever it may be?'

'I didn't do that. It was her. That journalist. Lorraine Temple.'

Banks slapped the table and immediately regretted it when Maggie jumped. 'Wrong,' he said. '*She* was only doing her job. Like it or not, that's what it was. Her job's to sell newspapers. You've got this all backwards, Maggie. You think the media's here to tell the truth and the police to lie.'

'You're confusing me now.' The kettle boiled and Maggie got up to make tea. She didn't offer Banks a cup, but when it was ready she poured him one automatically. He thanked her.

'All I'm saying, Maggie, is that you might be doing Lucy more harm than good by talking to the press. Look at what happened this time. You say it came out all wrong and that they practically said Lucy is as guilty as her husband. That's hardly helping her, is it?'

'But I *told* you. She twisted my words.'

'And I'm saying you should have expected that. It made a better story.'

'Then where *am* I supposed to go to tell the truth? Or to find it?'

'Christ, Maggie, if I knew the answer to that I'd—'

But before Banks could finish, his mobile rang. This time it was the PC on duty at the Infirmary. Lucy Payne had just been cleared for release, and she had a solicitor with her.

'Do you know anything about this solicitor?' Banks asked Maggie when he'd finished on the phone.

She smiled sheepishly. 'As a matter of fact, yes, I do.'

Banks said nothing, not trusting himself to respond in a civilized manner. Leaving his tea untouched, he bid Maggie Forrest a hurried farewell and dashed out to his car. He didn't even stop to talk to Annie Cabbot when he saw her walking out of number thirty-five, but managed only a quick wave before jumping in his Renault and roaring off.

•

Lucy Payne was sitting on the bed painting her toenails black when Banks walked in. She gave him a look and demurely pulled her skirt down over her thighs. The bandages were gone from her head and the bruises seemed to be healing well. She had rearranged her long black hair so it covered the patch the doctor had shaved for his stitches.

Another woman stood in the room, over by the window: the solicitor. Slight in stature, with chocolate brown hair cropped almost as closely as Banks's, and watchful, serious hazel eyes, she was dressed in a charcoal pinstriped jacket, matching skirt and a white blouse with some sort of ruffled front. She wore dark tights and shiny black pumps.

She walked over and held out her hand. 'Julia Ford. I'm Lucy's solicitor. I don't believe we've met.'

'A pleasure,' said Banks.

'This isn't the first time you've talked to my client, is it, Superintendent?'

'No,' said Banks.

'And the last time you were accompanied by a psychologist named Dr Fuller?'

'Dr Fuller's our consultant psychologist on the Chameleon task force,' said Banks.

'Just be careful, Superintendent, that's all. I'd have very good grounds to argue that anything Dr Fuller might have got from my client is inadmissible as evidence.'

'We weren't gathering evidence,' said Banks. 'Lucy was questioned as a witness, and as a *victim*. Not as a suspect.'

'A fine line, Superintendent, should matters change. And now?'

Banks glanced at Lucy, who had resumed painting her toenails, seeming indifferent to the banter between her solicitor and Banks. 'I wasn't aware you thought you needed a solicitor, Lucy,' he said.

Lucy looked up. 'It's in my best interests. They're discharging me this morning. Soon as the paperwork's done, I can go home.'

Banks looked at Julia Ford in exasperation. 'I hope you haven't encouraged her in this fantasy?'

Julia raised her eyebrows. 'I don't know what you're talking about.'

Banks turned back to Lucy. 'You can't go home, Lucy,' he explained. 'Your house is being taken apart brick by brick by forensic experts. Have you any concept of what happened there?'

'Of course I have,' said Lucy. 'Terry hit me. He knocked me out and put me in hospital.'

'But Terry's dead now, isn't he?'

'Yes. So?'

'That changes things, doesn't it?'

'Look,' said Lucy. 'I've been abused and I've just lost my husband. Now you're telling me I've lost my home, too?'

'For the time being.'

'Well, what am I supposed to do? Where am I supposed to go?'

'How about your foster parents, *Linda*?'

Lucy's look let Banks know that she hadn't missed the emphasis. 'I don't seem to have much choice, do I?'

'Anyway, it won't be a problem for a while yet,' Banks went on. 'We found traces of Kimberley Myers's blood on the sleeves of your dressing-gown, along with some yellow fibres under your fingernails. You've got a lot of explaining to do before you go anywhere.'

Lucy looked alarmed. 'What do you mean?'

Julia Ford narrowed her eyes and looked at Banks. 'What he means, Lucy, is that he's going to take you in to the police station for questioning.'

'Can he do that?'

'I'm afraid so, Lucy.'

'And can he keep me there?'

'Under the PACE regulations, he can, yes, if he's not satisfied with the answers you give him. For twenty-four hours. But there are very strict guidelines. You've got nothing to worry about.'

'You mean I could be in *prison* for a whole day? In a cell?'

'Don't be alarmed, Lucy,' said Julia, stepping over and touching her client's arm. 'Nothing bad will happen to you. Those days are gone, now. You'll be well looked after.'

'But I'll be in prison!'

'Possibly. It all depends.'

'But I *haven't done anything*!' She gave Banks an angry

look, black eyes burning like coals. 'I'm the victim here. Why are you picking on me?'

'Nobody's picking on you, Lucy,' said Banks. 'There's a lot of questions need answering, and we think you can help us.'

'I'll answer your questions. I'm not refusing to co-operate. You don't have to take me to the police station for that. Besides, I've already answered them.'

'Hardly. There's a lot more we need to know, and there are certain formalities, procedures to be followed. Anyway, it's all changed now that Terry's died, hasn't it?'

Lucy looked away. 'I don't know what you mean.'

'You can speak freely now. You don't have to be afraid of him.'

'Oh, I see.'

'What did you think I meant, Lucy?'

'Nothing.'

'That you could change your story? Just deny everything?'

'I told you. Nothing.'

'But there's the blood to explain now. And the yellow fibres. We know you were in the cellar. We can prove it.'

'I don't know anything about that. I don't remember.'

'Very convenient. Aren't you sorry Terry's dead, Lucy?'

Lucy packed her nail polish away in her handbag. 'Of course I am. But he beat me up. It was him who put me here, him who got me into all this trouble with the police. It's not *my* fault. None of it's my fault. I haven't done anything wrong. Why should I have to be the one who suffers?'

Banks shook his head and stood up. 'Maybe we'd better just go.'

Lucy looked over to Julia Ford.

'I'll come with you,' said Julia. 'I'll be present when you're questioned and near by in case you need me.'

Lucy managed a weak smile. 'But you won't stay in the cell with me?'

Julia smiled back, then looked at Banks. 'I'm afraid they don't make doubles, Lucy.'

'That's right,' said Banks. 'Like girls, do you, Lucy?'

'There was no need for that, Superintendent,' Julia Ford said. 'And I'll thank you to keep any more questions you might have until we're in the interview room.'

Lucy just glared at Banks.

'Anyway,' Julia Ford went on, turning back to Lucy. 'Let's not be pessimistic. It might not come to that.' She turned to Banks. 'Might I suggest, Superintendent, that we leave by a discreet exit? You can't have failed to notice the media presence.'

'It's a big story for them,' Banks said. 'But yes, that's a good idea. I've got another one, too.'

'Oh?'

'That we take Lucy to Eastvale for questioning. You and I know damn well that Millgarth will be a zoo once the press find out she's there. This way we've got a chance of avoiding all that chaos, at least for a while.'

Julia Ford thought for moment, then looked at Lucy. 'It's a good idea,' she said.

'Will you come to Eastvale with me? I'm scared.'

'Of course.' Julia looked at Banks. 'I'm sure the Superintendent here can recommend a decent hotel?'

•

'But how could she possibly know I'm seeing you?' Maggie asked Dr Susan Simms at the start of her session that afternoon.

'I've no idea, but you can be certain I didn't tell anyone. And I told her nothing.'

'I know,' said Maggie. 'Thank you.'

'Think nothing of it, dear. It's a matter of professional ethics. This implied support of yours for Lucy Payne, is it true?'

Maggie felt her anger bristle again as she remembered her argument with Banks that morning. She still felt upset by it. 'I think Lucy's been a victim of abuse, yes.'

Dr Simms remained silent for a while, gazing out of the window, then she shifted in her chair and said, 'Just be careful, Margaret. Just be careful. You seem to be under a lot of stress. Now, shall we begin? I believe last time we were talking about your family.'

Maggie remembered. It was their fourth session, and the first time they'd touched on Maggie's own family background. Which surprised her. She'd been expecting Freudian questions about her relationship with her father right from the start, even though Dr Simms had insisted she wasn't a Freudian analyst.

They were sitting in a small office overlooking Park Square, a peaceful, elegant bit of eighteenth-century Leeds. Birds sang in the trees amid the pink and white blossoms, and students sat on the grass reading or simply enjoying the sun again after yesterday's rain. Most of the humidity seemed to have cleared away and the air was crisp and warm. Dr Simms had her window open, and Maggie could smell flowers from the window-box; she didn't know what kind, but they were flowers all right, red and white and purple. She could just see the top of the town hall dome over the trees and elegant façades of the houses on the opposite side of the square.

The place was just like a doctor's office, Maggie thought,

or at least an old-style doctor's office, with solid desk, diplomas on the wall, fluorescent lights, filing cabinets and bookcases full of psychological journals and textbooks. There was no couch; Maggie and Dr Simms sat in armchairs, not facing each other, but at a slight angle so that eye contact was easy but not mandatory, co-operative rather than confrontational. Dr Simms had been recommended by Ruth, and so far she was turning out to be a real find. In her mid-fifties, solidly built, matronly even, and with a severe look about her, she always wore old-fashioned Laura Ashley-style clothes, and her blue-grey hair was lacquered into whorls and waves that looked razor-sharp. Appearances to the contrary, Dr Simms had the kindest, most compassionate manner Maggie could wish for, without being soft. For she certainly wasn't soft; sometimes she was downright prickly, especially if Maggie – whom she always called Margaret for some reason – got her defences up or started whimpering.

'There was never any violence in the home when we were growing up. My father was strict, but he never used his fists or his belt to discipline us. Neither my sister Fiona nor me.'

'So what *did* he do for discipline?'

'Oh, the usual things. Grounded us, stopped our pocket money, lectured us, that sort of thing.'

'Did he raise his voice?'

'No. I never heard him yell at anyone.'

'Did your mother have a violent temper?'

'Good Lord, no. I mean she might get mad and shout if Fiona or I did something annoying, like not tidying up our rooms, but it'd be all over and forgotten in no time.'

Dr Simms put her fist under her chin and rested on it. 'I see. Let's get back to Bill, shall we?'

'If you like.'

'No, Margaret, it's not for me to like. It's for you to want.'

Maggie shifted in her chair. 'Yes, all right.'

'You told me in our previous session that you'd seen signs of his aggressiveness before you were married. Can you tell me more about that?'

'Yes, but it wasn't directed towards me.'

'Towards whom was it directed? The world in general, perhaps?'

'No. Just some people. People who screwed up. Like waiters or delivery men.'

'Did he beat them up?'

'He got mad, lost his temper, yelled at them. Called them idiots, morons. What I meant was that he channelled a lot of aggression into his work.'

'Ah, yes. He's a lawyer, right?'

'Yes. For a big firm. And he wanted to make partner very badly.'

'He's competitive by nature?'

'Very. He was a high-school sports star, and he might have ended up playing professional football if he hadn't ripped his knee apart in a championship game. He still walks with a slight limp, but he hates it if anyone notices it and mentions it. It doesn't stop him playing with the firm's softball team. But I don't see what this has to do with anything.'

Dr Simms leaned forward and lowered her voice. 'Margaret, I want you to see, to understand, where your husband's anger and violence come from. They didn't come from you; they came from him. They didn't come out of your family background in any way, either. They came from his. Only when you see that, when you see that it was *his* problem and not yours, will you start to believe that it wasn't your fault, and will you find the strength and courage to go on and live your life as fully as you can, rather than continue in this shadow-existence you have at the moment.'

'But I already see that,' Maggie protested. 'I mean, I know it was *his* aggression, not mine.'

'But you don't *feel* it.'

Maggie felt disappointed; Dr Simms was right. 'Don't I?' she said. 'I suppose not.'

'Do you know anything about poetry, Margaret?'

'Not much, no. Only what we did at school, and one of my boyfriends at art college used to write me stuff. Terrible drivel, really. He just wanted to get in my pants.'

Dr Simms laughed. Another surprise, for it came out as a loud, horsy guffaw. 'Samuel Taylor Coleridge wrote a poem called "Dejection: An Ode". It was partly about his inability to *feel* anything, and one of the quotes that has always stuck in my mind was when he wrote about looking at the clouds, the moon and the stars and ended up saying, "I see, not feel, how beautiful they are." I think that applies to you, Margaret. And I think you know it. Intellectual awareness of something, through *reason*, does not guarantee emotional acceptance. And you are a very intellectual person, despite your obvious creative inclinations. If I were a Jungian, which I am not, I would probably classify you as the introverted, thinking type. Now tell me more about this courtship.'

'There's not much to tell.' A door opened and closed out in the corridor. Two male voices rose and fell. Then only the birdsongs and the sounds of distant traffic on the Headrow and Park Lane remained. 'I suppose he swept me off my feet,' she went on. 'It was about seven years ago, and I was just a young art school graduate without a career, still wet behind the ears, hanging out with the artsy crowd in bars and arguing philosophy in Queen Street West pubs and coffee houses, thinking one day some rich patron would appear and discover my genius. I'd had a few affairs in college, slept with a few boys, nothing satisfactory, then along came this tall, dark, intelligent, handsome man in an Armani suit who wanted to take me to concerts and expensive restaurants. It wasn't the money. That wasn't it at all. Not even the restaurants. I wasn't even eating much then. It was his style, his panache, I suppose. He dazzled me.'

'And did he prove to be the patron of the arts you'd been dreaming of?'

Maggie looked down at the scuffed knees of her jeans. 'Not really. Bill was never very much interested in the arts. Oh, we had all the requisite subscriptions: symphony, ballet, opera. But somehow I . . .'

'Somehow you what?'

'I don't know. Perhaps I'm being unfair. But I think maybe it was just some sort of a business thing. Being *seen*. Like going to a client's box at the Skydome. I mean, he'd be excited about going to the opera, for example, take ages getting dressed up in his tux and fuss about what he wanted me to wear, then we'd have drinks in the members' bar beforehand, rub shoulders with colleagues and clients, all the local bigwigs. But I just got the impression that the music itself *bored* him.'

'Did any problems manifest themselves early on in your relationship?'

Maggie twisted her sapphire ring around her finger, the 'freedom' ring she had bought after she had thrown Bill's wedding and engagement rings into Lake Ontario. 'Well,' she said, 'it's easy to identify things as problems in retrospect, isn't it? Claim that you saw it coming, or should have, after you've found out where things were leading. They might not have seemed strange at the time, might they?'

'Try.'

Maggie continued twisting at her ring. 'Well, I suppose the main problem was Bill's jealousy.'

'About what?'

'Most things, really. He was very possessive, he didn't like me talking to other men for too long at parties, that sort of thing. But mostly he was jealous of my friends.'

'The artists?'

'Yes. You see, he never had much time for them, he thought them all a bunch of deadbeats, losers, and he felt he'd somehow *rescued* me from them.' She laughed. 'And they, on their part, didn't want to mix with corporate lawyers in Armani suits.'

'But you continued to see your friends?'

'Oh, yes. Sort of.'

'And how did Bill react to this?'

'He used to make fun of them to me, put them down, criticize them. He called them pseudo-intellectuals, no-brainers and layabouts. If we ever met any of them when we were together, he'd just stand there, looking up at the sky, shifting from foot to foot, glancing at his Rolex, whistling. I can see him now.'

'Did you defend them?'

'Yes. For a while. Then there seemed no point.' Maggie remained silent for a moment, then she went on. 'You have to remember that I was head-over-heels in love with Bill. He took me to movie premieres. We'd go for weekends in New York, stay at the Plaza, take horse and buggy rides in Central Park, go to cocktail parties full of stockbrokers and CEOs, you name it. There was a romantic side to it all. Once we even flew down to LA for a movie premiere the firm's entertainment lawyers had been involved with. We went to the party, too, and Sean Connery was there. Can you believe it? I actually met *Sean Connery*!'

'How did *you* handle all this high living?'

'I fitted in well enough. I was good at mixing with them – businessmen, lawyers, entrepreneurs, the movers and shakers. Believe it or not, many of them are far more cultured than the artsy crowd thinks. A lot of them sponsored corporate art collections. My friends believed that everyone in a suit was dull and conservative, and a philistine to boot. But you can't always go by appearances. I knew that. I think they were being very immature about it all. I think Bill saw me as a positive enhancement to his career, but he saw my friends as dead weights that would drag me down with them if they could. Maybe him, too, if we weren't careful. And I didn't feel anywhere near as uncomfortable in his world as he did in mine. I began to feel I'd only been playing the *starving* artist role, anyway.'

'What do you mean by that?'

'Well, my dad's a pretty important architect, and we always moved in elevated circles. Travelled around the continent a fair bit on commissions, too, when I was younger, just after we emigrated from England. Sometimes, if it was school holidays, he'd take me with him. So I didn't come from a blue collar background or a bohemian one. Dad appreciates the arts, but he's very conservative. And we weren't poor. Anyway, as time went on, I suppose I began to agree with Bill. He wore down my defences, like he did in a lot of other ways. I mean, all my friends seemed to do was drift from one social security cheque to the next without making any attempt to *do* anything because it would compromise their precious art. The greatest sin in our crowd was to sell out.'

'Which you did?'

Maggie stared out of the window for a moment. The blossoms were falling from the trees in slow motion. She suddenly felt cold and hugged herself. 'Yes,' she said. 'I suppose I did. As far as my friends were concerned I was lost to them. I'd been seduced by the almighty dollar. And all because of Bill. At one of his firm's parties I met a small publisher who was looking for an illustrator for a children's book. I showed him my work and he loved it. I got the job, then that led to another, and so on.'

'How did Bill react to your success?'

'He was pleased at first. Thrilled. Proud that the publisher liked my work, proud when the book was published. He bought copies for all his nephews and nieces, his clients' kids. His boss. Dozens of copies. And he was pleased that it was because of him all this had happened. As he never ceased to tell me, it would never have happened if I'd chosen to stay with my deadbeat friends.'

'This was at first. What about later?'

Maggie felt herself shrinking in the chair, her voice becoming smaller. 'That was different. Later, after we were married and Bill still hadn't made partner, I think he started to resent my success. He started referring to art as my "little hobby" and suggested I might have to give it up at any time and start having babies.'

'But you chose not to have babies?'

'No. I had no choice. I can't have babies.' Maggie felt herself slipping down the rabbit hole, just like Alice, darkness closing around her.

'Margaret! Margaret!'

She could hear Dr Simms's voice only as if from a great distance, echoing. With a huge effort, she struggled up towards it, towards the light, and felt herself burst out like a drowning person from the water, gasping for air.

'Margaret, are you all right?'

'Yes. I'm . . . I . . . But it wasn't me,' she said, aware of the tears flowing down her cheeks. 'It *isn't* me who can't have babies. *Bill* can't. It's Bill. It's something to do with his sperm count.'

Dr Simms gave Maggie a little time to dry her eyes, calm down and compose herself.

When she had done so, Maggie laughed at herself. 'He used to have to masturbate into a Tupperware container and take it in for testing. Somehow that seemed so . . . well, Tupperware, I mean, it all seemed so *Leave it to Beaver.*'

'Pardon?'

'An old American TV programme. Mom at home, Pop at the office. Apple pie. Happy families. Perfect children.'

'I see. Couldn't you have adopted a child?'

Maggie was back out in the light now. Only it felt too bright. 'No,' she said. 'That wouldn't do for Bill. The child wouldn't be *his* then, you see. No more than if I'd had someone else's sperm in artificial insemination.'

'Did the two of you discuss what to do?'

'At first, yes. But not after he found out it was *his* physical problem and not mine. After that, if I ever mentioned children again, he hit me.'

'And around this time he came to resent your success?'

'Yes. Even to the point of committing little acts of sabotage so I'd be behind on a deadline. You know, throwing away some of my colours or brushes, misplacing an illustration or a package for the courier, accidentally wiping images from the computer, from *my* computer, forgetting to tell me about an important phone call, that sort of thing.'

'So at this time he wanted to have children but discovered that he couldn't father any, and he also wanted to be a partner in his law firm, but he didn't get to be?'

'That's right. But that's no excuse for what he did to me.'

Dr Simms smiled. 'True, Margaret. Very true. But it's a pretty volatile combination, don't you think? I'm not making excuses, but can you imagine the stress he must have been under, how it might have *triggered* his violent feelings?'

'I couldn't see it coming at the time. How could I?'

'No, you couldn't. No one could expect you to. It's as you said. Hindsight. Retrospect.' She leaned back in her chair, crossed her legs and looked at the clock. 'Now, I think that's enough for today, don't you?'

Now was the time. 'I've got a question,' Maggie blurted out. 'Not about me.'

Dr Simms raised her eyebrows and looked at her watch.

'It won't take a minute. Honest it won't.'

'All right,' said Dr Simms. 'Ask away.'

'Well, it's this friend of mine. Not really a friend, I suppose, because she's too young, just a schoolgirl, but she drops by, you know, on her way home from school.'

'Yes?'

'Claire's her name, Claire Toth. Claire was a friend of Kimberley Myers.'

'I know who Kimberley Myers was. I read the newspapers. Go on.'

'They were friends. They went to the same school. Both of them knew Terence Payne. He was their biology teacher.'

'Yes. Go on.'

'And she felt responsible, you know, for Kimberley. They were supposed to walk home together that night, but a boy asked Claire to dance. A boy she liked, and . . .'

'And her friend walked home alone. To her death?'

'Yes,' said Maggie.

'You said you had a question to ask me.'

'I haven't seen Claire since she told me this on Monday afternoon. I'm worried about her. Psychologically, I mean. What would something like this do to someone like her?'

'Not knowing the girl in question, I can't possibly say,' said Dr Simms. 'It depends on her inner resources, on her self-image, on family support, on many things. Besides, it seems to me that there are two separate issues here.'

'Yes?'

'First, the girl's proximity to the criminal and to one victim in particular, and second, her feeling of responsibility, of guilt. As far as the first is concerned, I can offer a few general considerations.'

'Please do.'

'First of all, tell me how *you* feel about it all.'

'Me?'

'Yes.'

'I . . . I don't know yet. Afraid, I suppose. Not so trusting. He was my neighbour, after all. I don't know. I haven't been able to work it all out yet.'

Dr Simms nodded. 'Your friend probably feels the same way. Mostly confused for the moment. Only she's younger than you, and she probably has fewer defences. She'll certainly be more mistrustful of people. After all, this man was her *teacher*, a figure of respect and authority. Handsome, well dressed, with a nice house and a pretty young wife. He didn't look at all like the sort of monster we usually associate in our minds with crimes such as these. And she'll experience a heightened sense of paranoia. She may not feel comfortable going out alone, for example, may feel she's being stalked or watched. Or her parents might not let her go out. Sometimes parents take control in these situations, especially if they feel they've been guilty of any sort of neglect.'

'So her parents might be keeping her at home? Keeping her from visiting *me*?'

'It's possible.'

'What else?'

'From what I can gather so far, these are sex crimes and as such they are bound to have some effect on a vulnerable young schoolgirl's burgeoning sexuality. Exactly what effect is hard to say. It takes different people different ways. Some girls might become more childlike, suppress their sexuality, because they think that will afford them some kind of protection. Others may even become more promiscuous because being good girls didn't help the victims. I can't tell you which way she'll go.'

'I'm sure Claire wouldn't become promiscuous.'

'She may become withdrawn and preoccupied with the case. I think it's most important that she doesn't keep these feelings bottled up, that she struggles to understand what happened. I know that's difficult, even for us adults, but we can help her.'

'How?'

'By accepting its effect on her but also reassuring her that it was some sort of aberration, not the natural course of things. There's little doubt the effects will be deep and long lasting, but she will have to learn how to readjust to the way her world-view has altered.'

'What do you mean?'

'We're always saying that teenagers feel immortal, but any immortality your friend felt she had will have been stripped away by what's happened. That's a hard adjustment to make, that what happened to someone close to you could happen to you, too. And the full horror of it hasn't even come out yet.'

'What can I do?'

'Probably nothing,' said Dr Simms. 'You can't make her come to you, but if she does you should encourage her to talk, be a good listener. But don't push her, and don't try to tell her how to feel.'

'Should she be seeing a psychologist?'

'Probably. But that's her decision. Or her parents'.'

'Could you recommend someone? I mean, if they're interested.'

Dr Simms wrote a name on a slip of paper. 'She's good,' she said. 'Now, off you go. I've got my next patient waiting.'

They arranged another appointment and Maggie walked out into Park Square thinking about Claire and Kimberley and human monsters. That numb sensation had come back, the feeling that the world was at a distance, through mirrors and filters, cotton wool, through the wrong end of the telescope. She felt like an alien in human form. She wanted to go back to where she came from, but she didn't know where it was any more.

She walked down to City Square, past the statue of the Black Prince and the nymphs bearing their torches, then she leaned against the wall near the bus-stop on Boar Lane and lit a cigarette. The elderly woman beside her gave her a curious look. Why was it, Maggie wondered, that she always felt worse after these sessions with Dr Simms than she did before she went?

The bus arrived. Maggie trod out her cigarette and got on.

11

The drive to Eastvale went smoothly enough. Banks ordered an unmarked car and driver from Millgarth and left through a side exit with Julia Ford and Lucy Payne. They didn't run into any reporters. During the journey Banks sat in the front with the driver, a young female DC, and Julia Ford and Lucy Payne sat in the back. Nobody spoke a word. Banks was preoccupied by the discovery of another body in the Paynes's back garden, news he had just received from Stefan Nowak on his mobile as they set off from the Infirmary. That made one body too many and by the sound of it, he didn't think this one was Leanne Wray's either.

Occasionally, Banks caught a glimpse of Lucy in the rearview mirror and saw that she was mostly gazing out of the window. He couldn't read her expression. Just to be on the safe side, they entered the Eastvale police station through the rear entrance. Banks settled Lucy and Julia in an interview room and went to his office, where he walked over to the window and lit a cigarette and prepared himself for the coming interview.

He had been so preoccupied with the extra body on the journey up that he had hardly noticed it was another gorgeous day out there. There were plenty of cars and coaches parked on the cobbled market square, family groups milling about, holding onto their children's hands, women with cardigans fastened loosely by the sleeves around their necks, just in case a cool breeze sprang up, clutching umbrellas against the possibility of rain. Why is it we English can never quite entrust ourselves to believe that fine weather will last? Banks wondered. We're always expecting the worst. That was why the forecasters covered all bases: sunny with cloudy periods and the chance of a shower.

The interview room smelled of disinfectant because its last inhabitant, a drunken seventeen-year-old joyrider, had puked up a takeaway pizza all over the floor. Other than that, the room was clean enough, though very little light filtered in through the high, barred window. Banks inserted tapes in the machine, tested them and then went through the immediate formalities of time, date and those present.

'Right, Lucy,' he said when he'd finished. 'Ready to begin?'

'If you like.'

'How long have you been living in Leeds?'

'What?'

Banks repeated the question. Lucy looked puzzled by it but said, 'Four years, more or less. Ever since I started working at the bank.'

'And you came from Hull, from your foster parents Clive and Hilary Liversedge?'

'Yes. You know that already.'

'Just getting the background clear, Lucy. Where did you live before then?'

Lucy started to fidget with her wedding ring. 'Alderthorpe,' she said quietly. 'I lived at number four Spurn Road.'

'And your parents?'

'Yes.'

'Yes what?'

'Yes, they lived there, too.'

Banks sighed. 'Don't play games with me, Lucy. This is a serious business.'

'Don't you think I know that?' Lucy snapped. 'You drag me out of hospital all the way up here for no reason, and then you start asking about my childhood. You're not a psychiatrist.'

'I'm just interested, that's all.'

'Well, it wasn't very interesting. Yes, they abused me, and yes I was taken into care. The Liversedges were good to me, but it's not as if they were my *real* parents or anything. When the time came, I wanted to go out on my own in the world, put my childhood behind me and make my own way. Is there anything wrong with that?'

'No,' said Banks. He wanted to find out more about Lucy's childhood, especially the events that occurred when she was twelve, but he knew he wasn't likely to find out much from her. 'Is that why you changed your name from Linda Godwin to Lucy Liversedge?'

'Yes. Reporters kept bothering me. The Liversedges arranged it with the social services.'

'What made you choose to move to Leeds?'

'That's where the job was.'

'The first one you applied for?'

'That I really wanted. Yes.'

'Where did you live?'

'I had a flat off Tong Road at first. When Terry got the job at Silverhill, we bought the house on The Hill. The one you say I can't go back to, even though it's my home. I suppose you expect me to keep making the mortgage payments while your men rip the place apart, too?'

'You moved in together before you were married?'

'We already knew we were getting married. It was such a

good deal at the time that we'd have been fools to turn it down.'

'When did you marry Terry?'

'Just last year. The twenty-second of May. We'd been going out together since the summer before.'

'How did you meet him?'

'What does that matter?'

'I'm just curious. Surely it's a harmless question.'

'In a pub.'

'Which pub?'

'I can't remember what it was called. It was a big one, though, with live music.'

'Where was it?'

'Seacroft.'

'Was he by himself?'

'I think so. Why?'

'Did he chat you up?'

'Not in so many words. I don't remember.'

'Did you ever stay at his flat?'

'Yes, of course I did. It wasn't wrong. We were in love. We were going to get married. We were engaged.'

'Even then?'

'It was love at first sight. You might not believe me, but it was. We'd only been going out two weeks when he bought me my engagement ring. It cost nearly a thousand pounds.'

'Did he have other girlfriends?'

'Not when we met.'

'But before?'

'I suppose so. I didn't make a fuss about it. I assumed he'd led a pretty normal life.'

'Normal?'

'Why not?'

'Did you ever see any evidence of other women in his flat?'

'No.'

'What were you doing in Seacroft when you lived off Tong Road? It's a long way.'

'We'd just finished a week's training course in town and one of the girls said it was a good place for a night out.'

'Had you heard of the man the papers at the time called the "Seacroft Rapist"?'

'Yes. Everybody had.'

'But it didn't stop you going to Seacroft.'

'You have to live your life. You can't let fear get the better of you, or a woman wouldn't even dare go out of the house alone.'

'That's true enough,' said Banks. 'So you never suspected that this man you met might be the Seacroft Rapist?'

'Terry? No, of course not. Why should I?'

'Was there nothing at all in Terry's behaviour that gave you cause for concern?'

'No. We were in love.'

'But he abused you. You admitted this the last time we talked.'

She looked away. 'That came later.'

'How much later?'

'I don't know. Christmas maybe.'

'Last Christmas?'

'Yes. Around then. But it wasn't like that all the time. Afterwards, he was wonderful. He always felt guilty. He'd buy me presents. Flowers. Bracelets. Necklaces. I really wish I had them with me now to remember him by.'

'In time, Lucy. So he always made up to you after he hit you?'

'Yes, he was wonderful to me for days.'

'Was he drinking more these past few months?'

'Yes. He was out more, too. I didn't see him as much.'

'Where was he?'

'I don't know. He didn't tell me.'

'Didn't you ever ask him?'

Lucy looked away demurely, turning her bruised side on him. Banks got the message.

'I think we can move on, can't we, Superintendent,' said Julia Ford. 'My client's clearly getting upset with this line of questioning.'

Pity for her, Banks wanted to say, but he had plenty more ground to cover. 'Very well.' He turned to Lucy again. 'Did you have anything to do with the abduction, rape and murder of Kimberley Myers?'

Lucy met his gaze, but he couldn't see anything in her dark eyes; if the eyes were the windows of the soul, then Lucy Payne's were made of tinted glass and her soul wore sunglasses. 'No, I didn't,' she said.

'What about Melissa Horrocks?'

'No. I had nothing to do with any of them.'

'How many were there, Lucy?'

'You know how many.'

'Tell me.'

'Five. That's what I read in the papers, anyway.'

'What did you do with Leanne Wray?'

'I don't understand.'

'Where is she, Lucy? Where's Leanne Wray? Where did you and Terry bury her? What made her different from the others?'

Lucy looked in consternation at Julia Ford. 'I don't know what he's talking about,' she said. 'Ask him to stop.'

'Superintendent,' Julia said, 'my client has already made

it clear she knows nothing about this person. I think you should move on.'

'Did your husband ever mention any of these girls?'

'No, Terry never mentioned any of them.'

'Did you ever go in that cellar, Lucy?'

'You've asked me all this before.'

'I'm giving you a chance to change your answer, to go on record.'

'I told you, I don't remember. I might have done, but I don't remember. I've got retrograde amnesia.'

'Who told you that?'

'My doctor at the hospital.'

'Dr Landsberg?'

'Yes. It's part of my post-traumatic shock disorder.'

It was the first Banks had heard of it. Dr Landsberg had told him she was no expert on the subject. 'Well, I'm very glad you can put a name to what's wrong with you. On how many occasions *might* you have gone down in the cellar, if you could remember?'

'Just the once.'

'When?'

'The day it happened. When I got put in hospital. Early last Monday morning.'

'So you admit that you *may* have gone down there?'

'If you say so. I can't remember. If I ever did go down, it was then.'

'It's not me who says so, Lucy. It's the scientific evidence. The lab found traces of Kimberley Myers's blood on the sleeves of your dressing-gown. How did it get there?'

'I . . . I don't know.'

'There's only two ways it could have got there: either *before* she was in the cellar or *after* she was in the cellar. Which is it, Lucy?'

'It must be after.'

'Why?'

'Because I never saw her before.'

'But she didn't live far away. Hadn't you seen her around?'

'In the street, maybe. Or the shops. Yes. But I never talked to her.'

Banks paused and shuffled some papers in front of him. 'So you admit now that you might have been in the cellar?'

'But I don't remember.'

'What do you think *might* have happened, hypothetically speaking?'

'Well, I might have heard a noise.'

'What sort of noise?'

'I don't know.' Lucy paused and put her hand to her throat. 'A scream, maybe.'

'The only screams Maggie Forrest heard were yours.'

'Well, maybe you could only hear it if you were inside the house. Maybe it came up from the cellar. When Maggie heard me I was in the hall.'

'You remember that? Being in the hall?'

'Only very vaguely.'

'Go on.'

'So I might have heard a noise and gone down to investigate.'

'Even though you knew it was Terry's private den and he'd kill you if you did?'

'Yes. Maybe I was disturbed enough.'

'By what?'

'By what I heard.'

'But the cellar was very well soundproofed, Lucy, and the door was closed when the police got there.'

'Then I don't know. I'm just trying to find a reason.'

'Go on. What might you have found there if you did go down?'

'That girl. I might have gone over to her to see if there was anything I could do.'

'What about the yellow fibres?'

'What about them?'

'They were from the plastic clothes-line that was wrapped around Kimberley Myers's neck. The pathologist determined ligature strangulation by that line as cause of death. Fibres were also embedded in Kimberley's throat.'

'I must have tried to get it off her.'

'Do you remember doing this?'

'No, I'm still imagining how it might have happened.'

'Go on.'

'Then Terry must have found me and chased me upstairs and hit me.'

'Why didn't he drag you back down the cellar and kill you, too?'

'I don't know. He was my husband. He loved me. He couldn't just kill me like . . .'

'Like some teenage girl?'

'Superintendent,' Julia Ford cut in. 'I don't think speculation about what Mr Payne did or didn't do is relevant here. My client says she *might* have gone down in the cellar and surprised her husband at . . . at whatever he was doing, and thus provoked him. That should explain your findings. It should also be enough.'

'But you said Terry would kill you if you went in the cellar. Why didn't he?' Banks persisted.

'I don't know. Maybe he was going to. Maybe he had something else to do first.'

'Like what?'

'I don't know.'

'Kill Kimberley?'

'Maybe.'

'But wasn't she already dead?'

'I don't know.'

'Get rid of her body?'

'Maybe. I don't know. I was unconscious.'

'Oh, come on, Lucy! This is rubbish,' said Banks. 'The next thing you'll be trying to convince me you did it while you were sleepwalking. *You* killed Kimberley Myers, didn't you, Lucy? You went down in the cellar and saw her lying there and you strangled her.'

'I didn't! Why would I do a thing like that?'

'Because you were jealous. Terry wanted Kimberley more than he wanted you. He wanted to keep her.'

Lucy banged the table with her fist. 'That's *not* true! You're making it up.'

'Well, why else did he have her staked out there naked on the mattress? To give her a biology lesson? It was quite a biology lesson, Lucy. He raped her repeatedly, both vaginally and anally. He forced her to fellate him. Then he – or *someone* – strangled her with a length of yellow plastic clothes-line.'

Lucy put her head in her hands and sobbed.

'Is this kind of gruesome detail really necessary?' asked Julia Ford.

'What's wrong?' Banks asked her. 'Afraid of the truth?'

'It's just a bit over the top, that's all.'

'*Over the top*? I'll tell you what's over the bloody top.' Banks pointed at Lucy. 'Kimberley's blood on the sleeves of *her* dressing-gown. Yellow fibres under *her* fingernails. *She* killed Kimberley Myers.'

'It's all circumstantial,' said Julia Ford. 'Lucy's already explained to you how it might have happened. She doesn't remember. That's not her fault. The poor woman was traumatized.'

'Either that or she's a damn good actress,' said Banks.

'Superintendent!'

'Banks turned back to Lucy. 'Who are the other girls, Lucy?'

'I don't know what you're talking about.'

'We've found two unidentified bodies in the back garden. Skeletal remains, at any rate. That makes six altogether, including Kimberley. We were only looking into five disappearances, and we haven't even found all of those yet. We don't know of these two. Who are they?'

'I've no idea.'

'Did you ever go out in the car with your husband and pick up a teenage girl?'

The change of direction seemed to shock Lucy into silence, but she soon found her voice and regained her composure. 'No, I did not.'

'So you knew nothing about the missing girls?'

'No. Only what I read in the papers. I told you. I didn't go in the cellar and Terry certainly didn't tell me. So how *could* I know?'

'How indeed?' Banks scratched the little scar beside his right eye. 'I'm more concerned with how you could possibly *not* have known. The man you're living with – your own husband – abducts and brings home *six* young girls that we know of so far, keeps them in the cellar for . . . God knows how long . . . while he rapes and tortures them, then he buries them either in the garden or in the cellar. And all this time you're living in the house, only one floor away, two at the most, and you expect me to believe you didn't know anything, didn't even *smell* anything? Do I look as if I was born yesterday, Lucy? I don't see how you could fail to know.'

'I told you I never went down there.'

'Didn't you notice when your husband was missing in the middle of the night?'

'No. I always sleep very heavily. I think Terry must have been giving me sleeping pills with my cocoa. That's why I never noticed anything.'

'We didn't find any sleeping pills at the house, Lucy.'

'He must have run out. That must be why I woke up on Monday morning and thought something was wrong. Or he forgot.'

'Did either of you have a prescription for sleeping tablets?'

'I didn't. I don't know if Terry did. Maybe he got them from a drug pusher.'

Banks made a note to look into the matter of sleeping tablets. 'Why do you think he might have forgotten to drug you *this* time? Why did you go down to the cellar *this* time?' he went on. 'What was so different about *this* time, about Kimberley? Was it because she was too close to home for comfort? Terry must have known he was taking a huge risk in abducting Kimberley, mustn't he? Was he obsessed with her, Lucy? Was that it? Were the others merely practice, substitutes until he could no longer stop himself from taking the one he really wanted? How did you feel about that, Lucy? That Terry wanted Kimberley more than you, more than life itself, more than freedom?'

Lucy put her hands to her ears. 'Stop it! It's lies, all lies! I don't know what you mean. I don't understand what's going on. Why are you persecuting me like this?' She turned to Julia Ford. 'Get me out of here now. Please! I don't have to stay and listen to any more of this, do I?'

'No,' said Julia Ford, standing up. 'You can leave whenever you like.'

'I don't think so.' Banks stood up and took a deep breath. 'Lucy Payne, I'm arresting you as an accessory in the murder of Kimberley Myers.'

'This is ludicrous,' shot Julia Ford. 'It's a travesty.'

'I don't believe your client's story,' said Banks. He turned to Lucy again. 'You don't have to say anything, Lucy, but if you fail to say something now that you later rely on in court it might be held against you. Do you understand?'

Banks opened the door and got two uniformed officers to take Lucy down to the custody officer. When they came towards her she turned pale.

'Please,' she said. 'I'll come back whenever you want. Please, I'm begging you, don't lock me all alone in a dark cell!'

For the first time in his dealings with her, Banks got the sense that Lucy Payne was genuinely afraid. He remembered what Jenny had told him about the 'Alderthorpe Seven'. *Kept in cages without food for days.* He almost faltered, but there was no going back now. He forced himself to remember Kimberley Myers spread-eagled on the bed in Lucy Payne's dark cellar. Nobody had given *her* a chance. 'The cells aren't dark, Lucy,' he said. 'They're well lit and very comfortable. They regularly get four stars in the police accommodation guide.'

Julia Ford gave him a disgusted look. Lucy shook her head. Banks nodded towards the officers. 'Take her to the cells.'

He'd managed it by the skin of his teeth, and he didn't even feel as good about it as he had thought he would, but he'd got Lucy Payne where he wanted her for twenty-four hours. *Twenty-four hours to find some real evidence against her.*

•

Annie felt only indifference towards Terence Payne's corpse laid out naked on the steel autopsy table. It was simply the shell, the deceptive outer human form of an aberration, a changeling, a demon. Come to think about it, though, she wasn't even certain she believed *that.* Terence Payne's evil was all too human. Over the centuries men had raped and mutilated women, whether as acts of plunder in wartime, for dark pleasures in the back alleys and cheap rooms of decaying cities, in the isolation of the countryside, or in the drawing rooms of the rich. It hardly needed a demon in human form to do what men themselves already did so well.

She turned her attention to events at hand: Dr Mackenzie's close examination of the exterior of Terence Payne's skull. Identity and time of death had not been a problem in this case: Payne had been pronounced dead by Dr Mogabe at Leeds General Infirmary at 8.13 p.m. the previous evening. Naturally, Dr Mackenzie would do a thorough job – his assistant had already carried out the weighing and measuring, and photographs and X-rays had been taken – indeed, Annie guessed Mackenzie to be the kind of doctor who would do a thorough post mortem on a man shot dead right in front of his very eyes. It didn't do to make assumptions.

The body was clean and ready for cutting, as there's no man cleaner than one who has just been through surgery. Luckily, the police surgeon had been dispatched to take fingernail scrapings, bloodstained clothing and blood samples when Payne had first arrived at the Infirmary, so no evidence had been lost owing to the scruples of hospital hygiene.

At the moment, Annie was interested only in the blows to Payne's head, and Dr Mackenzie was paying particular attention to the cranium before performing the full post mortem. They had already examined the fractured wrist and determined that it was broken by a blow from PC Janet Taylor's baton – which lay on the lab bench by the white-tiled wall – and there were also several defence bruises on Payne's arms, where he had tried to ward off PC Taylor's blows.

Unless Payne had been murdered by a nurse or doctor while he was in hospital, PC Janet Taylor's actions were most likely directly responsible for his death. What had yet to be determined was just *how* culpable she was. An emergency operation to relieve a subdural hematoma had complicated matters, Dr Mackenzie had told Annie, but it should be easy enough to separate the surgical procedure from the unskilled bludgeoning.

Payne's head had already been shaved before his surgery, which made the injuries easier to identify. After a close examination, Mackenzie turned to Annie and said, 'I'm not going to be able to tell you the exact sequence of blows, but there are some interesting clusters.'

'Clusters?'

'Yes. Come here. Look.'

Dr Mackenzie pointed towards Payne's left temple, which looked to Annie, with its shaved hair and bloody rawness, rather like a dead rat in a trap. 'There are at least three distinct wounds overlapping here,' Dr Mackenzie went on, tracing the outlines as he went, 'from the first one – this indentation here, followed by a later wound superimposed and a third, here, which overlaps parts of both.'

'Could they have been delivered in quick succession?' Annie asked, remembering what Janet Taylor had told her about the flurry of blows, and the way she had imagined it all herself when she had visited the scene.

'It's possible,' Dr Mackenzie admitted, 'but I'd say any one of these blows would have incapacitated him for a while, and perhaps changed his position in relation to his attacker.'

'Can you explain?'

Dr Mackenzie brought his hand around gently to the side of Annie's head and pushed. She went with the light pressure and stepped back, head turned. When he reached out again, his hand was closer to the back of her head. 'Had that been a real blow,' he said, 'you would have been turned even further away from me, and the blow would have stunned you. It might have taken you a little time to get back to the same position.'

'I see what you mean,' Annie said. 'So that would lead you to believe that perhaps other blows came in between?'

'Mmm. There's the angles to consider, too. If you look very closely at the indentations, you'll see that the first blow came when the victim was standing.' He glanced towards the baton. 'See. The wound is relatively smooth and even, allowing for the differences in height between PC Taylor and the victim. I've measured the baton, by the way, and matched it closely to each wound, and that, along with the X-rays gives me a better idea of the victim's position at the time of each blow.' He pointed again. 'At least one of those blows to the temple was delivered when the victim was on his knees. You can see the way the impression deepens. It's even clearer on the X-ray.'

Dr Mackenzie led Annie over to the X-ray viewer on the wall, slipped in a sheet of film and turned on the light. He was right. When he pointed to it, Annie could see how the wound was deeper towards the back, indicating that the baton had come down at an angle. They went back to the table.

'Could he have got up again after a blow like that?' Annie asked.

'It's possible. There's no telling with head wounds. People have been known to walk around for days with a bullet in their brains. The main problem would be the rate of blood loss. Head wounds bleed an awful lot. That's why we usually leave the brain until last in a post mortem. Most of the blood has drained off by then. Less messy.'

'What are you going to do with Payne's brain?' Annie asked. 'Keep it for scientific study?'

Dr Mackenzie snorted. 'I'd as soon read his character by the bumps on his head,' he said. 'And speaking of which . . .' He asked his assistants to turn the body over. Annie saw another raw, pulpy area at the back of Payne's head. She thought she could see splinters of bone sticking out, but realized she must be imagining things. Payne had been treated in hospital and they wouldn't leave bone splinters sticking out of the back of his head. There was also some evidence of surgical stitching, which probably gave the impression of splinters. She only shivered because it was cold in the room, she told herself.

'These wounds were almost certainly inflicted when the victim was at an inferior level, say on his hands and knees, and they were delivered from behind.'

'As if he were moving away from his attacker on all fours, looking for something?'

'I wouldn't know about that,' said Mackenzie. 'But it's possible.'

'It's just that at one point she says she hit him on the wrist and he dropped his machete, which she kicked into a corner. Apparently he went scrabbling after it on his hands and knees and she hit him again.'

'That would concur with this kind of injury,' Dr Mackenzie conceded, 'though I count three blows to the same general area: the brainstem, by the way, by far the most dangerous and vulnerable to attack.'

'She hit him there three times?'

'Yes.'

'Would he have been able to get up after that?'

'Again, I can't say. A weaker man might well have been dead by then. Mr Payne survived for three days. Perhaps he found his machete and got up again.'

'So that *is* a possible scenario?'

'I can't rule it out. But look at these.' Dr Mackenzie directed Annie's attention towards the deep depressions at the top of the skull. 'These two wounds, I can say with some certainty, were administered when the victim was in an inferior position to the attacker, perhaps sitting or squatting, given the angle, and they were administered with tremendous power.'

'What sort of power?'

Mackenzie stood back, raised both his arms high in the air, behind his head, and clasped his hands, then he brought them down as if wielding an imaginary hammer with all his might onto the head of an imaginary victim. 'Like that,' he said. 'And there was no resistance.'

Annie swallowed. *Damn.* This was turning into a real bugger of a case.

•

Elizabeth Bell, the social worker in charge of the 'Alderthorpe Seven' investigation, hadn't retired, but she had changed jobs and relocated to York, which made it easy for

Jenny to drop in on her after a quick stop by her office at the university. She found a narrow parking spot several doors away from the terrace house off Fulford Road, not far from the river, and managed to squeeze her car in without doing any damage.

Elizabeth answered the door as quickly as if she had been standing right behind it, though Jenny had been vague on the phone about her time of arrival. It hadn't mattered, Elizabeth said, as Friday was her day off this week, the kids were at school and she had ironing to catch up with.

'You must be Dr Fuller,' Elizabeth said.

'That's me. But call me Jenny.'

Elizabeth led Jenny inside. 'I still don't know what you want to see *me* about, but do come on in.' She led Jenny into a small living room, made even smaller by the ironing board and basket of laundry balanced on a chair. Jenny could smell the lemon detergent and fabric softener, along with that warm and comforting smell of freshly ironed clothes. The television was on, showing an old black and white thriller starring Jack Warner. Elizabeth cleared a pile of folded clothes from the armchair and bade Jenny sit.

'Excuse the mess,' she said. 'It's such a tiny house, but they're so expensive around here and we do so love the location.'

'Why did you move from Hull?'

'We'd been looking to move for a while, then Roger – that's my husband – got a promotion. He's a civil servant. Well, hardly all that civil, if you catch my drift.'

'What about you. Job, I mean?'

'Still the social. Only now I work down the benefits office. Do you mind if I carry on ironing while we talk? Only I've got to get it all done.'

'No. Not at all.' Jenny looked at Elizabeth. She was a tall, big-boned woman wearing jeans and a plaid button-down shirt. The knees of her jeans were stained, Jenny noticed, as if she had been gardening. Under her short, no-nonsense haircut, her face was hard and prematurely lined, but not without kindness, which showed in her eyes and in the expressions that suddenly softened the hardness as she spoke. 'How many children do you have?' Jenny asked.

'Only two. William and Pauline.' She nodded towards a photograph of two children that stood on the mantelpiece: smiling in a playground. 'Anyway, I'm intrigued. Why *are* you here? You didn't tell me very much over the telephone.'

'I'm sorry. I wasn't meaning to be mysterious, honestly. I'm here about the "Alderthorpe Seven". I understand you were involved?'

'How could I forget. Why do you want to know? It was all over ten years ago.'

'Nothing's ever all over in my line of work,' said Jenny. She had debated how much to tell Elizabeth and had even spoken with Banks on the phone about this. Useful as ever, he had said, 'As much as you have to, and as little as you need to.' Jenny had already asked Mr and Mrs Liversedge not to reveal Lucy's true origins or name to reporters, but it wouldn't be long before some bright spark came across a slip of paper or recognized a photo from the newspaper's obituary. She knew that she and Banks had a very narrow window of opportunity in which to operate before train-loads of media people got off at York and Hull, and even found their way to sleepy little Alderthorpe. She took a risk that Elizabeth Bell wasn't likely to tip them off, either.

'Can you keep a secret?' she asked.

Elizabeth looked up from the shirt she was ironing. 'If I have to. I have done before.'

'The person I'm interested in is Lucy Payne.'

'Lucy Payne?'

'Yes.'

'That name is familiar, but I'm afraid you'll have to jog my memory.'

'It's been in the news a lot recently. She was married to Terence Payne, the schoolteacher the police believe was responsible for the murder of six young girls.'

'Of course. Yes, I *did* see a mention in the paper, but I must admit that I don't follow such things.'

'Understandable. Anyway, Lucy's parents, Clive and Hilary Liversedge turn out to be *foster* parents. Lucy was one of the Alderthorpe Seven. You'd probably remember her as Linda Godwin.'

'Good heavens.' Elizabeth paused, holding the iron in mid-air, as if travelling back in her memory. 'Little Linda Godwin. The poor wee thing.'

'Perhaps now you can see why I asked you about keeping secrets?'

'The press would have a field day.'

'Indeed they would. Probably will, eventually.'

'They won't find out anything from me.'

A worthwhile risk, then. 'Good,' said Jenny.

'I think I'd better sit down.' Elizabeth propped the iron on its end and sat opposite Jenny. 'What do you want to know?'

'Whatever you can tell me. How did it all begin, for a start?'

'It was a local schoolteacher who tipped us off,' said Elizabeth. 'Maureen Nesbitt. She'd been suspicious about the state of some of the children for some time, and some of the things they said when they thought no one could overhear them. Then young Kathleen didn't show up for school for a week and nobody had a reasonable explanation.'

'That would be Kathleen Murray?'

'You know about her?'

'I just did a bit of background research among old newspapers at the library. I know that Kathleen Murray was the one who died.'

'Was murdered. Should have been the "Alderthorpe *Six*" as one of them was already dead by the time the whole thing blew up.'

'Where did Kathleen fit in?'

'There were two families involved: Oliver and Geraldine Murray, and Michael and Pamela Godwin. The Murrays had four children, ranging from Keith, aged eleven, to Susan, aged eight. The two in the middle were Dianne and Kathleen, aged ten and nine respectively. The Godwins had three children: Linda, at twelve, was the eldest, then came Tom, who was ten, and Laura, nine.'

'Good Lord, it sounds complicated.'

Elizabeth grinned. 'It gets worse. Oliver Murray and Pamela Godwin were brother and sister, and nobody was quite sure exactly who fathered whom. Extended family abuse. It's not as uncommon as it should be, especially in small, isolated communities. The families lived next door to one another in two semis in Alderthorpe, just far enough away from the other houses in the village to be guaranteed their privacy. It's a remote enough part of the world to begin with. Have you ever been there?'

'Not yet.'

'You should. Just to get the feel of the place. It's creepy.'

'I intend to. Were they true, then? The allegations.'

'The police would be able to tell you more about that. I was mostly responsible for separating the children and making sure they were cared for, getting them examined, and for fostering them, too, of course.'

'All of them?'

'I didn't do it all on my own, but I was in overall charge, yes.'

'Did any of them ever go back to their parents?'

'No. Oliver and Geraldine Murray were charged with Kathleen's murder and are still in jail, as far as I know. Michael Godwin committed suicide two days before the trial and his wife was declared unfit to stand trial. I believe she's still in care. A mental institution, I mean.'

'There's no doubt about who did what, then?'

'As I said, the police would know more about that than me, but . . . If ever I've come face to face with evil in my life, it was there, that morning.'

'What happened?'

'Nothing *happened*, it was just . . . I don't know . . . the aura around the place.'

'Did you go inside?'

'No. The police wouldn't let us. They said we'd only contaminate the scene. We had a van, a heated van, and they brought the children out to us.'

'What about the Satanic angle? I understand it didn't come up in court.'

'Wasn't necessary, the lawyers said. Would only confuse things.'

'Was there any evidence?'

'Oh, yes, but if you ask me it was nothing but a load of mumbo-jumbo to justify drinking, drug-taking and abusing the children. The police found cocaine and marijuana in both houses, you know, along with some LSD, Ketamine and Ecstasy.'

'Is that case why you gave up social work?'

Elizabeth paused before answering. 'Partly, yes. It was the straw that broke the camel's back, if you like. But I was already close to burning out long before that. It takes it out of you, it does, dealing with ill-treated kids all the time. You lose sight of the humanity, the dignity of life. Do you know what I mean?'

'I think so,' said Jenny. 'Spending too much time with criminals has a similar effect.'

'But these were children. They had no *choice*.'

'I see what you mean.'

'You meet some proper losers down at the benefits office, believe me, but it's not like childcare.'

'What state was Lucy in?'

'Same as the rest. Dirty, hungry, bruised.'

'Sexually abused?'

Elizabeth nodded.

'What was she like?'

'Linda? Or I suppose I'd better start calling her Lucy from now on, hadn't I? She was a sweet little thing. Shy and scared. Standing there with a blanket around her and that look on her face like a grubby little angel. She hardly said a word.'

'*Could* she speak?'

'Oh, yes. One of the children, Susan, I think, lost the use of her voice, but not Lucy. She'd been abused in just about every way imaginable, yet she was surprisingly resilient. She'd speak if she wanted to, but I never once saw her cry. In fact, she seemed to have assumed the role of care-giver to the younger ones, though she wasn't in a position to offer much in the way of care. She was the eldest, at least, so maybe she could offer them *some* comfort. You'd know more about this than I do, but I guessed she was repressing the full horror of what she'd been through, holding it back.

I often wondered what would become of her. I never suspected anything like this.'

'The problem is, Elizabeth—'

'Call me Liz, please. Everyone does.'

'Okay. Liz. The problem is that we just don't know what Lucy's role in all this is. She claims amnesia and she was certainly abused by her husband. We're trying to find out whether she knew anything about his other activities, or to what degree she might have been involved.'

'You can't be serious? Lucy involved in something like that? Surely her own experiences—'

'I know it sounds crazy, Liz, but the abused often become the abusers. It's all they know. Power, pain, withholding, tormenting. It's a familiar cycle. Studies have shown that abused children as young as eight or ten have gone on to abuse their younger siblings or neighbours.'

'But not Lucy, surely?'

'We don't know. That's why I'm asking questions, trying to fit the psychology together, build a profile of her. Is there anything more you can tell me?'

'Well, as I said, she was quiet, resilient, and the other children, the younger ones, seemed to defer to her.'

'Were they afraid of her?'

'I can't say I got that impression.'

'But they took notice of her?'

'Yes. She was definitely the boss.'

'What else can you tell me about Lucy's personality then?'

'Let me think . . . not much, really. She was a very private person. She'd only let you see what she wanted you to see. You have to realize that these children were probably as much, if not more, shaken up by the raid, by being taken from their parents so abruptly. That was all they knew, after all. It might have been hell, but it was a familiar hell. Lucy always seemed gentle, but like most children she could be cruel on occasion.'

'Oh?'

'I don't mean pulling the wings off flies or that sort of thing,' said Elizabeth. 'I assume that is the sort of thing you're looking for, isn't it?'

'Such early patterns of behaviour can be a useful guide, but I've always thought they were overrated. To be honest, I once pulled the wings off a fly myself. No, I just want to know about her. How could she be cruel, for example?'

'When we were arranging for foster parents, for example, you realize it was impossible to keep the siblings together, so they had to be split up. It was more important at the time that each child have a stable, possibly long-term, caring environment. Anyway, I remember Laura, in particular, Lucy's younger sister was upset, but all Lucy said was she'd just have to get used to it. The poor girl just wouldn't stop crying.'

'Where did she end up?'

'Laura? With a family in Hull, I believe. It's a long time ago, so forgive me if I don't remember all the details.'

'Of course. Can you tell me what happened to any of the other children at all?'

'I'm afraid I left there shortly after, so I never got to keep track of them. I often wish I had, but . . .'

'Is there anything more you can tell me?'

Elizabeth stood up and went back to her ironing. 'Not that I can think of.'

Jenny stood up, took her card from her purse and handed it over. 'If you think of anything at all . . .'

Elizabeth peered at the card and set it on the edge of the

ironing board. 'Yes, of course. I'm only too glad to have been of help.'

But she didn't look it, Jenny thought as she manoeuvred her car out of the tiny parking spot. Elizabeth Bell had looked like a woman forced to confront memories she would sooner forget. And Jenny didn't blame her. She didn't know if she'd learned anything much of value except confirmation that Satanic paraphernalia had been found in the cellar. Banks would certainly be interested in that. Tomorrow, she would go all the way to Alderthorpe and see if she could find anyone who knew the families before the investigation, and, as Elizabeth had suggested, to 'get the feel of the place'.

12

Banks hadn't had a break all day, had even missed his lunch interviewing Lucy Payne, so with no real plan in mind, around three o'clock that afternoon, he found himself wandering down an alley off North Market Street towards the Old Ship Inn, heavy with the recent news that the second body discovered in the back garden of thirty-five The Hill was definitely *not* Leanne Wray's.

Lucy Payne was being held in a cell in the basement of police headquarters and Julia Ford had booked herself in at the Burgundy, Eastvale's best, most expensive hotel. The task force and forensics people were working as fast and as hard as they could, and Jenny Fuller was probing Lucy's past – all looking for that one little chink in her armour, that one little piece of hard evidence that she was more involved with the killings than she let on. Banks knew that if they unearthed nothing more by noon tomorrow, he'd have to let her go. He had one more visit to make today: to talk to George Woodward, the detective inspector who had done most of the legwork on the Alderthorpe investigation, now retired and running a B & B in Withernsea. Banks glanced at his watch. It would take him about two hours: plenty of time to head out there after a drink and a bite to eat and still get back before too late.

The Old Ship was a shabby, undistinguished Victorian watering hole with a few benches scattered in the cobbled alley out front. Not much light got in, as the buildings all around were dark and high. Its claim to fame was that it was well hidden and known to be tolerant of under-age drinkers. Many an Eastvale lad, so Banks had heard, had sipped his first pint at the Old Ship well before his eighteenth birthday. The sign showed an old clipper ship, and the windows were of smoked, etched glass.

It wasn't very busy at that time of day, between the lunch hour and the after-work crowd. Indeed, the Old Ship wasn't busy very often at all, as few tourists liked the look of it, and most locals knew better places to drink. The interior was dim and the air stale and acrid with more than a hundred years' accumulated smoke and beer spills. Which made it all the more surprising that the barmaid was a pretty young girl with short, dyed red hair and an oval face, a smooth complexion, a bright smile and a cheerful disposition.

Banks leaned against the bar. 'I don't suppose there's any chance of a cheese and onion sandwich, is there?'

'Sorry,' she said. 'We don't serve food after two. Packet of chips – sorry, crisps – okay?'

'Better than nothing,' said Banks.

'What flavour?'

'Plain will do fine. And a pint of bitter shandy, too, please.'

As she was pouring the drink and Banks was dipping into a packet of rather soggy potato crisps, she kept glancing at him out of the corner of her eye and finally said, 'Aren't you the policeman who was here about that girl who disappeared a month or so ago?'

'Leanne Wray,' said Banks. 'Yes.'

'I thought so. I saw you here. You weren't the policeman I talked to, but you were here. Have you found her yet?'

'It's Shannon, isn't it?'

She smiled. 'You remember my name and you never even talked to me. I'm impressed.'

Shannon, Banks remembered from the statement taken by DC Winsome Jackman, was an American student taking a year off from her studies. She had already travelled around most of Europe and through relatives and, Banks suspected, a boyfriend, she had ended up spending a few months in Yorkshire, which she seemed to like. Banks guessed that she was working at the Old Ship, perhaps, because the manager wasn't concerned about visas and permits, and paid cash in hand. Probably not much of it, either.

Banks lit a cigarette and glanced around. A couple of old men sat smoking pipes by the window, not speaking, not making eye contact with each other. They seemed as if they might have been there since the place first opened in the nineteenth century. The floor was worn stone and the tables scored and wobbly. A watercolour of a huge sailing ship hung crookedly on one wall, and on the opposite one a series of framed charcoal sketches of sea-going scenes, quite good to Banks's untrained eye.

'I wasn't trying to be nosy,' Shannon said. 'I was only asking because I haven't seen you since and I've been reading about those girls in Leeds.' She gave a little shudder. 'It's horrible. I remember being in Milwaukee – that's where I'm from, Milwaukee, Wisconsin – when all the Jeffrey Dahmer stuff was going on. I was only a kid but I knew what it was all about and we were all scared and confused. I don't know how people can do things like that, do you?'

Banks looked at her, saw the innocence, the hope and the faith that her life would turn out to be worth living and that the world wasn't an entirely evil place, no matter what bad things happened in it. 'No,' he said. 'I don't.'

'So you haven't found her, then? Leanne?'

'No.'

'It's not that I knew her or anything. I only saw her once. But, you know, when something like that happens, like you think you might be the last person to have seen someone, well . . .' She rested her hand on her chest. 'It sort of sticks with you, if you know what I mean. I can't get the picture out of my mind. Her sitting over there by the fireplace.'

Banks thought of Claire Toth, whipping herself over Kimberley Myers's murder, and he knew that anyone remotely connected with what Payne had done felt tainted by it. 'I know what you mean,' he said.

One of the old men came up to the bar and plonked his half-pint glass down. Shannon filled it for him, he paid and went back to his chair. She wrinkled her nose. 'They're in here every day. You can set your watch by them. If one of them didn't turn up I'd have to call an ambulance.'

'When you say you can't get Leanne's image out of your mind, does that mean you've given any more thought to that evening?'

'Not really,' said Shannon. 'I mean, I thought . . . you know, that she'd been taken, like the others. That's what everyone thought.'

'I'm starting to believe that might not be the case,' said Banks, putting his fear into words for the first time. 'In fact, I'm beginning to think we might have been barking up the wrong tree on that one.'

'I don't understand.'

'Anyway,' Banks went on. 'I just thought I'd drop by, see if you remembered anything you forgot to mention before, that sort of thing. It's been a while.' And that, he knew, meant that any trail Leanne may have left would have gone cold. If they had screwed up in assuming too quickly that

Leanne Wray had been abducted by the same person, or persons, as Kelly Matthews and Samantha Foster, then any clues as to what had *really* happened could well have vanished for ever by now.

'I don't know how I can help,' said Shannon.

'Tell me,' said Banks, 'you say they were sitting over there, right?' He pointed to the table by the empty, tiled fireplace.

'Yes. Four of them. At that table.'

'Did they drink much?'

'No. I told the policewoman before. They only had a drink or two each. I didn't think she was old enough but the landlord tells us not to bother too much, unless it's *really* obvious.' She put her hand over her mouth. 'Shoot, I probably shouldn't have said that, should I?'

'Don't worry about it. We know all about Mr Parkinson's practices. And don't worry about what you told us before, Shannon. I know I could go and look it all up in the files if I wanted, but I want you to start again, as if it had never happened before.'

It was hard to explain to a civilian, but Banks needed the feel of investigating Leanne's disappearance as if it were a fresh crime. He didn't want to start by poring over old files in his office – though it would no doubt come to that if something didn't turn up soon – he wanted to start by revisiting the place where she had last been seen.

'Did Leanne seem intoxicated at all?' he asked.

'She was a bit giggly, a bit loud, as if maybe she wasn't used to the drink.'

'What was she drinking?'

'I can't remember. Not beer. Maybe wine, or it could have been Pernod, something like that.'

'Did you get the impression that the four of them had paired off? Anything along those lines?'

Shannon thought for a moment. 'No. Two of them were clearly a couple. You could tell by the way they were touching one another casually. I mean, it's not as if they were necking or anything. But the other two, Leanne and . . .'

'Mick Blair,' said Banks.

'I don't know their names. Anyway, I got the impression he might have been a bit keen and she was flirting a bit, maybe because of the drinks.'

'Was he bothering her at all?'

'Oh, no, nothing like that, or I'd have a made a point of saying so before. No, just the way I caught him looking at her once or twice. They seemed comfortable enough together, but as I say, I just thought maybe he fancied her and she was playing him along a bit, that's all.'

'You didn't mention this before.'

'It didn't seem important. Besides, nobody asked me. Back then, everyone was more concerned that she'd been abducted by a serial killer.'

True enough, Banks thought, with a sigh. Leanne's parents had been adamant that she was a good girl and would never, under any normal circumstances, break a curfew. So certain were they that she must have been attacked or abducted that their certainty influenced the investigation, and the police broke one of their cardinal rules: don't make assumptions until you've checked out every possible angle. People were also making noises about Kelly Matthews and Samantha Foster at the time, too, so Leanne's disappearance – another nice, well-adjusted teenager – became linked with theirs. And there was, of course, the matter of the abandoned shoulder-bag. In it were Leanne's inhaler, which she needed in case of an asthma attack, and her purse, which contained twenty-five pounds and a handful of change. It made no sense that she would throw away her money if she was running away from home. Surely she would need all she could get?

DC Winsome Jackman had questioned Shannon, and perhaps she should have asked more probing questions, but Banks couldn't blame Winsome for the omissions. She had discovered what mattered at the time: that the group had been well behaved, that they had caused no problems, that there had been no arguments, that they weren't drunk, and that there had been no unwelcome attention from strangers. 'What was their general mood?' Banks asked. 'Did they seem quiet, rambunctious, or what?'

'I don't remember anything unusual about them. They weren't causing any trouble, or I'm sure I'd have said. Usually you get that with people who know they're drinking under age. They know they're under sufferance, if you know what I mean, so they tend not to draw attention to themselves.'

Banks remembered the feeling well. At sixteen he had sat, proud and terrified, with his mate Steve in a poky little pub a mile or so from the estate where they both lived, drinking their first pints of bitter in a corner by the jukebox, smoking Park Drive tipped. They had felt like real grown-ups, but Banks also remembered being worried in case the police came around, or someone who knew them came in – one of his father's friends, for example – so they tried to fade into the woodwork as much as possible.

He sipped his shandy and crumpled up the crisp packet. Shannon took it from him and put it in the waste bin behind the bar.

'I do remember that they seemed excited about something just before they left, though,' Shannon added. 'I mean they were too far away for me to hear anything and they weren't really noisy about it, but I could tell someone had come up with a good idea for something to do.'

Banks hadn't heard about this before. 'You've no idea what it was?'

'No, it was just like, they were going, "Yeah, let's do that." Then a couple of minutes later they left.'

'What time was this?'

'Must have been about a quarter to eleven.'

'And they were *all* excited about this idea? Including Leanne?'

'I couldn't honestly separate out the reactions for you,' Shannon said with a frown. 'It was just a general sort of thing, as if someone had an idea for something to do and they all thought it would be fun.'

'This great idea, did you get the impression it was something they were going to do right then, after they left here?'

'I don't know. Perhaps. Why?'

Banks finished his drink. 'Because Leanne Wray had an eleven o'clock curfew,' he said. 'And according to her parents she never stayed out past her curfew. If she was planning on going off anywhere with them *after* they'd been here, she'd have missed it. There's something else, too.'

'What?'

'If they were all planning to do something, it means her friends all lied.'

Shannon thought for a moment. 'I see what you mean. But there was no reason to think she wasn't going home. She might have. I mean, it could have been just the three of them planning something. Look, I'm really sorry . . .

I mean, I never thought, you know, last time. I tried to remember everything that was important.'

'It's okay,' said Banks, smiling. 'Not your fault.' He looked at his watch. Time to head out for Withernsea. 'Must dash.'

'Oh. I'm leaving at the end of next week,' said Shannon. 'I mean, my last night's a week next Wednesday, you know, if you'd like to stop by for a drink, say goodbye.'

Banks didn't know how to take the invitation. Was it a come on? Surely not. Shannon couldn't have been a day over twenty-one. Still it was nice to think there was even the remotest chance that a younger girl fancied him. 'Thanks,' he said. 'I'm not sure I'll be able to make it, so in case I don't, I'll say *bon voyage* now.'

Shannon gave a little 'whatever' sort of shrug and Banks walked out into the dismal alley.

•

It was only mid-afternoon, but Annie would have sworn that Janet Taylor was drunk. Not totally, falling-down pissed, but emitting a slight buzz, fuzzy around the edges. She'd had a bit of experience with drunks at the artists' commune where she had grown up with her father, Ray. There had once, briefly, been an alcoholic writer, she remembered: a big, smelly man with rheumy eyes and a thick, matted beard. He hid bottles all over the place. Her father told her to stay away from him and once, when the man, whose name she couldn't remember, started talking to her, her father got angry and made him leave the room. It was one of the few times she had ever seen Ray really angry. He liked a drop or two of wine now and then, and no doubt he still smoked a bit of pot, but he wasn't a drunk or a drug addict. Most of the time he was consumed by his work, whatever painting it happened to be at the time, to the exclusion of pretty much everything, including Annie.

Janet's flat was a mess, with clothes strewn everywhere and half-full cups of tea on the windowsill and mantelpiece. It also smelled like a drunk's room, that peculiar mix of stale skin and the sweet and sour smell of booze. Gin, in Janet's case.

Janet slumped onto a wrinkled T-shirt and a pair of jeans on the armchair, leaving Annie to fend for herself. She cleared some newspapers off a hard-backed chair and sat.

'So what is it now?' Janet asked. 'You come to arrest me?'

'Not yet.'

'What, then? More questions?'

'You've heard Terence Payne died?'

'I've heard.'

'How are you doing, Janet?'

'How am I doing? Ha. That's a good one. Well, let me see.' She started counting off on her fingers as she spoke. 'Apart from not being able to sleep, apart from pacing the flat and feeling claustrophobic whenever it gets dark, apart from reliving the moment over and over again whenever I close my eyes, apart from the fact that my career's pretty much fucked, let me see . . . I feel just fine.'

Annie took a deep breath. She certainly wasn't there to make Janet feel any better, though in a way she wished she could. 'You know, you really should seek some sort of counselling, Janet. The Federation will—'

'No! No, I'm not seeing any shrinks. I'll not have them messing with my head. Not with all this shit going on. When they've done with me, I'll not know whether I'm coming or going. Imagine how that would look in court.'

Annie held her hands up. 'Okay. Okay. It's your choice.' She took some papers from her briefcase. 'I've attended

Terence Payne's post mortem, and there's a couple of things I'd like to go over on your statement.'

'Are you saying I was lying?'

'No, not at all.'

Janet ran her hand through her lifeless, greasy hair. 'Because I'm not a liar. I might have been a bit confused about the sequence of events – it all happened so fast – but I told it as I remember it.'

'Okay, Janet, that's fine. Look, in your statement you say you hit Payne three times on the left temple and once on his wrist, and that one of the blows to the temple was delivered two-handed.'

'Did I?'

'Yes. Is that correct?'

'I couldn't remember *exactly* how many times or where I hit him, but that seemed about right, yes. Why?'

'According to Dr Mackenzie's post mortem, you hit Payne *nine* times. Three on the temple, one to the wrist, one on the cheek, two to the base of the skull while he was crouching or kneeling, and two to the top of his head while he was squatting or sitting.'

Janet said nothing, and a jet from the airport streamed into the silence, filling it with the roar of engines and the promise of distant, exotic places. Anywhere but here, Annie was thinking, and she guessed that Janet probably felt the same. 'Janet?'

'What? I wasn't aware you'd asked me a question.'

'How do you respond to what I just said?'

'I don't know. I told you, I wasn't counting. I was just trying to save my life.'

'Are you sure you weren't acting out of revenge for Dennis?'

'What do you mean?'

'The number of blows, the position of the victim, the violence of the blows.'

Janet turned red. '*Victim!* Is that what you call the bastard? *Victim*. When Dennis was lying there on the floor with his life blood pumping away. You call Terence Payne a victim. How dare you!'

'I'm sorry, Janet, but that's the way a case would be presented in court, and you'd better get used to the idea.'

Janet said nothing.

'Why did you say what you did to the ambulance attendant?'

'What did I say?'

' "Is he dead? Did I kill the bastard?" What did you mean by that?'

'I don't know. I don't even remember saying it.'

'It could be construed as meaning you set out to kill him, do you see?'

'I suppose it could be twisted that way, yes.'

'Did you, Janet? Did you intend to kill Terence Payne?'

'No! I told you. I was just trying to save my life. Why can't you believe me?'

'What about the blows to the back of his head? When might those have occurred in the sequence of events?'

'I don't know.'

'Try harder. You can do better than that.'

'Maybe when he was bent over reaching for his machete.'

'Okay. But you don't remember delivering them?'

'No, but I suppose I must have done if you say so.'

'What about those two blows to the *top* of his head? Dr Mackenzie tells me they were delivered with a lot of force. They weren't just random hits.'

Janet shook her head. 'I don't know. I don't know.'

Annie leaned forward and held Janet's chin between

thumb and forefinger, looking into her blurry, scared eyes. 'Listen to me, Janet. Terence Payne was taller than you. By the angle and force of those blows, the *only* way they could have been delivered was if he was sitting and the attacker had plenty of time to take a huge, uninterrupted downward swing and . . . well, you get the picture. Come on, Janet. Talk to me. Believe it or not, I'm trying to help you.'

Janet twisted her chin from Annie's grip and looked away. 'What do you want me to say? I'd only get myself deeper in trouble.'

'Not true. You'll get nowhere if you're perceived as lying or covering up your actions. That'll only lead to perjury. The truth's your best defence. Do you think there's a person on that jury – if that's what it comes to – who won't sympathize with your predicament, even if you did admit to losing it for a few moments? Give yourself a break here, Janet.'

'What do you want me to say?'

'Tell the truth. Was that how it happened? Was he down and you just lost your temper, gave him one for Dennis? And, crack, there's another. Is that how it happened?'

Janet jumped up and began pacing, wringing her hands. 'So what if I did give him one or two for Dennis? It was nothing less than he deserved.'

'That's what you did? You remember now?'

Janet stopped and narrowed her eyes, then she poured herself two fingers of gin and knocked it back. 'Not clearly, no, but if you're telling me that's how it happened, I can hardly deny it, can I? Not in the face of the pathologist's evidence.'

'Pathologists can be wrong,' Annie said, though not, she thought, about the number, strength and angle of the blows.

'But who will they believe in court?'

'I've told you. If it comes to that you'll get a lot of sympathy. But it might not come to court.'

Janet sat down again, perched at the edge of the armchair. 'What do you mean?'

'It's up to the CPS. I'll be meeting with them on Monday. In the meantime, if you want to alter your statement at all before then, now's the time to do it.'

'It's no good,' said Janet, holding her head in her hands and weeping. 'I don't remember it clearly. It all seemed to happen so fast, it was over before I knew what was happening and Dennis . . . Dennis was dead, bleeding on my lap. That went on for ever, me telling him to hang on, trying to staunch the blood.' She looked at her hands as if seeing the same thing Lady Macbeth saw, what she couldn't wash away. 'But he wouldn't stop bleeding. I couldn't stop it from coming out. Maybe it happened as you said. Maybe that's the only way it could have happened. All I remember is the fear, the adrenalin, the—'

'The anger, Janet? Is that what you were going to say?'

Janet shot her a defiant glance. 'What if I was? Wasn't I right to feel anger?'

'I'm not here to judge you. I think I'd have been angry myself, maybe done exactly the same as you. But we've got to get this sorted. There's no way it'll simply disappear. As I say, the CPS might decide not to press charges. At the worst you'd be looking at excusable homicide, maybe even justifiable. We're not talking jail time here, Janet. Thing is, though, we can't hide it and it won't go away. There's got to be some action.' Annie spoke softly and clearly, as if to a frightened child.

'I hear what you're saying,' Janet said. 'It's like I'm some sort of sacrificial lamb tossed to the slaughter to appease public opinion.'

'Not at all.' Annie stood up. 'Public opinion is far more likely to be on your side. It's just procedure that has to be followed. Look, if you want to get in touch with me about anything, *anything* at all before Monday, here's my card.' She wrote her home and mobile numbers on the back.

'Thanks.' Janet took the card, glanced at it and set it on the coffee table.

'You know,' Annie said at the door. 'I'm not your enemy, Janet. Yes, I'd have to give evidence if it came to court, but I'm not against you.'

Janet gave her a twisted smile. 'Yeah, I know,' she said, reaching for the gin again. 'Life's a bitch, isn't it?'

'Sure is.' Annie smiled back. 'Then you die.'

•

'Claire! It's so nice to see you again. Come in.'

Claire Toth walked into Maggie's hall and followed her through to the front room, where she slouched on the sofa.

The first things Maggie noticed about her were how pale she was and that she had cut off all her beautiful long blonde hair. What was left lay jaggedly over her skull in a way that suggested she had cut it herself. She wasn't wearing her school uniform, but a pair of baggy jeans and a baggy sweat-shirt that hid all signs that she was an attractive young woman. She wore no make-up and her face was dotted with acne. Maggie remembered what Dr Simms had said about the possible reactions of Kimberley's close friends, that some might suppress their sexuality because they thought that would protect them from predators such as Terence Payne. It looked as if Claire was trying to do just that.

Maggie wondered if she should comment, but decided not to.

'Milk and cookies?' she asked.

Claire shook her head.

'What is it, sweetheart?' Maggie asked. 'What's wrong?'

'I don't know,' said Claire. 'I can't sleep. I just keep thinking of her. I just lie awake all night with it going through my head, what must have happened to her, what she must have felt like . . . I can't bear it. It's awful.'

'What do your parents say?'

Claire looked away. 'I can't talk to them. I . . . I thought, you know, you might understand better.'

'Let me get those cookies, anyway. I could do with one myself.' Maggie fetched two glasses of milk and a plate of chocolate chip cookies from the kitchen and put them down on the coffee table. Claire picked up her milk and sipped at it, then reached out and picked up a cookie.

'You read about me in the papers, then?' Maggie said.

Claire nodded.

'And what did you think?'

'At first I couldn't believe it. Not you. Then I realized it could be anybody, that you didn't have to be poor or stupid to be abused. Then I felt sorry for you.'

'Well, please don't do that,' said Maggie, trying on a smile. 'I stopped feeling sorry for myself a long time ago, and now I'm just getting on with life. All right?'

'Okay.'

'What sort of things do you think about? Do you want to tell me?'

'How terrible it must have been for Kim, with Mr Payne, you know, doing things to her. *Sex.* The police didn't say anything to the papers about it, but I *know* he did horrible things to her. I can just picture him there, doing it, hurting her, and Kim so helpless.'

'It's no use imagining what it was like, Claire. It won't do any good.'

'Do you think I don't know that? Do you think I do it on purpose?' She shook her head slowly. 'And I keep going over the details of that night in my mind. How I just said I was staying for a slow dance with Nicky and Kim said that was okay, she'd probably find somebody to walk home with but it wasn't very far anyway and the road was well lit. I should have known something would happen to her.'

'You couldn't know, Claire. How could you possibly know?'

'I *should* have. We knew about those girls, the ones who'd gone missing. We should have stuck together, been more careful.'

'Claire, listen to me: it's *not* your fault. And I know this sounds harsh, but if anyone should have been more careful, perhaps it's Kimberley. You can't be blamed for dancing with a boy. If she was concerned, then she should have made sure she had someone to walk home with her and not gone off alone.'

'Maybe she didn't.'

'What do you mean?'

'Maybe Mr Payne gave her a lift.'

'You told the police you didn't see him. You didn't, did you?'

'No. But he *could* have been waiting outside, couldn't he?'

'I suppose so,' Maggie admitted.

'I hate him. I'm glad he's dead. And I hate Nicky Gallagher. I hate all men.'

Maggie didn't know what to say to that. She could tell

Claire that she'd get over it in time, but a fat lot of good that would do. The best thing she could do, she decided, was have a talk with Mrs Toth and see if they could persuade Claire to go for counselling before things got worse. At least she seemed to *want* to talk about her thoughts and feelings, which was a good start.

'Was she conscious all the time he was doing stuff with her?' Claire asked. 'I mean, was she *aware* of him doing it to her?'

'Claire, stop it.' But Maggie was spared further debate by the phone. She listened, frowning, said a few words and then turned back to Claire, who managed to pull herself out of her absorption with Kimberley's ordeal for a moment and ask her who it was.

'It was the local television station,' Maggie said, wondering if she sounded as stunned as she felt.

A flicker of interest. 'What did they want?'

'They want me to go on the news show tonight.'

'What did you say?'

'I said yes,' said Maggie, as if she couldn't quite believe it herself.

'Cool,' said Claire, squeezing out a tiny smile.

•

There are many English seaside resorts that look as if they have seen better days. Withernsea looked as if it had never seen any good days at all. The sun was shining over the rest of the island, but you wouldn't know it at Withernsea. A vicious, cold rain slanted in from the iron sky, and waves from a North Sea the colour of stained underwear churned up dirty sand and pebbles on the beach. Set back from the front was a strip of gift shops, amusement arcades and bingo halls, their bright coloured lights garish and lurid in the gloomy afternoon, the bingo caller's amplified 'Number nine, doctor's orders!' pathetic as it sounded along the deserted promenade.

The whole thing reminded Banks of long ago childhood holidays at Great Yarmouth, Blackpool or Scarborough. July or August days when it seemed to rain nonstop for two weeks, and all he could do was wander the amusement arcades losing pennies in the one-armed bandits and watching the mechanical claw drop the shiny cigarette lighter just before it reached the winner's chute. He had never played bingo, but had often watched the hard-faced peroxide women sit there game after game chain-smoking and staring down at the little numbers on their cards.

On better days, and when he reached his teens, Banks would spend his time searching through the second-hand bookshops for the old Pan books of horror stories or steamy bestsellers such as *The Carpetbaggers* and *Peyton Place*. When he was thirteen or fourteen, feeling way too grown-up to be on holiday with his parents, he would wander off alone for the day, hanging around in coffee bars and browsing through the latest singles in Woolworths or a local record shop. Sometimes he would meet a girl in the same predicament, and he had had his first adolescent kisses and tentative gropings on these holidays.

Banks parked by the seafront and, without even stopping for a look at the water, hurried to the house directly across from him, where retired DI George Woodward now ran his B & B. The 'Vacancies' sign swung in the wind and creaked like a shutter on a haunted house. By the time Banks rang the front doorbell he was cold and soaked to the skin.

George Woodward was a dapper man with grey hair, bristly moustache and the watchful eyes of an ex-copper. There was also an aura of the hangdog about him, most noticeable as he looked over Banks's shoulder at the weather and shook his head slowly. 'I did suggest Torquay,' he said, 'but the wife's mother lives here in Withernsea.' He ushered Banks in. 'Ah, well, it's not that bad. You've just come on a miserable day, that's all. Early in the season, too. You should see it when the sun's shining and the place is full. A different world altogether.'

Banks wondered on which day of the year that momentous event occurred, but he kept silent. No point antagonizing George Woodward.

They were in a large room with a bay window and several tables, clearly the breakfast room where the lucky guests hurried down for their bacon and eggs every morning. The tables were laid out with white linen, but there were no knives and forks, and Banks wondered if the Woodwards had any guests at all at the moment. Without offering tea or anything stronger, George Woodward sat at one of the tables and bade Banks sit opposite.

'It's about Alderthorpe, is it, then?'

'Yes.' Banks had spoken with Jenny Fuller on his mobile on his way out to Withernsea and learned what Elizabeth Bell, the social worker, had to say. Now he was after the policeman's perspective.

'I always thought that would come back to haunt us one day.'

'How do you mean?'

'Damage like that. It doesn't go away. It festers.'

'I suppose you've got a point.' Like Jenny had with Elizabeth Bell, Banks decided he had to trust George Woodward. 'I'm here about Lucy Payne,' he said, watching Woodward's expression. 'Linda Godwin, as was. But that's between you and me for the moment.'

Woodward paled and whistled between his teeth. 'My God, I'd never have believed it. Linda Godwin?'

'That's right.'

'I saw her picture in the paper, but I didn't recognize her. The poor lass.'

'Not any more.'

'Surely you can't think she had anything to do with those girls?'

'We don't know what to think. That's the problem. She's claiming loss of memory. There's some circumstantial evidence, but not much. You know the sort of thing I mean.'

'What's your instinct?'

'That she's more involved than she's saying. Whether she's an accessory or not, I don't know.'

'You realize she was only a twelve-year-old girl when I met her?'

'Yes.'

'Twelve going on forty, the responsibility she had.'

'Responsibility?' Jenny had said something about Lucy taking care of the younger children; he wondered if this was what Woodward meant.

'Yes. She was the eldest. For Christ's sake, man, she had a ten-year-old brother who was being regularly buggered by his father and uncle and there wasn't a damn thing she could do about it. They were doing it to *her*, too. Can you even *begin* to imagine how all that made her feel?'

Banks admitted he couldn't. 'Mind if I smoke?' he asked.

'I'll get you an ashtray. You're lucky Mary's over at her mother's.' He winked. 'She'd never allow it.' Woodward produced a heavy glass ashtray from the cupboard by the door and surprised Banks by pulling a crumpled packet of Embassy Regal from the shirt pocket under his beige V-neck sweater. He then went on to surprise him even further by suggesting a wee dram. 'Nowt fancy, mind. Just Bell's.'

'Bell's would be fine,' said Banks. He'd have just the one, as he had a long drive home. The first sip, after they clinked glasses, tasted wonderful. It was everything to do with the cold rain lashing at the bay windows.

'Did you get to know Lucy at all?' he asked.

Woodward sipped his Bell's neat and grimaced. 'Barely spoke to her. Or any of the kids, for that matter. We left them to the social workers. We'd enough on our hands with the parents.'

'Can you tell me how it went down?'

Woodward ran his hand over his hair, then took a deep drag on his cigarette. 'Good Lord, this is going back a bit,' he said.

'Whatever you can remember.'

'Oh, I remember everything as if it was yesterday. That's the problem.'

Banks tapped some ash from his cigarette and waited for George Woodward to focus his memory on the one day he would probably sooner forget.

'It was pitch black when we went in,' Woodward began. 'And cold as a witch's tit. The eleventh of February, it was. 1990. There was me and Baz – Barry Stevens, my DS – in one car. The bloody heater didn't work properly, I remember, and we were almost blue with cold when we got to Alderthorpe. All the puddles were frozen. There were about three more cars and a van, for the social workers to isolate the kids, like. We were working off a tip from one of the local schoolteachers who'd got suspicious about some of the truancies, the way the kids looked and behaved and, especially, the disappearance of Kathleen Murray.'

'She's the one who was killed, right?'

'That's right. Anyway, there were a couple of lights on in the houses when we got there, and we marched straight up and bashed our way in – we had a warrant – and that was when we . . . we saw it.' He was silent for a moment, staring somewhere beyond Banks, beyond the bay window, beyond even the North Sea. Then he took another nip of whisky, coughed and went on. 'Of course, we didn't know who was who at first. The two households were mixed up and nobody knew who'd fathered who anyway.'

'What did you find?'

'Most of them were asleep until we bashed the doors in. They had a vicious dog, took a chunk out of Baz as we went in. Then we found Oliver Murray and Pamela Godwin – brother and sister – in a bed with one of the Godwin girls: Laura.'

'Lucy's sister.'

'Yes. Dianne Murray, the second eldest child was curled up safe and sound in a room with her brother Keith, but their sister, Susan, was sandwiched between the other two adults.' He swallowed. 'The place was a pigsty – both of them were – smelled terrible. Someone had knocked a hole through the living-room wall so they could travel back and forth without going outside and being seen.' He paused a moment to collect his thoughts. 'It's hard to get across the sense of squalor, of depravity you could feel there, but it was tangible, something you could touch and taste. I don't just mean the dirt, the stains, the smells, but more than that. A sort of spiritual squalor, if you catch my drift. Everyone was terrified, of course, especially the kids.' He shook his head. 'Sometimes, looking back, I wonder if we couldn't have done it some other way, some gentler way. I don't know. Too late for that now, anyroad.'

'I understand you found evidence of Satanic rituals?'

'In the cellar of the Godwin house, yes.'

'What did you find?'

'The usual. Incense, robes, books, pentagram, an altar – no doubt on which the virgin would be penetrated. Other occult paraphernalia. You know what my theory is?'

'No. What?'

'These people weren't witches or Satanists; they were just sick and cruel perverts. I'm sure they used the Satanism as an excuse to take drugs and dance and chant themselves into a frenzy. All that Satanic rigmarole, the candles, magic circles, robes, music, chanting and whatnot, it was just something to make it all seem like a game to the children. It was just something that played with their minds, like, didn't let the poor buggers know whether what they were doing was what was supposed to be happening – playing with Mummy and Daddy even if it hurt sometimes and they punished you when you were bad – or something way out, way over the top. It was both, of course. No wonder they couldn't understand. And all those trappings, they just helped turn it into a kid's game, ring around the roses, that's all.'

Satanic paraphernalia had also been found in the Paynes's cellar. Banks wondered if there was a connection. 'Did any of them profess any sort of belief in Satan at any time?'

'Oliver and Pamela tried to confuse the jury with some sort of gobbledygook about the Great Horned God and 666 at their trial, but nobody took a blind bit of notice of them. Trappings, that's all it were. A kid's game. Let's all go down in the cellar and dress up and play.'

'Where was Lucy?'

'Locked in a cage – we later found out it was a genuine Morrison shelter left over from the war – in the cellar of the Murray house along with her brother, Tom. It was where you got put if you misbehaved or disobeyed, we found out later. We never did find out what the two of them had done to get put there, though, because they wouldn't talk.'

'Wouldn't or couldn't?'

'Wouldn't. They wouldn't talk out against the adults, their parents. They'd been abused and messed up in their minds too long to dare put it into words.' He paused a moment. 'Sometimes, I don't think they could have expressed it all anyway, no matter how much they tried. I mean, where does a nine-year-old or an eleven-year-old find the language and points of reference she needs to explain something like that? They weren't just protecting their parents or shutting up in fear of them – it went deeper than that. Anyway, Tom and Linda . . . They were both naked and dirty, crawling in their own filth, looked as if they hadn't eaten for a couple of days – I mean, most of the children were malnourished and neglected, but they were worse. There was a bucket in the cage, and the smell . . . And Linda, well, she was twelve, and it showed. She was . . . I mean they'd made no provisions for . . . you know . . . time of the month. I'll never forget the look of shame and fear and defiance on that little kid's face when Baz and I walked in on them and turned the light on.'

Banks took a sip of Bell's, waited until it had burned all the way down, then asked, 'What did you do?'

'First off, we found some blankets for them, as much for warmth's sake as modesty's, because there wasn't much heat in the place, either.'

'After that?'

'We handed them over to the social workers.' He gave a little shudder. 'One of them couldn't handle it. Well-meaning young lass, thought she was tough, but she didn't have the stomach.'

'What did she do?'

'Went back to the car and wouldn't get out. Just sat there hunched up, shivering and crying. There was no one to pay her much mind as we all had our hands full. Me and Baz were mostly occupied with the adults.'

'Did they have much to say?'

'Nah. Surly lot. And Pamela Godwin – well there was clearly summat wrong with her. In the head. She didn't seem to have a clue what was going on. Kept on smiling and asking us if we wanted a cup of tea. Her husband, though, Michael, I'll never forget him. Greasy hair, straggly beard and that look in his dark eyes. You ever seen pictures of that American killer, Charles Manson?'

'Yes.'

'Like him. That's who Michael Godwin reminded me of: Charles Manson.'

'What did you do with them?'

'We arrested them all under the Protection of Children Act, to be going on with. They resisted arrest, of course. Picked up a few lumps and bruises.' He gave Banks a challenge-me-on-that-one-if-you-dare look. Banks didn't. 'Later, of course, we came up with a list of charges as long as your arm.'

'Including murder.'

'That was later, after we found Kathleen Murray's body.'

'When did you find her?'

'Later that day.'

'Where?'

'Out back in an old sack in the dustbin. I reckon they'd dumped her there until the ground softened a bit and they could bury her. You could see where someone had tried to dig a hole, but they'd given up, the earth was so hard. She'd been doubled over and been there long enough to freeze solid, so the pathologist had to wait till she thawed out before he could do the post mortem.'

'Were they all charged?'

'Yes. We charged all four adults with conspiracy.'

'And?'

'They were all committed for trial. Michael Godwin topped himself in his cell, and Pamela was found unfit to stand trial. The jury convicted the other two after a morning's deliberation.'

'What evidence did you have?'

'What do you mean?'

'Could anyone else have killed Kathleen?'

'Who?'

'I don't know. One of the other kids, maybe?'

Woodward's jaw tightened. 'You didn't see them,' he said. 'If you had, you wouldn't be making suggestions like that.'

'Did anyone suggest it at the time?'

He gave a harsh laugh. 'Believe it or not, yes. The adults had the gall to try and pin it on the boy, Tom. But nobody fell for that one, thank the Lord.'

'What about the evidence? How was she killed, for example?'

'Ligature strangulation.'

Banks held his breath. Another coincidence. 'With what?'

Woodward smiled as if laying down his trump card. 'Oliver Murray's belt. The pathologist matched it to the wound. He also found traces of Murray's semen in the girl's vagina and anus, not to mention unusual tearing. It looks as if they went too far that once. Maybe she was bleeding to death, I don't know, but they killed her – *he* killed her, with the knowledge and consent of the others, maybe even with their help, I don't know.'

'How did they plead? The Murrays?'

'What would you expect? Not guilty.'

'They never confessed?'

'No. People like that never do. They don't even think they've done anything wrong, they're so beyond the law, beyond what's normal for the rest of us folks. In the end, they got less than they deserved, in that they're still alive, but at least they're still locked up, out of harm's way. And that, Mr Banks, is the story of the Alderthorpe Seven.' Woodward put his palms on the table and stood up. He seemed less dapper and more weary than when Banks had first arrived. 'Now, if you'll excuse me, I've got the rooms to do before the missus comes back.'

It seemed like an odd time to be doing the rooms, Banks thought, especially as they were all probably vacant, but he sensed that Woodward had had enough, wanted to be alone and wanted, if he could, to get rid of the bad taste of his memories before his wife came home. Good luck to him. Banks couldn't think of anything more to ask, so he said his goodbyes, buttoned up and walked out into the rain. He could have sworn he felt a few lumps of hail stinging his bare head before he got into his car.

•

Maggie began to have doubts the moment she got in the taxi to the local television studio. Truth be told, she had been vacillating ever since she first got the call early that afternoon inviting her to participate in a discussion on domestic violence on the evening magazine show at six o'clock, after the news. A researcher had seen the article in the newspaper and thought Maggie would make a valuable guest.

This was not about Terence and Lucy Payne, the researcher had stressed, and their deeds were not to be discussed. It was an odd legal situation, she explained, that no one had yet been charged with the murders of the girls, and the main suspect was dead, but not proven guilty. Could you charge a dead man with murder? Maggie wondered.

As the taxi wound down Canal Road, over the bridge and under the viaduct to Kirkstall Road, where the rush-hour traffic was slow and heavy, Maggie felt the butterflies begin to flutter in her stomach. She remembered the newspaper article, how Lorraine Temple had twisted everything, and wondered again if she was doing the right thing or if she was simply walking back into the lions' den.

But she *did* have very good, strong reasons for doing it, she assured herself. In the first place, she wanted to atone for, even correct, the image the newspaper had given of Lucy Payne as being evil and manipulative, if she could slip it in somehow. Lucy was a *victim*, and the public should be made to realize that. Secondly, she wanted to rid herself of the mousy, nervous image Lorraine Temple had lumbered her with, both for her own sake and in order to get people to take her seriously. She didn't like being thought of as mousy and nervous, and she was damn well going to do something about it.

Finally, and this was the reason that pushed her to say yes, was the way that policeman, Banks, had come to the house shouting at her, insulting her intelligence and telling her what she could and couldn't do. *Damn him.* She'd show him. She'd show them all. She was feeling empowered now, and if it was her lot to become a spokeswoman for battered wives, then so be it; she was up to the task. Lorraine Temple had let the cat out of the bag about her past, anyway, so there was nothing more to hide; she might as well speak out and hope she could do some good for others in her position. No more mousy and nervous.

Julia Ford had phoned her that afternoon to tell her that Lucy was being detained in Eastvale for further questioning and would probably be kept there overnight. Maggie was outraged. What had Lucy done to deserve such treatment? Something was very much out of kilter in the whole business.

Maggie paid the taxi driver and kept the receipt. The TV people would reimburse her, they had said. She introduced herself at reception and the woman behind the desk called the researcher, Tina Driscoll, who turned out to be a cheerful slip of a lass in her early twenties with short bleached blonde hair and pale skin stretched tight over her high cheekbones. Like most of the other people Maggie saw as she followed Tina through the obligatory television studio maze, she was dressed in jeans and a white blouse.

'You're on after the poodle groomer,' Tina said, glancing at her watch. 'Should be about twenty past. Here's make-up.'

Tina ushered Maggie into a tiny room with chairs and mirrors and a whole array of powders, brushes and potions. 'Just here, love, that's right,' said the make-up artist, who introduced herself as Charley. 'Won't take a minute.' And she started dabbing and brushing away at Maggie's face. Finally, satisfied with the result, she said, 'Drop by when you've finished and I'll wipe it off in a jiffy.'

Maggie didn't see a great deal of difference, though she knew from her previous television experience that the studio lighting and cameras would pick up the subtle nuances. 'David will be conducting the interview,' said Tina, consulting her clipboard on their way to the green room. 'David', Maggie knew, was David Hartford, half of the male-female team that hosted the programme. The woman was called Emma Larson, and Maggie had been hoping that *she* would have been asking the questions. Emma had always come across as sympathetic on women's issues, but David Hartford, Maggie thought, had a cynical and derogatory tone to his questioning of anyone who was passionate about anything. He was also known to be provocative. Still, the way Maggie was feeling, she was quite willing to be provoked.

Maggie's fellow guests were waiting in the green room: the grave, bearded Dr James Bletchley, from the local hospital, DC Kathy Proctor of the domestic violence unit, and Michael Groves, a rather shaggy-looking social worker. Maggie realized she was the only 'victim' on the programme, Well, so be it. She could tell them what it was like to be on the receiving end.

They all introduced themselves and then a sort of nervous silence fell over the room, broken only when the poodle emitted a short yap at the entry of the producer, there to check that everyone was present and accounted for. For the remainder of the wait, Maggie chatted briefly with her fellow guests about things in general and watched the hubbub as people came and went and shouted questions at one another in the corridors outside. Like the other TV studio she had been in, this one also seemed to be in a state of perpetual chaos.

There was a monitor in the room, and they were able to watch the show's opening, the light banter of David and Emma and a recap of the day's main local news stories, including the death of a revered councillor, a proposed new roundabout for the city centre and a 'neighbours from hell' story from the Poplar Estate. During the commercial break after the poodle groomer, a set worker got them all in position on the armchairs and sofas, designed to give the feel of a cosy, intimate living room, complete with fake fireplace, wired up their mikes and disappeared. David Hartford made himself comfortable, in a position where he could see the guests without having to move too much, and where the cameras would show him to best advantage.

The silent countdown came to an end, David Hartford straightened his tie and put on his best smile, and they were off. Close up, Maggie thought, David's skin looked like pink plastic, and she imagined it would feel like a child's doll to the touch. His hair was also too impossibly black to be natural.

As soon as David started his introduction to the subject, he swapped his smile for a serious, concerned expression and turned first to Kathy, the policewoman, for a general idea of how many domestic complaints they got and how they dealt with them. After that, it was the social worker, Michael's, turn to talk about women's shelters. When David turned to Maggie for the first time, she felt her heart lurch in her chest. He was handsome in a TV host sort of way, but there was something about him that unnerved her. He didn't seem interested in the problems and the issues, but more in making something dramatically appealing out of it all, of which he was the focus. She supposed that was what television was all about when you came right down to it, making things dramatic and making presenters look good, but still it disturbed her.

He asked her when she first knew there was something wrong, and she briefly detailed the signs, the unreasonable demands, flashes of anger, petty punishments and, finally, the blows, right up to the time Bill broke her jaw, knocked out two of her teeth and put her in hospital for a week.

When Maggie had finished, he turned to the next question on his sheet: 'Why didn't you leave? I mean, you've just said you put up with this physical abuse for . . . how long . . . nearly two years? You're clearly an intelligent and resourceful woman. Why didn't you just get out?'

As Maggie sought the words to express why it didn't happen as simply as that, the social worker cut in and explained how easy it was for women to get trapped in the cycle of violence and how shame often prevented them from speaking out. Finally, Maggie found her voice.

'You're right,' she said to David. 'I could have left. As you say, I'm an intelligent and resourceful woman. I had a good job, good friends, a supportive family. I suppose part of it was that I thought it would go away, that we would work through it. I still loved my husband. Marriage wasn't something I was going to throw away lightly.' She paused, and when nobody else dived into the silence, said, 'Besides, it wouldn't have made any difference. Even after I did leave, he found me, stalked me, harassed me, assaulted me again. Even after the court order.'

This prompted David to go back to the policewoman and talk about how ineffective the courts were in protecting women at risk from abusive spouses, and Maggie had the chance to take stock of what she had said. She hadn't done too badly, she decided. It was hot under the studio lights and she felt her brow moisten with sweat. She hoped it wouldn't rinse away the make-up.

Next David turned to the doctor.

'Is domestic violence specifically directed from men to women, Dr Bletchley?' he asked.

'There are some cases of husbands being physically abused by their wives,' said the doctor, 'but relatively few.'

'I think you'll find, statistically,' Michael butted in, 'that male violence against women by far outstrips women's against men, almost enough to make female violence against men seem insignificant. It's built into our culture. Men hunt down and kill their ex-partners, for example, or commit familial massacres in a way that women do not.'

'But that aside,' David asked next, 'don't you think sometimes that a woman might overreact and ruin a man's life? I mean, once such accusations have been made, they are often very difficult to shake off, even if a court finds the person not guilty.'

'But isn't it worth the risk,' Maggie argued, 'if it saves the ones who really need saving?'

David smirked. 'Well, that's rather like saying what's hanging a few innocent people matter as long as we get the guilty ones, too, isn't it?'

'Nobody intentionally set out to hang innocent people,' Kathy pointed out.

'But, say, if a man retaliates in the face of extreme provocation,' David pressed on, 'isn't the woman still far more likely to be seen as the victim?'

'She *is* the victim,' Maggie said.

'That's like saying she asked for it,' Michael added. 'Just what kind of provocation justifies violence?'

'Are there not also women who actually like it rough?'

'Oh, don't be absurd,' said Michael. 'That's the same sort of thing as suggesting that women ask to be raped by the way they dress.'

'But there *are* masochistic personalities, aren't there, doctor?'

'You're talking about women who like their sex rough, yes?' said the doctor.

David seemed a little embarrassed by the directness of the question – clearly he was a man used to asking, not answering – but he nodded.

Dr Bletchley stroked his beard before answering. 'Well, to answer your question simply: yes, there are masochistic women, just as there are masochistic men, but you have to understand that we're dealing with a very tiny fragment of society here and not that section of society concerned with domestic violence.'

Obviously glad to be done with this line of questioning, David moved on to his next question, phrasing it carefully for Maggie. 'You've recently had some involvement with what's become rather a *cause célèbre* involving domestic abuse. Now, while we can't discuss the case directly for legal reasons, is there anything you *can* tell us about that situation?'

He looked hungry for an answer, Maggie thought. 'Someone confided in me,' she said. 'Confided that she was being abused by her husband. I offered advice, as much help and support as I could give.'

'But you didn't report it to the authorities.'

'It wasn't my place to do that.'

'What do you think of that, DC Proctor?'

'She's right. There's nothing we can do until the persons themselves report the matter.'

'Or until things come to a head, as they did in this instance?'

'Yes. That's often the unfortunate result of the way things work.'

'Thank you very much,' David said, about to wrap things up.

Maggie realized she had weakened at the end, got side-tracked, so she launched in, interrupting him, and said, 'If I might add just one more thing, it's that victims are not always treated with the care, respect and tenderness we all think they deserve. Right now, there's a young woman in the cells in Eastvale, a woman who until this morning was in hospital with injuries she sustained when her husband beat her last weekend. Why is this woman being persecuted like this?'

'Do you have an answer?' David asked. He was obviously pissed off at the interruption but excited by the possibility of controversy.

'I think it's because her husband's dead,' Maggie said. 'They think he killed some young girls, but he's dead and they can't exact their pound of flesh. That's why they're picking on her. That's why they're picking on Lucy.'

'Thank you very much,' David said, turning to the camera and bringing out his smile again. 'That just about wraps things up . . .'

There was silence when the programme ended and the technician removed their mikes, then the policewoman went over to Maggie and said, 'I think it was extremely ill advised of you to say what you did back there.'

'Oh, leave her alone,' said Michael. 'It's about time someone spoke out about it.'

The doctor had already left, and David and Emma were nowhere to be seen.

'Fancy a drink?' said Michael to Maggie, as they left the studio after having their make-up removed, but she shook her head. All she wanted to do was get a taxi home and climb into a nice warm bath with a good book. It might be the last bit of peace and quiet she got if there was a reaction to what she had said tonight. She didn't think she had broken any laws. After all, she hadn't said Terry was guilty of the killings, hadn't even mentioned his name, but she was also certain that the police could find something to charge her with if they wanted to. They seemed to be good at that.

And she wouldn't put it past Banks at all. Let them do it, she thought. Just let them make a martyr of her.

'Are you sure? Just a quick one.'

She looked at Michael and knew that all he wanted to do was probe her for more details. 'No,' she said. 'Thank you very much for the offer, but no. I'm going home.'

13

Banks found chaos outside Western Divisional Headquarters early on Saturday morning. Even at the back, where the entrance to the car park was located, reporters and camera-wielding television news teams pushed against one another and shouted out questions about Lucy Payne. Banks cursed to himself, turned off the Dylan CD halfway through 'Not Dark Yet' and edged his way carefully but firmly through the throng.

Inside, things were quieter. Banks slipped into his office and looked out of the window over the market square. More reporters. TV station vans with satellite dishes. The works. Someone had well and truly let the cat out of the bag. First, Banks walked into the detectives' squad room looking for answers. DCs Jackman and Templeton were at their desks, and Annie Cabbot was bending over the low drawer in the filing cabinet, a heartwarming sight in her tight black jeans, Banks thought, remembering they had a date that night. Dinner, video and . . .

'What the hell's going on out there?' he asked the room in general.

Annie looked up. 'Don't you know?'

'Know what?'

'Didn't you *see* her?'

'What are you talking about?'

Kevin Templeton and Winsome Jackman kept their heads down, leaving this one well alone.

Annie put her hands on her hips. 'Last night, on the television.'

'I was over in Withernsea interviewing a retired copper about Lucy Payne. What did I miss?'

Annie walked over to her desk and rested her hip against the edge. 'The neighbour, Maggie Forrest, was involved in a television discussion about domestic violence.'

'Oh, shit.'

'Indeed. She ended up by accusing us of persecuting Lucy Payne because we can't wreak our revenge on her husband and she informed the viewers in general that Lucy was being detained here.'

'Julia Ford,' Banks whispered.

'Who?'

'The lawyer. I'll bet she's the one told Maggie where we were holding Lucy. Christ, what a mess.'

'Oh, by the way,' Annie said with a smile. 'AC Hartnell's already phoned twice. Asked if you'd ring him as soon as you get in.'

Banks headed for his office. Before phoning Phil Hartnell, he opened his window as wide as it would go and lit a cigarette. Bugger the rules; it was shaping up to be one of those days, and it had only just begun. Banks should have known Maggie Forrest was a loose cannon, that his warning might well just egg her on to more foolish behaviour. But what else could he do about her? Not much, apparently. She hadn't committed a criminal offence, and certainly there was nothing to be gained by going around and telling her off again. Still, if he did happen to see her for any reason, he'd give her a piece of his mind. She had no idea what she was playing with.

When he calmed down, he sat at his desk and reached for

the phone, but it rang before he could pick it up and dial Hartnell's number.

'Alan? Stefan here.'

'I hope you've got some good news for me, Stefan, because the way this morning's going I could do with some.'

'That bad?'

'Getting that way.'

'Maybe this'll cheer you up, then. I just got the DNA comparison in from the lab.'

'And?'

'A match. Terence Payne was your Seacroft Rapist, all right.'

Banks slapped the desk. 'Excellent. Anything else?'

'Only minor points. The lads going through all the documents and bills taken from the house have found no evidence of sleeping tablets prescribed for either Terence or Lucy Payne and they didn't find any illegal ones, either.'

'As I thought.'

'They did find an electronics catalogue, though, from one of those places that put you on their mailing list when you buy something from them.'

'What did they buy?'

'There's no record of their buying anything on their credit cards, but we'll approach the company and get someone to go through the purchases, see if they used cash. And another thing: there were some marks on the floor of the cellar that on further investigation look rather like those a tripod would make. I've talked with Luke and he didn't use a tripod, so . . .'

'Someone else did.'

'Looks that way.'

'Then where the hell is it?'

'No idea.'

'Okay, Stefan, thanks for the good news. Keep looking.'

'Will do.'

As soon as he'd hung up, Banks dialled Hartnell's number. The man himself answered on the second ring.

'Area Commander Hartnell.'

'It's Alan,' said Banks. 'Heard you've been trying to get in touch with me.'

'Did you see it?'

'No. I've only just found out. The place is swarming with media.'

'Surprise, surprise. The stupid woman. What's the situation with Lucy Payne?'

'I talked to her yesterday, got nowhere.'

'Any more evidence?'

'Not evidence, as such.' Banks told him about the Seacroft Rapist DNA match, the possibility of a camcorder still being hidden somewhere on the Paynes's property, and his talk with George Woodward about the Satanic paraphernalia in Alderthorpe and the ligature strangulation of Kathleen Murray.

'It's nothing,' said Hartnell. 'Certainly not evidence against Lucy Payne. For Christ's sake, Alan, she was a victim of the most appalling abuse. I remember that Alderthorpe case. We don't want all that raked up. Think what it will look like if we start suggesting she killed her own bloody cousin when she was only twelve.'

'I thought I might use it to push her a bit, see where she goes.'

'You know as well as I do that blood and fibres aren't enough, and as far as evidence goes, they're all we've got. This speculation about her past will do nothing but gain her more sympathy from the public.'

'There are probably as many people outraged by the crimes and thinking maybe she had more to do with them than she admits.'

'Probably, but they're nowhere near as vocal as the people who've already been phoning Millgarth, believe me. Cut her loose, Alan.'

'But—'

'We caught our killer and he's dead. Let her go. We can't hold her any longer.'

Banks looked at his watch. 'We've still got four hours. Something might turn up.'

'Nothing will turn up in the next four hours, believe me. Release her.'

'What about surveillance?'

'Too bloody expensive. Tell the local police to keep an eye on her, and tell her to stick around, we might want to talk to her again.'

'If she's guilty, she'll disappear.'

'If she's guilty we'll find the evidence and then we'll find her.'

'Let me have one more shot at her first.' Banks held his breath as Hartnell paused at the other end.

'All right. Talk to her one more time. If she doesn't confess, let her go. But be bloody careful. I don't want any allegations of Gestapo interrogation tactics.'

Banks heard a knock at his door, put his hand over the mouthpiece and called out, 'Come in.'

Julia Ford entered and gave him a broad smile.

'No worry on that score, sir,' Banks said to Hartnell. 'Her lawyer will be present at all times.'

'Quite the zoo out there, isn't it?' Julia Ford said after Banks had hung up. The fine lines around her eyes crinkled when she smiled. She was wearing a different suit this morning – grey with a pearl blouse – but it looked every bit as business-like. Her hair looked shiny, as if fresh from the shower, and she had applied just enough make-up to take a few years off her age.

'Yes,' Banks answered. 'Looks as if someone tipped the entire British media off about Lucy's whereabouts.'

'Are you going to let her go?'

'Soon. I want another chat first.'

Julia sighed and opened the door for him. 'Ah, well. Once more unto the breach.'

•

Hull and beyond were parts of Yorkshire Jenny hardly knew at all. On her map there was a tiny village called Kilnsea right at the southern tip of land where the Humber joined the North Sea, just before a thin strip called Spurn Head, designated as a heritage coast, stuck out into the sea like a witch's crooked, wizened finger. It looked so desolate out there that Jenny shuddered just looking at the map, feeling the ceaseless cold wind and the biting salt spray she imagined were all one would find there.

Was it named Spurn Head because someone was spurned there once, she wondered, and her ghost lingered, walking the sands and wailing in the night, or because 'spurn' was a corruption of 'sperm' and it looked a bit like a sperm wiggling out to sea? It was probably something much more prosaic, like 'peninsula' in Viking. Jenny wondered if anybody ever went there. Birders perhaps; they were crazy enough to go anywhere in search of the elusive lesser speckled yellow tree warbler, or some such creature. It didn't look as if there were any holiday resorts in the region, except perhaps Withernsea, which Banks had visited yesterday. All the hot spots were much further north:

Bridlington, Filey, Scarborough, Whitby, all the way up to Saltburn and Redcar in Teeside.

It was a fine day: windy, but sunny with only an occasional high white cloud passing over. It wasn't exactly warm – definitely light jacket weather – but then it wasn't freezing, either. Jenny seemed to be the only car on the road beyond Patrington, where she stopped briefly for a cup of coffee and a look at St Patrick's church, reputed to be one of the finest village churches in England.

It was desolate country, mostly flat farmland, green fields and the occasional flash of bright yellow rapeseed. What villages she passed through were no more than mean assemblages of bungalows and the odd row of redbrick terraces. Soon, the surrealistic landscape of the North Sea Gas Terminal, with its twisted metal pipes and storage units, came into view, and Jenny headed up the coast towards Alderthorpe.

She had been thinking about Banks quite a lot during her journey and came to the conclusion that he wasn't happy. She didn't know why. Apart from Sandra's pregnancy, which was obviously upsetting to him for any number of reasons, he had everything to be thankful for. For a start, his career was back on track, and he had an attractive young girlfriend. At least she assumed that Annie was attractive.

But perhaps it was Annie who was making Banks unhappy? He had never seemed quite certain of their relationship whenever Jenny had questioned him. She had assumed that was mostly due to his innate evasiveness when it came to personal and emotional matters – like most men – but perhaps he was genuinely confused.

Not that she could do anything. She remembered how disappointed she had felt last year when he had accepted her dinner invitation and failed to turn up, or even phone. Jenny had sat there in her most seductive, silky outfit, duck à l'orange in the oven, ready to take a risk again, and waited and waited. At last he had phoned. He'd been called to a hostage situation. Well, it was definitely a good excuse, but it didn't do much to dispel her sense of disappointment and loss. Since then, they had been more circumspect with one another, neither willing to risk making an arrangement in case it got screwed up, but still she fretted about Banks and still, she admitted to herself, she wanted him.

The flat desolate landscape went on and on. How on earth could anybody live in such a remote and backward spot? Jenny wondered. She saw the sign pointing east: 'Alderthorpe ½ mile' and set off down the narrow unpaved track hoping to hell there was no one coming the other way. Still, the landscape was so open – hardly a tree in sight – that she could easily see someone coming from a long way away.

The half-mile seemed to go on for ever, as short distances often do on country roads. Then she saw a huddle of houses ahead, and she could smell the sea through her open window, though she couldn't see it yet. When she found herself turning left on to a paved street with bungalows on one side and rows of redbrick terrace houses on the other, she realized this must be Alderthorpe. There was a small post office cum general store with a rack of newspapers fluttering in the breeze, a greengrocer's and a butcher's, a squat gospel hall and a mean-looking pub called the Lord Nelson, and that was it.

Jenny pulled up behind a blue Citroen outside the post office and when she got out of the car she thought she could see curtains twitching over the road, feel curious eyes on her back as she opened the post-office door. *No one comes here*, she imagined the people thinking. *What could she possibly want?* Jenny felt as if she had walked into one of those lost village stories, the place that time forgot, and she had the illogical sense that by walking into it, she was lost too, and all memory of her in the real world was gone. Silly fool, she told herself, but she shivered, and it wasn't cold.

The bell pinged above her head, and she found herself in the kind of shop that she guessed had ceased to exist even before she was born, where jars of barley sugar rubbed shoulders with shoelaces and patent medicines on high shelves, and birthday cards stood on a rack next to the half-inch nails and tins of evaporated milk. It smelled both musty and fruity – pear drops, Jenny thought – and the light that filtered in from the street was dim and cast strips of shadow on the sales counter. There was a small post-office wicket, and the woman standing there in a threadbare brown coat turned and stared at Jenny when she entered. The post-mistress herself peered around her customer and adjusted her glasses. They had clearly been having a good natter and were none too thrilled at being interrupted.

'Can I help you?' the postmistress asked.

'I wondered if you could tell me where the old Murray and Godwin houses are,' Jenny asked.

'Why would you be wanting to know that?'

'It's to do with a job I'm doing.'

'Newspaper reporter, are you?'

'As a matter of fact, no. I'm a forensic psychologist.'

This stopped the woman in her tracks. 'It's Spurn Lane you want. Just over the street and down the lane to the sea. Last two semis. You can't miss them. Nobody's lived there for years.'

'Do you know if any of the children still live around here?'

'I've not seen hide nor hair of any of 'em since it happened.'

'What about the teacher, Maureen Nesbitt?'

'Lives in Easington. There's no school here.'

'Thank you very much.'

As she left, she heard the customer whisper, 'Forensic psychologist? Whatever's that when it's at home?'

'Sightseer,' muttered the postmistress. 'Ghoul, just like all the rest. Anyway, you were saying about Mary Wallace's husband . . .'

Jenny wondered how they would react when the media descended en masse, which they surely would do before long. It's not often a place such as Alderthorpe sees fame more than once in a lifetime.

She crossed the High Street, still feeling as if she were being watched, and found the unpaved lane that led east to the North Sea. Though there was a chill in the wind, the cloudless sky was such a bright piercing blue that she put on her sunglasses, remembering with a flutter of anger the day she bought them on Santa Monica pier, with Randy, the two-timing bastard.

There were about five or six bungalows on each side of Spurn Lane near the high street, but about fifty yards along, there was only rough ground. Jenny could see two dirty brick semis another fifty yards beyond that. They were certainly isolated from the village, which itself was isolated enough to begin with. She imagined that once the reporters and the television cameras had gone ten years ago, the silence and loneliness and sense of grief must have been devastating for the community, the questions and accusations screaming out loud in the air. Even the residents around The Hill, part of a suburb of a large, modern city, would be struggling to understand what had happened there for years, and many of the residents would need counselling. Jenny could only imagine what Alderthorpe folk probably thought of counselling.

As she approached the houses, she became more and more aware of the salt smell of the sea breeze and realized that it was out there, only yards away beyond the low dunes and marram grass. Villages along this coast had disappeared into the sea, Jenny had read; the sandy coastline was always shifting, and maybe in ten or twenty years time Alderthorpe would have vanished under water, too. It was a spooky thought.

The houses were beyond repair. The roofs had caved in and the broken windows and doors were boarded up. Here and there, people had spray-painted graffiti: 'ROT IN HELL', 'BRING BACK HANGING' and the simple, touching, 'KATHLEEN: WE WILL NOT FORGET'. Jenny found herself oddly moved as she stood there playing the voyeur.

The gardens were overgrown with weeds and shrubs, but she could make her way through the tangled undergrowth closer to the buildings. There wasn't much to see, and the doors had been so securely boarded up that she couldn't get inside even if she wanted to. In there, she told herself, Lucy Payne and six other children had been terrorized, raped, humiliated, tormented and tortured for God knew how many years before the death of one of them – Kathleen Murray – led the authorities to the door. Now the place was just a silent ruin. Jenny felt like a bit of a fraud standing there, the way she had in the cellar of The Hill. What could she possibly do or say to make sense of the horrors that occurred here? Her science, like all the rest, was inadequate.

Even so, she stood there for some time, then she walked around the buildings, noting that the back gardens were even more overgrown than the front. An empty clothes-line hung suspended between two rusty poles in one of the gardens.

As she was leaving, Jenny almost tripped over something in the undergrowth. At first she thought it was a root, but when she bent down and pulled aside the leaves and twigs, she saw a small teddy bear. It looked so dishevelled it could have been out there for years, could even have belonged to one of the Alderthorpe Seven, though Jenny doubted it. The police or the social services would have taken everything like that away, so it had probably been left later as a sort of tribute by a local child. When she picked it up, it felt soggy, and a beetle crawled out from a rip in its back onto her hand. Jenny let out a sharp gasp, dropped the teddy bear and headed quickly back to the village. She had intended to knock on a few doors and ask about the Godwins and the Murrays, but Alderthorpe had spooked her so much that she decided instead to head for Easington to talk to Maureen Nesbitt.

•

'Right, Lucy. Shall we start?'

Banks had turned on the tape recorders and tested them. This time they were in a slightly bigger and more salubrious interview room. In addition to Lucy and Julia Ford, Banks had invited DC Jackman along, too, though it wasn't her case, mostly to get her impressions of Lucy afterwards.

'I suppose so,' Lucy said in a resigned, sulky voice. She looked tired and shaken by her night in the cell, Banks thought, even though the cells were the most modern part of the station. The duty officer said she'd asked to have the light left on all night, so she couldn't have slept much.

'I hope you were comfortable last night,' he said.

'What do you care?'

'It's not my intention to cause you discomfort, Lucy.'

'Don't worry about me. I'm fine.'

Julia Ford tapped her watch. 'Can we get on with this, Superintendent Banks?'

Banks paused, then looked at Lucy. 'Let's talk a bit more about your background, shall we?'

'What's that got to do with anything?' Julia Ford butted in.

'If you'll allow me to ask my questions, you might find out.'

'If it distresses my client—'

'*Distresses your client!* The parents of five young girls are more than distressed.'

'That's irrelevant,' said Julia. 'It's nothing to do with Lucy.'

Banks ignored the lawyer and turned back to Lucy, who seemed disinterested by the discussion. 'Will you describe the cellar at Alderthorpe for me, Lucy?'

'The cellar?'

'Yes. Don't you remember it?'

'It was just a cellar,' Lucy said. 'Dark and cold.'

'Was there anything else down there?'

'I don't know. What?'

'Black candles, incense, a pentagram, robes. Wasn't there a lot of dancing and chanting down there, Lucy?'

Lucy closed her eyes. 'I don't remember. That wasn't me. That was Linda.'

'Oh, come on, Lucy. You can do better than that. Why is it that whenever we come to something you don't want to talk about, you always conveniently lose your memory?'

'Superintendent,' Julia Ford said. 'Remember my client has suffered retrograde amnesia due to post-traumatic shock.'

'Yes, yes, I remember. Impressive words.' Banks turned back to Lucy. 'You don't remember going into the cellar at The Hill, and you don't remember the dancing and chanting in the cellar at Alderthorpe. Do you remember the cage?'

Lucy seemed to draw in on herself.

'Do you?' Banks persisted. 'The old Morrison shelter.'

'I remember it,' Lucy whispered. 'It was where they put us when we were bad.'

'How were you bad, Lucy?'

'I don't understand.'

'Why were you in the cage when the police came? You and Tom. What had you done to get yourselves put there?'

'I don't know. It was never much. You never had to do much. If you didn't clean your plate – not that there was ever much on it to clean – or if you talked back or said no when they . . . when they wanted to . . . It was easy to get locked in the cage.'

'Do you remember Kathleen Murray?'

'I remember Kathleen. She was my cousin.'

'What happened to her?'

'They killed her.'

'Who did?'

'The grown-ups.'

'Why did they kill her?'

'I don't know. They just . . . she just died . . .'

'They said your brother Tom killed her.'

'That's ridiculous. Tom wouldn't kill anybody. Tom's gentle.'

'Do you remember how it happened?'

'I wasn't there. Just one day they told us Kathleen had gone away and she wouldn't be coming back. I knew she was dead.'

'How did you know?'

'I just knew. She cried all the time, she said she was going to tell. They always said they'd kill any of us if they thought we were going to tell.'

'Kathleen was strangled, Lucy.'

'Was she?'

'Yes. Just like the girls we found in your cellar. Ligature strangulation. Remember, those yellow fibres we found under your fingernails, along with Kimberley's blood?'

'Where are you going with this, Superintendent?' Julia Ford asked.

'There are a lot of similarities between the crimes. That's all.'

'But surely the killers of Kathleen Murray are behind bars?' Julia argued. 'It's got nothing to do with Lucy.'

'She was involved.'

'She was a victim.'

'Always the victim, eh, Lucy? The victim with the bad memory. How does it feel?'

'That's enough,' said Julia.

'It feels awful,' Lucy said in a small voice.

'What?'

'You asked how it feels, to be a victim with a bad memory. It feels awful. It feels like I have no self, like I'm lost, I have no control, like I don't count. I can't even remember the *bad* things that happened to me.'

'Let me ask you once more, Lucy: did you ever help your husband to abduct a young girl?'

'No, I didn't.'

'Did you ever harm any of the girls he brought home?'

'I never knew about them, not until last week.'

'Why did you get up and go down in the cellar on that particular night? Why not on any of the previous occasions when your husband was *entertaining* a young girl in the cellar of your house?'

'I never heard anything before. He must have drugged me.'

'We found no sleeping tablets in our search of the house, nor do either of you have a prescription for any.'

'He must have got them illegally. He must have run out. That's why I woke up.'

'Where would he get them?'

'School. There's all sorts of drugs in schools.'

'Lucy, did you know that your husband was a rapist when you met him?'

'Did I . . . what?'

'You heard me.' Banks opened the file in front of him. 'By our count he had already raped four women we know of before he met you at that pub in Seacroft. Terence Payne was the Seacroft Rapist. His DNA matches that left in the victims.'

'I . . . I . . .'

'You don't know what to say?'

'No.'

'How did you meet him, Lucy? None of your friends remember seeing you talk to him in the pub that night.'

'I told you. I was on my way out. It was a big pub with lots of rooms. We went into another bar.'

'Why should you be any different, Lucy?'

'I don't know what you mean.'

'I mean why didn't he follow you out into the street and rape you like he did with the others?'

'I don't know. How should I know?'

'You've got to admit it's strange, though, isn't it?'

'I told you, I don't know. He liked me. Loved me.'

'Yet he still continued to rape other young women *after*

he'd met you.' Banks consulted his file again. 'At least two more times, according to our account. And they're only the ones who reported it. Some women don't report it, you know. Too upset or too ashamed. See, they blame themselves.' Banks thought of Annie Cabbot and what she'd been through over two years ago.

'What's that got to do with me?'

'Why didn't he rape *you*?'

Lucy gave him an unfathomable look. 'Maybe he did.'

'Don't be absurd. No woman likes being raped and she's certainly not going to marry her rapist.'

'You'd be surprised what you can get used to if you've got no choice.'

'What do you mean, no choice?'

'What I say.'

'It was your choice to marry Terry, wasn't it? Nobody forced you to.'

'That's not what I mean.'

'Then what do you mean?'

'Never mind.'

'Come on.'

'Never mind.'

Banks shuffled his papers. 'What was it, Lucy? Did he tell you about what he'd done? Did it excite you? Did he recognize a kindred spirit? Your Hindley to his Brady?'

Julia Ford shot to her feet. 'That's *enough*, Superintendent. One more remark like that and this interview's over and I'll be reporting you.'

Banks ran his hand over his close-cropped hair. It felt spiky.

Winsome picked up the questioning. '*Did* he rape you, Lucy?' she asked, in her lilting Jamaican accent. 'Did your husband rape you?'

Lucy turned to look at Winsome and seemed to Banks to be calculating how to deal with this new factor in the equation.

'Of course not. I would never have married a rapist.'

'So you didn't know about him?'

'Of course I didn't.'

'Didn't you find *anything* odd about Terry? I mean, I never knew him, but it sounds to me as if there's enough there to give a person cause for concern.'

'He could be very charming.'

'Did he do or say *nothing* to make you suspicious in all the time you were together?'

'No.'

'But, somehow, you ended up married to a man who was not only a rapist but also an abductor and murderer of young girls. How can you explain that, Lucy? You've got to admit it's highly unusual, hard to believe.'

'I can't help that. And I can't explain it. That's just how it happened.'

'Did he like to play games, sexual games?'

'Like what?'

'Did he like tying you up? Did he like to *pretend* he was raping you?'

'We didn't do anything like that.'

Winsome gave Banks a signal to take over again, and her look mirrored his feelings; they were getting nowhere and Lucy Payne was probably lying.

'Where's the camcorder?' Banks asked.

'I don't know what you're talking about.'

'We found evidence in the cellar. A camcorder had been set up at the end of the bed. I think you liked to video what you were doing to the girls.'

'I didn't do anything to them. I've told you, I didn't go

down there, except maybe the once. I know nothing about any camcorder.'

'You never saw your husband with one?'

'No.'

'He never showed you any videos?'

'Only rented or borrowed ones.'

'We think we know where he bought the camcorder, Lucy. We can check.'

'Go ahead. I never saw one, never knew about any such thing.'

Banks paused and changed tack. 'You say you didn't play sexual games, Lucy, so what made you decide to dress up and act like a prostitute?' he asked.

'What?'

'Don't you remember?'

'Yes, but that wasn't it. I mean, I didn't . . . I wasn't on the *street* or anything. Who told you that?'

'Never mind. Did you pick up a man in a hotel bar for sex?'

'What if I did? It was just a lark, a dare.'

'So you did like games.'

'This was before I knew Terry.'

'So that makes it all right?'

'I'm not saying that. It was a lark, that's all.'

'What happened?'

Lucy gave a sly smile. 'Same as happened often enough if I let myself get chatted up in a pub. Only this time I got paid two hundred pounds. Like I said, it was a lark, that's all. Are you going to arrest me for prostitution?'

'Some lark,' said Banks.

Julia Ford looked a bit perplexed by the exchange but she said nothing.

Banks knew they were still going nowhere. Hartnell was

right: they had no real evidence against Lucy beyond the extreme weirdness of her relationship with Payne and the bloodstains and clothes-line fibres. Her answers might not make a lot of sense, but unless she confessed to aiding and abetting her husband in his murders, she was in the clear. He looked at her again. The bruises had almost faded to nothing and she looked quite innocent and lovely with her pale skin and long black hair, almost like a Madonna. The only thing that made Banks persist in his belief that there was far more to events than she would ever care to admit was her eyes: black, reflective, impermeable. He got the impression that if you stared into eyes like hers for too long you'd go mad. But that wasn't evidence; that was an overactive imagination. All of a sudden, he'd had enough. Surprising all three of them, he stood up so abruptly he almost knocked over his chair, said, 'You're free to go now, Lucy. Just don't go too far,' and hurried out of the interview room.

•

Easington was a pleasant change from Alderthorpe, Jenny thought as she parked her car near the pub at the centre of the village. Though still almost as remote from civilization, it seemed at least to be connected, to be a part of things in a way that Alderthorpe didn't.

Jenny found Maureen Nesbitt's address easily enough from the barmaid and soon found herself on the doorstep facing a suspicious woman with long white hair tied back in a blue ribbon, wearing a fawn cardigan and black slacks a little too tight for someone with such ample hips and thighs.

'Who are you? What do you want?'

'I'm a psychologist,' said Jenny. 'I want to talk to you about what happened in Alderthorpe.'

Maureen Nesbitt looked up and down the street, then turned back to face Jenny. 'Are you sure you're not a reporter?'

'I'm not a reporter.'

'Because they were all over me when it happened, but I told them nothing. Scavengers.' She pulled her cardie tighter over her chest.

'I'm not a reporter,' Jenny repeated, digging deep into her handbag for some sort of identification. The best she could come up with was her university library card. At least it identified her as Dr Fuller and as a member of the staff. Maureen scrutinized the card, clearly unhappy it didn't also bear a photograph, then she finally let Jenny in. Once inside, her manner changed completely, from grand inquisitor to gracious host, insisting on brewing a fresh pot of tea. The living room was small but comfortable, with only a couple of armchairs, a mirror above the fireplace and a glass-fronted cabinet full of beautiful crystal ware. Beside one of the armchairs was a small table, and on it lay a paperback of *Great Expectations* next to a half-full cup of milky tea. Jenny sat in the other chair.

When Maureen brought through the tray, including a plate of digestive biscuits, she said, 'I do apologize for my behaviour earlier. It's just that I've learned the hard way over the years. A little notoriety can quite change your life, you know.'

'Are you still teaching?'

'No. I retired three years ago.' She tapped the paperback. 'I promised myself that when I retired I would reread all my favourite classics.' She sat down. 'We'll just let the tea mash for a few minutes, shall we? I suppose you're here about Lucy Payne?'

'You know?'

'I've tried to keep up with them all over the years. I know that Lucy – Linda, as she was back then – lived with a couple called Liversedge near Hull, and then she got a job at a bank and went to live in Leeds, where she married Terence Payne. Last I heard this lunchtime was that the police just let her go for lack of evidence.'

Even Jenny hadn't heard that yet, but then she hadn't listened to the news that day. 'How do you know all this?' she asked.

'My sister works for the social services in Hull. You won't tell, will you?'

'Cross my heart.'

'So what do you want to know?'

'What were your impressions of Lucy?'

'She was a bright girl. Very bright. But easily bored, easily distracted. She was headstrong, stubborn, and once she'd made her mind up you couldn't budge her. Of course, you have to remember that she'd gone on to the local comprehensive at the time of the arrests. I only taught junior school. She was with us until she was eleven.'

'But the others were still there?'

'Yes. All of them. It's not as if there's a lot of choice when it comes to local schools.'

'I imagine not. Anything else you can remember about Lucy?'

'Not really.'

'Did she form any close friendships outside the immediate family?'

'None of them did. That was one of the odd things. They were a mysterious group and sometimes when you saw them together it gave you a creepy feeling, as if they had their own language and an agenda you knew nothing about. Have you ever read John Wyndham?'

'No.'

'You should. He's quite good. For a science-fiction writer, that is. Believe it or not, I encouraged my pupils to read just about anything they enjoyed, so long as they read something. Anyway, Wyndham wrote a book called *The Midwich Cuckoos* about a group of strange children fathered by aliens on an unsuspecting village.'

'That sounds vaguely familiar,' Jenny said.

'Perhaps you saw the film? It was called *Village of the Damned*.'

'That's it,' said Jenny. 'That one where the teacher planted a bomb to destroy the children and had to concentrate on a brick wall so they couldn't read his thoughts?'

'Yes. Well, it wasn't quite like that with the Godwins and the Murrays, but it still gave you that sort of feeling, the way they looked at you, waited in the corridor till you'd gone by before talking again. And they always seemed to speak in whispers. Linda, I remember, was very distressed when she had to leave and go to the comprehensive before the others, but I gather from her teacher there that she quickly got used to it. She has a strong personality, that girl, despite what happened to her, and she's adaptable.'

'Did she show any unusual preoccupations?'

'What do you mean?'

'Anything particularly morbid. Death? Mutilation?'

'Not so far as I noticed. She was . . . how shall I put this . . . an early developer and rather sexually aware for a girl of her age. On average girls peak in puberty at about twelve, but Lucy was beyond prepubescence at eleven. Her breasts were developing, for example.'

'Sexually active?'

'No. Well, as we now know she was being sexually abused in the home. But, no, not in the way you're suggesting. She was just sexually *there*. It was something people noticed about her and she wasn't above playing the little coquette.'

'I see.' Jenny made a note. 'And it was Kathleen's absence that led you to call in the authorities?'

'Yes.' Maureen looked away, towards the window, but she didn't look as if she was admiring the view. 'Not my finest moment,' she said, bending to pour the tea. 'Milk and sugar?'

'Yes, please. Thank you. Why?'

'I should have done something sooner, shouldn't I? It wasn't the first time I'd had my suspicions something was terribly wrong in those households. Though I never saw any bruises or clear outward signs of abuse, the children often looked undernourished and seemed timid. Sometimes – I know this is terrible – but they smelled, as if they hadn't bathed in days. Other children would stay away from them. They'd jump if you touched them, no matter how gently. I should have known.'

'What did you do?'

'Well, I talked with the other teachers, and we all agreed there was something odd about the children's behaviour. It turned out the social services already had their concerns, too. They'd been out to the houses once before but never got past the front door. I don't know if you know, but Michael Godwin had a particularly vicious Rottweiler. Anyway, when Kathleen Murray went absent without any reasonable explanation, they decided to act. The rest is history.'

'You say you've kept track of the children,' Jenny said. 'I'd really like to talk to some of them. Will you help me?'

Maureen paused a moment. 'If you like. But I don't think you'll get much out of them.'

'Do you know where they are, how they are?'

'Not all the details, no, but I can give you a general picture.'

Jenny sipped some tea and took out her notebook. 'Okay, I'm ready.'

14

'So what do you think of Lucy Payne?' Banks asked DC Winsome Jackman as they walked along North Market Street on their way to talk to Leanne Wray's parents.

Winsome paused before answering. Banks noticed several people gawp at her as they walked. She knew she was a token minority, she had told Banks when he interviewed her, brought in to fulfil a quota demanded in the aftermath of the Stephen Lawrence case. There were to be more police officers from minorities, the ruling stated, even in communities where those minorities were, to all extents, nonexistent: like West Indians in the Yorkshire Dales. But she also told him she didn't care about the tokenism and she'd do a damn good job anyway. Banks didn't doubt her for a moment. Winsome was ACC McLaughlin's golden girl, set for accelerated promotion and all its blessings; she'd probably be a superintendent before she was thirty-five. And Banks liked her. She was easy-going, had a wicked sense of humour, and she didn't let the race thing get in the way of doing her job, even when other people tried to put it in the way. He knew nothing about her personal life except that she enjoyed both climbing and spelunking – the very thought of which gave Banks a severe case of the heebie-jeebies – and that she lived in a flat on the fringe of the Eastvale student area. Whether she had a boyfriend, or a girlfriend, Banks had no idea.

'I think she might have been protecting her husband,'

Winsome said. 'She knew, or she suspected, and she kept quiet. Maybe she didn't even admit it to herself.'

'Do you think she was involved?'

'I don't know. I don't think so. I think she was attracted to the dark side, especially the sex, but I'd pull up short of assuming she was involved. Weird, yes. But a killer . . .?'

'Remember, Kathleen Murray died of ligature strangulation,' Banks said.

'But Lucy was only twelve then.'

'Makes you think, though, doesn't it? Isn't the house just down here?'

'Yes.'

They turned off North Market Street onto a grid of narrow streets opposite the community centre, where Sandra used to work. Seeing the place and remembering the times he dropped in on her there or waited to pick her up after work to go to a play or a film made Banks feel a pang of loss, but it passed. Sandra was gone now; far, far away from the wife he used to have.

They found the house, not at all far from the Old Ship – maybe ten or fifteen minutes' walk, and most of it along the busy, well-lit stretch of North Market Street, with its shops and pubs – and Banks knocked at the front door.

The first thing that assailed his senses as Christopher Wray opened the door was the smell of fresh paint. When Banks and Winsome stepped inside, he saw why. The Wrays were redecorating. All the wallpaper in the hallway had been stripped, and Mr Wray was painting the living-room ceiling cream. The furniture was covered with sheets.

'I'm sorry for the mess,' he apologized. 'Shall we go in the kitchen? Have you found Leanne yet?'

'No, not yet,' said Banks.

They followed him through to the small kitchen, where

he put the kettle on without even asking if they wanted a cup of tea. They all sat at the small kitchen table, and for the short time it took the kettle to boil, Mr Wray chatted on about the redecoration as if determined to avoid the real subject of their visit. Finally, tea made and poured, Banks decided it was time to steer things around to the subject of Leanne.

'I must say,' he began, 'that we're at a bit of a loss.'

'Oh?'

'As you know, our men have been working at the Payne house for days now. They've recovered six bodies, four of which have been identified, but none of the six is your daughter's. They're running out of places to look.'

'Does that mean Leanne might still be alive?' Wray asked, a gleam of hope in his eyes.

'It's possible,' Banks admitted. 'Though I've got to say, after all this time without contact, especially given the nationwide appeals on TV and in the press, I wouldn't hold out a lot of hope.'

'Then . . . what?'

'That's what we'd like to find out.'

'I don't see how I can help you.'

'Perhaps you can't,' Banks said, 'but the only thing to do when a case is stalled like this is to go right back to first principles. We've got to go over the ground we covered before and hope we see it from a new perspective this time.'

Wray's wife, Victoria, appeared in the doorway and looked puzzled to see Banks and Winsome enjoying a chat and a cup of tea with her husband. Wray jumped up. 'I thought you were resting, dear,' he said, giving her a peck on the cheek.

Victoria wiped the sleep from her eyes, though she looked to Banks as if she had spent at least a few minutes putting on her face before coming down. Her skirt and blouse were pure Harvey Nichols and her accent was what she thought sounded like upper class, though he could hear traces of Birmingham in it. She was an attractive woman in her early thirties, with a slim figure and a full head of shiny, natural brown hair that hung over her shoulders. She had a slightly retroussé nose, arched eyebrows and a small mouth, but the effect of the whole was rather more successful than one might imagine from the separate parts. Wray himself was about forty and pretty much medium in whatever category you might describe him, except for the chin, which slid down towards his throat before it even got started. They were an odd couple, Banks remembered thinking from the first time he had met them: he was a rather basic, down-to-earth bus driver and she was an affected social climber. What had drawn them together in the first place Banks had no idea, except perhaps that people who have suffered a great loss, as Christopher Wray had, might not necessarily be the best judges of their next move.

Victoria stretched, sat down and poured herself a cup of tea.

'How are you feeling?' her husband asked.

'Not bad.'

'You know you've got to be careful, in your condition. The doctor said so.'

'I know. I know.' She squeezed his hand. 'I'll be careful.'

'What condition's that?' Banks asked.

'My wife's expecting a baby, Superintendent.' Wray beamed.

Banks looked at Victoria. 'Congratulations,' he said.

She inclined her head in a queenly manner. Banks could hardly imagine Victoria Wray going through anything as messy and painful as childbirth, but life was full of surprises.

'How long?' he asked.

She patted her stomach. 'Almost four months.'

'So you were pregnant when Leanne went missing?'

'Yes. As a matter of fact, I'd just found out that morning.'

'What did Leanne think of it?'

Victoria looked down into her teacup. 'Leanne could be wilful and moody, Superintendent,' she said. 'She certainly wasn't quite as ecstatic as we hoped she would be.'

'Now, come on, love, that's not fair,' said Mr Wray. 'She'd have got used to it in time. I'm certain she would.'

Banks thought about the situation: Leanne's mother dies a slow and painful death from cancer. Shortly afterwards, her father remarries – to a woman Leanne clearly can't stand. Not long after that, the stepmother announces she's pregnant. You didn't need to be a psychologist to see that there was a situation ripe for disaster. It was a bit close to the bone for Banks, too, though he had hardly been in Leanne's position. Still, whether it's your father having a baby with your new stepmother or your estranged wife having one with the bearded Sean, the resulting feelings could be similar, perhaps even more intense in Leanne's case, given her age and her grief over her mother.

'So she wasn't happy with the news?'

'Not really,' Mr Wray admitted. 'But it takes time to get used to things like that.'

'You have to be at least willing to try first,' said Victoria. 'Leanne's too selfish for that.'

'Leanne was willing,' Mr Wray insisted.

'When did you tell her?' Banks asked.

'The morning of the day she disappeared.'

He sighed. 'Why didn't you tell us this when we interviewed you after Leanne's disappearance?'

Mr Wray looked surprised. 'Nobody asked. It didn't seem important. I mean it was a private family matter.'

'Besides,' said Victoria, 'it's bad luck to tell strangers until after three months.'

Were they really so thick or were they just playing at it? Banks wondered. Trying to keep his tone as calm and neutral as possible, reminding himself that they were the parents of a missing girl, he asked, 'What did she say?'

The Wrays looked at one another. 'Say? Nothing, really, did she, dear?' said Mr Wray.

'Acted up, is what she did,' said Victoria.

'Was she angry?'

'I suppose so,' said Mr Wray.

'Angry enough to punish you?'

'What do you mean?'

'Listen, Mr Wray,' Banks said, 'when you told us that Leanne was missing and we couldn't find her within a day or two, we were all of us willing to think the worst. Now, what you've just told us puts a different light on things.'

'It does?'

'If she was angry at you over her stepmother's pregnancy, then she might easily have run away to strike back.'

'But Leanne wouldn't run away,' Mr Wray said, slack-jawed. 'She loved me.'

'Maybe that's the problem,' Banks said. He didn't know if it was called the Electra complex, but he was thinking of the female version of the Oedipus complex: girl loves her father, then her mother dies, but instead of devoting himself to her, the father finds a new woman, and to make things worse, he makes her pregnant, threatening the entire stability of their relationship. He could easily see Leanne doing a bunk under circumstances like that. But the problem still remained that she would have to be a very uncaring child indeed not to let them know she was still alive after all the hue and cry about the missing girls, and she wouldn't have got far without her money and her inhaler.

'I think she'd probably be capable of it,' said Victoria. 'She could be cruel. Remember that time when she put castor oil in the coffee, the evening of my first book club meeting? Caroline Opley was sick all over her Margaret Atwood.'

'But that was early days, love,' Mr Wray protested. 'It all took a bit of getting used to for her.'

'I know. I'm only saying. And she didn't value things as she should have. She lost that silver—'

'Do you think she might have at least been angry enough to disobey her curfew?' Banks asked.

'Certainly,' answered Victoria without missing a beat. 'It's that boy you should be talking to. That Ian Scott. He's a drug dealer, you know.'

'Did Leanne take drugs?'

'Not to our knowledge,' said Mr Wray.

'But she could have done, Chris,' his wife went on. 'She obviously didn't tell us everything, did she? Who knows what she got up to when she was with those sorts of people.'

Christopher Wray put his hand over his wife's. 'Don't get excited, love. Remember what the doctor said.'

'I know.' Victoria stood up. She swayed a little. 'I think I need to go and lie down again for a while,' she said. 'But you mark my words, Superintendent, that's the one you should be looking at – Ian Scott. He's no good.'

'Thank you,' said Banks. 'I'll bear that in mind.'

When she'd gone, the silence stretched for a while. 'Is there anything else you can tell us?' Banks asked.

'No. No. I'm sure she wouldn't do . . . what you say. I'm sure something must have happened to her.'

'Why did you wait until morning to call the police? Had she done that sort of thing before?'

'Never. I would have told you if I thought that.'

'So why did you wait?'

'I wanted to call earlier.'

'Come on, Mr Wray,' said Winsome, touching his arm gently. 'You can tell us.'

He looked at her, his eyes beseeching, seeking forgiveness. 'I would have called the police, honest I would,' he said. 'She had never stayed out all night before.'

'But you'd had an argument, hadn't you?' Banks suggested. 'When she reacted badly to the news of your wife's pregnancy.'

'She asked me how could I . . . so soon after . . . after her mother. She was upset, crying, saying terrible things about Victoria, things she didn't mean, but . . . Victoria told her to get out if she wanted, and said she could stay out.'

'Why didn't you tell us this at the time?' Banks asked, though he knew the answer: embarrassment, that great social fear – something Victoria Wray would certainly be sensitive to – and not wanting the police involved in your private family arguments. The only way they had found out about the tension between Victoria and Leanne in the first place was through Leanne's friends, and Leanne clearly hadn't had time or chance to tell them about Victoria's pregnancy. Victoria Wray was the kind of woman, Banks thought, who would make the police use the tradesman's entrance, if they had a tradesman's entrance – and the fact that they didn't was probably an unbearable thorn in her side.

There were tears in Mr Wray's eyes. 'I couldn't,' he said. 'I just couldn't. We thought it was as you said, that perhaps she had stayed out all night to spite us, to demonstrate her anger. But no matter what, Superintendent, Leanne isn't a bad girl. She would have come back in the morning. I'm certain of that.'

Banks stood up. 'May we have another look at her room, Mr Wray? There may be something we missed.'

Wray looked puzzled. 'Yes, of course. But . . . I mean . . . it's been redone. There's nothing there.'

'You redecorated Leanne's room?' Winsome said.

He looked at her. 'Yes. We couldn't stand it with her gone. The memories. And now, with the new baby on the way . . .'

'What about her clothes?' Winsome asked.

'We gave them to the Oxfam shop.'

'Her books, belongings?'

'Them, too.'

Winsome shook her head. Banks asked, 'May we have a peek, anyway?'

They went upstairs. Wray was right. Not an object remained that indicated the room had ever belonged to a teenager like Leanne Wray. The tiny dresser, bedside drawers and matching wardrobe were all gone, as was her bed with the quilt bedspread, little bookcase, the few dolls left over from her childhood. Even the carpet was gone and the pop star posters had been ripped off the walls. Nothing remained. Banks could hardly believe his eyes. He could understand how people want to escape unpleasant memories, don't like being reminded of someone they've loved and lost, but all *this* just over a month after their daughter's disappearance, and without her body having been found?

'Thank you,' he said, indicating for Winsome to follow him down the stairs.

'Isn't that weird?' she said when they'd got outside. 'Makes you think, doesn't it?'

'Think what, Winsome?'

'That maybe Leanne *did* go home that night. And that maybe when they heard we were digging up the Paynes's garden, Mr Wray decided it was time for redecoration.'

'Hmm,' said Banks. 'Maybe you're right, or maybe people just have different ways of showing their grief. Either way, I think we'll be looking a bit more closely at the Wrays over the next few days. You can start by talking to their neighbours, see if they've seen or heard anything unusual.'

•

After her chat with Maureen Nesbitt, Jenny decided to visit Spurn Head itself before heading for home. Maybe a good long walk would help her think things over, blow the cobwebs away. Maybe it would also help her get rid of the eerie feeling she had had since Alderthorpe that she was being watched or followed. She couldn't explain it, but every time she turned suddenly to look over her shoulder, she *felt* rather than saw something slip into the shadows. It was irritating because she couldn't quite grasp whether she was being paranoid or whether it was a case of just because she was paranoid it didn't mean someone *wasn't* following her.

She was still feeling it.

Jenny paid her entrance fee and drove slowly along the narrow track to the car park, noticing an old lighthouse, half under water, and guessing that the sands had shifted since it was built and left it stranded there.

Jenny walked down to the beach. The place wasn't quite as desolate as she had imagined it to be. Just ahead, on a platform a little way out to sea, attached to the mainland by a narrow wooden bridge, were a dock and control centre for the Humber pilots, who guided the big tankers in from the

North Sea. Behind her stood the new lighthouse and a number of houses. Across the estuary, Jenny could see the docks and cranes of Grimsby and Immingham. Though the sun was shining, there was quite a breeze and Jenny felt the chill as she walked the sands around the point. The sea was an odd combination of colours – purple, brown, lavender, everything but blue, even in the sun.

There weren't many people around. Most of those who visited the area were serious birders, and the place was a protected wildlife sanctuary. Even so, Jenny saw a couple or two walking hand in hand, and one family with two small children. As she walked, she still couldn't shake off the feeling of being followed.

When the first tanker came around the head, it took her breath away. Because of the sharp curve, the huge shape seemed to appear there suddenly, moving very fast, and it filled her field of vision for a few moments, then one of the pilot boats near by guided it over the estuary towards Immingham docks. Another tanker followed only moments later.

As Jenny stood on the sand looking out over the broad waters, she thought of what Maureen Nesbitt had told her about the Alderthorpe Seven.

Tom Godwin, Lucy's younger brother, had stayed with his foster parents until he was eighteen, like Lucy, then he had gone to live with distant relatives in Australia, all thoroughly checked out by the social services, and he now worked on their sheep farm in New South Wales. By all accounts, Tom was a sturdy, quiet sort of boy, given to long walks alone and a sort of shyness that made him stutter in front of strangers. Often he woke up screaming from nightmares he couldn't remember.

Laura, Lucy's sister, was living in Edinburgh, where she

was studying medicine at the university, hoping to become a psychiatrist. Maureen said Laura was well adjusted, on the whole, after years of therapy, but there was still a timidity and reticence about her that might make it hard for her to face some of the more human challenges of her chosen profession. There was no doubt she was a brilliant and skilled pupil, but whether she could handle the daily pressures of psychiatry was another matter.

Of the three surviving Murray children, Susan had committed suicide, tragically, at the age of thirteen. Dianne was in a sort of halfway house for the mentally disturbed, suffering from severe sleep disorders and terrifying hallucinations. Keith, like Laura, was also a student, though Maureen reckoned he would be about graduation age by now. He had gone to the University of Durham to study history and English. He was still seeing a psychiatrist regularly and suffered from bouts of depression and anxiety attacks, especially in confined places, but he managed to function and do well in his studies.

And that was it: the sad legacy of Alderthorpe. Such blighted lives.

Jenny wondered if Banks wanted her to continue now that he'd let Lucy go. Maureen Nesbitt had said her best bets were clearly Keith Murray and Laura Godwin, and as Keith lived closer to Eastvale, she decided she would try to reach him first. But was there any more point to it all? She had to admit that she hadn't found any psychological evidence that significantly strengthened the case against Lucy. She felt every bit as inadequate as many officers on the task force thought all offender profilers were anyway.

Lucy *could* have sustained the kind of psychological damage that made her a compliant victim of Terence Payne's, but there again, she might not have. Different people subjected to the same horrors often go in completely different directions. Perhaps Lucy was truly a strong personality, strong enough to put the past behind her and get on with life. Jenny doubted that *anyone* had the strength to avoid at least some kind of psychological fallout from the events in Alderthorpe, but it was possible to heal, at least partially, over time, and to function on some level, as Tom, Laura and Keith had also demonstrated. They might be the walking wounded, but at least they were still walking.

When Jenny had covered half the circle of the head, she cut back through the long grass to the car park and set off down the narrow track. As she went, she noticed a blue Citroen in her rearview mirror and felt certain that she had seen it somewhere before. Telling herself to stop being so paranoid, she left the head and drove towards Patrington. When she'd got closer to the edges of Hull, she called Banks on her mobile.

He answered on the third ring. 'Jenny, where are you?'

'Hull. On my way home.'

'Find out anything interesting?'

'Plenty, but I'm not sure that it gets us any further. I'll try to put it all together into some sort of profile, if you want.'

'Please.'

'I just heard you had to let Lucy Payne go.'

'That's right. We got her out of a side exit without too much fuss, and her lawyer drove her straight to Hull. They did some shopping in the city centre, then Julia Ford, the lawyer, dropped Lucy off at the Liversedges'. They welcomed her with open arms.'

'That's where she is now?'

'Far as I know. The local police are keeping an eye on her for us. Where else can she go?'

'Where, indeed?' said Jenny. 'Does this mean it's over?'

'What?'

'My job.'

'No,' said Banks. 'Nothing's over yet.'

After Jenny had hung up, she checked her rearview mirror again. The blue Citroen was keeping its distance, allowing three or four other cars between them, but there was no doubt it was still back there on her tail.

•

'Annie, have you ever thought of having children?'

Banks felt Annie tense beside him in bed. They had just made love and were basking in the afterglow, the gentle rushing of the falls outside, the occasional night animal calling from the woods and Van Morrison's *Astral Weeks* drifting up from the stereo downstairs.

'I don't mean . . . well, not now. I mean, not you and me. But ever?'

Annie lay still and silent for a while. He felt her relax a little and stir against him. Finally, she said, 'Why do you ask?'

'I don't know. It's been on my mind. This case, the poor devils in the Murray and Godwin families, all the missing girls, not much more than kids, really. And the Wrays, her being pregnant.' And Sandra, he thought, but he hadn't told Annie about that yet.

'I can't say as I have,' Annie answered.

'Never?'

'Maybe I got short changed when it came to handing out the maternal instinct, I don't know. Or maybe it's to do with my own past. Anyway, it never came up.'

'Your past?'

'Ray. The commune. My mother dying so young.'

'But you said you were happy enough.'

'I was.' Annie sat up and reached for the glass of wine she had put on the bedside table. Her small breasts glowed in the dim light, smooth skin sloping down to the dark brown aureoles, slightly upturned where the nipples rose.

'Then why?'

'Good Lord, Alan, surely it's not every woman's duty in life to reproduce or to analyse why she doesn't want to. I'm not a freak, you know.'

'I know. Sorry.' Banks sipped some of his wine, lay back against the pillows. 'It's just . . . well, I had a bit of a shock the other day, that's all.'

'What?'

'Sandra.'

'What about her?'

'She's pregnant.' There, he'd done it. He didn't know why it should have been so difficult, or why he had the sharp, sudden feeling that he would have been wiser to have kept his mouth closed. He also wondered why he had told Jenny straight away but delayed so long before telling Annie. Partly it was because Jenny *knew* Sandra, of course, but there was more to it than that. Annie didn't seem to like the intimacy implied by details of Banks's life, and she had sometimes made him feel that sharing any part of his past was a burden to her. But he couldn't seem to help himself. Since splitting up with Sandra, he had become far more introspective and examined his life much more closely. He saw little point in being with someone if he couldn't share some of that.

At first, Annie said nothing, then she asked, 'Why didn't you tell me before?'

'I don't know.'

'How did you hear the news?'

'From Tracy, when we went to lunch in Leeds.'

'So Sandra didn't tell you herself?'

'You know as well as I do we don't communicate much.'

'Still, I would've thought . . . something like this.'

Banks scratched his cheek. 'Well, it just goes to show, doesn't it?'

Annie sipped more wine. 'Show what?'

'How far apart we've grown.'

'You seem upset by this, Alan.'

'Not really. Not *upset* so much as . . .'

'Disturbed?'

'Perhaps.'

'Why?'

'Just the thought of it. Of Tracy and Brian having a little brother or sister. Of . . .'

'Of what?'

'I was just thinking,' Banks said, turning towards her. 'I mean, it's something I haven't thought about in years, denied it, I suppose, but this has brought it all back.'

'All what back?'

'The miscarriage.'

Annie froze for a moment, then said, 'Sandra had a miscarriage?'

'Yes.'

'When was that?'

'Oh, years ago, when we were living in London. The kids were small, too small to understand.'

'What happened?'

'I was working undercover at the time. Drugs squad. You know what it's like, away for weeks at a time, can't contact your family. It was two days before my boss let *me* know.'

Annie nodded. Banks knew that she understood about the pressures and stresses of undercover work first hand; a knowledge of the job and its effects was one of the things they had in common. 'How did it happen?'

'Who knows? The kids were at school. She started bleeding. Thank God we had a helpful neighbour, or who knows what might have happened.'

'And you blame yourself for not being there?'

'She could have died, Annie. And we lost the baby. Everything might have gone just fine if I'd been there like any other father-to-be, helping out around the place. But Sandra had to do everything, for crying out loud, all the lifting, shopping, odd jobs, fetching and carrying. She was replacing a light bulb when she first started to feel funny. She could have fallen and broken her neck.' Banks reached for a cigarette. He didn't usually indulge in the 'one after' for Annie's sake, but this time he felt like it. He still asked, 'Is it okay?'

'Go ahead. I don't mind.' Annie sipped more wine. 'But thanks for asking. You were saying?'

Banks lit up and the smoke drifted away towards the half-open window. 'Guilt. Yes. But more than that.'

'What do you mean?'

'I was working drugs, like I said, spending most of my time on the streets or in filthy squats trying to get a lead to the big guys from their victims. Kids, for the most part, runaways, stoned, high, tripping, zonked out, whatever you care to call it. Some of them as young as ten or eleven. Half of them couldn't even tell you their own names. Or wouldn't. I don't know if you remember, but it was around the time the AIDS scare was growing. Nobody new for sure yet how bad it was, but there was a lot of scare-mongering. And everyone knew you got it through blood, from unprotected sex – mostly anal sex – and through sharing needles. Thing was, you lived in fear. You just didn't know if some small-time dealer was going to lunge at you with a dirty needle, or if some junkie's drool on your hand could give you AIDS.'

'I do know what you mean, Alan, though it was a bit before my time as a copper. But I'm not following. What has it got to do with Sandra's miscarriage?'

Banks sucked in some smoke, felt it burn on the way down and thought he ought to try stopping again. 'Probably nothing, but I'm just trying to give you some sense of the life I was living. I was in my early thirties, with a wife and two kids, another on the way, and I was spending my life in squalor, hanging out with scum. My own kids probably wouldn't have recognized me if they'd seen me in the street. The kids I saw were either dead or dying. I was a cop, not a social worker. I mean, I tried sometimes, you know, if I thought there was a chance a kid might listen, give up the life and go home, but that wasn't my job. I was there to get information and to track down the big players.'

'And?'

'Well, it's just that it has an effect on you, that's all. It changes you, warps you, alters your attitudes. You start out thinking you're an ordinary decent family man just doing a tough job, and you end up not really knowing what you are. Anyway, my first thought, when I heard Sandra was okay but that she'd had a miscarriage . . . Know what my first feeling was?'

'Relief?' said Annie.

Banks stared at her. 'What made you say that?'

She gave him a small smile. 'Common sense. It's what I'd feel – I mean if I'd been in *your* boots.'

Banks stubbed out the cigarette. He felt somehow deflated that his big revelation had seemed so obvious to Annie. He swirled some red wine around in his mouth to wash away the taste of smoke. Van Morrison was well into 'Madame George', riffing on the words. A cat howled in the woods, maybe the one that came for milk sometimes. 'Anyway,' he went on, 'that's what I felt: relief. And of course I felt guilty. Not for just not being there, but for being almost glad it happened. And relieved that we wouldn't have to go through it all again. The dirty nappies, the lack of sleep – not that I was getting much sleep anyway – the extra responsibility. Here was one life I didn't have to protect. Here was one extra responsibility I could easily live without.'

'It's not such an uncommon feeling, you know,' said Annie. 'It's not so terrible, either. It doesn't make you a monster.'

'I felt like one.'

'That's because you take too much on yourself. You always do. You're not responsible for all the world's ills and sins, not even a fraction of them. So Alan Banks is human; he isn't perfect. So he feels relief when he thinks he should feel grief. Do you think you're the only one that's happened to?'

'I don't know. I haven't asked anyone else.'

'Well, you're not. You just have to learn to live with your imperfections.'

'Like you do?'

Annie smiled and flicked a little wine at him. Luckily she was drinking white. 'What imperfections, you cheeky bastard?'

'Anyway, after that we decided no more kids and we never talked about it again.'

'But you've carried the guilt around ever since.'

'Yes, I suppose so. I mean, I don't think about it very

often, but this brought it all back. And do you know what else?'

'What?'

'I loved the job more. I never for a moment thought of giving it all up and becoming a used car salesman.'

Annie laughed. 'Just as well. I can't imagine you as the used car salesman type.'

'Or something else. Something with regular hours, less chance of catching AIDS.'

Annie reached out and stroked his cheek. 'Poor Alan,' she said, snuggling closer. 'Why don't you just try to put it all out of your mind. Just put everything out of your mind, everything except the moment, me, the music, the here and now.'

Van was getting into the meandering, sensuous 'Ballerina' and Banks felt Annie's lips, soft and moist, running over his chest, down his stomach, lingering, and he managed to do as she said when she reached her destination, but even as he gave himself up to the sensation of the moment, he still couldn't quite get the thought of dead babies out of his mind.

•

Maggie checked the locks and the windows for the second time before going to bed that Saturday night, and only when she was satisfied that all was secure did she take a glass of warm milk upstairs with her. She had hardly got halfway up when the telephone rang. At first, she wasn't going to answer it. Not at eleven o'clock on a Saturday night. It was probably a wrong number anyway. But curiosity got the better of her. She knew that the police had been forced to let Lucy go that morning, so it might be her, looking for help.

It wasn't. It was Bill. Maggie's heart started to beat fast, and she felt the room closing in on her.

'You're creating quite a stir over there, aren't you?' he said. 'Heroine and champion of battered wives everywhere. Or is that championess?'

Maggie felt herself shrinking, shrivelling, her heart squeezing into her throat. All her bravado, her *empowerment*, withered and died. She could hardly talk, hardly breathe. 'What do you want?' she whispered. 'How did you find out?'

'You underestimate your celebrity. You're not only in the *Globe* and the *Post*, you're in the *Sun* and the *Star*, too. Even a picture in the *Sun*, though it's not a very good one, unless you've changed a hell of a lot. They've been giving quite a bit of coverage to the "Chameleon" case, as they call it, comparing it to Bernardo and Homolka, naturally, and you seem to be caught right up in the thick of it.'

'What do you want?'

'Want? Me? Nothing.'

'How did you find me?'

'After the newspaper stories, it wasn't difficult. You had an old address book you forgot to take with you. Your friends were in it. Thirty-two, The Hill, Leeds. Am I right?'

'What do you want with me?'

'Nothing. Not at the moment, anyway. I just wanted to let you know that I know where you are, and I'm thinking of you. It must have been very interesting living across the street from a killer. What's Karla like?'

'It's Lucy. Leave me alone.'

'That's not very nice. We were married once, remember.'

'How could I forget?'

Bill laughed. 'Anyway, mustn't run up the firm's phone bill too much. I've been working very hard lately, and even my boss thinks I need a holiday. Just thought I'd let you know I might be taking a trip over to England soon. I don't know when. Might be next week, might be next month. But I think it'd be nice if we could get together for dinner or something, don't you?'

'You're sick,' Maggie said, and heard Bill chuckling as she hung up.

15

Banks had always thought that Sunday morning was a good time to put a little pressure on an unsuspecting villain. Sunday afternoon was good, too, after the papers, the pub and the roast beef and Yorkshire pud have put him in a good mood and he's stretched out in the armchair, newspaper over his head, enjoying a little snooze. But on Sunday morning, if they weren't particularly religious, people were either relaxed and all set to enjoy a day off, or they were hungover. Either way made for a good chat.

Ian Scott was definitely hungover.

His oily black hair stood in spikes on top and lay flat at the sides, plastered to his skull where he had lain on the pillow. One side of his pasty face was etched with crease marks. His eyes were bloodshot and he wore only a grubby vest and underpants.

'Can I come in, Ian?' said Banks, pushing gently past him before he got an answer. 'Won't take long.'

The flat reeked of last night's marijuana smoke and stale beer. Roaches still lay scattered in the ashtrays. Banks went over and opened the window as wide as it would go. 'Shame on you, Ian,' he said. 'A lovely spring morning like this, you ought to be out walking down by the river or having a crack at Fremlington Edge.'

'Bollocks,' said Ian, scratching those very items as he spoke.

Sarah Francis stumbled in from the bedroom, holding

her tousled hair back from her face and squinting through sleep-gummed eyes. She was wearing a white T-shirt with Donald Duck on the front, and nothing else. The T-shirt only came down to her hips.

'Shit,' she said, covering herself with her hands as best she could and dashing back into the bedroom.

'Enjoy the free show?' said Ian.

'Not particularly.' Banks tossed a heap of clothes from the chair nearest the window and sat down. Ian turned on the stereo, too loud, and Banks got up and turned it off. Ian sat down and sulked and Sarah came back in wearing a pair of jeans. 'You could have bloody warned me,' she grumbled to Ian.

'Shut up, you silly cunt,' he said.

Now Sarah sat down and sulked, too.

'Okay,' said Banks. 'Are we all comfortable? Can I begin?'

'I don't know what you want with us again,' said Ian. 'We told you everything that happened.'

'Well, it won't do any harm to go over it again, will it?'

Ian groaned. 'I don't feel well. I feel sick.'

'You should treat your body with more respect,' said Banks. 'It's a temple.'

'What do you want to know? Get it over with.'

'First off, I'm puzzled by something.'

'Well, you're the Sherlock, I'm sure you can work it out.'

'I'm puzzled by why you haven't asked me about Leanne.'

'What do you mean?'

'I'd hardly be back here interrupting your Sunday morning, would I, if Leanne had turned up dead and buried in a serial killer's garden?'

'What are you saying? Speak English.'

Sarah had curled herself into a foetal position in the other armchair and was watching the exchange intently.

'What I'm saying, Ian, is that you didn't ask about Leanne. That concerns me. Don't you care about her?'

'She was a mate, that's all. But it's nothing to do with us. We don't know what happened to her. Besides, I'd've got round to it eventually. My brain's not working properly yet.'

'Does it ever? Anyway, I'm beginning to think you do.'

'Do what?'

'Know something about what happened to Leanne.'

'That's rubbish.'

'Is it, really? Let's back up a bit. First off, we're pretty certain now that Leanne Wray wasn't one of the Chameleon's victims, as we had first thought.'

'Your mistake, isn't it?' said Ian. 'Don't come looking to us to bail you out.'

'Now, if that's not the case, then it stands to reason that something else happened to her.'

'You don't need to be a Sherlock to figure that one out.'

'Which, discounting the possibility of *another* stranger killing her, leaves three possibilities.'

'Oh, yeah? And what are those?'

Banks counted off on his fingers. 'One, that she ran away from home. Two, that she did go home on time and her parents did something to her. And three, the main reason I'm here, that she didn't, in fact, go home after you left the Old Ship. That the three of you stayed together and *you* did something to her.'

Ian Scott showed no expression but scorn as he listened, and Sarah started sucking on her thumb. 'We told you what happened,' Ian said. 'We told you what we did.'

'Yes,' said Banks. 'But the Riverboat was so busy the people we talked to were very vague about seeing you. They certainly weren't sure about the time and weren't even sure it was that Friday night.'

'But you've got the CCTV. For fuck's sake, what's Big Brother watching for if you can't believe what you see?'

'Oh, we believe what we see all right,' said Banks. 'But all we see is you, Sarah here and Mick Blair entering the Bar None shortly after half past twelve.'

'Well, there's no point going earlier. Things don't start to warm up till after midnight.'

'Yes, Ian, but that leaves over two hours unaccounted for. A lot can happen in two hours.'

'How was I to know I'd have to account for my every minute?'

'Two hours.'

'I told you. We walked around town a bit, dropped in at the Riverboat, then went to the Bar None. I don't know what fucking time it was.'

'Sarah?'

Sarah took her thumb from her mouth. 'What he says.'

'Is that how it usually goes?' Banks asked. 'What Ian says. Haven't you got a mind of your own?'

'What he says. We went to the Riverboat then to the Bar None. Leanne left us just before half past ten outside the Old Ship. We don't know what happened to her after that.'

'And Mick Blair went with you?'

'Yeah.'

'How did Leanne seem that night, Sarah?'

'Uh?'

'What sort of mood was she in?'

'All right, I suppose.'

'She wasn't upset about anything?'

'No. We were having a good time.'

'Leanne didn't confide anything in you?'

'Like what?'

'Oh, I don't know. Some problem with her stepmother, perhaps?'

'She was always having problems with that stuck-up bitch. I was sick of hearing about them.'

'Did she ever talk about running off?'

'Not to me. Not that I remember. Ian?'

'Nah. She just whined about the old cow, that's all. She hadn't the bottle to run away. If I was looking at somebody for it, I'd look at the stepmother first.'

'Somebody for what?'

'You know. If you think someone did something to Leanne, like.'

'I see. What was the idea that excited you all before you left the Old Ship?'

'I don't know what you mean,' said Ian.

'Oh, come on. We know you seemed excited by something you were going to do. What was it? Did it include Leanne?'

'We talked about going to the Bar None, but Leanne knew she couldn't come with us.'

'That's all?'

'What else could there be?'

'She didn't give you any hint that she might not be going straight home?'

'No.'

'Or that she might run off, teach her stepmother a lesson?'

'Dunno. Who can tell what's in a bitch's mind when it comes right down to it, hey?'

'Tut-tut, such language. You've been listening to too much hip-hop, Ian,' said Banks, standing to leave. 'Nice choice of partner, Sarah,' he said on his way out, noticing that Sarah Francis looked distinctly put out and, more to the point, even a little frightened. That might come in useful before too long, he thought.

•

'I just had to get out of the flat, that's all,' said Janet Taylor. 'I mean, I didn't want to drag you halfway across Yorkshire.'

'That's all right,' said Annie, with a smile. 'I don't live that far away. Besides, I like it here.'

Here was a rambling old pub on the edge of the moorland above Wensleydale, not far from Banks's cottage, with a solid reputation for Sunday lunch. Janet's call had come shortly after ten o'clock that morning, just as Annie was having a nap to make up for her lack of sleep at Banks's place. Their conversation had bothered her, kept her awake well into the small hours; she didn't like talking about babies.

Trust Banks to hit a nerve. What she also didn't like and didn't seem able to tell him about these personal revelations of his was that they pushed her into examining her own past and her own feelings far more than she felt ready to do right now. She wished he would just lighten up and take it easy.

Anyway, an open-air lunch was just the ticket. The air was pure, and there wasn't a cloud in the sky. From where they sat she could see the lush green dalesides criss-crossed with drystone walls, sheep wandering all over, baaing like crazy if any ramblers passed by. Down in the valley bottom, the river meandered and a group of cottages huddled around a village green, the square-towered church a little to one side, grey limestone bright in the midday sun. She thought she could see the tiny silhouettes of four people walking along the top of the high limestone scar over the dale. Christ, it would be good to be up there, all alone, not a care in the world.

But if the setting was ideal, she might have chosen a different companion. Despite the change of environment, Janet seemed distracted, forever flicking back the lock of hair that fell over her tired brown eyes. There was an unhealthy pallor about her that Annie guessed would take more than a lunch on the moors to dispel. Already Janet was on her second pint of lager and lime, and Annie had to bite her tongue not to say something about drink-driving. She was on her first half of bitter, might have another half, then coffee after lunch. Annie, who was a vegetarian, had ordered quiche and a salad, but she was pleased to see that Janet had ordered roast lamb; she looked as if she needed some meat on her bones.

'How are you doing?' Annie asked.

Janet laughed. 'Oh, about as well as can be expected.' She rubbed her forehead. 'I still can't get the sleep thing sorted out. You know, I keep replaying it, but I'm not sure if I'm seeing it the way it really happened.'

'What do you mean?'

'Well, in the replays I see his face.'

'Terry Payne's?'

'Yes, all twisted and contorted. Fearsome. But I don't think I remember seeing him clearly at the time. My mind must be filling in details.'

'Possibly.' Annie thought of her own ordeal, the rape carried out by three colleagues after celebrating her passing her sergeant's boards. At the time, she could have sworn she would remember every grunt and groan, every obscene facial expression and every sensation of him – the one who actually succeeded in penetrating her while the others held her down – forcing himself inside her as she struggled, tearing at her clothes, every drop of sweat that dripped from his face onto her skin, but she was surprised to find that much of it had faded, and it wasn't a memory she felt compelled to rerun for herself night after night. Perhaps she was tougher than she thought, or maybe she was compartmentalizing it, as someone had once told her she did, shutting out the pain and humiliation.

'You've changed your mind about the statement, then?' Annie asked. They were sitting far enough away that they couldn't be overheard if they spoke quietly. Not that any of the other diners looked as if they wanted to eavesdrop; they were all family groups talking loudly and laughing, trying to keep track of their adventurous children.

'I wasn't lying,' said Janet. 'I want you to know that, first off.'

'I know that.'

'I was just confused, that's all. My memory of that night's a bit shaky.'

'Understandable. But you do remember how many times you hit him?'

'No. All I'm saying is that it might have been more than I thought.'

Their meals arrived. Janet tucked in as if she hadn't eaten in a week, which she probably hadn't, and Annie picked at her food. The quiche was dry and the salad boring, but that was to be expected in a place that catered mostly for meat eaters. At least she could enjoy the view. A high plane left a figure of eight of white vapour-trail across the sky.

'Janet,' Annie went on. 'What do you want to change in your statement?'

'Well, you know, where I insisted I only hit him, what, two or three times?'

'Four.'

'Whatever. And the post mortem found . . . how many?'

'Nine blows.'

'Right.'

'Do you remember hitting him nine times?'

'No. That's not what I'm saying.' Janet sawed off a piece of lamb and chewed on it for a moment.

Annie ate some lettuce. 'What *are* you saying, Janet?'

'Just that, well, I suppose I lost it, that's all.'

'You're claiming diminished responsibility?'

'Not really. I mean, I knew what was going on, but I was scared and I was upset about Dennis, so I just . . . I don't know, maybe I should have stopped hitting him sooner, after I'd handcuffed him to the pipes.'

'You hit him after that?'

'I think so. Once or twice.'

'And you remember doing that?'

'I remember hitting him after I'd handcuffed him, yes. Thinking, this one's for Dennis, you bastard. I just don't remember how many times.'

'You realize you'll have to come to the station and revise your statement, don't you? I mean, it's okay just telling me here, now, like this, but it has to be done officially.'

Janet raised an eyebrow. 'Of course I know that. I'm still a copper, aren't I? I just wanted . . . you know . . .' She looked away out over the dale.

Annie thought she did know and that Janet was too embarrassed to say it. She wanted some company. She wanted someone who would at least try to understand her in a gorgeous setting on a beautiful day, before the three-ringed circus that was likely to be her life for the next while went into full swing.

•

Jenny Fuller and Banks had lunch together in the slightly less exotic Queen's Arms. The place was bursting at the seams with Sunday tourists, but they bagged a small table – so small there was hardly room for two roast beef and Yorkshire pud specials and the drinks – just before they stopped serving meals at two o'clock. Lager for Jenny and a pint of shandy for Banks because he had to conduct another interview that afternoon. He still looked tired, Jenny thought, and she guessed that the case had been keeping him awake at nights. That and his obvious discomfort over Sandra's pregnancy.

Jenny and Sandra had been friends. Not close, but both had been through harrowing experiences around the same time and these had created some sort of bond between them. Since her travels in America, though, Jenny hadn't seen much of Sandra and now she supposed she wouldn't see her again. If she had to choose sides, as people did, then she supposed she had chosen Alan's. She had thought he and Sandra had a solid marriage – after all, Alan had turned her down when she tried to seduce him and that had been a new experience for her – but clearly she was wrong. Never having been married herself, she would have been the first to confess that she knew little about such things, except that outward appearances often belie an inner turmoil.

So what had been going through Sandra's mind in that last little while was a mystery. Alan had said that he wasn't sure whether Sandra met Sean before or after they split up, or whether he was the real reason behind the separation. Jenny doubted it. Like most problems, it hadn't just happened overnight, or when someone else turned up on the scene. Sean was as much a symptom as anything, and an escape hatch. This business had probably been years in the making.

'The car,' Banks said.

'A blue Citroen.'

'Yes. I don't suppose you got the number?'

'I must admit it never crossed my mind the first time I saw it. I mean, why would I? It was in Alderthorpe and I parked behind it. Coming back from Spurn Head it always stayed too far behind for me to be able to see.'

'And you lost it where?'

'I didn't lose it. I noticed it stopped following me just after I got onto the M62 west of Hull.'

'And you never saw it again?'

'No.' Jenny laughed. 'I must admit I felt rather as if I was being run out of town. You know, like in those cowboy films.'

'You didn't get a glimpse of the driver at all?'

'No. Couldn't even tell if it was a man or a woman.'

'What next?'

'I've some university work to catch up on and some tutorials tomorrow. I could postpone them, but . . .'

'No, that's okay,' said Banks. 'Lucy Payne's out, anyway. No real rush.'

'Well, on Tuesday or Wednesday I'll see if I can talk to Keith Murray in Durham. Then there's Laura in Edinburgh. I'm developing a picture of Linda–Lucy, but it's still missing a few pieces.'

'Such as?'

'That's the problem. I'm not sure. I just get the feeling that I'm missing something.' She saw Banks's worried expression and slapped his arm. 'Oh, don't worry, I'll not go putting my intuitions into my profiles. This is just between you and me.'

'Okay.'

'I suppose you could call it the missing link. The link

between Linda's childhood and the possibility of Lucy's being involved in the abductions and murders.'

'There's the sexual abuse.'

'Yes, there's no doubt that many people who were abused become abusers themselves – it's a cycle – and, according to Maureen Nesbitt, Linda was sexually aware at eleven. But none of that's enough in itself. All I can say is that it *could* have created a psychopathology in Lucy that made her capable of becoming the compliant victim of a man like Terence Payne. People often repeat mistakes and bad choices. You just have to look at *my* history of relationships to see that.'

Banks smiled. 'You'll get it right one day.'

'Meet my knight in shining armour?'

'Is that what you want? Someone to fight your battles for you, then pick you up and carry you upstairs?'

'It's not a bad idea.'

'And I thought you were a feminist.'

'I am. It doesn't mean I might not fight his battles, pick him up and carry him upstairs the next day. All I'm saying is that the chance would be a fine thing. Anyway, can't a woman have her fantasies?'

'Depends where they lead. Has it occurred to you that Lucy Payne wasn't the compliant victim at all and that her husband was?'

'No, it hasn't. I've never come across such a case.'

'But not impossible?'

'In human psychology, nothing's impossible. Just very unlikely, that's all.'

'But supposing she were the powerful one, the dominant partner . . .'

'And Terence Payne was her sex slave, doing her bidding?'

'Something like that.'

'I don't know,' said Jenny. 'But I very much doubt it. Besides, even if it is true, it doesn't really get us any further, does it?'

'I suppose not. Just speculation. You mentioned that Payne might have used a camcorder when you visited the cellar, didn't you?'

'Yes.' Jenny sipped some lager and dabbed her lips with a paper serviette. 'It would be highly unusual in such a ritualized case of rape, murder and interment for the perpetrator *not* to keep some sort of record.'

'He had the bodies.'

'His trophies? Yes. And that probably explains why there was no further mutilation, no need to take a finger or a toe to remember them by. Payne had the whole body. But it's not just that. Someone like Payne would have needed more, something that enabled him to relive the events.'

Banks told her about the tripod marks and the electronics catalogue.

'So if he had one, where is it?' she asked.

'That's the question.'

'And why is it missing?'

'Another good question. Believe me, we're looking hard for it. If it's in that house, even if it's buried ten feet down, we'll find out. We won't leave a brick of that place standing until it's given up all its secrets.'

'*If* it's in the house.'

'Yes.'

'And there'll be tapes, too.'

'I haven't forgotten them.'

Jenny pushed her plate aside. 'I suppose I'd better go and get some work done.'

Banks looked at his watch. 'And I'd better go and see

Mick Blair.' He reached forward and touched her arm lightly. She was surprised at the tingle she felt. 'Take care, Jenny. Keep your eyes open, and if you see that car again phone me right away. Understand?'

Jenny nodded. Then she noticed someone she didn't know approaching them, walking with an easy, confident grace. An attractive young woman, tight jeans emphasizing her long and shapely legs, what looked like a man's white shirt hanging open over a red T-shirt. Chestnut hair cascaded in shiny waves to her shoulders, and the only flaw on her smooth complexion was a small mole to the right of her mouth. Even that wasn't so much an imperfection as a beauty spot. Her serious eyes were almond in shape and colour.

When she got to the table, she pulled up a chair and sat down without being invited. 'DI Cabbot,' she said, stretching out her hand. 'I don't think we've met.'

'Dr Fuller.' Jenny shook. Firm grasp.

'Ah, the famous Dr Fuller. A pleasure to meet you at last.'

Jenny felt tense. Was this woman, surely *the* Annie Cabbot, staking out her territory? Had she seen Banks touching her arm and thought something of it? Was she here to let Jenny know as subtly as possible to keep her hands off Banks? Jenny knew she was not bad when it came to the looks department, but she couldn't help feeling somehow *clumsy* and even a bit dowdy next to Annie. *Older*, too. Definitely older.

Annie smiled at Banks. 'Sir.'

Jenny could sense something between them. Sexual tension, yes, but it was more than that. Had they had a disagreement? All of a sudden the table was uncomfortable and she felt she had to leave. She picked up her bag and started rummaging for her car keys. Why did they always sink to the bottom and get lost among the hairbrushes, paper hankies and make-up?

'Don't let me interrupt your lunch,' said Annie, smiling again at Jenny, then turning to Banks, 'but I just happened to be in the station catching up on some paperwork after lunch. Winsome told me you were here and that she'd got a message for you. I said I'd deliver it.'

Banks raised his eyebrows. 'And?'

'It's from your mate Ken Blackstone in Leeds. It seems Lucy Payne's done a runner.'

Jenny gasped. 'What?'

'Local police dropped by her parents' house this morning just to make sure everything was okay. Turns out her bed hadn't been slept in.'

'Bloody hell,' said Banks. 'Another cock-up.'

'Just thought you'd want to know as soon as possible,' said Annie, untangling herself from the chair. She looked at Jenny. 'Nice to meet you.'

Then she walked out with the same elegant grace she had walked in with, leaving Banks and Jenny to sit and stare at one another.

•

Mick Blair, the fourth person in the group on the night Leanne Wray disappeared, lived with his parents in a semi in North Eastvale, near enough to the edge of town for a fine view over Swainsdale, but close enough to the centre for easy access. After Annie's revelation about Lucy Payne, Banks wondered whether he should change his plans, but he decided that Leanne Wray was still a priority and Lucy Payne was still a victim in the eyes of the law. Besides, there would be plenty of coppers keeping an eye open for her; it was the most they could do until, and unless, they had anything to charge her with.

Unlike Ian Scott, Mick had never been in trouble with the police, though Banks suspected he might well have been buying drugs from Ian. He had a slightly wasted look about him, not quite all there, and didn't seem to have much time for personal grooming. When Banks called after his lunch with Jenny that Sunday, Mick's parents were out visiting family, and Mick was slouching around in the living room listening to Nirvana loud on the stereo, wearing torn jeans and a black T-shirt with a picture of Kurt Cobain on it, above his birth and death dates.

'What do you want?' Mick asked, turning down the volume and flopping onto the sofa, hands behind his head.

'To talk about Leanne Wray.'

'We've already been over that.'

'Let's go over it again.'

'Why? Have you found out something new?'

'What would there be to find out?'

'I don't know. I'm just surprised at your coming here, that's all.'

'Was Leanne your girlfriend, Mick?'

'No. It wasn't like that.'

'She's an attractive girl. Didn't you fancy her?'

'Maybe. A bit.'

'But she wasn't having any of it?'

'It was early days, that's all.'

'What do you mean?'

'Some girls need a bit of time, a bit of working on. They don't all just jump into bed with you the first time you meet.'

'And Leanne needed time?'

'Yes.'

'How far had you got?'

'What do you mean?'

'How far? Holding hands? Necking? Tongue or no tongue?' Banks remembered his own adolescent gropings and the various stages you had to pass. After necking usually came touching above the waist, but with clothes on, then under the blouse but over the bra. After that, the bra came off, then it was below the waist, and so on until you got to go all the way. If you were lucky. With some girls it seemed to take for ever to move from one stage to another, and some might let you get below the waist but not go all the way. The whole negotiation was a minefield fraught with the danger of being dumped at every turn. Well, at least Leanne Wray hadn't been an easy conquest and, for some odd reason, Banks was glad to know that.

'We necked once in a while.'

'What about that Friday night, the thirty-first of March?'

'Nah. We were in a group, like, with Ian and Sarah.'

'You didn't neck with Leanne in the cinema?'

'Maybe.'

'Is that a yes or a no?'

'I suppose so.'

'Might you have had a falling out?'

'What are you getting at?'

Banks scratched the scar beside his right eye. 'It's like this, Mick. I come here to talk to you again, and it seems to bother you, but you don't ask me if we've found Leanne alive, or found her body yet. It was the same with Ian—'

'You've talked to Ian?'

'This morning. I'm surprised he didn't get straight on the phone to you.'

'He can't have been very worried.'

'Why should he be?'

'I don't know.'

'The thing is, you see, that you both *ought* to be asking me if we've found Leanne alive, or if we've found her body, or if we've identified her remains.'

'Why?'

'Why else would I come to talk to you?'

'How should I know?'

'But the fact that you *don't* ask makes me wonder if you know something you're not telling me.'

Mick folded his arms. 'I've told you everything I know.'

Banks leaned forward and held Mick's gaze. 'Know what? I think you're lying, Mick. I think you're all lying.'

'You can't prove anything.'

'What would I need to prove?'

'That I'm lying. I told you what happened. We went for a drink in the Old—'

'No. What you told us was that you went for coffee after the film.'

'Right. Well . . .'

'That was lying, wasn't it, Mick?'

'So what?'

'If you can do it once, you can do it again. In fact it gets easier the more you practise. What really happened that night, Mick? Why don't you tell me about it?'

'Nothing happened. I already told you.'

'Did you and Leanne have a fight? Did you hurt her? Maybe you didn't mean to. Where is she, Mick? You *know*, I'm certain of it.'

And Mick's expression told Banks that he *did* know, but it also told him that he wasn't going to confess to anything. Not today, at any rate. Banks felt pissed off and culpable at the same time. It was *his* fault that this line of inquiry hadn't been properly followed up. So fixated had he become on a serial killer abducting young girls, that he had ignored the basics of police work and not pushed hard enough at those in the position to know best what had happened to Leanne: the people she had been with at the time she disappeared. He should have followed up, knowing of Ian Scott's criminal record and that it involved drugs. But no. Leanne was put down as the third victim of the unidentified serial killer, another pretty young blonde victim, and that was that. Winsome Jackman had done a bit of follow-up work, but she had pretty much accepted the official story too. Banks's fault, all of it, just like Sandra's miscarriage. Just like bloody everything, it seemed sometimes.

'Tell me what happened,' Banks pushed again.

'I've told you. I've fucking told you!' Mick sat up abruptly. 'When we left the Old Ship, Leanne set off home. That was the last any of us saw of her. Some pervert must have got her. All right? That's what you thought, isn't it? Why are you changing your minds?'

'Ah, so you *are* curious,' Banks said, standing up. 'I'm sure you've been following the news. We've got the pervert who took and killed those girls – he's dead, so he can't tell us anything – but we found no trace of Leanne's body on the premises, and believe me we've taken the place apart.'

'Then it must've been some other pervert.'

'Come off it, Mick. The odds against one are wild enough, the odds against two are astronomical. No. It comes down to you. You, Ian and Sarah. The last people she was seen with. Now, I'm going to give you time to think about it, Mick, but I'll be back, you can count on that. Then we'll have a proper talk. No distractions. In the meantime, stick around. Enjoy the music.'

When Banks left, he paused just long enough at the garden gate to see Mick, silhouetted behind the lace curtains, jump up from the sofa and head over to the telephone.

16

The Monday morning sunlight spilled through Banks's kitchen window and glinted on the copper-bottomed pans hanging on the wall. Banks sat at his pine table with a cup of coffee, toast and marmalade, the morning newspaper spread out before him and Vaughan Williams's *Variations on a Theme by Thomas Tallis* playing on the radio. But he was neither reading nor listening.

He had been awake since before four, a million details dancing around in his mind, and though he felt dog-tired now, he knew he couldn't sleep. He would be glad when the Chameleon case was all over, when Gristhorpe was back at work, and when he could go back to his normal duties as a detective chief inspector. The responsibility of command over the past month and a half had exhausted him. He recognized the signs: lack of sleep, bad dreams, too much junk food, too much booze and too many cigarettes. He was reaching the same near-burnout state as he had been in when he left the Met for North Yorkshire years ago, hoping for a quieter life. He loved detective work, but it sometimes seemed that modern policing was a young man's game. Science, technology and changes in management structure hadn't simplified things; they had only made life more complicated. Banks realized that he had probably come to the limits of his ambition when he actually thought that morning, for the first time, about packing in the job altogether.

He heard the postman arrive and went out to pick up the letters from the floor. Among the usual collection of bills and circulars, there was a hand-addressed envelope from London, and Banks immediately recognized the neat, looping hand.

Sandra.

Heart beating just a little too fast for comfort, he carried the pile back into the kitchen. This was his favourite room in the cottage, mostly because he had dreamed about it before he had seen it, but what he read in Sandra's letter was enough to darken the brightest of rooms even more than his previous mood had darkened it.

Dear Alan,

I understand that Tracy told you Sean and I are expecting a baby. I wish she hadn't, but there it is, it's done now. I hope this knowledge will at least enable you to understand the need for expediency in the matter of our divorce, and that you will act accordingly.

Yours sincerely,

Sandra

That was it. Nothing more than a cold, formal note. Banks knew he hadn't been responding to the matter of the divorce with any great dispatch, but he hadn't seen any need for haste. Perhaps, deep down, he was stubbornly clinging to Sandra, and in some opaque and frightened part of his soul he was holding on to the belief that it was all just a nightmare or a mistake, and he would wake up one morning back in the Eastvale semi with Sandra beside him. Not that that was what he wanted, not any more, but he was at least willing to admit that he might harbour such irrational feelings.

Now this.

Banks put the letter aside, still feeling its chill. Why couldn't he just let go of this and move on, as Sandra clearly had done? Was it because of what he had told Annie, about his guilt over Sandra's miscarriage, about being glad that it happened? He didn't know; it all just felt too strange: his wife of over twenty years, mother of their children, now about to give birth to another man's child.

He tossed the letter aside, picked up his briefcase and headed out for the car.

He intended to go to Leeds later in the morning, but first he wanted to drop by his office, clear up some paperwork and have a word with Winsome. The drive to Eastvale from Gratly was, Banks had thought when he first made it, one of the most beautiful drives in the area: a narrow road about halfway up the daleside, with spectacular views of the valley bottom with its sleepy villages and meandering river to his left and the steeply rising fields with their drystone walls and wandering sheep to his right. But today he didn't even notice all this, partly because he did it so often, and partly because his thoughts were still clouded by Sandra's letter and a vague depression over his job.

After the chaos of the weekend, the police station was back to its normal level of activity; the reporters had disappeared, just as Lucy Payne had. Banks wasn't overly concerned about Lucy going missing, he thought as he closed his office door and turned on the radio. She would probably turn up again, and even if she didn't, there was no real cause for concern. Not unless they came up with some concrete evidence against her. At least in the meantime, they could keep track of her through ATM withdrawals and credit card transactions. No matter where she was, she would need money.

After he had finished the paperwork, Banks went into the

squad room. DC Winsome Jackman was sitting at her desk chewing on the end of a pencil.

'Winsome,' he said, remembering one of the details that had awoken him so early in the morning, 'I've got another job for you.'

And when he'd told her what he wanted her to do, he left by the back exit and set off for Leeds.

•

It was just after lunch when Annie entered the CPS offices, though she hadn't managed to grab a bite to eat herself yet. The Crown solicitor appointed to the case, Jack Whitaker, turned out to be younger than she had expected, late twenties or early thirties, she guessed, prematurely balding, and he spoke with a slight lisp. His handshake was firm, his palm just a little damp. His office was certainly far tidier than Stafford Oakes's in Eastvale, where every file was out of place and stained with an Olympic symbol of coffee rings.

'Any new developments?' he asked after Annie had sat down.

'Yes,' said Annie. 'PC Taylor changed her statement this morning.'

'May I?'

Annie handed him Janet Taylor's revised statement, and Whitaker read it over. When he'd finished, he slid the papers over the desk back towards Annie. 'What do you think?' she asked.

'I think,' Jack Whitaker said slowly, 'that we might be charging Janet Taylor with murder.'

'What?' Annie couldn't believe what she'd just heard. 'She acted as a policewoman in pursuit of her duty. I was thinking justifiable homicide, or at the very most, excusable. But *murder*?'

Whitaker sighed. 'Oh dear. I don't suppose you've heard the news then?'

'What news?' Annie hadn't turned on the radio when she drove down to Leeds, being far too preoccupied with Janet's case and her confused feelings about Banks to concentrate on news or chat.

'The jury came back on the John Hadleigh case just before lunch. You know, the Devon farmer.'

'I know about the Hadleigh case. What was the verdict?'

'Guilty of murder.'

'Jesus Christ,' said Annie. 'But even so, surely that's different entirely? I mean, Hadleigh was a civilian. He shot a burglar in the back. Janet Taylor—'

Whitaker held his hand up. 'The point is that it's a clear message. Given the Hadleigh verdict, we have to be *seen* to be acting fairly towards everyone. We can't afford to have the press screaming at us for going easy on Janet Taylor just because she's a policewoman.'

'So is it political?'

'Isn't it always? Justice must be seen to be done.'

'Justice?'

Whitaker raised his eyebrows. 'Listen,' he said, 'I can understand your sympathies, believe me, I can. But according to her statement, Janet Taylor handcuffed Terence Payne to a metal pipe *after* she had already subdued him, then she hit him twice with her baton. Hard. Think about it, Annie. That's deliberate. That's murder.'

'She didn't necessarily mean to kill him. There was no intent.'

'That's for a jury to decide. A good prosecutor could argue that she knew damn well what the effect of two more hard blows to the head would be after she'd already given him seven previous blows.'

'I can't believe I'm hearing this,' Annie said.

'No one's sorrier than I am,' said Whitaker.

'Except Janet Taylor.'

'Then she shouldn't have killed Terence Payne.'

'What the hell do you know? You weren't there, in that cellar, with your partner bleeding to death on the floor, a dead girl staked out on a mattress. You didn't have just seconds to react to a man coming at you with a machete. This is a bloody farce! It's politics, is all it is.'

'Calm down, Annie,' said Whitaker.

Annie stood up and paced, arms folded. 'Why should I? I don't feel calm. This woman has been going through hell. *I* provoked her into changing her statement because I thought it would go better for her in the long run than saying she couldn't remember. How does this make me look?'

'Is that all you're concerned about? How it makes you look?'

'Of course it's not.' Annie lowered herself slowly back into the chair. She still felt flushed and angry, her breath coming in sharp gasps. 'But it makes me look like a liar. It makes it look as if I tricked her. I don't like that.'

'You were only doing your job.'

'Only doing my job. Only obeying orders. Right. Thanks. That makes me feel a whole lot better.'

'Look, we might be able to get a bit of leeway here, Annie, but there'll have to be a trial. It'll all have to be a matter of public record. Above board. There'll be no sweeping it under the table.'

'That's not what I had in mind, anyway. What leeway?'

'I don't suppose Janet Taylor would plead guilty to murder.'

'Damn right she wouldn't, and I wouldn't advise her to.'

'It's not exactly a matter of *advising*. Besides, that's not your job. What do you think she *would* plead guilty to?'

'Excusable homicide.'

'It wasn't self-defence. Not when she crossed the line and delivered those final blows *after* Payne was rendered incapable of defending himself or of attacking her further.'

'What, then?'

'Voluntary manslaughter.'

'How long would she have to serve?'

'Between eighteen months and three years.'

'That's still a long time, especially for a copper in jail.'

'Not as long as John Hadleigh.'

'Hadleigh shot a kid in the back with a shotgun.'

'Janet Taylor beat a defenceless man about the head with a police baton, causing his death.'

'He was a serial killer.'

'She didn't know that at the time.'

'But he came at her with a machete!'

'And after she'd disarmed him, she used more force than necessary to subdue him, causing his death. Annie, it doesn't matter that he was a serial killer. It wouldn't matter if he'd been Jack the bloody Ripper.'

'He'd cut her partner. She was upset.'

'Well I'm certainly glad to hear she wasn't calm, cool and collected when she did it.'

'You know what I mean. There's no need for sarcasm.'

'Sorry. I'm sure the judge and jury will take the whole picture into account, her state of mind.'

Annie sighed. She felt sick. As soon as this farce was over she was getting the hell out of Complaints and Discipline, back to real police work, catching the villains.

'All right,' she said. 'What next?'

'You know what next, Annie. Find Janet Taylor. Arrest

her, take her to the police station and charge her with voluntary manslaughter.'

•

'Someone asking to see you, sir.'

Why was the fresh-faced PC who popped his head around the door of Banks's temporary office at Millgarth smirking? Banks wondered. 'Who is it?' he asked.

'You'd better see for yourself, sir.'

'Can't someone else deal with it?'

'She specifically asked to see someone in charge of the missing girls case, sir. Area Commander Hartnell's in Wakefield with the ACC, and DCI Blackstone's out. That leaves you, sir.'

Banks sighed. 'All right. Show her in.'

The PC smirked again and disappeared, leaving a distinct sense of smirk still in the air rather like the Cheshire cat's smile. A few moments later, Banks saw why.

She tapped very softly on his door and pushed it open so slowly that it creaked on its hinges, then she appeared before him. All five foot nothing of her. She was anorexically thin, and the harsh red of her lipstick and nail polish contrasted with the almost translucent paleness of her skin; her delicate features looked as if they were made out of porcelain carefully glued or painted on her moon-shaped face. Clutching a gold lamé handbag, she was wearing a bright green cropped top, which stopped abruptly just below her breasts – no more than goose pimples despite the push-up bra – and showed a stretch of pale, bare midriff and a belly-button ring, below which came a black PVC micro-skirt. She wore no tights and her pale thin legs stretched bare down to the knee-high and chunky platform heels that made her walk as if she were on stilts. Her expression showed fear and nervousness as her astonishingly lovely cobalt blue eyes roved restlessly about the stark office.

Banks would have put her down for a heroin-addicted prostitute, but he could see no needle tracks on her arms. That didn't mean she wasn't addicted to *something*, and it certainly didn't mean that she *wasn't* a prostitute. There are more ways of getting drugs into your system than through a needle. Something about her reminded him of Chief Constable Riddle's daughter, Emily, but it quickly passed. She bore more resemblance to the famous heroin-chic models of a few years ago.

'Are you the one?' she asked.

'What one?'

'The one in charge. I asked for the one in charge.'

'That's me. For my sins,' said Banks.

'What?'

'Never mind. Sit down.' She sat, slowly and suspiciously, eyes still flicking restlessly around the office, as if she were afraid someone was going to appear and strap her into her chair. It had obviously taken her a lot of courage to come this far. 'Can I get you some tea or coffee?' Banks asked.

She looked surprised at the offer. 'Er . . . yes. Please. Coffee would be nice.'

'How do you take it?'

'What?'

'The coffee? How do you want it?'

'Milk and plenty of sugar,' she said, as if unaware that it came any other way.

Banks phoned for two coffees – black for him – and turned back to her. 'What's your name?'

'Candy.'

'Really?'

'Why? What's wrong with it?'

'Nothing. Nothing, Candy. Ever been in a police station before?'

Fear flashed across Candy's delicate features. 'Why?'

'Just asking. You seem ill at ease.'

She managed a weak smile. 'Well, yes . . . Maybe I am. A little bit.'

'Relax. I won't eat you.'

Wrong choice of words, Banks realized, when he saw the lascivious, knowing look in her eye. 'I mean I won't harm you,' he corrected himself.

The coffee arrived, carried in by the same, still smirking PC. Banks was abrupt with him, resenting the kind of smug arrogance that the smirk implied.

'Okay, Candy,' said Banks after the first sip. 'Care to tell me what it's all about?'

'Can I smoke?' She opened her handbag.

'Sorry,' said Banks. 'No smoking anywhere in the station, otherwise I'd have one with you.'

'Maybe we could go outside?'

'I don't think that would be a good idea,' Banks said. 'Let's just get on with it.'

'It's just that I really like a ciggie with my coffee. I always have a smoke with my coffee.'

'Not this time. Why have you come to see me, Candy?'

She fidgeted a while longer, a sulky expression on her face, then shut the handbag and crossed her legs, clipping the underside of the desk with her platform and rattling it so much that Banks's coffee spilled over the rim of his mug and made a gathering stain on the pile of paper before him.

'Sorry,' she said.

'It's nothing.' Banks took out his handkerchief and wiped it up. 'You were going to tell me why you're here.'

'Was I?'

'Yes.'

'Well, look,' Candy said, leaning forward in her chair. 'First off, you have to grant me that immunization, or whatever. Or I won't say a word.'

'You mean immunity?'

She flushed. 'If that's what it's called. I didn't go to school much.'

'Immunity from what?'

'From prosecution.'

'But why would I want to prosecute you?'

Her eyes were everywhere but on Banks, hands twisting the bag on her bare lap. 'Because of what I do,' she said. 'You know . . . with men. I'm a prostitute, a tom.'

'Bloody hell,' said Banks. 'You could knock me over with a feather.'

Her eyes turned to him, shimmering with angry tears. 'There's no need to be sarky. I'm not ashamed of what I am. At least I don't go around locking up innocent people and letting the guilty go free.'

Banks felt like a shit. Sometimes he just didn't know when to hold his tongue. He had acted no better than the smirking PC when he insulted her with his sarcasm. 'I'm sorry, Candy,' he said. 'But I'm a very busy man. Can we get to the point? If you've got anything to tell me, then say it.'

'You promise?'

'Promise what?'

'You won't lock me up.'

'I won't lock you up. Cross my heart. Not unless you've come to confess a serious crime.'

She shot to her feet. 'I haven't done nothing!'

'All right. All right. Sit down, then. Take it easy.'

Candy sat slowly, careful with her platforms this time. 'I

came because you let her go. I wasn't going to come. I don't like the police. But you let her go.'

'Who's this about, Candy?'

'It's about that couple in the papers, the ones who took them young girls.'

'What about them?'

'Just that they . . . once . . . you know, they . . .'

'They picked *you* up?'

She looked down. 'Yes.'

'Both of them?'

'Yes.'

'How did it happen?'

'I was just, you know, out on the street, and they came by in a car. He did the talking and when we'd fixed it up they took me to a house.'

'When was this, Candy?'

'Last summer.'

'Do you remember the month?'

'August, I think. Late August. It was warm, anyway.'

Banks tried to work out the timing. The Seacroft rapes had stopped around the time the Paynes moved out of the area, about a year or so before Candy's experience. That left a period of about sixteen months before Payne abducted Kelly Matthews. Perhaps during that period he had been trying to sublimate his urges, relying on prostitutes? And Lucy's role?

'Where was the house?'

'The Hill. It's the same one that's in all the papers. I've *been* there.'

'Okay. What happened next?'

'Well, first we had a drink and they chatted to me, putting me at ease, like. They seemed a really nice couple.'

'And then?'

'What do you think?'

'I'd still like you to tell me.'

'He said let's go upstairs.'

'Just the two of you?'

'Yes. That's what I thought he meant at first.'

'Go on.'

'Well, we went up to the bedroom and I . . . you know . . . I got undressed. Well, partly. He wanted me to keep certain things on. Jewellery. My underwear. At first, anyway.'

'What happened next?'

'It was dark in there and you could only make out shadows. He made me lie down on the bed and the next thing I knew she was there, too.'

'Lucy Payne?'

'Yes.'

'On the bed with you?'

'Yes. Starkers.'

'Was she involved in what went on sexually?'

'Oh, yes. She knew what she was doing, all right. Proper little minx.'

'She never seemed to be coerced, a victim in any way?'

'Never. No way. She was in control. And she liked what was happening. She even came up with suggestions of her own . . . you know, different things to do. Different positions.'

'Did they hurt you?'

'Not really. I mean, they liked to play games, but they seemed to know how far to go.'

'What sort of games?'

'He asked me if I'd mind him tying me to the bed. He promised they weren't going to hurt me.'

'You let him do that?'

'They were paying well.'

'And they seemed nice?'

'Yes.'

Banks shook his head in amazement. 'Okay. Go on.'

'Don't judge me,' she said. 'You don't know anything about me or what I have to do, so don't you dare judge me!'

'Okay,' said Banks. 'Go on, Candy. They tied you to the bed.'

'She was doing something with hot candle wax. On my belly. My nipples. It hurt a bit, but it doesn't really hurt. You know what I mean?'

Banks hadn't experimented sexually with candle wax but he had spilled some on his hand on more than one occasion and knew the sensation, the brief flash of heat and pain followed by the quick cooling, the setting and drying, the way it pinched and puckered the skin. Not an entirely unpleasant sensation.

'Were you frightened?'

'A bit. Not really, though. I've known worse. But they were a team. That's what I'm telling you. That's why I came forward. I can't believe you've let her go.'

'We don't have any evidence against her, any evidence that she had anything to do with killing those girls.'

'But don't you see?' Candy pleaded. 'She's the same as him. They're a team. They do things together. *Everything together.*'

'Candy, I know it probably took you a lot of courage to come here and talk to me, but what you've said doesn't change things. We can't go and arrest her on—'

'On some *tom's* statement, you mean?'

'I wasn't going to say that. What I was going to say was that we can't just go and arrest her on the evidence of what you've just told me. You consented. You were paid for your services. They didn't hurt you beyond what you were prepared for. It's a risky profession you're in. You know that, Candy.'

'But surely what I've said makes a difference?'

'Yes, it makes a difference. To me. But we deal in facts, in evidence. I'm not doubting your word, that it happened, but even if we had it on video, it wouldn't make her a murderer.'

Candy paused for a moment, then she said, 'They did. Have it on video.'

'How do you know?'

'Because I saw the camera. They thought it was hidden behind a screen, but I could hear something, a whirring noise, and once when I got up to go to the toilet I glimpsed a video camera set up behind a screen. The screen had a hole in it.'

'We didn't find any videos at the house, Candy. And as I said, even if we had, it wouldn't change anything.' But the fact that Candy had *seen* a video camera interested Banks. Again, he had to ask himself where was it, and where were the tapes?

'So it's all for nothing, then? My coming here.'

'Not necessarily.'

'Yes, it is. You're not going to do anything. She's just as guilty as him, and you're going to let her get away with murder.'

'Candy, we've got no evidence against her. The fact that she joined in a threesome with her husband and you does *not* make her a murderer.'

'Then find some evidence.'

Banks sighed. 'Why did you come here?' he asked. 'Really. You girls never come forward voluntarily and talk to the police.'

'What do you mean, *you girls*? You're judging me again, aren't you?'

'Candy, for crying out loud . . . You're a tom. You told me yourself. You sell sex. I'm not judging your profession, but what I am saying is that girls who practise it rarely make themselves helpful to the police. So why are you here?'

She shot him a sly glance so full of humour and intelligence that Banks wanted to get on his soapbox and persuade her to go to university and get a degree. But he didn't. Then her expression quickly changed to one of sadness. 'You're right about my *profession*, as you call it,' she said. 'It's full of risks. Risk of getting some sexually transmitted disease. Risk of meeting the wrong kind of customer. The nasty kind. Things like that happen to us all the time. We deal with them. At the time, these two were no better or worse than anyone else. Better than some. At least they paid.' She leaned forward. 'But since I've read about them in the papers, what you found in the cellar.' She gave a little shudder and hugged her skinny shoulders. 'Girls go missing,' she went on. 'Girls like me. And nobody cares.'

Banks attempted to say something but she brushed it aside.

'Oh, you'll say you do. You'll say it doesn't matter who gets raped, beat up or murdered. But if it's some little butter-wouldn't-melt-in-her-knickers schoolgirl, you'll move heaven and earth to find out who did it. If it's someone like me . . . well . . . let's just say we're pretty much low priority. Okay?'

'If that's true, Candy, there are reasons,' said Banks. 'And it's not because we don't care.'

She studied him for a few moments and seemed to give him the benefit of the doubt. 'Maybe *you* do,' she said. 'Maybe you're different. And maybe there *are* reasons. Not that they get you off the hook. The point is, though, why I came and all that . . . not just that girls do go missing. Girls *have* gone missing. Well, one in particular.'

Banks felt the hairs bristle at the back of his neck. 'A girl you know? A friend of yours?'

'Not exactly a friend. You don't have many friends in this *profession*. But someone I knew, yes. Spent time with. Talked to. Had a drink with. Lent money to.'

'When did this happen?'

'I don't know exactly. Before Christmas.'

'Did you report it?'

Her cutting glance said he'd just gone down a lot in her estimation. Curiously, it mattered to him. 'Give me a break,' she said. 'Girls come and go all the time. Move on. Even give up the life sometimes, save up enough money, go to university, get a degree.'

Banks felt himself blush as she said the very thing that had crossed his mind some time ago. 'So what's to say this missing girl didn't just up and leave like the others?' he asked.

'Nothing,' said Candy. 'Maybe it's a wild goose chase.'

'But?'

'But you said that what I had to tell you wasn't evidence.'

'That's true.'

'It made you think, though, didn't it?'

'It gave me pause for thought. Yes.'

'Then what if this girl didn't just move on? What if something *did* happen to her? Don't you think you at least ought to look into that possibility? You never know, you might find some evidence there.'

'What you're saying makes sense, Candy, but did you ever see this girl with the Paynes?'

'Not exactly with them, no.'

'Did you see the Paynes at any time around her disappearance?'

'I did see them sometimes, cruising the streets. I can't remember the exact dates.'

'Around that time, though?'

'Yes.'

'Both of them?'

'Yes.'

'I'll need a name.'

'No problem. I know her name.'

'And not a name like Candy.'

'What's wrong with Candy?'

'I don't believe it's your own name.'

'Well, well. I can see why you're such an important detective. Actually, it's not. My real name is Hayley, which, if you ask me, is even worse.'

'Oh, I don't know. It's not that bad.'

'You can spare me the flattery. Don't you know us toms don't need to be flattered?'

'I didn't mean—'

She smiled. 'I know you didn't.' Then she leaned forward and rested her arms on the desk, her pale face only a foot or two away from his. He could smell bubblegum and smoke on her breath. 'But that girl who disappeared. I know her name. Her street name was Anna, but I know her *real* name. What do you think of that, Mr Detective?'

'I think we're in business,' said Banks, reaching for pad and pen.

She sat back and folded her arms. 'Oh, no. Not until I've had that cigarette.'

•

'What now?' asked Janet. 'I've already changed my statement.'

'I know,' said Annie, that sick feeling at the centre of her gut. Partly, it was due to Janet's stuffy flat, but only partly. 'I've been to talk to the CPS.'

Janet poured herself a shot of gin, neat, from an almost empty bottle. 'And?'

'And I'm supposed to arrest you and take you down to the station to charge you.'

'I see. What are you going to charge me with?'

Annie paused, took a deep breath, then said, 'The CPS wanted me to charge you with murder at first, but I managed to get them down to voluntary manslaughter. You'll have to talk to them about this, but I'm sure that if you plead guilty it'll go easy on you.'

The shock and the anger she had expected didn't come. Instead, Janet twisted a loose thread around her forefinger, frowned and took a sip of gin. 'It's because of the John Hadleigh verdict, isn't it? I heard it on the radio.'

Annie swallowed. 'Yes.'

'I thought so. A sacrificial lamb.'

'Look,' Annie went on, 'we can work this out. As I said, the CPS will probably work out a deal—'

Janet held up her hand. 'No.'

'What do you mean?'

'What part of no don't you understand?'

'Janet—'

'No. If the bastards want to charge me, let them. I'll not give them the satisfaction of pleading guilty to just doing my job.'

'This is no time for playing games, Janet.'

'What makes you think I'm playing games? I mean it. I'll plead innocent to any charges you care to bring.'

Annie felt a chill. 'Janet, listen to me. You can't do that.'

Janet laughed. She looked bad, Annie noticed: hair unwashed and unbrushed, pale skin breaking out in spots, a general haze of stale sweat and fresh gin. 'Don't be silly,' she said. 'Of course I can. The public want us to do our job, don't they? They want people to feel safe in their nice little middle-class beds at night, or when they're driving to work in the morning or going out for a drink in the evening. Don't they? Well, let them find out there's a price for keeping killers off the streets. No, Annie, I'll not plead guilty, not even to voluntary manslaughter.'

Annie leaned forward to put some emphasis into what she was saying. 'Think about this, Janet. It could be one of the most important decisions you ever make.'

'I don't think so. I already made that one in the cellar last week. But I have thought about it. I haven't thought about anything else for a week.'

'Your mind's made up?'

'Yes.'

'Do you think I want to do this, Janet?' Annie said, standing up.

Janet smiled at her. 'No, of course you don't. You're a decent enough person. You like to do the right thing, and you know as well as I do that this stinks. But when push comes to shove, you'll do your job. The bloody job. You know, I'm almost glad this has happened, glad to be out of it. The fucking hypocrites. Come on, get on with it.'

'Janet Taylor, I'm arresting you for the murder of Terence Payne. You do not have to say anything. But it may harm your defence if you do not mention, when questioned, something which you later rely on in court. Anything you do say may be given in evidence.'

•

When Annie suggested they meet for a drink somewhere other than the Queen's Arms, Banks felt immediately apprehensive. The Queen's Arms was their 'local'. It was where they always went for a drink after work. By naming another pub, the Pied Piper, a tourist haunt on Castle Hill, Annie was telling Banks she had a serious message to deliver, something beyond casual conversation, or so he believed. Either that or she was worried about Detective Superintendent Chambers finding out they were meeting.

He got there ten minutes early, bought a pint at the bar and sat at a table near the window, back to the wall. The view was spectacular. The formal gardens were a blaze of purple, scarlet and indigo, and across the river the tall trees of the Green, some of them still in blossom, blocked out most of the eyesore of the East End Estate. He could still see some of the grim maisonettes, and the two twelve-storey towerblocks stuck up as if they were giving the finger to the world, but he could also see beyond them to the lush plain with its fields of bright yellow rapeseed, and he even fancied he could make out the dark green humps of the Cleveland Hills in the far distance.

He could see the back of Jenny Fuller's house, too, facing the Green. Sometimes he worried about Jenny. She didn't seem to have much going on in her life apart from her work. She had joked about her bad relationships yesterday, but Banks had witnessed some of them, and they were no joke. He remembered the shock, disappointment and – yes – jealousy he had felt some years ago when he went to interrogate a loser called Dennis Osmond and saw Jenny poke her head around his bedroom door, hair in disarray, a thin dressing-gown slipping off her shoulders. He had also listened as she spilled out her woes over the unfaithful Randy. Jenny picked losers, cheats and generally unsuitable partners time after time. The sad thing was she knew it but it happened anyway.

Annie was fifteen minutes late, which was unlike her, and she lacked the usual spring in her step. When she got herself a drink and joined Banks at the table he could tell she was upset.

'Rough day?' he asked.

'You can say that again.'

Banks felt that he could have had a better one, too. Sandra's letter he could have done without, for a start. And while Candy's information was interesting, it was maddeningly lacking in the hard evidence he needed if he were to track down Lucy Payne and arrest her for anything other than kerb-crawling. That was the trouble; the odd things that trickled in – Lucy's childhood, the Satanic stuff in Alderthorpe, Kathleen Murray's murder, and now Candy's statement – were all disturbing and suggestive of more serious problems, but ultimately, as AC Hartnell had already pointed out, they added up to nothing.

'Anything in particular?' he asked.

'I just arrested Janet Taylor.'

'Let me guess: the Hadleigh verdict?'

'Yes. It seems everyone knew about it except me. The CPS wants justice to be seen to be done. It's just bloody politics, that's all.'

'Often is.'

Annie gave him a sour look. 'I know that, but it doesn't help.'

'They'll make a deal with her.'

Annie told him what Janet had just said.

'Should be an interesting trial, then. What did Chambers have to say?'

'He doesn't give a damn. He's just marking time till he gets his pension. I'm through with Complaints and Discipline. Soon as there's an opening in CID, I'm back.'

'And we'd be happy to have you, as soon as there is,' said Banks, smiling.

'Look, Alan,' Annie said, looking at the view through the window, 'there's something else I wanted to talk to you about.'

Just as he'd thought. He lit a cigarette. 'Okay. What is it?'

'It's just that . . . I don't know . . . this isn't working out. You and me. I think we should ease off. Cool it. That's all.'

'You want to end our relationship?'

'Not end it. Just change its focus, that's all. We can still be friends.'

'I don't know what to say, Annie. What's brought this on?'

'Nothing in particular.'

'Oh, come on. You can't just expect me to believe you suddenly decided for no apparent reason to chuck me.'

'I'm not chucking you. I told you. Things are just changing.'

'Okay. Are we going to continue going out for romantic dinners, to galleries and concerts together?'

'No.'

'Are we going to continue sleeping together?'

'No.'

'Then what, precisely, are we going to do together?'

'Be friends. You know, at work. Be supportive and stuff.'

'I'm already supportive and stuff. Why can't I be supportive and stuff and still sleep with you?'

'It's not that I don't like it, Alan. Sleeping with you. The sex. You know that.'

'I thought I did. Maybe you're just a damn good actress.'

Annie winced and swigged some beer. 'That's not fair. I don't deserve that. This isn't easy for me, you know.'

'Then why are you doing it? You know it's more than sex with us, anyway.'

'I *have* to.'

'No, you don't. Is it because of that conversation we had the other night? I wasn't trying to suggest that we should have children. That's the last thing I'd want right now.'

'I know. It wasn't that.'

'Was it to do with the miscarriage, what I told you I felt?'

'Christ, no. Maybe. Look, okay, I'll admit it threw me, but not in the way you think.'

'In what way, then?'

Annie paused, clearly uncomfortable, shifted in her chair and faced away from him, her voice low. 'It just made me think about things I'd rather not think about. That's all.'

'What things?'

'Do you have to know everything?'

'Annie, I care about you. That's why I'm asking.'

She ran her fingers through her hair, turned her eyes on him and shook her head. 'After the rape,' she said, 'over two years ago, well . . . he hadn't . . . the one who did it hadn't . . . Shit, this is more difficult than I thought.'

Banks felt understanding dawn on him. 'You got pregnant. That's what you're telling me, right? That's why this whole business with Sandra is bothering you so much.'

Annie smiled thinly. 'Perceptive of you.' She touched his hand and whispered, 'Yes. I got pregnant.'

'And?'

Annie shrugged. 'And I had an abortion. It wasn't my best moment, but it wasn't my worst. I didn't feel guilty afterwards. I didn't feel much of anything, in fact. But all this . . . I don't know . . . I just want to put it behind me, and being with you always seems to bring it all back, shove it right in my face.'

'Annie—'

'No. Let me finish. You've got too much baggage, Alan. Too much for me to handle. I thought it would get easier, go away maybe, but it hasn't. You can't let it go. You'll never let it go. Your marriage was such a big part of your life for so long that you can't. You're hurt and I can't console you. I don't do consoling well. Sometimes I just feel too overwhelmed by your life, your past, your problems, and all I want to do is crawl away and be on my own. I can't get any breathing space.'

Banks stubbed out his cigarette and noticed his hand was shaking a little. 'I didn't know you felt like that.'

'Well, that's why I'm telling you. I'm not good at commitment, at emotional closeness. Not yet, anyway. Maybe never. I don't know, but it's stifling me and scaring me.'

'Can't we work it out?'

'I don't want to work it out. I don't have the energy. This is not what I need in my life right now. That's the other reason.'

'What?'

'My career. This Janet Taylor fiasco aside, believe it or not, I do love police work and I do have an aptitude for it.'

'I know—'

'No, wait. Let me finish. What we've been doing is unprofessional. It's hard for me to believe that half the station doesn't already know what we're up to in private. I've heard the sniggers behind my back. Certainly all my colleagues in CID and Complaints and Discipline know. I think Chambers was also dropping a hint when he warned me you were a ladies' man. I wouldn't be surprised if ACC McLaughlin knows, too.'

'Relationships on the job aren't unusual and they certainly aren't illegal.'

'No, but they *are* seriously discouraged and frowned upon. I want to make chief inspector, Alan. Hell, I want to make superintendent, chief constable. Who knows? I've rediscovered my ambition.'

It was ironic, Banks thought, that Annie should rediscover her ambition just when he thought he had come to the limits of his. 'And I'm standing in your way?'

'Not standing in my way. Distracting me. I don't need any distractions.'

'All work and no play . . .'

'So I'll be dull for a while. It'll be a nice change.'

'So that's it, then? Just like that? Over. The end. Because I'm human and I've got a past that sometimes rears its ugly head, and because you've decided you want to put more effort into your career, we stop seeing each other?'

'If you want to put it like that, yes.'

'What other way is there to put it?'

Annie hurried her pint. Banks could tell she wanted to leave. Damn it, though, he was hurt and angry and he wasn't going to let her get off that easily.

'Are you sure there's nothing else?' he asked.

'Like what?'

'I don't know. You're not jealous of anyone, are you?'

'Jealous? Of whom? Why should I be?'

'Jenny, perhaps?'

'Oh, for crying out loud, Alan. No, I'm not jealous of Jenny. If I'm jealous of anyone, it's Sandra. Can't you see that? She's got more of a hold on you than anyone.'

'That's not true. Not any more.' But Banks remembered the letter, his feelings when he read the cold, business-like words. 'Is there someone else? Is that it?' he went on quickly.

'Alan, there's nobody else. Believe me. I've told you.

I don't have room for anyone in my life right now. I can't cope with anyone else's emotional demands.'

'What about sexual demands?'

'What do you mean?'

'It doesn't have to be emotional, sex, does it? I mean, if it's too much trouble to sleep with someone who actually cares a bit about you, maybe it'd be easier to pick up some stud in a bar for a quick anonymous fuck. No demands. You don't even have to tell one another your names. Is that what you want?'

'Alan, I don't know where you're going with this, but I'd like you to stop right there.'

Banks rubbed his temples. 'I'm just upset, Annie, that's all. I'm sorry. I've had a bad day, too.'

'I'm sorry about that. I really don't want to hurt you.'

He looked her in the eye. 'Then don't. No matter who you get involved with, you'll have to face things you want to avoid.'

He noticed the tears in her eyes. The only time he'd seen her cry before was when she told him about her rape. He reached out to touch her hand on the table, but she jerked it away. 'No. Don't.'

'Annie—'

'No.'

She stood up so abruptly that she banged the table hard and her drink spilled right onto Banks's lap, then she ran out of the pub before he could say another word. All he could do was sit there feeling the cold liquid seep through his trousers, aware of everyone's eyes on him, thankful only that they hadn't been in the Queen's Arms, where everyone knew him. And he'd thought the day couldn't get any worse.

17

After taking her last tutorial group and clearing up some paperwork, Jenny left her office at York early on Tuesday afternoon and headed for the A1 to Durham. The traffic was heavy, especially lorries and delivery vans, but at least it was a pleasant, sunny day, not pouring down with rain.

After talking to Keith Murray – if he agreed to talk to her – Jenny thought she would still have time to continue on to Edinburgh later in the afternoon and look up Laura Godwin. It would mean an overnight stay – either that or a long drive home in the dark – but she could worry about that later. She had an old student friend in the psychology department at the University of Edinburgh, and it might be fun to get together and catch up with one another's history. Not that Jenny's recent history was anything to write home about, she thought glumly, and now that she had met Banks's girlfriend, she decided there probably wasn't much hope for her there, either. Still, she was used to that by now; after all, they had known each other for seven years or more, and they hadn't once strayed beyond the bounds of propriety, more was the pity.

She still wasn't certain whether the Girlfriend had been jealous when she came over to them in the Queen's Arms. She must certainly have seen Banks touch Jenny's arm, and though it was merely a friendly, concerned gesture, it was open to misinterpretation, like so much body language. Was the Girlfriend the jealous kind? Jenny didn't know. Annie had seemed self-assured and poised, yet Jenny had sensed something in her attitude that made her feel strangely concerned for Banks, who was probably the only man she had ever met whom she worried about, wanted to protect. She didn't know why. He was independent, strong, private; perhaps he was more vulnerable than he let on, but he certainly wasn't the sort of person you went around feeling you needed to protect or mother.

A white van sped by on her outside lane just as she was turning off, and still lost in thought, she almost hit it. Luckily, instinct kicked in and she had time to swing back abruptly into her own lane without causing anyone else great distress, but she missed the turn-off she wanted. She honked her horn and cursed him out loud – impotent gestures, but all she could come up with – and drove on to the next junction.

When she had got off the A1, she switched the radio channel from a dreary Brahms symphony to some cheerful pop music, tunes she could hum along with and tap out the rhythm on the steering wheel.

Durham was an odd sort of place, Jenny had always thought. Though she had been born there, her parents had moved away when she was only three and she didn't remember it at all. Very early in her academic career she had applied for a job at the university, but she got pipped at the post by a man with more publications to his name. She would have liked living here, she thought, as she looked at the distant castle high on the hill and all the greenery surrounding it, but York suited her well enough and she had no desire to start applying for new jobs at this stage in her career.

She had found from her map that Keith Murray lived out by the university sports grounds, so she was able to bypass the central maze around the cathedral and colleges, the city's main tourist area. Even so, she still managed to get lost on a couple of occasions. There was a chance that Keith might be out at lectures, Jenny realized, though she remembered how few lectures she had attended when she was an undergraduate. If he was, she could wait until later if she had to, explore the city, have a pub lunch, and still be in plenty of time to get to Edinburgh to talk to Laura.

She pulled over into a small car park in front of some shops and consulted the map again. Not far away now. She just had to watch out for the one-way streets or she would end up back where she started.

On the second try, she got it right and pulled off the arterial road into an area of narrow streets. She was concentrating so much on finding the right street and the right house number, that she almost didn't see the car she parked behind until the last moment. When she did, her heart jumped into her throat. It was a blue Citroen.

Jenny told herself to be calm, that she couldn't be certain it was the *same* blue Citroen that had followed her around Holderness because she hadn't seen the number-plate. But it was the exact same model and she didn't believe in coincidences.

What should she do? Go ahead anyway? If the Citroen belonged to Keith Murray, what had he been doing at Alderthorpe and Spurn Head, and why had he followed her? Was he dangerous?

As Jenny was trying to make up her mind what to do, the front door of the house opened and two people walked over to the car: a young man with keys in his hand and a woman who looked remarkably like Lucy Payne. Just as Jenny decided to pull away, the young man saw her, said something to Lucy, then walked over and jerked open the driver's door of Jenny's car before she had time to lock it.

Well, she thought, you've well and truly done it now, this time, haven't you, Jenny?

•

There were no new developments at Millgarth, according to Ken Blackstone on the phone that morning. The SOCOs were getting to the point where there wasn't much left of the Payne house to take apart. Both gardens had been dug up to a depth of between six and ten feet and searched in a grid system. The concrete floors in the cellar and the garage had been ripped up by pneumatic drills. Almost a thousand exhibits had been bagged and labelled. The entire contents of the house had been stripped and taken away. The walls had been punched open at regular intervals. In addition to the crime scene specialists going over all the collected material, forensic mechanics had taken Payne's car apart looking for traces of the abducted girls. Payne may be dead, but a case still had to be answered and Lucy's role still had to be determined.

The only snippet of information about Lucy Payne was that she had withdrawn £200 from a cashpoint machine on Tottenham Court Road. It figured she would go to London if she wanted to disappear, Banks thought, remembering his search there for Chief Constable Riddle's daughter, Emily. Perhaps he would have to go and search for Lucy, too, although this time he would have all the resources of the Metropolitan Police at his disposal. Maybe it wouldn't come to that; maybe Lucy wasn't involved and would simply ease herself into a new identity and a new look in a new place and try to rebuild her shattered life. *Maybe.*

Banks looked again at the loose sheets of paper on his desk.

Katya Pavelic.

Katya, Candy's 'Anna', had been identified through dental records late the previous evening. Fortunately for Banks, she had suffered a toothache shortly before she disappeared and Candy had directed Katya to her own dentist. Katya had disappeared, according to Candy, sometime last November. At least, she remembered, the weather was cool and misty and the Christmas lights had recently been turned on in the city centre. That likely made Katya the victim before Kelly Matthews.

Certainly Candy, or Hayley Lyndon as she was called, had seen both Terence and Lucy Payne driving around the area on a number of occasions but she couldn't connect them directly with Katya. The circumstantial evidence was beginning to build up, though, and if Jenny's psychological probing into the old Alderthorpe wounds turned up anything interesting, then it might be time to reel Lucy in. For the moment, let her enjoy the illusion of freedom.

Katya Pavelic had come to England from Bosnia four years ago, when she was fourteen. Like so many young girls there she had been gang-raped by Serbian soldiers and then shot, saving herself only by playing dead under a pile of corpses until some Canadian UN peace-keepers found her three days later. Her wound was superficial and the blood had clotted. Her only problem was an infection and that had responded well to antibiotics. Various groups and individuals had seen that Katya got to England, but she was a disturbed and troublesome girl who soon ran away from her foster parents when she was sixteen, and they had tried in vain to find her and contact her ever since.

The irony wasn't lost on Banks. After having survived the

horrors of the Bosnian war, Katya Pavelic had ended up raped, murdered and buried in the Paynes's back garden. What was the bloody point of it all? he asked. As usual, he got no answer from the Supreme Ironist in the Sky, only a deep hollow laughter echoing through his brain. Sometimes, the pity and the horror of it all were almost too much for him to bear.

And there remained one more unidentified victim, the one who had been buried there the longest: a white woman in her late teens or early twenties, about five foot three inches tall, according to the forensic anthropologist, who was still conducting tests on the bones. There was little doubt in Banks's mind that she could easily be another prostitute victim and that might make the corpse hard to identify.

Banks had had one brainstorm and pulled in Terence Payne's teacher friend Geoff Brighouse to help him find the schoolteacher the two of them had taken up to their room at the convention. Luckily, Banks turned out to be wrong and she was still teaching in Aberdeen. Though she expressed some anger about her experience, she had kept quiet mostly because she didn't want to damage her teaching career and had written that one off to experience. She had also been very embarrassed and angry with herself for being so drunk and foolish as to go to a hotel room with two strange men after all the things she had read in the papers. She had almost fainted when Banks told her that the man who had coerced her into having anal sex was Terence Payne. She had only been on first name terms with the two and hadn't made the connection from the photo in the newspapers.

Banks opened his window onto another fine day in the market square, tourist buses pulling up already, disgorging their hordes onto the gleaming cobbles. A quick glance around the church's interior, a walk up to the castle, lunch at the Pied Piper – Banks felt depressed just thinking about what had happened there yesterday – then they'd pile back in the coach and be off to Castle Bolton or Devraulx Abbey. How he wished he could go on a long holiday. Maybe never come back.

The gold hands against the blue face of the church clock stood at five past ten. Banks lit a cigarette and planned out the rest of his day, plans that included Mick Blair, Ian Scott and Sarah Francis, not to mention the grieving parents, Christopher and Victoria Wray. Winsome had discovered nothing new from talking to the Wrays' neighbours, none of whom had either seen or heard anything unusual. Banks still had his suspicions about them, though he found it difficult to convince himself that they could actually have *killed* Leanne.

He had suffered yet another restless night, this time partly because of Annie. Now, the more he thought about her decision, the more sense it made. He didn't want to give her up, but if he were to be honest, it was best all round. Looking back at her on-again-off-again attitude towards their relationship, the way she bristled every time other aspects of his life came up, he realized that however much there had been, the relationship had also been a lot of grief, too. If she didn't like the way his past made her face details of her own, like the abortion, then perhaps she was right to end it. Time to move on and stay 'just friends', let her pursue her career and let him try to exorcise his personal demons.

Just as he was finishing his cigarette, DC Winsome Jackman tapped at his door and walked in looking particularly elegant in a tailored pinstripe suit over a white blouse.

The woman had clothes sense, Banks thought, unlike himself and unlike Annie Cabbot. He liked Annie's casual style – it was definitely *her* – but no one could accuse her of making a fashion statement. Anyway, best forget about Annie. He turned towards Winsome.

'Come in. Sit down.'

Winsome sat, crossing her long legs, sniffing accusingly and wrinkling her nose at the smoke.

'I know, I know,' Banks said. 'I'm going to stop soon, honestly.'

'That little job you asked me to do,' she said. 'I thought you'd like to know that your instinct was right. There was a car reported stolen from Disraeli Street between nine-thirty and eleven o'clock on the night Leanne Wray disappeared.'

'Was there, indeed? Isn't Disraeli Street just around the corner from the Old Ship Inn?'

'It is, sir.'

Banks sat down and rubbed his hands together. 'Tell me more.'

'Keeper's name is Samuel Gardner. I've spoken to him on the phone. Seems he parked there while he popped into the Cock and Bull on Palmerston Avenue, just for a pint of shandy, he stressed.'

'Of course. Perish the thought we should try to do him for drink driving two months after the event. What do you think, Winsome?'

Winsome shifted and crossed her legs the other way, straightening the hem of her skirt over her knees. 'I don't know, sir. Seems a bit of a coincidence, doesn't it?'

'That Ian Scott's in the neighbourhood?'

'Yes, sir. I know there are plenty of kids taking and driving away, but . . . well, the timing fits and the location.'

'Indeed it does. When did he report it missing?'

'Ten past eleven that night.'

'And when was it found?'

'Not until the next morning, sir. One of the beat constables came across it illegally parked down by the formal gardens.'

'That's not very far from the Riverboat, is it?'

'Ten minute walk, at the most.'

'You know, this is starting to look good, Winsome. I want you to go and have a word with this Samuel Gardner, see if you can find out any more from him. Put him at ease. Make it clear we don't give a damn whether he drank a whole bottle of whisky as long as he tells us everything he can remember about that night. And have the car taken into the police garage for a full forensic examination. I doubt we'll find anything after all this time, but Scott and Blair aren't likely to know that, are they?'

Winsome smiled wickedly. 'Doubt it very much, sir.'

Banks looked at his watch. 'When you've talked to Gardner and the car's safe in our care, have Mick Blair brought in. I think a little chat with him in one of the interview rooms might be very productive.'

'Right you are.'

'And have Sarah Francis brought in at the same time.'

'Okay.'

'And, Winsome.'

'Sir?'

'Make sure they see one another in passing, would you?'

'My pleasure, sir.' Winsome smiled, stood up and left the office.

•

'Look,' said Jenny, 'I haven't had any lunch yet. Instead of standing around here in the street, is there anywhere near by we can go?' Though her immediate fears had dispersed somewhat when the young man simply asked her who she was and what she wanted, without showing any particular inclination towards aggression, she still wanted to be with them in a public place, not up in the flat.

'There's a café down the road,' he said. 'We can go there if you want.'

'Fine.'

Jenny followed them back to the arterial road, crossed at the zebra and went into a corner café that smelled of bacon. She was supposed to be slimming – she was *always* supposed to be slimming – but she couldn't resist the smell and ordered a bacon butty and a mug of tea. The other two asked for the same and Jenny paid. Nobody objected. Poor students never do. Now that they were closer, sitting at an isolated table near the window, Jenny could see that she was mistaken. While the girl definitely resembled Lucy, had her eyes and mouth and the same shiny black hair, it *wasn't* her. There was something softer, more fragile, more *human* about this young woman, and her eyes weren't quite so black and impenetrable; they were intelligent and sensitive, though their depths flickered with horrors and fears Jenny could barely imagine.

'Laura, isn't it?' she said when they'd settled.

The young woman raised her eyebrows. 'Why, yes. How did you know?'

'It wasn't difficult,' Jenny said. 'You resemble your sister and you're with your cousin.'

Laura blushed. 'I'm only visiting him. It's not . . . I mean, I don't want you to get the wrong idea.'

'Don't worry,' said Jenny. 'I don't jump to conclusions.' Well, not *many*, she said to herself.

'Let's get back to my original question,' Keith Murray

cut in. He was more hard-edged than Laura and not one for small talk. 'That's who are you and why you're here. You might as well tell me what you were doing at Alderthorpe, too, while you're at it.'

Laura looked surprised. 'She was in Alderthorpe?'

'On Saturday. I followed her to Easington and then to Spurn Head. I turned back when she got to the M62.' He looked at Jenny again. 'Well?'

He was a good-looking young man, brown hair a little over his ears and collar, but professionally layered, slightly better dressed than most of the students she taught, in a light sports jacket and grey chinos, highly polished shoes. Clean shaven. Clearly a young lad who took some pride in his rather conservative appearance. Laura, in contrast, wore a shapeless sort of shift that hung around her in a haze of material and hid any claims she might have had to the kind of figure men like. There was a reticence and tentativeness about her that made Jenny want to reach out and tell her everything was fine, not to worry, she didn't bite. Keith also seemed very protective of her and Jenny wondered how their relationship had developed since Alderthorpe.

She told them who she was and what she was doing, about her forays into Lucy Payne's past, looking for answers to her present, and both Laura and Keith listened intently. When she had finished, they looked at one another, and she could tell they were communicating in some way that was beyond her. She couldn't tell what they were saying, and she didn't believe it was some sort of telepathic trick, just that whatever they had been through all those years ago had created a bond so strong and deep that it went beyond words.

'What makes you think you'll find any answers there?' Keith asked.

'I'm a psychologist,' Jenny said, 'not a psychiatrist, certainly not a Freudian, but I do believe that our past shapes us, makes us what we are.'

'And what *is* Linda, or Lucy, as she calls herself now?'

Jenny spread her hands. 'That's just it. I don't know. I was hoping you might be able to help.'

'Why should we help you?'

'I don't know,' said Jenny. 'Maybe there are some issues back then you still have to deal with yourselves.'

Keith laughed. 'If we lived to be a hundred we'd still have issues to deal with from *back then*,' he said. 'But what's that got to do with Linda?'

'She was with you, wasn't she? One of you.'

Keith and Laura looked at one another again and Jenny wished she knew what they were thinking. Finally, as if they had come to a decision, Laura said, 'Yes, she was *with* us, but in a way she was apart.'

'What do you mean, Laura?'

'Linda was the eldest, so she took care of us.'

Keith snorted.

'She *did*, Keith.'

'All right.'

Laura's lower lip trembled and for a moment Jenny thought she was going to cry. 'Go on, Laura,' she said. 'Please.'

'I know Linda was my sister,' Laura said, rubbing one hand against the top of her thigh, 'but there's three years between us and that's an awful lot when you're younger.'

'Tell me about it. My brother's three years older than me.'

'Well, you'll know what I mean, then. So I didn't really *know* Linda. In some ways, she was as distant as an adult to me, and just as incomprehensible. We played together when we were little, but the older we got, the more we drifted apart, especially with . . . you know . . . the way things were.'

'What was she like, though?'

'Linda? She was strange. Very distant. Very self-absorbed, even then. She liked to play games, and she could be cruel.'

'In what way?'

'If she didn't get her own way, or if you didn't do what she wanted, she could lie and get you in trouble with the adults. Get you put in the cage.'

'She did that?'

'Oh, yes,' said Keith. 'All of us got on her bad side at one time or another.'

'Sometimes we just didn't know if she was with us or them,' said Laura. 'But she could be kind. I remember her treating a cut I had once, putting some TCP on it so it didn't get infected. She was very gentle. And sometimes she even stuck up for us against them.'

'In what ways?'

'Little ways. If we were, you know, too weak to . . . or just . . . sometimes they listened to her. And she saved the kittens.'

'What kittens?'

'Our cat had kittens and D-D-Dad wanted to drown them but Linda took them and found them all homes.'

'She liked animals, then?'

'She adored them. She wanted to be a vet when she grew up.'

'Why didn't she?'

'I don't know. Maybe she wasn't clever enough. Or maybe she changed her mind.'

'But she was also their victim, too? The adults.'

'Oh, yes,' said Keith. 'We all were.'

'She was their favourite for a long time,' Laura added. 'That is, until she . . .'

'She what, Laura? Take your time.'

Laura blushed and looked away. 'Until she became a woman. When she was twelve. Then they weren't interested in her any more. Kathleen became their favourite then. She was only nine, like me, but they liked her better.'

'What was Kathleen like?'

Laura's eyes shone. 'She was . . . like a saint. She bore it all without complaining, everything those . . . those people did to us. Kathleen had some sort of inner light, some, I don't know, some spiritual quality that just shone out, but she was very f-f-fragile, very weak and she was always ill. She couldn't take the kind of punishments and beatings they dished out.'

'Like what?'

'The cage. And no food for days. She was too weak and frail to begin with.'

'Tell me,' said Jenny, 'why did none of you tell the authorities what was going on?'

Keith and Laura looked at one another in that intense way again. 'We didn't dare,' Keith said. 'They said they'd kill us if we ever told a soul.'

'And they were . . . they were family,' Laura added. 'I mean, you wanted your mummy and daddy to love you, didn't you, so you had to do, you know, what they wanted, you had to do what the grown-ups said or your d-d-daddy wouldn't love you any more.'

Jenny sipped some tea to cover her face for a moment. She wasn't sure whether anger or pity had brought the tears to her eyes but she didn't want Laura to see them.

'Besides,' Keith went on, 'we didn't know any different. How could we know life was different for other kids?'

'What about at school? You must have kept yourselves apart, been aware that you were *different*?'

'We kept apart, yes. We were told not to talk about what happened. It was *family*, and nobody else's business.'

'What were you doing in Alderthorpe?'

'I'm writing a book,' Keith said. 'A book about what happened. It's partly therapeutic and partly because I think people should know what goes on, so maybe it can be prevented from happening again.'

'Why did you follow me?'

'I thought you might be a reporter or something, poking about the place like that.'

'You'd better get used to that idea, Keith. It won't take them long to find out about Alderthorpe. I'm surprised they're not swarming around already.'

'I know.'

'So you thought I was a reporter. What were you going to do about me?'

'Nothing. I just wanted to see where you were going, make sure you were gone.'

'And what if I'd come back?'

Keith spread his hands, palms up. 'You did, didn't you?'

'Did you realize it was Linda as soon as the news about the Paynes broke?'

'I did, yes,' said Laura. 'It wasn't a good photo, but I knew she'd married Terry. I knew where she lived.'

'Did you ever get together, keep in touch?'

'We did until Susan committed suicide and Tom went to Australia. And Keith and I visit Dianne as often as we can. But as I said, Linda was always distant, older. I mean, we met up sometimes, for birthdays, that sort of thing, but I thought she was weird.'

'In what way?'

'I don't know. It was an evil thought. I mean, she'd suffered the same as we had.'

'But it seemed to have affected her in a different way,' Keith added.

'What way?'

'I didn't see her nearly as often as Laura did,' he went on, 'but she always gave me the impression that she was up to something bad, something deliciously evil. It was just the way she spoke, the hint of sin. She was secretive, so she never told us exactly what she was doing, but . . .'

'She was into some pretty weird stuff,' Laura said, blushing. 'S & M. That sort of thing.'

'She told you?'

'Once. Yes. She only did it to embarrass me. I'm not comfortable talking about sex.' She hugged herself and avoided Jenny's eyes.

'And Linda liked to embarrass you?'

'Yes. Tease me, I suppose.'

'Wasn't it a shock to you, what Terry had done, with Linda so close by, especially after the events of your childhood?'

'Of course it was,' said Keith. 'It still is. We're still trying to come to terms with it.'

'That's partly why I'm here,' said Laura. 'I needed to be with Keith. To talk. To decide what to do.'

'What do you mean, what to do?'

'But we didn't want to be rushed,' said Keith.

Jenny leaned forward. 'What is it?' she asked. 'What is it you need to do?'

They looked at one another again, and Jenny waited what seemed like ages before Keith spoke. 'We'd better tell her, don't you think?' he said.

'I suppose so.'

'Tell me what?'

'About what happened. That's what we've been trying to decide, you see. Whether we should tell.'

'But I'm sure you can understand,' Keith said, 'that we don't want the limelight any more. We don't want it all raked up again.'

'Your book will do that,' Jenny said.

'I'll deal with that when and if it happens.' He leaned forward. 'Anyway, you've sort of forced our hand, haven't you? We would probably have told someone soon, anyway, so it might as well be you, now.'

'I'm still not sure what you want to tell me,' Jenny said.

Laura looked at her, tears in her eyes. 'It's about Kathleen. Our parents didn't kill her, Tom didn't kill her. Linda killed her. Linda killed Kathleen.'

•

Mick Blair was surly when Banks and Winsome entered the interview room at 3.35 that afternoon. As well he might be, Banks thought. He had been dragged away from his job as an assistant in the Tandy shop in the Swainsdale Centre by two uniformed police officers and left waiting in the dingy room for over an hour. It was a wonder he wasn't screaming for his brief. Banks would have been.

'Just another little chat, Mick,' said Banks, smiling as he turned on the tape recorders. 'But we'll get it on record this time. That way you can be certain there's no funny business from us.'

'Very grateful, I'm sure,' said Blair. 'And why the hell did you have to keep me waiting so long?'

'Important police business,' said Banks. 'The bad guys just never stop.'

'What's Sarah doing here?'

'Sarah?'

'You know who I mean. Sarah Francis. Ian's girlfriend. I saw her in the corridor. What's she doing here?'

'Just answering our questions, Mick, the way I hope you will.'

'I don't know why you're wasting your time on me. I can't tell you anything you don't know already.'

'Don't underestimate yourself, Mick.'

'What's it about this time, then?' He eyed Winsome suspiciously.

'It's about the night Leanne Wray disappeared.'

'Again? But we've been over and over all that.'

'Yes, I know, but we haven't got to the truth yet. See, it's like peeling off the layers of an onion, Mick. All we've got so far is layer after layer of lies.'

'It's the truth. She left us outside the Old Ship and we went our separate ways. We didn't see her again. What else can I tell you?'

'The truth. Where the four of you went.'

'I've told you all I know.'

'You see, Mick,' Banks went on, 'Leanne was upset that day. She'd just heard some bad news. Her stepmother was going to have a baby. You might not understand why, but believe me, that upset her. So I should think that night she was in a rebellious mood, ready to say to hell with the curfew and let's have some fun. Make her parents suffer a bit at the same time. I don't know whose suggestion it was, maybe yours, but you decided to steal a car—'

'Now, wait a minute—'

'A car belonging to Mr Samuel Gardner, a blue Fiat Brava to be exact, which was parked just around the corner from the pub.'

'That's ridiculous! We never stole no car. You can't pin that on us.'

'Shut up and listen, Mick,' said Winsome. Blair looked at her, then swallowed and shut up. Winsome's expression was hard and unflinching, her eyes full of scorn and disgust.

'Where did you go on your little joyride, Mick?' Banks asked. 'What happened? What happened to Leanne? Was she giving you the come on? Did you think it was going to be your lucky night? Did you try it on with her and she changed her mind? Did you get a bit rough? Were you on drugs, Mick?'

'No! It's not true. None of it's true. She left us outside the pub.'

'You sound like a drowning man clinging to a bit of wood, Mick. Pretty soon you'll have to let go.'

'I'm telling the truth.'

'I don't think so.'

'Then prove it.'

'Listen, Mick,' said Winsome, standing up and pacing the small room. 'We've got Mr Gardner's car in the police garage right now and our forensics people are going over it inch by inch. Are you trying to tell us that they won't find anything?'

'I don't know what they'll find,' said Mick. 'How can I? I've never even seen the fucking car.'

Winsome stopped pacing and sat down. 'They're the best in the business, our forensics team. They don't even need fingerprints. If there's just one hair, they'll find it. And if it belongs to you, Ian, Sarah or Leanne, we've got you.' She held a finger up. 'One hair. Think about it, Mick.'

'She's right, you know,' said Banks. 'They *are* very good, these scientists. Me, I know bugger all about DNA and hair follicles, but these lads could find the exact spot on your head the hair came from.'

'We didn't steal no car.'

'I know what you're thinking,' Banks said.

'Mind reader, too, are you?'

Banks laughed. 'It doesn't take much. You're thinking, how long ago was it we took that car? It was the thirty-first of March. And what's today's date? It's the sixteenth of May. That's a month and a half. Surely there can't be any traces left by now? Surely the car must have been washed, the interior vacuumed? Isn't that what you're thinking, Mick?'

'I've told you. I don't know nothing about a stolen car.' He folded his arms and tried to look defiant. Winsome gave a grunt of disgust and impatience.

'DC Jackman's getting restless,' said Banks. 'And I wouldn't want to push her too far, if I were you.'

'You can't touch me. It's all on tape.'

'Touch you? Who said anything about touching you?'

'You're threatening me.'

'No. You've got it wrong, Mick. See, *I* want to get this all settled, get you back off to work, home in time for the evening news. Nothing I'd like better. But DC Jackman here is, well, let's just say that she'd be more than happy to see you in detention.'

'What do you mean?'

'In the cells, Mick. Downstairs. Overnight.'

'But I haven't done anything. You can't do that.'

'Was it Ian? Is that whose idea it was?'

'I don't know what you're talking about.'

'What happened to Leanne?'

'Nothing. I don't know.'

'I'll bet Sarah tells us it was all your fault.'

'I haven't done anything.'

'She'll want to protect her boyfriend, won't she, Mick? I'll bet she doesn't give a damn about you when the chips are down.'

'Stop it!'

Winsome looked at her watch. 'Let's just lock him up and go home,' she said. 'I'm getting fed up of this.'

'What do you think, Mick?'

'I've told you all I know.'

Banks looked at Winsome before turning back to Mick. 'I'm afraid, then, we're going to have to hold you on suspicion.'

'Suspicion of *what*?'

'Suspicion of the murder of Leanne Wray.'

Mick jumped to his feet. 'That's absurd. I didn't kill anyone. Nobody *murdered* Leanne.'

'How do you know that?'

'I mean *I* didn't murder Leanne. I don't know what happened to her. It's not my fault if somebody else killed her.'

'It is if you were there.'

'I wasn't there.'

'Then tell us the truth, Mick. Tell us what happened.'

'I've told you.'

Banks stood up and gathered his folders together. 'All right. We'll see what Sarah has to say. In the meantime, I want you to think about two things while you're in the cells for the night, Mick. Time can drag down there, especially in the wee hours, when all you've got for company is the drunk next door singing "Your Cheating Heart" over and over again, so it's nice to have something to think about, something to distract you.'

'What things?'

'First off, if you come clean with us, if you tell us the truth, if it was all Ian Scott's idea and if whatever happened to Leanne was down to Ian, then it'll go a lot easier with you.' He looked at Winsome. 'I could even see him walking away from this with little more than a reprimand, failing to report, or something minor like that, can't you, DC Jackman?'

Winsome grimaced, as if the idea of Mick Blair's getting off with less than murder appalled her.

'What's the other thing?' Mick asked.

'The other thing? Oh, yes. It's about Samuel Gardner.'

'Who?'

'The owner of the stolen car.'

'What about him?'

'Man's a slob, Mick. He *never* cleans his car. Inside or out.'

•

Jenny couldn't think of anything to say after what Keith and Laura had just told her. She sat with her mouth half open and an astonished expression on her face until her brain processed the information and she was able to continue. 'How do you know?' she asked.

'We saw her,' Keith said. 'We were with her. In a way, it was all of us. She was doing it for all of us but she was the only one had the guts to do it.'

'Are you certain about this?'

'Yes,' they said.

'This isn't something you've just remembered?' Like many of her colleagues, Jenny distrusted repressed memory syndrome and she wanted to make certain that was not what she was dealing with. Linda Godwin might have been kind to animals and never wet the bed or started a fire, but if she had killed when she was twelve, there was something seriously, pathologically wrong with her, and she could have killed again.

'No,' said Laura. 'We always knew. We just lost it for a while.'

'What do you mean?'

'It's like when you put something away where you can find it again easily, but then you don't remember where you put it,' said Keith.

Jenny understood that; it happened to her all the time.

'Or when you're carrying something and you remember you have to do something else, so you put it down on your way, and then you can't find it again,' Laura added.

'You say you were there?'

'Yes,' said Keith. 'We were in the room with her. We saw her do it.'

'And you've said nothing all these years?'

Laura and Keith just looked at her and she understood that they couldn't have said anything. How could they? They were too used to silence. And why would they? They were all victims of the Godwins and the Murrays. Why should Linda be singled out for more suffering?

'Is that why she was in the cage when the police came?'

'No. Linda was in the cage because it was her period,' Keith said. Laura blushed and turned away. 'Tom was in the cage with her because they thought *he* did it. They never suspected Linda.'

'But *why*?' asked Jenny.

'Because Kathleen just couldn't take any more,' said Laura. 'She was so weak, her spirit was almost gone. Linda killed her to s-s-save her. She *knew* what it was like to be in that position and she knew that Kathleen couldn't handle it. She killed her to save her further suffering.'

'Are you sure?' Jenny asked.

'What do you mean?'

'Are you certain that's why Linda killed her?'

'Why else?'

'Didn't you think it might have been because she was jealous? Because Kathleen was usurping *her* place?'

'No!' said Laura, scraping back her chair. 'That's horrible. How could you say something like that? She killed her to save her more suffering. She killed her out of k-k-kindness.'

One or two people in the café had noticed Laura's outburst and were looking over curiously at the table.

'Okay,' Jenny said. 'I'm sorry. I didn't mean to upset you.'

Laura looked at her and a note of defiant desperation came into her tone. 'She *could* be kind, you know. Linda *could* be kind.'

•

The old house was certainly full of noises, Maggie thought, and she was beginning to jump at almost every one: wood creaking as the temperature dropped after dark, a whistle of wind rattling at the windows, dishes shifting in the rack as they dried. It was Bill's phone call, of course, she told herself, and she tried the routines she used to calm herself – deep breathing, positive visualization – but the ordinary noises of the house continued to distract her from her work.

She put a CD compilation of Baroque classics in the stereo Ruth had set up in the studio, and that both cut out the disturbing sounds and helped her to relax.

She was working late on some sketches for 'Hansel and Gretel' because the following day she had to go to London to meet with her art director and discuss the project so far.

She also had an interview at Broadcasting House: a Radio 4 programme about domestic violence, naturally, but she was beginning to warm to being a spokesperson, and if anything she said could help anyone at all, then all the minor irritations, such as ignorant interviewers and provocative fellow guests, were worthwhile.

Bill already knew where she was, so she had no reason to worry about giving that away now. She wasn't going to run away. Not again. Despite his call and the way it had shaken her, she was determined to continue in her new role.

While she was in London, she would also try to get a ticket for a West End play she wanted to see and stay overnight at the modest little hotel her art director had recommended several visits ago.

Maggie turned back to her sketch. She was trying to capture the expression on the faces of Hansel and Gretel when they realized in the moonlight that the trail of crumbs they had left to lead them from the dangers of the forest to the safety of home had been eaten by birds. She liked the eerie effect she had created with the tree trunks, branches and shadows, which with just a little imagination could take the shapes of wild beasts and demons, but Hansel and Gretel's expressions still weren't quite right. They were only children, Maggie reminded herself, not adults, and their fear would be simple and natural, a look of abandonment and eyes on the verge of tears, not as complex as adult fear, which would include components of anger and the determination to find a way out. Very different facial expressions indeed.

In an earlier version of the sketch, Hansel and Gretel had come out looking a bit like younger versions of Terry and Lucy, Maggie thought, just as Rapunzel had resembled Claire, so she scrapped it. Now they were anonymous, faces she had probably once spotted in a crowd which, for whatever mysterious reason, had lodged in her unconscious.

Claire. The poor girl. That afternoon Maggie had talked with both Claire and her mother together, and they had agreed that Claire would try the psychologist Dr Simms had recommended. That was a start, at least, Maggie thought, though it might take Claire years to work through the psychological disturbance brought on by Terry Payne's acts, her friend's murder and her own sense of guilt and responsibility.

Pachelbel's 'Canon' played in the background and Maggie concentrated on her drawing, adding a little chiaroscuro effect here and a silvering of moonlight there. No need to make it too elaborate, as it would only serve as the model for a painting, but she needed these notes to herself to show her the way when she came to the final version. That would be different in some ways, of course, but would also retain many of the visual ideas she was having now.

When she heard the tapping over the music, she thought it was another noise the old house had come up with to scare her.

But when it stopped for a few seconds, then resumed at a slightly higher volume and faster rhythm, she turned off the stereo and listened.

Someone was knocking at the back door.

Nobody ever used the back door. It only led into a mean little lattice-work of ginnels and snickets that connected with the council estate behind The Hill.

Not Bill, surely?

No, Maggie reassured herself. Bill was in Toronto. Besides, the door was deadlocked, bolted and chained. She wondered if she should dial 999 right away, but then realized how silly she would look in the eyes of the police if it was Claire or Claire's mother. Or even the police themselves. She couldn't bear the idea of Banks hearing she had been such a fool.

Instead, she moved very slowly and quietly. Despite the anonymous creaks, the staircase was relatively silent underfoot, partly because of the thick pile carpet. She picked out one of Charles's golf clubs from the hall cupboard and, brandishing it ready to use, edged towards the kitchen door.

The knocking continued.

It was only when Maggie had got to within a few feet of the door that she heard the familiar woman's voice: 'Maggie, is that you? Are you there? Please let me in.'

She abandoned the golf club, turned on the kitchen light and fiddled with the various locks. When she finally got the door open, she was confused by what she saw. Appearance and voice didn't match. The woman had short, spiky blonde hair, was wearing a T-shirt under a soft black leather jacket and a pair of close-fitting blue jeans. She was carrying a small hold-all. Only the slight bruising by one eye and the impenetrable darkness of the eyes themselves told Maggie who it was, though it took several moments to process the information.

'Lucy. My God, it *is* you!'

'Can I come in?'

'Of course.' Maggie held the door open and Lucy Payne stepped into the kitchen.

'Only I've got nowhere to go and I wondered if you could put me up. Just for a couple of days or so, while I think of something.'

'Yes,' said Maggie, still feeling stunned. 'Yes, of course. Stay as long as you like. It's quite a new look. I didn't recognize you at first.'

Lucy gave a little twirl. 'Do you like it?'

'It's certainly different.'

Lucy laughed. 'Good,' she said. 'I don't want *anyone* else to know I'm here. Believe it or not, Maggie, but not everyone around here is as sympathetic towards me as you are.'

'I suppose not,' said Maggie, then she locked, bolted and put the chain on the door, turned out the kitchen light and led Lucy Payne into the living room.

18

'I just wanted to say I'm sorry,' Annie told Banks in his Eastvale office on Wednesday morning. He had just been glancing over the garage's report on Samuel Gardner's Fiat. They had, of course, found many hair traces in the car's interior, both human and animal, but they all had to be collected, labelled and sent to the lab, and it would take time to match them with the suspects, or with Leanne Wray. There were plenty of fingerprints, too – it was certainly true that Gardner had been a slob when it came to his car – but Vic Manson, fingerprints officer, could only hurry to a certain degree, and it wasn't fast enough for Banks's immediate needs.

Banks looked at Annie. 'Sorry for *what* exactly?'

'Sorry for making a scene in the pub, for acting like a fool.'

'Oh.'

'What did you think I meant?'

'Nothing.'

'No, come on. That I was sorry about what I said, about us? About ending the relationship?'

'I can always live in hope, can't I?'

'Oh, stop feeling sorry for yourself, Alan. It doesn't suit you.'

Banks opened up a paperclip. The sharp end pricked his finger and a tiny spot of blood dropped on his desk. Which fairy tale was that? he found himself wondering. *Sleeping*

Beauty? But he didn't fall asleep. Chance would be a fine thing.

'Now are we going to get on with life, or are you just going to sulk and ignore me? Because if you are, I'd like to know.'

Banks couldn't help but smile. She was right. He *had* been feeling sorry for himself. He had also decided that she was right about their relationship. Fine as it had been most of the time, and much as he would miss her intimate company, it was fraught with problems on both sides. So *tell* her, his inner voice prompted. Don't be a bastard. Don't put it all down to her, the whole burden. It was difficult; he wasn't used to talking about his feelings. He sucked his bleeding finger and said, 'I'm *not* going to sulk. Just give me a little time to get used to the idea, okay? I sort of enjoyed what we had.'

'So did I,' said Annie, with a hint of a smile tugging at the corners of her lips. 'Do you think it's any easier for me, just because I'm the one who's making the move? We want different things, Alan. *Need* different things. It's just not working.'

'You're right. Look, I promise I won't sulk or ignore you or put you down as long as you don't treat me like something nasty stuck on your shoe.'

'What on earth makes you think I'd do that?'

Banks was thinking of the letter from Sandra, which had made him feel exactly like that, but he was talking to Annie, he realized. Yes, she was right; things were well and truly screwed up. He shook his head. 'Ignore me, Annie. Friends and colleagues, okay?'

Annie narrowed her eyes and scrutinized him. 'I *do* care, you know.'

'I know you do.'

'That's part of the problem.'

'It'll get better. Over time. Sorry, I can't seem to think of anything to say but clichés. Maybe that's what they're for, situations like this? Maybe that's why there are so many of them. But don't worry, Annie, I mean what I say. I'll do the best I can to behave towards you with the utmost courtesy and respect.'

'Oh, bloody hell!' Annie said, laughing. 'You don't have to be so damn stuffy! A simple good morning, a smile and a friendly little chat in the canteen every now and then would be just fine.'

Banks felt his face burn, then he laughed with her. 'Right you are. How's Janet Taylor?'

'Stubborn as hell. I've tried to talk to her. The CPS has tried to talk to her. Her own lawyer has tried to talk to her. Even *Chambers* has tried to talk to her.'

'At least she's got a lawyer now.'

'The Federation sent someone over.'

'What's she being charged with?'

'They're going to charge her with voluntary manslaughter. If she pleads guilty with extenuating circumstances, there's every chance she'll get it down to excusable homicide.'

'And if she goes ahead as planned?'

'Who knows? It's up to the jury. They're either going to give her the same as they gave John Hadleigh, despite the vastly different circumstances, or they're going to take her job and her situation into account and give her the benefit of the doubt. I mean, the public doesn't want us hamstrung when it comes to doing our job, but they don't want us to get ideas above our station, either. They don't like to see us acting as if we're beyond the law. It's a toss up, really.'

'How's she bearing up?'

'She's not. She's just drinking.'

'Bugger.'

'Indeed. How about the Payne investigation?'

Banks told her what Jenny had discovered about Lucy's past.

Annie whistled. 'So what are you going to do?'

'Bring her in for questioning on the death of Kathleen Murray. If we can find her. It's probably a bloody waste of time – after all, it was over ten years ago and she was only twelve at the time – so I doubt we'll get anywhere with it, but who knows, it might open other doors if a little pressure is judiciously applied.'

'AC Hartnell won't like it.'

'I know that. He's already made his feelings clear.'

'Lucy Payne doesn't suspect you know so much about her past?'

'She has to be aware there was a chance the others would talk, or that we'd find out somehow. In that case, she may have already gone to ground.'

'Anything new on the sixth body?'

'No,' said Banks. 'But we'll find out who it is.' The fact that they couldn't identify the sixth victim nagged away at him. Like the other victims, she had been buried naked and no traces of clothing or personal belongings remained. Banks could only guess that Payne must have burned their clothes and disposed of any rings or watches somehow. He certainly hadn't kept them as trophies. The forensic anthropologist working on her remains had so far been able to tell him that she was a white female between the ages of eighteen and twenty-two and that she had died, like the others, of ligature strangulation. Horizontal striations in the tooth enamel indicated inconsistent nutrition during her early years. The regularity of the lines indicated possible seasonal swings in food supplies. Perhaps, like Katya, she had come from a war-torn country in Eastern Europe.

Banks had had a team keeping track of all mispers over the past few months and they were working overtime now, following up on reports. But if the victim were a prostitute, like Katya Pavelic, then the chances of finding out who she was were slim. Even so, Banks kept telling himself, she was *somebody's* daughter. Somewhere, somebody *must* be missing her. But perhaps not. There were plenty of people out there without friends or family, people who could die in their homes tomorrow and not be found until the rent was long overdue or the smell grew too bad for the neighbours to bear. There were refugees from Eastern Europe, like Katya, or kids who had left home to travel the world and might be anywhere from Katmandu to Kilimanjaro. He had to inure himself to the fact that they might *not* be able to identify the sixth victim for some time, if ever. But still it galled. She should have a name, an identity.

Annie stood up. 'Anyway, I've said what I came to say. Oh, and you'll probably be hearing very soon that I've made a formal request to come back to CID. Think there's any chance?'

'You can have my job, if you want.'

Annie smiled. 'You don't mean that.'

'Don't I? Anyway, I don't know if they've changed their minds about CID staffing levels, but I'll talk to Red Ron, if you think that'll help. We don't have a DI right now, so it's probably a good time to make your application.'

'Before Winsome catches up with me?'

'She's sharp, that lass.'

'Pretty, too.'

'Is she? I hadn't noticed.'

Annie stuck her tongue out at Banks and left his office.

Sad as he felt at the end of their brief romance, he felt some relief, too. He would no longer have to wonder from one day to the next whether they were on or off again; he had been given his freedom yet again, and freedom was a somewhat ambiguous gift.

'Sir?'

Banks looked up and saw Winsome framed in his doorway. 'Yes?'

'Just had a message from Steve Naylor, the custody sergeant downstairs.'

'Problem?'

'No, not at all.' Winsome smiled. 'It's Mick Blair. He wants to talk.'

Banks clapped his hands and rubbed them together. 'Excellent. Tell them to send him straight up. Our best interview room, I think, Winsome.'

•

When she was packed and ready to head for London, Maggie took Lucy a cup of tea in bed the following morning. It was the least she could do after all the poor woman had been through lately.

They had talked well into the previous night, emptying a bottle of white wine between them, and Lucy had hinted at what a terrible childhood she had suffered and how recent events had brought it all back to mind. She had also confided that she was afraid of the police, afraid they might try to fabricate some sort of evidence against her, and that she couldn't stand the thought of going to jail. Just one night in the cell had almost been too much for her to bear.

The police didn't like loose ends, she said, and in this case she was a very serious loose end indeed. She knew they had been watching her and had sneaked out of her foster parents' house after dark and taken the first train from Hull to York, then changed for London, where she had worked on changing her appearance, mostly through hair, make-up and a different style of dress. Maggie had to agree that the Lucy Payne she knew wouldn't have been seen dead in the kind of casual clothes she was wearing now, nor would she have worn the same, slightly tarty make-up. Maggie agreed to tell no one that Lucy was there, and if any of the neighbours saw her and asked who she was, she would tell them she was a distant relative just passing through.

Both bedrooms, the large and the small, overlooked The Hill, and when Maggie tapped on the door of the smaller room she had given Lucy and entered, she saw that Lucy was already standing by the window. Stark naked. She turned when Maggie entered with the tea. 'Oh, thank you. You're so kind.'

Maggie felt herself blush. She couldn't help but notice what a fine body Lucy had: the full, round breasts, taut, flat stomach, gently curving hips and smooth tapered thighs, the dark triangle between her legs. Lucy seemed completely unembarrassed by her own nakedness, but Maggie felt uncomfortable and tried to avert her eyes.

Luckily the curtains were still closed and the light was fairly dim, but Lucy had held them open a little at the top and had clearly been watching the activity across the street. It had let up a bit in the past couple of days, Maggie had noticed, but there was still a great deal of coming and going, and the front garden was still a complete mess.

'Have you seen what they've done over there?' said Lucy, coming forward and accepting the cup of tea. She got back into bed and covered herself with the thin white sheet. Maggie was grateful at least for that.

'Yes,' said Maggie.

'That's *my* house, and they've ruined it completely for me. I can't go back there now. Not *ever*.' Her lower lip trembled in anger. 'I saw through the door into the hall when someone came out. They've taken all the carpets, pulled up the floorboards. They've even punched big holes in the walls. They've just ruined it.'

'I suppose they were looking for things, Lucy. It's their job.'

'Looking for what? What more could they want? I'll bet they've taken all my nice things, too, all my jewellery and clothes. All my memories.'

'I'm sure you'll get it all back.'

Lucy shook her head. 'No. I don't want it all back. Not now. I thought I did, but now I've seen what they've done, it's tainted. I'll start over again. With what I've got.'

'Are you all right for money?' Maggie asked.

'Yes, thank you. We had a bit put away. I don't know what will happen to the house, the mortgage, but I doubt we'll be able to sell it in that state.'

'There must be some sort of compensation,' Maggie said. 'Surely they can't just take your house and not compensate you?'

'I wouldn't be surprised at *anything* they could do.' Lucy blew on the tea. Steam rose around her face.

'Look, I told you last night,' Maggie said, 'I have to go to London, just for a couple of days. Will you be all right here by yourself?'

'Yes. Of course. Don't worry about me.'

'There's plenty of food in the fridge and freezer, you know, if you don't want to go out or order in.'

'That's good, thank you,' said Lucy. 'I think I really would just like to stay in and shut out the world and watch television or something, try to take my mind off what's been happening.'

'There's plenty of video tapes in the cupboard under the TV in my bedroom,' said Maggie. 'Please feel free to watch them there whenever you want.'

'Thank you, Maggie. I will.'

Though there was a small television set in the living room, the only TV and video combination in the house was set up in the master bedroom, for some reason, and that was Maggie's room. Not that she wasn't thankful. She had often lain in bed unable to sleep and, when there was nothing suitable on television, had watched one of the love stories or romantic comedies Ruth seemed to favour, with actors such as Hugh Grant, Meg Ryan, Richard Gere, Tom Hanks, Julia Roberts and Sandra Bullock; they had helped her through many a long, hard night.

'Are you sure there isn't anything else you need?'

'I can't think of anything,' Lucy said. 'I just want to feel *safe* and comfortable so I can remember what it's like.'

'You'll be fine here. I'm really sorry I have to leave you so soon, but I'll be back before long. Don't worry.'

'It's okay, honest,' said Lucy. 'I didn't come here to interrupt your life or anything. You've got your work. I know that. I'm only asking for sanctuary for a short time, just till I get myself together.'

'What *are* you going to do?'

'No idea. I suppose I can change my name and get a job somewhere far away from here. Anyway, not to worry. You go to London and have a good time. I can take care of myself.'

'If you're sure.'

'I'm sure.' Lucy got out of bed again, put her cup of tea on the bedside table and went back towards the window.

There she stood, providing Maggie with a rear view of her finely toned body, looking out across the road at what used to be her home.

'I must dash, then,' said Maggie. 'The taxi will be here soon.'

'Bye,' said Lucy without turning round. 'Have a good time.'

•

'Okay, Mick,' said Banks. 'I understand you want to talk to us.'

After his night in the cells, Mick Blair didn't at all resemble the cocky teenager they had interviewed yesterday. In fact he looked like a frightened kid. Clearly the prospect of spending several years in a similar or worse facility had worked on his imagination. He had also, Banks knew through the custody sergeant, had a long telephone conversation with his parents shortly after his detention, and his manner had seemed to change after that. He had *not* asked for a lawyer. Not yet.

'Yeah,' he said. 'But first tell me what Sarah said.'

'You know I can't do that, Mick.'

In fact, Sarah Francis had told them nothing at all; she had remained as monosyllabic and as scared and surly as she had in Ian Scott's flat. But that didn't matter, as she had been mainly used as a lever against Mick, anyway.

Banks, Winsome and Mick were in the largest, most comfortable interview room. It had also been painted recently, and Banks could smell the paint from the institutional green walls. He still had nothing from the lab on Samuel Gardner's car, but Mick didn't know that. He said he wanted to talk, but if he decided to play coy again, Banks could always drop hints about fingerprints and hairs. He *knew* they had been in the car. It was something he should have checked at the time, with Ian Scott having a record for taking and driving away. Given Scott's other offence, he also had a good idea what the four of them had been up to.

'Would you like to make a statement, then?' Banks said. 'For the record.'

'Yes.'

'You've been made aware of all your rights?'

'Yes.'

'Okay, then, Mick, tell us what happened that night.'

'What you said yesterday, about it going easier with me . . .?'

'Yes?'

'You meant it, didn't you? I mean, whatever Sarah said, she might have been lying, you know, to protect herself and Ian.'

'The courts and the judges look favourably upon people who help the police, Mick. That's a fact. I'll be honest. I can't give you the exact details of what will happen – it depends on so many variables – but I *can* tell you that you'll have my support for leniency, and that should go some distance.'

Mick swallowed. He was about to rat on his friends. Banks had witnessed such moments before and knew how difficult it was, what conflicting emotions must be struggling for primacy inside Mick Blair's soul. Self-preservation usually won out, in Banks's experience, but sometimes at the cost of self-loathing. It was the same for him, the watcher; he wanted the information, and he had coaxed many a weak and sensitive suspect towards informing, but when he succeeded the taste of victory was often soured by the bile of disgust.

Not this time, though, Banks thought. He wanted to

know what had happened to Leanne Wray far more than he cared about Mick Blair's discomfort.

'You did steal that car, didn't you, Mick?' Banks began. 'We've already recovered a lot of hair samples and fingerprints. We'll find yours among them, won't we? And Ian's, Sarah's and Leanne's.'

'It was Ian,' Blair said. 'It was all Ian's idea. It was nothing to do with me. I can't even fucking drive.'

'What about Sarah?'

'Sarah? Ian says jump, Sarah asks how high.'

'And Leanne?'

'Leanne was all for it. She was in a pretty wild mood that night. I didn't know why. She said something about her stepmother, but I didn't know what the problem was. To be honest, I didn't really care. I mean, I didn't want to know about her family problems. We've all got problems, right?'

Indeed we have, thought Banks.

'You just wanted to get into her knickers, then?' said Winsome.

That seemed to shock Blair, coming from a woman, a beautiful woman at that, with a soft Jamaican accent.

'No! I mean, I liked her, yes. But I wasn't trying it on, honest. I wasn't trying to force her or anything like that.'

'What happened, Mick?' Banks asked.

'Ian said why don't we take a car and do some E and smoke a couple of spliffs and maybe drive up to Darlington and go clubbing.'

'What about Leanne's curfew?'

'She said fuck the curfew, it sounded like a great idea to her. Like I said, she was a bit wild that night. She'd had a couple of drinks. Not a lot, like, just a couple, but she didn't usually drink and it was just enough to loosen her up a bit. She wanted to have some fun.'

'And you thought you might get lucky?'

Again, Winsome's interjection seemed to confuse Blair. 'No. Yes. I mean, if she was willing. Okay, I fancied her. I thought, maybe . . . you know . . . she seemed different, more devil-may-care.'

'And you thought the drugs would make her even more willing?'

'No. I don't know.' He looked at Banks in annoyance. 'Look, do you want me to go on with this or not?'

'Go on.' Banks gave Winsome the signal to keep out of it for the time being. He could imagine the scenario easily enough: Leanne a little drunk, giggly, flirting with Blair a bit, as Shannon the barmaid had said, then Ian Scott offering Ecstasy in the car, maybe Leanne unsure about it, but Blair encouraging her, egging her on, hoping all the time to get her into bed. But all that was something they could deal with later on, if necessary, when they had established the circumstances of Leanne's disappearance.

'Ian stole the car,' Blair went on. 'I don't know anything about stealing cars, but he said he learned when he was a kid growing up on the East Side Estate.'

Banks knew all too well that stealing cars was one of the essential skills for kids growing up on the East Side Estate. 'Where did you go?'

'North. Like I said, we were going to Darlington. Ian knows the club scene up there. Soon as we set off Ian handed out the E and we all gobbled it up. Then Sarah rolled a spliff and we smoked that.'

Banks noticed that it was always someone else committing the illegal act, never Blair, but he filed that away for later. 'Had Leanne taken Ecstasy or smoked marijuana before?' he asked.

'Not to my knowledge. She always seemed a bit strait-laced to me.'

'But not that night?'

'No.'

'Okay. Go on. What happened?'

Mick looked down at the table and Banks could tell he was coming to the hard part. 'We hadn't got far out of Eastvale – maybe half an hour or so – when Leanne said she felt sick and she could feel her heart was beating way too fast. She was having trouble breathing. She used that inhaler thing she carried with her, but it didn't do any good. Made her worse, if you ask me. Anyway, Ian thought she was just panicking or hallucinating or something, so first he opened the car windows. It didn't do any good, though. Soon she was shaking and sweating. I mean, she was really scared. Me, too.'

'What did you do?'

'We were in the country by then, up on the moors above Lyndgarth, so Ian pulled off the road and stopped. We all got out and walked out on the moor. Ian thought the open spaces would be good for Leanne, a breath of fresh air, that maybe she was just getting claustrophobic in the car.'

'Did it help?'

Mick turned pale. 'No. Soon as we got out she was sick. I mean *really* sick. Then she collapsed. She couldn't breathe and she seemed to be choking.'

'Did you know she was asthmatic?'

'Like I said, I saw her use the inhaler in the car when she first started feeling weird.'

'And it didn't enter your mind that Ecstasy might be dangerous for an asthma sufferer, or that it might cause a bad reaction with the inhalant?'

'How could I know? I'm not a doctor.'

'No. But you *do* take Ecstasy – I doubt this was your first time – and you must have been aware of some of the adverse publicity. The Leah Betts story, for example, the girl who died about five years ago? A few others since.'

'I heard about them, yes, but I thought you just had to be careful about your body temperature when you were dancing. You know, like, drink plenty of water and be careful you don't dehydrate.'

'That's only one of the dangers. Did you give her the inhaler again when she became worse out on the moor?'

'We couldn't find it. It must have been back in the car, in her bag. Besides, it had only made her worse.'

Banks remembered viewing the contents of Leanne's shoulderbag, seeing the inhaler there among her personal items and doubting that she would have run away without it.

'Didn't it also cross your mind that she might have been choking on her own vomit?' he went on.

'I don't know, I never really . . .'

'What *did* you do?'

'That's just it. We didn't know what to do. We just tried to give her some breathing space, some air, you know, but all of a sudden she sort of twitched, and after that she didn't move at all.'

Banks let the silence stretch for a few moments, conscious only of their breathing and the soft electric hum of the tape machines.

'Why didn't you take her to the hospital?' he asked.

'It was too late! I told you. She was dead.'

'You were certain of that?'

'Yes. We checked her pulse, felt for a heartbeat, tried to see if she was breathing, but there was nothing. She was dead. It all happened so quickly. I mean, we were feeling the E, too, we were panicking a bit, not thinking clearly.'

Banks knew of at least three other recent Ecstasy-related deaths in the region, so Blair's account didn't surprise him too much. MDMA, short for methylenedioxy methamphetamine, was a popular drug with young people because it was cheap and kept you going all night at raves and clubs. It was believed to be safe, though Mick was right that you had to be careful about your water intake and body temperature, but it could also be particularly dangerous to people suffering from high blood pressure or asthma, like Leanne.

'Why didn't you take her to a hospital when you were all still in the car?'

'Ian said she'd be okay if we just got out and walked around for a while. He said he'd seen that kind of reaction before.'

'What did you do then, after you discovered she was dead?'

'Ian said we couldn't tell anyone what had happened, that we'd all go to jail.'

'So what *did* you do?'

'We carried her further out on the moor and buried her. I mean, there was a sort of sink hole, not very deep, by a bit of broken-down drystone wall, so we put her in there and we covered her up with stones and bracken. Nobody could find her unless they were *really* looking, and there weren't any public footpaths near by. Even the animals couldn't get to her. It was so desolate, the middle of nowhere.'

'And then?'

'Then we drove back to Eastvale. We were all badly shaken up, but Ian said we ought to be seen about the place, you know, acting natural, as if things were normal.'

'And Leanne's shoulder-bag?'

'That was Ian's idea. I mean, we'd all decided by then that we'd just say she left us outside the pub and set off home and that was the last we saw of her. I found her bag on the back seat of the car, and Ian said maybe if we dumped it in someone's garden near the Old Ship, the police would think she'd been picked up by a pervert or something.'

And indeed we did, thought Banks. One simple, spur-of-the-moment action, added to two other missing girls whose bags had also been found close to the scenes of their disappearances, and the entire Chameleon task force had been created. But not in time to save Melissa Horrocks or Kimberley Myers. He felt sick and angry.

There was mile after mile of moorland up beyond Lyndgarth, Banks knew, none of it farmed. Blair was right about the isolation, too. Only the occasional rambler crossed it, and then usually by the well-marked paths. 'Can you remember where you buried her?' he asked.

'I think so,' said Blair. 'I don't know about the exact spot, but within a couple of hundred yards. You'll know it when you see the old wall.'

Banks looked at Winsome. 'Get a search party together, would you, DC Jackman, and have young Mick here go out with them. Let me know the minute you find anything. And have Ian Scott and Sarah Francis picked up.'

Winsome stood up.

'That'll do for now,' Banks said.

'What'll happen to me?' Blair asked.

'I don't know, Mick,' said Banks. 'I honestly don't know.'

19

The interview had gone well, Maggie thought, as she walked out onto Portland Place. Behind her, Broadcasting House looked like the stern of a huge ocean liner. Inside, it had been a maze. She hadn't understood how anyone could find their way around, even if they had worked there for years. Thank the Lord the programme's researcher had met her in the lobby, then guided her through security to the entrails of the building.

It started to rain lightly, so Maggie ducked into Starbuck's. Sitting on a stool by the counter that stretched along the front window, sipping her latte and watching the people outside wrestle with their umbrellas, she reviewed her day. It was after three o'clock in the afternoon and the rush-hour seemed to have begun already. If it ever ended in London. The interview she had just given had focused almost entirely on the generalities of domestic abuse, things to watch out for, patterns to avoid falling into, rather than her own personal story, or that of her co-interviewee, an abused wife who had gone on to become a psychological counsellor. They had exchanged addresses and phone numbers and agreed to get in touch, then the woman had had to dash off to give another interview.

Lunch with Sally, the art director, had gone well, too. They had eaten at a rather expensive Italian restaurant near Victoria Station, and Sally had looked over the sketches, making helpful suggestions here and there. Mostly, though, they had talked about recent events in Leeds, and Sally had shown only the natural curiosity that anyone who happened to live across the street from a serial killer might expect. Maggie had been evasive when questioned about Lucy.

Lucy. The poor woman. Maggie felt guilty for leaving her alone in that big house on The Hill, right opposite where the nightmare of her own life had recently come to a head. Lucy had said she would be okay, but was she just trying to put a brave face on things?

Maggie hadn't been able to get tickets for the play she wanted to see. It was so popular it was sold out, even on a Wednesday. She thought she might book into the hotel anyway and go to the cinema instead, but the more she thought about it, and the more she looked out at the hordes of passing strangers, the more she thought she ought to be there for Lucy.

What she would do, she decided, was wait till the rain stopped – it only looked like a mild shower, and she could already see some blue clouds in the sky over the Langham Hilton across the road – do some shopping on Oxford Street and then head home in the early evening and surprise Lucy.

Maggie felt much better when she had decided to go home. After all, what was the point in going to the cinema by herself when Lucy needed someone to talk to, someone to help take her mind off her problems and help her decide what to do with her future?

When the rain had stopped completely, Maggie drained her latte and set out. She would buy Lucy a present, too, nothing expensive or ostentatious, but perhaps a bracelet or a necklace, something to mark her freedom. After all, as Lucy had said, the police had taken all her things and she didn't want them back now; she was about to start a new life.

•

It was late in the afternoon when Banks got the call to drive out to Wheaton Moor, north of Lyndgarth, and he took Winsome with him. She had done enough work on the Leanne Wray case to be there at the end. Most of the daffodils were gone, but white and pink blossoms covered the trees, and the hedgerows glowed with the burnished gold stars of celandines. Gorse flowered bright yellow all over the moors.

He parked as close as he could to the cluster of figures, but they still had almost a quarter of a mile to walk over the springy gorse and heather. Blair and the others had certainly carried Leanne a long way from civilization. Though the sun was shining and there were only a few high clouds, the wind was cold. Banks was glad of his sports jacket. Winsome was wearing calf-high leather boots and a herringbone jacket over her black poloneck sweater. She strode with grace and confidence, whereas Banks caught his ankle and stumbled every now and then in the thick gorse. Time to get out and exercise more, he told himself. And time to stop smoking.

They reached the team that Winsome had dispatched about three hours ago. Mick Blair was handcuffed to one of the uniformed officers, greasy hair blowing in the wind.

Another officer pointed down the shallow sink hole, and Banks saw part of a hand, most of the flesh eaten away, the white bone showing. 'We tried to disturb the scene as little as possible, sir,' the officer went on. 'I sent for the SOCOs and the rest of the team. They said they'd get here ASAP.'

Banks thanked him. He glanced back towards the road

and saw a car and a van pull up, figures get out and make their way across the rough moorland, some of them in white coveralls. The SOCOs had soon roped off an area of several yards around the mound of stones and Peter Darby, the local crime scene photographer got to work. Now all they needed was Dr Burns, the police surgeon. Dr Glendenning, the Home Office pathologist, would most likely conduct the PM, but he was too old and important to go scrambling across the moors any more. Dr Burns was skilled, Banks knew, and he already had plenty of experience of on-scene examinations.

It was another ten minutes before Dr Burns arrived. By then Peter Darby had finished photographing the scene intact and it was time to uncover the remains. This the SOCOs did slowly and carefully, so as not to disturb any evidence. Mick Blair had said that Leanne died after taking Ecstasy, but he could be lying; he could have tried to rape her and choked her when she didn't comply. Either way, they couldn't go around jumping to conclusions about Leanne. Not this time.

Banks began to feel that the whole thing was just too damn familiar, standing out there on the moors with his jacket flapping around him as men in white coveralls uncovered a body. Then he remembered Harold Steadman, the local historian they had found buried under a similar drystone wall below Crow Scar. That had been only his second case in Eastvale, back when the kids were still at school and he and Sandra were happily married, yet it seemed centuries ago now. He wondered what on earth a drystone wall was doing up here anyway, then realized it had probably marked the end of someone's property long ago, property that had now gone to moorland, overgrown with heather and gorse. The elements had done their work on the wall, and nobody had any interest in repairing it.

Stone by stone, the body was uncovered. As soon as he saw the blonde hair, Banks knew it was Leanne Wray. She was wearing the clothes she had gone missing in – jeans, white Nike trainers, T-shirt and a light suede jacket – and that was something in Blair's favour, Banks thought. Though there was some decomposition and evidence of insect and small animal activity – a missing finger on her right hand, for example – the cool weather had kept her from becoming a complete skeleton. In fact, despite the splitting of the skin to expose the muscle and fat on her left cheek, Banks was able to recognize Leanne's face from the photographs he had seen.

When the body was completely uncovered, everyone stood back as if they were at a funeral paying their last respects before the interment rather than at an exhumation. The moor was silent but for the wind whistling and groaning among the stones like lost souls. Mick Blair was crying, Banks noticed. Either that or the chill wind was making his eyes water.

'Seen enough, Mick?' he asked.

Mick sobbed, then abruptly turned away and vomited noisily and copiously into the gorse.

Banks's mobile rang as he turned away to go back to his car. It was Stefan Nowak and he sounded excited. 'Alan?'

'What is it, Stefan? Identified the sixth victim?'

'No. But I thought you'd like to know immediately. We've found Payne's camcorder.'

'Tell me where,' said Banks, 'and I'll be with you as fast as I possibly can.'

•

Maggie was tired when her train pulled into Leeds station around nine o'clock that evening, half an hour late owing to a cow in a tunnel outside Wakefield. Now she had an inkling of why the British complained so much about their trains.

There was a long queue at the taxi rank and Maggie only had a light hold-all to carry, so she decided to walk around the corner to Boar Lane and catch a bus. There were plenty of them that stopped within a short walk of The Hill. It was a pleasant evening, no sign of rain here, and there were still plenty of people on the streets. The bus soon came and she sat downstairs near the back. Two elderly women sat in front of her, just come from the bingo, one with hair that looked like a sort of blue haze sprinkled with glitter. Her perfume irritated Maggie's nose and made her sneeze, so she moved further back.

It was a familiar journey by now, and Maggie spent most of it reading another story in the new Alice Munro paperback she had bought in Charing Cross Road. She had also bought the perfect present for Lucy. It nestled in its little blue box in her hold-all. It was an odd piece of jewellery and had immediately caught her eye. Hanging on a thin silver chain was a circular silver disc about the size of a ten-pence piece. Inside the circle, made by a snake swallowing its own tail, was an image of the phoenix rising. Maggie hoped that Lucy would like and appreciate the sentiment.

The bus turned the last corner. Maggie rang the bell and got off near the top of The Hill. The streets were quiet and the western sky was smeared with the reds and purples of sunset. There was a slight chill in the air now, Maggie noticed, giving a little shiver. She saw Mrs Toth, Claire's mother, crossing The Hill with some fish and chips wrapped in newspaper and said hello, then turned to the steps.

She fumbled for her keys as she made her way up the dark

steps overhung with shrubbery. It was hard to see her way. A perfect place for an ambush, she thought, then wished she hadn't. Bill's telephone call still weighed on her mind.

The house seemed to be in darkness. Perhaps Lucy was out? Maggie doubted it. Then she got past the bushes and noticed a flickering light coming from the master bedroom. She was watching television. For a moment, Maggie felt the uncharitable wish that she had the house to herself. The knowledge that there was someone in her bedroom bothered her. But she had told Lucy she could watch television up there if she wanted, and she could hardly just march in and kick her out, tired as she was. Perhaps they should change rooms if Lucy wanted to watch television all the time? Maggie would be quite happy in the small bedroom for a few days.

She turned the key in the lock and went inside, then put down her bag and hung up her jacket before heading upstairs to tell Lucy she had decided to come back early. As she glided upstairs on the thick pile carpet she could hear sounds from the television but couldn't make out what they were. It sounded like somebody shouting. The bedroom door was slightly ajar, so without even thinking to knock Maggie simply pushed it open and walked in. Lucy lay sprawled on the bed naked. Well, that wasn't too much of a surprise after this morning's display, Maggie thought. But when she turned to see what was on television she didn't want to believe her eyes.

At first she thought it was just a porn movie, though why Lucy should be watching something like that and where she had got it from were beyond her, then she noticed the home-made quality, the makeshift lighting. It was some sort of cellar, and there was a girl who appeared to be tied to a bed. A man stood beside her playing with himself and shouting obscenities. Maggie recognized him. A woman lay with her head between the girl's legs and in the split second it took Maggie to register all this, the woman turned, licked her lips and grinned mischievously at the camera.

Lucy.

'Oh, no!' Maggie said, turning to Lucy, who was looking at her now with those dark, impenetrable eyes. Maggie put her hand to her mouth. She felt sick. Sick and afraid. She turned to leave but heard a sudden movement behind her, then felt a splitting pain at the back of her head and the world exploded.

•

The pond was gathering the evening light by the time Banks got there after taking Mick Blair back to Eastvale, making sure Ian Scott and Sarah Francis were under lock and key and picking up Jenny Fuller on his way out of town. Winsome and Sergeant Hatchley could take care of things at Eastvale until tomorrow morning.

The colours shimmered on the water's surface like an oil slick and the ducks, having noticed so much human activity, were keeping a polite and safe distance, and no doubt wondering where the expected chunks of bread had got to. The Panasonic Super 8 camcorder lay, still attached to its tripod, on a piece of cloth on the bank. DS Stefan Nowak and DCI Ken Blackstone had stayed with it until Banks could get there.

'Are you sure it's the one?' Banks asked Ken Blackstone.

Blackstone nodded. 'One of our enterprising young DCs succeeded in tracking down the branch where Payne bought it. He paid cash for it, on the third of March last year. The serial number checks out.'

'Any tapes?'

'One in the camera,' said Stefan. 'Ruined.'

'No chance of restoration?'

'All the king's horses . . .'

'Only the one? That's all?'

Stefan nodded. 'Believe me, the men went over every inch of the place.' He gestured to take in the area of the pond. 'If any tapes had been dumped here, we'd have found them by now.'

'So where are they?' Banks asked nobody in particular.

'If you want my guess,' said Stefan, 'I'd say whoever chucked the camcorder in the lake dubbed them onto VHS. There's some loss of quality, but it's the only way you can watch them on a regular VCR, without the camcorder.'

Banks nodded. 'Makes sense to me. Better take it to Millgarth and lock it up in the property room, though what good it's going to do us now, I don't know.'

Stefan bent to pick up the camera, wrapping it carefully in the cloth, as if it were a newborn baby. 'You never know.'

Banks noticed the pub sign about a hundred yards away: the Woodcutter's. It was a chain pub, that much he could tell even from a distance, but it was all there was in sight. 'It's been a long day and I haven't had my tea yet,' he said to Blackstone and Jenny after Stefan had driven off to Millgarth. 'Why don't we have a drink and toss a few ideas around?'

'You'll get no objection from me,' said Blackstone.

'Jenny?'

Jenny smiled. 'Not much choice, have I? I came in your car, remember? But count me in.'

They were soon settled at a corner table in the almost empty pub, which Banks found to his delight was still serving food. He ordered a beef burger and chips along with a pint of bitter. The jukebox wasn't so loud that they couldn't hear themselves talk, but it was loud enough to mask their conversation from any nearby tables.

'So what have we got?' Banks asked when he had his burger in front of him.

'A useless camcorder, by the looks of it,' said Blackstone.

'But what does it mean?'

'It means that someone – Payne, presumably – chucked it away.'

'Why?'

'Search me.'

'Come on, Ken, we can do better than this.'

Blackstone smiled. 'Sorry, it's been a long day for me, too.'

'It's an interesting question, though,' said Jenny. 'Why? And when?'

'Well, it has to have been before PCs Taylor and Morrisey entered the cellar,' said Banks.

'But Payne had a captive, remember,' said Blackstone. 'Kimberley Myers. Why on earth would he ditch his camera when he was doing exactly the sort of things we assume he liked to videotape? And what did he do with the dubbed VHS tapes, if Stefan's right about that?'

'I can't answer those questions,' Jenny said, 'but I can offer another way of looking at them.'

'I think I know what you're getting at,' said Banks.

'You do?'

'Uh-huh. Lucy Payne.' He took a bite of his beef burger. Not bad, he thought, but he was so hungry he would have eaten just about anything by then.

Jenny nodded slowly. 'Why have we still been assuming that this video business was all down to Terence Payne when we've been investigating Lucy as a possible partner in crime all along? Especially after what Laura and Keith told me about Lucy's past and what that young prostitute told Alan about Lucy's sexual proclivities. I mean, doesn't it make sense, psychologically, that she was just as involved as he was? Remember, the girls were killed in exactly the same way as Kathleen Murray: ligature strangulation.'

'Are you saying that *she* killed them?' Blackstone asked.

'Not necessarily. But if what Keith and Laura say is true, then Lucy might have seen herself acting as a deliverer, the way it appears she did with Kathleen.'

'A mercy killing? But you said earlier she killed Kathleen out of jealousy.'

'I said that jealousy certainly *could* have been a motive. One that her sister Laura didn't want to believe. But Lucy's motives could have been mixed. Nothing's simple in a personality like hers.'

'But why?' Blackstone went on. 'Even if it was her, why would she throw away the camera?'

Banks speared a chip and thought for a moment before answering: 'Lucy's terrified of jail. If she thought there was any chance of imminent capture – and it must have entered her mind after the first police visit and the connection between Kimberley Myers and Silverhill school – then might she not start making plans for self-preservation?'

'It all seems a bit far-fetched to me.'

'Not to me, Ken,' said Banks. 'Look at it from Lucy's point of view. She's not stupid. Brighter than her husband, I'd say. Terence Payne kidnaps Kimberley Myers that Friday night – he's out of control, becoming disorganized – but Lucy's still organized, she sees the end coming fast. First thing she does is get rid of as much evidence as possible, including the camcorder. Maybe that's what sets Terry against her, causes the row. Obviously she has no way of knowing that it will end the way it does, at the time it does, so she has to improvise, see which way the wind's blowing. If we find any traces of her being in the cellar—'

'Which we do.'

'Which we do,' Banks agreed, 'then she's got a believable explanation for that, too. She heard a noise and went to investigate, and surprise, surprise, look what she found. The fact that her husband clobbers her with a vase only helps her case.'

'And the tapes?'

'She wouldn't throw them away,' Jenny answered. 'Not if they were a record of what she – of what *they* – had done. The camera's nothing, merely a means to an end. You can buy another camera. But those tapes would be more valuable than diamonds to the Paynes because they're unique and they can't be replaced. They're her trophies. She could watch them over and over again and relive those moments with the victims in the cellar. It's the next best thing to the reality for her. She wouldn't throw them away.'

'Then where are they?' said Banks.

'And where is she?' said Jenny.

'Isn't it just remotely possible,' Banks suggested, pushing his plate aside, 'that the two questions have the same answer?'

•

Maggie woke up with a splitting headache and a feeling of nausea deep in the pit of her stomach. She felt weak and disoriented; didn't know at first where she was or how much time had gone by since she lost consciousness. The curtains were open and she could see it was dark outside. As things slowly came into focus, she realized she was still in her own bedroom. There was one bedside lamp turned on; the other lay in pieces on the floor. That must have been what Lucy hit her with, Maggie thought. She could feel something warm and sticky in her hair. Blood.

Lucy hit her! The sudden revelation shocked her closer to consciousness. She had seen the video, Lucy and Terry doing things to that poor girl, Lucy looking as if she were enjoying herself.

Maggie tried to move and found that her hands and feet were bound to the brass bed. She was tied up and spread-eagled, just like the girl on the video. She felt the panic rise in her. She thrashed around, trying to get loose, but only succeeding in making the bedsprings creak loudly. The door opened and Lucy came in. She was dressed in her jeans and T-shirt again.

Lucy shook her head slowly. 'Look what you made me do, Maggie,' she said. 'Just look at what you made me do. You said you weren't coming back for another day.'

'It was *you*,' Maggie said. 'On that video. It was you. It was vile, disgusting.'

'You weren't supposed to see that,' said Lucy, sitting at the edge of the bed and stroking Maggie's brow.

Maggie flinched.

Lucy laughed. 'Oh, don't worry, Maggie. Don't be such a prude. You're not my type anyway.'

'You killed them. You and Terry together.'

'You're wrong there,' said Lucy, getting up again and pacing the room, arms folded. 'Terry never killed anyone. He didn't have the bottle. Oh, he liked them tied up naked, all right. He liked to *do* things to them. Even *after* they were dead. But I had to do all the killing myself. Poor things. See, they could only take so much and then I had to put them to sleep. I was always gentle. Gentle as I could be.'

'You're insane,' said Maggie, thrashing around on the bed.

'Keep still!' Lucy sat on the bed again, but this time she didn't touch Maggie. 'Insane? I don't think so. Just because you can't understand me doesn't mean I'm insane. I'm different, true. I see things differently. I need different things. But I'm not insane.'

'But *why*?'

'I can't explain myself to you. I can't even explain myself to me.' She laughed again. 'Least of all to me. Oh, the psychiatrists and psychologists would try. They would dissect my childhood and toss around their theories, but even they know when it gets right down to it that they've got no explanations for someone like me. I just am. I happen. Like five-legged sheep and two-headed dogs. Call it what you will. Call me evil, if it helps you understand. More important right now, though, is how am I going to survive?'

'Why don't you just go? Run away. I won't say anything.'

Lucy gave her a sad smile. 'I wish that were true, Maggie. I wish things were as easy as that.'

'They are,' Maggie said. 'Go. Just go. Disappear.'

'I can't do that. You've seen the tape. You *know*. I can't let you walk around with that knowledge. Look, Maggie, I don't *want* to kill you, but I think I can. And I think I must. I promise I'll be every bit as gentle as I was with the others.'

'Why me?' Maggie whimpered. 'Why did you pick on me?'

'You? Easy. Because you were so willing to believe that I was a victim of domestic violence, just like you. True enough, Terry had been getting unpredictable and had lashed out on one or two occasions. It's an unfortunate thing that men like him lack the brains, but they don't lack for brawn. No matter, now. Do you know how I met him?'

'No.'

'He raped me. You don't believe me, I can tell. How

could you? How could anyone? But he did. I was walking to the bus-stop after I'd been to a pub with some friends and he dragged me in an alley and raped me. He had a knife.'

'He *raped* you and you *married* him? You didn't tell the police?'

Lucy laughed. 'He didn't know what he was getting into. I gave him the rape of his life. It might have taken him a while to realize it, but I was raping him as much as he was raping me. It wasn't my first time, Maggie. Believe me, I know *all* about rape. From experts. There was nothing he could do that hadn't been done to me before, time after time, by more than one person. He thought he was in control, but sometimes it's the victim who's *really* in control. We had a lot in common, we soon found out. Sexually. And in other ways. He kept on raping girls even after we were together. I encouraged him. I used to make him tell me all the details of what he'd done to them while we were fucking.'

'I don't understand.' Maggie was crying and trembling, no longer able to keep her horror and fear in check now she knew there was no chance of reasoning with Lucy.

'Of course you don't,' Lucy said soothingly. 'Why should you? But you've been useful, and I'd like to thank you for that. First you gave me somewhere to hide the tapes. I knew they were the only things that might incriminate me other than Terry and I didn't think he'd talk. Besides, he's dead now.'

'What do you mean about the tapes?'

'They were here all along, Maggie. Remember I came to see you that Sunday, before all hell broke loose?'

'Yes.'

'I brought them with me and hid them behind some boxes up in the loft when I went up to the toilet. You'd already told me you never went up there. Don't you remember?'

Maggie did remember. The loft was an airless, dusty place, she had discovered on her first and only look, which gave her the willies and aggravated her allergies. She must have mentioned it to Lucy when showing her around the house. 'Is that why you made friends with me, because you thought I might be useful?'

'I thought I might have need of a friend somewhere down the line, yes, a defender, even. And you *were* good. Thank you for all you've said on my behalf. Thank you for believing in me. I'm not enjoying this, you know. I get no pleasure from killing. It's a pity it has to end this way.'

'But it doesn't,' Maggie begged. 'Oh, God, please don't. Just go. I won't say anything. I promise.'

'Oh, you say that now, now that you're full of fear of death, but if I go, you won't feel that way any more and you'll tell the police everything.'

'I won't. I *promise.*'

'I wish I could believe you, Maggie, I really do.'

'It's true.'

Lucy took the belt off her jeans.

'What are you doing?'

'I told you, I'll be gentle. It's nothing to be frightened of, just a little pain, then you'll go to sleep.'

'No!'

Someone banged on the front door. Lucy froze and Maggie held her breath. 'Be quiet,' Lucy hissed, putting her hand over Maggie's mouth. 'They'll go away.'

But the banging continued. Then came a voice. 'Maggie! Open up, it's the police. We know you're in there. We spoke to your neighbour. She saw you come home. Open up, Maggie, we want to talk to you. It's very important.'

Maggie could see the fear in Lucy's expression. She struggled to shout, but the hand covered her mouth, almost cut off her breath.

'Is she with you, Maggie?' the voice continued. It was Banks, Maggie realized, the detective who had made her angry. If only he stayed, broke down the door and rescued her, she'd apologize; she'd do whatever he wanted. 'Is that who it is?' Banks went on. 'The blonde girl your neighbour saw. Is it Lucy? Did she change her appearance? If it's you, Lucy, we know all about Kathleen Murray. We've got a lot of questions for you. Maggie, come down and open up. If Lucy's with you, don't trust her. We think she hid the tapes in your house.'

'Be quiet,' Lucy said and went out of the room.

'I'm here!' Maggie immediately yelled at the top of her lungs, not sure if they could hear her or not. 'She's here, too. Lucy. She's going to kill me. Please help me!'

Lucy came back into the bedroom, but she didn't seem concerned by Maggie's screams. 'They're out back, too,' she said, crossing her arms. 'What can I do? I can't go to jail. I couldn't stand to be locked up in the cage for the rest of my days.'

'Lucy,' Maggie said as evenly as she could manage. 'Untie me and open the door. Let them in. I'm sure they'll be lenient. They'll see you need help.'

But Lucy wasn't listening. She had started pacing again and muttering to herself. All Maggie could catch was the word 'cage' again and again.

Then she heard an almighty crash from downstairs as the police broke the front door, then the sound of men running up the stairs.

'I'm up here!' she yelled.

Lucy looked at her, almost pitifully, Maggie thought, and

said, 'Try not to hate me too much,' then she took a run and dived through the bedroom window in a shower of glass.

Maggie screamed.

20

For someone who disliked hospitals as much as Banks did, he seemed to have spent more than enough time in the Infirmary over the past couple of weeks, he thought as he walked down the corridor to Maggie Forrest's private room on Thursday.

'Oh, it's you,' Maggie said when he knocked and walked in. She wouldn't look him in the eye, he noticed, but stared at the wall. The bandage over her forehead held the dressing at the back of her head in place. The wound had been a nasty one, requiring several stitches. She had also lost a lot of blood. When Banks had got to her, the pillow was soaked with it. According to the doctor, though, she was out of the woods and should be okay to go home in a day or so. Now she was being treated for delayed shock as much as anything. Looking at her, Banks thought of the day not so long ago when he first saw Lucy Payne in a hospital bed, one eye bandaged, the other assessing her situation, black hair spread out on the white pillow.

'Is that all the thanks I get?' he said.

'Thanks?'

'For bringing in the cavalry. It was my idea, you know. True, I was only doing my job, but people sometimes feel the need to add a word or two of personal thanks. Don't worry, I don't expect a tip or anything.'

'It's easy for you to be flippant, isn't it?'

Banks pulled up a chair and sat at her bedside. 'Maybe not as easy as you think. How are you?'

'Fine.'

'Really?'

'I'm all right. A bit sore.'

'It's hardly surprising.'

'Was it really you?'

'Was what really me?'

Maggie looked him in the eye for the first time. Hers were dulled with medication, but he could see pain and confusion there, along with something softer, something less definable. 'Who led the rescue party.'

Banks leaned back and sighed. 'I only blame myself that it took me so long,' he said.

'What do you mean?'

'I should have worked it out earlier. I had all the pieces. I just didn't put them together quickly enough, not until the SOCO team found the camcorder in the pond at the bottom of The Hill.'

'That's where it was?'

'Yes. Lucy must have dumped it there some time over that last weekend.'

'I go there sometimes to think and feed the ducks.' Maggie stared at the wall, then turned to face him again after a few seconds. 'Anyway, it's hardly your fault, is it? You're not a mind reader.'

'No? People sometimes expect me to be. But I suppose I'm not. Not in this case. We suspected from the start that there must have been a camcorder and tapes, and we knew she wouldn't part with the tapes easily. We also knew that the only person she was close to was you, and that she had visited your house the day before the domestic disturbance.'

'She couldn't have known what was going to happen.'

'No. But she knew things were coming to a head. She was working on damage control, and hiding the tapes was part of it. Where were they?'

'The loft,' Maggie said. 'She knew I didn't go up there.'

'And she knew she'd be able to get at them without too much trouble, that you were probably the only person in the whole country who'd give her house room. That was the other clue. There was really nowhere else for her to go. First we talked to your neighbours, and when Claire's mother told us you'd just got home and another neighbour said she'd seen a young woman knocking at your back door a couple of nights ago, it seemed to add up.'

'You must think I was *so* stupid to take her in.'

'Foolish maybe, naïve, but not necessarily stupid.'

'She just seemed so . . . so . . .'

'So much the victim?'

'Yes. I *wanted* to believe in her, needed to. Maybe as much for me as for her. I don't know.'

Banks nodded. 'She played the role well. She could do that because it was partially true. She'd had a lot of practice.'

'What do you mean?'

Banks told her about the Alderthorpe Seven and the murder of Kathleen Murray. When he had finished, Maggie turned pale, swallowed and lay back in silence, staring at the ceiling. It was a minute or so before she spoke again. 'She killed her cousin when she was only twelve?'

'Yes. That's partly what set us looking for her again. At last we had a bit of evidence that suggested she was more than she pretended to be.'

'But a lot of people have terrible childhoods,' said Maggie, some colour returning to her face. 'Perhaps not as terrible as that, but they don't all turn into killers. What was so different about Lucy?'

'I wish I knew the answer,' said Banks. 'Terry Payne was a rapist when they met, and Lucy had killed Kathleen. Somehow or other the two of them getting together the way they did created a special sort of chemistry, acted as a trigger. We don't know why. We'll probably never know.'

'And if they'd never met?'

Banks shrugged. 'It may never have happened. None of it. Terry finally gets caught for rape and put in jail, while Lucy goes on to marry a nice young man, have two point four children and become a bank manager. Who knows?'

'She told me that *she* killed the girls, that Terry didn't have the nerve.'

'Makes sense. She'd done it before. He hadn't.'

'She said she did it out of kindness.'

'Maybe she did. Or out of self-protection. Or out of jealousy. You can't expect her to understand her own motives any better than we can, or to tell the truth about them. With someone like Lucy it was probably some strange sort of combination of all three.'

'She also said they met because he raped her. Tried to rape her. I couldn't really understand. She said she raped him as much as he raped her.'

Banks shifted in his chair. He wished he could have a cigarette, even though he had determined to quit before the year was out. 'I can't explain it any more than you can, Maggie. I might be a policeman, and I might have seen a lot more of the dark side of human nature than you, but something like this . . . For someone with a past like Lucy's, who knows how topsy-turvy things can get? I should imagine that after the things that had been done to her in Alderthorpe, and given her peculiar sexual tastes, Terence Payne was a bit of a pussy cat to deal with.'

'She said to think of her as a five-legged sheep.'

The image took Banks back to his childhood, when the travelling fair came around at Easter and in autumn and set up on the local recreation ground. There were rides – Waltzers, Caterpillar, Dodgems and Speedway – and stalls where you could throw weighted darts at playing cards or shoot at tin figures with an air rifle to win a goldfish in a plastic bag full of water; there were flashing lights and crowds and loud music; but there was also the freak show, a tent set up on the edge of the fairground, where you paid your sixpence and went inside to see the exhibits. They were ultimately disappointing, not a genuine bearded lady, elephant man, spider woman or pinhead in sight. Those kinds of freaks Banks only saw later in Todd Browning's famous movie. None of these freaks were alive, for a start. They were deformed animals, stillborn or killed at birth, and they floated in the huge glass jars full of preserving fluid – a lamb with a fifth leg sticking out of its side; a kitten with horns; a puppy with two heads; a calf with no eye-sockets – the stuff that nightmares were made of.

'Despite what happened,' Maggie went on, 'I want you to know that I'm not going to let it turn me into a cynic. I know you think I'm naïve, but if that's the choice, I'd rather be naïve than bitter and untrusting.'

'You made a mistake in judgement and it almost got you killed.'

'Do you think she would have killed me if you hadn't come?'

'Do you?'

'I don't know. I've got a lot of thinking to do. But Lucy was . . . she was as much a victim as anything. You weren't there. You didn't hear her. She didn't *want* to kill me.'

'Maggie, for crying out loud, will you just listen to yourself! She murdered God knows how many young girls. She *would* have killed you, believe me. If I were you, I'd put the victim thing right out of my mind.'

'I'm not you.'

Banks took a deep breath and sighed. 'Lucky for both of us, isn't it? What will you do now?'

'Do?'

'Will you stay at The Hill?'

'Yes, I think so.' Maggie scratched at her bandages, then squinted at Banks. 'I don't really have anywhere else to go. And there's still my work, of course. Another thing I've discovered through all this is that I can also do some good. I can be a voice for people who don't have one, or who don't dare speak out. People listen to me.'

Banks nodded. He didn't say so, but he suspected that Maggie's very public championing of Lucy Payne might well tarnish her ability to act as a believable spokesperson for abused women. But perhaps not. About all you could say about the public, when it came right down to it, was that they were a fickle lot. Maybe Maggie would emerge as a heroine.

'Look, you'd better get some rest,' Banks said. 'I just wanted to see how you were. We'll want to talk to you in some detail later. But there's no hurry. Not now.'

'Isn't it all over?'

Banks looked into her eyes. He could tell she wanted it to be over, wanted to stand at a distance and think it through, get her life going again, work, good deeds, the lot. 'There still might be a trial,' he said.

'A trial? But I don't . . .'

'Haven't you heard?'

'Heard what?'

'I just assumed . . . oh, shit.'

'I've been pretty much out of it, what with the drugs and all. What is it?'

Banks leaned forward and rested his hand on her forearm. 'Maggie,' he said, 'I don't know how to say this any other way, but Lucy Payne isn't dead.'

Maggie recoiled from his touch and her eyes widened. 'Not dead? But I don't understand. I thought . . . I mean, she . . .'

'She jumped out of the window, yes, but the fall didn't kill her. Your front path is overgrown, and the bushes broke her fall. The thing is, though, she landed on the sharp edge of one of the steps and broke her back. It's serious. Very serious. There's severe damage to the spinal cord.'

'What does that mean?'

'The surgeons aren't sure of the full extent of her injuries yet – they've got a lot more tests to do – but they think she'll be paralysed from the neck down.'

'But Lucy's not dead?'

'No.'

'She'll be in a wheelchair?'

'If she survives.'

Maggie looked towards the window again. Banks could see tears glistening in her eyes. 'So she *is* in a cage, after all.'

Banks stood up to leave. He was finding Maggie's compassion for a killer of teenage girls difficult to take and didn't trust himself not to say something he'd regret. Just as he got to the door, he heard her small voice: 'Superintendent Banks?'

He turned, hand on doorknob. 'Yes?'

'Thank you.'

•

'Are you all right, love?'

'Yes, why shouldn't I be?' said Janet Taylor.

'Nothing,' the shopkeeper said, 'Only . . .'

Janet picked up her bottle of gin from the counter, paid him and walked out of the off-licence. What was up with him? she wondered. Had she suddenly sprouted an extra head or something? It was Saturday evening and she had hardly been out since her arrest and release on bail the previous Monday, but she didn't think she looked *that* different from the last time she'd been in the shop.

She climbed back up to her flat above the hairdresser's, and when she turned her key in the lock and walked inside she noticed the smell for the first time. And the mess. You didn't notice it so much when you were living in the midst of it, she thought, but you certainly did when you went out and came back to it. Dirty clothes lay strewn everywhere, unfinished coffee cups grew mould and the plant on the windowsill had wilted and died. The smell was of stale skin, rotting cabbage, sweat and gin. And some of it, she realized, turning her nose towards her armpit, came from her own body.

Janet looked in the mirror. It didn't surprise her to see the lank, lifeless hair and the dark bags under her eyes. After all, she had hardly slept since it happened. She didn't like to close her eyes because when she did, it all seemed to play over and over again inside her mind. The only times she could get any rest at all were when she'd had enough gin and passed out for an hour or two. No dreams came then, only oblivion, but as soon as she started to stir, the memory and the depression kicked in again.

She didn't really care what happened to her as long as the nightmares – sleeping and waking – went away. Let them kick her off the job, put her in jail, even. She didn't care as long as they also wiped out the memory of that morning in the cellar. Didn't they have machines or drugs that could do that, or was that only something she'd seen in a movie? Still, she was better off than Lucy Payne, she told herself. In a wheelchair for life, by the sound of it. But it was no less than she deserved. Janet remembered Lucy lying in the hall, blood pooling around her head wound, remembered her own concern for the abused woman, her anger at Dennis's male chauvinism. *Appearances.* Now she'd give anything to have Dennis back and thought even eternity in a wheelchair too slight a punishment for Lucy Payne.

Moving away from the mirror, Janet stripped off her clothes and tossed them on the floor. She would have a bath, she decided. Maybe it would make her feel better. First, she poured herself a large gin and took it into the bathroom with her. She put the plug in and turned on the taps, got the temperature right, poured in a capful of bubble bath. She looked at herself in the full-length mirror on the back of the bathroom door. Her breasts were starting to sag and the lard-coloured skin was creasing around her belly. She used to take good care of herself, work out at the police gym at least three times a week, go out for a run. Not for a couple of weeks, though.

Before dipping her toes into the water, she decided to bring the bottle and set it on the edge of the tub. She'd only have to get out and fetch it soon, anyway. Finally, she lay back and let the bubbles tickle her neck. At least she could clean herself. That would be a start. No more off-licence assistants asking her if she was all right because she smelled. As for the bags under her eyes, well they wouldn't go away overnight, but she would work on them. And on tidying up the flat.

On the other hand, she thought, after a good long sip of

gin, there were razor blades in the bathroom cabinet. All she had to do was stand up and reach for them. The water was good and hot. She was certain she would feel no pain. Just a quick slit on each wrist then put her arms underwater and let the blood seep out. It would be like going to sleep, only there would be no nightmares.

As she lay there wrapped in the warmth and softness of the bubble bath, her eyelids started to droop and she couldn't keep her eyes open. There she was again, in that stinking cellar with Dennis spurting blood all over the place and that maniac Payne coming at her with a machete. *What could she have done differently*? That seemed to be the question that nobody could, or would, answer for her. What *should* she have done?

She jerked to consciousness, gasping for breath, and at first the bathtub looked as if it were full of blood. She reached out for the gin, but she was clumsy and she knocked the bottle on the bathroom floor. It shattered on the tiles and spilled its precious contents.

Shit!

That meant she'd have to go out and buy more. She picked up the bathmat and shook it hard to get rid of any glass that might have lodged there, then she hauled herself out of the tub. When she stepped onto the mat, she underestimated her capacity for balance and stumbled a little. Her right foot hit the tiles and she felt the sting of glass on her sole. Janet winced with pain. Leaving a thin trail of blood on the bathroom floor, she negotiated her way into the living room without further injury, sat down and pulled out a couple of large slivers of glass, then she put on some old slippers and went back for peroxide and bandages. First she sat on the toilet seat and poured the peroxide as best she could over the sole of her foot. She almost screamed out in pain, but soon the waves abated and her foot just started to throb, then turn numb. She swathed it in bandages, then went to her bedroom and got dressed, putting on clean clothes and extra-thick socks.

She had to get out of the flat, she decided, and not just for as long as it took to go to the off-licence. A good drive would help keep her awake, the windows wide open, breeze blowing in her hair, rock music and chatter on the radio. Maybe she'd drop in on Annie Cabbot, the only decent copper among them. Or perhaps she'd drive out into the country and find a B & B where nobody knew who she was or what she had done, and stay a night or two. Anything to get away from this filthy, smelly place. She could pick up another bottle on the way. At least now she was clean, and no stuffy off-licence assistant was going to turn his nose up at her.

Janet hesitated a moment before she picked up her car keys, then pocketed them anyway. What more could they do to her? Add insult to injury and charge her with drink driving? Fuck the lot of them, Janet thought, laughing to herself as she limped down the stairs.

•

That same evening, three days since Lucy Payne had jumped out of Maggie Forrest's bedroom window, Banks was at home listening to *Thaïs* in his cosy living room with the melted-Brie ceiling and the blue walls. It was his first escape from the paperwork since he had visited Maggie Forrest in hospital on Thursday, and he was enjoying it immensely. Still uncertain about his future, he had decided that before making any major career decisions, he would first take a holiday and think things over. He had plenty of leave due and had already talked to Red Ron and picked up a few travel brochures. Now it was a matter of deciding *where* to go.

He had also spent quite a lot of time over the past couple of days standing at his office window looking down on the market square and thinking about Maggie Forrest, thinking about her conviction and her compassion, and now he was still thinking about her at home. Lucy Payne had tied Maggie to the bed and was about to strangle her with a belt when the police broke in. Yet Maggie still saw Lucy as the victim, and could shed tears for her. Was she a saint or a fool? Banks didn't know.

When he thought about the girls Lucy and Terry Payne had violated, terrorized and murdered – of Kelly Matthews, Samantha Foster, Melissa Horrocks, Kimberley Myers and Katya Pavelic – paralysis wasn't sufficient; it didn't *hurt* enough. But when he thought of Lucy's violent and abusive childhood at Alderthorpe, then a quick, clean death or a lifetime of solitary confinement seemed a more apt punishment.

As usual, what he thought didn't really matter, because the whole business was out of his hands, the judgement not his to make. Perhaps the best he could hope for was to put Lucy Payne out of his mind, which he would succeed in doing over time. Partially, at any rate. She would always be there – they all were, killers and victims – but in time she would fade and become a more shadowy figure than she was at the moment.

Banks had not forgotten the sixth victim. She had a name and unless her childhood was like Lucy Payne's, someone must have once loved her, held her and whispered words of comfort after a nightmare, perhaps, soothed away the pain when she fell and scraped her knee. He would have to be patient. The forensic experts were good at their jobs, and eventually her bones would yield up something that would lead to her identity.

Just as the famous 'Meditation' at the end of the first CD started, his phone rang. He was off duty and at first thought of not answering, but curiosity got the better of him, as it always did.

It was Annie Cabbot, and she sounded as if she were standing in the middle of a road, there was so much noise around her: voices, sirens, car brakes, people shouting orders.

'Annie, where the hell are you?'

'Roundabout on the Ripon Road, just north of Harrogate,' Annie said, shouting to make herself heard over the noise.

'What are you doing there?'

Somebody spoke to Annie, though Banks couldn't hear what was said. She answered abruptly and then came back on the line. 'Sorry, it's a bit chaotic down here.'

'What's going on?'

'I thought you ought to know. It's Janet Taylor.'

'What about her?'

'She ran into another car.'

'She what? How is she?'

'She's dead, Alan. *Dead.* They haven't been able to get her body out of the car yet, but they know she's dead. They got her handbag out and found my card in it.'

'Bloody hell.' Banks felt numb. 'How did it happen?'

'Can't say for sure,' Annie said. 'The person in the car behind her says she just seemed to speed up at the roundabout rather than slow down, and she hit the car that was going round. A mother driving her daughter home from a piano lesson.'

'Oh, Jesus Christ. What happened to them?'

'The mother's okay. Cuts and bruises. Shock.'

'The daughter?'

'It's touch and go. The paramedics suspect internal injuries, but they won't know till they get her to hospital. She's still stuck in the car.'

'Was Janet pissed?'

'Don't know yet. I wouldn't be surprised if drinking had something to do with it, though. And she was depressed. I don't know. She might have been trying to kill herself. If she did . . . it's . . .' Banks could sense Annie choking up.

'Annie, I know what you're going to say, but even if she did do it on purpose, it's not your fault. You didn't go down there in that cellar, see what she saw, do what she did. All you did was carry out an unbiased investigation.'

'Unbiased! Christ, Alan, I bent over backwards to be sympathetic towards her.'

'Whatever. It's not your fault.'

'Easy for you to say.'

'Annie, she was no doubt drunk, and she went off the road.'

'Maybe you're right. I can't believe that Janet would take someone else with her if she wanted to kill herself. But whichever way you look at it, drunk or not, suicide or not, it's still down to what happened, isn't it?'

'It happened, Annie. Nothing to do with you.'

'The politics. The fucking politics.'

'Do you want me to come down?'

'No, I'm okay.'

'Annie—'

'Sorry, got to go now. They're pulling the girl out of the car.' She hung up, leaving Banks holding the receiver and breathing quickly. Janet Taylor. Another casualty of the Paynes.

The first CD had finished and Banks had no real desire to listen to the second one after the news he had just heard. He poured himself two fingers of Laphroaig and took his cigarettes outside to his spot by the falls and, as the vivid orange and purple colours streaked the western sky, he drank a silent toast to Janet Taylor and to the nameless dead girl buried in the Paynes's garden.

But he hadn't been out there five minutes when he decided he should go to Annie, *had* to go, no matter what she had said. Their romantic relationship might be over, but he had promised to be her friend and give her support. If she didn't need that right now, when would she? He looked at his watch. It would take him an hour or so to get there, if he moved fast, and Annie would probably still be at the scene. Even if she'd gone, she would be at the hospital and he would be able to find her there easily enough.

He left the tumbler, still half full, on the low table and went to grab his jacket. Before he could put it on, the phone rang again. Thinking it was Annie calling back with more news, he answered. It was Jenny Fuller.

'I hope I haven't called at an awkward moment,' she said.

'I was just going out.'

'Oh. An emergency?'

'Sort of.'

'Only I was thinking we might have a drink and celebrate, you know, now it's all over.'

'That's a great idea, Jenny. I can't do it right now, though. I'll call you later, okay?'

'Story of my life.'

'Sorry. Got to go. I'll call. Promise.'

Banks could hear the disappointment in Jenny's voice, and he felt like a real bastard for being so abrupt with her – after all, she had worked on the case as hard as anyone – but he didn't want to explain about Janet Taylor and he didn't feel like celebrating anything.

Now it's all over, Jenny had said. Banks wondered if it would ever be all over, the aftermath of the Paynes's rampage, if it would ever cease taking its toll. Six teenage girls dead, one still unidentified. Kathleen Murray dead these ten years or more. PC Dennis Morrisey dead. Terence Payne dead. Lucy Payne in a wheelchair. Now Janet Taylor dead and a young girl seriously injured.

Banks checked for his keys and cigarettes, then headed out into the night.

ACKNOWLEDGEMENTS

I would like to thank my editor Patricia Lande Grader for her help in reshaping the unruly early drafts, and my wife Sheila Halladay for her perceptive and helpful comments. Also, many thanks to my agent Dominick Abel for all his hard work on my behalf and to Erika Schmid for her fine copy-editing.

As far as research goes, the usual crowd came through: Detective Sergeant Keith Wright, Detective Inspectors Claire Gormley and Alan Young, and Area Commander Philip Gormley. Any mistakes are entirely my own and are, of course, made in the interests of dramatic fiction. Also, thanks to Woitek Kubicki for his advice on Polish names.

A number of books proved invaluable in understanding the 'killer couple' phenomenon, and among those to which I owe my greatest debt of gratitude are Emlyn Williams, *Beyond Belief*; Brian Masters, *She Must Have Known*; Paul Britton, *The Jigsaw Man*; Gordon Burn, *Happy Like Murderers*; and Stephen Williams, *Invisible Darkness.*

THE CIVILIZATION OF THE RENAISSANCE IN ITALY

AN ESSAY

JACOB BURCKHARDT

PHAIDON · OXFORD

PHAIDON PRESS LIMITED, LITTLEGATE HOUSE,
ST EBBE'S STREET, OXFORD, OXI ISQ

FIRST PUBLISHED 1945
SECOND EDITION (PHOTOGRAPHICALLY REPRINTED) 1981

British Library Cataloguing in Publication Data

Burckhardt, Jacob
The civilization of the Renaissance in
Italy.—2nd ed—(Landmarks in art
history)
1. Italy—Civilization—1268–1559
I. Title II. Series

ISBN 0-7148-2140-3

PRINTED AND BOUND IN U.S.A. BY VAIL-BALLOU PRESS, INC.,
BINGHAMTON, N.Y.

THE CIVILIZATION OF THE RENAISSANCE IN ITALY

SUMMARY OF CONTENTS

PUBLISHER'S NOTE

This volume has been photographically reprinted from the first edition, published by Phaidon Press in 1945.

FOREWORD

In 1860, an obscure Swiss publisher issued, for the first time, 'The Civilization of the Renaissance in Italy'; the edition, comprising one thousand copies, was hard to sell. The author was Jacob Burckhardt, Professor of History at the Basel University, where he had lectured as 'ordinarius' for the past two years. The author did not receive any royalties or other payment from his publisher. He was then forty-two years old, three years younger than Bachofen, who was born in the same town, Basel.

Burckhardt's teachers had been Jacob Grimm, Boeckh and Ranke, three scholars alike famous for their new and fertilizing ideas as for their exquisite style. His first creative efforts were devoted to lyrical poetry and landscape painting. He had visited Italy six times. The last visit was in 1853–54, when he collected the material for his manual 'Cicerone', which he called 'an Instruction how to enjoy the works of art in Italy'; this was published five years before 'The Civilization of the Renaissance', and met with no greater success.

At this period Burckhardt enjoyed only local fame in Basel and Zurich on account of his lectures, which indeed covered the widest range imaginable. He had lectured on the History of Painting; the Springtime of the Middle Ages; about Tapestries; concerning the Supreme Power in the later Roman Empire; on Calderon, Rochefoucauld, Byron, Manzoni, Corneille, Rabelais and Schiller; about Gothic Monasteries; the Corpus Christi Festival in Viterbo, 1462; on Renaissance Art; on the Beauty of Landscapes; about the Conditions in Rome in the time of Gregory the Great; and on Greek Sculpture in the British Museum. It seems incredible that one man, and not a very old man at that, should know of all those things, and know them so well; better indeed than any one else in the Europe of that date; and no other scholar or writer had the gift of imparting his historical visions in so precise and vivid a style. Yet this brought little or no fame to Burckhardt, who, for his part, cared not for fame.

In later years, when fame came to him at last, Burckhardt was embarrassed and disquietened. He shrank from any publicity, even from the appreciation of fellow-scholars or the admiration of individuals. Nietzsche was perhaps the first to understand and appreciate his work—'The Civilization of the Renaissance' was one of the few modern books he admired; yet Nietzsche and Burckhardt were teachers at the same University for many years, and Burckhardt never made friends with him.

In 1868—a few months before Nietzsche came to Basel as Professor of Philology—Burckhardt's publisher sold the remainders and rights of

'The Civilization of the Renaissance', and of the 'Cicerone' as well, to a German publisher, who printed 1,650 copies. It took him five years to sell them and five more years to prepare the third edition.[1] *Burckhardt was not asked about the transfer of rights, nor did he receive any money. He did not protest and gave no consent; but eleven years later he mentioned in a letter to his new publisher that he was astonished that he should never have been consulted.*

Burckhardt intended originally to write a monumental history of the Middle Ages in a series of monographs, beginning with the age of Constantine the Great and ending with the Renaissance. He completed only the first and the last volumes of the Series, the 'Constantine' in 1853, and the 'Renaissance' in 1860;[2] *the one depicting the fall of antique civilization and the birth of the new culture of the West, the other the fall of the Middle Ages and the rise of modern times. In both books he arranged his abundant material somewhat like a poet or a historical novelist, not merely collecting facts which he thought to be 'characteristic' and placing them in due sequence but using a few impressive facts to build up a mosaic, artistically composed and full of colour. 'My starting point has to be a vision,' he wrote to a friend, 'otherwise I cannot do anything. Vision I call not only optical, but also spiritual realization; for instance, historical vision issuing from the old sources.' Burckhardt's method is philology lit by imagination.*

* * *

The present volume, in Middlemore's translation,[3] *is a complete and unabridged English rendering of the second original edition. The later editions are no longer the sole work of the author, who never looked into his books once they were published, and who loathed proof-correcting, leaving all work of 'revision' to younger scholars. In the case of his masterpiece, 'The Renaissance', the revision was carried out by a competent historian, who, however, tampered with the text and augmented the notes in a very scholarly but pedantic way. Our edition gives the authentic text of Burckhardt's great book, and the present editor has done no more than correct a few minor mistakes by a comparison with the first edition. The*

[1] During the next twenty years, however, 15,000 copies were sold, and, since 1928, when the copyright expired, the sales of the book in its original language may be estimated at something like half a million copies.

[2] The most important books of his later years are *The History of Renaissance Architecture and Decoration* (1867), *Rubens* (published in 1898, one year after his death), and *History of Greek Civilization*, in four volumes (1898–1902).

[3] First published in two volumes (1878)

Notes are abbreviated, as most of them refer to old books, well known to the specialist but inaccessible to the general public, or else to more recent authorities now out of date, or to Victorian editions of Italian writers now replaced by handier and more critical editions. All these Notes, placed in earlier editions at the end of the book, made the reading of the 'Renaissance' a toilsome task, as the perusal of a single page might be interrupted as often as twenty times. Only those Notes have been retained which throw fresh light upon the text or refer to books that are easily obtainable. I have quoted from the latest editions when I thought it helpful to the reader, and I have supplied English translations to all important Italian passages in the Notes. The few additions inserted are marked with an asterisk. The Notes are placed at the foot of the pages to facilitate study.

The hundred plates appended to this volume are designed to serve as a pictorial commentary. They are not selected for their artistic value—though they are mostly of the highest standard—but because they are characteristic of the life and manners of the period. Explanations are added to these illustrations, giving details about fashion, topography, dating and so on. It should be noted that the illustrations cover the same period as the text, i.e. the time from the birth of Dante to the death of Michelangelo, a period as long and at least as variegated as, for instance, the time from Watteau to Picasso, or from Milton to James Joyce.

It is hoped that this volume in handy form will be more useful than the earlier and bulkier editions.

London: 1944 L. GOLDSCHEIDER

CONTENTS

Part I

THE STATE AS A WORK OF ART

Part II

THE DEVELOPMENT OF THE INDIVIDUAL

Part III

THE REVIVAL OF ANTIQUITY

Part IV

THE DISCOVERY OF THE WORLD AND OF MAN

Part V

SOCIETY AND FESTIVALS

Part VI

MORALITY AND RELIGION

THE CIVILIZATION OF THE RENAISSANCE IN ITALY

PART I

THE STATE AS A WORK OF ART

INTRODUCTION

THIS work bears the title of an essay in the strictest sense of the word. No one is more conscious than the writer with what limited means and strength he has addressed himself to a task so arduous. And even if he could look with greater confidence upon his own researches, he would hardly thereby feel more assured of the approval of competent judges. To each eye, perhaps, the outlines of a given civilization present a different picture; and in treating of a civilization which is the mother of our own, and whose influence is still at work among us, it is unavoidable that individual judgement and feeling should tell every moment both on the writer and on the reader. In the wide ocean upon which we venture, the possible ways and directions are many; and the same studies which have served for this work might easily, in other hands, not only receive a wholly different treatment and application, but lead also to essentially different conclusions. Such indeed is the importance of the subject that it still calls for fresh investigation, and may be studied with advantage from the most varied points of view. Meanwhile we are content if a patient hearing is granted us, and if this book be taken and judged as a whole. It is the most serious difficulty of the history of civilization that a great intellectual process must be broken up into single, and often into what seem arbitrary categories, in order to be in any way intelligible. It was formerly our intention to fill up the gaps in this book by a special work on the 'Art of the Renaissance'—an intention, however, which we have been able to fulfil only in part.[1]

* [1] Burckhardt's *History of Architecture and Decoration of the Italian Renaissance* was first printed in 1867. His *Notes on Renaissance Sculpture* were posthumously published in 1934, as a part of Vol. XIII of his Collected Works. Of his intended *History of Renaissance Painting* three chapters only were finished: 'The Art Collectors', 'The Altar-piece', 'The Portrait'; in fact, three very fine essays, published in 1898, a year after the authors' death.

THE struggle between the Popes and the Hohenstaufen left Italy in a political condition which differed essentially from that of other countries of the West. While in France, Spain and England the feudal system was so organized that, at the close of its existence, it was naturally transformed into a unified monarchy, and while in Germany it helped to maintain, at least outwardly, the unity of the empire, Italy had shaken it off almost entirely. The Emperors of the fourteenth century, even in the most favourable case, were no longer received and respected as feudal lords, but as possible leaders and supporters of powers already in existence; while the Papacy, with its creatures and allies, was strong enough to hinder national unity in the future, but not strong enough itself to bring about that unity. Between the two lay a multitude of political units—republics and despots—in part of long standing, in part of recent origin, whose existence was founded simply on their power to maintain it.[2] In them for the first time we detect the modern political spirit of Europe, surrendered freely to its own instincts, often displaying the worst features of an unbridled egotism, outraging every right, and killing every germ of a healthier culture. But, wherever this vicious tendency is overcome or in any way compensated, a new fact appears in history—the State as the outcome of reflection and calculation, the State as a work of art. This new life displays itself in a hundred forms, both in the republican and in the despotic States, and determines their inward constitution, no less than their foreign policy. We shall limit ourselves to the consideration of the completer and more clearly defined type, which is offered by the despotic States.

The internal condition of the despotically governed States had a memorable counterpart in the Norman Empire of Lower Italy and Sicily, after its transformation by the Emperor Frederick II. Bred amid treason and peril in the neighbourhood of the Saracens, Frederick, the first ruler of the modern type who sat upon a throne, had early accustomed himself to a thoroughly objective treatment of affairs. His acquaintance with the internal condition and administration of the Saracenic States was close and intimate; and the mortal struggle in which he was engaged with the Papacy compelled him, no less than his adversaries, to bring into the field all the resources at his command. Frederick's measures (especially after the year 1231) are aimed at the complete destruction of the feudal State, at the

[2] The rulers and their dependants were together called 'lo stato', and this name afterwards acquired the meaning of the collective existence of a territory.

transformation of the people into a multitude destitute of will and of the means of resistance, but profitable in the utmost degree to the exchequer. He centralized, in a manner hitherto unknown in the West, the whole judicial and political administration. No office was henceforth to be filled by popular election, under penalty of the devastation of the offending district and of the enslavement of its inhabitants. The taxes, based on a comprehensive assessment, and distributed in accordance with Mohammedan usages, were collected by those cruel and vexatious methods without which, it is true, it is impossible to obtain any money from Orientals. Here, in short, we find, not a people, but simply a disciplined multitude of subjects; who were forbidden, for example, to marry out of the country without special permission, and under no circumstances were allowed to study abroad. The University of Naples was the first we know of to restrict the freedom of study, while the East, in these respects at all events, left its youth unfettered. It was after the examples of Mohammedan rules that Frederick traded on his own account in all parts of the Mediterranean, reserving to himself the monopoly of many commodities, and restricting in various ways the commerce of his subjects. The Fatimite Caliphs, with all their esoteric unbelief, were, at least in their earlier history, tolerant of all the differences in the religious faith of their people; Frederick, on the other hand, crowned his system of government by a religious inquisition, which will seem the more reprehensible when we remember that in the persons of the heretics he was persecuting the representatives of a free municipal life. Lastly, the internal police, and the kernel of the army for foreign service, was composed of Saracens who had been brought over from Sicily to Nocera and Lucera—men who were deaf to the cry of misery and careless of the ban of the Church. At a later period the subjects, by whom the use of weapons had long been forgotten, were passive witnesses of the fall of Manfred and of the seizure of the government by Charles of Anjou; the latter continued to use the system which he found already at work.

At the side of the centralizing Emperor appeared a usurper of the most peculiar kind; his vicar and son-in-law, Ezzelino da Romano. He stands as the representative of no system of government or administration, for all his activity was wasted in struggles for supremacy the eastern part of Upper Italy; but as a political type he was a f of no less importance for the future than his imperial Frederick. The conquests and usurpations which had hi place in the Middle Ages rested on real or pretended inheritance and other such claims, or else were effected against unbelievers and excommunicated persons. Here for the first time the attempt was openly made to found a throne by wholesale murder and endless barbarities, by the adoption, in short, of any means with a view to nothing but the end pursued. None of his successors, not even Cesare Borgia, rivalled the colossal guilt of Ezzelino; but the example once set was not forgotten, and his fall led to no return of justice among the nations, and served as no warning to future transgressors.

It was in vain at such a time that St. Thomas Aquinas, a born subject of Frederick, set up the theory of a constitutional monarchy, in which the prince was to be supported by an upper house named by himself, and a representative body elected by the people. Such theories found no echo outside the lecture-room, and Frederick and Ezzelino were and remain for Italy the great political phenomena of the thirteenth century. Their personality, already half legendary, forms the most important subject of 'The Hundred Old Tales', whose original composition falls certainly within this century.[3] In them Ezzelino is spoken of with the awe which all mighty impressions leave behind them. His person became the centre of a whole literature from the chronicle of eye-witnesses to the half-mythical tragedy of later poets.

DESPOTS OF THE FOURTEENTH CENTURY

The tyrannies, great and small, of the fourteenth century afford constant proof that examples such as these were not thrown away. Their misdeeds cried forth loudly and have been circumstantially told by historians. As States depending for existence on themselves alone, and scientifically organized with a view to this object, they present to us a higher interest than that of mere narrative.

The deliberate adaptation of means to ends, of which no prince [illegible] at time a conception, joined to almost absolute [illegible] nits of the State, produced among the despots [illegible] of life of a peculiar character. The chief secret [illegible] e hands of the prudent ruler lay in leaving the [illegible] as far as possible where he found it, or as he [illegible] The chief sources of income were: a land tax, [illegible]; definite taxes on articles of consumption and [illegible] nd imported goods; together with the private

[illegible] *Cento Novelle Antiche*, ed. 1525.

fortune of the ruling house. The only possible increase was derived from the growth of business and of general prosperity. Loans, such as we find in the free cities, were here unknown; a well-planned confiscation was held a preferable means of raising money, provided only that it left public credit unshaken—an end attained, for example, by the truly Oriental practice of deposing and plundering the director of the finances.

Out of this income the expenses of the little court, of the bodyguard, of the mercenary troops, and of the public buildings were met, as well as of the buffoons and men of talent who belonged to the personal attendants of the prince. The illegitimacy of his rule isolated the tyrant and surrounded him with constant danger; the most honourable alliance which he could form was with intellectual merit, without regard to its origin. The liberality of the northern princes of the thirteenth century was confined to the knights, to the nobility which served and sang. It was otherwise with the Italian despot. With his thirst for fame and his passion for monumental works, it was talent, not birth, which he needed. In the company of the poet and the scholar he felt himself in a new position, almost, indeed, in possession of a new legitimacy.

No prince was more famous in this respect than the ruler of Verona, Can Grande della Scala, who numbered among the illustrious exiles whom he entertained at his court representatives of the whole of Italy. The men of letters were not ungrateful. Petrarch, whose visits at the courts of such men have been so severely censured, sketched an ideal picture of a prince of the fourteenth century. He demands great things from his patron, the lord of Padua, but in a manner which shows that he holds him capable of them. 'Thou must not be the master but the father of thy subjects, and must love them as thy children; yea, as members of thy body. Weapons, guards, and soldiers thou mayest employ against the enemy—with thy subjects goodwill is sufficient. By citizens, of course, I mean those who love the existing order; for those who daily desire change are rebels and traitors, and against such a stern justice may take its course.'

Here follows, worked out in detail, the purely modern fiction of the omnipotence of the State. The prince is to take everything into his charge, to maintain and restore churches and public buildings, to keep up the municipal police, to drain the marshes, to look after the supply of wine and corn; so to distribute the taxes that the people can recognize their necessity; he is to support the sick and the helpless, and to give his protection and society to distinguished scholars, on whom his fame in after ages will depend.

But whatever might be the brighter sides of the system, and the merits of individual rulers, yet the men of the fourteenth century were not without a more or less distinct consciousness of the brief and uncertain tenure of most of these despotisms. Inasmuch as political institutions like these are naturally secure in proportion to the size of the territory in which they exist, the larger principalities were constantly tempted to swallow up the smaller. Whole hecatombs of petty rulers were sacrificed at this time to the Visconti alone. As a result of this outward danger an inward ferment was in ceaseless activity; and the effect of the situation on the character of the ruler was generally of the most sinister kind. Absolute power, with its temptations to luxury and unbridled selfishness, and the perils to which he was exposed from enemies and conspirators, turned him almost inevitably into a tyrant in the worst sense of the word. Well for him if he could trust his nearest relations! But where all was illegitimate, there could be no regular law of inheritance, either with regard to the succession or to the division of the ruler's property; and consequently the heir, if incompetent or a minor, was liable in the interest of the family itself to be supplanted by an uncle or cousin of more resolute character. The acknowledgment or exclusion of the bastards was a fruitful source of contest; and most of these families in consequence were plagued with a crowd of discontented and vindictive kinsmen. This circumstance gave rise to continual outbreaks of treason and to frightful scenes of domestic bloodshed, Sometimes the pretenders lived abroad in exile, and like the Visconti, who practised the fisherman's craft on the Lake of Garda, viewed the situation with patient indifference. When asked by a messenger of his rival when and how he thought of returning to Milan, he gave the reply, 'By the same means as those by which I was expelled, but not till his crimes have outweighed my own'. Sometimes, too, the despot was sacrificed by his relations, with the view of saving the family, to the public conscience which he had too grossly outraged. In a few cases the government was in the hands of the whole family, or at least the ruler was bound to take their advice; and here, too, the distribution of property and influence often led to bitter disputes.

The whole of this system excited the deep and persistent hatred of the Florentine writers of that epoch. Even the pomp and display with which the despot was perhaps less anxious to gratify his own vanity than to impress the popular imagination, awakened their keenest sarcasm. Woe to an adventurer if he fell into their hands, like the upstart Doge Agnello of Pisa (1364), who used to ride out with a golden sceptre, and show himself at the window of his house, 'as relics are shown', reclining on embroidered drapery and cushions, served like a pope or emperor, by kneeling attendants. More often, however, the old Florentines speak on this subject in a tone of lofty seriousness. Dante saw and characterized well the vulgarity and commonplace which marked the ambition of the new princes. 'What else mean their trumpets and their bells, their horns and their flutes, but "come, hangmen—come, vultures!"' The castle of the tyrant, as pictured by the popular mind, is lofty and solitary, full of dungeons and listening-tubes, the home of cruelty and misery. Misfortune is foretold to all who enter the service of the despot, who even becomes at last himself an object of pity: he must needs be the enemy of all good and honest men; he can trust no one, and can read in the faces of his subjects the expectation of his fall. 'As despotisms rise, grow, and are consolidated, so grows in their midst the hidden element which must produce their dissolution and ruin.' But the deepest ground of dislike has not been stated; Florence was then the scene of the richest development of human individuality, while for the despots no other individuality could be suffered to live and thrive but their own and that of their nearest dependants. The control of the individual was rigorously carried out, even down to the establishment of a system of passports.

The astrological superstitions and the religious unbelief of many of the tyrants gave, in the minds of their contemporaries, a peculiar colour to this awful and God-forsaken existence. When the last Carrara could no longer defend the walls and gates of the plague-stricken Padua, hemmed in on all sides by the Venetians (1405), the soldiers of the guard heard him cry to the devil 'to come and kill him'.

* * *

The most complete and instructive type of the tyranny of the fourteenth century is to be found unquestionably among the Visconti of Milan, from the death of the Archbishop Giovanni onwards (1354). The family likeness which shows itself between Bernabò and the worst of the Roman Emperors is unmistakable; the most important public object was the prince's boar-hunting; whoever interfered with it was put to death with torture, the terrified people were forced to maintain 5,000 boar-hounds, with strict responsibility for their health and safety. The taxes were extorted by every conceivable sort of compulsion; seven daughters of the prince received a dowry of 100,000 gold florins apiece; and an enormous treasure was collected. On the death of his wife (1384) an order was issued 'to the subjects' to share his grief, as once they had shared his joy, and to wear mourning for a year. The *coup de main* (1385) by which his nephew Giangaleazzo got him into his power—one of those brilliant plots which make the heart of even late historians beat more quickly—was strikingly characteristic of the man.

In Giangaleazzo that passion for the colossal which was common to most of the despots shows itself on the largest scale. He undertook, at the cost of 300,000 golden florins, the construction of gigantic dykes, to divert in case of need the Mincio from Mantua and the Brenta from Padua, and thus to render these cities defenceless. It is not impossible, indeed, that he thought of draining away the lagoons of Venice. He founded that most wonderful of all convents, the Certosa of Pavia, and the cathedral of Milan, 'which exceeds in size and splendour all the churches of Christendom'. The Palace in Pavia, which his father Galeazzo began and which he himself finished, was probably by far the most magnificent of the princely dwellings of Europe. There he transferred his famous library, and the great collection of relics of the saints, in which he placed a peculiar faith. It would have been strange indeed if a prince of this character had not also cherished the highest ambitions in political matters. King Wenceslaus made him Duke (1395); he was hoping for nothing less than the Kingdom of Italy or the Imperial crown, when (1402) he fell ill and died. His whole territories are said to have paid him in a single year, besides the regular contribution of 1,200,000 gold florins, no less than 800,000 more in extraordinary subsidies. After his death the dominions which he had brought together by every sort of violence fell to pieces; and for a time even the original nucleus could with difficulty be maintained by his successors. What might have become of his sons Giovanni Maria (died 1412) and Filippo Maria (died 1447), had they lived in a different country and among other traditions, cannot be said. But, as heirs of their house, they inherited that monstrous capital of cruelty and cowardice which had been accumulated from generation to generation.

Giovanni Maria, too, is famed for his dogs, which were no longer, however, used for hunting but for tearing human bodies. Tradition has preserved their names, like those of the bears of the Emperor Valentinian I. In May, 1409, when war was going on, and the starving populace cried to him in the streets, *Pace! Pace!* he let loose his mercenaries upon them, and 200 lives were sacrificed; under penalty of the gallows it was forbidden to utter the words *pace* and *guerra*, and the priests were ordered, instead of *dona nobis pacem*, to say *tranquillitatem!* At last a band of conspirators took advantage of the moment when Facino Cane, the chief Condottiere of the insane ruler, lay ill at Pavia, and cut down Giovanni Maria in the church of San Gottardo at Milan; the dying Facino on the same day made his officers swear to stand by the heir Filippo Maria, whom he himself urged his wife to take for a second husband. His wife, Beatrice di Tenda, followed his advice. We shall have occasion to speak of Filippo Maria later on.

And in times like these Cola di Rienzi was dreaming of founding on the rickety enthusiasm of the corrupt population of Rome a new State which was to comprise all Italy. By the side of rulers such as those whom we have described, he seems no better than a poor deluded fool.

DESPOTS OF THE FIFTEENTH CENTURY

The despotisms of the fifteenth century show an altered character. Many of the less important tyrants, and some of the greater, like the Scala and the Carrara, had disappeared, while the more powerful ones, aggrandized by conquest, had given to their systems each its characteristic development. Naples for example received a fresh and stronger impulse from the new Aragonese dynasty. A striking feature of this epoch is the attempt of the Condottieri to found independent dynasties of their own. Facts and the actual relations of things, apart from traditional estimates, are alone regarded; talent and audacity win the great prizes. The petty despots, to secure a trustworthy support, begin to enter the service of the larger States, and become themselves Condottieri, receiving in return for their services money and immunity for their misdeeds, if not an increase of territory. All, whether small or great, must exert themselves more, must act with greater caution and calculation, and must learn to refrain from too wholesale barbarities; only so much wrong is permitted by public opinion as is necessary for the end in view, and this the impartial bystander certainly finds no fault with. No trace is here visible of that half-religious loyalty by which the legitimate princes of the

West were supported; personal popularity is the nearest approach we can find to it. Talent and calculation are the only means of advancement. A character like that of Charles the Bold, which wore itself out in the passionate pursuit of impracticable ends, was a riddle to the Italians. 'The Swiss were only peasants, and if they were all killed, that would be no satisfaction for the Burgundian nobles who might fall in the war. If the Duke got possession of all Switzerland without a struggle, his income would not be 5,000 ducats the greater.' The mediæval features in the character of Charles, his chivalrous aspirations and ideals, had long become unintelligible to the Italians. The diplomatists of the South, when they saw him strike his officers and yet keep them in his service, when he maltreated his troops to punish them for a defeat, and then threw the blame on his counsellors in the presence of the same troops, gave him up for lost. Louis XI, on the other hand, whose policy surpasses that of the Italian princes in their own style, and who was an avowed admirer of Francesco Sforza, must be placed in all that regards culture and refinement far below these rulers.

Good and evil lie strangely mixed together in the Italian States of the fifteenth century. The personality of the ruler is so highly developed, often of such deep significance, and so characteristic of the conditions and needs of the time, that to form an adequate moral judgement on it is no easy task.

The foundation of the system was and remained illegitimate, and nothing could remove the curse which rested upon it. The imperial approval or investiture made no change in the matter, since the people attached little weight to the fact that the despot had bought a piece of parchment somewhere in foreign countries, or from some stranger passing through his territory. If the Emperor had been good for anything—so ran the logic of uncritical common sense—he would never have let the tyrant rise at all. Since the Roman expedition of Charles IV, the emperors had done nothing more in Italy than sanction a tyranny which had arisen without their help; they could give it no other practical authority than what might flow from an imperial charter. The whole conduct of Charles in Italy was a scandalous political comedy. Matteo Villani relates how the Visconti escorted him round their territory, and at last out of it; how he went about like a hawker selling his wares (privileges, etc.) for money; what a mean appearance he made in Rome, and how at the end, without even drawing the sword, he returned with replenished coffers across the Alps. Sigismund came, on the first occasion at least (1414), with the good intention of persuading John XXIII to take part in his council; it was on that journey, when Pope and Emperor were gazing from the lofty tower of Cremona on the panorama of Lombardy, that their host, the tyrant Gabrino Fondolo, was seized with the desire to throw them both over. On his second visit Sigismund came as a mere adventurer; for more than half a year he remained shut up in Siena, like a debtor in gaol, and only with difficulty, and at a later period, succeeded in being crowned in Rome. And what can be thought of Frederick III? His journeys to Italy have the air of holiday-trips or pleasure-tours made at the expense of those who wanted him to confirm their prerogatives, or whose vanity it flattered to entertain an emperor. The latter was the case with Alfonso of Naples, who paid 150,000 florins for the honour of an imperial visit. At Ferrara, on his second return from Rome (1469), Freberick spent a whole day without leaving his chamber, distributing no less than eighty titles; he created knights, counts, doctors, notaries—counts, indeed, of different degrees, as, for instance, counts palatine, counts with the right to create doctors up to the number of five, counts with the rights to legitimatize bastards, to appoint notaries, and so forth. The Chancellor, however, expected in return for the patents in question a gratuity which was thought excessive at Ferrara. The opinion of Borso, himself created Duke of Modena and Reggio in return for an annual payment of 4,000 gold florins, when his imperial patron was distributing titles and diplomas to all the little court, is not mentioned. The humanists, then the chief spokesmen of the age, were divided in opinion according to their personal interests, while the Emperor was greeted by some of them with the conventional acclamations of the poets of imperial Rome. Poggio confessed that he no longer knew what the coronation meant; in the old times only the victorious Imperator was crowned, and then he was crowned with laurel.

With Maximilian I begins not only the general intervention of foreign nations, but a new imperial policy with regard to Italy. The first step—the investiture of Lodovico il Moro with the duchy of Milan and the exclusion of his unhappy nephew—was not of a kind to bear good fruits. According to the modern theory of intervention, when two parties are tearing a country to pieces, a third may step in and take its share, and on this principle the empire acted. But right and justice could be invoked no longer. When Louis XII was expected in Genoa (1502), and the imperial eagle was removed from the hall of the ducal palace and replaced by painted lilies, the historian Senarega asked what, after all, was the meaning of the eagle which so many revolutions had spared, and what claims the empire had upon Genoa. No one knew more about the matter than the old phrase that Genoa was a *camera imperii*. In fact, nobody in Italy could give a clear answer to any such questions. At length when Charles V held Spain and the empire together, he was able by means of Spanish forces to make good imperial claims; but it is notorious that what he thereby gained turned to the profit, not of the empire, but of the Spanish monarchy.

* * *

Closely connected with the political illegitimacy of the dynasties of the fifteenth century was the public indifference to legitimate birth, which to foreigners—for example, to Comines—appeared so remarkable. The two things went naturally together. In northern countries, as in Burgundy, the illegitimate offspring were provided for by a distinct class of appanages, such as bishoprics and the like; in Portugal an illegitimate line maintained itself on the throne only by constant effort; in Italy, on the contrary, there no longer existed a princely house where, even in the direct line of descent, bastards were not patiently tolerated. The Aragonese monarchs of Naples belonged to the illegitimate line, Aragon itself falling to the lot of the brother of Alfonso I. The great Federigo of Urbino was, perhaps, no Montefeltro at all. When Pius II was on his way to the Congress of Mantua (1459), eight bastards of the house of Este rode to meet him at Ferrara, among them the reigning duke Borso himself and two illegitimate sons of his illegitimate brother and predecessor Lionello. The latter had also had a lawful wife, herself an illegitimate daughter of Alfonso I of Naples by an African woman. The bastards were often admitted to the succession where the lawful children were minors and the dangers of the situation were pressing; and a rule of seniority became recognized, which took no account of pure or impure birth. The fitness of the individual, his worth and capacity, were of more weight than all the laws and usages which prevailed elsewhere in the West. It was the age, indeed, in which the sons of the Popes were founding dynasties. In the sixteenth century, through the influence of foreign ideas and of the counter-reformation which then began, the who'e question was judged more strictly: Varchi discovers that the succession of the legitimate children 'is ordered by reason, and is the will of heaven from eternity'. Cardinal Ippolito de' Medici founded his claim to the lordship of Florence on the fact that he was perhaps the fruit of a lawful marriage, and at all events son of a gentlewoman, and not, like Duke Alessandro, of a servant girl. At this time began those morganatic marriages of affection which in the fifteenth century, on grounds either of policy or morality, would have had no meaning at all.

But the highest and the most admired form of illegitimacy in the fifteenth century was presented by the Condottiere, who, whatever may have been his origin, raised himself to the position of an independent ruler. At bottom, the occupation of Lower Italy by the Normans in the eleventh century was of this character. Such attempts now began to keep the peninsula in a constant ferment.

It was possible for a Condottiere to obtain the lordship of a district even without usurpation, in the case when his employer, through want of money or troops, provided for him in this way; under any circumstances the Condottiere, even when he dismissed for the time the greater part of his forces, needed a safe place where he could establish his winter quarters, and lay up his stores and provisions. The first example of a captain thus portioned is John Hawkwood, who was invested by Gregory XI with the lordship of Bagnacavallo and Cotignola. When with Alberigo da Barbiano Italian armies and leaders appeared upon the scene, the chances of founding a principality, or of increasing one already acquired, became more frequent. The first great bacchanalian outbreak of military ambition took place in the duchy of Milan after the death of Giangaleazzo (1402). The policy of his two sons was chiefly aimed at the destruction of the new despotisms founded by the Condottieri; and from the greatest of them, Facino Cane, the house of Visconti inherited, together with his widow, a long list of cities, and 400,000 golden florins, not to speak of the soldiers of her first husband whom Beatrice di Tenda brought with her. From henceforth that thoroughly immoral relation between the governments and their Condottieri, which is characteristic of the fifteenth century, became more and more common. An old story—one of those which are true and not true, everywhere and nowhere—describes it as follows: The citizens of a certain town (Siena seems to be meant) had once an officer in their service who had freed them from foreign aggression; daily they took counsel how to recompense him, and concluded that no reward in their power was great enough, not even if they made him lord of the city. At last one of them rose and said, 'Let us kill him and then worship him as our patron saint'. And so they did, following the example set by the Roman senate with Romulus. In fact, the Condottieri had reason to fear none so much as their employers; if they were successful, they became dangerous, and were put out of the way like Roberto Malatesta[4] just after the victory he had won for Sixtus IV (1482); if they failed, the vengeance of the Venetians on Carmagnola showed to what risks they were exposed (1432). It is characteristic of the moral aspect of the situation that the Condottieri had often to give their wives and children as hostages, and notwithstanding this, neither felt nor inspired confidence. They must have been heroes of abnegation, natures like Belisarius himself, not to be cankered by hatred and bitterness; only the most perfect goodness could save them from the most monstrous iniquity. No wonder then if we find them full of contempt for all sacred things, cruel and treacherous to their fellows—men who cared nothing whether or no they died under the ban of the Church. At the same time, and through the force of the same conditions, the genius and capacity of many among them attained the highest conceivable development, and won for them the admiring devotion of their followers; their armies are the first in modern history in which the personal credit of the leader is the one moving power. A brilliant example is shown in the life of Francesco Sforza; no prejudice of birth could prevent him from winning and turning to account when he needed it a boundless devotion from each individual with whom he had to deal; it happened more than once that his enemies laid down their arms at the sight of him, greeting him reverently with uncovered heads, each honouring in him 'the common father of the men-at-arms'. The race of the Sforza has this special interest, that from the very beginning of its history we seem able to trace its endeavours after the crown. The foundation of its fortune lay in the remarkable fruitfulness of the family; Francesco's father, Jacopo, himself a celebrated man, had twenty brothers and sisters, all brought up roughly at Cotignola, near Faenza, amid the perils of one of the endless Romagnole 'vendette' between their own house and that of the Pasolini. The family dwelling was a mere arsenal and fortress; the mother and daughters were as warlike as their kinsmen. In his thirteenth year Jacopo ran away and fled to Panicale to the Papal Condottiere Boldrino—the

*[4] But cf. Pastor, *History of the Popes*, Vol. ii, pp. 553 and 737.

man who even in death continued to lead his troops, the word of order being given from the bannered tent in which the embalmed body lay, till at last a fit leader was found to succeed him. Jacopo, when he had at length made himself a name in the service of different Condottieri, sent for his relations, and obtained through them the same advantages that a prince derives from a numerous dynasty. It was these relations who kept the army together when he lay a captive in the Castel dell'Uovo at Naples; his sister took the royal envoys prisoners with her own hands, and saved him by this reprisal from death. It was an indication of the breadth and the range of his plans that in monetary affairs Jacopo was thoroughly trustworthy; even in his defeats he consequently found credit with the bankers. He habitually protected the peasants against the licence of his troops, and reluctantly destroyed or injured a conquered city. He gave his well-known mistress, Lucia, the mother of Francesco, in marriage to another, in order to be free for a princely alliance. Even the marriages of his relations were arranged on a definite plan. He kept clear of the impious and profligate life of his contemporaries, and brought up his son Francesco to the three rules: 'Let other men's wives alone; strike none of your followers, or, if you do, send the injured man far away; don't ride a hard-mouthed horse, or one that drops his shoe.' But his chief source of influence lay in the qualities, if not of a great general, at least of a great soldier. His frame was powerful, and developed by every kind of exercise; his peasant's face and frank manners won general popularity; his memory was marvellous, and after the lapse of years could recall the names of his followers, the number of their horses, and the amount of their pay. His education was purely Italian: he devoted his leisure to the study of history, and had Greek and Latin authors translated for his use. Francesco, his still more famous son, set his mind from the first on founding a powerful State, and through brilliant generalship and a faithlessness which hesitated at nothing, got possession of the great city of Milan (1450).

His example was contagious. Æneas Sylvius wrote about this time: 'In our change-loving Italy, where nothing stands firm, and where no ancient dynasty exists, a servant can easily become a king'. One man in particular, who styles himself 'the man of fortune', filled the imagination of the whole country: Giacomo Piccinino, the son of Niccolò. It was a burning question of the day if he, too, would succeed in founding a princely house. The greater States had an obvious interest in hindering it, and even Francesco Sforza thought it would be all the better if the list of self-made sovereigns were not enlarged. But the troops and captains sent against him, at the time, for instance, when he was aiming at the lordship of Siena, recognized their interest in supporting him: 'If it were all over with him, we should have to go back and plough our fields'. Even while besieging him at Orbetello, they supplied him with provisions; and he got out of his straits with honour. But at last fate overtook him. All Italy was betting on the result, when (1465), after a visit to Sforza at Milan, he went to King Ferrante at Naples. In spite of the pledges given, and of his high connections, he was murdered in the Castel Nuovo. Even the Condottieri, who had obtained their dominions by inheritance, never felt themselves safe. When Roberto Malatesta and Federigo of Urbino died on the same day (1482), the one at Rome, the other at Bologna, it was found that each had recommended his State to the care of the other. Against a class of men who themselves stuck at nothing, everything was held to be permissible. Francesco Sforza, when quite young, had married a rich Calabrian heiress, Polissena Ruffo, Countess of Montalto, who bore him a daughter; an aunt poisoned both mother and child, and seized the inheritance.

From the death of Piccinino onwards, the foundations of new States by the Condottieri became a scandal not to be tolerated. The four great Powers, Naples, Milan, the Papacy, and Venice, formed among themselves a political equilibrium which refused to allow of any disturbance. In the States of the Church, which swarmed with petty tyrants, who in part were, or had been, Condottieri, the nephews of the Popes, since the time of Sixtus IV, monopolized the right to all such undertakings. But at the first sign of a political crisis, the soldiers of fortune appeared again upon the scene. Under the wretched administration of Innocent VIII it was near happening that a certain Boccalino, who had formerly served in the Burgundian army, gave himself and the town of Osimo, of which he was master, up to the Turkish forces; fortunately, through the intervention of Lorenzo the Magnificent, he proved willing to be paid off, and took himself away. In the year 1495, when the wars of Charles VIII had turned Italy upside down, the Condottiere Vidovero, of Brescia, made trial of his strength; he had already seized the town of Cesena and murdered many of the nobles and the burghers; but the citadel held out, and he was forced to withdraw. He then, at the head of a band lent him by another scoundrel, Pandolfo Malatesta of Rimini, son of the Roberto already spoken of, and Venetian Condottiere, wrested the town of Castelnuovo from the Archbishop of Ravenna. The Venetians, fearing that worse would follow, and urged also by the Pope, ordered Pandolfo, 'with the kindest intentions', to take an opportunity of arresting his good friend: the arrest was made. though 'with great regret', whereupon the order came to bring the prisoner to the gallows. Pandolfo was considerate enough to strangle him in prison, and then show his corpse to the people. The last notable example of such usurpers is the famous Castellan of Musso, who during the confusion in the Milanese territory which followed the battle of Pavia (1525), improvised a sovereignty on the Lake of Como.

THE SMALLER DESPOTISMS

It may be said in general of the despotisms of the fifteenth century that the greatest crimes are most frequent in the smallest States. In these, where the family was numerous and all the members wished to live in a manner befitting their rank, disputes respecting the inheritance were unavoidable. Bernardo Varano of Camerino put (1434) two of his brothers to death, wishing to divide their property among his sons. Where the ruler of a single town was distinguished by a wise, moderate, and humane government, and by zeal for intellectual culture, he was generally a member of some great family, or politically dependent on it. This was the case, for example, with Alessandro Sforza, Prince of Pesaro, brother of the great Francesco, and stepfather of Federigo of Urbino (d. 1473). Prudent in administration, just and affable in his rule, he enjoyed, after years of warfare, a tranquil reign, collected a noble library, and passed his leisure in learned or religious conversation. A man of the same class was Giovanni II Bentivoglio of Bologna (1463-1508), whose policy was determined by that of the Este and the Sforza. What ferocity and bloodthirstiness is found, on the other hand, among the Varani of Camerino, the Malatesta of Rimini, the Manfreddi of Faenza, and above all among the Baglioni of Perugia. We find a striking picture of the events in the last-named family towards the close of the fifteenth century, in the admirable historical narratives of Graziani and Matarazzo.

The Baglioni were one of those families whose rule never took the shape of an avowed despotism. It was rather a leadership exercised by means of their vast wealth and of their practical influence in the choice of public officers. Within the family one man was recognized as head; but deep and secret jealousy prevailed among the members of the different branches. Opposed to the Baglioni stood another aristocratic party, led by the family of the Oddi. In 1487 the city was turned into a camp, and the houses of the leading citizens swarmed with bravos; scenes of violence were of daily occurrence. At the burial of a German student, who had been assassinated, two colleges took arms against one another; sometimes the bravos of the different houses even joined battle in the public square. The complaints of the merchants and artisans were vain; the Papal Governors and *nipoti* held their tongues, or took themselves off on the first opportunity. At last the Oddi were forced to abandon Perugia, and the city became a beleaguered fortress under the absolute despotism of the Baglioni, who used even the cathedral as barracks. Plots and surprises were met with cruel vengeance; in the year 1491, after 130 conspirators, who had forced their way into the city, were killed and hung up at the Palazzo Comunale, thirty-five altars were erected in the square, and for three days mass was performed and processions held, to take away the curse which rested on the spot. A *nipote* of Innocent VIII was in open day run through in the street. A *nipote* of Alexander VI, who was sent to smooth matters over, was dismissed with public contempt. All the while the two leaders of the ruling house, Guido and Ridolfo, were holding frequent interviews with Suor Colomba of Rieti, a Dominican nun of saintly reputation and miraculous powers, who under penalty of some great disaster ordered them to make peace—naturally in vain. Nevertheless the chronicle takes the opportunity to point out the devotion and piety of the better men in Perugia during this reign of terror. When in 1494 Charles VIII approached, the Baglioni from Perugia and the exiles encamped in and near Assisi conducted the war with such ferocity that every house in the valley was levelled to the ground. The fields lay untilled, the peasants were turned into plundering and murdering savages, the fresh-grown bushes were filled with stags and wolves, and the beasts grew fat on the bodies of the slain, on so-called 'Christian flesh'. When Alexander VI withdrew (1495) into Umbria before Charles VIII, then returning from Naples, it occurred to him, when at Perugia, that he might now rid himself of the Baglioni once for all; he proposed to Guido a festival or tournament, or something else of the same kind, which would bring the whole family together. Guido, however, was of opinion 'that the most impressive spectacle of all would be to see the whole military force of Perugia collected in a body', whereupon the Pope abandoned his project. Soon after, the exiles made another attack in which nothing but the personal heroism of the Baglioni won them the victory. It was then that Simonetto Baglione, a lad of scarcely eighteen, fought in the square with a handful of followers against hundreds of the enemy: he fell at last with more than twenty wounds, but recovered himself when Astorre Baglione came to his help, and mounting on horseback in gilded armour with a falcon on his helmet, 'like Mars in bearing and in deeds, plunged into the struggle'.

At that time Raphael, a boy of twelve years of age, was at school under Pietro Perugino. The impressions of these days are perhaps immortalized in the small, early pictures of St. Michael and St. George: something of them, it may be, lives eternally in the large painting of St. Michael: and if Astorre Baglione has anywhere found his apotheosis, it is in the figure of the heavenly horseman in the Heliodorus.[5]

The opponents of the Baglioni were partly destroyed, partly scattered in terror, and were henceforth incapable of another enterprise of the kind. After a time a partial reconciliation took place, and some of the exiles were allowed to return. But Perugia became none the safer or more tranquil: the inward discord of the ruling family broke out in frightful excesses. An opposition was formed against Guido and Ridolfo and their sons Gianpaolo, Simonetto, Astorre, Gismondo, Gentile, Marcantonio and others, by two great-nephews, Grifone and Carlo Barciglia; the latter of the two was also nephew of Varano, Prince of Camerino, and brother-in-law of one of the former exiles, Gerolamo della Penna. In vain did Simonetto, warned by sinister presentiment, entreat his uncle on his knees to allow him to put Penna to death: Guido refused. The plot ripened suddenly on the occasion of the marriage of Astorre with Lavinia Colonna, at Midsummer, 1500. The festival began and lasted several days amid gloomy forebodings, whose deepening effect is admirably described by Matarazzo. Varano himself encouraged them with devilish ingenuity: he worked upon Grifone by the prospect of undivided authority, and by stories of an imaginary intrigue of his wife Zenobia

*[5] The two first-named pictures, painted *c.* 1502, are now in the Louvre; the large St. Michael, dated 1518, is in the same collection; the 'Heliodorus' is a part of the Vatican frescoes, finished in 1514. For reproductions of all of these paintings see the Phaidon Edition of Raphael.

with Gianpaolo. Finally each conspirator was provided with a victim. (The Baglioni lived all of them in separate houses, mostly on the site of the present castle.) Each received fifteen of the bravos at hand; the remainder were set on the watch. In the night of July 15 the doors were forced, and Guido, Astorre, Simonetto, and Gismondo were murdered; the others succeeded in escaping.

As the corpse of Astorre lay by that of Simonetto in the street, the spectators, 'and especially the foreign students', compared him to an ancient Roman, so great and imposing did he seem. In the features of Simonetto could still be traced the audacity and defiance which death itself had not tamed. The victors went round among the friends of the family, and did their best to recommend themselves; they found all in tears and preparing to leave for the country. Meantime the escaped Baglioni collected forces without the city, and on the following day forced their way in, Gianpaolo at their head, and speedily found adherents among others whom Barciglia had been threatening with death. When Grifone fell into their hands near Sant' Ercolano, Gianpaolo handed him over for execution to his followers. Barciglia and Penna fled to Varano, the chief author of the tragedy, at Camerino; and in a moment, almost without loss, Gianpaolo became master of the city.

Atalanta, the still young and beautiful mother of Grifone, who the day before had withdrawn to a country house with the latter's wife Zenobia and two children of Gianpaolo, and more than once had repulsed her son with a mother's curse, now returned with her daughter-in-law in search of the dying man. All stood aside as the two women approached, each man shrinking from being recognized as the slayer of Grifone, and dreading the malediction of the mother. But they were deceived: she herself besought her son to pardon him who had dealt the fatal blow, and he died with her blessing. The eyes of the crowd followed the two women reverently as they crossed the square with blood-stained garments. It was Atalanta for whom Raphael afterwards painted the world-famous 'Deposition', with which she laid her own maternal sorrows at the feet of a yet higher and holier suffering.

The cathedral, in the immediate neighbourhood of which the greater part of this tragedy had been enacted, was washed with wine and consecrated afresh. The triumphal arch, erected for the wedding, still remained standing, painted with the deeds of Astorre and with the laudatory verses of the narrator of these events, the worthy Matarazzo.

A legendary history, which is simply the reflection of these atrocities, arose out of the early days of the Baglioni. All the members of this family from the beginning were reported to have died an evil death—twenty-seven on one occasion together; their houses were said to have been once before levelled to the ground, and the streets of Perugia paved with the bricks—and more of the same kind. Under Paul III the destruction of their palaces really took place.

For a time they seemed to have formed good resolutions, to have brought their own party into order, and to have protected the public officials against the arbitrary acts of the nobility. But the old curse broke out again like a smouldering fire. In 1520 Gianpaolo was enticed to Rome under Leo X, and there beheaded; one of his sons, Orazio, who ruled in Perugia for a short time only, and by the most violent means, as the partisan of the Duke of Urbino (himself threatened by the Pope), once more repeated in his own family the horrors of the past. His uncle and three cousins were murdered, whereupon the Duke sent him word that enough had been done. His brother, Malatesta Baglione, the Florentine general, has made himself immortal by the treason of 1530; and Malatesta's son Ridolfo, the last of the house, attained, by the murder of the legate and the public officers in the year 1534, a brief but sanguinary authority.

We shall meet again with the names of the rulers of Rimini. Unscrupulousness, impiety, military skill, and high culture have been seldom combined in one individual as in Sigismondo Malatesta (d. 1467). But the accumulated crimes of such a family must at last outweigh all talent, however great, and drag the tyrant into the abyss. Pandolfo, Sigismondo's nephew, who has been mentioned already, succeeded in holding his ground, for the sole reason that the Venetians refused to abandon their Condottiere, whatever guilt he might be chargeable with; when his subjects (1497), after ample provocation, bombarded him in his castle at Rimini, and afterwards allowed him to escape, a Venetian commissioner brought him back, stained as he was with fratricide and every other abomination. Thirty years later the Malatesta were penniless exiles. In the year 1527, as in the time of Cesare Borgia, a sort of epidemic fell on the petty tyrants; few of them outlived this date, and none to their own good. At Mirandola, which was governed by insignificant princes of the house of Pico, lived in the year 1533 a poor scholar, Lilio Gregorio Giraldi, who had fled from the sack of Rome to the hospitable hearth of the aged Giovanni Francesco Pico, nephew of the famous Giovanni; the discussions as to the sepuchral monument which the prince was constructing for himself gave rise to a treatise, the dedication of which bears the date of April of this year. The postscript is a sad one—'In October of the same year the unhappy prince was attacked in the night and robbed of life and throne by his brother's son; and I myself escaped narrowly, and am now in the deepest misery.'

A near-despotism, without morals or principles, such as Pandolfo Petrucci exercised from after 1490 in Siena, then torn by faction, is hardly worth a closer consideration. Insignificant and malicious, he governed with the help of a professor of jurisprudence and of an astrologer, and frightened his people by an occasional murder. His pastime in the summer months was to roll blocks of stone from the top of Monte Amiata, without caring what or whom they hit. After succeeding, where the most prudent failed, in escaping from the devices of Cesare Borgia, he died at last forsaken and despised. His sons maintained a qualified supremacy for many years afterwards.

THE GREATER DYNASTIES

In treating of the chief dynasties of Italy, it is convenient to discuss the Aragonese, on account of its special character, apart from the rest. The feudal system, which from the days of the Normans had survived in the form of a territorial supremacy of the Barons, gave a distinctive colour to the political constitution of Naples; while elsewhere in Italy, excepting only in the southern part of the ecclesiastical dominion, and in a few other districts, a direct tenure of land prevailed, and no hereditary powers were permitted by the law. The great Alfonso, who reigned in Naples from 1435 onwards (d. 1458), was a man of another kind than his real or alleged descendants. Brilliant in his whole existence, fearless in mixing with his people, dignified and affable in intercourse, admired rather than blamed even for his old man's passion for Lucrezia d'Alagno, he had the one bad quality of extravagance, from which, however, the natural consequence followed. Unscrupulous financiers were long omnipotent at Court, till the bankrupt king robbed them of their spoils; a crusade was preached as a pretext for taxing the clergy; when a great earthquake happened in the Abruzzi, the survivors were compelled to make good the contributions of the dead. By such means Alfonso was able to entertain distinguished guests with unrivalled splendour; he found pleasure in ceaseless expense, even for the benefit of his enemies, and in rewarding literary work knew absolutely no measure. Poggio received 500 pieces of gold for translating Xenophon's 'Cyropædeia' into Latin.

Ferrante, who succeeded him, passed as his illegitimate son by a Spanish lady, but was not improbably the son of a half-caste Moor of Valencia. Whether it was his blood or the plots formed against his life by the barons which embittered and darkened his nature, it is certain that he was equalled in ferocity by none among the princes of his time. Restlessly active, recognized as one of the most powerful political minds of the day, and free from the vices of the profligate, he concentrated all his powers, among which must be reckoned profound dissimulation and an irreconcilable spirit of vengeance, on the destruction of his opponents. He had been wounded in every point in which a ruler is open to offence; for the leaders of the barons, though related to him by marriage, were yet the allies of his foreign enemies. Extreme measures became part of his daily policy. The means for this struggle with his barons, and for his external wars, were exacted in the same Mohammedan fashion which Frederick II had introduced: the Government alone dealt in oil and corn; the whole commerce of the country was put by Ferrante into the hands of a wealthy merchant, Francesco Coppola, who had entire control of the anchorage on the coast, and shared the profits with the King. Deficits were made up by forced loans, by executions and confiscations, by open simony, and by contributions levied on the ecclesiastical corporations. Besides hunting, which he practised regardless of all rights of property, his pleasures were of two kinds: he liked to have his opponents near him, either alive in well-guarded prisons, or dead and embalmed, dressed in the costume which they wore in their lifetime. He would chuckle in talking of the captives with his friends, and make no secret whatever of the museum of mummies. His victims were mostly men whom he had got into his power by treachery; some were even seized while guests at the royal table. His conduct to his prime minister, Antonello Petrucci, who had grown sick and grey in his service, and from whose increasing fear of death he extorted 'present after present', was literally devilish. At length a suspicion of complicity with the last conspiracy of the barons gave the pretext for his arrest and execution. With him died Coppola. The way in which all this is narrated in Caracciolo and Porzio makes one's hair stand on end.

The elder of the King's sons, Alfonso, Duke of Calabria, enjoyed in later years a kind of co-regency with his father. He was a savage, brutal profligate, who in point of frankness alone had the advantage of Ferrante, and who openly avowed his contempt for religion and its usages. The better and nobler features of the Italian despotisms are not to be found among the princes of this line; all that they possessed of the art and culture of their time served the purpose of luxury or display. Even the genuine Spaniards seem to have almost always degenerated in Italy; but the end of this cross-bred house (1494 and 1503) gives clear proof of a want of blood. Ferrante died of mental care and trouble; Alfonso accused his brother Federigo, the only honest member of the family, of treason, and insulted him in the vilest manner. At length, though he had hitherto passed for one of the ablest generals in Italy, he lost his head and fled to Sicily, leaving his son, the younger Ferrante, a prey to the French and to domestic treason. A dynasty which had ruled as this had done must at least have sold its life dear, if its children were ever to hope for a restoration. But, as Comines one-sidedly, and yet on the whole rightly observes on this occasion, '*Jamais homme cruel ne fut hardi*': there was never a more cruel man.

* * *

The despotism of the Dukes of Milan, whose government from the time of Giangaleazzo onwards was an absolute monarchy of the most thorough-going sort, shows the genuine Italian character of the fifteenth century. The last of the Visconti, Filippo Maria (1412–1447), is a character of peculiar interest, and of which fortunately an admirable description† has been left us. What a man of uncommon gifts and high position can be made by the passion of fear, is here shown with what may be called a mathematical completeness. All the resources of the State were devoted to the one end of securing his personal safety, though happily his cruel egotism did not degenerate into a purposeless thirst for blood. He lived in the Citadel of Milan, surrounded by magnificent gardens, arbours, and lawns. For years he never set foot in the city, making his excursions only in the country, where lay several of his splendid castles; the flotilla which, drawn by the swiftest horses, conducted him to them along canals constructed for the purpose, was so arranged as to allow of the application of the most rigorous etiquette. Whoever entered the citadel was watched by a hundred eyes; it was forbidden even to stand at the window, lest signs should be given to those without. All who were admitted among the personal followers of the Prince were subjected to a series of the

† Petri Candidi Decembrii Vita Phil. Mariae Vicecomitis (Muratori, Scriptores rerum Italicarum, Milan 1750, vol. xx).

strictest examinations; then, once accepted, were charged with the highest diplomatic commissions, as well as with the humblest personal services—both in this Court being alike honourable. And this was the man who conducted long and difficult wars, who dealt habitually with political affairs of the first importance, and every day sent his plenipotentiaries to all parts of Italy. His safety lay in the fact that none of his servants trusted the others, that his Condottieri were watched and misled by spies, and that the ambassadors and higher officials were baffled and kept apart by artificially nourished jealousies, and in particular by the device of coupling an honest man with a knave. His inward faith, too, rested upon opposed and contradictory systems; he believed in blind necessity, and in the influence of the stars, and offering prayers at one and the same time to helpers of every sort; he was a student of the ancient authors, as well as of French tales of chivalry. And yet the same man, who would never suffer death to be mentioned in his presence, and caused his dying favourites to be removed from the castle, that no shadow might fall on the abode of happiness, deliberately hastened his own death by closing up a wound, and, refusing to be bled, died at last with dignity and grace.

His son-in-law and successor, the fortunate Condottiere Francesco Sforza (1450–1466), was perhaps of all the Italians of the fifteenth century the man most after the heart of his age. Never was the triumph of genius and individual power more brilliantly displayed than in him; and those who would not recognize his merit were at least forced to wonder at him as the spoilt child of fortune. The Milanese claimed it openly as an honour to be governed by so distinguished a master; when he entered the city the thronging populace bore him on horseback into the cathedral, without giving him the chance to dismount. Let us listen to the balance-sheet of his life, in the estimate of Pope Pius II, a judge in such matters: 'In the year 1459, when the Duke came to the congress at Mantua, he was 60 (really 58) years old; on horseback he looked like a young man; of a lofty and imposing figure, with serious features, calm and affable in conversation, princely in his whole bearing, with a combination of bodily and intellectual gifts unrivalled in our time, unconquered on the field of battle—such was the man who raised himself from a humble position to the control of an empire. His wife was beautiful and virtuous, his children were like the angels of heaven; he was seldom ill, and all his chief wishes were fulfilled. And yet he was not without misfortune. His wife, out of jealousy, killed his mistress; his old comrades and friends, Troilo and Brunoro, abandoned him and went over to King Alfonso; another, Ciarpollone, he was forced to hang for treason; he had to suffer it that his brother Alessandro set the French upon him; one of his sons formed intrigues against him, and was imprisoned; the March of Ancona, which he had won in war, he lost again the same way. No man enjoys so unclouded a fortune that he has not somewhere to struggle with adversity. He is happy who has but few troubles.' With this negative definition of happiness the learned Pope dismisses the reader. Had he been able to see into the future, or been willing to stop and discuss the consequences of an uncontrolled despotism, one pervading fact would not have escaped his notice—the absence of all guarantee for the future. Those children, beautiful as angels, carefully and thoroughly educated as they were, fell victims, when they grew up, to the corruption of a measureless egotism. Galeazzo Maria (1466–1476), solicitous only of outward effect, took pride in the beauty of his hands, in the high salaries he paid, in the financial credit he enjoyed, in his treasure of two million pieces of gold, in the distinguished people who surrounded him, and in the army and birds of chase which he maintained. He was fond of the sound of his own voice, and spoke well, most fluently, perhaps, when he had the chance of insulting a Venetian ambassador. He was subject to caprices, such as having a room painted with figures in a single night; and, what was worse, to fits of senseless debauchery and of revolting cruelty to his nearest friends. To a handful of enthusiasts, he seemed a tyrant too bad to live; they murdered him, and thereby delivered the State into the power of his brothers, one of whom, Lodovico il Moro, threw his nephew into prison, and took the government into his own hands. From this usurpation followed the French intervention, and the disasters which befell the whole of Italy.

Lodovico Sforza, called 'il Moro', the Moor, is the most perfect type of the despot of that age, and, as a kind of natural product, almost disarms our moral judgement. Notwithstanding the profound immorality of the means he employed, he used them with perfect ingeniousness; no one would probably have been more astonished than himself to learn that for the choice of means as well as of ends a human being is morally responsible; he would rather have reckoned it as a singular virtue that, so far as possible, he had abstained from too free a use of the punishment of death. He accepted as no more than his due the almost fabulous respect of the Italians for his political genius. In 1496 he boasted that the Pope Alexander was his chaplain, the Emperor Maximilian his Condottiere, Venice his chamberlain, and the King of France his courier, who must come and go at his bidding. With marvellous presence of mind he weighed, even in his last extremity (1499), all possible means of escape, and at length he decided, to his honour, to trust to the goodness of human nature; he rejected the proposal of his brother, the Cardinal Ascanio, who wished to remain in the Citadel of Milan, on the ground of a former quarrel: 'Monsignore, take it not ill, but I trust you not, brother though you be'; and appointed to the command of the castle, 'that pledge of his return', a man to whom he had always done good, but who nevertheless betrayed him. At home the Moor was a good and useful ruler, and to the last he reckoned on his popularity both in Milan and in Como. In later years (after 1496) he had overstrained the resources of his State, and at Cremona had ordered, out of pure expediency, a respectable citizen, who had spoken against the new taxes, to be quietly strangled. Since that time, in holding audiences, he kept his visitors away from his person by means of a bar, so that in conversing with him they were compelled to speak at the top of their voices. At his court, the most brilliant in Europe, since that of Burgundy had ceased to exist, immorality of the worst kind was prevalent; the daughter was sold by the father, the wife by the husband, the sister by the brother. The Prince himself was incessantly active, and, as son of his own deeds, claimed relationship with all who, like himself, stood on their personal merits—with scholars, poets, artists, and musicians. The academy which he founded[6] served rather for his own purposes than for the instruction of scholars; nor was it the fame of the distinguished men who surrounded him which he heeded, so much as their society and their services. It is certain that Bramante was scantily paid at first; Leonardo, on the other hand, was up to 1496 suitably remunerated—and besides, what kept him at the court, if not his own free will? The world lay open to him, as perhaps to no other mortal man of that day; and if proof were wanting of the loftier element in the nature of Lodovico il Moro, it is found in the long stay of the enigmatic master at his court. That afterwards Leonardo entered the service of Cesare Borgia and Francis I was probably due to the interest he felt in the unusual and striking character of the two men.

*[6] This is based on Amoretti, *Memorie storiche sulla vita di Lionardo da Vinci*, Milan, 1804, pp. 35 and 83, but this *accademia* was not an Academy of Art; for more details see note 10, p. 6, of the Phaidon Edition of *Leonardo da Vinci*.

After the fall of the Moor, his sons were badly brought up among strangers. The elder, Massimiliano, had no resemblance to him; the younger, Francesco, was at all events not without spirit. Milan, which in those years changed its rulers so often, and suffered so unspeakably in the change, endeavoured to secure itself against a reaction. In the year 1512 the French, retreating before the arms of Maximilian and the Spaniards, were induced to make a declaration that the Milanese had taken no part in their expulsion, and, without being guilty of rebellion, might yield themselves to a new conqueror. It is a fact of some political importance that in such moments of transition the unhappy city, like Naples at the flight of the Aragonese, was apt to fall a prey to gangs of (often highly aristocratic) scoundrels.

The house of Gonzaga at Mantua and that of Montefeltro of Urbino were among the best ordered and richest in men of ability during the second half of the fifteenth century. The Gonzaga were a tolerably harmonious family; for a long period no murder had been known among them, and their dead could be shown to the world without fear.[7] The Marquis Francesco Gonzaga and his wife, Isabella of Este, in spite of some few irregularities, were a united and respectable couple, and brought up their sons to be successful and remarkable men at a time when their small but most important State was exposed to incessant danger. That Francesco, either as statesman or as soldier, should adopt a policy of exceptional honesty, was what neither the Emperor, nor Venice, nor the King of France could have expected or desired; but certainly since the battle of the Taro (1495), so far as military honour was concerned, he felt and acted as an Italian patriot, and imparted the same spirit to his wife. Every deed of loyalty and heroism, such as the defence of Faenza against Cesare Borgia, she felt as a vindication of the honour of Italy. Our judgement of her does not need to rest on the praises of the artists and writers who made the fair princess a rich return for her patronage; her own letters show her to us as a woman of unshaken firmness, full of kindliness and humorous observation. Bembo, Bandello, Ariosto, and Bernardo Tasso sent their works to this court, small and powerless as it was, and empty as they found its treasury. A more polished and charming circle

*[7] What follows is taken from 'The Correspondence of Isabella', with Appendices, publ. by d'Arco in *Arch. stor. ital.* Vol. III, pp. 206–326; and in *Dell' Arte e degli Artefici di Mantova* (2 vols., 1857–58); English translations of many of Isabella d'Este's letters are to be found in *Isabella d'Este, Marchioness of Mantua*, by Julia Cartwright, 2 vols., London, 1903, 3rd edition 1915.

was not to be seen in Italy, since the dissolution (1508) of the old Court of Urbino; and in one respect, in freedom of movement, the society of Ferrara was inferior to that of Mantua. In artistic matters Isabella had an accurate knowledge, and the catalogue of her small but choice collection can be read by no lover of art without emotion.

In the great Federigo (1444–1482), whether he were a genuine Montefeltro or not, Urbino possessed a brilliant representative of the princely order. As a Condottiere he shared the political morality of soldiers of fortune, a morality of which the fault does not rest with them alone; as ruler of his little territory he adopted the plan of spending at home the money he had earned abroad, and taxing his people as lightly as possbile. Of him and his two successors, Guidobaldo and Francesco Maria, we read: 'They erected buildings, furthered the cultivation of the land, lived at home, and gave employment to a large number of people: their subjects loved them'. But not only the State, but the court too, was a work of art and organization, and this in every sense of the word. Federigo had 500 persons in his service; the arrangements of the court were as complete as in the capitals of the greatest monarchs, but nothing was wasted; all had its object, and all was carefully watched and controlled. The court was no scene of vice and dissipation: it served as a school of military education for the sons of other great houses, the thoroughness of whose culture and instruction was made a point of honour by the Duke. The palace which he built, if not one of the most splendid, was classical in the perfection of its plan; there was placed the greatest of his treasures, the celebrated library. Feeling secure in a land where all gained profit or employment from his rule, and where none were beggars, he habitually went about unarmed and almost unaccompanied; alone among the princes of his time he ventured to walk in an open park, and to take his frugal meals in an open chamber, while Livy, or in time of fasting some devotional work, was read to him. In the course of the same afternoon he would listen to a lecture on some classical subject, and thence would go to the monastery of the Clarisses and talk of sacred things through the grating with the abbess. In the evening he would overlook the martial exercises of the young people of his court on the meadow of San Francesco, known for its magnificent view, and saw to it well that all the feats were done in the most perfect manner. He strove always to be affable and accessible to the utmost degree, visiting the artisans who worked for him in their shops, holding frequent audiences, and, if possible, attending to the requests of each individual on the same day that they were presented. No wonder that the people, as he walked along the street, knelt down and cried: 'Dio ti mantenga, signore!' He was called by thinking people 'the light of Italy'. His gifted son Guidobaldo, visited by sickness and misfortune of every kind, was able at the last (1508) to give his State into the safe hands of his nephew Francesco Maria (*nipote* also of Pope Julius II), who at least succeeded in preserving the territory from any permanent foreign occupation. It is remarkable with what confidence Guidobaldo yielded and fled before Cesare Borgia and Francesco before the troops of Leo X; each knew that his restoration would be all the easier and the more popular the less the country suffered through a fruitless defence. When Lodovico made the same calculation at Milan, he forgot the many grounds of hatred which existed against him. The court of Guidobaldo has been made immortal as the high school of polished manners by Baldassare Castiglione, who represented his eclogue Thyrsis before and in honour of that society (1506), and who afterwards (1508) laid the scene of the dialogue of his 'Cortigiano' in the circle of the accomplished Duchess Elisabetta Gonzaga.

The government of the family of Este at Ferrara, Modena, and Reggio displays curious contrasts of violence and popularity. Within the palace frightful deeds were perpetrated; a princess was beheaded (1425) for alleged adultery with a stepson; legitimate and illegitimate children fled from the court, and even abroad their lives were threatened by assassins sent in pursuit of them (1471). Plots from without were incessant; the bastard of a bastard tried to wrest the crown from the lawful heir, Ercole I: this latter is said afterwards (1493) to have poisoned his wife on discovering that she, at the instigation of her brother Ferrante of Naples, was going to poison him. This list of tragedies is closed by the plot of two bastards against their brothers, the ruling Duke Alfonso I and Cardinal Ippolito (1506), which was discovered in time, and punished with imprisonment for life. The financial system in this State was of the most perfect kind, and necessarily so, since none of the large or second-rate powers of Italy were exposed to such danger and stood in such constant need of armaments and fortifications. It was the hope of the rulers that the increasing prosperity of the people would keep pace with the increasing weight of taxation, and the Marquis Niccolo (d. 1441) used to express the wish that his subjects might be richer than the people of other countries. If the rapid increase of the population be a measure of prosperity actually attained, it is certainly a fact of importance that in 1497, notwithstanding the considerable extension of the capital, no houses were to be let. Ferrara is the first really modern city in Europe; large and well-built quarters sprang up at the bidding of the ruler: here, by the concentration of the official classes and the active promotion of trade, was formed for the first time a true capital; wealthy fugitives from all parts of Italy, Florentines especially, settled and built their palaces at Ferrara. But the indirect taxation, at all events, must have reached a point at which it could only just be borne. The Government, it is true, took measures of alleviation which were also adopted by other Italian despots, such as Galeazzo Maria Sforza: in time of famine, corn was brought from a distance and seems to have been distributed gratuitously; but in ordinary times it compensated itself by the monopoly, if not of corn, of many other of the necessaries of life—fish, salt, meat, fruit and vegetables, which last were carefully planted on and near the walls of the city. The most considerable source of income, however, was the annual sale of public offices, a usage which was common throughout Italy, and about the working of which at Ferrara we have more precise information. We read, for example, that at the new year 1502 the majority of the officials bought their places at 'prezzi salati' (pungent prices); public servants of the most various kinds, custom-house officers, bailiffs (massari), notaries, 'podestà', judges, and even governors of provincial towns are quoted by name. As one of the 'devourers of the people' who paid dearly for their places, and who were 'hated worse than the devil', Tito Strozza—let us hope not the famous Latin poet—is mentioned. About the same time every year the dukes were accustomed to make a round of visits in Ferrara, the so-called 'andar per ventura', in which they took presents from, at any rate, the more wealthy citizens. The gifts, however, did not consist of money, but of natural products.

It was the pride of the duke for all Italy to know that at Ferrara the soldiers received their pay and the professors at the University their salary not a day later than it was due; that the soldiers never dared lay arbitrary hands on citizen or peasant; that the town was impregnable to assault; and that vast sums of coined money were stored up in the citadel. To keep two sets of accounts seemed unnecessary: the Minister of Finance was at the same time manager of the ducal household. The buildings erected by Borso (1430–1471), by

Ercole I (till 1505), and by Alfonso I (till 1534), were very numerous, but of small size; they are characteristic of a princely house which, with all its love of splendour—Borso never appeared but in embroidery and jewels—indulged in no ill-considered expense. Alfonso may perhaps have foreseen the fate which was in store for his charming little villas, the Belvedere with its shady gardens, and Montana with its fountains and beautiful frescoes.

It is undeniable that the dangers to which these princes were constantly exposed developed in them capacities of a remarkable kind. In so artificial a world only a man of consummate address could hope to succeed; each candidate for distinction was forced to make good his claims by personal merit and show himself worthy of the crown he sought. Their characters are not without dark sides; but in all of them lives something of those qualities which Italy then pursued as its ideal. What European monarch of the time laboured for his own culture as, for instance, Alfonso I? His travels in France, England, and the Netherlands were undertaken for the purpose of study: by means of them he gained an accurate knowledge of the industry and commerce of these countries. It is ridiculous to reproach him with the turner's work which he practised in his leisure hours, connected as it was with his skill in the casting of cannon, and with the unprejudiced freedom with which he surrounded himself by masters of every art. The Italian princes were not, like their contemporaries in the North, dependent on the society of an aristocracy which held itself to be the only class worth consideration, and which infected the monarch with the same conceit. In Italy the prince was permitted and compelled to know and to use men of every grade in society; and the nobility, though by birth a caste, were forced in social intercourse to stand upon their personal qualifications alone. But this is a point which we shall discuss more fully in the sequel.

The feeling of the Ferrarese towards the ruling house was a strange compound of silent dread, of the truly Italian sense of well-calculated interest, and of the loyalty of the modern subject: personal admiration was transferred into a new sentiment of duty. The city of Ferrara raised in 1451 a bronze equestrian statue to their Prince Niccolò, who had died ten years earlier; Borso (1454) did not scruple to place his own statue, also of bronze, but in a sitting posture, hard by in the market; in addition to which the city, at the beginning of his reign, decreed to him a 'marble triumphal pillar'. A citizen who, when abroad in Venice, had spoken ill of Borso in public, was informed against on his return home, and condemned to banishment and the confiscation of his goods; a loyal subject was with difficulty restrained from cutting him down before the tribunal itself, and with a rope round his neck the offender went to the duke and begged for a full pardon. The government was well provided with spies, and the duke inspected personally the daily list of travellers which the innkeepers were strictly ordered to present. Under Borso, who was anxious to leave no distinguished stranger unhonoured, this regulation served a hospitable purpose; Ercole I used it simply as a measure of precaution. In Bologna, too, it was then the rule, under Giovanni II Bentivoglio, that every passing traveller who entered at one gate must obtain a ticket in order to go out at another. An unfailing means of popularity was the sudden dismissal of oppressive officials. When Borso arrested in person his chief and confidential counsellors, when Ercole I removed and disgraced a tax-gatherer who for years had been sucking the blood of the people, bonfires were lighted and the bells were pealed in their honour. With one of his servants, however, Ercole let things go too far. The director of the police, or by whatever name we should choose to call him (Capitano di Giustizia), was Gregorio Zampante of Lucca—a native being unsuited for an office of this kind. Even the sons and brothers of the duke trembled before this man; the fines he inflicted amounted to hundreds and thousands of ducats, and torture was applied even before the hearing of a case: bribes were accepted from wealthy criminals, and their pardon obtained from the duke by false representations. Gladly would the people have paid any sum to their ruler for sending away the 'enemy of God and man'. But Ercole had knighted him and made him godfather to his children; and year by year Zampante laid by 2,000 ducats. He dared only eat pigeons bred in his own house, and could not cross the street without a band of archers and bravos. It was time to get rid of him; in 1496 two students and a converted Jew whom he had mortally offended, killed him in his house while taking his siesta, and then rode through the town on horses held in waiting, raising the cry, 'Come out! come out! we have slain Zampante!' The pursuers came too late, and found them already safe across the frontier. Of course it now rained satires—some of them in the form of sonnets, others of odes.

It was wholly in the spirit of this system that the sovereign imposed his own respect for useful servants on the court and on the people. When in 1469 Borso's privy councillor Lodovico Casella died, no court of law or place of business in the city, and no lecture-room at the University, was allowed to be open: all had to follow the body to San Domenico, since the duke intended to be present. And, in fact, 'the first of the house of Este who attended the corpse of a subject' walked, clad in black, after the coffin, weeping, while behind him came the relatives of Casella, each conducted by one of the gentlemen of the court: the body of the plain citizen was carried by nobles from the church into the cloister, where it was buried. Indeed this official sympathy with princely emotion first came up in the Italian States. At the root of the practice may be a beautiful, humane sentiment; the utterance of it, especially in the poets, is, as a rule, of equivocal sincerity. One of the youthful poems of Ariosto, on the Death of Leonora of Aragon, wife of Ercole I, contains besides the inevitable graveyard flowers, which are scattered in the elegies of all ages, some thoroughly modern features: 'This death had given Ferrara a blow which it would not get over for years: its benefactress was now its advocate in heaven, since earth was not worthy of her; truly the angel of Death did not come to her, as to us common mortals, with blood-stained scythe, but fair to behold (onesta), and with so kind a face that every fear was allayed.' But we meet, also, with sympathy of a different kind. Novelists, depending wholly on the favour of their patrons, tell us the love-stories of the prince, even before his death, in a way which, to later times, would seem the height of indiscretion, but which then passed simply as an innocent compliment. Lyrical poets even went so far as to sing the illicit flames of their lawfully married lords, *e.g.* Angelo Poliziano, those of Lorenzo the Magnificent, and Gioviano Pontano, with a singular gusto, those of Alfonso of Calabria. The poem in question betrays unconsciously the odious disposition of the Aragonese ruler; in these things too, he must needs be the most fortunate, else woe be to those who are more successful! That the greatest artists, for example Leonardo, should paint the mistresses of their patrons was no more than a matter of course.

But the house of Este was not satisfied with the praises of others; it undertook to celebrate itself. In the Palazzo Schifanoia Borso caused himself to be painted in a series of historical representations, and Ercole (from 1472 on) kept the anniversary of his accession to the throne by a procession which was compared to the feast of Corpus Christi; shops were closed as on Sunday; in the centre of the line walked all the members of the princely house (bastards included) clad in embroidered robes. That the crown was the fountain of honour and authority, that all personal distinction flowed from it alone, had been long expressed at this court by the Order of the Golden Spur—an order which had nothing in common with mediæval chivalry. Ercole I added to the spur a sword, a gold-laced mantle, and a grant of money, in return for which there is no doubt that regular service was required.

The patronage of art and letters for which this court has obtained a world-wide reputation, was exercised through the University, which was one of the most perfect in Italy, and by the gift of places in the personal or official service of the prince; it involved consequently no additional expense. Boiardo, as a wealthy country gentleman and high official, belonged to this class. At the time when Ariosto began to distinguish himself, there existed no court, in the true sense of the word, either at Milan or Florence, and soon there was none either at Urbino or at Naples. He had to content himself with a place among the musicians and jugglers of Cardinal Ippolito till Alfonso took him into his service. It was otherwise at a later time with Torquato Tasso, whose presence at court was jealously sought after.

THE OPPONENTS OF THE DESPOTS

In face of this centralized authority, all legal opposition within the borders of the State was futile. The elements needed for the restoration of a republic had been for ever destroyed, and the field prepared for violence and despotism. The nobles, destitute of political rights, even where they held feudal possessions, might call themselves Guelphs or Ghibellines at will, might dress up their bravos in padded hose and feathered caps or how else they pleased; thoughtful men like Machiavelli knew well enough that Milan and Naples were too 'corrupt' for a republic. Strange judgements fell on these two so-called parties, which now served only to give official sanction to personal and family disputes. An Italian prince, whom Agrippa of Nettesheim advised to put them down, replied that their quarrels brought him in more than 12,000 ducats a year in fines. And when in the year 1500, during the brief return of Lodovico il Moro to his States, the Guelphs of Tortona summoned a part of the neighbouring French army into the city, in order to make an end once for all of their opponents, the French certainly began by plundering and ruining the Ghibellines, but finished by doing the same to the Guelphs, till Tortona was utterly laid waste. In Romagna, the hotbed of every ferocious passion, these two names had long lost all political meaning. It was a sign of the political delusion of the people that they not seldom believed the Guelphs to be the natural allies of the French and the Ghibellines of the Spaniards. It is hard to see that those who tried to profit by this error got much by doing so. France, after all her interventions, had to abandon the peninsula at last, and what became of Spain, after she had destroyed Italy, is known to every reader.

But to return to the despots of the Renaissance. A pure and simple mind, we might think, would perhaps have argued that, since all power is derived from God, these princes, if they were loyally and honestly supported by all their subjects, must in time themselves improve and lose all traces of their violent origin. But from characters and imaginations inflamed by passion and ambition, reasoning of this kind could not be expected. Like bad physicians, they thought to cure the disease by removing the symptoms, and fancied that if the tyrant were put to death, freedom would follow of itself. Or else, without reflecting even to this extent, they sought only to give a vent to the universal hatred, or to take vengeance for some family misfortune or personal affront. Since the governments were absolute, and free from all legal restraints, the opposition chose its weapons with equal freedom. Boccaccio declares openly: 'Shall I call the tyrant king or prince, and obey him loyally as my lord? No, for he is the enemy of the commonwealth. Against him I may use arms, conspiracies, spies, ambushes and fraud; to do so is a sacred and necessary work. There is no more acceptable sacrifice than the blood of a tyrant.' We need not occupy ourselves with individual cases; Machiavelli, in a famous chapter of his 'Discorsi', treats of the conspiracies of ancient and modern times from the days of the Greek tyrants downwards, and classifies them with cold-blooded indifference according to their various plans and results. We need make but two observations, first on the murders committed in church, and next on the influence of classical antiquity. So well was the tyrant guarded that it was almost impossible to lay hands upon him elsewhere than at solemn religious services; and on no other occasion was the whole family to be found assembled together. It was thus that the Fabrianese murdered (1435) the members of their ruling house, the Chiavelli, during high mass, the signal being given by the words of the Creed, 'Et incarnatus est'. At Milan the Duke Giovan Maria Visconti (1412) was assassinated at the entrance of the church of San Gottardo, Galeazzo Maria Sforza (1476) in the church of Santo Stefano, and Lodovico il Moro only escaped (1484) the daggers of the adherents of the widowed Duchess Bona, through entering the church of Sant' Ambrogio by another door than that by which he was expected. There was no intentional impiety in the act; the assassins of Galeazzo did not fail to pray before the murder to the patron saint of the church, and to listen devoutly to the first mass. It was, however, one cause of the partial failure of the conspiracy of the Pazzi against Lorenzo and Giuliano Medici (1478), that the brigand Montesecco, who had bargained to commit the murder at a banquet, declined to undertake it in the Cathedral of Florence. Certain of the clergy 'who were familiar with the sacred place, and consequently had no fear' were induced to act in his stead.

As to the imitation of antiquity, the influence of which on moral, and more especially on political, questions we shall often refer to, the example was set by the rulers themselves, who, both in their conception of the State and in their personal conduct, took the old Roman empire avowedly as their model. In like manner their opponents, when they set to work with a deliberate theory, took pattern by the ancient tyrannicides. It may be hard to prove that in the main point—in forming the resolve itself—they consciously followed a classical example; but the appeal to antiquity was no mere phrase. The most striking disclosures have been left us with respect to the murderers of Galeazzo Sforza—Lampugnani, Olgiati, and Visconti. Though all three had personal ends to serve, yet their enterprise may be partly ascribed to a more general reason. About this time Cola de' Montani, a humanist and professor of eloquence, had awakened among many of the young Milanese nobility a vague passion for glory and patriotic achievements, and had mentioned to Lampugnani and Olgiati his hope of delivering Milan. Suspicion was soon aroused against him: he was banished from the city, and his pupils were abandoned to the fanaticism he had excited. Some ten days before the deed they met together and took a solemn oath in the monastery of Sant' Ambrogio. 'Then,' says Olgiati, 'in a remote corner I raised my eyes before the picture of the patron saint, and implored his help for ourselves and for all *his* people.' The heavenly protector of the city was called on to bless the undertaking, as was afterwards St. Stephen, in whose church it was fulfilled. Many of their comrades were now informed of the plot, nightly meetings were held in the house of Lampugnani, and the conspirators practised for the murder with the sheaths of their daggers. The attempt was successful, but Lampugnani was killed on the spot by the attendants of the duke; the others were captured: Visconti was penitent, but Olgiati through all his tortures maintained that the deed was an acceptable offering to God, and exclaimed while the executioner was breaking his ribs, 'Courage, Girolamo! thou wilt long be remembered; death is bitter, but glory is eternal.'

But however idealistic the object and purpose of such conspiracies may appear, the manner in which they were conducted betrays the influence of that worst of all conspirators, Catiline—a man in whose thoughts freedom had no place whatever. The annals of Siena tell us expressly that the conspirators were students of Sallust, and the fact is indirectly confirmed by the confession of Olgiati. Elsewhere, too, we meet with the name of Catiline, and a more attractive pattern of the conspirator, apart from the end he followed, could hardly be discovered.

Among the Florentines, whenever they got rid of, or tried to get rid of, the Medici, tyrannicide was a practice universally accepted and approved. After the flight of the Medici in 1494, the bronze group of Donatello—Judith with the dead Holofernes—was taken from their collection and placed before the Palazzo della Signoria, on the spot where the 'David' of Michelangelo now stands, with the inscription, 'Exemplum salutis publicæ cives posuere 1495'. No example was more popular than that of the younger Brutus, who, in Dante, lies with Cassius and Judas Iscariot in the lowest pit of hell, because of his treason to the empire. Pietro Paolo Boscoli, whose plot against Giuliano, Giovanni, and Giulio Medici failed (1513), was an enthusiastic admirer of Brutus, and in order to follow his steps, only waited to find a Cassius. Such a partner he met with in Agostino Capponi. His last utterances in prison—a striking evidence of the religious feeling of the time—show with what an effort he rid his mind of these classical imaginations, in order to die like a Christian. A friend and the confessor both had to assure him that St. Thomas Aquinas condemned conspirators absolutely; but the confessor afterwards admitted to the same friend that St. Thomas drew a distinction and permitted conspiracies against a tyrant who had forced himself on a people against their will.

After Lorenzino Medici had murdered the Duke Alessandro (1537), and then escaped, an apology for the deed appeared,[8] which is probably his own work, and certainly composed in his interest, and in which he praises tyrannicide as an act of the highest merit; on the supposition that Alessandro was a legitimate Medici, and, therefore,

[8] See Roscoe, *Lorenzo de'Medici*, Vol. IV, Appendix 12.

related to him, if only distantly, he boldly compares himself with Timoleon, who slew his brother for his country's sake. Others, on the same occasion, made use of the comparison with Brutus, and that Michelangelo himself, even late in life, was not unfriendly to ideas of this kind, may be inferred from his bust of Brutus in the Bargello. He left it unfinished, like nearly all his works, but certainly not because the murder of Cæsar was repugnant to his feeling, as the couplet beneath declares.

A popular radicalism in the form in which it is opposed to the monarchies of later times, is not to be found in the despotic States of the Renaissance. Each individual protested inwardly against despotism but was disposed to make tolerable or profitable terms with it rather than to combine with others for its destruction. Things must have been as bad as at Camerino, Fabriano, or Rimini, before the citizens united to destroy or expel the ruling house. They knew in most cases only too well that this would but mean a change of masters. The star of the Republics was certainly on the decline.

THE REPUBLICS: VENICE AND FLORENCE

The Italian municipalities had, in earlier days, given signal proof of that force which transforms the city into the State. It remained only that these cities should combine in a great confederation; and this idea was constantly recurring to Italian statesmen, whatever differences of form it might from time to time display. In fact, during the struggles of the twelfth and thirteenth centuries, great and formidable leagues actually were formed by the cities; and Sismondi is of opinion that the time of the final armaments of the Lombard confederation against Barbarossa (from 1168 on) was the moment when a universal Italian league was possible. But the more powerful States had already developed characteristic features which made any such scheme impracticable. In their commercial dealings they shrank from no measures, however extreme, which might damage their competitors; they held their weaker neighbours in a condition of helpless dependence—in short, they each fancied they could get on by themselves without the assistance of the rest, and thus paved the way for future usurpation. The usurper was forthcoming when long conflicts between the nobility and the people, and between the different factions of the nobility, had awakened the desire for a strong government, and when bands of mercenaries ready and willing to sell their aid to the highest bidder had superseded the general levy of the citizens which party leaders now found unsuited to their purposes. The tyrants destroyed the freedom of most of the cities; here and there they were expelled, but not thoroughly, or only for a short time; and they were always restored, since the inward conditions were favourable to them, and the opposing forces were exhausted.

Among the cities which maintained their independence are two of deep significance for the history of the human race: Florence, the city of incessant movement, which has left us a record of the thoughts and aspirations of each and all who, for three centuries, took part in this movement, and Venice, the city of apparent stagnation and of political secrecy. No contrast can be imagined stronger than that which is offered us by these two, and neither can be compared to anything else which the world has hitherto produced.

* * *

Venice recognized itself from the first as a strange and mysterious creation—the fruit of a higher power than human ingenuity. The solemn foundation of the city was the subject of a legend: on March 25, 413, at midday, emigrants from Padua laid the first stone at the Rialto, that they might have a sacred, inviolable asylum amid the devastations of the barbarians. Later writers attributed to the founders the presentiment of the future greatness of the city; M. Antonio Sabellico, who has celebrated the event in the dignified flow of his hexameters, makes the priest who completes the act of consecration cry to heaven, 'When we hereafter attempt great things, grant us prosperity! Now we kneel before a poor altar; but if our vows are not made in vain, a hundred temples, O God, of gold and marble shall arise to Thee.' The island city at the end of the fifteenth century was the jewel-casket of the world. It is so described by the same Sabellico, with its ancient cupolas, its leaning towers, its inlaid marble façades, its compressed splendour, where the richest decoration did not hinder the practical employment of every corner of space. He takes us to the crowded Piazza before San Giacometto at the Rialto, where the business of the world is transacted, not amid shouting and confusion, but with the subdued hum of many voices; where in the porticoes round the square and in those of the adjoining streets sit hundreds of moneychangers and goldsmiths, with endless rows of shops and warehouses above their heads. He describes the great Fondaco of the Germans beyond the bridge, where their goods and their dwellings lay, and before which their ships are drawn up side by side in the canal; higher up is a whole fleet laden with wine and oil, and parallel with it, on the shore swarming with porters, are the vaults of the merchants; then from the Rialto to the square of St. Mark come the inns and the perfumers' cabinets. So he conducts the reader from one quarter of the city to another till he comes at last to the two hospitals, which were among those institutions of public utility nowhere so numerous as at Venice. Care for the people, in peace as well as in war, was characteristic of this government, and its attention to the wounded, even to those of the enemy, excited the admiration of other States.

Public institutions of every kind found in Venice their pattern; the pensioning of retired servants was carried out systematically, and included a provision for widows and orphans. Wealth, political security, and acquaintance with other countries, had matured the understanding of such questions. These slender fair-haired[9] men, with quiet cautious steps and deliberate speech, differed but slightly in costume and bearing from one another; ornaments, especially pearls, were reserved for the women and girls. At that time the general prosperity, notwithstanding the losses sustained from the Turks, was still dazzling; the stores of energy which the city possessed, and the prejudice in its favour diffused throughout Europe, enabled it at a much later time to survive the heavy blows inflicted upon it by the discovery of the sea route to the Indies, by the fall of the Mamelukes in Egypt, and by the war of the League of Cambrai.

Sabellico, born in the neighbourhood of Tivoli, and accustomed to the frank loquacity of the scholars of his day, remarks elsewhere with some astonishment, that the young nobles who came of a morning to hear his lectures could not be prevailed upon to enter into political discussions: 'When I ask them what people think, say, and expect about this or that movement in Italy, they all answer with one voice that they know nothing about the matter.' Still, in spite of the strict imposition of the State, much was to be learned from the more corrupt members of the aristocracy by those who were willing to pay enough for it. In the last quarter of the fifteenth century there were traitors among the highest officials; the popes, the Italian princes, and even the second-rate Condottieri in the service of the

*[9] Geiger remarked here, in a later edition of this book, that Venetians usually wore their hair short, which fashion was different from the vogue in Florence, Milan and other cities. Erasmus in his *Colloquy of the Soldier and the Carthusian:* 'Many noble Venetians shave their heads all over.'

government had informers in their pay, sometimes with regular salaries; things went so far that the Council of Ten found it prudent to conceal important political news from the Council of the Pregadi, and it was even supposed that Lodovico il Moro had control of a definite number of votes among the latter. Whether the hanging of single offenders and the high rewards—such as a life-pension of sixty ducats paid to those who informed against them—were of much avail, it is hard to decide; one of the chief causes of this evil, the poverty of many of the nobility, could not be removed in a day. In the year 1492 a proposal was urged by two of that order, that the State should spend 70,000 ducats for the relief of those poorer nobles who held no public office; the matter was near coming before the Great Council, in which it might have had a majority, when the Council of Ten interfered in time and banished the two proposers for life to Nicosia in Cyprus. About this time a Soranzo was hanged, though not in Venice itself, for sacrilege, and a Contarini put in chains for burglary; another of the same family came in 1499 before the Signory, and complained that for many years he had been without an office, that he had only sixteen ducats a year and nine children, that his debts amounted to sixty ducats, that he knew no trade and had lately been turned into the streets. We can understand why some of the wealthier nobles built houses, sometimes whole rows of them, to provide free lodging for their needy comrades. Such works figure in wills among deeds of charity.

But if the enemies of Venice ever founded serious hopes upon abuses of this kind, they were greatly in error. It might be thought that the commercial activity of the city, which put within reach of the humblest a rich reward for their labour, and the colonies on the eastern shores of the Mediterranean would have diverted from political affairs the dangerous elements of society. But had not the political history of Genoa, notwithstanding similar advantages, been of the stormiest? The cause of the stability of Venice lies rather in a combination of circumstances which were found in union nowhere else. Unassailable from its position, it had been able from the beginning to treat of foreign affairs with the fullest and calmest reflection, and ignore nearly altogether the parties which divided the rest of Italy, to escape the entanglement of permanent alliances, and to set the highest price on those which it thought fit to make. The keynote of the Venetian character was, consequently, a spirit of proud and contemptuous isolation, which, joined to the hatred felt for the city by the other States of Italy, gave rise to a strong sense of solidarity within. The inhabitants meanwhile were united by the most powerful ties of interest in dealing both with the colonies and with the possessions on the mainland, forcing the population of the latter, that is, of all the towns up to Bergamo, to buy and sell in Venice alone. A power which rested on means so artificial could only be maintained by internal harmony and unity; and this conviction was so widely diffused among the citizens that conspirators found few elements to work upon. And the discontented, if there were such, were held so far apart by the division between the noble and the burgher that a mutual understanding was not easy. On the other hand, within the ranks of the nobility itself, travel, commercial enterprise, and the incessant wars with the Turks saved the wealthy and dangerous from that fruitful source of conspiracies—idleness. In these wars they were spared, often to a criminal extent, by the general in command, and the fall of the city was predicted by a Venetian Cato, if this fear of the nobles 'to give one another pain' should continue at the expense of justice. Nevertheless this free movement in the open air gave the Venetian aristocracy, as a whole, a healthy bias.

And when envy and ambition called for satisfaction, an official victim was forthcoming and legal means and authorities were ready. The moral torture which for years the Doge Francesco Foscari (d. 1457) suffered before the eyes of all Venice is a frightful example of a vengeance possible only in an aristocracy. The Council of Ten, which had a hand in everything, which disposed without appeal of life and death, of financial affairs and military appointments, which included the Inquisitors among its number, and which overthrew Foscari, as it had overthrown so many powerful men before—this Council was yearly chosen afresh from the whole governing body, the Gran Consiglio, and was consequently the most direct expression of its will. It is not probable that serious intrigues occurred at these elections, as the short duration of the office and the accountability which followed rendered it an object of no great desire. But violent and mysterious as the proceedings of this and other authorities might be, the genuine Venetian courted rather than fled their sentence, not only because the Republic had long arms, and if it could not catch him might punish his family, but because in most cases it acted from rational motives and not from a thirst for blood. No State, indeed, has ever exercised a greater moral influence over its subjects, whether abroad or at home. If traitors were to be found among the Pregadi, there was ample compensation for this in the fact that every Venetian away from home was a born spy for his government. It was a matter of course that the Venetian cardinals at Rome sent home news of the transactions of the secret papal consistories. The Cardinal Domenico Grimani had the dispatches intercepted in the neighbourhood of Rome (1500) which Ascanio Sforza was sending to his brother Lodovico il Moro, and forwarded them to Venice; his father, then exposed to a serious accusation, claimed public credit for this service of his son before the Gran Consiglio, in other words, before all the world.

The conduct of the Venetian government to the Condottieri in its pay has been spoken of already. The only further guarantee of their fidelity which could be obtained lay in their great number, by which treachery was made as difficult as its discovery was easy. In looking at the Venetian army list, one is only surprised that among forces of such miscellaneous composition any common action was possible. In the catalogue for the campaign of 1495 we find 15,526 horsemen, broken up into a number of small divisions. Gonzaga of Mantua alone had as many as 1,200, and Gioffredo Borgia 740; then follow six officers with a contingent of 600 to 700, ten with 400, twelve with 400 to 200, fourteen or thereabouts with 200 to 100, nine with 80, six with 50 to 60, and so forth. These forces were partly composed of old Venetian troops, partly of veterans led by Venetian city or country nobles; the majority of the leaders were, however, princes and rulers of cities or their relatives. To these forces must be added 24,000 infantry—we are not told how they were raised or commanded—with 3,300 additional troops, who probably belonged to the special services. In time of peace the cities of the mainland were wholly unprotected or occupied by insignificant garrisons. Venice relied, if not exactly on the loyalty, at least on the good sense of its subjects; in the war of the League of Cambrai (1509) it absolved them, as is well known, from their oath of allegiance, and let them compare the amenities of a foreign occupation with the mild government to which they had been accustomed. As there had been no treason in their desertion of St. Mark, and consequently no punishment was to be feared, they returned to their old masters with the utmost eagerness. This war, we may remark parenthetically, was the result of a century's outcry against the Venetian desire for aggrandizement. The Venetians, in fact, were not free from the mistake of those over-clever people who will credit their opponents with no irrational and inconsiderate conduct. Misled by this optimism, which is, perhaps, a peculiar weakness of aristocracies, they had utterly ignored not only the preparations of Mohammed II for the capture of Constantinople, but even the armaments of Charles VIII, till the unexpected blow fell at last. The League of Cambrai was an event of the same character, in so far as it was clearly opposed to the interests of the two chief members, Louis XII and Julius II. The hatred of all Italy against the victorious city seemed to be concentrated in the mind of the Pope, and to have blinded him to the evils of foreign intervention; and as to the policy of Cardinal d'Amboise and his king, Venice ought long before to have recognized it as a piece of malicious imbecility, and to have been thoroughly on its guard. The other members of the League took part in it from that envy which may be a salutary corrective to great wealth and power, but which in itself is a beggarly sentiment. Venice came out of the conflict with honour, but not without lasting damage.

A power whose foundations were so complicated, whose activity and interests filled so wide a stage, cannot be imagined without a systematic oversight of the whole, without a regular estimate of means and burdens, of profits and losses. Venice can fairly make good its claim to be the birthplace of statistical science, together, perhaps, with Florence, and followed by the more enlightened despotisms. The feudal state of the Middle Ages knew of nothing more than catalogues of signorial rights and possessions (urbaria); it looked on production as a fixed quantity, which it approximately is, so long as we have to do with landed property only. The towns, on the other hand, throughout the West must from very early times have treated production, which with them depended on industry and commerce, as exceedingly variable; but even in the most flourishing times of the Hanseatic League, they never got beyond a simple commercial balance-sheet. Fleets, armies, political power and influence fall under the debit and credit of a trader's ledger. In the Italian States a clear political consciousness, the pattern of Mohammedan administration, and the long and active exercise of trade and commerce, combined to produce for the first time a true science of statistics. The absolute monarchy of Frederick II in Lower Italy was organized with the sole object of securing a concentrated power for the death-struggle in which he was engaged. In Venice, on the contrary, the supreme objects were the enjoyment of life and power, the increase of inherited advantages, the creation of the most lucrative forms of industry, and the opening of new channels for commerce.

The writers of the time speak of these things with the greatest freedom. We learn that the population of the city amounted in the year 1422 to 190,000 souls; the Italians were, perhaps, the first to reckon, not according to hearths, or men able to bear arms, or people able to walk, and so forth, but according to 'animæ', and thus to get the most neutral basis for further calculation. About this time, when the Florentines wished to form an alliance with Venice against Filippo Maria Visconti, they were for the moment refused, in the belief, resting on accurate commercial returns, that a war between Venice and Milan, that is, between seller and buyer, was foolish. Even if the duke simply increased his army, the Milanese, through the heavier taxation they must pay, would become worse customers. 'Better let the Florentines be defeated, and then, used as they are to the life of a free city, they will settle with us and bring their silk and woollen industry with them, as the Lucchese did in their distress.' The speech of the dying Doge Mocenigo (1423) to a few of the senators whom he had sent for to his bedside is still more remarkable. It contains the chief elements of a statistical account of the whole resources of Venice. I cannot say whether or where a thorough elucidation of this perplexing document exists; by way of illustration, the following facts may be quoted. After repaying a war-loan of four million ducats, the public debt ('il monte') still amounted to six million ducats; the current trade (it seems) to ten millions, which yielded, the text informs us, a profit of four millions. The 3,000 'navigli', the 300 'navi', and the 45 galleys were manned respectively by 17,000, 8,000 and 11,000 seamen (more than 200 for each galley). To these must be added 16,000 shipwrights. The houses in Venice were valued at seven millions, and brought in a rent of half a million.[10] There were 1,000 nobles whose incomes ranged from 70 to 4,000 ducats. In another passage the ordinary income of the State in that same year is put at 1,100,000 ducats; through the disturbance of trade caused by the wars it sank about the middle of the century to 800,000 ducats.

If Venice, by this spirit of calculation, and by the practical turn

[10] Here all the houses, and not merely those owned by the State, are meant. The latter, however, sometimes yielded enormous rents. (*Vasari, in the *Life of Sansovino:* 'Not long after Jacopo saw that by removing a house in the Merceria leading to the Rialto near the Clock-tower, paying only twenty-six ducats rent, he could make a street to the Spadaria, increasing the rents of the houses and shops all round; and so he had the house pulled down; making a gain of one hundred and fifty ducats a year.' According to Cecchetti, the value of the houses in Venice was more than three and a half million ducats in 1425.)

which she gave it, was the first fully to represent one important side of modern political life, in that culture, on the other hand, which Italy then prized most highly she did not stand in the front rank. The literary impulse, in general, was here wanting, and especially that enthusiasm for classical antiquity which prevailed elsewhere.[11] The aptitude of the Venetians, says Sabellico, for philosophy and eloquence was in itself not smaller than that for commerce and politics. George of Trebizond, who, in 1459, laid the Latin translation of Plato's Laws at the feet of the Doge, was appointed professor of philology with a yearly salary of 150 ducats, and finally dedicated his 'Rhetoric' to the Signoria. If, however, we look through the history of Venetian literature which Francesco Sansovino has appended to his well-known book, we shall find in the fourteenth century almost nothing but history, and special works on theology, jurisprudence, and medicine; and in the fifteenth century, till we come to Ermolao Barbaro and Aldo Manuzio, humanistic culture is, for a city of such importance, most scantily represented. The library which Cardinal Bessarion bequeathed to the State (1468) narrowly escaped dispersion and destruction. Learning could be had at the University of Padua, where, however, physicians and jurists—the latter for their opinion on points of law—received by far the highest pay. The share of Venice in the poetical creations of the country was long insignificant, till, at the beginning of the sixteenth century, her deficiencies were made good. Even the art of the Renaissance was imported into the city from without, and it was not before the end of the fifteenth century that she learned to move in this field with independent freedom and strength. But we find more striking instances still of intellectual backwardness. This Government, which had the clergy so thoroughly in its control, which reserved to itself the appointment to all important ecclesiastical offices, and which, one time after another, dared to defy the court of Rome, displayed an official piety of a most singular kind. The bodies of saints and other relics imported from Greece after the Turkish conquest were bought at the greatest sacrifices and received by the Doge in solemn procession.[12] For the coat without a seam it was decided (1455) to offer

[11] This dislike seems to have amounted to positive hatred in Pope Paul II, who called the humanists heretics one and all.

[12] When the body of St. Luke was brought from Bosnia, a dispute arose with the Benedictines of Santa Giustina at Padua, who claimed to possess it already and the Pope had to decide between the two parties.

10,000 ducats, but it was not to be had. These measures were not the fruit of any popular excitement, but of the tranquil resolutions of the heads of the Government, and might have been omitted without attracting any comment, and at Florence, under similar circumstances, would certainly have been omitted. We shall say nothing of the piety of the masses, and of their firm belief in the indulgences of an Alexander VI. But the State itself, after absorbing the Church to a degree unknown elsewhere, had in truth a certain ecclesiastical element in its composition, and the Doge, the symbol of the State, appeared in twelve great processions ('andate') in a half-clerical character. They were almost all festivals in memory of political events, and competed in splendour with the great feasts of the Church; the most brilliant of all, the famous marriage with the sea, fell on Ascension Day.

The most elevated political thought and the most varied forms of human development are found united in the history of Florence, which in this sense deserves the name of the first modern State in the world. Here the whole people are busied with what in the despotic cities is the affair of a single family. That wondrous Florentine spirit, at once keenly critical and artistically creative, was incessantly transforming the social and political condition of the State, and as incessantly describing and judging the change. Florence thus became the home of political doctrines and theories, of experiments and sudden changes, but also, like Venice, the home of statistical science, and alone and above all other States in the world, the home of historical representation in the modern sense of the phrase. The spectacle of ancient Rome and a familiarity with its leading writers were not without influence; Giovanni Villani confesses that he received the first impulse to his great work at the jubilee of the year 1300,[13] and began it immediately on his return home. Yet how many among the 200,000 pilgrims of that year may have been like him in gifts and tendencies and still did not write the history of their native cities! For not all of them could encourage themselves with the thought: 'Rome is sinking; my native city is rising, and ready to achieve great things, and therefore I wish to relate its past history, and hope to continue the story to the present time, and as long as my life shall last.' And besides the witness to its past, Florence obtained through its historians something further—a greater fame than fell to the lot of any other city of Italy.

[13] The year 1300 is also a fixed date in Dante's *Divina Comedia.*

Our present task is not to write the history of this remarkable State, but merely to give a few indications of the intellectual freedom and independence for which the Florentines were indebted to this history.

In no other city of Italy were the struggles of political parties so bitter, of such early origin, and so permanent. The descriptions of them, which belong, it is true, to a somewhat later period, give clear evidence of the superiority of Florentine criticism.

And what a politician is the great victim of these crises, Dante Alighieri, matured alike by home and by exile! He uttered his scorn of the incessant changes and experiments in the constitution of his native city in ringing verses, which will remain proverbial so long as political events of the same kind recur[14]; he addressed his home in words of defiance and yearning which must have stirred the hearts of his countrymen. But his thoughts ranged over Italy and the whole world; and if his passion for the Empire, as he conceived it, was no more than an illusion, it must yet be admitted that the youthful dreams of a newborn political speculation are in his case not without a poetical grandeur. He is proud to be the first who trod this path,[15] certainly in the footsteps of Aristotle, but in his own way independently. His ideal emperor is a just and humane judge, dependent on God only, the heir of the universal sway of Rome to which belonged the sanction of nature, of right and of the will of God. The conquest of the world was, according to this view, rightful, resting on a divine judgement between Rome and the other nations of the earth, and God gave his approval to this empire, since under it He became Man, submitting at His birth to the census of the Emperor Augustus, and at His death to the judgement of Pontius Pilate. We may find it hard to appreciate these and other arguments of the same kind, but Dante's passion never fails to carry us with him. In his letters he appears as one of the earliest publicists,[16] and is perhaps the first layman to publish political tracts in this form. He began early. Soon after the death of Beatrice he addressed a pamphlet on the State of Florence 'to the Great ones of the Earth', and the public utterances of his later years, dating from the time of his banishment, are all

[14] *Purgatorio*, VI, at the end.

[15] *De Monarchia*, I, 1. (*English translation by Philip H. Wicksteed in the Temple Classics.)

[16] Dante wished to keep the Pope as well as the Emperor always in Italy. See his letter written during the conclave of Carpentras, 1314. (*A translation of the Latin Works of Dante, Temple Classics, London, 1940, Epistolæ VI–VIII, pp. 316–339.)

directed to emperors, princes, and cardinals. In these letters and in his book *De Vulgari Eloquentia* (About the Vernacular) the feeling, bought with such bitter pains, is constantly recurring that the exile may find elsewhere than in his native place an intellectual home in language and culture, which cannot be taken from him. On this point we shall have more to say in the sequel.

To the two Villani, Giovanni as well as Matteo, we owe not so much deep political reflection as fresh and practical observations, together with the elements of Florentine statistics and important notices of other States. Here too trade and commerce had given the impulse to economic as well as political science. Nowhere else in the world was such accurate information to be had on financial affairs. The wealth of the Papal court at Avignon, which at the death of John XXII amounted to twenty-five millions of gold florins, would be incredible on any less trustworthy authority. Here only, at Florence, do we meet with colossal loans like that which the King of England contracted from the Florentine houses of Bardi and Peruzzi, who lost to his Majesty the sum of 1,365,000 gold florins (1338)—their own money and that of their partners—and nevertheless recovered from the shock. Most important facts are here recorded as to the condition of Florence at this time:[17] the public income (over 300,000 gold florins) and expenditure; the population of the city, here only roughly estimated, according to the consumption of bread, in 'bocche', *i.e.* mouths, put at 90,000, and the population of the whole territory; the excess of 300 to 500 male children among the 5,800 to 6,000 annually baptized;[18] the schoolchildren, of whom 8,000 to 10,000 learned reading, 1,000 to 1,200 in six schools arithmetic; and besides these, 600 scholars who were taught Latin grammar and logic in four schools. Then follow the statistics of the churches and monasteries; of the hospitals, which held more than a thousand beds; of the wool trade, with most valuable details; of the mint, the provisioning of the city, the public officials, and so on.[19] Incidentally we learn many curious facts; how, for instance, when the public funds ('monte') were first established, in the year 1353, the Franciscans spoke from the pulpit in favour of the measure, the Dominicans and

[17] In Machiavelli's *History of Florence* (book II, chapter 42) we read that 96,000 persons died of the plague in 1348.

[18] The priest put aside a black bean for every boy, and a white one for every girl. This was the only means of registration.

[19] There was already a permanent fire brigade in Florence.

Augustinians against it. The economic results of the black death were and could be observed and described nowhere else in all Europe as in this city.[20] Only a Florentine could have left it on record how it was expected that the scanty population would have made everything cheap, and how instead of that labour and commodities doubled in price; how the common people at first would do no work at all, but simply give themselves up to enjoyment, how in the city itself servants and maids were not to be had except at extravagant wages; how the peasants would only till the best lands, and left the rest uncultivated; and how the enormous legacies bequeathed to the poor at the time of the plague seemed afterwards useless, since the poor had either died or had ceased to be poor. Lastly, on the occasion of a great bequest, by which a childless philanthropist left six 'denarii' to every beggar in the city, the attempt is made to give a comprehensive statistical account of Florentine mendicancy.

This statistical view of things was at a later time still more highly cultivated at Florence. The noteworthy point about it is that, as a rule, we can perceive its connection with the higher aspects of history, with art, and with culture in general. An inventory of the year 1422 mentions, within the compass of the same document, the seventy-two exchange offices which surrounded the 'Mercato Nuovo'; the amount of coined money in circulation (two million golden florins); the then new industry of gold spinning; the silk wares; Filippo Brunellesco, then busy in digging classical architecture from its grave; and Leonardo Aretino, secretary of the republic, at work at the revival of ancient literature and eloquence; lastly, it speaks of the general prosperity of the city, then free from political conflicts, and of the good fortune of Italy, which had rid itself of foreign mercenaries. The Venetian statistics quoted above which date from about the same year, certainly give evidence of larger property and profit and of a more extensive scene of action; Venice had long been mistress of the seas before Florence sent out its first galleys (1422) to Alexandria. But no reader can fail to recognize the higher spirit of the Florentine documents. These and similar lists recur at intervals of ten years, systematically arranged and tabulated, while elsewhere we find at best occasional notices. We can form an approximate estimate of the property and the business of the first Medici; they paid for charities, public buildings, and taxes from 1434 to 1471 no less than

[20] The best authority for the plague itself is the famous description by Boccaccio at the beginning of the *Decameron*.

663,755 gold florins, of which more than 400,000 fell on Cosimo alone, and Lorenzo Magnifico was delighted that the money had been so well spent. In 1478 we have again a most important and in its way complete view of the commerce and trades of this city, some of which may be wholly or partly reckoned among the fine arts—such as those which had to do with damasks and gold or silver embroidery, with woodcarving and 'intarsia', with the sculpture of arabesques in marble and sandstone, with portraits in wax, and with jewellery and work in gold. The inborn talent of the Florentines for the systematization of outward life is shown by their books on agriculture, business, and domestic economy, which are markedly superior to those of other European people in the fifteenth century. It has been rightly decided to publish selections of these works, although no little study will be needed to extract clear and definite results from them. At all events, we have no difficulty in recognizing the city, where dying parents begged the government in their wills to fine their sons 1,000 florins if they declined to practise a regular profession.

For the first half of the sixteenth century probably no State in the world possesses a document like the magnificent description of Florence by Varchi. In descriptive statistics, as in so many things besides, yet another model is left to us, before the freedom and greatness of the city sank into the grave.

This statistical estimate of outward life is, however, uniformly accompanied by the narrative of political events to which we have already referred.

Florence not only existed under political forms more varied than those of the free States of Italy and of Europe generally, but it reflected upon them far more deeply. It is a faithful mirror of the relations of individuals and classes to a variable whole. The pictures of the great civic democracies in France and in Flanders, as they are delineated in Froissart, and the narratives of the German chroniclers of the fourteenth century, are in truth of high importance; but in comprehensiveness of thought and in the rational development of the story, none will bear comparison with the Florentines. The rule of the nobility, the tyrannies, the struggles of the middle class with the proletariat, limited and unlimited democracy, pseudo-democracy, the primacy of a single house, the theocracy of Savonarola, and the mixed forms of government which prepared the way for the Medicean despotism—all are so described that the inmost motives of the actors are laid bare to the light.[21] At length Machiavelli in his Florentine history (down to 1492) represents his native city as a living organism and its development as a natural and individual process; he is the first of the moderns who has risen to such a conception. It lies without our province to determine whether and in what points Machiavelli may have done violence to history, as is notoriously the case in his life of Castruccio Castracani—a fancy picture of the typical despot. We might find something to say against every line of the 'Storie Fiorentine', and yet the great and unique value of the whole would remain unaffected. And his contemporaries and successors, Jacopo Pitti, Guicciardini, Segni, Varchi, Vettori, what a circle of illustrious names! And what a story it is which these masters tell us! The great and memorable drama of the last decades of the Florentine republic is here unfolded. The voluminous record of the collapse of the highest and most original life which the world could then show may appear to one but as a collection of curiosities, may awaken in another a devilish delight at the shipwreck of so much nobility and grandeur, to a third may seem like a great historical assize; for all it will be an object of thought and study to the end of time. The evil which was for ever troubling the peace of the city was its rule over once powerful and now conquered rivals like Pisa—a rule of which the necessary consequence was a chronic state of violence. The only remedy, certainly an extreme one and which none but Savonarola could have persuaded Florence to accept, and that only with the help of favourable chances, would have been the well-timed dissolution of Tuscany into a federal union of free cities. At a later period this scheme, then no more than the dream of a past age, brought (1548) a patriotic citizen of Lucca to the scaffold. From this evil and from the ill-starred Guelph sympathies of Florence for a foreign prince, which familiarized it with foreign intervention, came

[21] In regard to prices and wealth in Italy, in default of other means of investigation, I am only able to bring together some scattered facts picked up here and there. Obvious exaggerations are ignored. The gold coins worth referring to are the ducat, the sequin, the 'fiorino d'oro', and the 'scudo d'oro'. The value of all of them is nearly the same, 11 to 12 Swiss francs. (*The florin or ducat weighed ⅛ oz., and its standard value was put at 24 carats. It was worth about half a guinea, or approximately $1.50, but its purchasing power was at least £5. Lorenzo di Giovanni de'Medici, the brother of Cosimo, left at his death (1440) 235,137 florins. About 1460 the Patriarch of Aquilea, Lodovico Patavino, who possessed 200,000 ducats, was called 'well-nigh the richest of all Italians'. Between 1400 and 1580 Francesco Sansovino assumes a 50% depreciation in the value of money.)

all the disasters which followed. But who does not admire the people which was wrought up by its venerated preacher to a mood of such sustained loftiness that for the first time in Italy it set the example of sparing a conquered foe, while the whole history of its past taught nothing but vengeance and extermination? The glow which melted patriotism into one with moral regeneration may seem, when looked at from a distance, to have soon passed away; but its best results shine forth again in the memorable siege of 1529–30. They were 'fools', as Guicciardini then wrote, who drew down this storm upon Florence, but he confesses himself that they achieved things which seemed incredible; and when he declares that sensible people would have got out of the way of the danger, he means no more than that Florence ought to have yielded itself silently and ingloriously into the hands of its enemies. It would no doubt have preserved its splendid suburbs and gardens, and the lives and prosperity of countless citizens; but it would have been the poorer by one of its greatest and most ennobling memories.

In many of their chief merits the Florentines are the pattern and the earliest type of Italians and modern Europeans generally; they are so also in many of their defects. When Dante compares the city which was always mending its constitution with the sick man who is continually changing his posture to escape from pain, he touches with the comparison a permanent feature of the political life of Florence. The great modern fallacy that a constitution can be made, can be manufactured by a combination of existing forces and tendencies, was constantly cropping up in stormy times; even Machiavelli is not wholly free from it. Constitutional artists were never wanting who by an ingenious distribution and division of political power, by indirect elections of the most complicated kind, by the establishment of nominal offices, sought to found a lasting order of things, and to satisfy or to deceive the rich and the poor alike. They naïvely fetch their examples from classical antiquity, and borrow the party names 'ottimati', 'aristocrazia',[22] as a matter of course. The world since then has become used to these expressions and given them a conventional European sense, whereas all former party names were purely national, and either characterized the cause at issue or sprang from the caprice of accident. But how a name colours or discolours a political cause!

But of all who thought it possible to construct a State, the greatest

[22] The latter first in 1527, after the expulsion of the Medici.

beyond all comparison was Machiavelli. He treats existing forces as living and active, takes a large and accurate view of alternative possibilities, and seeks to mislead neither himself nor others. No man could be freer from vanity or ostentation; indeed, he does not write for the public, but either for princes and administrators or for personal friends. The danger for him does not lie in an affectation of genius or in a false order of ideas, but rather in a powerful imagination which he evidently controls with difficulty. The objectivity of his political judgement is sometimes appalling in its sincerity; but it is the sign of a time of no ordinary need and peril, when it was a hard matter to believe in right, or to credit others with just dealing. Virtuous indignation at his expense is thrown away on us, who have seen in what sense political morality is understood by the statesmen of our own century. Machiavelli was at all events able to forget himself in his cause. In truth, although his writings, with the exception of very few words, are altogether destitute of enthusiasm, and although the Florentines themselves treated him at last as a criminal, he was a patriot in the fullest meaning of the word. But free as he was, like most of his contemporaries, in speech and morals, the welfare of the State was yet his first and last thought.

His most complete programme for the construction of a new political system at Florence is set forth in the memorial to Leo X, composed after the death of the younger Lorenzo Medici, Duke of Urbino (d. 1519), to whom he had dedicated his 'Prince'. The State was by that time in extremities and utterly corrupt, and the remedies proposed are not always morally justifiable; but it is most interesting to see how he hopes to set up the republic in the form of a moderate democracy, as heiress to the Medici. A more ingenious scheme of concessions to the Pope, to the Pope's various adherents, and to the different Florentine interests, cannot be imagined; we might fancy ourselves looking into the works of a clock. Principles, observations, comparisons, political forecasts, and the like are to be found in numbers in the 'Discorsi', among them flashes of wonderful insight. He recognizes, for example, the law of a continuous though not uniform development in republican institutions, and requires the constitution to be flexible and capable of change, as the only means of dispensing with bloodshed and banishments. For a like reason, in order to guard against private violence and foreign interference—'the death of all freedom'—he wishes to see introduced a judicial procedure ('accusa') against hated citizens, in place of which Florence had hitherto had nothing but the court of scandal. With a masterly hand the tardy and involuntary decisions are characterized which at critical moments play so important a part in republican States. Once, it is true, he is misled by his imagination and the pressure of events into unqualified praise of the people, which chooses its officers, he says, better than any prince, and which can be cured of its errors by 'good advice'. With regard to the Government of Tuscany, he has no doubt that it belongs to his native city, and maintains, in a special 'Discorso' that the reconquest of Pisa is a question of life or death; he deplores that Arezzo, after the rebellion of 1502, was not razed to the ground; he admits in general that Italian republics must be allowed to expand freely and add to their territory in order to enjoy peace at home, and not to be themselves attacked by others, but declares that Florence had always begun at the wrong end, and from the first made deadly enemies of Pisa, Lucca, and Siena, while Pistoia, 'treated like a brother', had voluntarily submitted to her.

★ ★ ★

It would be unreasonable to draw a parallel between the few other republics which still existed in the fifteenth century and this unique city—the most important workshop of the Italian, and indeed of the modern European spirit. Siena suffered from the gravest organic maladies, and its relative prosperity in art and industry must not mislead us on this point. Æneas Sylvius looks with longing from his native town over to the 'merry' German imperial cities, where life is embittered by no confiscations of land and goods, by no arbitrary officials, and by no political factions. Genoa scarcely comes within range of our task, as before the time of Andrea Doria it took almost no part in the Renaissance. Indeed, the inhabitant of the Riviera was proverbial among Italians for his contempt of all higher culture. Party conflicts here assumed so fierce a character, and disturbed so violently the whole course of life, that we can hardly understand how, after so many revolutions and invasions, the Genoese ever contrived to return to an endurable condition. Perhaps it was owing to the fact that all who took part in public affairs were at the same time almost without exception active men of business. The example of Genoa shows in a striking manner with what insecurity wealth and vast commerce, and with what internal disorder the possession of distant colonies, are compatible.

FOREIGN POLICY

As the majority of the Italian States were in their internal constitution works of art, that is, the fruit of reflection and careful adaptation, so was their relation to one another and to foreign countries also a work of art. That nearly all of them were the result of recent usurpations, was a fact which exercised as fatal an influence in their foreign as in their internal policy. Not one of them recognized another without reserve; the same play of chance which had helped to found and consolidate one dynasty might upset another. Nor was it always a matter of choice with the despot whether to keep quiet or not. The necessity of movement and aggrandizement is common to all illegitimate powers. Thus Italy became the scene of a 'foreign policy' which gradually, as in other countries also, acquired the position of a recognized system of public law. The purely objective treatment of international affairs, as free from prejudice as from moral scruples, attained a perfection which sometimes is not without a certain beauty and grandeur of its own. But as a whole it gives us the impression of a bottomless abyss.

Intrigues, armaments, leagues, corruption and treason make up the outward history of Italy at this period. Venice in particular was long accused on all hands of seeking to conquer the whole peninsula, or gradually so to reduce its strength that one State after another must fall into her hands. But on a closer view it is evident that this complaint did not come from the people, but rather from the courts and official classes, which were commonly abhorred by their subjects, while the mild government of Venice had secured for it general confidence. Even Florence, with its restive subject cities, found itself in a false position with regard to Venice, apart from all commercial jealousy and from the progress of Venice in Romagna. At last the League of Cambrai actually did strike a serious blow at the State which all Italy ought to have supported with united strength.

The other States, also, were animated by feelings no less unfriendly, and were at all times ready to use against one another any weapon which their evil conscience might suggest. Lodovico il Moro, the Aragonese kings of Naples, and Sixtus IV—to say nothing of the smaller powers—kept Italy in a constant perilous agitation. It would have been well if the atrocious game had been confined to Italy; but it lay in the nature of the case that intervention and help should at last be sought from abroad—in particular from the French and the Turks.

The sympathies of the people at large were throughout on the side of France. Florence had never ceased to confess with shocking *naïvete* its old Guelph preference for the French. And when Charles VIII actually appeared on the south of the Alps, all Italy accepted him with an enthusiasm which to himself and his followers seemed unaccountable.[23] In the imagination of the Italians, to take Savonarola for an example, the ideal picture of a wise, just, and powerful saviour and ruler was still living, with the difference that he was no longer the emperor invoked by Dante, but the Capetian king of France. With his departure the illusion was broken; but it was long before all understood how completely Charles VIII, Louis XII, and Francis I had mistaken their true relation to Italy, and by what inferior motives they were led. The princes, for their part, tried to make use of France in a wholly different way. When the Franco-English wars came to an end, when Louis XI began to cast about his diplomatic nets on all sides, and Charles of Burgundy to embark on his foolish adventures, the Italian Cabinets came to meet them at every point. It became clear that the intervention of France was only a question of time, even if the claims on Naples and Milan had never existed, and that the old interference with Genoa and Piedmont was only a type of what was to follow. The Venetians, in fact, expected it as early as 1462. The mortal terror of the Duke Galeazzo Maria of Milan during the Burgundian war, in which he was apparently the ally of Charles as well as of Louis, and consequently had reason to dread an attack from both, is strikingly shown in his correspondence. The plan of an equilibrium of the four chief Italian powers, as understood by Lorenzo the Magnificent, was but the assumption of a cheerful optimistic spirit, which had outgrown both the recklessness of an experimental policy and the superstitions of Florentine Guelphism, and persisted in hoping for the best. When Louis XI offered him aid in the war against Ferrante of Naples and Sixtus IV, he replied, 'I cannot set my own advantage above the safety of all Italy; would to God it never came into the mind of the French kings to try their strength in this country! Should they ever do so, Italy is lost.' For the other princes, the King of France was alternately a bugbear to themselves and their enemies, and they threatened to call him in whenever they saw no more convenient way out of their difficulties. The Popes, in their turn, fancied that they could make use of France without any danger to

[23] Comines, *Charles VIII*, chapter 10: The French were considered *comme saints*.

themselves, and even Innocent VIII imagined that he could withdraw to sulk in the North, and return as a conqueror to Italy at the head of a French army.

Thoughtful men, indeed, foresaw the foreign conquest long before the expedition of Charles VIII. And when Charles was back again on the other side of the Alps, it was plain to every eye that an era of intervention had begun. Misfortune now followed on misfortune; it was understood too late that France and Spain, the two chief invaders, had become great European powers, that they would be no longer satisfied with verbal homage, but would fight to the death for influence and territory in Italy. They had begun to resemble the centralized Italian States, and indeed to copy them, only on a gigantic scale. Schemes of annexation or exchange of territory were for a time indefinitely multiplied. The end, as is well known, was the complete victory of Spain, which, as sword and shield of the counter-reformation, long held Papacy among its other subjects. The melancholy reflections of the philosophers could only show them how those who had called in the barbarians all came to a bad end.

Alliances were at the same time formed with the Turks too, with as little scruple or disguise; they were reckoned no worse than any other political expedients. The belief in the unity of Western Christendom had at various times in the course of the Crusades been seriously shaken, and Frederick II had probably outgrown it. But the fresh advance of the Oriental nations, the need and the ruin of the Greek Empire, had revived the old feeling, though not in its former strength, throughout Western Europe. Italy, however, was a striking exception to this rule. Great as was the terror felt for the Turks, and the actual danger from them, there was yet scarcely a government of any consequence which did not conspire against other Italian States with Mohammed II and his successors. And when they did not do so, they still had the credit of it; nor was it worse than the sending of emissaries to poison the cisterns of Venice, which was the charge brought against the heirs of Alfonso, King of Naples. From a scoundrel like Sigismondo Malatesta nothing better could be expected than that he should call the Turks into Italy. But the Aragonese monarchs of Naples, from whom Mohammed—at the instigation, we read, of other Italian governments, especially of Venice—had once wrested Otranto (1480), afterwards hounded on the Sultan Bajazet II against the Venetians. The same charge was brought against Lodovico il Moro. 'The blood of the slain, and the misery of the prisoners in the hands of the Turks, cry to God for vengeance against him,' says the State historian. In Venice, where the government was informed of everything, it was known that Giovanni Sforza, ruler of Pesaro, the cousin of Lodovico, had entertained the Turkish ambassadors on their way to Milan. The two most respectable among the Popes of the fifteenth century, Nicholas V and Pius II, died in the deepest grief at the progress of the Turks, the latter indeed amid the preparations for a crusade which he was hoping to lead in person; their successors embezzled the contributions sent for this purpose from all parts of Christendom, and degraded the indulgences granted in return for them into a private commercial speculation. Innocent VIII consented to be gaoler to the fugitive Prince Djem, for a salary paid by the prisoner's brother Bajazet II, and Alexander VI supported the steps taken by Lodovico il Moro in Constantinople to further a Turkish assault upon Venice (1498), whereupon the latter threatened him with a Council. It is clear that the notorious alliance between Francis I and Soliman II was nothing new or unheard of.

Indeed, we find instances of whole populations to whom it seemed no particular crime to go over bodily to the Turks. Even if it were only held out as a threat to oppressive governments, this is at least a proof that the idea had become familiar. As early as 1480 Battista Mantovano gives us clearly to understand that most of the inhabitants of the Adriatic coast foresaw something of this kind, and that Ancona in particular desired it. When Romagna was suffering from the oppressive government of Leo X, a deputy from Ravenna said openly to the Legate, Cardinal Giulio Medici: 'Monsignore, the honourable Republic of Venice will not have us, for fear of a dispute with the Holy See; but if the Turk comes to Ragusa we will put ourselves into his hands.'

It was a poor but not wholly groundless consolation for the enslavement of Italy then begun by the Spaniards, that the country was at least secured from the relapse into barbarism which would have awaited it under the Turkish rule. By itself, divided as it was, it could hardly have escaped this fate.

If, with all these drawbacks, the Italian statesmanship of this period deserves our praise, it is only on the ground of its practical and unprejudiced treatment of those questions which were not affected by fear, passion, or malice. Here was no feudal system after the northern fashion, with its artificial scheme of rights; but the power which each possessed he held in practice as in theory. Here was no attendant nobility to foster in the mind of the prince the mediæval sense of honour with all its strange consequences; but princes and counsellors were agreed in acting according to the exigencies of the particular case and to the end they had in view. Towards the men whose services were used and towards allies, come from what quarter they might, no pride of caste was felt which could possibly estrange a supporter; and the class of the Condottieri, in which birth was a matter of indifference, shows clearly enough in what sort of hands the real power lay; and lastly, the government, in the hands of an enlightened despot, had an incomparably more accurate acquaintance with its own country and with that of its neighbours than was possessed by northern contemporaries, and estimated the economical and moral capacities of friend and foe down to the smallest particular. The rulers were, notwithstanding grave errors, born masters of statistical science. With such men negotiation was possible; it might be presumed that they would be convinced and their opinion modified when practical reasons were laid before them. When the great Alfonso of Naples was (1434) a prisoner of Filippo Maria Visconti, he was able to satisfy his gaoler that the rule of the House of Anjou instead of his own at Naples would make the French masters of Italy; Filippo Maria set him free without ransom and made an alliance with him. A northern prince would scarcely have acted in the same way, certainly not one whose morality in other respects was like that of Visconti. What confidence was felt in the power of self-interest is shown by the celebrated visit (1478) which Lorenzo Magnifico, to the universal astonishment of the Florentines, paid the faithless Ferrante at Naples—a man who would certainly be tempted to keep him a prisoner, and was by no means too scrupulous to do so. For to arrest a powerful monarch, and then to let him go alive, after extorting his signature and otherwise insulting him, as Charles the Bold did to Louis XI at Peronne (1468), seemed madness to the Italians; so that Lorenzo was expected to come back covered with glory, or else not to come back at all. The art of political persuasion was at this time raised to a point—especially by the Venetian ambassadors—of which northern nations first obtained a conception from the Italians, and of which the official addresses give a most imperfect idea. These are mere pieces of humanistic rhetoric. Nor, in spite of an otherwise ceremonious etiquette was there in case of need any lack of rough and frank speaking in diplomatic intercourse. A man like Machiavelli appears in his 'Legazioni' in an almost pathetic light. Furnished with scanty instructions, shabbily equipped, and treated as an agent of inferior rank, he never loses his gift of free and wide observation or his pleasure in picturesque description.

A special division of this work will treat of the study of man individually and nationally, which among the Italians went hand in hand with the study of the outward conditions of human life.

WAR AS A WORK OF ART

It must here be briefly indicated by what steps the art of war assumed the character of a product of reflection. Throughout the countries of the West the education of the individual soldier in the Middle Ages was perfect within the limits of the then prevalent system of defence and attack: nor was there any want of ingenious inventors in the arts of besieging and of fortification. But the development both of strategy and of tactics was hindered by the character and duration of military service, and by the ambition of the nobles, who disputed questions of precedence in the face of the enemy, and through simple want of discipline caused the loss of great battles like Crécy and Maupertuis. Italy, on the contrary, was the first country to adopt the system of mercenary troops, which demanded a wholly different organization; and the early introduction of firearms did its part in making war a democratic pursuit, not only because the strongest castles were unable to withstand a bombardment, but because the skill of the engineer, of the gunfounder, and of the artillerist—men belonging to another class than the nobility—was now of the first importance in a campaign. It was felt, with regret, that the value of the individual, which had been the soul of the small and admirably organized bands of mercenaries, would suffer from these novel means of destruction, which did their work at a distance; and there were Condottieri who opposed to the utmost the introduction at least of the musket, which had lately been invented in Germany. We read that Paolo Vitelli, while recognizing and himself adopting the cannon, put out the eyes and cut off the hands of the captured 'schioppettieri' (arquebusiers) because he held it unworthy that a gallant, and it might be noble, knight should be wounded and laid low by a common, despised foot soldier. On the whole, however, the new discoveries were accepted and turned to useful account, till the Italians became the teachers of all Europe, both in the building of fortifications and in the means of attacking them. Princes like Federigo of Urbino and Alfonso of Ferrara acquired a mastery of the subject compared to which the knowledge even of Maximilian I appears superficial. In Italy, earlier than elsewhere, there existed a comprehensive science and art of military affairs; here, for the first time, that impartial delight is taken in able generalship for its own sake, which might, indeed, be expected from the frequent change of party and from the wholly unsentimental mode of action of the Condottieri. During the Milano-Venetian war of 1451 and 1452, between Francesco Sforza and Jacopo Piccinino, the headquarters of the latter were attended by the scholar Gian Antonio Porcellio dei Pandoni, commissioned by Alfonso of Naples to write a report of the campaign. It is written, not in the purest, but in a fluent Latin, a little too much in the style of the humanistic bombast of the day, is modelled on Cæsar's Commentaries, and interspersed with speeches, prodigies, and the like. Since for the past hundred years it had been seriously disputed whether Scipio Africanus or Hannibal was the greater, Piccinino through the whole book must needs be called Scipio and Sforza Hannibal. But something positive had to be reported too respecting the Milanese army; the sophist presented himself to Sforza, was led along the ranks, praised highly all that he saw, and promised to hand it down to posterity. Apart from him the Italian literature of the day is rich in descriptions of wars and strategic devices, written for the use of educated men in general as well as of specialists, while the contemporary narratives of northerns, such as the 'Burgundian War' by Diebold Schilling, still retain the shapelessness and matter-of-fact dryness of a mere chronicle. The greatest *dilettante* who has ever treated in that character of military affairs, Machiavelli, was then busy writing his 'Arte della Guerra'. But the development of the individual soldier found its most complete expression in those public and solemn conflicts between one or more pairs of combatants which were practised long before the famous 'Challenge of Barletta' (1503). The victor was assured of the praises of poets and scholars, which were denied to the northern warrior. The result of these combats was no longer regarded as a Divine judgement, but as a triumph of personal merit, and to the minds of the spectators seemed to be both the decision of an exciting competition and a satisfaction for the honour of the army or the nation.

It is obvious that this purely rational treatment of warlike affairs allowed, under certain circumstances, of the worst atrocities, even in the absence of a strong political hatred, as, for instance, when the plunder of a city had been promised to the troops. After the forty days' devastation of Piacenza, which Sforza was compelled to permit to his soldiers (1477), the town long stood empty, and at last had to be peopled by force. Yet outrages like these were nothing compared with the misery which was afterwards brought upon Italy by foreign troops, and most of all by the Spaniards, in whom perhaps a touch of oriental blood, perhaps familiarity with the spectacles of the Inquisition, had unloosed the devilish element of human nature. After seeing them at work at Prato, Rome, and elsewhere, it is not easy to take any interest of the higher sort in Ferdinand the Catholic and Charles V who knew what these hordes were, and yet unchained them. The mass of documents which are gradually brought to light from the cabinets of these rulers will always remain an important source of historical information; but from such men no fruitful political conception can be looked for.

THE PAPACY

The Papacy and the dominions of the Church are creations of so peculiar a kind that we have hitherto, in determining the general characteristics of Italian States, referred to them only occasionally. The deliberate choice and adaptation of political expedients, which gives so great an interest to the other States, is what we find least of all at Rome, since here the spiritual power could constantly conceal or supply the defects of the temporal. And what fiery trials did this State undergo in the fourteenth and the beginning of the fifteenth century, when the Papacy was led captive to Avignon! All, at first, was thrown into confusion; but the Pope had money, troops, and a great statesman and general, the Spaniard Albornoz, who again brought the ecclesiastical State into complete subjection. The danger of a final dissolution was still greater at the time of the schism, when neither the Roman nor the French Pope was rich enough to reconquer the newly-lost State; but this was done under Martin V, after the unity of the Church was restored, and done again under Eugenius IV, when the same danger was renewed. But the ecclesiastical State was and remained a thorough anomaly among the powers of Italy; in and near Rome itself, the Papacy was defied by the great families of the Colonna, Orsini, Savelli and Anguillara; in Umbria, in the Marches, and in Romagna, those civic republics had almost ceased to exist, for whose devotion the Papacy had shown so little gratitude; their place had been taken by a crowd of princely dynasties, great or small, whose loyalty and obedience signified little. As self-dependent powers, standing on their own merits, they have an interest of their own; and from this point of view the most important of them have already been discussed.

Nevertheless, a few general remarks on the Papacy can hardly be dispensed with. New and strange perils and trials came upon it in the course of the fifteenth century, as the political spirit of the nation began to lay hold upon it on various sides, and to draw it within the sphere of its action. The least of these dangers came from the populace or from abroad; the most serious had their ground in the characters of the Popes themselves.

Let us, for this moment, leave out of consideration the countries beyond the Alps. At the time when the Papacy was exposed to mortal danger in Italy, it neither received nor could receive the slightest assistance either from France, then under Louis XI, or from England, distracted by the Wars of the Roses, or from the then disorganized Spanish monarchy, or from Germany, but lately betrayed at the Council of Basle. In Italy itself there was a certain number of instructed and even uninstructed people whose national vanity was flattered by the Italian character of the Papacy; the personal interests of very many depended on its having and retaining this character; and vast masses of the people still believed in the virtue of the Papal blessing and consecration;[24] among them notorious transgressors like Vitelozzo Vitelli, who still prayed to be absolved by Alexander VI, when the Pope's son had him strangled. But all these grounds of sympathy put together would not have sufficed to save the Papacy from its enemies, had the latter been really in earnest, and had they known how to take advantage of the envy and hatred with which the institution was regarded.

And at the very time when the prospect of help from without was so small, the most dangerous symptoms appeared within the Papacy itself. Living as it now did, and acting in the spirit of the secular Italian principalities, it was compelled to go through the same dark experiences as they; but its own exceptional nature gave a peculiar colour to the shadows.

As far as the city of Rome itself is concerned, small account was taken of its internal agitations, so many were the Popes who had returned after being expelled by popular tumult, and so greatly did

[24] For the impression made by the blessing of Eugenius IV in Florence see his Life in the *Vespasiano Memoirs* (*English Edition by Waters, London, 1926, p. 27).

the presence of the Curia minister to the interests of the Roman people. But Rome not only displayed at times a specific anti-papal radicalism, but in the most serious plots which were then contrived, gave proof of the working of unseen hands from without. It was so in the case of the conspiracy of Stefano Porcari against Nicholas V (1453), the very Pope who had done most for the prosperity of the city. Porcari aimed at the complete overthrow of the papal authority, and had distinguished accomplices, who, though their names are not handed down to us, are certainly to be looked for among the Italian governments of the time. Under the pontificate of the same man, Lorenzo Valla concluded his famous declamation against the gift of Constantine with the wish for the speedy secularization of the States of the Church.

The Catilinarian gang with which Pius II had to contend (1460) avowed with equal frankness their resolution to overthrow the government of the priests, and its leader, Tiburzio, threw the blame on the soothsayers, who had fixed the accomplishment of his wishes for this very year. Several of the chief men of Rome, the Prince of Taranto, and the Condottiere Jacopo Piccinino, were accomplices and supporters of Tiburzio. Indeed, when we think of the booty which was accumulated in the palaces of wealthy prelates—the conspirators had the Cardinal of Aquileia especially in view—we are surprised that, in an almost unguarded city, such attempts were not more frequent and more successful. It was not without reason that Pius II preferred to reside anywhere rather than in Rome, and even Paul II was exposed to no small anxiety through a plot formed by some discharged abbreviators, who, under the command of Platina, besieged the Vatican for twenty days. The Papacy must sooner or later have fallen a victim to such enterprises, if it had not stamped out the aristocratic factions under whose protection these bands of robbers grew to a head.

This task was undertaken by the terrible Sixtus IV. He was the first Pope who had Rome and the neighbourhood thoroughly under his control, especially after his successful attack on the House of Colonna, and consequently, both in his Italian policy and in the internal affairs of the Church, he could venture to act with a defiant audacity, and to set at nought the complaints and threats to summon a council which arose from all parts of Europe. He supplied himself with the necessary funds by simony, which suddenly grew to unheard-of proportions, and which extended from the appointment of cardinals down to the granting of the smallest favours. Sixtus himself had not obtained the papal dignity without recourse to the same means.

A corruption so universal might sooner or later bring disastrous consequences on the Holy See, but they lay in the uncertain future. It was otherwise with nepotism, which threatened at one time to destroy the Papacy altogether. Of all the 'nipoti', Cardinal Pietro Riario enjoyed at first the chief and almost exclusive favour of Sixtus. He soon drew upon him the eyes of all Italy, partly by the fabulous luxury of his life, partly through the reports which were current of his irreligion and his political plans. He bargained with Duke Galeazzo Maria of Milan (1473), that the latter should become King of Lombardy, and then aid him with money and troops to return to Rome and ascend the papal throne; Sixtus, it appears, would have voluntarily yielded to him. This plan, which, by making the Papacy hereditary, would have ended in the secularization of the papal State, failed through the sudden death of Pietro. The second 'nipote', Girolamo Riario, remained a layman, and did not seek the Pontificate. From this time the 'nipoti', by their endeavours to found principalities for themselves, became a new source of confusion to Italy. It had already happened that the Popes tried to make good their feudal claims on Naples in favour of their relatives, but since the failure of Calixtus III, such a scheme was no longer practicable, and Girolamo Riario, after the attempt to conquer Florence (and who knows how many other places) had failed, was forced to content himself with founding a State within the limits of the papal dominions themselves. This was in so far justifiable as Romagna, with its princes and civic despots, threatened to shake off the papal supremacy altogether, and ran the risk of shortly falling a prey to Sforza or the Venetians, when Rome interfered to prevent it. But who, at times and in circumstances like these, could guarantee the continued obedience of 'nipoti' and their descendants, now turned into sovereign rulers, to Popes with whom they had no further concern? Even in his lifetime the Pope was not always sure of his own son or nephew, and the temptation was strong to expel the 'nipote' of a predecessor and replace him by one of his own. The reaction of the whole system on the Papacy itself was of the most serious character; all means of compulsion, whether temporal or spiritual, were used without scruple for the most questionable ends, and to these all the other objects of the Apostolic See were made subordinate. And when they were attained, at whatever cost of revolutions and proscriptions, a dynasty was founded which had no stronger interest than the destruction of the Papacy.

At the death of Sixtus, Girolamo was only able to maintain himself in his usurped principality of Forlì and Imola by the utmost exertions of his own, and by the aid of the House of Sforza, to which his wife belonged. In the conclave (1484) which followed the death of Sixtus —that in which Innocent VIII was elected—an incident occurred which seemed to furnish the Papacy with a new external guarantee. Two cardinals, who, at the same time, were princes of ruling houses, Giovanni d'Aragona, son of King Ferrante, and Ascanio Sforza, brother of Lodovico il Moro, sold their votes with shameless effrontery; so that, at any rate, the ruling houses of Naples and Milan became interested, by their participation in the booty, in the continuance of the papal system. Once again, in the following conclave, when all the cardinals but five sold themselves, Ascanio received enormous sums in bribes, not without cherishing the hope that at the next election he would himself be the favoured candidate.

Lorenzo the Magnificent, on his part, was anxious that the House of Medici should not be sent away with empty hands. He married his daughter Maddalena to the son of the new Pope—the first who publicly acknowledged his children—Franceschetto Cibo, and expected not only favours of all kinds for his own son, Cardinal Giovanni, afterwards Leo X, but also the rapid promotion of his son-in-law. But with respect to the latter, he demanded impossibilities. Under Innocent VIII there was no opportunity for the audacious nepotism by which States had been founded, since Franceschetto himself was a poor creature who, like his father the Pope, sought power only for the lowest purpose of all—the acquisition and accumulation of money. The manner, however, in which father and son practised this occupation must have led sooner or later to a final catastrophe—the dissolution of the State. If Sixtus had filled his treasury by the sale of spiritual dignities and favours, Innocent and his son, for their part, established an office for the sale of secular favours, in which pardons for murder and manslaughter were sold for large sums of money. Out of every fine 150 ducats were paid into the papal exchequer, and what was over to Franceschetto. Rome, during the latter part of this pontificate, swarmed with licensed and unlicensed assassins; the factions, which Sixtus had begun to put down, were again as active as ever; the Pope, well guarded in the

Vatican, was satisfied with now and then laying a trap, in which a wealthy misdoer was occasionally caught. For Franceschetto the chief point was to know by what means, when the Pope died, he could escape with well-filled coffers. He betrayed himself at last, on the occasion of a false report (1490) of his father's death; he endeavoured to carry off all the money in the papal treasury, and when this proved impossible, insisted that, at all events, the Turkish prince, Djem, should go with him, and serve as a living capital, to be advantageously disposed of, perhaps to Ferrante of Naples. It is hard to estimate the political possibilities of remote periods, but we cannot help asking ourselves the question if Rome could have survived two or three pontificates of this kind. Also with reference to the believing countries of Europe, it was imprudent to let matters go so far that not only travellers and pilgrims, but a whole embassy of Maximilian, King of the Romans, were stripped to their shirts in the neighbourhood of Rome, and that envoys had constantly to turn back without setting foot within the city.

Such a condition of things was incompatible with the conception of power and its pleasures which inspired the gifted Alexander VI (1492–1503), and the first event that happened was the restoration, at least provisionally, of public order, and the punctual payment of every salary.

Strictly speaking, as we are now discussing phases of Italian civilization, this pontificate might be passed over, since the Borgias are no more Italian than the House of Naples. Alexander spoke Spanish in public with Cesare; Lucrezia, at her entrance to Ferrara, where she wore a Spanish costume, was sung to by Spanish buffoons; their confidential servants consisted of Spaniards, as did also the most ill-famed company of the troops of Cesare in the war of 1500; and even his hangman, Don Micheletto, and his poisoner, Sebastiano Pinzon Cremonese, seem to have been of the same nation. Among his other achievements, Cesare, in true Spanish fashion, killed, according to the rules of the craft, six wild bulls in an enclosed court. But the Roman corruption, which seemed to culminate in this family, was already far advanced when they came to the city.

What they were and what they did has been often and fully described. Their immediate purpose, which, in fact, they attained, was the complete subjugation of the pontifical State. All the petty despots, who were mostly more or less refractory vassals of the Church, were expelled or destroyed; and in Rome itself the two great factions were annihilated, the so-called Guelph Orsini as well as the so-called Ghibelline Colonna. But the means employed were of so frightful a character that they must certainly have ended in the ruin of the Papacy, had not the contemporaneous death of both father and son by poison suddenly intervened to alter the whole aspect of the situation. The moral indignation of Christendom was certainly no great source of danger to Alexander; at home he was strong enough to extort terror and obedience; foreign rulers were won over to his side, and Louis XII even aided him to the utmost of his power. The mass of the people throughout Europe had hardly a conception of what was passing in Central Italy. The only moment which was really fraught with danger—when Charles VIII was in Italy—went by with unexpected fortune, and even then it was not the Papacy as such that was in peril, but Alexander, who risked being supplanted by a more respectable Pope. The great, permanent, and increasing danger for the Papacy lay in Alexander himself, and, above all, in his son Cesare Borgia.

In the nature of the father, ambition, avarice, and sensuality were combined with strong and brilliant qualities. All the pleasures of power and luxury he granted himself from the first day of his pontificate in the fullest measure. In the choice of means to this end he was wholly without scruple; it was known at once that he would more than compensate himself for the sacrifices which his election had involved, and that the simony of the seller would far exceed the simony of the buyer. It must be remembered that the vice-chancellorship and other offices which Alexander had formerly held had taught him to know better and turn to more practical account the various sources of revenue than any other member of the Curia. As early as 1494, a Carmelite, Adam of Genoa, who had preached at Rome against simony, was found murdered in his bed with twenty wounds. Hardly a single cardinal was appointed without the payment of enormous sums of money.

But when the Pope in course of time fell under the influence of his son Cesare Borgia, his violent measures assumed that character of devilish wickedness which necessarily reacts upon the ends pursued. What was done in the struggle with the Roman nobles and with the tyrants of Romagna exceeded in faithlessness and barbarity even that measure to which the Aragonese rulers of Naples had already accustomed the world; and the genius for deception was also greater. The manner in which Cesare isolated his father, murdering brother,

brother-in-law, and other relations or courtiers, whenever their favour with the Pope or their position in any other respect became inconvenient to him, is literally appalling. Alexander was forced to acquiesce in the murder of his best-loved son, the Duke of Gandia, since he himself lived in hourly dread of Cesare.

What were the final aims of the latter? Even in the last months of his tyranny, when he had murdered the Condottieri at Sinigaglia, and was to all intents and purposes master of the ecclesiastical State (1503), those who stood near him gave the modest reply that the Duke merely wished to put down the factions and the despots, and all for the good of the Church only; that for himself he desired nothing more than the lordship of the Romagna, and that he had earned the gratitude of all the following Popes by ridding them of the Orsini and Colonna. But no one will accept this as his ultimate design. The Pope Alexander himself, in his discussions with the Venetian ambassador, went further than this, when committing his son to the protection of Venice: 'I will see to it,' he said, 'that one day the Papacy shall belong either to him or to you.' Cesare indeed added that no one could become Pope without the consent of Venice, and for this end the Venetian cardinals had only to keep well together. Whether he referred to himself or not we are unable to say; at all events, the declaration of his father is sufficient to prove his designs on the pontifical throne. We further obtain from Lucrezia Borgia a certain amount of indirect evidence, in so far as certain passages in the poems of Ercole Strozza may be the echo of expressions which she as Duchess of Ferrara may easily have permitted herself to use. Here, too, Cesare's hopes of the Papacy are chiefly spoken of; but now and then a supremacy over all Italy is hinted at, and finally we are given to understand that as temporal ruler Cesare's projects were of the greatest, and that for their sake he had formerly surrendered his cardinalate. In fact, there can be no doubt whatever that Cesare, whether chosen Pope or not after the death of Alexander, meant to keep possession of the pontifical State at any cost, and that this, after all the enormities he had committed, he could not as Pope have succeeded in doing permanently. He, if anybody, could have secularized the States of the Church, and he would have been forced to do so in order to keep them. Unless we are much deceived, this is the real reason of the secret sympathy with which Machiavelli treats the great criminal; from Cesare, or from nobody, could it be hoped that he 'would draw the steel from the wound', in other words, annihilate the Papacy—the source of all foreign intervention and of all the divisions of Italy. The intriguers who thought to divine Cesare's aims, when holding out to him hopes of the Kingdom of Tuscany, seem to have been dismissed with contempt.

But all logical conclusions from his premises are idle, not because of the unaccountable genius, which in fact characterized him as little as it did Wallenstein, but because the means which he employed were not compatible with any large and consistent course of action. Perhaps, indeed, in the very excess of his wickedness some prospect of salvation for the Papacy may have existed even without the accident which put an end to his rule.

Even if we assume that the destruction of the petty despots in the pontifical State had gained for him nothing but sympathy, even if we take as proof of his great projects the army composed of the best soldiers and officers in Italy, with Leonardo da Vinci as chief engineer, which followed his fortunes in 1502, other facts nevertheless bear such a character of unreason that our judgement, like that of contemporary observers, is wholly at a loss to explain them. One fact of this kind is the devastation and maltreatment of the newly-won State, which Cesare still intended to keep and to rule over. Another is the condition of Rome and of the Curia in the last decades of the pontificate. Whether it were that father and son had drawn up a formal list of proscribed persons, or that the murders were resolved upon one by one, in either case the Borgias were bent on the secret destruction of all who stood in their way or whose inheritance they coveted. Of this, money and movable goods formed the smallest part; it was a much greater source of profit for the Pope that the incomes of the clerical dignitaries in question were suspended by their death, and that he received the revenues of their offices while vacant, and the price of these offices when they were filled by the successors of the murdered men. The Venetian ambassador Paolo Capello reported in the year 1500: 'Every night four or five murdered men are discovered—bishops, prelates and others—so that all Rome is trembling for fear of being destroyed by the Duke (Cesare).' He himself used to wander about Rome in the night-time with his guards, and there is every reason to believe that he did so not only because, like Tiberius, he shrank from showing his now repulsive features by daylight, but also to gratify his insane thirst for blood, perhaps even on persons unknown to him.

As early as the year 1499 the despair was so great and so general that many of the Papal guards were waylaid and put to death. But those whom the Borgias could not assail with open violence fell victims to their poison. For the cases in which a certain amount of discretion seemed requisite, a white powder of an agreeable taste was made use of, which did not work on the spot, but slowly and gradually, and which could be mixed without notice in any dish or goblet. Prince Djem had taken some of it in a sweet draught, before Alexander surrendered him to Charles VIII (1495), and at the end of their career father and son poisoned themselves with the same powder by accidentally tasting a sweetmeat intended for a wealthy cardinal. The official epitomizer of the history of the Popes, Onofrio Panvinio, mentions three cardinals, Orsini, Ferrerio and Michiel, whom Alexander caused to be poisoned, and hints at a fourth, Giovanni Borgia, whom Cesare took into his own charge—though probably wealthy prelates seldom died in Rome at that time without giving rise to suspicions of this sort. Even tranquil scholars who had withdrawn to some provincial town were not out of reach of the merciless poison. A secret horror seemed to hang about the Pope; storms and thunderbolts, crushing in walls and chambers, had in earlier times often visited and alarmed him; in the year 1500, when these phenomena were repeated, they were held to be 'cosa diabolica'. The report of these events seems at last, through the well-attended jubilee of 1500, to have been carried far and wide throughout the countries of Europe, and the infamous traffic in indulgences did what else was needed to draw all eyes upon Rome. Besides the returning pilgrims, strange white-robed penitents came from Italy to the North, among them disguised fugitives from the Papal State, who are not likely to have been silent. Yet none can calculate how far the scandal and indignation of Christendom might have gone, before they became a source of pressing danger to Alexander. 'He would,' says Panvinio elsewhere, 'have put all the other rich cardinals and prelates out of the way, to get their property, had he not, in the midst of his great plans for his son, been struck down by death.' And what might not Cesare have achieved if, at the moment when his father died, he had not himself been laid upon a sickbed! What a conclave would that have been, in which, armed with all his weapons, he had extorted his election from a college whose numbers he had judiciously reduced by poison—and this at a time when there was no French army at hand! In pursuing such a hypothesis the imagination loses itself in an abyss.

Instead of this followed the conclave in which Pius III was elected, and, after his speedy death, that which chose Julius II—both elections the fruits of a general reaction.

Whatever may have been the private morals of Julius II, in all essential respects he was the saviour of the Papacy. His familiarity with the course of events since the pontificate of his uncle Sixtus had given him a profound insight into the grounds and conditions of the Papal authority. On these he founded his own policy, and devoted to it the whole force and passion of his unshaken soul. He ascended the steps of St. Peter's chair without simony and amid general applause, and with him ceased, at all events, the undisguised traffic in the highest offices of the Church. Julius had favourites, and among them were some the reverse of worthy, but a special fortune put him above the temptation to nepotism. His brother, Giovanni della Rovere, was the husband of the heiress of Urbino, sister of the last Montefeltro, Guidobaldo, and from this marriage was born, in 1491, a son, Francesco Maria della Rovere, who was at the same time Papal 'nipote' and lawful heir to the duchy of Urbino. What Julius elsewhere acquired, either on the field of battle or by diplomatic means, he proudly bestowed on the Church, not on his family; the ecclesiastical territory, which he found in a state of dissolution, he bequeathed to his successor completely subdued, and increased by Parma and Piacenza. It was not his fault that Ferrara too was not added to the dominions of the Church. The 700,000 ducats which were stored up in the Castel Sant' Angelo were to be delivered by the governor to none but the future Pope. He made himself heir of the cardinals, and, indeed, of all the clergy who died in Rome, and this by the most despotic means; but he murdered or poisoned none of them. That he should himself lead his forces to battle was for him an unavoidable necessity, and certainly did him nothing but good at a time when a man in Italy was forced to be either hammer or anvil, and when personality was a greater power than the most indisputable right. If despite all his high-sounding 'Away with the barbarians!' he nevertheless contributed more than any man to the firm settlement of the Spaniards in Italy, he may have thought it a matter of indifference to the Papacy, or even, as things stood, a relative advantage. And to whom, sooner than to Spain, could the Church look for a sincere and lasting respect, in an age when the princes of Italy cherished none but sacrilegious projects against her? Be this as it may, the powerful, original nature, which could swallow no anger and conceal no genuine good-will, made on the whole the impression most desirable in his situation—that of the 'Pontefice terribile'.[25] He could even, with comparatively clear conscience, venture to summon a council to Rome, and so bid defiance to that outcry for a council which was raised by the opposition all over Europe. A ruler of this stamp needed some great outward symbol of his conceptions; Julius found it in the reconstruction of St. Peter's. The plan of it, as Bramante wished to have it, is perhaps the grandest expression of power in unity which can be imagined. In other arts besides architecture the face and the memory of the Pope live on in their most ideal form, and it is not without significance that even the Latin poetry of those days gives proof of a wholly different enthusiasm for Julius than that shown for his predecessors. The entry into Bologna, at the end of the 'Iter Julii Secundi' by the Cardinal Adriano da Corneto, has a splendour of its own, and Giovan Antonio Flaminio, in one of the finest elegies, appealed to the patriot in the Pope to grant his protection to Italy.

In a constitution of his Lateran Council, Julius had solemnly denounced the simony of the Papal elections. After his death in 1513, the money-loving cardinals tried to evade the prohibition by proposing that the endowments and offices hitherto held by the chosen candidate should be equally divided among themselves, in which case they would have elected the best-endowed cardinal, the incompetent Raphael Riario. But a reaction, chiefly arising from the younger members of the Sacred College, who, above all things, desired a liberal Pope, rendered the miserable combination futile; Giovanni Medici was elected—the famous Leo X.

We shall often meet with him in treating of the noonday of the Renaissance; here we wish only to point out that under him the Papacy was again exposed to great inward and outward dangers. Among these we do not reckon the conspiracy of the Cardinals Petrucci, De Sauli, Riario, and Corneto (1517), which at most could have occasioned a change of persons, and to which Leo found the true antidote in the unheard-of creation of thirty-one new cardinals, a measure which had the additional advantage of rewarding, in some cases at least, real merit.

* [25] *Terribile* cannot be translated by terrible or horrifying; it is a superlative of *fiero* (vehement, proud) and *magnanimo*, and points to a superhuman and heroic greatness of mind, but sometimes merely indicates an intensive irritability. Contemporary writers referred to Michelangelo's *terribilità;* Symonds explains this word as 'a passionate violence of temper'.

But some of the paths which Leo allowed himself to tread during the first two years of his office were perilous to the last degree. He seriously endeavoured to secure, by negotiation, the kingdom of Naples for his brother Giuliano, and for his nephew Lorenzo a powerful North Italian State, to comprise Milan, Tuscany, Urbino and Ferrara. It is clear that the Pontifical State, thus hemmed in on all sides, would have become a mere Medicean appanage, and that, in fact, there would have been no further need to secularize it.

The plan found an insuperable obstacle in the political conditions of the time. Giuliano died early. To provide for Lorenzo, Leo undertook to expel the Duke Francesco Maria della Rovere from Urbino, but reaped from the war nothing but hatred and poverty, and was forced, when in 1519 Lorenzo followed his uncle to the grave, to hand over the hard-won conquests to the Church. He did on compulsion and without credit what, if it had been done voluntarily, would have been to his lasting honour. What he attempted against Alfonso of Ferrara, and actually achieved against a few petty despots and Condottieri, was assuredly not of a kind to raise his reputation. And this was at a time when the monarchs of the West were yearly growing more and more accustomed to political gambling on a colossal scale, of which the stakes were this or that province of Italy. Who could guarantee that, since the last decades had seen so great an increase of their power at home, their ambition would stop short of the States of the Church? Leo himself witnessed the prelude of what was fulfilled in the year 1527; a few bands of Spanish infantry appeared—of their own accord, it seems—at the end of 1520, on the borders of the Pontifical territory, with a view to laying the Pope under contribution, but were driven back by the Papal forces. The public feeling, too, against the corruptions of the hierarchy had of late years been drawing rapidly to a head, and men with an eye for the future, like the younger Pico della Mirandola, called urgently for reform. Meantime Luther had already appeared upon the scene.

Under Adrian VI (1521–23), the few and timid improvements, carried out in the face of the great German Reformation, came too late. He could do little more than proclaim his horror of the course which things had taken hitherto, of simony, nepotism, prodigality, brigandage, and profligacy. The danger from the side of the Lutherans was by no means the greatest; an acute observer from Venice, Girolamo Negro, uttered his fears that a speedy and terrible disaster would befall the city of Rome itself.

Under Clement VII the whole horizon of Rome was filled with vapours, like that leaden veil which the sirocco drew over the Campagna, and which made the last months of summer so deadly. The Pope was no less detested at home than abroad. Thoughtful people were filled with anxiety, hermits appeared upon the streets and squares of Rome, foretelling the fate of Italy and of the world, and calling the Pope by the name of Antichrist; the faction of the Colonna raised its head defiantly; the indomitable Cardinal Pompeo Colonna, whose mere existence was a permanent menace to the Papacy, ventured to surprise the city in 1526, hoping, with the help of Charles V, to become Pope then and there, as soon as Clement was killed or captured. It was no piece of good fortune for Rome that the latter was able to escape to the Castel Sant' Angelo, and the fate for which he himself was reserved may well be called worse than death.

By a series of those falsehoods which only the powerful can venture on, but which bring ruin upon the weak, Clement brought about the advance of the Germano-Spanish army under Bourbon and Frundsberg (1527). It is certain that the Cabinet of Charles V intended to inflict on him a severe castigation, and that it could not calculate beforehand how far the zeal of its unpaid hordes would carry them. It would have been vain to attempt to enlist men in Germany without paying any bounty, if it had not been well known that Rome was the object of the expedition. It may be that the written orders to Bourbon will be found some day or other, and it is not improbable that they will prove to be worded mildly. But historical criticism will not allow itself to be led astray. The Catholic King and Emperor owed it to his luck and nothing else that Pope and cardinals were not murdered by his troops. Had this happened, no sophistry in the world could clear him of his share in the guilt. The massacre of countless people of less consequence, the plunder of the rest, and all the horrors of torture and traffic in human life, show clearly enough what was possible in the 'Sacco di Roma'.

Charles seems to have wished to bring the Pope, who had fled a second time to the Castel Sant' Angelo, to Naples, after extorting from him vast sums of money, and Clement's flight to Orvieto must have happened without any connivance on the part of Spain. Whether the Emperor ever thought seriously of the secularization of the States of the Church, for which everybody was quite prepared, and whether he was really dissuaded from it by the representations of Henry VIII of England, will probably never be made clear.

But if such projects really existed, they cannot have lasted long: from the devastated city arose a new spirit of reform both in Church and State. It made itself felt in a moment. Cardinal Sadoleto, one witness of many, thus writes: 'If through our suffering a satisfaction is made to the wrath and justice of God, if these fearful punishments again open the way to better laws and morals, then is our misfortune perhaps not of the greatest. . . . What belongs to God He will take care of; before us lies a life of reformation, which no violence can take from us. Let us so rule our deeds and thoughts as to seek in God only the true glory of the priesthood and our own true greatness and power.'

In point of fact, this critical year, 1527, so far bore fruit that the voices of serious men could again make themselves heard. Rome had suffered too much to return, even under a Paul III, to the gay corruption of Leo X.

The Papacy, too, when its sufferings became so great, began to excite a sympathy half religious and half political. The kings could not tolerate that one of their number should arrogate to himself the rights of Papal gaoler, and concluded (August 18, 1527) the Treaty of Amiens, one of the objects of which was the deliverance of Clement. They thus, at all events, turned to their own account the unpopularity which the deeds of the Imperial troops had excited. At the same time the Emperor became seriously embarrassed, even in Spain, where the prelates and grandees never saw him without making the most urgent remonstrances. When a general deputation of the clergy and laity, all clothed in mourning, was projected, Charles, fearing that troubles might arise out of it, like those of the insurrection quelled a few years before, forbade the scheme. Not only did he not dare to prolong the maltreatment of the Pope, but he was absolutely compelled, even apart from all considerations of foreign politics, to be reconciled with the Papacy, which he had so grievously wounded. For the temper of the German people, which certainly pointed to a different course, seemed to him, like German affairs generally, to afford no foundation for a policy. It is possible, too, as a Venetian maintains, that the memory of the sack of Rome lay heavy on his conscience, and tended to hasten that expiation which was sealed by the permanent subjection of the Florentines to the Medicean family of which the Pope was a member. The 'nipote' and new Duke, Alessandro Medici, was married to the natural daughter of the Emperor.

In the following years the plan of a Council enabled Charles to keep the Papacy in all essential points under his control, and at one and the same time to protect and to oppress it. The greatest danger of all—secularization—the danger which came from within, from the Popes themselves and their 'nipoti', was adjourned for centuries by the German Reformation. Just as this alone had made the expedition against Rome (1527) possible and successful, so did it compel the Papacy to become once more the expression of a world-wide spiritual power, to raise itself from the soulless debasement in which it lay, and to place itself at the head of all the enemies of this reformation. The institution thus developed during the latter years of Clement VII, and under Paul III, Paul IV, and their successors, in the face of the defection of half Europe, was a new, regenerated hierarchy, which avoided all the great and dangerous scandals of former times, particularly nepotism, with its attempts at territorial aggrandizement, and which, in alliance with the Catholic princes, and impelled by a newborn spiritual force, found its chief work in the recovery of what had been lost. It only existed and is only intelligible in opposition to the seceders. In this sense it can be said with perfect truth that the moral salvation of the Papacy is due to its mortal enemies. And now its political position, too, though certainly under the permanent tutelage of Spain, became impregnable; almost without effort it inherited, on the extinction of its vassals, the legitimate line of Este and the house of Della Rovere, the duchies of Ferrara and Urbino. But without the Reformation—if, indeed, it is possible to think it away—the whole ecclesiastical State would long ago have passed into secular hands.

PATRIOTISM

In conclusion, let us briefly consider the effect of these political circumstances on the spirit of the nation at large.

It is evident that the general political uncertainty in Italy, during the fourteenth and fifteenth centuries, was of a kind to excite in the better spirits of the time a patriotic disgust and opposition. Dante and Petrarch, in their day, proclaimed loudly a common Italy, the object of the highest efforts of all her children. It may be objected that this was only the enthusiasm of a few highly instructed men, in which the mass of the people had no share; but it can hardly have been otherwise even in Germany, although in name at least that country was united, and recognized in the Emperor one supreme head. The first patriotic utterances of German literature, if we except some verses of the 'Minnesänger', belong to the humanists of the time of Maximilian I and after, and read like an echo of Italian declamations. And yet, as a matter of fact, Germany had been long a nation in a truer sense than Italy ever was since the Roman days. France owes the consciousness of its national unity mainly to its conflicts with the English, and Spain has never permanently succeeded in absorbing Portugal, closely related as the two countries are. For Italy, the existence of the ecclesiastical State, and the conditions under which alone it could continue, were a permanent obstacle to national unity, an obstacle whose removal seemed hopeless. When, therefore, in the political intercourse of the fifteenth century, the common fatherland is sometimes emphatically named, it is done in most cases to annoy some other Italian State. But those deeply serious and sorrowful appeals to national sentiment were not heard again till later, when the time for unity had gone by, when the country was inundated with Frenchmen and Spaniards. The sense of local patriotism may be said in some measure to have taken the place of this feeling, though it was but a poor equivalent for it.

PART II

THE DEVELOPMENT OF THE INDIVIDUAL

PERSONALITY

IN the character of these States, whether republics or despotisms, lies, not the only, but the chief reason for the early development of the Italian. To this it is due that he was the firstborn among the sons of modern Europe.

In the Middle Ages both sides of human consciousness—that which was turned within as that which was turned without—lay dreaming or half awake beneath a common veil. The veil was woven of faith, illusion, and childish prepossession, through which the world and history were seen clad in strange hues. Man was conscious of himself only as a member of a race, people, party, family, or corporation—only through some general category. In Italy this veil first melted into air; an *objective* treatment and consideration of the State and of all the things of this world became possible. The *subjective* side at the same time asserted itself with corresponding emphasis; man became a spiritual *individual*,[26] and recognized himself as such. In the same way the Greek had once distinguished himself from the barbarian, and the Arab had felt himself an individual at a time when other Asiatics knew themselves only as members of a race. It will not be difficult to show that this result was due above all to the political circumstances of Italy.

In far earlier times we can here and there detect a development of free personality which in Northern Europe either did not occur at all, or could not display itself in the same manner. The band of audacious wrongdoers in the tenth century described to us by Liudprand, some of the contemporaries of Gregory VII (for example, Benzo of Alba), and a few of the opponents of the first Hohenstaufen, show us characters of this kind. But at the close of the thirteenth century Italy began to swarm with individuality; the ban laid upon human personality was dissolved; and a thousand figures meet us each in its own special shape and dress. Dante's great poem would have been impossible in any other country of Europe, if only for the

[26] Observe the expressions *uomo singolare* and *uomo unico* for the higher and highest stages of individual development.

reason that they all still lay under the spell of race. For Italy the august poet, through the wealth of individuality which he set forth, was the most national herald of his time. But this unfolding of the treasures of human nature in literature and art—this many-sided representation and criticism—will be discussed in separate chapters; here we have to deal only with the psychological fact itself. This fact appears in the most decisive and unmistakable form. The Italians of the fourteenth century knew little of false modesty or of hypocrisy in any shape; not one of them was afraid of singularity, of being and seeming[27] unlike his neighbours.

Despotism, as we have already seen, fostered in the highest degree the individuality not only of the tyrant or Condottiere himself, but also of the men whom he protected or used as his tools—the secretary, minister, poet, and companion. These people were forced to know all the inward resources of their own nature, passing or permanent; and their enjoyment of life was enhanced and concentrated by the desire to obtain the greatest satisfaction from a possibly very brief period of power and influence.

But even the subjects whom they ruled over were not free from the same impulse. Leaving out of account those who wasted their lives in secret opposition and conspiracies, we speak of the majority who were content with a strictly private station, like most of the urban population of the Byzantine empire and the Mohammedan States. No doubt it was often hard for the subjects of a Visconti to maintain the dignity of their persons and families, and multitudes must have lost in moral character through the servitude they lived under. But this was not the case with regard to individuality; for political impotence does not hinder the different tendencies and manifestations of private life from thriving in the fullest vigour and variety. Wealth and culture, so far as display and rivalry were not forbidden to them, a municipal freedom which did not cease to be considerable, and a Church which, unlike that of the Byzantine or of the Mohammedan world, was not identical with the State—all these conditions undoubtedly favoured the growth of individual thought, for which the necessary leisure was furnished by the cessation of party conflicts. The private man, indifferent to politics, and busied partly with serious pursuits, partly with the interests of a *dilettante*, seems to have been first fully formed in these despotisms of the fourteenth century. Documentary evidence

[27] By the year 1390 there was no longer any prevailing fashion of dress for men at Florence, each preferring to clothe himself in his own way.

cannot, of course, be required on such a point. The novelists, from whom we might expect information, describe to us oddities in plenty, but only from one point of view and in so far as the needs of the story demand. Their scene, too, lies chiefly in the republican cities.

In the latter, circumstances were also, but in another way, favourable to the growth of individual character. The more frequently the governing party was changed, the more the individual was led to make the utmost of the exercise and enjoyment of power. The statesmen and popular leaders, especially in Florentine history, acquired so marked a personal character that we can scarcely find, even exceptionally, a parallel to them in contemporary history, hardly even in Jacob van Arteveldt.

The members of the defeated parties, on the other hand, often came into a position like that of the subjects of the despotic States, with the difference that the freedom or power already enjoyed, and in some cases the hope of recovering them, gave a higher energy to their individuality. Among these men of involuntary leisure we find, for instance, an Agnolo Pandolfini (d. 1446), whose work on domestic economy is the first complete programme of a developed private life. His estimate of the duties of the individual as against the dangers and thanklessness of public life is in its way a true monument of the age.

Banishment, too, has this effect above all, that it either wears the exile out or develops whatever is greatest in him. 'In all our more populous cities,' says Gioviano Pontano, 'we see a crowd of people who have left their homes of their own free will; but a man takes his virtues with him wherever he goes.' And, in fact, they were by no means only men who had been actually exiled, but thousands left their native place voluntarily, because they found its political or economic condition intolerable. The Florentine emigrants at Ferrara and the Lucchese in Venice formed whole colonies by themselves.

The cosmopolitanism which grew up in the most gifted circles is in itself a high stage of individualism. Dante, as we have already said, finds a new home in the language and culture of Italy, but goes beyond even this in the words, 'My country is the whole world'. And when his recall to Florence was offered him on unworthy conditions, he wrote back: 'Can I not everywhere behold the light of the sun and the stars; everywhere meditate on the noblest truths, without appearing ingloriously and shamefully before the city and the people? Even my bread will not fail me.' The artists exult no less defiantly in their freedom from the constraints of fixed residence. 'Only he who has learned everything,' says Ghiberti,[28] 'is nowhere a stranger; robbed of his fortune and without friends, he is yet the citizen of every country, and can fearlessly despise the changes of fortune.' In the same strain an exiled humanist writes: 'Wherever a learned man fixes his seat, there is home'.[29]

An acute and practised eye might be able to trace, step by step, the increase in the number of complete men during the fifteenth century. Whether they had before them as a conscious object the harmonious development of their spiritual and material existence, is hard to say; but several of them attained it, so far as is consistent with the imperfection of all that is earthly. It may be better to renounce the attempt at an estimate of the share which fortune, character, and talent had in the life of Lorenzo il Magnifico. But look at a personality like that of Ariosto, especially as shown in his satires. In what harmony are there expressed the pride of the man and the poet, the irony with which he treats his own enjoyments, the most delicate satire, and the deepest goodwill!

When this impulse to the highest individual development was combined with a powerful and varied nature, which had mastered all the elements of the culture of the age, then arose the 'all-sided man'—'l'uomo universale'—who belonged to Italy alone. Men there were of encyclopædic knowledge in many countries during the Middle Ages, for this knowledge was confined within narrow limits; and even in the twelfth century there were universal artists, but the problems of architecture were comparatively simple and uniform, and in sculpture and painting the matter was of more importance than the form. But in Italy at the time of the Renaissance, we find artists who in every branch created new and perfect works, and who also made the greatest impression as men. Others, outside the arts they practised, were masters of a vast circle of spiritual interests.

Dante, who, even in his lifetime, was called by some a poet, by others a philosopher, by others a theologian,[30] pours forth in all his writings a stream of personal force by which the reader, apart from

* [28] In *secondo commentario*, being Ghiberti's autobiography; see the complete translation of it in the Phaidon Edition of *Ghiberti*. The paragraph to which Burckhardt refers is actually a quotation from Vitruvius's *Architecture*, VI, 2.

[29] *Codri Urcei Vita*, Bologna, 1502.

[30] Boccaccio, *Vita di Dante*. (*English translation by Philip H. Wicksteed, in The King's Classics, London, 1904.)

the interest of the subject, feels himself carried away. What power of will must the steady, unbroken elaboration of the *Divine Comedy* have required! And if we look at the matter of the poem, we find that in the whole spiritual or physical world there is hardly an important subject which the poet has not fathomed, and on which his utterances —often only a few words—are not the most weighty of his time. For the visual arts he is of the first importance, and this for better reasons than the few references to contemporary artists—he soon became himself the source of inspiration.[31]

The fifteenth century is, above all, that of the many-sided men. There is no biography which does not, besides the chief work of its hero, speak of other pursuits all passing beyond the limits of dilettantism. The Florentine merchant and statesman was often learned in both the classical languages; the most famous humanists read the Ethics and Politics of Aristotle to him and his sons; even the daughters of the house were highly educated. It is in these circles that private education was first treated seriously. The humanist, on his side, was compelled to the most varied attainments, since his philological learning was not limited, as it is now, to the theoretical knowledge of classical antiquity, but had to serve the practical needs of daily life. While studying Pliny, he made collections of natural history; the geography of the ancients was his guide in treating of modern geography, their history was his pattern in writing contemporary chronicles, even when composed in Italian; he not only translated the comedies of Plautus, but acted as manager when they were put on the stage; every effective form of ancient literature down to the dialogues of Lucian he did his best to imitate; and besides all this, he acted as magistrate, secretary and diplomatist—not always to his own advantage.

But among these many-sided men, some, who may truly be called all-sided, tower above the rest. Before analysing the general phases of life and culture of this period, we may here, on the threshold of the fifteenth century, consider for a moment the figure of one of these giants—Leon Battista Alberti (b. 1404, d. 1472). His biography, which is only a fragment, speaks of him but little as an artist, and makes no mention at all of his great significance in the history of architecture. We shall now see what he was, apart from these special claims to distinction.

[31] The angels which he drew on tablets at the anniversary of the death of Beatrice (*Vita Nuova*) may have been more than the work of a dilettante. Leonardo Aretino says he drew 'egregiamente', and was a great lover of music.

In all by which praise is won, Leon Battista was from his childhood the first. Of his various gymnastic feats and exercises we read with astonishment how, with his feet together, he could spring over a man's head; how, in the cathedral, he threw a coin in the air till it was heard to ring against the distant roof; how the wildest horses trembled under him. In three things he desired to appear faultless to others, in walking, in riding, and in speaking. He learned music without a master, and yet his compositions were admired by professional judges. Under the pressure of poverty, he studied both civil and canonical law for many years, till exhaustion brought on a severe illness. In his twenty-fourth year, finding his memory for words weakened, but his sense of facts unimpaired, he set to work at physics and mathematics. And all the while he acquired every sort of accomplishment and dexterity, cross-examining artists, scholars and artisans of all descriptions, down to the cobblers, about the secrets and peculiarities of their craft. Painting and modelling he practised by the way, and especially excelled in admirable likenesses from memory. Great admiration was excited by his mysterious 'camera obscura',[32] in which he showed at one time the stars and the moon rising over rocky hills, at another wide landscapes with mountains and gulfs receding into dim perspective, and with fleets advancing on the waters in shade or sunshine. And that which others created he welcomed joyfully, and held every human achievement which followed the laws of beauty for something almost divine. To all this must be added his literary works, first of all those on art, which are landmarks and authorities of the first order for the Renaissance of Form, especially in architecture; then his Latin prose writings—novels and other works—of which some have been taken for productions of antiquity; his elegies, eclogues, and humorous dinner-speeches. He also wrote an Italian treatise on domestic life in four books; and even a funeral oration on his dog. His serious and witty sayings were thought worth collecting, and specimens of them, many columns long, are quoted in his biography. And all that he had and knew he imparted, as rich natures always do, without the least reserve, giving away his chief discoveries for nothing. But the deepest spring of his nature has yet to be spoken of—the sympathetic intensity with which

[32] Other inventions, especially an attempt at a flying-machine, had been made about 880 by the Andalusian Abul Abbas Kasim ibn Firnas. (*See Guayangos, *History of the Muhammedan Dynasties in Spain*, London, 1840, Vol. I, p. 148 *et seq.* and 425–7.)

he entered into the whole life around him. At the sight of noble trees and waving cornfields he shed tears; handsome and dignified old men he honoured as 'a delight of nature', and could never look at them enough. Perfectly formed animals won his goodwill as being specially favoured by nature; and more than once, when he was ill, the sight of a beautiful landscape cured him. No wonder that those who saw him in this close and mysterious communion with the world ascribed to him the gift of prophecy. He was said to have foretold a bloody catastrophe in the family of Este, the fate of Florence and that of the Popes many years beforehand, and to be able to read in the countenances and the hearts of men. It need not be added that an iron will pervaded and sustained his whole personality; like all the great men of the Renaissance, he said, 'Men can do all things if they will'.

And Leonardo da Vinci was to Alberti as the finisher to the beginner, as the master to the *dilettante*. Would only that Vasari's work were here supplemented by a description like that of Alberti! The colossal outlines of Leonardo's nature can never be more than dimly and distantly conceived.

GLORY

To this inward development of the individual corresponds a new sort of outward distinction—the modern form of glory.

In the other countries of Europe the different classes of society lived apart, each with its own mediæval caste sense of honour. The poetical fame of the Troubadours and Minnesänger was peculiar to the knightly order. But in Italy social equality had appeared before the time of the tyrannies or the democracies. We there find early traces of a general society, having, as will be shown more fully later on, a common ground in Latin and Italian literature; and such a ground was needed for this new element in life to grow in. To this must be added that the Roman authors, who were now zealously studied, are filled and saturated with the conception of fame, and that their subject itself—the universal empire of Rome—stood as a permanent ideal before the minds of Italians. From henceforth all the aspirations and achievements of the people were governed by a moral postulate, which was still unknown elsewhere in Europe.

Here, again, as in all essential points, the first witness to be called is Dante. He strove for the poet's garland with all the power of his soul.[33]

[33] *Paradiso*, XXV, at the beginning.

As publicist and man of letters, he laid stress on the fact that what he did was new, and that he wished not only to be, but to be esteemed the first in his own walks.[34] But in his prose writings he touches also on the inconveniences of fame; he knows how often personal acquaintance with famous men is disappointing, and explains how this is due partly to the childish fancy of men, partly to envy, and partly to the imperfections of the hero himself. And in his great poem he firmly maintains the emptiness of fame, although in a manner which betrays that his heart was not free from the longing for it. In Paradise the sphere of Mercury is the seat of such blessed ones[35] as on earth strove after glory and thereby dimmed 'the beams of true love'. It is characteristic that the lost souls in hell beg of Dante to keep alive for them their memory and fame on earth,[36] while those in Purgatory only entreat his prayers and those of others for their deliverance.[37] And in a famous passage,[38] the passion for fame—'lo gran disio dell'eccellenza' (the great desire of excelling)—is reproved for the reason that intellectual glory is not absolute, but relative to the times, and may be surpassed and eclipsed by greater successors.

The new race of poet-scholars which arose soon after Dante quickly made themselves masters of this fresh tendency. They did so in a double sense, being themselves the most acknowledged celebrities of Italy, and at the same time, as poets and historians, consciously disposing of the reputation of others. An outward symbol of this sort of fame was the coronation of the poets, of which we shall speak later on.

A contemporary of Dante, Albertinus Musattus or Mussatus, crowned poet at Padua by the bishop and rector, enjoyed a fame which fell little short of deification. Every Christmas Day the doctors and students of both colleges at the University came in solemn procession before his house with trumpets and, it seems, with burning tapers, to salute him and bring him presents. His reputation lasted till, in 1318, he fell into disgrace with the ruling tyrant of the House of Carrara.

This new incense, which once was offered only to saints and heroes, was given in clouds to Petrarch, who persuaded himself in his later

[34] *De vulgari eloquentia*, I, 1; and *De Monarchia*, I, 1.

[35] *Paradiso*, VI, 112 *et seq.*

[36] E.g. *Inferno*, VI, 89; XIII, 53; XVI, 85; XXXI, 127.

[37] *Purgatorio*, V, 70, 87, 133; VI, 26; VIII, 71; XI, 31; XIII, 147.

[38] *Purgatorio*, XI, 85–117.

years that it was but a foolish and troublesome thing. His letter 'To Posterity' is the confession of an old and famous man, who is forced to gratify the public curiosity. He admits that he wishes for fame in the times to come, but would rather be without it in his own day. In his dialogue on fortune and misfortune, the interlocutor, who maintains the futility of glory, has the best of the contest. But, at the same time, Petrarch is pleased that the autocrat of Byzantium knows him as well by his writings as Charles IV knows him. And in fact, even in his lifetime, his fame extended far beyond Italy. And the emotion which he felt was natural when his friends, on the occasion of a visit to his native Arezzo (1350), took him to the house where he was born, and told him how the city had provided that no change should be made in it. In former times the dwellings of certain great saints were preserved and revered in this way, like the cell of St. Thomas Aquinas in the Dominican convent at Naples, and the Portiuncula of St. Francis near Assisi; and one or two great jurists also enjoyed the half-mythical reputation which led to this honour. Towards the close of the fourteenth century the people at Bagnolo, near Florence, called an old building the 'Studio of Accursius' (died in 1260), but, nevertheless, suffered it to be destroyed. It is probable that the great incomes and the political influence which some jurists obtained as consulting lawyers made a lasting impression on the popular imagination.

To the cult of the birthplaces of famous men must be added that of their graves, and, in the case of Petrarch, of the spot where he died. In memory of him Arquà became a favourite resort of the Paduans, and was dotted with graceful little villas. At this time there were no 'classic spots' in Northern Europe, and pilgrimages were only made to pictures and relics. It was a point of honour for the different cities to possess the bones of their own and foreign celebrities; and it is most remarkable how seriously the Florentines, even in the fourteenth century—long before the building of Santa Croce—laboured to make their cathedral a Pantheon. Accorso, Dante, Petrarch, Boccaccio, and the jurist Zanobi della Strada were to have had magnificent tombs there erected to them. Late in the fifteenth century, Lorenzo il Magnifico applied in person to the Spoletans, asking them to give up the corpse of the painter Fra Filippo Lippi for the cathedral, and received the answer that they had none too many ornaments to the city, especially in the shape of distinguished people, for which reason they begged him to spare them; and, in fact, he had to be content with erecting a cenotaph. And even Dante, in spite of all the applications to which Boccaccio urged the Florentines with bitter emphasis, remained sleeping tranquilly in San Francesco at Ravenna, 'among ancient tombs of emperors and vaults of saints, in more honourable company than thou, O Florence, couldst offer him'. It even happened that a man once took away unpunished the lights from the altar on which the crucifix stood, and set them by the grave, with the words, 'Take them; thou art more worthy of them than He, the Crucified One!' (Franco Sacchetti, Novella 121.)

And now the Italian cities began again to remember their ancient citizens and inhabitants. Naples, perhaps, had never forgotten its tomb of Virgil, since a kind of mythical halo had become attached to the name.

The Paduans, even in the sixteenth century, firmly believed that they possessed not only the genuine bones of their founder, Antenor, but also those of the historian Livy. 'Sulmona,' says Boccaccio, 'bewails that Ovid lies buried far away in exile; and Parma rejoices that Cassius sleeps within its walls.' The Mantuans coined a medal in 1257 with the bust of Virgil, and raised a statue to represent him. In a fit of aristocratic insolence, the guardian of the young Gonzaga, Carlo Malatesta, caused it to be pulled down in 1392, and was afterwards forced, when he found the fame of the old poet too strong for him, to set it up again.[39] Even then, perhaps, the grotto, a couple of miles from the town, where Virgil was said to have meditated, was shown to strangers, like the 'Scuola di Virgilio' at Naples. Como claimed both the Plinys for its own, and at the end of the fifteenth century erected statues in their honour, sitting under graceful baldachins on the façade of the cathedral.

History and the new topography were now careful to leave no local celebrity unnoticed. At the same period the northern chronicles only here and there, among the list of popes, emperors, earthquakes, and comets, put in the remark, that at such a time this or that famous man 'flourished'. We shall elsewhere have to show how, mainly under the influence of this idea of fame, an admirable biographical literature was developed. We must here limit ourselves to the local patriotism of the topographers who recorded the claims of their native cities to distinction.

In the Middle Ages, the cities were proud of their saints and of the bones and relics in their churches. With these the panegyrist of Padua

*[39] Cf. G. Voigt, *Die Wiederbelebung des klassischen Altertums*, I, 575.

in 1450, Michele Savonarola, begins his list; from them he passes to 'the famous men who were no saints, but who, by their great intellect and force (*virtus*) deserve to be added (*adnecti*) to the saints'—just as in classical antiquity the distinguished man came close upon the hero. The further enumeration is most characteristic of the time. First comes Antenor, the brother of Priam, who founded Padua with a band of Trojan fugitives; King Dardanus, who defeated Attila in the Euganean hills, followed him in pursuit, and struck him dead at Rimini with a chessboard; the Emperor Henry IV, who built the cathedral; a King Marcus, whose head was preserved in Monselice; then a couple of cardinals and prelates as founders of colleges, churches, and so forth; the famous Augustinian theologian, Fra Alberto; a string of philosophers beginning with Paolo Veneto and the celebrated Pietro of Abano; the jurist Paolo Padovano; then Livy and the poets Petrarch, Mussato, Lovato. If there is any want of military celebrities in the list, the poet consoles himself for it by the abundance of learned men whom he has to show, and by the more durable character of intellectual glory, while the fame of the soldier is buried with his body, or, if it lasts, owes its permanence only to the scholar. It is nevertheless honourable to the city that foreign warriors lie buried here by their own wish, like Pietro de' Rossi of Parma, Filippo Arcelli of Piacenza, and especially Gattemelata of Narni (d. 1443), whose brazen equestrian statue, 'like a Cæsar in triumph', already stood by the church of the Santo. The author then names a crowd of jurists and physicians, nobles 'who had not only, like so many others, received, but deserved, the honour of knighthood'. Then follows a list of famous mechanicians, painters, and musicians, and in conclusion the name of a fencing-master Michele Rosso, who, as the most distinguished man in his profession, was to be seen painted in many places.

By the side of these local temples of fame, which myth, legend, popular admiration, and literary tradition combined to create, the poet-scholars built up a great Pantheon of world-wide celebrity. They made collections of famous men and famous women, often in direct imitation of Cornelius Nepos, the pseudo-Suetonius, Valerius Maximus, Plutarch (*Mulierum virtutes*), Jerome (*De viris illustribus*), and others: or they wrote of imaginary triumphal processions and Olympian assemblies, as was done by Petrarch in his 'Trionfo della Fama', and Boccaccio in the 'Amorosa Visione', with hundreds of names, of which three-fourths at least belong to antiquity and the rest to the Middle Ages. By and by this new and comparatively modern element was treated with greater emphasis; the historians began to insert descriptions of character, and collections arose of the biographies of distinguished contemporaries, like those of Filippo Villani, Vespasiano Fiorentino, Bartolommeo Fazio, and lastly of Paolo Giovio.

The North of Europe, until Italian influence began to tell upon its writers—for instance, on Trithemius, the first German who wrote the lives of famous men—possessed only either legends of the saints, or descriptions of princes and churchmen partaking largely of the character of legends and showing no traces of the idea of fame, that is, of distinction won by a man's personal efforts. Poetical glory was still confined to certain classes of society, and the names of northern artists are only known to us at this period in so far as they were members of certain guilds or corporations.

The poet-scholar in Italy had, as we have already said, the fullest consciousness that he was the giver of fame and immortality, or, if he chose, of oblivion. Boccaccio complains of a fair one to whom he had done homage, and who remained hard-hearted in order that he might go on praising her and making her famous, and he gives her a hint that he will try the effect of a little blame. Sannazaro, in two magnificent sonnets, threatens Alfonso of Naples with eternal obscurity on account of his cowardly flight before Charles VIII. Angelo Poliziano seriously exhorts (1491) King John of Portugal to think betimes of his immortality in reference to the new discoveries in Africa, and to send him materials to Florence, there to be put into shape (*operosius excolenda*), otherwise it would befall him as it had befallen all the others whose deeds, unsupported by the help of the learned, 'lie hidden in the vast heap of human frailty'. The king, or his humanistic chancellor, agreed to this, and promised that at least the Portuguese chronicles of African affairs should be translated into Italian, and sent to Florence to be done into Latin. Whether the promise was kept is not known. These pretensions are by no means so groundless as they may appear at first sight; for the form in which events, even the greatest, are told to the living and to posterity is anything but a matter of indifference. The Italian humanists, with their mode of exposition and their Latin style, had long the complete control of the reading world of Europe, and till last century the Italian poets were more widely known and studied than those of any other nation. The baptismal name of the Florentine Amerigo Vespucci was given, on account of his book of travels, to a new quarter of the globe, and if Paolo Giovio, with all his superficiality and graceful caprice, promised himself immortality, his expectation has not latogether been disappointed.

Amid all these preparations outwardly to win and secure fame, the curtain is now and then drawn aside, and we see with frightful evidence a boundless ambition and thirst after greatness, regardless of all means and consequences. Thus, in the preface to Machiavelli's Florentine history, in which he blames his predecessors Leonardo, Aretino and Poggio for their too considerate reticence with regard to the political parties in the city: 'They erred greatly and showed that they understood little the ambition of men and the desire to perpetuate a name. How many who could distinguish themselves by nothing praiseworthy, strove to do so by infamous deeds!' Those writers did not consider that actions which are great in themselves, as is the case with the actions of rulers and of States, always seem to bring more glory than blame, of whatever kind they are and whatever the result of them may be. In more than one remarkable and dreadful undertaking the motive assigned by serious writers is the burning desire to achieve something great and memorable. This motive is not a mere extreme case of ordinary vanity, but something dæmonic, involving a surrender of the will, the use of any means, however atrocious, and even an indifference to success itself. In this sense, for example, Machiavelli conceives the character of Stefano Porcari; of the murderers of Galeazzo Maria Sforza (1476), the documents tell us about the same; and the assassination of Duke Alessandro of Florence (1537) is ascribed by Varchi himself to the thirst for fame which tormented the murderer Lorenzino Medici. Still more stress is laid on this motive by Paolo Giovio. Lorenzino, according to him, pilloried by a pamphlet of Molza, broods over a deed whose novelty shall make his disgrace forgotten, and ends by murdering his kinsman and prince. These are characteristic features of this age of overstrained and despairing passions and forces, and remind us of the burning of the temple of Diana at Ephesus in the time of Philip of Macedon.

RIDICULE AND WIT

The corrective, not only of this modern desire for fame, but of all highly developed individuality, is found in ridicule, especially when expressed in the victorious form of wit. We read in the Middle Ages how hostile armies, princes, and nobles, provoked one another with symbolical insult, and how the defeated party was loaded with symbolical outrage. Here and there, too, under the influence of classical literature, wit began to be used as a weapon in theological disputes, and the poetry of Provence produced a whole class of satirical compositions. Even the Minnesänger, as their political poems show, could adopt this tone when necessary.[40] But wit could not be an independent element in life till its appropriate victim, the developed individual with personal pretensions, had appeared. Its weapons were then by no means limited to the tongue and the pen, but included tricks and practical jokes—the so-called 'burle' and 'beffe'—which form a chief subject of many collections of novels.

The 'Hundred Old Novels', which must have been composed about the end of the thirteenth century, have as yet neither wit, the fruit of contrast, nor the 'burla', for their subject; their aim is merely to give simple and elegant expression to wise sayings and pretty stories or fables. But if anything proves the great antiquity of the collection, it is precisely this absence of satire. For with the fourteenth century comes Dante, who, in the utterance of scorn, leaves all other poets in the world far behind, and who, if only on account of his great picture of the deceivers,[41] must be called the chief master of colossal comedy. With Petrarch begin the collections of witty sayings after the pattern of Plutarch (Apophthegmata, etc.).

What stores of wit were concentrated in Florence during this century is most characteristically shown in the novels of Franco Sacchetti. These are, for the most part, not stories but answers, given under certain circumstances—shocking pieces of *naïveté*, with which silly folks, court jesters, rogues, and profligate women make their retort. The comedy of the tale lies in the startling contrast of this real or assumed *naïveté* with conventional morality and the ordinary relations of the world—things are made to stand on their heads. All means of picturesque representation are made use of, including the

[40] The Middle Ages are also rich in so-called satirical poems; the satire, however, is not personal, but is aimed at classes, professions, and whole populations, and it easily assumes the didactic tone. The spirit of this literature is best represented by *Reynard the Fox*, in all its forms among the different nations of the West. For this branch of French literature see a new and admirable work by Lenient, *La Satire en France au Moyen-âge*, Paris, 1860, and the equally excellent continuation, *La Satire en France, ou la littérature militante au XVI Siècle*, Paris, 1866.

[41] *Inferno*, XXI, XXII. The only possible parallel is Aristophanes.

introduction of certain North Italian dialects. Often the place of wit is taken by mere insolence, clumsy trickery, blasphemy, and obscenity; one or two jokes told of Condottieri are among the most brutal and malicious which are recorded. Many of the 'burle' are thoroughly comic, but many are only real or supposed evidence of personal superiority, of triumph over another. How much people were willing to put up with, how often the victim was satisfied with getting the laugh on his side by a retaliatory trick, cannot be said; there was much heartless and pointless malice mixed up with it all, and life in Florence was no doubt often made unpleasant enough from this cause. The inventors and retailers of jokes soon became inevitable figures, and among them there must have been some who were classical—far superior to all the mere court-jesters, to whom competition, a changing public, and the quick apprehension of the audience, all advantages of life in Florence, were wanting. Some Florentine wits went starring among the despotic courts of Lombardy and Romagna, and found themselves much better rewarded than at home, where their talent was cheap and plentiful. The better type of these people is the amusing man (l'uomo piacevole), the worse is the buffoon and the vulgar parasite who presents himself at weddings and banquets with the argument, 'If I am not invited, the fault is not mine.' Now and then the latter combine to pluck a young spendthrift, but in general they are treated and despised as parasites, while wits of higher position bear themselves likes princes, and consider their talent as something sovereign. Dolcibene, whom Charles IV had pronounced to be the 'king of Italian jesters', said to him at Ferrara: 'You will conquer the world, since you are my friend and the Pope's; you fight with the sword, the Pope with his bulls, and I with my tongue.' This is no mere jest, but the foreshadowing of Pietro Aretino.

The two most famous jesters about the middle of the fifteenth century were a priest near Florence, Arlotto (1483), for more refined wit ('facezie'), and the court-fool of Ferrara, Gonnella, for buffoonery. We can hardly compare their stories with those of the Parson of Kalenberg and Till Eulenspiegel, since the latter arose in a different and half-mythical manner, as fruits of the imagination of a whole people, and touch rather on what is general and intelligible to all, while Arlotto and Gonnella were historical beings, coloured and shaped by local influences. But if the comparison be allowed, and extended to the jests of the non-Italian nations, we shall find in general that the joke in the French *fabliaux*, as among the Germans, is chiefly directed to the attainment of some advantage or enjoyment; while the wit of Arlotto and the practical jokes of Gonnella are an end in themselves, and exist simply for the sake of the triumph of production. (Till Eulenspiegel again forms a class by himself, as the personified quiz, mostly pointless enough, of particular classes and professions.) The court-fool of the Este retaliated more than once by his keen satire and refined modes of vengeance.

The type of the 'uomo piacevole' and the 'buffone' long survived the freedom of Florence. Under Duke Cosimo flourished Barlacchia, and at the beginning of the seventeenth century Francesco Ruspoli and Curzio Marignolli. In Pope Leo X, the genuine Florentine love of jesters showed itself strikingly. This prince, whose taste for the most refined intellectual pleasures was insatiable, endured and desired at his table a number of witty buffoons and jack-puddings, among them two monks and a cripple; at public feasts he treated them with deliberate scorn as parasites, setting before them monkeys and crows in the place of savoury meats. Leo, indeed, showed a peculiar fondness for the 'burla'; it belonged to his nature sometimes to treat his own favourite pursuits—music and poetry—ironically, parodying them with his factotum, Cardinal Bibbiena. Neither of them found it beneath him to fool an honest old secretary till he thought himself a master of the art of music. The Improvisatore, Baraballo of Gaeta, was brought so far by Leo's flattery that he applied in all seriousness for the poet's coronation on the Capitol. On the feast of St. Cosmas and St. Damian, the patrons of the House of Medici, he was first compelled, adorned with laurel and purple, to amuse the papal guests with his recitations, and at last, when all were ready to split with laughter, to mount a gold-harnessed elephant in the court of the Vatican, sent as a present to Rome by Emmanuel the Great of Portugal, while the Pope looked down from above through his eyeglass.[42] The brute, however, was so terrified by the noise of the trumpets and kettledrums, and the cheers of the crowd, that there was no getting him over the bridge of Sant' Angelo.

[42] The eye-glass I not only infer from Raphael's portrait, where it can be explained as a magnifier for looking at the miniatures in the prayer-book, but from a statement of Pellicanus, according to which Leo views an advancing procession of monks through a 'specillum' (cf. *Züricher Taschenbuch* for 1858, p. 177), and from the 'cristallus concava', which, according to Paolo Giovio, he used when hunting.

The parody of what is solemn or sublime, which here meets us in the case of a procession, had already taken an important place in poetry.[43] It was naturally compelled to choose victims of another kind than those of Aristophanes, who introduced the great tragedians into his plays. But the same maturity of culture which at a certain period produced parody among the Greeks, did the same in Italy. By the close of the fourteenth century, the love-lorn wailings of Petrarch's sonnets and others of the same kind were taken off by caricaturists; and the solemn air of this form of verse was parodied in lines of mystic twaddle. A constant invitation to parody was offered by the 'Divine Comedy', and Lorenzo il Magnifico wrote the most admirable travesty in the style of the 'Inferno' (Simposio or I Beoni). Luigi Pulci obviously imitates the Improvisatori in his 'Morgante', and both his poetry and Boiardo's are in part, at least, a half-conscious parody of the chivalrous poetry of the Middle Ages. Such a caricature was deliberately undertaken by the great parodist Teofilo Folengo (about 1520). Under the name of Limerno Pitocco, he composed the 'Orlandino', in which chivalry appears only as a ludicrous setting for a crowd of modern figures and ideas. Under the name of Merlinus Coccaius he described the journeys and exploits of his fantastic vagabonds (also in the same spirit of parody) in half-Latin hexameters, with all the affected pomp of the learned Epos of the day ('Opus Macaronicorum'). Since then caricature has been constantly, and often brilliantly, represented on the Italian Parnassus.

About the middle period of the Renaissance a theoretical analysis of wit was undertaken, and its practical application in good society was regulated more precisely. The theorist was Gioviano Pontano. In his work on speaking, especially in the third and fourth books, he tries by means of the comparison of numerous jokes or 'facetiæ' to arrive at a general principle. How wit should be used among people of position is taught by Baldassare Castiglione in his 'Cortigiano'. Its chief function is naturally to enliven those present by the repetition of comic or graceful stories and sayings; personal jokes, on the contrary, are discouraged on the ground that they wound unhappy

[43] We find it also in visual art, e.g. in the famous engraving parodying the group of the Laocoön as three monkeys, but here parody seldom went beyond sketches and the like, though much, it is true, may have been destroyed. Caricature, again, is something different. Leonardo, in the grotesque faces in the Biblioteca Ambrosiana, represents what is hideous when and because it is comical, and exaggerates the ludicrous element at pleasure.

people, show too much honour to wrong-doers, and make enemies of the powerful and the spoiled children of fortune; and even in repetition, a wide reserve in the use of dramatic gestures is recommended to the gentleman. Then follows, not only for purposes of quotation, but as patterns for future jesters, a large collection of puns and witty sayings, methodically arranged according to their species, among them some that are admirable. The doctrine of Giovanni della Casa, some twenty years later, in his guide to good manners, is much stricter and more cautious; with a view to the consequences, he wishes to see the desire of triumph banished altogether from jokes and 'burle'. He is the herald of a reaction, which was certain sooner or later to appear.

Italy had, in fact, become a school for scandal, the like of which the world cannot show, not even in France at the time of Voltaire. In him and his comrades there was assuredly no lack of the spirit of negation; but where, in the eighteenth century, was to be found the crowd of suitable victims, that countless assembly of highly and characteristically developed human beings, celebrities of every kind, statesmen, churchmen, inventors, and discoverers, men of letters, poets and artists, all of whom then gave the fullest and freest play to their individuality? This host existed in the fifteenth and sixteenth centuries, and by its side the general culture of the time had educated a poisonous brood of impotent wits, of born critics and railers, whose envy called for hecatombs of victims; and to all this was added the envy of the famous men among themselves. In this the philologists notoriously led the way—Filelfo, Poggio, Lorenzo Valla, and others—while the artists of the fifteenth century lived in peaceful and friendly competition with one another. The history of art may take note of the fact.

Florence, the great market of fame, was in this point, as we have said, in advance of other cities. 'Sharp eyes and bad tongues' is the description given of the inhabitants. An easy-going contempt of everything and everybody was probably the prevailing tone of society. Machiavelli, in the remarkable prologue to his 'Mandragola', refers rightly or wrongly the visible decline of moral force to the general habit of evil-speaking, and threatens his detractors with the news that he can say sharp things as well as they. Next to Florence comes the Papal court, which had long been a rendezvous of the bitterest and wittiest tongues. Poggio's 'Facetiæ' are dated from the Chamber of Lies (*bugiale*) of the apostolic notaries; and when we remember the number of disappointed place-hunters, of hopeless competitors and enemies of the favourites, of idle, profligate prelates there assembled, it is intelligible how Rome became the home of the savage pasquinade as well as of more philosophical satire. If we add to this the widespread hatred borne to the priests, and the well-known instinct of the mob to lay any horror to the charge of the great, there results an untold mass of infamy. Those who were able, protected themselves best by contempt both of the false and true accusations, and by brilliant and joyous display. More sensitive natures sank into utter despair when they found themselves deeply involved in guilt, and still more deeply in slander. In course of time calumny became universal, and the strictest virtue was most certain of all to challenge the attacks of malice. Of the great pulpit orator, Fra Egidio of Viterbo, whom Leo made a cardinal on account of his merits, and who showed himself a man of the people and a brave monk in the calamity of 1527, Giovio gives us to understand that he preserved his ascetic pallor by the smoke of wet straw and other means of the same kind. Giovio is a genuine Curial in these matters. He generally begins by telling his story, then adds that he does not believe it, and then hints at the end that perhaps after all there may be something in it. But the true scapegoat of Roman scorn was the pious and moral Adrian VI. A general agreement seemed to be made to take him only on the comic side. He fell out from the first with the formidable Francesco Berni, threatening to have thrown into the Tiber not, as people said, the statue of Pasquino, but the writers of the satires themselves. The vengeance for this was the famous 'Capitolo' against Pope Adriano, inspired not exactly by hatred, but by contempt for the comical Dutch barbarian; the more savage menaces were reserved for the cardinals who had elected him. The plague, which then was prevalent in Rome, was ascribed to him; Berni and others sketch the environment of the Pope with the same sparkling untruthfulness with which the modern *feuilletoniste* turns black into white, and everything into anything. The biography which Paolo Giovio was commissioned to write by the cardinal of Tortosa, and which was to have been a eulogy, is for anyone who can read between the lines an unexampled piece of satire. It sounds ridiculous—at least for the Italians of that time—to hear how Adrian applied to the Chapter of Saragossa for the jawbone of St. Lambert; how the devout Spaniards decked him out till he looked 'like a right well-dressed Pope'; how he came in a confused and tasteless procession from

Ostia to Rome, took counsel about burning or drowning Pasquino, would suddenly break off the most important business when dinner was announced; and lastly, at the end of an unhappy reign, how he died of drinking too much beer—whereupon the house of his physician was hung with garlands by midnight revellers, and adorned with the inscription, 'Liberatori Patriæ S.P.Q.R.' It is true that Giovio had lost his money in the general confiscation of public funds, and had only received a benefice by way of compensation because he was 'no poet', that is to say, no pagan. But it was decreed that Adrian should be the last great victim. After the disaster which befell Rome in 1527, slander visibly declined along with the unrestrained wickedness of private life.

★ ★ ★

But while it was still flourishing was developed, chiefly in Rome, the greatest railer of modern times, Pietro Aretino. A glance at his life and character will save us the trouble of noticing many less distinguished members of his class.

We know him chiefly in the last thirty years of his life (1527–56), which he passed in Venice, the only asylum possible for him. From hence he kept all that was famous in Italy in a kind of state of siege, and here were delivered the presents of the foreign princes who needed or dreaded his pen. Charles V and Francis I both pensioned him at the same time, each hoping that Aretino would do some mischief to the other. Aretino flattered both, but naturally attached himself more closely to Charles, because he remained master in Italy. After the Emperor's victory at Tunis in 1535, this tone of adulation passed into the most ludicrous worship, in observing which it must not be forgotten that Aretino constantly cherished the hope that Charles would help him to a cardinal's hat. It is probable that he enjoyed special protection as Spanish agent, as his speech or silence could have no small effect on the smaller Italian courts and on public opinion in Italy. He affected utterly to despise the Papal court because he knew it so well; the true reason was that Rome neither could nor would pay him any longer. Venice, which sheltered him, he was wise enough to leave unassailed. The rest of his relations with the great is mere beggary and vulgar extortion.

Aretino affords the first great instance of the abuse of publicity to such ends. The polemical writings which a hundred years earlier Poggio and his opponents interchanged, are just as infamous in their tone and purpose, but they were not composed for the press, but for a sort of private circulation. Aretino made all his profit out of a complete publicity, and in a certain sense may be considered the father of modern journalism. His letters and miscellaneous articles were printed periodically, after they had already been circulated among a tolerably extensive public.[44]

Compared with the sharp pens of the eighteenth century, Aretino had the advantage that he was not burdened with principles, neither with liberalism nor philanthropy nor any other virtue, nor even with science; his whole baggage consisted of the well-known motto, 'Veritas odium parit'. He never, consequently, found himself in the false position of Voltaire, who was forced to disown his 'Pucelle' and conceal all his life the authorship of other works. Aretino put his name to all he wrote, and openly gloried in his notorious 'Ragionamenti'. His literary talent, his clear and sparkling style, his varied observation of men and things, would have made him a considerable writer under any circumstances, destitute as he was of the power of conceiving a genuine work of art, such as a true dramatic comedy; and to the coarsest as well as the most refined malice he added a grotesque wit so brilliant that in some cases it does not fall short of that of Rabelais.

In such circumstances, and with such objects and means, he set to work to attack or circumvent his prey. The tone in which he appealed to Clement VII not to complain or to think of vengeance, but to forgive, at the moment when the wailings of the devastated city were ascending to the Castel Sant' Angelo, where the Pope himself was a prisoner, is the mockery of a devil or a monkey. Sometimes, when he is forced to give up all hope of presents, his fury breaks out into a savage howl, as in the 'Capitolo' to the Prince of Salerno, who after paying him for some time refused to do so any longer. On the other hand, it seems that the terrible Pierluigi Farnese, Duke of Parma, never took any notice of him at all. As this gentleman had probably renounced altogether the pleasures of a good reputation, it was not easy to cause him any annoyance; Aretino tried to do so by comparing his personal appearance to that of a constable, a miller, and a baker.

[44] The fear which he caused to men of mark, especially artists, by these means, cannot here be described. The propaganda weapon of the German Reformation was chiefly the pamphlet dealing with events as they occurred; Aretino is a journalist in the sense that he has within himself a perpetual occasion for writing.

Aretino is most comical of all in the expression of whining mendicancy, as in the 'Capitolo' to Francis I; but the letters and poems made up of menaces and flattery cannot, notwithstanding all that is ludicrous in them, be read without the deepest disgust. A letter like that one of his written to Michelangelo in November, 1545, is alone of its kind; along with all the admiration he expresses for the 'Last Judgement' he charges him with irreligion, indecency, and theft from the heirs of Julius II, and adds in a conciliating postcript, 'I only want to show you that if you are "divino", I am not "d'acqua" '.† Aretino laid great stress upon it—whether from the insanity of conceit or by way of caricaturing famous men—that he himself should be called divine, as one of his flatterers had already begun to do; and he certainly attained so much personal celebrity that his house at Arezzo passed for one of the sights of the place. There were indeed whole months during which he never ventured to cross his threshold at Venice, lest he should fall in with some incensed Florentine like the younger Strozzi. Nor did he escape the cudgels and the daggers of his enemies, although they failed to have the effect which Berni prophesied him in a famous sonnet. Aretino died in his house, of apoplexy.

The differences he made in his modes of flattery are remarkable: in dealing with non-Italians he was grossly fulsome; people like Duke Cosimo of Florence he treated very differently. He praised the beauty of the then youthful prince, who in fact did share this quality with Augustus in no ordinary degree; he praised his moral conduct, with an oblique reference to the financial pursuits of Cosimo's mother, Maria Salviati, and concluded with a mendicant whine about the bad times and so forth. When Cosimo pensioned him, which he did liberally, considering his habitual parsimony—to the extent, at least, of 160 ducats a year—he had doubtless an eye to Aretino's dangerous character as Spanish agent. Aretino could ridicule and revile Cosimo, and in the same breath threaten the Florentine agent that he would obtain from the Duke his immediate recall; and if the Medicean prince felt himself at last to be seen through by Charles V he would naturally not be anxious that Aretino's jokes and rhymes against him should circulate at the Imperial court. A curiously qualified piece of flattery was that addressed to the notorious Marquis of Marignano, who as Castellan of Musso had attempted to found an independent State. Thanking him for the gift of a hundred crowns, Aretino

† A rather stupid play on the words *divino* (divine) and *di vino* (of wine).

writes: 'All the qualities which a prince should have are present in you, and all men would think so, were it not that the acts of violence inevitable at the beginning of all undertakings cause you to appear a trifle rough (*aspro*).'

It has often been noticed as something singular that Aretino only reviled the world, and not God also. The religious belief of a man who lived as he did is a matter of perfect indifference, as are also the edifying writings which he composed for reasons of his own.[45] It is in fact hard to say why he should have been a blasphemer. He was no professor, or theoretical thinker or writer; and he could extort no money from God by threats or flattery, and was consequently never goaded into blasphemy by a refusal. A man like him does not take trouble for nothing.

It is a good sign for the present spirit of Italy that such a character and such a career have become a thousand times impossible. But historical criticism will always find in Aretino an important study.

[45] He may have done so either in the hope of obtaining the red hat or from fear of the new activity of the Inquisition, which he had ventured to attack bitterly in 1535, but which, after its reorganization in 1542, received a new lease of life, and soon silenced every opposing voice.

PART III

THE REVIVAL OF ANTIQUITY

INTRODUCTORY

NOW that this point in our historical view of Italian civilization has been reached, it is time to speak of the influence of antiquity, the 'new birth' of which has been one-sidedly chosen as the name to sum up the whole period. The conditions which have been hitherto described would have sufficed, apart from antiquity, to upturn and to mature the national mind; and most of the intellectual tendencies which yet remain to be noticed would be conceivable without it. But both what has gone before and what we have still to discuss are coloured in a thousand ways by the influence of the ancient world; and though the essence of the phenomena might still have been the same without the classical revival, it is only with and through this revival that they are actually manifested to us. The Renaissance would not have been the process of world-wide significance which it is, if its elements could be so easily separated from one another. We must insist upon it, as one of the chief propositions of this book, that it was not the revival of antiquity alone, but its union with the genius of the Italian people, which achieved the conquest of the western world. The amount of independence which the national spirit maintained in this union varied according to circumstances. In the modern Latin literature of the period, it is very small, while in the visual arts, as well as in other spheres, it is remarkably great; and hence the alliance between two distant epochs in the civilization of the same people, because concluded on equal terms, proved justifiable and fruitful. The rest of Europe was free either to repel or else partly or wholly to accept the mighty impulse which came forth from Italy. Where the latter was the case we may as well be spared the complaints over the early decay of mediæval faith and civilization. Had these been strong enough to hold their ground, they would be alive to this day. If those elegiac natures which long to see them return could pass but one hour in the midst of them, they would gasp to be back in modern air. That in a great historical process of this kind flowers of exquisite beauty may perish, without being made immortal in poetry or tradition, is undoubtedly true; nevertheless, we cannot wish the process undone. The general result of it consists in this—that by the side of the Church which had hitherto held the countries of the West together (though it was unable to do so much longer) there arose a new spiritual influence which, spreading itself abroad from Italy, became the breath of life for all the more instructed minds in Europe. The worst that can be said of the movement is, that it was anti-popular, that through it Europe became for the first time sharply divided into the cultivated and uncultivated classes. The reproach will appear groundless when we reflect that even now the fact, though clearly recognized, cannot be altered. The separation, too, is by no means so cruel and absolute in Italy as elsewhere. The most artistic of her poets, Tasso, is in the hands of even the poorest.

The civilization of Greece and Rome, which, ever since the fourteenth century, obtained so powerful a hold on Italian life, as the source and basis of culture, as the object and ideal of existence, partly also as an avowed reaction against preceding tendencies—this civilization had long been exerting a partial influence on mediæval Europe, even beyond the boundaries of Italy. The culture of which Charlemagne was a representative was, in face of the barbarism of the seventh and eighth centuries, essentially a Renaissance, and could appear under no other form. Just as in the Romanesque architecture of the North, beside the general outlines inherited from antiquity, remarkable direct imitations of the antique also occur, so too monastic scholarship had not only gradually absorbed an immense mass of materials from Roman writers, but the style of it, from the days of Einhard onwards, shows traces of conscious imitation.

But the resuscitation of antiquity took a different form in Italy from that which it assumed in the North. The wave of barbarism had scarcely gone by before the people, in whom the former life was but half effaced, showed a consciousness of its past and a wish to reproduce it. Elsewhere in Europe men deliberately and with reflection borrowed this or the other element of classical civilization; in Italy the sympathies both of the learned and of the people were naturally engaged on the side of antiquity as a whole, which stood to them as a symbol of past greatness. The Latin language, too, was easy to an Italian, and the numerous monuments and documents in which the country abounded facilitated a return to the past. With this tendency other elements—the popular character which time had now greatly modified, the political institutions imported by the Lombards from Germany, chivalry and other northern forms of civilization, and the influence of religion and the Church—combined to produce the modern Italian spirit, which was destined to serve as the model and ideal for the whole western world.

How antiquity influenced the visual arts, as soon as the flood of barbarism had subsided, is clearly shown in the Tuscan buildings of the twelfth and in the sculptures of the thirteenth centuries. In poetry, too, there will appear no want of similar analogies to those who hold that the greatest Latin poet of the twelfth century, the writer who struck the keynote of a whole class of Latin poems, was an Italian. We mean the author of the best pieces in the so-called 'Carmina Burana'. A frank enjoyment of life and its pleasures, as whose patrons the gods of heathendom are invoked, while Catos and Scipios hold the place of the saints and heroes of Christianity, flows in full current through the rhymed verses. Reading them through at a stretch, we can scarcely help coming to the conclusion that an Italian, probably a Lombard, is speaking; in fact, there are positive grounds for thinking so. To a certain degree these Latin poems of the 'Clerici vagantes' of the twelfth century, with all their remarkable frivolity, are, doubtless, a product in which the whole of Europe had a share; but the writer of the song 'De Phyllide et Flora' and the 'Æstuans Interius' can have been a northerner as little as the polished Epicurean observer to whom we owe 'Dum Dianæ vitrea sero lampas oritur'. Here, in truth, is a reproduction of the whole ancient view of life, which is all the more striking from the mediæval form of the verse in which it is set forth. There are many works of this and the following centuries, in which a careful imitation of the antique appears both in the hexameter and pentameter of the metre and in the classical, often mythological, character of the subject, and which yet have not anything like the same spirit of antiquity about them. In the hexametric chronicles and other works of Guglielmus Apuliensis and his successors (from about 1100), we find frequent traces of a diligent study of Virgil, Ovid, Lucan, Statius, and Claudian; but this classical form is, after all, a mere matter of archæology, as is the classical subject in compilers like Vincent of Beauvais, or in the mythological and allegorical writer, Alanus ab Insulis. The Renaissance, however, is not a fragmentary imitation or compilation, but a new birth; and the signs of this are visible in the poems of the unknown 'Clericus' of the twelfth century.

But the great and general enthusiasm of the Italians for classical antiquity did not display itself before the fourteenth century. For this a development of civic life was required, which took place only in Italy, and there not till then. It was needful that noble and burgher should first learn to dwell together on equal terms, and that a social world should arise which felt the want of culture, and had the leisure and the means to obtain it. But culture, as soon as it freed itself from the fantastic bonds of the Middle Ages, could not at once and without help find its way to the understanding of the physical and intellectual world. It needed a guide, and found one in the ancient civilization, with its wealth of truth and knowledge in every spiritual interest. Both the form and the substance of this civilization were adopted with admiring gratitude; it became the chief part of the culture of the age. The general condition of the country was favourable to this transformation. The mediæval empire, since the fall of the Hohenstaufen, had either renounced, or was unable to make good, its claims on Italy. The Popes had migrated to Avignon. Most of the political powers actually existing owed their origin to violent and illegitimate means. The spirit of the people, now awakened to self-consciousness, sought for some new and stable ideal on which to rest. And thus the vision of the world-wide empire of Italy and Rome so possessed the popular mind that Cola di Rienzi could actually attempt to put it in practice. The conception he formed of his task, particularly when tribune for the first time, could only end in some extravagant comedy; nevertheless, the memory of ancient Rome was no slight support to the national sentiment. Armed afresh with its culture, the Italian soon felt himself in truth citizen of the most advanced nation in the world.

It is now our task to sketch this spiritual movement, not indeed in all its fullness, but in its most salient features, and especially in its first beginnings.[46]

[46] For particulars we must refer the reader to Roscoe, *Lorenzo Magnifico* and *Leo X*, as well as to Voigt, *Enea Silvio* (Berlin, 1856–63). To obtain a general idea of the extent of studies at the beginning of the sixteenth century we cannot do better than turn to the *Commentarii Urbani* of Raphael Volaterranus (ed. Basle, 1544, fol. 16, etc.), which shows how antiquity formed the introduction and chief matter of study in every branch of knowledge from geography and local history, the lives of great and famous men, popular philosophy, morals and the special sciences, down to the analysis of the whole of Aristotle, with which the work closes. To understand its significance as an authority for the history of culture, we must compare it with all the earlier encyclopædias. A complete and circumstantial account of the matters is given in G. Voigt's admirable work, *Die Wiederbelebung des klassischen Altertums oder Das erste Jahrhundert des Humanismus*, Berlin, 1859 (3rd edition, 2 vols., 1893).

THE RUINS OF ROME

Rome itself, the city of ruins, now became the object of a wholly different sort of piety from that of the time when the 'Mirabilia Romæ' and the collection of William of Malmesbury were composed. The imaginations of the devout pilgrim, or of the seeker after marvels and treasures, are supplanted in contemporary records by the interests of the patriot and the historian. In this sense we must understand Dante's words, that the stones of the walls of Rome deserve reverence, and that the ground on which the city is built is more worthy than men say. The jubilees, incessant as they were, have scarcely left a single devout record in literature properly so called. The best thing that Giovanni Villani brought back from the jubilee of the year 1300 was the resolution to write his history which had been awakened in him by the sight of the ruins of Rome. Petrarch gives evidence of a taste divided between classical and Christian antiquity. He tells us how often with Giovanni Colonna he ascended the mighty vaults of the Baths of Diocletian, and there in the transparent air, amid the wide silence with the broad panorama stretching far around them, they spoke, not of business or political affairs, but of the history which the ruins beneath their feet suggested, Petrarch appearing in these dialogues as the partisan of classical, Giovanni of Christian antiquity; then they would discourse of philosophy and of the inventors of the arts. How often since that time, down to the days of Gibbon and Niebuhr, have the same ruins stirred men's minds to the same reflections!

This double current of feeling is also recognizable in the 'Dittamondo' of Fazio degli Uberti, composed about the year 1360—a description of visionary travels, in which the author is accompanied by the old geographer Solinus, as Dante was by Virgil. They visit Bari in memory of St. Nicholas, and Monte Gargano of the archangel Michael, and in Rome the legends of Aracoeli and of Santa Maria in Trastevere are mentioned. Still, the pagan splendour of ancient Rome unmistakably exercises a greater charm upon them. A venerable matron in torn garments—Rome herself is meant—tells them of the glorious past, and gives them a minute description of the old triumphs; she then leads the strangers through the city, and points out to them the seven hills and many of the chief ruins—'che comprender potrai, quanto fui bella'.

Unfortunately this Rome of the schismatic and Avignonese popes was no longer, in respect of classical remains, what it had been some generations earlier. The destruction of 140 fortified houses of the Roman nobles by the senator Brancaleone in 1257 must have wholly altered the character of the most important buildings then standing: for the nobles had no doubt ensconced themselves in the loftiest and best-preserved of the ruins.[47] Nevertheless, far more was left than we now find, and probably many of the remains had still their marble incrustation, their pillared entrances, and their other ornaments, where we now see nothing but the skeleton of brickwork. In this state of things, the first beginnings of a topographical study of the old city were made.

In Poggio's walks through Rome the study of the remains themselves is for the first time more intimately combined with that of the ancient authors and inscriptions—the latter he sought out from among all the vegetation in which they were imbedded—the writer's imagination is severely restrained, and the memories of Christian Rome carefully excluded. The only pity is that Poggio's work was not fuller and was not illustrated with sketches. Far more was left in his time than was found by Raphael eighty years later. He saw the tomb of Cæcilia Metella and the columns in front of one of the temples on the slope of the Capitol, first in full preservation, and then afterwards half destroyed, owing to that unfortunate quality which marble possesses of being easily burnt into lime. A vast colonnade near the Minerva fell piecemeal a victim to the same fate. A witness in the year 1443 tells us that this manufacture of lime still went on: 'which is a shame, for the new buildings are pitiful, and the beauty of Rome is in its ruins'. The inhabitants of that day, in their peasant's cloaks and boots, looked to foreigners like cowherds; and in fact the cattle were pastured in the city up to the Banchi. The only social gatherings were the services at church, on which occasion it was possible also to get a sight of the beautiful women.

In the last years of Eugenius IV (d. 1447) Blondus of Forlì wrote his 'Roma Instaurata', making use of Frontinus and of the old 'Libri Regionali', as well as, it seems, of Anastasius. His object is not only the

[47] Parenthetically we may quote foreign evidence that Rome in the Middle Ages was looked upon as a quarry. The famous Abbot Sugerius, who about 1140 was in search of lofty pillars for the rebuilding of St. Denis, thought at first of nothing less than getting hold of the granite monoliths of the Baths of Diocletian, but afterwards changed his mind. Charlemagne was doubtless more modest in his requirements.

description of what existed, but still more the recovery of what was lost. In accordance with the dedication to the Pope, he consoles himself for the general ruin by the thought of the precious relics of the saints in which Rome was so rich.

With Nicholas V (1447–1455) that new monumental spirit which was distinctive of the age of the Renaissance appeared on the papal throne. The new passion for embellishing the city brought with it on the one hand a fresh danger for the ruins, on the other a respect for them, as forming one of Rome's claims to distinction. Pius II was wholly possessed by antiquarian enthusiasm, and if he speaks little of the antiquities of Rome, he closely studied those of all other parts of Italy, and was the first to know and describe accurately the remains which abounded in the districts for miles around the capital. It is true that, both as priest and cosmographer, he was interested alike in classical and Christian monuments and in the marvels of nature. Or was he doing violence to himself when he wrote that Nola was more highly honoured by the memory of St. Paulinus than by all its classical reminiscences and by the heroic struggle of Marcellus? Not, indeed, that his faith in relics was assumed; but his mind was evidently rather disposed to an inquiring interest in nature and antiquity, to a zeal for monumental works, to a keen and delicate observation of human life. In the last years of his Papacy, afflicted with the gout and yet in the most cheerful mood, he was borne in his litter over hill and dale to Tusculum, Alba, Tibur, Ostia, Falerii, and Otriculum, and whatever he saw he noted down. He followed the Roman roads and aqueducts, and tried to fix the boundaries of the old tribes which had dwelt round the city. On an excursion to Tivoli with the great Federigo of Urbino the time was happily spent in talk on the military system of the ancients, and particularly on the Trojan war. Even on his journey to the Congress of Mantua (1459) he searched, though unsuccessfully, for the labyrinth of Clusium mentioned by Pliny, and visited the so-called villa of Virgil on the Mincio. That such a Pope should demand a classical Latin style from his abbreviators, is no more than might be expected. It was he who, in the war with Naples, granted an amnesty to the men of Arpinum, as countrymen of Cicero and Marius, after whom many of them were named. It was to him alone, as both judge and patron, that Blondus could dedicate his 'Roma Triumphans', the first great attempt at a complete exposition of Roman antiquity.

Nor was the enthusiasm for the classical past of Italy confined at this period to the capital. Boccaccio had already called the vast ruins of Baiæ 'old walls, yet new for modern spirits'; and since his time they were held to be the most interesting sight near Naples. Collections of antiquities of all sorts now became common. Ciriaco of Ancona (d. 1457) travelled not only through Italy, but through other countries of the old Orbis terrarum, and brought back countless inscriptions and sketches. When asked why he took all this trouble, he replied, 'To wake the dead'. The histories of the various cities of Italy had from the earliest times laid claim to some true or imagined connection with Rome, had alleged some settlement or colonization which started from the capital; and the obliging manufacturers of pedigrees seem constantly to have derived various families from the oldest and most famous blood of Rome. So highly was the distinction valued, that men clung to it even in the light of the dawning criticism of the fifteenth century. When Pius II was at Viterbo he said frankly to the Roman deputies who begged him to return, 'Rome is as much my home as Siena, for my House, the Piccolomini, came in early times from the capital to Siena, as is proved by the constant use of the names Æneas and Sylvius in my family'. He would probably have had no objection to be held a descendant of the Julii. Paul II, a Barbo of Venice, found his vanity flattered by deducing his House, notwithstanding an adverse pedigree, according to which it came from Germany, from the Roman Ahenobarbus, who had led a colony to Parma, and whose successors had been driven by party conflicts to migrate to Venice. That the Massimi claimed descent from Q. Fabius Maximus, and the Cornaro from the Cornelii, cannot surprise us. On the other hand, it is a strikingly exceptional fact for the sixteenth century that the novelist Bandello tried to connect his blood with a noble family of Ostrogoths.

To return to Rome. The inhabitants, 'who then called themselves Romans', accepted greedily the homage which was offered them by the rest of Italy. Under Paul II, Sixtus IV and Alexander VI, magnificent processions formed part of the Carnival, representing the scene most attractive to the imagination of the time—the triumph of the Roman Imperator. The sentiment of the people expressed itself naturally in this shape and others like it. In this mood of public feeling, a report arose on April 18, 1485, that the corpse of a young Roman lady of the classical period—wonderfully beautiful and in perfect preservation—had been discovered. Some Lombard masons digging out an ancient tomb on an estate of the convent of Santa

Maria Nuova, on the Appian Way, beyond the tomb of Cæcilia Metella, were said to have found a marble sarcophagus with the inscription, 'Julia, daughter of Claudius'. On this basis the following story was built. The Lombards disappeared with the jewels and treasure which were found with the corpse in the sarcophagus. The body had been coated with an antiseptic essence, and was as fresh and flexible as that of a girl of fifteen the hour after death. It was said that she still kept the colours of life, with eyes and mouth half open. She was taken to the palace of the 'Conservatori' on the Capitol; and then a pilgrimage to see her began. Among the crowd were many who came to paint her; 'for she was more beautiful than can be said or written, and, were it said or written, it would not be believed by those who had not seen her'. By order of Innocent VIII she was secretly buried one night outside the Pincian Gate; the empty sarcophagus remained in the court of the 'Conservatori'. Probably a coloured mask of wax or some other material was modelled in the classical style on the face of the corpse, with which the gilded hair of which we read would harmonize admirably. The touching point in the story is not the fact itself, but the firm belief that an ancient body, which was now thought to be at last really before men's eyes, must of necessity be far more beautiful than anything of modern date.

Meanwhile the material knowledge of old Rome was increased by excavations. Under Alexander VI the so-called 'Grotesques', that is, the mural decorations of the ancients, were discovered, and the Apollo of the Belvedere was found at Porto d'Anzio. Under Julius II followed the memorable discoveries of the Laocoön, of the Venus of the Vatican, of the Torso of the Cleopatra.[48] The palaces of the nobles and the cardinals began to be filled with ancient statues and fragments. Raphael undertook for Leo X that ideal restoration of the whole ancient city which his (or Castiglione's) celebrated letter (1518 or 1519) speaks of. After a bitter complaint over the devastations which had not even then ceased, and which had been particularly frequent under Julius II, he beseeches the Pope to protect the few relics which were left to testify to the power and greatness of that divine soul of antiquity whose memory was inspiration to all who were capable of higher things. He then goes on with penetrating judgement to lay the foundations of a comparative history of art, and concludes

[48] As early as Julius II excavations were made in the hope of finding statues (Vasari, in *Vita di Giovanni da Udine*).

by giving the definition of an architectural survey which has been accepted since his time; he requires the ground plan, section and elevation separately of every building that remained. How archæology devoted itself after his day to the study of the venerated city and grew into a special science, and how the Vitruvian Academy at all events proposed to itself great aims, cannot here be related. Let us rather pause at the days of Leo X, under whom the enjoyment of antiquity combined with all other pleasures to give to Roman life a unique stamp and consecration. The Vatican resounded with song and music, and their echoes were heard through the city as a call to joy and gladness, though Leo did not succeed thereby in banishing care and pain from his own life, and his deliberate calculation to prolong his days by cheerfulness was frustrated by an early death. The Rome of Leo, as described by Paolo Giovio, forms a picture too splendid to turn away from, unmistakable as are also its darker aspects—the slavery of those who were struggling to rise; the secret misery of the prelates, who, notwithstanding heavy debts, were forced to live in a style befitting their rank; the system of literary patronage, which drove men to be parasites or adventurers; and, lastly, the scandalous maladministration of the finances of the State. Yet the same Ariosto who knew and ridiculed all this so well, gives in the sixth satire a longing picture of his expected intercourse with the accomplished poets who would conduct him through the city of ruins, of the learned counsel which he would there find for his own literary efforts, and of the treasures of the Vatican library. These, he says, and not the long-abandoned hope of Medicean protection, were the baits which really attracted him, if he were again asked to go as Ferrarese ambassador to Rome.

But the ruins within and outside Rome awakened not only archæological zeal and patriotic enthusiasm, but an elegiac or sentimental melancholy. In Petrarch and Boccaccio we find touches of this feeling. Poggio Bracciolini often visited the temple of Venus and Roma, in the belief that it was that of Castor and Pollux, where the senate used so often to meet, and would lose himself in memories of the great orators Crassus, Hortensius, Cicero. The language of Pius II, especially in describing Tivoli, has a thoroughly sentimental ring, and soon afterwards (1467) appeared the first pictures of ruins, with a commentary by Polifilo.[49] Ruins of mighty arches and colonnades,

[49] Franciscus Colonna, *Polifili Hypnerotomachia*, printed by Aldo Manuzio at Venice in 1499. (*Five woodcuts from Polifilo are reproduced in the

half hid in plane-trees, laurels, cypresses and brushwood, figure in his pages. In the sacred legends it became the custom, we can hardly say how, to lay the scene of the birth of Christ in the ruins of a magnificent palace. That artificial ruins became afterwards a necessity of landscape gardening is only a practical consequence of this feeling.

THE CLASSICS

But the literary bequests of antiquity, Greek as well as Latin, were of far more importance than the architectural, and indeed than all the artistic remains which it had left. They were held in the most absolute sense to be the springs of all knowledge. The literary conditions of that age of great discoveries have often been set forth; no more can here be attempted than to point out a few less-known features of the picture.

Great as was the influence of the old writers on the Italian mind in the fourteenth century and before, yet that influence was due rather to the wide diffusion of what had long been known than to the discovery of much that was new. The most popular Latin poets, historians, orators and letter-writers, together with a number of Latin translations of single works of Aristotle, Plutarch, and a few other Greek authors, constituted the treasure from which a few favoured individuals in the time of Petrarch and Boccaccio drew their inspiration. The former, as is well known, owned and kept with religious care a Greek Homer, which he was unable to read. A complete Latin translation of the Iliad and Odyssey, though a very bad one, was made at Petrarch's suggestion, and with Boccaccio's help, by a Calabrian Greek, Leonzio Pilato. But with the fifteenth century began the long list of new discoveries, the systematic creation of libraries by means of copies, and the rapid multiplication of translations from the Greek.

Had it not been for the enthusiasm of a few collectors of that age, who shrank from no effort or privation in their researches, we should certainly possess only a small part of the literature, especially that of the Greeks, which is now in our hands. Pope Nicholas V, when only a simple monk, ran deeply into debt through buying manuscripts

Picture Book No. 25 of the Victoria and Albert Museum, *Fifteenth-Century Italian Book Illustrations*. See also J. W. Appell, 'Facsimiles of 168 Wood-cuts in the *Polifili Hypnerotomachia*', with an introductory notice and description, London, 1889.)

or having them copied. Even then he made no secret of his passion for the two great interests of the Renaissance, books and buildings. As Pope he kept his word. Copyists wrote and spies searched for him through half the world. Perotto received 500 ducats for the Latin translation of Polybius; Guarino, 1,000 gold florins for that of Strabo, and he would have been paid 500 more but for the death of the Pope. Filelfo was to have received 10,000 gold florins for a metrical translation of Homer, and was only prevented by the Pope's death from coming from Milan to Rome. Nicholas left a collection of 5,000 or, according to another way of calculating, of 9,000 volumes, for the use of the members of the Curia, which became the foundation of the library of the Vatican. It was to be preserved in the palace itself, as its noblest ornament, like the library of Ptolemy Philadelphus at Alexandria. When the plague (1450) drove him and his court to Fabriano, whence then, as now, the best paper was procured, he took his translators and compilers with him, that he might run no risk of losing them.

The Florentine Niccolò Niccoli, a member of that accomplished circle of friends which surrounded the elder Cosimo de' Medici, spent his whole fortune in buying books. At last, when his money was all gone, the Medici put their purse at his disposal for any sum which his purpose might require. We owe to him the later books of Ammianus Marcellinus, the 'De Oratore' of Cicero, and other works; he persuaded Cosimo to buy the best manuscript of Pliny from a monastery at Lübeck. With noble confidence he lent his books to those who asked for them, allowed all comers to study them in his own house, and was ready to converse with the students on what they had read. His collection of 800 volumes, valued at 6,000 gold florins, passed after his death, through Cosimo's intervention, to the monastery of San Marco, on the condition that it should be accessible to the public.

Of the two great book-finders, Guarino and Poggio, the latter, on the occasion of the Council of Constance and acting partly as the agent of Niccoli, searched industriously among the abbeys of South Germany. He there discovered six orations of Cicero, and the first complete Quintilian, that of St. Gallen, now at Zürich; in thirty-two days he is said to have copied the whole of it in a beautiful handwriting. He was able to make important additions to Silius Italicus, Manilius, Lucretius, Valerius Flaccus, Asconius Pedianus, Columella, Celsus, Aulus Gellius, Statius, and others; and with the help of

Leonardo Aretino he unearthed the last twelve comedies of Plautus, as well as the Verrine orations.

The famous Greek, Cardinal Bessarion, in whom patriotism was mingled with a zeal for letters, collected, at a great sacrifice, 600 manuscripts of pagan and Christian authors. He then looked round for some receptacle where they could safely lie until his unhappy country, if she ever regained her freedom, could reclaim her lost literature. The Venetian government declared itself ready to erect a suitable building, and to this day the Biblioteca Marciana retains a part of these treasures.

The formation of the celebrated Medicean library has a history of its own, into which we cannot here enter. The chief collector for Lorenzo il Magnifico was Johannes Lascaris. It is well known that the collection, after the plundering in the year 1494, had to be recovered piecemeal by the Cardinal Giovanni Medici, afterwards Leo X.

The library of Urbino, now in the Vatican, was wholly the work of the great Federigo of Montefeltro (p. 29 sq.). As a boy he had begun to collect; in after years he kept thirty or forty 'scrittori' employed in various places, and spent in the course of time no less than 30,000 ducats on the collection. It was systematically extended and completed, chiefly by the help of Vespasiano, and his account of it forms an ideal picture of a library of the Renaissance. At Urbino there were catalogues of the libraries of the Vatican, of St. Mark at Florence, of the Visconti at Pavia, and even of the library at Oxford. It was noted with pride that in richness and completeness none could rival Urbino. Theology and the Middle Ages were perhaps most fully represented. There was a complete Thomas Aquinas, a complete Albertus Magnus, a complete Bonaventura. The collection, however, was a many-sided one, and included every work on medicine which was then to be had. Among the 'moderns' the great writers of the fourteenth century—Dante and Boccaccio, with their complete works—occupied the first place. Then followed twenty-five select humanists, invariably with both their Latin and Italian writings and with all their translations. Among the Greek manuscripts the Fathers of the Church far outnumbered the rest; yet in the list of the classics we find all the works of Sophocles, all of Pindar, and all of Menander. The last codex must have quickly disappeared from Urbino, else the philologists would have soon edited it.

We have, further, a good deal of information as to the way in which manuscripts and libraries were multiplied. The purchase of an ancient manuscript, which contained a rare, or the only complete, or the only existing text of an old writer, was naturally a lucky accident of which we need take no further account. Among the professional copyists those who understood Greek took the highest place, and it was they especially who bore the honourable name of 'scrittori'. Their number was always limited, and the pay they received very large. The rest, simply called 'copisti', were partly mere clerks who made their living by such work, partly schoolmasters and needy men of learning, who desired an addition to their income. The copyists at Rome in the time of Nicholas V were mostly Germans or Frenchmen—'barbarians' as the Italian humanists called them, probably men who were in search of favours at the papal court, and who kept themselves alive meanwhile by this means. When Cosimo de' Medici was in a hurry to form a library for his favourite foundation, the Badia below Fiesole, he sent for Vespasiano, and received from him the advice to give up all thoughts of purchasing books, since those which were worth getting could not be had easily, but rather to make use of the copyists; whereupon Cosimo bargained to pay him so much a day, and Vespasiano, with forty-five writers under him, delivered 200 volumes in twenty-two months. The catalogue of the works to be copied was sent to Cosimo by Nicholas V, who wrote it with his own hand. Ecclesiastical literature and the books needed for the choral services naturally held the chief place in the list.

The handwriting was that beautiful modern Italian which was already in use in the preceding century, and which makes the sight of one of the books of that time a pleasure. Pope Nicholas V, Poggio, Gianozzo Manetti, Niccolò Niccoli, and other distinguished scholars, themselves wrote a beautiful hand, and desired and tolerated none other. The decorative adjuncts, even when miniatures formed no part of them, were full of taste, as may be seen especially in the Laurentian manuscripts, with the light and graceful scrolls which begin and end the lines. The material used to write on, when the work was ordered by great or wealthy people, was always parchment; the binding, both in the Vatican and at Urbino, was a uniform crimson velvet with silver clasps. Where there was so much care to show honour to the contents of a book by the beauty of its outward form, it is intelligible that the sudden appearance of printed books was greeted at first with anything but favour. Federigo of Urbino 'would have been ashamed to own a printed book'.

But the weary copyists—not those who lived by the trade, but the many who were forced to copy a book in order to have it—rejoiced at the German invention. It was soon applied in Italy to the multiplication first of the Latin and then of the Greek authors, and for a long period nowhere but in Italy, yet it spread with by no means the rapidity which might have been expected from the general enthusiasm for these works. After a while the modern relation between author and publisher began to develop itself, and under Alexander VI, when it was no longer easy to destroy a book, as Cosimo could make Filelfo promise to do, the prohibitive censorship made its appearance.

* * *

The growth of textual criticism which accompanied the advancing study of languages and antiquity belongs as little to the subject of this book as the history of scholarship in general. We are here occupied, not with the learning of the Italians in itself, but with the reproduction of antiquity in literature and life. One word more on the studies themselves may still be permissible.

Greek scholarship was chiefly confined to Florence and to the fifteenth and the beginning of the sixteenth centuries. The impulse which had proceeded from Petrarch and Boccaccio, superficial as was their own acquaintance with Greek, was powerful, but did not tell immediately on their contemporaries, except a few; on the other hand, the study of Greek literature died out about the year 1520 with the last of the colony of learned Greek exiles, and it was a singular piece of fortune that northerners like Erasmus, the Stephani, and Budæus had meanwhile made themselves masters of the language. That colony had begun with Manuel Chrysoloras and his relation John, and with George of Trebizond. Then followed, about and after the time of the conquest of Constantinople, John Argyropulos, Theodore Gaza, Demetrios Chalcondylas, who brought up his sons Theophilos and Basilios to be excellent Hellenists, Andronikos Kallistos, Marcos Musuros and the family of the Lascaris, not to mention others. But after the subjection of Greece by the Turks was completed, the succession of scholars was maintained only by the sons of the fugitives and perhaps here and there by some Candian or Cyprian refugee. That the decay of Hellenistic studies began about the time of the death of Leo X was due partly to a general change of intellectual attitude, and to a certain satiety of classical influences which now made itself felt; but its coincidence with the death of the

Greek fugitives was not wholly a matter of accident. The study of Greek among the Italians appears, if we take the year 1500 as our standard, to have been pursued with extraordinary zeal. Many of those who then learned the language could still speak it half a century later, in their old age, like the Popes Paul III and Paul IV. But this sort of mastery of the study presupposes intercourse with native Greeks.

Besides Florence, Rome and Padua nearly always maintained paid teachers of Greek, and Verona, Ferrara, Venice, Perugia, Pavia and other cities occasional teachers. Hellenistic studies owed a priceless debt to the press of Aldo Manuzio at Venice, where the most important and voluminous writers were for the first time printed in the original. Aldo ventured his all in the enterprise; he was an editor and publisher whose like the world has rarely seen.

Along with this classical revival, Oriental studies now assumed considerable proportions. The controversial writings of the great Florentine statesman and scholar, Giannozzo Manetti (d. 1459) against the Jews afford an early instance of a complete mastery of their language and science. His son Agnolo was from his childhood instructed in Latin, Greek and Hebrew. The father, at the bidding of Nicholas V, translated the whole Bible afresh, as the philologists of the time insisted on giving up the 'Vulgata'.

Many other humanists devoted themselves before Reuchlin to the study of Hebrew, among them Pico della Mirandola, who was not satisfied with a knowledge of the Hebrew grammar and Scriptures, but penetrated into the Jewish Cabbalah and even made himself as familiar with the literature of the Talmud as any Rabbi.[50]

Among the Oriental languages, Arabic was studied as well as Hebrew. The science of medicine, no longer satisfied with the older Latin translations of the great Arab physicians, had constant recourse to the originals, to which an easy access was offered by the Venetian consulates in the East, where Italian doctors were regularly kept. Hieronimo Ramusio, a Venetian physician, translated a great part of Avicenna from the Arabic and died at Damascus in 1486. Andrea Mongaio of Belluno lived long at Damascus for the purpose of studying Avicenna, learnt Arabic, and emended the author's text.

★[50] Cf. Steinschneider and Cassel, *Jüdische Typographie*, in Ersch and Gruber's *Real-Enzyclopädie*, Section 2, Vol. XXVIII, p. 34 *et seq.*, and *Catal. Bodl.* by Steinschneider, pp. 2821, 2866: probably the first books printed with Hebrew types. See also Steinschneider's *Letteratura italiana dei Giudei*, Rome, 1884.

The Venetian government afterwards appointed him professor of this subject at Padua.

We must here linger for a moment over Pico della Mirandola, before passing on to the general effects of humanism. He was the only man who loudly and vigorously defended the truth and science of all ages against the one-sided worship of classical antiquity. He knew how to value not only Averroës and the Jewish investigators, but also the scholastic writers of the Middle Ages, according to the matter of their writings. In one of his writings he makes them say, 'We shall live for ever, not in the schools of word-catchers, but in the circle of the wise, where they talk not of the mother of Andromache or of the sons of Niobe, but of the deeper causes of things human and divine; he who looks closely will see that even the barbarians had intelligence (*mercurium*), not on the tongue but in the breast'. Himself writing a vigorous and not inelegant Latin, and a master of clear exposition, he despised the purism of pedants and the current over-estimate of borrowed forms, especially when joined, as they often are, with one-sidedness, and involving indifference to the wider truth of the things themselves. Looking at Pico, we can guess at the lofty flight which Italian philosophy would have taken had not the counter-reformation annihilated the higher spiritual life of the people.

THE HUMANISTS

Who now were those who acted as mediators between their own age and a venerated antiquity, and made the latter a chief element in the culture of the former?

They were a crowd of the most miscellaneous sort, wearing one face today and another tomorrow; but they clearly felt themselves, and it was fully recognized by their time that they formed, a wholly new element in society. The 'clerici vagantes' of the twelfth century may perhaps be taken as their forerunners—the same unstable existence, the same free and more than free views of life, and the germs at all events of the same pagan tendencies in their poetry. But now, as competitor with the whole culture of the Middle Ages, which was essentially clerical and was fostered by the Church, there appeared a new civilization, founding itself on that which lay on the other side of the Middle Ages. Its active representatives became influential because they knew what the ancients knew, because they tried to write as the ancients wrote, because they began to think, and soon to feel, as the ancients thought and felt. The tradition to which they devoted themselves passed at a thousand points into genuine reproduction.

Some modern writers deplore the fact that the germs of a far more independent and essentially national culture, such as appeared in Florence about the year 1300, were afterwards so completely swamped by the humanists. There was then, we are told, nobody in Florence who could not read; even the donkey-men sang the verses of Dante; the best Italian manuscripts which we possess belonged originally to Florentine artisans; the publication of a popular encyclopædia, like the 'Tesoro' of Brunetto Latini, was then possible; and all this was founded on a strength and soundness of character due to the universal participation in public affairs, to commerce and travel, and to the systematic reprobation of idleness. The Florentines, it is urged, were at that time respected and influential throughout the whole world, and were called in that year, not without reason, by Pope Boniface VIII, 'the fifth element'. The rapid progress of humanism after the year 1400 paralysed native impulses. Henceforth men looked only to antiquity for the solution of every problem, and consequently allowed literature to turn into mere quotation. Nay, the very fall of civil freedom is partly ascribed to all this, since the new learning rested on obedience to authority, sacrificed municipal rights to Roman law, and thereby both sought and found the favour of the despots.

These charges will occupy us now and then at a later stage of our inquiry, when we shall attempt to reduce them to their true value, and to weigh the losses against the gains of this movement. For the present we must confine ourselves to showing how the civilization even of the vigorous fourteenth century necessarily prepared the way for the complete victory of humanism, and how precisely the greatest representatives of the national Italian spirit were themselves the men who opened wide the gate for the measureless devotion to antiquity in the fifteenth century.

To begin with Dante. If a succession of men of equal genius had presided over Italian culture, whatever elements their natures might have absorbed from the antique, they still could not fail to retain a characteristic and strongly-marked national stamp. But neither Italy nor Western Europe produced another Dante, and he was and remained the man who first thrust antiquity into the foreground of national culture. In the 'Divine Comedy' he treats the ancient and the Christian worlds, not indeed as of equal authority, but as parallel to one another. Just as, at an earlier period of the Middle Ages, types and antitypes were sought in the history of the Old and New Testaments, so does Dante constantly bring together a Christian and a pagan illustration of the same fact. It must be remembered that the Christian cycle of history and legend was familiar, while the ancient was relatively unknown, was full of promise and of interest, and must necessarily have gained the upper hand in the competition for public sympathy when there was no longer a Dante to hold the balance between the two.

Petrarch, who lives in the memory of most people nowadays chiefly as a great Italian poet, owed his fame among his contemporaries far rather to the fact that he was a kind of living representative of antiquity, that he imitated all styles of Latin poetry, endeavoured by his voluminous historical and philosophical writings not to supplant but to make known the works of the ancients, and wrote letters that, as treatises on matters of antiquarian interest, obtained a reputation which to us is unintelligible, but which was natural enough in an age without handbooks.

It was the same with Boccaccio. For two centuries, when but little was known of the 'Decameron' north of the Alps, he was famous all over Europe simply on account of his Latin compilations on mythology, geography and biography. One of these, 'De Genealogia Deorum', contains in the fourteenth and fifteenth books a remarkable appendix, in which he discusses the position of the then youthful humanism with regard to the age. We must not be misled by his exclusive references to 'poesia', as closer observation shows that he means thereby the whole mental activity of the poet-scholars.[51] This it is whose enemies he so vigorously combats—the frivolous ignoramuses who have no soul for anything but debauchery; the sophistical theologian, to whom Helicon, the Castalian fountain, and the grove of Apollo were foolishness; the greedy lawyers, to whom poetry was a superfluity, since no money was to be made by it; finally the mendicant friars, described periphrastically, but clearly enough, who made free with their charges of paganism and immorality. Then follows the defence of poetry, the praise of it, and especially of the deeper and allegorical meanings which we must always attribute to it, and of that calculated obscurity which is intended to repel the dull minds of the ignorant.

[51] 'Poeta', even in Dante (*Vita Nuova*), means only a writer of Latin verses, while for Italian poets the expressions '*Rimatore, Dicitore per rima*' are used. It is true that the names and ideas became mixed in course of time.

And finally, with a clear reference to his own scholarly work,[52] the writer justifies the new relation in which his age stood to paganism. The case was wholly different, he pleads, when the Early Church had to fight its way among the heathen. Now—praised be Jesus Christ!—true religion was strengthened, paganism destroyed, and the victorious Church in possession of the hostile camp. It was now possible to touch and study paganism almost (*fere*) without danger. This is the argument invariably used in later times to defend the Renaissance.

There was thus a new cause in the world and a new class of men to maintain it. It is idle to ask if this cause ought not to have stopped short in its career of victory, to have restrained itself deliberately, and conceded the first place to purely national elements of culture. No conviction was more firmly rooted in the popular mind than that antiquity was the highest title to glory which Italy possessed.

There was a symbolical ceremony peculiar to the first generation of poet-scholars which lasted on into the fifteenth and sixteenth centuries, though losing the higher sentiment which inspired it—the coronation of the poets with the laurel wreath. The origin of this custom in the Middle Ages is obscure, and the ritual of the ceremony never became fixed. It was a public demonstration, an outward and visible expression of literary enthusiasm, and naturally its form was variable. Dante, for instance, seems to have understood it in the sense of a half-religious consecration; he desired to assume the wreath in the baptistery of San Giovanni, where, like thousands of other Florentine children, he had received baptism.[53] He could, says his biographer, have anywhere received the crown in virtue of his fame, but desired it nowhere but in his native city, and therefore died uncrowned. From the same source we learn that the usage was till then uncommon, and was held to be inherited by the ancient Romans from the Greeks. The most recent source to which the practices could be referred is to be found in the Capitoline contests of musicians, poets, and other artists, founded by Domitian in imitation of the Greeks and celebrated every five years, which may possibly have

[52] Boccaccio, in a later letter to Jacobus Pizinga (*Opere Volgari*, Vol. XVI), confines himself more strictly to poetry properly so called. And yet he only recognizes as poetry that which treated of antiquity, and ignores the Troubadours.

[53] Boccaccio, in his *Vita di Dante:* 'In Florence alone, and over the font of San Giovanni, was Dante disposed to take the crown, to the end that, where he had taken his first name by baptism, in that same place he might take his second name by coronation.' Cf. also *Paradiso*, XXV, 7–12.

survived for a time the fall of the Roman Empire; but as few other men would venture to crown themselves, as Dante desired to do, the question arises, to whom did this office belong? Albertino Mussato was crowned at Padua in 1310 by the bishop and the rector of the University. The University of Paris, the rector of which was then a Florentine (1341), and the municipal authorities of Rome, competed for the honour of crowning Petrarch. His self-elected examiner, King Robert of Anjou, would have liked to perform the ceremony at Naples, but Petrarch preferred to be crowned on the Capitol by the senator of Rome. This honour was long the highest object of ambition, and so it seemed to Jacobus Pizinga, an illustrious Sicilian magistrate. Then came the Italian journey of Charles IV, whom it amused to flatter the vanity of ambitious men, and impress the ignorant multitude by means of gorgeous ceremonies. Starting from the fiction that the coronation of poets was a prerogative of the old Roman emperors, and consequently was no less his own, he crowned (May 15, 1355) the Florentine scholar, Zanobi della Strada, at Pisa, to the great disgust of Boccaccio, who declined to recognize this 'laurea Pisana' as legitimate. Indeed, it might be fairly asked with what right this stranger, half Slavonic by birth, came to sit in judgement on the merits of Italian poets. But from henceforth the emperors crowned poets wherever they went on their travels; and in the fifteenth century the popes and other princes assumed the same right, till at last no regard whatever was paid to place or circumstances. In Rome, under Sixtus IV, the academy of Pomponius Lætus gave the wreath on its own authority. The Florentines had the good taste not to crown their famous humanists till after death. Carlo Aretino and Leonardo Aretino were thus crowned; the eulogy of the first was pronounced by Matteo Palmieri, of the latter by Giannozzo Manetti, before the members of the council and the whole people, the orator standing at the head of the bier, on which the corpse lay clad in a silken robe. Carlo Aretino was further honoured by a tomb in Santa Croce, which is among the most beautiful in the whole course of the Renaissance.

UNIVERSITIES AND SCHOOLS

The influence of antiquity on culture, of which we have now to speak, presupposes that the new learning had gained possession of the universities. This was so, but by no means to the extent and with the results which might have been expected.

Few of the Italian universities[54] show themselves in their full vigour till the thirteenth and fourteenth centuries, when the increase of wealth rendered a more systematic care for education possible. At first there were generally three sorts of professorships—one for civil law, another for canonical law, the third for medicine; in course of time professorships of rhetoric, of philosophy, and of astronomy were added, the last commonly, though not always, identical with astrology. The salaries varied greatly in different cases. Sometimes a capital sum was paid down. With the spread of culture, competition became so active that the different universities tried to entice away distinguished teachers from one another, under which circumstances Bologna is said to have sometimes devoted the half of its public income (20,000 ducats) to the university. The appointments were as a rule made only for a certain time, sometimes for only half a year, so that the teachers were forced to lead a wandering life, like actors. Appointments for life were, however, not unknown. Sometimes the promise was exacted not to teach elsewhere what had already been taught at one place. There were also voluntary, unpaid professors.

Of the chairs which have been mentioned, that of rhetoric was especially sought by the humanist; yet it depended only on his familiarity with the matter of ancient learning whether or no he could aspire to those of law, medicine, philosophy, or astronomy. The inward conditions of the science of the day were as variable as the outward conditions of the teacher. Certain jurists and physicians received by far the largest salaries of all, the former chiefly as consulting lawyers for the suits and claims of the State which employed them. In Padua a lawyer of the fifteenth century received a salary of 1,000 ducats, and it was proposed to appoint a celebrated physician with a yearly payment of 2,000 ducats, and the right of private practice, the same man having previously received 700 gold florins at Pisa. When the jurist Bartolommeo Socini, professor at Pisa, accepted

[54] Bologna, as is well known, was older than the other universities. Pisa flourished in the fourteenth century, fell through the wars with Florence, and was afterwards restored by Lorenzo il Magnifico, 'ad solatium veteris amissæ libertatis', as Giovio says. The university of Florence, which existed as early as 1321, with compulsory attendance for the natives of the city, was founded afresh after the Black Death in 1348, and endowed with an income of 2,500 gold florins, fell again into decay, and was refounded in 1357. The chair for the explanation of Dante, established in 1373 at the request of many citizens, was afterwards commonly united with the professorship of philology and rhetoric, as when Filelfo held it.

a Venetian appointment at Padua, and was on the point of starting on his journey, he was arrested by the Florentine government and only released on payment of bail to the amount of 18,000 gold florins. The high estimation in which these branches of science were held makes it intelligible why distinguished philologists turned their attention to law and medicine, while on the other hand specialists were more and more compelled to acquire something of a wide literary culture. We shall presently have occasion to speak of the work of the humanists in other departments of practical life.

Nevertheless, the position of the philologists, as such, even where the salary was large, and did not exclude other sources of income, was on the whole uncertain and temporary, so that one and the same teacher could be connected with a great variety of institutions. It is evident that change was desired for its own sake, and something fresh expected from each newcomer, as was natural at a time when science was in the making, and consequently depended to no small degree on the personal influence of the teacher. Nor was it always the case that a lecturer on classical authors really belonged to the university of the town where he taught. Communication was so easy, and the supply of suitable accommodation, in monasteries and elsewhere, was so abundant, that a private appointment was often practicable. In the first decades of the fifteenth century, when the University of Florence was at its greatest brilliance, when the courtiers of Eugenius IV, and perhaps even of Martin V thronged the lecture-room, when Carlo Aretino and Filelfo were competing for the largest audience, there existed, not only an almost complete university among the Augustinians of Santo Spirito, not only an association of scholars among the Camaldolesi of the Angeli, but individuals of mark, either singly or in common, arranged to provide philosophical and philological teaching for themselves and others. Linguistic and antiquarian studies in Rome had next to no connection with the university (Sapienza), and depended almost exclusively either on the favour of individual popes and prelates, or on the appointments made in the Papal chancery. It was not till Leo X (1513) that the great reorganization of the Sapienza took place, which now had eighty-eight lecturers, among whom there were the most able men of Italy, reading and interpreting the classics. But this new brilliancy was of short duration. We have already spoken briefly of the Greek professorships in Italy.

To form an accurate picture of the method of scientific instruction then pursued, we must turn away our eyes as far as possible from our present academic system. Personal intercourse between the teachers and the taught, public disputations, the constant use of Latin and often of Greek, the frequent changes of lecturers and the scarcity of books, gave the studies of that time a colour which we cannot represent to ourselves without effort.

There were Latin schools in every town of the least importance, not by any means merely as preparatory to higher education, but because, next to reading, writing, and arithmetic, the knowledge of Latin was a necessity; and after Latin came logic. It is to be noted particularly that these schools did not depend on the Church, but on the municipality; some of them, too, were merely private enterprises.

This school system, directed by a few distinguished humanists, not only attained a remarkable perfection of organization, but became an instrument of higher education inthe modern sense of the phrase. With the education of the children of two princely houses in North Italy institutions were connected which may be called unique of their kind.

At the court of Giovan Francesco Gonzaga at Mantua (1407–1444) appeared the illustrious Vittorino da Feltre, one of those men who devote their whole life to an object for which their natural gifts constitute a special vocation.

He directed the education of the sons and daughters of the princely house, and one of the latter became under his care a woman of learning. When his reputation extended far and wide over Italy, and members of great and wealthy families came from long distances, even from Germany, in search of his instructions, Gonzaga was not only willing that they should be received, but seems to have held it an honour for Mantua to be the chosen school of the aristocratic world. Here for the first time gymnastics and all noble bodily exercises were treated along with scientific instruction as indispensable to a liberal education. Besides these pupils came others, whose instruction Vittorino probably held to be his highest earthly aim, the gifted poor, whom he supported in his house and educated, 'per l'amore di Dio', along with the highborn youths who here learned to live under the same roof with untitled genius. Gonzaga paid him a yearly salary of 300 gold florins, and contributed to the expenses caused by the poorer pupils. He knew that Vittorino never saved a penny for himself, and doubtless realized that the education of the poor was the unexpressed condition of his presence. The establishment was conducted on strictly religious lines, stricter indeed than many monasteries.

More stress was laid on pure scholarship by Guarino of Verona (1370–1460), who in the year 1429 was called to Ferrara by Niccolò d'Este to educate his son Lionello, and who, when his pupil was nearly grown up in 1436, began to teach at the university of eloquence and of the ancient languages. While still acting as tutor to Lionello, he had many other pupils from various parts of the country, and in his own house a select class of poor scholars, whom he partly or wholly supported. His evening hours till far into the night were devoted to hearing lessons or to instructive conversation. His house, too, was the home of a strict religion and morality. It signified little to him or to Vittorino that most of the humanists of their day deserved small praise in the matter of morals or religion. It is inconceivable how Guarino, with all the daily work which fell upon him, still found time to write translations from the Greek and voluminous original works.

Not only in these two courts, but generally throughout Italy, the education of the princely families was in part and for certain years in the hands of the humanists, who thereby mounted a step higher in the aristocratic world. The writing of treatises on the education of princes, formerly the business of theologians, fell now within their province.

From the time of Pier Paolo Vergerio the Italian princes were well taken care of in this respect, and the custom was transplanted into Germany by Æneas Sylvius, who addressed detailed exhortations to two young German princes of the House of Habsburg on the subject of their further education, in which they are both urged, as might be expected, to cultivate and nurture humanism. Perhaps Æneas was aware that in addressing these youths he was talking in the air, and therefore took measures to put his treatise into public circulation. But the relations of the humanists to the rulers will be discussed separately.

PROPAGATORS OF ANTIQUITY

We have here first to speak of those citizens, mostly Florentines, who made antiquarian interests one of the chief objects of their lives, and who were themselves either distinguished scholars, or else distinguished *dilettanti* who maintained the scholars. They were of peculiar significance during the period of transition at the beginning of the fifteenth century, since it was in them that humanism first showed itself practically as an indispensable element in daily life. It was not till after this time that the popes and princes began seriously to occupy themselves with it.

Niccolò Niccoli and Giannozzo Manetti have been already spoken of more than once. Niccoli is described to us by Vespasiano as a man who would tolerate nothing around him out of harmony with his own classical spirit. His handsome long-robed figure, his kindly speech, his house adorned with the noblest remains of antiquity, made a singular impression. He was scrupulously cleanly in everything, most of all at table, where ancient vases and crystal goblets stood before him on the whitest linen. The way in which he won over a pleasure-loving young Florentine to intellectual interests is too charming not to be here described. Piero de' Pazzi, son of a distinguished merchant, and himself destined to the same calling, fair to behold, and much given to the pleasures of the world, thought about anything rather than literature. One day, as he was passing the Palazzo del Podestà, Niccolò called the young man to him, and although they had never before exchanged a word, the youth obeyed the call of one so respected. Niccolò asked him who his father was. He answered, 'Messer Andrea de' Pazzi'. When he was further asked what his pursuit was, Piero replied, as young people are wont to do, 'I enjoy myself' ('attendo a darmi buon tempo'). Niccolò said to him, 'As son of such a father, and so fair to look upon, it is a shame that thou knowest nothing of the Latin language, which would be so great an ornament to thee. If thou learnest it not, thou wilt be good for nothing, and as soon as the flower of youth is over, wilt be a man of no consequence' (*virtù*). When Piero heard this, he straightway perceived that it was true, and said that he would gladly take pains to learn, if only he had a teacher. Whereupon Niccolò answered that he would see to that. And he found him a learned man for Latin and Greek, named Pontano, whom Piero treated as one of his own house, and to whom he paid 100 gold florins a year. Quitting all the pleasures in which he had hitherto lived, he studied day and night, and became a friend of all learned men and a noble-minded statesman. He learned by heart the whole Æneid and many speeches of Livy, chiefly on the way between Florence and his country house at Trebbio. Antiquity was represented in another and higher sense by Giannozzo Manetti (1393–1459). Precocious from his first years, he was hardly more than a child when he had finished his apprenticeship in commerce and became book-keeper in a bank. But soon the life he led seemed to him empty and perishable, and he began to yearn after science, through which alone man can secure immortality. He then busied himself with books as few laymen had done before him, and became, as has been said, one of the most profound scholars of his time. When appointed by the government as its representative magistrate and tax-collector at Pescia and Pistoia, he fulfilled his duties in accordance with the lofty ideal with which his religious feeling and humanistic studies combined to inspire him. He succeeded in collecting the most unpopular taxes which the Florentine State imposed, and declined payment for his services. As provincial governor he refused all presents, abhorred all bribes, checked gambling, kept the country well supplied with corn, was indefatigable in settling lawsuits amicably, and did wonders in calming inflamed passions by his goodness. The Pistoiese were never able to discover to which of the two political parties he leaned. As if to symbolize the common rights and interests of all, he spent his leisure hours in writing the history of the city, which was preserved, bound in a purple cover, as a sacred relic in the town hall. When he took his leave the city presented him with a banner bearing the municipal arms and a splendid silver helmet.

For further information as to the learned citizens of Florence at this period the reader must all the more be referred to Vespasiano, who knew them all personally, because the tone and atmosphere in which he writes, and the terms and conditions on which he mixed in their society, are of even more importance than the facts which he records. Even in a translation, and still more in the brief indications to which we are here compelled to limit ourselves, this chief merit of his book is lost. Without being a great writer, he was thoroughly familiar with the subject he wrote on, and had a deep sense of its intellectual significance.

If we seek to analyse the charm which the Medici of the fifteenth century, especially Cosimo the Elder (d. 1464) and Lorenzo the Magnificent (d. 1492) exercised over Florence and over all their contemporaries, we shall find that it lay less in their political capacity than in their leadership in the culture of the age. A man in Cosimo's position—a great merchant and party leader, who also had on his side all the thinkers, writers and investigators, a man who was the first of the Florentines by birth and the first of the Italians by culture—such a man was to all intents and purposes already a prince. To Cosimo belongs the special glory of recognizing in the Platonic philosophy the fairest flower of the ancient world of thought,[55] of inspiring his

[55] What was known of Plato before can only have been fragmentary. A strange discussion on the antagonism of Plato and Aristotle took place at Ferrara in 1438, between Ugo of Siena and the Greeks who came to the Council.

friends with the same belief, and thus of fostering within humanistic circles themselves another and a higher resuscitation of antiquity. The story is known to us minutely. It all hangs on the calling of the learned Johannes Argyropulos, and on the personal enthusiasm of Cosimo himself in his last years, which was such that the great Marsilio Ficino could style himself, as far as Platonism was concerned, the spiritual son of Cosimo. Under Pietro Medici, Ficino was already at the head of a school; to him Pietro's son and Cosimo's grandson, the illustrious Lorenzo, came over from the Peripatetics. Among his most distinguished fellow-scholars were Bartolommeo Valori, Donato Acciaiuoli, and Pierfilippo Pandolfini. The enthusiastic teacher declares in several passages of his writings that Lorenzo had sounded all the depths of the Platonic philosophy, and had uttered his conviction that without Plato it would be hard to be a good Christian or a good citizen. The famous band of scholars which surrounded Lorenzo was united together, and distinguished from all other circles of the kind, by this passion for a higher and idealistic philosophy. Only in such a world could a man like Pico della Mirandola feel happy. But perhaps the best thing of all that can be said about it is, that, with all this worship of antiquity, Italian poetry found here a sacred refuge, and that of all the rays of light which streamed from the circle of which Lorenzo was the centre, none was more powerful than this. As a statesman, let each man judge him as he pleases; a foreigner will hesitate to pronounce what in the fate of Florence was due to human guilt and what to circumstances, but no more unjust charge was ever made than that in the field of culture Lorenzo was the protector of mediocrity, that through his fault Leonardo da Vinci and the mathematician Fra Luca Pacioli lived abroad, and that Toscanella, Vespucci, and others remained at least unsupported. He was not, indeed, a man of universal mind; but of all the great men who have striven to favour and promote spiritual interests, few certainly have been so many-sided, and in none probably was the inward need to do so equally deep.

The age in which we live is loud enough in proclaiming the worth of culture, and especially of the culture of antiquity. But the enthusiastic devotion to it, the recognition that the need of it is the first and greatest of all needs, is nowhere to be found in such a degree as among the Florentines of the fifteenth and the early part of the sixteenth centuries. On this point we have indirect proof which precludes all doubt. It would not have been so common to give the daughters of the house a share in the same studies, had they not been held to be the noblest of earthly pursuits; exile would not have been turned into a happy retreat, as was done by Palla Strozzi; nor would men who indulged in every conceivable excess have retained the strength and the spirit to write critical treatises on the Natural History of Pliny like Filippo Strozzi. Our business here is not to deal out either praise or blame, but to understand the spirit of the age in all its vigorous individuality.

Besides Florence, there were many cities of Italy where individuals and social circles devoted all their energies to the support of humanism and the protection of the scholars who lived among them. The correspondence of that period is full of references to personal relations of this kind. The feeling of the instructed classes set strongly and almost exclusively in this direction.

But it is now time to speak of humanism at the Italian courts. The natural alliance between the despot and the scholar, each relying solely on his personal talent, has already been touched upon; that the latter should avowedly prefer the princely courts to the free cities, was only to be expected from the higher pay which he there received. At a time when the great Alfonso of Aragon seemed likely to become master of all Italy, Æneas Sylvius wrote to another citizen of Siena: 'I had rather that Italy attained peace under his rule than under that of the free cities, for kingly generosity rewards excellence of every kind.' Too much stress has latterly been laid on the unworthy side of this relation, and the mercenary flattery to which it gave rise, just as formerly the eulogies of the humanists led to a too favourable judgement on their patrons. Taking all things together, it is greatly to the honour of the latter that they felt bound to place themselves at the head of the culture of their age and country, one-sided though this culture was. In some of the popes, the fearlessness of the consequences to which the new learning might lead strikes us as something truly, but unconsciously, imposing. Nicholas V was confident of the future of the Church, since thousands of learned men supported her. Pius II was far from making such splendid sacrifices for humanism as were made by Nicholas, and the poets who frequented his court were few in number; but he himself was much more the personal head of the republic of letters than his predecessor, and enjoyed his position without the least misgiving. Paul II was the first to dread and mistrust the culture of his secretaries, and his three successors, Sixtus, Innocent, and Alexander, accepted dedications and allowed themselves to be sung to the hearts' content of the poets—there even existed a 'Borgiad', probably in hexameters—but were too busy elsewhere, and too occupied in seeking other foundations for their power, to trouble themselves much about the poet-scholars. Julius II found poets to eulogize him, because he himself was no mean subject for poetry, but he doesnot seem to have troubled himself much about them. He was followed by Leo X, 'as Romulus by Numa'—in other words, after the warlike turmoil of the previous pontificate, a new one was hoped for wholly given to the muses. Enjoyment of elegant Latin prose and melodious verse was part of the programme of Leo's life, and his patronage certainly had the result that his Latin poets have left us a living picture of that joyous and brilliant spirit of the Leonine days, with which the biography of Jovius is filled, in countless epigrams, elegies, odes, and orations. Probably in all European history there is no prince who, in proportion to the few striking events of his life, has received such manifold homage. The poets had access to him chiefly about noon, when the musicians had ceased playing; but one of the best among them tells us how they also pursued him when he walked in his garden or withdrew to the privacy of his chamber, and if they failed to catch him there, would try to win him with a mendicant ode or elegy, filled, as usual, with the whole population of Olympus. For Leo, prodigal of his money, and disliking to be surrounded by any but cheerful faces, displayed a generosity in his gifts which was fabulously exaggerated in the hard times that followed. His reorganization of the Sapienza has been already spoken of. In order not to underrate Leo's influence on humanism we must guard against being misled by the toy-work that was mixed up with it, and must not allow ourselves to be deceived by the apparent irony with which he himself sometimes treated these matters. Our judgement must rather dwell on the countless spiritual possibilities which are included in the word 'stimulus', and which, though they cannot be measured as a whole, can still, on closer study, be actually followed out in particular cases. Whatever influence in Europe the Italian humanists have had since 1520 depends in some way or other on the impulse which was given by Leo. He was the Pope who in granting permission to print the newly found Tacitus, could say that the great writers were a rule of life and a consolation in misfortune; that helping learned men and obtaining excellent books had ever been one of his highest aims; and that he now thanked heaven that he could benefit the human race by furthering the publication of this book.

The sack of Rome in the year 1527 scattered the scholars no less than the artists in every direction, and spread the fame of the great departed Mæcenas to the farthest boundaries of Italy.

Among the secular princes of the fifteenth century, none displayed such enthusiasm for antiquity as Alfonso the Great of Aragon, King of Naples. It appears that his zeal was thoroughly unaffected, and that the monuments and writings of the ancient world made upon him, from the time of his arrival in Italy, an impression deep and powerful enough to reshape his life. With strange readiness he surrendered the stubborn Aragon to his brother, and devoted himself wholly to his new possessions. He had in his service, either successively or together, George of Trebizond, the younger Chrysoloras, Lorenzo Valla, Bartolommeo Fazio and Antonio Panormita, of whom the two latter were his historians; Panormita daily instructed the King and his court in Livy, even during military expeditions. These men cost him yearly 20,000 gold florins. He gave Panormita 1,000 for his work; Fazio received for the 'Historia Alfonsi', besides a yearly income of 500 ducats, a present of 1,500 more when it was finished, with the words, 'It is not given to pay you, for your work would not be paid for if I gave you the fairest of my cities; but in time I hope to satisfy you.' When he took Giannozzo Manetti as his secretary on the most brilliant conditions, he said to him, 'My last crust I will share with you.' When Giannozzo first came to bring the congratulations of the Florentine government on the marriage of Prince Ferrante, the impression he made was so great, that the King sat motionless on the throne, 'like a brazen statue, and did not even brush away a fly, which had settled on his nose at the beginning of the oration'. His favourite haunt seems to have been the library of the castle at Naples, where he would sit at a window overlooking the bay, and listen to learned debates on the Trinity. For he was profoundly religious, and had the Bible, as well as Livy and Seneca, read to him, till after fourteen perusals he knew it almost by heart. Who can fully understand the feeling with which he regarded the suppositious remains of Livy at Padua? When, by dint of great entreaties, he obtained an arm-bone of the skeleton from the Venetians, and received it with solemn pomp at Naples, how strangely Christian and pagan sentiment must have been blended in his heart! During a campaign in the Abruzzi, when the distant Sulmona, the birthplace of Ovid, was pointed out to him, he saluted the spot and returned thanks to its tutelary genius. It gladdened him to make good the prophecy of the great poet as to his future fame. Once indeed, at his famous entry into the conquered city of Naples (1443) he himself chose to appear before the world in ancient style. Not far from the market a breach forty ells wide was made in the wall, and through this he drove in a gilded chariot like a Roman Triumphator. The memory of the scene is preserved by a noble triumphal arch of marble in the Castello Nuovo. His Neapolitan successors inherited as little of this passion for antiquity as of his other good qualities.

Alfonso was far surpassed in learning by Federigo of Urbino, who had but few courtiers around him, squandered nothing, and in his appropriation of antiquity, as in all other things, went to work considerately. It was for him and for Nicholas V that most of the translations from the Greek, and a number of the best commentaries and other such works, were written. He spent much on the scholars whose services he used, but spent it to good purpose. There were no traces of a poets' court at Urbino, where the Duke himself was the most learned in the whole court. Classical antiquity, indeed, only formed a part of his culture. An accomplished ruler, captain, and gentleman, he had mastered the greater part of the science of the day, and this with a view to its practical application. As a theologian, he was able to compare Scotus with Aquinas, and was familiar with the writings of the old Fathers of the Eastern and Western Churches, the former in Latin translations. In philosophy, he seems to have left Plato altogether to his contemporary Cosimo, but he knew thoroughly not only the Ethics and Politics of Aristotle but the Physics and some other works. The rest of his reading lay chiefly among the ancient historians, all of whom he possessed; these, and not the poets, 'he was always reading and having read to him'.

The Sforza, too, were all of them men of more or less learning and patrons of literature; they have been already referred to in passing. Duke Francesco probably looked on humanistic culture as a matter of course in the education of his children, if only for political reasons. It was felt universally to be an advantage if a prince could mix with the most instructed men of his time on an equal footing. Lodovico il Moro, himself an excellent Latin scholar, showed an interest in intellectual matters which extended far beyond classical antiquity.

Even the petty rulers strove after similar distinctions, and we do them injustice by thinking that they only supported the scholars at their courts as a means of diffusing their own fame. A ruler like Borso of Ferrara, with all his vanity, seems by no means to have looked for immortality from the poets, eager as they were to propitiate him with a 'Borseid' and the like. He had far too proud a sense of his own position as a ruler for that. But intercourse with learned men, interest in antiquarian matters, and the passion for elegant Latin correspondence were necessities for the princes of that age. What bitter complaints are those of Duke Alfonso, competent as he was in practical matters, that his weakliness in youth had forced him to seek recreation in manual pursuits only! or was this merely an excuse to keep the humanists at a distance? A nature like his was not intelligible even to contemporaries.

Even the most insignificant despots of Romagna found it hard to do without one or two men of letters about them. The tutor and secretary were often one and the same person, who sometimes, indeed, acted as a kind of court factotum. We are apt to treat the small scale of these courts as a reason for dismissing them with a too ready contempt, forgetting that the highest spiritual things are not precisely matters of measurement.

Life and manners at the court of Rimini must have been a singular spectacle under the bold pagan Condottiere Sigismondo Malatesta. He had a number of scholars around him, some of whom he provided for liberally, even giving them landed estates, while others earned at least a livelihood as officers in his army. In his citadel—'arx Sismundea'—they used to hold discussions, often of a very venomous kind, in the presence of the 'rex', as they termed him. In their Latin poems they sing his praises and celebrate his amour with the fair Isotta, in whose honour and as whose monument the famous rebuilding of San Francesco at Rimini took place—'Divæ Isottæ Sacrum'. When the humanists themselves came to die, they were laid in or under the sarcophagi with which the niches of the outside walls of the church were adorned, with an inscription testifying that they were laid here at the time when Sigismundus, the son of Pandulfus, ruled. It is hard for us nowadays to believe that a monster like this prince felt learning and the friendship of cultivated people to be a necessity of life; and yet the man who excommunicated him, made war upon him, and burnt him in effigy, Pope Pius II, says: 'Sigismondo knew history and had a great store of philosophy; he seemed born to all that he undertook'.

REPRODUCTION OF ANTIQUITY: EPISTOLOGRAPHY: LATIN ORATORS

There were two purposes, however, for which the humanist was as indispensable to the republics as to princes or popes, namely, the official correspondence of the State, and the making of speeches on public and solemn occasions.

Not only was the secretary required to be a competent Latinist, but conversely, only a humanist was credited with the knowledge and ability necessary for the post of secretary. And thus the greatest men in the sphere of science during the fifteenth century mostly devoted a considerable part of their lives to serve the State in this capacity. No importance was attached to a man's home or origin. Of the four great Florentine secretaries who filled the office between 1427 and 1465, three belonged to the subject city of Arezzo, namely, Leonardo (Bruni), Carlo (Marzuppini), and Benedetto Accolti; Poggio was from Terra Nuova, also in Florentine territory. For a long period, indeed, many of the highest offices of State were on principle given to foreigners. Leonardo, Poggio, and Giannozzo Manetti were at one time or another private secretaries to the popes, and Carlo Aretino was to have been so. Biondo of Forlì, and, in spite of everything, at last even Lorenzo Valla, filled the same office. From the time of Nicholas V and Pius II onwards, the Papal chancery continued more and more to attract the ablest men, and this was still the case even under the last popes of the fifteenth century, little as they cared for letters. In Platina's 'History of the Popes', the life of Paul II is a charming piece of vengeance taken by a humanist on the one Pope who did not know how to behave to his chancery—to that circle 'of poets and orators who bestowed on the Papal court as much glory as they received from it'. It is delightful to see the indignation of these haughty gentlemen, when some squabble about precedence happened, when, for instance, the 'Advocati consistoriales' claimed equal or superior rank to theirs. The Apostle John, to whom the 'Secreta cœlestia' were revealed; the secretary of Porsenna, whom Mucius Scævola mistook for the king; Mæcenas, who was private secretary to Augustus; the archbishops, who in Germany were called chancellors, are all appealed to in turn. 'The apostolic secretaries have the most weighty business of the world in their hands. For who but they decide on matters of the Catholic faith, who else combat heresy, re-establish peace, and mediate between great monarchs; who but they write the statistical accounts of Christendom? It it they who astonish kings, princes, and nations by what comes forth from the Pope. They write commands and instructions for the legates, and receive their orders only from the Pope, on whom they wait day and night.' But the highest summit of glory was only attained by the two famous secretaries and stylists of Leo X: Pietro Bembo and Jacopo Sadoleto.

All the chanceries did not turn out equally elegant documents. A leathern official style, in the impurest of Latin, was very common. In the Milanese documents preserved by Corio there is a remarkable contrast between this sort of composition and the few letters written by members of the princely house, which must have been written, too, in moments of critical importance. They are models of pure Latinity. To maintain a faultless style under all circumstances was a rule of good breeding, and a result of habit.

The letters of Cicero, Pliny, and others, were at this time diligently studied as models. As early as the fifteenth century a great mass of manuals and models for Latin correspondence had appeared (as offshoots of the great grammatical and lexicographic works), a mass which is astounding to us even now when we look at them in the libraries. But just as the existence of these helps tempted many to undertake a task to which they had no vocation, so were the really capable men stimulated to a more faultless excellence, till at length the letters of Politian, and at the beginning of the sixteenth century those of Pietro Bembo, appeared, and took their place as unrivalled masterpieces, not only of Latin style in general, but also of the more special art of letter-writing.

Together with these there appeared in the sixteenth century the classical style of Italian correspondence, at the head of which stands Bembo again. Its form is wholly modern, and deliberately kept free from Latin influence, and yet its spirit is thoroughly penetrated and possessed by the ideas of antiquity.

But at a time and among a people where 'listening' was among the chief pleasures of life, and where every imagination was filled with the memory of the Roman senate and its great speakers, the orator occupied a far more brilliant place than the letter-writer. Eloquence had shaken off the influence of the Church, in which it had found a refuge during the Middle Ages, and now became an indispensable element and ornament of all elevated lives. Many of the social hours which are now filled with music were then given to Latin or Italian oratory, with results which every reader can imagine.

The social position of the speaker was a matter of perfect indifference; what was desired was simply the most cultivated humanistic talent. At the court of Borso of Ferrara, the Duke's physician, Girolamo da Castello, was chosen to deliver the congratulatory address on the visits of Frederick III and of Pius II. Married laymen ascended the pulpits of the churches at any scene of festivity or mourning, and even on the feast-days of the saints. It struck the non-Italian members of the Council of Basle as something strange that the Archbishop of Milan should summon Æneas Sylvius, who was then unordained, to deliver a public discourse at the feast of Saint Ambrose; but they suffered it in spite of the murmurs of the theologians, and listened to the speaker with the greatest curiosity.

Let us glance for a moment at the most frequent and important occasions of public speaking.

It was not for nothing, in the first place, that the ambassadors from one State to another received the title of orators. Whatever else might be done in the way of secret negotiation, the envoy never failed to make a public appearance and deliver a public speech, under circumstances of the greatest possible pomp and ceremony. As a rule, however numerous the embassy might be, one individual spoke for all; but it happened to Pius II, a critic before whom all were glad to be heard, to be forced to sit and listen to a whole deputation, one after another. Learned princes who had the gift of speech were themselves fond of discoursing in Latin or Italian. The children of the House of Sforza were trained to this exercise. The boy Galeazzo Maria delivered in 1455 a fluent speech before the Great Council at Venice, and his sister Ippolita saluted Pope Pius II with a graceful address at the Congress of Mantua (1459). Pius himself through all his life did much by his oratory to prepare the way for his final elevation to the Papal chair. Great as he was both as scholar and diplomatist, he would probably never have become Pope without the fame and the charm of his eloquence. 'For nothing was more lofty than the dignity of his oratory.' Without doubt this was a reason why multitudes held him to be the fittest man for the office even before his election.

Princes were also commonly received on public occasions with speeches, which sometimes lasted for hours. This happened of course only when the prince was known as a lover of eloquence,[56] or wished to pass for such, and when a competent speaker was present, whether university professor, official, ecclesiastic, physician, or court-scholar.

Every other political opportunity was seized with the same eagerness, and according to the reputation of the speaker, the concourse of the lovers of culture was great or small. At the yearly change of public officers, and even at the consecration of new bishops, a humanist was sure to come forward, and sometimes addressed his audience in hexameters or Sapphic verses. Often a newly appointed official was himself forced to deliver a speech more or less relevant to his department, as, for instance, on justice; and lucky for him if he were well up in his part! At Florence even the Condottieri, whatever their origin or education might be, were compelled to accommodate themselves to the popular sentiment, and on receiving the insignia of their office, were harangued before the assembled people by the most learned secretary of state. It seems that beneath or close to the Loggia de' Lanzi—the porch where the government was wont to appear solemnly before the people—a tribune or platform (*rostra, ringhiera*) was erected for such purposes.

Anniversaries, especially those of the death of princes, were commonly celebrated by memorial speeches. Even the funeral oration strictly so called was generally entrusted to a humanist, who delivered it in church, clothed in a secular dress; nor was it only princes, but officials, or persons otherwise distinguished, to whom this honour was paid. This was also the case with the speeches delivered at weddings or betrothals, with the difference that they seem to have been made in the palace, instead of in church, like that of Filelfo at the betrothal of Anna Sforza to Alfonso of Este in the castle of Milan. It is still possible that the ceremony may have taken place in the chapel of the castle. Private families of distinction no doubt also employed such wedding orators as one of the luxuries of high life. At Ferrara, Guarino was requested on these occasions to send some one or other of his pupils. The clergy performed only the purely religious ceremonies at weddings and funerals.

The academical speeches, both those made at the installation of a new teacher and at the opening of a new course of lectures, were

[56] Charles V, when unable on one occasion to follow the flourishes of a Latin orator at Genoa, whispered in the ear of Paolo Giovio: 'Ah, my tutor Adrian was right when he told me I should be chastened for my childish idleness in learning Latin.'

delivered by the professor himself, and treated as occasions of great rhetorical display. The ordinary university lectures also usually had an oratorical character.

With regard to forensic eloquence, the quality of the audience determined the form of speech. In case of need it was enriched with all sorts of philosophical and antiquarian learning.

As a special class of speeches we may mention the address made in Italian on the battlefield, either before or after the combat. Federigo of Urbino was esteemed a classic in this style; he used to pass round among his squadrons as they stood drawn up in order of battle, inspiring them in turn with pride and enthusiasm. Many of the speeches in the military historians of the fifteenth century, as for instance in Porcellius (p. 63), may be, in part at least, imaginary, but may be also in part faithful representations of words actually spoken. The addresses again which were delivered to the Florentine Militia, organized in 1506 chiefly through the influence of Machiavelli, and which were spoken first at reviews, and afterwards at special annual festivals, were of another kind. They were simply general appeals to the patriotism of the hearers, and were addressed to the assembled troops in the church of each quarter of the city by a citizen in armour, sword in hand.

Finally, the oratory of the pulpit began in the fifteenth century to lose its distinctive peculiarities. Many of the clergy had entered into the circle of classical culture, and were ambitious of success in it. The street-preacher Bernardino da Siena, who even in his lifetime passed for a saint and who was worshipped by the populace, was not above taking lessons in rhetoric from the famous Guarino, although he had only to preach in Italian. Never indeed was more expected from preachers than at that time—especially from the Lenten preachers; and there were not a few audiences which could not only tolerate, but which demanded a strong dose of philosophy from the pulpit. But we have here especially to speak of the distinguished occasional preachers in Latin. Many of their opportunities had been taken away from them, as has been observed, by learned laymen. Speeches on particular saints' days, at weddings and funerals, or at the installation of a bishop, and even the introductory speech at the first mass of a clerical friend, or the address at the festival of some religious order, were all left to laymen. But at all events at the Papal court in the fifteenth century, whatever the occasion might be, the preachers were generally monks. Under Sixtus IV, Giacomo da

Volterra regularly enumerates these preachers, and criticizes them according to the rules of the art. Fedra Inghirami, famous as an orator under Julius II, had at least received holy orders and was canon at St. John Lateran; and besides him, elegant Latinists were now common enough among the prelates. In this matter, as in others, the exaggerated privileges of the profane humanists appear lessened in the sixteenth century—on which point we shall presently speak more fully.

What now was the subject and general character of these speeches? The national gift of eloquence was not wanting to the Italians of the Middle Ages, and a so-called 'rhetoric' belonged from the first to the seven liberal arts; but so far as the revival of the ancient methods is concerned, this merit must be ascribed, according to Filippo Villani, to the Florentine Bruno Casini, who died of the plague in 1348. With the practical purpose of fitting his countrymen to speak with ease and effect in public, he treated, after the pattern of the ancients, invention, declamation, bearing, and gesticulation, each in its proper connection. Elsewhere too we read of an oratorical training directed solely to practical application. No accomplishment was more highly esteemed that the power of elegant improvisation in Latin. The growing study of Cicero's speeches and theoretical writings, of Quintilian and of the imperial panegyrists, the appearance of new and original treatises, the general progress of antiquarian learning, and the stores of ancient matter and thought which now could and must be drawn from—all combined to shape the character of the new eloquence.

This character nevertheless differed widely according to the individual. Many speeches breathe a spirit of true eloquence, especially those which keep to the matter treated of; of this kind is the mass of what is left to us of Pius II. The miraculous effects produced by Giannozzo Manetti point to an orator the like of whom has not been often seen. His great audiences as envoy before Nicholas V and before the Doge and Council of Venice were events not to be soon forgotten. Many orators, on the contrary, would seize the opportunity, not only to flatter the vanity of distinguished hearers, but to load their speeches with an enormous mass of antiquarian rubbish. How it was possible to endure this infliction for two and even three hours, can only be understood when we take into account the intense interest then felt in everything connected with antiquity, and the rarity and defectiveness of treatises on the subject at a time when printing was but little diffused Such orations had at least the value which we have claimed (p. 122) for many of Petrarch's letters. But some speakers went too far. Most of Filelfo's speeches are an atrocious patchwork of classical and biblical quotations, tacked on to a string of commonplaces, among which the great people he wishes to flatter are arranged under the head of the cardinal virtues, or some such category, and it is only with the greatest trouble, in his case and in that of many others, that we can extricate the few historical notices of any value which they really contain. The speech, for instance, of a scholar and professor of Piacenza at the reception of the Duke Galeazzo Maria, in 1467, begins with Julius Cæsar, then proceeds to mix up a mass of classical quotations with a number from an allegorical work by the speaker himself, and concludes with some exceedingly indiscreet advice to the ruler. Fortunately it was late at night, and the orator had to be satisfied with handing his written panegyric to the prince. Filelfo begins a speech at a betrothal with the words: 'Aristotle, the peripatetic'. Others start with P. Cornelius Scipio, and the like, as though neither they nor their hearers could wait a moment for a quotation. At the end of the fifteenth century public taste suddenly improved, chiefly through Florentine influence, and the practice of quotation was restricted within due limits. Many works of reference were now in existence, in which the first comer could find as much as he wanted of what had hitherto been the admiration of princes and people.

As most of the speeches were written out beforehand in the study, the manuscripts served as a means of further publicity afterwards. The great extemporaneous speakers, on the other hand, were attended by shorthand writers. We must further remember that not all the orations which have come down to us were intended to be actually delivered. The panegyric, for example, of the elder Beroaldus on Lodovico il Moro was presented to him in manuscript. In fact, just as letters were written addressed to all conceivable persons and parts of the world as exercises, as formularies, or even to serve a controversial end, so there were speeches for imaginary occasions to be used as models for the reception of princes, bishops, and other dignitaries.

For oratory, as for the other arts, the death of Leo X (1521) and the sack of Rome (1527) mark the epoch of decadence. Giovio, but just escaped from the desolation of the eternal city, described, not impartially, but on the whole correctly, the causes of this decline:

'The plays of Plautus and Terence, once a school of Latin style for the educated Romans, are banished to make room for Italian comedies. Graceful speakers no longer find the recognition and reward which they once did. The Consistorial advocates no longer prepare anything but the introductions to their speeches, and deliver the rest—a confused muddle—on the inspiration of the moment. Sermons and occasional speeches have sunk to the same level. If a funeral oration is wanted for a cardinal or other great personage, the executors do not apply to the best orators in the city, to whom they would have to pay a hundred pieces of gold, but they hire for a trifle the first impudent pedant whom they come across, and who only wants to be talked of, whether for good or ill. The dead, they say, is none the wiser if an ape stands in a black dress in the pulpit, and beginning with a hoarse, whimpering mumble, passes little by little into a loud howling. Even the sermons preached at great Papal ceremonies are no longer profitable, as they used to be. Monks of all orders have again got them into their hands, and preach as if they were speaking to the mob. Only a few years ago a sermon at mass before the Pope might easily lead the way to a bishopric.'

THE TREATISE, AND HISTORY IN LATIN

From the oratory and the epistolary writings of the humanists, we shall here pass on to their other creations, which were all, to a greater or less extent, reproductions of antiquity.

Among these must be placed the treatise, which often took the shape of a dialogue. In this case it was borrowed directly from Cicero. In order to do anything like justice to this class of literature—in order not to throw it aside at first sight as a bore—two things must be taken into consideration. The century which escaped from the influence of the Middle Ages felt the need of something to mediate between itself and antiquity in many questions of morals and philosophy; and this need was met by the writer of treatises and dialogues. Much which appears to us as mere commonplace in their writings, was for them and their contemporaries a new and hard-won view of things upon which mankind had been silent since the days of antiquity. The language too, in this form of writing, whether Italian or Latin, moved more freely and flexibly than in historical narrative, in letters, or in oratory, and thus became in itself the source of a special pleasure. Several Italian compositions of this kind still hold their place as patterns of style. Many of these works have been, or will be mentioned on account of their contents; we here refer to them as a class. From the time of Petrarch's letters and treatises down to near the end of the fifteenth century, the heaping up of learned quotations, as in the case of the orators, is the main business of most of these writers. Subsequently the whole style, especially in Italian, was purified, until, in the 'Asolani' of Bembo, and the 'Vita Sobria' of Luigi Cornaro, a classical perfection was reached. Here too the decisive fact was this, that antiquarian matter of every kind had meantime begun to be deposited in encyclopædic works (now printed), and no longer stood in the way of the essayist.

It was inevitable too that the humanistic spirit should control the writing of history. A superficial comparison of the histories of this period with the earlier chronicles, especially with works so full of life, colour, and brilliancy as those of the Villani, will lead us loudly to deplore the change. How insipid and conventional appear by their side the best of the humanists, and particularly their immediate and most famous successors among the historians of Florence, Leonardo Aretino and Poggio! The enjoyment of the reader is incessantly marred by the sense that, in the classical phrases of Fazio, Sabellico, Foglietta, Senarega, Platina in the chronicles of Mantua, Bembo in the annals of Venice, and even of Giovio in his histories, the best local and individual colouring and the full sincerity of interest in the truth of events have been lost. Our mistrust is increased when we hear that Livy, the pattern of this school of writers, was copied just where he is least worthy of imitation—on the ground, namely, 'that he turned a dry and naked tradition into grace and richness'. In the same place we meet with the suspicious declaration that it is the function of the historian—just as if he were one with the poet—to excite, charm, or overwhelm the reader. We ask ourselves finally, whether the contempt for modern things, which these same humanists sometimes avowed openly must not necessarily have had an unfortunate influence on their treatment of them. Unconsciously the reader finds himself looking with more interest and confidence on the unpretending Latin and Italian annalists, like those of Bologna and Ferrara, who remained true to the old style, and still more grateful does he feel to the best of the genuine chroniclers who wrote in Italian—to Marino Sanuto, Corio, and Infessura—who were followed at the beginning of the sixteenth century by that new and illustrated band of great national historians who wrote in their mother tongue.

Contemporary history, no doubt, was written far better in the language of the day than when forced into Latin. Whether Italian was also more suitable for the narrative of events long past, or for historical research, is a question which admits, for that period, of more answers than one. Latin was, at that time, the 'Lingua franca' of instructed people, not only in an international sense, as a means of intercourse between Englishmen, Frenchmen, and Italians, but also in an interprovincial sense. The Lombard, the Venetian, and the Neapolitan modes of writing, though long modelled on the Tuscan, and bearing but slight traces of the dialect, were still not recognized by the Florentines. This was of less consequence in local contemporary histories, which were sure of readers at the place where they were written, than in the narratives of the past, for which a larger public was desired. In these the local interests of the people had to be sacrificed to the general interests of the learned. How far would the influence of a man like Biondo of Forlì have reached if he had written his great monuments of learning in the dialect of the Romagna? They would have assuredly sunk into neglect, if only through the contempt of the Florentines, while written in Latin they exercised the profoundest influence on the whole European world of learning. And even the Florentines in the fifteenth century wrote Latin, not only because their minds were imbued with humanism, but in order to be more widely read.

Finally, there exist certain Latin essays in contemporary history which stand on a level with the best Italian works of the kind. When the continuous narrative after the manner of Livy—that Procrustean bed of so many writers—is abandoned, the change is marvellous. The same Platina and Giovio, whose great histories we only read because and so far as we must, suddenly come forward as masters in the biographical style. We have already spoken of Tristano Caracciolo, of the biographical works of Fazio and of the Venetian topography of Sabellico, and others will be mentioned in the sequel.

The Latin treatises on past history were naturally concerned, for the most part, with classical antiquity. What we are most surprised to find among these humanists are some considerable works on the history of the Middle Ages. The first of this kind was the chronicle of Matteo Palmieri (449–1449), beginning where Prosper Aquitanus ceases. On opening the 'Decades' of Biondo of Forlì, we are surprised to find a universal history, 'ab inclinatione Romanorum imperii', as in Gibbon, full of original studies on the authors of each century, and occupied, through the first 300 folio pages, with early mediæval history down to the death of Frederick II. And this when in Northern countries nothing more was current than chronicles of the popes and emperors, and the 'Fasciculus temporum'. We cannot here stay to show what writings Biondo made use of, and where he found his materials, though this justice will some day be done to him by the historians of literature. This book alone would entitle us to say that it was the study of antiquity which made the study of the Middle Ages possible, by first training the mind to habits of impartial historical criticism. To this must be added, that the Middle Ages were now over for Italy, and that the Italian mind could the better appreciate them, because it stood outside them. It cannot, nevertheless, be said that it at once judged them fairly, let alone with piety. In the arts a strong prejudice established itself against all that those centuries had created, and the humanists date the new era from the time of their own appearance. 'I begin,' says Boccaccio, 'to hope and believe that God has had mercy on the Italian name, since I see that His infinite goodness puts souls into the breasts of the Italians like those of the ancients—souls which seek fame by other means than robbery and violence, but rather on the path of poetry, which makes men immortal.' But this narrow and unjust temper did not preclude investigation in the minds of the more gifted men, at a time, too, when elsewhere in Europe any such investigation would have been out of the question. A historical criticism of the Middle Ages was practicable, just because the rational treatment of all subjects by the humanists had trained the historical spirit. In the fifteenth century this spirit had so far penetrated the history even of the individual cities of Italy that the stupid fairy tales about the origin of Florence, Venice, and Milan vanished, while at the same time, and long after, the chronicles of the North were stuffed with this fantastic rubbish, destitute for the most part of all poetical value, and invented as late as the fourteenth century.

The close connection between local history and the sentiment of glory has already been touched on in reference to Florence. Venice would not be behindhand. Just as a great rhetorical triumph of the Florentines would cause a Venetian embassy to write home post-haste for an orator to be sent after them, so too the Venetians felt the need of a history which would bear comparison with those of

Leonardo Aretino and Poggio. And it was to satisfy this feeling that, in the fifteenth century, the 'Decades' of Sabellico appeared, and in the sixteenth the 'Historia rerum Venetarum' of Pietro Bembo, both written at the express charge of the republic, the latter a continuation of the former.

The great Florentine historians at the beginning of the sixteenth century were men of a wholly different kind from the Latinists Bembo and Giovio. They wrote Italian, not only because they could not vie with the Ciceronian elegance of the philologists, but because, like Machiavelli, they could only record in a living tongue the living results of their own immediate observations—and we may add in the case of Machiavelli, of his observation of the past—and because, as in the case of Guicciardini, Varchi, and many others, what they most desired was, that their view of the course of events should have as wide and deep a practical effect as possible. Even when they only write for a few friends, like Francesco Vettori, they feel an inward need to utter their testimony on men and events, and to explain and justify their share in the latter.

And yet, with all that is characteristic in their language and style, they were powerfully affected by antiquity, and, without its influence, would be inconceivable. They were not humanists, but they had passed through the school of humanism and have in them more of the spirit of the ancient historians than most of the imitators of Livy. Like the ancients, they were citizens who wrote for citizens.

ANTIQUITY AS THE COMMON SOURCE

We cannot attempt to trace the influence of humanism in the special sciences. Each has its own history, in which the Italian investigators of this period, chiefly through their rediscovery of the results, attained by antiquity,[57] mark a new epoch, with which the modern period of the science in question begins with more or less distinctness. With regard to philosophy, too, we must refer the reader to the special historical works on the subject. The influence of the old philosophers on Italian culture will appear at times immense, at times inconsiderable; the former, when we consider how the doctrines of Aristotle, chiefly drawn from the Ethics and Politics—both widely diffused at an early period—became the common property of educated

[57] In fact, it was then held that Homer alone contained the whole of the arts and sciences—that he was an encyclopædia.

Italians, and how the whole method of abstract thought was governed by him; the latter, when we remember how slight was the dogmatic influence of the old philosophies, and even of the enthusiastic Florentine Platonists, on the spirit of the people at large. What looks like such an influence is generally no more than a consequence of the new culture in general, and of the special growth and development of the Italian mind. When we come to speak of religion, we shall have more to say on this head. But in by far the greater number of cases, we have to do, not with the general culture of the people, but with the utterances of individuals or of learned circles; and here, too, a distinction must be drawn between the true assimilation of ancient doctrines and fashionable make-believe. For with many, antiquity was only a fashion, even among very learned people.

Nevertheless, all that looks like affectation to our age, need not then have actually been so. The giving of Greek and Latin names to children, for example, is better and more respectable than the present practice of taking them, especially the female names, from novels. When the enthusiasm for the ancient world was greater than for the saints, it was simple and natural enough that noble families called their sons Agamemnon, Tydeus, and Achilles, and that a painter named his son Apelles and his daughter Minerva.[58] Nor will it appear unreasonable that, instead of a family name, which people were often glad to get rid of, a well-sounding ancient name was chosen. A local name, shared by all residents in the place, and not yet transformed into a family name, was willingly given up, especially when its religious associations made it inconvenient. Filippo da San Gimignano called himself Callimachus. The man, misunderstood and insulted by his family, who made his fortune as a scholar in foreign cities, could afford, even if he were a Sanseverino, to change his name to Julius Pomponius Lætus. Even the simple translation of a name into Latin or Greek, as was almost uniformly the custom in Germany, may be excused to a generation which spoke and wrote Latin, and which needed names that could be not only declined, but used with facility in verse and prose. What was blameworthy and ridiculous

[58] Vasari, in the Life of Sodoma and in that of Garofalo (ed. Le Monnier, XI, pp. 189, 257). It is not surprising that the profligate women of Rome took the most sonorous ancient names—Julia, Lucretia, Cassandra, Portia, Virginia, Penthesilea, under which they appear in Aretino. It was, perhaps, then that the Jews took the names of the great Semitic enemies of the Romans—Hannibal, Hamilcar, Hasdrubal—which even now they commonly bear in Rome.

was the change of half a name, baptismal or family, to give it a classical sound and a new sense. Thus Giovanni was turned into Jovianus or Janus, Pietro to Petreius or Pierius, Antonio to Aonius, Sannazaro to Syncerus, Luca Grasso to Lucius Crassus. Ariosto, who speaks with such derision of all this, lived to see children called after his own heroes and heroines.

Nor must we judge too severely the latinization of many usages of social life, such as the titles of officials, of ceremonies, and the like, in the writers of the period. As long as people were satisfied with a simple, fluent Latin style, as was the case with most writers from Petrarch to Æneas Sylvius, this practice was not so frequent and striking; it became inevitable when a faultless, Ciceronian Latin was demanded. Modern names and things no longer harmonized with the style, unless they were first artificially changed. Pedants found a pleasure in addressing municipal counsellors as 'Patres Conscripti', nuns as 'Virgines Vestales', and entitling every saint 'Divus' or 'Deus'; but men of better taste, such as Paolo Giovio, only did so when and because they could not help it. But as Giovio does it naturally, and lays no special stress upon it, we are not offended if, in his melodious language, the cardinals appear as 'Senatores', their dean as 'Princeps Senatus', excommunication as 'Dirae', and the carnival as 'Lupercalia'. The example of this author alone is enough to warn us against drawing a hasty inference from these peculiarities of style as to the writer's whole mode of thinking.

The history of Latin composition cannot here be traced in detail. For fully two centuries the humanists acted as if Latin were, and must remain, the only language worthy to be written. Poggio deplores that Dante wrote his great poem in Italian; and Dante, as is well known, actually made the attempt in Latin, and wrote the beginning of the 'Inferno' first in hexameters. The whole future of Italian poetry hung on his not continuing in the same style, but even Petrarch relied more on his Latin poetry than on the Sonnets and 'Canzoni', and Ariosto himself was desired by some to write his poem in Latin. A stronger coercion never existed in literature; but poetry shook it off for the most part, and it may be said, without the risk of too great optimism, that it was well for Italian poetry to have had both means of expressing itself. In both something great and characteristic was achieved, and in each we can see the reason why Latin or Italian was chosen. Perhaps the same may be said of prose. The position and influence of Italian culture throughout the world depended on the fact that certain subjects were treated in Latin—'urbi et orbi'—while Italian prose was written best of all by those to whom it cost an inward struggle not to write in Latin.

From the fourteenth century Cicero was recognized universally as the purest model of prose. This was by no means due solely to a dispassionate opinion in favour of his choice of language, of the structure of his sentences, and of his style of composition, but rather to the fact that the Italian spirit responded fully and instinctively to the amiability of the letter-writer, to the brilliancy of the orator, and to the lucid exposition of the philosophical thinker. Even Petrarch recognized clearly the weakness of Cicero as a man and a statesman, though he respected him too much to rejoice over them. After Petrarch's time, the epistolary style was formed entirely on the pattern of Cicero; and the rest, with the exception of the narrative style, followed the same influence. Yet the true Ciceronianism, which rejected every phrase which could not be justified out of the great authority, did not appear till the end of the fifteenth century, when the grammatical writings of Lorenzo Valla had begun to tell on all Italy, and when the opinions of the Roman historians of literature had been sifted and compared. Then every shade of difference in the style of the ancients was studied with closer and closer attention till the consoling conclusion was at last reached that in Cicero alone was the perfect model to be found, or, if all forms of literature were to be embraced, in 'that immortal and almost heavenly age of Cicero'. Men like Pietro Bembo and Pierio Valeriano now turned all their energies to this one object. Even those who had long resisted the tendency, and had formed for themselves an archaic style from the earlier authors, yielded at last, and joined in the worship of Cicero. Longolius, at Bembo's advice, determined to read nothing but Cicero for five years long, and finally took an oath to use no word which did not occur in this author. It was this temper which broke out at last in the great war among the scholars, in which Erasmus and the elder Scaliger led the battle.

For all the admirers of Cicero were by no means so one-sided as to consider him the only source of language. In the fifteenth century, Politian and Ermolao Barbaro made a conscious and deliberate effort to form a style of their own, naturally on the basis of their 'overflowing' learning, and our informant of this fact, Paolo Giovio, pursued the same end. He first attempted, not always successfully, but often with remarkable power and elegance, and at no small cost of effort, to reproduce in Latin a number of modern, particularly of æsthetic, ideas. His Latin characteristics of the great painters and sculptors of his time contain a mixture of the most intelligent and of the most blundering interpretation. Even Leo X, who placed his glory in the fact, 'ut lingua latina nostro pontificatu dicatur facta auctior', was inclined to a liberal and not too exclusive Latinity, which, indeed, was in harmony with his pleasure-loving nature. He was satisfied if the Latin which he had to read and to hear was lively, elegant, and idiomatic. Then, too, Cicero offered no model for Latin conversation, so that here other gods had to be worshipped beside him. The want was supplied by representations of the comedies of Plautus and Terence, frequent both in and out of Rome, which for the actors were an incomparable exercise in Latin as the language of daily life. A few years later, in the pontificate of Paul II, the learned Cardinal of Teano (probably Niccolò Forteguerra of Pistoia) became famous for his critical labours in this branch of scholarship. He set to work upon the most defective plays of Plautus, which were destitute even of a list of the characters, and went carefully through the whole remains of this author, chiefly with an eye to the language. Possibly it was he who gave the first impulse for the public representations of these plays. Afterwards Pomponius Lætus took up the same subject, and acted as producer when Plautus was put on the stage in the houses of great churchmen. That these representations became less common after 1520, is mentioned by Giovio, as we have seen, among the causes of the decline of eloquence.

We may mention, in conclusion, the analogy between Ciceronianism in literature and the revival of Vitruvius by the architects in the sphere of art. And here, too, the law holds good which prevails elsewhere in the history of the Renaissance, that each artistic movement is preceded by a corresponding movement in the general culture of the age. In this case, the interval is not more than about twenty years, if we reckon from Cardinal Adrian of Corneto (1505?) to the first avowed Vitruvians.

NEO-LATIN POETRY

The chief pride of the humanists is, however, their modern Latin poetry. It lies within the limits of our task to treat of it, at least in so far as it serves to characterize the humanistic movement.

How favourable public opinion was to that form of poetry, and how nearly it supplanted all others, has been already shown. We may be very sure that the most gifted and highly developed nation then existing in the world did not renounce the use of a language such as the Italian out of mere folly and without knowing what they were doing. It must have been a weighty reason which led them to do so.

This cause was the devotion to antiquity. Like all ardent and genuine devotion it necessarily prompted men to imitation. At other times and among other nations we find many isolated attempts of the same kind. But only in Italy were the two chief conditions present which were needful for the continuance and development of neo-Latin poetry: a general interest in the subject among the instructed classes, and a partial re-awakening of the old Italian genius among the poets themselves—the wondrous echo of a far-off strain. The best of what is produced under these conditions is not imitation, but free production. If we decline to tolerate any borrowed forms in art, if we either set no value on antiquity at all, or attribute to it some magical and unapproachable virtue, or if we will pardon no slips in poets who were forced, for instance, to guess or to discover a multitude of syllabic quantities, then we had better let this class of literature alone. Its best works were not created in order to defy criticism, but to give pleasure to the poet and to thousands of his contemporaries.

The least success of all was attained by the epic narratives drawn from the history or legends of antiquity. The essential conditions of a living epic poetry were denied, not only to the Romans who now served as models, but even to the Greeks after Homer. They could not be looked for among the Latins of the Renaissance. And yet the 'Africa' of Petrarch probably found as many and as enthusiastic readers and hearers as any epos of modern times. Purpose and origin of the poem are not without interest. The fourteenth century recognized with sound historical sense that the time of the second Punic war had been the noonday of Roman greatness; and Petrarch could not resist writing of this time. Had Silius Italicus been then discovered, Petrarch would probably have chosen another subject; but as it was, the glorification of Scipio Africanus the Elder was so much in accordance with the spirit of the fourteenth century, that another poet, Zanobi di Strada, also proposed to himself the same task, and only from respect for Petrarch withdrew the poem with which he had already made great progress. If any justification were sought for the 'Africa', it lies in the fact that in Petrarch's time and afterwards Scipio was as much an object of public interest as if he were then alive, and that he was regarded as greater than Alexander, Pompey, and Cæsar. How many modern epics treat of a subject at once so popular, so historical in its basis, and so striking to the imagination? For us, it is true, the poem is unreadable. For other themes of the same kind the reader may be referred to the histories of literature.

A richer and more fruitful vein was discovered in expanding and completing the Greco-Roman mythology. In this too, Italian poetry began early to take a part, beginning with the 'Teseid' of Boccaccio, which passes for his best poetical work. Under Martin V, Maffeo Vegio wrote in Latin a thirteenth book to the Æneid; besides which we meet with many less considerable attempts, especially in the style of Claudian—a 'Meleagris', a 'Hesperis', and so forth. Still more curious were the newly-invented myths, which peopled the fairest regions of Italy with a primæval race of gods, nymphs, genii, and even shepherds, the epic and bucolic styles here passing into one another. In the narrative or conversational eclogue after the time of Petrarch, pastoral life was treated in a purely conventional manner, as a vehicle of all possible feelings and fancies; and this point will be touched on again in the sequel.[59] For the moment, we have only to do with the new myths. In them, more clearly than anywhere else, we see the double significance of the old gods to the men of the Renaissance. On the one hand, they replace abstract terms in poetry, and render allegorical figures superfluous; and, on the other, they serve as free and independent elements in art, as forms of beauty which can be turned to some account in any and every poem. The example was boldly set by Boccaccio, with his fanciful world of gods and shepherds who people the country round Florence in his 'Ninfale d'Ameto' and 'Ninfale Fiesolano'. Both these poems were written in Italian. But the masterpiece in this style was the 'Sarca' of Pietro Bembo, which tells how the river-god of that name wooed the nymph Garda; of the brilliant marriage feast in a cave of Monte Baldo; of the prophecies of Manto, daughter of Tiresias; of the birth of the child Mincius; of the founding of Mantua, and of the future glory of Virgil, son of Mincius and of Magia, nymph of Andes. This humanistic rococo is set forth by Bembo in verses of great beauty, concluding with an address to Virgil, which any poet might envy him. Such works are often slighted as mere declamation. This is a matter of taste on which we are all free to form our own opinion.

[59] The brilliant exceptions, where rural life is treated realistically, will also be mentioned below.

Further, we find long epic poems in hexameters on biblical or ecclesiastical subjects. The authors were by no means always in search of preferment or of papal favour. With the best of them, and even with less gifted writers, like Battista Mantovano, the author of the 'Parthenice', there was probably an honest desire to serve religion by their Latin verses—a desire with which their half-pagan conception of Catholicism harmonized well enough. Gyraldus goes through a list of these poets, among whom Vida, with his 'Christiad' and Sannazaro, with his three books, 'De partu Virginis' hold the first place. Sannazaro (b. 1458, d. 1530) is impressive by the steady and powerful flow of his verse, in which Christian and pagan elements are mingled without scruple, by the plastic vigour of his description, and by the perfection of his workmanship. He could venture to introduce Virgil's fourth Eclogue into his song of the shepherds at the manger without fearing a comparison. In treating of the unseen world, he sometimes gives proofs of a boldness worthy of Dante, as when King David in the Limbo of the Patriarchs rises up to sing and prophesy, or when the Eternal, sitting on the throne clad in a mantle shining with pictures of all the elements, addresses the heavenly host. At other times he does not hesitate to weave the whole classical mythology into his subject, yet without spoiling the harmony of the whole, since the pagan deities are only accessory figures, and play no important part in the story. To appreciate the artistic genius of that age in all its bearings, we must not refuse to notice such works as these. The merit of Sannazaro will appear the greater, when we consider that the mixture of Christian and pagan elements is apt to disturb us much more in poetry than in the visual arts. The latter can still satisfy the eye by beauty of form and colour, and in general are much more independent of the significance of the subject than poetry. With them, the imagination is interested chiefly in the form, with poetry, in the matter. Honest Battista Mantovano, in his calendar of the festivals, tried another expedient. Instead of making the gods and demigods serve the purposes of sacred history, he put them, as the Fathers of the Church did, in active opposition to it. When the angel Gabriel salutes the Virgin at Nazareth, Mercury flies after him from Carmel, and listens at the door. He then announces the result of his eavesdropping to the assembled gods, and stimulates them thereby to desperate resolutions. Elsewhere, it is true, in his writings, Thetis, Ceres, Æolus, and other pagan deities pay willing homage to the glory of the Madonna.

The fame of Sannazaro, the number of his imitators, the enthusiastic homage which was paid to him by the greatest men, all show how dear and necessary he was to his age. On the threshold of the Reformation he solved for the Church the problem, whether it were possible for a poet to be a Christian as well as a classic; and both Leo and Clement were loud in their thanks for his achievements.

And, finally, contemporary history was now treated in hexameters or distichs, sometimes in a narrative and sometimes in a panegyrical style, but most commonly to the honour of some prince or princely family. We thus meet with a Sforziad, a Borseid, a Laurentiad, a Borgiad, a Trivulziad, and the like. The object sought after was certainly not attained; for those who became famous and are now immortal owe it to anything rather than to this sort of poems, for which the world has always had an ineradicable dislike, even when they happen to be written by good poets. A wholly different effect is produced by smaller, simpler and more unpretentious scenes from the lives of distinguished men, such as the beautiful poem on Leo X's 'Hunt at Palo', or the 'Journey of Julius II' by Adrian of Corneto. Brilliant descriptions of hunting-parties are found in Ercole Strozzi, in the above-mentioned Adrian, and in others; and it is a pity that the modern reader should allow himself to be irritated or repelled by the adulation with which they are doubtless filled. The masterly treatment and the considerable historical value of many of these most graceful poems guarantee to them a longer existence than many popular works of our own day are likely to attain.

In general, these poems are good in proportion to the sparing use of the sentimental and the general. Some of the smaller epic poems, even of recognized masters, unintentionally produce, by the ill-timed introduction of mythological elements, an impression that is indescribably ludicrous. Such, for instance, is the lament of Ercole Strozzi on Cesare Borgia. We there listen to the complaint of Roma, who had set all her hopes on the Spanish Popes, Calixtus III and Alexander VI, and who saw her promised deliverer in Cesare. His history is related down to the catastrophe of 1503. The poet then asks the Muse what were the counsels of the gods at that moment, and Erato tells how, upon Olympus. Pallas took the part of the Spaniards, Venus of the Italians, how both then embrace the knees of Jupiter, how thereupon he kisses them, soothes them, and explains to them that he can do nothing against the fate woven by the Parcæ, but that the divine promises will be fulfilled by the child of the House of

Este-Borgia.[60] After relating the fabulous origin of both families, he declares that he can confer immortality on Cesare as little as he could once, in spite of all entreaties, on Memnon or Achilles; and concludes with the consoling assurance that Cesare, before his own death, will destroy many people in war. Mars then hastens to Naples to stir up war and confusion, while Pallas goes to Nepi, and there appears to the dying Cesare under the form of Alexander VI. After giving him the good advice to submit to his fate and be satisfied with the glory of his name, the papal goddess vanishes 'like a bird'.

Yet we should needlessly deprive ourselves of an enjoyment which is sometimes very great, if we threw aside everything in which classical mythology plays a more or less appropriate part. Here, as in painting and sculpture, art has often ennobled what is in itself purely conventional. The beginnings of parody are also to be found by lovers of that class of literature, e.g. in the Macaroneid—to which the comic Feast of the Gods, by Giovanni Bellini, forms an early parallel.

Many, too, of the narrative poems in hexameters are merely exercises, or adaptations of histories in prose, which latter the reader will prefer, where he can find them. At last, everything—every quarrel and every ceremony—came to be put into verse, and this even by the German humanists of the Reformation. And yet it would be unfair to attribute this to mere want of occupation, or to an excessive facility in stringing verses together. In Italy, at all events, it was rather due to an abundant sense of style, as is further proved by the mass of contemporary reports, histories, and even pamphlets, in the 'terza rima'. Just as Niccolò da Uzzano published his scheme for a new constitution, Machiavelli his view of the history of his own time, a third, the life of Savonarola, and a fourth the siege of Piombino by Alfonso the Great, in this difficult metre, in order to produce a stronger effect, so did many others feel the need of hexameters, in order to win their special public. What was then tolerated and demanded, in this shape, is best shown by the didactic poetry of the time. Its popularity in the fifteenth century is something astounding. The most distinguished humanists were ready to celebrate in Latin hexameters the most commonplace, ridiculous, or disgusting themes, such as the making of gold, the game of chess, the management of silkworms, astrology, and venereal diseases (*morbus gallicus*), to say nothing of many long

[60] This was Ercole II of Ferrara, born April 4, 1508, probably either shortly before or shortly after the composition of this poem. '*Nascere, magne puer, matri expectate patrique*', is said near the end.

Italian poems of the same kind. Nowadays this class of poem is condemned unread, and how far, as a matter of fact, they are really worth the reading, we are unable to say. One thing is certain: epochs far above our own in the sense of beauty—the Renaissance and the Greco-Roman world—could not dispense with this form of poetry. It may be urged in reply, that it is not the lack of a sense of beauty, but the greater seriousness and the altered method of scientific treatment which renders the poetical form inappropriate, on which point it is unnecessary to enter.

One of these didactic works has of late years been occasionally republished—the 'Zodiac of Life', by Marcellus Palingenius (Pier Angelo Manzolli), a secret adherent of Protestantism at Ferrara, written about 1528. With the loftiest speculations on God, virtue, and immortality, the writer connects the discussion of many questions of practical life, and is, on this account, an authority of some weight in the history of morals. On the whole, however, his work must be considered as lying outside the boundaries of the Renaissance, as is further indicated by the fact that, in harmony with the serious didactic purpose of the poem, allegory tends to supplant mythology.

But it was in lyric, and more particularly in elegiac poetry, that the poet-scholar came nearest to antiquity; and next to this, in epigram.

In the lighter style, Catullus exercised a perfect fascination over the Italians. Not a few elegant Latin madrigals, not a few little satires and malicious epistles, are mere adaptations from him; and the death of parrots and lapdogs is bewailed, even where there is no verbal imitation, in precisely the tone and style of the verses on Lesbia's sparrow. There are short poems of this sort, the date of which even a critic would be unable to fix, in the absence of positive evidence that they are works of the fifteenth and sixteenth centuries.

On the other hand, we can find scarcely an ode in the Sapphic or Alcaic metre, which does not clearly betray its modern origin. This is shown mostly by a rhetorical verbosity, rare in antiquity before the time of Statius, and by a singular want of the lyrical concentration which is indispensable to this style of poetry. Single passages in an ode, sometimes two or three strophes together, may look like an ancient fragment; but a longer extract will seldom keep this character throughout. And where it does so, as, for instance, in the fine Ode to Venus, by Andrea Navagero, it is easy to detect a simple paraphrase of ancient masterpieces. Some of the ode-writers take the saints for their subject, and invoke them in verses tastefully modelled after the pattern of analogous odes of Horace and Catullus. This is the manner of Navagero, in the Ode to the Archangel Gabriel, and particularly of Sannazaro (p. 155), who goes still further in his appropriation of pagan sentiment. He celebrates above all his patron saint, whose chapel was attached to his lovely villa on the shores of Posilippo, 'there where the waves of the sea drink up the stream from the rocks, and surge against the walls of the little sanctuary'. His delight is in the annual feast of St. Nazzaro, and the branches and garlands with which the chapel is hung on this day seem to him like sacrificial gifts. Full of sorrow, and far off in exile, at St. Nazaire, on the banks of the Loire, with the banished Federigo of Aragon, he brings wreaths of box and oak leaves to his patron saint on the same anniversary, thinking of former years, when all the youth of Posilippo used to come forth to greet him on flower-hung boats, and praying that he may return home.

Perhaps the most deceptive likeness to the classical style is borne by a class of poems in elegiacs or hexameters, whose subject ranges from elegy, strictly so called, to epigram. As the humanists dealt most freely of all with the text of the Roman elegiac poets, so they felt themselves most at home in imitating them. The elegy of Navagero addressed to the Night, like other poems of the same age and kind, is full of points which remind us of his model; but it has the finest antique ring about it. Indeed Navagero always begins by choosing a truly poetical subject, which he then treats, not with servile imitation, but with masterly freedom, in the style of the Anthology, of Ovid, of Catullus, or of the Virgilian eclogues. He makes a sparing use of mythology, only, for instance, to introduce a sketch of country life, in a prayer to Ceres and other rural divinities. An address to his country, on his return from an embassy to Spain, though left unfinished, might have been worthy of a place beside the 'Bella Italia, amate sponde' of Vincenzo Monti, if the rest had been equal to this beginning:

> 'Salve cura Deûm, mundi felicior ora,
> Formosae Veneris dulces salvete recessus;
> Ut vos post tantos animi mentisque labores
> Aspicio lustroque libens, ut munere vestro
> Sollicitas toto depello e pectore curas!'

The elegiac or hexametric form was that in which all higher sentiment found expression, both the noblest patriotic enthusiasm and the most elaborate eulogies on the ruling houses, as well as the tender melancholy of a Tibullus. Francesco Maria Molza, who rivals Statius and Martial in his flattery of Clement VII and the Farnesi, gives us in his elegy to his 'comrades', written from a sick-bed, thoughts on death as beautiful and genuinely antique as can be found in any of the poets of antiquity, and this without borrowing anything worth speaking of from them. The spirit and range of Roman elegy were best understood and reproduced by Sannazaro, and no other writer of his time offers us so varied a choice of good poems in this style as he. We shall have occasion now and then to speak of some of these elegies in reference to the matter they treat of.

The Latin epigram finally became in those days an affair of serious importance, since a few clever lines, engraved on a monument or quoted with laughter in society, could lay the foundation of a scholar's celebrity. This tendency showed itself early in Italy. When it was known that Giudo da Polenta wished to erect a monument at Dante's grave, epitaphs poured in from all directions, 'written by such as wished to *show themselves*, or to honour the dead poet, or to win the favour of Polenta'. On the tomb of the Archbishop Giovanni Visconti (d. 1354), in the Cathedral at Milan, we read at the foot of thirty-six hexameters: 'Master Gabrius de Zamoreis of Parma, Doctor of Laws, wrote these verses.' In course of time, chiefly under the influence of Martial, and partly of Catullus, an extensive literature of this sort was formed. It was held the greatest of all triumphs, if an epigram was mistaken for a genuine copy from some old marble, or if it was so good that all Italy learned it by heart, as happened in the case of some of Bembo's. When the Venetian government paid Sannazaro 600 ducats for a eulogy in three distichs, no one thought it an act of generous prodigality. The epigram was prized for what it was, in truth, to all the educated classes of that age—the concentrated essence of fame. Nor, on the other hand, was any man then so powerful as to be above the reach of a satirical epigram, and even the most powerful needed, for every inscription which they set before the public eye, the aid of careful and learned scholars, lest some blunder or other should qualify it for a place in the collections of ludicrous epitaphs. Epigraphy and literary epigrams began to link up; the former was based on a most diligent study of the ancient monuments.

The city of epigrams and inscriptions was, above all others, Rome. In this state without hereditary honours, each man had to look after his own immortality, and at the same time found the epigram an effective weapon against competitors. Pius II enumerates with satisfaction the distichs which his chief poet Campanus wrote on any event of his government which could be turned to poetical account. Under the following popes satirical epigrams came into fashion, and reached, in the opposition to Alexander VI and his family, the highest pitch of defiant invective. Sannazaro, it is true, wrote his verses in a place of comparative safety, but others in the immediate neighbourhood of the court ventured on the most reckless attacks. On one occasion when eight threatening distichs were found fastened to the doors of the library, Alexander strengthened his guard by 800 men; we can imagine what he would have done to the poet if he had caught him. Under Leo X, Latin epigrams were like daily bread. For complimenting or for reviling the Pope, for punishing enemies and victims, named or unnamed, for real or imaginary subjects of wit, malice, grief, or contemplation, no form was held more suitable. On the famous group of the Virgin with Saint Anne and the Child, which Andrea Sansovino carved for Sant' Agostino, no fewer than 120 persons wrote Latin verses, not so much, it is true, from devotion, as from regard for the patron who ordered the work. This man, Johann Goritz of Luxemburg, papal referendary of petitions, not only held a religious service on the feast of Saint Anne, but gave a great literary dinner in his garden on the slopes of the Capitol. It was then worth while to pass in review, in a long poem 'De poetis urbanis', the whole crowd of singers who sought their fortune at the court of Leo. This was done by Franciscus Arsillus—a man who needed the patronage neither of pope nor prince, and who dared to speak his mind, even against his colleagues. The epigram survived the pontificate of Paul III only in a few rare echoes, while epigraphy continued to flourish till the seventeenth century, when it perished finally of bombast.

In Venice, also, this form of poetry had a history of its own, which we are able to trace with the help of the 'Venezia' of Francesco Sansovino. A standing task for the epigram-writers was offered by the mottoes (Brievi) on the pictures of the Doges in the great hall of the ducal palace—two or four hexameters, setting forth the most noteworthy facts in the government of each. In addition to this, the tombs of the Doges in the fourteenth century bore short inscriptions in prose, recording merely facts, and beside them turgid hexameters or leonine verses. In the fifteenth century more care was taken with the style; in the sixteenth century it is seen at its best; and then soon after came pointless antithesis, prosopopœia, false pathos, praise of abstract qualities—in a word, affectation and bombast. A good many traces of satire can be detected, and veiled criticism of the living is implied in open praise of the dead. At a much later period we find a few instances of deliberate recurrence to the old, simple style.

Architectural works and decorative works in general were constructed with a view to receiving inscriptions, often in frequent repetition; while the Northern Gothic seldom, and with difficulty, offered a suitable place for them, and in sepulchral monuments, for example, left free only the most exposed parts—namely the edges.

By what has been said hitherto we have, perhaps, failed to convince the reader of the characteristic value of this Latin poetry of the Italians. Our task was rather to indicate its position and necessity in the history of civilization. In its own day, a caricature of it appeared—the so-called macaronic poetry. The masterpiece of this style, the 'opus macaronicorum', was written by Merlinus Coccaius (Teofilo Folengo of Mantua). We shall now and then have occasion to refer to the matter of this poem. As to the form—hexameter and other verses, made up of Latin words and Italian words with Latin endings—its comic effect lies chiefly in the fact that these combinations sound like so many slips of the tongue, or like the effusions of an over-hasty Latin 'improvisatore'. The German imitations do not give the smallest notion of this effect.

FALL OF THE HUMANISTS IN THE SIXTEENTH CENTURY

After a brilliant succession of poet-scholars had, since the beginning of the fourteenth century, filled Italy and the world with the worship of antiquity, had determined the forms of education and culture, had often taken the lead in political affairs and had, to no small extent, reproduced ancient literature—at length in the sixteenth century, before their doctrines and scholarship had lost hold of the public mind, the whole class fell into deep and general disgrace. Though they still served as models to the poets, historians and orators, personally no one would consent to be reckoned of their number. To the two chief accusations against them—that of malicious self-conceit, and that of abominable profligacy—a third charge of irreligion was now loudly added by the rising powers of the Counter-reformation.

Why, it may be asked, were not these reproaches, whether true or false, heard sooner? As a matter of fact, they were heard at a very early period, but the effect they produced was insignificant, for the plain reason that men were far too dependent on the scholars for their knowledge of antiquity—that the scholars were personally the possessors and diffusers of ancient culture. But the spread of printed editions of the classics, and of large and well-arranged handbooks and dictionaries, went far to free the people from the necessity of personal intercourse with the humanists, and, as soon as they could be but partly dispensed with, the change in popular feeling became manifest. It was a change under which the good and bad suffered indiscriminately.

The first to make these charges were certainly the humanists themselves. Of all men who ever formed a class, they had the least sense of their common interests, and least respected what there was of this sense. All means were held lawful, if one of them saw a chance of supplanting another. From literary discussion they passed with astonishing suddenness to the fiercest and the most groundless vituperation. Not satisfied with refuting, they sought to annihilate an opponent. Something of this must be put to the account of their position and circumstances; we have seen how fiercely the age, whose loudest spokesmen they were, was borne to and fro by the passion for glory and the passion for satire. Their position, too, in practical life was one that they had continually to fight for. In such a temper they wrote and spoke and described one another. Poggio's works alone contain dirt enough to create a prejudice against the whole class—and these 'Opera Poggii' were just those most often printed, on the north as well as on the south side of the Alps. We must take care not to rejoice too soon, when we meet among these men a figure which seems immaculate; on further inquiry there is always a danger of meeting with some foul charge, which, even if it is incredible, still discolours the picture. The mass of indecent Latin poems in circulation, and such things as ribaldry on the subject of one's own family, as in Pontano's dialogue 'Antonius', did the rest to discredit the class. The sixteenth century was not only familiar with all these ugly symptoms, but had also grown tired of the type of the humanist. These men had to pay both for the misdeeds they had done, and for the excess of honour which had hitherto fallen to their lot. Their evil fate willed it that the greatest poet of the nation, Ariosto, wrote of them in a tone of calm and sovereign contempt.

Of the reproaches which combined to excite so much hatred, many were only too well founded. Yet a clear and unmistakable tendency to strictness in matters of religion and morality was alive in many of the philologists, and it is a proof of small knowledge of the period, if the whole class is condemned. Yet many, and among them the loudest speakers, were guilty.

Three facts explain and perhaps diminish their guilt: the overflowing excess of fervour and fortune, when the luck was on their side; the uncertainty of the future, in which luxury or misery depended on the caprice of a patron or the malice of an enemy; and finally, the misleading influence of antiquity. This undermined their morality, without giving them its own instead; and in religious matters, since they could never think of accepting the positive belief in the old gods, it affected them only on the negative and sceptical side. Just because they conceived of antiquity dogmatically—that is, took it as the model for all thought and action—its influence was here pernicious. But that an age existed which idolized the ancient world and its products with an exclusive devotion was not the fault of individuals. It was the work of an historical providence, and all the culture of the ages which have followed, and of the ages to come, rests upon the fact that it was so, and that all the ends of life but this one were then deliberately put aside.

The career of the humanists was, as a rule, of such a kind that only the strongest characters could pass through it unscathed. The first danger came, in some cases, from the parents, who sought to turn a precocious child into a miracle of learning, with an eye to his future position in that class which then was supreme. Youthful prodigies, however, seldom rise above a certain level; or, if they do, are forced to achieve their further progress and development at the cost of the bitterest trials. For an ambitious youth, the fame and the brilliant position of the humanists were a perilous temptation; it seemed to him that he too 'through inborn pride could no longer regard the low and common things of life'. He was thus led to plunge into a life of excitement and vicissitude, in which exhausting studies, tutorships, secretaryships, professorships, offices in princely households, mortal enmities and perils, luxury and beggary, boundless admiration and boundless contempt, followed confusedly one upon the other, and in which the most solid worth and learning were often pushed aside by superficial impudence. But the worst of all was, that the position of the humanist was almost incompatible with a fixed home, since it either made frequent changes of dwelling necessary for a livelihood, or so affected the mind of the individual that he could never be happy for long in one place. He grew tired of the people, and had no peace among the enmities which he excited, while the people themselves in their turn demanded something new. Much as this life reminds us of the Greek sophists of the Empire, as described to us by Philostratus, yet the position of the sophists was more favourable. They often had money, or could more easily do without it than the humanists, and as professional teachers of rhetoric, rather than men of learning, their life was freer and simpler. But the scholar of the Renaissance was forced to combine great learning with the power of resisting the influence of ever-changing pursuits and situations. Add to this the deadening effect of licentious excess, and—since do what he might, the worst was believed of him—a total indifference to the moral laws recognized by others. Such men can hardly be conceived to exist without an inordinate pride. They needed it, if only to keep their heads above water, and were confirmed in it by the admiration which alternated with hatred in the treatment they received from the world. They are the most striking examples and victims of an unbridled subjectivity.

The attacks and the satirical pictures began, as we have said, at an early period. For all strongly marked individuality, for every kind of distinction, a corrective was at hand in the national taste for ridicule. And in this case the men themselves offered abundant and terrible materials which satire had but to make use of. In the fifteenth century, Battista Mantovano, in discoursing of the seven monsters, includes the humanists, with many others, under the head 'Superbia'. He describes how, fancying themselves children of Apollo, they walk along with affected solemnity and with sullen, malicious looks, now gazing at their own shadow, now brooding over the popular praise they hunted after, like cranes in search of food. But in the sixteenth century the indictment was presented in full. Besides Ariosto, their own historian Gyraldus gives evidence of this, whose treatise, written under Leo X, was probably revised about the year 1540. Warning examples from ancient and modern times of the moral disorder and the wretched existence of the scholars meet us in astonishing abundance, and along with these, accusations of the most serious nature are brought formally against them. Among these are anger, vanity, obstinacy, self-adoration, a dissolute private life, immorality of all descriptions, heresy, atheism; further, the habit of speaking without conviction, a sinister influence on government, pedantry of speech, thanklessness towards teachers, and abject flattery of the great, who first give the scholar a taste of their favours and then leave him to starve. The description is closed by a reference to the golden age, when no such thing as science existed on the earth. Of these charges, that of heresy soon became the most dangerous, and Gyraldus himself, when he afterwards republished a perfectly harmless youthful work, was compelled to take refuge beneath the mantle of Duke Ercole II of Ferrara, since men now had the upper hand who held that people had better spend their time on Christian themes than on mythological researches. He justifies himself on the ground that the latter, on the contrary, were at such a time almost the only harmless branches of study, as they deal with subjects of a perfectly neutral character.

But if it is the duty of the historian to seek for evidence in which moral judgement is tempered by human sympathy, he will find no authority comparable in value to the work so often quoted of Pierio Valeriano, 'On the Infelicity of the Scholar'. It was written under the gloomy impressions left by the sack of Rome, which seems to the writer, not only the direct cause of untold misery to the men of learning, but, as it were, the fulfilment of an evil destiny which had long pursued them. Pierio is here led by a simple and, on the whole, just feeling. He does not introduce a special power, which plagued the men of genius on account of their genius, but he states facts, in which an unlucky chance often wears the aspect of fatality. Not wishing to write a tragedy or to refer events to the conflict of higher powers, he is content to lay before us the scenes of everyday life. We are introduced to men who, in times of trouble, lose first their incomes and then their places; to others who, in trying to get two appointments, miss both; to unsociable misers who carry about their money sewn into their clothes, and die mad when they are robbed of it; to others, who accept well-paid offices, and then sicken with a melancholy longing for their lost freedom. We read how some died young of a plague or fever, and how the writings which had cost them so much toil were burnt with their bed and clothes; how others lived in terror of the murderous threats of their colleagues; how one was slain by a covetous servant, and another caught by highwaymen on a journey, and left to pine in a dungeon, because unable to pay his ransom. Many died of unspoken grief for the insults they received and the prizes of which they were defrauded. We are told how a Venetian died because of the death of his son, a youthful prodigy; and how mother and brothers followed, as if the lost child drew them all after him. Many, especially Florentines, ended their lives by suicide; others through the secret justice of a tyrant. Who, after all, is happy?—and by what means? By blunting all feeling for such misery? One of the speakers in the dialogue in which Pierio clothed his argument, can give an answer to these questions—the illustrious Gasparo Contarini, at the mention of whose name we turn with the expectation to hear at least something of the truest and deepest which was then thought on such matters. As a type of the happy scholar, he mentions Fra Urbano Valeriano of Belluno, who was for years a teacher of Greek at Venice, who visited Greece and the East, and towards the close of his life travelled, now through this country, now through that, without ever mounting a horse; who never had a penny of his own, rejected all honours and distinctions, and after a gay old age, died in his eighty-fourth year, without, if we except a fall from a ladder, having ever known an hour of sickness. And what was the difference between such a man and the humanists? The latter had more free will, more subjectivity, than they could turn to purposes of happiness. The mendicant friar, who had lived from his boyhood in the monastery, and never eaten or slept except by rule, ceased to feel the compulsion under which he lived. Through the power of this habit he led, amid all outward hardships, a life of inward peace, by which he impressed his hearers far more than by his teaching. Looking at him, they could believe that it depends on ourselves whether we bear up against misfortune or surrender to it. 'Amid want and toil he was happy, because he willed to be so, because he had contracted no evil habits, was not capricious, inconstant, immoderate; but was always contented with little or nothing.' If we heard Contarini himself, religious motives would no doubt play a part in the argument—but the practical philosopher in sandals speaks plainly enough. An allied character, but placed in other circumstances, is that of Fabio Calvi of Ravenna, the commentator of Hippocrates. He lived to a great age in Rome, eating only pulse 'like the Pythagoreans', and dwelt in a hovel little better than the tub of Diogenes. Of the pension which Pope Leo gave him, he spent enough to keep body and soul together, and gave the rest away. He was not a healthy man, like Fra Urbano, nor is it likely that, like him, he died with a smile on his lips. At the age of ninety, in the sack of Rome, he was dragged away by the Spaniards, who hoped for a ransom, and died of hunger in a hospital. But his name has passed into the kingdom of the immortals, for Raphael loved the old man like a father, and honoured him as a teacher, and came to him for advice in all things. Perhaps they discoursed chiefly of the projected restoration of ancient Rome, perhaps of still higher matters. Who can tell what a share Fabio may have had in the conception of the School of Athens, and in other great works of the master?

We would gladly close this part of our essay with the picture of some pleasing and winning character. Pomponius Lætus, of whom we shall briefly speak, is known to us principally through the letter of his pupil Sabellicus, in which an antique colouring is purposely given to his character. Yet many of its features are clearly recognizable. He was a bastard of the House of the Neapolitan Sanseverini, princes of Salerno, whom he nevertheless refused to recognize, writing, in reply to an invitation to live with them, the famous letter: 'Pomponius Lætus cognatis et propinquis suis salutem. Quod petitis fieri non potest. Valete.'† An insignificant little figure, with small, quick eyes, and quaint dress, he lived, during the last decades of the fifteenth century, as professor in the University of Rome, either in his cottage in a garden on the Esquiline hill, or in his vineyard on the Quirinal. In the one he bred his ducks and fowls; the other he cultivated according to the strictest precepts of Cato, Varro, and Columella. He spent his holidays in fishing or bird-catching in the Campagna, or in feasting by some shady spring or on the banks of the Tiber. Wealth and luxury he despised. Free himself from envy and uncharitable speech, he would not suffer them in others. It was only against the hierarchy that he gave his tongue free play, and passed, till his latter years, for a scorner of religion altogether. He was involved in the persecution of the humanists begun by Pope Paul II, and surrendered to this pontiff by the Venetians; but no means could be found to wring unworthy confessions from him. He was afterwards befriended and supported by popes and prelates, and when his house was plundered in the disturbances under Sixtus IV, more was collected for him than he had lost. No teacher was more conscientious. Before daybreak he was to be seen descending the Esquiline with his lantern, and on reaching his lecture-room found it always filled to overflowing. A stutter compelled him to speak with care, but his delivery was even and effective. His few works

† 'Pomponius Lætus wishes good health to all his kinsfolk. What you ask for cannot be done. Good-bye.'

give evidence of careful writing. No scholar treated the text of ancient authors more soberly and accurately. The remains of antiquity which surrounded him in Rome touched him so deeply that he would stand before them as if entranced, or would suddenly burst into tears at the sight of them. As he was ready to lay aside his own studies in order to help others, he was much loved and had many friends; and at his death, even Alexander VI sent his courtiers to follow the corpse, which was carried by the most distinguished of his pupils. The funeral service in the Aracœli was attended by forty bishops and by all the foreign ambassadors.

It was Lætus who introduced and conducted the representations of ancient, chiefly Plautine, plays in Rome. Every year, he celebrated the anniversary of the foundation of the city by a festival, at which his friends and pupils recited speeches and poems. Such meetings were the origin of what acquired, and long retained, the name of the Roman Academy. It was simply a free union of individuals, and was connected with no fixed institution. Besides the occasions mentioned, it met at the invitation of a patron, or to celebrate the memory of a deceased member, as of Platina. At such times, a prelate belonging to the academy would first say mass; Pomponio would then ascend the pulpit and deliver a speech; someone else would then follow him and recite an elegy. The customary banquet, with declamations and recitations, concluded the festival, whether joyous or serious, and the academicians, notably Platina himself, early acquired the reputation of epicures. At other times, the guests performed farces in the old Atellan style. As a free association of very varied elements, the academy lasted in its original form down to the sack of Rome, and included among its hosts Angelus Coloccius, Johannes Corycius and others. Its precise value as an element in the intellectual life of the people is as hard to estimate as that of any other social union of the same kind; yet a man like Sadoleto reckoned it among the most precious memories of his youth. A large number of other academies appeared and passed away in many Italian cities, according to the number and significance of the humanists living in them, and to the patronage bestowed by the great and wealthy. Of these we may mention the Academy of Naples, of which Jovianus Pontanus was the centre, and which sent out a colony to Lecce, and that of Pordenone, which formed the court of the Condottiere Alviano. The circle of Lodovico il Moro, and its peculiar importance for that prince, has been already spoken of.

About the middle of the sixteenth century, these associations seem to have undergone a complete change. The humanists, driven in other spheres from their commanding position, and viewed askance by the men of the Counter-reformation, lost the control of the academies: and here, as elsewhere, Latin poetry was replaced by Italian. Before long every town of the least importance had its academy, with some strange, fantastic name, and its own endowment and subscriptions. Besides the recitation of verses, the new institutions inherited from their predecessors the regular banquets and the representation of plays, sometimes acted by the members themselves, sometimes under their direction by young amateurs, and sometimes by paid players. The fate of the Italian stage, and afterwards of the opera, was long in the hands of these associations.

PART IV

THE DISCOVERY OF THE WORLD AND OF MAN

JOURNEYS OF THE ITALIANS

FREED from the countless bonds which elsewhere in Europe checked progress, having reached a high degree of individual development and been schooled by the teachings of antiquity, the Italian mind now turned to the discovery of the outward universe, and to the representation of it in speech and form.

On the journeys of the Italians to distant parts of the world, we can here make but a few general observations. The Crusades had opened unknown distances to the European mind, and awakened in all the passion for travel and adventure. It may be hard to indicate precisely the point where this passion allied itself with, or became the servant of, the thirst for knowledge; but it was in Italy that this was first and most completely the case. Even in the Crusades the interest of the Italians was wider than that of other nations, since they already were a naval power and had commercial relations with the East. From time immemorial the Mediterranean Sea had given to the nations that dwelt on its shores mental impulses different from those which governed the peoples of the North; and never, from the very structure of their character, could the Italians be adventurers in the sense which the word bore among the Teutons. After they were once at home in all the eastern harbours of the Mediterranean, it was natural that the most enterprising among them should be led to join that vast international movement of the Mohammedans which there found its outlet. A new half of the world lay, as it were, freshly discovered before them. Or, like Polo of Venice, they were caught in the current of the Mongolian peoples, and carried on to the steps of the throne of the Great Khan. At an early period, we find Italians sharing in the discoveries made in the Atlantic Ocean; it was the Genoese who, in the thirteenth century, found the Canary Islands. In the same year, 1291, when Ptolemais, the last remnant of the Christian East, was lost, it was again the Genoese who made the first known attempt to find a sea-passage to the East Indies. Columbus himself is but the greatest of a long list of Italians who, in the service of the western nations, sailed into distant seas. The true discoverer, however, is not the man who first chances to stumble upon anything, but the man who finds what he has sought. Such a one alone stands in a link with the thoughts and interests of his predecessors, and this relationship will also determine the account he gives of his search. For which reason the Italians, although their claim to be the first comers on this or that shore may be disputed, will yet retain their title to be pre-eminently the nation of discoverers for the whole latter part of the Middle Ages. The fuller proof of this assertion belongs to the special history of discoveries. Yet ever and again we turn with admiration to the august figure of the great Genoese, by whom a new continent beyond the ocean was demanded, sought and found; and who was the first to be able to say: 'il mondo è poco'—the world is not so large as men have thought. At the time when Spain gave Alexander VI to the Italians, Italy gave Columbus to the Spaniards. Only a few weeks before the death of that pope Columbus wrote from Jamaica his noble letter (July 7, 1503) to the thankless Catholic kings, which the ages to come can never read without profound emotion. In a codicil to his will, dated Valladolid, May 4, 1506, he bequeathed to 'his beloved home, the Republic of Genoa, the prayer-book which Pope Alexander had given him, and which in prison, in conflict, and in every kind of adversity, had been to him the greatest of comforts'. It seems as if these words cast upon the abhorred name of Borgia one last gleam of grace and mercy.

The development of geographical and allied sciences among the Italians must, like the history of their voyages, be touched upon but very briefly. A superficial comparison of their achievements with those of other nations shows an early and striking superiority on their part. Where, in the middle of the fifteenth century, could be found, anywhere but in Italy, such a union of geographical, statistical, and historical knowledge as was found in Æneas Sylvius? Not only in his great geographical work, but in his letters and commentaries, he describes with equal mastery landscapes, cities, manners, industries and products, political conditions and constitutions, wherever he can use his own observation or the evidence of eye-witnesses. What he takes from books is naturally of less moment. Even the short sketch of that valley in the Tyrolese Alps where Frederick III had given him a benefice, and still more his description of Scotland, leaves untouched none of the relations of human life, and displays a power and method of unbiased observation and comparison impossible in any but a countryman of Columbus, trained in the school of the ancients. Thousands saw and, in part, knew what he did, but they felt no impulse to draw a picture of it, and were unconscious that the world desired such pictures.

In geography[61] as in other matters, it is vain to attempt to distinguish how much is to be attributed to the study of the ancients, and how much to the special genius of the Italians. They saw and treated the things of this world from an objective point of view, even before they were familiar with ancient literature, partly because they were themselves a half-ancient people, and partly because their political circumstances predisposed them to it; but they would not so rapidly have attained to such perfection had not the old geographers shown them the way. The influence of the existing Italian geographies on the spirit and tendencies of the travellers and discoverers was also inestimable. Even the simple 'dilettante' of a science—if in the present case we should assign to Æneas Sylvius so low a rank—can diffuse just that sort of general interest in the subject which prepares for new pioneers the indispensable groundwork of a favourable predisposition in the public mind. True discoverers in any science know well what they owe to such mediation.

THE NATURAL SCIENCES IN ITALY

For the position of the Italians in the sphere of the natural sciences, we must refer the reader to the special treatises on the subject, of which the only one with which we are familiar is the superficial and depreciatory work of Libri. The dispute as to the priority of particular discoveries concerns us all the less, since we hold that, at any time, and among any civilized people, a man may appear who, starting with very scanty preparation, is driven by an irresistible impulse into the path of scientific investigation, and through his native gifts achieves the most astonishing success. Such men were Gerbert of Rheims and Roger Bacon. That they were masters of the whole knowledge of the age in their several departments was a natural

[61] In the sixteenth century Italy continued to be the home of geographical literature, at the time when the discoverers themselves belonged almost exclusively to the countries on the shores of the Atlantic. (*Cf. Oskar Peschel, Abhandlungen zur Erd- und Völkerkunde, Leipzig, 1878; and K. Müller, Mappae Mundi, Stuttgart, 1898.)

consequence of the spirit in which they worked. When once the veil of illusion was torn asunder, when once the dread of nature and the slavery to books and tradition were overcome, countless problems lay before them for solution. It is another matter when a whole people takes a natural delight in the study and investigation of nature, at a time when other nations are indifferent, that is to say, when the discoverer is not threatened or wholly ignored, but can count on the friendly support of congenial spirits. That this was the case in Italy is unquestionable. The Italian students of nature trace with pride in the 'Divine Comedy' the hints and proofs of Dante's scientific interest in nature. On his claim to priority in this or that discovery or reference, we must leave the men of science to decide; but every layman must be struck by the wealth of his observations on the external world, shown merely in his picture and comparisons. He, more than any other modern poet, takes them from reality, whether in nature or human life, and uses them never as mere ornament, but in order to give the reader the fullest and most adequate sense of his meaning. It is in astronomy that he appears chiefly as a scientific specialist, though it must not be forgotten that many astronomical allusions in his great poem, which now appear to us learned, must then have been intelligible to the general reader. Dante, learning apart, appeals to a popular knowledge of the heavens, which the Italians of his day, from the mere fact that they were a nautical people, had in common with the ancients. This knowledge of the rising and setting of the constellations has been rendered superfluous to the modern world by calendars and clocks, and with it has gone whatever interest in astronomy the people may once have had. Nowadays, with our schools and handbooks, every child knows—what Dante did not know—that the earth moves round the sun; but the interest once taken in the subject itself has given place, except in the case of astronomical specialists, to the most absolute indifference.

The pseudo-science which dealt with the stars proves nothing against the inductive spirit of the Italians of that day. That spirit was but crossed, and at times overcome, by the passionate desire to penetrate the future. We shall recur to the subject of astrology when we come to speak of the moral and religious character of the people.

The Church treated this and other pseudo-sciences nearly always with toleration; and showed itself actually hostile even to genuine science only when a charge of heresy together with necromancy was also in question—which certainly was often the case. A point which it would be interesting to decide is this: whether and in what cases the Dominican (and also the Franciscan) Inquisitors in Italy were conscious of the falsehood of the charges, and yet condemned the accused, either to oblige some enemy of the prisoner or from hatred to natural science, and particularly to experiments. The latter doubtless occurred, but it is not easy to prove the fact. What helped to cause such persecutions in the North, namely, the opposition made to the innovators by the upholders of the received official, scholastic system of nature, was of little or no weight in Italy. Pietro of Abano, at the beginning of the fourteenth century, is well known to have fallen a victim to the envy of another physician, who accused him before the Inquisition of heresy and magic; and something of the same kind may have happened in the case of his Paduan contemporary, Giovannino Sanguinacci, who was known as an innovator in medical practice. He escaped, however, with banishment. Nor must it be forgotten that the inquisitorial power of the Dominicans was exercised less uniformly in Italy than in the North. Tyrants and free cities in the fourteenth century treated the clergy at times with such sovereign contempt that very different matters from natural science went unpunished. But when, with the fifteenth century, antiquity became the leading power in Italy, the breach it made in the old system was turned to account by every branch of secular science. Humanism, nevertheless, attracted to itself the best strength of the nation, and thereby, no doubt, did injury to the inductive investigation of nature. Here and there the Inquisition suddenly started into life, and punished or burned physicians as blasphemers or magicians. In such cases it is hard to discover what was the true motive underlying the condemnation. But even so, Italy, at the close of the fifteenth century, with Paolo Toscanelli, Luca Pacioli and Leonardo da Vinci, held incomparably the highest place among European nations in mathematics and the natural sciences, and the learned men of every country, even Regiomontanus and Copernicus, confessed themselves its pupils. This glory survived the Counter-reformation, and even today the Italians would occupy the first place in this respect if circumstances had not made it impossible for the greatest minds to devote themselves to tranquil research.

A significant proof of the widespread interest in natural history is found in the zeal which showed itself at an early period for the collection and comparative study of plants and animals. Italy claims to be the first creator of botanical gardens, though possibly they may have served a chiefly practical end, and the claim to priority may be itself disputed. It is of far greater importance that princes and wealthy men, in laying out their pleasure-gardens, instinctively made a point of collecting the greatest possible number of different plants in all their species and varieties. Thus in the fifteenth century the noble grounds of the Medicean Villa Careggi appear from the descriptions we have of them to have been almost a botanical garden, with countless specimens of different trees and shrubs. Of the same kind was a villa of the Cardinal Trivulzio, at the beginning of the sixteenth century, in the Roman Campagna towards Tivoli, with hedges made up of various species of roses, with trees of every description—the fruit-trees especially showing an astonishing variety—with twenty different sorts of vines and a large kitchen-garden. This is evidently something very different from the score or two of familiar medicinal plants which were to be found in the garden of any castle or monastery in Western Europe. Along with a careful cultivation of fruit for the purposes of the table, we find an interest in the plant for its own sake, on account of the pleasure it gives to the eye. We learn from the history of art at how late a period this passion for botanical collections was laid aside, and gave place to what was considered the picturesque style of landscape-gardening.

The collections, too, of foreign animals not only gratified curiosity, but served also the higher purposes of observation. The facility of transport from the southern and eastern harbours of the Mediterranean, and the mildness of the Italian climate, made it practicable to buy the largest animals of the south, or to accept them as presents from the Sultans. The cities and princes were especially anxious to keep live lions, even where a lion was not, as in Florence, the emblem of the State. The lions' den was generally in or near the government palace, as in Perugia and Florence; in Rome, it lay on the slope of the Capitol. The beasts sometimes served as executioners of political judgements, and no doubt, apart from this, they kept alive a certain terror in the popular mind. Their condition was also held to be ominous of good or evil. Their fertility, especially, was considered a sign of public prosperity, and no less a man than Giovanni Villani thought it worth recording that he was present at the delivery of a lioness. The cubs were often given to allied States and princes, or to Condottieri as a reward of their valour. In addition to the lions, the

Florentines began very early to keep leopards, for which a special keeper was appointed. Borso of Ferrara used to set his lion to fight with bulls, bears, and wild boars.

By the end of the fifteenth century, however, true menageries (serragli), now reckoned part of the suitable appointments of a court, were kept by many of the princes. 'It belongs to the position of the great,' says Matarazzo, 'to keep horses, dogs, mules, falcons, and other birds, court-jesters, singers, and foreign animals.' The menagerie at Naples, in the time of Ferrante, contained even a giraffe and a zebra, presented, it seems, by the ruler of Baghdad. Filippo Maria Visconti possessed not only horses which cost him each 500 or 1,000 pieces of gold, and valuable English dogs, but a number of leopards brought from all parts of the East; the expense of his hunting-birds, which were collected from the countries of Northern Europe, amounted to 3,000 pieces of gold a month. King Emanuel the Great of Portugal knew well what he was about when he presented Leo X with an elephant and a rhinoceros. It was under such circumstances that the foundations of a scientific zoology and botany were laid.

A practical fruit of these zoological studies was the establishment of studs, of which the Mantuan, under Francesco Gonzaga, was esteemed the first in Europe. All interest in, and knowledge of the different breeds of horses is as old, no doubt, as riding itself, and the crossing of the European with the Asiatic must have been common from the time of the Crusades. In Italy, a special inducement to perfect the breed was offered by the prizes at the horse-races held in every considerable town in the peninsula. In the Mantuan stables were found the infallible winners in these contests, as well as the best military chargers, and the horses best suited by their stately appearance for presents to great people. Gonzaga kept stallions and mares from Spain, Ireland, Africa, Thrace, and Cilicia, and for the sake of the last he cultivated the friendship of the Sultans. All possible experiments were here tried, in order to produce the most perfect animals.

Even human menageries were not wanting. The famous Cardinal Ippolito Medici, bastard of Giuliano, Duke of Nemours, kept at his strange court a troop of barbarians who talked no less than twenty different languages, and who were all of them perfect specimens of their races. Among them were incomparable *voltigeurs* of the best blood of the North African Moors, Tartar bowmen, Negro wrestlers, Indian divers, and Turks, who generally accompanied the Cardinal on his hunting expeditions. When he was overtaken by an early death (1535), this motley band carried the corpse on their shoulders from Itri to Rome, and mingled with the general mourning for the open-handed Cardinal their medley of tongues and violent gesticulations.

These scattered notices of the relations of the Italians to natural science, and their interest in the wealth and variety of the products of nature, are only fragments of a great subject. No one is more conscious than the author of the defects in his knowledge on this point. Of the multitude of special works in which the subject is adequately treated, even the names are but imperfectly known to him.

DISCOVERY OF THE BEAUTY OF LANDSCAPE

But outside the sphere of scientific investigation, there is another way to draw near to nature. The Italians are the first among modern peoples by whom the outward world was seen and felt as something beautiful.[62]

The power to do so is always the result of a long and complicated development, and its origin it not easily detected, since a dim feeling of this kind may exist long before it shows itself in poetry and painting and thereby becomes conscious of itself. Among the ancients, for example, art and poetry had gone through the whole circle of human interests, before they turned to the representation of nature, and even then the latter filled always a limited and subordinate place. And yet, from the time of Homer downwards, the powerful impression made by nature upon man is shown by countless verses and chance expressions. The Germanic races, which founded their States on the ruins of the Roman Empire, were thoroughly and specially fitted to understand the spirit of natural scenery; and though Christianity compelled them for a while to see in the springs and mountains, in the lakes and woods, which they had till then revered, the working of evil demons, yet this transitional conception was soon outgrown. By the year 1200, at the height of the Middle Ages, a genuine, hearty enjoyment of the external world was again in existence, and found lively expression in the minstrelsy of different nations, which gives evidence of the sympathy felt with all the simple phenomena of nature—spring with its flowers, the green fields and the woods. But these pictures are all foreground without perspective.

[62] It is hardly necessary to refer the reader to the famous chapters on this subject in Humboldt's *Kosmos*, Vol. II.

Even the crusaders, who travelled so far and saw so much, are not recognizable as such in their poems. The epic poetry, which describes armour and costumes so fully, does not attempt more than a sketch of outward nature; and even the great Wolfram von Eschenbach scarcely anywhere gives us an adequate picture of the scene on which his heroes move. From these poems it would never be guessed that their noble authors in all countries inhabited or visited lofty castles, commanding distant prospects. Even in the Latin poems of the wandering clerks, we find no traces of a distant view—of landscape properly so called—but what lies near is sometimes described with a glow and splendour which none of the knightly minstrels can surpass. What picture of the Grove of Love can equal that of the Italian poet—for such we take him to be— of the twelfth century?

'Immortalis fieret
Ibi manens homo;
Arbor ibi quaelibet
Suo gaudet pomo;
Viae myrrha, cinnamo
Fragrant, et amomo—
Conjectari poterat
Dominus ex domo' etc.

To the Italian mind, at all events, nature had by this time lost its taint of sin, and had shaken off all trace of demoniacal powers. Saint Francis of Assisi, in his Hymn to the Sun, frankly praises the Lord for creating the heavenly bodies and the four elements.

But the unmistakable proofs of a deepening effect of nature on the human spirit begin with Dante. Not only does he awaken in us by a few vigorous lines the sense of the morning air and the trembling light on the distant ocean, or of the grandeur of the storm-beaten forest, but he makes the ascent of lofty peaks, with the only possible object of enjoying the view—the first man, perhaps, since the days of antiquity who did so. In Boccaccio we can do little more than infer how country scenery affected him; yet his pastoral romances show his imagination to have been filled with it. But the significance of nature for a receptive spirit is fully and clearly displayed by Petrarch—one of the first truly modern men. That clear soul—who first collected from the literature of all countries evidence of the origin and progress of the sense of natural beauty, and himself, in his 'Aspects of Nature', achieved the noblest masterpiece of description—Alexander von Humboldt has not done full justice to Petrarch; and following in the steps of the great reaper, we may still hope to glean a few ears of interest and value.

Petrarch was not only a distinguished geographer—the first map of Italy is said to have been drawn by his direction—and not only a reproducer of the sayings of the ancients, but felt himself the influence of natural beauty. The enjoyment of nature is, for him, the favourite accompaniment of intellectual pursuits; it was to combine the two that he lived in learned retirement at Vaucluse and elsewhere, that he from time to time fled from the world and from his age. We should do him wrong by inferring from his weak and undeveloped power of describing natural scenery that he did not feel it deeply. His picture, for instance, of the lovely Gulf of Spezia and Porto Venere, which he inserts at the end of the sixth book of the 'Africa', for the reason that none of the ancients or moderns had sung of it, is no more than a simple enumeration, but Petrarch is also conscious of the beauty of rock scenery, and is perfectly able to distinguish the picturesqueness from the utility of nature. During his stay among the woods of Reggio, the sudden sight of an impressive landscape so affected him that he resumed a poem which he had long laid aside. But the deepest impression of all was made upon him by the ascent of Mont Ventoux, near Avignon. An indefinable longing for a distant panorama grew stronger and stronger in him, till at length the accidental sight of a passage in Livy, where King Philip, the enemy of Rome, ascends the Hæmus, decided him. He thought that what was not blamed in a grey-headed monarch, might well be *excused* in a young man of private station. The ascent of a mountain for its own sake was unheard of, and there could be no thought of the companionship of friends or acquaintances. Petrarch took with him only his younger brother and two country people from the last place where he halted. At the foot of the mountain an old herdsman besought him to turn back, saying that he himself had attempted to climb it fifty years before, and had brought home nothing but repentance, broken bones, and torn clothes, and that neither before nor after had anyone ventured to do the same. Nevertheless, they struggled forward and upward, till the clouds lay beneath their feet, and at last they reached the top. A description of the view from the summit would be looked for in vain, not because the poet was insensible to it, but, on the contrary, because the impression was too overwhelming. His whole past life, with all its follies, rose before his mind; he remembered that ten years ago that day he had quitted Bologna a young man, and turned a longing gaze towards his native country; he opened a book which then was his constant companion, the 'Confessions' of St. Augustine, and his eye fell on the passage in the tenth chapter, 'and men go forth, and admire lofty mountains and broad seas, and roaring torrents, and the ocean, and the course of the stars, and forget their own selves while doing so'. His brother, to whom he read these words, could not understand why he closed the book and said no more.

Some decades later, about 1360, Fazio degli Uberti describes, in his rhyming geography, the wide panorama from the mountains of Auvergne, with the interest, it is true, of the geographer and antiquarian only, but still showing clearly that he himself had seen it. He must, however, have ascended far higher peaks, since he is familiar with facts which only occur at a height of 10,000 feet or more above the sea—mountain-sickness and its accompaniments—of which his imaginary comrade Solinus tries to cure him with a sponge dipped in an essence. The ascents of Parnassus and Olympus, of which he speaks, are perhaps only fictions.

In the fifteenth century, the great masters of the Flemish school, Hubert and Jan van Eyck, suddenly lifted the veil from nature. Their landscapes are not merely the fruit of an endeavour to reflect the real world in art, but have, even if expressed conventionally, a certain poetical meaning—in short, a soul. Their influence on the whole art of the West is undeniable, and extended to the landscape-painting of the Italians, but without preventing the characteristic interest of the Italian eye for nature from finding its own expression.

On this point, as in the scientific description of nature, Æneas Sylvius is again one of the most weighty voices of his time. Even if we grant the justice of all that has been said against his character, we must nevertheless admit that in few other men was the picture of the age and its culture so fully reflected, and that few came nearer to the normal type of the men of the early Renaissance. It may be added parenthetically, that even in respect to his moral character he will not be fairly judged, if we listen solely to the complaints of the German Church, which his fickleness helped to baulk of the Council it so ardently desired.

He here claims our attention as the first who not only enjoyed the magnificence of the Italian landscape, but described it with enthusiasm down to its minutest details. The ecclesiastical State and the south of

Tuscany—his native home—he knew thoroughly, and after he became Pope he spent his leisure during the favourable season chiefly in excursions to the country. Then at last the gouty man was rich enough to have himself carried in a litter across the mountains and valleys; and when we compare his enjoyments with those of the Popes who succeeded him, Pius, whose chief delight was in nature, antiquity, and simple, but noble, architecture, appears almost a saint. In the elegant and flowing Latin of his 'Commentaries' he freely tells us of his happiness.

His eye seems as keen and practised as that of any modern observer. He enjoys with rapture the panoramic splendour of the view from the summit of the Alban Hills—from the Monte Cavo—whence he could see the shores of St. Peter from Terracina and the promontory of Circe as far as Monte Argentaro, and the wide expanse of country round about, with the ruined cities of the past, and with the mountain-chains of Central Italy beyond; and then his eye would turn to the green woods in the hollows beneath and the mountain-lakes among them. He feels the beauty of the position of Todi, crowning the vineyards and olive-clad slopes, looking down upon distant woods and upon the valley of the Tiber, where towns and castles rise above the winding river. The lovely hills about Siena, with villas and monasteries on every height, are his own home, and his descriptions of them are touched with a peculiar feeling. Single picturesque glimpses charm him too, like the little promontory of Capo di Monte that stretches out into the Lake of Bolsena. 'Rocky steps,' we read, 'shaded by vines, descend to the water's edge, where the evergreen oaks stand between the cliffs, alive with the song of thrushes.' On the path round the Lake of Nemi, beneath the chestnuts and fruit-trees, he feels that here, if anywhere, a poet's soul must awake—here in the hiding-place of Diana! He often held consistories or received ambassadors under huge old chestnut-trees, or beneath the olives on the greensward by some gurgling spring. A view like that of a narrowing gorge, with a bridge arched boldly over it, awakens at once his artistic sense. Even the smallest details give him delight through something beautiful, or perfect, or characteristic in them—the blue fields of waving flax, the yellow gorse which covers the hills, even tangled thickets, or single trees, or springs, which seem to him like wonders of nature.

The height of his enthusiasm for natural beauty was reached during his stay on Monte Amiata, in the summer of 1462, when plague and heat made the lowlands uninhabitable. Half-way up the mountain, in the old Lombard monastery of San Salvatore, he and his court took up their quarters. There, between the chestnuts which clothe the steep declivity, the eye may wander over all Southern Tuscany, with the towers of Siena in the distance. The ascent of the highest peak he left to his companions, who were joined by the Venetian envoy; they found at the top two vast blocks of stone one upon the other—perhaps the sacrificial altar of a prehistoric people—and fancied that in the far distance they saw Corsica and Sardinia rising above the sea. In the cool air of the hills, among the old oaks and chestnuts, on the green meadows where there were no thorns to wound the feet, and no snakes or insects to hurt or to annoy, the Pope passed days of unclouded happiness. For the 'Segnatura', which took place on certain days of the week, he selected on each occasion some new shady retreat 'novos in convallibus fontes et novas inveniens umbras, quæ dubiam facerent electionem'. At such times the dogs would perhaps start a great stag from his lair, who, after defending himself a while with hoofs and antlers, would fly at last up the mountain. In the evening the Pope was accustomed to sit before the monastery on the spot from which the whole valley of the Paglia was visible, holding lively conversations with the cardinals. The courtiers, who ventured down from the heights on their hunting expeditions, found the heat below intolerable, and the scorched plains like a very hell, while the monastery, with its cool, shady woods, seemed like an abode of the blessed.

All this is genuine modern enjoyment, not a reflection of antiquity. As surely as the ancients themselves felt in the same manner, so surely, nevertheless, were the scanty expressions of the writers whom Pius knew insufficient to awaken in him such enthusiasm.

The second great age of Italian poetry, which now followed at the end of the fifteenth and the beginning of the sixteenth centuries, as well as the Latin poetry of the same period, is rich in proofs of the powerful effect of nature on the human mind. The first glance at the lyric poets of that time will suffice to convince us. Elaborate descriptions of natural scenery, it is true, are very rare, for the reason that, in this energetic age, the novels, and the lyric or epic poetry had something else to deal with. Boiardo and Ariosto paint nature vigorously, but as briefly as possible, and with no effort to appeal by their descriptions to the feelings of the reader, which they endeavour to reach solely by their narrative and characters. Letter-writers and the authors of philosophical dialogues are, in fact, better evidence of the growing love of nature than the poets. The novelist Bandello, for example, observes rigorously the rules of his department of literature; he gives us in his novels themselves not a word more than is necessary on the natural scenery amid which the action of his tales takes place, but in the dedications which always precede them we meet with charming descriptions of nature as the setting for his dialogues and social pictures. Among letter-writers, Aretino unfortunately must be named as the first who has fully painted in words the splendid effect of light and shadow in an Italian sunset.

We sometimes find the feeling of the poets, also, attaching itself with tenderness to graceful scenes of country life. Tito Strozzi, about the year 1480, describes in a Latin elegy the dwelling of his mistress. We are shown an old ivy-clad house, half hidden in trees, and adorned with weather-stained frescoes of the saints, and near it a chapel much damaged by the violence of the River Po, which flowed hard by; not far off, the priest ploughs his few barren roods with borrowed cattle. This is no reminiscence of the Roman elegists, but true modern sentiment; and the parallel to it—a sincere, unartificial description of country life in general—will be found at the end of this part of our work.

It may be objected that the German painters at the beginning of the sixteenth century succeeded in representing with perfect mastery these scenes of country life, as, for instance, Albrecht Dürer, in his engraving of the Prodigal Son. But it is one thing if a painter, brought up in a school of realism, introduces such scenes, and quite another thing if a poet, accustomed to an ideal or mythological framework, is driven by inward impulse into realism. Besides which, priority in point of time is here, as in the descriptions of country life, on the side of the Italian poets.

DISCOVERY OF MAN

To the discovery of the outward world the Renaissance added a still greater achievement, by first discerning and bringing to light the full, whole nature of man.[63]

This period, as we have seen, first gave the highest development to individuality, and then led the individual to the most zealous and thorough study of himself in all forms and under all conditions. Indeed, the development of personality is essentially involved in the recognition of it in oneself and in others. Between these two great

[63] These striking expressions are taken from the Introduction to the seventh volume of Michelet's *Histoire de France*.

processes our narrative has placed the influence of ancient literature because the mode of conceiving and representing both the individual and human nature in general was defined and coloured by that influence. But the power of conception and representation lay in the age and in the people.

The facts which we shall quote in evidence of our thesis will be few in number. Here, if anywhere in the course of this discussion, the author is conscious that he is treading on the perilous ground of conjecture, and that what seems to him a clear, if delicate and gradual, transition in the intellectual movement of the fourteenth and fifteenth centuries, may not be equally plain to others. The gradual awakening of the soul of a people is a phenomenon which may produce a different impression on each spectator. Time will judge which impression is the most faithful.

Happily the study of the intellectual side of human nature began, not with the search after a theoretical psychology—for that, Aristotle still sufficed—but with the endeavour to observe and to describe. The indispensable ballast of theory was limited to the popular doctrine of the four temperaments, in its then habitual union with the belief in the influence of the planets. Such conceptions may remain ineradicable in the minds of individuals, without hindering the general progress of the age. It certainly makes on us a singular impression, when we meet them at a time when human nature in its deepest essence and in all its characteristic expressions was not only known by exact observation, but represented by an immortal poetry and art. It sounds almost ludicrous when an otherwise competent observer considers Clement VII to be of a melancholy temperament, but defers his judgement to that of the physicians, who declare the Pope of a sanguine-choleric nature; or when we read that the same Gaston de Foix, the victor of Ravenna, whom Giorgione painted and Bambaia carved, and whom all the historians describe, had the saturnine temperament. No doubt those who use these expressions mean something by them; but the terms in which they tell us their meaning are strangely out of date in the Italy of the sixteenth century.

As examples of the free delineation of the human spirit, we shall first speak of the great poets of the fourteenth century.

If we were to collect the pearls from the courtly and knightly poetry of all the countries of the West during the two preceding centuries, we should have a mass of wonderful divinations and single pictures of the inward life, which at first sight would seem to rival the poetry of the Italians. Leaving lyrical poetry out of account, Godfrey of Strassburg gives us, in 'Tristram and Isolt', a representation of human passion, some features of which are immortal. But these pearls lie scattered in the ocean of artificial convention, and they are altogether something very different from a complete objective picture of the inward man and his spiritual wealth.

Italy, too, in the thirteenth century had, through the 'Trovatori', its share in the poetry of the courts and of chivalry. To them is mainly due the 'Canzone', whose construction is as difficult and artificial as that of the songs of any northern minstrel. Their subject and mode of thought represents simply the conventional tone of the courts, be the poet a burgher or a scholar.

But two new paths at length showed themselves, along which Italian poetry could advance to another and a characteristic future. They are not the less important for being concerned only with the formal and external side of the art.

To the same Brunetto Latini—the teacher of Dante—who, in his 'Canzoni', adopts the customary manner of the 'Trovatori', we owe the first-known 'versi sciolti', or blank hendecasyllabic verses, and in his apparent absence of form, a true and genuine passion suddenly showed itself. The same voluntary renunciation of outward effect, through confidence in the power of the inward conception, can be observed some years later in fresco-painting, and later still in painting of all kinds, which began to cease to rely on colour for its effect, using simply a lighter or darker shade. For an age which laid so much stress on artificial form in poetry, these verses of Brunetto mark the beginning of a new epoch.[64]

About the same time, or even in the first half of the thirteenth century, one of the many strictly balanced forms of metre, in which Europe was then so fruitful, became a normal and recognized form in Italy—the sonnet. The order of rhymes and even the number of lines varied for a whole century, till Petrarch fixed them permanently. In this form all higher lyrical and meditative subjects, and at a later time subjects of every possible description, were treated, and the madrigals, the sestine, and even the 'Canzoni' were reduced to a subordinate place. Later Italian writers complain, half jestingly, half

[64] Blank verse became at a later time the usual form for dramatic compositions. Trissino, in the dedication of his *Sofonisba* to Leo X, expressed the hope that the Pope would recognize this style for what it was—as better, nobler, and *less easy* than it looked. Roscoe, *Leone X*, ed. Bossi, viii, 174.

resentfully, of this inevitable mould, this Procrustean bed, to which they were compelled to make their thoughts and feelings fit. Others were, and still are, quite satisfied with this particular form of verse, which they freely use to express any personal reminiscence or idle sing-song without necessity or serious purpose. For which reason there are many more bad or insignificant sonnets than good ones.

Nevertheless, the sonnet must be held to have been an unspeakable blessing for Italian poetry. The clearness and beauty of its structure, the invitation it gave to elevate the thought in the second and more rapidly moving half, and the ease with which it could be learned by heart, made it valued even by the greatest masters. In fact, they would not have kept it in use down to our own century had they not been penetrated with a sense of its singular worth. These masters could have given us the same thoughts in other and wholly different forms. But when once they had made the sonnet the normal type of lyrical poetry, many other writers of great, if not the highest, gifts, who otherwise would have lost themselves in a sea of diffusiveness, were forced to concentrate their feelings. The sonnet became for Italian literature a condenser of thoughts and emotions such as was possessed by the poetry of no other modern people.

Thus the world of Italian sentiment comes before us in a series of pictures, clear, concise, and most effective in their brevity. Had other nations possessed a form of expression of the same kind, we should perhaps have known more of their inward life; we might have had a number of pictures of inward and outward situations—reflexions of the national character and temper—and should not be dependent for such knowledge on the so-called lyrical poets of the fourteenth and fifteenth centuries, who can hardly ever be read with any serious enjoyment. In Italy we can trace an undoubted progress from the time when the sonnet came into existence. In the second half of the thirteenth century the 'Trovatori della transizione', as they have been recently named, mark the passage from the Troubadours to the poets —that is, to those who wrote under the influence of antiquity. The simplicity and strength of their feeling, the vigorous delineation of fact, the precise expression and rounding off of their sonnets and other poems, herald the coming of a Dante. Some political sonnets of the Guelphs and Ghibellines (1260–1270) have about them the ring of his passion, and others remind us of his sweetest lyrical notes.

Of his own theoretical view of the sonnet, we are unfortunately ignorant, since the last books of his work, 'De vulgari eloquentia', in which he proposed to treat of ballads and sonnets, either remained unwritten or have been lost. But, as a matter of fact, he has left us in his Sonnets and 'Canzoni' a treasure of inward experience. And in what a framework he has set them! The prose of the 'Vita Nuova', in which he gives an account of the origin of each poem, is as wonderful as the verses themselves, and forms with them a uniform whole, inspired with the deepest glow of passion. With unflinching frankness and sincerity he lays bare every shade of his joy and his sorrow, and moulds it resolutely into the strictest forms of art. Reading attentively these Sonnets and 'Canzoni' and the marvellous fragments of the diary of his youth which lie between them, we fancy that throughout the Middle Ages the poets have been purposely fleeing from themselves, and that he was the first to seek his own soul. Before his time we meet with many an artistic verse; but he is the first artist in the full sense of the word—the first who consciously cast immortal matter into an immortal form. Subjective feeling has here a full objective truth and greatness, and most of it is so set forth that all ages and peoples can make it their own. Where he writes in a thoroughly objective spirit, and lets the force of his sentiment be guessed at only by some outward fact, as in the magnificent sonnets 'Tanto gentile', etc., and 'Vede perfettamente', etc., he seems to feel the need of excusing himself. The most beautiful of these poems really belongs to this class—the 'Deh peregrini che pensosi andate'. ('Oh, pilgrims, walking deep in thoughts', from *Vita Nuova.*) Even apart from the 'Divine Comedy', Dante would have marked by these youthful poems the boundary between mediævalism and modern times. The human spirit had taken a mighty step towards the consciousness of its own secret life.

The revelations in this matter which are contained in the 'Divine Comedy' itself are simply immeasurable; and it would be necessary to go through the whole poem, one canto after another, in order to do justice to its value from this point of view. Happily we have no need to do this, as it has long been a daily food of all the countries of the West. Its plan, and the ideas on which it is based, belong to the Middle Ages, and appeal to our interest only historically; but it is nevertheless the beginning of all modern poetry, through the power and richness shown in the description of human nature in every shape and attitude.[65]

From this time forward poetry may have experienced unequal

[65] For Dante's psychology, the beginning of *Purg.* iv, is one of the most important passages. See also the parts of the *Convito* bearing on the subject.

fortunes, and may show, for half a century together, a so-called relapse. But its nobler and more vital principle was saved for ever; and whenever in the fourteenth, fifteenth, and in the beginning of the sixteenth centuries, an original mind devotes himself to it, he represents a more advanced stage than any poet out of Italy, given—what is certainly not always easy to settle satisfactorily—an equality of natural gifts to start with.

Here, as in other things in Italy, culture—to which poetry belongs—precedes the visual arts and, in fact, gives them their chief impulse. More than a century elapsed before the spiritual element in painting and sculpture attained a power of expression in any way analogous to that of the 'Divine Comedy'. How far the same rule holds good for the artistic development of other nations,[66] and of what importance the whole question may be, does not concern us here. For Italian civilization it is of decisive weight.

The position to be assigned to Petrarch in this respect must be settled by the many readers of the poet. Those who come to him in the spirit of a cross-examiner, and busy themselves in detecting the contradictions between the poet and the man, his infidelities in love, and the other weak sides of his character, may perhaps, after sufficient effort, end by losing all taste for his poetry. In place, then, of artistic enjoyment, we may acquire a knowledge of the man in his 'totality'. What a pity that Petrarch's letters from Avignon contain so little gossip to take hold of, and that the letters of his acquaintances and of the friends of these acquaintances have either been lost or never existed! Instead of Heaven being thanked when we are not forced to inquire how and through what struggles a poet has rescued something immortal from his own poor life and lot, a biography has been stitched together for Petrarch out of these so-called 'remains', which reads like an indictment. But the poet may take comfort. If the printing and editing of the correspondence of celebrated people goes on for another half-century as it has begun in England and Germany, he will have illustrious company enough sitting with him on the stool of repentance.

Without shutting our eyes to much that is forced and artificial in his poetry, where the writer is merely imitating himself and singing on in the old strain, we cannot fail to admire the marvellous

[66] The portraits of Van Eyck and his school would prove the contrary for the North. They remained for a long period far in advance of all descriptions in words.

abundance of pictures of the inmost soul—descriptions of moments of joy and sorrow which must have been thoroughly his own, since no one before him gives us anything of the kind, and on which his significance rests for his country and for the world. His verse is not in all places equally transparent; by the side of his most beautiful thoughts stands at times some allegorical conceit or some sophistical trick of logic, altogether foreign to our present taste. But the balance is on the side of excellence.

Boccaccio, too, in his imperfectly-known Sonnets, succeeds sometimes in giving a most powerful and effective picture of his feeling. The return to a spot consecrated by love (Son. 22), the melancholy of spring (Son. 33), the sadness of the poet who feels himself growing old (Son. 65), are admirably treated by him. And in the 'Ameto' he has described the ennobling and transfiguring power of love in a manner which would hardly be expected from the author of the 'Decameron'. In the 'Fiammetta' we have another great and minutely-painted picture of the human soul, full of the keenest observation, though executed with anything but uniform power, and in parts marred by the passion for high-sounding language and by an unlucky mixture of mythological allusions and learned quotations. The 'Fiammetta', if we are not mistaken, is a sort of feminine counterpart to the 'Vita Nuova' of Dante, or at any rate owes its origin to it.

That the ancient poets, particularly the elegists, and Virgil, in the fourth book of the Æneid, were not without influence on the Italians of this and the following generation is beyond a doubt; but the spring of sentiment within the latter was nevertheless powerful and original. If we compare them in this respect with their contemporaries in other countries, we shall find in them the earliest complete expression of modern European feeling. The question, be it remembered, is not to know whether eminent men of other nations did not feel as deeply and as nobly, but who first gave documentary proof of the widest knowledge of the movements of the human heart.

Why did the Italians of the Renaissance do nothing above the second rank in tragedy? That was the field on which to display human character, intellect, and passion, in the thousand forms of their growth, their struggles, and their decline. In other words: why did Italy produce no Shakespeare? For with the stage of other northern countries besides England the Italians of the sixteenth and seventeenth centuries had no reason to fear a comparison; and with the Spaniards they could not enter into competition, since Italy had long lost all traces of religious fanaticism, treated the chivalrous code of honour only as a form, and was both too proud and too intelligent to bow down before its tyrannical and illegitimate masters. We have therefore only to consider the English stage in the period of its brief splendour.

It is an obvious reply that all Europe produced but one Shakespeare, and that such a mind is the rarest of Heaven's gifts. It is further possible that the Italian stage was on the way to something great when the Counter-reformation broke in upon it, and, aided by the Spanish rule over Naples and Milan, and indirectly over almost the whole peninsula, withered the best flowers of the Italian spirit. It would be hard to conceive of Shakespeare himself under a Spanish viceroy, or in the neighbourhood of the Holy Inquisition at Rome, or even in his own country a few decades later, at the time of the English Revolution. The stage, which in its perfection is a late product of every civilization, must wait for its own time and fortune.

We must not, however, quit this subject without mentioning certain circumstances which were of a character to hinder or retard a high development of the drama in Italy, till the time for it had gone by.

As the most weighty of these causes we must mention without doubt that the scenic tastes of the people were occupied elsewhere, and chiefly in the mysteries and religious processions. Throughout all Europe dramatic representations of sacred history and legend form the origin of the secular drama; but Italy, as will be shown more fully in the sequel, had spent on the mysteries such a wealth of decorative splendour as could not but be unfavourable to the dramatic element. Out of all the countless and costly representations, there sprang not even a branch of poetry like the 'Autos Sagramentales' of Calderón and other Spanish poets, much less any advantage or foundation for the secular drama.

And when the latter did at length appear, it at once gave itself up to magnificence of scenic effects, to which the mysteries had already accustomed the public taste to far too great an extent. We learn with astonishment how rich and splendid the scenes in Italy were, at a time when in the North the simplest indication of the place was thought sufficient. This alone might have had no such unfavourable effect on the drama, if the attention of the audience had not been drawn away from the poetical conception of the play partly by the splendour of the costumes, partly and chiefly by fantastic interludes (Intermezzi).

That in many places, particularly in Rome and Ferrara, Plautus and

Terence, as well as pieces by the old tragedians, were given in Latin or in Italian, that the academies of which we have already spoken, made this one of their chief objects, and that the poets of the Renaissance followed these models too servilely, were all untoward conditions for the Italian stage at the period in question. Yet I hold them to be of secondary importance. Had not the Counter-reformation and the rule of foreigners intervened, these very disadvantages might have been turned into useful means of transition. At all events, by the year 1520 the victory of the mother-tongue in tragedy and comedy was, to the great disgust of the humanists, as good as won. On this side, then, no obstacle stood in the way of the most developed people in Europe, to hinder them from raising the drama, in its noblest forms, to be a true reflexion of human life and destiny. It was the Inquisitors and Spaniards who cowed the Italian spirit, and rendered impossible the representation of the greatest and most sublime themes, most of all when they were associated with patriotic memories. At the same time, there is no doubt that the distracting 'Intermezzi' did serious harm to the drama. We must now consider them a little more closely.

When the marriage of Alfonso of Ferrara with Lucrezia Borgia was celebrated, Duke Ercole in person showed his illustrious guests the 110 costumes which were to serve at the representation of five comedies of Plautus, in order that all might see that not one of them was used twice. But all this display of silk and camlet was nothing to the ballets and pantomimes which served as interludes between the acts of the Plautine dramas. That, in comparison, Plautus himself seemed mortally dull to a lively young lady like Isabella Gonzaga, and that while the play was going on everybody was longing for the interludes, is quite intelligible, when we think of the picturesque brilliancy with which they were put on the stage. There were to be seen combats of Roman warriors, who brandished their weapons to the sound of music, torch-dances executed by Moors, a dance of savages with horns of plenty, out of which streamed waves of fire—all as the ballet of a pantomime in which a maiden was delivered from a dragon. Then came a dance of fools, got up as Punches, beating one another with pigs' bladders, with more of the same kind. At the Court of Ferrara they never gave a comedy without 'its' ballet (Moresca). In what style the 'Amphitruo' of Plautus was there represented (1491, at the first marriage of Alfonso with Anna Sforza), is doubtful. Possibly it was given rather as a pantomime with music than as a drama. In any case, the accessories were more considerable than the play itself. There was a choral dance of ivy-clad youths, moving in intricate figures, done to the music of a ringing orchestra; then came Apollo, striking the lyre with the plectrum, and singing an ode to the praise of the House of Este; then followed, as an interlude within an interlude, a kind of rustic farce, after which the stage was again occupied by classical mythology—Venus, Bacchus and their followers—and by a pantomime representing the judgement of Paris. Not till then was the second half of the fable of Amphitruo performed, with unmistakable references to the future birth of a Hercules of the House of Este. At a former representation of the same piece in the courtyard of the palace (1487), 'a paradise with stars and other wheels', was constantly burning, by which is probably meant an illumination with fireworks, that, no doubt, absorbed most of the attention of the spectators. It was certainly better when such performances were given separately, as was the case at other courts. We shall have to speak of the entertainments given by the Cardinal Pietro Riario, by the Bentivogli at Bologna, and by others, when we come to treat of the festivals in general.

This scenic magnificence, now become universal, had a disastrous effect on Italian tragedy. 'In Venice formerly,' writes Francesco Sansovino, about 1570, 'besides comedies, tragedies by ancient and modern writers were put on the stage with great pomp. The fame of the scenic arrangements (*apparati*) brought spectators from far and near. Nowadays, performances are given by private individuals in their own houses, and the custom has long been fixed of passing the carnival in comedies and other cheerful entertainments.' In other words, scenic display had helped to kill tragedy.

The various starts or attempts of these modern tragedians, among which the 'Sofonisba' of Trissino (1515) was the most celebrated, belong into the history of literature. The same may be said of genteel comedy, modelled on Plautus and Terence. Even Ariosto could do nothing of the first order in this style. On the other hand, popular prose-comedy, as treated by Machiavelli, Bibbiena, and Aretino, might have had a future, if its matter had not condemned it to destruction. This was, on the one hand, licentious to the last degree, and on the other, aimed at certain classes in society, which, after the middle of the sixteenth century, ceased to afford a ground for public attacks. If in the 'Sofonisba' the portrayal of character gave place to brilliant declamation, the latter, with its half-sister caricature, was used far too freely in comedy also.

The writing of tragedies and comedies, and the practice of putting both ancient and modern plays on the stage, continued without intermission; but they served only as occasions for display. The national genius turned elsewhere for living interest. When the opera and the pastoral fable came up, these attempts were at length wholly abandoned.

One form of comedy only was and remained national—the unwritten, improvised 'Commedia dell' Arte'. It was of no great service in the delineation of character, since the masks used were few in number and familiar to everybody. But the talent of the nation had such an affinity for this style, that often in the middle of written comedies the actors would throw themselves on their own inspiration, so that a new mixed form of comedy came into existence in some places. The plays given in Venice by Burchiello, and afterwards by the company of Armonio, Val. Zuccato, Lod. Dolce, and others, were perhaps of this character. Of Burchiello we know expressly that he used to heighten the comic effect by mixing Greek and Slavonic words with the Venetian dialect. A complete 'Comedia dell' Arte', or very nearly so, was represented by Angelo Beolco, known as 'Il Ruzzante' (1502–42), whose customary masks were Paduan peasants, with the names Menato, Vezzo, Billora, etc. He studied their dialect when spending the summer at the villa of his patron Luigi Cornaro (Aloysius Cornelius) at Codevico. Gradually all the famous local masks made their appearance, whose remains still delight the Italian populace at our day: Pantalone, the Doctor, Brighella, Pulcinella, Arlecchino, and the rest. Most of them are of great antiquity, and possibly are historically connected with the masks in the old Roman farces; but it was not till the sixteenth century that several of them were combined in one piece. At the present time this is less often the case; but every great city still keeps to its local mask—Naples to the Pulcinella, Florence to the Stentorello, Milan to its often so admirable Meneghino.

This is indeed scanty compensation for a people which possessed the power, perhaps to a greater degree than any other, to reflect and contemplate its own highest qualities in the mirror of the drama. But this power was destined to be marred for centuries by hostile forces, for whose predominance the Italians were only in part responsible. The universal talent for dramatic representation could not indeed be uprooted, and in music Italy long made good its claim to supremacy in Europe. Those who can find in this world of sound a compensation for the drama, to which all future was denied, have, at all events, no meagre source of consolation.

But perhaps we can find in epic poetry what the stage fails to offer us. Yet the chief reproach made against the heroic poetry of Italy is precisely on the score of the insignificance and imperfect representation of its characters.

Other merits are allowed to belong to it, among the rest, that for three centuries it has been actually read and constantly reprinted, while nearly the whole of the epic poetry of other nations has become a mere matter of literary or historical curiosity. Does this perhaps lie in the taste of the readers, who demand something different from what would satisfy a northern public? Certainly, without the power of entering to some degree into Italian sentiment, it is impossible to appreciate the characteristic excellence of these poems, and many distinguished men declare that they can make nothing of them. And in truth, if we criticize Pulci, Boiardo, Ariosto, and Berni solely with an eye to their thought and matter, we shall fail to do them justice. They are artists of a peculiar kind, who write for a people which is distinctly and eminently artistic.

The mediæval legends had lived on after the gradual extinction of the poetry of chivalry, partly in the form of rhyming adaptations and collections, and partly of novels in prose. The latter was the case in Italy during the fourteenth century; but the newly-awakened memories of antiquity were rapidly growing up to a gigantic size, and soon cast into the shade all the fantastic creations of the Middle Ages. Boccaccio, for example, in his 'Visione Amorosa', names among the heroes in his enchanted palace Tristram, Arthur, Galeotto, and others, but briefly, as if he were ashamed to speak of them; and following writers either do not name them at all, or name them only for purposes of ridicule. But the people kept them in its memory, and from the people they passed into the hands of the poets of the fifteenth century. These were now able to conceive and represent their subjects in a wholly new manner. But they did more. They introduced into it a multitude of fresh elements, and in fact recast it from beginning to end. It must not be expected of them that they should treat such subjects with the respect once felt for them. All other countries must envy them the advantage of having a popular interest of this kind to appeal to; but they could not without hypocrisy treat these myths with any respect.

Instead of this, they moved with victorious freedom in the new field which poetry had won. What they chiefly aimed at seems to have been that their poems, when recited, should produce the most harmonious and exhilarating effect. These works indeed gain immensely when they are repeated, not as a whole, but piecemeal, and with a slight touch of comedy in voice and gesture. A deeper and more detailed portrayal of character would do little to enhance this effect; though the reader may desire it, the hearer, who sees the rhapsodist standing before him, and who hears only one piece at a time, does not think about it at all. With respect to the figures, which the poet found ready made for him, his feeling was of a double kind; his humanistic culture protested against their mediæval character, and their combats as counterparts of the battles and tournaments of the poet's own age exercised all his knowledge and artistic power, while at the same time they called forth all the highest qualities in the reciter. Even in Pulci, accordingly, we find no parody, strictly speaking, of chivalry, nearly as the rough humour of his paladins at times approaches it. By their side stands the ideal of pugnacity—the droll and jovial Morgante—who masters whole armies with his bell-clapper, and who is himself thrown into relief by contrast with the grotesque and most interesting monster Margutte. Yet Pulci lays no special stress on these two rough and vigorous characters, and his story, long after they had disappeared from it, maintains its singular course. Boiardo treats his characters with the same mastery, using them for serious or comic purposes as he pleases; he has his fun even out of supernatural beings, whom he sometimes intentionally depicts as louts. But there is one artistic aim which he pursues as earnestly as Pulci, namely, the lively and exact description of all that goes forward. Pulci recited his poem, as one book after another was finished, before the society of Lorenzo il Magnifico, and in the same way Boiardo recited his at the court of Ercole of Ferrara. It may be easily imagined what sort of excellence such an audience demanded, and how little thanks a profound exposition of character would have earned for the poet. Under these circumstances the poems naturally formed no complete whole, and might just as well be half or twice as long as they now are. Their composition is not that of a great historical picture, but rather that of a frieze, or of some rich festoon entwined among groups of picturesque figures. And precisely as in the figures or tendrils of a frieze we do not look for minuteness of execution in the individual forms, or for distant perspectives and different planes, so we must as little expect anything of the kind from these poems.

The varied richness of invention which continually astonishes us, most of all in the case of Boiardo, turns to ridicule all our school definitions as to the essence of epic poetry. For that age, this form of literature was the most agreeable diversion from archæological studies, and, indeed, the only possible means of re-establishing an independent class of narrative poetry. For the versification of ancient history could only lead to the false tracks which were trodden by Petrarch in his 'Africa', written in Latin hexameters, and a hundred and fifty years later by Trissino in his 'Italy delivered from the Goths', composed in 'versi sciolti'—a never-ending poem of faultless language and versification, which only makes us doubt whether this unlucky alliance has been more disastrous to history or to poetry.

And whither did the example of Dante beguile those who imitated him? The visionary 'Trionfi' of Petrarch were the last of the works written under this influence which satisfy our taste. The 'Amorosa Visione' of Boccaccio is at bottom no more than an enumeration of historical or fabulous characters, arranged under allegorical categories. Others preface what they have to tell with a baroque imitation of Dante's first canto, and provide themselves with some allegorical comparison, to take the place of Virgil. Uberti, for example, chose Solinus for his geographical poem—the 'Dittamondo'—and Giovanni Santi, Plutarch for his encomium on Federigo of Urbino. The only salvation of the time from these false tendencies lay in the new epic poetry which was represented by Pulci and Boiardo. The admiration and curiosity with which it was received, and the like of which will perhaps never fall again to the lot of epic poetry to the end of time, is a brilliant proof of how great was the need of it. It is idle to ask whether that epic ideal which our own day has formed from Homer and the 'Nibelungenlied' is or is not realized in these works; an ideal of their own age certainly was. By their endless descriptions of combats, which to us are the most fatiguing part of these poems, they satisfied, as we have already said, a practical interest of which it is hard for us to form a just conception—as hard, indeed, as of the esteem in which a lively and faithful reflection of the passing moment was then held.

Nor can a more inappropriate test be applied to Ariosto than the degree in which his 'Orlando Furioso'[67] serves for the representation of character. Characters, indeed, there are, and drawn with an affectionate care; but the poem does not depend on these for its effect,

[67] First edition, 1516.

and would lose, rather than gain, if more stress were laid upon them. But the demand for them is part of a wider and more general desire which Ariosto fails to satisfy as our day would wish it satisfied. From a poet of such fame and such mighty gifts we would gladly receive something better than the adventures of Orlando. From him we might have hoped for a work expressing the deepest conflicts of the human soul, the highest thoughts of his time on human and divine things—in a word, one of those supreme syntheses like the 'Divine Comedy' or 'Faust'. Instead of which he goes to work like the visual artists of his own day, not caring for originality in our sense of the word, simply reproducing a familiar circle of figures, and even, when it suits his purpose, making use of the details left him by his predecessors. The excellence which, in spite of all this, can nevertheless be attained, will be the more incomprehensible to people born without the artistic sense, the more learned and intelligent in other respects they are. The artistic aim of Ariosto is brilliant, living action, which he distributes equally through the whole of his great poem. For this end he needs to be excused, not only from all deeper expression of character, but also from maintaining any strict connection in his narrative. He must be allowed to take up lost and forgotten threads when and where he pleases; his heroes must come and go, not because their character, but because the story requires it. Yet in this apparently irrational and arbitrary style of composition he displays a harmonious beauty, never losing himself in description, but giving only such a sketch of scenes and persons as does not hinder the flowing movement of the narrative. Still less does he lose himself in conversation and monologue, but maintains the lofty privilege of the true epos, by transforming all into living narrative. His pathos does not lie in the words, not even in the famous twenty-third and following cantos, where Roland's madness is described. That the love-stories in the heroic poem are without all lyrical tenderness, must be reckoned a merit, though from a moral point of view they cannot always be approved. Yet at times they are of such truth and reality, notwithstanding all the magic and romance which surrounds them, that we might think them personal affairs of the poet himself. In the full consciousness of his own genius, he does not scruple to interweave the events of his own day into the poem, and to celebrate the fame of the house of Este in visions and prophecies. The wonderful stream of his octaves bears it all forward in even and dignified movement.

With Teofilo Folengo, or, as he here calls himself, Limerno

Pitocco, the parody of the whole system of chivalry attained the end it had so long desired. But here comedy, with its realism, demanded of necessity a stricter delineation of character. Exposed to all the rough usage of the half-savage street-lads in a Roman country town, Sutri, the little Orlando grows up before our eyes into the hero, the priest-hater, and the disputant. The conventional world which had been recognized since the time of Pulci and had served as a framework for the epos, here falls to pieces. The origin and position of the paladins is openly ridiculed, as in the tournament of donkeys in the second book, where the knights appear with the most ludicrous armament. The poet utters his ironical regrets over the inexplicable faithlessness which seems implanted in the house of Gano of Mainz, over the toilsome acquisition of the sword Durindana, and so forth. Tradition, in fact, serves him only as a substratum for episodes, ludicrous fancies, allusions to events of the time (among which some, like the close of cap. vi. are exceedingly fine), and indecent jokes. Mixed with all this, a certain derision of Ariosto is unmistakable, and it was fortunate for the 'Orlando Furioso' that the 'Orlandino', with its Lutheran heresies, was soon put out of the way by the Inquisition. The parody is evident when (cap. VI, 28) the house of Gonzaga is deduced from the paladin Guidone, since the Colonna claimed Orlando, the Orsini Rinaldo, and the house of Este—according to Ariosto—Ruggiero as their ancestors. Perhaps Ferrante Gonzaga, the patron of the poet, was a party to this sarcasm on the house of Este.

That in the 'Jerusalem Delivered' of Torquato Tasso the delineation of character is one of the chief tasks of the poet, proves only how far his mode of thought differed from that prevalent half a century before. His admirable work is a true monument of the Counter-reformation which had meanwhile been accomplished, and of the spirit and tendency of that movement.

BIOGRAPHY IN THE MIDDLE AGES AND IN THE RENAISSANCE

Outside the sphere of poetry also, the Italians were the first of all European nations who displayed any remarkable power and inclination accurately to describe man as shown in history, according to his inward and outward characteristics.

It is true that in the Middle Ages considerable attempts were made in the same direction; and the legends of the Church, as a kind of standing biographical task, must, to some extent, have kept alive the interest and the gift for such descriptions. In the annals of the monasteries and cathedrals, many of the churchmen, such as Meinwerk of Paderborn, Godehard of Hildesheim, and others, are brought vividly before our eyes; and descriptions exist of several of the German emperors, modelled after old authors—particularly Suetonius—which contain admirable features. Indeed these and other profane 'vitae' came in time to form a continuous counterpart to the sacred legends. Yet neither Einhard nor Wippo nor Radevicus can be named by the side of Joinville's picture of St. Louis, which certainly stands almost alone as the first complete spiritual portrait of a modern European nature. Characters like St. Louis are rare at all times, and his was favoured by the rare good fortune that a sincere and naïve observer caught the spirit of all the events and actions of his life, and represented it admirably. From what scanty sources are we left to guess at the inward nature of Frederick II or of Philip the Fair. Much of what, till the close of the Middle Ages, passed for biography, is properly speaking nothing but contemporary narrative, written without any sense of what is individual in the subject of the memoir.

Among the Italians, on the contrary, the search for the characteristic features of remarkable men was a prevailing tendency; and this it is which separates them from the other western peoples, among whom the same thing happens but seldom, and in exceptional cases. This keen eye for individuality belongs only to those who have emerged from the half-conscious life of the race and become themselves individuals.

Under the influence of the prevailing conception of fame an art of comparative biography arose which no longer found it necessary, like Anastasius, Agnellus, and their successors, or like the biographers of the Venetian doges, to adhere to a dynastic or ecclesiastical succession. It felt itself free to describe a man if and because he was remarkable. It took as models Suetonius, Nepos (the 'viri illustres'), and Plutarch, so far as he was known and translated; for sketches of literary history, the lives of the grammarians, rhetoricians, and poets, known to us as the 'Appendices' to Suetonius, seem to have served as patterns, as well as the widely-read life of Virgil by Donatus.

It has already been mentioned that biographical collections—lives of famous men and famous women—began to appear in the fourteenth century. Where they do not describe contemporaries, they are naturally dependent on earlier narratives. The first great original effort is the life of Dante by Boccaccio. Lightly and rhetorically written, and full, as it is, of arbitrary fancies, this work nevertheless gives us a lively sense of the extraordinary features in Dante's nature. Then follow, at the end of the fourteenth century, the 'vite' of illustrious Florentines, by Filippo Villani. They are men of every calling: poets, jurists, physicians, scholars, artists, statesmen, and soldiers, some of them then still living. Florence is here treated like a gifted family, in which all the members are noticed in whom the spirit of the house expresses itself vigorously. The descriptions are brief, but show a remarkable eye for what is characteristic, and are noteworthy for including the inward and outward physiognomy in the same sketch. From that time forward, the Tuscans never ceased to consider the description of man as lying within their special competence, and to them we owe the most valuable portraits of the Italians of the fifteenth and sixteenth centuries. Giovanni Cavalcanti, in the appendices to his Florentine history, written before the year 1450, collects instances of civil virtue and abnegation, of political discernment and of military valour, all shown by Florentines. Pius II gives in his 'Commentaries' valuable portraits of famous contemporaries; and not long ago a separate work of his earlier years, which seems preparatory to these portraits, but which has colours and features that are very singular, was reprinted. To Jacopo of Volterra we owe piquant sketches of members of the Curia in the time of Sixtus IV. Vespasiano Fiorentino has often been referred to already, and as a historical authority a high place must be assigned to him; but his gift as a painter of character is not to be compared with that of Machiavelli, Niccolò Valori, Guicciardini, Varchi, Francesco Vettori, and others, by whom European historical literature has probably been as much influenced in this direction as by the ancients. It must not be forgotten that some of these authors soon found their way into northern countries by means of Latin translations. And without Giorgio Vasari of Arezzo and his all-important work, we should perhaps to this day have no history of Northern art, or of the art of modern Europe, at all.

Among the biographers of North Italy in the fifteenth century, Bartolommeo Fazio of Spezia holds a high rank. Platina, born in the territory of Cremona, gives us, in his 'Life of Paul II', examples of biographical caricatures. The description of the last Visconti, written by Piercandido Decembrio—an enlarged imitation of Suetonius—is of special importance. Sismondi regrets that so much trouble has been spent on so unworthy an object, but the author would hardly have been equal to deal with a greater man, while he was thoroughly competent to describe the mixed nature of Filippo Maria, and in and through it to represent with accuracy the conditions, the forms, and the consequences of this particular kind of despotism. The picture of the fifteenth century would be incomplete without this unique biography, which is characteristic down to its minutest details. Milan afterwards possessed, in the historian Corio, an excellent portrait-painter; and after him came Paolo Giovio of Como, whose larger biographies and shorter 'Elogia' have achieved a world-wide reputation, and become models for subsequent writers in all countries. It is easy to prove by a hundred passages how superficial and even dishonest he was; nor from a man like him can any high and serious purpose be expected. But the breath of the age moves in his pages, and his Leo, his Alfonso, his Pompeo Colonna, live and act before us with such perfect truth and reality, that we seem admitted to the deepest recesses of their nature.

Among Neapolitan writers, Tristano Caracciolo, so far as we are able to judge, holds indisputably the first place in this respect, although his purpose was not strictly biographical. In the figures which he brings before us, guilt and destiny are wondrously mingled. He is a kind of unconscious tragedian. That genuine tragedy which then found no place on the stage, 'swept by' in the palace, the street, and the public square. The 'Words and Deeds of Alfonso the Great', written by Antonio Panormita during the lifetime of the king, are remarkable as one of the first of such collections of anecdotes and of wise and witty sayings.

The rest of Europe followed the example of Italy in this respect but slowly, although great political and religious movements had broken so many bonds, and had awakened so many thousands to new spiritual life. Italians, whether scholars or diplomatists, still remained, on the whole, the best source of information for the characters of the leading men all over Europe. It is well known how speedily and unanimously in recent times the reports of the Venetian embassies in the sixteenth and seventeenth centuries have been recognized as authorities of the first order for personal description. Even autobiography takes here and there in Italy a bold and vigorous flight, and puts before us, together with the most varied incidents of external life, striking revelations of the inner man. Among other nations, even in Germany at the time of the Reformation, it deals only with outward experiences, and leaves us to guess at the spirit within from the style of the narrative. It seems as though Dante's 'Vita Nuova', with the inexorable truthfulness which runs through it, had shown his people the way.

The beginnings of autobiography are to be traced in the family histories of the fourteenth and fifteenth centuries, which are said to be not uncommon as manuscripts in the Florentine libraries—unaffected narratives written for the sake of the individual or of his family, like that of Buonaccorso Pitti.

A profound self-analysis is not to be looked for in the 'Commentaries' of Pius II. What we here learn of him as a man seems at first sight to be chiefly confined to the account which he gives of the various steps in his career. But further reflection will lead us to a different conclusion with regard to this remarkable book. There are men who are by nature mirrors of what surrounds them. It would be irrelevant to ask incessantly after their convictions, their spiritual struggles, their inmost victories and achievements. Æneas Sylvius lived wholly in the interest which lay near, without troubling himself about the problems and contradictions of life. His Catholic orthodoxy gave him all the help of this kind which he needed. And at all events, after taking part in every intellectual movement which interested his age, and notably furthering some of them, he still at the close of his earthly course retained character enough to preach a crusade against the Turks, and to die of grief when it came to nothing.

Nor is the autobiography of Benvenuto Cellini, any more than that of Pius II, founded on introspection. And yet it describes the whole man—not always willingly—with marvellous truth and completeness. It is no small matter that Benvenuto, whose most important works have perished half finished, and who, as an artist, is perfect only in his little decorative speciality, but in other respects, if judged by the works of him which remain, is surpassed by so many of his greater contemporaries—that Benvenuto as a man will interest mankind to the end of time. It does not spoil the impression when the reader often detects him bragging or lying; the stamp of a mighty, energetic, and thoroughly developed nature remains. By his side our modern autobiographers, though their tendency and moral character may stand much higher, appear incomplete beings. He is a man who can do all and dares do all, and who carries his measure in himself. Whether we like him or not, he lives, such as he was, as a significant type of the modern spirit.

Another man deserves a brief mention in connection with this subject—a man who, like Benvenuto, was not a model of veracity: Girolamo Cardano of Milan (b. 1500). His little book, 'De propria vita', will outlive and eclipse his fame in philosophy and natural science, just as Benvenuto's Life, though its value is of another kind, has thrown his works into the shade. Cardano is a physician who feels his own pulse, and describes his own physical, moral, and intellectual nature, together with all the conditions under which it had developed, and this, to the best of his ability, honestly and sincerely. The work which he avowedly took as his model—the 'Confessions' of Marcus Aurelius—he was able, hampered as he was by no stoical maxims, to surpass in this particular. He desires to spare neither himself nor others, and begins the narrative of his career with the statement that his mother tried, and failed, to procure abortion. It is worth remark that he attributes to the stars which presided over his birth only the events of his life and his intellectual gifts, but not his moral qualities; he confesses (cap. 10) that the astrological prediction that he would not live to the age of forty or fifty years did him much harm in his youth. But there is no need to quote from so well-known and accessible a book; whoever opens it will not lay it down till the last page. Cardano admits that he cheated at play, that he was vindictive, incapable of all compunction, purposely cruel in his speech. He confesses it without impudence and without feigned contrition, without even wishing to make himself an object of interest, but with the same simple and sincere love of fact which guided him in his scientific researches. And, what is to us the most repulsive of all, the old man, after the most shocking experiences and with his confidence in his fellow-men gone, finds himself after all tolerably happy and comfortable. He has still left him a grandson, immense learning, the fame of his works, money, rank and credit, powerful friends, the knowledge of many secrets, and, best of all, belief in God. After this, he counts the teeth in his head, and finds that he has fifteen.

Yet when Cardano wrote, Inquisitors and Spaniards were already busy in Italy, either hindering the production of such natures, or, where they existed, by some means or other putting them out of the way. There lies a gulf between this book and the memoirs of Alfieri.

Yet it would be unjust to close this list of autobiographers without listening to a word from one man who was both worthy and happy. This is the well-known philosopher of practical life, Luigi Cornaro, whose dwelling at Padua, classical as an architectural work, was at the same time the home of all the muses. In his famous treatise 'On the Sober Life', he describes the strict regimen by which he succeeded, after a sickly youth, in reaching an advanced and healthy age, then of eighty-three years. He goes on to answer those who despise life after the age of sixty-five as a living death, showing them that his own life had nothing deadly about it. 'Let them come and see, and wonder at my good health, how I mount on horseback without help, how I run upstairs and up hills, how cheerful, amusing, and contented I am, how free from care and disagreeable thoughts. Peace and joy never quit me. . . . My friends are wise, learned, and distinguished people of good position, and when they are not with me I read and write, and try thereby, as by all other means, to be useful to others. Each of these things I do at the proper time, and at my ease, in my dwelling, which is beautiful and lies in the best part of Padua, and is arranged both for summer and winter with all the resources of architecture, and provided with a garden by the running water. In the spring and autumn, I go for awhile to my hill in the most beautiful part of the Euganean mountains, where I have fountains and gardens, and a comfortable dwelling; and there I amuse myself with some easy and pleasant chase, which is suitable to my years. At other times I go to my villa on the plain; there all the paths lead to an open space, in the middle of which stands a pretty church; an arm of the Brenta flows through the plantations—fruitful, well-cultivated fields, now fully peopled, which the marshes and the foul air once made fitter for snakes than for men. It was I who drained the country; then the air became good, and people settled there and multiplied, and the land became cultivated as it now is, so that I can truly say: "On this spot I gave to God an altar and a temple, and souls to worship Him". This is my consolation and my happiness whenever I come here. In the spring and autumn, I also visit the neighbouring towns, to see and converse with my friends, through whom I make the acquaintance of other distinguished men, architects, painters, sculptors, musicians, and cultivators of the soil. I see what new things they have done, I look again at what I know already, and learn much that is of use to me. I see palaces, gardens, antiquities, public grounds, churches, and fortifications. But what most of all delights me when I travel, is the beauty of the country and the places, lying now on the plain, now on the slopes of the hills, or on the banks of rivers and streams, surrounded by gardens and villas. And these enjoyments are not diminished through weakness of the eyes or the ears; all my senses (thank God!) are in the best condition, including the sense of taste; for I enjoy more the simple food which I now take in moderation, than all the delicacies which I ate in my years of disorder.'

After mentioning the works he had undertaken on behalf of the republic for draining the marshes, and the projects which he had constantly advocated for preserving the lagoons, he thus concludes:

'These are the true recreations of an old age which God has permitted to be healthy, and which is free from those mental and bodily sufferings to which so many young people and so many sickly older people succumb. And if it be allowable to add the little to the great, to add jest to earnest, it may be mentioned as a result of my moderate life, that in my eighty-third year I have written a most amusing comedy, full of blameless wit. Such works are generally the business of youth, as tragedy is the business of old age. If it is reckoned to the credit of the famous Greek that he wrote a tragedy in his seventy-third year, must I not, with my ten years more, be more cheerful and healthy than he ever was? And that no consolation may be wanting in the overflowing cup of my old age, I see before my eyes a sort of bodily immortality in the persons of my descendants. When I come home I see before me, not one or two, but eleven grandchildren, between the ages of two and eighteen, all from the same father and mother, all healthy, and, so far as can already be judged, all gifted with the talent and disposition for learning and a good life. One of the younger I have as my playmate (buffoncello), since children from the third to the fifth year are born to tricks; the elder ones I treat as my companions, and, as they have admirable voices, I take delight in hearing them sing and play on different instruments. And I sing myself, and find my voice better, clearer, and louder than ever. These are the pleasures of my last years. My life, therefore, is alive, and not dead; nor would I exchange my age for the youth of such as live in the service of their passions.'

In the 'Exhortation' which Cornaro added at a much later time, in his ninety-fifth year, he reckons it among the elements of his happiness that his 'Treatise' had made many converts. He died at Padua in 1565, at the age of over a hundred years.

This national gift did not, however, confine itself to the criticism and description of individuals, but felt itself competent to deal with the qualities and characteristics of whole peoples. Throughout the

Middle Ages the cities, families, and nations of all Europe were in the habit of making insulting and derisive attacks on one another, which, with much caricature, contained commonly a kernel of truth. But from the first the Italians surpassed all others in their quick apprehension of the mental differences among cities and populations. Their local patriotism, stronger probably than in any other mediæval people, soon found expression in literature, and allied itself with the current conception of 'Fame'. Topography became the counterpart of biography; while all the more important cities began to celebrate their own praises in prose and verse, writers appeared who made the chief towns and districts the subject partly of a serious comparative description, partly of satire, and sometimes of notices in which jest and earnest are not easy to be distinguished. Next to some famous passages in the 'Divine Comedy', we have here the 'Dittamondo' of Uberti (about 1360). As a rule, only single remarkable facts and characteristics are here mentioned: the Feast of the Crows at Sant' Apollinare in Ravenna, the springs at Treviso, the great cellar near Vicenza, the high duties at Mantua, the forest of towers at Lucca. Yet mixed up with all this, we find laudatory and satirical criticisms of every kind. Arezzo figures with the crafty disposition of its citizens, Genoa with the artificially blackened eyes and teeth (?) of its women, Bologna with its prodigality, Bergamo with its coarse dialect and hard-headed people. In the fifteenth century the fashion was to belaud one's own city even at the expense of others. Michele Savonarola allows that, in comparison with his native Padua, only Rome and Venice are more splendid, and Florence perhaps more joyous—by which our knowledge is naturally not much extended. At the end of the century, Jovianus Pontanus, in his 'Antonius', writes an imaginary journey through Italy, simply as a vehicle for malicious observations. But in the sixteenth century we meet with a series of exact and profound studies of national characteristics, such as no other people of that time could rival. Machiavelli sets forth in some of his valuable essays the character and the political condition of the Germans and French in such a way that the born northerner, familiar with the history of his own country, is grateful to the Florentine thinker for his flashes of insight. The Florentines begin to take pleasure in describing themselves; and basking in the well-earned sunshine of their intellectual glory, their pride seems to attain its height when they derive the artistic pre-eminence of Tuscany among Italians, not from any special gifts of nature, but from hard, patient work. The homage of famous men from other parts of Italy, of which the sixteenth Capitolo of Ariosto is a splendid example, they accepted as a merited tribute to their excellence.

Of an admirable description of the Italians, with their various pursuits and characteristics, though in a few words and with special stress laid on the Lucchese, to whom the work was dedicated, we can give only the title: *Forcianae Questiones*, by Ortensio Landi, Naples, 1536. Leandro Alberti is not so fruitful as might be expected in his description of the character of the different cities. A 'Commentario' (by Ortensio Landi, Venice, 1553) contains among many absurdities some valuable information on the unfortunate conditions prevailing about the middle of the century.

To what extent this comparative study of national and local characteristics may, by means of Italian humanism, have influenced the rest of Europe, we cannot say with precision. To Italy, at all events, belongs the priority in this respect, as in the description of the world in general.

DESCRIPTION OF THE OUTWARD MAN

But the discoveries made with regard to man were not confined to the spiritual characteristics of individuals and nations; his outward appearance was in Italy the subject of an entirely different interest from that shown in it by northern peoples.

Of the position held by the great Italian physicians with respect to the progress of physiology, we cannot venture to speak; and the artistic study of the human figure belongs, not to a work like the present, but to the history of art. But something must here be said of that universal education of the eye, which rendered the judgement of the Italians as to bodily beauty or ugliness perfect and final.

On reading the Italian authors of that period attentively, we are astounded at the keenness and accuracy with which outward features are seized, and at the completeness with which personal appearance in general is described. Even today the Italians, and especially the Romans, have the art of sketching a man's picture in a couple of words. This rapid apprehension of what is characteristic is an essential condition for detecting and representing the beautiful. In poetry, it is true, circumstantial description may be a fault, not a merit, since a single feature, suggested by deep passion or insight, will often awaken in the reader a far more powerful impression of the figure described. Dante gives us nowhere a more splendid idea of his

Beatrice than where he only describes the influence which goes forth from her upon all around. But here we have not to treat particularly of poetry, which follows its own laws and pursues its own ends, but rather of the general capacity to paint in words real or imaginary forms.

In this Boccaccio is a master—not in the 'Decameron', where the character of the tales forbids lengthy description, but in the romances, where he is free to take his time. In his 'Ameto' he describes a blonde and a brunette much as an artist a hundred years later would have painted them—for here, too, culture long precedes art. In the account of the brunette—or, strictly speaking, of the less blonde of the two—there are touches which deserve to be called classical. In the words 'la spaziosa testa e distesa' lies the feeling for grander forms, which go beyond a graceful prettiness; the eyebrows with him no longer resemble two bows, as in the Byzantine ideal, but a single wavy line; the nose seems to have been meant to be aquiline; the broad, full breast, the arms of moderate length, the effect of the beautiful hand, as it lies on the purple mantle—all this foretells the sense of beauty of a coming time, and unconsciously approaches to that of classical antiquity. In other descriptions Boccaccio mentions a flat (not mediævally rounded) brow, a long, earnest, brown eye, and round, not hollowed neck, as well as—in a very modern tone— the 'little feet' and the 'two roguish eyes' of a black-haired nymph.

Whether the fifteenth century has left any written account of its ideal of beauty, I am not able to say. The works of the painters and sculptors do not render such an account as unnecessary as might appear at first sight, since possibly, as opposed to their realism, a more ideal type might have been favoured and preserved by the writers. In the sixteenth century Firenzuola came forward with his remarkable work on female beauty. We must clearly distinguish in it what he had learned from old authors or from artists, such as the fixing of proportions according to the length of the head, and certain abstract conceptions. What remains is his own genuine observation, illustrated with examples of women and girls from Prato. As his little work is a kind of lecture, delivered before the women of this city—that is to say, before very severe critics—he must have kept pretty closely to the truth. His principle is avowedly that of Zeuxis and of Lucian—to piece together an ideal beauty out of a number of beautiful parts. He defines the shades of colour which occur in the hair and skin, and gives to the 'biondo' the preference, as the most beautiful colour for the hair, understanding by it a soft yellow, inclining to brown. He requires that the hair should be thick, long, and locky; the forehead serene, and twice as broad as high; the skin bright and clear (candida), but not of a dead white (bianchezza); the eyebrows dark, silky, most strongly marked in the middle, and shading off towards the ears and the nose; the white of the eye faintly touched with blue, the iris not actually black, though all the poets praise 'occhi neri' as a gift of Venus, despite that even goddesses were known for their eyes of heavenly blue, and that soft, joyous, brown eyes were admired by everybody. The eye itself should be large and full, and brought well forward; the lids white, and marked with almost invisible tiny red veins; the lashes neither too long, nor too thick, nor too dark. The hollow round the eye should have the same colour as the cheek. The ear, neither too large nor too small, firmly and neatly fitted on, should show a stronger colour in the winding than in the even parts, with an edge of the transparent ruddiness of the pomegranate. The temples must be white and even, and for the most perfect beauty ought not to be too narrow.[68] The red should grow deeper as the cheek gets rounder. The nose, which chiefly determines the value of the profile, must recede gently and uniformly in the direction of the eyes; where the cartilage ceases, there may be a slight elevation, but not so marked as to make the nose aquiline, which is not pleasing in women; the lower part must be less strongly coloured than the ears, but not of a chilly whiteness, and the middle partition above the lips lightly tinted with red. The mouth, our author would have rather small, and neither projecting to a point, nor quite flat, with the lips not too thin, and fitting neatly together; an accidental opening, that is, when the woman is neither speaking nor laughing, should not display more than six upper teeth. As delicacies of detail, he mentions a dimple in the upper lip, a certain fullness of the under lip, and a tempting smile in the left corner of the mouth—and so on. The teeth should not be too small, regular, well marked off from one another, and of the colour of ivory; and the gums must not be too dark or even like red velvet. The chin is to be round, neither pointed nor curved outwards, and growing slightly

[68] Referring to the fact that the appearance of the temples can be altogether changed by the arrangement of the hair, Firenzuola makes a comical attack on the overcrowding of the hair with flowers, which causes the head to 'look like a lot of pinks or a quarter of goat on the spit'. He is, as a rule, thoroughly at home in caricature.

red as it rises; its glory is the dimple. The neck should be white and round and rather long than short, with the hollow and the Adam's apple but faintly marked; and the skin at every movement must show pleasing lines. The shoulders he desires broad, and in the breadth of the bosom sees the first condition of its beauty. No bone may be visible upon it, its fall and swell must be gentle and gradual, its colour 'candidissimo'. The leg should be long and not too hard in the lower parts, but still not without flesh on the shin, which must be provided with white, full calves. He likes the foot small, but not bony, the instep (it seems) high, and the colour white as alabaster. The arms are to be white, and in the upper parts tinted with red; in their consistence fleshy and muscular, but still soft as those of Pallas, when she stood before the shepherd on Mount Ida—in a word, ripe, fresh, and firm. The hand should be white, especially towards the wrist, but large and plump, feeling soft as silk, the rosy palm marked with a few, but distinct and not intricate lines; the elevations in it should be not too great, the space between thumb and forefinger brightly coloured and without wrinkles, the fingers long, delicate, and scarcely at all thinner towards the tips, with nails clear, even, not too long nor too square, and cut so as to show a white margin about the breadth of a knife's back.

Æsthetic principles of a general character occupy a very subordinate place to these particulars. The ultimate principles of beauty, according to which the eye judges 'senza appello', are for Firenzuola a secret, as he frankly confesses; and his definitions of 'Leggiadria', 'Grazia', 'Vaghezza', 'Venustà', 'Aria', 'Maestà', are partly, as has been remarked, philological, and partly vain attempts to utter the unutterable. Laughter he prettily defines, probably following some old author, as a radiance of the soul.

The literature of all countries can, at the close of the Middle Ages, show single attempts to lay down theoretic principles of beauty; but no other work can be compared to that of Firenzuola. Brantome, who came a good half-century later, is a bungling critic by his side, because governed by lasciviousness and not by a sense of beauty.

DESCRIPTION OF HUMAN LIFE

Among the new discoveries made with regard to man, we must reckon, in conclusion, the interest taken in descriptions of the daily course of human life.

The comical and satirical literature of the Middle Ages could not dispense with pictures of everyday events. But it is another thing, when the Italians of the Renaissance dwelt on this picture for its own sake—for its inherent interest—and because it forms part of that great, universal life of the world whose magic breath they felt everywhere around them. Instead of and together with the satirical comedy, which wanders through houses, villages, and streets, seeking food for its derision in parson, peasant, and burgher, we now see in literature the beginnings of a true *genre*, long before it found any expression in painting. That *genre* and satire are often met with in union, does not prevent them from being wholly different things.

How much of earthly business must Dante have watched with attentive interest, before he was able to make us see with our own eyes all that happened in his spiritual world. The famous pictures of the busy movement in the arsenal at Venice, of the blind men laid side by side before the church door, and the like, are by no means the only instances of this kind: for the art, in which he is a master, of expressing the inmost soul by the outward gesture, cannot exist without a close and incessant study of human life. (Cf. Inferno xxi, 1–6, Purgatorio xiii, 61–66.) The poets who followed rarely came near him in this respect, and the novelists were forbidden by the first laws of their literary style to linger over details. Their prefaces and narratives might be as long as they pleased, but what we understand by *genre* was outside their province. The taste for this class of description was not fully awakened till the time of the revival of antiquity.

And here we are again met by the man who had a heart for everything—Æneas Sylvius. Not only natural beauty, not only that which has an antiquarian or a geographical interest, finds a place in his descriptions, but any living scene of daily life. Among the numerous passages in his memoirs in which scenes are described which hardly one of his contemporaries would have thought worth a line of notice, we will here only mention the boat-race on the Lake of Bolsena. We are not able to detect from what old letter-writer or story-teller the impulse was derived to which we owe such lifelike pictures. Indeed, the whole spiritual communion between antiquity and the Renaissance is full of delicacy and of mystery.

To this class belong those descriptive Latin poems of which we have already spoken—hunting-scenes, journeys, ceremonies, and so forth. In Italian we also find something of the same kind, as, for example, the descriptions of the famous Medicean tournament by Politian and

Luca Pulci. The true epic poets, Luigi Pulci, Boiardo, and Ariosto, are carried on more rapidly by the stream of their narrative; yet in all of them we must recognize the lightness and precision of their descriptive touch as one of the chief elements of their greatness. Franco Sacchetti amuses himself with repeating the short speeches of a troop of pretty women caught in the woods by a shower of rain.

Other scenes of moving life are to be looked for in the military historians. In a lengthy poem, dating from an earlier period, we find a faithful picture of a combat of mercenary soldiers in the fourteenth century, chiefly in the shape of the orders, cries of battle, and dialogue with which it is accompanied.

But the most remarkable productions of this kind are the realistic descriptions of country life, which are found most abundantly in Lorenzo il Magnifico and the poets of his circle.

Since the time of Petrarch, an unreal and conventional style of bucolic poetry had been in vogue, which, whether written in Latin or Italian, was essentially a copy of Virgil. Parallel to this, we find the pastoral novel of Boccaccio and other works of the same kind down to the 'Arcadia' of Sannazaro, and later still, the pastoral comedy of Tasso and Guarini. They are works whose style, whether poetry or prose, is admirably finished and perfect, but in which pastoral life is only an ideal dress for sentiments which belong to a wholly different sphere of culture.

But by the side of all this there appeared in Italian poetry, towards the close of the fifteenth century, signs of a more realistic treatment of rustic life. This was not possible out of Italy; for here only did the peasant, whether labourer or proprietor, possess human dignity, personal freedom, and the right of settlement, hard as his lot might sometimes be in other respects. The difference between town and country is far from being so marked here as in northern countries. Many of the smaller towns are peopled almost exclusively by peasants who, on coming home at nightfall from their work, are transformed into townfolk. The masons of Como wandered over nearly all Italy; the child Giotto was free to leave his sheep and join a guild at Florence; everywhere there was a human stream flowing from the country into the cities, and some mountain populations seemed born to supply this current. It is true that the pride and local conceit supplied poets and novelists with abundant motives for making game of the 'villano', and what they left undone was taken charge of by the comic improvisers. But nowhere do we find a trace of that brutal and contemptuous class-hatred against the 'vilains' which inspired the aristocratic poets of Provence, and often, too, the French chroniclers. On the contrary, Italian authors of every sort gladly recognize and accentuate what is great or remarkable in the life of the peasant. Gioviano Pontano mentions with admiration instances of the fortitude of the savage inhabitants of the Abruzzi, in the biographical collections and in the novelists we meet with the figure of the heroic peasant-maiden who hazards her life to defend her family and her honour.[69]

Such conditions made the poetical treatment of country life possible. The first instance we shall mention is that of Battista Mantovano, whose eclogues, once much read and still worth reading, appeared among his earliest works about 1480. They are a mixture of real and conventional rusticity, but the former tends to prevail. They represent the mode of thought of a well-meaning village clergyman, not without a certain leaning to liberal ideas. As Carmelite monk, the writer may have had occasion to mix freely with the peasantry.

But it is with a power of a wholly different kind that Lorenzo il Magnifico transports himself into the peasant's world. His 'Nencia di Barberino' reads like a crowd of genuine extracts from the popular songs of the Florentine country, fused into a great stream of octaves. The objectivity of the writer is such that we are in doubt whether the speaker—the young peasant Vallera, who declares his love to Nencia—awakens his sympathy or ridicule. The deliberate contrast to the conventional eclogue is unmistakable. Lorenzo surrenders himself purposely to the realism of simple, rough country life, and yet his work makes upon us the impression of true poetry.

The 'Beca da Dicomano' of Luigi Pulci is an admitted counterpart to the 'Nencia' of Lorenzo. But the deeper purpose is wanting. The 'Beca' is written not so much from the inward need to give a picture of popular life, as from the desire to win the approbation of the educated Florentine world by a successful poem. Hence the greater and more deliberate coarseness of the scenes, and the indecent jokes.

[69] On the condition of the Italian peasantry in general, and especially of the details of that condition in several provinces, we are unable to particularize more fully. The proportions between freehold and leasehold property, and the burdens laid on each in comparison with those borne at the present time, must be gathered from special works which we have not had the opportunity of consulting. In stormy times the country people were apt to have appalling relapses into savagery.

Nevertheless, the point of view of the rustic lover is admirably maintained.

Third in this company of poets comes Angelo Poliziano, with his 'Rusticus' in Latin hexameters. Keeping clear of all imitation of Virgil's Georgics, he describes the year of the Tuscan peasant, beginning with the late autumn, when the countryman gets ready his new plough and prepares the seed for the winter. The picture of the meadows in spring is full and beautiful, and the 'Summer' has fine passages; but the vintage-feast in autumn is one of the gems of modern Latin poetry. Politian wrote poems in Italian as well as Latin, from which we may infer that in Lorenzo's circle it was possible to give a realistic picture of the passionate life of the lower classes. His gipsy's love-song is one of the earliest products of that wholly modern tendency to put oneself with poetic consciousness into the position of another class. This had probably been attempted for ages with a view to satire, and the opportunity for it was offered in Florence at every carnival by the songs of the maskers. But the sympathetic understanding of the feeling of another class was new; and with it the 'Nencia' and this 'Canzone zingaresca' mark a new starting-point in the history of poetry.

Here, too, we must briefly indicate how culture prepared the way for artistic development. From the time of the 'Nencia', a period of eighty years elapses to the rustic genre-painting of Jacopo Bassano and his school.

In the next part of this work we shall show how differences of birth had lost their significance in Italy. Much of this was doubtless owing to the fact that men and mankind were here first thoroughly and profoundly understood. This one single result of the Renaissance is enough to fill us with everlasting thankfulness. The logical notion of humanity was old enough—but here the notion became a fact.

The loftiest conceptions on this subject were uttered by Pico della Mirandola in his Speech on the Dignity of Man, which may justly be called one of the noblest of that great age. God, he tells us, made man at the close of the creation, to know the laws of the universe, to love its beauty, to admire its greatness. He bound him to no fixed place, to no prescribed form of work, and by no iron necessity, but gave him freedom to will and to love. 'I have set thee,' says the Creator to Adam, 'in the midst of the world, that thou mayst the more easily behold and see all that is therein. I created thee a being neither heavenly nor earthly, neither mortal nor immortal only, that thou mightest be free to shape and to overcome thyself. Thou mayst sink into a beast, and be born anew to the divine likeness. The brutes bring from their mother's body what they will carry with them as long as they live; the higher spirits are from the beginning, or soon after, what they will be for ever. To thee alone is given a growth and a development depending on thine own free will. Thou bearest in thee the germs of a universal life.'

PART V

SOCIETY AND FESTIVALS

EQUALITY OF CLASSES

EVERY period of civilization which forms a complete and consistent whole manifests itself not only in political life, in religion, art, and science, but also sets its characteristic stamp on social life. Thus the Middle Ages had their courtly and aristocratic manners and etiquette, differing but little in the various countries of Europe, as well as their peculiar forms of middle-class life.

Italian customs at the time of the Renaissance offer in these respects the sharpest contrasts to mediævalism. The foundation on which they rest is wholly different. Social intercourse in its highest and most perfect form now ignored all distinctions of caste, and was based simply on the existence of an educated class as we now understand the word. Birth and origin were without influence, unless combined with leisure and inherited wealth. Yet this assertion must not be taken in an absolute and unqualified sense, since mediæval distinctions still sometimes made themselves felt to a greater or less degree, if only as a means of maintaining equality with the aristocratic pretensions of the less advanced countries of Europe. But the main current of the time went steadily towards the fusion of classes in the modern sense of the phrase.

The fact was of vital importance that, from certainly the twelfth century onwards, the nobles and the burghers dwelt together within the walls of the cities. The interests and pleasures of both classes were thus identified, and the feudal lord learned to look at society from another point of view than that of his mountain castle. The Church, too, in Italy never suffered itself, as in northern countries, to be used as a means of providing for the younger sons of noble families. Bishoprics, abbacies, and canonries were often given from the most unworthy motives, but still not according to the pedigrees of the applicants; and if the bishops in Italy were more numerous, poorer, and, as a rule, destitute of all sovereign rights, they still lived in the cities where their cathedrals stood, and formed, together with their chapters, an important element in the cultivated society of the place. In the age of despots and absolute princes which followed, the nobility in most of the cities had the motives and the leisure to give themselves up to a private life free from the political danger and adorned with all that was elegant and enjoyable, but at the same time hardly distinguishable from that of the wealthy burgher. And after the time of Dante, when the new poetry and literature were in the hands of all Italy,[70] when to this was added the revival of ancient culture and the new interest in man as such, when the successful Condottiere became a prince, and not only good birth, but legitimate birth, ceased to be indispensable for a throne, it might well seem that the age of equality had dawned, and the belief in nobility vanished for ever.

From a theoretical point of view, when the appeal was made to antiquity, the conception of nobility could be both justified and condemned from Aristotle alone. Dante, for example,[71] derives from Aristotle's definition, 'Nobility rests on excellence and inherited wealth', his own saying, 'Nobility rests on personal excellence or on that of forefathers'. But elsewhere he is not satisfied with this conclusion. He blames himself,[72] because even in Paradise, while talking with his ancestor Cacciaguida, he made mention of his noble origin, which is but a mantle from which time is ever cutting something away, unless we ourselves add daily fresh worth to it. And in the 'Convito'[73] he disconnects 'nobile' and 'nobiltà' from every condition of birth, and identifies the idea with the capacity for moral and intellectual eminence, laying a special stress on high culture by calling 'nobiltà' the sister of 'filosofia'.

And as time went on, the greater the influence of humanism on the Italian mind, the firmer and more widespread became the conviction that birth decides nothing as to the goodness or badness of a man. In the fifteenth century this was the prevailing opinion. Poggio, in his dialogue 'On nobility', agrees with his interlocutors—Niccolò Niccoli, and Lorenzo Medici, brother of the great Cosimo—that there is no other nobility than that of personal merit. The keenest shafts of his ridicule are directed against much of what vulgar prejudice thinks indispensable to an aristocratic life. 'A man is all

[70] This was the case long before printing. A large number of manuscripts, and among them the best, belonged to Florentine artisans. If it had not been for Savonarola's great bonfire, many more of them would be left.

[71] *De monarchia*, ii. cap. 3.

[72] *Paradiso*, xvi. at the beginning.

[73] *Convito*, nearly the whole *Trattato*, iv., and elsewhere.

the farther removed from true nobility, the longer his forefathers have plied the trade of brigands. The taste for hawking and hunting savours no more of nobility than the nests and lairs of the hunted creatures of spikenard. The cultivation of the soil, as practised by the ancients, would be much nobler than this senseless wandering through the hills and woods, by which men make themselves liker to the brutes than to the reasonable creatures. It may serve well enough as a recreation, but not as the business of a lifetime.' The life of the English and French chivalry in the country or in the woody fastnesses seems to him thoroughly ignoble, and worst of all the doings of the robber-knights of Germany. Lorenzo here begins to take the part of the nobility, but not—which is characteristic—appealing to any natural sentiment in its favour, but because Aristotle in the fifth book of the Politics recognizes the nobility as existent, and defines it as resting on excellence and inherited wealth. To this Niccoli retorts that Aristotle gives this not as his own conviction, but as the popular impression; in this Ethics, where he speaks as he thinks, he calls him noble who strives after that which is truly good. Lorenzo urges upon him vainly that the Greek word for nobility (Eugeneia) means good birth; Niccoli thinks the Roman word 'nobilis' (i.e. remarkable) a better one, since it makes nobility depend on a man's deeds.[74] Together with these discussions, we find a sketch of the conditions of the nobles in various parts of Italy. In Naples they will not work, and busy themselves neither with their own estates nor with trade and commerce, which they hold to be discreditable; they either loiter at home or ride about on horseback. The Roman nobility also despise trade, but farm their own property; the cultivation of the land even opens the way to a title;[75] it is a respectable but boorish nobility. In Lombardy the nobles live upon the rent of their inherited estates; descent and the abstinence from any regular calling constitute nobility. In Venice, the 'nobili', the ruling caste, were all merchants. Similarly in Genoa the nobles and non-nobles were alike merchants and sailors, and only separated by their birth; some few of the former, it is true, still lurked as brigands in their mountain castles. In Florence a part of the old

[74] This contempt of noble birth is common among the humanists. See the severe passages in Æn. Sylvius, *Opera*, pp. 84 (*Hist. bohem.* cap. 2) and 640 (*Stories of Lucretia and Euryalus*).

[75] Throughout Italy it was universal that the owner of large landed property stood on an equality with the nobles.

nobility had devoted themselves to trade; another, and certainly by far the smaller part, enjoyed the satisfaction of their titles, and spent their time, either in nothing at all, or else in hunting and hawking.[76]

The decisive fact was, that nearly everywhere in Italy, even those who might be disposed to pride themselves on their birth could not make good the claims against the power of culture and of wealth, and that their privileges in politics and at court were not sufficient to encourage any strong feeling of caste. Venice offers only an apparent exception to this rule, for there the 'nobili' led the same life as their fellow-citizens, and were distinguished by few honorary privileges. The case was certainly different at Naples, which the strict isolation and the ostentatious vanity of its nobility excluded, above all other causes, from the spiritual movement of the Renaissance. The traditions of mediæval Lombardy and Normandy, and the French aristocratic influences which followed, all tended in this direction; and the Aragonese government, which was established by the middle of the fifteenth century, completed the work, and accomplished in Naples what followed a hundred years later in the rest of Italy—a social transformation in obedience to Spanish ideas, of which the chief features were the contempt for work and the passion for titles. The effect of this new influence was evident, even in the smaller towns, before the year 1500. We hear complaints from La Cava that the place had been proverbially rich, as long as it was filled with masons and weavers; whilst now, since instead of looms and trowels nothing but spurs, stirrups and gilded belts was to be seen, since everybody was trying to become Doctor of Laws or of Medicine, Notary, Officer or Knight, the most intolerable poverty prevailed. In Florence an analogous change appears to have taken place by the time of Cosimo, the first Grand Duke; he is thanked for adopting the young people, who now despise trade and commerce, as knights of his order of St. Stephen.[77] This goes straight in the teeth

[76] The severe judgement of Machiavelli (*Discorsi*, I. 55) refers only to those of the nobility who still retained feudal rights, and who were thoroughly idle and politically mischievous. Agrippa of Nettesheim, who owes his most remarkable ideas chiefly to his life in Italy, has a chapter on the nobility and princes (*De Incert. et Vanit. Scient.* cap. 80), the bitterness of which exceeds anything to be met with elsewhere, and is due to the social ferment then prevailing in the North.

[77] In North Italy the Spanish rule brought about the same results. Bandello, parte ii. nov. 40, dates from this period.

of the good old Florentine custom,[78] by which fathers left property to their children on the condition that they should have some occupation. But a mania for titles of a curious and ludicrous sort sometimes crossed and thwarted, especially among the Florentines, the levelling influence of art and culture. This was the passion for knighthood, which became one of the most striking follies of the day, at a time when the dignity itself had lost every shadow of significance.

'A few years ago,' writes Franco Sacchetti, towards the end of the fourteenth century, 'everybody saw how all the workpeople down to the bakers, how all the wool-carders, usurers, money-changers and blackguards of all description, became knights. Why should an official need knighthood when he goes to preside over some little provincial town? What has this title to do with any ordinary bread-winning pursuit? How art thou sunken, unhappy dignity! Of all the long list of knightly duties, what single one do these knights of ours discharge? I wished to speak of these things that the reader might see that knighthood is dead. And as we have gone so far as to confer the honour upon dead men, why not upon figures of wood and stone, and why not upon an ox?' The stories which Sacchetti tells by way of illustration speak plainly enough. There we read how Bernabò Visconti knighted the victor in a drunken brawl, and then did the same derisively to the vanquished; how German knights with their decorated helmets and devices were ridiculed—and more of the same kind. At a later period Poggio makes merry over the many knights of his day without a horse and without military training. Those who wished to assert the privilege of the order, and ride out with lance and colours, found in Florence that they might have to face the government as well as the jokers.

On considering the matter more closely, we shall find that this belated chivalry, independent of all nobility of birth, though partly the fruit of an insane passion for titles, had nevertheless another and a better side. Tournaments had not yet ceased to be practised, and no one could take part in them who was not a knight. But the combat in the lists, and especially the difficult and perilous tilting with the lance, offered a favourable opportunity for the display of strength, skill, and courage, which no one, whatever might be his

[78] When, in the fifteenth century, Vespasiano Fiorentino implies that the rich should not try to increase their inherited fortune, but should spend their whole annual income, this can only, in the mouth of a Florentine, refer to the great landowners.

origin, would willingly neglect in an age which laid such stress on personal merit.

It was in vain that from the time of Petrarch downwards the tournament was denounced as a dangerous folly. No one was converted by the pathetic appeal of the poet: 'In what book do we read that Scipio and Cæsar were skilled at the joust?' The practice became more and more popular in Florence. Every honest citizen came to consider his tournament—now, no doubt, less dangerous than formerly—as a fashionable sport. Franco Sacchetti has left us a ludicrous picture of one of these holiday cavaliers—a notary seventy years old. He rides out on horseback to Peretola, where the tournament was cheap, on a jade hired from a dyer. A thistle is stuck by some wag under the tail of the steed, who takes fright, runs away, and carries the helmeted rider, bruised and shaken, back into the city. The inevitable conclusion of the story is a severe curtain-lecture from the wife, who is not a little enraged at these break-neck follies of her husband.[79]

It may be mentioned in conclusion that a passionate interest in this sport was displayed by the Medici, as if they wished to show—private citizens as they were, without noble blood in their veins—that the society which surrounded them was in no respect inferior to a Court. Even under Cosimo (1459), and afterwards under the elder Pietro, brilliant tournaments were held at Florence. The younger Pietro neglected the duties of government for these amusements and would never suffer himself to be painted except clad in armour. The same practice prevailed at the Court of Alexander VI, and when the Cardinal Ascanio Sforza asked the Turkish Prince Djem how he liked the spectacle, the barbarian replied with much discretion that such combats in his country only took place among slaves, since then, in the case of accident, nobody was the worse for it. The Oriental was unconsciously in accord with the old Romans in condemning the manners of the Middle Ages.

Apart, however, from this particular prop of knighthood, we find here and there in Italy, for example at Ferrara, orders of courtiers whose members had a right to the title of *Cavaliere*.

[79] This is one of the oldest parodies of the tournament. Sixty years passed before Jacques Cœur, the burgher-minister of finance under Charles VII, placed a relief of a tournament of donkeys in the courtyard of his palace at Bourges (about 1450). The most brilliant of all these parodies—the second canto of the *Orlandino*—was not published till 1526.

But, great as were individual ambitions, and the vanities of nobles and knights, it remains a fact that the Italian nobility took its place in the centre of social life, and not at the extremity. We find it habitually mixing with other classes on a footing of perfect equality, and seeking its natural allies in culture and intelligence. It is true that for the courtier a certain rank of nobility was required, but this exigence is expressly declared to be caused by a prejudice rooted in the public mind—'per l'opinion universale'—and never was held to imply the belief that the personal worth of one who was not of noble blood was in any degree lessened thereby, nor did it follow from this rule that the prince was limited to the nobility for his society. It meant simply that the perfect man—the true courtier—should not be wanting in any conceivable advantage, and therefore not in this. If in all the relations of life he was specially bound to maintain a dignified and reserved demeanour, the reason was not found in the blood which flowed in his veins, but in the perfection of manner which was demanded from him. We are here in the presence of a modern distinction, based on culture and on wealth, but on the latter solely because it enables men to devote their life to the former, and effectually to promote its interests and advancement.

COSTUMES AND FASHIONS

But in proportion as distinctions of birth ceased to confer any special privilege, was the individual himself compelled to make the most of his personal qualities, and society to find its worth and charm in itself. The demeanour of individuals, and all the higher forms of social intercourse, became ends pursued with a deliberate and artistic purpose.

Even the outward appearance of men and women and the habits of daily life were more perfect, more beautiful, and more polished than among the other nations of Europe. The dwellings of the upper classes fall rather within the province of the history of art; but we may note how far the castle and the city mansion in Italy surpassed in comfort, order, and harmony the dwellings of the northern noble. The style of dress varied so continually that it is impossible to make any complete comparison with the fashions of other countries, all the more because since the close of the fifteenth century imitations of the latter were frequent. The costumes of the time, as given us by the Italian painters, are the most convenient, and the most pleasing to the eye which were then to be found in Europe; but we cannot be sure if they represent the prevalent fashion, or if they are faithfully reproduced by the artist. It is nevertheless beyond a doubt that nowhere was so much importance attached to dress as in Italy. The nation was, and is, vain; and even serious men among it looked on a handsome and becoming costume as an element in the perfection of the individual. At Florence, indeed, there was a brief period when dress was a purely personal matter, and every man set the fashion for himself, and till far into the sixteenth century there were exceptional people who still had the courage to do so; and the majority at all events showed themselves capable of varying the fashion according to their individual tastes. It is a symptom of decline when Giovanni della Casa warns his readers not to be singular or to depart from existing fashions. Our own age, which, in men's dress at any rate, treats uniformity as the supreme law, gives up by so doing far more than it is aware of. But it saves itself much time, and this, according to our notions of business, outweighs all other disadvantages.

In Venice and Florence at the time of the Renaissance there were rules and regulations prescribing the dress of the men and restraining the luxury of the women. Where the fashions were more free, as in Naples, the moralists confess with regret that no difference can be observed between noble and burgher. They further deplore the rapid changes of fashion, and—if we rightly understand their words—the senseless idolatry of whatever comes from France, though in many cases the fashions which were received back from the French were originally Italian. It does not further concern us how far these frequent changes, and the adoption of French and Spanish ways, contributed to the national passion for external display; but we find in them additional evidence of the rapid movement of life in Italy in the decades before and after the year 1500.

We may note in particular the efforts of the women to alter their appearance by all the means which the toilette could afford. In no country of Europe since the fall of the Roman Empire was so much trouble taken to modify the face, the colour of the skin and the growth of the hair, as in Italy at this time. All tended to the formation of a conventional type, at the cost of the most striking and transparent deceptions. Leaving out of account costume in general, which in the fourteenth century[80] was in the highest degree varied in colour and

[80] On the Florentine women, see the chief references in Giovanni Villani, x. 10 and 152 (Regulations as to dress and their repeal); Matteo Villani, i. 4 (Extravagant living in consequence of the plague). In the celebrated edict

loaded with ornament, and at a later period assumed a character of more harmonious richness, we here limit ourselves more particularly to the toilette in the narrower sense.

No sort of ornament was more in use than false hair, often made of white or yellow silk.[81] The law denounced and forbade it in vain, till some preacher of repentance touched the worldly minds of the wearers. Then was seen, in the middle of the public square, a lofty pyre (talamo), on which, besides lutes, dice-boxes, masks, magical charms, song-books, and other vanities, lay masses of false hair, which the purging fires soon turned into a heap of ashes. The ideal colour sought for both natural and artificial hair was blond. And as the sun was supposed to have the power of making the hair this colour, many ladies would pass their whole time in the open air on sunshiny days. Dyes and other mixtures were also used freely for the same purpose. Besides all these, we meet with an endless list of beautifying waters, plasters, and paints for every single part of the face—even for the teeth and eyelids—of which in our day we can form no conception. The ridicule of the poets, the invectives of the preachers, and the experience of the baneful effects of these cosmetics on the skin, were powerless to hinder women from giving their faces an unnatural form and colour. It is possible that the frequent and splendid representations of Mysteries,[82] at which hundreds of people appeared painted and masked, helped to further this practice in daily life. It is certain that it was widespread, and that the countrywomen vied in this respect with their sisters in the towns. It was vain to preach that such decorations were the mark of the courtesan; the most honourable matrons, who all the year round never touched paint, used it nevertheless on holidays when they showed themselves in public. But whether we look on this bad habit as a remnant of barbarism, to which the painting of savages is a parallel, or as a consequence of the desire for perfect youthful beauty in feature and in colour, as the art and

on fashions of the year 1330, embroidered figures only were allowed on the dresses of women, to the exclusion of those which were painted (*dipinto*). What was the nature of these decorations appears doubtful.

[81] Tours of real hair were called 'capelli morti'. For an instance of false teeth made of ivory, and worn, though only for the sake of clear articulation, by an Italian prelate, see Anshelm, *Berner Chronik*, iv. p. 30 (1508).

[82] Cennino Cennini, *Trattato della Pittura*, gives in cap. 161 a recipe for painting the face, evidently for the purpose of mysteries or masquerades, since, in cap. 162, he solemnly warns his readers against the general use of cosmetics and the like.

complexity of the toilette would lead us to think—in either case there was no lack of good advice on the part of the men.

The use of perfumes, too, went beyond all reasonable limits. They were applied to everything with which human beings came into contact. At festivals even the mules were treated with scents and ointments, and Pietro Aretino thanks Cosimo I for a perfumed roll of money.

The Italians of that day lived in the belief that they were more cleanly than other nations. There are in fact general reasons which speak rather for than against this claim. Cleanliness is indispensable to our modern notion of social perfection, which was developed in Italy earlier than elsewhere. That the Italians were one of the richest of existing peoples, is another presumption in their favour. Proof, either for or against these pretensions, can of course never be forthcoming, and if the question were one of priority in establishing rules of cleanliness, the chivalrous poetry of the Middle Ages is perhaps in advance of anything that Italy can produce. It is nevertheless certain that the singular neatness and cleanliness of some distinguished representatives of the Renaissance, especially in their behaviour at meals, was noticed expressly,[83] and that 'German' was the synonym in Italy for all that is filthy. The dirty habits which Massimiliano Sforza picked up in the course of his German education, and the notice they attracted on his return to Italy, are recorded by Giovio. It is at the same time very curious that, at least in the fifteenth century, the inns and hotels were left chiefly in the hands of Germans, who probably, however, made their profit mostly out of the pilgrims journeying to Rome. Yet the statements on this point may refer mainly to the country districts, since it it notorious that in the great cities Italian hotels held the first place. The want of decent inns in the country may also be explained by the general insecurity of life and property.

To the first half of the sixteenth century belongs the manual of politeness which Giovanni della Casa, a Florentine by birth, published under the title 'Il Galateo'. Not only cleanliness in the strict sense of the word, but the dropping of all the habits which we consider unbecoming, is here prescribed with the same unfailing tact with

★[83] The use of handkerchiefs was quite general for ladies in Venice, towards the end of the sixteenth century. According to M. Guedemann (*Gesch. d. Erziehungswesens und d. Kultur d. abendländischen Juden*, Vienna, 1880–88) the handkerchief or *fazzoletto* is already mentioned by a Jewish-Italian writer of the thirteenth century.

which the moralist discerns the highest ethical truths. In the literature of other countries the same lessons are taught, though less systematically, by the indirect influence of repulsive descriptions.[84]

In other respects also, the 'Galateo' is a graceful and intelligent guide to good manners—a school of tact and delicacy. Even now it may be read with no small profit by people of all classes, and the politeness of European nations is not likely to outgrow its precepts. So far as tact is an affair of the heart, it has been inborn in some men from the dawn of civilization, and acquired through force of will by others; but the Italians were the first to recognize it as a universal social duty and a mark of culture and education. And Italy itself had altered much in the course of two centuries. We feel at their close that the time for practical jokes between friends and acquaintances—for 'burle' and 'beffe'—was over in good society, that the people had emerged from the walls of the cities and had learned a cosmopolitan politeness and consideration. We shall speak later on of the intercourse of society in the narrower sense.

Outward life, indeed, in the fifteenth and the early part of the sixteenth centuries, was polished and ennobled as among no other people in the world. A countless number of those small things and great things which combine to make up what we mean by comfort, we know to have first appeared in Italy. In the well-paved streets of the Italian cities, driving was universal, while elsewhere in Europe walking or riding was the custom, and at all events no one drove for amusement. We read in the novelists of soft, elastic beds, of costly carpets and bedroom furniture, of which we hear nothing in other countries. We often hear especially of the abundance and beauty of the linen. Much of all this is drawn within the sphere of art. We note with admiration the thousand ways in which art ennobles luxury, not only adorning the massive sideboard or the light brackets with noble vases, clothing the walls with the movable splendour of tapestry, and covering the toilet-table with numberless graceful trifles, but absorbing whole branches of mechanical work—especially carpentering—into its province. All Western Europe, as soon as its wealth enabled it to do so, set to work in the same way at the close of the Middle Ages. But its efforts produced either childish and fantastic toy-work, or were bound by the chains of a narrow and purely Gothic art, while the Renaissance moved freely, entering into the

[84] Comp. e.g. the passages in Sebastian Brant's *Narrenschiff*, in the Colloquies of Erasmus, in the Latin poem *Grobianus*, etc.

spirit of every task it undertook and working for a far larger circle of patrons and admirers than the northern artists. The rapid victory of Italian decorative art over northern in the course of the sixteenth century is due partly to this fact, though partly the result of wider and more general causes.

LANGUAGE AND SOCIETY

The higher forms of social intercourse, which here meet us as a work of art—as a conscious product and one of the highest products of national life—have no more important foundation and condition than language. In the most flourishing period of the Middle Ages, the nobility of Western Europe had sought to establish a 'courtly' speech for social intercourse as well as for poetry. In Italy, too, where the dialects differed so greatly from one another, we find in the thirteenth century a so-called 'Curiale', which was common to the courts and to the poets. It is of decisive importance for Italy that the attempt was there seriously and deliberately made to turn this into the language of literature and society. The introduction to the 'Cento Novelle Antiche', which were put into their present shape before 1300, avows this object openly. Language it here considered apart from its uses in poetry; its highest function is clear, simple, intelligent utterance in short speeches, epigrams, and answers. This faculty was admired in Italy, as nowhere else but among the Greeks and Arabs: 'how many in the course of a long life have scarcely produced a single "bel parlare".'

But the matter was rendered more difficult by the diversity of the aspects under which it was considered. The writings of Dante transport us into the midst of the struggle. His work 'On the Italian Language' is not only of the utmost importance for the subject itself, but is also the first complete treatise on any modern language. His method and results belong to the history of linguistic science, in which they will always hold a high place. We must here content ourselves with the remark that long before the appearance of this book the subject must have been one of daily and pressing importance, that the various dialects of Italy had long been the objects of eager study and dispute, and that the birth of the one ideal language was not accomplished without many throes.

Nothing certainly contributed so much to this end as the great poem of Dante. The Tuscan dialect became the basis of the new national speech.[85] If this assertion may seem to some to go too far, as foreigners we may be excused, in a matter on which much difference of opinion prevails, for following the general belief.

Literature and poetry probably lost more than they gained by the contentious purism which was long prevalent in Italy, and which marred the freshness and vigour of many an able writer. Others, again, who felt themselves masters of this magnificent language, were tempted to rely upon its harmony and flow, apart from the thought which it expressed. A very insignificant melody, played upon such an instrument, can produce a very great effect. But however this may be, it is certain that socially the language had great value. It was, as it were, the crown of a noble and dignified behaviour, and compelled the gentleman, both in his ordinary bearing and in exceptional moments to observe external propriety. No doubt this classical garment, like the language of Attic society, served to drape much that was foul and malicious; but it was also the adequate expression of all that is noblest and most refined. But politically and nationally it was of supreme importance, serving as an ideal home for the educated classes in all the States of the divided peninsula. Nor was it the special property of the nobles or of any one class, but the poorest and humblest might learn it if they would. Even now—and perhaps more than ever—in those parts of Italy where, as a rule, the most unintelligible dialect prevails, the stranger is often astonished at hearing pure and well-spoken Italian from the mouths of peasants or artisans, and looks in vain for anything analogous in France or in Germany, where even the educated classes retain traces of a provincial speech. There is certainly a larger number of people able to read in Italy than we should be led to expect from the condition of many parts of the country—as for instance, the States of the Church—in other respects; but what is more important is the general and undisputed respect for pure language and pronunciation as something precious and sacred. One part of the country after another came to adopt the classical dialect officially. Venice, Milan, and Naples did so at the noontime of Italian literature, and partly through its influences. It was not till the

[85] The gradual progress which this dialect made in literature and social intercourse could be tabulated without difficulty by a native scholar. It could be shown to what extent in the fourteenth and fifteenth centuries the various dialects kept their places, wholly or partly, in correspondence, in official documents, in historical works, and in literature generally. The relations between the dialects and a more or less impure Latin, which served as the official language, would also be discussed.

present century that Piedmont became of its own free will a genuine Italian province by sharing in this chief treasure of the people—pure speech.[86] The dialects were from the beginning of the sixteenth century purposely left to deal with a certain class of subjects, serious as well as comic,[87] and the style which was thus developed proved equal to all its tasks. Among other nations a conscious separation of this kind did not occur till a much later period.

The opinion of educated people as to the social value of language is fully set forth in the 'Cortigiano'.[88] There were then persons, at the beginning of the sixteenth century, who purposely kept to the antiquated expressions of Dante and the other Tuscan writers of his time, simply because they were old. Our author forbids the use of them altogether in speech, and is unwilling to permit them even in writing, which he considers a form of speech. Upon this follows the admission that the best style of speech is that which most resembles good writing. We can clearly recognize the author's feeling that people who have anything of importance to say must shape their own speech, and that language is something flexible and changing because it is something living. It is allowable to make use of any expression, however ornate, as long as it is used by the people; nor are non-Tuscan words, or even French and Spanish words forbidden, if custom has once applied them to definite purposes.[89] Thus care and intelligence will produce a language, which, if not the pure old Tuscan, is still Italian, rich in flowers and fruit like a well-kept garden. It belongs to the

[86] Tuscan, it is true, was read and written long before this in Piedmont—but very little reading and writing was done at all.

[87] The place, too, of the dialect in the usage of daily life was clearly understood. Gioviano Pontano ventured especially to warn the Prince of Naples against the use of it. The last Bourbons were notoriously less scrupulous in this respect. For the way in which a Milanese Cardinal who wished to retain his native dialect in Rome was ridiculed, see Bandello, parte ii. nov. 31.

[88] Bald. Castiglione, *Il Cortigiano*, i. fol. 27 sqq. Throughout the dialogue we are able to gather the personal opinion of the writer.

[89] There was a limit, however, to this. The satirists introduce bits of Spanish, and Folengo (under the pseudonym Limerno Pitocco, in his *Orlandino*) of French, but only by way of ridicule. It is an exceptional fact that a street in Milan, which at the time of the French (1500 to 1512, 1515 to 1522) was called Rue Belle, now bears the name Rugabella. The long Spanish rule has left no traces on the language, and but rarely the name of some governor in streets and public buildings. It was not till the eighteenth century that, together with French modes of thought, many French words and phrases found their way into Italian. The purism of our century is still busy in removing them.

completeness of the 'Cortigiano' that his wit, his polished manners, and his poetry, must be clothed in this perfect dress.

When style and language had once become the property of a living society, all the efforts of purists and archaists failed to secure their end. Tuscany itself was rich in writers and talkers of the first order, who ignored and ridiculed these endeavours. Ridicule in abundance awaited the foreign scholar who explained to the Tuscans how little they understood their own language. The life and influence of a writer like Machiavelli was enough to sweep away all these cobwebs. His vigorous thoughts, his clear and simple mode of expression wore a form which had any merit but that of the 'Trecentisti'. And on the other hand there were too many North Italians, Romans, and Neapolitans, who were thankful if the demand for purity of style in literature and conversation was not pressed too far. They repudiated, indeed, the forms and idioms of their dialect; and Bandello, with what a foreigner might suspect to be false modesty, is never tired of declaring: 'I have no style; I do not write like a Florentine, but like a barbarian; I am not ambitious of giving new graces to my language; I am a Lombard, and from the Ligurian border into the bargain.' But the claims of the purists were most successfully met by the express renunciation of the higher qualities of style, and the adoption of a vigorous, popular language in their stead. Few could hope to rival Pietro Bembo who, though born in Venice, nevertheless wrote the purest Tuscan, which to him was a foreign language, or the Neapolitan Sannazaro, who did the same. But the essential point was that language, whether spoken or written, was held to be an object of respect. As long as this feeling was prevalent, the fanaticism of the purists—their linguistic congresses and the rest of it[90]—did little harm. Their bad influence was not felt till much later, when the original power of Italian literature relaxed and yielded to other and far worse influences. At last it became possible for the Accademia della Crusca to treat Italian like a dead language. But this association proved so helpless that it could not even hinder the invasion of Gallicism in the eighteenth century.

This language—loved, tended, and trained to every use—now served as the basis of social intercourse. In northern countries, the nobles and the princes passed their leisure either in solitude, or in

[90] Such a congress appears to have been held at Bologna at the end of 1531 under the presidency of Bembo. See the letter of Claud. Tolomei, in Firenzuola, *Opere*, vol. ii. append. p. 231 sqq.

hunting, fighting, drinking, and the like; the burghers in games and bodily exercises, with a mixture of literary or festive amusements. In Italy there existed a neutral ground, where people of every origin, if they had the needful talent and culture, spent their time in conversation and the polished interchange of jest and earnest. As eating and drinking formed a small part of such entertainments,[91] it was not difficult to keep at a distance those who sought society for these objects. If we are to take the writers of dialogues literally, the loftiest problems of human existence were not excluded from the conversation of thinking men, and the production of noble thoughts was not, as was commonly the case in the North, the work of solitude, but of society. But we must here limit ourselves to the less serious side of social intercourse—to the side which existed only for the sake of amusement.

SOCIAL ETIQUETTE

This society, at all events at the beginning of the sixteenth century, was a matter of art; and had, and rested on, tacit or avowed rules of good sense and propriety, which are the exact reverse of all mere etiquette. In less polished circles, where society took the form of a permanent corporation, we meet with a system of formal rules and a prescribed mode of entrance, as was the case with those wild sets of Florentine artists of whom Vasari tells us that they were capable of giving representations of the best comedies of the day.[92] In the easier intercourse of society it was not unusual to select some distinguished lady as president, whose word was law for the evening. Everybody knows the introduction to Boccaccio's 'Decameron', and looks on the presidency of Pampinea as a graceful fiction. That it was so in this particular case is a matter of course; but the fiction was nevertheless based on a practice which often occurred in reality. Firenzuola, who

[91] Luigi Cornaro complains about 1550 (at the beginning of his *Trattato della Vita Sobria*) that latterly Spanish ceremonies and compliments, Lutheranism and gluttony had been gaining ground in Italy. With moderation in respect to the entertainment offered to guests, the freedom and ease of social intercourse disappeared.

[92] Vasari, xii. 9 and 11, *Vita di Rustici*. For the School for Scandal of needy artists, see xi. 216 sqq. *Vita d'Aristotile*. Machiavelli's *Capitoli* for a circle of pleasure-seekers (*Opere minori*, p. 407) are a ludicrous caricature of these social statutes. The well-known description of the evening meeting of artists in Rome in Benvenuto Cellini, i. cap. 30, is incomparable.

nearly two centuries later (1523) prefaces his collection of tales in a similar manner, with express reference to Boccaccio, comes assuredly nearer to the truth when he puts into the mouth of the queen of the society a formal speech on the mode of spending the hours during the stay which the company proposed to make in the country. The day was to begin with a stroll among the hills passed in philosophical talk; then followed breakfast,[93] with music and singing, after which came the recitation, in some cool, shady spot, of a new poem, the subject of which had been given the night before; in the evening the whole party walked to a spring of water where they all sat down and each one told a tale; last of all came supper and lively conversation 'of such a kind that the women might listen to it without shame and the men might not seem to be speaking under the influence of wine'. Bandello, in the introductions and dedications to single novels, does not give us, it is true, such inaugural discourses as this, since the circles before which the stories are told are represented as already formed; but he gives us to understand in other ways how rich, how manifold, and how charming the conditions of society must have been. Some readers may be of opinion that no good was to be got from a world which was willing to be amused by such immoral literature. It would be juster to wonder at the secure foundations of a society which, notwithstanding these tales, still observed the rules of order and decency, and which knew how to vary such pastimes with serious and solid discussion. The need of noble forms of social intercourse was felt to be stronger than all others. To convince ourselves of it, we are not obliged to take as our standard the idealized society which Castiglione depicts as discussing the loftiest sentiments and aims of human life at the court of Guidobaldo of Urbino, and Pietro Bembo at the castle of Asolo. The society described by Bandello, with all the frivolities which may be laid to its charge, enables us to form the best notion of the easy and polished dignity, of the urbane kindliness, of the intellectual freedom, of the wit and the graceful dilettantism, which distinguished these circles. A significant proof of the value of such circles lies in the fact that the women who were the centres of them could become famous and illustrious without in any way compromising their reputation. Among the patronesses of Bandello, for example, Isabella Gonzaga (born an Este) was talked of unfavourably not through any fault

[93] Which must have been taken about 10 or 11 o'clock. See Bandello, parte ii. nov. 10.

of her own, but on account of the too-free-lived young ladies who filled her court. Giulia Gonzaga Colonna, Ippolita Sforza married to a Bentivoglio, Bianca Rangona, Cecilia Gallerana, Camilla Scarampa, and others, were either altogether irreproachable, or their social fame threw into the shade whatever they may have done amiss. The most famous woman of Italy, Vittoria Colonna (b. 1490, d. 1547), the friend of Castiglione and Michelangelo, enjoyed the reputation of a saint. It is hard to give such a picture of the unconstrained intercourse of these circles in the city, at the baths, or in the country, as will furnish literal proof of the superiority of Italy in this respect over the rest of Europe. But let us read Bandello, and then ask ourselves if anything of the same kind would have been possible, say, in France, before this kind of society was there introduced by people like himself. No doubt the supreme achievements of the human mind were then produced independently of the help of the drawing-room. Yet it would be unjust to rate the influence of the latter on art and poetry too low, if only for the reason that society helped to shape that which existed in no other country—a widespread interest in artistic production and an intelligent and critical public opinion. And apart from this society of the kind we have described was in itself a natural flower of that life and culture which was then purely Italian, and which since then has extended to the rest of Europe.

In Florence society was powerfully affected by literature and politics. Lorenzo the Magnificent was supreme over his circle, not, as we might be led to believe, through the princely position which he occupied, but rather through the wonderful tact he displayed in giving perfect freedom of action to the many and varied natures which surrounded him. We see how gently he dealt with his great tutor Politian, and how the sovereignty of the poet and scholar was reconciled, though not without difficulty, with the inevitable reserve prescribed by the approaching change in the position of the house of Medici and by consideration for the sensitiveness of the wife. In return for the treatment he received, Politian became the herald and the living symbol of Medicean glory. Lorenzo, after the fashion of a true Medici, delighted in giving an outward and artistic expression to his social amusements. In his brilliant improvisation—the Hawking Party—he gives us a humorous description of his comrades, and in the Symposium a burlesque of them, but in both cases in such a manner that we clearly feel his capacity for more serious companionship.[94] Of this intercourse his correspondence and the records of his literary and philosophical conversation give ample proof. Some of the social unions which were afterwards formed in Florence were in part political clubs, though not without a certain poetical and philosophical character. Of this kind was the so-called Platonic Academy which met after Lorenzo's death in the gardens of the Rucellai.

At the courts of the princes, society naturally depended on the character of the ruler. After the beginning of the sixteenth century they became few in number, and these few soon lost their importance. Rome, however, possessed in the unique court of Leo X a society to which the history of the world offers no parallel.

EDUCATION OF THE 'CORTIGIANO'

It was for this society—or rather for his own sake—that the 'Cortigiano', as described to us by Castiglione, educated himself. He was the ideal man of society, and was regarded by the civilization of that age as its choicest flower; and the court existed for him rather than he for the court. Indeed, such a man would have been out of place at any court, since he himself possessed all the gifts and the bearing of an accomplished ruler, and because his calm supremacy in all things, both outward and spiritual, implied a too independent nature. The inner impulse which inspired him was directed, though our author does not acknowledge the fact, not to the service of the prince, but to his own perfection. One instance will make this clear. In time of war the courtier refuses even useful and perilous tasks, if they are not beautiful and dignified in themselves, such as, for instance, the capture of a herd of cattle; what urges him to take part in war is not duty but 'l'onore'. The moral relation to the prince, as described in the fourth book, is singularly free and independent. The theory of well-bred love-making, set forth in the third book, is full of delicate psychological observation, which perhaps would be more in place in a treatise on human nature generally; and the magnificent praise of ideal love, which occurs at the end of the fourth book, and

[94] The title 'Simposio' is inaccurate; it should be called, 'The Return from the Vintage'. Lorenzo, in a parody of Dante's Hell, gives an amusing account of his meeting in the Via Faenza all his good friends coming back from the country more or less tipsy. There is a most comical picture in the eighth chapter of Piovano Arlotto, who sets out in search of his lost thirst, armed with dry meat, a herring, a piece of cheese, a sausage, and four sardines.

which rises to a lyrical elevation of feeling, has no connection whatever with the special object of the work. Yet here, as in the 'Asolani' of Bembo, the culture of the time shows itself in the delicacy with which this sentiment is represented and analysed. It is true that these writers are not in all cases to be taken literally; but that the discourses they give us were actually frequent in good society, cannot be doubted, and that it was no affectation, but genuine passion, which appeared in this dress, we shall see further on.

Among outward accomplishments, the so-called knightly exercises were expected in thorough perfection from the courtier, and besides these much that could only exist at courts highly organized and based on personal emulation, such as were not to be found out of Italy. Other points obviously rest on an abstract notion of individual perfection. The courtier must be at home in all noble sports, among them running, leaping, swimming and wrestling; he must, above all things, be a good dancer and, as a matter of course, an accomplished rider. He must be master of several languages, at all events of Latin and Italian; he must be familiar with literature and have some knowledge of the fine arts. In music a certain practical skill was expected of him, which he was bound, nevertheless, to keep as secret as possible. All this is not to be taken too seriously, except what relates to the use of arms. The mutual interaction of these gifts and accomplishments results in the perfect man, in whom no one quality usurps the place of the rest.

So much is certain, that in the sixteenth century the Italians had all Europe for their pupils both theoretically and practically in every noble bodily exercise and in the habits and manners of good society. Their instructions and their illustrated books on riding, fencing, and dancing served as the model to other countries. Gymnastics as an art, apart both from military training and from mere amusement, was probably first taught by Vittorino da Feltre and after his time became essential to a complete education. The important fact is that they were taught systematically, though what exercises were most in favour, and whether they resembled those now in use, we are unable to say. But we may infer, not only from the general character of the people, but from positive evidence which has been left for us, that not only strength and skill, but grace of movement was one of the main objects of physical training. It is enough to remind the reader of the great Federigo of Urbino directing the evening games of the young people committed to his care.

The games and contests of the popular classes did not differ essentially from those which prevailed elsewhere in Europe. In the maritime cities boat-racing was among the number, and the Venetian regattas were famous at an early period.[95] The classical game of Italy was and is the ball; and this was probably played at the time of the Renaissance with more zeal and brilliancy than elsewhere. But on this point no distinct evidence is forthcoming.

MUSIC

A few words on music will not be out of place in this part of our work.[96] Musical composition down to the year 1500 was chiefly in the hands of the Flemish school, whose originality and artistic dexterity were greatly admired. Side by side with this, there nevertheless existed an Italian school, which probably stood nearer to our present taste. Half a century later came Palestrina, whose genius still works powerfully among us. We learn among other facts that he was a great innovator; but whether he or others took the decisive part in shaping the musical language of the modern world lies beyond the judgement of the unprofessional critic. Leaving on one side the history of musical composition, we shall confine ourselves to the position which music held in the social life of the day.

[95] They are said to have arisen through the rowing out to the Lido, where the practice with the crossbow took place. The great regatta on the feast of St. Paul was prescribed by law from 1315 onwards. In early times there was much riding in Venice, before the streets were paved and the level wooden bridges turned into arched stone ones. Petrarch (*Epist. Seniles*, iv. 2) describes a brilliant tournament held in 1364 on the square of St. Mark, and Doge Steno, about the year 1400, has as fine a stable as any prince in Italy. But riding in the neighbourhood of the square was prohibited as a rule after the year 1291. At a later time, of course, the Venetians had the name of bad riders.

[96] On Dante's position with regard to music, and on the music to Petrarch's and Boccaccio's poems, see Trucchi, *Poesie Ital. inedite*, ii. p. 139. Out of Italy it was still hardly allowable for persons of consequence to be musicians; at the Flemish court of the young Charles V a serious dispute took place on the subject. A remarkable and comprehensive passage on music is to be found, where we should not expect it, in the *Macaroneide Phant.* xx. It is a comic description of a quartette from which we see that Spanish and French songs were often sung, that music already had its enemies (1520), and that the orchestra of Leo X and the still earlier composer, Josquin des Prés, whose principal works are mentioned, were the chief subjects of enthusiasm in the musical world of that time. The same writer (Folengo) displays in his *Orlandino*, published under the name of Limerno Pitocco, a musical fanaticism of a thoroughly modern sort.

A fact most characteristic of the Renaissance and of Italy is the specialization of the orchestra, the search for new instruments and modes of sound, and, in close connection with this tendency, the formation of a class of 'virtuosi', who devoted their whole attention to particular instruments or particular branches of music.

Of the more complex instruments, which were perfected and widely diffused at a very early period, we find not only the organ, but a corresponding string instrument, the 'gravicembalo' or 'clavicembalo'. Fragments of these, dating from the beginning of the fourteenth century have come down to our own days, adorned with paintings from the hands of the greatest masters. Among other instruments the first place was held by the violin, which even then conferred great celebrity on the successful player. At the court of Leo X, who, when cardinal, had filled his house with singers and musicians, and who enjoyed the reputation of a critic and performer, the Jew Giovan Maria del Corneto and Jacopo Sansecondo were among the most famous. The former received from Leo the title of count and a small town; the latter has been taken to be the Apollo in the Parnassus of Raphael. In the course of the sixteenth century, celebrities in every branch of music appeared in abundance, and Lomazzo (1584) names the three most distinguished masters of the art of singing, of the organ, the lute, the lyre, the 'viola da gamba', the harp, the cithern, the horn, and the trumpet, and wishes that their portraits might be painted on the instruments themselves.[97] Such many-sided comparative criticism would have been impossible anywhere but in Italy, although the same instruments were to be found in other countries.

The number and variety of these instruments is shown by the fact that collections of them were now made from curiosity. In Venice, which was one of the most musical cities of Italy, there were several such collections, and when a sufficient number of performers happened to be on the spot, a concert was at once improvised. In one of these museums there was a large number of instruments, made after

[97] Lomazzo (*Trattato dell'Arte della Pittura*, etc., p. 347), speaking of the lyre, mentions Leonardo da Vinci and Alfonso (Duke?) of Ferrara. The author includes in his work all the celebrities of the age, among them several Jews. The most complete list of the famous musicians of the sixteenth century, divided into an earlier and a later generation, is to be found in Rabelais, in the 'New Prologue' to the fourth book. A virtuoso, the blind Francesco of Florence (d. 1390), was crowned at Venice with a wreath of laurel by the King of Cyprus.

ancient pictures and descriptions, but we are not told if anybody could play them, or how they sounded. It must not be forgotten that such instruments were often beautifully decorated, and could be arranged in a manner pleasing to the eye. We thus meet with them in collections of other rarities and works of art.

The players, apart from the professional performers, were either single amateurs, or whole orchestras of them, organized into a corporate Academy. Many artists in other branches were at home in music, and often masters of the art. People of position were averse to wind instruments, for the same reason which made them distasteful to Alcibiades and Pallas Athene. In good society singing, either alone or accompanied with the violin, was usual; but quartettes of string instruments were also common, and the 'clavicembalo' was liked on account of its varied effects. In singing, the solo only was permitted, 'for a single voice is heard, enjoyed, and judged far better'. In other words, as singing, notwithstanding all conventional modesty, is an exhibition of the individual man of society, it is better that each should be seen and heard separately. The tender feelings produced in the fair listeners are taken for granted, and elderly people are therefore recommended to abstain from such forms of art, even though they excel in them. It was held important that the effect of the song should be enhanced by the impression made on the sight. We hear nothing, however, of the treatment in these circles of musical composition as an independent branch of art. On the other hand it happened sometimes that the subject of the song was some terrible event which had befallen the singer himself.

This dilettantism, which pervaded the middle as well as the upper classes, was in Italy both more widespread and more genuinely artistic than in any other country of Europe. Wherever we meet with a description of social intercourse, there music and singing are always and expressly mentioned. Hundreds of portraits show us men and women, often several together, playing or holding some musical instrument, and the angelic concerts represented in the ecclesiastical pictures prove how familiar the painters were with the living effects of music. We read of the lute-player Antonio Rota, at Padua (d. 1549), who became a rich man by his lessons, and published a handbook to the practice of the lute.

At a time when there was no opera to concentrate and monopolize musical talent, this general cultivation of the art must have been something wonderfully varied, intelligent, and original. It is another question how much we should find to satisfy us in these forms of music, could they now be reproduced for us.

EQUALITY OF MEN AND WOMEN

To understand the higher forms of social intercourse at this period, we must keep before our minds the fact that women stood on a footing of perfect equality with men. We must not suffer ourselves to be misled by the sophistical and often malicious talk about the assumed inferiority of the female sex, which we meet with now and then in the dialogues of this time, nor by such satires as the third of Ariosto, who treats woman as a dangerous grown-up child, whom a man must learn how to manage, in spite of the great gulf between them. There is, indeed, a certain amount of truth in what he says. Just because the educated woman was on a level with the man, that communion of mind and heart which comes from the sense of mutual dependance and completion, could not be developed in marriage at this time, as it has been developed later in the cultivated society of the North.

The education given to women in the upper classes was essentially the same as that given to men. The Italian, at the time of the Renaissance, felt no scruple in putting sons and daughters alike under the same course of literary and even philological instruction. Indeed, looking at this ancient culture as the chief treasure of life, he was glad that his girls should have a share in it. We have seen what perfection was attained by the daughters of princely houses in writing and speaking Latin. Many others must at least have been able to read it, in order to follow the conversation of the day, which turned largely on classical subjects. An active interest was taken by many in Italian poetry, in which, whether prepared or improvised, a large number of Italian women, from the time of the Venetian Cassandra Fedele onwards (about the close of the fifteenth century), made themselves famous. One, indeed, Vittoria Colonna, may be called immortal. If any proof were needed of the assertion made above, it would be found in the manly tone of this poetry. Even the love-sonnets and religious poems are so precise and definite in their character, and so far removed from the tender twilight of sentiment, and from all the dilettantism which we commonly find in the poetry of women, that we should not hesitate to attribute them to male authors, if we had not clear external evidence to prove the contrary.

For, with education, the individuality of women in the upper classes was developed in the same way as that of men. Till the time of the Reformation, the personality of women out of Italy, even of the highest rank, comes forward but little. Exceptions like Isabella of Bavaria, Margaret of Anjou, and Isabella of Castille, are the forced result of very unusual circumstances. In Italy, throughout the whole of the fifteenth century, the wives of the rulers, and still more those of the Condottieri, have nearly all a distinct, recognizable personality, and take their share of notoriety and glory. To these came gradually to be added a crowd of famous women of the most varied kind; among them those whose distinction consisted in the fact that their beauty, disposition, education, virtue, and piety, combined to render them harmonious human beings. There was no question of 'woman's rights' or female emancipation, simply because the thing itself was a matter of course. The educated woman, no less than the man, strove naturally after a characteristic and complete individuality. The same intellectual and emotional development which perfected the man, was demanded for the perfection of the woman. Active literary work, nevertheless, was not expected from her, and if she were a poet, some powerful utterance of feeling, rather than the confidences of the novel or the diary, was looked for. These women had no thought of the public; their function was to influence distinguished men, and to moderate male impulse and caprice.

The highest praise which could then be given to the great Italian women was that they had the mind and the courage of men. We have only to observe the thoroughly manly bearing of most of the women in the heroic poems, especially those of Boiardo and Ariosto, to convince ourselves that we have before us the ideal of the time. The title 'virago', which is an equivocal compliment in the present day, then implied nothing but praise. It was borne in all its glory by Caterina Sforza, wife and afterwards widow of Girolamo Riario, whose hereditary possession, Forlì, she gallantly defended first against his murderers, and then against Cesare Borgia. Though finally vanquished, she retained the admiration of her countrymen and the title 'prima donna d'Italia'. This heroic vein can be detected in many of the women of the Renaissance, though none found the same opportunity of showing their heroism to the world. In Isabella Gonzaga this type is clearly recognizable.

Women of this stamp could listen to novels like those of Bandello, without social intercourse suffering from it. The ruling genius of society was not, as now, womanhood, or the respect for certain presuppositions, mysteries, and susceptibilities, but the consciousness of energy, of beauty, and of a social state full of danger and opportunity. And for this reason we find, side by side with the most measured and polished social forms, something our age would call immodesty, forgetting that by which it was corrected and counterbalanced—the powerful characters of the women who were exposed to it.

That in all the dialogues and treatises together we can find no absolute evidence on these points is only natural, however freely the nature of love and the position and capacities of women were discussed.

What seems to have been wanting in this society were the young girls who, even when not brought up in the monasteries, were still carefully kept away from it. It is not easy to say whether their absence was the cause of the greater freedom of conversation, or whether they were removed on account of it.

Even the intercourse with courtesans seems to have assumed a more elevated character, reminding us of the position of the Hetairae in classical Athens. The famous Roman courtesan Imperia was a woman of intelligence and culture, had learned from a certain Domenico Campana the art of making sonnets, and was not without musical accomplishments. The beautiful Isabella de Luna, of Spanish extraction, who was reckoned amusing company, seems to have been an odd compound of a kind heart with a shockingly foul tongue, which latter sometimes brought her into trouble. At Milan, Bandello knew the majestic Caterina di San Celso, who played and sang and recited superbly. It is clear from all we read on the subject that the distinguished people who visited these women, and from time to time lived with them, demanded from them a considerable degree of intelligence and instruction, and that the famous courtesans were treated with no slight respect and consideration. Even when relations with them were broken off, their good opinion was still desired, which shows that departed passion had left permanent traces behind. But on the whole this intellectual intercourse is not worth mentioning by the side of that sanctioned by the recognized forms of social life, and the traces which it has left in poetry and literature are for the most part of a scandalous nature. We may well be astonished that among the 6,800 persons of this class, who were to be found in Rome in 1490—that is, before the appearance of syphilis—scarcely a single woman seems to have been remarkable for any higher gifts. Those whom we have mentioned all belong to the period which immediately followed. The mode of life, the morals and the philosophy of the public women, who with all their sensuality and greed were not always incapable of deeper passions, as well as the hypocrisy and devilish malice shown by some in their later years, are best set forth by Giraldi, in the novels which form the introduction to the 'Hecatommithi'. Pietro Aretino, in his 'Ragionamenti', gives us rather a picture of his own depraved character than of this unhappy class of women as they really were.

The mistresses of the princes, as has been pointed out, were sung by poets and painted by artists, and thus have become personally familiar to their contemporaries and to posterity. But we hardly know more than the name of Alice Perries; and of Clara Dettin, the mistress of Frederick the Victorious, and of Agnes Sorel we have only a half-legendary story. With the concubines of the Renaissance monarchs—Francis I and Henry II—the case is different.

DOMESTIC LIFE

After treating of the intercourse of society, let us glance for a moment at the domestic life of this period. We are commonly disposed to look on the family life of the Italians at this time as hopelessly ruined by the national immorality, and this side of the question will be more fully discussed in the sequel. For the moment we must content ourselves with pointing out that conjugal infidelity has by no means so disastrous an influence on family life in Italy as in the North, so long at least as certain limits are not overstepped.

The domestic life of the Middle Ages was a product of popular morals, or if we prefer to put it otherwise, a result of the inborn tendencies of national life, modified by the varied circumstances which affected them. Chivalry at the time of its splendour left domestic economy untouched. The knight wandered from court to court, and from one battlefield to another. His homage was given systematically to some other woman than his own wife, and things went how they might at home in the castle. The spirit of the Renaissance first brought order into domestic life, treating it as a work of deliberate contrivance. Intelligent economical views, and a rational style of domestic architecture served to promote this end. But the chief cause of the change was the thoughtful study of all questions relating to social intercourse, to education, to domestic service and organization.

The most precious document on this subject is the treatise on the management of the home by Agnolo Pandolfini (actually written by L. B. Alberti, d. 1472). He represents a father speaking to his grown-up sons, and initiating them into his method of administration. We are introduced into a large and wealthy household, which, if governed with moderation and reasonable economy, promises happiness and prosperity for generations to come. A considerable landed estate, whose produce furnishes the table of the house, and serves as the basis of the family fortune, is combined with some industrial pursuit, such as the weaving of wool or silk. The dwelling is solid and the food good. All that has to do with the plan and arrangement of the house is great, durable and costly, but the daily life within it is as simple as possible. All other expenses, from the largest in which the family honour is at stake, down to the pocket-money of the younger sons, stand to one another in a rational, not a conventional relation. Nothing is considered of so much importance as education, which the head of the house gives not only to the children, but to the whole household. He first develops his wife from a shy girl, brought up in careful seclusion, to the true woman of the house, capable of commanding and guiding the servants. The sons are brought up without any undue severity,[98] carefully watched and counselled, and controlled 'rather by authority than by force'. And finally the servants are chosen and treated on such principles that they gladly and faithfully hold by the family.

One feature of that book must be referred to, which is by no means peculiar to it, but which it treats with special warmth—the love of the educated Italian for country life. In northern countries the nobles lived in the country in their castles, and the monks of the higher orders in their well-guarded monasteries, while the wealthiest burghers dwelt from one year's end to another in the cities. But in Italy, so far as the neighbourhood of certain towns at all events was concerned, the security of life and property was so great, and the passion for a country residence was so strong, that men were willing

[98] A thorough history of 'flogging' among the Germanic and Latin races, treated with some psychological power, would be worth volumes of dispatches and negotiations. When, and through what influence, did flogging become a daily practice in the German household? Not till after Walther sang: '*Nieman kan mit gerten kindes zuht beherten*' (Nobody can educate a child by using the rod). In Italy beating ceased early: a child of seven was no longer beaten. (*About flogging in England, see Heinrich Heine's *English Fragments*, 1861, p. 64.)

to risk a loss in time of war. Thus arose the villa, the country-house of the well-to-do citizen. This precious inheritance of the old Roman world was thus revived, as soon as the wealth and culture of the people were sufficiently advanced.

Pandolfini finds at his villa a peace and happiness, for an account of which the reader must hear him speak himself. The economical side of the matter is that one and the same property must, if possible, contain everything—corn, wine, oil, pasture-land and woods, and that in such cases the property was paid for well, since nothing needed then to be got from the market. But the higher enjoyment derived from the villa is shown by some words of the introduction: 'Round about Florence lie many villas in a transparent atmosphere, amid cheerful scenery, and with a splendid view; there is little fog and no injurious winds; all is good, and the water pure and healthy. Of the numerous buildings many are like palaces, many like castles costly and beautiful to behold.' He is speaking of those unrivalled villas, of which the greater number were sacrificed, though vainly, by the Florentines themselves in the defence of their city in 1529.

In these villas, as in those on the Brenta, on the Lombard hills, at Posilippo and on the Vomero, social life assumes a freer and more rural character than in the palaces within the city. We meet with charming descriptions of the intercourse of the guests, the hunting-parties, and all the open-air pursuits and amusements. But the noblest achievements of poetry and thought are sometimes also dated from these scenes of rural peace.

FESTIVALS

It is by no arbitrary choice that in discussing the social life of this period, we are led to treat of the processions and shows which formed part of the popular festivals. The artistic power of which the Italians of the Renaissance gave proof on such occasions, was attained only by means of that free intercourse of all classes which formed the basis of Italian society. In Northern Europe the monasteries, the courts, and the burghers had their special feasts and shows as in Italy; but in the one case the form and substance of these displays differed according to the class which took part in them, in the other an art and culture common to the whole nation stamped them with both a higher and a more popular character. The decorative architecture, which served to aid in these festivals, deserves a chapter to itself in the history of art, although our imagination can only form a picture of it from the descriptions which have been left to us. We are here more especially concerned with the festival as a higher phase in the life of the people, in which its religious, moral, and poetical ideas took visible shape. The Italian festivals in their best form mark the point of transition from real life into the world of art.

The two chief forms of festal display were originally here, as elsewhere in the West, the Mystery, or the dramatization of sacred history and legend, and the Procession, the motive and character of which was also purely ecclesiastical.

The performances of the Mysteries in Italy were from the first more frequent and splendid than elsewhere, and were most favourably affected by the progress of poetry and of the other arts. In the course of time not only did the farce and the secular drama branch off from the Mystery, as in other countries of Europe, but the pantomime also, with its accompaniments of singing and dancing, the effect of which depended on the richness and beauty of the spectacle.

The Procession, in the broad, level, and well-paved streets of the Italian cities, was soon developed into the 'Trionfo', or train of masked figures on foot and in chariots, the ecclesiastical character of which gradually gave way to the secular. The processions at the Carnival and at the feast of Corpus Christi were alike in the pomp and brilliancy with which they were conducted, and set the pattern afterwards followed by the royal or princely progresses. Other nations were willing to spend vast sums of money on these shows, but in Italy alone do we find an artistic method of treatment which arranged the processions as a harmonious and significative whole.

What is left of these festivals is but a poor remnant of what once existed. Both religious and secular displays of this kind have abandoned the dramatic element—the costumes—partly from dread of ridicule, and partly because the cultivated classes, which formerly gave their whole energies to these things, have for several reasons lost their interest in them. Even at the Carnival, the great procession of masks are out of fashion. What still remains, such as the costumes adopted in imitation of certain religious confraternities, or even the brilliant festival of Santa Rosalia at Palermo, shows clearly how far the higher culture of the country has withdrawn from such interests.

The festivals did not reach their full development till after the decisive victory of the modern spirit in the fifteenth century, unless perhaps Florence was here, as in other things, in advance of the rest of Italy. In Florence, the several quarters of the city were, in early times, organized with a view to such exhibitions, which demanded no small expenditure of artistic effort. Of this kind was the representation of Hell, with a scaffold and boats in the Arno, on the 1st of May, 1304, when the Ponte alla Carraia broke down under the weight of the spectators. That at a later time the Florentines used to travel through Italy as directors of festivals (festaiuoli), shows that the art was early perfected at home.

In setting forth the chief points of superiority in the Italian festivals over those of other countries, the first that we shall have to remark is the developed sense of individual characteristics, in other words, the capacity to invent a given mask, and to act the part with dramatic propriety. Painters and sculptors not merely did their part towards the decoration of the place where the festival was held, but helped in getting up the characters themselves, and prescribed the dress, the paints, and the other ornaments to be used. The second fact to be pointed out is the universal familiarity of the people with the poetical basis of the show. The Mysteries, indeed, were equally well understood all over Europe, since the biblical story and the legends of the saints were the common property of Christendom; but in all other respects the advantage was on the side of Italy. For the recitations, whether of religious or secular heroes, she possessed a lyrical poetry so rich and harmonious that none could resist its charm. The majority, too, of the spectators—at least in the cities—understood the meaning of mythological figures, and could guess without much difficulty at the allegorical and historical, which were drawn from sources familiar to the mass of Italians.

This point needs to be more fully discussed. The Middle Ages were essentially the ages of allegory. Theology and philosophy treated their categories as independent beings, and poetry and art had but little to add, in order to give them personality. Here all the countries of the West were on the same level. Their world of ideas was rich enough in types and figures, but when these were put into concrete shape, the costume and attributes were likely to be unintelligible and unsuited to the popular taste. This, even in Italy, was often the case, and not only so during the whole period of the Renaissance, but down to a still later time. To produce the confusion, it was enough if a predicate of the allegorical figures was wrongly translated by an attribute. Even Dante is not wholly free from such errors, and, indeed, he prides himself on the obscurity of his allegories in general. Petrarch, in his 'Trionfi', attempts to give clear, if short, descriptions of at all events the figures of Love, of Chastity, of Death, and of Fame. Others again load their allegories with inappropriate attributes. In the Satires of Vinciguerra, for example, Envy is depicted with rough, iron teeth, Gluttony as biting its own lips, and with a shock of tangled hair, the latter probably to show its indifference to all that is not meat and drink. We cannot here discuss the bad influence of these misunderstandings on the plastic arts. They, like poetry, might think themselves fortunate if allegory could be expressed by a mythological figure—by a figure which antiquity saved from absurdity—if Mars might stand for war, and Diana for the love of the chase.

Nevertheless art and poetry had better allegories than these to offer, and we may assume with regard to such figures of this kind as appeared in the Italian festivals, that the public required them to be clearly and vividly characteristic, since its previous training had fitted it to be a competent critic. Elsewhere, particularly at the Burgundian court, the most inexpressive figures, and even mere symbols, were allowed to pass, since to understand, or to seem to understand them, was a part of aristocratic breeding. On the occasion of the famous 'Oath of the Pheasant' in the year 1454, the beautiful young horsewoman, who appears as 'Queen of Pleasure', is the only pleasing allegory. The huge epergnes, with automatic or even living figures within them, are either mere curiosities or are intended to convey some clumsy moral lesson. A naked female statue guarding a live lion was supposed to represent Constantinople and its future saviour, the Duke of Burgundy. The rest, with the exception of a Pantomime—Jason in Colchis—seems either too recondite to be understood or to have no sense at all. Olivier de la Marche, to whom we owe the description of the scene (Mémoires, ch. 29), appeared costumed as 'The Church', in a tower on the back of an elephant, and sang a long elegy on the victory of the unbelievers.

But although the allegorical element in the poetry, the art, and the festivals of Italy is superior both in good taste and in unity of conception to what we find in other countries, yet it is not in these qualities that it is most characteristic and unique. The decisive point of superiority lay rather in the fact that, besides the personifications of abstract qualities, historical representatives of them were introduced in great number—that both poetry and plastic art were accustomed to represent famous men and women. The 'Divine Comedy', the 'Trionfi' of Petrarch, the 'Amorosa Visione' of Boccaccio—all of them works constructed on this principle—and the great diffusion of culture which took place under the influence of antiquity, had made the nation familiar with this historical element. These figures now appeared at festivals, either individualized, as definite masks, or in groups, as characteristic attendants on some leading allegorical figure. The art of grouping and composition was thus learnt in Italy at a time when the most splendid exhibitions in other countries were made up of unintelligible symbolism or unmeaning puerilities.

Let us begin with that kind of festival which is perhaps the oldest of all—the Mysteries. They resembled in their main features those performed in the rest of Europe. In the public squares, in the churches and in the cloisters, extensive scaffolds were constructed, the upper story of which served as a Paradise to open and shut at will, and the ground-floor often as a Hell, while between the two lay the stage properly so-called, representing the scene of all the earthly events of the drama. In Italy, as elsewhere, the biblical or legendary play often began with an introductory dialogue between Apostles, Prophets, Sibyls, Virtues, and Fathers of the Church, and sometimes ended with a dance. As a matter of course the half-comic 'Intermezzi' of secondary characters were not wanting in Italy, yet this feature was hardly so broadly marked as in northern countries. The artificial means by which figures were made to rise and float in the air—one of the chief delights of these representations—were probably much better understood in Italy than elsewhere; and at Florence in the fourteenth century the hitches in these performances were a stock subject of ridicule. Soon afterwards Brunellesco invented for the Feast of the Annunciation in the Piazza San Felice a marvellous apparatus consisting of a heavenly globe surrounded by two circles of angels, out of which Gabriel flew down in a machine shaped like an almond. Cecca, too, devised mechanisms for such displays. The spiritual corporations or the quarters of the city which undertook the charge and in part the performance of these plays spared, at all events in the larger towns, no trouble and expense to render them as perfect and artistic as possible. The same was no doubt the case at the great court festivals, when Mysteries were acted as well as pantomimes and secular dramas. The court of Pietro Riario and that of Ferrara were assuredly not wanting in all that human invention could produce. When we picture to ourselves the theatrical talent and the splendid costumes of the actors, the scenes constructed in the style of the architecture of the period, and hung with garlands and tapestry, and in the background the noble buildings of an Italian piazza, or the slender columns of some great courtyard or cloister, the effect is one of great brilliance. But just as the secular drama suffered from this passion for display, so the higher poetical development of the Mystery was arrested by the same cause. In the texts which are left we find for the most part the poorest dramatic groundwork, relieved now and then by a fine lyrical or rhetorical passage, but no trace of the grand symbolic enthusiasm which distinguishes the 'Autos Sagramentales' of Calderon.

In the smaller towns, where the scenic display was less, the effect of these spiritual plays on the character of the spectators may have been greater. We read that one of the great preachers of repentance of whom more will be said later on, Roberto da Lecce, closed his Lenten sermons during the plague of 1448, at Perugia, with a representation of the Passion. The piece followed the New Testament closely. The actors were few, but the whole people wept aloud. It is true that on such occasions emotional stimulants were resorted to which were borrowed from the crudest realism. We are reminded of the pictures of Matteo da Siena, or of the groups of clay-figures by Guido Mazzoni, when we read that the actor who took the part of Christ appeared covered with weals and apparently sweating blood, and even bleeding from a wound in the side.

The special occasions on which these mysteries were performed, apart from the great festivals of the Church, from princely weddings, and the like, were of various kinds. When, for example, St. Bernardino of Siena was canonized by the Pope (1450), a sort of dramatic imitation of the ceremony (rappresentazione) took place, probably on the great square of his native city, and for two days there was feasting with meat and drink for all comers. We are told that a learned monk celebrated his promotion to the degree of Doctor of Theology by giving a representation of the legend about the patron saint of the city. Charles VIII had scarcely entered Italy before he was welcomed at Turin by the widowed Duchess Bianca of Savoy with a sort of half-religious pantomime, in which a pastoral scene first symbolized the Law of Nature, and then a procession of patriarchs the Law of Grace. Afterwards followed the story of Lancelot of the lake, and that 'of Athens'. And no sooner had the King reached Chieri than he was received with another pantomime, in which a woman in childbed was shown surrounded by distinguished visitors.

If any church festival was held by universal consent to call for exceptional efforts, it was the feast of Corpus Christi, which in Spain gave rise to a special class of poetry. We possess a splendid description of the manner in which that feast was celebrated at Viterbo by Pius II in 1462. The procession itself, which advanced from a vast and gorgeous tent in front of San Francesco along the main street to the Cathedral, was the least part of the ceremony. The cardinals and wealthy prelates had divided the whole distance into parts, over which they severally presided, and which they decorated with curtains, tapestry, and garlands. Each of them had also erected a stage of his own, on which, as the procession passed by, short historical and allegorical scenes were represented. It is not clear from the account whether all the characters were living beings or some merely draped figures; the expense was certainly very great. There was a suffering Christ amid singing cherubs, the Last Supper with a figure of St. Thomas Aquinas, the combat between the Archangel Michael and the devils, fountains of wine and orchestras of angels, the grave of Christ with all the scene of the Resurrection, and finally, on the square before the Cathedral, the tomb of the Virgin. It opened after High Mass and Benediction, and the Mother of God ascended singing to Paradise, where she was crowned by her Son, and led into the presence of the Eternal Father.

Among these representations in the public street, that given by the Cardinal Vice-Chancellor Roderigo Borgia, afterwards Pope Alexander VI, was remarkable for its splendour and obscure symbolism. It offers an early instance of the fondness for salvos of artillery which was characteristic of the house of Borgia.

The account is briefer which Pius II gives us of the procession held the same year in Rome on the arrival of the skull of St. Andrew from Greece. There, too, Roderigo Borgia distinguished himself by his magnificence; but this festival has a more secular character than the other, as, besides the customary choirs of angels, other masks were exhibited, as well as 'strong men', who seemed to have performed various feats of muscular prowess.

Such representations as were wholly or chiefly secular in their character were arranged, especially at the more important princely courts, mainly with a view to splendid and striking scenic effects. The subjects were mythological or allegorical, and the interpretation commonly lay on the surface. Extravagances, indeed, were not wanting—gigantic animals from which a crowd of masked figures suddenly emerged, as at Siena in the year 1465, when at a public reception a ballet of twelve persons came out of a golden wolf; living table ornaments, not always, however, showing the tasteless exaggeration of the Burgundian Court—and the like. Most of them showed some artistic or poetical feeling. The mixture of pantomime and drama at the Court of Ferrara has been already referred to in the treating of poetry. The entertainments given in 1473 by the Cardinal Pietro Riario at Rome when Leonora of Aragon, the destined bride of Prince Hercules of Ferrara, was passing through the city, were famous far beyond the limits of Italy. The plays acted were mysteries on some ecclesiastical subject, the pantomimes, on the contrary, were mythological. There were represented Orpheus with the beasts, Perseus and Andromeda, Ceres drawn by dragons, Bacchus and Ariadne by panthers, and finally the education of Achilles. Then followed a ballet of the famous lovers of ancient times, with a troop of nymphs, which was interrupted by an attack of predatory centaurs, who in their turn were vanquished and put to flight by Hercules. The fact, in itself a trifle, may be mentioned as characteristic of the taste of the time, that the human beings who at all festivals appeared as statues in niches or on pillars and triumphal arches, and then showed themselves to be alive by singing or speaking, wore their natural complexion and a natural costume, and thus the sense of incongruity was removed; while in the house of Riario there was exhibited a living child, gilt from head to foot, who showered water round him from a spring.

Brilliant pantomimes of the same kind were given at Bologna, at the marriage of Annibale Bentivoglio with Lucrezia of Este. Instead of the orchestra, choral songs were sung, while the fairest of Diana's nymphs flew over to the Juno Pronuba, and while Venus walked with a lion—which in this case was a disguised man—among a troop of savages. The decorations were a faithful representation of a forest. At Venice, in 1491, the princesses of the house of Este were met and welcomed by the Bucentaur, and entertained by boat-races and a splendid pantomime, called 'Meleager', in the court of the ducal palace. At Milan Leonardo da Vinci directed the festivals of the Duke and of some leading citizens. One of his machines, which must have rivalled that of Brunellesco, represented the heavenly bodies with all their movements on a colossal scale. Whenever a planet approached Isabella, the bride of the young Duke, the divinity whose name it bore stepped forth from the globe, and sang some verses written by the court-poet Bellincioni (1490). At another festival (1493) the model of the equestrian statue of Francesco Sforza appeared with other objects under a triumphal arch on the square before the castle. We read in Vasari of the ingenious automata which Leonardo invented to welcome the French kings as masters of Milan. Even in the smaller cities great efforts were sometimes made on these occasions. When Duke Borso came in 1453 to Reggio, to receive the homage of the city, he was met at the gate by a great machine, on which St. Prospero, the patron saint of the town, appeared to float, shaded by a baldachin held by angels, while below him was a revolving disc with eight singing cherubs, two of whom received from the saint the sceptre and keys of the city, which they then delivered to the Duke, while saints and angels held forth in his praise. A chariot drawn by concealed horses now advanced, bearing an empty throne, behind which stood a figure of Justice attended by a genius. At the corners of the chariot sat four grey-headed lawgivers, encircled by angels with banners; by its side rode standard-bearers in complete armour. It need hardly be added that the goddess and the genius did not suffer the Duke to pass by without an address. A second car, drawn by a unicorn, bore a Caritas with a burning torch; between the two came the classical spectacle of a car in the form of a ship, moved by men concealed within it. The whole procession now advanced before the Duke. In front of the Church of St. Pietro, a halt was again made. The saint, attended by two angels, descended in an aureole from the façade, placed a wreath of laurel on the head of the Duke, and then floated back to his former position. The clergy provided another allegory of a purely religious kind. Idolatry and Faith stood on two lofty pillars, and after Faith, represented by a beautiful girl, had uttered her welcome, the other column fell to pieces with the lay figure upon it. Further on, Borso was met by a Cæsar with seven beautiful women, who were presented to him as the Virtues which he was exhorted to pursue. At last the Cathedral was reached, but after the service the Duke again took his seat on a lofty golden throne, and a second time received the homage of some of the masks already mentioned. To conclude all, three angels flew down from an adjacent building, and, amid songs of joy, delivered to him palm branches, as symbols of peace.

Let us now give a glance at those festivals the chief feature of which was the procession itself.

There is no doubt that from an early period of the Middle Ages the religious processions gave rise to the use of masks. Little angels accompanied the sacrament or the sacred pictures and reliques on their way through the streets; or characters in the Passion—such as Christ with the cross, the thieves and the soldiers, or the faithful women—were represented for public edification. But the great feasts of the Church were from an early time accompanied by a civic procession, and the *naïveté* of the Middle Ages found nothing unfitting in the many secular elements which it contained. We may mention especially the naval car (*carrus navalis*), which had been inherited from pagan times, and which, as an instance already quoted shows, was admissible at festivals of very various kinds, and is associated with one of them in particular—the Carnival. Such ships, decorated with all possible splendour, delighted the eyes of spectators long after the original meaning of them was forgotten. When Isabella of England met her bridegroom, the Emperor Frederick II, at Cologne, she was met by a number of such chariots, drawn by invisible horses, and filled with a crowd of priests who welcomed her with music and singing.

But the religious processions were not only mingled with secular accessories of all kinds, but were often replaced by processions of clerical masks. Their origin is perhaps to be found in the parties of actors who wound their way through the streets of the city to the place where they were about to act the mystery; but it is possible that at an early period the clerical procession may have constituted itself as a distinct species. Dante described the 'Trionfo' of Beatrice, with the twenty-four Elders of the Apocalypse, with the four mystical Beasts, with the three Christian and four Cardinal Virtues, and with Saint Luke, Saint Paul, and other Apostles, in a way which almost forces us to conclude that such processions actually occurred before his time. We are chiefly led to this conclusion by the chariot in which Beatrice drives, and which in the miraculous forest of the vision would have been unnecessary or rather out of place. It is possible, on the other hand, that Dante looked on the chariot as a symbol of victory and triumph, and that his poem rather served to give rise to these processions, the form of which was borrowed from the triumph of the Roman Emperors. However this may be, poetry and theology continued to make free use of the symbol. Savonarola in his 'Triumph of the Cross' represents Christ on a Chariot of Victory, above his head the shining sphere of the Trinity, in his left hand the Cross, in his right the Old and New Testaments; below him the Virgin Mary; on both sides the Martyrs and Doctors of the Church with open books; behind him all the multitude of the saved; and in the distance the countless host of his enemies—emperors, princes, philosophers, heretics—all vanquished, their idols broken, and their books burned. A great picture of Titian, which is known only as a woodcut, has a good deal in common with this description. The ninth and tenth of Sabellico's thirteen Elegies on the Mother of God contain a minute account of her triumph, richly adorned with allegories, and especially interesting from that matter-of-fact air which also characterizes the realistic painting of the fifteenth century.

Nevertheless, the secular 'Trionfi' were far more frequent than the religious. They were modelled on the procession of the Roman Imperator, as it was known from the old reliefs and the writings of ancient authors. The historical conceptions then prevalent in Italy, with which these shows were closely connected, have already been discussed (p. 87).

We now and then read of the actual triumphal entrance of a victorious general, which was organized as far as possible on the ancient pattern, even against the will of the hero himself. Francesco Sforza had the courage (1450) to refuse the triumphal chariot which had been prepared for his return to Milan, on the ground that such things were monarchial superstitions. Alfonso the Great, on his entrance into Naples (1443), declined the wreath of laurel, which Napoleon did not disdain to wear at his coronation in Notre-Dame. For the rest, Alfonso's procession, which passed by a breach in the wall through the city to the cathedral, was a strange mixture of antique, allegorical, and purely comic elements. The car, drawn by four white horses, on which he sat enthroned, was lofty and covered with gilding; twenty patricians carried the poles of the canopy of cloth of gold which shaded his head. The part of the procession which the Florentines then present in Naples had undertaken was composed of elegant young cavaliers, skilfully brandishing their lances, of a chariot with the figure of Fortune, and of seven Virtues on horseback. The goddess herself, in accordance with the inexorable logic of allegory to which even the painters at that time conformed, wore hair only on the front part of her head, while the back part was bald, and the genius who sat on the lower steps of the car, and who symbolized the fugitive character of fortune, had his feet immersed in a basin of water. Then followed, equipped by the same Florentines, a troop of horsemen in the costumes of various nations, dressed as foreign princes and nobles, and then, crowned with laurel and standing above a revolving globe, a Julius Cæsar, who explained to the king in Italian verse the meaning of the allegories, and then took his place in the procession. Sixty Florentines, all in purple and scarlet, closed this splendid display of what their home could achieve. Then a band of Catalans advanced on foot, with lay figures of horses fastened on to them before and behind, and engaged in a mock combat with a body of Turks, as though in derision of the Florentine sentimentalism. Last of all came a gigantic tower, the door guarded by an angel with a drawn sword; on it stood four Virtues, who each addressed the king with a song. The rest of the show had nothing specially characteristic about it.

At the entrance of Louis XII into Milan in the year 1507 we find, besides the inevitable chariot with Virtues, a living group representing Jupiter, Mars, and a figure of Italy caught in a net. After which came a car laden with trophies, and so forth.

And when there were in reality no triumphs to celebrate, the poets found a compensation for themselves and their patrons. Petrarch and Boccaccio had described the representation of every sort of fame as attendants each of an allegorical figure; the celebrities of past ages were now made attendants of the prince. The poetess Cleofe Gabrielli of Gubbio paid this honour to Borso of Ferrara. She gave him seven queens—the seven liberal arts—as his handmaids, with whom he mounted a chariot; further, a crowd of heroes, distinguished by names written on their foreheads; then followed all the famous poets; and after them the gods driving in their chariots. There is, in fact, at this time simply no end to the mythological and allegorical charioteering, and the most important work of art of Borso's time—the frescoes in the Palazzo Schifanoia—shows us a whole frieze filled with these motives.[99] Raphael, when he had to paint the Camera della Segnatura, found this mode of artistic thought completely vulgarized and worn out. The new and final consecration which he gave to it will remain a wonder to all ages.

The triumphal processions, strictly speaking, of victorious generals, formed the exception. But all the festive processions, whether they celebrated any special event or were mainly held for their own sakes,

[99] Old paintings of similar scenes are by no means rare, and no doubt often represent masquerades actually performed. The wealthy classes soon became accustomed to drive in chariots at every public solemnity. We read that Annibale Bentivoglio, eldest son of the ruler of Bologna, returned to the palace after presiding as umpire at the regular military exercises, 'cum triumpho more romano'.

assumed more or less the character and nearly always the name of a 'Trionfo'. It is a wonder that funerals were not also treated in the same way.

It was the practice, both at the Carnival and on other occasions, to represent the triumphs of ancient Roman commanders, such as that of Paulus Æmilius under Lorenzo the Magnificent at Florence, and that of Camillus on the visit of Leo X. Both were conducted by the painter Francesco Granacci. In Rome, the first complete exhibition of this kind was the triumph of Augustus after the victory over Cleopatra, under Paul II, where, besides the comic and mythological masks, which, as a matter of fact, were not wanting in the ancient triumphs, all the other requisites were to be found—kings in chains, tablets with decrees of the senate and people, a senate clothed in the ancient costume, praetors, aediles, and quaestors, four chariots filled with singing masks, and, doubtless, cars laden with trophies. Other processions rather aimed at setting forth, in a general way, the universal empire of ancient Rome; and in answer to the very real danger which threatened Europe from the side of the Turks, a cavalcade of camels bearing masks representing Ottoman prisoners, appeared before the people. Later, at the Carnival of the year 1500, Cesare Borgia, with a bold allusion to himself, celebrated the triumph of Julius Cæsar, with a procession of eleven magnificent chariots, doubtless to the scandal of the pilgrims who had come for the Jubilee. Two 'Trionfi', famous for their taste and beauty, were given by rival companies in Florence, on the election of Leo X to the Papacy. One of them represented the three Ages of Man, the other the Ages of the World, ingeniously set forth in five scenes of Roman history, and in two allegories of the golden age of Saturn and of its final return. The imagination displayed in the adornment of the chariots, when the great Florentine artists undertook the work, made the scene so impressive that such representations became in time a permanent element in the popular life. Hitherto the subject cities had been satisfied merely to present their symbolical gifts—costly stuffs and wax-candles—on the day when they annually did homage. The guild of merchants now built ten chariots, to which others were afterwards to be added, not so much to carry as to symbolize the tribute, and Andrea del Sarto, who painted some of them, no doubt did his work to perfection. These cars, whether used to hold tribute or trophies, now formed part of all such celebrations, even when there was not much money to be laid out. The Sienese announced, in 1477, the alliance between Ferrante and Sixtus IV, with which they themselves were associated, by driving a chariot round the city, with 'one clad as the goddess of peace standing on a hauberk and other arms'.

At the Venetian festivals the processions, not on land but on water, were marvellous in their fantastic splendour. The sailing of the Bucentaur to meet the Princesses of Ferrara in the year 1491 seems to have been something belonging to fairyland. Countless vessels with garlands and hangings, filled with the richly dressed youth of the city, moved in front; genii with attributes symbolizing the various gods, floated on machines hung in the air; below stood others grouped as tritons and nymphs; the air was filled with music, sweet odours, and the fluttering of embroidered banners. The Bucentaur was followed by such a crowd of boats of every sort that for a mile all round (*octo stadia*) the water could not be seen. With regard to the rest of the festivities, besides the pantomime mentioned above, we may notice as something new a boat-race of fifty powerful girls. In the sixteenth century the nobility were divided into corporations with a view to these festivals, whose most noteworthy feature was some extraordinary machine placed on a ship. So, for instance, in the year 1541, at the festival of the 'Sempiterni', a round 'universe' floated along the Grand Canal, and a splendid ball was given inside it. The Carnival, too, in this city was famous for its dances, processions, and exhibitions of every kind. The Square of St. Mark was found to give space enough not only for tournaments, but for 'Trionfi', similar to those common on the mainland. At a festival held on the conclusion of peace, the pious brotherhoods ('scuole') took each its part in the procession. There, among golden chandeliers with red candles, among crowds of musicians and winged boys with golden bowls and horns of plenty, was seen a car on which Noah and David sat together enthroned; then came Abigail, leading a camel laden with treasures, and a second car with a group of political figures—Italy sitting between Venice and Liguria—and on a raised step three female symbolical figures with the arms of the allied princes. This was followed by a great globe with the constellations, as it seems, round it. The princes themselves, or rather their bodily representatives, appeared on other chariots with their servants and their coats of arms, if we have rightly interpreted our author.

The Carnival, properly so called, apart from these great triumphal marches, had nowhere, perhaps, in the fifteenth century so varied a character as in Rome. There were races of every kind—of horses, asses, buffaloes, old men, young men, Jews, and so on. Paul II entertained the people in crowds before the Palazzo di Venezia, in which he lived. The games in the Piazza Navona, which had probably never altogether ceased since the classical times, were remarkable for their warlike splendour. We read of a sham fight of cavalry, and a review of all the citizens in arms. The greatest freedom existed with regard to the use of masks, which were sometimes allowed for several months together. Sixtus IV ventured, in the most populous part of the city—at the Campofiore and near the Banchi—to make his way through crowds of masks, though he declined to receive them as visitors in the Vatican. Under Innocent VIII, a discreditable usage, which had already appeared among the Cardinals, attained its height. In the Carnival of 1491, they sent one another chariots full of splendid masks, of singers, and of buffoons, chanting scandalous verses. They were accompanied by men on horseback. Apart from the Carnival, the Romans seem to have been the first to discover the effect of a great procession by torchlight. When Pius II came back from the Congress of Mantua in 1459, the people waited on him with a squadron of horsemen bearing torches, who rode in shining circles before his palace. Sixtus IV, however, thought it better to decline a nocturnal visit of the people, who proposed to wait on him with torches and olive-branches.

But the Florentine Carnival surpassed the Roman in a certain class of processions, which have left their mark even in literature. Among a crowd of masks on foot and on horseback appeared some huge, fantastic chariots, and upon each an allegorical figure or group of figures with the proper accompaniments, such as Jealousy with four spectacled faces on one head; the four temperaments with the planets belonging to them; the three Fates; Prudence enthroned above Hope and Fear, which lay bound before her; the four Elements, Ages, Winds, Seasons, and so on; as well as the famous chariot of Death with the coffins, which presently opened. Sometimes we meet with a splendid scene from classical mythology—Bacchus and Ariadne, Paris and Helen, and others. Or else a chorus of figures forming some single class or category, as the beggars, the hunters and nymphs, the lost souls who in their lifetime were hardhearted women, the hermits, the astrologers, the vagabonds, the devils, the sellers of various kinds of wares, and even on one occasion 'il popolo', the people as such, who all reviled one another in their songs. The songs, which still remain and have been collected, give the explanation of the masquerade sometimes in a pathetic, sometimes in a humorous, and sometimes in an excessively indecent tone. Some of the worst in this respect are attributed to Lorenzo the Magnificent, probably because the real author did not venture to declare himself. However this may be, we must certainly ascribe to him the beautiful song which accompanied the masque of Bacchus and Ariadne, whose refrain still echoes to us from the fifteenth century, like a regretful presentiment of the brief splendour of the Renaissance itself:

'Quanto è bella giovinezza,
Che si fugge tuttavia!
Chi vuol esser lieto, sia:
Di doman non c'è certezza.'[100]

★ 100 The meaning of these verses is roughly this: 'Youth is beautiful, but it flies away! Who would be cheerful, let him be; of the morrow there is no certainty.'

PART VI

MORALITY AND RELIGION

MORALITY AND JUDGEMENT

THE relation of the various peoples of the earth to the supreme interests of life, to God, virtue, and immortality, may be investigated up to a certain point, but can never be compared to one another with absolute strictness and certainty. The more plainly in these matters our evidence seems to speak, the more carefully must we refrain from unqualified assumptions and rash generalizations.

This remark is especially true with regard to our judgement on questions of morality. It may be possible to indicate many contrasts and shades of difference among different nations, but to strike the balance of the whole is not given to human insight. The ultimate truth with respect to the character, the conscience, and the guilt of a people remains for ever a secret; if only for the reason that its defects have another side, where they reappear as peculiarities or even as virtues. We must leave those who find pleasure in passing sweeping censures on whole nations, to do so as they like. The people of Europe can maltreat, but happily not judge one another. A great nation, interwoven by its civilization, its achievements, and its fortunes with the whole life of the modern world, can afford to ignore both its advocates and its accusers. It lives on with or without the approval of theorists.

Accordingly, what here follows is no judgement, but rather a string of marginal notes, suggested by a study of the Italian Renaissance extending over some years. The value to be attached to them is all the more qualified as they mostly touch on the life of the upper classes, with respect to which we are far better informed in Italy than in any other country in Europe at that period. But though both fame and infamy sound louder here than elsewhere, we are not helped thereby in forming an adequate moral estimate of the people.

What eye can pierce the depths in which the character and fate of nations are determined?—in which that which is inborn and that which has been experienced combine to form a new whole and a fresh nature?—in which even those intellectual capacities which at first sight we should take to be most original are in fact evolved late and slowly? Who can tell if the Italian before the thirteenth century possessed that flexible activity and certainty in his whole being—that play of power in shaping whatever subject he dealt with in word or in form, which was peculiar to him later? And if no answer can be found to these questions, how can we possibly judge of the infinite and infinitely intricate channels through which character and intellect are incessantly pouring their influence one upon the other. A tribunal there is for each one of us, whose voice is our conscience; but let us have done with these generalities about nations. For the people that seems to be most sick the cure may be at hand; and one that appears to be healthy may bear within it the ripening germs of death, which the hour of danger will bring forth from their hiding-place.

MORALITY AND IMMORALITY

At the beginning of the sixteenth century, when the civilization of the Renaissance had reached its highest pitch, and at the same time the political ruin of the nation seemed inevitable, there were not wanting serious thinkers who saw a connexion between this ruin and the prevalent immorality. It was not one of those methodistical moralists who in every age think themselves called to declaim against the wickedness of the time, but it was Machiavelli, who, in one of his best-considered works, said openly: 'We Italians are irreligious and corrupt above others.' Another man would perhaps have said, 'We are individually highly developed; we have outgrown the limits of morality and religion which were natural to us in our undeveloped state, and we despise outward law, because our rulers are illegitimate, and their judges and officers wicked men'. Machiavelli adds, 'because the Church and her representatives set us the worst example'.

Shall we add also, 'because the influence exercised by antiquity was in this respect unfavourable'? The statement can only be received with many qualifications. It may possibly be true of the humanists, especially as regards the profligacy of their lives. Of the rest it may perhaps be said with some approach to accuracy that, after they became familiar with antiquity, they substituted for holiness—the Christian ideal of life—the cult of historical greatness. We can understand, therefore, how easily they would be tempted to consider those faults and vices to be matters of indifference, in spite of which their heroes were great. They were probably scarcely conscious of this themselves, for if we are summoned to quote any statement of doctrine on this subject, we are again forced to appeal to humanists like Paolo Giovio, who excuses the perjury of Giangaleazzo Visconti, through which he was enabled to found an empire, by the example of Julius Cæsar. The great Florentine historians and statesmen never stoop to these slavish quotations, and what seems antique in their deeds and their judgements is so because the nature of their political life necessarily fostered in them a mode of thought which has some analogy with that of antiquity.

Nevertheless, it cannot be denied that Italy at the beginning of the sixteenth century found itself in the midst of a grave moral crisis, out of which the best men saw hardly any escape.

Let us begin by saying a few words about that moral force which was then the strongest bulwark against evil. The highly gifted man of that day thought to find it in the sentiment of honour. This is that enigmatic mixture of conscience and egotism which often survives in the modern man after he has lost, whether by his own fault or not, faith, love, and hope. This sense of honour is compatible with much selfishness and great vices, and may be the victim of astonishing illusions; yet, nevertheless, all the noble elements that are left in the wreck of a character may gather around it, and from this fountain may draw new strength. It has become, in a far wider sense than is commonly believed, a decisive test of conduct in the minds of the cultivated Europeans of our own day, and many of those who yet hold faithfully by religion and morality are unconsciously guided by this feeling in the gravest decisions of their lives.

It lies without the limits of our task to show how the men of antiquity also experienced this feeling in a peculiar form, and how, afterwards, in the Middle Ages, a special sense of honour became the mark of a particular class. Nor can we here dispute with those who hold that conscience, rather than honour, is the motive power. It would indeed be better and nobler if it were so; but since it must be granted that even our worthier resolutions result from 'a conscience more or less dimmed by selfishness', it is better to call the mixture by its right name. It is certainly not always easy, in treating of the Italian of this period, to distinguish this sense of honour from the passion for fame, into which, indeed, it easily passes. Yet the two sentiments are essentially different.

There is no lack of witnesses on this subject. One who speaks plainly may here be quoted as a representative of the rest. We read in the recently published 'Aphorisms' of Guicciardini: 'He who esteems honour highly succeeds in all that he undertakes, since he fears neither trouble, danger, nor expense; I have found it so in my own case, and may say it and write it; vain and dead are the deeds of men which have not this as their motive.' It is necessary to add that, from what is known of the life of the writer, he can here be only speaking of honour, and not of fame. Rabelais has put the matter more clearly than perhaps any Italian. We quote him, indeed, unwillingly in these pages. What the great, baroque Frenchman gives us is a picture of what the Renaissance would be without form and without beauty. But his description of an ideal state of things in the Thelemite monastery is decisive as historical evidence. In speaking of his gentlemen and ladies of the Order of Free Will, he tells us as follows:

'En leur reigle n'estoit que ceste clause: Fay ce que vouldras. Parce que gens liberes, bien nayz, bien instruictz, conversans en compaignies honnestes, ont par nature ung instinct et aguillon qui tousjours les poulse à faictz vertueux, et retire de vice: lequel ilz nommoyent honneur.'

This is that same faith in the goodness of human nature which inspired the men of the second half of the eighteenth century, and helped to prepare the way for the French Revolution. Among the Italians, too, each man appeals to this noble instinct within him, and though with regard to the people as a whole—chiefly in consequence of the national disasters—judgements of a more pessimistic sort became prevalent, the importance of this sense of honour must still be rated highly. If the boundless development of individuality, stronger than the will of the individual, be the work of a historical providence, not less so is the opposing force which then manifested itself in Italy. How often, and against what passionate attacks of selfishness it won the day, we cannot tell, and therefore no human judgement can estimate with certainty the absolute moral value of the nation.

A force which we must constantly take into account in judging of the morality of the more highly developed Italian of this period, is that of the imagination. It gives to his virtues and vices a peculiar colour, and under its influence his unbridled egotism shows itself in its most terrible shape.

The force of his imagination explains, for example, the fact that he was the first gambler on a large scale in modern times. Pictures of future wealth and enjoyment rose in such lifelike colours before his eyes, that he was ready to hazard everything to reach them. The Mohammedan nations would doubtless have anticipated him in this respect, had not the Koran, from the beginning, set up the prohibition against gambling as a chief safeguard of public morals, and directed the imagination of its followers to the search after buried treasures. In Italy, the passion for play reached an intensity which often threatened or altogether broke up the existence of the gambler. Florence had already, at the end of the fourteenth century, its Casanova—a certain Buonaccorso Pitti, who, in the course of his incessant journeys as merchant, political agent, diplomatist and professional gambler, won and lost sums so enormous that none but princes like the Dukes of Brabant, Bavaria, and Savoy, were able to compete with him. That great lottery-bank, which was called the Court of Rome, accustomed people to a need of excitement, which found its satisfaction in games of hazard during the intervals between one intrigue and another. We read, for example, how Franceschetto Cibo, in two games with the Cardinal Raffaello Riario, lost no less than 14,000 ducats, and afterwards complained to the Pope that his opponent had cheated him. Italy has since that time been the home of the lottery.

It was to the imagination of the Italians that the peculiar character of their vengeance was due. The sense of justice was, indeed, one and the same throughout Europe, and any violation of it, so long as no punishment was inflicted, must have been felt in the same manner. But other nations, though they found it no easier to forgive, nevertheless forgot more easily, while the Italian imagination kept the picture of the wrong alive with frightful vividness.[101] The fact that, according to the popular morality, the avenging of blood is a duty—a duty often performed in a way to make us shudder—gives to this passion a peculiar and still firmer basis. The government and the tribunals recognize its existence and justification, and only attempt to keep it within certain limits. Even among the peasantry, we read of Thyestean banquets and mutual assassination on the widest scale. Let us look at an instance.

In the district of Acquapendente three boys were watching cattle, and one of them said: 'Let us find out the way how people are hanged.' While one was sitting on the shoulders of the other, and

[101] This opinion of Stendhal (*La Chartreuse de Parme*) seems to me to rest on profound psychological observation.

the third, after fastening the rope round the neck of the first, was tying it to an oak, a wolf came, and the two who were free ran away and left the other hanging. Afterwards they found him dead, and buried him. On the Sunday his father came to bring him bread, and one of the two confessed what had happened, and showed him the grave. The old man then killed him with a knife, cut him up, brought away the liver, and entertained the boy's father with it at home. After dinner, he told him whose liver it was. Hereupon began a series of reciprocal murders between the two families, and within a month thirty-six persons were killed, women as well as men.

And such 'vendette', handed down from father to son, and extending to friends and distant relations, were not limited to the lower classes, but reached to the highest. The chronicles and novels of the period are full of such instances, especially of vengeance taken for the violation of women. The classic land for these feuds was Romagna, where the 'vendetta' was interwoven with intrigues and party divisions of every conceivable sort. The popular legends present an awful picture of the savagery into which this brave and energetic people had relapsed. We are told, for instance, of a nobleman at Ravenna, who had got all his enemies together in a tower, and might have burned them; instead of which he let them out, embraced them, and entertained them sumptuously; whereupon shame drove them mad, and they conspired against him. Pious and saintly monks exhorted unceasingly to reconciliation, but they can scarcely have done more than restrain to a certain extent the feuds already established; their influence hardly prevented the growth of new ones. The novelists sometimes describe to us this effect of religion—how sentiments of generosity and forgiveness were suddenly awakened, and then again paralysed by the force of what had once been done and could never be undone. The Pope himself was not always lucky as a peacemaker. Pope Paul II desired that the quarrel between Antonio Caffarello and the family of Alberino should cease, and ordered Giovanni Alberino and Antonio Caffarello to come before him, bade them kiss one another, and threatened them with a fine of 2,000 ducats if they renewed this strife, and two days after Antonio was stabbed by the same Giacomo Alberino, son of Giovanni, who had wounded him once before; and the Pope was full of anger, and confiscated the goods of Alberino, and destroyed his houses, and banished father and son from Rome. The oaths and ceremonies by which reconciled enemies attempted to guard themselves against a relapse, are sometimes utterly horrible. When the parties of the 'Nove' and the 'Popolari' met and kissed one another by twos in the cathedral at Siena on New Year's Eve, 1494, an oath was read by which all salvation in time and eternity was denied to the future violator of the treaty—'an oath more astonishing and dreadful than had ever yet been heard'. The last consolations of religion in the hour of death were to turn to the damnation of the man who should break it. It is clear, however, that such a ceremony rather represents the despairing mood of the mediators than offers any real guarantee of peace, inasmuch as the truest reconciliation is just that one which has least need of it.

This personal need of vengeance felt by the cultivated and highly placed Italian, resting on the solid basis of an analogous popular custom, naturally displays itself under a thousand different aspects, and receives the unqualified approval of public opinion, as reflected in the works of the novelists. All are at one on the point that, in the case of those injuries and insults for which Italian justice offered no redress, and all the more in the case of those against which no human law can ever adequately provide, each man is free to take the law into his own hands. Only there must be art in the vengeance, and the satisfaction must be compounded of the material injury and moral humiliation of the offender. A mere brutal, clumsy triumph of force was held by public opinion to be no satisfaction. The whole man with his sense of fame and of scorn, not only his fist, must be victorious.

The Italian of that time shrank, it is true, from no dissimulation in order to attain his ends, but was wholly free from hypocrisy in matters of principle. In these he attempted to deceive neither himself nor others. Accordingly, revenge was declared with perfect frankness to be a necessity of human nature. Cool-headed people declared that it was then most worthy of praise when it was disengaged from passion, and worked simply from motives of expedience, 'in order that other men may learn to leave us unharmed'. Yet such instances must have formed only a small minority in comparison with those in which passion sought an outlet. This sort of revenge differs clearly from the avenging of blood, which has already been spoken of; while the latter keeps more or less within the limits of retaliation—the 'ius talionis'—the former necessarily goes much further, not only requiring the sanction of the sense of justice, but craving admiration, and even striving to get the laugh on its own side.

Here lies the reason why men were willing to wait so long for their revenge. A 'bella vendetta' demanded as a rule a combination of circumstances for which it was necessary to wait patiently. The gradual ripening of such opportunities is described by the novelists with heartfelt delight.

There is no need to discuss the morality of actions in which plaintiff and judge are one and the same person. If this Italian thirst for vengeance is to be palliated at all, it must be by proving the existence of a corresponding national virtue, namely gratitude. The same force of imagination which retains and magnifies wrong once suffered, might be expected also to keep alive the memory of kindness received. It is not possible, however, to prove this with regard to the nation as a whole, though traces of it may be seen in the Italian character of today. The gratitude shown by the inferior classes for kind treatment, and the good memory of the upper for politeness in social life, are instances of this.

This connexion between the imagination and the moral qualities of the Italian repeats itself continually. If, nevertheless, we find more cold calculation in cases where the Northerner rather follows his impulses, the reason is that individual development in Italy was not only more marked and earlier in point of time, but also far more frequent. Where this is the case in other countries, the results are also analogous. We find, for example, that the early emancipation of the young from domestic and paternal authority is common to North America with Italy. Later on, in the more generous natures, a tie of freer affection grows up between parents and children.

It is, in fact, a matter of extreme difficulty to judge fairly of other nations in the sphere of character and feeling. In these respects a people may be developed highly, and yet in a manner so strange that a foreigner is utterly unable to understand it. Perhaps all the nations of the West are in this point equally favoured.

But where the imagination has exercised the most powerful and despotic influence on morals is in the illicit intercourse of the two sexes. It is well known that prostitution was freely practised in the Middle Ages, before the appearance of syphilis. A discussion, however, on these questions does not belong to our present work. What seems characteristic of Italy at this time, is that here marriage and its rights were more often and more deliberately trampled underfoot than anywhere else. The girls of the higher classes were carefully secluded, and of them we do not speak. All passion was directed to the married women.

Under these circumstances it is remarkable that, so far as we know, there was no diminution in the number of marriages, and that family life by no means underwent that disorganization which a similar state of things would have produced in the North. Men wished to live as they pleased, but by no means to renounce the family, even when they were not sure that it was all their own. Nor did the race sink, either physically or mentally, on this account; for that apparent intellectual decline which showed itself towards the middle of the sixteenth century may be certainly accounted for by political and ecclesiastical causes, even if we are not to assume that the circle of achievements possible to the Renaissance had been completed. Notwithstanding their profligacy, the Italians continued to be, physically and mentally, one of the healthiest and best-born populations in Europe,[102] and have retained this position, with improved morals, down to our own time.

When we come to look more closely at the ethics of love at the time of the Renaissance, we are struck by a remarkable contrast. The novelists and comic poets give us to understand that love consists only in sensual enjoyment, and that to win this, all means, tragic or comic, are not only permitted, but are interesting in proportion to their audacity and unscrupulousness. But if we turn to the best of the lyric poets and writers of dialogues, we find in them a deep and spiritual passion of the noblest kind, whose last and highest expression is a revival of the ancient belief in an original unity of souls in the Divine Being. And both modes of feeling were then genuine, and could co-exist in the same individual. It is not exactly a matter of glory, but it is a fact, that, in the cultivated man of modern times, this sentiment can be not merely unconsciously present in both its highest and lowest stages, but may also manifest itself openly, and even artistically. The modern man, like the man of antiquity, is in this respect too a microcosm, which the mediæval man was not and could not be.

To begin with the morality of the novelists. They treat chiefly, as we have said, of married women, and consequently of adultery.

The opinion mentioned above of the equality of the two sexes is of great importance in relation to this subject. The highly developed and cultivated woman disposes of herself with a freedom unknown

[102] It is true that when the Spanish rule was fully established the population fell off to a certain extent. Had this fact been due to the demoralization of the people, it would have appeared much earlier.

in Northern countries; and her unfaithfulness does not break up her life in the same terrible manner, so long as no outward consequences follow from it. The husband's claim on her fidelity has not that firm foundation which it acquires in the North through the poetry and passion of courtship and betrothal. After the briefest acquaintance with her future husband, the young wife quits the convent or the paternal roof to enter upon a world in which her character begins rapidly to develop. The rights of the husband are for this reason conditional, and even the man who regards them in the light of a 'ius quæsitum' thinks only of the outward conditions of the contract, not of the affections. The beautiful young wife of an old man sends back the presents and letters of a youthful lover, in the firm resolve to keep her honour (honestà). 'But she rejoiced in the love of the youth for his great excellence; and she perceived that a noble woman may love a man of merit without loss to her honour.' But the way is short from such a distinction to a complete surrender.

The latter seems indeed as good as justified when there is unfaithfulness on the part of the husband. The woman, conscious of her own dignity, feels this not only as a pain, but also as a humiliation and deceit, and sets to work, often with the calmest consciousness of what she is about, to devise the vengeance which the husband deserves. Her tact must decide as to the measure of punishment which is suited to the particular case. The deepest wound, for example, may prepare the way for a reconciliation and a peaceful life in the future, if only it remain secret. The novelists, who themselves undergo such experiences or invent them according to the spirit of the age, are full of admiration when the vengeance is skilfully adapted to the particular case, in fact, when it is a work of art. As a matter of course, the husband never at bottom recognizes this right of retaliation, and only submits to it from fear or prudence. Where these motives are absent, where his wife's unfaithfulness exposes him or may expose him to the derision of outsiders, the affair becomes tragical, and not seldom ends in murder or other vengeance of a violent sort. It is characteristic of the real motive from which these deeds arise, that not only the husbands, but the brothers[103] and the father of the

[103] A shocking instance of vengeance taken by a brother at Perugia in the year 1455 is to be found in the chronicle of Graziani (*Arch. Stor.* xvi. p. 629). The brother forces the gallant to tear out the sister's eyes, and then beats him from the place. It is true that the family was a branch of the Oddi, and the lover only a rope-maker.

woman feel themselves not only justified in taking vengeance, but bound to take it. Jealousy, therefore, has nothing to do with the matter, moral reprobation but little; the real reason is the wish to spoil the triumph of others. 'Nowadays,' says Bandello, 'we see a woman poison her husband to gratify her lusts, thinking that a widow may do whatever she desires. Another, fearing the discovery of an illicit amour, has her husband murdered by her lover. And though fathers, brothers, and husbands arise to extirpate the shame with poison, with the sword, and by every other means, women still continue to follow their passions, careless of their honour and their lives.' Another time, in milder strain, he exclaims: 'Would that we were not daily forced to hear that one man has murdered his wife because he suspected her of infidelity; that another has killed his daughter, on account of a secret marriage; that a third has caused his sister to be murdered, because she would not marry as he wished! It is great cruelty that we claim the right to do whatever we list, and will not suffer women to do the same. If they do anything which does not please us, there we are at once with cords and daggers and poison. What folly it is of men to suppose their own and their house's honour depend on the appetite of a woman!' The tragedy in which such affairs commonly ended was so well known that the novelist looked on the threatened gallant as a dead man, even while he went about alive and merry. The physician and lute-player Antonio Bologna had made a secret marriage with the widowed Duchess of Amalfi, of the house of Aragon. Soon afterwards her brother succeeded in securing both her and her children, and murdered them in a castle. Antonio, ignorant of their fate, and still cherishing the hope of seeing them again, was staying at Milan, closely watched by hired assassins, and one day in the society of Ippolita Sforza sang to the lute the story of his misfortunes. A friend of the house, Delio, 'told the story up to this point to Scipione Atellano, and added that he would make it the subject of a novel, as he was sure that Antonio would be murdered'. The manner in which this took place, almost under the eyes of both Delio and Atellano, is movingly described by Bandello.

Nevertheless, the novelists habitually show a sympathy for all the ingenious, comic, and cunning features which may happen to attend adultery. They describe with delight how the lover manages to hide himself in the house, all the means and devices by which he communicates with his mistress, the boxes with cushions and sweetmeats in which he can be hidden and carried out of danger. The deceived husband is described sometimes as a fool to be laughed at, sometimes as a bloodthirsty avenger of his honour; there is no third situation except when the woman is painted as wicked and cruel, and the husband or lover is the innocent victim. It may be remarked, however, that narratives of the latter kind are not strictly speaking novels, but rather warning examples taken from real life.

When in the course of the sixteenth century Italian life fell more and more under Spanish influence, the violence of the means to which jealousy had recourse perhaps increased. But this new phase must be distinguished from the punishment of infidelity which existed before, and which was founded in the spirit of the Italian Renaissance itself. As the influence of Spain declined, these excesses of jealousy declined also, till towards the close of the seventeenth century they had wholly disappeared, and their place was taken by that indifference which regarded the 'Cicisbeo' as an indispensable figure in every household, and took no offence at one or two contemporary lovers ('Patiti').

But who can undertake to compare the vast sum of wickedness which all these facts imply, with what happened in other countries? Was the marriage-tie, for instance, really more sacred in France during the fifteenth century than in Italy? The 'fabliaux' and farces would lead us to doubt it, and rather incline us to think that unfaithfulness was equally common, though its tragic consequences were less frequent, because the individual was less developed and his claims were less consciously felt than in Italy. More evidence, however, in favour of the Germanic peoples lies in the fact of the social freedom enjoyed among them by girls and women, which impressed Italian travellers so pleasantly in England and in the Netherlands. And yet we must not attach too much importance to this fact. Unfaithfulness was doubtless very frequent, and in certain cases led to a sanguinary vengeance. We have only to remember how the northern princes of that time dealt with their wives on the first suspicion of infidelity.

But it was not merely the sensual desire, not merely the vulgar appetite of the ordinary man, which trespassed upon forbidden ground among the Italians of that day, but also the passion of the best and noblest; and this, not only because the unmarried girl did not appear in society, but also because the man, in proportion to the completeness of his own nature, felt himself most strongly attracted by the woman whom marriage had developed. These are the men who struck the loftiest notes of lyrical poetry, and who have attempted in their treatises and dialogues to give us an idealized image of the devouring passion—'l'amor divino'. When they complain of the cruelty of the winged god, they are not only thinking of the coyness or hard-heartedness of the beloved one, but also of the unlawfulness of the passion itself. They seek to raise themselves above this painful consciousness by that spiritualization of love which found a support in the Platonic doctrine of the soul, and of which Pietro Bembo is the most famous representative. His thoughts on this subject are set forth by himself in the third book of the 'Asolani', and indirectly by Castiglione, who puts in his mouth the splendid speech with which the fourth book of the 'Cortigiano' concludes. Neither of these writers was a stoic in his conduct, but at that time it meant something to be at once a famous and a good man, and this praise must be accorded to both of them; their contemporaries took what these men said to be a true expression of their feeling, and we have not the right to despise it as affectation. Those who take the trouble to study the speech in the 'Cortigiano' will see how poor an idea of it can be given by an extract. There were then living in Italy several distinguished women, who owed their celebrity chiefly to relations of this kind, such as Giulia Gonzaga, Veronica da Correggio, and, above all, Vittoria Colonna. The land of profligates and scoffers respected these women and this sort of love—and what more can be said in their favour? We cannot tell how far vanity had to do with the matter, how far Vittoria was flattered to hear around her the sublimated utterances of hopeless love from the most famous men in Italy. If the thing was here and there a fashion, it was still no trifling praise for Vittoria that she, at least, never went out of fashion, and in her latest years produced the most profound impressions. It was long before other countries had anything similar to show.

In the imagination then, which governed this people more than any other, lies one general reason why the course of every passion was violent, and why the means used for the gratification of passion were often criminal. There is a violence which cannot control itself because it is born of weakness; but in Italy we find what is the corruption of powerful natures. Sometimes this corruption assumes a colossal shape, and crime seems to acquire almost a personal existence of its own.

The restraints of which men were conscious were but few. Each individual, even among the lowest of the people, felt himself inwardly emancipated from the control of the State and its police, whose title to respect was illegitimate, and itself founded on violence; and no man believed any longer in the justice of the law. When a murder was committed, the sympathies of the people, before the circumstances of the case were known, ranged themselves instinctively on the side of the murderer. A proud, manly bearing before and at the execution excited such admiration that the narrator often forgets to tell us for what offence the criminal was put to death. But when we add to this inward contempt of law and to the countless grudges and enmities which called for satisfaction, the impunity which crime enjoyed during times of political disturbance, we can only wonder that the State and society were not utterly dissolved. Crises of this kind occurred at Naples, during the transition from the Aragonese to the French and Spanish rule, and at Milan, on the repeated expulsions and returns of the Sforzas; at such times those men who have never in their hearts recognized the bonds of law and society, come forward and give free play to their instincts of murder and rapine. Let us take, by way of example, a picture drawn from a humbler sphere.

When the Duchy of Milan was suffering from the disorders which followed the death of Galeazzo Maria Sforza, about the year 1480, all safety came to an end in the provincial cities. This was the case in Parma, where the Milanese Governor, terrified by threats of murder, consented to throw open the gaols and let loose the most abandoned criminals. Burglary, the demolition of houses, public assassination and murders, were events of everyday occurrence. At first the authors of these deeds prowled about singly, and masked; soon large gangs of armed men went to work every night without disguise. Threatening letters, satires, and scandalous jests circulated freely; and a sonnet in ridicule of the Government seems to have roused its indignation far more than the frightful condition of the city. In many churches the sacred vessels with the host were stolen, and this fact is characteristic of the temper which prompted these outrages. It is impossible to say what would happen now in any country of the world, if the government and police ceased to act, and yet hindered by their presence the establishment of a provisional authority; but what then occurred in Italy wears a character of its own, through the great share which the personal hatred and revenge had in it. The impression, indeed, which Italy at this period makes on us is, that even in quiet times great crimes were commoner than in other countries. We may, it is true, be misled by the fact that we have far fuller details on such matters here than elsewhere, and that the same force of imagination, which gives a special character to crimes actually committed, causes much to be invented which never really happened. The amount of violence was perhaps as great elsewhere. It is hard to say for certain, whether in the year 1500 men were any safer, whether human life was any better protected, in powerful, wealthy Germany, with its robber knights, extortionate beggars, and daring highwaymen. But one thing is certain, that premeditated crimes, committed professionally and for hire by third parties, occurred in Italy with great and appalling frequency.

So far as regards brigandage, Italy, especially in the more fortunate provinces, such as Tuscany, was certainly not more, and probably less, troubled than the countries of the North. But the figures which do meet us are characteristic of the country. It would be hard, for instance, to find elsewhere the case of a priest, gradually driven by passion from one excess to another, till at last he came to head a band of robbers. That age offers us this example among others. On August 12, 1495, the priest Don Niccolò de' Pelagati of Figarolo was shut up in an iron cage outside the tower of San Giuliano at Ferrara. He had twice celebrated his first mass; the first time he had the same day committed murder, but afterwards received absolution at Rome; he then killed four people and married two wives, with whom he travelled about. He afterwards took part in many assassinations, violated women, carried others away by force, plundered far and wide, and infested the territory of Ferrara with a band of followers in uniform, extorting food and shelter by every sort of violence. When we think of what all this implies, the mass of guilt on the head of this one man is something tremendous. The clergy and monks had many privileges and little supervision, and among them were doubtless plenty of murderers and other malefactors—but hardly a second Pelagati. It is another matter, though by no means creditable, when ruined characters sheltered themselves in the cowl in order to escape the arm of the law, like the corsair whom Masuccio knew in a convent at Naples. What the real truth was with regard to Pope John XXIII in this respect, is not known with certainty.

The age of the famous brigand chief did not begin till later, in the seventeenth century, when the political strife of Guelph and Ghibelline, of Frenchman and Spaniard, no longer agitated the country. The robber then took the place of the partisan.

In certain districts of Italy, where civilization had made little progress, the country people were disposed to murder any stranger who fell into their hands. This was especially the case in the more remote parts of the Kingdom of Naples, where the barbarism dated probably from the days of the Roman 'latifundia', and when the stranger and the enemy ('hospes' and 'hostis') were in all good faith held to be one and the same. These people were far from being irreligious. A herdsman once appeared in great trouble at the confessional, avowing that, while making cheese during Lent, a few drops of milk had found their way into his mouth. The confessor, skilled in the customs of the country, discovered in the course of his examination that the penitent and his friends were in the practice of robbing and murdering travellers, but that, through the force of habit, this usage gave rise to no twinges of conscience within them. We have already mentioned to what a degree of barbarism the peasants elsewhere could sink in times of political confusion.

A worse symptom than brigandage of the morality of that time was the frequency of paid assassination. In that respect Naples was admitted to stand at the head of all the cities of Italy. 'Nothing,' says Pontano, 'is cheaper here than human life.' But other districts could also show a terrible list of these crimes. It is hard, of course, to classify them according to the motives by which they were prompted, since political expediency, personal hatred, party hostility, fear, and revenge, all play into one another. It is no small honour to the Florentines, the most highly developed people of Italy, that offences of this kind occurred more rarely among them than anywhere else, perhaps because there was a justice at hand for legitimate grievances which was recognized by all, or because the higher culture of the individual gave him different views as to the right of men to interfere with the decrees of fate. In Florence, if anywhere, men were able to feel the incalculable consequences of a deed of blood, and to understand how uncertain the author of a so-called profitable crime is of any true and lasting gain. After the fall of Florentine liberty, assassination, especially by hired agents, seems to have rapidly increased, and continued till the government of Grand Duke Cosimo I de' Medici had attained such strength that the police were at last able to repress it.

Elsewhere in Italy paid crimes were probably more or less frequent in proportion to the number of powerful and solvent buyers. Impossible as it is to make any statistical estimate of their amount, yet if only a fraction of the deaths which public report attributed to violence were really murders, the crime must have been terribly frequent. The worst example of all was set by princes and governments, who without the faintest scruple reckoned murder as one of the instruments of their power. And this, without being in the same category with Cesare Borgia. The Sforzas, the Aragonese monarchs, and, later on, the agents of Charles V resorted to it whenever it suited their purpose. The imagination of the people at last became so accustomed to facts of this kind that the death of any powerful man was seldom or never attributed to natural causes. There were certainly absurd notions current with regard to the effect of various poisons. There may be some truth in the story of that terrible white powder used by the Borgias, which did its work at the end of a definite period, and it is possible that it was really a 'venenum atterminatum' which the Prince of Salerno handed to the Cardinal of Aragon, with the words: 'In a few days you will die, because your father, King Ferrante, wished to trample upon us all'. But the poisoned letter which Caterina Riario sent to Pope Alexander VI would hardly have caused his death even if he had read it; and when Alfonso the Great was warned by his physicians not to read in the Livy which Cosimo de' Medici had presented to him, he told them with justice not to talk like fools. Nor can that poison with which the secretary of Piccinino wished to anoint the sedan-chair of Pius II have affected any other organ than the imagination. The proportion which mineral and vegetable poisons bore to one another, cannot be ascertained precisely. The poison with which the painter Rosso Fiorentino destroyed himself (1541) was evidently a powerful acid, which it would have been impossible to administer to another person without his knowledge. The secret use of weapons, especially of the dagger, in the service of powerful individuals, was habitual in Milan, Naples, and other cities. Indeed, among the crowds of armed retainers who were necessary for the personal safety of the great, and who lived in idleness, it was natural that outbreaks of this mania for blood should from time to time occur. Many a deed of horror would never have been committed, had not the master known that he needed but to give a sign to one or other of his followers.

Among the means used for the secret destruction of others—so far, that is, as the intention goes—we find magic, practised, however, sparingly. Where 'maleficii', 'malie', and so forth, are mentioned, they appear rather as a means of heaping up additional terror on the head of some hated enemy. At the courts of France and England in the fourteenth and fifteenth centuries, magic, practised with a view to the death of an opponent, plays a far more important part than in Italy. In this country, finally, where individuality of every sort attained its highest development, we find instances of that ideal and absolute wickedness which delights in crimes for their own sake, and not as means to an end, or at any rate as means to ends for which our psychology has no measure.

Among these appalling figures we may first notice certain of the 'Condottieri', such as Braccio da Montone, Tiberto Brandolino, and that Werner von Urslingen whose silver hauberk bore the inscription: 'The enemy of God, of pity and of mercy.' This class of men offers us some of the earliest instances of criminals deliberately repudiating every moral restraint. Yet we shall be more reserved in our judgement of them when we remember that the worst part of their guilt—in the estimate of those who record it—lay in their defiance of spiritual threats and penalties, and that to this fact is due that air of horror with which they are represented as surrounded. In the case of Braccio, the hatred of the Church went so far that he was infuriated at the sight of monks at their psalms, and had them thrown down from the top of a tower; but at the same time 'he was loyal to his soldiers and a great general'. As a rule, the crimes of the 'Condottieri' were committed for the sake of some definite advantage, and must be attributed to a position in which men could not fail to be demoralized. Even their apparently gratuitous cruelty had commonly a purpose, if it were only to strike terror. The barbarities of the House of Aragon, as we have seen, were mainly due to fear and to the desire for vengeance. The thirst for blood on its own account, the devilish delight in destruction, is most clearly exemplified in the case of the Spaniard Cesare Borgia, whose cruelties were certainly out of all proportion to the end which he had in view. In Sigismondo Malatesta, tyrant of Rimini, the same disinterested love of evil may also be detected. It is not only the Court of Rome, but the verdict of history, which convicts him of murder, rape, adultery, incest, sacrilege, perjury and treason, committed not once but often. The most shocking crime of all—the unnatural attempt on his own son Roberto, who frustrated it with his drawn dagger—may have been the result not merely of moral corruption, but perhaps of some magical or astrological superstition. The same conjecture has been made to account for the rape of the Bishop of Fano by Pierluigi Farnese of Parma, son of Paul III.

* * *

If we now attempt to sum up the principal features in the Italian character of that time, as we know it from a study of the life of the upper classes, we shall obtain something like the following result. The fundamental vice of this character was at the same time a condition of its greatness, namely, excessive individualism. The individual first inwardly casts off the authority of a State which, as a fact, is in most cases tyrannical and illegitimate, and what he thinks and does is, rightly or wrongly, now called treason. The sight of victorious egotism in others drives him to defend his own right by his own arm. And, while thinking to restore his inward equilibrium, he falls, through the vengeance which he executes, into the hands of the powers of darkness. His love, too, turns mostly for satisfaction to another individuality equally developed, namely, to his neighbour's wife. In face of all objective facts, of laws and restraints of whatever kind, he retains the feeling of his own sovereignty, and in each single instance forms his decision independently, according as honour or interest, passion or calculation, revenge or renunciation, gain the upper hand in his own mind.

If therefore egotism in its wider as well as narrower sense is the root and fountain of all evil, the more highly developed Italian was for this reason more inclined to wickedness than the members of other nations of that time.

But this individual development did not come upon him through any fault of his own, but rather through an historical necessity. It did not come upon him alone, but also, and chiefly, by means of Italian culture, upon the other nations of Europe, and has constituted since then the higher atmosphere which they breathe. In itself it is neither good nor bad, but necessary; within it has grown up a modern standard of good and evil—a sense of moral reponsibility—which is essentially different from that which was familiar to the Middle Ages.

But the Italian of the Renaissance had to bear the first mighty surging of a new age. Through his gifts and his passions, he has become the most characteristic representative of all the heights and all the depths of his time. By the side of profound corruption appeared human personalities of the noblest harmony, and an artistic splendour which shed upon the life of man a lustre which neither antiquity nor mediævalism could or would bestow upon it.

RELIGION IN DAILY LIFE

The morality of a people stands in the closest connection with its consciousness of God, that is to say, with its firmer or weaker faith in the divine government of the world, whether this faith looks on the world as destined to happiness or to misery and speedy destruction.[104] The infidelity then prevalent in Italy is notorious, and whoever takes the trouble to look about for proofs, will find them by the hundred. Our present task, here as elsewhere, is to separate and discriminate; refraining from an absolute and final verdict.

The belief in God at earlier times had its source and chief support in Christianity and the outward symbol of Christianity, the Church. When the Church became corrupt, men ought to have drawn a distinction, and kept their religion in spite of all. But this is more easily said than done. It is not every people which is calm enough, or dull enough, to tolerate a lasting contradiction between a principle and its outward expression. But history does not record a heavier responsibility than that which rests upon the decaying Church. She set up as absolute truth, and by the most violent means, a doctrine which she had distorted to serve her own aggrandizement. Safe in the sense of her inviolability, she abandoned herself to the most scandalous profligacy, and, in order to maintain herself in this state, she levelled mortal blows against the conscience and the intellect of nations, and drove multitudes of the noblest spirits, whom she had inwardly estranged, into the arms of unbelief and despair.

Here we are met by the question: Why did not Italy, intellectually so great, react more energetically against the hierarchy; why did she not accomplish a reformation like that which occurred in Germany, and accomplish it at an earlier date?

A plausible answer has been given to this question. The Italian mind, we are told, never went further than the denial of the hierarchy, while the origin and the vigour of the German Reformation was due to its positive religious doctrines, most of all to the doctrines of justification by faith and of the inefficacy of good works.

It is certain that these doctrines only worked upon Italy through

[104] On which point feeling differs according to the place and the people. The Renaissance prevailed in times and cities where the tendency was to enjoy life heartily. The general darkening of the spirits of thoughtful men did not begin to show itself till the time of the foreign supremacy in the sixteenth century.

Germany, and this not till the power of Spain was sufficiently great to root them out without difficulty, partly by itself and partly by means of the Papacy, and its instruments.[105] Nevertheless, in the earlier religious movements of Italy, from the Mystics of the thirteenth century down to Savonarola, there was a large amount of positive religious doctrine which, like the very definite Christianity of the Huguenots, failed to achieve success only because circumstances were against it. Mighty events like the Reformation elude, as respects their details, their outbreak and their development, the deductions of the philosophers, however clearly the necessity of them as a whole may be demonstrated. The movements of the human spirit, its sudden flashes, its expansions and its pauses, must for ever remain a mystery to our eyes, since we can but know this or that of the forces at work in it, never all of them together.

The feeling of the upper and middle classes in Italy with regard to the Church at the time when the Renaissance culminated, was compounded of deep and contemptuous aversion, of acquiescence in the outward ecclesiastical customs which entered into daily life, and of a sense of dependence on sacraments and ceremonies. The great personal influence of religious preachers may be added as a fact characteristic of Italy.

That hostility to the hierarchy, which displays itself more especially from the time of Dante onwards in Italian literature and history, has been fully treated by several writers. We have already (p. 132) said something of the attitude of public opinion with regard to the Papacy. Those who wish for the strongest evidence which the best authorities offer us, can find it in the famous passages of Machiavelli's 'Discorsi', and in the unmutilated edition of Guicciardini. Outside the Roman Curia, some respect seems to have been felt for the best men among the bishops, and for many of the parochial clergy. On the other hand, the mere holders of benefices, the canons and the monks were held in almost universal suspicion, and were often the objects of the most scandalous aspersions, extending to the whole of their order.

It has been said that the monks were made the scapegoats for the

[105] What is termed the spirit of the Counter-Reformation was developed in Spain some time before the Reformation itself, chiefly through the sharp surveillance and partial reorganization of the Church under Ferdinand and Isabella. The principal authority on this subject is Gomez, *Life of Cardinal Ximenez*, in Rob. Belus, *Rer. Hispan. Scriptores*, 3 vols., 1581.

whole clergy, for the reason that none but they could be ridiculed without danger. But this is certainly incorrect. They are introduced so frequently in the novels and comedies, because these forms of literature need fixed and well-known types where the imagination of the reader can easily fill up an outline. Besides which, the novelists do not as a fact spare the secular clergy.[106] In the third place, we have abundant proof in the rest of Italian literature that men could speak boldly enough about the Papacy and the Court of Rome. In works of imagination we cannot expect to find criticism of this kind. Fourthly, the monks, when attacked, were sometimes able to take a terrible vengeance.

It is nevertheless true that the monks were the most unpopular class of all, and that they were reckoned a living proof of the worthlessness of conventual life, of the whole ecclesiastical organization, of the system of dogma, and of religion altogether, according as men pleased, rightly or wrongly, to draw their conclusions. We may also assume that Italy retained a clearer recollection of the origin of the two great mendicant orders than other countries, and had not forgotten that they were the chief agents in the reaction against what is called the heresy of the thirteenth century, that is to say, against an early and vigorous movement of the modern Italian spirit. And that spiritual police which was permanently entrusted to the Dominicans certainly never excited any other feeling than secret hatred and contempt.

After reading the 'Decameron' and the novels of Franco Sacchetti, we might imagine that the vocabulary of abuse directed at the monks and nuns was exhausted. But towards the time of the Reformation this abuse became still fiercer. To say nothing of Aretino, who in the 'Ragionamenti' uses conventual life merely as a pretext for giving free play to his own poisonous nature, we may quote one author at typical of the rest—Masuccio, in the first ten of his fifty novels. They are written in a tone of the deepest indignation, and with the purpose to make this indignation general; and are dedicated to men in the highest position, such as King Ferrante and Prince Alfonso of Naples. The stories are many of them old, and some of them familiar to

[106] Bandello prefaces ii. nov. i. with the statement that the vice of avarice was more discreditable to priests than to any other class of men, since they had no families to provide for. On this ground he justifies the disgraceful attack made on a parsonage by two soldiers or brigands at the orders of a young gentleman, on which occasion a sheep was stolen from the stingy and gouty old priest. A single story of this kind illustrates the ideas in which men lived and acted better than all the dissertations in the world.

readers of Boccaccio. But others reflect, with a frightful realism, the actual state of things at Naples. The way in which the priests befool and plunder the people by means of spurious miracles, added to their own scandalous lives, is enough to drive any thoughtful observer to despair. We read of the Minorite friars who travelled to collect alms: 'They cheat, steal, and fornicate, and when they are at the end of their resources, they set up as saints and work miracles, one displaying the cloak of St. Vincent, another the handwriting of St. Bernardino, a third the bridle of Capistrano's donkey.' Others 'bring with them confederates who pretend to be blind or afflicted with some mortal disease, and after touching the hem of the monk's cowl, or the relics which he carries, are healed before the eyes of the multitude. All then shout "Misericordia", the bells are rung, and the miracle is recorded in a solemn protocol.' Or else the monk in the pulpit is denounced as a liar by another who stands below among the audience; the accuser is immediately possessed by the devil, and then healed by the preacher. The whole thing was a pre-arranged comedy, in which, however, the principal with his assistant made so much money that he was able to buy a bishopric from a Cardinal, on which the two confederates lived comfortably to the end of their days. Masuccio makes no great distinction between Franciscans and Dominicans, finding the one worth as much as the other. 'And yet the foolish people lets itself be drawn into their hatreds and divisions, and quarrels about them in public places, and calls itself "franceschino" or "domenichino".' The nuns are the exclusive property of the monks. Those of the former who have anything to do with the laity, are prosecuted and put in prison, while others are wedded in due form to the monks, with the accompaniments of mass, a marriage-contract, and a liberal indulgence in food and wine. 'I myself,' says the author, 'have been there not once, but several times, and seen it all with my own eyes. The nuns afterwards bring forth pretty little monks or else use means to hinder that result. And if anyone charges me with falsehood, let him search the nunneries well, and he will find there as many little bones as in Bethlehem at Herod's time.' These things, and the like, are among the secrets of monastic life. The monks are by no means too strict with one another in the confessional, and impose a Paternoster in cases where they would refuse all absolution to a layman as if he were a heretic. 'Therefore may the earth open and swallow up the wretches alive, with those who protect them!' In another place Masuccio, speaking of the fact that the influence of the monks depends chiefly on the dread of another world, utters the following remarkable wish: 'The best punishment for them would be for God to abolish Purgatory; they would then receive no more alms, and would be forced to go back to their spades.'

If men were free to write, in the time of Ferrante, and to him, in this strain, the reason is perhaps to be found in the fact that the king himself had been incensed by a false miracle which had been palmed off on him. An attempt had been made to urge him to a persecution of the Jews, like that carried out in Spain and imitated by the Popes, by producing a tablet with an inscription bearing the name of St. Cataldus, said to have been buried at Taranto, and afterwards dug up again. When he discovered the fraud, the monks defied him. He had also managed to detect and expose a pretended instance of fasting, as his father, Alfonso, had done before him. The Court, certainly, was no accomplice in maintaining these blind superstitions.

We have been quoting from an author who wrote in earnest, and who by no means stands alone in his judgement. All the Italian literature of that time is full of ridicule and invective aimed at the begging friars. It can hardly be doubted that the Renaissance would soon have destroyed these two Orders, had it not been for the German Reformation and the Counter-Reformation which intervened. Their saints and popular preachers could hardly have saved them. It would only have been necessary to come to an understanding at a favourable moment with a Pope like Leo X, who despised the Mendicant Orders. If the spirit of the age found them ridiculous or repulsive, they could no longer be anything but an embarrassment to the Church. And who can say what fate was in store for the Papacy itself, if the Reformation had not saved it?

The influence which the Father Inquisitor of a Dominican monastery was able habitually to exercise in the city where it was situated, was in the latter part of the fifteenth century just considerable enough to hamper and irritate cultivated people, but not strong enough to extort any lasting fear or obedience.[107] It was no longer possible to punish men for their thoughts, as it once was, and those whose tongues wagged most impudently against the clergy could easily keep clear of heretical doctrine. Except when some powerful party had an end to serve, as in the case of Savonarola, or when there

[107] The story in Vasari, v. p. 120, *Vita di Sandro Botticelli*, shows that the Inquisition was sometimes treated jocularly. It is true that the 'Vicario' here mentioned may have been the archbishop's deputy instead of the inquisitor's.

was a question of the use of magical arts, as was often the case in the cities of North Italy, we seldom read at this time of men being burnt at the stake. The Inquisitors were in some instances satisfied with the most superficial retraction, in others it even happened that the victim was saved out of their hands on the way to the place of execution. In Bologna (1452) the priest Niccolò da Verona had been publicly degraded on a wooden scaffold in front of San Domenico as a wizard and profaner of the sacraments, and was about to be led away to the stake, when he was set free by a gang of armed men, sent by Achille Malvezzi, a noted friend of heretics and violator of nuns. The legate, Cardinal Bessarion, was only able to catch and hang one of the party; Malvezzi lived on in peace.

It deserves to be noticed that the higher monastic orders—e.g. Benedictines, with their many branches—were, notwithstanding their great wealth and easy lives, far less disliked than the mendicant friars. For ten novels which treat of 'frati', hardly one can be found in which a 'monaco' is the subject and the victim. It was no small advantage to these orders that they were founded earlier, and not as an instrument of police, and that they did not interfere with private life. They contained men of learning, wit, and piety, but the average has been described by a member of it, Firenzuola, who says: 'These well-fed gentlemen with the capacious cowls do not pass their time in barefooted journeys and in sermons, but sit in elegant slippers with their hands crossed over their paunches, in charming cells wainscoted with cyprus-wood. And when they are obliged to quit the house, they ride comfortably, as if for their amusement, on mules and sleek, quiet horses. They do not overstrain their minds with the study of many books, for fear lest knowledge might put the pride of Lucifer in the place of monkish simplicity.'

Those who are familiar with the literature of the time, will see that we have only brought forward what is absolutely necessary for the understanding of the subject.[108] That the reputation attaching to the monks and the secular clergy must have shattered the faith of multitudes in all that is sacred is, of course, obvious.

And some of the judgements which we read are terrible; we will quote one of them in conclusion, which has been published only lately and is but little known. The historian Guicciardini, who was for many years in the service of the Medicean Popes, says (1529) in

[108] Pius II was on principle in favour of the abolition of the celibacy of the clergy.

his Aphorisms': 'No man is more disgusted than I am with the ambition, the avarice, and the profligacy of the priests, not only because each of these vices is hateful in itself, but because each and all of them are most unbecoming in those who declare themselves to be men in special relations with God, and also because they are vices so opposed to one another, that they can only co-exist in very singular natures. Nevertheless, my position at the Court of several Popes forced me to desire their greatness for the sake of my own interest. But, had it not been for this, I should have loved Martin Luther as myself, not in order to free myself from the laws which Christianity, as generally understood and explained, lays upon us, but in order to see this swarm of scoundrels (questa caterva di scelerati) put back into their proper place, so that they may be forced to live either without vices or without power.'

The same Guicciardini is of opinion that we are in the dark as to all that is supernatural, that philosophers and theologians have nothing but nonsense to tell us about it, that miracles occur in every religion and prove the truth of none in particular, and that all of them may be explained as unknown phenomena of nature. The faith which moves mountains, then common among the followers of Savonarola, is mentioned by Guicciardini as a curious fact, but without any bitter remark.

Notwithstanding this hostile public opinion, the clergy and the monks had the great advantage that the people were used to them, and that their existence was interwoven with the everyday existence of all. This is the advantage which every old and powerful institution possesses. Everybody had some cowled or frocked relative, some prospect of assistance or future gain from the treasure of the Church; and in the centre of Italy stood the Court of Rome, where men sometimes became rich in a moment. Yet it must never be forgotten that all this did not hinder people from writing and speaking freely. The authors of the most scandalous satires were themselves mostly monks or beneficed priests. Poggio, who wrote the 'Facetiae', was a clergyman; Francesco Berni, the satirist, held a canonry; Teofilo Folengo, the author of the 'Orlandino', was a Benedictine, certainly by no means a faithful one; Matteo Bandello, who held up his own order to ridicule, was a Dominican, and nephew of a general of this order. Were they encouraged to write by the sense that they ran no risks? Or did they feel an inward need to clear themselves personally from the infamy which attached to their order? Or were they moved by that selfish pessimism which takes for its maxim, 'it will last our time'? Perhaps all of these motives were more or less at work. In the case of Folengo, the unmistakable influence of Lutheranism must be added.

The sense of dependence on rites and sacraments, which we have already touched upon in speaking of the Papacy (p. 65), is not surprising among that part of the people which still believed in the Church. Among those who were more emancipated, it testifies to the strength of youthful impressions, and to the magical force of traditional symbols. The universal desire of dying men for priestly absolution shows that the last remnants of the dread of hell had not, even in the case of one like Vitellozzo, been altogether extinguished. It would hardly be possible to find a more instructive instance than this. The doctrine taught by the Church of the 'character indelibilis' of the priesthood, independently of the personality of the priest, had so far borne fruit that it was possible to loathe the individual and still desire his spiritual gifts. It is true, nevertheless, that there were defiant natures like Galeotto of Mirandola, who died unabsolved in 1499, after living for sixteen years under the ban of the Church. All this time the city lay under an interdict on his account, so that no mass was celebrated and no Christian burial took place.

A splendid contrast to all this is offered by the power exercised over the nation by its great Preachers of Repentance. Other countries of Europe were from time to time moved by the words of saintly monks, but only superficially, in comparison with the periodical upheaval of the Italian conscience. The only man, in fact, who produced a similar effect in Germany during the fifteenth century, was an Italian, born in the Abruzzi, named Giovanni Capistrano. Those natures which bear within them this religious vocation and this commanding earnestness, wore then in Northern countries an intuitive and mystical aspect. In the South they were practical and expansive, and shared in the national gift of oratorical skill. The North produced an 'Imitation of Christ', which worked silently, at first only within the walls of the monastery, but worked for the ages; the South produced men who made on their fellows an immediate and mighty but passing impression.

This impression consisted chiefly in the awakening of the conscience. The sermons were moral exhortations, free from abstract notions and full of practical application, rendered more impressive by the saintly and ascetic character of the preacher, and by the miracles which, even against his will, the inflamed imagination of the people attributed to him.[109] The most powerful argument used was not the threat of Hell and Purgatory, but rather the living results of the 'maledizione', the temporal ruin wrought on the individual by the curse which clings to wrong-doing. The grieving of Christ and the Saints has its consequences in this life. And only thus could men, sunk in passion and guilt, be brought to repentance and amendment—which was the chief object of these sermons.

Among these preachers were Bernardino da Siena, Alberto da Sarzana, Jacopo della Marca, Giovanni Capistrano, Roberto da Lecce and others; and finally, Girolamo Savonarola. No prejudice of the day was stronger than that against the mendicant friar, and this they overcame. They were criticized and ridiculed by a scornful humanism; but when they raised their voices, no one gave heed to the humanists. The thing was no novelty, and the scoffing Florentines had already in the fourteenth century learned to caricature it whenever it appeared in the pulpit. But no sooner did Savonarola come forward than he carried the people so triumphantly with him, that soon all their beloved art and culture melted away in the furnace which he lighted. Even the grossest profanation done to the cause by hypocritical monks, who got up an effect in the audience by means of confederates, could not bring the thing itself into discredit. Men kept on laughing at the ordinary monkish sermons, with their spurious miracles and manufactured relics; but did not cease to honour the great and genuine preachers. These are a true speciality of the fifteenth century.

The Order—generally that of St. Francis, and more particularly the so-called Observantines—sent them out according as they were wanted. This was commonly the case when there was some important public or private feud in a city, or some alarming outbreak of violence, immorality, or disease. When once the reputation of a preacher was made, the cities were all anxious to hear him even without any special occasion. He went wherever his superiors sent him. A special form of this work was the preaching of a Crusade against the Turks; but here we have to speak more particularly of the exhortations to repentance.

[109] Capistrano, for instance, contented himself with making the sign of the cross over the thousands of sick persons brought to him, and with blessing them in the name of the Trinity and of his master St. Bernardino, after which some of them not unnaturally got well. The Brescian chronicle puts it in this way, 'He worked fine miracles, yet not so many as were told of him'.

The order of these, when they were treated methodically, seems to have followed the customary list of the deadly sins. The more pressing, however, the occasion is, the more directly does the preacher make for his main point. He begins perhaps in one of the great churches of the Order, or in the cathedral. Soon the largest piazza is too small for the crowds which throng from every side to hear him, and he himself can hardly move without risking his life. The sermon is commonly followed by a great procession; but the first magistrates of the city, who take him in their midst, can hardly save him from the multitude of women who throng to kiss his hands and feet, and cut off fragments from his cowl.

The most immediate consequences which follow from the preacher's denunciations of usury, luxury, and scandalous fashions, are the opening of the gaols—which meant no more than the discharge of the poorest debtors—and the burning of various instruments of luxury and amusement, whether innocent or not. Among these are dice, cards, games of all kinds, written incantations, masks, musical instruments, song-books, false hair, and so forth. All these would then be gracefully arranged on a scaffold ('talamo'), a figure of the devil fastened to the top, and then the whole set on fire.

Then came the turn of the more hardened consciences. Men who had long never been near the confessional, now acknowledged their sins. Ill-gotten gains were restored, and insults which might have borne fruit in blood retracted. Orators like Bernardino of Siena entered diligently into all the details of the daily life of men, and the moral laws which are involved in it. Few theologians nowadays would feel tempted to give a morning sermon 'on contracts, restitutions, the public debt ("monte"), and the portioning of daughters', like that which he once delivered in the Cathedral at Florence. Imprudent speakers easily fell into the mistake of attacking particular classes, professions, or offices, with such energy that the enraged hearers proceeded to violence against those whom the preacher had denounced. A sermon which Bernardino once preached in Rome (1424) had another consequence besides a bonfire of vanities on the Capitol: 'After this,' we read, 'the witch Finicella was burnt, because by her diabolical arts she had killed many children and bewitched many other persons; and all Rome went to see the sight.'

But the most important aim of the preacher was, as has been already said, to reconcile enemies and persuade them to give up thoughts of vengeance. Probably this end was seldom attained till towards the close of a course of sermons, when the tide of penitence flooded the city, and when the air resounded with the cry of the whole people: 'Misericordia!' Then followed those solemn embracings and treaties of peace, which even previous bloodshed on both sides could not hinder. Banished men were recalled to the city to take part in these sacred transactions. It appears that these 'Paci' were on the whole faithfully observed, even after the mood which prompted them was over; and then the memory of the monk was blessed from generation to generation. But there were sometimes terrible crises like those in the families Della Valle and Crocè in Rome (1482), where even the great Roberto da Lecce raised his voice in vain. Shortly before Holy Week he had preached to immense crowds in the square before the Minerva. But on the night before Maundy Thursday a terrible combat took place in front of the Palazzo della Valle, near the Ghetto. In the morning Pope Sixtus gave orders for its destruction, and then performed the customary ceremonies of the day. On Good Friday Roberto preached again with a crucifix in his hand; but he and his hearers could do nothing but weep.

Violent natures, which had fallen into contradictions with themselves, often resolved to enter a convent, under the impression made by these men. Among such were not only brigands and criminals of every sort, but soldiers without employment. This resolve was stimulated by their admiration of the holy man, and by the desire to copy at least his outward position.

The concluding sermon is a general benediction, summed up in the words: 'la pace sia con voi!' Throngs of hearers accompany the preacher to the next city, and there listen for a second time to the whole course of sermons.

The enormous influence exercised by these preachers made it important, both for the clergy and for the government, at least not to have them as opponents; one means to this end was to permit only monks or priests who had received at all events the lesser consecration, to enter the pulpit, so that the Order or Corporation to which they belonged was, to some extent, responsible for them. But it was not easy to make the rule absolute, since the Church and pulpit had long been used as a means of publicity in many ways, judicial, educational, and others, and since even sermons were sometimes delivered by humanists and other laymen. There existed, too, in Italy, a dubious class of persons who were neither monks nor priests, and who yet had renounced the world—that is to say, the numerous class of hermits who appeared from time to time in the pulpit on their own authority, and often carried the people with them. A case of this kind occurred at Milan in 1516, after the second French conquest, certainly at a time when public order was much disturbed. A Tuscan hermit, Hieronymus of Siena, possibly an adherent of Savonarola, maintained his place for months together in the pulpit of the Cathedral, denounced the hierarchy with great violence, caused a new chandelier and a new altar to be set up in the church, worked miracles, and only abandoned the field after a long and desperate struggle. During the decades in which the fate of Italy was decided, the spirit of prophecy was unusually active, and nowhere where it displayed itself was it confined to any one particular class. We know with what a tone of true prophetic defiance the hermits came forward before the sack of Rome. In default of any eloquence of their own, these men made use of messengers with symbols of one kind or another, like the ascetic near Siena (1496), who sent a 'little hermit', that is a pupil, into the terrified city with a skull upon a pole, to which was attached a paper with a threatening text from the Bible.

Nor did the monks themselves scruple to attack princes, governments, the clergy, or even their own order. A direct exhortation to overthrow a despotic house, like that uttered by Jacopo Bussolaro at Pavia in the fourteenth century, hardly occurs again in the following period: but there is no want of courageous reproofs, addressed even to the Pope in his own chapel, and of naïve political advice given in the presence of rulers who by no means held themselves in need of it. In the Piazza del Castello at Milan, a blind preacher from the Incoronata —consequently an Augustinian—ventured in 1494 to exhort Lodovico il Moro from the pulpit: 'My lord, beware of showing the French the way, else you will repent it.' There were further prophetic monks who, without exactly preaching political sermons, drew such appalling pictures of the future that the hearers almost lost their senses. After the election of Leo X, in the year 1513, a whole association of these men, twelve Franciscan monks in all, journeyed through the various districts of Italy, of which one or other was assigned to each preacher. The one who appeared in Florence, Fra Francesco da Montepulciano, struck terror into the whole people. The alarm was not diminished by the exaggerated reports of his prophecies which reached those who were too far off to hear him. After one of his sermons he suddenly died 'of pain in the chest'. The people thronged in such numbers to kiss the feet of the corpse that it had to be secretly buried in the night. But the newly awakened spirit of prophecy, which seized upon even women and peasants, could not be controlled without great difficulty. 'In order to restore to the people their cheerful humour, the Medici—Giuliano, Leo's brother, and Lorenzo—gave on St. John's Day, 1514, those splendid festivals, tournaments, processions, and hunting-parties, which were attended by many distinguished persons from Rome, and among them, though disguised, no less than six cardinals.'

But the greatest of the prophets and apostles had already been burnt in Florence in the year 1498—Fra Girolamo Savonarola of Ferrara. We must content ourselves with saying a few words respecting him.[110]

The instrument by means of which he transformed and ruled the city of Florence (1494–8) was his eloquence. Of this the meagre reports that are left to us, which were taken down mostly on the spot, give us evidently a very imperfect notion. It was not that he possessed any striking outward advantages, for voice, accent, and rhetorical skill constituted precisely his weakest side; and those who required the preacher to be a stylist, went to his rival Fra Mariano da Genazzano. The eloquence of Savonarola was the expression of a lofty and commanding personality, the like of which was not seen again till the time of Luther. He himself held his own influence to be the result of a divine illumination, and could therefore, without presumption, assign a very high place to the office of the preacher, who, in the great hierarchy of spirits, occupies, according to him, the next place below the angels.

This man, whose nature seemed made of fire, worked another and greater miracle than any of his oratorical triumphs. His own Dominican monastery of San Marco, and then all the Dominican monasteries of Tuscany, became like-minded with himself, and undertook voluntarily the work of inward reform. When we reflect what the monasteries then were, and what measureless difficulty attends the least change where monks are concerned, we are doubly astonished at so complete a revolution. While the reform was still in progress

[110] M. Perrens, *Jérôme Savonarole*, 2 vols., Paris, 1856, perhaps the most systematic and sober of all the many works on the subject. P. Villari, *La Storia di Girol. Savonarola* (second edition, 2 vols., 8vo., Firenze, Lemonnier, 1887. *Both editions have been translated into English; the first in 1863, with an Appendix containing the Documents; the second in 1888, with many additions but leaving out the Documents.)

large numbers of Savonarola's followers entered the Order, and thereby greatly facilitated his plans. Sons of the first houses in Florence entered San Marco as novices.

This reform of the Order in a particular province was the first step to a national Church, in which, had the reformer himself lived longer, it must infallibly have ended. Savonarola, indeed, desired the regeneration of the whole Church, and near the end of his career sent pressing exhortations to the great potentates urging them to call together a Council. But in Tuscany his Order and party were the only organs of his spirit—the salt of the earth—while the neighbouring provinces remained in their old condition. Fancy and asceticism tended more and more to produce in him a state of mind to which Florence appeared as the scene of the kingdom of God upon earth.

The prophecies, whose partial fulfilment conferred on Savonarola a supernatural credit, were the means by which the ever-active Italian imagination seized control of the soundest and most cautious natures At first the Franciscans of the Osservanza, trusting in the reputation which had been bequeathed to them by St. Bernardino of Siena, fancied that they could compete with the great Dominican. They put one of their own men into the Cathedral pulpit, and outbid the Jeremiads of Savonarola by still more terrible warnings, till Piero de' Medici, who then still ruled over Florence, forced them both to be silent. Soon after, when Charles VIII came to Italy and the Medici were expelled, as Savonarola had clearly foretold, he alone was believed in.

It must be frankly confessed that he never judged his own premonitions and visions critically, as he did those of others. In the funeral oration on Pico della Mirandola, he deals somewhat harshly with his dead friend. Since Pico, notwithstanding an inner voice which came from God, would not enter the Order, he had himself prayed to God to chasten him for his disobedience. He certainly had not desired his death, and alms and prayers had obtained the favour that Pico's soul was safe in Purgatory. With regard to a comforting vision which Pico had upon his sickbed, in which the Virgin appeared and promised him that he should not die, Savonarola confessed that he had long regarded it as a deceit of the Devil, till it was revealed to him that the Madonna meant the second and eternal death. If these things and the like are proofs of presumption, it must be admitted that this great soul at all events paid a bitter penalty for his fault. In his last days Savonarola seems to have recognized the vanity of his visions and prophecies. And yet enough inward peace was left to him to enable him to meet death like a Christian. His partisans held to his doctrine and predictions for thirty years longer.

He only undertook the reorganization of the State for the reason that otherwise his enemies would have got the government into their own hands. It is unfair to judge him by the semi-democratic constitution of the beginning of the year 1495, which was neither better nor worse than other Florentine constitutions.

He was at bottom the most unsuitable man who could be found for such a work. His idea was a theocracy, in which all men were to bow in blessed humility before the Unseen, and all conflicts of passion were not even to be able to arise. His whole mind is written in that inscription on the Palazzo della Signoria, the substance of which was his maxim as early as 1495, and which was solemnly renewed by his partisans in 1527: 'Jesus Christus Rex populi Florentini S.P.Q. decreto creatus.' He stood in no more relation to mundane affairs and their actual conditions than any other inhabitant of a monastery. Man, according to him, has only to attend to those things which make directly for his salvation.

This temper comes out clearly in his opinions on ancient literature: 'The only good thing which we owe to Plato and Aristotle, is that they brought forward many arguments which we can use against the heretics. Yet they and other philosophers are now in Hell. An old woman knows more about the Faith than Plato. It would be good for religion if many books that seem useful were destroyed. When there were not so many books and not so many arguments ("ragioni naturali") and disputes, religion grew more quickly than it has done since.' He wished to limit the classical instruction of the schools to Homer, Virgil and Cicero, and to supply the rest from Jerome and Augustine. Not only Ovid and Catullus, but Terence and Tibullus, were to be banished. This may be no more than the expressions of a nervous morality, but elsewhere in a special work he admits that science as a whole is harmful. He holds that only a few people should have to do with it, in order that the tradition of human knowledge may not perish, and particularly that there may be no want of intellectual athletes to confute the sophisms of the heretics. For all others, grammar, morals, and religious teaching ('litterae sacrae') suffice. Culture and education would thus return wholly into the charge of the monks, and as, in his opinion, the 'most learned and the most pious' are to rule over the States and empires, these rulers would also be monks. Whether he really foresaw this conclusion, we need not inquire.

A more childish method of reasoning cannot be imagined. The simple reflection that the newborn antiquity and the boundless enlargement of human thought and knowledge which was due to it, might give splendid confirmation to a religion able to adapt itself thereto, seems never even to have occurred to the good man. He wanted to forbid what he could not deal with by any other means. In fact, he was anything but liberal, and was ready, for example, to send the astrologers to the same stake at which he afterwards himself died.

How mighty must have been the soul which dwelt side by side with this narrow intellect! And what a flame must have glowed within him before he could constrain the Florentines, possessed as they were by the passion for knowledge and culture, to surrender themselves to a man who could thus reason!

How much of their heart and their worldliness they were ready to sacrifice for his sake is shown by those famous bonfires by the side of which all the 'talami' of Bernardino da Siena and others were certainly of small account.

All this could not, however, be effected without the agency of a tyrannical police. He did not shrink from the most vexatious interferences with the much-prized freedom of Italian private life, using the espionage of servants on their masters as a means of carrying out his moral reforms. That transformation of public and private life which the Iron Calvin was but just able to effect at Geneva with the aid of a permanent state of siege necessarily proved impossible at Florence, and the attempt only served to drive the enemies of Savonarola into a more implacable hostility. Among his most unpopular measures may be mentioned those organized parties of boys, who forced their way into the houses and laid violent hands on any objects which seemed suitable for the bonfire. As it happened that they were sometimes sent away with a beating, they were afterwards attended, in order to keep up the figment of a pious 'rising generation', by a bodyguard of grown-up persons.

On the last day of the Carnival in the year 1497, and on the same day the year after, the great 'Auto da Fé' took place on the Piazza della Signoria. In the centre of it rose a high pyramid of several tiers, like the 'rogus' on which the Roman Emperors were commonly burned. On the lowest tier were arranged false beards, masks, and carnival disguises; above came volumes of the Latin and Italian poets, among others Boccaccio, the 'Morgante' of Pulci, and Petrarch, partly in the form of valuable printed parchments and illuminated manuscripts; then women's ornaments and toilet articles, scents, mirrors, veils and false hair; higher up, lutes, harps, chessboards, playing-cards; and finally, on the two uppermost tiers, paintings only, especially of female beauties, partly fancy-pictures, bearing the classical names of Lucretia, Cleopatra, or Faustina, partly portraits of the beautiful Bencina, Lena Morella, Bina and Maria de' Lenzi. On the first occasion a Venetian merchant who happened to be present offered the Signoria 22,000 gold florins for the objects on the pyramid; but the only answer he received was that his portrait, too, was painted, and burned along with the rest. When the pile was lighted, the Signoria appeared on the balcony, and the air echoed with song, the sound of trumpets, and the pealing of bells. The people then adjourned to the Piazza di San Marco, where they danced round in three concentric circles. The innermost was composed of monks of the monastery, alternating with boys, dressed as angels; then came young laymen and ecclesiastics; and on the outside, old men, citizens, and priests, the latter crowned with wreaths of olive.

All the ridicule of his victorious enemies, who in truth had no lack of justification or of talent for ridicule, was unable to discredit the memory of Savonarola. The more tragic the fortunes of Italy became, the brighter grew the halo which in the recollection of the survivors surrounded the figure of the great monk and prophet. Though his predictions may not have been confirmed in detail, the great and general calamity which he foretold was fulfilled with appalling truth.

Great, however, as the influence of all these preachers may have been, and brilliantly as Savonarola justified the claim of the monks to this office, nevertheless the order as a whole could not escape the contempt and condemnation of the people. Italy showed that she could give her enthusiasm only to individuals.

STRENGTH OF THE OLD FAITH

If, apart from all that concerns the priests and the monks, we attempt to measure the strength of the old faith, it will be found great or small according to the light in which it is considered. We have spoken already of the need felt for the Sacraments as something indispensable. Let us now glance for a moment at the position of faith and worship in daily life. Both were determined partly by the habits of the people and partly by the policy and example of the rulers.

All that has to do with penitence and the attainment of salvation by means of good works was in much the same stage of development or corruption as in the North of Europe, both among the peasantry and among the poorer inhabitants of the cities. The instructed classes were sometimes influenced by the same motives. Those sides of popular Catholicism which had their origin in the old pagan ways of invoking, rewarding, and propitiating the gods have fixed themselves ineradicably in the consciousness of the people. The eighth eclogue of Battista Mantovano, which has already been quoted elsewhere, contains the prayer of a peasant to the Madonna, in which she is called upon as the special patroness of all rustic and agricultural interests. And what conceptions they were which the people formed of their protectress in heaven! What was in the mind of the Florentine woman who gave 'ex voto' a keg of wax to the Annunziata, because her lover, a monk, had gradually emptied a barrel of wine without her absent husband finding it out! Then, too, as still in our own days, different departments of human life were presided over by their respective patrons. The attempt has often been made to explain a number of the commonest rites of the Catholic Church as remnant of pagan ceremonies, and no one doubts that many local and popular usages, which are associated with religious festivals, are forgotten fragments of the old pre-Christian faiths of Europe. In Italy, on the contrary, we find instances in which the affiliation of the new faith to the old seems consciously recognized. So, for example, the custom of setting out food for the dead four days before the feast of the Chair of St. Peter, that is to say, on February 18, the date of the ancient Feralia. Many other practices of this kind may then have prevailed and have since then been extirpated. Perhaps the paradox is only apparent if we say that the popular faith in Italy had a solid foundation just in proportion as it was pagan.

The extent to which this form of belief prevailed in the upper classes can to a certain point be shown in detail. It had, as we have said in speaking of the influence of the clergy, the power of custom and early impressions on its side. The love for ecclesiastical pomp and display helped to confirm it, and now and then there came one of those epidemics of revivalism, which few even among the scoffers and the sceptics were able to withstand.

But in questions of this kind it is perilous to grasp too hastily at absolute results. We might fancy, for example, that the feeling of educated men towards the relics of the saints would be a key by which some chambers of their religious consciousness might be opened. And in fact, some difference of degree may be demonstrable, though by no means as clearly as might be wished. The Government of Venice in the fifteenth century seems to have fully shared in the reverence felt throughout the rest of Europe for the remains of the bodies of the saints. Even strangers who lived in Venice found it well to adapt themselves to this superstition. If we can judge of scholarly Padua from the testimony of its topographer Michele Savonarola, things must have been much the same there. With a mixture of pride and pious awe, Michele tells us how in times of great danger the saints were heard to sigh at night along the streets of the city, how the hair and nails on the corpse of a holy nun in Santa Chiara kept continually growing, and how the same corpse, when any disaster was impending, used to make a noise and lift up the arms. When he sets to work to describe the chapel of St. Anthony in the Santo, the writer loses himself in ejaculations and fantastic dreams. In Milan the people at least showed a fanatical devotion to relics; and when once, in the year 1517, the monks of San Simpliciano were careless enough to expose six holy corpses during certain alterations of the high altar, which event was followed by heavy floods of rain, the people attributed the visitation to this sacrilege, and gave the monks a sound beating whenever they met them in the street. In other parts of Italy, and even in the case of the Popes themselves, the sincerity of this feeling is much more dubious, though here, too, a positive conclusion is hardly attainable. It is well known amid what general enthusiasm Pius II solemnly deposited the head of the Apostle Andrew, which had been brought from Greece, and then from San Maura, in the Church of St. Peter (1462); but we gather from his own narrative that he only did it from a kind of shame, as so many princes were competing for the relic. It was not till afterwards that the idea struck him of making Rome the common refuge for all the remains of the saints which had been driven from their own churches. Under Sixtux IV, the population of the city was still more zealous in this cause than the Pope himself, and the magistracy (1483) complained bitterly that Sixtus had sent to Louis XI, the dying King of France, some specimens of the Lateran relics. A courageous voice was raised about this time at Bologna, advising the sale of the skull of St. Dominic to the King of Spain, and the application of the money to some useful public object. But those who had the least reverence of all for the relics were the Florentines. Between the decision to honour their saint, St. Zanobi, with a new sarcophagus and the final execution of the project by Ghiberti, ten years elapsed (1432–42), and then it only happened by chance, because the master had executed a smaller order of the same kind with great skill (1428).

Perhaps through being tricked by a cunning Neapolitan abbess (1352), who sent them a spurious arm of the patroness of the Cathedral, Santa Reparata, made of wood and plaster, they began to get tired of relics. Or perhaps it would be truer to say that their æsthetic sense turned them away in disgust from dismembered corpses and mouldy clothes. Or perhaps their feeling was rather due to that sense of glory which thought Dante and Petrarch worthier of a splendid grave than all the twelve apostles put together. It is probable that throughout Italy, apart from Venice and from Rome, the condition of which latter city was exceptional, the worship of relics had long been giving way to the adoration of the Madonna, at all events to a greater extent than elsewhere in Europe; and in this fact lies indirect evidence of an early development of the æsthetic sense.

It may be questioned whether in the North, where the vastest cathedrals are nearly all dedicated to Our Lady, and where an extensive branch of Latin and indigenous poetry sang the praises of the Mother of God, a greater devotion to her was possible. In Italy, however, the number of miraculous pictures of the Virgin was far greater, and the part they played in the daily life of the people much more important. Every town of any size contained a quantity of them, from the ancient, or ostensibly ancient, paintings by St. Luke, down to the works of contemporaries, who not seldom lived to see the miracles wrought by their own handiwork. The work of art was in these cases by no means as harmless as Battista Mantovano thinks; sometimes it suddenly acquired a magical virtue. The popular craving for the miraculous, especially strong in women, may have been fully satisfied by these pictures, and for this reason the relics been less regarded. It cannot be said with certainty how far the respect for genuine relics suffered from the ridicule which the novelisy aimed at the spurious. The attitude of the educated classes in Italy towards Mariolatry, or the worship of the Virgin, is more clearly recognizable than towards the worship of images. One cannot but be struck with the fact that in Italian literature Dante's 'Paradise' is the last poem in honour of the Virgin, while among the people hymns in her praise have been constantly produced down to our own day. The names of Sannazaro and Sabellico and other writers of Latin poems prove little on the other side, since the object with which they wrote was chiefly literary. The poems written in Italian in the fifteenth and at the beginning of the sixteenth centuries, in which we meet with genuine religious feeling, such as the hymns of Lorenzo the Magnificent, and the sonnets of Vittoria Colonna and of Michelangelo might have been just as well composed by Protestants. Besides the lyrical expression of faith in God, we chiefly notice in them the sense of sin, the consciousness of deliverance through the death of Christ, the longing for a better world. The intercession of the Mother of God is only mentioned by the way. The same phenomenon is repeated in the classical literature of the French at the time of Louis XIV. Not till the time of the Counter-Reformation did Mariolatry reappear in the higher Italian poetry. Meanwhile the visual arts had certainly done their utmost to glorify the Madonna. It may be added that the worship of the saints among the educated classes often took an essentially pagan form.

We might thus critically examine the various sides of Italian Catholicism at this period, and so establish with a certain degree of probability the attitude of the instructed classes towards popular faith. Yet an absolute and positive result cannot be reached. We meet with contrasts hard to explain. While architects, painters, and sculptors were working with restless activity in and for the churches, we hear at the beginning of the sixteenth century the bitterest complaints of the neglect of public worship and of these churches themselves.

It is well known how Luther was scandalized by the irreverence with which the priests in Rome said Mass. And at the same time the feasts of the Church were celebrated with a taste and magnificence of which Northern countries had no conception. It looks as if this most imaginative of nations was easily tempted to neglect everyday things, and as easily captivated by anything extraordinary.

It is to this excess of imagination that we must attribute the epidemic of religious revivals, upon which we shall again say a few words. They must be clearly distinguished from the excitement called forth by the great preachers. They were rather due to general public calamities, or to the dread of such.

In the Middle Ages all Europe was from time to time flooded by these great tides, which carried away whole peoples in their waves.

The Crusades and the Flagellant revival are instances. Italy took part in both of these movements. The first great companies of Flagellants appeared, immediately after the fall of Ezzelino and his house, in the neighbourhood of the same Perugia which has been already spoken of as the headquarters of the revivalist preachers. Then followed the Flagellants of 1310 and 1334, and then the great pilgrimage without scourging in the year 1399, which Corio has recorded. It is not impossible that the Jubilees were founded partly in order to regulate and render harmless this sinister passion for vagabondage which seized on the whole populations at times of religious excitement. The great sanctuaries of Italy, such as Loreto and others, had meantime become famous, and no doubt diverted a certain part of this enthusiasm.

But terrible crises had still at a much later time the power to reawaken the glow of mediæval penitence, and the conscience-stricken people, often still further appalled by signs and wonders, sought to move the pity of Heaven by wailings and scourgings. So it was at Bologna when the plague came in 1457, and so in 1496 at a time of internal discord at Siena, to mention two only out of countless instances. No more moving scene can be imagined than that which we read of at Milan in 1529, when famine, plague, and war conspired with Spanish extortion to reduce the city to the lowest depths of despair. It chanced that the monk who had the ear of the people, Fra Tommaso Nieto, was himself a Spaniard. The Host was borne along in a novel fashion, amid barefooted crowds of old and young. It was placed on a decorated bier, which rested on the shoulders of four priests in linen garments—an imitation of the Ark of the Covenant which the children of Israel once carried round the walls of Jericho. Thus did the afflicted people of Milan remind their ancient God of His old covenant with man; and when the procession again entered the cathedral, and it seemed as if the vast building must fall in with the agonized cry of 'Misericordia!', many who stood there may have believed that the Almighty would indeed subvert the laws of nature and of history, and send a miraculous deliverance.

There was one government in Italy, that of Duke Ercole I of Ferrara, which assumed the direction of public feeling, and compelled the popular revivals to move in regular channels. At the time when Savonarola was powerful in Florence, and the movement which he began spread far and wide among the population of Central Italy, the people of Ferrara voluntarily entered on a general fast (at the beginning of 1496). A Lazarist announced from the pulpit the approach of a season of war and famine such as the world had never seen; but the Madonna had assured some pious people that these evils might be avoided by fasting. Upon this, the court itself had no choice but to fast, but it took the conduct of the public devotions into its own hands. On Easter Day, the 3rd of April, a proclamation on morals and religion was published, forbidding blasphemy, prohibiting games, sodomy, concubinage, the letting of houses to prostitutes or panders, and the opening of all shops on feast-days, excepting those of the bakers and greengrocers. The Jews and Moors, who had taken refuge from the Spaniards at Ferrara, were now again compelled to wear the yellow O upon the breast. Contraveners were threatened, not only with the punishments already provided by law, but also 'with such severer penalties as the Duke might think good to inflict'. After this, the Duke and the court went several days in succession to hear sermons in church, and on the 10th of April all the Jews in Ferrara were compelled to do the same. On the 3rd of May, the director of police, Zampante, sent the crier to announce that whoever had given money to the police-officers in order not to be denounced as a blasphemer, might, if he came forward, have it back with a further indemnification. These wicked officers, he said, had extorted as much as two or three ducats from innocent persons by threatening to lodge an information against them. They had then mutually informed against one another, and so had all found their way into prison. But as the money had been paid precisely in order not to have to do with Zampante, it is probable that his proclamation induced few people to come forward. In the year 1500, after the fall of Lodovico il Moro, when a similar outbreak of popular feeling took place, Ercole ordered a series of nine processions, in which there were 4,000 children dressed in white, bearing the standard of Jesus. He himself rode on horseback, as he could not walk without difficulty. An edict was afterwards published of the same kind as that of 1496. It is well known how many churches and monasteries were built by this ruler. He even sent for a live saint, the Suor Colomba, shortly before he married his son Alfonso to Lucrezia Borgia (1502). A special messenger fetched the saint with fifteen other nuns from Viterbo, and the Duke himself conducted her on her arrival at Ferrara into a convent prepared for her reception. We shall probably do him no injustice if we attribute all these measures very largely to political calculation. To the conception of government formed by the House of Este, this employment of religion for the ends of statecraft belongs by a kind of logical necessity.

RELIGION AND THE SPIRIT OF THE RENAISSANCE

But in order to reach a definite conclusion with regard to the religious sense of the men of this period, we must adopt a different method. From their intellectual attitude in general, we can infer their relation both to the Divine idea and to the existing religion of their age.

These modern men, the representatives of the culture of Italy, were born with the same religious instincts as other mediæval Europeans. But their powerful individuality made them in religion, as in other matters, altogether subjective, and the intense charm which the discovery of the inner and outer universe exercised upon them rendered them markedly worldly. In the rest of Europe religion remained, till a much later period, something given from without, and in practical life egotism and sensuality alternated with devotion and repentance. The latter had no spiritual competitors, as in Italy, or only to a far smaller extent.

Further, the close and frequent relations of Italy with Byzantium and the Mohammedan peoples had produced a dispassionate tolerance which weakened the ethnographical conception of a privileged Christendom. And when classical antiquity with its men and institutions became an ideal of life, as well as the greatest of historical memories, ancient speculation and scepticism obtained in many cases a complete mastery over the minds of Italians.

Since, again, the Italians were the first modern people of Europe who gave themselves boldly to speculations on freedom and necessity, and since they did so under violent and lawless political circumstances, in which evil seemed often to win a splendid and lasting victory, their belief in God began to waver, and their view of the government of the world became fatalistic. And when their passionate natures refused to rest in the sense of uncertainty, they made a shift to help themselves out with ancient, Oriental, or mediæval superstition. They took to astrology and magic.

Finally, these intellectual giants, these representatives of the Renaissance, show, in respect to religion, a quality which is common in youthful natures. Distinguishing keenly between good and evil, they yet are conscious of no sin. Every disturbance of their inward harmony they feel themselves able to make good out of the plastic resources of their own nature, and therefore they feel no repentance. The need of salvation thus becomes felt more and more dimly, while the ambitions and the intellectual activity of the present either shut out altogether every thought of a world to come, or else caused it to assume a poetic instead of a dogmatic form.

When we look on all this as pervaded and often perverted by the all-powerful Italian imagination, we obtain a picture of that time which is certainly more in accordance with truth than are vague declamations against modern paganism. And closer investigation often reveals to us that underneath this outward shell much genuine religion could still survive.

The fuller discussion of these points must be limited to a few of the more essential explanations.

That religion should again become an affair of the individual and of his own personal feeling was inevitable when the Church became corrupt in doctrine and tyrannous in practice, and is a proof that the European mind was still alive. It is true that this showed itself in many different ways. While the mystical and ascetical sects of the North lost no time in creating new outward forms for their new modes of thought and feeling, each individual in Italy went his own way, and thousands wandered on the sea of life without any religious guidance whatever. All the more must we admire those who attained and held fast to a personal religion. They were not to blame for being unable to have any part or lot in the old Church, as she then was; nor would it be reasonable to expect that they should all of them go through that mighty spiritual labour which was appointed to the German reformers. The form and aim of this personal faith, as it showed itself in the better minds, will be set forth at the close of our work.

The worldliness, through which the Renaissance seems to offer so striking a contrast to the Middle Ages, owed its first origin to the flood of new thoughts, purposes, and views, which transformed the mediæval conception of nature and man. The spirit is not in itself more hostile to religion than that 'culture' which now holds its place, but which can give us only a feeble notion of the universal ferment which the discovery of a new world of greatness then called forth. This worldliness was not frivolous, but earnest, and was ennobled by art and poetry. It is a lofty necessity of the modern spirit that this attitude, once gained, can never again be lost, that an irresistible impulse forces us to the investigation of men and things, and that we must hold this inquiry to be our proper end and work. How soon and by what paths this search will lead us back to God, and in what ways the religious temper of the individual will be affected by it, are questions which cannot be met by any general answer. The Middle Ages, which spared themselves the trouble of induction and free inquiry, can have no right to impose upon us their dogmatical verdict in a matter of such vast importance.

To the study of man, among many other causes, was due the tolerance and indifference with which the Mohammedan religion was regarded. The knowledge and admiration of the remarkable civilization which Islam, particularly before the Mongol inundation, had attained, was peculiar to Italy from the time of the Crusades. This sympathy was fostered by the half-Mohammedan government of some Italian princes, by dislike and even contempt for the existing Church, and by constant commercial intercourse with the harbours of the Eastern and Southern Mediterranean. It can be shown that in the thirteenth century the Italians recognized a Mohammedan ideal of nobleness, dignity, and pride, which they loved to connect with the person of a Sultan. A Mameluke Sultan is commonly meant; if any name is mentioned, it is the name of Saladin. Even the Osmanli Turks, whose destructive tendencies were no secret, gave the Italians only half a fright, and a peaceable accord with them was looked upon as no impossibility.

The truest and most characteristic expression of this religious indifference is the famous story of the Three Rings, which Lessing has put into the mouth of his Nathan, after it had been already told centuries earlier, though with some reserve, in the 'Hundred Old Novels' (nov. 72 or 73), and more boldly in Boccaccio (Decamerone, i, nov. 3). In what language and in what corner of the Mediterranean it was first told can never be known; most likely the original was much more plain-spoken than the two Italian adaptations. The religious postulate on which it rests, namely Deism, will be discussed later on in its wider significance for this period. The same idea is repeated, though in a clumsy caricature, in the famous proverb of the 'three who have deceived the world, that is, Moses, Christ, and Mohammed'. If the Emperor Frederick II, in whom this saying is said to have originated, really thought so, he probably expressed himself with more wit. Ideas of the same kind were also current in Islam.

At the height of the Renaissance, towards the close of the fifteenth century, Luigi Pulci offers us an example of the same mode of thought in the 'Morgante Maggiore'. The imaginary world of which his story treats is divided, as in all heroic poems of romance, into a Christian and a Mohammedan camp. In accordance with the mediæval temper, the victory of the Christian and the final reconciliation among the combatants was attended by the baptism of the defeated Islamites, and the Improvisatori, who preceded Pulci in the treatment of these subjects, must have made free use of this stock incident. It was Pulci's object to parody his predecessors, particularly the worst among them, and this he does by the invocations of God, Christ, and the Madonna, with which each canto begins; and still more clearly by the sudden conversions and baptisms, the utter senselessness of which must have struck every reader or hearer. This ridicule leads him further to the confession of his faith in the relative goodness of all religions, which faith, notwithstanding his profession of orthodoxy, rests on an essentially theistic basis. In another point, too, he departs widely from mediæval conceptions. The alternatives in past centuries were: Christian, or else Pagan and Mohammedan; orthodox believer or heretic. Pulci draws a picture of the Giant Margutte who, disregarding each and every religion, jovially confesses to every form of vice and sensuality, and only reserves to himself the merit of having never broken faith. Perhaps the poet intended to make something of this—in his way—honest monster, possibly to have led him into virtuous paths by Morgante, but he soon got tired of his own creation, and in the next canto brought him to a comic end. Margutte has been brought forward as a proof of Pulci's frivolity; but he is needed to complete the picture of the poetry of the fifteenth century. It was natural that it should somewhere present in grotesque proportions the figure of an untamed egotism, insensible to all established rule, and yet with a remnant of honourable feeling left. In other poems sentiments are put into the mouths of giants, fiends, infidels, and Mohammedans which no Christian knight would venture to utter.

Antiquity exercised an influence of another kind than that of Islam, and this not through its religion, which was but too much like the Catholicism of this period, but through its philosophy. Ancient literature, now respected as something incomparable, is full of the victory of philosophy over religious tradition. An endless number of systems and fragments of systems were suddenly presented to the Italian mind, not as curiosities or even as heresies, but almost with the authority of dogmas, which had now to be reconciled rather than discriminated. In nearly all these various opinions and doctrines a certain kind of belief in God was implied; but taken altogether they formed a marked contrast to the Christian faith in a Divine government of the world. And there was one central question, which mediæval theology had striven in vain to solve, and which now urgently demanded an answer from the wisdom of the ancients, namely, the relation of Providence to the freedom or necessity of the human will. To write the history of this question even superficially from the fourteenth century onwards, would require a whole volume. A few hints must here suffice.

If we take Dante and his contemporaries as evidence, we shall find that ancient philosophy first came into contact with Italian life in the form which offered the most marked contrast to Christianity, that is to say, Epicureanism. The writings of Epicurus were no longer preserved, and even at the close of the classical age a more or less one-sided conception had been formed of his philosophy. Nevertheless, that phase of Epicureanism which can be studied in Lucretius, and especially in Cicero, is quite sufficient to make men familiar with a godless universe. To what extent his teaching was actually understood, and whether the name of the problematic Greek sage was not rather a catchword for the multitude, it is hard to say. It is probable that the Dominican Inquisition used it against men who could not be reached by a more definite accusation. In the case of sceptics born before the time was ripe, whom it was yet hard to convict of positive heretical utterances, a moderate degree of luxurious living may have sufficed to provoke the charge. The word is used in this conventional sense by Giovanni Villani, when he explains the Florentine fires of 1115 and 1117 as a Divine judgement on heresies, among others, 'on the luxurious and gluttonous sect of Epicureans'. The same writer says of Manfred, 'His life was Epicurean, since he believed neither in God, nor in the Saints, but only in bodily pleasure.'

Dante speaks still more clearly in the ninth and tenth cantos of the 'Inferno'. That terrible fiery field covered with half-opened tombs, from which issued cries of hopeless agony, was peopled by the two great classes of those whom the Church had vanquished or expelled in the thirteenth century. The one were heretics who opposed the Church by deliberately spreading false doctrine; the other were

Epicureans, and their sin against the Church lay in their general disposition, which was summed up in the belief that the soul dies with the body. The Church was well aware that this one doctrine, if it gained ground, must be more ruinous to her authority than all the teachings of the Manichæans and Paterines, since it took away all reason for her interference in the affairs of men after death. That the means which she used in her struggles were precisely what had driven the most gifted natures to unbelief and despair was what she naturally would not herself admit.

Dante's loathing of Epicurus, or of what he took to be his doctrine, was certainly sincere. The poet of the life to come could not but detest the denier of immortality; and a world neither made nor ruled by God, no less than the vulgar objects of earthly life which the system appeared to countenance, could not but be intensely repugnant to a nature like his. But if we look closer, we find that certain doctrines of the ancients made even on him an impression which forced the biblical doctrine of the Divine government into the background, unless, indeed, it was his own reflection, the influence of opinions then prevalent, or loathing for the injustice that seemed to rule this world, which made him give up the belief in a special Providence. His God leaves all the details of the world's government to a deputy, Fortune, whose sole work it is to change and change again all earthly things, and who can disregard the wailings of men in unalterable beatitude. Nevertheless, Dante does not for a moment fail to insist on the moral responsibility of man; he believes in free will.

The belief in the freedom of the will, in the popular sense of the words, has always prevailed in Western countries. At all times men have been held responsible for their actions, as though this freedom were a matter of course. The case is otherwise with the religious and philosophical doctrine, which labours under the difficulty of harmonizing the nature of the will with the laws of the universe at large. We have here to do with a question of more or less, which every moral estimate must take into account. Dante is not wholly free from those astrological superstitions which illumined the horizon of his time with deceptive light, but they do not hinder him from rising to a worthy conception of human nature. 'The stars,' he makes his Marco Lombardo say ('Purgatorio', xvi, 73), 'the stars give the first impulse to your actions, but a light is given you to know good and evil, and free will, which, if it endure the strain in its first battlings with the heavens, at length gains the whole victory, if it be well nurtured.'

Others might seek the necessity which annulled human freedom in another power than the stars, but the question was henceforth an open and inevitable one. So far as it was a question for the schools or the pursuit of isolated thinkers, its treatment belongs to the historian of philosophy. But inasmuch as it entered into the consciousness of a wider public, it is necessary for us to say a few words respecting it.

The fourteenth century was chiefly stimulated by the writings of Cicero, who, though in fact an eclectic, yet, by his habit of setting forth the opinions of different schools, without coming to a decision between them, exercised the influence of a sceptic. Next in importance came Seneca, and the few works of Aristotle which had been translated into Latin. The immediate fruit of these studies was the capacity to reflect on great subjects, if not in direct opposition to the authority of the Church, at all events independently of it.

In the course of the fifteenth century the works of antiquity were discovered and diffused with extraordinary rapidity. All the writings of the Greek philosophers which we ourselves possess were now, at least in the form of Latin translations, in everybody's hands. It is a curious fact that some of the most zealous apostles of this new culture were men of the strictest piety, or even ascetics. Fra Ambrogio Camaldolese, as a spiritual dignitary chiefly occupied with ecclesiastical affairs, and as a literary man with the translation of the Greek Fathers of the Church, could not repress the humanistic impulse, and at the request of Cosimo de' Medici, undertook to translate Diogenes Laertius into Latin. His contemporaries, Niccolò Niccoli, Giannozzo Manetti, Donato Acciaiuoli, and Pope Nicholas V, united to a many-sided humanism profound biblical scholarship and deep piety. In Vittorino da Feltre the same temper has been already noticed. The same Maffeo Vegio, who added a thirteenth book to the Æneid, had an enthusiasm for the memory of St. Augustine and his mother, Monica, which cannot have been without a deeper influence upon him. The result of all these tendencies was that the Platonic Academy at Florence deliberately chose for its object the reconciliation of the spirit of antiquity with that of Christianity. It was a remarkable oasis in the humanism of the period.

This humanism was in fact pagan, and became more and more so as its sphere widened in the fifteenth century. Its representatives, whom we have already described as the advance guard of an unbridled individualism, display as a rule such a character that even their religion, which is sometimes professed very definitely, becomes a matter of indifference to us. They easily got the name of atheists, if they showed themselves indifferent to religion and spoke freely against the Church; but not one of them ever professed, or dared to profess, a formal, philosophical atheism. If they sought for any leading principle, it must have been a kind of superficial rationalism—a careless inference from the many and contradictory opinions of antiquity with which they busied themselves, and from the discredit into which the Church and her doctrines had fallen. This was the sort of reasoning which was near bringing Galeotto Martio to the stake, had not his former pupil, Pope Sixtus IV, perhaps at the request of Lorenzo de' Medici, saved him from the hands of the Inquisition. Galeotto had ventured to write that the man who lived uprightly, and acted according to the natural law born within him, would go to heaven, whatever nation he belonged to.

Let us take, by way of example, the religious attitude of one of the smaller men in the great army. Codrus Urceus was first the tutor of the last Ordelaffo, Prince of Forlì, and afterwards for many years professor at Bologna. Against the Church and the monks his language is as abusive as that of the rest. His tone in general is reckless to the last degree, and he constantly introduces himself in all his local history and gossip. But he knows how to speak to the edification of the true God-Man, Jesus Christ, and to commend himself by letter to the prayers of a saintly priest. On one occasion, after enumerating the follies of the pagan religions, he thus goes on: 'Our theologians, too, quarrel about "the guinea-pig's tail", about the Immaculate Conception, Antichrist, Sacraments, Predestination, and other things, which were better let alone than talked of publicly.' Once, when he was not at home, his room and manuscripts were burnt. When he heard the news he stood opposite a figure of the Madonna in the street, and cried to it: 'Listen to what I tell you; I am not mad, I am saying what I mean. If I ever call upon you in the hour of my death, you need not hear me or take me among your own, for I will go and spend eternity with the devil.' After which speech he found it desirable to spend six months in retirement at the home of a woodcutter. With all this, he was so superstitious that prodigies and omens gave him incessant frights, leaving him no belief to spare for the immortality of the soul. When his hearers questioned him on the matter, he answered that no one knew what became of a man, of his soul *or* his spirit, after death, and the talk about another life was only fit to frighten old women. But when he came to die, he commended in his will his soul *or* his spirit to Almighty God, exhorted his weeping pupils to fear the Lord, and especially to believe in immortality and future retribution, and received the Sacrament with much fervour. We have no guarantee that more famous men in the same calling, however significant their opinions may be, were in practical life any more consistent. It is probable that most of them wavered inwardly between incredulity and a remnant of the faith in which they were brought up, and outwardly held for prudential reasons to the Church.

Through the connexion of rationalism with the newly born science of historical investigation, some timid attempts at biblical criticism may here and there have been made. A saying of Pius II has been recorded, which seems intended to prepare the way for such criticism: 'Even if Christianity were not confirmed by miracles, it ought still to be accepted on account of its morality.' The legends of the Church, in so far as they contained arbitrary versions of the biblical miracles, were freely ridiculed, and this reacted on the religious sense of the people. Where Judaizing heretics are mentioned, we must understand chiefly those who denied the Divinity of Christ, which was probably the offence for which Giorgio da Novara was burnt at Bologna about the year 1500. But again at Bologna in the year 1497 the Dominican Inquisitor was forced to let the physician Gabriele da Salò, who had powerful patrons, escape with a simple expression of penitence, although he was in the habit of maintaining that Jesus was not God, but son of Joseph and Mary, and conceived in the usual way; that by his cunning he had deceived the world to its ruin; that he may have died on the cross on account of crimes which he had committed; that his religion would soon come to an end; that his body was not really contained in the sacrament, and that he performed his miracles, not through any divine power, but through the influence of the heavenly bodies. This latter statement is most characteristic of the time: Faith is gone, but magic still holds its ground.

With respect to the moral government of the world, the humanists seldom get beyond a cold and resigned consideration of the prevalent violence and misrule. In this mood the many works 'On Fate,' or whatever name they bear, are written. They tell of the turning of the wheel of Fortune, and of the instability of earthly, especially political, things. Providence is only brought in because the writers would still be ashamed of undisguised fatalism, of the avowal of their ignorance, or of useless complaints. Gioviano Pontano ingeniously illustrates the nature of that mysterious something which men call Fortune by a hundred incidents, most of which belonged to his own experience. The subject is treated more humorously by Æneas Sylvius, in the form of a vision seen in a dream. The aim of Poggio, on the other hand, in a work written in his old age, is to represent the world as a vale of tears, and to fix the happiness of various classes as low as possible. This tone became in future the prevalent one. Distinguished men drew up a debit and credit of the happiness and unhappiness of their lives, and generally found that the latter outweighed the former. The fate of Italy and the Italians, so far as it could be told in the year 1510, has been described with dignity and almost elegiac pathos by Tristan Caracciolo. Applying this general tone of feeling to the humanists themselves, Pierio Valeriano afterwards composed his famous treatise. Some of these themes, such as the fortunes of Leo X, were most suggestive. All the good that can be said of him politically has been briefly and admirably summed up by Francesco Vettori; the picture of Leo's pleasures is given by Paolo Giovio and in the anonymous biography; and the shadows which attended his prosperity are drawn with inexorable truth by the same Pierio Valeriano.

We cannot, on the other hand, read without a kind of awe how men sometimes boasted of their fortune in public inscriptions. Giovanni II Bentivoglio, ruler of Bologna, ventured to carve in stone on the newly built tower by his palace that his merit and his fortune had given him richly of all that could be desired—and this a few years before his expulsion. The ancients, when they spoke in this tone, had nevertheless a sense of the envy of the gods. In Italy it was probably the Condottieri who first ventured to boast so loudly of their fortune.

But the way in which resuscitated antiquity affected religion most powerfully, was not through any doctrines or philosophical system, but through a general tendency which it fostered. The men, and in some respects the institutions, of antiquity were preferred to those of the Middle Ages, and in the eager attempt to imitate and reproduce them, religion was left to take care of itself. All was absorbed in the admiration for historical greatness. To this the philologians added many special follies of their own, by which they became the mark for general attention. How far Paul II was justified in calling his

Abbreviators and their friends to account for their paganism, is certainly a matter of great doubt, as his biographer and chief victim, Platina, has shown a masterly skill in explaining his vindictiveness on other grounds, and especially in making him play a ludicrous figure. The charges of infidelity, paganism, denial of immortality, and so forth, were not made against the accused till the charge of high treason had broken down. Paul, indeed, if we are correctly informed about him, was by no means the man to judge of intellectual things. It was he who exhorted the Romans to teach their children nothing beyond reading and writing. His priestly narrowness of views reminds us of Savonarola, with the difference that Paul might fairly have been told that he and his like were in great part to blame if culture made men hostile to religion. It cannot, nevertheless, be doubted that he felt a real anxiety about the pagan tendencies which surrounded him. And what, in truth, may not the humanists have allowed themselves at the court of the profligate pagan, Sigismondo Malatesta? How far these men, destitute for the most part of fixed principle, ventured to go, depended assuredly on the sort of influences they were exposed to. Nor could they treat of Christianity without paganizing it. It is curious, for instance, to notice how far Gioviano Pontano carried this confusion. He speaks of a saint not only as 'divus', but as 'deus'; the angels he holds to be identical with the genii of antiquity; and his notion of immortality reminds us of the old kingdom of the shades. This spirit occasionally appears in the most extravagant shapes. In 1526, when Siena was attacked by the exiled party, the worthy Canon Tizio, who tells us the story himself, rose from his bed on the 22nd of July, called to mind what is written in the third book of Macrobius, celebrated Mass, and then pronounced against the enemy the curse with which his author had supplied him, only altering 'Tellus mater teque Jupiter obtestor' into 'Tellus teque Christe Deus obtestor'. After he had done this for three days, the enemy retreated. On the one side, these things strike us as an affair of mere style and fashion; on the other, as a symptom of religious decadence.

INFLUENCE OF ANCIENT SUPERSTITION

But in another way, and that dogmatically, antiquity exercised a perilous influence. It imparted to the Renaissance its own forms of superstition. Some fragments of this had survived in Italy all through the Middle Ages, and the resuscitation of the whole was thereby made so much the more easy. The part played by the imagination in the process need not be dwelt upon. This only could have silenced the critical intellect of the Italians.

The belief in a Divine government of the world was in many minds destroyed by the spectacle of so much injustice and misery. Others, like Dante, surrendered at all events this life to the caprices of chance, and if they nevertheless retained a sturdy faith, it was because they held that the higher destiny of man would be accomplished in the life to come. But when the belief in immortality began to waver, then Fatalism got the upper hand, or sometimes the latter came first and had the former as its consequence.

The gap thus opened was in the first place filled by the astrology of antiquity, or even of the Arabs. From the relation of the planets among themselves and to the signs of the zodiac, future events and the course of whole lives were inferred, and the most weighty decisions were taken in consequence. In many cases the line of action thus adopted at the suggestion of the stars may not have been more immoral than that which would otherwise have been followed. But too often the decision must have been made at the cost of honour and conscience. It is profoundly instructive to observe how powerless culture and enlightenment were against this delusion; since the latter had its support in the ardent imagination of the people, in the passionate wish to penetrate and determine the future. Antiquity, too, was on the side of astrology.

At the beginning of the thirteenth century this superstition suddenly appeared in the foreground of Italian life. The Emperor Frederick II always travelled with his astrologer Theodorus; and Ezzelino da Romano with a large, well-paid court of such people, among them the famous Guido Bonatto and the long-bearded Saracen, Paul of Baghdad. In all important undertakings they fixed for him the day and the hour, and the gigantic atrocities of which he was guilty may have been in part practical inferences from their prophecies. Soon all scruples about consulting the stars ceased. Not only princes, but free cities, had their regular astrologers, and at the universities, from the fourteenth to the sixteenth century, professors of this pseudo-science were appointed, and lectured side by side with the astronomers. The Popes[111] commonly made no secret of their stargazing, though Pius II, who also despised magic, omens, and

[111] About 1260, Pope Alexander IV compelled a Cardinal (and shamefaced astrologer) Bianco to bring out a number of political prophecies.

the interpretation of dreams, is an honourable exception. Even Leo X seems to have thought the flourishing condition of astrology a credit to his pontificate, and Paul III never held a Consistory till the stargazers had fixed the hour.

It may fairly be assumed that the better natures did not allow their actions to be determined by the stars beyond a certain point, and that there was a limit where conscience and religion made them pause. In fact, not only did pious and excellent people share the delusion, but they actually came forward to profess it publicly. One of these was Maestro Pagolo of Florence, in whom we can detect the same desire to turn astrology to moral account which meets us in the late Roman Firmicus Maternus. His life was that of a saintly ascetic. He ate almost nothing, despised all temporal goods, and only collected books. A skilled physician, he only practised among his friends, and made it a condition of his treatment that they should confess their sins. He frequented the small but famous circle which assembled in the Monastery of the Angeli around Fra Ambrogio Camaldolese. He also saw much of Cosimo the Elder, especially in his last years; for Cosimo accepted and used astrology, though probably only for objects of lesser importance. As a rule, however, Pagolo only interpreted the stars to his most confidential friends. But even without this severity of morals, the astrologers might be highly respected and show themselves everywhere. There were also far more of them in Italy than in other European countries, where they only appeared at the great courts, and there not always. All the great householders in Italy, when the fashion was once established, kept an astrologer, who, it must be added, was not always sure of his dinner. Through the literature of this science, which was widely diffused even before the invention of printing, a dilettantism also grew up which as far as possible followed in the steps of the masters. The worst class of astrologers were those who used the stars either as an aid or a cloak to magical arts.

Yet apart from the latter, astrology is a miserable feature in the life of that time. What a figure do all these highly gifted, many-sided, original characters play, when the blind passion for knowing and determining the future dethrones their powerful will and resolution! Now and then, when the stars send them too cruel a message, they manage to brace themselves up, act for themselves, and say boldly: 'Vir sapiens dominabitur astris'—the wise man is master of the stars—and then again relapse into the old delusion.

In all the better families the horoscope of the children was drawn as a matter of course, and it sometimes happened that for half a lifetime men were haunted by the idle expectation of events which never occurred.[112] The stars were questioned whenever a great man had to come to any important decision, and even consulted as to the hour at which any undertaking was to be begun. The journeys of princes, the reception of foreign ambassadors,[113] the laying of the foundation-stones of public buildings, depended on the answer. A striking instance of the latter occurs in the life of the aforenamed Guido Bonatto, who by his personal activity and by his great systematic work on the subject deserves to be called the restorer of astrology in the thirteenth century. In order to put an end to the struggle of the Guelphs and Ghibellines at Forlì, he persuaded the inhabitants to rebuild the city walls and to begin the works under a constellation indicated by himself. If then two men, one from each party, at the same moment put a stone into the foundation, there would henceforth and for ever be no more party divisions in Forlì. A Guelph and a Ghibelline were selected for this office; the solemn moment arrived, each held the stone in his hands, the workmen stood ready with their implements. Bonatto gave the signal, and the Ghibelline threw down his stone on to the foundation. But the Guelph hesitated, and at last refused to do anything at all, on the ground that Bonatto himself had the reputation of a Ghibelline and might be devising some mysterious mischief against the Guelphs. Upon which the astrologer addressed him: 'God damn thee and the Guelph party, with your distrustful malice! This constellation will not appear above our city for 500 years to come.' In fact God soon afterwards did destroy the Guelphs of Forlì, but now, writes the chronicler about 1480, the two parties are thoroughly reconciled, and their very names are heard no longer.

Nothing that depended upon the stars was more important than decisions in time of war. The same Bonatto procured for the great Ghibelline leader Guido da Montefeltro a series of victories, by

[112] The father of Piero Capponi, himself an astrologer, put his son into trade lest he should get the dangerous wound in the head which threatened him. The physician and astrologer Pierleoni of Spoleto believed that he would be drowned, avoided in consequence all watery places, and refused brilliant positions offered him at Venice and Padua.

[113] For instances in the life of Lodovico il Moro, see Senarega, in Murat. xxiv. And yet his father, the great Francesco Sforza, had despised astrology, and his grandfather Giacomo had not at any rate followed its warnings.

telling him the propitious hour for marching. When Montefeltro was no longer accompanied by him[114] he lost the courage to maintain his despotism, and entered a Minorite monastery, where he lived as a monk for many years till his death. In the war with Pisa in 1362, the Florentines commissioned their astrologer to fix the hour for the march, and almost came too late through suddenly receiving orders to take a circuitous route through the city. On former occasions they had marched out by the Via di Borgo Santi Apostoli, and the campaign had been unsuccessful. It was clear that there was some bad omen connected with the exit through this street against Pisa, and consequently the army was now led out by the Porta Rossa. But as the tents stretched out there to dry had not been taken away, the flags—another bad omen—had to be lowered. The influence of astrology in war was confirmed by the fact that nearly all the Condottieri believed in it. Jacopo Caldora was cheerful in the most serious illness, knowing that he was fated to fall in battle, which in fact happened. Bartolommeo Alviano was convinced that his wounds in the head were as much a gift of the stars as his military command. Niccolò Orsini-Pitigliano asked the physicist and astrologer Alessandro Benedetto to fix a favourable hour for the conclusion of his bargain with Venice (1495). When the Florentines on June 1, 1498, solemnly invested their new Condottiere Paolo Vitelli with his office, the Marshal's staff which they handed him was, at his own wish, decorated with pictures of the constellations.

Sometimes it is not easy to make out whether in important political events the stars were questioned beforehand, or whether the astrologers were simply impelled afterwards by curiosity to find out the constellation which decided the result. When Giangaleazzo Visconti by a master-stroke of policy took prisoner his uncle Bernabò, with the latter's family (1385), we are told by a contemporary that Jupiter, Saturn and Mars stood in the house of the Twins, but we cannot say if the deed was resolved on in consequence. It is also probable that the advice of the astrologers was often determined by political calculation not less than by the course of the planets.

[114] When constellations which augured victory appeared, Bonatto ascended with his book and astrolabe to the tower of San Mercuriale above the Piazza, and when the right moment came gave the signal for the great bell to be rung. Yet it was admitted that he was often wide of the mark, and foresaw neither his own death nor the fate of Montefeltro. Not far from Cesena he was killed by robbers, on his way back to Forlì from Paris and from Italian universities where he had been lecturing.

All Europe, through the latter part of the Middle Ages, had allowed itself to be terrified by predictions of plagues, wars, floods, and earthquakes, and in this respect Italy was by no means behind other countries. The unlucky year 1494, which for ever opened the gates of Italy to the stranger, was undeniably ushered in by many prophecies of misfortune—only we cannot say whether such prophecies were not ready for each and every year.

This mode of thought was extended with thorough consistency into regions where we should hardly expect to meet with it. If the whole outward and spiritual life of the individual is determined by the facts of his birth, the same law also governs groups of individuals and historical products—that is to say, nations and religions; and as the constellation of these things changes, so do the things themselves. The idea that each religion has its day, first came into Italian culture in connection with these astrological beliefs. The conjunction of Jupiter with Saturn brought forth, we are told, the faith of Israel; that of Jupiter and Mars, the Chaldean; with the Sun, the Egyptian; with Venus, the Mohammedan; with Mercury, the Christian; and the conjunction of Jupiter with the Moon will one day bring forth the religion of Antichrist. Cecco d'Ascoli had already blasphemously calculated the nativity of Christ, and deduced from it his death upon the Cross. For this he was burnt at the stake in 1327, at Florence. Doctrines of this sort ended by simply darkening men's whole perceptions of spiritual things.

So much more worthy then of recognition is the warfare which the clear Italian spirit waged against this army of delusions. Notwithstanding the great monumental glorification of astrology, as in the frescoes in the Salone at Padua, and those in Borso's summer palace (Schifanoia) at Ferrara, notwithstanding the shameless praises of even such a man as the elder Beroaldus, there was no want of thoughtful and independent minds to protest against it. Here, too, the way had been prepared by antiquity, but it was their own common sense and observation which taught them what to say. Petrarch's attitude towards the astrologers, whom he knew by personal intercourse, is one of bitter contempt; and no one saw through their system of lies more clearly than he. The novels, from the time when they first began to appear—from the time of the 'Cento novelle antiche', are almost always hostile to the astrologers. The Florentine chroniclers bravely keep themselves free from the delusions which, as part of historical tradition, they are compelled to record. Giovanni Villani says more than once, 'No constellation can subjugate either the free will of man, or the counsels of God.' Matteo Villani declares astrology to be a vice which the Florentines had inherited, along with other superstitions, from their pagan ancestors, the Romans. The question, however, did not remain one for mere literary discussion, but the parties for and against disputed publicly. After the terrible floods of 1333, and again in 1345, astrologers and theologians discussed with great minuteness the influence of the stars, the will of God, and the justice of his punishments. These struggles never ceased throughout the whole time of the Renaissance, and we may conclude that the protestors were in earnest, since it was easier for them to recommend themselves to the great by defending, than by opposing astrology.

In the circle of Lorenzo the Magnificent, among his most distinguished Platonists, opinions were divided on this question. Marsilio Ficino defended astrology, and drew the horoscope of the children of the house, promising the little Giovanni, afterwards Leo X, that he would one day be Pope. Pico della Mirandola, on the other hand, made an epoch in the subject by his famous refutation. He detects in this belief the root of all impiety and immorality. If the astrologer, he maintains, believes in anything at all, he must worship not God, but the planets, from which all good and evil are derived. All other superstitions find a ready instrument in astrology, which serves as handmaid to geomancy, chiromancy, and magic of every kind. As to morality, he maintains that nothing can more foster evil than the opinion that heaven itself is the cause of it, in which case the faith in eternal happiness and punishment must also disappear. Pico even took the trouble to check off the astrologers inductively, and found that in the course of a month three-fourths of their weather prophecies turned out false. But his main achievement was to set forth, in the Fourth Book, a positive Christian doctrine of the freedom of the will and the government of the universe, which seems to have made a greater impression on the educated classes throughout Italy than all the revivalist preachers put together. The latter, in fact, often failed to reach these classes.

The first result of his book was that the astrologers ceased to publish their doctrines, and those who had already printed them were more or less ashamed of what they had done. Gioviano Pontano, for example, in his book on Fate, had recognized the science, and in a great work of his had expounded the whole theory of it in the style of the old Firmicus, ascribing to the stars the growth of every bodily and spiritual quality. He now in his dialogue 'Ægidius' surrendered, if not astrology, at least certain astrologers, and sounded the praises of free will, by which man is enabled to know God. Astrology remained more or less in fashion, but seems not to have governed human life in the way it formerly had done. The art of painting, which in the fifteenth century had done its best to foster the delusion, now expressed the altered tone of thought. Raphael, in the cupola of the Cappella Chigi, represents the gods of the different planets and the starry firmament, watched, however, and guided by beautiful angel-figures, and receiving from above the blessing of the Eternal Father. There was also another cause which now began to tell against astrology in Italy. The Spaniards took no interest in it, not even the generals, and those who wished to gain their favour declared open war against the half-heretical, half-Mohammedan science. It is true that Guicciardini writes in the year 1529: 'How happy are the astrologers, who are believed if they tell one truth to a hundred lies, while other people lose all credit if they tell one lie to a hundred truths.' But the contempt for astrology did not necessarily lead to a return to the belief in Providence. It could as easily lead to an indefinite Fatalism.

In this respect, as in others, Italy was unable to make its own way healthily through the ferment of the Renaissance, because the foreign invasion and the Counter-Reformation came upon it in the middle. Without such interfering causes its own strength would have enabled it thoroughly to get rid of these fantastic illusions. Those who hold that the onslaught of the strangers and the Catholic reactions were necessities for which the Italian people was itself solely responsible, will look on the spiritual bankruptcy which they produced as a just retribution. But it is a pity that the rest of Europe had indirectly to pay so large a part of the penalty.

The belief in omens seems a much more innocent matter than astrology. The Middle Ages had everywhere inherited them in abundance from the various pagan religions; and Italy did not differ in this respect from other countries. What is characteristic of Italy is the support lent by humanism to the popular superstition. The pagan inheritance was here backed up by a pagan literary development.

The popular superstition of the Italians rested largely on premonitions and inferences drawn from ominous occurrences, with which a good deal of magic, mostly of an innocent sort, was connected. There was, however, no lack of learned humanists who boldly ridiculed these delusions, and to whose attacks we partly owe the knowledge of them. Gioviano Pontano, the author of the great astrological work already mentioned above, enumerates with pity in his 'Charon' a long string of Neapolitan superstitions—the grief of the women when a fowl or goose caught the pip; the deep anxiety of the nobility if a hunting falcon did not come home, or if a horse sprained its foot; the magical formulæ of the Apulian peasants, recited on three Saturday evenings, when mad dogs were at large. The animal kingdom, as in antiquity, was regarded as specially significant in this respect, and the behaviour of the lions, leopards, and other beasts kept by the State gave the people all the more food for reflection, because they had come to be considered as living symbols of the State. During the siege of Florence, in 1529, an eagle which had been shot at fled into the city, and the Signoria gave the bearer four ducats because the omen was good. Certain times and places were favourable or unfavourable, or even decisive one way or the other, for certain actions. The Florentines, so Varchi tells us, held Saturday to be the fateful day on which all important events, good as well as bad, commonly happened. Their prejudice against marching out to war through a particular street has been already mentioned. At Perugia one of the gates, the 'Porta Eburnea', was thought lucky, and the Baglioni always went out to fight through it. Meteors and the appearance of the heavens were as significant in Italy as elsewhere in the Middle Ages, and the popular imagination saw warring armies in an unusual formation of clouds, and heard the clash of their collision high in the air. The superstition became a more serious matter when it attached itself to sacred things, when figures of the Virgin wept or moved the eyes, or when public calamities were associated with some alleged act of impiety, for which the people demanded expiation. In 1478, when Piacenza was visited with a violent and prolonged rainfall, it was said that there would be no dry weather till a certain usurer, who had been lately buried in San Francesco, had ceased to rest in consecrated earth. As the bishop was not obliging enough to have the corpse dug up, the young fellows of the town took it by force, dragged it round the streets amid frightful confusion, and at last threw it into the Po. Even Politian accepted this point of view in speaking of Giacomo Pazzi, one of the chiefs of the conspiracy of 1478, in Florence, which is called after his family. When he was put to death, he devoted his soul to Satan with fearful words. Here, too, rain followed and threatened to ruin the harvest; here, too, a party of men, mostly peasants, dug up the body in the church, and immediately the clouds departed and the sun shone—'so gracious was fortune to the opinion of the people', adds the great scholar. The corpse was first cast into unhallowed ground, the next day dug up, and after a horrible procession through the city thrown into the Arno.

These facts and the like bear a popular character, and might have occurred in the tenth, just as well as in the sixteenth century. But now comes the literary influence of antiquity. We know positively that the humanists were peculiarly accessible to prodigies and auguries, and instances of this have been already quoted. If further evidence were needed, it would be found in Poggio. The same radical thinker who denied the rights of noble birth and the inequality of men, not only believed in all the mediæval stories of ghosts and devils, but also in prodigies after the ancient pattern, like those said to have occurred on the last visit of Pope Eugenius IV to Florence. 'Near Como there were seen one evening four thousand dogs, who took the road to Germany; these were followed by a great herd of cattle, and these by an army on foot and horseback, some with no heads and some with almost invisible heads, and then a gigantic horseman with another herd of cattle behind him.' Poggio also believes in a battle of magpies and jackdaws. He even relates, perhaps without being aware of it, a well-preserved piece of ancient mythology. On the Dalmatian coast a Triton had appeared, bearded and horned, a genuine sea-satyr, ending in fins and a tail; he carried away women and children from the shore, till five stout-hearted washerwomen killed him with sticks and stones. A wooden model of the monster, which was exhibited at Ferrara, makes the whole story credible to Poggio. Though there were no more oracles, and it was no longer possible to take counsel of the gods, yet it became again the fashion to open Virgil at hazard, and take the passage hit upon as an omen ('Sortes Virgilianae'). Nor can the belief in dæmons current in the later period of antiquity have been without influence on the Renaissance. The work of Iamblichus or Abammon on the Mysteries of the Egyptians, which may have contributed to this result, was printed in a Latin translation at the end of the fifteenth century. The Platonic Academy at Florence was not free from these and other neoplatonic delusions of the Roman decadence. A few words must here be given to the belief in dæmons and to the magic which was connected with this belief.

The popular faith in what is called the spirit-world was nearly the same in Italy as elsewhere in Europe. In Italy as elsewhere there were ghosts, that is, reappearances of deceased persons; and if the view taken of them differed in any respect from that which prevailed in the North, the difference betrayed itself only in the ancient name 'ombra'. Even nowadays if such a shade presents itself, a couple of Masses are said for its repose. That the spirits of bad men appear in a dreadful shape, is a matter of course, but along with this we find the notion that the ghosts of the departed are universally malicious. The dead, says the priest in a novel of Bandello, kill the little children. It seems as if a certain shade was here thought of as separate from the soul, since the latter suffers in Purgatory, and when it appears, does nothing but wail and pray. At other times what appears is not the ghost of a man, but of an event—of a past condition of things. So the neighbours explained the diabolical appearances in the old palace of the Visconti near San Giovanni in Conca, at Milan, since here it was that Bernabò Visconti had caused countless victims of his tyranny to be tortured and strangled, and no wonder if there were strange things to be seen. One evening a swarm of poor people with candles in their hands appeared to a dishonest guardian of the poor at Perugia, and danced round about him; a great figure spoke in threatening tones on their behalf—it was St. Alò, the patron saint of the poorhouse. These modes of belief were so much a matter of course that the poets could make use of them as something which every reader would understand. The appearance of the slain Lodovico Pico under the walls of the besieged Mirandola is finely represented by Castiglione. It is true that poetry made the freest use of these conceptions when the poet himself had outgrown them.

Italy, too, shared the belief in dæmons with the other nations of the Middle Ages. Men were convinced that God sometimes allowed bad spirits of every class to exercise a destructive influence on parts of the world and of human life. The only reservation made was that the man to whom the Evil One came as tempter, could use his free will to resist. In Italy the dæmonic influence, especially as shown in natural events, easily assumed a character of poetical greatness. In the night before the great inundation of the Val d'Arno in 1333, a pious hermit above Vallombrosa heard a diabolical tumult in his cell, crossed himself, stepped to the door, and saw a crowd of black and terrible knights gallop by in armour. When conjured to stand, one of them said: 'We go to drown the city of Florence on account of its sins, if God will let us.' With this, the nearly contemporary vision at Venice (1340) may be compared, out of which a great master of the Venetian school, probably Giorgione, made the marvellous picture of a galley full of dæmons, which speeds with the swiftness of a bird over the stormy lagoon to destroy the sinful island-city, till the three saints, who have stepped unobserved into a poor boatman's skiff, exorcized the fiends and sent them and their vessel to the bottom of the waters. [Finished by Palma Vecchio. Venice, Accademia, 516.]

To this belief the illusion was now added that by means of magical arts it was possible to enter into relations with the evil ones, and use their help to further the purposes of greed, ambition, and sensuality. Many persons were probably accused of doing so before the time when it was actually attempted by many; but when the so-called magicians and witches began to be burned, the deliberate practice of the black art became more frequent. With the smoke of the fires in which the suspected victims were sacrificed, were spread the narcotic fumes by which numbers of ruined characters were drugged into magic; and with them many calculating imposters became associated.

The primitive and popular form in which the superstition had probably lived on uninterruptedly from the time of the Romans, was the art of the witch (*strega*). The witch, so long as she limited herself to mere divination, might be innocent enough, were it not that the transition from prophecy to active help could easily, though often imperceptibly, be a fatal downward step. She was credited in such a case not only with the power of exciting love or hatred between man and woman, but also with purely destructive and malignant arts, and was especially charged with the sickness of little children, even when the malady obviously came from the neglect and stupidity of the parents. It is still questionable how far she was supposed to act by mere magical cermonies and formulæ, or by a conscious alliance with the fiends, apart from the poisons and drugs which she administered with a full knowledge of their effect.

The more innocent form of the superstition, in which the mendicant friar could venture to appear as the competitor of the witch, is shown in the case of the witch of Gaeta whom we read of in Pontano. His traveller Suppatius reaches her dwelling while she is giving audience to a girl and a serving-maid, who come to her with a black hen, nine eggs laid on a Friday, a duck, and some white thread—for it is the third day since the new moon. They are then sent away, and bidden to come again at twilight. It is to be hoped that nothing worse than divination is intended. The mistress of the servant-maid is pregnant by a monk; the girl's lover has proved untrue and has gone into a monastery. The witch complains: 'Since my husband's death I support myself in this way, and should make a good thing of it, since the Gaetan women have plenty of faith, were it not that the monks balk me of my gains by explaining dreams, appeasing the anger of the saints for money, promising husbands to the girls, men-children to the pregnant women, offspring to the barren, and besides all this visiting the women at night when their husbands are away fishing, in accordance with the assignations made in daytime at church.' Suppatius warns her against the envy of the monastery, but she has no fear, since the guardian of it is an old acquaintance of hers.

But the superstition further gave rise to a worse sort of witches, namely those who deprived men of their health and life. In these cases the mischief, when not sufficiently accounted for by the evil eye and the like, was naturally attributed to the aid of powerful spirits. The punishment, as we have seen in the case of Finicella, was the stake; and yet a compromise with fanaticism was sometimes practicable. According to the laws of Perugia, for example, a witch could settle the affair by paying down 400 pounds. The matter was not then treated with the seriousness and consistency of later times. In the territories of the Church, at Norcia (Nursia), the home of St. Benedict in the upper Apennines, there was a perfect nest of witches and sorcerers, and no secret was made of it. It is spoken of in one of the most remarkable letters of Æneas Sylvius, belonging to his earlier period. He writes to his brother: 'The bearer of this came to me to ask if I knew of a Mount of Venus in Italy, for in such a place magical arts were taught, and his master, a Saxon and a great astronomer, was anxious to learn them. I told him that I knew of a Porto Venere not far from Carrara, on the rocky coast of Liguria, where I spent three nights on the way to Basle; I also found that there was a mountain called Eryx, in Sicily, which was dedicated to Venus, but I did not know whether magic was taught there. But it came into my mind while talking, that in Umbria, in the old Duchy (Spoleto), near the town of Nursia, there is a cave beneath a steep rock, in which water flows. There, as I remember to have heard, are witches (striges), dæmons, and nightly shades, and he that has the courage can see and speak to ghosts (spiritus), and learn magical arts.[115] I have not

[115] In the fourteenth century there existed a kind of hell-gate near Ansedonia in Tuscany. It was a cave, with footprints of men and animals in the sand, which whenever they were effaced, reappeared the next day.

seen it, nor taken any trouble about it, for that which is learned with sin is better not learned at all.' He nevertheless names his informant, and begs his brother to take the bearer of the letter to him, should he be still alive. Æneas goes far enough here in his politeness to a man of position, but personally he was not only freer from superstition than his contemporaries, but he also stood a test on the subject which not every educated man of our own day could endure. At the time of the Council of Basle, when he lay sick of the fever for seventy-five days at Milan, he could never be persuaded to listen to the magic doctors, though a man was brought to his bedside who a short time before had marvellously cured 2,000 soldiers of fever in the camp of Piccinino. While still an invalid, Æneas rode over the mountains to Basle, and got well on the journey.

We learn something more about the neighbourhood of Norcia through the necromancer who tried to get Benvenuto Cellini into his power. A new book of magic was to be consecrated, and the best place for the ceremony was among the mountains in that district. The master of the magician had once, it is true, done the same thing near the Abbey of Farfa, but had there found difficulties which did not present themselves at Norcia; further, the peasants in the latter neighbourhood were trustworthy people who had had practice in the matter, and who could afford considerable help in case of need. The expedition did not take place, else Benvenuto would probably have been able to tell us something of the impostor's assistants. The whole neighbourhood was then proverbial. Aretino says somewhere of an enchanted well, 'there dwell the sisters of the sibyl of Norcia and the aunt of the Fata Morgana'. And about the same time Trissino could still celebrate the place in his great epic with all the resources of poetry and allegory as the home of authentic prophecy.

After the notorious Bull of Innocent VIII (1484), witchcraft and the persecution of witches grew into a great and revolting system. The chief representatives of this system of persecution were German Dominicans; and Germany and, curiously enough, those parts of Italy nearest Germany were the countries most afflicted by this plague. The bulls and injunctions of the Popes themselves refer, for example, to the Dominican Province of Lombardy, to Cremona, to the dioceses of Brescia and Bergamo. We learn from Sprenger's famous theoretico-practical guide, the 'Malleus Maleficarum', that forty-one witches were burnt at Como in the first year after the publication of the bull; crowds of Italian women took refuge in the territory of the

Archduke Sigismund, where they believed themselves to be still safe. Witchcraft ended by taking firm root in a few unlucky Alpine valleys, especially in the Val Camonica; the system of persecution had succeeded in permanently infecting with the delusion those populations which were in any way predisposed for it. This essentially German form of witchcraft is what we should think of when reading the stories and novels of Milan or Bologna. That it did not make further progress in Italy is probably due to the fact that here a highly developed 'stregheria' was already in existence, resting on a different set of ideas. The Italian witch practised a trade, and needed for it money and, above all, sense. We find nothing about her of the hysterical dreams of the Northern witch, of marvellous journeys through the air, of Incubus and Succubus; the business of the 'strega' was to provide for other people's pleasure. If she was credited with the power of assuming different shapes, or of transporting herself suddenly to distant places, she was so far content to accept this reputation, as her influence was thereby increased; on the other hand, it was perilous for her when the fear of her malice and vengeance, and especially of her power for enchanting children, cattle, and crops, became general. Inquisitors and magistrates were then most thoroughly in accord with popular wishes if they burnt her.

By far the most important field for the activity of the 'strega' lay, as has been said, in love-affairs, and included the stirring up of love and of hatred, the producing of abortion, the pretended murder of the unfaithful man or woman by magical arts, and even the manufacture of poisons. Owing to the unwillingness of many persons to have to do with these women, a class of occasional practitioners arose who secretly learned from them some one or other of their arts, and then used this knowledge on their own account. The Roman prostitutes, for example, tried to enhance their personal attractions by charms of another description in the style of the Horatian Canidia. Aretino may not only have known, but have also told the truth about them in this particular. He gives a list of the loathsome messes which were to be found in their boxes—hair, skulls, ribs, teeth, dead men's eyes, human skin, the navels of little children, the soles of shoes and pieces of clothing from tombs. They even went themselves to the graveyard and fetched bits of rotten flesh, which they slyly gave their lovers to eat—with more that is still worse. Pieces of the hair and nails of the lover were boiled in oil stolen from the ever-burning lamps in the church. The most innocuous of their charms was to make a heart of glowing ashes, and then to pierce it while singing:

'Prima che'l fuoco spenghi,
Fa ch'a mia porta venghi;
Tal ti punga mio amore
Quale io fo questo cuore.

There were other charms practised by moonshine, with drawings on the ground, and figures of wax or bronze, which doubtless represented the lover, and were treated according to circumstances.

These things were so customary that a woman who, without youth and beauty, nevertheless exercised a powerful charm on men, naturally became suspected of witchcraft. The mother of Sanga, secretary to Clement VII, poisoned her son's mistress, who was a woman of this kind. Unfortunately the son died too, as well as a party of friends who had eaten of the poisoned salad.

Next comes, not as helper, but as competitor to the witch, the magician or enchanter—'incantatore'—who was still more familiar with the most perilous business of the craft. Sometimes he was as much or more of an astrologer than of a magician; he probably often gave himself out as an astrologer in order not to be prosecuted as a magician, and a certain astrology was essential in order to find out the favourable hour for a magical process. But since many spirits are good or indifferent, the magician could sometimes maintain a very tolerable reputation, and Sixtus IV, in the year 1474, had to proceed expressly against some Bolognese Carmelites, who asserted in the pulpit that there was no harm in seeking information from the dæmons. Very many people believed in the possibility of the thing itself; an indirect proof of this lies in the fact that the most pious men believed that by prayer they could obtain visions of good spirits. Savonarola's mind was filled with these things; the Florentine Platonists speak of a mystic union with God; and Marcellus Palingenius gives us to understand clearly enough that he had to do with consecrated spirits. The same writer is convinced of the existence of a whole hierarchy of bad dæmons, who have their seat from the moon downwards, and are ever on the watch to do some mischief to nature and human life. He even tells of his own personal acquaintance with some of them, and as the scope of the present work does not allow of a systematic exposition of the then prevalent belief in spirits, the narrative of Palingenius may be given as one instance out of many.

At San Silvestro, on Soracte, he had been receiving instruction from a pious hermit on the nothingness of earthly things and the worthlessness of human life; and when the night drew near he set out on his way back to Rome. On the road, in the full light of the moon, he was joined by three men, one of whom called him by name, and asked him whence he came. Palingenius made answer: 'From the wise man on the mountain.' 'O fool,' replied the stranger, 'dost thou in truth believe that anyone on earth is wise? Only higher beings (Divi) have wisdom, and such are we three, although we wear the shapes of men. I am named Saracil, and these two Sathiel and Jana. Our kingdom lies near the moon, where dwell that multitude of intermediate beings who have sway over earth and sea.' Palingenius then asked, not without an inward tremor, what they were going to do at Rome. The answer was: 'One of our comrades, Ammon, is kept in servitude by the magic arts of a youth from Narni, one of the attendants of Cardinal Orsini; for mark it, O men, there is proof of your own immortality therein, that you can control one of us: I myself, shut up in crystal, was once forced to serve a German, till a bearded monk set me free. This is the service which we wish to render at Rome to our friend, and he shall also take the opportunity of sending one or two distinguished Romans to the nether world.' At these words a light breeze arose, and Sathiel said: 'Listen, our messenger is coming back from Rome, and this wind announces him.' And then another being appeared, whom they greeted joyfully and then asked about Rome. His utterances are strongly anti-papal: Clement VII was again allied with the Spaniards and hoped to root out Luther's doctrines, not with arguments, but by the Spanish sword. This is wholly in the interest of the dæmons, whom the impending bloodshed would enable to carry away the souls of thousands into hell. At the close of this conversation, in which Rome with all its guilt is represented as wholly given over to the Evil One, the apparitions vanish, and leave the poet sorrowfully to pursue his way alone. [Zodiacus Vitae, x, 770.]

Those who would form a conception of the extent of the belief in those relations to the dæmons which could be openly avowed in spite of the penalties attaching to witchcraft, may be referred to the much-read work of Agrippa of Nettesheim 'On secret Philosophy'. He seems originally to have written it before he was in Italy, but in the dedication to Trithemius he mentions Italian authorities among others, if only by way of disparagement. In the case of equivocal persons like Agrippa, or of the knaves and fools into whom the majority of the rest may be divided, there is little that is interesting in the system they profess, with its formulæ, fumigations, ointments, and the rest of it. But this system was filled with quotations from the superstitions of antiquity, the influence of which on the life and the passions of Italians is at times most remarkable and fruitful. We might think that a great mind must be thoroughly ruined, before it surrendered itself to such influences; but the violence of hope and desire led even vigorous and original men of all classes to have recourse to the magician, and the belief that the thing was feasible at all weakened to some extent the faith, even of those who kept at a distance, in the moral order of the world. At the cost of a little money and danger it seemed possible to defy with impunity the universal reason and morality of mankind, and to spare oneself the intermediate steps which otherwise lie between a man and his lawful or unlawful ends.

Let us here glance for a moment at an older and now decaying form of superstition. From the darkest period of the Middle Ages, or even from the days of antiquity, many cities of Italy had kept the remembrance of the connection of their fate with certain buildings, statues, or other material objects. The ancients had left records of consecrating priests or Telestæ, who were present at the solemn foundation of cities, and magically guaranteed their prosperity by erecting certain monuments or by burying certain objects (Telesmata). Traditions of this sort were more likely than anything else to live on in the form of popular, unwritten legend; but in the course of centuries the priest naturally became transformed into the magician, since the religious side of his function was no longer understood. In some of the Virgilian miracles at Naples, the ancient remembrance of one of these Telestæ is clearly preserved, his name being in course of time supplanted by that of Virgil. The enclosing of the mysterious picture of the city in a vessel is neither more nor less than a genuine ancient Telesma; and Virgil, as founder of Naples, is but the officiating priest who took part in the ceremony, presented in another dress. The popular imagination went on working at these themes, till Virgil became also responsible for the brazen horse, for the heads at the Nolan gate, for the brazen fly over another gate, and even for the Grotto of Posilippo —all of them things which in one respect or other served to put a magical constraint upon fate, and the first two of which seemed to determine the whole fortune of the city. Mediæval Rome also preserved confused recollections of the same kind. At the church of Sant' Ambrogio at Milan, there was an ancient marble Hercules; so long, it was said, as this stood in its place, so long would the Empire last. That of the Germans is probably meant, as the coronation of their emperors at Milan took place in this church. The Florentines were convinced that the temple of Mars, afterwards transformed into the Baptistery, would stand to the end of time, according to the constellation under which it had been built; they had, as Christians, removed from it the marble equestrian statue; but since the destruction of the latter would have brought some great calamity on the city—also according to a constellation—they set it upon a tower by the Arno. When Totila conquered Florence, the statue fell into the river, and was not fished out again till Charlemagne refounded the city. It was then placed on a pillar at the entrance to the Ponte Vecchio, and on this spot Buondelmonti was slain in 1215. The origin of the great feud between Guelph and Ghibelline was thus associated with the dreaded idol. During the inundation of 1333 the statue vanished for ever.

But the same Telesma reappears elsewhere. Guido Bonatto, already mentioned, was not satisfied, at the refounding of the walls of Forlì, with requiring certain symbolic acts of reconciliation from the two parties. By burying a bronze or stone equestrian statue, which he had produced by astrological or magical arts, he believed that he had defended the city from ruin, and even from capture and plunder. When Cardinal Albornoz was governor of Romagna some sixty years later, the statue was accidentally dug up and then shown to the people, probably by the order of the Cardinal, that it might be known by what means the cruel Montefeltro had defended himself against the Roman Church. And again, half a century later, when an attempt to surprise Forlì had failed, men began to talk afresh of the virtue of the statue, which had perhaps been saved and reburied. It was the last time that they could do so; for a year later Forlì was really taken. The foundation of buildings all through the fifteenth century was associated not only with astrology but also with magic. The large number of gold and silver medals which Paul II buried in the foundation of his buildings was noticed, and Platina was by no means displeased to recognize an old pagan Telesma in the fact. Neither Paul nor his biographer were in any way conscious of the mediæval religious significance of such an offering.

But this official magic, which in many cases only rests on hearsay, was comparatively unimportant by the side of the secret arts practised for personal ends.

The form which these most often took in daily life is shown by

Ariosto in his comedy of the necromancers. His hero is one of the many Jewish exiles from Spain, although he also gives himself out for a Greek, an Egyptian, and an African, and is constantly changing his name and costume. He pretends that his incantations can darken the day and lighten the darkness, that he can move the earth, make himself invisible, and change men into beasts; but these vaunts are only an advertisement. His true object is to make his account out of unhappy and troubled marriages, and the traces which he leaves behind him in his course are like the slime of a snail, or often like the ruin wrought by a hailstorm. To attain his ends he can persuade people that the box in which a lover is hidden is full of ghosts, or that he can make a corpse talk. It is at all events a good sign that poets and novelists could reckon on popular applause in holding up this class of men to ridicule. Bandello not only treats this sorcery of a Lombard monk as a miserable, and in its consequences terrible, piece of knavery, but he also describes with unaffected indignation the disasters which never cease to pursue the credulous fool. 'A man hopes with "Solomon's Key" and other magical books to find the treasures hidden in the bosom of the earth, to force his lady to do his will, to find out the secret of princes, and to transport himself in the twinkling of an eye from Milan to Rome. The more often he is deceived, the more steadfastly he believes. . . . Do you remember the time, Signor Carlo, when a friend of ours, in order to win a favour of his beloved, filled his room with skulls and bones like a churchyard?' The most loathsome tasks were prescribed—to draw three teeth from a corpse or a nail from its finger, and the like; and while the hocus-pocus of the incantation was going on, the unhappy participants sometimes died of terror.

Benvenuto Cellini did not die during the well-known incantation (1532) in the Colosseum at Rome,[116] although both he and his companions witnessed no ordinary horrors; the Sicilian priest, who probably expected to find him a useful coadjutor in the future, paid him the compliment as they went home of saying that he had never met a man of so sturdy a courage. Every reader will make his own reflections on the proceedings themselves. The narcotic fumes and the fact that the imaginations of the spectators were predisposed for all possible terrors, are the chief points to be noticed, and explain why the lad who formed one of the party, and on whom they made most impression, saw much more than the others. But it may be inferred that Benvenuto himself was the one whom it was wished to impress,

[116] Autobiography, I, cap. 64.

since the dangerous beginning of the incantation can have had no other aim than to arouse curiosity. For Benvenuto had to think before the fair Angelica occurred to him; and the magician told him afterwards that love-making was folly compared with the finding of treasures. Further, it must not be forgotten that it flattered his vanity to be able to say, 'The dæmons have kept their word, and Angelica came into my hands, as they promised, just a month later' (I, cap. 68). Even on the supposition that Benvenuto gradually lied himself into believing the whole story, it would still be permanently valuable as evidence of the mode of thought then prevalent.

As a rule, however, the Italian artists, even 'the odd, capricious, and eccentric' among them, had little to do with magic. One of them, in his anatomical studies, may have cut himself a jacket out of the skin of a corpse, but at the advice of his confessor he put it again into the grave. Indeed the frequent study of anatomy probably did more than anything else to destroy the belief in the magical influence of various parts of the body, while at the same time the incessant observation and representation of the human form made the artist familiar with a magic of a wholly different sort.

In general, notwithstanding the instances which have been quoted, magic seems to have been markedly on the decline at the beginning of the sixteenth century—that is to say, at a time when it first began to flourish vigorously out of Italy; and thus the tours of Italian sorcerers and astrologers in the North seem not to have begun till their credit at home was thoroughly impaired. In the fourteenth century it was thought necessary carefully to watch the lake on Mount Pilatus, near Scariotto, to hinder the magicians from there consecrating their books. In the fifteenth century we find, for example, that the offer was made to produce a storm of rain, in order to frighten away a besieged army; and even then the commander of the besieged town—Niccolô Vitelli in Città di Castello—had the good sense to dismiss the sorcerers as godless persons. In the sixteenth century no more instances of this official kind appear, although in private life the magicians were still active. To this time belongs the classic figure of German sorcery, Dr. Johann Faust; the Italian ideal, on the other hand, Guido Bonatto, dates back to the thirteenth century.

It must nevertheless be added that the decrease of the belief in magic was not necessarily accompanied by an increase of the belief in a moral order, but that in many cases, like the decaying faith in astrology, the delusion left behind it nothing but a stupid fatalism.

One or two minor forms of this superstition, pyromancy, chiromancy and others, which obtained some credit as the belief in sorcery and astrology was declining, may be here passed over, and even the pseudo-science of physiognomy has by no means the interest which the name might lead us to expect. For it did not appear as the sister and ally of art and psychology, but as a new form of fatalistic superstition, and, what it may have been among the Arabs, as the rival of astrology. The author of a physiognomical treatise, Bartolommeo Cocle, who styled himself a 'metoposcopist', and whose science, according to Giovio, seemed like one of the most respectable of the free arts, was not content with the prophecies which he made to the many people who daily consulted him, but wrote also a most serious 'catalogue of such whom great dangers to life were awaiting'. Giovio, although grown old in the free thought of Rome—'in hac luce romana'—is of opinion that the predictions contained therein had only too much truth in them. We learn from the same source how the people aimed at in these and similar prophecies took vengeance on a seer. Giovanni Bentivoglio caused Lucas Gauricus to be five times swung to and fro against the wall, on a rope hanging from a lofty, winding staircase, because Lucas had foretold to him the loss of his authority. Ermes Bentivoglio sent an assassin after Cocle, because the unlucky metoposcopist had unwillingly prophesied to him that he would die an exile in battle. The murderer seems to have derided the dying man in his last moments, saying that Cocle himself had foretold him he would shortly commit an infamous murder. The reviver of chiromancy, Antioco Tiberto of Cesena, came by an equally miserable end at the hands of Pandolfo Malatesta of Rimini, to whom he had prophesied the worst that a tyrant can imagine, namely, death in exile and in the most grievous poverty. Tiberto was a man of intelligence, who was supposed to give his answers less according to any methodical chiromancy than by means of his shrewd knowledge of mankind; and his high culture won for him the respect of those scholars who thought little of his divination.

Alchemy, in conclusion, which is not mentioned in antiquity till quite late under Diocletian, played only a very subordinate part at the best period of the Renaissance. Italy went through the disease earlier, when Petrarch in the fourteenth century confessed, in his polemic against it, that gold-making was a general practice. Since then that particular kind of faith, devotion, and isolation which the practice of alchemy required became more and more rare in Italy, just when

Italian and other adepts began to make their full profit out of the great lords in the North. Under Leo X the few Italians who busied themselves with it were called 'ingenia curiosa', and Aurelio Augurelli, who dedicated to Leo X, the great despiser of gold, his didactic poem on the making of the metal, is said to have received in return a beautiful but empty purse. The mystic science which besides gold sought for the omnipotent philosopher's stone, is a late northern growth, whch had its rise in the theories of Paracelsus and others.

GENERAL SPIRIT OF DOUBT

With these superstitions, as with ancient modes of thought generally, the decline in the belief of immortality stands in the closest connection. This question has the widest and deepest relations with the whole development of the modern spirit.

One great source of doubt in immortality was the inward wish to be under no obligations to the hated Church. We have seen that the Church branded those who thus felt as Epicureans. In the hour of death many doubtless called for the sacraments, but multitudes during their whole lives, and especially during their most vigorous years, lived and acted on the negative supposition. That unbelief on this particular point must often have led to a general scepticism, is evident of itself, and is attested by abundant historical proof. These are the men of whom Ariosto says: 'Their faith goes no higher than the roof'. In Italy, and especially in Florence, it was possible to live as an open and notorious unbeliever, if a man only refrained from direct acts of hostility against the Church. The confessor, for instance, who was sent to prepare a political offender for death, began by inquiring whether the prisoner was a believer, 'for there was a false report that he had no belief at all'.

The unhappy transgressor here referred to—the same Pierpaolo Boscoli who has been already mentioned—who in 1513 took part in an attempt against the newly restored family of the Medici, is a faithful mirror of the religious confusion then prevalent. Beginning as a partisan of Savonarola, he became afterwards possessed with an enthusiasm for the ancient ideals of liberty, and for paganism in general; but when he was in prison his early friends regained the control of his mind, and secured for him what they considered a pious ending. The tender witness and narrator of his last hours is one of the artistic family of the Della Robbia, the learned philologist Luca.

'Ah,' sighs Boscoli, 'get Brutus out of my head for me, that I may go my way as a Christian.' 'If you will,' answers Luca, 'the thing is not difficult; for you know that these deeds of the Romans are not handed down to us as they were, but idealized (con arte accresciute).' The penitent now forces his understanding to believe, and bewails his inability to believe voluntarily. If he could only live for a month with pious monks he would truly become spiritually minded. It comes out that these partisans of Savonarola knew their Bible very imperfectly; Boscoli can only say the Paternoster and Ave Maria, and earnestly begs Luca to exhort his friends to study the sacred writings, for only what a man has learned in life does he possess in death. Luca then reads and explains to him the story of the Passion according to the Gospel of St. John; the poor listener, strange to say, can perceive clearly the Godhead of Christ, but is perplexed at His manhood; he wishes to get as firm a hold of it 'as if Christ came to meet him out of a wood'. His friend thereupon exhorts him to be humble, since this was only a doubt sent him by the Devil. Soon after it occurs to the penitent that he has not fulfilled a vow made in his youth to go on pilgrimage to the Impruneta; his friend promises to do it in his stead. Meantime the confessor—a monk, as was desired, from Savonarola's monastery—arrives, and after giving him the explanation quoted above of the opinion of St. Thomas Aquinas on tyrannicide, exhorts him to bear death manfully. Boscoli makes answer: 'Father, waste no time on this; the philosophers have taught it me already; help me to bear death out of love to Christ.' What follows—the communion, the leave-taking and the execution—is very touchingly described; one point deserves special mention. When Boscoli laid his head on the block, he begged the executioner to delay the stroke for a moment: 'During the whole time since the announcement of the sentence he had been striving after a close union with God, without attaining it as he wished, and now in this supreme moment he thought that by a strong effort he could give himself wholly to God.' It is clearly some half-understood expression of Savonarola which was troubling him.

If we had more confessions of this character the spiritual picture of the time would be richer by many important features which no poem or treatise has preserved for us. We should see more clearly how strong the inborn religious instinct was, how subjective and how variable the relation of the individual to religion, and what powerful enemies and competitors religion had. That men whose inward condition is of this nature, are not the men to found a new church, is evident; but the history of the Western spirit would be imperfect without a view of that fermenting period among the Italians, while other nations, who have had no share in the evolution of thought, may be passed over without loss. But we must return to the question of immortality.

If unbelief in this respect made such progress among the more highly cultivated natures, the reason lay partly in the fact that the great earthly task of discovering the world and representing it in word and form, absorbed most of the higher spiritual faculties. We have already spoken of the inevitable worldliness of the Renaissance. But this investigation and this art were necessarily accompanied by a general spirit of doubt and inquiry. If this spirit shows itself but little in literature, if we find, for example, only isolated instances of the beginnings of biblical criticism, we are not therefore to infer that it had no existence. The sound of it was only overpowered by the need of representation and creation in all departments—that is, by the artistic instinct; and it was further checked, whenever it tried to express itself theoretically, by the already existing despotism of the Church. This spirit of doubt must, for reasons too obvious to need discussion, have inevitably and chiefly busied itself with the question of the state of man after death.

And here came in the influence of antiquity, and worked in a twofold fashion on the argument. In the first place men set themselves to master the psychology of the ancients, and tortured the letter of Aristotle for a decisive answer. In one of the Lucianic dialogues of the time, Charon tells Mercury how he questioned Aristotle on his belief in immortality, when the philosopher crossed in the Stygian boat; but the prudent sage, although dead in the body and nevertheless living on, declined to compromise himself by a definite answer—and centuries later how was it likely to fare with the interpretation of his writings? All the more eagerly did men dispute about his opinion and that of others on the true nature of the soul, its origin, its pre-existence, its unity in all men, its absolute eternity, even its transformations; and there were men who treated of these things in the pulpit. The dispute was warmly carried on even in the fifteenth century; some proved that Aristotle taught the doctrine of an immortal soul; others complained of the hardness of men's hearts, who would not believe that there was a soul at all, till they saw it sitting down on a chair before them; Filelfo, in his funeral oration on Francesco Sforza, brings forward a long list of opinions of ancient and even of Arab philosophers in favour of immortality, and closes the mixture, which covers a folio page and a half of print, with the words, 'Besides all this we have the Old and New Testaments, which are above all truth.' Then came the Florentine Platonists with their master's doctrine of the soul, supplemented at times, as in the case of Pico, by Christian teaching. But the opposite opinion prevailed in the instructed world. At the beginning of the sixteenth century the stumbling-block which it put in the way of the Church was so serious that Leo X set forth a Constitution at the Lateran Council in 1513, in defence of the immortality and individuality of the soul, the latter against those who asserted that there was but one soul in all men. A few years later appeared the work of Pomponazzo, in which the impossibility of a philosophical proof of immortality is maintained; and the contest was now waged incessantly with replies and 'apologies', till it was silenced by the Catholic reaction. The pre-existence of the soul in God, conceived more or less in accordance with Plato's theory of ideas, long remained a common belief, and proved of service even to the poets. The consequences which followed from it as to the mode of the soul's continued existence after death were not more closely considered.

There was a second way in which the influence of antiquity made itself felt, chiefly by means of that remarkable fragment of the sixth book of Cicero's 'Republic', known by the name of Scipio's Dream. Without the commentary of Macrobius it would probably have perished like the rest of the second part of the work; it was now diffused in countless manuscript copies, and, after the discovery of typography, in a printed form and edited afresh by various commentators. It is the description of a transfigured hereafter for great men, pervaded by the harmony of the spheres. This pagan heaven, for which many other testimonies were gradually extracted from the writings of the ancients, came step by step to supplant the Christian heaven in proportion as the ideal of fame and historical greatness threw into the shade the ideal of the Christian life, without, nevertheless, the public feeling being thereby offended as it was by the doctrine of personal annihilation after death. Even Petrarch founds his hope chiefly on this Dream of Scipio, on the declarations found in other Ciceronian works, and on Plato's 'Phædo', without making any mention of the Bible. 'Why,' he asks elsewhere, 'should not I as a Catholic share a hope which was demonstrably cherished by the heathen?' Soon afterwards Coluccio Salutati wrote his 'Labours of Hercules' (still existing in manuscript), in which it is proved at the end that the valorous man, who has well endured the great labours of earthly life, is justly entitled to a dwelling among the stars. If Dante still firmly maintained that the great pagans, whom he would have gladly welcomed in Paradise, nevertheless must not come beyond the Limbo at the entrance to Hell, the poetry of a later time accepted joyfully the new liberal ideas of a future life. Cosimo the Elder, according to Bernardo Pulci's poem on his death, was received in heaven by Cicero, who had also been called the 'Father of his country', by the Fabii, by Curius, Fabricius and many others; with them he would adorn the choir where only blameless spirits sing.

But in the old writers there was another and less pleasing picture of the world to come—the shadowy realms of Homer and of those poets who had not sweetened and humanized the conception. This made an impression on certain temperaments. Gioviano Pontano somewhere attributes to Sannazaro the story of a vision which he beheld one morning early while half awake. He seemed to see a departed friend, Ferrandus Januarius, with whom he had often discoursed on the immortality of the soul, and whom he now asked whether it was true that the pains of Hell were really dreadful and eternal. The shadow gave an answer like that of Achilles when Odysseus questioned him. 'So much I tell and aver to thee, that we who are parted from earthly life have the strongest desire to return to it again.' He then saluted his friend and disappeared.

It cannot but be recognized that such views of the state of man after death partly presuppose and partly promote the dissolution of the most essential dogmas of Christianity. The notion of sin and of salvation must have almost entirely evaporated. We must not be misled by the effects of the great preachers of repentance or by the epidemic revivals which have been described above. For even granting that the individually developed classes had shared in them like the rest, the cause of their participation was rather the need of emotional excitement, the rebound of passionate natures, the horror felt at great national calamities, the cry to heaven for help. The awakening of the conscience had by no means necessarily the sense of sin and the felt need of salvation as its consequence, and even a very severe outward penance did not perforce involve any repentance in the Christian meaning of the word. When the powerful natures of the Renaissance tell us that their principle is to repent of nothing, they may have in their minds only matters that are morally indifferent, faults of unreason or imprudence; but in the nature of the case this contempt for repentance must extend to the sphere of morals, because its origin, namely the consciousness of individual force, is common to both sides of human nature. The passive and contemplative form of Christianity, with its constant reference to a higher world beyond the grave, could no longer control these men. Machiavelli ventured still further, and maintained that it could not be serviceable to the State and to the maintenance of public freedom.

The form assumed by the strong religious instinct which, notwithstanding all, survived in many natures, was Theism or Deism, as we may please to call it. The latter name may be applied to that mode of thought which simply wiped away the Christian element out of religion, without either seeking or finding any other substitute for the feelings to rest upon. Theism may be considered that definite heightened devotion to the one Supreme Being which the Middle Ages were not acquainted with. This mode of faith does not exclude Christianity, and can either ally itself with the Christian doctrines of sin, redemption, and immortality, or else exist and flourish without them.

Sometimes this belief presents itself with childish *naïveté* and even with a half-pagan air, God appearing as the almighty fulfiller of human wishes. Agnolo Pandolfini tells us how, after his wedding, he shut himself in with his wife, and knelt down before the family altar with the picture of the Madonna, and prayed, not to her, but to God, that He would vouchsafe to them the right use of their property, a long life in joy and unity with one another, and many male descendants: 'For myself I prayed for wealth, honour, and friends; for her blamelessness, honesty, and that she might be a good housekeeper.' When the language used has a strong antique flavour, it is not always easy to keep apart the pagan style and the theistic belief.

This temper sometimes manifests itself in times of misfortune with a striking sincerity. Some addresses to God are left us from the latter period of Firenzuola, when for years he lay ill of fever, in which, though he expressly declares himself a believing Christian, he shows that his religious consciousness is essentially theistic. His sufferings seem to him neither as the punishment of sin, nor as preparation for a higher world; they are an affair between him and God only, who has put the strong love of life between man and his despair. 'I curse, but only curse Nature, since Thy greatness forbids me to utter Thy name. . . . Give me death, Lord, I beseech Thee, give it me now!'

In these utterances and the like, it would be vain to look for a conscious and consistent Theism; the speakers partly believed themselves to be still Christians, and for various other reasons respected the existing doctrines of the Church. But at the time of the Reformation, when men were driven to come to a distinct conclusion on such points, this mode of thought was accepted with a fuller consciousness; a number of the Italian Protestants came forward as Anti-Trinitarians and Socinians, and even as exiles in distant countries made the memorable attempt to found a church on these principles. From the foregoing exposition it will be clear that, apart from humanistic rationalism, other spirits were at work in this field.

One chief centre of theistic modes of thought lay in the Platonic Academy at Florence, and especially in Lorenzo il Magnifico himself. The theoretical works and even the letters of these men show us only half their nature. It is true that Lorenzo, from his youth till he died, expressed himself dogmatically as a Christian, and that Pico was drawn by Savonarola's influence to accept the point of view of a monkish ascetic. But in the hymns of Lorenzo, which we are tempted to regard as the highest product of the spirit of this school, an unreserved Theism is set forth—a Theism which strives to treat the world as a great moral and physical Cosmos. While the men of the Middle Ages look on the world as a vale of tears, which Pope and Emperor are set to guard against the coming of Antichrist; while the fatalists of the Renaissance oscillate between seasons of overflowing energy and seasons of superstition or of stupid resignation, here, in this circle of chosen spirits, the doctrine is upheld that the visible world was created by God in love, that it is the copy of a pattern pre-existing in Him, and that He will ever remain its eternal mover and restorer. The soul of man can by recognizing God draw Him into its narrow boundaries, but also by love of Him expand itself into the Infinite—and this is blessedness on earth.

Echoes of mediæval mysticism here flow into one current with Platonic doctrines and with a characteristically modern spirit. One of the most precious fruits of the knowledge of the world and of man here comes to maturity, on whose account alone the Italian Renaissance must be called the leader of modern ages.

THE CIVILIZATION OF THE RENAISSANCE IN PICTURES

SELECTED AND EXPLAINED BY
LUDWIG GOLDSCHEIDER

I. A CONDOTTIERE. VERROCCHIO'S COLLEONE MONUMENT IN VENICE

VIEW OF A MEDIAEVAL ITALIAN TOWN, BY AMBROGIO LORENZETTI

3. THE PIAZZA DELLA SIGNORIA IN FLORENCE, 1498.
BY AN UNKNOWN TUSCAN PAINTER

4. VIEW OF FLORENCE, 1530. BY GIORGIO VASARI

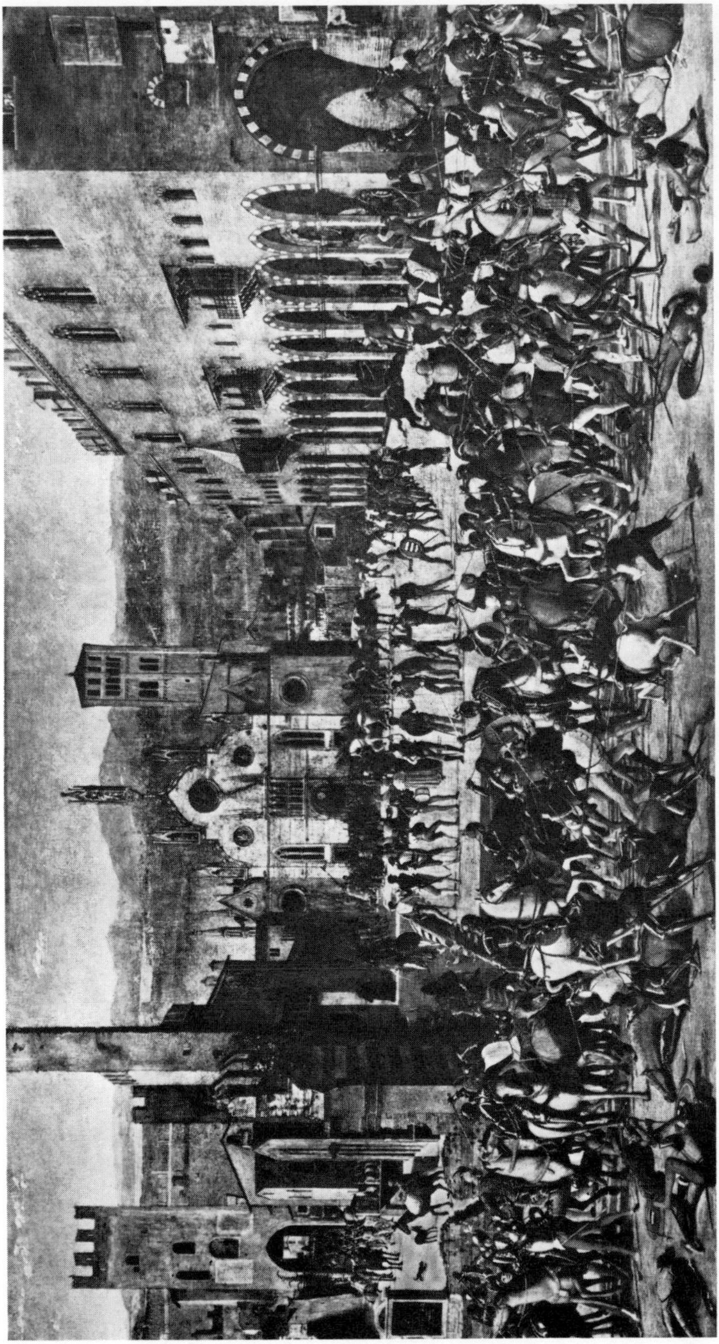

5. THE PIAZZA SORDELLO IN MANTUA, 1494. BY DOMENICO MORONE

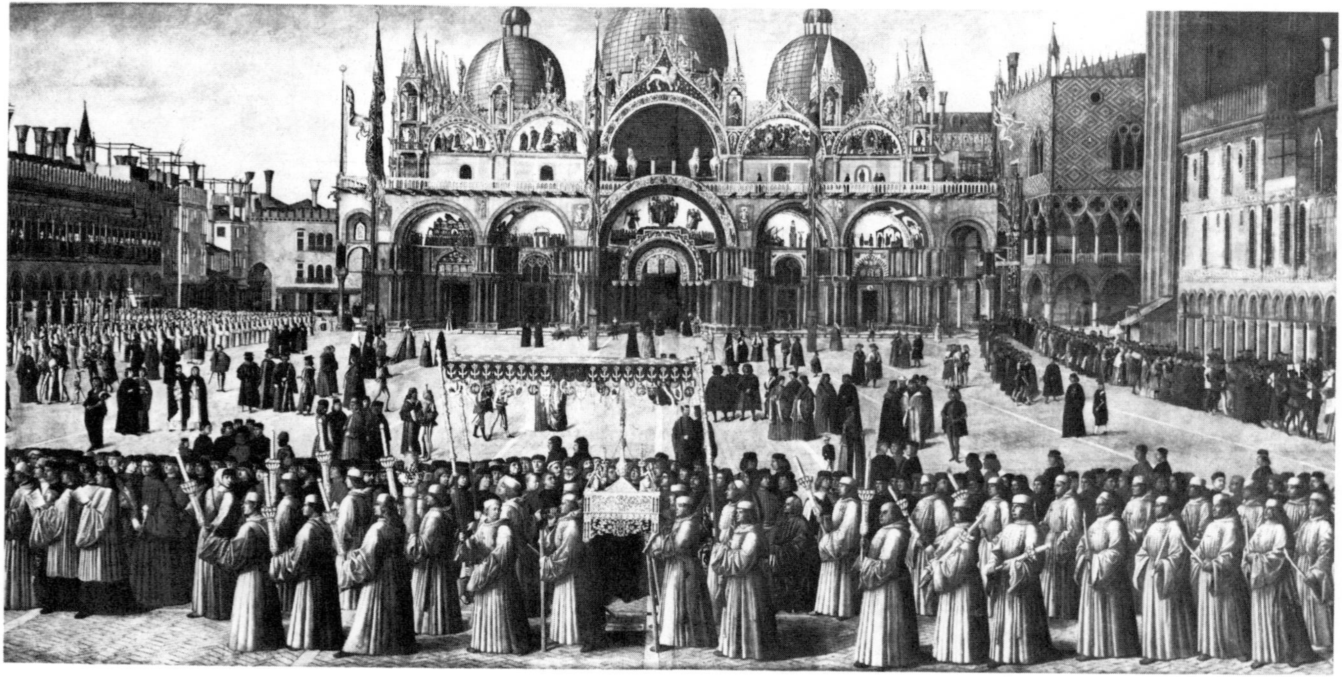

6. A PROCESSION IN FRONT OF ST. MARK'S BASILICA IN VENICE, 1496. BY GENTILE BELLINI

7. A RENAISSANCE PALACE IN VENICE. THE CA D'ORO, 1436

8. THE TOWN HALL OF SIENA

9. A CORNER OF THE DUCAL PALACE AND BELL TOWER IN VENICE

10. PALAZZO DI PARTE GUELFA, FLORENCE

11. THE ENTRANCE OF THE CASINO MEDICEO IN FLORENCE, 1576

12. THE ENTRANCE OF THE CERTOSA DI PAVIA, MILAN

13. THE TRIUMPHAL ARCH OF ALFONSO OF ARAGON, NAPLES

14. THE COURTYARD OF A RENAISSANCE PALACE.
PALAZZO FARNESE IN ROME, BY MICHELANGELO

15. RENAISSANCE DECORATION OF A GOTHIC CHURCH.
THE CHOIR OF THE FRARI CHURCH IN VENICE

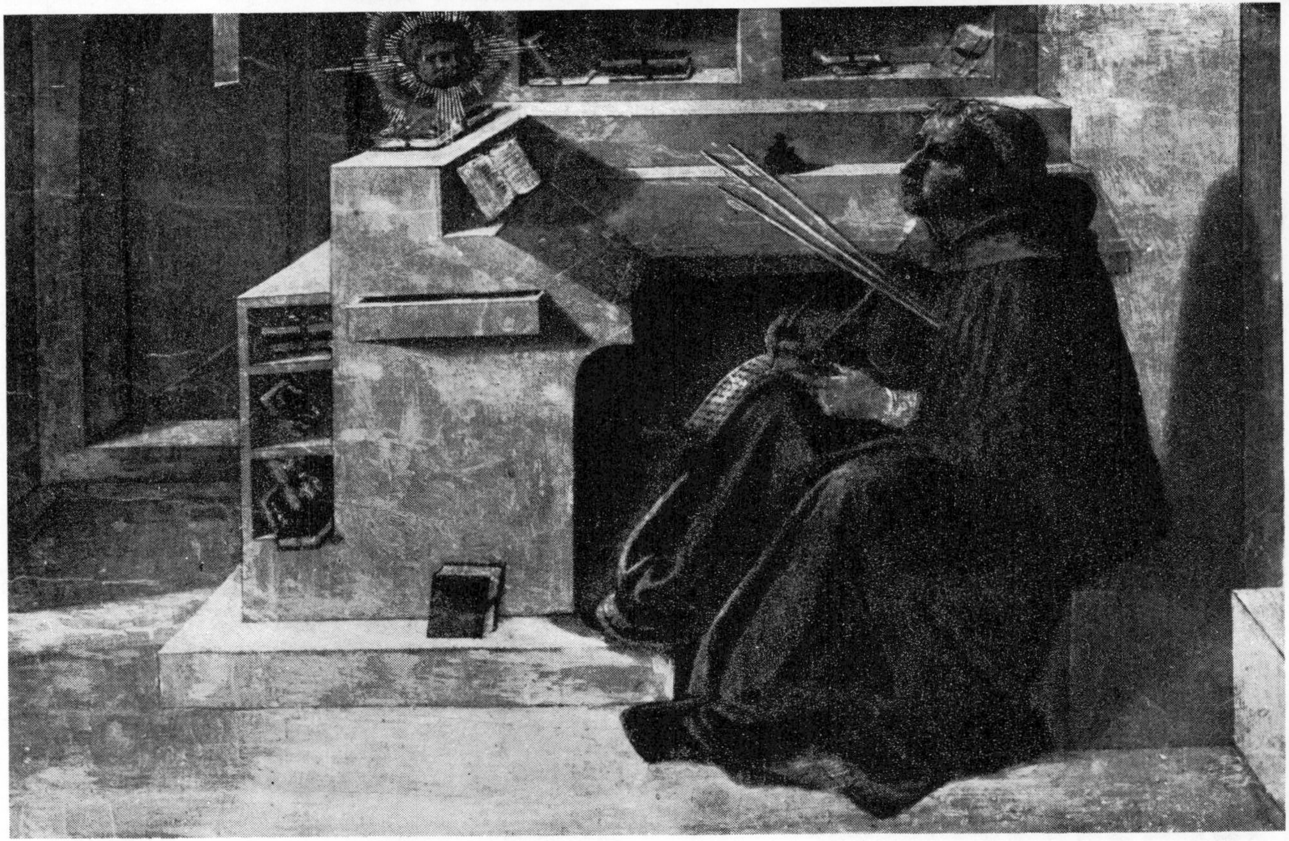

17. WRITING DESK OF A SCHOLAR, 1438. 'ST. AUGUSTINE IN HIS STUDY' BY FILIPPO LIPPI

18. A BEDROOM IN FERRARA, *c.* 1530. 'VISION OF A SAINT', BY BATTISTA DOSSI

19. A VENETIAN BEDROOM, *c.* 1570. ATTRIBUTED TO PARIS BORDONE

20. RENAISSANCE FURNITURE, 16TH CENTURY. (*a*) A FLORENTINE 'CASSAPANCA' OR SETTEE. (*b*) A SIENESE 'CASSONE' OR MARRIAGE COFFER. (*c*) A FLORENTINE 'CASSONE'

21. FLORENTINE CABINET, USED AS STRONG-BOX, 16TH CENTURY

22. A MAJOLICA PLATE
FROM A SERVICE MADE FOR ISABELLA D'ESTE

23. A MANTELPIECE, *c.* 1520. BY BENEDETTO ROVEZZANO

24. IVORY COMBS, 15TH AND 16TH CENTURY

25. SURGICAL INSTRUMENTS, 16TH CENTURY

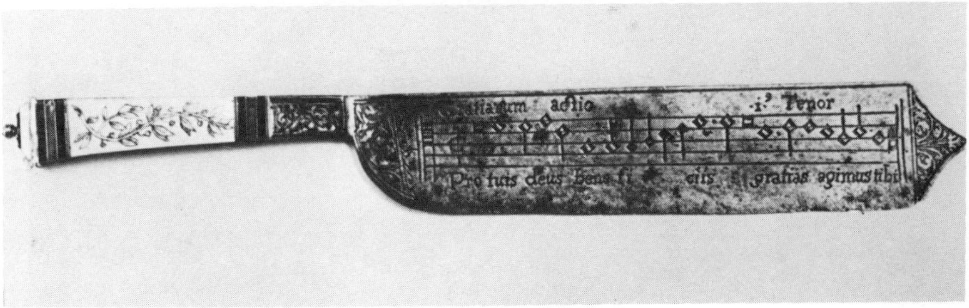

26. TABLE-KNIFE WITH A HANDLE OF IVORY AND EBONY, 16TH CENTURY

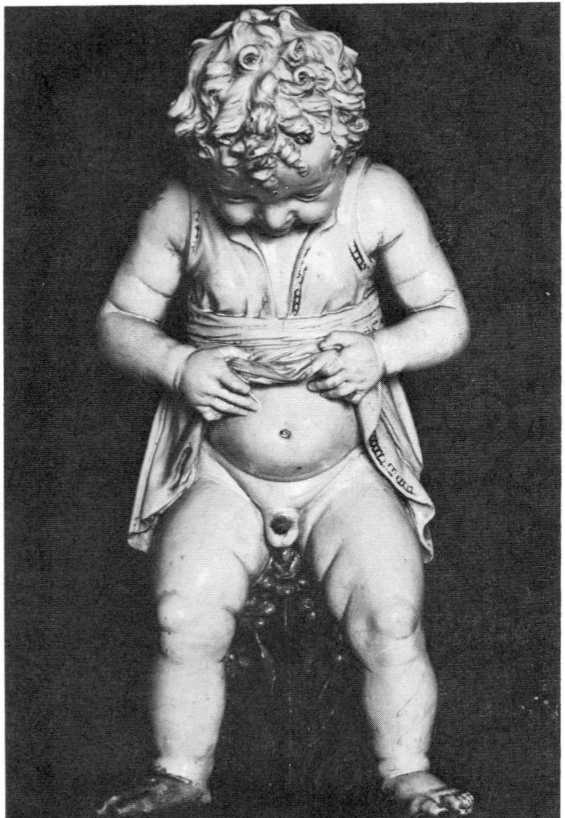

27. TWO SMALL RENAISSANCE FOUNTAINS. (*a*) POLYCHROME TERRACOTTA, BY ANDREA DELLA ROBBIA. (*b*) BRONZE, BY ANDREA DEL VERROCCHIO

28. TWO FAIENCE POTS FROM A PHARMACY, 15TH CENTURY

29. LARGE BRONZE CANDELABRUM
BY ANDREA RICCIO, 1516

30. TWO BRONZE INKSTANDS. BY ANDREA RICCIO

31. SILVER CROZIER. MADE FOR POPE CLEMENT VII

32. BENVENUTO CELLINI'S GOLDEN SALT-CELLAR.
MADE FOR KING FRANCIS I, 1543

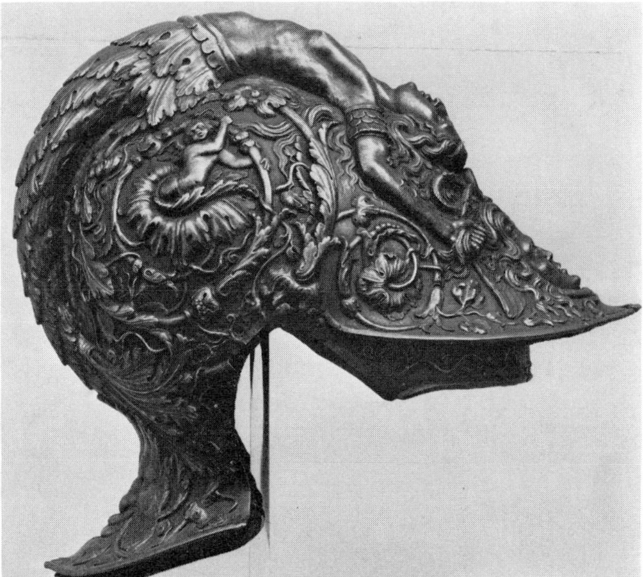

33. CASQUE.
MADE BY FILIPPO NEGROLI OF MILAN, PROBABLY FOR FRANCIS I, 1543

34. THE ERECTION OF AN EARLY RENAISSANCE CHURCH:
THE TEMPIO MALATESTIANO IN RIMINI.
DRAWING BY GIOVANNI DI BARTOLO BETTINI, *c.* 1463

35 A LOCKSMITH (OR GOLDSMITH?) AND HIS APPRENTICE ENGRAVING

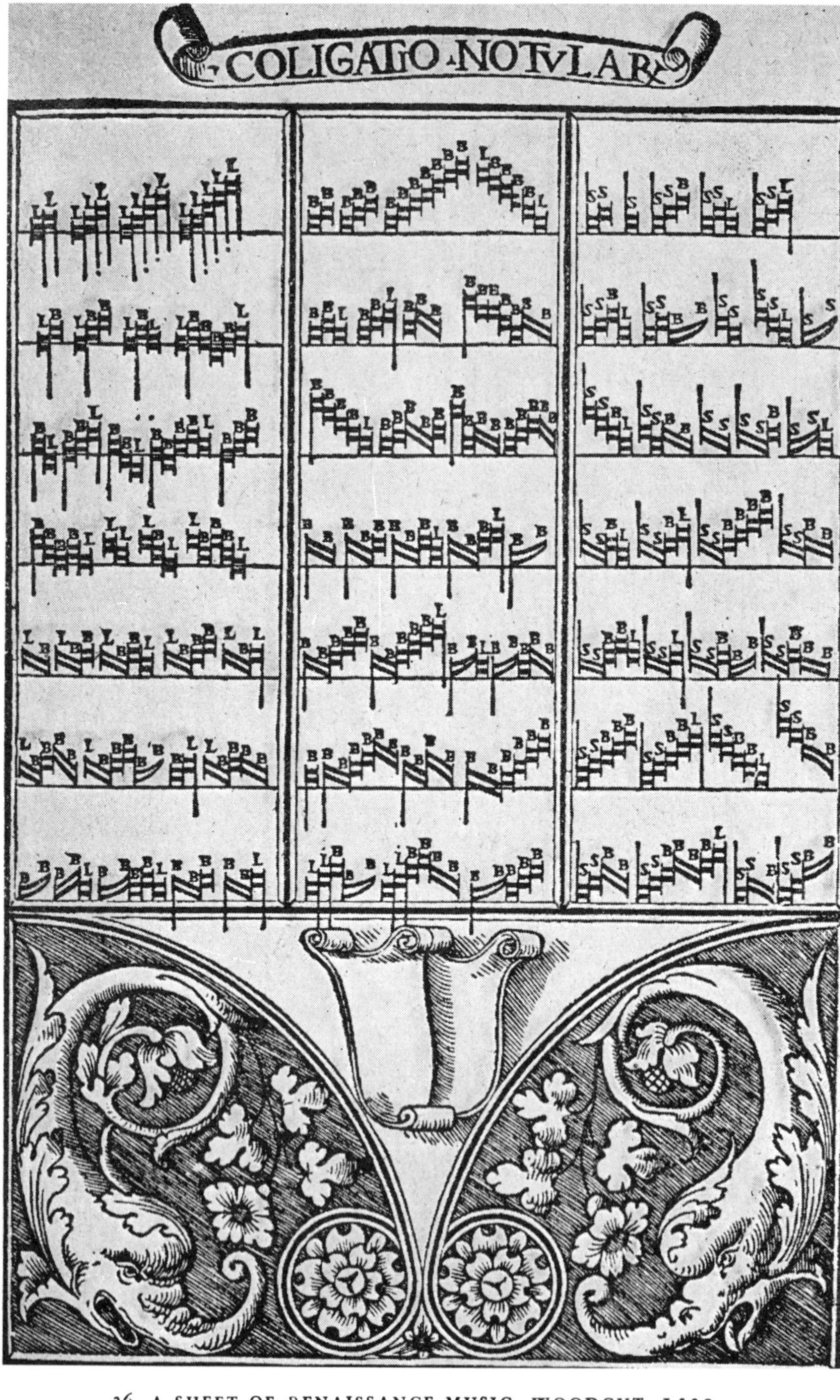

36. A SHEET OF RENAISSANCE MUSIC. WOODCUT, 1539

INTER
mortaliũ res arduã
quidem ac difficiles
unum illud mihi se
per difficillimũ est ui
sum: Reuerende ac p
stantissime uir Ioan
nes Episcope Varadi
ne Serenissimi & semper Augusti Mat
thię Pannonię Regis eiusq Illustrissimi
filij ducis Ioannis hoc loco uices gerẽs: Ma
gnifici ac splendidissimi oratores: Illustris
sime princeps mi Ioannes Galeaci: Reue
rendissime ecclesię Romanę Antistes Pri
cepsq inclyte Ascani maria: & tu Bona i
ter claras mulieres clarissima: Illud inquã
mihi semper difficillimũ est uisũ, cũ quis
ĩfrequẽti pręstantissimorũ uirorũ cõspe
ctu alijs omnibus silentibus de rebus
magnis ac pręclaris uerba esset facturus
Quod cũ ego quandoq re ipsa didicerĩ
quippe qui iussu tuo dux mi ornatissĩe

37. PAGE OF A BOOK, DESIGNED FOR MATTHIAS CORVINUS, KING OF HUNGARY. BY AN UNKNOWN MILANESE MINIATURIST

38. PERFORMANCE OF A COMEDY BY PLAUTUS. WOODCUT, 1511

39. PERFORMANCE OF A MIRACLE-PLAY, EARLY 16TH CENTURY. 'ASSUMPTION OF THE VIRGIN', BY GIROLAMO DA VICENZA

40. TWO ARCHITECTURAL VIEWS, DESIGNED FOR THE THEATRE OR IMITATING STAGE-SETTINGS.

41. THE STAGE OF THE TEATRO OLIMPICO AT VICENZA. CONSTRUCTED BY ANDREA PALLADIO, 1579

42. THE HUMANIST: PORTRAIT OF PETRARCH.
BY ANDREA DEL CASTAGNO

43. THE CONDOTTIERE: FARINATA DEGLI UBERTI. BY ANDREA DEL CASTAGNO

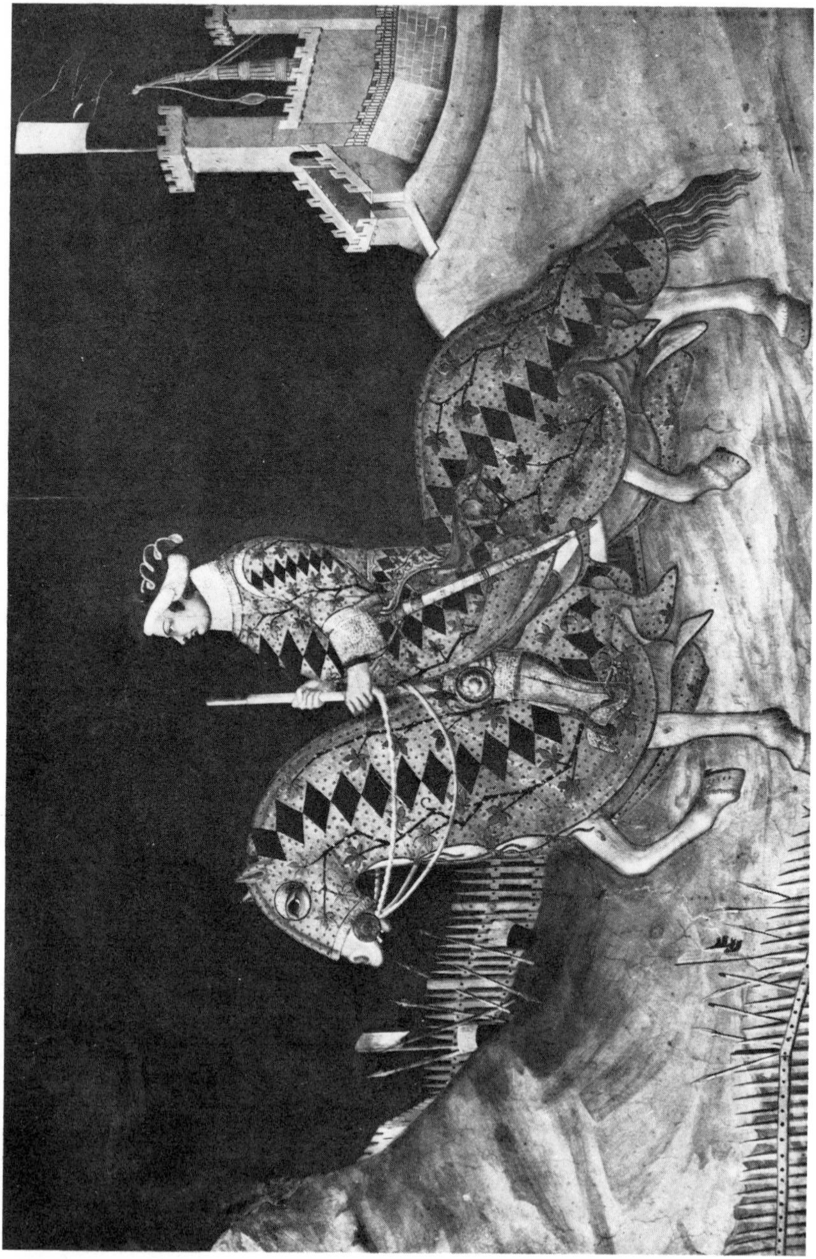

44. A KNIGHT IN FRONT OF HIS CASTLE. BY SIMONE MARTINI, 1328

45. FLORENTINE NOBLEMEN IN A STREET NEAR THE CATHEDRAL.
BY AN UNKNOWN FLORENTINE PAINTER, *c.* 1440

46. VENETIAN YOUTH. BRONZE, ATTRIBUTED TO ANTONIO RIZZO

47. YOUNG FLORENTINE LADY. TERRACOTTA, BY LUCA DELLA ROBBIA

48. A WIDOW. TERRACOTTA, PERHAPS BY ANTONIO POLLAIUOLO

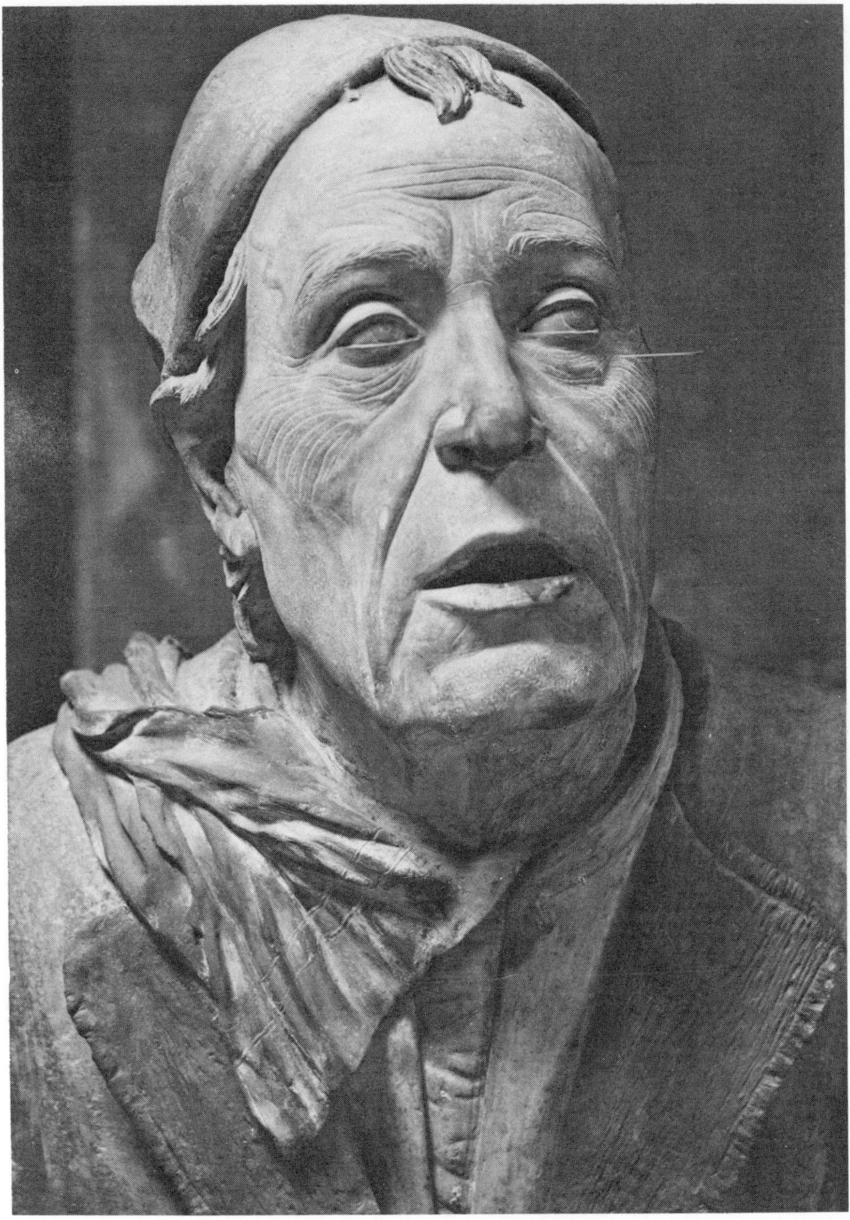

49. NATURALISTIC PORTRAIT OF AN OLD MAN.
POLYCHROME CLAY, BY GUIDO MAZZONI, 1490

50. A GENTLEWOMAN WITH A HORN-SHAPED HEAD-DRESS.
BY LORENTINO D'AREZZO

51. A YOUNG FLORENTINE LADY OF FASHION. BY PAOLO UCCELLO

52. FLORENTINE LADY IN A BROCADE DRESS
BY DOMENICO GHIRLANDAIO

53. YOUNG LADY DRESSED IN MANY-COLOURED BROCADE. ATTRIBUTED TO ANTONIO POLLAIUOLO

54. DEATH MASK OF LORENZO DE' MEDICI, CALLED IL MAGNIFICO. PLASTER, CAST IN 1492

55. LORENZO DE' MEDICI.
POLYCHROME STUCCO, ATTRIBUTED TO ORSINO

56. CLEMENT VII AS A CARDINAL. BY SEBASTIANO DEL PIOMBO

57. CHRISTOPHER COLUMBUS. BY SEBASTIANO DEL PIOMBO, 1519

58. POPE ALEXANDER VI.
MARBLE, ATTRIBUTED TO PASQUALE DA CARAVAGGIO

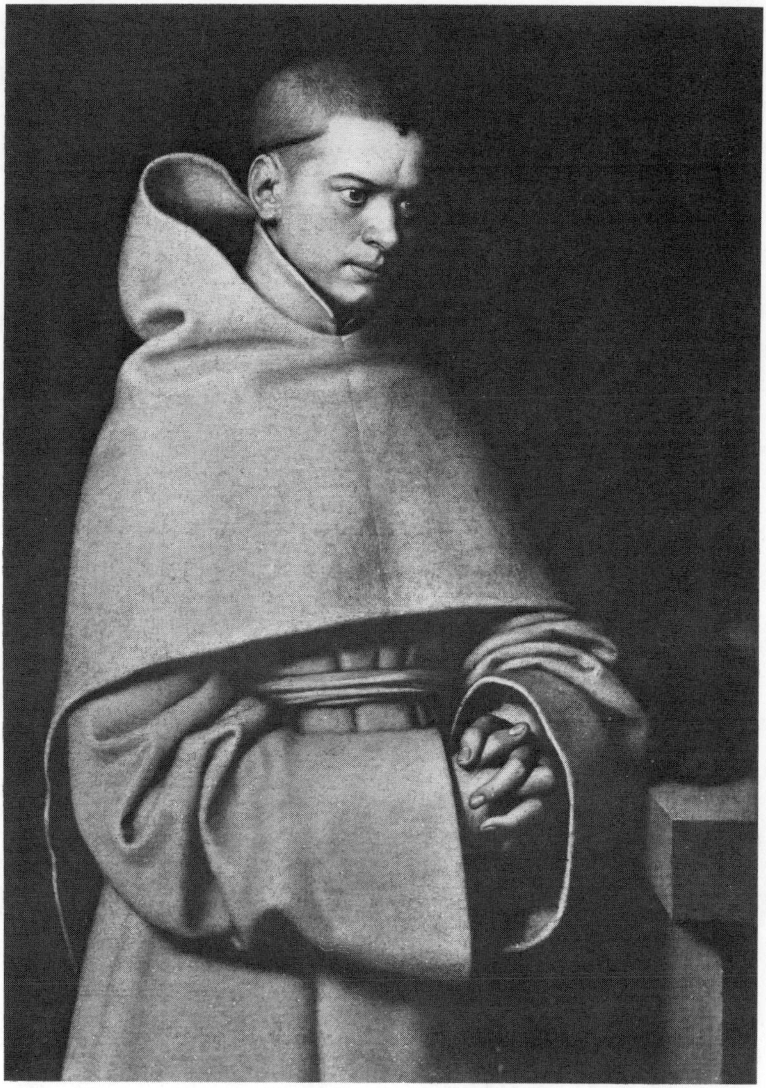

59. PORTRAIT OF A YOUNG MONK. BY SOFONISBA ANGUISSOLA

60. THE DOGE OF VENICE: PORTRAIT OF LEONARDO LOREDANO. ATTRIBUTED TO GENTILE BELLINI

61. A FLORENTINE GENERAL: PORTRAIT OF MALATESTA BAGLIONE OF PERUGIA. BY PARMIGIANINO

62. PORTRAIT OF A SCHOLAR AT HIS WRITING-DESK
BY FRANCIABIGIO, 1522

63. TWO ARCHITECTS AT WORK.
BY AN UNKNOWN ITALIAN PAINTER, 1555

64. THE YOUNG MUSICIAN.
BY AN UNKNOWN PAINTER OF THE SCHOOL OF PARMA

65. A SCULPTOR. BY ANDREA DEL SARTO

66. THE DUCHESS OF URBINO. BY FEDERICO BAROCCI

67. PORTRAIT OF A FLORENTINE GENTLEMAN, DRESSED AFTER THE SPANISH FASHION. ATTRIBUTED TO PONTORMO

68. PORTRAIT OF A WOMAN,
CALLED 'THE NURSE OF THE MEDICI CHILDREN'. BY PARIS BORDONE

69. PORTRAIT OF A YOUNG ROMAN BOURGEOIS WOMAN.
BY SEBASTIANO DEL PIOMBO, 1512

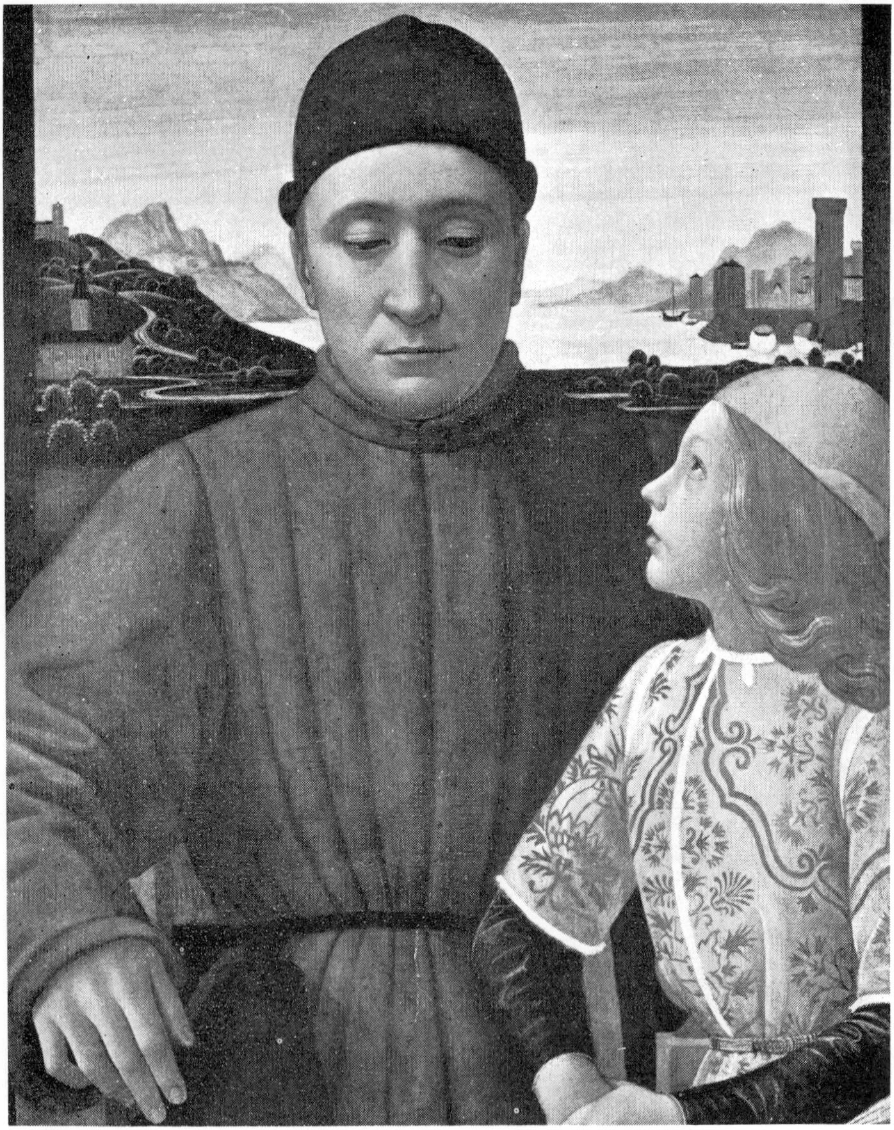

70. A FLORENTINE GENTLEMAN AND HIS GRANDSON.
PORTRAIT OF FRANCESCO SASSETTI, BY DOMENICO GHIRLANDAIO

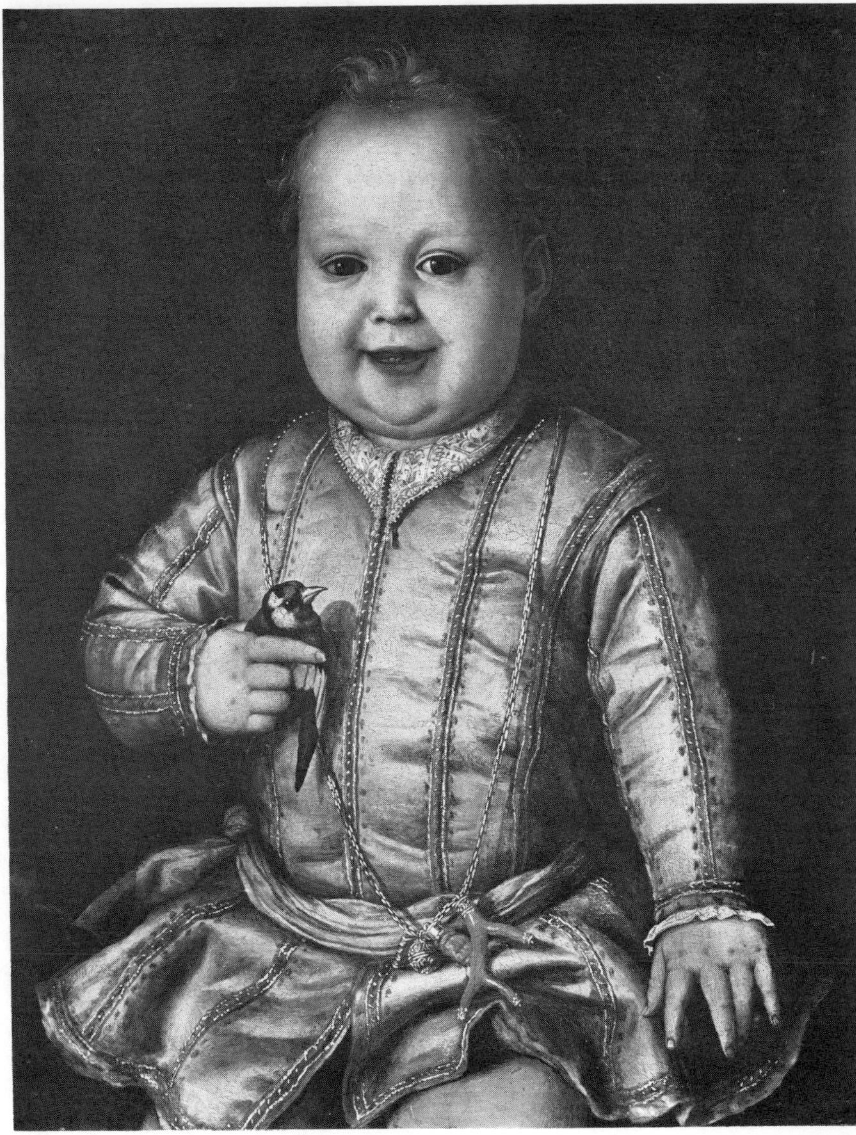

71. A LITTLE BOY IN HUNTING HABIT.
PORTRAIT OF DON GARCIA DE' MEDICI, BY BRONZINO

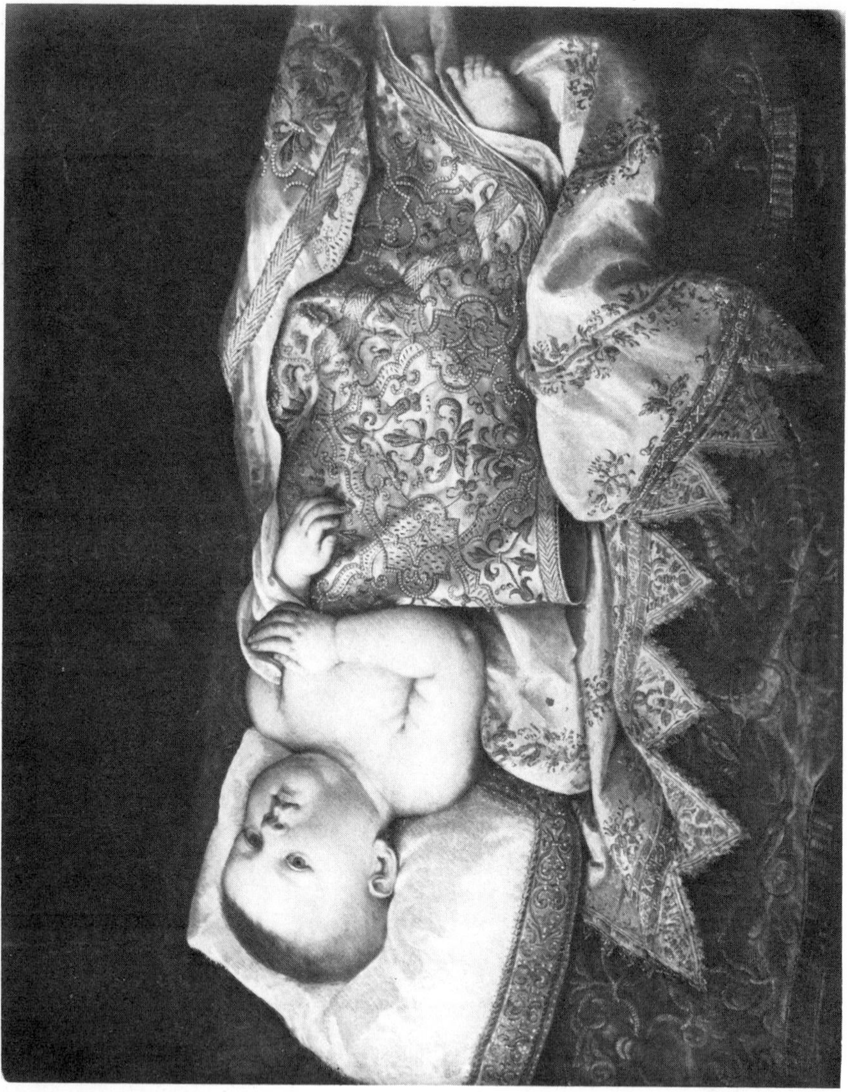

72. A BABY IN HIS BED. PORTRAIT OF LEOPOLDO DE' MEDICI, BY TIBERIO TITI

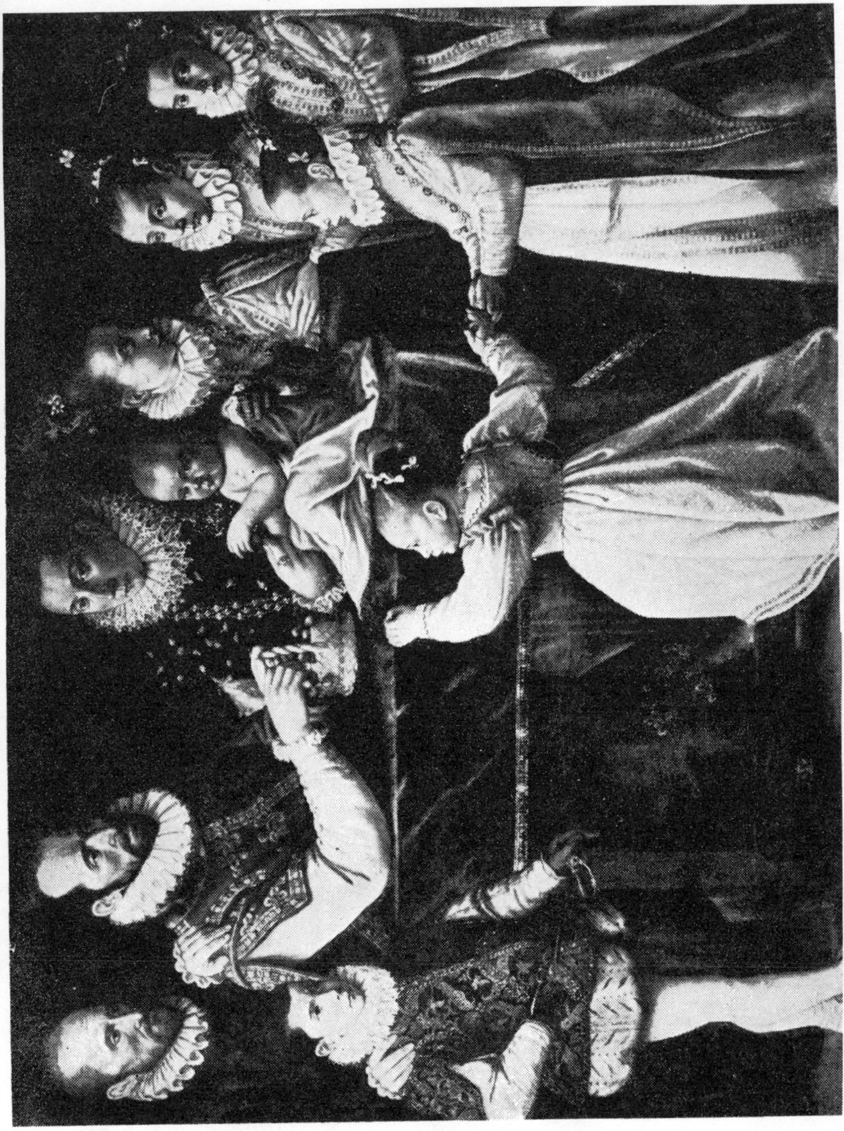

73. PORTRAIT OF A ROMAN FAMILY, 1581. THE COLONNA FAMILY,
BY SCIPIONE PULZONE

74. MARQUIS LODOVICO GONZAGA AND HIS FAMILY.
BY ANDREA MANTEGNA

TEMPLA DOMVM EXPOSITIS: VICOS FORA MOENIA PONTES:
VIRGINEAM TRIVII QVOD REPARARIS AQVAM.
PRISCA LICET NAVTIS STATVAS DARE COMMODA PORTVS:
ET VATICANVM CINGERE SIXTE IVGVM:
PLVS TAMEN VRBS DEBET: NAM QVAE SQVALORE LATEBAT:
CERNITVR IN CELEBRI BIBLIOTHECA LOCO.

75. POPE SIXTUS IV AND HIS COURT. BY MELOZZO DA FORLI

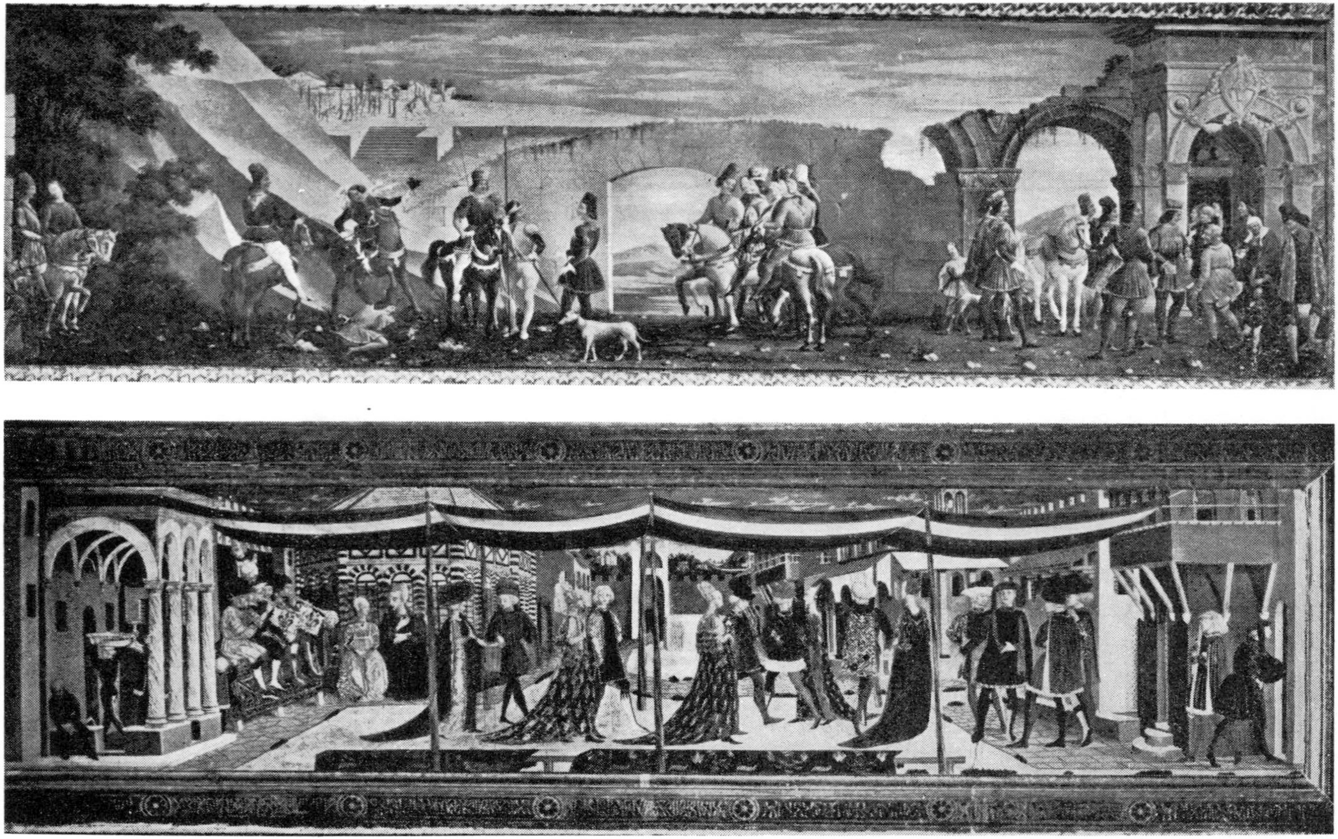

76. SCENES FROM THE LIFE OF THE FLORENTINE ARISTOCRACY. FRONT PANELS FROM TWO CASSONI, FIFTEENTH CENTURY. (*a*) A HUNTING PARTY. (*b*) THE ADIMARI NUPTIALS, 1420

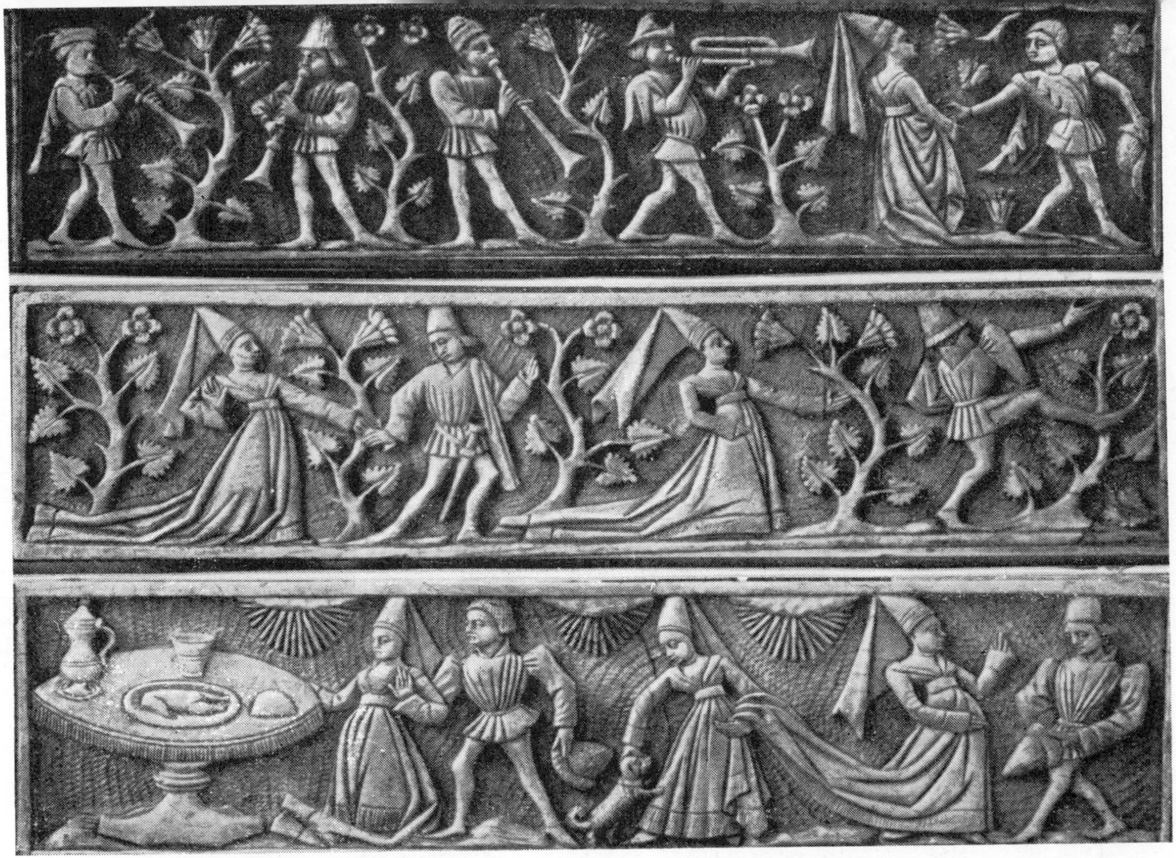

77. THE DANCE. DETAILS FROM A FLORENTINE IVORY CHESSBOARD

78. TWO VENETIAN COURTESANS ON A BALCONY.
BY VITTORE CARPACCIO

79. PORTRAIT OF A COURTESAN. BY BARTOLOMMEO VENETO

80. WOMEN BATHING. 'THE LETTER OF URIAH', BY FRANCIABIGIO, 1523

81. A FEAST AT VENICE. 'THE MARRIAGE AT CANA', BY PAOLO VERONESE, 1563

83–84. PEASANT'S LIFE IN THE FIFTEENTH CENTURY. (*a*) A PEASANT REAPING CORN. POLYCHROME TERRACOTTA, BY LUCA DELLA ROBBIA. (*b*) A VINTAGER, ATTRIBUTED TO FRANCESCO DEL COSSA

85. YOUNG FLORENTINES PLAYING 'CIVETTINO'.
BY AN UNKNOWN TUSCAN PAINTER, *c.* 1430

86. FAMILY LIFE IN THE SIXTEENTH CENTURY. MIDDLE-PIECE OF A TAPESTRY, WOVEN IN FLANDERS AFTER A FLORENTINE CARTOON

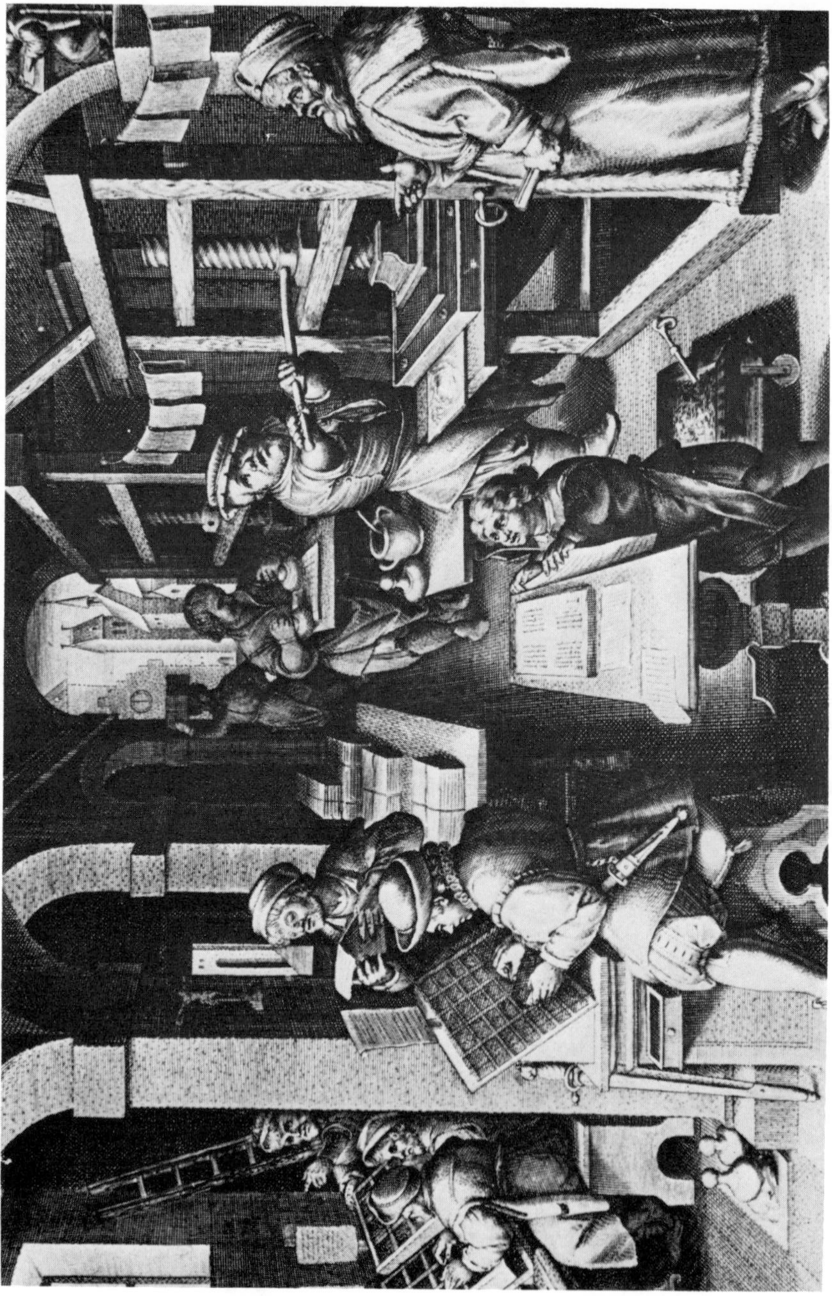

87. FLORENTINE PRINTING-OFFICE, *c.* 1570.

88. A SUGAR FACTORY AT FLORENCE, *c.* 1570.
ETCHING AFTER A DRAWING BY GIOVANNI STRADANO

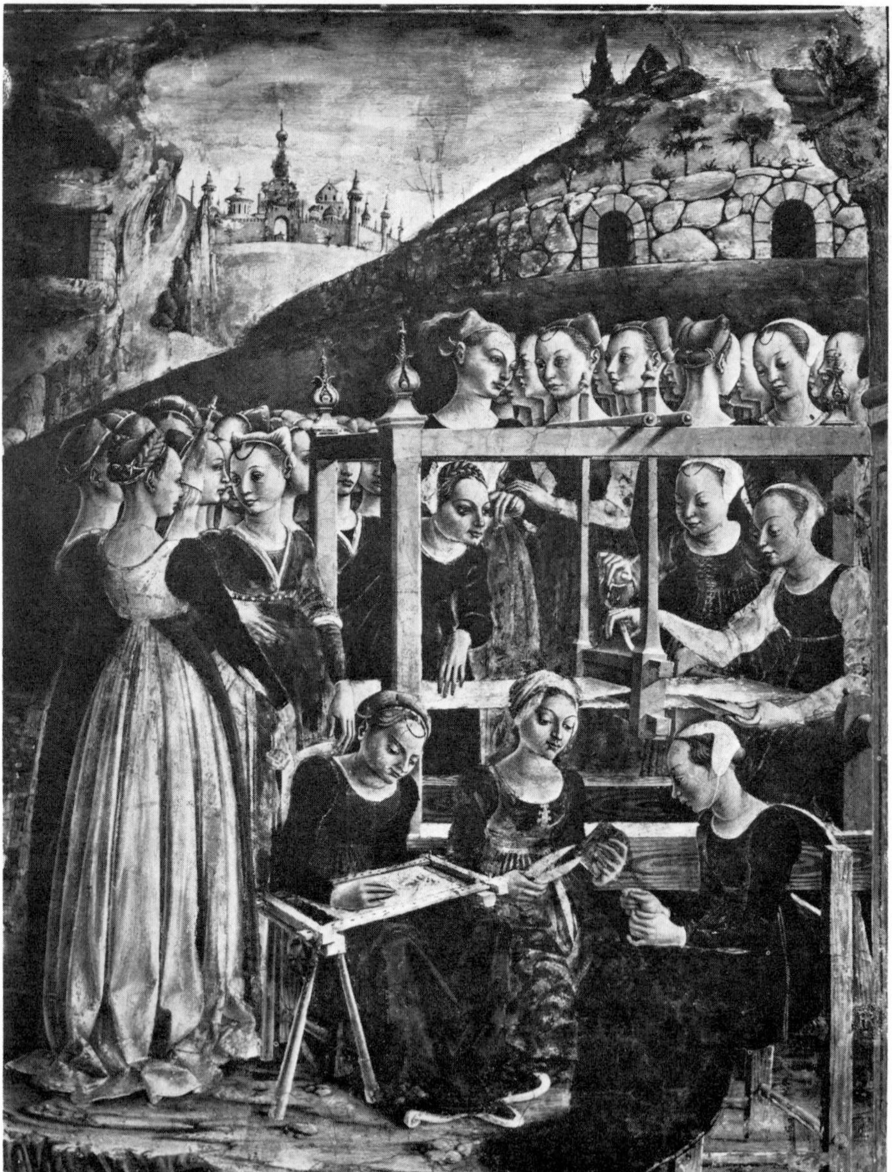

89. WOMEN WEAVING AND EMBROIDERING.
BY FRANCESCO COSSA, 1470

90. THE LABORATORY OF A CHEMIST. BY GIOVANNI STRADANO, 1570

92. A UNIVERSITY LECTURE. BY LAURENTIUS VOLTALINA

93. BRICKLAYER, STONEMASON, ARCHITECT, SCULPTOR. MARBLE RELIEF BY NANNI DI BANCO

94. A VENETIAN EMBASSY AT CAIRO, 1512.
BY A FOLLOWER OF GENTILE BELLINI, PROBABLY NICCOLÒ MANSUETI

95. RECEPTION OF AN ENGLISH EMBASSY IN VENICE. 'THE ARRIVAL OF THE AMBASSADORS AT THE COURT OF KING MAURUS', BY VITTORE CARPACCIO

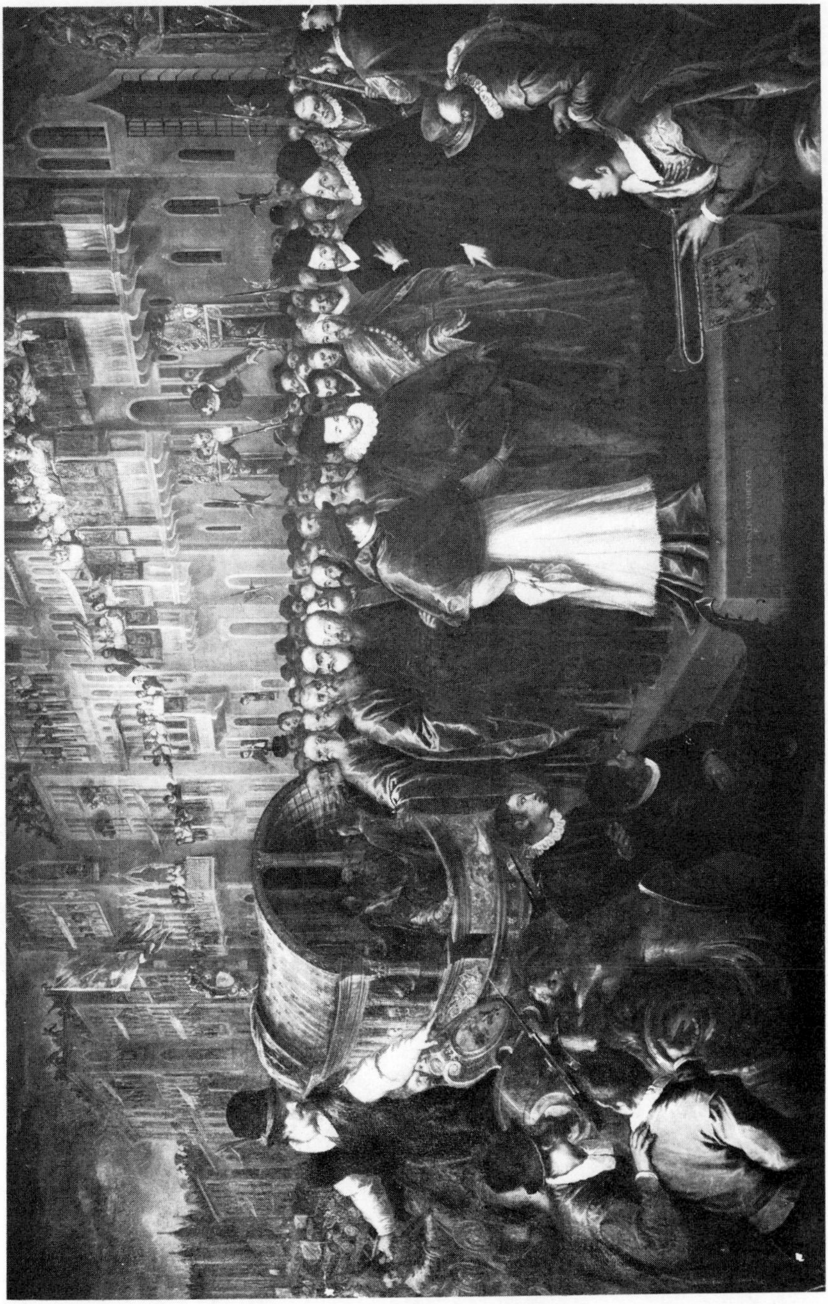

96. RECEPTION OF HENRY III, KING OF POLAND AND FRANCE, IN VENICE, 1574.
BY PALMA GIOVANE

97. CARICATURE: AN UGLY OLD MAN.
BY LEONARDO DA VINCI

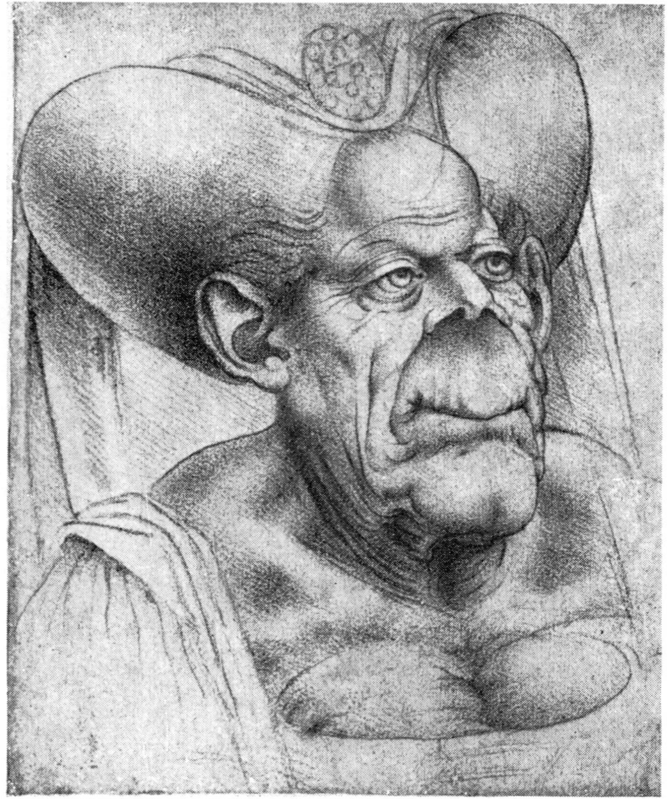

98. CARICATURE: BUST OF A HIDEOUS OLD WOMAN.
BY A PUPIL OF LEONARDO

99. CARICATURE OF TIPPLERS AND MUSICIANS. BY AN UNKNOWN VENETIAN PAINTER
c. 1590

100. CARICATURE OF THE SINGER RABBATIN DE GRIFFI AND HIS WIFE SPILLA POMINA. BY ANNIBALE CARRACCI

NOTES ON THE PLATES

1. ANDREA DEL VERROCCHIO: COLLEONE MONUMENT. VENICE, IN FRONT OF THE CHURCH OF SAN GIOVANNI E PAOLO

Verrocchio began his work on this monument in Florence when Leonardo was still an assistant in his workshop; the model was finished in 1481, and thereafter Verrocchio lived permanently in Venice. He died there in 1488 of the effects of a cold caught in casting the bronze horse. The monument was finished by Alessandro Leopardi in 1496.

The Renaissance, in imitating antique hero worship, also imitated the antique equestrian monuments. Curiously enough, the two most beautiful equestrian monuments of the Renaissance—and perhaps the most beautiful of all periods—Donatello's Gattamelata and Verrocchio's Colleone, are not dedicated to kings or princes, but to unscrupulous *condottieri*, or captains of mercenaries.

2. AMBROGIO LORENZETTI: VIEW OF A MEDLÆVAL ITALIAN TOWN, *c.* 1340. SIENA, ACADEMY

The town is situated on a lake; many of the houses are built as small fortresses with high turrets; on the right is a castle surrounded by walls. Many Italian towns preserved their mediæval appearance well into the noon of the Renaissance; others, especially the richer ones, were constantly being rebuilt, thus obliterating every trace of Gothic style.

3. UNKNOWN TUSCAN PAINTER: THE PIAZZA DELLA SIGNORIA. FLORENCE, MUSEUM OF SAN MARCO

The picture shows the square between the Town Hall of Florence and the Cathedral, with the scene of the burning of Savonarola in 1498. Another copy of this painting is in the Palazzo Corsini in Florence, which is thought to be the original.

The cells 12–14 on the upper floor of the Convent of San Marco were once Savonarola's abode; this picture is kept in cell 12. (The next cell is reproduced as plate 16.)

4. GIORGIO VASARI: PANORAMA OF FLORENCE, WITH THE CAMP OF THE PRINCE OF ORANGE IN THE SIEGE OF 1529–30. FRESCO IN THE PALAZZO VECCHIO AT FLORENCE, SALA DI CLEMENTE VII

Charles V besieged and occupied Florence in 1530, when he restored the Medici; Michelangelo helped as a fortification engineer in defending his native town.

5. DOMENICO MORONE: THE BATTLE OF THE BONACOLSI AND GONZAGA. 1494. MANTUA, CASTELLO DI CORTE

The painting is actually in the Museo Patrio, which occupies the ground floor of the Castello. The picture shows the centre of Mantua at the end of the fifteenth century, the time of Isabella d'Este; note the old Cathedral and the Gothic palaces of the Bonacolsi, the predecessors of the Gonzaga.

6. GENTILE BELLINI: THE CORPUS CHRISTI PROCESSION IN VENICE. 1496. VENICE, ACADEMY

The Corpus Christi Procession, the most solemn religious festival in Venice, was celebrated on the 3rd of June in every year. The Doge and the Council of Ten, together with the most honoured guests, watched the procession from the Ducal Palace (at the right of the painting) and from the Library (on the left). The latter is of course the old building, used since 1468, and not the new one, finished by Jacopo Sansovino in 1553.

The main front of St. Mark's basilica, in the centre of the background, is depicted here as it appeared at the end of the fifteenth century: the vaulted portals are still decorated with Byzantine mosaics, which were replaced by more modern work in Titian's time; the semicircular gable-heads were gilded, and so were the famous bronze horses above the main door. The buildings forming the right side of the Piazza were then in one line with the Campanile. The Doge and his suite are just leaving through the 'Porta della Carta'. The foreground is filled by white-robed ecclesiastics, carrying candles.

7. THE CÁ D'ORO IN VENICE

Built in 1427–36, at the same time as the Doge's Palace. 'This is,' as Venturi said, 'a typical model of mature Venetian Gothic with *loggias*, adorned almost like sacred standards with crosses and *quadrilobi*, in rows over the Grand Canal as though waiting for the triumphal galleys of the Republic.'

8. THE PALAZZO COMMUNALE OF SIENA

The Palazzo Communale or Town Hall of Siena contained the official residence of the Podestá, the council chamber and the prison. The bell tower of the Palazzo was always thought to be one of the most beautiful in all Italy.

9. A CORNER OF THE PALAZZO DUCALE AND OF THE CAMPANILE IN VENICE

The Campanile is not old. It collapsed twice: first in an earthquake of 1512, and then in 1902. What we see now is a true *copy* of the old tower. The Doge's Palace is an early Renaissance building; it consists of a long balcony over an arcade, and a heavy two-storied superstructure. The earliest part of the Palazzo Ducale dates from the first half of the fourteenth century; the west wing was finished in 1438.

10. PALAZZO DI PARTE GUELFA, FLORENCE

This court house of the 'capitani' of the Guelph party, the enemies of the Ghibellines, was erected in the fourteenth century; it was extended by Brunelleschi in 1418–31, and rebuilt by Vasari, in 1555–57. It is now destroyed.

11. THE ENTRANCE TO THE CASINO MEDICEO IN FLORENCE

This small palace was built in 1576 by Bernardo Buontalenti on the site of the Medici Gardens, where once Lorenzo il Magnifico kept many of his art treasures, and where Leonardo da Vinci, Sansovino and Michelangelo, and many other artists began to study sculpture. Here Grand Duke Francesco I de' Medici resided.

12. THE ENTRANCE TO THE CERTOSA DI PAVIA (CARTHUSIAN CONVENT OR CHARTERHOUSE)

The Church, of which a part is seen through the doorway, was begun in 1451 by Guiniforte Solari; according to Burckhardt, it is the most beautiful of all Renaissance churches.

13. THE TRIUMPHAL ARCH OF ALFONSO OF ARAGON. CASTEL NUOVO, NAPLES

Erected about 1453–80 by Luciano and Francesco Laurana, Pietro di Martino, Paolo Romano, Domenico Gagini, and others. This triumphal arch is—together with Leone Battista Alberti's 'Tempio Malatestiano' (1446–55)—the first monument of the Renaissance which revived antique architectural forms.

14. COURTYARD OF THE PALAZZO FARNESE, ROME

Begun by Michelangelo in 1547 and finished by Vignola and Giacomo della Porta in 1589.

15. THE CHOIR OF THE CHURCH OF S. MARIA GLORIOSA DEI FRARI, VENICE

In the foreground are the marble screens by Andrea Vicentino, 1475; on the high altar is Titian's 'Assunta', 1516–18. The church was built from 1330 to 1417.

16. SAVONAROLA'S CELL IN THE MONASTERY OF SAN MARCO AT FLORENCE, *c.* 1490

This is Cell 13 of the Monastery, which is now converted into a museum. On the wall is hanging a portrait of Savonarola, painted by Fra Bartolommeo, who lived in the cloister from 1500 onwards and painted a large number of pictures for it. Another monk who lived and painted here was Fra Angelico, who covered the walls of the monastery with frescoes during a period of ten years.

17. FILIPPO LIPPI: ST. AUGUSTINE IN HIS STUDY, 1438. FLORENCE UFFIZI

This is a part of the predella of an altar-piece which Gherardo Barbadori ordered for his chapel in Santo Spirito, on March 8, 1437. The altar-painting is now in the Louvre, and the three parts of the predella are in the Uffizi.

18. BATTISTA DOSSI: VISION OF A SAINT, *c.* 1530. FLORENCE, UFFIZI

This small and very charming genre painting shows a room in a house at Ferrara. The large bed has a velvet cover and a velvet canopy. The straight-backed chair is apparently covered with the same material.

19. ATTRIBUTED TO PARIS BORDONE: VENETIAN NURSERY, *c.* 1570. HANOVER, KESTNER MUSEUM

20A. FLORENTINE 'CASSAPANCA', *c.* 1550. FLORENCE, MUSEO NAZIONALE

The Cassapanca, from which our sofa is derived, was a specifically Florentine piece of furniture, and in vogue between 1460 and 1560. It was used as a seat and therefore often covered with cushions; it also served as a chest to hold clothing and linen.

20B. CASSONE, WOOD, WITH PAINTED PANELS (SOLOMON AND THE QUEEN OF SHEBA). SIENESE, *c.* 1480. LONDON, VICTORIA AND ALBERT MUSEUM

20C. CASSONE, WOOD, CARVED AND GILDED. FLORENTINE, *c.* 1540. FLORENCE, MUSEO NAZIONALE

The Cassoni, or marriage coffers, are nearly always of the finest craftsmanship, and the best artists, including Botticelli, were not averse from decorating them with paintings. In the early fifteenth century they were merely intended to hold the linen and dresses of the bride; but later on they were filled with precious articles of adornment. The marriage coffer of Giovanna de'Medici, for instance, contained a hood embroidered with gold, a fringed Milanese hat, eight pairs of silk stockings, four pairs of gloves, a cape of silver and pearls, many robes with trains of brocade, velvet edged with fur, shoes embroidered with gold and trimmed with sable, a diamond necklace, and other jewellery.

21. CABINET, USED AS A STRONG BOX, CARVED WOOD. FLORENTINE, *c.* 1560. FLORENCE, MUSEO NAZIONALE

22. MAJOLICA PLATE FROM A SERVICE MADE FOR ISABELLA D'ESTE, DUCHESS OF FERRARA, BY NICOLA PELLIPARIO. LONDON, VICTORIA AND ALBERT MUSEUM

The story of Hippolytus and Phaedra is depicted on the plate: at the right Phaedra making advances to her stepson; at the left Hippolytus going a-hunting, and driving along the Troezenian shore in his chariot. In the middle Isabella's coat-of-arms, with a scroll of music underneath. On the barrier, in front, Isabella's motto is inscribed: '*Nec spe nec metu*'—neither by hope nor fear; and XXV.II, another of her devices, signifying that all the sects (*sette*) of her enemies were conquered (*vinte*).

23. A MANTELPIECE, MARBLE AND SANDSTONE, BY BENEDETTO ROVEZZANO, *c.* 1520. FROM THE PALAZZO BORGHERINI. FLORENCE, MUSEO NAZIONALE

There is a work by Rovezzano at St. Paul's in London: the sarcophagus which holds the body of Nelson. Rovezzano visited England in 1524, to execute the sepulchre for Wolsey. After the Cardinal's fall, Charles I wanted the sarcophagus for himself; but after his death Parliament took the bronze ornaments of the marble coffin and melted them down for warlike purposes. Since 1805, however, it stands in the crypt of St. Paul's as Nelson's sepulchre.

24. COMBS, IVORY, FIFTEENTH AND SIXTEENTH CENTURIES, FLORENCE, MUSEO NAZIONALE

The upper comb, still rather Gothic in style, shows a lady with a little dog, and a man holding her hand, with a fiddler behind them; a woman winding a garland, a man kneeling before her and offering her flowers, and two other love scenes.

On the other comb, which is of a later date, Venus is depicted sitting on a throne, and Cupid with a kerchief round his eyes, aiming his arrow towards a winged heart in the clouds.

25. SURGICAL INSTRUMENTS IN A LEATHER CASE, SIXTEENTH CENTURY. LONDON, BRITISH MUSEUM

26. TABLE KNIFE WITH A HANDLE OF IVORY AND EBONY, SIXTEENTH CENTURY. LONDON, VICTORIA AND ALBERT MUSEUM

Engraved on the blade is the tenor part of a 'grace', a song of thanksgiving before and after meals.

27. TWO SMALL RENAISSANCE FOUNTAINS:
(*a*) TERRACOTTA, PAINTED IN WHITE, GREEN, YELLOW AND BLUE, GILDED AND GLAZED. BY ANDREA DELLA ROBBIA, *c.* 1470. BERLIN MUSEUM. (*b*) BRONZE, EXECUTED BY ANDREA DEL VERROCCHIO FOR THE MEDICI VILLA AT CAREGGI. *c.* 1470. FLORENCE, PALAZZO VECCHIO

28. TWO FAIENCE POTS FROM A PHARMACY, DECORATED WITH PORTRAITS, FIFTEENTH CENTURY. PARIS, MUSÉE DE CLUNY

29. ANDREA RICCIO: LARGE CANDELABRUM. BRONZE, 1507–16. PADUA, IL SANTO (CHURCH OF ST. ANTHONY)

This famous candlestick, ten feet high, stands in the choir of the Church, at the left side of Donatello's Bronze Altar (Madonna and Child between St. Francis and Anthony and four other saints).

30. ANDREA RICCIO: TWO INKSTANDS, BRONZE, *c.* 1520:
(*a*) NEW YORK, METROPOLITAN MUSEUM. (*b*) LONDON, WALLACE COLLECTION

31. CROZIER (PASTORAL STAFF), SILVER, GILT METAL AND JEWELS. MADE FOR POPE CLEMENT VII, *c.* 1525. FLORENCE, MUSEO NAZIONALE

32. BENVENUTO CELLINI: SALT-CELLAR, MADE FOR FRANCIS I, 1539–43. VIENNA MUSEUM

Gold; cast, embossed, chased, parcel-gilt, enamelled. The two reclining figures represent the Sea and the Earth. Next to Neptune is a vessel for salt, shaped like a ship; next to Tellus a container for pepper in the form of a triumphal arch.

This is certainly the most famous of all salt-cellars ever produced, and Cellini tells at length in his autobiography how he worked on it for four years.

33. CASQUE, DATED 1543, MADE BY FILIPPO DE NEGROLI, A MILANESE ARMOURER PROBABLY FOR FRANCIS I. NEW YORK, METROPOLITAN MUSEUM

34. THE ERECTION OF AN EARLY RENAISSANCE CHURCH: THE TEMPIO MALATESTIANO IN RIMINI, DESIGNED BY LEONE BATTISTA ALBERTI. PEN DRAWING LIGHTLY COLOURED, BY GIOVANNI DI BARTOLO BETTINI, *c.* 1463. OXFORD, BODLEIAN LIBRARY

35. A LOCKSMITH (OR GOLDSMITH?) AND HIS APPRENTICE. ENGRAVING, *c.* 1467. LONDON, BRITISH MUSEUM

One of the 'Tarocchi' (Playing-cards) wrongly attributed to Baldini, who —according to Vasari—was Botticelli's collaborator. Most of the Tarocchi were not actually used for games, but formed a series of didactic prints; they were invented in Venice or Ferrara and show either allegorical figures (the spheres, the virtues, the arts), or depict the life of all classes and professions (Cf. Hind, Catalogue of Early Italian Engravings, 1910, pp. 217–235.)

36. A SHEET OF MUSIC. WOODCUT IN 'TOSCANELLO IN MUSICA DI MESSER PIERO AARON', PRINTED IN VENICE, 1539. FLORENCE, BIBLIOTECA NAZIONALE

37. PAGE OF A BOOK, DESIGNED FOR KING MATTHIAS CORVINUS, BY AN UNKNOWN MILANESE MINIATURIST, ABOUT 1485. VOLTERRA, GUARNACCI MUSEUM

38. PERFORMANCE OF A COMEDY BY PLAUTUS. WOODCUT IN THE PLAUTUS EDITION PRINTED IN VENICE, 1511. VIENNA, STATE LIBRARY

The view is taken from the stage, the actor in the centre is seen from the back; a second actor is about to enter through a curtained opening at the right; another curtained entrance at the left. There are two rows of spectators apparently, and two galleries.

39. ASSUMPTION OF THE VIRGIN, *c.* 1510. BY GIROLAMO DA VICENZA (SIGNED ON THE BALCONY). LONDON, NATIONAL GALLERY

Some compositions by Italian Renaissance painters and sculptors, e.g. Donatello's Padua reliefs—are inspired by contemporary religious performances. In this panel the scene is a courtyard enclosed by altar railings towards the front, and flanked by large buildings; on a balcony at the left, musicians. In the middle a canopied bier is erected, the scene for 'The Death of the Virgin'. Above, a golden glory is suspended, in which 'The Assumption of the Virgin' takes place. Similar theatrical machinery floating through the air is often mentioned by Venetian and Florentine writers: e.g. by Vasari in the Life of Brunelleschi.

40. LUCIANO LAURANA: TWO ARCHITECTURAL VIEWS, *c.* 1475. (*a*) BERLIN MUSEUM. (*b*) URBINO, DUCAL PALACE

Tempera paintings, designed for the theatre of imitating stage settings. The paintings were also ascribed to Piero della Francesca and Francesco di Giorgio. The best architects and painters of the Renaissance did not disdain to lend their hands as occasional stage designers; even sketches by Leonardo da Vinci are preserved.

41. THE STAGE OF THE TEATRO OLIMPICO AT VICENZA

The Theatre at Vincenza was begun by Andrea Palladio in 1579, and finished after his death by Vinc. Scamozzi in 1584. Palladio followed the rules given by Vitruvius for the construction of antique theatres; and the first play performed in Palladio's theatre in 1584 was the *Oedipus Tyrannus* by Sophocles. The theatre of Vicenza has five doors in a façade of symmetrical, palatial buildings. Through the gates sloping lanes are visible.

42. ANDREA DEL CASTAGNO: PETRARCH, *c.* 1450–55. FLORENCE, SANT'APOLLONIA. See note to plate 43.

43. ANDREA DEL CASTAGNO: THE CONDOTTIERE FARINATA DEGLI UBERTI, *c.* 1450–55. FLORENCE, SANT'APOLLONIA

The Cenacolo (Refectory) of Sant'Apollonia, which was previously a convent, now contains the Castagno Museum. The complete set of the 'Uomini famosi' consists of nine pictures (two of them are reproduced here as plates 42–43). The series includes Dante, Boccaccio, and the Condottiere Pippo Spano. The paintings were originally frescoes in the Pandolfini Villa at Legnaio, but are now transferred to canvas and much restored.

44. SIMONE MARTINI: EQUESTRIAN PORTRAIT OF GUIDORICCIO DA FOGLIANO. SIENA, TOWN HALL

Palazzo Pubblico, Sala del Mappamondo. Dated 1328. The knight is wearing a fur cap, and over his armour a 'capuccio' with a pattern showing the emblems of his coat-of-arms: rhombs and sprigs ('fogliani'); the trappings of his horse show the same emblems.

45. FLORENTINE NOBLEMEN IN A STREET NEAR THE CATHEDRAL. DETAIL OF A CASSONE FRONT, *c.* 1440. FLORENCE, ACADEMY

The complete Cassone painting is reproduced here as plate 76B. The marriage took place in 1420, but the painting is certainly later. This detail reproduction is interesting as a fashion plate; note, e.g. the different kinds of headgear; the young man at the left wears a hat with a rim of ermine after the French fashion. Though the marriage was celebrated in June and in a city as hot as Florence, the men's cloaks are lined with fur.

46. ATTRIBUTED TO ANTONIO RIZZO: VENETIAN YOUTH. BRONZE, *c.* 1490. VENICE, CORRER MUSEUM

Sometimes ascribed to Andrea Riccio. Note the curious tour of hair which also appears in portraits by Alvise Vivarini and Giovanni Bellini; this hair-dress was probably a wig.

47. LUCA DELLA ROBBIA: FLORENTINE LADY. TERRACOTTA BUST, POLYCHROME AND GLAZED, *c.* 1470. FLORENCE, MUSEO NAZIONALE

The hair is covered by a transparent hood, leaving the temples free; on top of it is a veil, cut like two palm leaves, fastened to the crown of the head with a brooch. A double string of pearls is wound along the rim of the hair and the ears backward to the nape.

48. FEMALE PORTRAIT BUST. TERRACOTTA, *c.* 1480. FLORENCE, MUSEO NAZIONALE

This portrait is obviously worked up from a death mask; but it is certainly not a portrait of Caterina Sforza, as some expert suggested. Whoever the woman was, she was a widow, as is proved by the way in which the veil is wrapped round her head.

The bust was once wrongly ascribed to Donatello and to Vecchietta. It shows much affinity with Antonio Pollaiuolo's bronze head of Pope Sixtus IV (on his monument in St. Peter's in Rome), which is also worked from a death mask.

49. GUIDO MAZZONI: PORTRAIT OF AN OLD MAN. POLYCHROME CLAY, 1490. NAPLES, MONTE OLIVETO

Detail of a group, 'The Deposition'. Vasari thought this naturalistic head a portrait of the poet Jacopo Sannazaro.

50. LORENTINO D'AREZZO: A GENTLEWOMAN WITH A HORN-SHAPED HEAD-DRESS, *c.* 1450. NATIONAL GALLERY, MELBOURNE

Formerly wrongly attributed to Piero della Francesca, and thought to be a portrait of Isotta da Rimini; also wrongly attributed to Paolo Uccello and to a follower of Filippo Lippi. The forehead of the lady is shaved (or the hair depilated with tweezers) to make it look larger; the hair hanging out from the ends of the horns is false. The costume is embroidered with pearls and gold, the sleeves are figured velvet, and the jewellery is especially beautiful—even for the Renaissance, which never saw such insipid trinkets as our age calls precious; but in those days men like Ghiberti, Pollaiuolo, Leonardo and Michelangelo designed jewellery.

51. PAOLO UCCELLO: A YOUNG FLORENTINE LADY OF FASHION, *c.* 1460. BOSTON, ISABELLA STEWART GARDNER MUSEUM

The forehead is depilated, and the headgear is adorned with pearls. The attribution of this painting to Uccello (Hendy, L. Venturi and Tietze) is contested; it is also ascribed to the Master of the Castello Nativity (Offner) and to the Master of the Karlsruhe Adoration (Pudelko); and even to Francesco di Giorgio (Berenson).

52. DOMENICO GHIRLANDAIO: FLORENTINE LADY IN A YELLOW BROCADE DRESS, *c.* 1488. FLORENCE, CHOIR OF SANTA MARIA NOVELLA

This detail from the fresco 'Birth of the Virgin' is a portrait of Ludovica Tornabuoni, at the age of about sixteen. (The Tornabuoni, one of the noblest families of Florence, were friends of the Medici and enemies of Savonarola.)

53. ANTONIO POLLAIUOLO: YOUNG LADY DRESSED IN MANY-COLOURED BROCADE, *c.* 1470. BERLIN MUSEUM. (ATTRIBUTED BY BODE TO DOMENICO VENEZIANO)

54. DEATH MASK OF LORENZO DE' MEDICI, CALLED IL MAGNIFICO. PLASTER, CAST IN 1492. FLORENCE, SOCIETÀ COLUMBARIA

55. PORTRAIT OF LORENZO DE'MEDICI. BERLIN MUSEUM

Polychrome stucco bust, probably executed by a follower of Verrocchio from a death-mask of Lorenzo, who died in 1492. Of this impressive portrait bust at least six copies are extant, including one in the possession of Lord Taunton, Bridgwater, and one in the National Gallery, Washington (Clarence H. Mackay Collection). Lorenzo de'Medici, called 'il Magnifico', was one of the 'Makers of Florence', a protector of the arts, and a contemporary of all the great Florentine artists between Leonardo da Vinci and Michelangelo. (This stucco bust is probably by Orsino Benintendi. Cf. Vasari-Milanesi, III, 372 *seq.*, and Cruttwell, Verrocchio, p. 99.)

56. SEBASTIANO DEL PIOMBO: PORTRAIT OF CLEMENT VII AS A CARDINAL, *c.* 1520. NAPLES, MUSEO NAZIONALE

57. SEBASTIANO DEL PIOMBO: PORTRAIT OF CHRISTOPHER COLUMBUS, 1519. NEW YORK, METROPOLITAN MUSEUM

This is a posthumous portrait, as Columbus died in 1506.

58. ATTRIBUTED TO PASQUALE DA CARAVAGGIO: PORTRAIT OF POPE ALEXANDER VI. MARBLE, *c.* 1492. BERLIN MUSEUM

59. SOFONISBA ANGUISSOLA: PORTRAIT OF A YOUNG MONK, *c.* 1570. RICHMOND, COOK COLLECTION

60. GENTILE BELLINI: THE DOGE OF VENICE, *c.* 1505. BERGAMO, CARRARA ACADEMY

This portrait, though of much inferior quality to the other portrait of the Doge (by Gentile's brother, Giovanni, at the National Gallery), is perhaps the more interesting as it is so little known.

61. PARMIGIANINO: PORTRAIT OF MALATESTA BAGLIONE OF PERUGIA. VIENNA MUSEUM

Malatesta Baglione was Commissionary-General of the Florentine militia during the siege of 1529–30 (cf. plate 4).

62. FRANCIABIGIO: PORTRAIT OF A YOUNG SCHOLAR AT HIS WRITING-DESK, 1522. BERLIN MUSEUM

This portrait is interesting from the standpoint of fashion. The young man is dressed in a black garment with wide sleeves, and his white shirt, with a loose upturned collar, comes out of a kind of corset. His big beret is also black.

63. TWO ARCHITECTS AT WORK. BY AN UNKNOWN ITALIAN PAINTER, 1555. NAPLES, MUSEO NAZIONALE

64. THE YOUNG MUSICIAN. BY AN UNKNOWN PAINTER OF THE SCHOOL OF PARMA *c.* 1540. MADRID, PRADO MUSEUM

65. ANDREA DEL SARTO: PORTRAIT OF A SCULPTOR, *c.* 1520. LONDON, NATIONAL GALLERY

66. FEDERICO BAROCCI: THE DUCHESS OF URBINO, *c.* 1580. NAPLES, FILANGIERI MUSEUM

67. ATTRIBUTED TO PONTORMO: PORTRAIT OF A NOBLEMAN DRESSED AFTER THE SPANISH FASHION, *c.* 1550. CASSEL, GALLERY

68. PARIS BORDONE: 'LA BALIA DI CASA MEDICI', *c.* 1560. FLORENCE, PITTI GALLERY

69. SEBASTIANO DEL PIOMBO: PORTRAIT OF A YOUNG ROMAN BOURGEOIS WOMAN 1512. FLORENCE, UFFIZI

70. DOMENICO GHIRLANDAIO: FRANCESCO SASSETTI AND HIS GRANDSON, *c.* 1470. NEW YORK, METROPOLITAN MUSEUM (BACHE COLLECTION)

The Sassettis, a rich Florentine merchant family, were faithful supporters of the Medici interests.

71. BRONZINO: A LITTLE BOY IN HUNTING HABIT, *c.* 1560. FLORENCE, UFFIZI

Portrait of Don Garcia de'Medici, son of the Grand Duke Cosimo I.

72. TIBERIO TITI: A BABY IN ITS BED. FLORENCE, PITTI GALLERY

Portrait of Leopoldo de'Medici.

73. SCIPIONE PULZONE: PORTRAIT OF THE COLONNA FAMILY, 1581. ROME, COLONNA GALLERY

The children's ages are added; the boy at the left, dressed in brocade and holding the sword-hilt with his gloved hand, is seven; the girl in the middle, in a silken dress with a train, is three; and the little lady at the right, with a very stiff frill and wearing feathers in her hair and a chain of jewels across her breast, is six.

74. ANDREA MANTEGNA: MARQUIS LODOVICO GONZAGA AND HIS FAMILY, *c.* 1473. MANTUA, CAMERA DEGLI SPOSI IN THE CASTELLO DI CORTE

75. MELOZZO DA FORLÌ: POPE SIXTUS IV AND HIS COURT, *c.* 1477. VATICAN, PINACOTECA

This fresco decorated originally the first room of the library of Pope Sixtus IV, and represents the inauguration of the old library. Behind the Pope stands Cardinal Pietro Riario, his favourite nephew; before him his other nephew, Cardinal Giuliano della Rovere, the later Pope Julius II. The kneeling figure is Bartolommeo Platina, Librarian of the Vaticana and author of a history of the Popes. On the left, Girolamo Riario, Count of Imola, and Giovanni della Rovere, Prefect of Rome, both good soldiers and nephews of the Pope.

This fresco, which in a way contains the character of a whole period, is a canon of nepotism.

76. TWO FLORENTINE CASSONE FRONTS WITH SCENES FROM THE LIFE OF THE ARISTOCRACY, FIFTEENTH CENTURY

(*a*) A Hunting Party. Florence, Pitti Gallery.
(*b*) The Adimari Nuptials. Florence, Academy. (Cf. plate 45.)

77. DETAILS OF AN IVORY CHESSBOARD, FLORENTINE, EARLY FIFTEENTH CENTURY. FLORENCE, MUSEO NAZIONALE

78. VITTORE CARPACCIO: TWO VENETIAN COURTESANS ON A BALCONY OR THE ROOF OF THEIR HOUSE, *c.* 1505. VENICE, CORRER MUSEUM

The two women, sitting on the 'altana' of their house—some writers contend that they are not courtesans but quite respectable people—have assembled a little menagerie around them. The dresses show a very low neck. On top of their own hair the ladies wear curls of false hair, and the hair is dyed the brightest yellow. Very interesting are the shoes; the woman in front has taken hers off and they are standing at the left, next to the ugly little page and the peacock. These shoes have very high, wedged heels, a kind of socle or cothurnus. The lady in the background, holding a handkerchief in a limp hand, has her shoes on, and the dress is falling in clumsy folds around the soles which are about eight inches thick.

79. BARTOLOMMEO VENETO: PORTRAIT OF A COURTESAN, *c.* 1520. FRANKFORT a M. STAEDEL INSTITUTE

The hair is stiffened with gum and gilded. Note the beautiful jewellery, the garland and the pendant.

80. FRANCIABIGIO: THE LETTER OF URIAH, 1523. DRESDEN GALLERY

81. PAOLO VERONESE: THE MARRIAGE AT CANA, 1563. PARIS, LOUVRE

The scene of this religious painting is obviously taken from luxurious contemporary Venetian life, depicting a sumptuous meal in a palatial court-yard. It contains many portraits—of Veronese himself playing the violoncello, Tintoretto the viola, Titian the contra-bass, Jacopo Bassano the flute; there are also portraits of Paolo Veronese's brother, of Pietro Aretino, and of some courtesans. For painting a similar picture Veronese was summoned before the Tribunal of the Inquisition in 1573.

82. BEEKEEPERS AT WORK. MINIATURE IN A VIRGIL MANUSCRIPT BY THE SO-CALLED MASTER OF THE VITÆ IMPERATORUM, MILAN, *c.* 1460. OXFORD, BODLEIAN LIBRARY

83. LUCA DELLA ROBBIA: A PEASANT REAPING CORN. DETAIL OF A TERRACOTTA ROUNDEL, ENAMELLED IN BLUE AND WHITE, *c.* 1440. LONDON, VICTORIA AND ALBERT MUSEUM

84. ATTRIBUTED TO FRANCESCO DEL COSSA (RECENTLY ALSO TO ANGELO DEL MACCAGNINO OF SIENA): ALLEGORY OF AUTUMN, *c.* 1470. BERLIN MUSEUM

Once in the session-room of the Inquisition in the Dominican Convent at Ferrara.

85. YOUNG FLORENTINES PLAYING 'CIVETTINO', BY AN UNKNOWN FLORENTINE PAINTER, *c.* 1430. FLORENCE, UFFIZI

The 'civettino' or 'Fop' was a Handy Pandy Game, played in the squares and streets of Florence, mostly by young men of birth and manners, 'and their movements partook of the graceful steps of a minuet and the elegant postures of the gymnasium'. The various costumes in this small painting are worth noticing. The man at the left has a fur-lined jacket, and a 'capuccio', which is a cap with a muffler sewn on to it. The man at the right wears a short, sleeveless cape, of the sort then fashionable in Milan. The man in the background is dressed after the Venetian fashion in a short overcoat with very wide sleeves that are narrow at the wrists. The trousers of the players consist of two separate leggings which show the shirt in the middle and are fixed with ribbons to the doublet. The little boys in the foreground have no trousers on at all. The game is being played by three young men; the one in the middle is standing on the feet of the two others. The iron rods and brackets on the buildings are for hanging woollen cloth pieces to dry after dyeing.

86. FAMILY LIFE IN THE SIXTEENTH CENTURY. MIDDLE-PIECE OF A TAPESTRY WOVEN IN FLANDERS AFTER A FLORENTINE CARTOON; ONCE IN THE POSSESSION OF THE MEDICI. FLORENCE, GALLERIA DEGLI ARAZZI

In the background a fireplace, men playing cards, a curtained bed, and a balcony with a view to the street; in the foreground an old man with a chafing-dish, a boy working the bellows, and women winding yarn.

87. FLORENTINE PRINTING OFFICE, *c.* 1570. ETCHING AFTER A DRAWING BY GIOVANNI STRADANO. LONDON, BRITISH MUSEUM

Design for an engraving in 'Nova Reperta', a book of plates on new inventions, published at Antwerp by Philip Galle, without date. Stradano (Jan von der Straet), a painter born in Bruges, lived in Florence from about 1554, and was employed as a designer for the tapestry works which Cosimo de'Medici had founded. In 1570 he decorated the 'studiolo' of Francesco I de'Medici in the Palazzo Vecchio. Stradano, who lived fifty years in Florence, became an Italian painter, but he preserved his Netherlandish sense of naturalistic observation and painted pictures of the activities in Florentine workshops which were strictly true to life; he was a forerunner of baroque and modern painting as far as his themes are concerned.

88. A SUGAR FACTORY AT FLORENCE, *c.* 1570. ETCHING AFTER A DRAWING BY GIOVANNI STRADANO FOR 'NOVA REPERTA'. LONDON, BRITISH MUSEUM

Cf. note on plate 87.

89. FRANCESCO COSSA: WOMEN WEAVING AND EMBROIDERING, 1470. DETAIL OF A FRESCO IN THE PALAZZO SCHIFANOIA AT FERRARA

90. GIOVANNI STRADANO: THE LABORATORY OF A CHEMIST, 1570. FRESCO IN THE 'STUDIOLO' OF GRAND DUKE I FRANCESCO DE'MEDICI IN THE PALAZZO VECCHIO AT FLORENCE

Cf. note on plate 87.

91. BARTOLOMMEO PASSEROTTI: A LECTURE ON ANATOMY, *c.* 1570. ROME, BORGHESE GALLERY

92. LAURENTIUS VOLTALINA: A UNIVERSITY LECTURE, *c.* 1420. PAINTING ON PARCHMENT. BERLIN, PRINT ROOM

This small water-colour painting shows Henricus de Alemannia, a German professor, reading the Ethics before twenty-four students in an open courtyard at Bologna.

93. NANNI DI BANCO: THE WORKSHOP OF A SCULPTOR, *c.* 1412. MARBLE RELIEF. FLORENCE, OR SAN MICHELE

From left to right: bricklayer; a stonemason drilling a small pillar; an architect working with compasses and square at a capital; at the right end the sculptor—a self-portrait of Nanni di Banco—chiselling the figure of a putto.

94. A VENETIAN EMBASSY AT CAIRO. PARIS, LOUVRE

This painting, dated 1512, is by a follower of Gentile Bellini (who died in 1507), probably by Niccolò Mansueti. The name of the Venetian ambassador was Domenico Trevisano, procurator of San Marco; the Sultan of Egypt was Abul Feth Kansu Ghuree. The scene of the reception of the embassy is at the gates of Cairo.

95. VITTORE CARPACCIO: RECEPTION OF AN ENGLISH EMBASSY IN VENICE, *c.* 1495. VENICE, ACADEMY

A part of Carpaccio's Ursula paintings, 'The Arrival of the Ambassadors at the Court of King Maurus'. The scene is actually not Brittany, as the legend suggests, but the Lido of Venice. King Maurus is depicted like a Doge sitting with his four councillors. (See Ludwig and Molmenti, 'Carpaccio', p. 88.)

96. PALMA GIOVANE: RECEPTION OF HENRY III, KING OF POLAND AND FRANCE, IN VENICE, 1574. DRESDEN GALLERY

Large representational paintings like this were executed probably very true to life. Their aim is not very different from the topical illustrations in modern periodicals or the cinema newsreels. But there is one very important difference: those report painters did not work for the day alone; on the contrary they strove to impart eternal memory to a passing moment of history by means of the highest art.

97. LEONARDO DA VINCI: CARICATURE OF AN UGLY OLD MAN. PEN AND INK DRAWING, *c.* 1490. MILAN, AMBROSIANA

98. PUPIL OF LEONARDO DA VINCI (PROBABLY FRANCESCO MELZI): CARICATURE OF A HIDEOUS OLD WOMAN. RED CHALK DRAWING, *c.* 1490. WINDSOR CASTLE, ROYAL LIBRARY

99. CARICATURE OF TIPPLERS AND MUSICIANS. OIL PAINTING BY AN UNKNOWN VENETIAN MASTER, ABOUT 1590 (WRONGLY ASCRIBED TO PIETRO DELLA VECCHIA). TRIESTE, COLLECTION POLLITZER

100. ATTRIBUTED TO ANNIBALE CARRACCI: CARICATURE OF THE SINGER RABBATIN DE GNIFFI AND HIS WIFE SPILLA POMINA. PEN AND INK DRAWING, *c.* 1580. STOCKHOLM, NATIONAL MUSEUM

INDEX